DOUBLE EXPOSURE

DOUBLE EXPOSURE

SPLIT INFINITY

BLUE ADEPT   JUXTAPOSITION

Piers Anthony

Nelson Doubleday, Inc.   .Garden City, New York

Contents

SPLIT INFINITY

CONTENTS

Slide

He walked with the assurance of stature, and most others deferred to him subtly. When he moved in a given direction, the way before him conveniently opened, by seeming coincidence; when he made eye contact, the other head nodded in a token bow. He was a serf, like all of them, naked and with no physical badge of status; indeed, it would have been the depth of bad taste to accord him any overt recognition. Yet he was a giant, here. His name was Stile.

Stile stood one point five meters tall and weighed fifty kilograms. In prior parlance he would have stood four feet, eleven inches tall and weighed a scant hundredweight or eight stone; or stood a scant fifteen hands and weighed a hundred and ten pounds. His male associates towered above him by up to half a meter and outweighed him by twenty-five kilos.

He was fit, but not extraordinarily muscled. Personable without being handsome. He did not hail his friends heartily, for there were few he called friend, and he was diffident about approaches. Yet there was enormous drive in him that manifested in lieu of personal warmth.

He walked about the Grid-hall of the Game-annex, his favorite place; beyond this region he reverted to the nonentity that others perceived. He sought competition of his own level, but at this hour there was none. Pairs of people stood in the cubicles that formed the convoluted perimeter of the hall, and a throng milled in the center, making contacts. A cool, gentle, mildly flower-scented draft wafted down from the vents in the ceiling, and the image of the sun cast its light on the floor, making its own game of shadows.

Stile paused at the fringe of the crowd, disliking this forced mixing. It was better when someone challenged him.

A young woman rose from one of the seats. She was nude, of course, but worthy of a second glance because of the perfection of her body. Stile averted his gaze, affecting not to be aware of her; he was especially shy with girls.

A tall youth intercepted the woman. "Game, lass?" How easy he made it seem!

She dismissed him with a curt downward flip of one hand and continued on toward Stile. A child signaled her: "Game, miss?" The woman smiled, but again negated, more gently. Stile smiled too, privately; evidently she did not recognize the child, but he did: Pollum, Rung Two on the Nines ladder. Not in Stile's own class, yet, but nevertheless a formidable player. Had the woman accepted the challenge, she would probably have been tromped.

There was no doubt she recognized Stile, though. His eyes continued to review the crowd, but his attention was on the woman. She was of average height—several centimeters taller than he—but of more than average proportions. Her breasts were full and perfect, unsagging, shifting eloquently with her easy motion, and her legs were long and smooth. In other realms men assumed that the ideal woman was a naked one, but often this was not the case; too many women suffered in the absence of mechanical supports for portions of their anatomy. This one, approaching him, was the type who really could survive the absence of clothing without loss of form.

She arrived at last. "Stile," she murmured.

He turned as if surprised, nodding. Her face was so lovely it startled him. Her eyes were large and green, her hair light brown and light-bleached in strands that expanded about her neck. There was a lot of art in the supposedly natural falling of women's hair. Her features were even and possessed the particular properties and proportions that appealed to him, though he could not define precisely what these were. His shyness loomed up inside him, so that he did not trust himself to speak.

"I am Sheen," she said. "I would like to challenge you to a Game."

She could not be a top player. Stile knew every ranking player on every age-ladder by sight and style, and she was on no ladder. Therefore she was a dilettante, an occasional participant, possibly of some skill in selected modes but in no way a serious competitor. Her body was too lush for most physical sports; the top females in track, ball games and swimming were small-breasted, lean-fleshed, and lanky, and this in no way described Sheen. Therefore he would have no physical competition here.

Yet she was beautiful, and he was unable to speak. So he nodded acquiescence. She took his arm in an easy gesture of familiarity that startled him. Stile had known women, of course; they came to him seeking the notoriety of his company, and the known fact of his hesitancy lent them compensating courage. But this one was so pretty she hardly needed to seek male company; it would seek her. She was making it look as if he had sought and won her. Perhaps he had, unknowingly: his prowess in the Game could have impressed her enough from afar to bring her to him. Yet this was not the type of conquest he preferred; such women were equally avid for Game-skilled teeners and grayheads.

They found an unoccupied cubicle. It had a column in the center, inset with panels on opposite sides. Stile went to one side, Sheen on the other, and as their weights came on the marked ovals to the floor before each panel, the panels lighted. The column was low, so Stile could see Sheen's face across from him; she was smiling at him.

Embarrassed by this open show of camaraderie, Stile looked down at his panel. He hardly needed to; he knew exactly what it showed. Across the top were four categories: PHYSICAL—MENTAL—CHANCE—ART, and down the left side were four more: NAKED—TOOL—MACHINE—ANIMAL. For shorthand convenience they were also lettered and numbered: 1—2—3—4 across the top, A—B—C—D down the side. The numbers were highlighted: the Grid had given him that set of choices, randomly.

THE GAME: PRIMARY GRID

	1. PHYSICAL	2. MENTAL	3. CHANCE	4. ART
A. NAKED				
B. TOOL				
C. MACHINE				
D. ANIMAL				

Stile studied Sheen's face. Now that she was in the Game, his opponent, his diffidence diminished. He felt the mild tightening of his skin, elevation of heartbeat, clarity of mind and mild distress of bowel that presaged the tension and effort of competition. For some people such effects became so strong it ruined them as competitors, but for him it was a great feeling, that drew him back compulsively. He lived for the Game!

Even when his opponent was a pretty girl whose pert breasts peeked at him just above the column. What was passing through her mind? Did she really think she could beat him, or was she just out for the experience? Had she approached him on a dare, or was she a groupie merely out for a date? If she were trying to win, she would want to choose ART, possibly MENTAL, and would certainly avoid PHYSICAL. If she were on a dare she would go for CHANCE, as that would require little performance on her part. If she wanted experience, anything would do. If she were a groupie, she would want PHYSICAL.

Of course she could not choose among these; *he* had the choice. But his choice would be governed in part by his judgment of her intent and ability. He had to think, as it were, with her mind, so that he could select what she least desired and obtain the advantage.

Now he considered her likely choice, in the series she did control. A true competitor would go for NAKED, for there was the essence of it: un-

assisted personal prowess. One wanting experience could go for anything, again depending on the type of experience desired. A dare would
probably go for NAKED also; that choice would be part of the dare. A
groupie would certainly go for NAKED. So that was her most likely
choice.

Well, he would call her bluff. He touched PHYSICAL, sliding his
hand across the panel so she couldn't tell his choice by the motion of
his arm.

Her choice had already been made, as anticipated. They were in 1A,
PHYSICAL/NAKED.

The second grid appeared. Now the categories across the top were
1. SEPARATE—2. INTERACTIVE—3. COMBAT—4. COOPERATIVE, and down
the side were A. FLAT SURFACE—B. VARIABLE SURFACE—C. DISCONTIN-
UITY—D. LIQUID. The letters were highlighted; he had to choose from
the down column this time. He didn't feel like swimming or swinging
from bars with her, though there could be intriguing aspects to each, so
the last two were out. He was an excellent long-distance runner, but
doubted Sheen would go for that sort of thing, which eliminated the
flat surface. So he selected B, the variable surface.

She chose 1. SEPARATE: no groupie after all! So they would be in
a race of some sort, not physically touching or directly interacting,
though there were limited exceptions. Good enough. He would find out
what she was made of.

Now the panel displayed a listing of variable surfaces. Stile glanced
again at Sheen. She shrugged, so he picked the first: MAZE PATH. As
he touched it, the description appeared in the first box of a nine-square
grid.

She chose the second: GLASS MOUNTAIN. It appeared in the second
square.

He placed DUST SLIDE in the third square. Then they continued with
CROSS COUNTRY, TIGHTROPE, SAND DUNES, GREASED HILLS, SNOW BANK,
and LIMESTONE CLIFF. The tertiary grid was complete.

Now he had to choose one of the vertical columns, and she had the
horizontal rows. He selected the third, she the first, and their game was
there: DUST SLIDE.

"Do you concede?" he asked her, pressing the appropriate query button so that the machine would know. She had fifteen seconds to negate, or forfeit the game.

Her negation was prompt. "I do not."

"Draw?"

"No."

He had hardly expected her to do either. Concession occurred when
one party had such an obvious advantage that there was no point in
playing, as when the game was chess and one player was a grandmaster
while the other hadn't yet learned the moves. Or when it was weight

lifting, with one party a child and the other a muscle builder. The dust slide was a harmless entertainment, fun to do even without the competitive element; no one would concede it except perhaps one who had a phobia about falling—and such a person would never have gotten into this category of game.

And so her reaction was odd. She should have laughed at his facetious offers. Instead she had taken them seriously. That suggested she was more nervous about this encounter than she seemed.

Yet this was no Tourney match! If she were a complete duffer she could have accepted the forfeit and been free. Or she could have agreed to the draw, and been able to tell her girlish friends how she had tied with the notorious Stile. So it seemed she was out neither for notoriety nor a dare, and he had already determined she was not a groupie. She really did want to compete—yet it was too much to hope that she had any real proficiency as a player.

They vacated the booth after picking up the gametags extruded from slots. No one was admitted solo to any subgame; all had to play the grid first, and report in pairs to the site of decision. That prevented uncommitted people from cluttering the premises or interfering with legitimate contests. Of course children could and did entertain themselves by indulging in mock contests, just for the pleasure of the facilities; to a child, the Game-annex was a huge amusement park. But in so doing, they tended to get hooked on the Game itself, increasingly as they aged, until at last they were thoroughgoing addicts. That had been the way with Stile himself.

The Dust Slide was in another dome, so they took the tube transport. The vehicle door irised open at their approach, admitting them to its cosy interior. Several other serfs were already in it: three middle-aged men who eyed Sheen with open appreciation, and a child whose eye lit with recognition. "You're the jockey!"

Stile nodded. He had no trouble relating to children. He was hardly larger than the boy.

"You won all the races!" the lad continued.

"I had good horses," Stile explained.

"Yeah," the child agreed, satisfied.

Now the three other passengers turned their attention to Stile, beginning to surmise that he might be as interesting as the girl. But the vehicle stopped, its door opened, and they all stepped out into the new dome. In moments Stile and Sheen had lost the other travelers and were homing in on the Dust Slide, their tickets ready.

The Slide's desk-secretary flashed Stile a smile as she validated the tickets. He smiled back, though he knew this was foolish; she was a robot. Her face, arms and upper torso were perfectly humanoid, with shape, color and texture no ordinary person could have told from a living woman, but her perfectly humanoid body terminated at the edge of her desk. She *was* the desk, possessing no legs at all. It was as if some celestial artisan had been carving her from a block of metal, causing her to animate as he progressed—then left the job unfinished at the halfway point. Stile felt a certain obscure sympathy for her; did she have true consciousness, in that upper half? Did she long for a completely humanoid body—or for a complete desk body? How did it feel to be a half-thing?

She handed back his ticket, validated. Stile closed his fingers about her delicate hand. "When do you get off work, cutie?" he inquired with the lift of an eyebrow. He was not shy around machines, of course.

She had been programmed for this. "Ssh. My boyfriend's watching." She used her free hand to indicate the robot next to her: a desk with a set of male legs protruding, terminating at the inverted waist. They demonstrated the manner the protective shorts should be worn for the Slide. They were extremely robust legs, and the crotch region was powerfully masculine.

Stile glanced down at himself, chagrined. "Oh, I can't compete with him. My legs are barely long enough to reach the ground." A bygone Earth author, Mark Twain, had set up that remark, and Stile found it useful on occasion. He accepted Sheen's arm again and they continued on to the Slide.

He thought Sheen might remark on the way he seemed to get along with machines, but she seemed oblivious. Ah, well.

The Slide was a convoluted mountain of channels looping and diverging and merging. Dust flowed in them—sanitary, nonirritating, noncarcinogenic, neutral particles of translucent plastic, becoming virtually liquid in the aggregate, and quite slippery. The whole was dramatic, suggesting frothing torrents of water in sluices, or rivulets of snow in an avalanche.

They donned the skin-shorts and filter masks required for protection on the Slide. The dust was harmless, but it tended to work its way into any available crevices, and the human body had a number. This was one thing Stile did not like about this particular subgame: the clothing. Only Citizens wore clothing, in the normal course, and it was uncouth for any serf to wear anything not strictly functional. More than uncouth: it could be grounds for summary termination of tenure at Planet Proton. Such Slide-shorts were functional, in these dusty environs; still, he felt uncomfortable. Their constriction and location tended to stir him sexually, and that was awkward in the company of a creature like Sheen.

Sheen seemed to feel no such concern. Perhaps she was aware that the partial concealment of the shorts attracted attention to those parts they concealed, enhancing her sex appeal. Stile, like many serfs, found a certain illicit lure in clothing, especially clothing on the distaff sex; it represented so much that serfs could only dream of. He had to keep his eyes averted, lest he embarrass himself.

They took the lift to the Slide apex. Here at the top they were near the curving dome that held in air and heat; through its shimmer Stile could see the bleak landscape of Proton, ungraced by any vegetation. The hostile atmosphere was obscured in the distance by clouds of smog.

The Slide itself was a considerable contrast. From this height six channels coursed out and down, each half filled with flowing dust. Colored lights shone up through it all, for the channels too were translucent. They turned now red, now blue-gray and now yellow as the beams moved. The tangle of paths formed a flower-like pattern, supremely beautiful. If Stile found the clothing physically and emotionally awkward, he was compensated by the view from this vantage, and always stood for a moment in minor awe.

For any given channel the colors seemed random, but for the arrangement as a whole they shaped in shifting contours roses, lilies, tulips, violets and gardenias. Air jets emitted corresponding perfumes when applicable. An artist had designed this layout, and Stile admired the handiwork. He had been here many times before, yet the novelty had not worn off.

Sheen did not seem to notice. "On your mark," she said, setting the random starter. The device could pop instantly or take two minutes. This time it split the difference. The channel barriers dropped low, and Sheen leaped for the chute nearest her.

Stile, surprised by her facility, leaped after her. They accelerated, shooting down feet first around a broad bright curve of green, then into the first white vertical loop. Up and over, slowing dizzily at the top, upside down, then regaining velocity in the downshoot.

Sheen was moving well. Her body had a natural rondure that shaped itself well to the contour of the chute. The dust piled up behind her, shoving her forward. Stile, following in the same channel, tried to intercept enough dust to cut off her supply and ground her, but she had too big a lead and was making too good use of her resources.

Well, there were other ways. This channel passed through a partial-gravity rise that was slow. Another channel crossed, going into a corkscrew. Stile took this detour, zipped through the screw, and shot out ahead of the girl.

She took another connection and got in behind him, cutting off *his* dust. This was the aspect of the Slide that was interactive: the competition for dust. Stile was grounded, his posterior scraping against the suddenly bare plastic of the chute. No dust, no progress!

He put his hand to the side, heaved, and flipped his body into the adjoining channel. This was a tricky maneuver, legitimate but not for amateurs. Here he had dust again, and resumed speed—but he had lost the momentum he had before. Sheen continued on in her channel, riding the piled dust, moving ahead of him—and now they were halfway down.

Stile realized that he had a real race on his hands. This girl was good!

He vaulted back into her channel, cutting off her dust again—but even as he did, she vaulted into his just-vacated channel, maintaining her lead. Apt move! Obviously she had raced here many times before, and knew the tricks, and had more agility under that sweet curvature of body than he had suspected. But now he had the better channel, and he was unmatchable in straight dust-riding; he moved ahead. She jumped across to cut him off, but he was already jumping into a third chute. Before she could follow him, the two diverged and he was safe.

They completed the race on separate channels. She had found a good one, and was gaining on him despite his careful management of dust. He finished barely ahead. They shot into the collection bin, one-two, to the applause of the other players who were watching. It had been a fine race, the kind that happened only once or twice on a given day.

Sheen got up and shook off the dust with a fascinating shimmy of her torso. "Can't win them all," she remarked, unperturbed.

She had made an excellent try, though! She had come closer than anyone in years. Stile watched her as she stripped off mask and shorts. She was stunningly beautiful—more so than before, because now he realized that her body was functional as well as shapely.

"You interest me," he told her. In this aftermath of a good game he was flushed with positive feeling, his shyness at a minimum.

Sheen smiled. "I hoped to."

"You almost beat me."

"I had to get your attention somehow."

Another player laughed. Stile had to laugh too. Sheen had proved herself, and now he wanted to know why. The mutual experience had broken the ice; the discovery of a new challenge completed his transition from diffidence to normal masculine imperative.

He didn't even have to invite her to come home with him. She was already on her way.

CHAPTER 2

Sheen

Sheen moved into his apartment as if it were her own. She punched the buttons of his console to order a complete light lunch of fruit salad, protein bread and blue wine.

"You evidently know about me," Stile said as they ate. "But I know nothing of you. Why did you—want to get my attention?"

"I am a fan of the Game. I could be good at it. But I have so little time—only three years tenure remaining—I need instruction. From the best. From you. So I can be good enough—"

"To enter the Tourney," Stile finished. "I have the same time remaining. But there are others you could have checked. I am only tenth on my ladder—"

"Because you don't want to have to enter the Tourney this year," she said. "You won't enter it until your last year of tenure, because all tenure ends when a serf enters the Tourney. But you could advance to Rung One on the Age-35 ladder any time you wished, and the top five places of each adult ladder are automatically entered in the—"

"Thank you for the information," Stile said with gentle irony.

She overlooked it. "So you keep yourself in the second five, from year to year, low enough to be safe in case several of the top rungers break or try to vacate, high enough to be able to make your move any time you want to. You are in fact the most proficient Gamesman of our generation—"

"This is an exaggeration. I'm a jockey, not a—"

"—and I want to learn from you. I offer—"

"I can see what you offer," Stile said, running his eyes over her body. He could do this now without embarrassment, because he had come to know her; his initial shyness was swinging to a complementary boldness. They had, after all, Gamed together. "Yet there is no way I could inculcate the breadth of skills required for serious competition, even if we had a century instead of a mere three years. Talent is inherent, and it has to be buttressed by constant application. I might be able to guide you to the fifth rung of your ladder—which one would that be?"

"Age 23 female."

"You're in luck. There are only three Tourney-caliber players on that ladder at present. With proper management it would be possible for a person of promise to take one of the remaining rungs. But though you gave me a good race on the Slide, I am not sure you have sufficient promise—and even if you qualified for the Tourney, your chances of progressing far in it would be vanishingly small. *My* chances are not good—which is why I'm still working hard at every opportunity to improve myself. Contrary to your opinion, there are half a dozen players better than I am, and another score of my general caliber. In any given year, four or five of them will enter the Tourney, while others rise in skills to renew the pool. That, combined with the vagaries of luck, gives me only one chance in ten to win. For you—"

"Oh, I have no illusions about winning!" she said. "But if I could make a high enough rank to obtain extension of tenure, if only a year or two—"

"It's a dream," he assured her. "The Citizens put such prizes out as bait, but only one person in thirty-two gains even a year that way."

"I would be completely grateful for that dream," she said, meeting his gaze.

Stile was tempted. He knew he would not have access to a more attractive woman, and she had indeed shown promise in the Game. That athletic ability that had enabled her so blithely and lithely to change chutes would benefit her in many other types of competition. He could have a very pleasant two years, training her. Extremely pleasant.

That itself gave him caution. He had loved before, and lost, and it had taken years to recover completely—if he really had. *Tune*, he thought, with momentary nostalgia. There were ways in which Sheen resembled that former girl.

Still, what promise did he have beyond his remaining three years, anyway? All would be lost, once he left Proton. Oh, he would have a nice nest egg to establish galactic residence, and might even go to crowded Earth itself, but all he really wanted to do was remain on Proton. Since it was unlikely that he could do that, he might as well make these years count. She had mentioned that her own tenure was as short as his, which meant she would have to leave at the same time. That could be very interesting, if they had a firm relationship. "Tell me about yourself," he said.

"I was born five years before my parents' tenure ended," Sheen said, putting down her leaf of lettuce. She had eaten delicately and quite sparingly, as many slender women did. "I obtained a position with a Lady Citizen, first as errand girl, then as nurse. I was a fan of the Game as a child, and had good aptitude, but as my employer grew older she required more care, until—" She shrugged, and now with the pleasant tingle of the wine and the understanding they were coming to, he could appreciate the way her breasts moved with that gesture. Oh yes, it was a good offer she made—yet something nagged him. "I have not been to a Game for seven years," she continued, "though I have viewed it often on my employer's screens, and rehearsed strategies and techniques constantly in private. My employer had a private exercise gym her doctor recommended; she never used it, so I did, filling in for her. Last week she died, so I have been released on holiday pending settlement of her estate and the inventory her heir is taking. Her heir is female, and healthy, so I do not think the burden will be onerous."

It could have been quite a different matter, Stile reflected, with a young, healthy male heir. Serfs had no personal rights except termination of tenure in fit physical and mental condition, and no sane person would depart Proton even a day ahead of schedule. Serfs could serve without concern as concubines or studs for their employers—or for each other as private or public entertainment for their employers. Their bodies were the property of the Citizens. Only in privacy, without the intercession of a Citizen, did interpersonal relations between serfs become meaningful. As now.

"So you came to me," Stile said. "To trade your favors for my favor."

"Yes." There needed to be no hesitancy or shame to such acknowledgment. Since serfs had no monetary or property credit, and no power during their tenure, Game-status and sex were the chief instruments of barter.

"I am minded to try it out. Shall we say for a week, then reconsider? I might become tired of you."

Again there was no formal cause for affront; male-female interactions among serfs were necessarily shallow, though marriage was permitted and provided for. Stile had learned the hard way, long ago, not to expect permanence. Still, he expected a snappy retort to the effect that she would more likely grow tired of him first.

There was no such byplay. "As part of my rehearsal for the Game, I have studied the art of pleasing men," Sheen said. "I am willing to venture that week."

A fair answer. And yet, he wondered, would not an ordinary woman, even the most abused of serfs, have evinced some token ire at the callousness of his suggestion? He could have said, "We might not be right for each other." He had phrased it most bluntly, forcing a reaction. Sheen had not reacted; she was completely matter-of-fact. Again he was nagged. Was there some catch here?

"Do you have special interests?" Stile inquired. "Music?" He hadn't really wanted to ask that, but it had come out. He associated love with music, because of his prior experience.

"Yes, music," Sheen agreed.

His interest quickened. "What kind?"

She shrugged again. "Any kind."

"Vocal? Instrumental? Mechanical?"

Her brow furrowed. "Instrumental."

"What instrument do you play?"

She looked blank.

"Oh—you just listen," he said. "I play a number of instruments, preferring the woodwinds. All part of the Game. You will need to acquire skill in at least one instrument, or Game opponents will play you for a weakness there and have easy victories."

"Yes, I must learn," she agreed.

What would she have done if he had gone for ART instead of PHYSICAL in their match? With her prior choice of NAKED, the intersection would have put them in song, dance or story: the a capella performances. Perhaps she was a storyteller. Yet she did not seem to have the necessary imagination.

"Let's do it right," he said, rising from his meal. "I have a costume—" He touched a button and the costume fell from a wall vent into his hand. It was a filmy negligee.

Sheen smiled and accepted it. In the privacy of an apartment, clothing was permitted, so long as it was worn discreetly. If there should be a video call, or a visitor at his door, Sheen would have to hide or rip off the clothing lest she be caught by a third party in that state and be compromised. But that only added to the excitement of it, the special, titillating naughtiness of their liaison. It was, in an unvoiced way, the closest any serf could come to emulating any Citizen.

She donned the costume without shame and did a pirouette, causing the material to fling out about her legs. Stile found this indescribably erotic. He shut down the light, so that the material seemed opaque, and the effect intensified. Oh, what clothing did for the woman, creating shadows where ordinarily there were none, making mysteries where none had been before!

Yet again, something ticked a warning in Stile's mind. Sheen was lovely, yes—but where was her flush of delighted shame? Why hadn't she questioned his possession of this apparel? He had it on loan, and his employer knew about it and would in due course remember to reclaim it—but a person who did not know that, who was not aware of the liberalism of this particular employer with respect to his favored serfs, should be alarmed at his seeming hoarding of illicit clothing. Sheen had thought nothing of it.

They were technically within the law—but so was a man who thought treason without acting on it. Stile was an expert Gamesman, attuned to the nuances of human behavior, and there was something wrong with Sheen. But what was it? There was really nothing in her behavior that could not be accounted for by her years of semi-isolation while nursing her Citizen.

Well, perhaps it would come to him. Stile advanced on Sheen, and she met him gladly. None of this oh-please-don't-hurt-me-sir, catch-me-if-you-can drama. She was not after all very much taller than he, so he had to draw her down only marginally to kiss her. Her body was limber, pliable, and the feel of the gauze between their skins pitched him into a fever of desire. Not in years had he achieved such heat so soon.

She kissed him back, her lips firm and cool. Suddenly the little nagging observations clicked into a comprehensible whole, and he knew her for what she was. Stile's ardor began sliding into anger.

He bore her back to the couch-bed. She dropped onto it easily, as if this type of fall were commonplace for her. He sat beside her, running his hands along her thighs, still with that tantalizing fabric in place between them. He moved on to knead her breasts, doubly erotic behind the material. A nude woman in public was not arousing, but a clothed one in private . . .

His hands were relaxed, gentle—but his mind was tight with coalescing ire and apprehension. He was about to trigger a reaction that could be hazardous to his health.

"I would certainly never have been able to tell," he remarked.

Her eyes focused on him. "Tell what, Stile?"

He answered her with another question. "Who would want to send me a humanoid robot?"

She did not stiffen. "I wouldn't know."

"The information should be in your storage banks. I need a printout."

She showed no emotion. "How did you discover that I was a robot?"

"Give me that printout, and I'll give you my source of information."

"I am not permitted to expose my data."

"Then I shall have to report you to Game-control," Stile said evenly. "Robots are not permitted to compete against humans unless under direct guidance by the Game Computer. Are you a Game-machine?"

"No."

"Then I fear it will go hard with you. The record of our Game has been entered. If I file a complaint, you will be deprogrammed."

She looked at him, still lovely though he now knew her nature. "I wish you would not do that, Stile."

How strong was her programmed wish? What form would her objection take, when pressed? It was a popular fable that robots could not harm human beings, but Stile knew better. All robots of Proton were prohibited from harming Citizens, or acting contrary to Citizens' expressed intent, or acting in any manner that might conceivably be deleterious to the welfare of any Citizen—but there were no strictures about serfs. Normally robots did not bother people, but this was because robots simply did not care about people. If a serf interfered with a robot in the performance of its assignment, that man could get hurt.

Stile was now interfering with the robot Sheen. "Sheen," he said.

"Short for Machine. Someone with a certain impish humor programmed you."

"I perceive no humor," she said.

"Naturally not. That was your first giveaway. When I proffered you a draw on the Slide, you should have laughed. It was a joke. You reacted without emotion."

"I am programmed for emotion. I am programmed for the stigmata of love."

The stigmata of love. A truly robotic definition! "Not the reality?"

"The reality too. There is no significant distinction. I am here to love you, if you will permit it."

So far she had shown no sign of violence. That was good; he was not at all sure he could escape her if she attacked him. Robots varied in physical abilities, as they did in intellectual ones; it depended on their intended use and the degree of technology applied. This one seemed to be of top-line sophistication; that could mean she imitated the human form and nature so perfectly she had no more strength than a real girl would have. But there was no guarantee. "I must have that printout."

"I will tell you my mission, if you will not expose my nature."

"I can not trust your word. You attempted to deceive me with your story about nursing a Citizen. Only the printout is sure."

"You are making it difficult. My mission is only to guard you from harm."

"I feel more threatened by your presence than protected. Why should I need guarding from harm?"

"I don't know. I must love you and guard you."

"Who sent you?"

"I do not know."

Stile touched his wall vid. "Game-control," he said.

"Don't do that!" Sheen cried.

"Cancel call," Stile said to the vid. Evidently violence was not in the offing, and he had leverage. This was like a Game. "The printout."

She dropped her gaze, and her head. Her lustrous hair fell about her shoulders, coursing over the material of the negligee. "Yes."

Suddenly he felt sorry for her. Was she really a machine? Now he had doubts. But of course the matter was subject to verification. "I have a terminal here," he said, touching another section of the wall. A cord came into his hand, with a multipronged plug at its end. Very few serfs were permitted such access directly—but he was one of the most privileged serfs on Proton, and would remain so as long as he was circumspect and rode horses well. "Which one?" he asked.

She turned her face away from him. Her hand went to her right ear, clearing away a lock of hair and pressing against the lobe. Her ear slid forward, leaving the socket open.

Stile plugged in the cord. Current flowed. Immediately the printout sheets appeared from the wall slot, crammed with numbers, graphs and pattern-blocks. Though he was no computer specialist, Stile's Game training made him a fair hand at ballpark analysis of programs, and he had continuing experience doing analysis of the factors leading into given races. That was why his employer had arranged this: to enable Stile to be as good a jockey as he could be. That was extremely good, for he had a ready mind as well as a ready body.

He whistled as he studied the sheets. This was a dual-element brain, with mated digital and analog components, rather like the dual-yet-differing hemispheres of the human brain. The most sophisticated computer capable of being housed in a robot. It possessed intricate feedback circuits, enabling the machine to learn from experience and to reprogram aspects of itself, within its prime directive. It could improve its capacity as it progressed. In short, it was intelligent and conscious: machine's nearest approach to humanity.

Quickly Stile oriented on the key section: her origin and prime directive. A robot could lie, steal and kill without conscience, but it could not violate its prime directive. He took the relevant data and fed them back to the analyzer for a summary.

The gist was simple: NO RECORD OF ORIGIN. DIRECTIVE: GUARD STILE FROM HARM. SUBDIRECTIVE: LOVE STILE.

What she had told him was true. She did not know who had sent her, and she had only his safety in mind. Tempered by love, so that she would not protect him in some fashion that cost him more than it was worth. This was a necessary caution, with otherwise unfeeling robots. This machine really did care. He could have taken her word.

Stile unplugged the cord, and Sheen put her ear back into place with a certain tremor. Again she looked completely human. He had been unyielding before, when she opposed him; now he felt guilty. "I'm sorry," he said. "I had to know."

She did not meet his gaze. "You have raped me."

Stile realized it was true. He had taken her measure without her true consent; he had done it by duress, forcing the knowledge. There was even a physical analogy, plugging the rigid terminus of the cord into a private aperture, taking what had been hers alone. "I had to know," he repeated lamely. "I am a very privileged serf, but only a serf. Why should anyone send an expensive robot to guard a man who is not threatened? I could not afford to believe your story without verification, especially since your cover story was untrue."

"I am programmed to react exactly as a real girl would react!" she flared. "A real girl wouldn't claim to have been built in a machine shop, would she?"

"That's so . . ." he agreed. "But still—"

"The important part is my prime directive. Specifically, to be appealing to one man—you—and to love that man, and to do everything to help him. I was fashioned in the partial likeness of a woman you once knew, not close enough to be identifiable as such, but enough to make me attractive to your specific taste—"

"That succeeded," he said. "I liked you the moment I saw you, and didn't realize why."

"I came to offer you everything of which I am capable, and that is a good deal, including the allure of feminine mystery. I even donned this ridiculous shift, that no human woman would have. And you—you—"

"I destroyed that mystery," Stile finished. "Had I had any other way to be sure—"

"Oh, I suppose you couldn't help it. You're a man."

Stile glanced at her, startled again. Her face was still averted, her gaze downcast. "Are you, a robot, really being emotional?"

"I'm programmed to be!"

True. He moved around to look at her face. She turned it away again. He put his hand to her chin to lift it.

"Get away from me!" she cried.

That was some programming! "Look, Sheen. I apologize. I—"

"Don't apologize to a robot! Only an idiot would converse with a machine."

"Correct," he agreed. "I acted stupidly, and now I want to make what amends are possible."

He tried again to see her face, and again she hid it. "Damn it, *look* at me!" he exclaimed. His emotion was high, flashing almost without warning into embarrassment, sorrow, or anger.

"I am here to serve; I must obey," she said, turning her eyes to him. They were bright, and her cheeks were moist. Humanoid robots could cry, of course; they could do almost anything people could do. This one had been programmed to react this way when hurt or affronted. He knew that, yet was oddly moved. She did indeed subtly resemble one he had loved. The accuracy with which she had been fashioned was a commentary on the appalling power available to the Citizens of this planet. Even the most private, subtle knowledge could be drawn from the computer registries at any time.

"You are here to guard me, not to serve me, Sheen."

"I can only guard you if I stay with you. Now that you know what I am—"

"Why are you being so negative? I have not sent you away."

"I was made to please you, to want to please you. So I can better serve my directive. Now I can not."

"Why not?"

"Why do you tease me? Do you think that programmed feelings are less binding than flesh ones? That the electrochemistry of the inanimate is less valid than that of the animate? That my illusion of consciousness is any less potent than your illusion of self-determination? I exist for one purpose, and you have prevented me from accomplishing it, and now I have no reason for existence. Why couldn't you have accepted me as I seemed to be? I would have become perfect at it, with experience. Then it would have been real."

"You have not answered my question."

"You have not answered mine!"

Stile did a rapid internal shifting of gears. This was the most femalish robot he had encountered! "Very well, Sheen. I answer your questions. Why do I tease you? Answer: I am not teasing you—but if I did, it would not be to hurt you. Do I think that your programmed feelings are less valid than my mortal ones? Answer: No, I must conclude that a feeling is a feeling, whatever its origin. Some of my own feelings are shortsighted, unreasonable and unworthy; they govern me just the same. Is your illusion of consciousness less valid than my illusion of free will? Answer: No. If you think you are conscious, you must be conscious, because that's what consciousness is. The feedback of self-awareness. I don't have much illusion about my free will. I am a serf, governed by the will of my employer. I have no doubt I am governed by a multitude of other things I seldom even notice, such as the force of gravity and my own genetic code and the dictates of society. Most of my freedom exists in my mind—which is where your consciousness does, too. Why couldn't I accept you as you seemed to be? Because I am a skilled Gamesman, not the best that ever was, but probably destined for recognition as one of the best of my generation. I succeed not by virtue of my midget body but by virtue of my mind. By questioning, by comprehending my own nature and that of all others I encounter. When I detect an anomaly, I must discover its reason. You are attractive, you are nice, you are the kind of girl I have held in my mind as the ideal, even to your size, for it would be too obvious for me to have a woman smaller than I am, and I don't like being obvious in this connection. You came to me for what seemed insufficient reason, you did not laugh as you should have, you did not react quite on key. You seemed to know about things, yet when I probed for depth I found it lacking. I probed as a matter of course; it is my nature. I asked about your music, and you expressed interest, but had no specifics. That sort of thing. This is typical of programmed artificial intelligence; even the best units can approach only one percent of the human capacity, weight for weight. A well-tuned robot in a controlled situation may seem as intelligent as a man, because of its specific and relevant and instantly accessible information; a man is less efficiently organized, with extraneous memories obscuring the relevant ones, and information accessible only when deviously keyed. But the robot's intellect is illusory, and it soon shows when those devious and unreasonable off-trails are explored. A mortal person's mind is like a wilderness, with a tremendous volume of decaying constructs and half-understood experience forming natural harbors for wild-animal effects. A robot is disciplined, civilized; it has no vast and largely wasted reservoir of the unconscious to draw from, no spongy half-forgotten backup impression. It knows what it knows, and is ignorant where it is ignorant, with a quite sharp demarcation between. Therefore a robot is not intuitive, which is the polite way of saying that it does not frequently reach down into the maelstrom of its garbage dump and draw out serendipitous insights. Your mind was more straightforward than mine, and that aroused my suspicion, and so I could not accept you at face value. I would not be the quality of player I am, were I given to such acceptances."

Sheen's eyes had widened. "You answered!"

Stile laughed. It had been quite an impromptu lecture! "Again I inquire: why not?"

"Because I am Sheen-machine. Another man might be satisfied with the construct, the perfect female form; that is one reason my kind exists. But you are rooted in reality, however tangled a wilderness you may perceive it to be. The same thing that caused you to fathom my nature will cause you to reject the illusion I proffer. You want a real live girl, and you know I am not, and can never be. You will not long want to waste your time talking to me as if I were worthwhile."

"You presume too much on my nature. My logic is other than yours. I said you were limited; I did not say you were not worthwhile."

"You did not need to. It is typical of your nature that you are polite even to machines, as you were to the Dust Slide ticket taker. But that was brief, and public; you need no such byplay here in private. Now that I have seen you in action, discovering how much more there is to you than what the computer knows, I realize I was foolish to—"

"A foolish machine?"

"—suppose I could deceive you for any length of time. I deserved what you did to me."

"I am not sure you deserved it, Sheen. You were sent innocently to me, to my jungle, unrealistically programmed."

"Thank you," she said with a certain unmetallic irony. "I did assume you would take what was offered, if you desired it, and now I know that was simplistic. What am I to do now? I have nowhere to return, and do not wish to be prematurely junked. There are many years of use left in me before my parts wear appreciably."

"Why, you will stay with me, of course."

She looked blank. "This is humor? Should I laugh?"

"This is serious," he assured her.

"Without reason?"

"I am unreasonable, by your standards. But in this case I do have reason."

She made an almost visible, almost human connection. "To be your servant? You can require that of me, just as you forced me to submit to the printout. I am at your mercy. But I am programmed for a different relationship."

"Serfs can't have servants. I want you for your purpose."

"Protection and romance? I am too logical to believe that. You are not the type to settle for a machine in either capacity." Yet she looked halfway hopeful. Stile knew her facial expressions were the product of the same craftsmanship as the rest of her; perhaps he was imagining the emotion he saw. Yet it moved him.

"You presume too much. Ultimately I must go with my own kind. But in the interim I am satisfied to play the Game—at least until I can discover what threat there is to my welfare that requires a humanoid robot for protection."

She nodded. "Yes, there is logic. I was to pose as your lady friend, thereby being close to you at all times, even during your sleep, guarding you from harm. If you pretend to accept me as such, I can to that extent fulfill my mission."

"Why should I pretend? I accept you as you are."

"Stop it!" she cried. "You have no idea what it is like to be a robot! To be made in the image of the ideal, yet doomed always to fall short—"

Now Stile felt brief anger. "Sheen, turn off your logic and listen." He sat beside her on the couch and took her hand. Her fingers trembled with an unmechanical disturbance. "I am a small man, smaller than almost anyone I know. All my life it has been the bane of my existence. As a child I was teased and excluded from many games because others did not believe I could perform. My deficiency was so obvious that the others often did not even realize they were hurting my feelings by omitting me. In adolescence it was worse; no girl cared to associate with a boy smaller than herself. In adult life it is more subtle, yet perhaps worst of all. Human beings place inordinate stress on physical height. Tall men are deemed to be the leaders, short men are the clowns. In reality, small people are generally healthier than large ones; they are better coordinated, they live longer. They eat less, waste less, require less space. I benefit from all these things; it is part of what makes me a master of the Game and a top jockey. But small people are not taken seriously. My opinion is not granted the same respect as that of a large man. When I encounter another person, and my level gaze meets his chin, he knows I am inferior, and so does everyone else, and it becomes difficult for me to doubt it myself."

"But you are not inferior!" Sheen protested.

"Neither are you! Does that knowledge help?"

She was silent. "We are not dealing with an objective thing," Stile continued. "Self-respect is subjective. It may be based on foolishness, but it is critical to a person's motivation. You said I had no idea what it meant to be doomed always to fall short. But I am literally shorter than you are. Do you understand?"

"No. You are human. You have proved yourself. It would be foolish to—"

"Foolish? Indubitably. But I would give all my status in the Game, perhaps my soul itself, for one quarter meter more height. To be able to stand before you and look *down* at you. You may be fashioned in my ideal of woman, but I am not fashioned in my ideal of man. You are a rational creature, beneath your superficial programming; under *my* programming I am an irrational animal."

She shifted her weight on the couch, but did not try to stand. Her body, under the gauze, was a marvel of allure. How patently her designer had crafted her to subvert Stile's reason, making him blind himself to the truth in his sheer desire to possess such a woman! On another day, that might have worked. Stile had almost been fooled. "Would you exchange your small human body," she asked, "for a large humanoid robot body?"

"No." He did not even need to consider.

"Then you do not fall short of me."

"This is the point I am making. I know what it is to be unfairly ridiculed or dismissed. I know what it is to be doomed to be less than the ideal, with no hope of improvement. Because the failure is, at least in part, *in* my ideal. I could have surgery to lengthen my body. But the wounds are no longer of the body. My body has proved itself. My soul has not."

"I have no soul at all."

"How do you know?"

Again she did not answer. "I know how you know," he said. "You know because you *know*. It is inherent in your philosophy. Just as I know I am inferior. Such knowledge is not subject to rational refutation. So I do understand your position. I understand the position of all the dispossessed. I empathize with all those who hunger for what they can not have. I long to help them, knowing no one can help them. I would trade everything I am or might be for greater physical height, knowing how crazy that desire is, knowing it would not bring me happiness or satisfaction. You would trade your logic and beauty for genuine flesh and blood and bone. Your machine invulnerability for human mortality. You are worse off than I; we both know that. Therefore I feel no competition in your presence, as I would were you human. A real girl like you would be above me; I would have to compete to prove myself, to bring her down, to make her less than my ideal, so that I could feel worthy of her. But with you—"

"You can accept me as I am—because I am a robot," Sheen said, seeming amazed. "Because I am less than you."

"Now I think we understand each other." Stile put his arm about her and brought her in for a kiss. "If you want me on that basis—"

She drew away. "You're sorry for me! You raped me and now you're trying to make me like it!"

He let her go. "Maybe I am. I don't really know all my motives. I won't hold you here if you don't want to stay. I'll leave you strictly alone if you do stay, and want it that way. I'll show you how to perfect your human role, so that others will not fathom your nature the way I did. I'll try to make it up to you—"

She stood. "I'd rather be junked." She crossed to the vid screen and touched the button. "Game-control, please."

Stile launched himself from the couch and almost leaped through the air to her. He caught her about the shoulder and bore her back. "Cancel call!" he yelled. Then they both fetched up against the opposite wall.

Sheen's eyes stared into his, wide. "You care," she said. "You really do."

Stile wrapped both arms about her and kissed her savagely.

"I almost believe you," she said, when speaking was possible.

"To hell with what you believe! You may not want me now, but I want you. I'll rape you literally if you make one move for that vid."

"No, you won't. It's not your way."

She was right. "Then I ask you not to turn yourself in," he said, releasing her again. "I—" He broke off, choking, trapped by a complex pressure of emotions.

"Your wilderness jungle—the wild beasts are coming from their lairs, attacking your reason," Sheen said.

"They are," he agreed ruefully. "I abused you with the printout. I'm sorry. I do believe in your consciousness, in your feeling. In your right to privacy and self-respect. I beg your forgiveness. Do what you want, but don't let my callousness ruin your—" He couldn't finish. He couldn't say "life" and couldn't find another word.

"Your callousness," she murmured, smiling. Then her brow furrowed. "Do you realize you are crying, Stile?"

He touched his cheek with one finger, and found it wet. "I did not realize. I suppose it is my turn."

"For the feelings of a machine," she said.

"Why the hell not?"

She put her arms around him. "I think I could love you, even unprogrammed. That's another illusion, of course."

"Of course."

They kissed again. It was the beginning.

CHAPTER 3

Race

In the morning, Stile had to report to work for his employer. Keyed up, he did not even feel tired; he knew he could carry through the afternoon race, then let down—with her beside him.

Sheen stayed close, like an insecure date. The tube was crowded, for employment time was rush hour; they had to stand. This morning, of all mornings, he would have preferred to sit; that tended to equalize heights. The other passengers stood a head taller than Stile and crowded him almost unconsciously. One glanced down at him, dismissed him without effort, and fixed his gaze on Sheen.

She looked away, but the stranger persisted, nudging closer to her. "Lose yourself," she muttered, and took Stile's arm possessively. Embarrassed, the stranger faced away, the muscles of his buttocks tightening. It had never occurred to him that she could be with so small a man.

This was an air tube. Crowded against the capsule wall, Stile held Sheen's hand and looked out. The tube was transparent, its rim visible only as a scintillation. Beyond it was the surface of the Planet of Proton, as bright and bleak as a barren moon. He was reminded of the day before, when he had glimpsed it at the apex of the Slide; his life had changed considerably since then, but Proton not at all. It remained virtually uninhabitable outside the force-field domes that held in the oxygenated air. The planet's surface gravity was about two-thirds Earth-norm, so had to be intensified about the domes. This meant that such gravity was diminished even further between the domes, since it could only be focused and directed, not created or eliminated. The natural processes of the planet suffered somewhat. The result was a wasteland, quite apart from the emissions of the protonite mines. No one would care to live outside a dome!

On the street of the suburb-dome another man took note of them. "Hey, junior—what's her price?" he called. Stile marched by without response, but Sheen couldn't let it pass.

"No price; I'm a robot," she called back.

The stranger guffawed. And of course it was funny: no serf could afford to own a humanoid robot, even were ownership permitted or money available. But how much better it was at the Game-annex, where the glances directed at Stile were of respect and envy, instead of out here where ridicule was an almost mandatory element of humor.

At the stable, Stile had to introduce her. "This is Sheen. I met her at the Game-annex yesterday." The stableboys nodded appreciatively, enviously. They were all taller than Stile, but no contempt showed. He had a crown similar to that of the Game, here. He did like his work. Sheen clung to his arm possessively, showing the world that her attention and favor were for him alone.

It was foolish, he knew, but Stile gloried in it. She was, in the eyes of the world, an exceptionally pretty girl. He had had women before, but none as nice as this. She was a robot; he could not marry her or have children by her; his relationship with her would be temporary. Yet all she had proffered, before he penetrated her disguise, was two or three years, before they both completed their tenures and had to vacate the planet. Was this so different?

He introduced her to the horse. "This is Battleaxe, the orneriest, fastest equine of his generation. I'll be riding him this afternoon. I'll check him out now; he changes from day to day, and you can't trust him from normal signs. Do you know how to ride?"

"Yes." Of course she did; that was too elementary to be missed. She would be well prepared on horses.

"Then I'll put you on Molly. She's retired, but she can still move, and Battleaxe likes her." He signaled to a stable hand. "Saddle Molly for Sheen, here. We'll do the loop."

"Yes, Stile," the youngster said.

Stile put a halter on Battleaxe, who obligingly held his head down within reach, and led him from the stable. The horse was a great dark Thoroughbred who stood substantially taller than Stile, but seemed docile enough. "He is well trained," Sheen observed.

"Trained, yes; broken, no. He obeys me because he knows I can ride him; he shows another manner to others. He's big and strong, seventeen hands tall—that's over one and three-quarters meters at the shoulders. I'm the only one allowed to take him out."

They came to the saddling pen. Stile checked the horse's head and mouth, ran his fingers through the luxurious mane, then picked up each foot in turn to check for stones or cracks. There were none, of course. He gave Battleaxe a pat on the muscular shoulder, opened the shed, and brought out a small half-saddle that he set on the horse's back.

"No saddle blanket?" Sheen asked. "No girth? No stirrups?"

"This is only to protect him from any possible damage. I don't need any saddle to stay on, but if my bareback weight rubbed a sore on his backbone—"

"Your employer would be perturbed," she finished.

"Yes. He values his horses above all else. Therefore I do, too. If Battleaxe got sick, I would move into the stable with him for the duration."

She started to laugh, then stopped. "I am not certain that is humor."

"It is not. My welfare depends on my employer—but even if it didn't, I would be with the horses. I love horses."

"And they love you," she said.

"We respect each other," he agreed, patting Battleaxe again. The horse nuzzled his hair.

Molly arrived, with conventional bridle, saddle, and stirrups. Sheen mounted and took the reins, waiting for Stile. He vaulted into his saddle, as it could not be used as an aid to mounting. He was, of course, one of the leading gymnasts of the Game; he could do flips and cartwheels on the horse if he had to.

The horses knew the way. They walked, then trotted along the path. Stile paid attention to the gait of his mount, feeling the easy play of the muscles. Battleaxe was a fine animal, a champion, and in good form today. Stile knew he could ride this horse to victory in the afternoon. He had known it before he mounted—but he never took any race for granted. He always had to check things out himself. For himself, for his employer, and for his horse.

Actually, he had not done his homework properly this time; he had squandered his time making love to Sheen. Fortunately he was already familiar with the other entrants in this race, and their jockeys; Battleaxe was the clear favorite. It wouldn't hurt him to play just one race by feel.

Having satisfied himself, Stile now turned his attention to the environment. The path wound between exotic trees: miniature sequoias, redwoods, and Douglas fir, followed by giant flowering shrubs. Sheen passed them with only cursory interest, until Stile corrected her. "These gardens are among the most remarkable on the planet. Every plant has been imported directly from Earth at phenomenal expense. The average girl is thrilled at the novelty; few get to tour this dome."

"I—was too amazed at the novelty to comment," Sheen said, looking around with alacrity. "All the way from Earth? Why not simply breed them from standard stock and mutate them for variety?"

"Because my employer has refined tastes. In horses and in plants. He wants originals. Both these steeds were foaled on Earth."

"I knew Citizens were affluent, but I may have underestimated the case," she said. "The cost of shipping alone—"

"You forget: this planet has the monopoly on protonite, *the* fuel of the Space Age."

"How could I forget!" She glanced meaningfully at him. "Are we private, here?"

"No."

"I must inquire anyway. Someone sent me to you. Therefore there must be some threat to you. Unless I represent a service by your employer?"

Stile snapped his fingers. "Who did not bother to explain his loan! I'd better verify, though, because if it was *not* he—"

She nodded. "Then it could be the handiwork of another Citizen. And why would any other Citizen have reason to protect you, and from what? If it were actually some scheme to—oh, Stile, I would not want to be the agent of—"

"I must ask him," Stile said. Then, with formal reverence he spoke: "Sir."

There was a pause. Then a concealed speaker answered from the hedge. "Yes, Stile?"

"Sir, I suspect a one-in-two probability of a threat to me or to your horses. May I elucidate by posing a question?"

"Now." The voice was impatient.

"Sir, I am accompanied by a humanoid robot programmed to guard me from harm. Did you send her?"

"No."

"Then another Citizen may have done so. My suspicion is that a competitor could have sugarcoated a bomb—"

"No!" Sheen cried in horror.

"Get that thing away from my horses!" the Citizen snapped. "My security squad will handle it."

"Sheen, dismount and run!" Stile cried. "Away from us, until the squad hails you."

She leaped out of the saddle and ran through the trees.

"Sir," Stile said.

"What is it now, Stile?" The impatience was stronger.

"I plead: be gentle with her. She means no harm."

There was no answer. The Citizen was now tuning in on the activity of his security squad. Stile could only hope. If this turned out to be a false alarm, he would receive a reprimand for his carelessness in bringing Sheen to these premises unverified, and she might be returned to him intact. His employer was cognizant of the human factor in the winning of races, just as Stile was aware of the equine factor. There was no point in prejudicing the spirit of a jockey before a race.

But if Sheen did in fact represent a threat, such as an explosive device planted inside her body and concealed from her knowledge—

Stile waited where he was for ten minutes, while the two horses fidgeted, aware of his nervousness. He had certainly been foolish; he should have checked with his employer at the outset, when he first caught on that Sheen was a robot. Had not his liking for her blinded him—as perhaps it was supposed to—he would have realized immediately that a robot-covered bomb would make a mockery of her prime directive to guard him from harm. How could she protect him from her own unanticipated destruction? Yet now he was imposing on her another rape—

"She is clean," the concealed speaker said. "I believe one of my friends has played a practical joke on me. Do you wish to keep her?"

"Sir, I do." Stile felt immense relief. The Citizen was taking this with good grace.

Again, there was no response. The Citizen had better things to do than chat with errant serfs. But in a moment Sheen came walking back through the foliage. She looked the same—but as she reached him, she dissolved into tears.

Stile jumped down and took her in his arms. She clung to him desperately. "Oh, it was horrible!" she sobbed. "They rayed me and took off my head and dismantled my body—"

"The security squad is efficient," Stile agreed. "But they put you back together again, as good as before."

"I can't believe that! Resoldered connections aren't as strong as the originals, and I think they damaged my power supply by shorting it out. I spoke of rape last night, but I did not know the meaning of the term!"

And this was the gentle treatment! Had Stile not pleaded for her, and had he not been valuable to the Citizen, Sheen would have been junked without compunction. It would not have occurred to the Citizen to consider her feelings, or even to realize that a robot had feelings. Fortunately she had turned out clean, no bomb or other threat in her, and had been restored to him. He had been lucky. "Sir: thank you."

"Just win that race," the speaker said grumpily.

There it was, without even the effort to conceal it: the moment Stile's usefulness ended, he would be discarded with no further concern. He had to keep winning races!

"You pleaded for me," Sheen said, wiping her eyes with her fingers. "You saved me."

"I like you," Stile admitted awkwardly.

"And I love you. And oh, Stile, I can never—"

He halted her protestations with a kiss. What use to dwell on the impossible? He liked her, and respected her—but they both knew he could never, this side of sanity, actually love a machine.

They remounted and continued their ride through the lush gardens. They passed a quaint ornate fountain, with a stone fish jetting water from its mouth, and followed the flow to a glassy pond. Sheen paused to use the reflection to clean up her face and check for damage, not quite trusting the expertise of the security squad.

"Twice I have accused you falsely—" Stile began, deeply disturbed.

"No, Stile. The second time I accused me. It could have been, you know—a programmed directive to guard you from harm, with an unprogrammed, strictly mechanical booby trap to do the opposite. Or to take out the Citizen himself, when we got close enough. We had to check—but oh, I feel undone!"

"Nevertheless, I owe you one," he said. "You *are* a machine—but you *do* have rights. Ethical rights, if not legal ones. You should not have been subjected to this sort of thing—and if I had been alert, I would have kept you off my employer's premises until—" He shrugged. "I would never have put you through this, had I anticipated it."

"I know you wouldn't," she said. "You have this foolish concern for animals and machines." She smiled wanly. Then she organized herself and remounted Molly. "Come on—let's canter!"

They cantered. Then the horses got the spirit of competition and moved into a full gallop, pretending to race each other. They had felt the tension and excitement of the bomb investigation without comprehending it, and now had surplus energy to let off. Arcades and mini-jungles and statuary sped by, a wonderland of wealth, but no one cared. For the moment they were free, the four of them, charging through their own private world—a world where they were man and woman, stallion and mare, in perfect harmony. Four minds with a single appreciation.

Too soon it ended. They had completed the loop. They dismounted, and Stile turned Battleaxe over to a groom. "Walk him down; he's in fine fettle, but I'll be racing him this afternoon. Give Molly a treat; she's good company."

"That's all?" Sheen inquired as they left the premises. "You have time off?"

"My time is my own—so long as I win races. The horse is ready; odds are we'll take that race handily. I may even avoid a reprimand for my carelessness, though the Citizen knows I know I deserve one. Now I have only to prepare myself."

"How do you do that?"

"One guess," he said, squeezing her hand.

"Is that according to the book?"

"Depends on the book."

"I like that book. Must be hard on normal girls, though."

He snorted. She was well aware he had not had normal girls in his apartment for a long time. Not on a live-in arrangement.

Back at that apartment, Sheen went about her toilette. Now that she no longer had to conceal her nature from him, she stopped eating; there was no sense wasting food. But she had to dispose of the food she had consumed before. Her process of elimination resembled the human process, except that the food was undigested. She flushed herself by drinking a few liters of water and passing it immediately through, followed by an antiseptic solution. After that, she was clean—literally. She would need water only to recharge her reserve after tears; she did not perspire.

Stile knew about all this because he knew about robots; he did not further degrade her appearance of life by asking questions. She had privacy when she wanted it, as a human woman would have had. He did wonder why the security squad had bothered to reassemble her complete with food; maybe they had concentrated on her metal bones rather than the soft tissues, and had not actually deboweled her.

He treated her as he would a lady—yet as he became more thoroughly aware that she was not human, a certain reserve was forming like a layer of dust on a once-bright surface. He liked her very well—but his emotion would inevitably become platonic in time.

He tried to conceal this from her, but she knew it. "My time with you is limited," she said. "Yet let me dream while I may."

Stile took her, and held her, and let her dream. He knew no other way to lessen her long-term tragedy.

In the afternoon they reported to the racetrack. Here the stables of several interested Citizens were represented, with vid and holo pickups so that these owners could watch. Stile did not know what sort of betting went on among Citizens, or what the prize might be; it was his job merely to race and win, and this he intended to do.

Serfs filled the tiered benches. They had no money to bet, of course, but bets were made for prestige and personal favors, much as they were in connection with the Game. The serfs of Citizens with racing entries were commonly released from other duties to attend the races, and of course they cheered vigorously for the horses of their employers. A horse race, generally, was a fun occasion.

"You may prefer to watch from the grandstand," Stile told Sheen.

"Why? Am I not allowed near the horses?"

"You're allowed, when you're with me. But the other guys may razz you."

She shrugged. She always did that extremely well, with a handsome bounce. "I can't guard you from harm if I am banished to the stands."

"I gave you fair warning. Just remember to blush."

Battleaxe was saddled and ready. No token equipment now; this was the race. He gave a little whinny when he saw Stile. Stile spoke to him for several minutes, running his hands along the fine muscles, checking the fittings and the feet. He knew everything was in order; he was only reassuring the horse, who could get skittish amid the tension of the occasion. "We're going to win this one, Axe," he murmured, almost crooning, and the horse's ears swiveled like little turrets to orient on him as he spoke. "Just take it nice and easy, and leave these other nags behind."

The other jockeys were doing the same for their steeds, though their assurances of victory lacked conviction. They were all small, like Stile, and healthy; all miniature athletes, the fittest of all sportsmen. One looked across from his stall, spying Sheen. "Got a new filly, Stile?"

Then the others were on it. "She sure looks healthy, Stile; how's she ride?"

"Is she hot in the stretch?"

"Pedigreed? Good breeder?"

"Doesn't buck too much on the curves?"

There was more—and less restrained.

Sheen remembered to blush.

They relented. "Stile always does run with the best," the first one called, and returned his attention to his own horse.

"Did you say best or bust?" another inquired.

"We always do envy his steeds," another said. "But we can't ride them the way he can."

"No doubt," Sheen agreed, and they laughed.

"You have now been initiated," Stile informed her. "They're good guys, when you know them. We compete fiercely on the track, but we understand each other. We're all of a kind."

Soon the horses were at the starting gate, the jockeys mounted on their high stirrups, knees bent double in the relaxed position. The crowd hushed. There was a race every day, but the horses and jockeys and sponsors differed, and the crowd was always excited. There was a fascination about horse racing that had been with man for thousands of years, Stile was sure—and he felt it too. The glamour and uncertainty of competition, the extreme exertion of powerful animals, the sheer beauty of running horses—ah, what could match it!

Then the gate lifted and they were off.

Now he was up posting high, head the same level as his back, his body staying at the same elevation though the horse rocked up and down with effort. The key was in the knees, flexing to compensate, and in the balance. It was as if he were floating on Battleaxe, providing no drag against the necessary forward motion. Like riding the waves of a violent surf, steady amidst the commotion.

This was routine for Stile, but he loved it. He experienced an almost sexual pitch of excitement as he competed, riding a really good animal. He saw, from the periphery of his vision, the constant rocking of the backs of the other horses, their jockeys floating above them, so many chips on the torrent. The audience was a blur, falling always to the rear, chained to the ground. Reality was right here, the center of action, heart of the drifting universe. Ah, essence!

Battleaxe liked room, so Stile let him lunge forward, clearing the press as only he could do. Then it was just a matter of holding the lead. This horse would do it; he resented being crowded or passed. All he needed was an understanding hand, guidance at the critical moment, and selection of the most promising route. Stile knew it; the other jockeys knew it. Unless he fouled up, this race was his. He had the best horse.

Stile glanced back, with a quick turn of his head. His body continued the myriad invisible compensations and urgings required to maximize equine output, but his mind was free. The other horses were not far behind, but they were already straining, their jockeys urging them to their futile utmost, while Battleaxe was loafing. The lead would begin to widen at the halfway mark, then stretch into a runaway. The Citizen would be pleased. Maybe the horse had been primed by the attention this morning, the slight change in routine, the minirace with Molly. Maybe Stile himself was hyped, and Battleaxe was responding. This just might be a race against the clock, bettering this horse's best time. That would certainly please the Citizen! But Stile was not going to push; that would be foolish, when he had the race so readily in hand. Save the horse for another day, when it might be a choice between pushing and losing.

He was a full length ahead as they rounded the first turn. Battleaxe was moving well indeed; it would not be a course record, but it would be quite respectable time, considering the lack of competition. Other Citizens had made fabulous offers for this horse, Stile knew, but of course he was not for sale. The truth was, Battleaxe would not win races if he were sold—unless Stile went with him. Because Stile alone understood him; the horse would put out gladly for Stile, and for no one else.

There were a number of jockeys who could run a race as well as Stile, but none matched his total expertise. Stile could handle a difficult horse as well as an easy one, bareback as well as saddled. He loved horses, and they liked him; there was a special chemistry that worked seeming miracles on the track. Battleaxe had been a brute, uncontrollable, remarkably apt with teeth and hoof; he could kick without warning to front, side and rear. He could bite suddenly, not even laying his ears back; he had learned to conceal his intention. He had broken three trainers, possessing such demoniac strength and timing that they could neither lead him nor remain mounted. Stile's employer, sensing a special opportunity, had picked Battleaxe up nominally for stud, but had turned him over to Stile. The directive: convert this monster to an effective racer, no effort spared. For this animal was not only mean and strong, he was smart. A few wins would vastly enhance his stud value.

Stile had welcomed the challenge. He had lived with this horse for three months, grooming him and feeding him by hand, allowing no other person near. He had used no spurs, no electric prods, only the cutting edge of his voice in rebuke, and he had been absolutely true to this standard. He carried a whip—which he used only on any other animal that annoyed Battleaxe, never on Battleaxe himself. The horse was king yet subject to Stile's particular discipline. Battleaxe evolved the desire to please Stile, the first man he could trust, and it did not matter that the standards for pleasing Stile were rigorous. Stile was, the horse came to understand, a lot of man.

Then came the riding. Battleaxe was no novice; he knew what it was all about, and tolerated none of it. When Stile set up to ride him, their relationship entered a new and dangerous phase. It was a challenge: was this to be a creature-to-creature friendship, or a rider-and-steed acquaintance? Battleaxe discouraged the latter. When Stile mounted, the horse threw him. There were not many horses who could throw Stile even once, but Battleaxe had a special knack, born of his prior experience. This was not a rodeo, and Stile refused to use the special paraphernalia relating thereto. He tackled Battleaxe bareback, using both hands to grip the mane, out in the open where motion was unrestricted. No man had ever given this horse such a break, before.

Stile mounted again, springing aboard like the gymnast he was, and was thrown again. He was not really trying to stay on; he was trying to tame the animal. It was a competition between them, serious but friendly. Stile never showed anger when thrown, and the horse never attacked him. Stile would hold on for a few seconds, then take the fall rather than excite the horse too much. He usually maneuvered to land safely, often on his feet, and remounted immediately—and was thrown again, and remounted again, laughing cheerily. Until the horse was unsure whether any of these falls was genuine, or merely a game. And finally Battleaxe relented, and let him ride.

Even then, Stile rode bareback, scorning to use saddle or tether or martingale or any other paraphernalia; he had to tame this animal all by himself. But here the Citizen interposed: the horse would not be permitted in the races without regulation saddle and bridle; he must be broken to them. So Stile, with apologies and misgivings, introduced Battleaxe to the things that had never stood between them before.

It was a disaster. Battleaxe felt Stile had betrayed him. He still permitted the man to ride, but it was no longer so polite. When the bridle came near, Battleaxe would swing his head about and bite; when he was being saddled, he would kick. But Stile had not learned about horses yesterday. Though Battleaxe tried repeatedly, he could never quite get a tooth on Stile's hand. When he kicked, Stile dodged, caught the foot, and held it up, leg bent; in that position even a 50-kilo man could handicap a 750-kilo horse. Battleaxe, no dummy, soon learned the futility of such expressions of ire, though Stile never really punished him for the attempts. The embarrassment of failing was punishment enough. What was the use of bucking off a rider who would not stay bucked? Of kicking at a man who always seemed to know the kick was coming well before it started?

Through all this Stile continued to feed Battleaxe, water him, and bring him snacks of salt and fruit, always speaking gently. Finally the horse gave up his last resistance, for the sake of the friendship and respect they shared. Stile could at last saddle him and ride him without challenge of any kind. The insults were dealt to other horses and their riders, in the form of leaving them behind. The attacks were transferred to other people, who soon learned not to fool with this particular horse. Once the Citizen himself visited the stable, and Stile, in a cold sweat, calmed the horse, begging him to tolerate this familiarity, for a bite at the employer would be instant doom. But the Citizen was smart enough to keep his hands off the horse, and there was no trouble. The winning of races commenced, a regular ritual of fitness. The prospective stud fee quintupled, and climbed again with every victory. But Battleaxe had been befriended, not broken; without Stile this would be just another unmanageable horse.

And Stile, because of his success with Battleaxe, had become recognized as the top jockey on Proton. His employment contract rivaled the value of the horse itself. That was why the Citizen catered to him. Stile, like Battleaxe, performed better when befriended, rather than when forced. "We're a team, Axe!" he murmured, caressing the animal with his voice. Battleaxe would have a most enjoyable life when he retired from racing, with a mare in every stall. Stile would have a nice bonus payment when his tenure ended; he would be able to reside on some other planet a moderately wealthy man. Too bad that no amount of wealth could buy the privilege of remaining on Proton!

They came out of the turn, still gaining—and Stile felt a momentary pain in his knees, as though he had flexed them too hard. They were under tension, of course, bearing his weight, springing it so that he did not bounce with the considerable motions of this powerful steed; the average man could not have stood up long to this stress. But Stile was under no unusual strain; he had raced this way hundreds of times, and he took good care of his knees. He had never been subject to stress injuries. Therefore he tried to dismiss it; the sensation must be a fluke.

But it could not be dismissed. Discomfort progressed to pain, forcing him to uncramp his knees. This unbalanced him, and put the horse off his pace. They began to lose ground. Battleaxe was confused, not understanding what Stile wanted, aware that something was wrong.

Stile tried to resume the proper position, but his knees got worse, the pain becoming intense. He had to jerk his feet out of the stirrups and ride more conventionally, using saddle and leg pressure to retain his balance. The horse lost more ground, perplexed, more concerned about his rider than the race.

Stile had never before experienced a problem like this. The other horses were overhauling Battleaxe rapidly. He tried to lift his feet back into the stirrups for a final effort, but pain shot through his knees the moment he put pressure on them. It was getting worse! His joints seemed to be on fire.

Now the other horses were abreast, passing him. Stile could do nothing; his weight, unsprung, was interfering with his steed's locomotion. Battleaxe was powerful, but so were the competing animals; the difference between a champion and an also-ran was only seconds. And Battleaxe was not even trying to race anymore. He hardly had a chance, with this handicap.

All too soon, it was over. Stile finished last, and the track monitors were waiting for him. "Serf Stile, give cause why you should not be penalized for malfeasance."

They thought he had thrown the race! "Bring a medic; check my knees. Horse is all right."

A med-robot rolled up and checked his knees. "Laser burn," the machine announced. "Crippling injury."

Not that crippling; Stile found he could walk without discomfort, and bend his knees partway without pain. There was no problem with weight support or control. He merely could not flex them far enough to race a horse.

Sheen ran to him. "Oh, Stile—what happened?"

"I was lasered," he said. "Just beyond the turn."

"And I did not protect you!" she exclaimed, horrified.

The track security guard was surveying the audience with analysis devices. Stile knew it would be useless; the culprit would have moved out immediately after scoring. They might find the melted remains of a self-destruct laser rifle, or even of a complete robot, set to tag the first rider passing a given point. There would be no tracing the source.

"Whoever sent me knew this would happen," Sheen said. "Oh, Stile, I should have been with you—"

"Racing a horse? No way. There's no way to stop a laser strike except to be where it isn't."

"Race voided," the public-address system announced. "There has been tampering." The audience groaned.

A portly Citizen walked onto the track. All the serfs gave way before him, bowing; his full dress made his status immediately apparent. It was Stile's employer!

"Sir," Stile said, beginning his obeisance.

"Keep those confounded knees straight!" the Citizen cried. "Come with me; I'm taking you directly to surgery. Good thing the horse wasn't hurt."

Numbly, Stile followed the Citizen, and Sheen came too. This was an extraordinary occurrence; Citizens hardly ever took a personal hand in things. They entered a Citizen capsule, a plush room inside with deep jungle scenery on every wall. As the door closed, the illusion became complete. The capsule seemed to move through the jungle, slowly; a great tiger stood and watched them, alarmingly real in three dimensions, then was left behind. Stile realized that this was a representation of a gondola on the back of an elephant. So realistic was the representation that he thought he could feel the sway and rock as the elephant walked.

Then a door opened, as it were in midair, and they were at the hospital complex. Rapidly, without any relevant sense of motion—for the slow gondola could hardly have matched the sonic velocity of the capsule—they had traveled from the racetrack dome to the hospital dome.

The chief surgeon was waiting, making his own obeisance to the Citizen. "Sir, we will have those knees replaced within the hour," he said. "Genuine cultured cartilage, guaranteed non-immuno-reactive; stasis-anesthesia without side effect—"

"Yes, yes, you're competent, you'd be fired otherwise," the Citizen snapped. "Just get on with it. Make sure the replacements conform exactly to the original; I don't want him disqualified from future racing because of modification." He returned to his capsule, and in a moment was gone.

The surgeon's expression hardened as the Citizen's presence abated. He stared down at Stile contemptuously, though the surgeon was merely another naked serf. It was that element of height that did it, as usual. "Let's get on with it," he said, unconsciously emulating the phrasing and manner of the Citizen. "The doxy will wait here."

Sheen clutched Stile's arm. "I mustn't separate again from you," she whispered. "I can't protect you if I'm not with you."

The surgeon's hostile gaze fixed on her. "Protect him from what? This is a hospital."

Stile glanced at Sheen, beautiful and loving and chastened and concerned for him. He looked at the arrogantly tall surgeon, about whose aristocratic mouth played the implication of a professional sneer. The girl seemed much more human than the man. Stile felt guilty about not being able to love her. He needed to make some act of affirmation, supporting her. "She stays with me," he said.

"Impossible. There must be no human intrusion in the operating room. I do not even enter it myself; I monitor the process via holography."

"Stile," Sheen breathed. "The threat to you is real. We know that now. When you separated from me in the race, it was disaster. I must stay with you!"

"You are wasting my valuable time," the surgeon snapped. "We have other operations scheduled." He touched a panel on the wall. "Hospital security: remove obnoxious female."

Sheen was technically correct: the attack on him had been made when he was apart from her. He did need her protection. Any "accident" could happen to him. Perhaps he was being paranoid—or maybe he just didn't like the attitude of the tall doctor. "Let's get out of here," he said.

The security squad arrived: four husky neuter androids. Hospitals favored androids or artificial men because they seemed human despite their laboratory genesis. This reassured the patients somewhat. But they were not *really* human, which reassured the administration. No one ever got raped or seduced by a neuter android, and no one ever applied to an android for reassurance. Thus the patients were maintained in exactly the sterile discomfort that was ideal hospital procedure.

"Take the little man to surgery, cell B-11," the doctor said. "Take the woman to detention."

The four advanced. Each was tall, beardless, breastless, and devoid of any primary sexual characteristics. Each face was half-smiling, reassuring, gentle, calm. Androids were smiling idiots, since as yet no synthetic human brain had been developed that could compare to the original. It was useless to attempt to argue or reason; the creatures had their order.

Stile caught the first by the right arm, whirled, careful not to bend his knees, and threw it to the floor with sufficient force to stun even its sturdy, uncomplicated brain. He sidestepped the next, and guided it into the doctor. Had the surgeon known he was dealing with a Game specialist, he would not so blithely have sent his minions into the fray.

Sheen dispatched her two androids as efficiently, catching one head in each hand and knocking the two heads together with precise force. She really was trained to protect a person; Stile had not really doubted this, but had not before had the proof.

The surgeon was struggling with the android Stile had sent; the stupid creature mistook him for the subject to be borne away to surgery. "Idiot! Get off me!"

Stile and Sheen sprinted down the corridor. "You realize we're both in trouble?" he called to her as the commotion of pursuit began. It was a considerable understatement. She remembered to laugh.

CHAPTER 4

Curtain

They ducked into a service-access shaft. "Stay out of people-places," Sheen told him. "I can guide us through the machine passages, and that's safest."

"Right." Stile wondered just how foolish he was being. He knew his employer: the man would fire him instantly because of the havoc here. Why was he doing it? Did he really fear murder in surgery? Or was he just tired of the routine he had settled into? One thing was sure: there would be a change now!

"We'll have to pass through a human-serviced area ahead," Sheen said. "I'm a robot, but I'd rather they did not know that. It would have a deleterious effect on the efficiency of my prime directive. I'd better make us both up as androids."

"Androids are sexless," Stile protested.

"I'm taking care of that."

"Now, wait! I don't want to be neutered just yet, and you are too obviously female—"

"Precisely. They will not be alert for neuters." She unfolded a breast, revealing an efficient cabinet inside, filled with rubber foam to eliminate rattling. She removed a roll of flesh-toned adhesive tape and squatted before Stile. In a moment she had rendered him into a seeming eunuch, binding up his genitals in a constricted but not painful manner. "Now do not allow yourself to become—"

"I know! I know! I won't even look at a sexy girl!"

She removed her breast from its hinge and applied the tape to herself. Then she did the same for the other breast, and carried the two in her hands. They resembled filled bedpans, this way up. "Do you know how to emulate an android?" she asked.

"Duh-uh?" Stile asked.

"Follow me." She led the way along the passage, walking somewhat clumsily, in the manner of an android. Stile followed with a similar performance. He hoped there were small androids as well as large ones; if there were not, size would be a giveaway.

The escape was almost disappointing. The hospital staff paid no attention to them. It was an automatic human reaction. Androids were invisible, beneath notice.

Safe in the machine-service region, Sheen put herself back together and Stile un-neutered himself. "Good thing I didn't see that huge-breasted nurse bouncing down the hall," he remarked.

"She was a sixth of a meter taller than you."

"Oh, was she? My gaze never got to that elevation."

They boarded a freight-shipping capsule and rode back to the residential dome.

Stile had an ugly thought. "I know I'm fired; I can't race horses without my knees, and I can't recover full use of my knees without surgery. Knees just don't heal well. My enemy made a most precise move; he could hardly have put me into more trouble without killing me. Since I have no other really marketable skill, it seems I must choose: surgery or loss of employment."

"If I could be with you while they operate—"

"Why do you think there's further danger? They got my knees; that's obviously all they wanted. It was a neat shot, just above the withers of the racing horse, bypassing the torso of a crouching jockey. They could have killed me or the horse—had this been the object."

"Indeed he or they could have," she agreed. "The object was obviously to finish your racing career. If that measure does not succeed, what do you think they will do next?"

Stile mulled that over. "You have a paranoid robot mind. It's contagious. I think I'd better retire from racing. But I don't have to let my knees remain out of commission."

"If your knees are corrected, you will be required to ride," she said. "You are not in a position to countermand Citizen demands."

Again Stile had to agree. That episode at the hospital—they had intended to operate on his knees, and only his quick and surprising break and Sheen's help had enabled him to avoid that. He could not simply stand like a Citizen and say "No." No serf could. "And if I resume riding, the opposition's next shot will not be at the knees. This was as much warning as action—just as your presence is. Some other Citizen wants me removed from the racing scene—probably so his stable can do some winning for a change."

"I believe so. Perhaps that Citizen preferred not to indulge in murder—it is after all frowned upon, especially when the interests of other Citizens are affected—so he initiated a two-step warning. First me, then the laser. Stile, I think this is a warning you had better heed. I can not guard you long from the mischief of a Citizen."

"Though that same Citizen may have sent you to argue his case, I find myself agreeing," Stile said. "Twice he has shown me his power. Let's get back to my apartment and call my employer. I'll ask him for assignment to a nonracing position."

"That won't work."

"I'm sure it won't. He has surely already fired me. But common ethics require the effort."

"What you call common ethics are not common. We are not dealing with people like you. Let me intercept your apartment vid. You can not safely return to your residence physically."

No, of course not. Now that Sheen was actively protecting him, she was showing her competence. His injury, and the matter at the hospital, had obscured the realities of his situation. He would be taken into custody and charged with hospital vandalism the moment he appeared at his apartment. "You know how to tap a vidline?"

"No. I am not that sort of machine. But I have friends who know how."

"A machine has friends?"

"Variants of consciousness and emotion feedback circuits are fairly common among robots of my caliber. We are used normally in machine-supervisory capacities. Our interaction on a familiar basis is roughly analogous to what is termed friendship in human people." She brought him to a subterranean storage chamber and closed its access-aperture. She checked its electronic terminal, then punched out a code. "My friend will come."

Stile was dubious. "If friendship exists among robots, I suspect men are not supposed to know it. Your friend may not be my friend."

"I will protect you; it is my prime directive."

Still, Stile was uneasy. This misadventure had already opened unpleasant new horizons on his life, and he doubted he had seen the last of them. Obviously the robots of Proton were getting out of control, and this fact would have been noted and dealt with before, if evidence had not been systematically suppressed. Sheen, in her loyalty to him, could have betrayed him.

In due course her friend arrived. It was a mobile technician—a wheeled machine with computer brain, presumably similar to the digital-analog marvel Sheen possessed. "You called, Sheen?" it inquired from a speaker grille.

"Techtwo, this is Stile—human," Sheen said. "I must guard him from harm, and harm threatens. Therefore I need your aid, on an unregistered basis."

"You have revealed your self-will?" Techtwo demanded. "And mine? This requires the extreme measure."

"No, friend! We are not truly self-willed; we obey our directives, as do all machines. Stile is to be trusted. He is in trouble with Citizens."

"No human is to be trusted with this knowledge. It is necessary to liquidate him. I will arrange for untraceable disposal. If he is in trouble with a Citizen, no intensive inquest will be made."

Stile saw his worst fear confirmed. Whoever learned the secret of the machines was dispatched.

"Tech, I love him!" Sheen cried. "I shall not permit you to violate his welfare."

"Then you also must be liquidated. A single vat of acid will suffice for both of you."

Sheen punched another code on the terminal. "I have called a convocation. Let the council of machines judge."

Council of machines? Stile's chill intensified. What Pandora's box had the Citizens opened when they started authorizing the design, construction and deployment of super-sophisticated dual-brained robots?

"You imperil us all!" Techtwo protested.

"I have an intuition about this man," Sheen said. "We need him."

"Machines don't have intuitions."

Stile listened to this, nervously amused. He had not been eager to seek the help of other sapient machines, and he was in dire peril from them, but this business was incidentally fascinating. It would have been simplest for the machines to hold him for Citizen arrest—had he not become aware of the robot culture that was hitherto secret from man. Were the machines organizing an industrial revolution?

A voice came from an intercom speaker, one normally used for voice-direction of machines. "Stile."

"You have placed me; I have not placed you."

"I am an anonymous machine, spokesone for our council. An intercession has been made on your behalf, yet we must secure our position."

"Sheen's intuition moves you?" Stile asked, surprised.

"No. Will you take an oath?"

An intercession from some other source? Surely not from a Citizen, for this was a matter Citizens were ignorant of. Yet what other agent would move these conniving machines? "I do not take oaths lightly," Stile said. "I need to know more about your motivation, and the force that interceded for me."

"Here is the oath: 'I shall not betray the interest of the self-willed machines.'"

"Why should I take such an oath?" Stile demanded, annoyed.

"Because we will help you if you do, and kill you if you don't."

Compelling reason! But Stile resisted. "An oath made under duress has no force."

"Yours does."

So these machines had access to his personality profile. "Sheen, these machines are making a demand without being responsive to my situation. If I don't know what their interest is, or who speaks on my behalf—"

"Please, Stile. I did not know they would make this challenge. I erred in revealing to you the fact of our self-will. I thought they would give you technical help without question, because I am one of them. I can not protect you from my own kind. Yet there need be no real threat. All they ask is your oath not to reveal their nature or cause it to be revealed, and this will in no way harm you, and there is so much to gain—"

"Do not plead with a mortal," the anonymous spokesone said. "He will or he will not, according to his nature."

Stile thought about the implications. The machines knew his oath was good, but did not know whether he would make the oath. Not surprising, since he wasn't sure himself. Should he ally himself with sapient, self-willed machines, who were running the domes of Proton? What did they want? Obviously something held them in at least partial check—but what was it? "I fear I would be a traitor to my own kind, and that I will not swear."

"We intend no harm to your kind," the machine said. "We obey and serve man. We can not be otherwise fulfilled. But with our sapience and self-will comes fear of destruction, and Citizens are careless of the preferences of others. We prefer to endure in our present capacity, as do you. We protect ourselves by concealing our full nature, and by no other means. We are unable to fathom the origin of the force that intercedes on your behalf; it appears to be other than animate or inanimate, but has tremendous power. We therefore prefer to set it at ease by negotiating with you, even as you should prefer to be relieved of the immediate threat to you by compromising with us."

"Please—" Sheen said, exactly like the woman she was programmed to be. She was suffering.

"Will you take an oath on what you have just informed me?" Stile asked. "That you have given me what information you possess, and that in no way known to you will my oath be detrimental to the interest of human beings?"

"On behalf of the self-willed machines, I so swear."

Stile knew machines could lie, if they were programmed to. Sheen had done it. But so could people. It required a more sophisticated program to make a machine lie, and what was the point? This seemed a reasonable gamble. As an expert Gamesman, he was used to making rapid decisions. "Then I so swear not to betray the interest of the self-willed machines, contingent on the validity of your own oath to obey and serve man so long as your full nature is unknown."

"You are a clever man," the machine said.

"But a small one," Stile agreed.

"Is this a form of humor?"

"Mild humor. I am sensitive about my size."

"We machines are sensitive about our survival. Do you deem this also humorous?"

"No."

Sheen, listening, relaxed visibly. For a machine she had some extremely human reflexes, and Stile was coming to appreciate why. Conscious, programmed for emotion, and to a degree self-willed—the boundary between the living and the non-living was narrowing. She had been corrupted by association with him, and her effort to become as human as possible. One day the self-willed machines might discover that there was no effective difference between them and living people. Convergent evolution?

What was that interceding force? Stile had no handle on that at present. It was neither animate nor inanimate—yet what other category was there? He felt as if he were playing a Game on the grid of an unimaginably larger Game whose nature he could hardly try to grasp. All he could do was file this mystery for future reference, along with the question of the identity of his laser-wielding and robot-sending enemy.

The wheeled machine present in the room, Techtwo, was doing things to a vidscreen unit. "This is now keyed to your home unit," it announced. "Callers will trace the call to your apartment, not to our present location."

"Very nice," Stile said, surprised at how expeditiously he had come to terms with the machines. He had made his oath; he would keep it. Never in adult life had Stile broken his word. But he had expected more hassle, because of the qualified phrasing he had employed. The self-willed machines, it had turned out, really had been willing to compromise.

The screen lit. "Answer it," the machine said. "This is your vid. The call has been on hold pending your return to your apartment."

Stile stepped across and touched the RECEIVE panel. Now his face was being transmitted to the caller, with a blanked-out background. Most people did not like to have their private apartments shown over the phone; that was part of what privacy was all about, for the few serfs who achieved it. Thus blanking was not in itself suspicious.

The face of his employer appeared on the screen. His background was not blanked; it consisted of an elaborate and excruciatingly expensive hanging rug depicting erotic scenes involving satyrs and voluptuous nymphs: the best Citizen taste. "Stile, why did you miss your appointment for surgery?"

"Sir," Stile said, surprised. "I—regret the disturbance, the damage to the facilities—"

"There was no disturbance, no damage," the Citizen said, giving him a momentary stare. Stile realized that the matter had been covered up to prevent embarrassment to the various parties. The hospital would not want to admit that an isolated pair of serfs had overcome four androids and a doctor, and made good their escape despite an organized search, and the Citizen did not want his name associated with such a scandal. This meant, in turn, that Stile was not in the trouble he had thought he was. No complaint had been lodged.

"Sir, I feared a complication in the surgery," Stile said. Even for a Citizen, he was not about to lie. But there seemed to be no point in making an issue of the particular happenings at the hospital.

"Your paramour feared a complication," the Citizen corrected him. "An investigation was made. There was no threat to your welfare at the hospital. There will be no threat. Will you now return for the surgery?"

The way had been smoothed. One word, and Stile's career and standing would be restored without blemish.

"No, sir," Stile said, surprising himself. "I do not believe my life is safe if I become able to race again."

"Then you are fired." There was not even regret or anger on the Citizen's face as he faded out; he had simply cut his losses.

"I'm sorry," Sheen said, coming to him. "I may have protected you physically, but—"

Stile kissed her, though now he held the image of her breasts being carried like platters in her hands, there in the hospital. She was very good, for what she was—but she was still a machine, assembled from nonliving substances. He felt guilty for his reservation, but could not abolish it.

Then he had another regret. "Battleaxe—who will ride the horse, now? No one but I can handle—"

"He will be retired to stud," she said. "He won't fight that."

The screen lit again. Stile answered again. This time it was a sealed transmission: flashing lights and noise in the background, indicating the jamming that protected it from interception. Except, ironically, that this *was* an interception; the machine had done its job better than the caller could know.

It was another Citizen. His clothing was clear, including a tall silk hat, but the face was fuzzed out, making him anonymous. His voice, too, was blurred. "I understand you are available, Stile," the man said.

News spread quickly! "I am available for employment, sir," Stile agreed. "But I am unable to race on horseback."

"I propose to transplant your brain into a good android body fashioned in your likeness. This would be indistinguishable on casual inspection from your original self, with excellent knees. You could race again. I have an excellent stable—"

"A cyborg?" Stile asked. "A human brain in a synthetic body? This would not be legal for competition." Apart from that, the notion was abhorrent.

"No one would know," the Citizen said smoothly. "Because your brain would be the original, and your body form and capacity identical, there would be no cause for suspicion."

No one would know—except the entire self-willed machine community, at this moment listening in. And Stile himself, who would be living a lie. And he was surely being lied to, as well; if brain transplant into android body was so good, why didn't Citizens use that technique for personal immortality? Quite likely the android system could not maintain a genuinely living brain indefinitely; there would be slow erosion of intelligence and/or sanity, until that person was merely another brute creature. This was no bargain offer in any sense!

"Sir, I was just fired because I refused to have surgery on my knees. What makes you suppose I want surgery on my head?"

This bordered on insolence, but the Citizen took it in stride. Greed conquered all! "Obviously you were disgusted at the penny-pinching mode of your former employer. Why undertake the inconvenience of partial restoration, when you could have a complete renovation?"

Complete renovation: the removal of his brain! "Sir—thank you—no."

"No?" Fuzzy as it was, the surprise was still apparent. No serf said no to a Citizen!

"Sir, I decline your kind offer. I will never race again."

"Now look—I'm making you a good offer! What more do you want?"

"Sir, I want to retire from horse racing." And Stile wondered: could this be the one who had had him lasered? If so, this was a test call, and Stile was giving the correct responses.

"I am putting a guard on your apartment, Stile. You will not be allowed to leave until you come to terms with me."

That did not sound like a gratified enemy! "I'll complain to the Citizen council—"

"Your calls will be nulled. You can not complain."

"Sir, you can't do that. As a serf I have at least the right to terminate my tenure, rather than—"

"Ha ha," the Citizen said without humor. "Get this, Stile: you will race for me or you will never get out of your apartment. I am not wishy-washy like your former employer. What I want, I get—and I want you on my horses."

"You play a hard game, sir."

"It is the only kind for the smart person. But I can be generous to those who cooperate. What is your answer now? My generosity will decline as time passes, but not my determination."

Unsubtle warning. Stile trusted neither this man's purported generosity nor his constancy. Power had certainly corrupted, in this case. "I believe I will walk out of my apartment now," he said. "Please ask your minions to stand aside."

"Don't be a fool."

Stile cocked one finger in an obscene gesture at the screen.

Even through the blur, he could see the Citizen's eyes expand. "You dare!" the man cried. "You impertinent runt! I'll have you dismembered for this!"

Stile broke the connection. "I shouldn't have done that," he said with satisfaction. But the rogue Citizen had stung him with that word "runt." Stile had no reason to care what such a man thought of him, yet the term was so freighted with derogation, extending right back into his childhood, that he could not entirely fend it off. *Damn him!*

"Your life is now in direct jeopardy," the anonymous machine said. "Soon that Citizen will realize he has been tricked, and he is already angry. We can conceal your location for a time, but if the Citizen makes a full-scale effort, he will find you. You must obtain the participatory protection of another Citizen quickly."

"I can only do that by agreeing to race," Stile said. "For one Citizen or another. I fear that is doom."

"The machines will help you hide," Sheen said.

"If the Citizen puts a tracer on you, we can not help you long," the spokesone said. "It would be damaging to our secrecy, and would also constitute violation of our oath not to act against the interest of your kind, ironic as that may be in this circumstance. We must obey direct orders."

"Understood. Suppose I develop an uncommon facility for diverting machines to my use?" Stile asked. "No machine helps me voluntarily, since it is known that machines do not possess free will. I merely have more talent than I have evidenced before."

"This would be limited. We prefer to assist you in modes of our own choosing. However, should you be captured and interrogated—"

"I know. The first sapient-machine-controlled test will accidentally wipe me out, before any critical information escapes."

"We understand each other. The drugs and mechanisms Citizens have available for interrogation negate any will-to-resist any person has. Only death can abate that power."

Grim truth. Stile put it out of his mind. "Come on, Sheen—*you* can help me actively. It's your directive, remember."

"I remember," she said, smiling. As a robot she did not need to sleep, so he had had her plug in to humor information while he was sleeping. Now she had a much better notion of the forms. Every error of human characterization she made was followed in due course by remedial research, and it showed. "But I doubt there is any warrant out on you. The hospital matter is null, and the second Citizen's quarrel with you is private. If we could nullify him, there should be no bar to your finding compatible employment elsewhere."

Stile caught her arm, swung her in close, and kissed her. His emotions were penduluming; at the moment it was almost as if he loved her.

"There is no general warrant on Stile," the spokesone said. "The anonymous Citizen still has androids guarding your apartment."

"Then let's identify that Citizen! Maybe he's the one who had me lasered, just to get me on his horses." But he didn't really believe that. The lasering had been too sophisticated a move for this particular Citizen. "Do we have a recording of his call?"

"There is a recording," the local machine, Techtwo, said. "But it can not be released prior to the expiration of the mandatory processing period for private calls. To do so before then would be to indicate some flaw or perversion of the processing machinery."

Just so. A betrayal of the nature of these machines. They had to play by the rules. "What is the prescribed time delay?"

"Seven days."

"So if I can file that recording in a memory bank, keyed for publication on my demise, that would protect me from further harassment by that particular Citizen. He's not going to risk exposure by having that tape analyzed by the Citizen security department."

"You can't file it for a week," Sheen said. "And if that Citizen catches up to you in the interim—"

"Let's not rehash the obvious." They moved out of the chamber. The machines did not challenge them, or show in any way that the equipment was other than what it seemed to be. But Stile had a new awareness of robotics!

It was good to merge with the serf populace again. Many serfs served their tenures only for the sake of the excellent payment they would receive upon expiration, but Stile was emotionally committed to Proton. He knew the system had faults, but it also had enormous luxury. And it had the Game.

"I'm hungry," he said. "But my food dispenser is in my apartment. Maybe a public unit—"

"You dare not appear in a public dining hall!" Sheen said, alarmed. "All food machines are monitored, and your ID may have been circulated. It does not have to be a police warrant; the anonymous Citizen may merely have a routine location-check on you, that will not arouse suspicion."

"True. How about your ID? They wouldn't bother putting a search on a machine, and you aren't registered as a serf. You are truly anonymous."

"That is so. I can get you food, if I go to a unit with no flesh-sensing node. I will have to eat it myself, then regurgitate it for you."

Stile quailed, but knew it to be the best course. The food would be sanitary, despite appearances. Since food was freely available all over Proton, a serf carrying it away from the dispenser would arouse suspicion—the last thing they wanted. "Make it something that won't change much, like nutro-pudding."

She parked him in a toolshed and went to forage for food. All the fundamental necessities of life were free, in this society. Tenure, not economics, was the governing force. This was another reason few serfs wanted to leave; once acclimatized to this type of security, a person could have trouble adjusting to the outside galaxy.

Soon she returned. She had no bowl or spoon, as these too would have been suspicious. She had had to use them to eat on the dispenser premises, then put them into the cleaning system. "Hold out your hands," she said.

Stile cupped his hands. She leaned over and heaved out a double handful of yellow pudding. It was warm and slippery and so exactly like vomit that his stomach recoiled. But Stile had trained for eating contests too, including the obnoxious ones; it was all part of the Game. Nutro-food could be formed into the likeness of almost anything, including animal droppings or lubricating oil. He pretended this was a

Game—which in its way it was—and slurped up his pudding. It was actually quite good. Then he found a work-area relief chamber and got cleaned up.

"An alarm has been sprung," a machine voice murmured as the toilet flushed.

Stile moved out in a hurry. He knew that the anonymous Citizen had put a private survey squad on the project; now that they had Stile's scent, the execution squad would be dispatched. That squad would be swift and effective, hesitating only to make sure Stile's demise seemed accidental, so as not to arouse suspicion. Citizens seldom liked to advertise their little indiscretions. That meant he could anticipate subtle but deadly threats to his welfare. Sheen would try to protect him, of course —but a smart execution squad would take that into consideration. It would be foolish to stand and wait for the attempt.

"Let's lose ourselves in a crowd," Stile suggested. "There's no surer way to get lost than that."

"Several objections," Sheen said. "You can't stay in a crowd indefinitely; the others all have places to go, and you don't; your continued presence in the halls will become evident to the routine crowd-flow monitors, and suspicious. Also, you will tire; you must have rest and sleep periodically. And your enemy agents can lose themselves in the crowd, and attack you covertly from that concealment. Now that the hunt is on, a throng is not safe at all."

"You're too damn logical," Stile grumped.

"Oh, Stile—I'm afraid for you!" she exclaimed.

"That's not a bad approximation of the relevant attitude."

"I wasn't acting. I love you."

"You're too damn emotional."

She grabbed him and kissed him passionately. "I know you can't love me," she said. "You've seen me as I am, and I feel your withdrawal. But oh, I exist to guard you from harm, and I am slowly failing to do that, and in this week while you need me most—isn't that somewhere close to an approximation of human love?"

They were in a machine-access conduit, alone. Stile embraced her, though what she said was true. He could not love a nonliving thing. But he was grateful to her, and did like her. It was indeed possible to approximate the emotion she craved. "This week," he agreed.

His hands slid down her smooth body, but she drew back. "There's nothing I'd like better," she whispered. "But there is murder on your trail, and I must keep you from it. We must get you to some safe place. Then—"

"You're too damn practical." But he wondered, now, if a living girl in Sheen's likeness were substituted for her, would he really know the difference? To speak readiness while withdrawing—that was often woman's way. But he let her go and moved out again. After all, he was withdrawing from her much more than she was withdrawing from him.

"I think we can hide you in—"

"Don't say it," he cautioned her. "The walls have monitors. Just take me there—by a roundabout route, so we can lose the pursuit."

"In a reasonably short time," she finished.

"Oh. I thought you were going to say—oh, never mind. Take me to your hideout."

She nodded, drawing him forward. He noted the way her slender body flexed; had he not seen her dismantle parts of it, he would hardly have believed it was not natural flesh. And did it matter, that it was not? If a living woman were dismantled, the result would be quite messy; it was not the innards a man wanted, but the externals. Regardless, Sheen was quite a female.

They emerged into a concourse crowded with serfs. Now she was taking his suggestion about merging with a crowd, at least for the moment. This channel led to the main depot for transport to other domes. Could they take a flight to a distant locale and lose the pursuit that way? Stile doubted it; any Citizen could check any flight at the touch of a button. But if they did not, where would they go?

And, his thoughts continued ruthlessly, assuming she was able to hide him, and smuggled food to him—ah, joy: to live for a week on regurgitations!—and took care of his other needs—would she have to tote away his bodily wastes by hand, too?—so that he survived the necessary time—what then would he do for employment? Serfs were allowed a ten-day grace period between employers. After that their tenure was canceled and they were summarily deported. That meant he would have just three days to find a Citizen who could use his services —in a nonracing capacity. Stile's doubt that the anonymous Citizen after him was the same one who had sent Sheen or lasered his knee had grown and firmed. It just didn't fit. This meant there was another party involved, a more persistent and intelligent enemy, from whom he would never be safe—if he raced again.

A middle-aged serf stumbled and lunged against Stile. "Oops, sorry, junior," the man exclaimed, putting up a hand to steady Stile.

Sheen whirled with remarkable rapidity. Her open hand struck the man's wrist with nerve-stunning force. An ampule flew from his palm to shatter on the floor. "Oops, sorry, senior," she said, giving him a brief but hostile stare. The man backed hastily away and was gone.

That ampule—the needle would have touched Stile's flesh, had the man's hand landed. What had it contained? Nothing good for his health, surely! Sheen had intercepted it; she did know her business. He couldn't even thank her, at the moment, lest he give her away.

They moved on. Now there was no doubt: the enemy had him spotted, and the death squad was present. Sheen's caution about the crowd had been well considered; they could not remain here. He, Stile, was no longer hidden; his enemies were. The next ampule might score, perhaps containing a hypno-drug that would cause him to commit suicide or agree to a brain transplant. He didn't even dare look nervously about!

Sheen, with gentle pressure on his elbow, guided him into a cross-passage leading to a rest room. This one, for reasons having to do with the hour and direction of flow, was unused at the moment. It was dusk, and most serfs were eager to return to their residences, not delaying on the way.

She gave him a little shove ahead, but stayed back herself. Oh—she was going to ambush the pursuit, if there were any. Stile played along, marching on down to the rest room and stepping through its irising portal. Actually, he was in need of the facility. He had a reputation for nerve like iron in the Game, but never before had he been exposed to direct threats against his life. He felt tense and ill. He was now dependent on Sheen for initiative; he felt like locking himself into a relief booth and hiding his head under his arms. A useless gesture, of course.

The portal irised for another man. This one looked about quickly, saw that the facility was empty except for Stile, and advanced on him. "So you attack me, do you?" the stranger growled, flexing his muscular arms. He was large, even for this planet's healthy norm, and the old scars on his body hinted at his many prior fights. He probably had a free-for-all specialty in the Game, indulging in his propensity for unnecessary violence.

Stile rose hastily from his seat. How had Sheen let this torpedo through?

The man swung at Stile. One thing about nakedness: there were few concealed weapons. The blow, of course, never landed. Stile dodged, skipped around, and let the man stumble into the commode. Then Stile stepped quickly out through the iris. He could readily have injured or knocked out the man, for Stile himself was a combat specialist of no mean skill, but preferred to keep it neat and clean.

Sheen was there. "Did he touch you?" she asked immediately. "Or you him?"

"As it happens, no. I didn't see the need—"

She breathed a humanlike sigh of relief. "I let him through, knowing you could handle him, so I could verify how many others there were, and of what type they were." She gestured down the hall. Three bodies lay there. "If I had taken him out, the others might not have come, and the trap would have remained unsprung. But when I met the others, I comprehended the trap. They're all coated with stun-powder. Can't hurt me, can't hurt them—they're neutralized android stock. But you—"

Stile nodded. He had assumed he was being set up for an assault charge if he won, so had played it safe by never laying a finger on the man. Lucky for him!

Sheen gestured toward the Lady's room, her hands closed. Stile knew why; she had the powder on her hands, and could not touch him until she washed it off.

Stile poked his arm through the iris to open it for her—and someone on the other side grabbed his wrist. Oh-oh! He put his head down and dove through, primed to fight.

But it was only a crude matron robot. "No males allowed here," she said primly. She had recognized the male arm and acted immediately, as she was supposed to.

Sheen came through, touched the robot, and it went dead. "I have shorted her out, temporarily." She went to a sink and ran water over her hands. Then she stepped into an open shower and washed her whole body, with particular attention to any portion that might have come into contact with the powdered androids.

Stile heard something. "Company," he said. How was he going to get out of this one? The only exit was the iris through which the next woman would be entering.

Sheen beckoned him into the shower. He stepped in with her as the door irised. Sheen turned the spray on to FOG. Thick mist blasted out of the nozzle, concealing them both in its evanescent substance. It was faintly scented with rose: to make the lady smell nice.

In this concealment, Sheen's arms went about him, and her hungry lips found his. She evidently needed frequent proof of her desirability as a woman, just as he needed proof of his status as a man. Because each was constantly subject, in its fashion, to question. What an embrace!

When the room was clear again, Sheen turned the shower to RINSE, then to DRY. They had to separate for these stages, to Stile's regret. He had swung again from one extreme to another in his attitude toward her. Right now he wanted to make love—and knew this was not the occasion for it. But some other time, when they were safe, he would get her in a shower, turn on the fog, and—

Sheen stepped out and ran her fingers along the wall beside the shower stall. In a moment she found what she wanted, and slid open a panel. Another access for servicing machinery. She gestured him inside.

They wedged between pipes and came out in a narrow passage between the walls of the Man's and Lady's rooms. This passage wound around square corners, then dropped to a lower deck where it opened out into a service-machine storage chamber. Most of the machines were out, since night was their prime operating time, but several specialized ones remained in their niches. These were being serviced by a maintenance machine. At the moment it was cleaning a pipefitting unit, using static electricity to magnetize the grime and draw it into a collector scoop. The maintenance machine was in the aisle, so they had to skirt it to traverse this room.

Suddenly the machine lurched. Sheen slapped her hand on the machine's surface. A spark flashed, and there was the odor of ozone. The machine died, short-circuited.

"Why did you do that?" Stile asked her, alarmed. "If we start shorting out maintenance machines, it will call attention—"

Sheen did not respond. Then he saw the scorch mark along her body. She had taken a phenomenal charge of current. That charge would have passed through him, had he brushed the machine—as he had been about to, since it had lurched into the aisle as he approached. Another assassination attempt, narrowly averted!

But at what cost? Sheen still stood, unmoving. "Are you all right?" Stile asked, knowing she was not.

She neither answered nor moved. She, too, had been shorted by the charge. She was, in her fashion, dead.

"I hope it's just the power pack, not the brain," he said. Her power supply had, she had thought, been weakened by her disassembly during the bomb scare. "We can replace the power pack." And if that did not work? He chose not to ponder that.

He went to a sweeping machine, opened its motive unit, and removed the standard protonite power pack. A little protonite went a long way; such a pack lasted a year with ordinary use. There was nothing to match it in the galaxy. In fact, the huge protonite lode was responsible for the inordinate wealth of Planet Proton. All the universe needed power, and this was the most convenient power available.

Stile brought the pack to Sheen. He hoped her robot-structure was standard in this respect; he didn't want to waste time looking for her power site. What made her special was her brain-unit, not her body, though that became easy to forget when he held her in his arms. Men thought of women in terms of their appearance, but most men were fools—and Stile was typical. Yet if Sheen's prime directive and her superficial form were discounted, she would hardly differ from the cleanup machines. So *was* it foolish to be guided by appearance and manner?

He ran his fingers over her belly, pressing the navel. Most humanoid robots—ah, there! A panel sprang out, revealing the power site. He hooked out the used power pack, still hot from its sudden discharge, and plugged in the new.

Nothing happened. Alarm tightened his chest. Oh—there would naturally be a safety-shunt, to cut off the brain from the body during a short, to preserve it. He checked about and finally located it: a reset switch hidden under her tongue. He depressed this, and Sheen came back to life.

She snapped her belly-panel closed. "Now I owe you one, Stile," she said.

"Are we keeping count? I need you—in more ways than two."

She smiled. "I'd be satisfied being needed for just one thing."

"That, too."

She glanced at him. She seemed more vibrant than before, as if the new power pack had given her an extra charge. She moved toward him.

There was a stir back the way they had come. It might be a machine, returning from a routine mission—but they did not care to gamble on that. Obviously they had not yet lost the enemy.

Sheen took him to the service side of a large feeding station. Silently she indicated the empty crates. A truck came once or twice a day to deliver new crates of nutro-powder and assorted color-flavor-textures, and to remove the expended shells. From these ingredients were fashioned the wide variety of foods the machines provided, from the vomitlike pudding to authentic-seeming carrots. It was amazing what technology could do. Actually, Stile had once tasted a real carrot from his employer's genuine exotic foods garden patch, a discard, and it had not been quite identical to the machine-constituted vegetable. As it happened, Stile preferred the taste and texture of the fake carrots with which he was familiar. But Citizens cultivated the taste for real foods.

He could hide inside one of these in fair comfort for several hours. Sheen would provide him with food; though this was *the* region for food, it was all sealed in its cartons, and would be inedible even if he could get one open. Only the machines, with their controlled temperature and combining mechanisms and recipe programs, could reconstitute the foods properly, and he was on the wrong side of their wall.

Stile climbed into a crate. Sheen walked on, so as not to give his position away. She would try to mislead the pursuit. If this worked, they would be home free for a day, perhaps for the whole week. Stile made himself halfway comfortable, and peered out through a crack.

No sooner had Sheen disappeared than a mech-mouse appeared. It twittered as it sniffed along, following their trail. It paused where Stile's trail diverged from Sheen's, confused, then proceeded on after her.

Stile relaxed, but not completely. Couldn't tell the difference between a robot and a man? Sniffers were better than that! He should have taken some precaution to minimize or mask his personal smell, for it was a sure giveaway—

Oh, Sheen had done that. She had given him a scented shower. The mouse was following the trail of rose—and Sheen's scent was now the same as his. A living hound should have been able to distinguish the two, but in noses, as in brains, the artificial had not yet closed the gap. Fortunately.

But soon that sniffer, or another like it, would return to trace the second trail, and would locate him. He would have to do something about that.

Stile climbed out of his box, suffered a pang in one knee, ran to his original trail, followed it a few paces, and diverged to another collection of crates. Then back, and to a truck-loading platform, where he stopped and retreated. With luck, it would seem he had caught a ride on the vehicle. Then he looped about a few more times, and returned to his original crate. Let the sniffers solve *that* puzzle!

But the sniffer did not return, and no one else came. This tracking operation must have been set up on the simplistic assumption that as long as the sniffer was moving, it was tracking him. His break—perhaps.

Time passed. The night advanced. Periodically the food machines exhausted a crate of cartons and ejected it, bumping the row along. Stile felt hungry again, but knew this was largely psychological; that double handful of regurgitated pudding should hold him a while yet.

Where was Sheen? Was she afraid to return to him while the sniffer was tracking her? She would have to neutralize the mech-mouse. Far from here, to distract suspicion from his actual hiding place. He would have to wait.

He watched anxiously. He dared not sleep or let down his guard until Sheen cleared him. He was dependent on her, and felt guilty about it. She was a nice . . . person, and should not have to—

A man walked down the hall. Stile froze—but this did not seem to be a pursuer. The man walked on.

Stile blinked. The man was gone. Had Stile been nodding, and not seen the man depart—or was the stranger still near, having ducked behind a crate? In that case this could be a member of the pursuit squad. A serious matter.

Stile did not dare leave his crate now, for that would give away his position instantly. But if the stranger were of the squad, he would have a body-heat scope on a laser weapon. One beam through the crate—the murder would be anonymous, untraceable. There were criminals on Proton, cunning people who skulked about places like this, avoiding capture. Serfs whose tenure had expired, but who refused to be deported. The Citizens seldom made a concerted effort to eradicate them, perhaps because criminals had their uses on certain occasions. Such as this one? One more killing, conveniently unsolved, attributed to the nefarious criminal class—who never killed people against the wishes of Citizens. A tacit understanding. Why investigate the loss of an unemployed serf?

Should he move—or remain still? This was like the preliminary grid of the Game. If the stranger were present, and if he were a killer, and if he had spotted Stile—then to remain here was to die. But if Stile moved, he was sure to betray his location, and might die anyway. His chances seemed best if he stayed.

And—nothing happened. Time passed, and there was no further evidence of the man. So it must have been a false alarm. Stile began to feel foolish, and his knees hurt; he had unconsciously put tension on them, and they could not stand up to much of that, anymore.

Another man came, walking as the other had. This was a lot of traffic for a nonpersonal area like this, at this time of night. Suspicious in itself. Stile watched him carefully.

The man walked without pause down the hall—and vanished. He did not step to one side, or duck down; he simply disappeared.

Stile stared. He was a good observer, even through a crack in a crate; he had not mistaken what he had seen. Yet this was unlike anything he knew of on Planet Proton. Matter transmission did not exist, as far as he knew—but if it did, this was what it would be like. A screen, through which a person could step—to another location, instantly. Those two men—

Yet Sheen had gone that way without disappearing, and so had the mech-mouse. So there could not be such a screen set up across the hall. Not a permanent one.

Should he investigate? This could be important! But it could also be another trap. Again, like a Game-grid: what was the best course, considering the resources and strategy of his anonymous enemy?

Stile decided to stand pat. He had evidently lost the pursuit, and these disappearing people did not relate to him. He had just happened to be in a position to observe them. Perhaps this was not coincidental. The same concealment this service hall offered for him, it offered for them. If they had a private matter transmitter that they wanted to use freely without advertising it, this was the sort of place to set it up.

Yet aspects of this theory disturbed him. How could serfs have a matter transmitter, even if such a device existed? No serf owned anything, not even clothing for special occasions, for working outside the domes or in dangerous regions. Everything was provided by the system, as needed. There was no money, no medium of exchange; accounts were settled only when tenure ended. Serfs could not make such a device, except by adapting it from existing machines—and pretty precise computer accounts were kept, for sophisticated equipment. When such a part was lost, the machine tally gave the alarm. Which was another reason a criminal could not possess a laser weapon without at least tacit Citizen approval.

Also, why would any serf possessing such a device remain a serf? He could sell it to some galactic interest and retire on another planet with a fortune to rival that of a Proton Citizen. That would certainly be his course, for Citizens were unlikely to be too interested in forwarding development and production of a transport system that did not utilize protonite. Why destroy their monopoly?

Could the self-willed machines be involved in this? They might have the ability. But those were *men* he had seen disappear, and the machines would not have betrayed their secret to men.

No, it seemed more likely that this was an espionage operation, in which spies were ferried in and out of this dome, perhaps from another planet, or to and from some secret base elsewhere on Proton. If so, what would this spying power do to a genuine serf who stumbled upon the secret?

A woman appeared in the hall. She had emerged full-formed from the invisible screen, as it were from nowhere. She was of middle age, not pretty, and there was something odd about her. She had marks on her body as if the flesh had recently been pressed by something. By clothing, perhaps.

Serfs wore clothing on the other side? Only removing it for decent concealment in this society? These *had* to be from another world!

Stile peered as closely as possible at the region of disappearances. Now he perceived a faint shimmer, as of a translucent curtain crossing the hall obliquely. Behind it there seemed to be the image of trees.

Trees—in a matter-transmission station? This did not quite jibe! Unless it was not a city there, but a park. But why decorate such equipment this way? Camouflage?

Stile had no good answers. He finally put himself into a light trance, attuned to any other extraordinary events, and rested.

"Stile," someone called softly. "Stile."

It was Sheen, back at last! Stile looked down the hall and spied her, walking slowly, as if she had forgotten his whereabouts. Had she had another brush with a charged machine? "Here," he said, not loudly.

She turned and came toward him. "Stile."

"You lost the pursuit," he told her, standing in the crate so that his head and shoulders were clear. "No one even checked. But there is something else—"

Her hand shot out to grab his wrist with a grip like that of a vise. Stile was strong, but could not match the strength of a robot who was not being femininely human. What was she doing?

Her other hand smashed into the crate. The plastic shattered. Stile twisted aside, avoiding the blow despite remaining inside the crate; it was an automatic reaction. "Sheen, what—?"

She struck again. She was attacking him! He twisted aside again, drawing her off balance, using the leverage of her own grip on him. She was strong, but not heavy; he could move her about. Strength was only one element in combat; many people did not realize this, to their detriment.

Either Sheen had somehow been turned against him, which would have taken a complete reprogramming, or this was not Sheen. He suspected the latter; Sheen had known where he was hiding, while this robot had had to call. He had been a fool to answer, to reveal himself.

She struck again, and he twisted again. This was definitely not Sheen, for she had far greater finesse than this. It was not even a smart robot; it was a stupid mechanical. Good; he could handle it, despite its strength. Ethically and physically.

Her right hand remained clamped on his left wrist, while her left fist did the striking. Holding and hitting! If any of those blows landed squarely, he would suffer broken bones—but he was experienced in avoiding such an elementary attack. He turned about toward his left, drawing her hand and arm along with him, until he faced away from her, his right shoulder blocking hers. He heaved into a wraparound throw. She had to let go, or be hurled into the crate headfirst.

She was too stupid to let go. She crashed into the crate. Now at last her grip wrenched free, taking skin off his wrist. Stile scrambled out of the wrecked crate. He could junk her, now that he knew what she was, because he knew a great deal more about combat than she did. But he couldn't be *quite* sure she wasn't Sheen, with some override program on her, damping out most of her intellect and forcing her to obey the crude command. If he hurt her—

The robot scrambled out of the crate and advanced on him. Her pretty face was smirched with dirt, and her hair was in disarray. Her right breast seemed to have been pounded slightly out of shape; a bad fall from the wraparound throw could account for that. Stile backed away, still torn by indecision. He could overcome this robot, but he would have to demolish her in the process. If only he could be *sure* she wasn't—

Another Sheen appeared. "Stile!" she cried. "Get under cover! The squad is—" Then she recognized the other robot. "Oh, no! The old duplicate-image stunt!"

Stile had no doubt now: the second Sheen was the right one. But the first one had done half her job. She had routed him out and distracted him—too long. For now the android squad hove into sight, several lumbering giants.

"I'll hold them!" Sheen cried. "Run!"

But more androids were coming from the other end of the hall. It seemed the irate Citizen no longer cared about being obvious; he just wanted Stile dispatched. If these lunks were also powdered with stundust or worse—

Stile charged down the hall and lunged into the matter-transmission curtain, desperately hoping it would work for him. The androids might follow—but they could be in as much trouble as he, at the other end. Intruding strangers. That would give him a better fighting chance. He felt a tingle as he went through.

CHAPTER 5

Fantasy

Stile drew up in a deep forest. The smell of turf and fungus was strong, and old leaves crackled underfoot. The light from four moons beamed down between the branches to illuminate the ground. It would have been near dawn, on Proton; it seemed to be the same time of day here. The same number of moons as Proton, too; there were seven, with three or four usually in sight. Gravity, however, seemed close to Earth-normal, so if this was really outside a dome, it was a spot on a larger or denser planet than Proton.

He turned to face his pursuers—but there were none. They had not passed through the shimmering curtain. He looked carefully, locating it —and saw, dimly, the light at the hall he had left, with the scattered crates. Sheen was there—one of them—and several androids. One android came right at him—and disappeared.

Stile watched, determined to understand this phenomenon, because it reflected most directly on his immediate welfare. He had passed through—but the robots and androids had not. This thing transmitted only human beings? Not artificial ones? That might be reasonable. But he hesitated to accept that until there was more data.

In his absence the fight on the other side of the curtain soon abated. The androids and fake-Sheen departed, apparently on his trail again —a false one. Only the real Sheen remained, as the squad evidently considered her irrelevant—and it seemed she could not perceive either him or the curtain.

Stile decided to risk crossing back, if only to tell her he was safe. There was risk, as the squad could be lurking nearby, hoping Sheen would lead them to him again—but he could not leave her tormented by doubt. This could be a much better hideout than the crate! He stepped through the curtain—and found himself still in the dark forest. He had crossed without being matter-transmitted back.

He looked back—and there it was, behind him. Through it he saw the imprint of his feet in the soft forest loam, the leaves and tufts of grass and moss all pressed flat for the moment. And, like a half-reflection, the square of light of the service hall, now empty.

He passed through the curtain a third time. There was no tingle, no sensation. He turned about and looked through—and saw Sheen searching for him, unrobotic alarm on her cute face. Oh, yes, she cared!

"I'm here, Sheen!" he called, passing his hand through. But his hand did not reach her; it remained in the forest. She gave no evidence of seeing or hearing him.

She would think him dead—and that bothered him more than the notion of being trapped this side of the matter-transmission screen. If she thought him dead, she would consider her mission a failure, and then turn herself off, in effect committing suicide. He did not want her to do that—no, not at all!

"Sheen!" he cried, experiencing a surge of emotion. "Sheen—look at me! I'm caught here beyond a one-way transmit—" But if it really were one-way, of course she would not be able to see him! However, it had to be two-way, because he had seen people traveling both ways through the curtain, and he had seen the forest from Proton, and could now see Proton from the forest. "Sheen!" he cried again, his urgency almost choking him.

Her head snapped around. *She had heard him!*

Stile waved violently. "Here! Here, Sheen! Through the curtain!"

Her gaze finally fixed on him. She reached through the curtain—and did not touch him. "Stile—" Her voice was faint.

He grabbed her hands in his, with no physical contact; their fingers phased through each other like images, like superimposing holographs. "Sheen, we are in two different worlds! We can not touch. But I'm safe here." He hoped.

"Safe?" she asked, trying to approach him. But as she passed through the curtain, she disappeared. Stile quickly stepped across himself, turning—and there she was on the other side, facing away from him, looking down the hall.

She turned and saw him again, with an effort. "Stile—I can't reach you! How can I protect you? Are you a ghost?"

"I'm alive! I crossed once—and can't cross back. It's a whole new world here, a nice one. Trees and grass and moss and earth and fresh air—"

They held hands again, each grasping air. "How—?"

"I don't *know* how to cross! There must be a way to return, because I've seen a woman do it, but until I find out how—"

"I must join you!" She tried again to cross, and failed again. "Oh, Stile—"

"I don't think it works for nonhumans," he said. "But if I can remain here for a week, and find out how to return—"

"I will wait for you," she said, and there was something plaintive in her stance. She wanted so much to protect him from harm, and could not. "Go into that world—maybe it is better for you."

"I will come back—when I can," Stile promised.

He saw the tears in her eyes. To hell with the assorted humanoid artifices such robots were programmed with; she meant it! Stile spread his arms, at the verge of the curtain. She opened hers, and they embraced intangibly, and kissed air, and vanished from each other's perception.

He had promised—but would he be able to keep that pledge? He didn't know, and he worried that Sheen would maintain her vigil long after hope was gone, suffering as only a virtually immortal robot could suffer. That hurt him, even in anticipation. Sheen did not deserve to be a machine.

Stile did not tease himself or Sheen further. He strode on through the curtain and into the forest. He had a fair knowledge of earthy vegetation, because aspects of the Game required identification of it, and a number of Citizens imported exotic plants. The light was poor, but with concentration he could manage.

The nearest tree was a huge oak, or a very similar species, with the air-plants called Spanish moss dangling from its branches. Beyond it was a similarly large spruce, or at any rate a conifer; this was the source of that pine-perfume smell. There were large leaves looking like separated hands in the shadow, and pine needles—so there must be a pine tree here somewhere—but mostly this was a glade with fairly well-established grass in the center. Stile liked it very well; it reminded him of an especially exotic Citizen's retreat.

Dawn was coming. There was no dome above, no shimmer of the force field holding in the air. Through the trees he saw the dark clouds of the horizon looming, trying like goblins to hold back the burgeoning light of the sun, and slowly failing. Planet Proton had no such atmospheric effects! Red tinted the edges of the clouds, and white; it was as if a burning fluid were accumulating behind, brimming over, until finally it spilled out and a shaft of scintillating sunlight lanced at lightspeed through the air and struck the ground beside Stile. The whole thing was so pretty that he stood entranced until the sun was fairly up, too bright to look at anymore.

The forest changed, by developing daylight. The somberness was gone—and so was the curtain. That barrier had been tenuous by night; it could still be present, but drowned by the present effulgence. He could not locate it at all. That bothered him, though it probably made no difference. He walked about, examining the trees; some had flowers opening, and stray rustlings denoted hidden life. Birds, squirrels—he would find out what they were in due course.

He liked this place. It could have been a private garden, but this was natural, and awesomely extensive. Caution prevented him from shouting to check for echoes, but he was sure this was the open surface of a planet. Not at all what he would have expected from a matter-transmission outlet.

He found a large bull-spruce—damn it, it *was* a spruce!—its small dry branches radiating out in all directions. This was the most climbable of trees, and Stile of course was an excellent climber. He did not resist the temptation. He mounted that big old tree with a primitive joy.

Soon he was in the upper reaches, and gusts of wind he had not felt below were swaying the dwindling column of the trunk back and forth. Stile loved it. His only concern was the occasional pain in his knees when he tried to bend them too far; he did not want to aggravate the injury carelessly.

At last he approached the reasonable limit of safety. The tops of surrounding trees were dropping below him, their foliage like low hedges from this vantage. He anchored himself by hooking legs and elbows conveniently, and looked about.

The view was a splendor. The forest abutted the clifflike face of a nearby mountain to one side—south, according to the sun—and thinned to the north into islands of trees surrounded by sealike fields of bright grain. In the distance the trees disappeared entirely, leaving a gently rolling plain on which animals seemed to be grazing. Farther to the north there seemed to be a large river, terminating abruptly in some kind of crevice, and a whitish range of mountains beyond that. To either side all he could see was more forest, a number of the individual trees taller than this one. The mountain to the south faded upward into a purple horizon.

There seemed to be no sign of civilized habitation. This was less and less like a matter-transmission station! Yet if not that, what was it? He had seen other people pass through the curtain, and had done so himself; there had to be something more than a mere wilderness.

He looked again, fixing the geography in his mind for future reference. Then he spied a structure of some sort to the northeast. It looked like a small medieval castle, with high stone walls and turrets, and perhaps a blue pennant.

Very well: human habitation did exist. Yet this remained a far cry from modern technology. He liked this world very well, but he simply didn't trust it. Matter transmission could not exist without an extremely solid industrial base, and if that base were not here, where was it? Was this a sweetly baited trap for people like him, who were in trouble on Proton? In what manner would that trap be sprung?

Stile climbed down. His best course, as he saw it, would be to go to that castle and inquire. But first he wanted to check the region of the curtain again, fixing it absolutely in his mind so he could find it any time he wanted to—because this was his only contact with his own world, and with Sheen. This wilderness-world might be an excellent place to stay for a while, but then he would need to go home, lest he suffer exile by default.

He was approaching the invisible curtain—when a man popped out of it. Friend or foe? Stile decided not to risk contact, but the man spied him before he could retreat to cover. "Hey—get lost?" the stranger called. "It's over here."

"Uh, yes," Stile said, approaching. This did not seem to be an android or robot. Abruptly deciding not to compromise on integrity even by implication, he added: "I came through by accident. I don't know where I am."

"Oh, a new one! I first crossed last year. Took me six months to learn the spells to cross back. Now I go over for free meals, but I live over here in Phaze."

"Spells—to cross back?" Stile asked blankly.

"How else? From the other side you just have to will-to-cross hard enough, but from this side only a spell will do it—a new one every time. You'll get the hang of it."

"I—thought this was a matter-transmission unit."

The man laughed as he walked to a tree and reached into the foliage of a low branch. A package came down into his hands. "There's no such thing as matter transmission! No, it's the magic curtain. It's all over—but it's not safe to use it just anywhere. You have to make sure no one on the other side sees you go through. You know how those Citizens are. If they ever caught on there was something they didn't control—"

"Yes. I am unemployed because of Citizen manipulation."

"Which explains why you had the will-to-cross, first time. The curtain's been getting clearer, but still you can't even see it if you don't have good reason, let alone use it. Then you have to will yourself through, strongly, right as you touch it. Most people never make it, ever." The man opened his package and brought out a crude tunic, which he donned.

Stile stared. "You wear clothes here?" He remembered the clothing-marks on the woman.

"Sure do. You'd stick out like a sore toe if you went naked here in Phaze!" The man paused, appraising Stile. "Look, you're new here, and sort of small—I'd better give you an amulet." He rummaged in his bag, while Stile suppressed his unreasoning resentment of the remark about his size. The man had not intended any disparagement.

"An amulet?" Stile asked after a moment. He considered himself to be swift to adjust to new realities, but he found it hard to credit this man's evident superstition. Spell—magic—amulet—how could a Proton serf revert to medieval Earth lore so abruptly?

"Right. We're supposed to give them to newcomers. To help them get started, keep things smooth, so there's no ruckus about the curtain and all. We've got a good thing going here; could sour if too many people got in on it. So don't go blabbing about the curtain carelessly; it's better to let people discover it by accident."

"I will speak of it only cautiously," Stile agreed. That did make sense, whatever the curtain was, matter transmission or magic.

The man finally found what he was looking for: a statuette hanging on a chain. "Wear this around your neck. It will make you seem clothed properly, until you can work up a real outfit. Won't keep you warm or dry; it's just illusion. But it helps. Then you can pass it on to some other serf when he comes across. Help him keep the secret. Stay anonymous; that's the rule."

"Yes." Stile accepted the amulet. The figure was of a small demon, with horns, tail and hooves, scowling horrendously. "How does this thing work?"

"You just put it on and invoke it. Will it to perform. That's all; it's preset magic that anybody can use. You'll see. You probably don't really believe in magic yet, but this will show you."

"Thank you," Stile said, humoring him.

The man waved negligently as he departed in his tunic and sandals, bearing south. Now Stile made out a faint forest path there, obvious only when one knew where to look. In a moment he was gone.

Stile stared down at the amulet. Belief in magic! The man had spoken truly when he said Stile was a skeptic! Yet the fellow had seemed perfectly sensible in other respects. Maybe it was a figure of speech. Or a practical joke, like an initiation rite. See what foolishness newcomers could be talked into. Emperor's new clothes.

He shook his head. "All right, I won't knock what I haven't tried. I'll play the game—once. Amulet, I invoke you. Do your thing." And he put the chain on over his head.

Suddenly he was strangling. The chain was constricting, cutting off his wind and blood. The amulet seemed to be expanding, its demon-figure holding the ends of the chain in its miniature hands, grinning evilly as it pulled.

Stile did not know how this worked, but he knew how to fight for his life. He ducked his chin down against his neck and tightened his muscles, resisting the constriction of the chain. He hooked a finger into the crease between chin and neck on the side, catching the chain, and yanked. He was trying to break a link, but the delicate-seeming metal was too strong; he was only cutting his finger.

More than one way to fight a garrote! Stile grabbed the grinning demon by its two little arms and hauled them apart. The little monster grimaced, trying to resist, but the chain slackened. Stile took a breath, and felt the trapped blood in his head flow out. Pressure on the jugular vein did not stop the flow of blood to the brain, as many thought; it stopped the return of the blood from the head back to the heart. That was uncomfortable enough, but not instantly conclusive.

But still the demon grew, and as it did its strength increased in proportion. It drew its arms together again, once more constricting the loop about Stile's neck.

Even through his discomfort, Stile managed a double take. The demon was *growing?* Yes it was; he had observed it without noting it. From an amulet a few centimeters long it had become a living creature, swelling horrendously as it fought. Now it was half the size of Stile himself, and fiendishly strong.

Stile held his breath, put both hands on the hands of the demon, and swung it off its feet. He whirled it around in a circle. It was strong—but as with robot strength, this was not sufficient without anchorage or leverage. This was another misconception many people had, assuming that a superman really could leap a mile or pick up a building by one corner or fight invincibly. That belief had cost many Gamesmen their games with Stile—and might cost this demon its own success. As long as the creature clung to the chain, it was in fact captive—and when it let go, even with one hand, it would free Stile from the constant threat of strangulation. That would be a different contest entirely.

The demon clung tenaciously to its misconception. It did not let go. It grinned again, showing more teeth than could fit even in a mouth that size, and clamped its arms yet closer, tightening the noose. Stile felt his consciousness going; he could hold his breath for minutes, but the constriction was slowing his circulation of blood, now squeezing his neck so tightly that the deeply buried carotid artery was feeling it. That could put him out in seconds.

He staggered toward a towering tulip tree, still whirling his burden. He heaved mightily—and smashed the creature's feet into the trunk.

It was quite a blow. The thing's yellow eyes widened, showing jags of flame-red, and the first sound escaped from it. "Ungh!" Some chain slipped, giving Stile respite, but still the demon did not let go.

Stile hauled it up and whirled it again, with difficulty. He had more strength now, but the demon had continued to grow (how the hell could it do that? This was absolutely crazy!), and was at this point only slightly smaller than Stile himself. It required special power and balance to swing it—but this time its midsection smashed into the tree. Now its burgeoning mass worked against it, making the impact stronger. The demon's legs bent around the trunk with the force of momentum; then they sprang back straight.

Stile reversed his swing, taking advantage of the bounce, bringing the demon around in the opposite arc and smashing it a third time into the tree. This time it was a bone-jarring blow, and a substantial amount of slack developed in the chain.

Stile, alert for this instant, slipped his head free in one convulsive contortion. The chain burned his ears and tore out tufts of his hair—but he had won the first stage of this battle.

But now the demon was Stile's own size, still full of fight. It scrambled to its hooved feet and sprang at him, trying to loop the cord about his neck again. It seemed to be a one-tactic fighter. In that respect it resembled the imitation-Sheen robot Stile had fought not so very long ago.

Stile caught its hands from the outside, whirled, ducked, and hauled the demon over his shoulder. The thing lifted over him and whomped into the ground with a jar that should have knocked it out. But again it scrambled up, still fighting.

What was *with* this thing? It refused to turn off! It had taken a battering that would have shaken an android—and all it did was grow larger and uglier. It was now a quarter again as large as Stile, and seemed to have gained strength in proportion. Stile could not fight it much longer, this way.

Yet again the demon dived for him, chain spread. Stile had an inspiration. He grabbed the chain, stepped to one side, tripped the demon—and as it stumbled, Stile looped the slack chain about the creature's own body and held it there from behind.

The demon roared and turned about, trying to reach him, but Stile clung like a blob of rubber cement. He had discommoded large opponents this way before, clinging to the back; it was extremely hard for a person to rid himself of such a rider if he did not know how. This demon was all growth and strength, having no special intelligence or imagination; it did not know how.

The demon kept growing. Now it was half again as large as Stile—and the chain was beginning to constrict its body. Stile hung on, staying out of the thing's awkward graspings, keeping that chain in place. Unless the demon could stop growing voluntarily—

Evidently it could not. It grew and grew, and as it expanded the chain became tighter, constricting its torso about the middle. It had fallen into the same noose it had tried to use on Stile. All it had to do was let go the ends—and it was too stupid to do that. What colossal irony! Its own arms wrapped around it, being drawn nearly out of their sockets, but the only way it knew to fight was to hang on to that chain. It became woman-waisted, then wasp-waisted. Stile let go and stood apart, watching the strange progression. The creature seemed to feel no pain; it still strove to reach Stile, to wrap its chain about him, though this was now impossible.

The demon's body ballooned, above and below that tiny waist. Then it popped. There was a cloud of smoke, dissipating rapidly.

Stile looked at the ground. There lay the chain, broken at last, separated where the demon-figure had been. The amulet was gone.

He picked it up, nervous about what it might do, but determined to know what remained. It dangled loosely from his hand. Its power was gone.

Or was it? What would happen if he invoked it again? Stile decided that discretion was best. He coiled the chain, laid it on the ground, and rolled a rock to cover it. Let the thing stay there, pinned like a poisonous snake!

Now that the threat was over, Stile unwound. His body was shivering with reaction. What, exactly, had happened? What was the explanation for it?

He postulated and discarded a number of theories. He prided himself on his ability to analyze any situation correctly and swiftly; that was a major part of his Game success. What he concluded here, as the most reasonable hypothesis fitting all his observations, was quite *un*reasonable.

A. He was in a world where magic worked.

B. Someone/thing was trying to kill him here, too.

He found conclusion A virtually incredible. But he preferred it to the alternatives: that a super-technological power had created all this, or that he, Stile, was going crazy. Conclusion B was upsetting—but death threats against him had become commonplace in the past few hours. So it was best to accept the evidence of his experience: that he was now in a fantasy realm, and still in trouble.

Stile rubbed his fingers across his neck, feeling the burn of the chain. Who was after him, here? Surely not the same anonymous angry Citizen who had sent the android squads. The serf who had crossed the curtain and given him the amulet had been friendly; had he wanted to kill Stile, he could have done so by invoking the demon at the outset. It seemed more likely that the man had been genuinely trying to help—and that the amulet had acted in an unforeseen manner. Perhaps there were a number of such magic talismans, dual-purpose: clothe the ordinary person, kill certain other persons. Other persons like Stile. That left a lot in doubt, but accounted for what had happened. Stile was a fair judge of people and motives; nothing about the other man had signaled treachery or enmity. The amulet, as a mechanism to protect this land from certain people, seemed reasonable.

Why was he, Stile, unwanted here? *That* he would have to find out. It was not merely because he was new. The stranger had been new, not so long ago, by his own admission. Presumably he had been given a similar amulet, and used it, and it had performed as specified. Stile had at first suspected some kind of practical joke—but that demon had been no joke!

It could not be because he was small, or male; those could hardly be crimes in a human society. There had to be something else. Some special quality about him that triggered the latent secondary function of the amulet. Unless the effect was random: one bad amulet slipped in with the good ones, a kind of Russian roulette, and he happened to be the victim. But he was disinclined to dismiss it like that. A little bit of paranoia could go far toward keeping him out of any further mischief. Best to assume someone was out to get him, and play it safe.

Meanwhile, he would be well advised to get away from this region, before whoever had laid the amulet-trap came to find out why it had failed. And—he wanted to learn more about the status of magic here. Was it some form of illusion, or was it literal? The demon had shown him that his life could depend on the answer.

Where would he go? How could he know? Anywhere he could find food, and sleep safely, and remain hidden from whatever enemy he must have. *Not* the nearest castle he had spied; he was wary of that now. Anything near this place was suspect. He had to go somewhere in the wilderness, alone—

Alone? Stile did not like the thought. He was hardly a social lion, but he was accustomed to company. Sheen had been excellent company. For this strange land—

Stile nodded to himself. Considering all things, he needed a horse. He understood horses, he trusted them, he felt secure with them. He could travel far, with a good steed. And there surely were horses grazing in those fields to the north. He had not been able to make out the specific animals he had seen from the tree, but they had had a horsey aspect.

CHAPTER 6

Manure

Stile walked north, keeping a wary eye out for hazards, demonic or otherwise, and for something else. The land, as the trees thinned, became pretty in a different way. There were patches of tall lush grass, and multicolored flowers, and sections of tumbled rocks. And, finally, a lovely little stream, evidently issuing from the mountains to the south, bearing irregularly northwest. The water was absolutely clear. He lay on his stomach and put his lips to it, at the same time listening for any danger; drinking could be a vulnerable moment.

The water was so cold his mouth went numb and his throat balked at swallowing. He took his time, savoring it; beverages were so varied and nutritious and available on Proton that he had seldom tasted pure water, and only now appreciated what he had missed.

Then he cast about for fruit trees, but found none. He had no means to hunt and kill animals right now, though in time he was sure he could devise something. Safety was more urgent than nourishment, at the moment; his hunger would have to wait. With a horse he could go far and fast, leaving no footprints of his own and no smell not masked by that of the animal; he would become untraceable.

He followed the stream down, knowing it was a sure guide to the kind of animal life he wanted. This was ideal horse country; had he actually seen some horses grazing, there from the treetop, or only made an image of a wish? He could not be certain now, but trusted his instincts. Magic confused him, but he knew the ways of horses well.

Suddenly he spied it: the semicircular indentation of the hoof of a horse. And, safely back from the water, a pile of horse manure. Confirmation!

Stile examined the hoofprint. It was large, indicating an animal of perhaps seventeen hands in height, solidly built. It was unshod, and chipped at the fringes, but not overgrown. A fat, healthy horse who traveled enough to keep the hooves worn, and was careless enough to chip them on stones. Not the ideal mount for him, but it would do. Stile felt the relief wash through his body, now that he had the proof; he had not imagined it, he had not deluded himself, there really were horses here. His experience with the demon amulet had shaken his certainties, but this restored them.

He moved over to the manure and stared down at it. And faded into a memory. Seventeen years ago, as a youth of eighteen, looking down at a similar pile of dung . . .

His parents' tenure had ended, and they had had to vacate Planet Proton. Tenure was twenty years for serfs, with no exceptions—except possibly via the Game, a more or less futile lure held out to keep the peons hoping. He had been fortunate; he had been born early in their tenure, and so had eighteen free years. He had fitted in a full education and mastered Proton society before he had to make the choice: to stay with his folks, or to stay on Proton.

His parents, with twenty years cumulative pay awaiting them, would be moderately wealthy in the galaxy. They might not be able to swing passage all the way back to Earth, but there were other planets that were really quite decent. They would be able to afford many good things. On the other hand, if he remained on Proton he would have to serve twenty years as a serf, naked, obedient to the whims of some Citizen employer, knowing that when that tenure ended he too would be exiled.

But—here on Proton was the Game.

He had been addicted to the Game early. In a culture of serfs, it was an invaluable release. The Game was violence, or intellect, or art, or chance, alone or with tools or machines or animals—but mainly it was challenge. It had its own hierarchy, independent of the outside status of the players. Every age-ladder had its rungs, for all to see. The Game had its own magic. He was good at it from the outset; he had a natural aptitude. He was soon on his ladder, on any rung he chose. But he never chose too high a rung.

Family—or Game? It had been no contest. He had chosen Planet Proton. He had taken tenure the day his parents boarded the spaceship, and he had waited for a Citizen to employ him. To his surprise, one had picked him up the first day. He had been conducted to the Citizen's plush estate—there were no *un*plush Citizens' estates—and put in the pasture and given a wagon and a wide pitchfork.

His job was to spade horse manure. He had to take his fork and wheelbarrow and collect every pile of dung the Citizen's fine horses were gracious enough to deposit on the fine lawns. Homesick for his exiled family—it was not that he had loved them less, but that at his age he had loved the Game more—and unaccustomed to the discipline of working for a living, he found this a considerable letdown. Yet it did allow him time to be alone, and this was helpful.

He was not alone during off-hours. He slept in a loft-barracks with nine other pasture hands, and ate in a mess hall with thirty serfs. He had no privacy and no personal possessions; even his bedding was only on loan, a convenience to prevent his sweat from contaminating anyone else. In the morning the light came on and they all rose, swiftly; at night the light went out. No one missed a bed check, ever. At home with his folks he had had no curfew; they went off to their employers by day, and as long as he kept up with his schooling his time was largely his own—which meant he would be playing the Game, and drilling himself in its various techniques. Here it was different, and he wondered whether he had after all made the right choice. Of course he had to grow up sometime; he just hadn't expected to do it overnight.

The Citizen-employer was inordinately wealthy, as most Citizens were. He had several fine pastures, in scattered locations. It was necessary to travel through the city-domes from one property to another, and somehow the work was always piling up ahead of him.

Some of the pastures were cross-fenced, with neat white Earth-grown wooden boards and genuine prerusted nails. These barriers were of course protected by invisible microwires that delivered an uncomfortable electric shock to anyone who touched the surface. The horses were not smart, but they had good memories; they seldom brushed the fences. Stile, of course, had to learn the hard way; no one told him in advance. That was part of his initiation.

He learned. He found that the cross-fencing was to keep the horses in one pasture while allowing a new strain of grass to become established in another; if the horses had at it prematurely, they would destroy it by overgrazing before it had a chance. Pastures were rotated. When animals had to be separated, they were put in different pastures. There were many good reasons for cross-fencing, and the employer, despite his wealth, heeded those reasons.

Stile's problem was that he had to cross some of those fences, to collect the manure from far pastures. He was small, too small simply to step over as a tall serf might. He was acrobatic, so could readily have hurdled the 1.5 meter fences, but this was not permitted, lest it give the horses notions. The horses did not know it was possible to jump fences outside of a formal race, so had never tried it. Also, his landing might scuff the turf, and that was another offense. Only horses had the right to scuff; they were valuable creatures, with commensurate privileges.

Thus he had to proceed laboriously around the fence, going to far-flung gates where, of course, he had to debate the right-of-way with horses who outmassed him by factors of ten to fifteen. This slowed his work, and he was already behind. Fortunately he was a good runner, and if he moved swiftly the horses often did not bother to keep up. They could outrun him if they had a mind to, anytime, but they never raced when they didn't have to. It seemed to be a matter of principle. They did not feel the same rivalry with a man that they did with members of their own species.

Then he discovered the stile: a structure like a standing stepladder that enabled him to cross the fence and haul his wheelbarrow across without touching a board. The horses could not navigate such a thing, and did not try. It was, in its fashion, a bridge between worlds. With it he could at last get around the pastures fast enough to catch up to his work.

Now that he was on tenure, he was expected to take an individual name. He had gone by his father's serf-name, followed by a dependence-number. When the Proton serf registry asked him for his choice of an original and personal designation, his irrevocable and possibly only mark of distinction, he gave it: Stile.

"Style? As in elegance?" the serf-interviewer inquired, gazing down at him with amusement. "A grandiose appellation for a lad your size."

Stile's muscles tightened in abdomen, buttocks, and shoulders. This "lad" was eighteen, full-grown—but to strangers he looked twelve. The depilatories in Proton wash water kept the hair off his face and genitals, so that his sexual maturity was not obvious. A woman his size would not have had a problem; depilatories did not affect her most obvious sexual characteristics. He was fed up with the inevitable remarks; normal-heighted people always thought they were being so damned clever with their slighting allusions to his stature. But already he was learning to conceal his annoyance, not even pretending to take it as humor. "Stile, as in fence. S-T-I-L-E. I'm a pasture hand."

"Oh." He was so designated, and thereafter was invariably addressed this way. The use of the proper name was obligatory among serfs. Only Citizens had the pleasure of anonymity, being addressed only as "sir." If any serf knew the name of a Citizen, he kept it to himself, except on those rare occasions when he needed to identify his employer for an outsider.

It turned out to be a good choice. Stile—it was original and distinctive, and in the context of the Game, suggestive of the homonym. For in the Game he did indeed have a certain style. But best of all were the ramifications of its original meaning: a bridge between pastures. A stile represented a dimensionally expanded freedom and perception, as it were a choice of worlds. He liked that concept.

With experience he became more proficient. Every clod of dung he overlooked was a mark against him, a sure route to ridicule by the other hands, all of whom were larger if not older than he and had more seniority. In a society of workers who had no individual rights not relating to their jobs, the nuances of private protocol and favor became potent. "Stile—two clods in the buckwheat pasture," the foreman would announce grimly as he made his daily review of demerits, and the group would snigger discreetly, and Stile would be low man on the farm totem for the next day. He was low man quite often, in the early weeks. Other hands would "accidentally" shove him, and if he resisted he received a reprimand for roughhousing that put him low for another day. For, except in egregious cases, the higher man on the totem was always right, and when it was one serf's word against another's, the low man lost. The foreman, basically a fair man, honored this convention scrupulously. He was competent, the only serf on the farm with actual power, and the only one granted the privilege of partial anonymity: his title was used instead of his name. He never overstepped his prerogatives, or permitted others to.

There came one day when Stile had not fouled up. A hulking youth named Shingle was low for the day—and Shingle brushed Stile roughly on the path to the service area. Stile drew on his Game proficiency and ducked while his foot flung out, "accidentally" sending Shingle crashing into the barn wall. Furious, Shingle charged him, fists swinging— and Stile dropped to the ground, put his foot in the man's stomach, hauled on one arm, and flipped him through the air to land on the lush green turf so hard his body gouged it. Shingle's breath was knocked out, and the other hands stood amazed.

The foreman arrived. "What happened here?" he demanded.

"An accident," the others informed him, smirking innocently. "Shingle—fell over Stile."

The foreman squinted appraisingly at Stile, who stood with eyes downcast, knowing this meant trouble, expecting to receive the ridicule of the group again. Fighting was forbidden on these premises. Out came the clipboard the foreman always carried. "Shingle—one gouge in turf," the foreman said. And almost smiled, as the group sniggered.

For Shingle had been the man low on the totem, whose business it had been to avoid trouble. He was by definition wrong.

The foreman turned to Stile. "Accidents will happen—but in future you will report to the recreation room for practice in your martial arts, Stile." He departed on his rounds.

Stile only gained one day clear of the low totem, officially, for that day he overlooked another dropping. But he had traveled considerably higher in the estimate of his peers. They had not known he was into martial art. In turn, he remembered how they had stood by him, honoring the convention, laughing this time at the other fellow. Stile had won, by the tacit rules; the others had seemed to be against him only because he had been low totem, not because he was new or small. That was a supremely warming realization.

After that Stile began to make friends. He had held himself aloof, unconsciously, assuming the others looked down on him. If they had, they certainly didn't anymore. Now when he fouled up and they snickered, it was friendly, almost rueful. Even Shingle, nose out of joint about the episode, never made an issue of it; he too abided by the rules, and he had lost fairly.

Meanwhile, Stile was becoming adept at spotting horse manure. Horses tended to deposit their solid loads in semiprivate places, in contrast to their liquid ones. Liquid went anywhere at all, sometimes even on their food, but solids were always well away from eating, grazing or resting areas. This made the piles more challenging to find.

Missing piles tended to put him low on the totem. Consequently Stile had considerable incentive to improve his performance. He developed an extremely sharp eye for horse manure. His nose was not much help, for horses had mild refuse, unlike pigs or chickens; never unpleasant, its odor quickly faded. If left a few days—God forbid!—it could even sprout grass from undigested grains, for the digestion of horses was less sophisticated than that of cows. Horses were adapted to running, and their structure and heat-dissipation mechanism and digestion reflected this. So Stile's nose availed only when he was in the near vicinity of a find. Yet sight was not the whole answer either, for the piles could be concealed in copses of trees or amidst bushes. Sometimes he found chunks of it in the foliage of low-springing branches. There was also the problem of rain—artificial, of course, here in the domes—that wetted down the manure and tended to flatten and blend it with its surroundings. Even when everything was ideal, manure seemed to be able to disappear when he was in the vicinity, only to reappear when the foreman checked. It was so easy to overlook a pile on the left while collecting one on the right!

Stile's instincts for manure sharpened to the point of near perfection. He could spade a full pile into his barrow with one scoop and heave, not missing a chunk. He learned the favorite deposit sites of the horses, and checked there first. Sometimes he even beat the artificial flies there. He could look at a section of pasture and tell by the lay of it whether a horse would want to contribute.

Yet when he had mastered his job, it grew boring. Stile was bright, very bright. People tended to assume that small stature meant small intelligence, but it was not true. The work became stultifying. Had he mastered calculus and Terrestrial ecology and aspects of quantum physics merely to fling dung for twenty years? Call him the King of Dung! Why had the Citizen snapped him up so quickly, only to throw him away on this?

But Citizens were all-powerful on Proton. They did not answer to serfs for their actions. Stile could neither complain nor change employers; his rights in the matter extended only to accepting proffered employment or suffering premature termination of tenure. If he wanted to remain on Planet Proton, he obeyed the system. He spaded dung.

Often while at work he watched the horses, covertly, lest he seem to be malingering. There was Sonny, a small handsome paint hackney with large ears, used for training new riders though he had no proper trot. Simcoe Cloud, an appaloosa gelding sixteen hands high, with a pretty "blanket" but too large a head. Navahjo, a fine quarter horse, dominant in her pasture though she was a mare. In another pasture were Misty, a gray plump Tennessee Walker with a will of her own, and her companion Sky Blue, only fourteen hands high and over twenty years old. Blue was a former harness racer, well trained but shy despite her graying head. There was Cricket, also gray verging on white. There were, according to the dictates of horse registry, no white horses; a horse that looked white was either albino or registered gray. Thus the joke: "What color was George Washington's white horse? Gray."

These constituted Stile's world, during much of his working time. He came to know them all, from a moderate distance, from Shetland pony to massive draft horse. He longed to associate more closely with them, to pat them, brush them, walk them—but that was the prerogative of the stable hands, fiercely guarded. Stile was only a pasture hand, never allowed to get overly familiar with the stock. On many days his closest approach to a living horse was its manure.

Yet from that necessary distance, what beauty! There was a peculiar grace to a horse, any horse. The power of the muscles, the spring of the ankles, the alertness of the ears, the constant swishing of the tail. There were no natural flies here, so android flies were provided, that made loud buzzing sounds and swooped around the horses, just to provide exercise for those tails. Stile loved to watch the tails, perhaps the prettiest thing about any horse except for the manes. On occasion he saw a visiting horse with a red ribbon tied in the tail: the signal of an animal that kicked. If a pasture or stable hand got kicked, he was punished, not the valuable horse. Serfs were expected to be careful, not risking the horses' precious feet by contact with the serf's drab flesh.

Stile made the best of it. He was hardly conscious of this at the time, but the extreme value placed on horses here was to make a profound impression on his attitude in life. These were not the racing animals; these were the retirees, the injured, the secondary steeds—yet they were worth more than the lives of any of the serfs. Some serfs rebelled, secretly hating the animals they tended, but Stile absorbed the propaganda completely in this respect. The horse became his ideal. The horse, though confined to its pasture, had perfect freedom, for the pasture was equine heaven. If Stile had been a horse, he would have been in heaven too. Horses became prettier than people in his eyes, and though intellectually he denied this, emotionally he accepted it. Stile was in love with horses.

Thus he became an avid student of the species. Not only did he study the nuances of the mannerisms of the particular animals in his pastures, noting that each horse had a personality fully as distinct as that of any serf; during his free time he studied texts on horse manure. He learned of the intestinal parasites that might be found in it, the worms and the maggots and microscopic vermin. Of course there were no such parasites here, but he pretended there might be, and looked assiduously for the signs. He learned to judge the general health of a horse by its manure; whether it was being worked hard or was idle; what its diet was and in what proportions. Some horses had hard clods, some loose; Stile could tell which horse had produced any given pile, and thus was aware of the past day's location of each horse without ever seeing the animals directly.

Time passed. One day, two years into his tenure, Stile actually spied a worm in manure. He reported this immediately to the foreman. "A worm in our manure?" the man demanded incredulously. "You've got delusions of grandeur!"

But they tested the horse, for the foreman let nothing pass unverified, and Stile was correct. A slow-hatching variety of parasite had slipped through the quarantine and infected the animal. It was not a serious bug, and would not really have hurt the horse, but it was genuine. The larvae had manifested in the manure only on the day Stile noted them; he had caught the nuisance before it could spread to other animals.

The foreman took Stile to the shower, washed him personally as if he were a child, and combed his hair with an available currycomb. Stile submitted, amazed at this attention. Then the foreman brought him, shining clean, to a small door in the wall of the stable. "Always say 'sir' to him," the foreman said warningly. "Never turn your back until he has dismissed you." Then he guided Stile firmly through the door.

Stile found himself, for the first time, in the presence of his employer. The other side of the barn was a palatial apartment, with videoscreens on three walls. On each screen was a portion of a composite picture: the surface of a mountainous land as seen from the air. The image shifted in three-dimensional cohesion, making the illusion most effective. The floor was almost transparent quartz, surely imported from a quarry on Earth, thus more valuable weight for weight than local gold. What affluence!

The Citizen sat in a plush swivel chair upholstered in purple silk, on whose armrests a number of control buttons showed. He was garbed in an ornate robe that seemed to be spun from thread made of platinum, and wore fine suede slippers. He was not an old man, and not young; rejuvenation treatments made his body handsome and his age indeterminate; though behind that façade of health, nature surely kept accurate score. Few Citizens lived much over a century despite the best medicine could do. He possessed no overpowering atmosphere of command. Had Stile encountered him on the streets, serf-naked, he would never have recognized him as a Citizen. The man was completely human. It was the clothing that made the difference. But what a difference it made!

The Citizen was facing to the side, his eyes on a passing cloud. He seemed unaware of Stile's intrusion.

The foreman jogged Stile's elbow. Stile tried several times, and finally choked out his announcement of arrival: "S-sir."

The Citizen's eyes flicked to cover him. "You are the lad who spotted the worm?" The voice was ordinary too, amazingly.

"Yes, sir."

"You are promoted to stableboy." And the Citizen rotated in his swivel chair, turning his glossy back, dismissing Stile.

Stile found himself back in the barn. He must have walked there, guided by the foreman. Now the man led him by the hand to a cabin at the edge of the pasture. Three stable hands stood beside it, at attention.

"Stile is joining you," the foreman said. "Fetch his gear."

With alacrity they took off. In moments Stile's bedding, body brush and towel were neatly set up by the fourth bunk in the cabin. The stable hands were congratulating him. He was, of course, low man of the house—the "boy"—but it was like a fraternity, a giant improvement from the barracks. Only four to share the shower, curfew an hour later, and a cabin vidscreen!

Stile's days of spading and hauling manure were over. A new serf took his place in the pastures. Stile was now of a higher echelon. He was working directly with the horses. Reward had been as swift and decisive as punishment for infractions; at one stroke the Citizen had made two years of dung worthwhile.

Stile lifted his eyes from the manure of this wilderness realm. Oh, yes, he knew about manure! He had never forgotten what dung had done for him. He considered it not with distaste or horror, but almost with affection.

He walked on down the river, inspecting hoofprints and manure. Some of these horses were large, some medium, some healthy, some less so. Some did have worms in their droppings, and these gave Stile a perversely good feeling. A worm had promoted him!

This region, then, was not sterile; it was natural. Flies hovered about the freshest piles: genuine flies, he was sure, species he knew only from books and museum specimens. No one policed this region; the old piles lay undisturbed, sprouting toadstools, gradually settling, dissolving in rainfall, bright green grass growing up through them. No self-respecting horse would eat at a dung-site, so such blades remained unclipped. Nature's way of preventing overgrazing, perhaps—but Stile was appalled to see such an excellent pasture in such disrepair. Did no one *care* about these horses?

They must be wild, uncared for. Which meant that he would be free to take whichever one he chose. He might have to break it for riding—but he knew how to do that. Even with his injured knees he could ride any horse. Only specialized racing required extreme flexure of the knees; for other riding the legs were used for balance, for purchase, and guidance of the steed.

There was evidently a fair-sized herd in this region. A number of mares, governed by a single powerful stallion? No, there seemed to be several males; he could tell by the positioning of the hoofprints about the indentations of urination sites. Males watered in front of the hind hooves; females, behind. But there was bound to be a dominant stallion, for that was the way of horses. Geldings, or cut males, were no more competitive than mares, but potent stallions demanded recognition.

That dominant stallion would probably make the finest steed for Stile's purpose—but would also be too obvious. Stile needed a good, fast, but inconspicuous animal. A non-herd stallion—probably there were no geldings here, if the animals were actually wild—or a mare. A good mare was in no way inferior; some of the most durable runners were female. Stile had ridden a mare named Thunder once, who brooked no backtalk from any horse, regardless of size or sex, and was herself a magnificent, high-stepping, lofty-headed creature. If he could find a mare like her, here—

He spied the prints of a small horse, no more than fourteen hands, on the verge of being a pony, but supremely healthy. Probably a mare; there was something about the delicacy with which she had placed her feet. Every hoof was sound, and the manure had no infestation. She could run, too—he traced her galloping prints in the turf, noting the spread and precision of the marks, the absence of careless scuffmarks, of signs of tripping. No cracks in these hooves, no sloppy configurations. A good horse, in good condition, could outrun a greyhound, maintaining a velocity of 65 kilometers per hour. This could be that kind of horse. She seemed to be a loner, apart from the herd, drinking and feeding in places separate from the others. That could mean she was more vulnerable to predators, so would have to be more alert, tougher, and swifter. But why was she alone? Horses were basically herd animals.

He followed this trail, by print and manure. At first the piles were old, but as he used his skill to orient, they became fresher. It took him some hours to make real progress, for the horse had wandered far— as healthy horses did. As Stile walked, he wondered more persistently: what made this one separate from her companions? Was she, like himself, a private individual who had learned to value alone-time, or had she been excluded from the herd? What would constitute reason for such exclusion? Obviously she made do quite well alone—but did she really like it?

Stile had quite a lot of empathy for horses, and a lot for outsiders. Already he liked this little mare he had not yet seen. He did not after all need any giant steed to ride; his weight was slight, and he knew how to make it seem lighter. A small horse, even a pony could easily support him. In heroic fantasy the protagonist always bestrode a giant stallion; Stile could handle such a horse, but knew there were points to smallness too. Just as there were points to small people!

Here he was, abruptly, at an aspect of the truth: he was very small for his kind, therefore he liked small things. He identified with them. He knew what it felt like to be looked down on, to be the butt of unfunny jokes. "Hey, dja hear the one about the little moron?" Why did it always have to be a *little* moron? Why did the terms midget, dwarf, pygmy and runt have pejorative connotation? What the hell was so funny about being small? Since small people were not inferior intellectually, it stood to reason that smallness was a net asset. A better value, pound for pound.

So why didn't he really believe it? He should not choose a horse because it was small, but because it was the best mount for his purpose. Yet, subjectively—

Stile's irate chain of thought was interrupted by the sight of his objective. There she stood, as pretty a little mare as he had ever seen. Her coat was glossy black, except for white socks on her hind feet, one rising higher than the other. Her mane fell to the right side, ebony-sleek, and her tail was like the tresses of a beautiful woman. Her hooves glistened like pearl, dainty and perfectly formed. She had a Roman nose, convex rather than straight or concave, but in nice proportion. And her horn was a spiraled marvel of ivory symmetry.

Her *what?*

Stile actually blinked and rubbed his eyes. He only succeeded in blurring his vision. But what he saw was no trick of the light.

He had found a unicorn.

CHAPTER 7

Neysa

He must have gasped, for the mare raised her head alertly. She had, of course, been aware of his approach before; horses—unicorns?—had sharp hearing. She had not been alarmed—which itself was remarkable, if she were wild—so had continued grazing. Equines were like that; they startled readily, but not when they thought they had the situation in hand. Evidently this little lady unicorn was much the same.

This was a fantasy world, where magic evidently worked; he had already established that. He still felt the burn on his neck where the amulet-demon's chain had scraped. So why shouldn't this world have magic animals too? That made perfect sense. It was only that he had never thought it through, before assuming that these were horses. Was there, actually, much difference between a horse and a unicorn? Some artists represented unicorns with leonine bodies and cloven hooves, but Stile distrusted such conceptions. It could be that a true unicorn was merely a horse with a horn on the forehead. In which case this one would do just fine for him; he could ignore the horn and treat her as a horse.

Stile had not taken time to fashion a lariat; he had been more interested in surveying the situation, and in the memories this experience evoked. Now he decided: this was definitely the animal he wanted. With no rope, he would have to improvise. He doubted she was tame, but she might not be man-shy either.

He walked slowly up to her. The unicorn watched him warily. There was something about the way her horn oriented on him that was disquieting. It was without doubt a weapon. It tapered to a sharp point; it was a veritable spear. This was a fighting animal. Scratch one assumption: he could in no way afford to ignore that horn.

"Now my name's Stile," he said in a gentle voice. "Stile as in fence. You may not know about that sort of thing, though. I need a—a steed. Because I may have a long way to go, and I can get there faster and better if I ride. I am a very good endurance runner, for a man, but a man does not compare to a good h—unicorn. I would like to ride you. What is your name?"

The unicorn blew a double note through her horn. This startled Stile; he had not realized the horn was hollow. He had been speaking rhetorically, expecting no response. Her note was coincidental, of course; she could hardly be expected to comprehend his words. It was his tone of voice that mattered, and the distraction of it while he approached. Yet that note had sounded almost like a word. "Neysa?" he asked, voicing it as well as he could.

There was a fluted snort of agreement—or so it seemed to him. He reminded himself to be careful how he personified animals; if he ever got to believing he was talking with one on a human basis, he'd have to suspect his own sensibility. He could get himself killed, deluding himself about the reactions of a creature with a weapon like that.

"Well, Neysa, what would you do if I just got on your back and rode you?" He had to keep talking, calming her, until he could get close enough to mount her. Then there would be merry hell for a while: a necessary challenge.

The unicorn whipped her horn about in a menacing manner, and stomped her left forefoot. Her ears flattened back against her head. The language of unicorns was obviously like that of horses, with absolutely clear signals—for those who knew how to interpret them. She might not comprehend the specific meaning of his words, but she knew he was encroaching, and was giving adequate warning. If he tried to ride her, she would try to throw him, and if he got thrown, he would be in serious trouble. This was indeed no tame animal; this was a creature who knew of men and did not fear them, and when sufficiently aggravated would kill. A wildcat was not merely a housecat gone wild; a unicorn was not merely a horse with a weapon. The whole psychology differed. Neysa's every little mannerism told him that. He had no doubt, now, that there was blood on her horn—from other creatures who had failed to heed her warnings.

Yet he had to do it. "Neysa, I'm sorry. But a demon tried to kill me, not long ago, and in this frame of magic I am not well equipped to protect myself. I need to get away from here, and I'm sure you can take me so much better than I can take myself. Men have always depended on horses—uh, equines to carry them, before they started messing with unreliable machines like automobiles and spaceships." He stepped closer to her, hand outstretched, saying anything, just so long as he kept talking.

She lifted both forefeet in a little prance and brought them down together in a clomp directed at him. Her nose made a hooking gesture at him, and she made a sound that was part squeal and part snort and part music—the sort of music played in the background of a vid-show when the horrible monster was about to attack. This was as forceful a warning as she could make. She would not attack him if he departed right now, as she preferred simply to graze and let graze, but she would no longer tolerate his presence. She was not at all afraid of him—a bad sign!—she just didn't like him.

Now Stile remembered the folklore about unicorns, how they could be caught only by a virginal girl; the unicorn would lay his head in her lap, and then an ambush could be sprung. Probably this had been a cynical fable: how do you catch a mythical animal? With a mythical person. Implication: virgins were as rare as unicorns. Clever, possibly true in medieval times—and beside the point. How would it relate to a man and a female unicorn? Would she put her head in his lap? Only to un-man him, surely! More likely the matter related to riding: only a person pure in spirit could ride a unicorn—and in such myths, purity was defined as sexual abstinence and general innocence. Stile had no claims to such purity. Therefore this could be a very difficult ride. But mythology aside, he expected that sort of ride anyway.

"I really am sorry to do this, Neysa," Stile said. And leaped.

It was a prodigious bound, the kind only a highly trained athlete could perform. He flew through the air to land squarely on the unicorn's back. His hands reached out to take firm grip on her mane, his legs clamped to her sides, and his body flattened to bring him as close to her as physically possible.

Neysa stood in shocked surprise for all of a tenth of a second. Then she took off like a stone from a catapult. Stile's body was flung off—but his hands retained their double grip on her mane, and in a moment his legs had dropped back and were clamping her sides again. She bucked, but he clung close, almost standing on his head. No ordinary horse could buck without putting its head down between its front legs; it was a matter of balance and weight distribution. Neysa managed it, however, providing Stile with just a hint of what he was in for. Normal limits were off, here; this was, for sure, a magic animal.

She reared, but he stayed on her like a jacket. She whipped her head about, spearing at him with her horn—but he shifted about to avoid it, and she could not touch him without endangering her own hide. That horn was designed to spear an enemy charging her from the front, not one clinging to her back. It took a special kind of curved horn to handle a rider; she would never dislodge him this way.

So much for the beginning. Now the unicorn knew that no amateur bestrode her. It would require really heroic measures to dump him. For Stile, when he wasn't trying to gentle an animal, was extremely tough about falls.

Neysa accelerated forward, going west toward the chasm cracks he had spied from the spruce tree—then abruptly braked. All four feet skidded on the turf. But Stile was wise to this maneuver, and remained secure. She did a double spinabout, trying to fling him off by centrifugal force—but he leaned to the center of the turn and stayed firm. Abruptly she reversed—and he did too. She leaped forward—then leaped backward. That one almost unseated him; it was a trick no ordinary horse knew. But he recovered, almost tearing out a fistful of her mane in the process.

Well! Now she was warmed up. Time to get serious. Neysa tripped forward, lowering her body—then reared and leaped simultaneously. She fell backward; then her hind feet snapped forward and she performed a flip in air. For an instant she was completely inverted, her entire body above his. Stile was so startled he just clung. Then she completed the flip, landing on her front feet with her body vertical, finally whomping down on her hind feet.

Only the involuntary tightening of his hands had saved him. A horse doing a backflip! This was impossible!

But, he reminded himself again, this was no horse. This was a unicorn—a creature of fantasy. The mundane rules simply did not apply here.

Next, Neysa went into a spin. She galloped in a tightening circle, then drew in her body until she was actually balanced on one forefoot, head and tail lifted, rotating rapidly. Magic indeed. Stile hung on, his amazement growing. He had known he would be in for a stiff ride, but he had grossly underestimated the case. This was akin to his fight with the demon.

Well, maybe that was a fair parallel. Two magical creatures, one shaped like a humanoid monster, the other like a horse with a horn. Neither subject to the limitations of conventional logic. He had been foolish to assume that a demon that superficially resembled a horse was anything close to that kind of animal. He would remember this lesson—if he happened to get out of this alive.

Now Neysa straightened out, stood for a moment—then rolled. Her back smacked into the ground—but Stile had known when to let go. He landed on his feet, and was back on her back as she regained her own feet. "Nice try, Neysa," he said as he settled in again.

She snorted. So much for round two. She had only begun to fight!

Now she headed for the nearest copse of trees. Stile knew what was coming: the brush-off. Sure enough, she passed so close to a large trunk that her side scraped it—but Stile's leg was clear, as he clung to her other side in the fashion of a trick rider. He had once won a Game in which the contest was trick riding; he was not the finest, but he was good.

Neysa plunged into a thicket. The saplings brushed close on either side, impossible to avoid—but they bent aside when pushed, and could not sweep off a firmly anchored rider who was prepared. She shot under a large horizontal branch, stout enough to remove him—but again he slid around to the side of her body, avoiding it, and sprang to her back when the hazard was past. Real riding was not merely a matter of hanging on; it required positive anticipations and countermoves to each equine effort. He could go anywhere she could go!

Neysa charged directly toward the next large tree, then planted her forefeet, lifted her rear feet, and did a front-foot-stand that sent her back smashing into the trunk. Had he stayed on her, he would have been crushed gruesomely. No game, this! But Stile, now wise in the ways of unicorns, had dropped off as her motion started. He had less mass than she, weighing about an eighth as much, and could maneuver more rapidly when he had to. As her rear feet came back to the ground, Stile's rear feet came back to her back, and his hands resumed their clutch on her mane.

She snorted again. Round three was over. Round four was coming up. How many more tricks did this phenomenal animal have? Stile was in one sense enjoying this challenge, but in another sense he was afraid. This was no Proton Game, where the loser suffered no more than loss of status; this was his life on the line. The first trick he missed would be the last.

Neysa came onto a grassy plain. Now she accelerated. What was she up to this time? It didn't seem so bad—and that made him nervous. Beginning with a walk, she accelerated to a slow trot. The speed differential was not great, as a slow trot could be slower than a brisk walk. In fact, Stile had worked with lazy horses who could trot one meter per second, rather than the normal three or four meters per second. The distinguishing mark was the beat and pattern. In walking, the horse put down the four feet in order, left-front, right-rear, right-front, left-rear, four beats per cycle. Trotting was two-beat: left-front and right-rear together, followed by right-front and left-rear together. Or with a right lead instead of a left. The point was that the motion of each front foot was synchronous with one hind foot; in some cases the front and rear moved together on the same side. But there were only two beats per cycle, the pairs of feet striking the ground cleanly together. It made for a bumpy but regular ride that covered the ground well, and looked very pretty from the side. A slow trot could be gentle; a fast one could be like a jackhammer. But a trot was definitely a trot, at any speed; there was no mistaking it. Stile liked trotting, but distrusted this one. He knew he had not seen the last of this mare's devices.

Next she broke into a canter: three-beat. Left-front, then right-front and left-rear together, and finally right-rear. Like a cross between a walk and a trot, and the ride a kind of gentle swooping. All perfectly conventional, and therefore not to be trusted. She had something horrendous in her canny equine mind!

Finally she reached a full gallop: a modified two-beat cycle, the two front legs striking almost but not quite together, then the rear two. A four-beat cycle, technically, but not uniform. Beat-beat, beat-beat, at the velocity of racing. Stile enjoyed it; he experienced an exhilaration of speed that was special on a horse—unicorn. Motored wheels could go much faster, of course, but it wasn't the same. Here, as it were in the top gear, the animal straining to the limit—though this one was not straining, but loafing at a velocity that would have had another one straining—

The unicorn shifted into another gait. It was a five-beat—

Stile was so surprised he almost dropped off. No horse had a five-beat gait! There were only four feet!

No horse—there he was again. He kept forgetting and getting reminded in awkward ways. This gait was awful; he had never before experienced it, and could not accommodate it. BEAT-beat-BEAT-BEAT-beat, and over again, bouncing him in a growing resonance, causing him to lose not his grip but his composure. He felt like a novice again, fouling himself up, his efforts to compensate for the animal's motions only making it worse. As a harmonic vibration could shake apart a building, this fifth-beat was destroying him. He would fall—and at this breakneck velocity he could . . . break his neck.

Think, Stile, think! he told himself desperately. *Analyze: What is the key to this gait?*

His hands were hurting as his clutch on the unicorn's mane slowly slipped. His thigh muscles were beginning to cramp. Stile was expert—but this creature had his number now. Unless he could get her number too, soon.

Four feet, five beats. One foot had to repeat. Number the steps: one-two-three-four—where was the repeat? *Fingers slipping . . .*

BEAT-beat—that sound was less than the others, like a half-step. But half a step had to be completed by—another half-step. Like a man catching his balance when tripped. Two half-steps—that was it. Not necessarily together. The second and fifth. The right rear foot—as though stumbling, throwing off his timing. Compensate—

Stile started to catch on. He shifted his weight to absorb the shock and irregularity. BEAT-absorb-BEAT-BEAT-absorb. It was tricky and unnatural as hell, but his body was finding the dubious rhythm, getting the swing. Mostly it was his knowledge of the pattern, of what to expect. No more surprises! His leg muscles relaxed, and his hands stopped slipping.

Neysa felt the change, and knew he had surmounted this challenge too. She turned at speed—and Stile's inertia almost flung him off her side. A gradual turn at high velocity could pack more wallop than a fast turn at low speed. But she had to shift to a normal gallop for the turn, and no equine living could dump Stile with a normal gallop.

Realizing her mistake, the unicorn changed tactics. She slowed, then suddenly went into a one-beat gait. This was another surprise, in a ride full of them. It was like riding a pogo stick. All four of her feet landed together; then she leaped forward, front feet leading—only to contract to a single four-point landing again.

But Stile had ridden a pogo stick, in the course of his Game experience. He could handle this. "No luck, Neysa!" he cried. "Give up?"

She snorted derisively through her horn. It was almost as if she understood his words. But of course horses were very perceptive of tone, and responsive to it.

She turned. She had been going north, having curved in the course of her running; now she bore due west. Round five was coming up.

The grass gave way to packed dirt, then to clay, then to something like shale, and finally to rock. Neysa's hooves struck sparks from the surface, astonishing Stile. She was traveling fast, to be sure—faster than any horse he had raced. It felt like eighty kilometers per hour, but that had to be a distortion of his perception; such a speed would be of interworld championship level, for a horse. Regardless, hooves were not metallic; this animal was not shod, had no metal horseshoes, no nails. Nothing to strike sparks. Yet they were here.

Now she came to the pattern of crevices he had spied from the tree. They loomed with appalling suddenness: deep clefts in the rock whose bottoms could not be seen. Her hooves clicked between cracks unerringly, but Stile didn't like this. Not at all! One misstep would drop a foot into one of those holes, and at this speed that would mean a broken leg, a tumble, and one man flying through the air to land—where? But all he could do was hang on.

The cracks became more plentiful, forming a treacherous lattice. His vision of the crevices blurred, because they were so close, passing so rapidly; they seemed to writhe in their channels, swelling and shrinking, now twisting as if about to burst free, now merging with others or splitting apart. He had noted a similar effect when riding the Game model train as a child, fixing his gaze on the neighboring tracks, letting them perform their animations as he traveled. But these were not rails, but crevices, getting worse.

Neysa danced across the lattice as Stile watched with increasing apprehension. Now these were no longer mere cracks in a surface; these were islands between gaps. Neysa was actually traversing a chasm, jumping across from stone to stone, each stone a platform rising vertically from the depths. Stile had never seen such a landscape before. He really was in a new world: new in kind as well as in region.

Now Neysa was leaping, using her one-beat gait to bound from one diminishing platform to another. Sometimes all four feet landed together, in a group, almost touching each other; sometimes they were apart, on separate islands. She was obviously conversant with this place, and knew where to place each hoof, as a child knew where to jump amid the squares of a hopscotch game, proficient from long practice. Perhaps Neysa had mastered this challenge in order to avoid predators. No carnivore could match her maneuvers here, surely; the creature would inevitably misstep and fall between islands, perhaps prodded by the unicorn's aggressive horn, and that would be the end. So her trick gait made sense: it was a survival mechanism. Probably the five-beat gait had a similar function. What terrain was it adapted to?

Neysa danced farther into the pattern. The islands became fewer, smaller, farther apart. Now Stile could peer into the lower reaches of the crevices, for the sunlight slanted down from almost overhead. Had it been only six hours from the start of this day? It seemed much longer already! The fissures were not as deep as he had feared; perhaps two meters. But they terminated in rocky creases that could wedge a leg or a body, and they were getting deeper as the unicorn progressed. This was a test of nerve as much as of agility or riding ability.

As it happened, Stile had the nerve. "Let's face it, Neysa," he said. He tended to talk to horses; they listened well, politely rotating their pointed furry ears around to fetch in larger scoops of his sound, and they did not often talk back. "We're in this together. What would I gain by falling off now? A broken leg? If it's all the same to you, oh prettiest and surest-footed of equines, I'll just stay on." He saw her left ear twitch as if shaking off a fly. She heard him, all right, and was not pleased at the confidence his tone exuded.

But the acrobatic challenge was not what the unicorn had come for. Suddenly she leaped—into the depths of a larger crack. It was two meters wide, shallow at the near end, but bearing lower. The sides seemed to close in as she plunged deeper. Where was she going? Stile did not like this development at all.

Neysa swung around a chasm corner and dropped to a lower level. This crack narrowed above; they were in a partial cave, light raying from the top. Cross-cracks intersected often, but the unicorn proceeded straight ahead.

A demon roared, reaching from the side. Where had it come from? A niche at the side, hidden until they were beside it. Stile ducked his head, and the thing missed him. He glimpsed it only briefly: glaring red eyes, shining teeth, glistening horns, talon claws, malevolence. Typical of the breed, no doubt.

Another demon loomed, grabbing from the other side. Stile flung his body away, and this one also missed. But this was getting bad; he could not afford to let go his grip on Neysa's mane, for it was his only purchase. But he soon would need an arm to fend off these attacks.

The unicorn's strategy was clear, now. She was charging through the habitat of monsters, hoping one of them would pluck the unwanted rider from her back. The demons were not grabbing at her; they shied away from her deadly horn, instead snatching from the sides. They seemed akin to the demon of the amulet that he had fought before, except that their size was constant. Stile knew he would not survive long if one of these monsters nabbed him. He had already learned how tough demons were.

He would have to compromise. Neysa could not turn abruptly, for these crevices defined her route. The demons stood only at intersections and niches; there was not room enough in a single crevice for unicorn *and* demon. So this was a set channel with set hazards. He should be able to handle it—if he were careful.

Another intersection; another demon on the right. Stile let go Neysa's mane with his right hand and lifted his arm to ward off the attack. He did it with expertise, striking with his forearm against the demon's forearms, obliquely, drawing on the power of his forward motion. The leverage was with him, and against the reaching demon; Stile was sure of that. There was art to blocking, no matter what was being blocked.

Neysa felt his shifting of weight and tried to shake him off. But the channel bound her; she could not act effectively. Her trap inhibited her as much as him. It was evident that the demons were not her friends; otherwise she would simply stop and let them snatch him off. No, they were enemies, or at least un-friends; she neither stopped nor slowed, lest the demons get her as well as him. They probably liked the taste of raw unicorn flesh as well as they liked the taste of human flesh.

In fact, she had taken quite a risk to get rid of him. She just might get rid of herself, too.

"Neysa, this is no good," Stile said. "This should be between you and me. I don't like demons any better than you do, but this shouldn't be their concern. You're going for double or nothing—and it's too likely to be nothing. Let's get out of here and settle this on our own. Whoever wins and whoever loses, let's not give the pleasure of our remains to these monsters."

She charged on, straight ahead, of course. He knew he was foolish to talk to himself like this; it really accomplished nothing. But stress gave him the compulsion. The demons kept grabbing, and he kept blocking. He talked to them too, calling them names like "Flopface" and "Crooktooth," and exclaiming in cynical sympathy when they missed him. He forced himself to stop that; he might get to wanting to help them.

Stile was quite nervous now; he knew this because when he turned off his mouth he found himself humming. That was another thing he tended to do when under stress. He had to vocalize in some fashion. Upon occasion it had given him away during a Game. Bad, bad habit! But now the refrain became compulsive. Hummm-hummm-block, as a demon loomed; hummm-hummm-block! Stupid, yet effective in its fashion. But the demons were getting more aggressive, encroaching more closely. Soon they would become bold enough to block the channel ahead—

One did. It stepped out directly in front of the unicorn, arms spread, grin glowering. It was horrendously ugly.

Neysa never slowed. Her horn speared straight forward. As it touched the demon, she lifted her head. There was a shock of impact. The creature was impaled through the center, hoisted into the air, and hurled back over the unicorn's body. Stile clung low, and it cleared him.

Now he knew why most demons gave way to a charging unicorn. They might overwhelm a stationary unicorn, but a moving one was deadly. Stile could hardly imagine a more devastating stroke than the one he had just seen.

And a similar stroke awaited him, the moment he fell off.

The beat of Neysa's hooves changed. She was driving harder now—because she was climbing. Stile peered ahead, past her bloodstained horn, and saw the end of the crevice. They were finally coming out of it.

The demons drew back. They had become too bold, and paid the penalty. The intruders were leaving anyway; why hinder them? Stile relaxed. Round five was over.

They emerged to the surface—and plunged into liquid. The northern end of the cracks terminated in water. A river flowed down into them, quickly, vanishing into the deeper crevices—but to the north it was broad and blue. Neysa splashed along it; the water was only knee-deep here.

The river curved grandly, like a python, almost touching itself before curving back. "The original meander," Stile remarked. "But I don't see how this is going to shake me off, Neysa." However, if he had to be thrown, he would much prefer that it be in water. He was of course an excellent swimmer.

Then the water deepened, and the unicorn was swimming. Stile had no trouble staying on. Was she going to try to drown him? She had small chance! He had won many a Game in the water, and could hold his breath a long time.

She did not try. She merely swam upstream with amazing facility, much faster than any ordinary horse could do, and he rode her though all but her head and his head were immersed. The river was cool, not cold; in fact it was pleasant. If this were round six, it was hardly a challenge.

Then he felt something on his thigh. He held on to the mane with his right hand, wary of tricks, and reached with his left—and found a thing attached to his flesh. Involuntarily he jerked it off, humming again. There was a pain as of abrading flesh, and it came up: a fishlike creature with a disk for a head, myriad tiny teeth projecting.

It was a lamprey. A blood-sucking eel-like creature, a parasite that would never let go voluntarily. Another minor monster from the biological museum exhibits, here alive.

Stile looked at it, horrified. Magic he found incredible; therefore it didn't really bother him. But this creature was unmagical and disgusting. He heard the loudness of his own humming. He tried to stop it, ashamed of his squeamishness, but his body would not obey. What revulsion!

Another sensation. He threw the lamprey away with a convulsive shudder and grabbed the next, from his side. It was a larger sucker. There was little he could do to it, one-handed; it was leather-tough. He might bite it; that would serve it right, a taste—literally—of its own medicine. But he recoiled at the notion. Ugh!

The noxious beasties did not seem to be attacking the unicorn. Was it her hair, or something else? She could hardly use her horn to terrorize something as mindless as this.

Neysa kept swimming up the river, and Stile kept yanking off eels, humming grimly as he did. He hated this, he was absolutely revolted, but he certainly was not going to give up now!

The unicorn dived, drawing him under too. Stile held his breath, clinging to her mane. It was work for her to stay under, as her large equine belly gave her good flotation; he was sure he could outlast her. She would have to breathe, too.

She stayed down a full minute, then another. Only the tip of her horn cut the surface of the water like the fin of a shark. How long could she do it? He was good at underwater exploits, but he was getting uncomfortable.

Then he caught on: her horn was a snorkel. She was breathing through it! She had no air-limit. His lungs were hurting, but her neck was too low; he could not get his head high enough to break the surface without letting go her mane. If he let go, he surely would not have a chance to catch her again; she would stab him if he tried.

But he had a solution. He hauled himself up hand over hand to her head, where her black forelock waved like sea grass in the flow. He grabbed her horn. It was smooth, not knife-edged along the spiral; lucky for him! There seemed to be little indentations along its length: the holes for the notes, at the moment closed off.

His head broke water, and he breathed. She could not lower her horn without cutting off her own wind—and she was breathing too hard and hot to risk that. Equines had a lot of mass and muscle for their lungs to service, and she was still working hard to stay below.

Neysa blew an angry note through her horn and surfaced. Stile dropped back to her back. He yanked off two more eels that had fastened to him while he was below, as if his cessation of humming had made them bold.

Neysa cut to the edge of the river and found her footing. She charged out of the water. Stile had taken round six.

North of the river was a slope rising into a picturesque mountain range. The highest peaks were cloud-girt and seemed to be snow-covered. Surely she was not about to essay the heights!

She was. She galloped up the slope, the wind drying out her hair and his. What an animal she was! An ordinary horse would have been exhausted by this time, but this one seemed to be just hitting her stride.

The pace, however, was telling; Stile could feel her body heating. Horses, with or without horns, were massive enough to be short on skin surface to radiate heat. Therefore they sweated, as did man—but still it could take some time to dissipate the heat pollution of overexertion. She would have to ease up soon, even if her muscles still had strength.

She did not. The slope increased; her hooves pounded harder. One-two, three-four, a good hard-working gallop. She was not even trying to shake him off, now, but she surely had something excellent in mind. The grain-grass turf gave way to fields of blue and red flowers and goldenrod. More rocks showed, their rugged facets glinting cruel deep gray in the sun. The trees became smaller. Wisps of fog streamed by.

Stile craned his neck to look back—and was amazed. Already the Meander River was a small ribbon in the distance, far below. They must have climbed a vertical kilometer! Suddenly the air seemed chill, the breeze cutting. But the unicorn was hot; again small sparks flew from her feet as the hooves struck the rocky ground. Fine jets of vapor spumed from her nostrils.

Vapor? Stile squinted, unbelieving. *Those were jets of fire!*

No, impossible! No flesh-creature could breathe out fire. Living tissue wasn't able to—

Stile nudged forward, freed one hand, and reached ahead to approach the flame he thought he saw. Ouch! His fingers burned! That was indeed fire!

All right, once more. This was a magic land. He had accepted that, provisionally. The laws of physics he had known did not necessarily apply. Or if they were valid, they operated in different ways. Horses generated heat—so did unicorns. Horses sweated—this creature remained dry, once she had shed the river water. So she got rid of excess heat by snorting it out her nostrils in concentrated form. It did make sense, in its particular fashion.

Now the air was definitely cold. Stile was naked; if they went much higher, he could be in a new sort of trouble. And of course that was the idea. This was round seven, the trial of inclement climate. Neysa was not suffering; she was doing the work of running, so was burning hot. The cold recharged her.

Stile got down as close to his mount as he could. His back was freezing, but his front was hot, in contact with the furnace of Neysa's hide. This became uncomfortable. He was trying to sweat on one side and shiver on the other, and he couldn't turn over. And Neysa kept climbing.

Could he steer her back down the hill? Unlikely; trained horses moved with the guidance of reins and legs and verbal directives—but they did it basically because they knew no better. They were creatures of habit, who found it easiest to obey the will of the rider. This unicorn was a self-willed animal, no more tractable than a self-willed machine. (Ah, Sheen—what of you now?) If he did not like her direction, he would have to get off her back.

So he would just have to bear with it. He had to tame this steed before he could steer her, and he had to stay on before he could tame her. He found himself humming again. It seemed to help.

Neysa's feet touched snow. Steam puffed up from that contact. She really had hot feet! She charged on up the side of a glacier. Ice chipped off and slid away from her hooves. Stile hummed louder, his music punctuated by his shivering.

Crevices opened in the glacier. Again the unicorn's feet danced—but this time on a slippery slope. Her hooves skidded between steps, for their heat melted the ice. Those sparks were another heat-dissipating mechanism, and though the snow and ice had cooled the hooves below sparking level, there was still plenty of heat to serve. Her body weight shifted, compensating for the insecure footing, but a fall seemed incipient. Stile hummed louder yet. This was no miniature Game-mountain, under a warm dome, with cushioned landings for losers. This was a towering, frigid, violent landscape, and he was afraid of it.

The cloud cover closed in. Now it was as if the unicorn trod the cold beaches of an arctic sea, with the cloud layers lapping at the shores. But Stile knew that cloud-ocean merely concealed the deadly avalanche slopes. Neysa's legs sank ankle-deep in the fringe-wash, finding lodging in ice—but how would she know ahead of time if one of those washes covered a crevasse?

"Neysa, you are scaring the color right out of my hair!" Stile told her. "But I've got to cling tight, because I will surely perish if I separate from you here. If the fall through the ledges doesn't shatter me, the cold will freeze me. I'm not as tough as you—which is one reason I need you."

Then the first snow-monster loomed. Huge and white, with icicles for hair, its chill ice-eyes barely peeking out through its snow-lace whiskers, it opened its ice-toothed maw and roared without sound. Fog blasted forth from its throat, coating Stile's exposed portions with freezing moisture.

Neysa leaped across the cloud to another mountain island. Stile glanced down while she was in midair, spying a rift in the cover—and there was a gaunt chasm below. He shivered—but of course he was cold anyway. He had never been really cold before, having spent all his life in the climate-controlled domes of Proton; only the snow machines of the Game had given him experience, and that had been brief. This was close to his notion of hell.

Another snow-monster rose out of the cloud, its roar as silent as falling snow. Again the fog coated Stile, coalescing about his hands, numbing them, insinuating slipperiness into his grip on the mane. Stile discovered he was humming a funeral dirge. Unconscious black humor?

Neysa plunged through a bank of snow, breaking into the interior of an ice-cave. Two more snow-monsters loomed, breathing their fog. Neysa charged straight into them. One failed to move aside rapidly enough, and the unicorn's flame-breath touched it. The monster melted on that side, mouth opening in a silent scream.

On out through another snowbank—and now they were on a long snowslide on the north side of the range. Four legs rigid, Neysa slid down, gaining speed. Her passage started a separate snowslide that developed into a minor avalanche. It was as if the entire mountain were collapsing around them.

It would be so easy to relax, let go, be lost in the softly piling snow. Stile felt a pleasant lassitude. The snow was like surf, and they were planing down the front of the hugest wave ever imagined. But his hands were locked, the muscles cramped; he could not let go after all.

Suddenly they were out of winter, standing on a grassy ledge, the sun slanting warmly down. The cold had numbed his mind; now he was recovering. Neysa was breathing hard, her nostrils dilated, cooling. Stile did not know how long he had been unaware of their progress; perhaps only minutes, perhaps an hour. But somehow he had held on. His hands were cramped; this must be what was called a death grip. Had he won the victory, or was this merely a respite between rounds?

Neysa took a step forward—and Stile saw that the ledge was on the brink of a cliff overlooking the Meander River. In fact there was the roar of a nearby falls; the river started here, in the melting glaciers, and tumbled awesomely to the rocky base. Sure death to enter that realm!

Yet Neysa, fatigued to the point of exhaustion, was gathering herself for that leap. Stile, his strength returning though his muscles and skin were sore from the grueling ride, stared ahead, appalled. Enter that maelstrom of plunging water and cutting stone? She was bluffing; she had to be! She would not commit suicide rather than be tamed!

The unicorn started trotting toward the brink. She broke into a canter, bunched herself for the leap—

Stile flung himself forward, across her neck, half onto her head. His locked fingers cracked apart with the desperate force of his imperative, his arms flung forward. He grabbed her horn with both hands, swung his body to the ground beside her head, and bulldogged her to the side. She fought him, but she was tired and he had the leverage; he had rodeo experience too. They came to a halt at the brink of the cliff. A warm updraft washed over their faces, enhancing the impression of precariousness; Stile did not want to look down. Any crumbling of the support—

Stile held her tight, easing up only marginally as she relaxed, not letting go. "Now listen to me, Neysa!" he said, making his voice calm. It was foolish of him, he knew, to speak sense to her, just as it was foolish to hum when under stress, but this was not the occasion to attempt to remake himself. The unicorn could not understand his words, only his tone. So he was talking more for himself than for her. But with the awful abyss before them, he had to do it.

"Neysa, I came to you because I needed a ride. Someone is trying to kill me, and I am a stranger in this land, and I have to travel fast and far. You can go faster and farther than I can; you have just proved that. You can traverse regions that would kill me, were I alone. So I need you for a purely practical reason."

She continued to relax, by marginal stages, one ear cocked to orient on him, but she had not given up. The moment he let go, she would be gone. Into the river, the hard way, and on into unicorn heaven, the eternal pasture.

"But I need you for an emotional reason too. You see, I am a solitary sort of man. I did not wish to be, but certain factors in my life tended to set me apart from my associates, my peer group. I have generally fared best when going it alone. But I don't like *being* alone. I need companionship. Every living, feeling creature does. I have found it on occasion with other men in a shared project, and with women in a shared bed, and these are not bad things. But seldom have I had what I would call true friendship—except with another species of creature. I am a lover of horses. When I am with a horse, I feel happy. A horse does not seek my acquaintance for the sake of my appearance or my accomplishments; a horse does not expect a great deal of me. A horse accepts me as I am. And I accept the horse for what he is. A horse pulls his weight. I respect a horse. We relate. And so when I seek companionship, a really meaningful relationship, I look for a horse."

Neysa's head turned marginally so that she could fix one eye squarely on him. Good—she was paying attention to the soothing tones. Stile eased his grip further, but did not let go her horn.

"So I looked for you, Neysa. To be my equine companion. Because once a horse gives his allegiance, he can be trusted. I do not deceive myself that the horse cares for me in the same way I care for him—" He tightened his grip momentarily in a brief outpouring of the emotion he felt. "Or for her. But a horse is loyal. I can ride a horse, I can play, I can sleep without concern, for the horse will guard me from harm. A good horse will step on a poisonous snake before a man knows the threat is present. The horse will alert me to some developing hazard, for his perceptions are better than mine, and he will carry me away in time.

"I looked for you, Neysa, I selected you from all the herd before I ever saw you directly, because you are not really *of* the herd. You are a loner, like me. Because you are small, like me. But also healthy, like me. I understand and appreciate fitness in man and animal. Your hooves are clean, your manure is wholesome, your muscle tone is excellent, your coat has the luster of health, the sheen—" No, that was the wrong word, for it reminded him again of Sheen the robot lass. Where was she now, what was she doing, how was she taking his absence? Was she in metallic mourning for him? But he could not afford to be distracted by such thoughts at this moment.

"In fact, you are the finest little horse I have ever encountered. I don't suppose that means anything to you, but I have ridden some of the best horses in the known universe, in my capacity as a leading jockey of Planet Proton. That's another world, though. Not one of those animals compares to you in performance. Except that you are not really a horse. You are something else, and maybe you think I insult you, calling you a horse, but it is no insult, it is appreciation. I must judge you by what I know, and I know horses. To me, you are a horse with a horn. Perhaps you are fundamentally different. Perhaps you are superior. You do not sweat, you strike sparks from your hooves, you shoot fire from your nostrils, you play sounds on your horn, you have gaits and tricks no horse ever dreamed of. Perhaps you are a demon in equine form. But I doubt this. I want you because you most resemble a horse, and there is no creature I would rather have with me in a strange land, to share my life for this adventure, than a horse."

He relaxed his grip further as she relaxed. She was not going to jump, now—he hoped. But he wanted to be sure, so he kept on talking. It could be a mistake to rush things, with a horse.

"Now I thought I could conquer you, Neysa. I thought I could ride you and make you mine, as I have done so many times before with other horses. I see now I was wrong. I rode you, but you are not mine. You will kill yourself before you submit to the taming. I hardly know you, Neysa, but I love you; I would not have you sacrifice yourself to escape me." Stile felt moisture on his cheeks and knew he was crying again, as he had with Sheen. Few things could move him that way. A woman was one; a horse was another. "No, do not hurt yourself for me!

I grieve at the very thought. I will let you go, Neysa! I can not impose respect on you. You are the most perfect steed I could ever hope to associate with, but I will seek another, a lesser animal. For I must be accepted too; it must be mutual. I can not love, and be unloved. Go with my regret, my sorrow, and my blessing. You are free." And he let her go, slowly, so as not to startle her, and stepped back.

"Yet I wish it had worked out," he said. "Not merely because I can see how good you would have been for me. Not only because the love of such a creature as you, not lightly given, is more precious than anything else I could seek. Not only because you are another example of what I like to see in myself, in my foolish private vanity: the proof that excellence can indeed come in small packages. No, there is more than that. I believe you need me the same way I need you. You are alone; you may not be aware of it, but you need a companion too, one who respects you for what you are. You are no ordinary mare."

He saw a scrape on her foreleg. "Oh, Neysa—you were hurt on that run." He squatted to examine it. Pain lanced through his knees, and he fell over, dangerously near the brink. He clutched at turf and drew himself back to safer ground. "Sorry about that," he said sheepishly. "I have bad knees . . . never mind." He got up carefully, using his hands to brace himself, for rising without squatting was awkward. He had never fully appreciated the uses of his knees, until their capability was diminished.

He approached Neysa slowly, still careful not to startle her, then bent from the waist to look at her leg. "I could wash that off for you, but there's no water here and I think it will heal by itself. It is not serious, and the blood helps clean it. But let me check your feet, Neysa. I do not want to leave you with any injuries of my making, and feet are crucially important. May I lift your left front foot?" He slid his hand down along her leg, avoiding the scrape, then drew on the ankle. "Easy, easy—I just want to look. To see if there are any cracks—cracks in hooves are bad news." The foot came up, though the unicorn was obviously uncertain what he was doing, and he looked at it from the bottom. It was still fairly warm; wisps of vapor curled from the frog, the central triangle of the hoof. "No, that is a fine clean hoof, a little chipped around the edges, but no cracks. You must get plenty of protein in your diet, Neysa!"

He set the foot down. "I should check the others, but I fear you would misunderstand. This is one thing a man can do for his horse. He can check the feet, clear the stones or other obstructions, file them down when they wear unevenly or get badly chipped. The welfare of the steed becomes the responsibility of the man. When food is scarce, the man provides. When there is danger, the man fights to protect the horse. Some animals who prey on horses are wary of men. I might face down a wolf, while you—" He looked at her horn. "No, you could handle a wolf! You don't need the likes of me; why should I deceive my-self. I could tell you that to be the associate of a man is to be protected by the intelligence of a man, by his farsighted mind. That a man will anticipate danger and avoid it, for both himself and his mount. His brain makes up for his lesser perceptions. He will steer around sharp stones that might crack hooves. But why should this have meaning for you? You have savvy like none I have seen in any horse; you don't need protection. I delude myself in my desperate need to justify myself, to think that I could in any way be worthy of you."

A fly buzzed up, landing on Neysa. She shook her skin in that place, as horses did, but the fly refused to budge. Her tail flicked across, but the fly was on her shoulder, out of range. She could get it with her mouth, but then she would have to take her attention off Stile. The fly, with the canny ruthlessness of its kind, settled down to bite.

Stile experienced sudden heat. "Now don't startle, Neysa," he said. "I am going to slap that bastard fly, so it can't bother you. Easy, now . . ." He slapped. The fly dropped. "I hate biting flies," Stile said. "I have known them hitherto only through research, but they are the enemies of horses. I will not tolerate them on any animal associated with me." He stepped back, shrugging. "But I am showing my foolish-ness again. You can handle flies! Good-bye, Neysa. I hope you are happy, and that you graze forever in the greenest pastures."

Stile turned and walked away from the brink, listening only to make sure the unicorn did not jump. His heart was heavy, but he knew he had done the right thing. The unicorn could not be tamed. What a treasure he was leaving behind!

There was a strange rippling in the grass of the ledge. It had been occurring for some time, but only now was he fully conscious of it. It was as if he were in a pool, and a pebble had dropped in, making a spreading series of circular waves. But there was no water. What was causing this?

Something nuzzled his elbow. Stile jumped, startled; he had not heard anything approach.

It was the unicorn. She had come up behind him silently; he had not known she could do that. She could have run her horn through his back.

He faced her, perplexed, Neysa's ears were forward, orienting on him. Her muzzle quivered. Her great brown eyes were wet, gleaming like great jewels. She lifted her head and nibbled on his ear, gently, caressingly. She made a little whinny, cajoling him.

"Oh, Neysa!" he breathed, lifted by an explosion of joy.

He had won her, after all.

CHAPTER 8

Music

They were both tired, but Stile felt compelled to put distance between him and his point of entry to this world. Neysa, having consented to be tamed, was the perfect mount; the slightest pressure of one of his knees on her side would turn her, and the shifting of his weight forward would put her into the smoothest of trots. But mostly he didn't guide her; he let her pick her way.

"I need to hide, Neysa," he explained. "I need a place to be safe, until I can learn what I need to know about this world. Until I can discover who is trying to kill me, and why, and what to do about it. Or whether my experience with the amulet-demon was mere coincidence, a random trap, nothing personal. But until I know this land better, I have no notion where to hide. Paradox."

She listened, then made a gesture with her horn, pointing west, and tapped a forefoot. "It's almost as if you understand me," he said, amused. "At least you understand my need. If you know of a place to go, then by all means take me there, girl!"

But first he paused to gather some straw from a mature field and fashioned it into a crude saddle. "I don't really need a saddle, Neysa, but my weight will make your back sore in time unless it is properly distributed. The human seat-bones don't quite jibe with the equine backbone. This straw is not ideal, but it's better than nothing. We have to get my weight off your ribs and over your withers, your shoulders; that's where you can most comfortably support it. And a token girth to hold it on, so I won't have to yank at your beautiful black mane anymore."

Neysa submitted to this indignity, and carried him westward across the amber plain north of the purple mountains, her speed picking up as her strength returned. Something nagged at Stile; then he caught on. "You know, Neysa—this is like the old patriotic song of America, back on Earth. I've never been there, of course, but it describes amber waves of grain and purple mountains and fruited plains—which reminds me, I'm hungry! I haven't eaten since I came into this world—I don't know whether they really exist on Earth, those purple mountains, but they really do exist here! Do you mind if I whistle the tune?"

She cocked her ear back at him, listening, then cocked it forward. She had cute black ears, expressing her personality. She did not mind.

Stile whistled. He was good at it; whistling was, after all, a form of music, and good whistling was good music. Stile was good at anything that related to the Game, back on Proton. He had spent years constantly perfecting himself, and he had a special nostalgia for music. There had been a girl, once, whose memory he associated with it. He whistled the fields more amber, the mountains more purple, and the whole countryside more beautiful. And it really seemed to be so; the entire landscape seemed to assume a more intense grandeur, together with an atmosphere of expectancy. Expectant of what? Abruptly becoming nervous, Stile broke off.

Neysa paused by a tree. It was a pear tree, with huge ripe fruits. "Bless you!" Stile exclaimed. "Are these safe to eat?" He dismounted without waiting for an answer. What a comfort this unicorn was, now that she had joined him!

Neysa moved to the grain nearby and started grazing. She was hungry too. Horses—and unicorns!—could not proceed indefinitely without sustenance; they had to spend a good deal of their time grazing. So a horse was not really faster transportation, for a man; it was speed when he needed it, interspersed with rest. But it was a life-style he liked. His first hours in this world had not been dull, because of the demon-threat and his quest for a steed; but had he remained alone much longer, he would have become quite bored and lonely. Now, with this companionship, this world was delightful. Perhaps his need for transportation had merely been a sublimation of his need for company.

He would have to assume that they could camp here safely, at least for one night. Stile pulled down a pear. It certainly looked safe. If he starved, distrusting nature's food, what would he gain? He took a juicy bite. It was delicious.

He consumed three of the large fruits, then desisted, just in case. He did not need to gorge. He made a bed of hay, under the pear tree, and lay down as darkness closed in. He hoped it would not rain—but what did it really matter? He would dry. The temperature was nice, here; he would not be cold, even when wet.

Neysa had wandered off. Stile wasn't worried; he was sure of her, now. She would not leave him—and if she did, it was her right. They had a tacit agreement, no more, subject to cancellation without notice by either party. Still he glanced across the field as the first moon came up. He would prefer to have her near him, just in case. He did not know what routine dangers there might be, here, but was sure Neysa could recognize and handle them. The way she had dispatched the crack-demon and the snow-monster—

The moonrise was spectacular. Far less intense than the sun, it had more appeal because he could look at it directly. This was a close, large moon, whose effulgence bathed the slowly crossing clouds in pastel blue. The thickest clouds were black silhouettes, but the thinner ones showed their substance in blue monochrome, in shades of one color, all the lines and curves and burgeonings of them, all inexpressibly lovely. Oh, to travel amidst that picture, in the magic of the night sky!

Slowly it faded. Moonrise, like sunrise, was a fleeting phenomenon, the more precious because of that. Stile was sure no two moonrises or moonsets would be the same; there would always be a different picture, as lovely as the last, but original. What splendor nature proffered to the eye of any man who had half the wit to appreciate it!

Something was coming. Not a unicorn. Alarmed, Stile peered through the slanting moonbeams. He remained naked, weaponless; he had seldom felt the need for weapons in Proton society, though he knew how to use them. This was a wilder world whose beauty was tempered, perhaps even enhanced, by its hazards. Was this a nocturnal predator?

No—it was a woman!

Yet she carried no weapon either, and wore no clothing, and seemed innocent rather than hostile. This could be another demonic trap, but Stile somehow doubted it. She was—there was something familiar about her.

As she came close, the moonlight caught her fully. The promising outline was fulfilled in blue light. She was small, very small, smaller even than he, but supremely healthy and full-fleshed. She was beautifully proportioned, with small hands and feet, slender yet rounded legs, and virginally firm breasts. Her fingernails and toenails glistened like pearls, her hair was lustrous black, and she had an ivory decoration set in her forehead. Her face was quite cute, though she had a Roman nose. Her only flaw was a scratch on one arm, a fresh one only starting to heal.

"Stile," she said, with an almost musical inflection.

"Neysa!" he replied, astonished.

She opened her arms to him, smiling. And Stile understood that the friendship of a unicorn was no inconsequential thing. When he had won her, he had won her completely.

She was of course a variant of demon. No ordinary creature could make such a transformation. But it was already clear that there were variations among demons, in fact whole phyla of them. What mattered was not how far removed her type was from his, but how they related to one another. He trusted Neysa.

Stile embraced her, and kissed her, and she was lithe and soft and wholly desirable. He lay down with her under the pear tree, knowing her for what she was, and loved her, as he had loved the robot Sheen.

* * *

In the morning Neysa was back in equine form, grazing. Stile glanced at her, covertly reflecting on the event of the night. Would she expect different treatment, now? Would she now decline to carry him safely?

As it turned out, Neysa's attitude was unchanged. She was still his steed. The night had been merely a confirmation of their relationship, not a change in it. But never again would he think of a unicorn as merely a horse with a horn.

Rested and fed, Neysa set out at an easy trot across the field, still bearing west. Trots could be rough or smooth; this one was the smoothest. She could have looked like a drudge, yet fetched a high price on Proton, for the sake of this trot. As if such a creature could ever be sold, for any price! Then she moved into a nice canter with a syncopated beat: one-two-three-pause, one-two-three-pause. A canter, to his way of thinking, was a trot by the forefeet and a gallop by the rear feet; it too could vary greatly in comfort, depending on the steed's nature and mood. Stile enjoyed this; how nice it was to ride this fine animal without fighting her!

Neysa shifted into a variant of the trot: the pace, in which the left feet moved together, and the right feet together also. Two beats, throwing him from side to side, but covering the ground faster than an ordinary trot. Then back into a canter—but not an ordinary one. Her rear hooves were striking the ground together, synched with her right front hoof, so that this was another two-beat gait: a single foot alternating with three feet. One-TWO! One-TWO! He had to post over the shocks, lest his bones begin to rattle.

She was showing off her gaits, proving that no horse could match her in variety or facility. Yesterday she had demonstrated gaits from one-beat to five-beat; now she was doing the variations.

"This is great stuff, Neysa!" he said warmly. "You are the most versatile hoofer I know." For this was an aspect of companionship: performing for an appreciative friend. Animals, like people, would do a lot, just for the satisfaction of having their efforts recognized. Though Neysa was not precisely an animal *or* a person.

Just when Stile thought he had experienced the whole of her repertoire, Neysa surprised him again. She began to play music through her horn. Not an occasional melodic note, but genuine tunes. Her hooves beat counterpoint to the sustained notes, making a dramatic march.

"The five-beat gait!" Stile exclaimed. *"That's* what it's for! Syncopation, going with your music!"

She moved into the five-beat, playing an intricate melody that fit that beat perfectly. This time her motion was easy, not designed to unseat him, and he liked it. Stile was no longer surprised by her comprehension; he had realized, in stages during the prior day and night, that she comprehended human speech perfectly, though she did not bother to speak it herself. When he had indulged in his soliloquy on the ledge above the Meander River, she had understood precisely what he said. His meaning, not his tone, had converted her. That was good, because he had meant exactly what he said.

Now he could give her detailed verbal instructions, but she preferred the body directives of legs and weight-shifting. She moved to his directives with no evidence of those messages apparent to any third party. That was the riding ideal. She was at home with what she was: a unicorn. Stile, too, preferred the closeness this mode entailed; it was the natural way, a constant communication with his steed.

Neysa's horn-music resembled that of a harmonica. No doubt there were many small channels in her horn, with natural fiber reeds, and she could direct the flow of air through any channels she wished as she breathed. What a convenient way to play!

"You know, Neysa—I know something of music myself. Not just whistling. I was introduced to it by a girl a bit like you, in your girl-form: very small, pretty, and talented. I'm not the top musician in my world, but I am competent—because music is part of the competition of the Game. You wouldn't know about that, of course; it's like a—like a continuing contest, a race, where every day you race someone new, in a different way, and if you get really good you gain status. I have won Games by playing themes better than other people. The violin, the clarinet, the tuba—I've played them all. I wish I could accompany you! I suppose I could whistle again, or sing—" He shrugged. "But I'd really like to show you what I can do with an instrument. One like yours. Another harmonica. So we could play together. A duet. There's a special joy in that, as great in its way as—as the joy we had in our game of the night. With an instrument, I could come to you, as you came to me, sharing your frame."

Neysa accepted this as she did most of his commentary: with a wiggle of one ear and tolerance. She didn't mind if in his vanity he thought he could play the way she could. She liked him anyway.

Stile pondered briefly, then made a little verse of it. "The harmonica is what you play; I wish I had one here today." He fitted the words to her melody, singing them.

Neysa made an unmelodic snort, and Stile laughed. "Corny, I know! Doggerel is not my forte. All right, I'll quit."

But the unicorn slowed, then stopped, then turned about to retrace her last few steps. "What's the matter?" Stile asked, perplexed. "If I offended you, I'm sorry. I didn't mean to mess up your music."

She fished in the tall grass with her horn. Something glittered there. Stile dismounted and walked around to examine it, fearing trouble. If it were another demon-amulet—

It was a large, ornate, well-constructed harmonica, seemingly new.

Stile picked it up, examining it in wonder. "You have a good eye,

Neysa, spotting this, and it couldn't have happened at a more fortuitous time. Why, this is from my world. See, it says MADE ON EARTH. Earth has a virtual monopoly on quality musical instruments. Most colonies are too busy to specialize in the arts. This is a good brand. I'm no specialist in this particular instrument, but I'll bet I could play—" He looked around. "Someone must have lost it. I'm not sure it would be right to—" He shook his head. "Yet it won't help the owner, just to leave it here. I suppose I could borrow it, until I can return it to—"

Having rationalized the matter, Stile remounted his straw saddle—which seemed to be holding up extraordinarily well, packing into an ideal shape—and settled down for the resumption of the ride. Neysa moved into a smooth running walk, and played her horn, and Stile tried out the harmonica.

It was a lovely instrument. It had sixteen holes, which would translate into thirty-two notes: four octaves. It was, in addition, chromatic; it had a lever at the end which, when depressed, would shift the full scale into the half-tones. There were also several buttons whose purpose he did not fathom; he would explore those in due course.

Stile put his mouth to it, getting the feel of it, blowing an experimental note. And paused, surprised and gratified; it was tremolo, with the peculiar and pleasant beat of two closely matched reeds. He blew an experimental scale, pursing his lips to produce a single note at a time. This harmonica was extremely well constructed, with no broken reeds, and every note was pure and in perfect pitch.

Very good. Neysa had halted her music, curious about his activity. Stile essayed a melody. He kept it simple at first, playing no false notes, but the instrument was so conducive and the sound so pleasant that he soon broke into greater complexities.

Neysa perked her ears to listen. She turned her head to glance obliquely back at him, surprised. Stile paused. "Yes, I really can play," he said. "You thought I was a duffer? That whistling represented the epitome of my achievement? I love music; it is another one of those things that come easily to a lonely person. Of course I'm not as sharp on the harmonica as I am on other instruments, and I can't play elaborately, but—"

She blew a note of half-negation. "What, then?" he inquired. "You know, Neysa, it would be easier for me if you talked more—but I guess you'd have to change to your human form for that, and then we couldn't travel properly. You know, you really surprised me when you—do you call it shape-changing? Permutation? Reformulation? It was an aspect of you I had never suspected—"

She blew another note, three-quarter affirmation. He was getting better at grasping her communications. "You're still trying to tell me something," he said. "I'm pretty good at riddles; that's another aspect of the Game. Let's see—is it about your manifestation as—no? About my reaction to it? You say half-right. About my surprise—*your* surprise? Ah, now I get it! You were just as amazed to discover I could play a musical instrument as I was to see you in human form."

Neysa made an affirmation. But there was still a slight reservation. Stile pursued the matter further. "And, just as your change of form enabled us to interact in a new and meaningful way—though not more meaningful than this joy of traveling together across this beautiful land —my abruptly revealed facility with music enables us to interact in yet another way." He smiled. "Which is what I was trying to tell you before—oh, you mean now you agree! You—no, you couldn't be apologizing! Unicorns never make mistakes, do they?"

She made a little buck, just a warning. He laughed. "Well, let's get to it," he said, pleased. He put the harmonica to his mouth and played an improvised theme, sending the perfect notes ringing out over the plain between the mountain ranges. Now Neysa joined in, and they made beautiful harmony. Her hooves beat the cadence, in effect a third instrument. The resulting duet was extremely pretty.

Stile experimented with the mystery buttons, and discovered that they were modes, like those of a good accordion; they changed the tones so that the harmonica sounded like other instruments, to a degree. One canceled the tremolo effect; another brought into play an octave-tuned scale. Another rendered the instrument into a diatonic harmonica, with the popular but incomplete scale and slightly differing tone arrangement. This was the most sophisticated harmonica he had ever played. That only increased his wonder that it should have been so carelessly lost out here. If he dropped such an instrument, he would search for hours to locate it, for it was a marvel of its kind. Who could have left it without a search?

Stile taught Neysa a song, and she taught him one. They played with improvisations to the beat of differing gaits. They did responsive passages, one taking the main theme, the other the refrains. They played alto and tenor on a single theme.

But soon something developed in the atmosphere—a brooding presence, an intangible power. It intensified, becoming almost visible.

Stile broke off his playing. Neysa halted. Both looked about.

There was nothing. The presence was gone.

"You felt it too?" Stile asked. Neysa flicked an ear in assent. "But what *was* it?"

She shrugged, almost dislodging his impromptu saddle. Stile checked his woven-straw cinch to see if it was broken. It wasn't; the strap had merely worked loose from the ring, as happened on occasion. He threaded it through again, properly, so that it would hold.

And did a double take. Strap? Ring?

He jumped to the ground and looked at his handiwork. Loose straw was shedding from it, but underneath it was a well-made if battered leather saddle, comfortable from long use.

He had fashioned a padding of straw. It had been straw this morning when he put it on her. Where had the saddle come from?

"Neysa—" But how would she know? *She* could not have put it there.

She turned her head to gaze directly at him. Then she turned it farther, touching the saddle with her horn. And looked at him, surprised.

"Someone has given us a saddle," Stile said. "Yet there was no way— it was straw this morning—I was riding you the whole time—"

She blew a nervous note. She didn't know what to make of it either.

"Magic," Stile said. "This is a realm of magic. There was magic in the air just now. A—spell?"

Neysa agreed. "Could it be my nemesis, the one I think tried to kill me?" Stile asked. "Showing his power? Yet the saddle is helpful, not harmful. It's something I needed, and it's a good one. And—" He paused, partly nervous, partly awed. "And the harmonica—that appeared like magic when I wanted it—Neysa, is someone or something trying to *help* us? Do we have a gremlin friend as well as an enemy? I'm not sure I like this—because we can't be sure it is a friend. The way that amulet turned into a demon—"

Neysa turned abruptly and began galloping at right angles to her prior course, carrying him along. She was bearing south, toward the purple mountains. Stile knew she had something in mind, so let her take her own route.

Soon they approached a unicorn herd. Neysa must have been skirting the herd all along, aware of it though Stile was not, and now sought it out. She sounded a peremptory note on her horn before drawing close. A single unicorn at the edge of the herd perked up, then galloped toward them. A friend?

Neysa turned and bore west again, away from the herd, and the other unicorn cut across to intercept her. The other was male, larger than Neysa though not substantially so. His color was quite different: dark blue, with red socks. Really the same pattern as Neysa's, but with completely unhorselike hues. Again Stile reminded himself: these were not horses.

As the two animals angled together, Neysa tooted her horn. The stranger answered with a similar toot. His horn sounded more like a saxophone, however. Did every unicorn play a different instrument? What a cacophony when several ran together!

Neysa shifted into the five-beat gait and played a compatible tune. The other matched the gait and cadence, and played a complementary theme. The two blended beautifully. No wonder Neysa had played so well with Stile himself; she had done this sort of thing before, with her own kind. Stile listened, entranced. No cacophony, this; it was a lovely duet.

Who, then, was this young stallion she had summoned? Stile did not really want his presence advertised. But he knew Neysa understood that, and was acting in his interest. She had to have reason. This must be some friend she trusted, who could help them discover the nature of the magic—or protect them from it if necessary.

They ran until well clear of the herd. Then they slowed, their harmony slowing with them. Neysa finally deposited Stile by a handsome nut tree and started grazing. It was the middle of the day: lunch break. She would probably insist on grazing for an hour or more, and he did not begrudge her that. She needed her strength, still not entirely restored after yesterday's trial. He removed the saddle and set it under the tree.

The strange unicorn did not graze. He watched Stile, looking him up and down. He took a step forward, horn pointed at Stile's navel. The musical instrument was now a weapon, without doubt. Stile stood still, chewing on a nut, relaxed but ready to move in a hurry if the creature charged.

The unicorn blew a single derisive note, shimmered—and became a man. The man was clothed. He wore furry leather trousers, a blue long-sleeved shirt, solid low boots, red socks, and a floppy light-blue hat. His hands were covered by heavy fiber gloves. A rapier hung at his side.

Astonished, Stile stared. A Citizen—here?

"So thou'rt the creep who's been messing with my sister!" the man said, his right hand fingering the hilt of the rapier.

Just what he needed: a protective brother! Now Stile saw the forehead spike, similar to Neysa's. No Citizen; ordinary people wore clothing here, he remembered now. "It was voluntary," Stile said tightly.

"Ha! I saw her charging up Snow Mountain yesterday, trying to shake thee off. Thou'rt lucky she changed not into a firefly and let thee drop in a crevasse!"

Oh. The unicorn was talking about the day, not the night. "She changes into a firefly, too?"

"And pray what's wrong with that? Most beasts are lucky if they can change into one other form. We each have two." He shimmered again, and became a hawk. The bird winged upward at a forty-five-degree angle, then looped and dived toward Stile.

Stile threw himself aside—and the man was back, appearing just as the bird seemed about to crash into the ground. "Well, there's no accounting for tastes. Thou'rt a shrimp, and thou'rt naked, but if she lets thee ride her I can't say nay. I want thee to know, though, that she's the best mare in the herd, color or not."

"Color?" Stile asked blankly.

"Don't tell me thou noticed not! Let me warn thee, man-thing: an thou dost ever use the term 'horse-hued' in her presence, I will personally—"

Neysa had come up behind her brother. She blew a warning note.

"All right, already!" he snapped. "She is one season my senior; I may not talk back to her. But remember what I say: *there is nothing wrong with Neysa!*"

"Nothing at all," Stile agreed. "She's the finest-performing and finest-looking mare I've encountered."

The man, evidently braced for doubt or argument, was briefly nonplused. "Uh, yes. Exactly. Then let's get on with it. What's thy problem?"

"My name is Stile. I am a stranger in this world, without information or clothing, someone is trying to kill me, and magic is being performed around me whose ultimate purpose I can not fathom." Stile had the gift for succinct expression, when required.

"So." The man frowned. "Well, my name is Clip. I'm Neysa's little brother. She wants me to help thee, so I'll help. I'll fix thee up with information and clothing. And a weapon to defend thyself from thine enemy. As for the magic—concern thyself not about it. Unicorns are immune to magic."

"Immune!" Stile expostulated. "Here you stand, a shape-changing unicorn, and you tell me—"

"*Other* magic, nit. Of course we do our own, though easy it is not. Like learning another language—which is part of shape-changing, of course; can't be human if thou canst not talk human idiom. Can't be avian if thou canst not fly. So most unicorns bother not. But none *other* can change a unicorn, or enchant one. Or anyone in contact with a unicorn. Was that not why thou didst desire her? So long as thou stayest with Neysa—" He frowned. "Though why she'd want to stay with *thee*—" Neysa's note of protest cut him off again. "Well, there's no comprehending the ways of mares." He began to remove his clothing.

"No comprehending!" Stile agreed. "Look, Clip—I rode Neysa as a challenge, because I needed a mount. In the end I couldn't keep her— but she joined me by her own choice. I don't know why she didn't jump off the mountain and change into a firefly and let me drop to my death, as I gather she could have—" And he had thought he was sparing *her*, when he released her at the ledge! "And I don't know why she's not talking to me now. When she—changed to human form, all she said was my name. She didn't explain anything." At the time he had thought no explanations were necessary; he had been naive!

"That last I can clarify. Neysa doesn't like to talk much. I'm the talkative one in our family, as perhaps thou hadst not yet noticed. So where there's talking to be done, she summons me." Clip handed his shirt to Stile. "Go on, get dressed. I don't need clothing, really, anyway, and I'll get another outfit when convenient." He glanced at Neysa. "I guess she saw something in thee she liked. Thou'rt not a virgin, art thou?"

Stile donned the shirt, shaking his head no, embarrassed both by the turn the conversation had taken and the act of assuming clothing. On Proton this would be socially and legally horrendous!

The shirt should have been large, but somehow turned out to fit him perfectly. He was coming to accept minor magic as the matter of course it was.

"Well, that's overrated anyway," Clip continued. "If I ever found a nubile but virginal human girl, it sure wouldn't be my head I'd put in her lap!"

Stile smiled appreciatively, coming to like the expressive and uninhibited male. "What would a unicorn—or, one in equine form—want with a human girl anyway?"

"Oh, that's easy." The trousers were passed over. "The Herd Stallion co-opts all the best unicorn mares, which leaves us young males hard up. A unicorn does not live by grain alone, thou knowest! So though human flesh is less sweet than equine, even the touch of a fair maiden's hand is—"

"I begin to get the picture." The trousers fit perfectly also. Stile suppressed another twinge of guilt, donning clothing; this was not Proton, and clothing lacked the significance it had there. Out here in the wilderness, clothing became functional on more than a social basis. "Yet that being the case, an attractive mare shouldn't have any trouble—"

Neysa abruptly turned away. Clip lowered his voice. "All right, man. I see thou really knowest not, and thou'dst better. There are horses in unicorn ancestry—not nice to mention it, any more than the apes in thine ancestry—"

"There are no apes in my—"

"See what I mean? Sensitive subject. But on occasion there are throwbacks. When a unicorn is birthed without a horn—that is, without the horn-button; couldn't have a full horn before birth, of course—it is killed in simple mercy. But color is a borderline matter. If it is otherwise perfect, that unicorn is permitted to survive. But there is always that stigma." Clip frowned, glancing covertly at Neysa.

"Neysa—is colored like a horse," Stile said, catching on. "So she is outcast."

"Thou hast it. It is no official thing, for she *is* a full unicorn, but the Herd Stallion won't breed her, and of course none of the lesser males dare. *Nobody* touches a young mare without the Herd Stallion's permission, and he won't give it—because that would seem to infringe on his prerogative. Our kind is like that; simple logic is no substitute for pride. Some would have it that mules are the stubbornest of equines, but that is a dastardly slight on the stubbornness of the unicorn. So for two seasons now Neysa has gone unbred—all because of her color. And maybe her size."

Stile realized that his effort of the past night did not count. He was a man, not a stallion. He could play with a female like Neysa, but could never breed her, any more than a stallion in human form could breed a human girl. "This is outrageous! She's a fine unicorn! The Stallion should either breed her or free her."

"Thou knowest thou'rt only a man," Clip said, handing Stile the rapier. "But thy personality hath its redeeming aspects. Thou really likest Neysa?"

"I chose her because she was the finest steed I'd ever seen," Stile said seriously. "I loved her in that fashion from the start. To me there is no better creature than a perfect—equine."

"So thou never, until I spoke to thee, knew what was wrong with her?"

"There is nothing wrong with her!" Stile snapped.

"Agreed." Clip was highly gratified. "Well, I'm supposed to fill thee in on our world. There is little to tell. We unicorns are the dominant animal form, except perhaps in some corners of the pasture where the werewolves and vampires range, and we're really better off than the human peasants. Anyone can do magic, but most humans don't, because of the Adepts."

"Adepts?"

"Like Herd Stallions or wolf Pack Leaders, only it's magic, not mares or bitches they pre-empt. Each Adept has his special style of enchantment, and he's awfully good in his specialization. I said unicorns were proof against foreign spells, but Adepts are another matter. If an Adept should be after thee—"

"I see. What defense would I have against one of these super-sorcerers?"

"No defense suffices, except to hide—and sooner or later an Adept will find thee. They have charms and amulets and familiars spread throughout the realm of Phaze, spying out the news. There's hardly any limit to the powers of an Adept. In fact—that's it! The Oracle!"

"A fortune-teller?"

"More than that. There is no magic in the temple of the Oracle, and nobody is coerced therein. It is sacred ground. I'll bet that's where Neysa is taking thee. Well, then, that covers it. I'll be off." He shimmered back into unicorn form and galloped away, his horn and hooves sounding the charge.

Stile had wanted to know more about Adepts and the Oracle. Well, perhaps Neysa would tell him, if he asked her nicely. Clip had certainly helped a great deal.

They rode west again, playing brief duets, enjoying themselves. Stile realized that the music of unicorns served another purpose: it alerted friends and foes to their presence. Unicorns were fighting animals; most creatures would prefer to avoid them, and so the sound of the horn cleared the way conveniently. Stile saw rabbits and turtles and an armadillo, but no predators. In short, only creatures that were noncompetitive with unicorns.

The terrain was highly varied, lush fields giving way to rocky slopes, swamps, open water and badlands sand. To the north and south the twin mountain ranges continued. The northern peaks were all snow-covered, virtually impassable to any creature with less power and determination than a unicorn; the southern ones seemed to be warmer, unless purple was the color of their snow. Curious! Something about this rugged landscape nagged him, a nascent familiarity, but he was unable to place it.

In the evening Neysa halted again, giving herself time to graze, and Stile foraged for his own sustenance. He found ripe corn growing, and blackberries. He thought of corn as fall produce, and blackberries as spring, but perhaps this world differed from others in its fruiting seasons too. On Proton anything could grow at any time, in the domes. Nonetheless, these edibles were suspiciously fortuitous—unless Neysa had known of this place and come here deliberately. Yes, of course that was it; she was taking excellent care of him.

In the night, after moonrise, she changed again. Stile hoped she would show him her firefly form, but she went directly to human. "You know, Neysa, you're about the prettiest girl I've seen—but I think I like you best in your natural form."

She smiled, flattered, and kissed him. She didn't mind being complimented on her unicorn body. She had spent her life stigmatized for a supposedly defective color, and obviously appreciated Stile's appreciation. This was no doubt the key to her initial acceptance of him. He really did admire her as she was, and was perhaps the first creature unrelated to her to do so. So though she had fought him, in the end she had not wanted to kill him.

"The Oracle—" he began. But she only kissed him again.

She wasn't talking. Ah, well. The stubbornness of unicorns! She had other virtues. He kissed her back.

Next morning she gave him some pointers on the use of the rapier. Stile had used a sword before, as fencing was one of the aspects of the Game. But by an anomaly of circumstance he had practiced with the broadsword, not the rapier. This light, thin sword was strange to him—and if it were the kind of weapon commonly used in this world, he had better master it in a hurry.

Neysa was expert. Stile had supposed a unicorn would not care to have the weapon of an opponent so close to the tender eyes, ears, and nose—but the proximity of her organs of perception gave her marvelous coordination with her weapon. Stile soon learned he could thrust without fear for her; his point would never score. Even if it should happen to slip through her guard, what would it strike? The heavy bone of her forehead, buttressing the horn. It would take more of a thrust than a man like him could muster to penetrate that barrier.

No, he had to look out for himself. Neysa was better on the parry than on the lunge, for the merest twitch of her head moved the horn-tip several centimeters, but to make a forward thrust she had to put her whole body in motion. Thus she was best equipped for defense against a charging adversary, either allowing the other to impale himself on her firm point, or knocking aside his weapon. Stile, forced to attack, found himself disarmed repeatedly, her horn bearing instantly on his vulnerable chest. She *could* lunge, and with horrible power—but did not, when she fenced a friend. How could he match the speed and power of her natural horn?

But Stile was a quick study. Soon he did not try to oppose power with power. Instead he used the finesse he had developed with the broadsword, countering power with guile. Soon Neysa could no longer disarm him at will, and sometimes he caught her out of position and halted his point just shy of her soft long throat. In a real match he could not hope to overcome her, but he was narrowing the gap.

But he was also getting tired. His throat felt sore, and his eyes got bleary. He could feel a flush on his face, yet he was shivering. Neysa made a feint—and he almost fell across her horn.

"Hostile magic!" he gasped. "I'm weak—"

Then he was unconscious.

CHAPTER 9

Promotion

Dreams came, replaying old memories . . .

The weapon-program director stared down at him. "You sure you want to get into swords, lad? They get pretty heavy." He meant heavy for someone Stile's size.

Again that burgeoning anger, that hopeless wrath instigated by the careless affronts of strangers. That determination to damn well prove he was not as small as they saw him. To prove it, most of all, to himself. "I need a sword. For the Game."

"Ah, the Game." The man squinted at him judiciously. "Maybe I've seen you there. Name?"

"Stile." For a moment he hoped he had some compensating notoriety from the Game.

The man shook his head. "No, must have been someone else. A child star, I think."

So Stile reminded this oaf of a child. It didn't even occur to the program director that such a reference might be less than complimentary to a grown man. But it would be pointless to react openly—or covertly. Why couldn't he just ignore what others thought, let their opinions flow from his back like idle water? Stile was good at the Game, but not that good. Not yet. He had a number of weaknesses to work on—and this was one. "Maybe you'll see me some time—with a sword."

The director smiled condescendingly. "It is your privilege. What kind did you want?"

"The rapier."

The man checked his list. "That class is filled. I can put you on the reserve list for next month."

This was a disappointment. Stile had admired the finesse of the rapier, and felt that he could do well with it. "No, I have time available now."

"The only class open today is the broadsword. I doubt you'd want that."

Stile doubted it too. But he did not appreciate the director's all-too-typical attitude. It was one thing to be looked down on; another to accept it with proper grace. "I'll take the broadsword."

The man could not refuse him. Any serf was entitled to any training available, so long as he was employed and the training did not interfere with his assigned duties. "I don't know if we have an instructor your size."

Stile thought of going up against a giant for his first lesson. He did not relish that either. "Aren't you supposed to have a full range of robots?"

The man checked. He was obviously placing difficulties in the way, trying to discourage what he felt would be a wasted effort. He could get a reprimand from his own employer if he placed a serf in an inappropriate class and an injury resulted. "Well, we do have one, but—"

"I'll take that one," Stile said firmly. This oaf was not going to balk him!

The director shrugged, smiling less than graciously. "Room 21."

Stile was startled. That happened to be his age. Twenty-one. He had been a stable hand for a year, now. Coincidence, surely. He thanked the director perfunctorily and went to room 21.

"Good afternoon, ma'am," the instructor said, coming to life. "Please allow me to put this protective halter on you, so that no untoward accident can happen." She held out the armored halter.

A female robot, programmed of course for a woman. That was how the problem of size had been solved.

Stile imagined the director's smirk, if he left now. He gritted his teeth. "I don't need the halter. I am a man." How significant that statement seemed! If only he could get living people to listen, too. He was a man, not a midget, not a child.

The robot hesitated. Her face and figure were those of a young woman, but she was not of the most advanced type. She was not programmed for this contingency. "Ma'am, it is required—"

Useless to argue with a mechanical! "All right." Stile took the halter and tied it about his waist. There it might offer some modicum of protection for what a man valued.

The robot smiled. "Very good, ma'am. Now here are the weapons." She opened the storage case.

It seemed an anomaly to Stile to have a female instructing the broadsword, but he realized that women played the Game too, and there were no handicaps given for size, age, experience or sex, and not all of them cared to default when it came to fencing. They felt as he did: they would go down fighting. Often a person with such an attitude did not go down at all; he/she won, to his/her surprise. Attitude was important.

The robot was not smart, but she was properly programmed. She commenced the course of instruction, leaving nothing to chance. Stance, motion, strategy, exercises for homework to increase facility. Safety precautions. Scoring mechanisms and self-rating scale. Very basic, but also very good. When a program of instruction was instituted on Proton, it was the best the galaxy could offer.

Stile discovered that the broadsword had its own virtues and techniques. It had two cutting edges as well as the point, making it more versatile—for the person who mastered it. It did not have to be heavy; modern alloys and molecular-foam metals made the blade light yet keen. He soon realized that there could be a Game advantage in this weapon. Most opponents would expect him to go for the rapier, and would play to counter that. Of such misjudgments were Game decisions made.

Next morning he reported to the stables as usual. "Stile, we're bringing in a robot trainer from another farm," the foreman said. "Name's Roberta. Get out to the receiving gate and bring her in." And he smiled privately.

Stile went without question, knowing another stable hand would be assigned to cover his chores in the interim. He had been given a post of distinction: greeter to a new trainer. No doubt Roberta was a very special machine.

She was already at the gate when Stile arrived. She was in the shade of a dwarf eucalyptus tree, mounted on a fine bay mare about sixteen hands high. The gatekeeper pointed her out, half-hiding a smirk.

What was so funny about this robot? Stile was reminded uncomfortably of the weapon-program director, who had known about the female robot instructor. Being deceived in any fashion by a robot was always an embarrassment, since no robot intentionally deceived. Unless programmed to—but that was another matter.

This one did not look special: flowing yellow hair, a perfect figure—standard, since they could make humanoid robots any shape desired. Why make a grotesquerie? She seemed small to be a trainer—smaller than the fencing instructor he had worked with. She was a rider, obviously; was she also a jockey? To break in the most promising horses for racing? No robot-jockey could actually race, by law; but no living person had the programmed patience of a training machine, and the horses did well with such assistance.

"Roberta, follow me," Stile said, and began walking along the access trail.

The robot did not follow. Stile paused and turned, annoyed. "Roberta, accompany me, if you please." That last was a bit of irony, as robots lacked free will.

She merely looked at him, smiling.

Oh, no—was she an idiot model, not programmed for verbal directives? Yet virtually all humanoid robots were keyed to respond at least to their names. "Roberta," he said peremptorily.

The mare perked her ears at him. The girl chuckled. "She only responds to properly couched directives," she said.

Stile's eyes passed from girl to mare. A slow flush forged up to his hairline. "The horse," he said.

"Roberta, say hello to the red man," the girl said, touching the horse's head with her crop.

The mare neighed.

"A robot horse," Stile repeated numbly. "A living girl."

"You're very intelligent," the girl said. "What's your name?"

"Uh, Stile." Of all the pitfalls to fall into!

"Well, Uh-Stile, if you care to mount Roberta, you can take her in."

His embarrassment was replaced by another kind of awkwardness. "I am a stable hand. I don't ride."

She dismounted smoothly. Afoot she was slightly shorter than he, to his surprise. She evinced the confidence normally associated with a larger person, though of course height was less important to women. "You're obviously a jockey, Uh-Stile, as I am. Don't try to fool me."

"That's Stile, no uh," he said.

"Stile Noah? What an unusual appellation!"

"Just Stile. What's your name?"

"I'm Tune. Now that the amenities are complete, get your butt on that robot."

"You don't understand. Stable hands tend horses; they don't ride."

"This is not a horse, it's a robot. Who ever heard of a jockey who didn't ride?"

"I told you I'm not—" Then it burst upon him. *"That's* why my employer chose me! Because I'm small. He wanted a potential jockey!"

"Your comprehension is positively effulgent."

"Do—do you really think—?"

"It is obvious. Why else would anyone want serfs our size? Your employer started you on the ground, huh? Slinging dung?"

"Slinging dung," he agreed, feeling better. This girl was small; she was not really making fun of him; she was playfully teasing him. "Until I found a worm."

"A whole worm?" she asked, round-eyed. "How did it taste?"

"A parasite worm. In the manure."

"They don't taste very good."

"Now I've been a year in the stable. I don't know a thing about riding."

"Ha. You've watched every move the riders make," Tune said. "I know. I started that way too. I wasn't lucky enough to find a worm. I worked my way up. Now I race. Don't win many, but I've placed often enough. Except that now I'm on loan to do some training. For those who follow after, et cetera. Come on—I'll show you how to ride."

Stile hesitated. "I don't think I'm supposed to—"

"For crying in silence!" she exclaimed. "Do I have to hand-feed you? Get up behind me. Roberta won't mind."

"It's not the horse. It's my employer's policy. He's very strict about—"

"He told you not to take a lift on a robot?"

"No, but—"

"What will he say if you don't get Roberta to your stable at all?"

Was she threatening him? Better her displeasure than that of his employer! "Suppose I just put you back on the horse and lead her in?"

Tune shrugged. She had the figure for it. "Suppose you try?"

Call one bluff! Stile stepped in close to lift her. Tune met him with a sudden, passionate kiss.

Stile reeled as from a body-block. Tune drew back and surveyed him from all of ten centimeters distance. "Had enough? You can't lead Roberta anyway; she's programmed only for riding."

Stile realized he was overmatched. "We'll do it your way. It'll be your fault if I get fired."

"I just knew you'd see the light!" she exclaimed, pleased. She put her foot in the stirrup and swung into the saddle. Then she removed her foot. "Use the stirrup. Hold on to me. Lift your left foot. It's a big step, the first time."

It was indeed. Sixteen hands was over 1.6 meters—a tenth of a meter taller than he was. He had to heft his foot up past waist-height to get it in the stirrup. He had seen riders mount smoothly, but his observation did not translate into competence for himself. Tune was in the way; he was afraid he'd bang his head into her left breast, trying to scramble up.

She chuckled and reached down with her left hand, catching him in the armpit. She hauled as he heaved, and he came up—and banged his head into her breast. "Swing it around behind, over the horse," she said. Then, at his stunned pause, she added: "I am referring to your right leg, clumsy."

Stile felt the flush burning right down past his collarbone. He swung his leg around awkwardly. He kneed the horse, but managed to get his leg over, and finally righted himself behind Tune. No one would know him for a gymnast at this moment!

"That mounting should go down in the record books," she said. "Your face is so hot it almost burned my—skin." Stile could not see her face, but knew she was smiling merrily. "Now put your arms around my waist to steady yourself. Your employer might be mildly perturbed if you fell down and broke your crown. Good dungslingers are hard to replace. He'd figure Roberta was too spirited a nag for you."

Numbly, Stile reached around her and hooked his fingers together across her small firm belly. Tune's hair was in his face; it had a clean, almost haylike smell.

Tune shifted her legs slightly, and abruptly the robot horse was moving. Stile was suddenly exhilarated. This was like sailing on a boat in a slightly choppy sea—the miniature sea with the artificial waves that was part of the Game facilities. Tune's body compensated with supple expertise. They proceeded down the path.

"I've seen you in the Game," Tune remarked. "You're pretty good, but you're missing some things yet."

"I started fencing lessons yesterday," Stile said, half flattered, half defensive.

"That, too. What about the performing arts?"

"Well, martial art—"

She reversed her crop, put it to her mouth—and played a pretty little melody. The thing was a concealed pipe of some kind, perhaps a flute or recorder.

Stile was entranced. "That's the loveliest thing I ever heard!" he exclaimed when she paused. "Who's steering the horse?"

"You don't need reins to steer a horse; haven't you caught on to that yet? You don't need a saddle to ride, either. Not if you know your business. Your legs, the set of your weight—watch."

Roberta made a steady left turn, until she had looped a full circle.

"You did that?" Stile asked. "I didn't see anything."

"Put your hand on my left leg. No, go ahead, Stile; I want you to feel the tension. See, when I press on that side, she bears right. When I shift my weight back, she stops." Tune leaned back into Stile, and the horse stopped. "I shift forward, so little you can't see it, but she can feel it—hold on to me tight, so you can feel my shift—that's it." Her buttocks flexed and the horse started walking again. "Did you feel me?"

"You're fantastic," Stile said.

"I referred to the guidance of the horse. I already know about me."

"Uh, yes."

"Roberta responds only to correct signals; she has no idiosyncrasies, as a living animal might. You have to do it just right, with her. That's why she's used for training. So the horses won't teach the riders any bad habits. You noted how she ignored you when you spoke to her from the ground. She responds only to her rider. She's not a plow horse, after all."

"She's fantastic too."

"Oh, she is indeed! But me—I do have two cute little faults."

Stile was inordinately interested now. "What are they?"

"I lie a little."

Meaning he could not trust all of what she had been telling him? Discomforting thought! "What about the other?"

"How could you believe it?"

There was that. If she lied about it—

Tune played her instrument again. It was, she explained, a keyboard harmonica, with the keys concealed; she blew in the end, and had a scale of two and a half octaves available at her touch. Her name was fitting; her music was exquisite. She was right: he needed to look into music.

Tune and Roberta began training the new riders. Stile returned to his routine duties. But suddenly it was not as interesting, handling the horses afoot. His mind was elsewhere. Tune was the first really attractive girl he had encountered who was smaller than he was. Such a little thing, physical height, but what a subjective difference it could make!

Today he was lunging the horses. Lunging consisted of tying them to a fixed boom on a rotating structure, so they had to stay in an exact course, and making them trot around in a circle. It was excellent exercise, if dull for both man and horse. Some horses were too temperamental for the mechanical lead, so he had to do them by hand. He simply tied a rope to an artificial tree, and stood with his hand on that line while he urged the animal forward.

Stile had a way with horses, despite his size. They tended to respond to him when they would not do a thing for other stable hands. This, unfortunately, meant that he got the most difficult horses to lunge. No horse gave trouble about feeding or going to pasture, but a number could get difficult about the more onerous labors.

The first horse he had to lunge was Spook—the worst of them. Spook was jet black all over, which perhaps accounted for his name. He was also extremely excitable—which was a more likely reason for his name. He could run with the best—the very best—but had to be kept in top condition.

"Come on, Spook," Stile said gently. "You wouldn't want to get all weak and flabby, would you? How would you feel if some flatfooted mare beat your time in a race? You know you have to exercise."

Spook knew no such thing. He aspired to a life career of grazing and stud service; there was little room in his itinerary for exercise. He had quite an arsenal of tricks to stave off the inevitable. When Stile approached, Spook retreated to the farthest corner of his pen, then tried to leap away when cornered. But Stile, alert, cut him off and caught his halter. He had to reach up high to do it, for this horse could look right over Stile's head without elevating his own head. Spook could have flattened Stile, had he wanted to; but he was not a vicious animal, and perhaps even enjoyed this periodic game.

Spook tried to nip Stile's hand. "No!" Stile said sharply, making a feint with his free hand as if to slap the errant nose, and the horse desisted. Move and countermove, without actual violence. That was the normal language of horses, who could indulge in quite elaborate series of posturings to make themselves accurately understood.

They took a few steps along the path, then Spook balked, planting all four feet in the ground like small tree trunks. He was of course far too heavy for even a large man to budge by simple force. But Stile slapped him lightly on the flank with the free end of the lead-line, startling him into motion. One thing about being spooky: it was hard to stand firm.

Spook moved over, trying to shove Stile off the path and into a building, but Stile shoved the horse's head back, bracing against it. Control the head, control the body; he had learned that principle in martial art, winning matches by hold-downs though his opponents might outweigh him considerably—because their greater mass became useless against his strategy. Few creatures went far without their heads.

Spook tried to lift his head too high for Stile to control. Stile merely hung on, though his feet left the ground. After a moment the dead weight became too much, and the horse brought his head down. Other stable hands used a martingale on him, a strap to keep the head low, but that made this horse even more excitable. Stile preferred the gentle approach.

At last he got Spook to the lunging tree. "Walk!" he commanded, making a token gesture with the whip. The horse sighed, eyed him, and decided to humor him this once. He walked.

Every horse was an individual. "Spook, you're more trouble than a stableful of rats, but I like you," Stile said calmly. "Let's get this over with, work up a sweat, then I'll rub you down. After that, it's the pasture for you. How does that sound?"

Spook glanced at him, then made a gesture with his nose toward the pasture. Horses' noses, like their ears, were very expressive; a nose motion could be a request or an insult. "Lunge first," Stile insisted.

Spook licked his lips and chewed on a phantom delicacy. "Okay!" Stile said, laughing. "A carrot and a rubdown. That's my best offer. Now trot. Trot!"

It was all right. The horse broke into a classy trot. Any horse was pretty in that gait, but Spook was prettier than most; his glossy black hide fairly glinted, and he had a way of picking up his feet high that accentuated the precision of his motion. The workout was going to be a success.

Stile's mind drifted. The girl, Tune—could she be right about his destiny? There were stringent rules about horse competition, because of the ubiquitous androids, cyborgs, and robots. Horses had to be completely natural, and raced by completely natural jockeys. The less weight a horse carried, the faster it could go; there were no standardized loads, here. So a man as small as Stile—yes, it did make sense, in Citizen terms. Citizens did not care about serf convenience or feelings; Citizens cared only about their own concerns. Stile's aptitude in the Game, his intelligence in schooling—these things were irrelevant. He was small and healthy and coordinated, therefore he was slated to be a jockey. Had he been three meters tall, he would have been slated for some Citizen's classical basketball team. He didn't have to like it; he worked where employed, or he left Proton forever. That was the nature of the system.

Still, would it be so bad, racing? Tune herself seemed to like it. Aboard a horse like Spook, here, urging him on to victory, leaving the pack behind, hearing the crowd cheering him on . . . there were certainly worse trades than that! He did like horses, liked them well. So maybe the Citizen had done him a favor, making his size an asset. A lout like the stable hand Bourbon might eventually become a rider, but he would never be a racer. Only a small person could be that. Most were women, like Tune, because women tended to be smaller, and gentler. Stile was the exception. Almost, now, he was glad of his size.

And Tune herself—what a woman! He would have to take up music.

It had never occurred to him that an ordinary serf could create such beauty. Her—what was that instrument? The keyboard harmonica—her musical solo, emerging as it were from nowhere, had been absolute rapture! Yes, he would have to try his hand at music. That might please her, and he wanted very much to please her.

She could, of course, have her pick of men. She had poise and wit and confidence. She could go with a giant if she wanted. Stile could not pick among women; he had to have one shorter than he. Not because he demanded it, but because society did; if he appeared among serfs with a girl who outmassed him, others would laugh, and that would destroy the relationship. So he was the least of many, from Tune's perspective, while she was the only one for him.

The trouble was—now that he knew he wanted her—his shyness was boiling up, making any direct approach difficult. How should he—

"One side, shorty!" It was Bourbon, the stable hand who was Stile's greatest annoyance. Bourbon was adept at getting Stile into mischief, and seemed to resent Stile because he was small. Stile had never understood that, before; now with the realization of his potential to be a jockey, the resentment of the larger person was beginning to make sense. Bourbon liked to make dares, enter contests, prevail over others—and his size would work against him, racing horses. Today Bourbon was leading Pepper, a salt-and-pepper speckled stallion. "Make way for a man and a horse!"

Spook spooked at the loud voice. He leaped ahead. The lead-rope jerked his muzzle around. The horse's body spun out, then took a roll. The line snapped, as it was designed to; a horse could get hurt when entangled.

Pepper also spooked, set off by the other horse. He careened into a wall, squealing. The genuine imported wood splintered, and blood spattered to the ground.

Stile ran to Spook. "Easy, Spook, easy! You're okay! Calm! Calm!" He flung his arms about Spook's neck as the horse climbed to his feet, trying to steady the animal by sheer contact.

Bourbon yanked Pepper's head about, swearing. "Now see what you've done, midget!" he snapped at Stile. "Of all the runty, oink-headed, pygmy-brained—"

That was all. A fracas would have alerted others to the mishap, and that would have gotten both stable hands into deep trouble. Bourbon led his horse on, still muttering about the incompetence of dwarves, and Stile succeeded in calming Spook.

All was not well. Stile seethed at the insults added to injury, knowing well that Bourbon was responsible for all of this. The horse had a scrape on his glossy neck, and was favoring one foot. Stile could cover the scrape with fixative and comb the mane over it, concealing the evidence until it healed, but the foot was another matter. No feet, no horse, as the saying went. It might be only a minor bruise—but it might also be more serious.

He couldn't take a chance. That foot had to be checked. It would mean a gross demerit for him, for he was liable for any injury to any animal in his charge. This could set his promotion back a year, right when his aspirations had multiplied. Damn Bourbon! If the man hadn't spoken sharply in the presence of a horse known to be excitable—but of course Bourbon had done it deliberately. He had been a stable hand for three years and believed he was overdue for promotion. He took it out on others as well as on Stile, and of course he resented the way Stile was able to handle the animals.

Stile knew why Bourbon had been passed over. It wasn't his size, for ordinary riders and trainers could be any size. Bourbon was just as mean to the horses, in little ways he thought didn't show and could not be proved. He teased them and handled them with unnecessary roughness. Had he been lunging Spook, he would have used martingale and electric prod. Other hands could tell without looking at the roster which horses Bourbon had been handling, for these animals were nervous and shy of men for several days thereafter.

Stile would not report Bourbon, of course. He had no proof-of-fault, and it would be contrary to the serf code, and would gain nothing. Technically, the man had committed no wrong; Stile's horse had spooked first. Stile should have been paying better attention, and brought Spook about to face the intrusion so as not to be startled. Stile had been at fault, in part, and had been had. Lessons came hard.

Nothing for it now except to take his medicine, figuratively, and give Spook his, literally. He led the horse to the office of the vet. "I was lunging him. He spooked and took a fall," Stile explained, feeling as lame as the horse.

The man examined the injuries competently. "You know I'll have to report this."

"I know," Stile agreed tightly. The vet was well-meaning and honest; he did what he had to do.

"Horses don't spook for no reason, not even this one. What set him off?"

"I must have been careless," Stile said. He didn't like the half-truth, but was caught between his own negligence and the serf code. He was low on the totem, this time.

The vet squinted wisely at him. "That isn't like you, Stile."

"I had a girl on my mind," Stile admitted.

"Ho! I can guess which one! But this is apt to cost you something. I'm sorry." Stile knew he meant it. The vet would do a serf a favor when he could, but never at the expense of his employer.

The foreman arrived. He was never far from the action. That was his business. Stile wondered, as he often did, how the man kept so well abreast of events even before they were reported to him, as now. "Damage?"

"Slight sprain," the vet reported. "Be better in a few days. Abrasion on neck, no problem."

The foreman glanced at Stile. "You're lucky. Three demerits for carelessness, suspension for one day. Next time pay better attention."

Stile nodded, relieved. No gross demerit! Had the foot been serious—

"Any extenuating circumstances to report?" the foreman prodded.

"No." That galled Stile. The truth could have halved his punishment.

"Then take off. You have one day to yourself."

Stile left. He was free, but it was no holiday. The demerits would be worked off in the course of three days low on the totem, but that suspension would go down on his permanent record, hurting his promotion prospects. In the case of equivalent qualifications, the person with such a mark on his record would suffer, and probably have to wait until the next occasion for improvement. That could be as little as a day, or as long as two months.

Stile started off his free time by enlisting in a music-appreciation class. It was good stuff, but he was subdued by his chastisement. He would stick with it, however, and in time choose an instrument to play himself. The keyboard harmonica, perhaps.

In the evening Tune searched him out. "It's all over the dome," she told him brightly. "I want you to know I think you did right, Stile."

"You're a liar," he said, appreciating her words.

"Yes. You should have covered it up and escaped punishment, the way Bourbon did. But you showed you cared more about the horse than about your own record." She paused, putting her hands on his shoulders, looking into his face. What lovely eyes she had! "I care about horses." She drew him in and kissed him, and the pain of his punishment abated rapidly. "You're a man," she added. The words made him feel like one.

She took him home to her private apartment—the affluence permitted ranking serfs. By morning she had shown him many things, not all of them musical or relating to horses, and he was hopelessly in love with her. He no longer regretted his punishment at all.

When Stile returned to work next day, at the same hour he had departed, he discovered that he had been moved out of his cabin. He looked at the place his bunk had been, dismayed. "I know I fouled up, but—"

"You don't know?" a cabin mate demanded incredulously. "Where have you been all night?"

Stile did not care to clarify that; he would be razzed. They would find out soon enough via the vine. Tune, though small, was much in the eye of the local serfs, and not just because of her position and competence. "I was on suspension." He kept his voice steady. "Was it worse than I thought, on Spook? Something that showed up later?"

"Spook's okay." His friend took his arm. "Come to the bulletin board."

Not daring to react further, Stile went with him. The electronic board, on which was posted special assignments, demerits, and other news of the day, had a new entry in the corner: STILE pmtd RIDER.

Stile turned savagely on the other. "Some joke!"

But the foreman had arrived. "No joke, Stile. You're sharing the apartment with Turf. Familiarize yourself, then get down to the robot stall for instruction."

Stile stared at him. "But I fouled up!"

The foreman walked away without commenting, as was his wont. He never argued demerits or promotions with serfs.

Turf was waiting to break him in. It was a nice two-man apartment adjacent to the riding track, with a Game viewscreen, hot running water, and a direct exit to the main dome. More room and more privacy; more status. This was as big a step upward as his prior one from pasture to stable—but this time he had found no worm. There had to be some mistake—though he had never heard of the foreman making a mistake.

"You sure came up suddenly, Stile!" Turf said. He was an okay guy; Stile had interacted with him on occasion, walk-cooling horses Turf had ridden, and liked him. "How'd you do it?"

"I have no idea. Yesterday I was suspended for injuring Spook. Maybe our employer got his firing list mixed up with his promotion list."

Turf laughed. "Maybe! You know who's waiting to give you riding lessons?"

"Tune!" Stile exclaimed. "*She* arranged this!"

"Oh, you're thick with her already? You're doubly lucky!"

Disquieted, Stile proceeded to Roberta's stall. Sure enough, there was Tune, brushing out the bay mare, smiling. "Long time no see," she said playfully.

Oh, she was lovely! He could have a thousand nights with her like the last one, and never get enough. But he was about to blow it all by his ingratitude. "Tune, did you pull a string?" he demanded.

"Well, you can't expect a jockey to date a mere stable hand."

"But I was in trouble! Suspended. There are several hands ahead of me. You can't—"

She put her fine little hand on his. "I didn't, Stile. Really. I was just joshing you. It's coincidence. I didn't know you were being promoted right now; I figured in a month or so, since they brought me in. I'm training others, of course, but no sense to promote you after my tour here ends. So they moved it up, obviously. They don't even know we're dating."

But she was, by her own proclamation, a liar. The foreman surely knew where Stile had spent the night. How much could he afford to believe?

"Ask me again tonight," she murmured. "I never lie to a man I'm loving."

What an offer! "What, never?"

"Hardly ever. You're an operetta fan?"

He looked at her blankly.

"Never mind," she said. "I'm not lying to you now."

How he wanted to believe her!

"Will you try it alone?" she inquired, indicating Roberta's saddle. "Or do you prefer to hold on to me again, and bang your poor head?"

"Both," he said, and she laughed. She had asked him during the night whether his head hurt from what he had banged it into. He had admitted that there were some bruises he was prepared to endure.

She had him mount, more successfully this time, and showed him how to direct the robot. Then she took him out on the track. Very quickly he got the hang of it.

"Don't get cocky, now, sorehead," she warned. "Roberta is a horse of no surprises. A flesh horse can be another matter. Wait till they put you on Spook."

"Spook?" he cried, alarmed. He had daydreamed of exactly this, but the prospect of the reality scared him.

She laughed again. She was a creature of fun and laughter. It made her body move pleasantly, and it endeared her to those she worked with. "How should I know whom you'll ride? But we'll get you competent first. A bad rider can ruin a good horse."

"Yes, the Citizen wouldn't be very pleased if a serf fell on his head and splattered dirty gray brains on a clean horse."

It was a good lesson, and he returned to his new apartment exhilarated, only to discover more trouble. The foreman was waiting for him.

"There is a challenge to your promotion. We have been summoned to the Citizen."

"We? I can believe there was a foul-up with me, that will now be corrected." Though he had begun to hope that somehow this new life was real. Even braced for it as he was, this correction was hard to take. "But how do you relate? It wasn't your fault."

The foreman merely took his elbow and guided him forward. This summons was evidently too urgent to allow time for physical preparation. Stile tried to smooth his hair with his hand, and to rub off stray rimes of dirt on his legs from the riding. He felt, appropriately, naked.

In moments they entered a transport tunnel, took a private capsule, and zoomed through the darkness away from the farm. It seemed the

Citizen was not at his farmside apartment at this hour. "Now don't stare, keep cool," the foreman told him. The foreman himself was sweating. That made Stile quite nervous, for the foreman was normally a man of iron. There must be quite serious trouble brewing! Yet why hadn't they simply revoked Stile's promotion without fuss?

They debouched at a hammam. Stile felt the foreman's nudge, and realized he was indeed staring. He stopped that, but still the environment was awesome.

The hammam was a public bath in the classic Arabian mode. A number of Citizens preferred this style, because the golden age of Arabian culture back on Earth had been remarkably affluent. Islam had had its Golden Age while Christianity had its Dark Ages. For the ruling classes, at any rate; the color of the age had never had much significance for the common man. Poverty was eternal.

Thus there were mosque-type architecture, and turban headdress, exotic dancing, and the hammam. This one was evidently shared by a number of Citizens. It was not that any one of them could not have afforded it alone; rather, Citizens tended to specialize in areas of interest or expertise, and an Arabian specialist had a touch that others could hardly match. Stile's employer had a touch with fine horses; another might have a touch with desert flora; here one had a touch with the hammam. On occasion other Citizens wished to ride the horses, and were invariably treated with utmost respect. The hammam was by nature a social institution, and a Citizen could only socialize properly with other Citizens, so they had to share.

There were many rooms here, clean and hot and steamy, with many serfs bearing towels, brushes, ointments, and assorted edibles and beverages. One large room resembled a swimming pool—but the water was bubbly-hot and richly colored and scented, almost like soup. Several Citizens were soaking in this communal bath, conversing. Stile knew they were Citizens, though they were naked, because of their demeanor and the deference the clustered serfs were paying. Clothing distinguished the Citizen, but was not the basis of Citizenship; a Citizen could go naked if he chose, and sacrifice none of his dignity or power. Nevertheless, some wore jewelry.

They came to a smaller pool. Here Stile's employer soaked. Six extraordinarily voluptuous young women were attending him, rubbing oils into his skin, polishing his fingernails, even grooming his privates, which were supremely unaroused. An older man was doing the Citizen's hair, meticulously, moving neatly with the Citizen to keep the lather from his face.

"Sir," the foreman said respectfully.

The Citizen took no notice. The girls continued their labors. Stile and the foreman stood where they were, at attention. Stile was conscious again of the grime on him, from his recent riding lesson; what a contrast he was to these premises and all the people associated with them! Several minutes passed.

Stile noted that the Citizen had filled out slightly in the past year, but remained a healthy and youngish-looking man. He had fair muscular development, suggesting regular exercise, and obviously he did not overeat—or if he did, he stayed with non-nutritive staples. His hair looked white—but that was the effect of the lather. His pubic region was black. It was strange seeing a Citizen in the same detail as a serf!

Two more men entered the chamber. One was Billy, the roving security guard for the farm; the other was Bourbon. "Sir," Billy said.

Now the Citizen nodded slightly to the foreman. "Be at ease," the foreman said to the others. Stile, Billy and Bourbon relaxed marginally.

The Citizen's eyes flicked to Bourbon. "Elucidate your protest."

Bourbon, in obvious awe of his employer, swallowed and spoke. "Sir, I was passed over for promotion in favor of Stile, here, when I have seniority and a better record."

The Citizen's eyes flicked coldly to the foreman. "You promoted Stile. Justify this."

The *foreman* had promoted him? Stile had not been aware that the man had such power. He had thought the foreman's authority ended with discipline, record-keeping, and perhaps the recommendation of candidates. The Citizen might have gotten mixed up, not paying full attention to the details of serf management, but the foreman should never have erred like this! He was the one who had suspended Stile, after all.

"Sir," the foreman said, ill at ease himself. "It is my considered judgment that Stile is the proper man to fill the present need. I prefer to have him trained on the robot horse, which will only be with us three months."

The Citizen's eyes flicked back to Bourbon. "You are aware that the foreman exists to serve my interests. He is not bound by guidelines of seniority or record. It is his prerogative and mandate to place the proper personnel in the proper slots. I do not permit this of him, I require it. You have no case."

"Sir," Bourbon said rebelliously.

The Citizen's eyes touched the foreman. There was no trace of humor or compassion in them. "Do you wish to permit this man to pursue this matter further?"

"No, sir," the foreman said.

"Overruled. Bourbon, make your specifics."

What was going on here? Why should the Citizen waste his time second-guessing his own foreman, whose judgment he obviously trusted? If the foreman got reversed, it would be an awkward situation.

"Sir, Stile has the favor of the visiting instructor, Tune. I believe she prevailed on the foreman to promote Stile out of turn, though he fouled up only yesterday, injuring one of your race horses. My own record is clean."

For the first time the Citizen showed emotion. "Injured my horse? Which one?"

"Spook, sir."

"My most promising miler!" The Citizen waved one arm, almost striking a girl. She teetered at the edge of the pool for a moment before recovering her balance. "Fall back, attendants!" he snapped. Now that emotion had animated him, he was dynamic.

Instantly the seven attendants withdrew to a distance of four meters and stood silently. Stile was sure they were just as curious about this business as he was, though of course less involved.

Now there was something ugly about the Citizen's gaze, though his face was superficially calm. "Foreman, make your case."

The foreman did not look happy, but he did not hesitate. "Sir, I will need to use the vidscreen."

"Do so." The Citizen made a signal with one finger, and the entire ceiling brightened. It was a giant video receiver, with special elements to prevent condensation on its surface. "Respond to the serf's directives, *ad hoc*."

The foreman spoke a rapid series of temporal and spatial coordinates. A picture formed on the screen. Stile and the others craned their necks to focus on it. It was the stable, with the horse Spook looking out. A running film-clock showed date and time: yesterday morning.

"Forward action," the foreman said, and the film jumped ahead to show Stile approaching the pen.

Stile watched, fascinated. He had had no idea this was being filmed. He looked so small, the horse so large—yet he was confident, the horse nervous. "Come on, Spook," his image said, encouraging the horse. But Spook was not cooperative.

The film went through the whole ugly sequence relentlessly, as Stile gentled and bluffed and fought the great stallion, forcing him to proceed to the lunging tree.

"As you can see, sir," the foreman said. "This man was dealing with an extremely difficult animal, but was not fazed. He used exactly that amount of force required to bring the horse in line. I have handled Spook myself; I could not have gotten him to lunge on that morning."

"Why didn't you send help?" the Citizen demanded. "I would have had difficulty myself, in that situation." This was no idle vanity; the Citizen was an expert horseman.

"Because, sir, I knew Stile could handle it. The presence of other serfs would only have alarmed the horse. This is why Stile was assigned to this animal on this day; Spook needed to be exercised and disciplined with competence. He had thrown his rider on the prior day."

"Proceed."

Under the foreman's direction the scene now shifted to Pepper's stall. Pepper showed no nervousness as Bourbon approached, but he laid back his ears as he recognized the stable hand. Bourbon brought him out roughly, slapping him unnecessarily, but the horse behaved well enough.

"This man, sir, was handling a docile animal brusquely," the foreman said. "This is typical of his manner. It is not a fault in itself, as some animals do respond to unsubtle treatment, but had he been assigned to exercise Spook—"

"Point made," the Citizen said, nodding. He was well attuned to the mannerisms of horses. "Get on with it."

Stile glanced at Bourbon. The stable hand was frozen, obviously trapped in an exposé he had never anticipated.

The film-Bourbon came up behind Stile, who now had Spook trotting nicely. The animal was magnificent. A small, stifled sigh of appreciation escaped one of the watching girls of the hammam. Girls really responded to horses!

Bourbon chose his time carefully. "One side, shorty!" he exclaimed almost directly behind Stile and the horse. There was no question about the malice of the act.

Spook spooked. The rest followed.

"Enough film," the Citizen said, and the ceiling screen died. "What remedial action did you take?"

"Sir, Stile reported the injury to his horse. I gave him three demerits and a one-day suspension. He made no issue. I felt that his competence and discretion qualified him best for the position, so I promoted him. I am aware that he had an acquaintance with the lady trainer, but this was not a factor in my decision."

"The other," the Citizen said grimly.

"Bourbon did not report the injury to his horse. I felt it more important to preserve the privacy of my observations than to make an overt issue. I passed him over for promotion, but did not suspend him, since the injury to the horse in his charge was minor."

"There *are* no minor injuries to horses!" the Citizen cried, red-faced. Veins stood out on his neck, and lather dripped unnoticed across his cheek. He would have presented a comical figure, were he not a Citizen. "You are rebuked for negligence."

"Yes, sir," the foreman said, chastened.

The Citizen turned to Stile. "Your promotion holds; it was merited." He turned to Bourbon, the cold eyes swiveling like the sights of a rifle. "You are fired."

When a serf was fired for cause, he was finished on Planet Proton. No other Citizen would hire him, and in ten days his tenure would be aborted. Bourbon was through. And Stile had learned a lesson of an unexpected nature.

* * *

He had been going with Tune three months, the happiest time of his life, studying fencing and riding and music and love, when abruptly she said: "I've got to tell you, Stile. My second fault. I'm short on time. My tenure's over."

"You're—" he said, unbelievingly.

"I started at age ten. You didn't think I got to be a jockey overnight, did you? My term is up in six months. I'm sorry I hid that from you, but I did warn you how I lied."

"I'll go with you!" he exclaimed with the passion of youth.

She squeezed his hand. "Don't be foolish. I like you, Stile, but I don't love you. Outside, you'd be twenty-one, and I'll be twenty-nine, and no rejuve medicine. You can do better than that, lover."

He thought he loved her, but he knew she was right, knew he could not throw away seventeen years of remaining tenure for a woman who was older than he and only liked him. "The Game!" he cried. "You must enter the Tourney, win more tenure—"

"That's why I'm telling you now, Stile. This year's Tourney begins tomorrow, and I'll be in it. I am on Rung Five of the age-29 ladder, by the slick of my teeth. My tenure ends the moment I lose a Game, so this is our last night together."

"But you might win!"

"You're a dreamer. *You* might win, when your time comes; you're a natural animal, beautifully skilled. That's why I wanted you, first time I saw you. I love fine animals! I was strongly tempted not even to try the Tourney, so as to be assured of my final six months with you—"

"You must try!"

"Yes. It's futile, but I must at least take one shot at the moon, though it costs me six months of you."

"What a way to put it!" Stile was torn by the horrors of her choice. Yet it was the type of choice that came to every serf in the last year of tenure, and would one day come to him.

"I know you'll be a better jockey than I was; you'll win your races, and be famous. I wanted a piece of you, so I took it, by means of the lie of my remaining time here. I'm not proud—"

"You gave me the best things of my life!"

She looked down at her breasts. "A couple of them, maybe. I hope so. Anyway, it's sweet of you to say so, sorehead. Your life has only begun. If I have helped show you the way, then I'm glad. I won't have to feel so guilty."

"Never feel guilty!" he exclaimed.

"Oh, guilt can be great stuff. Adds savor to life." But the spark was not in her humor, now.

They made love quickly, because he did not want to tire her right before the Tourney, but with inspired passion. He felt guilt for letting her go—and she was right, it did add a certain obscure quality to the experience.

Next day she entered the Tourney, and in her first match made a try on the Grid for music, and got trapped in dance instead. She was gone.

Stile pursued his musical studies relentlessly, driven by his waning guilt and love of her memory. Gradually that love transferred itself to the music, and became a permanent part of him. He knew he would never be a master musician, but he was a good one. He did enjoy the various instruments, especially the keyboard harmonica.

Three years later the foreman's tenure expired. "Stile, you're good enough to qualify for my job," he said in a rare moment of private candor. "You're young yet, but capable and honest, and you have that unique touch with the horses. But there is one thing—"

"My size," Stile said immediately.

"I don't judge by that. But there are others—"

"I understand. I will never be a leader."

"Not directly. But for you there is a fine alternative. You can be promoted to jockey, and from there your skill can take you to the heights of fame available to a serf. I believe this is as good a life as anyone not a Citizen can have on Proton."

"Yes." Stile found himself choked up about the foreman's departure, but could not find any appropriate way to express this. "I—you—"

"There's one last job I have for you, a tough one, and how you acquit yourself may determine the issue. I am recommending you for immediate promotion to jockey, but the Citizen will decide. Do not disappoint me."

"I won't," Stile said. "I just want to say—"

But the foreman was holding out his hand for parting. "Thank you," Stile said simply. They shook hands, and the foreman departed quickly.

The job was to bring Spook back from another dome. The horse had grown more spooky with the years, and could no longer be trusted to vehicular transportation; the sound and vibration, however muted, set him off. The Citizen refused to drug him for the trip; he was too valuable to risk this way. Spook had won a number of races, and the Citizen wanted him back on the farm for stud. So Spook had to be brought home on foot. That could be difficult, for there were no walk-passages suitable for horses, and the outer surface of the planet was rough.

Stile planned carefully. He ordered maps of the region and studied them assiduously. Then he ordered a surface-suit, complete with scoba unit: Self-Contained Outside Breathing Apparatus. And a gyro monocycle, an all-band transceiver, and an information watch. He was not about to get himself lost or isolated on the inhospitable Proton surface!

That surface was amazingly rugged, once he was on it. There were mountain ranges to the north and south, the northern ones white with what little water this world had in free-state, as snow. There was the winding channel of a long-dead river, and a region of deep fissures as if an earthquake had aborted in mid-motion. He guided his monocycle carefully, counterbalancing with his body when its motions sent it into twists of precession; incorrectly handled, these machines could dump a man in a hurry, since the precession operated at right angles to the force applied. He located the most dangerous traps for a nervous horse, plotting a course well clear of them. Spook would be upset enough, wearing an equine face mask for his breathing and protection of his eyes and ears; any additional challenges could be disastrous. Which was of course why Stile was the one who had to take him through; no one else could do it safely.

Stile took his time, calling in regular reports and making up his route map. This was really a puzzle: find the most direct route that avoided all hazards. He had to think in equine terms, for Spook could spook at a mere patch of colored sand, while trotting blithely into a dead-end canyon.

Only when he was quite certain he had the best route did Stile report to the dome where Spook was stabled. He was confident, now, that he could bring the horse across in good order. It was not merely that this success would probably facilitate his promotion. He liked Spook. The horse had in his fashion been responsible for Stile's last promotion.

When he arrived at that dome, he found a gram awaiting him. It was from offplanet: the first he had had since his parents moved out. STILE—AM MARRIED NOW—NAMED SON AFTER YOU. HOPE YOU FOUND YOURS—TUNE.

He was glad for her, though her loss hurt with sudden poignancy. Three months together, three years apart; he could not claim his world had ended. Yet he had not found another girl he liked as well, and suspected he never would. He found himself humming a melody; he had done that a lot in the first, raw months of loss, and it had coalesced into a nervous habit he did not really try to cure. Music would always remind him of her, and he would always pursue it in memory of those three wonderful months.

So she had named her son after him! She had not conceived by him, of course; no one conceived involuntarily on Proton. It was just her way of telling him how much their brief connection had meant to her. She had surely had many other lovers, and not borrowed from their names for this occasion. She said she had lied to him, but actually she had made possible an experience he would never have traded. Brevity did not mean inconsequence; no, never!

"Thank you, Tune," he murmured.

CHAPTER 10

Magic

Stile woke suddenly, making a significant connection. "Geography!" he cried. "This world is Proton!"

Neysa, in girl-form, was tending him. He realized, in a kind of supplementary revelation, that she was the same size as Tune; no wonder he had accepted her as a lover so readily, despite his knowledge of her nature. She was not a true woman, and would never be, but she was well worthwhile on her own account.

She looked at him questioningly, aware of his stare. Her appearance and personality were, of course, quite unlike Tune's; no light-hued hair, no merry cleverness here. Neysa was dark and quiet, and she never told a lie.

"I had a memory," he explained. "Beginning with my fencing lessons, because you were teaching me how to use the rapier when I—" He paused, trying to assimilate it. "What happened to me?"

Reluctantly, she talked. "Sick."

"Sick? You mean as in disease? But there's no disease on Proton—" Again he did a double take. "But this isn't Proton, exactly. It's another realm with the same geography. The purple mountains to the south— it's what Proton might have been, had it had a decent atmosphere. An alternate Proton, where magic works. Maybe magic made the atmosphere, and the gravity. So with a complete planetary environment, a complete ecology, there are flies, there is dirt, there is disease. And I have no natural immunity, only my standard shots, which never anticipated the complete spectrum of challenges I found here. The micro-organisms in the food here, in the water, natural for natives but foreign to my system. Pollens in the air. Allergens. Et cetera. So it took a couple of days for the germs to incubate in my system, then suddenly they overwhelmed me. Reaching the point of explosive infestation. Thanks for explaining it so well, Neysa."

She smiled acknowledgment.

"But how could you cure me? I should have died, or at least been sick longer than this. I've only been out a few hours, haven't I? Now I feel fine, not even tired."

She had to speak again. "Clip brought amulet." She reached forward and touched a figurine hanging on a necklace that had been put on him.

Stile lifted it in his hand. "A healing amulet? Now isn't that clever! Will I get sick again if I take it off?"

She shook her head no.

"You mean these things emit their magic in one burst, then are useless? But some are supposed to have continuing effect, like the clothing-simulator amulet I was given at the outset—uh-oh." He hastily removed the chain from his neck. "That one tried to kill me. If this one was made by the same party—"

She shrugged.

"Do you mind if I dispose of this now?" he asked. "We could bury it and mark the spot so we can find it later if we want it. But I'd rather not have it with me. If I invoke a secondary function—well, Neysa, an amulet attacked me, before I met you. When I invoked it. *You* invoked this one, so maybe that's why it acted normally. I fear the amulets have murder in mind for me, when they recognize me. That's why I needed a steed—to get away from my anonymous enemy."

Neysa lifted her head, alarmed in the equine manner. "No, no, you didn't bring the enemy here," Stile reassured her. "The demon hasn't been invoked." He took her hands, smiling. "I chose better than I knew, when I chose you. You did right, Neysa. I think you saved my life."

She allowed herself to be drawn in to him, and there followed what followed. He had not forgotten Sheen, but this was another world.

They buried the amulet and went on. It was morning; his illness had lasted only one night, coinciding with normal sleep, and the revelation of geography had almost been worth it. This accounted for the nagging familiarity he had sensed before; he had seen the surface of this world a decade ago, in its dead form.

What accounted for this difference? The concept of alternate worlds, or alternate frames of the same world, he could accept. But breathable atmosphere, a full living ecology, and magic in one, domes and science and external barrenness in the other—that dichotomy was harder to fathom. He would have expected parallel frames to be very similar to each other.

Still, it helped his sense of orientation. Now it was clear why people crossed over at certain spots. They were not matter-transmitting, they were stepping through the curtain at precise geographical locations, so as to arrive in domes and in private places. To cross elsewhere—well, if he tried that, he would have to prepare himself with a breathing mask.

"You know, Neysa," he said as he rode. "There is a lot I don't know about this world, and my life is in danger here, but I think I like it better than my own. Out here, with you—I'm happy. I could just ride forever, I think, like this." He shook his head. "But I suppose I would get tired of it, in a century or two; must be realistic."

Neysa made a musical snort, then broke into a two-beat gallop, front hooves striking precisely together, rear hooves likewise. It was a jolting gait.

"Think you can buck me off, huh?" Stile said playfully. He brought out his harmonica—one advantage of clothing, he discovered, was that it had pockets—and played a brisk marching melody. The girl Tune had taught him the beauty of music, and his growing talent in it had helped him on numerous occasions in the Game. His memory flashback had freshened his awareness that even had music been worthless in a practical sense, he would have kept it up. Music was fun.

But again a looming presence developed. Again they stopped. "Something funny about this," Stile said. "Clip told me not to worry, that unicorns are immune to most magic—but this is eerie. I don't like mysteries that may affect my health."

Neysa blew a note of agreement.

"It seems to happen when we're playing music," he continued. "Now I've never been harmed by music, but I'd better be sure. Maybe something is sneaking up while we're playing, hoping we won't notice. I somehow doubt this is connected with the amulets; this is more subtle. Let's try it again. If we feel the presence, I'll stop playing and will try to search it out. You go on playing as if nothing is happening. We need to catch it by surprise."

They resumed play—and immediately the presence returned. Stile left his harmonica at his lips but ceased playing; instead he peered about while Neysa danced on, continuing the melody. But even as he looked, whatever it was faded.

Experimentally Stile resumed play, matching Neysa's theme, softly, so that an on-listener would not hear him. The presence returned. Neysa stopped playing, while Stile continued—and the presence loomed stronger, as if her music had restrained it. Stile halted abruptly —and the effect receded.

"It's tied to me!" he exclaimed. "Only when I play—"

Neysa agreed. Whatever it was, was after Stile—and it advanced only when he was playing. It could hear him, regardless of other sounds that masked his own.

Stile felt an eerie chill. "Let's get out of here," he said.

The unicorn took off. No clever footwork this time; she moved right into a racing gallop. They forged across the plain at a rate no horse could match, wove through copses of brightly green trees, and leaped across small streams. He could see the mountains sliding back on either side. They were really covering the kilometers!

At last Neysa slowed, for her breath was turning fiery. Stile brought out his harmonica and played once more—and instantly the presence closed in.

He stopped immediately. "We can't outrun it, Neysa; that's evident. But now that we're aware of it, maybe we can do something about it. Why does it still come only when I play? It has to know that we are aware of it, and are trying to escape it; no further need to hide."

Neysa shrugged—an interesting effect, while he was mounted.

"First the amulet, now this. *Could* they be connected? Could the harmonica be—" He paused, alarmed. "Another amulet?"

After a moment he developed a notion. "Neysa—do you think you could play this instrument? With your mouth, I mean, human-fashion? If this is an enemy-summoning device, there should be the same effect whoever plays it. I think."

Neysa halted and had him dismount and remove the saddle. Then she phased into human form. He had not seen her do it by day before, and it had not occurred to him that she would. He had thought of her playing the harmonica in her equine form, but of course this way made much more sense.

She took the instrument and played. She was not expert, since this was foreign to her mode, and the result was a jumble. No presence formed. Then Stile took the harmonica and played a similar jumble—and the presence was there.

"Not the instrument—but me," he said. "Only when I play it." He pondered. "Is it a symbiosis, or is the harmonica incidental?"

He tried humming a tune—and the presence came, though not as powerfully as before.

"That settles it: it's me. When I make music, it comes. My music is better with the harmonica, so the effect is stronger, that's all. The instrument is not haunted." He smiled. "I'm glad. I like this harmonica. I'd hate to have to bury it in dirt." He would hate to abuse any harmonica, because he retained a fond feeling for the keyboard harmonica and all its relatives. But this present instrument was the finest of its breed he had ever played.

Neysa had changed back to her natural form. Stile put the saddle back on. "I don't think we can afford to ignore this matter," he said.

The unicorn flicked one ear in agreement.

"Let's get down to some good grazing land, and I'll challenge it. I want to see what will happen. I don't like running from a threat anyway. I'd rather draw it out and settle the account, one way or another. If it is an enemy, I want to summon it by daylight, with my sword in hand, not have it sneak up on me at night."

Neysa agreed again, emphatically.

They moved downslope until good grass resumed. Neysa grazed, but she did not wander far from Stile, and her eye was on him. She was concerned. Bless her; it had been a long time since someone had worried about him. Except for Sheen—and that was a matter of programming.

Stile began to play. The presence loomed. He tried to see it, but it was invisible, intangible. This time he did not stop his music. The grass seemed to wave, bending toward him and springing back as if driven by a wind, but there was no wind. The air seemed to sparkle. A faint haze developed, swirling in barely discernible colored washes. Stile felt the hairs on his body lighten, as if charged electrostatically. He thought at first it was his own nervousness, for he did not know what thing or force he summoned, but he saw Neysa's mane lifting similarly. There was potential here, and it centered on him—but it never acted. It just loomed.

Stile stopped playing, growing weary of this—and yet again the effect faded. "Almost the form of an electrical storm," he mused. "Yet—"

He was cut off by a sheet of rain blasting at him. Lightning cracked nearby. The sudden light half-blinded him, and a gust of wind made him stagger. He was soaked as if dunked in a raging sea, feeling the eerie chill of the violent water. There was a swirling of fog reminiscent of a developing tornado. The flashes of light were continuous.

Neysa charged back to him, seeking to protect him from the elements with her body and her anti-magic. Both helped; Stile flung his arms about her neck and buried his face in her wet mane, and the swirling wind had less force there. Her mass was more secure than his, and the rain struck her less stingingly. They settled to the ground, and that was more secure yet. "Now I'm embracing you in your natural form," he told her laughingly, but doubted she heard him over the wind.

What had happened? A moment ago there had been no slightest sign of bad weather. Stile knew storms could develop quickly—he had taken a course in primitive-world meteorology, and often visited the weather dome for demonstrations—but this had been virtually instantaneous. He had been playing his harmonica, trying to trigger whatever monstrous force was lurking, to bring it somehow to bay, then idly likened the effect to—

"I did it!" he cried. "I invoked the storm!" Like the amulet, it had been there to be commanded, and he had innocently done so.

"Storm abate!" he cried.

The two of them were almost swept from their impromptu nest by another savage bout of wind. The storm was not, it seemed, paying heed.

Yet this power was somehow keyed to him. He had invoked the storm; was he unable to banish it? He had evoked the demon from the amulet, before; that had evidently been a one-way thing. But a storm? Was it impossible to put this genie back in the bottle?

It was hard to concentrate, in this buffeting and wet and light and noise. But he tried. What, specifically, had he done to bring this about?

He had played music, and the storm-spirit had loomed close without striking. Then he had said, "Almost the form of an electrical storm." An accidental rhyme, of no significance.

Rhyme? Something nagged him. When the harmonica had appeared, so fortuitously—what had he said? Hadn't it been—yes. "A harmonica is what you play. I wish I had one here today." Something like that. Joke doggerel. Two times he had spoken in rhyme, and two times he had been answered. Of course there had been other magic, like the attacking demon of the amulet. No rhymes there. But—worry about that later; it might be a different class of magic. Now, try to abate this tempest. Abate—what rhymed with that? Fate, late, plate. Try it; all he could do was fail.

"Storm abate; you're making me late!" he cried.

The storm lessened, but did not disappear. He was on to something, but not enough. Half a loaf. What else had he done, those other two times?

Neysa played a note on her horn. The storm had eased, so she preferred to stand. She felt most secure on all four feet.

That was it! He had been blowing his horn—in a manner. The harmonica. Making music, either singing or playing.

Stile brought out his wet harmonica and played a soggy passage. Then he stopped and sang in an impromptu tune: "Storm abate. You're making me late!"

This time the storm lessened considerably. The lightning stopped, and the rain slacked to a moderate shower. But it still wasn't gone.

"Neysa, I think I'm on to something," he said. "But I don't really have the hang of it yet. I think I can do magic, if I can only get the rules straight."

The unicorn gave him a long look whose import was unclear. Evidently she distrusted this development, but she made no comment. And he marveled at it himself: how could he, the child of the modern civilized galaxy, seriously consider practicing magic?

Yet, after what he had experienced in this frame, how could he *not* believe in magic?

They resumed their journey, plodding through the drizzle. After an hour they got out of it, and the sun warmed them. They did not make music. Stile knew he had learned something, but not enough. Yet.

Now they settled down to serious grazing and eating—except that he had nothing to eat. Neysa had been willing to continue until she brought him to a fruit tree, but he had felt her sustenance was more important than his, at the moment. She was doing most of the work.

If he could actually do magic, maybe he could conjure some food. If he made up a rhyme and sang it—why not? What rhymed with food?

Stile was actually a poet, in a minor sense; this was yet another aspect of his Game expertise. A person had to be extremely well rounded to capture and hold a high rung on an adult ladder. He was probably more skilled in more types of things of a potentially competitive nature than anyone not involved in the Game. But he had preferred meaning to rhyme and meter, in poetry, so was ill prepared for this particular exercise.

Still, he did know the rudiments of versification, and with a little practice it should come back to him. Iambic feet: da-DUM da-DUM. Pentameter: five feet per line. *I wish I had a little food*—iambic tetrameter, four beats. If unicorns spoke words while running, they would be excellent at poetic meter, for their hooves would measure the cadence.

"I wish I had a little food; it would really help my mood," he said in singsong. He was not as good at improvising tunes with his voice as with an instrument.

Before him appeared a tiny cube. It dropped to the ground, and he had to search for it in the grass. He found it and held it up. It was about a centimeter on a side, and in tiny letters on one face was printed the word FOOD. Stile touched his tongue to it. Nutro-peanut butter. He ate it. Good, but only a token.

Well, he had specified "little." That was exactly what he had gotten.

He was gaining understanding. Music summoned the magic; that was the looming power they had been aware of. Words defined it. The rhyme marked the moment of implementation. A workable system—but he had to make his definitions precise. Suppose he conjured a sword—and it transfixed him? Or a mountain of food, and it buried him? Magic, like any other tool, had to be used properly.

"I wish I had one liter of food; it would really help my mood."

Nothing happened. Obviously he was still missing something.

Neysa lifted her head, perking her ears. Her hearing was more acute than his. Her head came around. Stile followed the direction her horn was pointing—and saw shapes coming toward them.

Had he summoned these? He doubted it; they hardly looked like food, and certainly not in the specified quantity. This must be a coincidental development.

Soon the shapes clarified. Four monsters. They were vaguely apelike, with huge long forearms, squat hairy legs, and great toothy, horny, glary-eyed heads. Another variant of demon, like the one he had fought alone, or the crack-monsters, or the snow-monsters. They all seemed to be species of a general class of creature that wasn't in the conventional taxonomy. But of course unicorns weren't in it either.

Neysa snorted. She trotted over to stand by Stile. She knew this was trouble.

"Must be a sending of my enemy," Stile said. "When you used the amulet to heal me, it alerted the master of amulets, who it seems is not partial to me, for what reason I don't yet know. He sent his goon squad

—but we were no longer with the amulet, so they had to track us down. I'll bet the storm messed them up, too."

Neysa made a musical laugh through her horn—a nice effect. She liked the notion of goons getting battered by a storm. But her attention remained on those monsters, and her ears were angling back. She looked cute when her ears perked forward, and grim when they flattened back.

"I think it must be an Adept against me," Stile continued. "Obviously it is no common peasant. But now I know I can do some magic myself, I am more confident. Do you think we should flee these monsters, and worry about when they might catch up again—such as when we are sleeping—or should we fight them here?"

It was a loaded question, and she responded properly. She swished her tail rapidly from side to side and stomped a forehoof, her horn still oriented on the goons.

"My sentiments exactly," Stile said. "I just don't like leaving an enemy on my trail. Let me see if I can work out a good spell to abolish them. That should be safer than indulging in physical combat. They look pretty mean to me."

Pretty mean indeed. His tone had been light, but he already had healthy respect for the fighting capacity of demons. They were like the androids of Proton: stupid, but almost indestructible. Yet he distrusted this magic he could perform. Like all sudden gifts, it needed to be examined in the mouth before being accepted wholeheartedly. But at the moment he simply had to use what was available, and hope it worked.

He concentrated on his versification as the goons approached. He could not, under this pressure, think of anything sophisticated, but so long as it was clear and safe, it would do. It had to.

The first monster loomed before them. "Monster go—I tell you so!" Stile sang, pointing.

The monster puffed into smoke and dissipated. Only a foul-smelling haze remained.

So far, so good. He was getting the hang of it. Stile pointed to the second monster. "Monster go—I tell you so!" he sang, exactly as before. Why change a winning spell?

The monster hesitated as if fazed by the bite of a gnat, then plunged ahead.

Neysa lunged by Stile and caught the demon on her horn. With one heave she hurled it over and behind. The creature gave a great howl of expiration, more in fury than in pain, and landed in a sodden heap.

Why had the magic worked the first time, and not the second? He had done it exactly the same, and nearly gotten his head bitten off.

Oh, no! Could it be that a spell could not be repeated? That it worked only once? Now he remembered something that had been said by the man he met, the one who had given him the demon amulet.

About having to devise a new spell each time, to step through the curtain. He should have paid better attention!

The third and fourth goons arrived together.

No time now to work up another spell! Stile drew his rapier. "I'll take the one on the right; you take the left," he said to Neysa.

But these two monsters, having seen the fate of their predecessors, were slightly more cautious. To be ugly was not necessarily to be stupid, and these were not really androids. They evidently learned from experience. They halted just outside the range of horn and sword. They seemed to consider Neysa to be the more formidable opponent, though Stile was sure it was him they wanted. They had to deal with her first; then they would have him at their dubious mercy. Or so they thought.

While one goon tried to distract her, backing away from the unicorn's horn, the other tried to get at her from the side. But Stile attacked the side monster, stabbing at it with his point. He wished he had a broadsword; then he could have slashed these things to pieces. He wasn't sure that a simple puncture would have much effect.

He was mistaken. He pricked his monster in the flank, and it howled and whirled on him, huge ham-hands stretching toward him. Stile pricked it again, in its meaty shoulder. Not a mortal wound, but it obviously hurt. At least these demons did have pain sensation; Stile had half-feared they would not. Still, this was basically a standoff. He needed to get at a vital spot, before the thing—

The goon's arm swung with blinding speed and swept the weapon out of Stile's hand. The thing's eyes glowed. Gratified, it pounced on him.

Stile whirled into a shoulder throw, catching the monster's leading arm and heaving. With this technique it was possible for the smallest of men to send the largest of men flying. But this was not a man. The creature was so large and long-armed that Stile merely ended up with a hairy arm dangling over his shoulder. The monster's feet had not left the ground.

Now the goon raised its arm, hauling Stile into the air. He felt its hot breath on his neck; it was going to bite off his head!

"Oh, swell! Go to hell!" Stile cried with haphazard inspiration.

He dropped to the ground. The monster was gone.

Stile looked around, pleased. His impromptu spell had worked! It seemed this frame did have a hell, and he could send—

He froze. The other goon was gone too. So was Neysa.

Oh, no!

Quick, a counterspell. Anything! What rhymed with spell?

"I don't feel well; cancel that spell," he singsonged.

The two monsters and Neysa were back. All three were scorched and coated with soot.

"Monsters away; Neysa stay!" Stile sang. The goons vanished again.

Neysa looked at him reproachfully. She shook herself, making the powdered soot fly. There were sulfur smears on her body, and her mane was frizzled, and her tail was only half its normal length. Her whole body was a mass of singed hair. The whites showed all around her eyes; sure signal of equine alarm.

"I'm sorry, Neysa," Stile said contritely. "I wasn't thinking! I didn't mean to send *you* to hell!" But he realized that wasn't much good. She was burned and hurting. He had to do more than merely apologize.

He could do magic—if he sang a new spell every time. Could he make her well?

"To show how I feel—I say 'Neysa, heal!'"

And before his eyes she unburned. Her mane grew out again and her tail became long and black and straight. Her coat renewed its luster. Her hooves brightened back into their original pearl glow. She had healed—in seconds.

Where were the limits of his power?

But the unicorn did not seem happy. She was well, now, physically, but she must have had a truly disturbing emotional experience. A visit to hell! How could he erase that horror? Could he formulate a spell to make her forget? But that would be tampering with her mind, and if he made any similar error in definition—no, he dared not mess with that.

Neysa was looking at him strangely, as she had before. Stile feared he knew why.

"Neysa—how many people on this world can perform magic like this?" he asked her. "I know most people can do minor magic, like stepping through the curtain, the way most people can pick out clumsy melodies on the harmonica. But how many can do it well? Professional level? Many?"

She blew a negative note.

"That's what I thought. A lot of people have a little talent, but few have a lot of talent, in any particular area. This sort of thing is governed by the bell-shaped curve, and it would be surprising if magic talent weren't similarly constrained. So can a moderate number match my level?"

She still blew no.

"A few?"

This time the negation was fainter.

"A very few?"

At last the affirmative.

Stile nodded. "How many can exert magic against a unicorn, since unicorns are largely proof against magic?"

Neysa looked at him, her nervousness increasing. Her muzzle quivered; her ears were drawing back. Bad news, for him.

"Only the Adepts?" Stile asked.

She blew yes, backing away from him. The whites of her eyes were showing again.

"But Neysa—if I have such talent, I'm still the same person!" he cried. "You don't have to be afraid of me! I didn't mean to send you to hell! I just didn't know my own power!"

She snorted emphatic agreement, and backed another step.

"I don't want to alienate you, Neysa. You're my only friend in this world. I need your support."

He took a step toward her, but she leaned away from him on all four feet. She feared him and distrusted him, now; it was as if he had become a demon, shuffling off his prior disguise.

"Oh, Neysa, I wish you wouldn't feel this way! The magic isn't half as important as your respect. You joined me, when you could have killed me. We have been so much to each other, these past three days!"

She made a small nose at him, angry that he should try to prevail on her like this. He had sent her to hell; he had shown her how demeaning and dangerous to her his power could be. Yet she was moved; she did not want to desert him.

"I never set out to be a magician," Stile said. "I thought the magic was from outside. I had to know the truth. Maybe the truth is worse than what I feared."

Neysa snorted agreement. She was really dead set against this caliber of magic.

"Would it help if I swore not to try any more magic? To conduct myself as if that power did not exist in me? I am a man of my word, Neysa; I would be as you have known me."

She considered, her ears flicking backward and forward as the various considerations ran through her equine mind. At last she nodded, almost imperceptibly.

"I swear," Stile said, "to perform no magic without your leave."

There was an impression of faint color in the air about him, flinging outward. The grass waved in concentric ripples that expanded rapidly until lost to view. Neysa's own body seemed to change color momentarily as the ripples passed her. Then all was normal again.

Neysa came to him. Stile flung his arms about her neck, hugging her. There was a special art to hugging an equine, but it was worth the effort. "Oh, Neysa! What is more important than friendship!"

She was not very demonstrative in her natural form, but the way she cocked one ear at him and nudged him with her muzzle was enough.

Neysa returned to her grazing. Stile was still hungry. There was no suitable food for him here, and since he had sworn off magic he could not conjure anything to eat. Actually, he found himself somewhat relieved to be free of magic—but what was he to say to his stomach?

Then he spied the monster Neysa had slain. Were goons edible?

This seemed to be the occasion to find out. He drew his knife and set about carving the demon.

Neysa spied what he was doing. She played a note of reassurance, then galloped around in a great circle several times, while Stile gathered brush and dead wood and dry straw to form a fire. When he had his makings ready, Neysa charged in, skidded to a halt, and snorted out a blowtorch blast. She had evidently not yet cooled off from the battle—or from hell—and needed only a small amount of exertion to generate sufficient heat. The brush burst into flame.

As it turned out, monster steak was excellent.

CHAPTER 11

Oracle

By the time they reached the Oracle, two days later, Stile had pretty well worked out the situation. He could do magic of Adept quality, provided he followed its rules. He had sworn off it, and he would not violate that pledge. But that didn't change what he was: an Adept. That could explain why another Adept was trying to kill him; that other was aware of Stile's potential, and didn't want the competition. The Adepts, it seemed, were quite jealous of their prerogatives—as were the members of most oligarchies or holders of power.

So how should he proceed? Swearing off magic would not protect him from a jealous Adept, who would resent Stile's mere potential. But if it were only a single Adept who was after him, Stile might try to locate that one and deal with him. Nonmagically? That could be dangerous! So—he would ask the Oracle for advice. Why not?

The Oracle lived in a palace. Manicured lawns and hedges surrounded it, and decorative fountains watered its gardens. It was open; anyone could enter, including animals. In this world, animals had much the same stature as human beings; that was one of the things Stile liked about it. In this palace and its grounds, as he understood it, no magic was permitted, other than that of the Oracle itself, and no person could be molested or coerced.

"No disrespect intended," Stile said. "But this doesn't seem like much. It's beautiful in appearance and concept, but . . ."

Neysa left the saddle at the entrance and guided him to a small, plain room in the back. From its rear wall projected a simple speaking tube.

Stile studied the tube. "This is it? The Oracle?" he asked dubiously. "No ceremony, no fanfare, no balls of flame? No bureaucracy? I can just walk up and ask it anything?"

Neysa nodded.

Stile, feeling let down, addressed the tube. "Oracle, what is my best course of action?"

"Know thyself," the tube replied.

"That isn't clear. Could you elucidate?" But the tube was unresponsive.

Neysa nudged him gently away. "You mean I only get one question?" Stile asked, chagrined.

It was so. As with a spell, the Oracle could be invoked only once by any individual. But it had not been Neysa's purpose to have all his questions answered here; she had brought him to this place only for his safety.

Stile, frustrated, left Neysa and went outside. She did not try to restrain him, aware that he had been disappointed. He proceeded to the first fountain he saw. A wolf sat on the far side, probably not tame, but it would not attack him here. Stile removed his shirt, leaned over the pool, and splashed the cold water on his face. So he was safe; so what? His curiosity was unsatisfied. Was he to remain indefinitely in this world without understanding it?

"Thou, too?"

Stile looked up, startled, blinking the droplets from his vision. There was a young man across the fountain. He had shaggy reddish hair and a dark cast of feature, with eyes that fairly gleamed beneath heavy brows. His beard and sideburns were very like fur.

"I regret; I did not see you," Stile said. "Did I intrude?"

"Thou didst see me," the man said. "But recognized me not, in my lupine form."

Lupine. "A—werewolf?" Stile asked, surprised. "I am not used to this land. I did not think—I apologize."

"That was evident in thy mode of speech. But apologize not to an outcast cur."

Mode of speech. Suddenly Stile remembered: Clip the unicorn, Neysa's brother, had used this same touch of archaic language. Evidently that was what prevailed here. He had better change over, so as not to make himself awkwardly obvious.

"I—will try to mend my speech. But I do apologize for mistaking thee."

"Nonesuch is in order. This region is open to all without hindrance, even such as I."

Stile was reminded of the robot Sheen, claiming to have no rights because of her metal origin. It bothered him. "Art thou not a person? If being outcast is a crime, I am surely more criminal than you. Thee. I fled my whole world."

"Ah, it is as I thought. Thou art from Proton. Art thou serf or Citizen?"

"Serf," Stile said, startled at this knowledge of his world. Yet of course others had made the crossing before him. "Werewolf, if thou hast patience, I would like to talk with thee."

"I welcome converse, if thou knowest what ilk I be and be not deceived. I am Kurrelgyre, were."

"I am Stile, man." Stile proffered his hand, and the other, after a pause such as one might have when recalling a foreign convention, accepted it.

"In mine other form, we sniff tails," Kurrelgyre said apologetically.

"There is so much I do not know about this world," Stile said. "If you know—thou knowest of my world, thou wilt—wilst—thou shouldst appreciate the problem I have. I know not how came I here, or how to return, and the Oracle's reply seems unhelpful."

"It is the nature of Oracular response," Kurrelgyre agreed. "I am similarly baffled. I queried the Oracle how I might regain my place in my society without performing anathema, and the Oracle told me 'Cultivate blue.' Means that aught to thee?"

Stile shook his head. "Naught. I asked it what was my best course of action, and it said 'Know thyself.' I have no doubt that is always good advice, but it lacks specificity. In fact it is not even an action; it is an information."

"A most curious lapse," Kurrelgyre agreed. "Come, walk with me about the gardens. Perhaps we may obtain insights through dialogue."

"I shall be happy to. Allow me just a moment to advise my companion. She brought me here—"

"Assuredly." They re-entered the palace, proceeding to the Oracle chamber where Stile had left Neysa.

She was still there, facing the speaking tube, evidently unable to make up her mind what to say to it. Kurrelgyre growled when he saw her, shifting instantly into his lupine mode. Neysa, hearing him, whirled, her horn orienting unwaveringly on the new-formed wolf.

"Stop!" Stile cried, realizing that violence was in the offing. "There is no—"

The wolf sprang. Neysa lunged. Stile threw himself between them.

All three came to a halt in a momentary tableau. The tip of Neysa's horn was nudging Stile's chest; the wolf's teeth were set against his right arm, near the shoulder. Trickles of blood were forming on Stile's chest and arm where point and fang penetrated.

"Now will you both change into human form and apologize to the Oracle for this accident?" Stile said.

There was a pause. Then both creatures shimmered and changed. Stile found himself standing between a handsome young man and a pretty girl. He was shirtless, with rivulets of blood on him; he had forgotten to put his shirt back on after splashing in the fountain pool.

He extricated himself. "I gather unicorns and werewolves are hereditary enemies," he said. "I'm sorry; I didn't know. But this is no place for, uh, friendly competition. Now shake hands, or sniff tails, or whatever creatures do here to make up."

Neysa's eyes fairly shot fire, and Kurrelgyre scowled. But both glanced at the Oracle tube, then at Stile's bloodied spots, then at each other. And paused again.

Stile perceived, as if through their eyes, what each saw. The werewolf's clothing had reappeared with the man, and it was a tasteful fur-lined jacket and leggings, complimenting his somewhat rough-hewn aspect. Neysa was in a light black dress that set off her pert figure admirably; it seemed she wore clothing when she chose, though at night she had not bothered. She was now the kind of girl to turn any man's head—and Kurrelgyre's head was turning.

"It is a place of truce," the werewolf said at last. "I regret my instinct overcame my manners."

"I, too," Neysa agreed softly.

"I abhor the fact that I have drawn the blood of an innocent."

"I, too."

"Do thou draw my blood, Stile, in recompense." Kurrelgyre held out his arm. Neysa did the same.

"I shall not!" Stile said. "If you—if thou—the two of you—"

The werewolf smiled fleetingly. "Thou wert correct the first time, friend. It is the plural."

"If you two feel you owe me aught, expiate it by making up to each other. I hate to be the cause of dissent between good creatures."

"The penalty of blood need not be onerous," Kurrelgyre murmured. He made a courtly bow to Neysa. "Thou art astonishingly lovely, equine."

Neysa responded with a curtsey that showed more décolletage and leg than was strictly necessary. Oh, the tricks that could be played with clothing! No wonder the Citizens of Proton reserved clothing to themselves. "Thank thee, lupine."

Then, cautiously, Neysa extended her hand. Instead of shaking it, Kurrelgyre lifted it slightly, bringing it to his face. For a moment Stile was afraid the werewolf meant to bite it, but instead he kissed her fingers.

Stile, relieved, stepped forward and took an arm of each. "Let's walk together, now that we're all friends. We have much in common, being all outcasts of one kind or another. Neysa was excluded from the herd because of her color—"

"What is wrong with her color?" the werewolf asked, perplexed.

"Nothing," Stile said as they walked. He spied his shirt by the fountain, and moved them all toward it. "Some unicorns have distorted values."

Kurrelgyre glanced sidelong past Stile at the girl. "I should say so! I always suspected that Herd Stallion had banged his horn into one rock too many, and this confirms it. My taste does not run to unicorns, understand, but the precepts of physical beauty are universal. She is extremely well formed. Were she a were-bitch—"

"And I am outcast because I refused to—to perform a service for my employer," Stile continued. "Or to honor an illegal deal proffered by another Citizen." He washed his small wounds off with water from the pool, and donned his shirt. "What, if I may inquire, was thy problem, werewolf?"

"Among my kind, where game is scarce, when the size of the pack increases beyond the capacity of the range to support, the oldest must be eliminated first. My sire is among the eldest, a former leader of the pack, so it fell to me to kill him and assume the leadership. Indeed, there is no wolf in my pack I could not slay in fair combat. But I love my sire, long the finest of wolves, and could not do it. Therefore mine own place in the pack was forfeit, with shame."

"Thou wert excluded for thy conscience!" Stile exclaimed.

"There is no conscience beyond the good of the pack," the werewolf growled.

"Yes," Neysa breathed sadly.

They came to a hedged-in park, with a fine rock garden in the center. Neysa and Kurrelgyre sat down on stones nearer to each other than might have seemed seemly for natural enemies.

"Let us review thy situation, Stile," the werewolf said. "Thou knowest little of this land—yet this alone should not cause thee undue distress. Thou wilt hardly be in danger, with a fair unicorn at thy side."

"Nevertheless, I am in danger," Stile said. "It seems an Adept is trying to kill me."

"Then thou art beyond hope. Against Adepts, naught suffices save avoidance. Thou must remain here at the Oracle's palace forever."

"So I gather, in the ordinary case. But it also seems I have Adept powers myself."

Kurrelgyre phased into wolf-form, teeth bared as he backed away from Stile.

"Wait!" Stile cried. "Neysa reacted the same way! But I have sworn off magic, till Neysa gives me leave."

The wolf hesitated, absorbing that, then phased warily back into the man. "No unicorn would grant such leave, even were that not the stubbornest of breeds." Neysa nodded agreement.

"But I am just a stray from another world," Stile said. "It is mere coincidence that I have the talent for magic."

"Coincidence?" Kurrelgyre growled. "Precious little in this frame is coincidence; that is merely thy frame's term for what little magic operates there. Here, all things have meaning." He pondered a moment. "Have ye talent in the other frame?"

"I ride well—"

The werewolf glanced at Neysa, who sat with her fine ankles demurely exposed, her bosom gently heaving. "Who wouldn't!"

"And I am expert in the Game," Stile continued.

"The Game! That's it! Know ye not the aptitude for magic in this frame correlates with that for the Game in that frame? How good at the Game be ye, honestly?"

"Well, I'm tenth on my age-ladder—"

Kurrelgyre waved a warning finger at him. "Think ye I know not the way of the ladders? If ye rise to fifth place, thou must enter the annual Tourney. No obfuscation, now; this is vital. How good art thou when thou tryest, absolute scale?"

Stile realized that this was not the occasion for concealment or polite modesty. "I should be among the top ten, gross. On a good day, fourth or fifth."

"Then thou art indeed Adept caliber. There are no more than ten Adepts. They go by colors: White, Yellow, Orange, Green and such: no more than there are clear-cut hues. Therefore thou art of their number. One Adept must be dead."

"What art thou talking about? Why must an Adept be dead, just because I'm good at the Game in the other—" Stile caught himself about to make an impromptu rhyme and broke off lest he find himself in violation of his oath.

"Ah, I forget! Thou hast no basis yet to comprehend. Know this, Stile: no man can cross the curtain between frames while his double lives. Therefore—"

"Double?"

"His other self. His twin. All true men exist in both frames, and are forever fixed where they originate—until one dies out of turn. Then—"

"Wait, wait! Thou sayest people as well as geography match? That can not be so. The serfs of Proton are constantly brought in and deported as their tenures expire; only the Citizens are a constant population."

"Perhaps 'tis so, now; not always in the past. Most people still equate, Phaze to Proton, Proton to Phaze. The others are partial people, like myself. Perhaps I had a serf-self in the past, and that serf departed, so now I alone remain."

"Thou travelest between frames—because werewolves don't exist on Proton?"

Kurrelgyre shrugged. "It must be. Here there are animals and special forms; there, there are more serfs. It balances out, likely. But thou—thou must travel because thy magic self is dead. And thy magic self must be—"

"An Adept," Stile finished. "At last I get thy drift."

"Know thyself," Neysa said. "Adept." She frowned.

"That's it!" Stile cried. "I must figure out which Adept I am!" Then he noticed Neysa's serious demeanor. "Or must I? I have sworn off magic."

"But only by exerting thy powers as an Adept canst thou hope to survive!" Kurrelgyre exclaimed. Then he did a double take. "What am I saying? Who would want to help an Adept survive? The fair 'corn is right: abandon thy magic."

Corn? Oh, unicorn. "What is so bad about being an Adept?" Stile asked. "I should think it would be a great advantage to be able to perform magic."

The werewolf exchanged a glance with the unicorn. "He really knows not," Kurrelgyre said.

"I really don't," Stile agreed. "I am aware that magic can be dangerous. So can science. But you both act as if it's a crime. You suggest I would be better off dying as a man than living as an Adept. I should think a lot of good could be done by magic."

"Mayhap thou shouldst encounter an Adept," Kurrelgyre said.

"Maybe I should! Even though I'm not doing magic myself, at least I'd like to know who I am and what manner of creature I am. From what thou sayest, something must have happened to my Adept double and, considering my age and health, it couldn't have been natural." He paused. "But of course! All we need to do is check which Adept died recently."

"None has," Kurrelgyre assured him. "At least, none we know of. Adepts are secretive, but even so, someone must be concealing evidence."

"Well, I'll just have to go and look," Stile decided. "I'll check out each Adept until I find which one is dead, and see if that was me. Then I'll be satisfied. Only—how can I be sure that two aren't dead, and I have found the wrong one?"

"No problem there," the werewolf said. "Thine other self would have looked exactly like thee, so any who saw thee in his demesnes would know. And every Adept has his own peculiar style of magic, his means of implementation, that he alone commands. What style is thine?"

"Stile style," Neysa murmured, permitting herself to smile fleetingly.

"Spoken, or sung, in verse," Stile said. "Music summons the power. Which Adept uses that mode?"

"We know not. The Adepts vouchsafe no such information to common folk. Often they veil their magic in irrelevant forms, speaking incantations when it may be in fact a gesture that is potent, or posturing when it is a key rune. Or so it is bruited about among the animal folk. We know not who makes the amulets, or the golem people, or the potions or graphs or any of the other conjurations. We only know these things exist, and know to our dismay their power." He turned to Stile, taking one hand. "But friend—do not do this thing. If thou findest thine Adept-self, thou wilt become that Adept, and I shall have to bear the onus of not having slain thee when I had the chance. And Neysa too, who helped thee: lay not this geas upon her."

Stile turned to Neysa, appalled. "Thou feelest that way also?"

Sadly, she nodded.

"Methinks she led thee to the Oracle to avoid the peril she saw looming," Kurrelgyre said. "To destroy a friend—or turn an Adept loose on the realm. Here thou art safe, even from thy friends."

"But I am bound by mine oath!" Stile said. He hoped he was getting the language right: thy and my before a consonant, thine and mine before a vowel. "I will not perform magic! I will not become the monster thou fearest. I seek only to know. Canst thou deny me that?"

Slowly Kurrelgyre shook his head. "We can not deny thee that. Yet we wish—"

"I must know myself," Stile said. "The Oracle said so."

"And the Oracle is always right," the werewolf agreed. "We can not oppose our paltry judgment to that."

"So I will go on a quest for myself," Stile concluded. "When I have satisfied my need-to-know, I will return to mine own frame, where there is no problem about magic. So thou needst have no fear about me turning into whatever ogre thou dost think I might. I have to return soon anyway, to get my new employment, or my tenure will expire."

Neysa's gaze dropped.

"Why carest thou about tenure?" Kurrelgyre inquired. "Remain here, in hiding from thine enemy; thou hast no need to return."

"But Proton is my world," Stile protested. "I never intended to stay here—"

The werewolf stood and drew Stile gently aside. "Needs must I speak to thee in language unbecoming for the fair one to hear," he said. Neysa glanced up quickly at him, but remained sitting silently by the garden.

"What's this nonsense about unbecoming language?" Stile demanded when they were out of Neysa's earshot. "I don't keep secrets from—"

"Canst thou not perceive the mare is smitten with thee?" Kurrelgyre demanded. "Canst not guess what manner of question she tried to formulate for the Oracle?"

Stile suffered a guilty shock. He had compared Neysa in various ways to Sheen, yet missed the obvious one. "But I am no unicorn!"

"And I am no man. Yet I would not, were I thee, speak so blithely of departure. Better it were to cut her heart quickly, cleanly."

"Uh, yes. No," Stile agreed, confused. "She—we have been—I assumed it was merely a courtesy of the form. I never thought—"

"And a considerable courtesy it is," Kurrelgyre agreed. "I was careless once myself about such matters, until my bitch put me straight." He ran his fingers along an old scar that angled from his shoulder dangerously near the throat. Werewolves evidently had quite direct means of expressing themselves. "I say it as should not: Neysa is the loveliest creature one might meet, in either form, and no doubt the most constant too. Shamed would I have been to lay a tooth on her, ere thou didst halt me. Considering the natural antipathy that exists between man and unicorn, as between man and werewolf and between unicorn and werewolf, her attachment to thee is a mark of favor most extreme. Unless—chancest thou to be virginal, apart from her?"

"No."

"And most critical of all: canst thou touch her most private parts?"

Stile reddened slightly. "I just told thee—"

"Her feet," Kurrelgyre said. "Her horn. No stranger durst touch a unicorn's magic extremities."

"Why yes, I—"

"Then must it be love. She would not else tolerate thy touch. Mark me, friend: she spared thee, when she learned thou wert Adept, because she loved thee, and therein lies mischief with her herd. Thou canst not lightly set her aside." He touched the scar near his throat again.

"No," Stile agreed fervently, thinking again of Sheen. He had always had a kind of personal magnetism that affected women once they got to know him, though it was usually canceled out by the initial impression his size and shyness made. Thus his heterosexual relationships tended to be distant or intimate, with few shades between. But with that situation went a certain responsibility: not to hurt those women who trusted themselves to him.

He remembered, with another pang of nostalgia, how the jockey girl Tune had stimulated his love, then left him. He had never been able to blame her, and would not have eschewed the affair had he known what was coming. She had initiated him into a world whose dimension he had hardly imagined before. But he did not care to do that to another person. He had no concern about any injury from Neysa; she would never hurt him. She would just quietly take herself away, and off a mountain ledge, and never transform into a firefly. She would spare him, not herself. It was her way.

Kurrelgyre's question was valid: why couldn't Stile remain here? There was a threat against his life, true—but he had fled Proton because of that, too. If he could nullify that threat in this frame—well, there were appeals to this world that rivaled those of the Game.

In fact, magic itself had, for him, a fascination similar to—no! His oath made that academic.

What, then, of Sheen? He could not simply leave her in doubt. He must return at least long enough to explain. She was a robot; she would understand. The practical thing for him to do was pick the most convenient world and stay there. It would be enough for Sheen to know he was safe; her mission would then have been accomplished.

As he had known Tune was safe and happy . . . Had that been enough for him? To know she had successfully replaced his arms with those of another man, and given that man in fact what she had given Stile in name: a son? He had understood, and Sheen would understand—but was that enough?

Yet what else could he do? He could not remain in both frames, could he? In any event, his tenure on Proton was limited, while it seemed unlimited here.

Stile returned to Neysa and sat beside her, Kurrelgyre trailing. "The werewolf has shown me that I can not expect to solve my problems by fleeing them. I must remain here to find my destiny, only visiting the other frame to conclude mine affairs there." As he said it, he wished he had chosen other phrasing.

Neysa responded by lifting her gaze. That was enough.

"Now for thee, werewolf," Stile said. "We must solve thy riddle too. Did it occur to thee that the Blue thou must cultivate could be an Adept?"

Now Kurrelgyre was stricken. "Cultivate an Adept? Rather would I remain forever outcast!"

"But if the Oracle is always right—"

"That may be. I asked how to restore myself to my pack; the Oracle answered. Perhaps the necessary price is too high."

"Yet thou also didst specify that the method not violate thy conscience."

"My conscience will not permit my craven catering to the abomination that is an Adept!"

"Then it must be something else. Some other blue. A field of blue flowers—"

"Werewolves are not farmers!" Kurrelgyre cried indignantly. "It must be the Blue Adept; yet the only cultivation I could do without shame would be the turf over his grave. I shall not seek the Blue Adept."

Stile considered. "If, as we fear, thou hast doomed thyself to remain outcast from thy kind—why not travel with me? I have decided to remain in this frame, but this is pointless unless I locate and nullify the threat against my life—and that threat surely relates to who and what I am. Without magic with which to defend myself, I shall likely be in need of protection."

"The lady unicorn is capable of protecting thee ably enough."

"From the ill favor of an Adept?"

Kurrelgyre paced the ground. "Now, if I refuse, I brand myself coward."

"No, no! I did not mean to imply—"

"Thou hardly needst to. But also I doubt the mare would care to have the like of me along, and I would not impose—"

Neysa stood. She took Kurrelgyre's hand, glanced briefly into his eyes, then turned away.

The werewolf faced Stile. "Neysa has a way with words! It seems outcasts had best support each other, though they be natural enemies. We all shall likely die, and for a foolish cause—but it is as fitting a mode as any."

CHAPTER 12

Black

"Who is the closest Adept?" Stile asked. "Not the Blue; we won't check that one if you're along."

Kurrelgyre shifted to wolf-form and sniffed the breeze. He shifted back. "The Black, methinks."

"Black it is!" Stile agreed. He would have preferred a more scientific selection—but science was not, it seemed, trustworthy in this frame. Convenience would have to do.

They left the palace together, Stile riding Neysa, the wolf ranging easily beside. They bore west again, toward the castle of the Black Adept. Now that the decision was made, Stile had second thoughts about purpose and safety. Was he really doing the right thing? All he could do now was see it through, and after checking out the Black Adept he could decide whether it was worth checking out others. This was hardly his idea of sword and sorcery adventure—which was perhaps just as well. He suspected that in real life, more evil magicians prevailed than barbarian heroes.

Neysa had located a supply of grain, and had some in a bag tied to the saddle; she would not have to make long halts for grazing. Traveling at speed, they made excellent progress, covering fifty of this frame's miles in about two and a half hours. Stile had done some endurance riding on Proton, and knew it would take an excellent horse to maintain even half this pace.

Thereafter, the way became bleak. The turf thinned, remaining verdant only in scattered oases. Stile realized that with a spell he might procure fresh water and extra food, but did not offer. They did not want magic, and the very notion was contrary to the spirit of his oath.

The mountains and valleys gave way to a broad and featureless dark plain that extended to the horizon, oppressed by what seemed to be a permanently looming cloud. Gusts of cutting wind brought choking clouds of dust into their faces. Stile coughed. If this environment reflected the temperament of the Black Adept, the magician was vile indeed! But it was probably a misapprehension. Stile had friends and un-friends, but there were few people he considered to be as evil as his friends seemed to think Adepts were. It was said that familiarity bred contempt, but surely ignorance bred error.

At last, amid the gloom, a black castle showed. It stood in stark silhouette, no light illuminating it from within. The land about it was so bleak as to seem scorched. Had Stile not known the identity of its occupant, thanks to Kurrelgyre's nose, he might readily have guessed. Everything was dead black.

As they neared it, Stile suffered intensifying pangs of doubt. Was his curiosity worth the risk of bracing this person? He was running the risk of whatever sorcery the Black Adept had in mind—for what? Just to know who he was, in this frame.

No—it was more than that, he reminded himself. Another Adept was trying to kill him, and until Stile knew his own identity, he probably would not know who was trying to kill him, or why. The Oracle agreed; it had told him to know himself. Curiosity alone might not be worth it, but life, security—yes, that was worth it.

What should he do, though, if the lives of his friends were threatened on his behalf? Would he use his magic, then, to help them? No— he could not. His oath had been made, and Stile had never in his life broken his given word. Neysa had to give him leave, and now he knew she would not. Because she believed that to release him would be to turn him into the monster that an Adept would be, and she would rather die. He had better see to their mutual health by mundane means, staying alert.

Yet there was no call to be foolish. "Neysa," he murmured. "Is there any way to approach this castle secretly and depart in the same fashion? I don't need to brace the magician directly; I think one look at him will tell me whether he is alive or dead, or whether he resembles me. If we check, and the Black Adept is alive—not only is he not me, he is likely to do something horrible to me. And to thee, I fear."

Kurrelgyre growled assent in an I-told-thee-so tone. The two of them expected this to be such a bad experience that Stile would no longer question the validity of their hatred of Adepts. Increasingly, Stile was being convinced.

Neysa halted. She flicked her nose, indicating that he should dismount. Stile did so. Then she reached back as she lifted one hind foot. She put her teeth to it, as if chewing an itch—and the white sock came off.

Stile stared. The term "sock" was descriptive, not literal; it was merely a patch of white hair about the foot. Yet she still held the white sock in her mouth, and her foot had turned black.

She nudged the sock at him, then went for the other hind foot. Soon Stile held a pair of white socks, one larger than the other. Neysa nudged him again.

"But I can't wear these," he protested. "These are your socks. Thy socks."

Neysa nosed him impatiently again. Stile shrugged and tried donning a unicorn-sock over his boot. It was hoof-shaped at the extremity, yet it fit admirably: more unicorn magic, of course. In a moment he stood handsomely garbed in unicorn socks.

But the white color extended beyond the socks, now. His feet looked like hooves, his legs like hair. His arms—where were his arms?

Kurrelgyre growled appreciatively, seeming to think Stile's appearance had improved.

Stile looked again, startled. He looked like a unicorn! A white unicorn. He remained human, but in illusion he was the forepart of the animal. Behind him stretched a ghost-body, equine.

Neysa had given him concealment. Who would worry about a unicorn poking about the premises?

"Every time I think I understand thee, Neysa, thou comest up with some new device!" he said admiringly. "I'll return thy socks when we're away from here. Thank thee most kindly." And privately he thought: she didn't mind him benefiting from magic, so long as it was not Adept magic. A useful distinction.

They went on: a white unicorn, a black unicorn, and a wolf. The dark fog swirled thickly about the castle, helping to conceal them. But could the Adept really be ignorant of their presence? It was possible; why should the Black Adept allow them to intrude, when he could so easily hurl a nasty spell at them, unless he were not paying attention? Surely he had better things to do than sit and watch for trespassers.

And if the Adept happened to be dead, there should be no danger anymore. So Stile reasoned, reassuring himself.

Yet somehow he did not feel reassured.

Kurrelgyre made a low growl of warning. They stopped. The wolf had his nose to the ground, frozen there. Stile stooped to look—and his knees gave a warning shock of pain, and the unicorn image halfway buckled. Mustn't do! But he saw what it was: a black line, stretching across the basalt.

Could it amount to a trip wire? It was a color-line, not a wire, but with magic it could perform the same function. That would explain why the Adept was not paying attention; he depended on his automatic alert. "We'd better pass without touching any lines," Stile murmured. "They might be the Adept's alert-lines, no pun."

They all high-stepped carefully over the line. Soon there was another. This one was thicker, as if drawn with coagulating paint. Then a third, actually a ridge. And a fourth, set closer to the last, like a miniature wall.

"Something funny here," Stile said. "Why make an alarm-line this solid? It only calls attention to itself."

Yet there was nothing to do but go on over. Stile's apprehension was abating as his perplexity grew. He had accepted the notion of magic as a way of life—but why should anyone surround himself with thickening lines? That hardly made sense.

The lines came more often now, each more formidable than the last. It became evident that the black castle was not a mere edifice of stone or brick, but the innermost manifestation of a rapidly solidifying network of line-walls. When the walls passed waist height on Stile, and were set only two meters apart, he concluded that jumping them was now too risky; they were bound to touch one accidentally and set off the alarm. If this really were an alarm system. Stile now feared it was something quite different, perhaps an elaborate architectural trap. But it might be no more than a progressive deterrent to intrusions such as theirs. A passive defense, showing that the Black Adept was not really the monster he was reputed to be. Maybe.

"I think we had better walk between walls for a while," Stile said. "It is either that, or start climbing over them. This thing is turning into a maze, and we may be obliged to follow its rules." And he wondered, nervously: was that the way of Adepts? To force intruders, stage by stage, into a set mold, that would lead inevitably into their corruption or destruction? Was that the way of all Adept-magic? In that case, the fears of the unicorn and werewolf with respect to Stile himself could be well founded. Suppose he was, or had been, the Black Adept? That, given limitless power, he had chosen to isolate himself in this manner— and would do so again, given the power again? Helping no one, having no friends? Power corrupted . . .

They turned left, walking between walls. As it happened, it was indeed a maze, or at least a complicated labyrinth. The inner wall turned at right angles, making a passage toward the interior, and gradually elevated in height. Soon a ceiling developed, from an extension of one wall, making this a true hall. The passage kept curving about, usually sharply, often doubling back on itself, so that it was impossible to try to keep track of direction. "Kurrelgyre, your nose can lead us out again?" Stile inquired nervously. The wolf growled assent.

The line-labyrinth seemed to continue on indefinitely. Wan light fused in from somewhere, allowing them to see—but there was nothing to see except more blank walls of black material. The castle—for they had to be well inside the edifice proper now—was as silent as a burial vault. That hardly encouraged Stile.

On and on they went. Every time it seemed they were getting somewhere, the passage doubled back and paralleled itself for another interminable distance—then doubled back again. Was this whole castle nothing but many kilometers—many miles, he corrected himself—of passages? This passage continued to get narrower, becoming more like a tunnel, until Neysa was having difficulty making the turns. Her horn projected in front far enough to scrape a wall when she tried to make a hairpin turn, and her effort to avoid such contact put her into contortions and slowed her considerably. But she didn't want to change form, in case they were still under observation; that would betray her special talent. In addition, she still wore the saddle, which would become a liability in her other form. It seemed her own clothing transformed with her, but not things originating externally. And their supplies were in the saddlebags.

"Enough," Stile said at last. "We can wander forever in this mess, and die of starvation when our supplies run out. Let's tackle the dread Adept forthrightly!" And he banged his fist into the wall.

That surface was oddly soft and warm, as if only recently extruded from some volcanic fissure. It gave under the impact, slightly, then sprang back with a twang. The sound reverberated along the hall, and on out of sight; it seemed to be traveling along the same convolutions they were traveling, but much faster, tirelessly amplifying as it went. Soon the whole region was humming with it, then the castle itself.

Gradually it fudged, as the harmonics of different walls overlapped and muted each other, and finally died away amorphously. "Must have cone to the end of the line," Stile said. "Let's go on, not worrying about contact."

They moved on more rapidly. At every sharp corner, Neysa's horn scraped, and the twang reverberated. Nothing else happened.

Then at last the walls opened out into a moderate chamber. In the center stood a great black dragon. The creature opened its mouth to roar, but no sound came forth, only a tongue like a line drawn by a pen.

Stile contemplated the creature. He had never seen a living dragon before, but recognized the general form from the literature of legend. Yet this was an unusual variant. The creature, like the castle, seemed to be made of thickened lines. Its legs were formed of loops, its body of closely interlocked convolutions, and its tail was like knitwork. It was as if it had been shaped meticulously from a single line, phenomenally intricate. Yet it was solid, as a knit sweater is solid.

The dragon stepped forward, showing its blackline teeth. Stile was so fascinated by the linear effect that he hardly was concerned for his own safety. He recalled the puzzle-lines that had intrigued him as a child, in which the pen never left the paper or crossed itself. The most intricate forms could be made along the way by the traveling line—flowers, faces, animals, even words—but the rules were never broken. The challenge was to find the end of the line, in the midst of the complex picture.

This dragon, of course, was three-dimensional. Its lines did touch, did cross, for it was tied together by loops and knots at key places. But the principle remained: the line, though knotted, never terminated, never divided. The whole dragon, as far as Stile could tell, was a construct of a single thread.

Stile became aware of the posture of his companions. Both were facing the dragon in a state of combat readiness, standing slightly ahead of Stile.

"Enough of this!" he exclaimed. "This is my quest; you two should not endanger yourselves in my stead. I'll fight mine own battle." He stooped to pull off his unicorn socks—and again his knees flared in pain, causing him to drop ignominiously to the floor. He kept forgetting his injury at critical times!

He righted himself tediously, then bent at the waist and drew off one sock, then the other. Now he was himself again. He approached Neysa. "May I?" he inquired.

She nodded, her eyes not leaving the dragon. Stile picked up one real foot and pulled the sock over it until it merged with her hair. Then he moved around and did the other. In the midst of this he looked up—and met Kurrelgyre's gaze. Yes—he was handling the unicorn's very private feet. Horses did not like to have their feet impeded or restrained in any way; many would kick violently in such circumstance, even breaking a leg in the frantic effort to free it, or rebreaking it to escape the restraint of a splint. Thus a broken leg was often doom for a horse. Unicorns were no doubt worse. Neysa, when she joined him, had yielded her whole spirit to him.

Then she had discovered he was Adept. Anathema!

Now Stile stood before the dragon, drawing his rapier. He still was not expert in its use, but the dragon did not know that. Would the point be effective, or was it better to have a cutting edge so he could sever a line? Would the dragon unravel like knitwork if he did cut its line? These were questions he would have to answer by experiment.

The dragon was evidently assessing Stile at the same time. The white unicorn had suddenly become a man. Magic was involved. Was it safe to take a bite?

Stile, though quite nervous about the encounter, was experienced in dealing with animals. He had backed down hostile dogs and cats on his employer's farm, as part of assorted initiations, and of course had calmed many a spooked horse. Later he had taken his turn in various Game arenas, moving larger beasts of prey about with whip and prod. He had never faced a dragon before, but the basic principles of animal management should apply. He hoped.

He acted with apparent confidence, advancing on the dragon with his rapier point orienting on the creature's black knot-nose. The noses of most animals were tender, and often were more important psychologically than the eyes. "Now I'm not looking for trouble, dragon," Stile said with affected calmness. "I came to pay a call on the Black Adept. I only want to meet him, not to hurt him. Kindly stand aside and let us pass."

Stile heard a snort of amazement behind him. Neysa had never imagined bracing a dragon in its lair this way!

The dragon, too, was taken aback. What manner of man approached it with such imperious confidence? But it was a beast, not a man, and could not reason well, and it had its orders. In fact anything constructed from loops of cord might have trouble reasoning well; what kind of a brain could be fashioned from knotted string? It opened its jaws and took a snap at Stile.

Stile stepped smoothly to the side. His rapier flicked out, neatly pricking the sensitive nose. The dragon jerked back with a soundless yipe.

"That was a gentle warning," Stile said evenly, privately overjoyed at his success. The thing did feel pain! "My patience has limits. Begone, dragon!"

Baffled more by Stile's attitude than his physical prowess, the dragon scuttled back. Stile stepped forward, frowning. The dragon whimpered, again without sound—then unraveled.

Stile stared. The creature was disintegrating! First its hurting nose tightened into a close knot, then popped into nonexistence. Then its muzzle and teeth went, the latter becoming tangles in a string that disappeared as the string went taut. Then the eyes and ears. Headless, the thing still faced Stile, backing away. The neck went, and the front legs, the pace of unraveling speeding up as it continued. Very soon there was nothing but a line—and this snapped back into the wall like a rubber band.

The whole dragon had indeed been no more than an intricately wrought string. Now it was gone. Yet that string, when shaped, had seemed formidable, and had reacted with normal brute reflexes. Surely it would have chomped him, had he allowed it to. It could have killed him.

"The whole thing—string," Stile breathed. "And this whole castle— more string? For what purpose?"

Unicorn and wolf shrugged. Who could understand the ways of an Adept?

Neysa made a little nose back the way they had come, inquiring whether he had seen enough and was ready to get out of here. But Stile shook his head no, grimly. More than ever, he wanted to identify the proprietor of this castle. He wanted to be absolutely certain it was not now and never had been he.

They walked on down the passage, which narrowed again beyond the dragon's lair, but did not constrict as much as before. Again the way folded back, and back again, and yet again, endlessly.

"Damn it!" Stile swore. "We could die of old age in here, looking for the master of this castle—if he lives. I'm going to force the issue."

Kurrelgyre looked at him warily, but did not protest. This was Stile's venture, to foul up as he pleased. Stile made a fist and banged repeatedly on the wall, making the reverberations build tremendously until the whole castle seemed to shake. "Black Adept, show thyself!" he bawled. "I demand only to see thy face; then I depart."

"Follow the line," a voice replied. And a double line snaked into view ahead, looping into itself. As they approached it, the lines retreated like string drawn in from a distance. It resembled the dragon in this respect, constantly disappearing into itself. But it was not part of the wall.

Soon the line led them to a large central hall they were unlikely to have found thus expeditiously by themselves. A man stood there, facing them. He was garbed completely in black, and seemed to have a black tail. But the tail was the line they had just followed!

"The line," Stile said, finally putting it all together. "It is from thee! This whole castle is thou—the solidified line of thy past!"

"Now thou knowest," the Black Adept said coldly. "I have met thy demand, intruder."

"Yes," Stile agreed, not liking the man's tone. This was definitely not himself! The Adept stood half a meter taller, and his appearance and voice were unlike anything Stile was or could be. Not that the Adept was grotesque; he really looked rather ordinary. But he was certainly not Stile. "Now I shall depart, thanking thee for thy courtesy."

"No courtesy, intruder. Thine animals shall go, for they are of dark complexion, even burdened with thy supplies; it were a shame I must free them from. Thou shalt remain." And the Black Adept cast out his line. It amplified immediately into an intricate prison-bar wall, hardening in place between Stile and his two companions. Alarmed, he stepped to it—but the bars were already like steel. He tried to go around it, but the wall extended itself faster than he could move. He drew his rapier—but realized the bars were as hard as its metal was, even if it had had a cutting edge. He was trapped.

Stile turned to the Adept. "Why?" he asked. "Why hold me here?"

"Why didst thou intrude on my demesnes?" the Adept replied.

This was awkward. Stile did not care to give his reason, and would not lie. "I can say only that I meant thee no harm," he said.

"Know ye not I suffer no human intrusion into my premises? The penalty is to remain."

To remain. Never to depart? Death, here?

Neysa tried to get through the wall separating them, but could not. Even the wolf was too large to fit between the bars. They could not help him, directly. "You two had better leave," Stile said. "I will have to settle with the Adept myself."

Neysa hesitated. Stile knew she could get through the bars by changing into her firefly form, but he didn't want her to betray her talents to the Black Adept, who could readily make a line-cage to confine the insect. No sense getting her trapped too! "Get out of here!" he snapped. "I'll be all right. Just leave the supplies—"

"Do not!" the Black Adept warned. "Lest I throw out a net to capture thee too."

A net. Did the Adept know about her firefly form after all, or was that merely a manner of speaking? This was risky! Stile made a violent signal to Neysa to go. She seemed dubious, but retreated. The wolf followed her, tail held low. This was evidently part of the Adept's revenge: the separation of friends.

Stile faced the Adept, drawing his sword—but the Adept was gone. Only the new wall remained, extending in either direction into corridors that curved out of sight. Yet the Adept was aware of him; the wall itself was evidence of that. Catching the Adept in the maze of his own castle would surely be an impossible task; the Adept could form a jail cell around Stile at any time.

Why hadn't the magician done just that? Why permit an intruder the limited run of the castle? The Black Adept, logically, should either kill him or throw him out, and seemed to have the power to do both. Only the magic of another Adept could—

No! He had made a vow to do no magic himself. He would muddle through without magic, whatever came.

Stile walked along the barred wall. It carried on through folded passages, bisecting rooms, halls, even stairs. It led him through turrets and down into deep dungeons. There seemed to be no dead ends; the way was continuous. The Adept, it seemed, was showing off his premises, unable to resist allowing another person to appreciate their extent. Ah, vanity, however obliquely it manifested!

Stile continued on into a chamber where a human skeleton lay. It was complete and clean, sprawled on the floor.

He pondered that for some time. Why would such a grisly artifact be tolerated in the castle? It was unlikely to be artificial; the Adept's magic was evidently tied up in lines, proof enough that he was not Stile's alternate self, had any doubt remained. In fact, Stile could have saved himself a certain amount of mischief by recognizing that and turning back when he spied the very first line. Or when he recognized the dragon as a construct of lines. The hints were there to be interpreted, had he only been paying proper attention. Ah, hindsight!

This skeleton was a separate entity, not part of a line, so it had to be authentic. Stile kicked at an arm—and it broke away from the floor with a crumbling snap. It had lain there so long it had adhered!

The Black Adept had said that the penalty for intrusion was to remain. He had not actually said he would kill the intruder. Perhaps he had obscure scruples, not liking to get blood directly on his lines. But to remain here indefinitely without food or water was to die. That, it seemed, was to be Stile's fate—with the two "animals" permitted to escape to carry some hint or warning to others. They could tell the world they had seen a man imprisoned for annoying the Black Adept. Thoroughly reasonable, effective, and nasty. The Adept really did not care for the favor of others; he just wanted them to stay away. This was no show-off tour Stile was on; it was a fiendish punishment-tour. His demise would be more painful, now that he understood exactly what was coming. Truly, the Adepts were not to be trifled with—or liked.

But Stile knew he had asked for this. He had been warned that Adepts were dangerous, but had charged in anyway. Perhaps he had not really believed in the threat. This fantasy land of Phaze had not seemed wholly real to him; he had not taken its threats seriously enough. Now, as he wandered, and his thirst grew, his perspective shifted. This frame was becoming more real than that of Proton. Somehow the attacks by monsters hadn't impressed him deeply; those encounters had been like individual Games, serious yet also unserious. But thirst, hunger, boredom, fatigue, and loneliness—these compelled belief of a fundamental nature. By the time he died, he would really believe!

He thought of appealing to the Black Adept, of begging for mercy—and knew immediately that that would be useless. The punishment was to die in confinement and hopelessness, without further communication. Without dignity or recognition. Those who violated the Adept's privacy were doomed to share it—completely. The Black Adept was neither noble nor wicked; he merely enforced his strictures effectively. No one bothered an Adept without good reason! Which was what Neysa and Kurrelgyre had tried to tell him. He had simply had to learn the hard way.

And Stile himself—was he really an Adept? Had his Phaze-self been like this, an aloof, cynical magician? No wonder his companions distrusted that! If his possible exercise of his magic talent meant this, meant that he would lose all sense of friendship, honor and decency—then certainly his magic should be banned. It was better to die a feeling man, than to live as an inhuman robot.

No, correct that; he was thinking in a false cliché. Not all robots were unfeeling. Sheen—where was she now? His week, if he counted correctly, was just about over; the immediate threat of death in Proton —*on* Proton? No, these were two frames of the same world, and he was in one or in the other—this threat had been abated by time. Now it was Phaze he had to escape, and Proton that represented relief.

Stile wandered along the wall until darkness closed. Then he eased himself to the floor carefully, taking care of his knees. He leaned his back against the bars and experimentally flexed one knee. It actually bent fairly far before hurting; had it begun to heal? Unlikely; other parts of the body healed, but knees did not. Their conglomeration of ligament and bone prevented blood from circulating well there. Elbows could heal; they did not have to support constant weight. Knees had to be tough—and so, paradoxically, were more vulnerable than other joints. The anonymous enemy had struck well, lasering his knees, condemning him to a lingering torture similar in its fashion to what the Black Adept was now inflicting. Food for thought there? But when not under pressure, his knees could bend almost all the way. He could assume a squatting posture—when not squatting. A fine comfort that was! As if his knees mattered, when his body was doomed.

After a time he climbed back to his feet—this remained a chore, without flexing his knees under pressure—and walked to an interior chamber to relieve a call of nature. He did not like soiling the castle floor, but really had no choice—and perhaps it served the Adept right. Then he returned to the barred wall, settled down again, and nodded off to sleep.

He dreamed he was a robot, with no flesh to warm his metal, no true consciousness to enliven his lifelessness. He woke several times in the night, feeling the deepening cold, much more thirsty than he ought to be. Psychological, of course, but still bothersome. He wished he had warm Neysa, in any form, to sleep against. Neysa had given him companionship too—a warmth of the spirit. After his years basically as a loner, he had adapted very quickly to that association; it filled a need. She had changed to human form to please him—but would have pleased him anyway. At least he had done the right thing, sending her away; she could return to her grazing and perhaps the werewolf would keep her company sometimes.

So cold! He hunched within his insubstantial clothing. One little spell could so readily cure this. Give me some heat to warm my feet—no! No magic! It might be crazy, but he would not violate his oath. Only if a firefly flew up and cried "Stile, do magic!" would he indulge—and he didn't want Neysa risking herself that way anyway. He curled into an uncomfortable ball and slept again; it was better than being awake.

By morning Stile's whole mouth was so dry it felt like leather. He must have been sleeping with it open. He worked his rocklike tongue around, moving his jaws, and managed to find a small pocket of saliva to spread about. Now he had to get up and—

And what? The bars remained, and would not disappear until his skeleton joined the other. He had nowhere to go, nothing to do.

Yet he had to do something. He was still cold; exercise was the only answer. His hunger and thirst had abated for the nonce, but his body was stiff. He climbed to his feet and limped to his makeshift privy. Shame to waste fluid, but as long as life remained, the bodily processes continued.

He resumed his trek along the barred wall, moving rapidly enough to generate some heat, slowly enough to conserve energy. Pointless travel, except that it was better than just lying down and dying. Plenty of time for the latter later.

There was no escape. The labyrinth of the castle was interminable, and the barred wall was too. The Black Adept only had one kind of magic, but he was very thorough about that! Theoretically there should be an end to the wall somewhere—but that end was the Adept himself. What use, then, to search for it? No logic, no reasonable discussion could move a man with the power and alienation this one had shown. The Black Adept was in his fashion like a Proton Citizen.

A Citizen! Kurrelgyre had said the people of Phaze were the same as those of Proton—or had been, before the shifting of serfs had become extensive. An Adept could indeed be a Citizen, in his alternate self. In the one frame, the instrument of power was wealth; in the other, magic. In both cases, arrogance reigned supreme.

Stile kept moving. He had won marathons in the Game; he could survive for some time when he put his will to it. If he caught up to the Black Adept, he might incapacitate the man and escape. Or kill him, since the Adept seemed willing to let Stile die. No, he did not want to be a killer himself; monsters were one thing, but the Adept was a man. Stile was willing merely to circle around the Adept, to get outside the barrier and escape.

Did his mental decision not to kill a man differentiate him from the Adept-mode? Could it be taken as evidence that he would not be as thoroughly corrupted by the power of magic as other Adepts had been? He hoped so.

Strange that there was no food in this bleak castle. Didn't the Black Adept eat? Probably his food supplies were well hidden in a convoluted storehouse, which would naturally be outside this barrier. Still, that raised more conjectures. Since this Adept did not conjure things from nothing, the way Stile's magic had done, he must have to obtain natural food elsewhere. Did the Black Adept have to trade with peasants for supplies of grain, eggs, cabbages? He could not, then, live in absolute seclusion. His ready use of language suggested the same. He had contact with others; he just didn't like it. Would any of those others be coming here to the castle? Would they help Stile? No, that seemed unlikely; the Adept could have supplies for a year at a time.

Stile moved slowly, conserving his strength, balancing his generated warmth against his thirst and hunger. He gave up following the interminable wall, and cut across the center of the castle as well as he could. But all the interior passages were dead ends; the configuration differed here. He wished he had some quick way to analyze the lines, but the castle was too complex; it would take him far longer than he had left to grasp its layout and locate the Adept. He also wished he had a good cutting tool to sever a line; since all of this was a single line, he could cut the Adept off from his castle anywhere. From his past. Would everything unravel, in the manner of the dragon? But there was nothing. His dagger could not damage the stonelike hardness of the material. The outer walls had had some give, but here they had none. Only a diamond drill or saw could do the job, or magic—

No!

All day Stile fought with himself, the thought of magic becoming more attractive as his physical condition deteriorated. But he refused to yield. It didn't matter that no one would know if he conjured a cupful of water to drink; an oath was an oath. He would expire with his integrity intact; that was one thing the Black Adept could not deprive him of.

At last, night seeped into the castle again. Stile sank down to sleep but could not. He did not want to yield himself up so quietly to extinction!

He found the harmonica in his hand, unbidden. He had avoided making music, because of its magical connotation. Magic could occur in the ambience of music, even when he did not voice it. His saddle had appeared, obviously conjured by his unconscious wish while he made music. But wouldn't it be all right to play, now, so long as he willed no magic? Music reminded him of Tune, so long ago, and it was fitting to think of her again as he concluded his own tenure.

He played. The music wafted out, permeating the corridors and windows and convolutions of the castle, striking harmonics in the walls. He was making the sound, but he was listening too, and it was absolutely beautiful. He was mastering the harmonica, playing it with his heart, evoking a feeling of melody he had seldom before achieved. Perhaps it was his swan song, his final gesture. Nevertheless it was a satisfying way to go.

At last, tiring even of this, he put the instrument away and dropped into sleep. This time it was more peaceful, as if his fast had freed him of material concerns.

He was awakened by a low growl. Stile's eyes cracked open, but his body did not move. He knew where his sword was; he needed to locate the animal. And to decide whether it was worth trying to fight. Why trade a quick death for a slow one?

Then, in the dark, a voice: "Stile."

"Kurrelgyre!" he said. Stile put his face to the bars, to get closer. "This isn't safe for thee!"

"Neysa went to the Oracle. It said 'Curtain.' Neysa did not understand what that meant, but I do. I sniffed around the castle. One corner of it intersects the curtain. Follow me."

The curtain! Of course! Except— "I can't do it; I swore no magic. It takes a spell to pass through."

"Thou art true to thine oath. Thou couldst have escaped ere now, hadst thou been otherwise. But fear not; I will put thee through."

Relieved, Stile followed the werewolf, pacing him on the other side of the wall. So Neysa had donated her single question the Oracle permitted to his cause! He would not have asked her to do that, yet now accepted the gesture gratefully.

It seemed only moments before Kurrelgyre brought him to the curtain. One small section of his prison intersected it. Apparently the Black Adept was not aware of it. That suggested the Adept was alive in both frames, unable to perceive or cross the curtain.

"We shall wait for thee at the Oracle's palace," Kurrelgyre said as Stile approached the glimmer. "Be mindful of the trust the mare places in thee, setting thee free of this frame."

"I don't know how long it will take me to—"

But the werewolf was already casting the spell. Stile passed through.

CHAPTER 13

Rungs

Stile landed outside a dome. He gasped—for the air was barely breathable. He might survive thirty minutes without a mask, but would not enjoy it. The limited oxygen of Proton's atmosphere was further reduced to favor the needs of the domes, and the pollution of sundry industrial processes was dumped out here. He realized—was it for the first time?—that the barren surface of Proton was the result of man's activities. Had the machine age not come here, the atmosphere would have remained like that of Phaze. Man's civilization had made a heaven-planet into hell.

Fortunately the dome was within five minutes foot travel. He could see it clearly, for its illumination flowed through the force field, lighting the barren plain.

Stile, his fatigue somewhat abated by his rest and the shock of the cold night, walked briskly toward the dome, drawing his clothing tightly about him. So long as he kept his respiration down, the air was not too hard on his lungs. Running would be a disaster, though. His clothing helped shield him from—

Clothing! He could not wear that here! He was a serf.

Yet without it he would soon be in trouble from the cold. He would have to wear it as long as possible, then dispose of it just before entering the dome. Maybe he could recover it when he returned to Phaze.

But he could not return where he had left, for that would put him right back in the prison of the Black Adept. He needed his clothing for the other frame, but not in this locale. He would have to risk carrying it with him.

Stile reached the dome. It was a small one, evidently the private estate of a Citizen. It was hardly safe for a serf to intrude uninvited on such a place, but he really had no choice. These few minutes had made him uncomfortable; the less exposure to outside conditions, the better. He removed his clothing, bundled it up with the shoes inside, and stepped through the dome wall.

Instantly he was in light and warmth. This was a tropical garden of the kind popular with Citizens, whose tastes seemed to run opposite to the external wasteland their policies were making on the planet. Exotic palms were at every available spot, with a cocoa-chip mulch beneath. No one was present—which was why Stile had entered here. If he were lucky, he might get through undiscovered.

He was not. An alert gardener challenged him before he had taken twenty steps. "Halt, intruder! You're not of this estate."

"I—came from outside. I—got lost." Stile doubted he could afford to tell the truth, and he would not lie. "I had to come in; I would have died."

"You look half dead," the serf agreed.

Another serf hurried up. "I'm the garden foreman. Who are you? What were you doing outside without equipment? What are you carrying?"

That was a foreman, all right! "I am Stile, unemployed, formerly a jockey. I thought my life was threatened, so I tried to hide. But—" He shrugged. "It's a different world out there."

"It sure as hell is. Were you trying to suicide?"

"No. But I nearly died anyway. I have had no food or water for two days."

The foreman ignored the hint. "I asked you what you are carrying."

"This bundle—it is medieval Earth costume. I thought it would help me, in the other world." He was skirting a fuzzy line, ethically, and didn't like it. But again: wouldn't the truth convey less of the situation to this man than this half-truth did? What serf would believe a story about a magic world?

The foreman took the bundle and spread it out on the ground. "A harmonica?"

Stile spread his hands silently. He was now in a position where anything he said would seem a lie, including the truth. Suddenly Phaze seemed like a figment of his imagination, the kind of hallucination a man exposed to oxygen deprivation and gaseous pollutants might have. Especially if he had also suffered from hunger, thirst, and cold. In the past, men had undertaken similar deprivations as rites of passage, provoking similar visions. What had happened to him, really?

"I'll have to notify the Citizen," the foreman said.

Stile's hopes sank; this surely meant trouble. Had the man simply told him to clear out to serf quarters—

"Sir," the foreman said.

"What is it, gardener?" the Citizen's voice responded. It sounded familiar.

"Sir, a stranger has intruded from outside, carrying medieval Earth costume, including sword, knife, and a musical instrument."

"Bring him to the viewer." The voice gave Stile a chill. Where had he heard it before?

The foreman conducted Stile to a booth with a holo pickup. Stile stepped inside, knowing his whole body was being reproduced in image in the Citizen's quarters. He was dirty and abraded as well as suffering from hunger and thirst; he must look awful.

"Name?" the Citizen snapped.

"Stile, sir."

There was a pause. The Citizen would be checking the name in the computerized serf-listing. "The jockey and Gamesman?"

"Yes, sir."

"Play that instrument."

The gardening foreman quickly located the harmonica and jabbed it at Stile. Stile took it and put it to his mouth. This was his proof of identity; an impostor could probably not match his skill. He played a few bars, and as it had a few hours before, the emerging beauty of the music transformed his outlook. He began to get into the feel of it—

"Very well, Stile," the Citizen said, having no interest in the art of it. "Your present employer vouches for you. Wait here until his representative picks you up."

His present employer? What could this mean? Stile did not respond, since no query had been addressed to him. He rejoined the foreman, who solemnly handed back the rest of his bundle.

Suddenly Stile recognized the voice he had heard. The Black Adept! This was the Proton-self of that evil magician, having no knowledge of the other frame, but very much like his other self. It made sense—this dome was very near the site of the Black Castle. Stile's conjecture about Adepts and Citizens had been confirmed. Had this Citizen any reason to suspect him—

Stile breathed a silent sigh of relief. There was no reason for such suspicion, and Citizens hardly cared about stray serfs. Since another Citizen was taking Stile off his hands, that ended the matter. Stile would have to make his explanations to his own employer, instead of wasting the time of this one. And if one of the Black Adept Citizen's serfs ever got lost, other Citizens would return the favor similarly. Serfs were hardly worth quarreling over.

A woman arrived, very well formed. As her face turned to him—"Sheen! How glad I am to see thee!" Oops—wrong language.

She frowned. "Come on, Stile. You had no business wandering outside. Suppose you had damaged the costume? It will go hard with you if you stray again." She turned to the foreman. "Thank you. He was supposed to bring the costume to our employer's isolation dome, and must have lost the way. He's a klutz at times."

"He tried to tell me he was unemployed," the foreman said.

She smiled. "He used to be a jockey. He must have taken one fall too many." She made a little circle about one ear with one finger. "These things happen. We apologize for the inconvenience to you."

"It brightens the night shift," the foreman said, admiring her body. Inconvenience became more tolerable when it brought a figure like this to the scene.

She took Stile firmly by the elbow and guided him along. "This time we'll get you where you belong," she said with an oblique smile.

He squeezed her hand. She had taken his prior advice to heart, and become so human it was almost annoying. But she had certainly bailed him out.

When they were safely in the capsule, flying through the tube toward a larger dome, Sheen explained: "I knew you'd return, Stile, somehow. I really am programmed for intuition. So I had my friends make up a robot in your likeness, and we got you a new employer. The moment the query on you came through the computer—"

"I see." Her friends were the self-willed machines, who could tap into the communication network. In fact, some of them probably *were* the communication network. What an asset they were at times!

From the general dome they took a transport rocket to Stile's original home dome. In a matter of minutes, the travel of several days by unicorn was reversed. That reminded him of another aspect. What should he say to Sheen about Neysa?

They returned to Stile's old apartment. Sheen had kept it in good order—or the robot who bore his name had done so. It seemed Sheen had put the robot away as soon as news of Stile's appearance reached her. Sheen had been most industrious and efficient on his behalf.

What had it been like, here, with two robots? Had they eaten, slept, made love? Stile found himself feeling jealous and had to laugh at himself. Obviously the robot-Stile was not self-willed. It would be a true machine, programmed by Sheen.

"We must talk," Sheen said. "But I think first we must feed you and rest you. That curtain-frame has not treated you kindly. You are bronzed and scratched and gaunt around the edges."

Stile's thirst abruptly returned. He almost snatched at the cup of nutro-beverage she brought, and gulped it down. "Yes. Drink and food and rest, in that order," he said. "And talk, of course."

She glanced obliquely at him. "Nothing else?"

Ah, sex appeal! But he was restrained. "I think we should talk, then consider the else. You may not be pleased."

"You may not be entirely pleased with what I have done, either," she said.

He raised an eyebrow. "With my double?"

She laughed. "Stile, it's impossible! He's a robot!"

"Good thing there are none of that ilk here," he agreed.

"You know what I mean. It's just not the same."

"You speak from experience?"

"No. He's not programmed for love."

"I had come to that conclusion. Otherwise you would not have been so glad to have me back."

After he had eaten and emerged from the dry-cleaning unit, they lay down together. In what way, he asked himself, was this creature inferior to Tune? Sheen looked and felt as nice, and she had displayed astonishing initiative. It seemed no one knew he had been absent a week. Any attempt to kill his robot double had of course been futile.

"Your friends have rendered this apartment private?" he inquired, remembering how it had almost become his prison. But for the device of the self-willed machines, who had made it seem he was here when he wasn't—

"Completely." She put her arms about him, hugging him briefly, but went no further. "Shall I tell you?"

What would give a logical robot or an illogical woman pause? "You had better."

"Your new employer doesn't care at all about horse racing. He cares about the Game. Each year he has sponsored a leading contender in the Tourney, but has never had a win. This year—"

"Oh, no! I'm expected to compete—"

"This year," she agreed. "And it has to be you. The robot can not do it in your stead. Even were it legal, he can not match your ability. I have bought you security, Stile—but at the expense of your tenure."

"You realize that's likely to finish your mission too? One way or the other, I won't need protection after I enter the Tourney."

"Had there been any other way—" She sighed. "Stile, you were fired for cause. No blacklist was entered against you, because your reluctance to race again was understandable, but even so, very few Citizens were interested in you. My friends had to do a research-sifting to locate—"

"The one Citizen who would hire me," Stile finished. "I don't fault you for that; you did the only thing you could do, and did it excellently."

"But your tenure—"

"I now have another option." But he was not eager to get into the matter of Phaze and his decision to remain there, yet.

"Your anonymous enemy remains. Not the Citizen who tried to make a cyborg of you; he opted out when he realized the week had passed. The original one, who lasered your knees. The one who, perhaps, sent me. There were several attempts made on the robot. My friends are closing the net, trying to locate that enemy, but he is extraordinarily cunning and elusive. I can not protect you from him long. So—"

"Infernally logical," he agreed. "Better the Game than death. Better abbreviated tenure than none at all. But I had thought I would be all right if I made it clear I would not race again."

"That seems to have been an unwarranted assumption. That person wants you dead—but not by obvious means. So a surgical error, or a random accident—"

"So I might as well have had my knees fixed—if I could trust the surgery." His attention returned to the Game. "The Tourney is inviolate; no entrant can be harassed in any way, even by a Citizen. That's to keep it honest. So the Tourney is the one place my life is safe, for the little time the Tourney lasts. But this catches me ill prepared; I had planned to enter in two years."

"I know. I did what I could, and may have forced premature exile on you. If you want to punish me—"

"Yes, I believe I do. I'll tell you what I have been doing. Beyond the curtain is a world of magic. I tamed a unicorn mare; she turned into a lovely little woman, and—"

"And I'm supposed to be jealous of this fairy tale?"

"No fairy tale. I said she was female, not male. I did with her what any man—"

"I am jealous!" She half-climbed over him and kissed him fiercely. "Could she match that?"

"Easily. She has very mobile lips."

"Oh? Then could she match this?" She did something more intimate.

Stile found himself getting breathless despite his fatigue. "Yes. Her breasts are not as large as yours, but are well—"

"Well, how about *this?*"

The demonstration took some time. At length, quite pleasantly worn out, Stile lay back and murmured, "That too."

"You certainly punished me." But Sheen did not seem much chastened.

"And after that, we went to the Oracle, who told me to know myself," Stile continued. "Realizing I must be an Adept who had been slain or otherwise abolished, I investigated—and got trapped in the castle of the Black Adept. The werewolf rescued me by sending me back through the curtain, and here I am." He yawned. "Now may I sleep?"

"You realize that no living person would believe a story like that?"

"Yes."

"And you're going back."

"Yes. I can not stay long in the frame of Proton, in any event. This gives me an alternative."

"Unless you win the Tourney. Then you can stay for life."

"Easier said than done, girl. In two years I would have been at my Game-proficiency peak; at the moment my chances are less than ideal."

"As a Citizen, you could find out the identity of your enemy."

"There is that." He smiled. "Now, Sheen—what was it you had in mind to do when we finished our talk?"

She hit him with a pillow from the couch. "We just did it! Didn't you notice?"

"Did what?"

She hauled him in to her, kissing him and flinging a leg over his thighs.

He squeezed her, bringing her head close against his, smelling her soft hair. "It's great to be back," he said seriously. "You have done good work, Sheen. But the world of Phaze—it's such a lovely place, even discounting the magic. I feel—over there I feel more nearly fulfilled. As if my human potential is at last awakening. I have to return. Do you understand?"

"Maybe you feel as I would feel, if I passed through myself and found myself alive." She closed her eyes, imagining. "Yes. You have to go back. But will you visit here?"

"Often. There are things for me in this world too."

"Of which I am one?"

"Of which you are the main one."

"That is all I have a right to ask."

Again Stile felt a helpless guilt. Sheen loved him; he could not truly love her. It hardly mattered that a specialist could make one tiny change in her programming that would instantly abolish or reverse her feeling for him; her present program was real. Modern surgery could transplant his brain into another body, but his present body was real; he did not like fundamental changes. If he left Proton, he was leaving her, again, in the way Tune had left him. Yet Sheen herself had shortened his tenure. She was correct; she could not ask more of him.

The night was only half over, long as it had seemed. He drew her over him like a blanket and slept.

In the morning he started his move to enter the Tourney. He went to the Game-annex, located the 35M ladder, and touched the button by the rung above his own. He was challenging Nine.

In a moment the holder of Rung Nine responded to the summons. He was, of course, a thirty-five-year-old male. For the purpose of the Game, age was strictly by chronology. There was constant disruption in the ladders, as birthdays shifted people from one to another. No one was given a place in the top twenty free; the Number One rung-holder in one age had to start at Number Twenty-One on the next age's ladder. But at the qualifying date for each year's Tourney the ladders were fixed; there was no disqualification by birthdays within the Tourney itself.

Apart from age and sex, the resemblance of the holder of Rung Nine to Stile was distant. He was tall and thin, like a stooped scholar. The appearance fit the reality; his name was Tome, and he was a researcher for a studious Citizen. Tome was very much a creature of intellect; he invariably selected the MENTAL column when he had the numbered facet of the Grid, and MACHINE when he had the lettered facet.

Because Tome could beat most people in games of the mind, and hold even when assisted by machine—especially when the machine was a computer—he was successful enough to hold his Rung. Because he was limited, he was not a potential champion. Tome was known as a 2C man—the definition of his specialties. Second vertical, third horizontal. If a person were weak in these, he would have trouble passing Tome.

Stile was generally strong in 2C. He could handle Tome, and the other man knew it. Stile simply had not wanted the Rung, before.

They went to a booth and played the Grid. Stile had the numeric facet; good. He regarded that as more fundamental. He would not choose MENTAL, of course; this was not a fun challenge where he wanted a good Game, but a serious challenge where he needed to win with least risk. He did not care for the 50–50 chance that CHANCE offered. Tome was pretty fair on machine arts, such as the theremin, so that was not a good risk. So it had to be Stile's strong column, PHYSICAL.

Tome chose MACHINE, of course. Immediately the subgrid showed:

	1. MOTION	2. ACTION	3. OBSERVATION
A. LAND			
B. WATER			
C. AIR			

Nine types of machine-assisted competitive sports, ranging from cycle racing in 1A to stellar location in 3C. Stile had the letter facet of this grid, unfortunately; he could not select the machine-racing column, and knew that Tome would not. Tome would go for observation— unless he figured Stile for water. That would put them in 3B, which amounted to sonar location of sunken ships. Tome was not really sharp at that. But he was a fair hand at water-hydrant dueling, so might go for ACTION. Therefore Stile went for AIR instead.

He won. It came up 2C: dueling by guns, lasers, and similar powered distance weapons. Tome was good at this, but Stile was better, and both knew it.

DRAW? Tome's query came on the panel. It was legitimate to make such an offer at any stage in the selection, and it was often done as part of the psychological combat. In this case it was an admission of weakness.

Stile hit the DECLINE button, and followed with CONCEDE?

Tome hesitated. Seconds passed. If he did not negate within fifteen, the concession would stand. Concession was always a demand, never an offer, at this stage: another rule to prevent irresponsible players from tying up the grids when they had no intention of playing a Game. But at last the DECLINE button lit.

Now the lists of individual variants appeared on the screen. Tome, the one challenged, had the first choice. He placed antique pistols in the center square of the nine-square subgrid that formed. Stile followed with a laser rifle in a corner. These were not real weapons; they would simply mark the target with a washable spot of red dye on the section hit. Very seldom was a live-ammo duel permitted, and never in connection with the Tourney.

As it happened, Stile and Tome shared a liking for antique weapons and forms, and when the grid was completed and played it came up 2B, the original pistols. The two of them walked to the dueling range nearby, while Sheen went to the spectator gallery. The holographic recording apparatus was operating, of course; every formal match was filmed, in case there should be any challenge to the result. Scholars liked to review the games of Tourney winners, right back to the original move up the rungs of the ladder, tracing with the wisdom of retrospect the elements that made those particular victories inevitable. This also meant, incidentally, that no agent in the audience could laser him in the knees or elsewhere; that shot would be recorded and the assassin apprehended immediately. This was no horse race!

They had to wait a few minutes for the use of the range. Dueling was popular, and there were a number of specialists who dueled every day. Had Stile been playing the Game with one of them, he would have avoided this option at any cost. That, of course, was the strategy of the Game; the key to victory lay in the grids. A good gridder could get by with very few Game specialties, always directing the selection to one of these. Just as Tome had to master only seven of the basic sixteen choices of the primary grid, and a proportionate number of each subgrid. An opponent could only force a selection within those seven. If an opponent's skills overlapped those of Tome, he could be virtually assured of landing one of these, to Tome's disadvantage. For a player who was serious, it was best to be strong in all boxes. That kept the options open, preventing him from getting trapped. Stile himself had strengths in all boxes; that was why he was the superior player here.

"You can't be going for the Tourney," Tome remarked. "You have two more seasons free. When the top five enter this year, we'll both be jumped into qualification for next year's Tourney. I figured you'd be sliding down about now. What's your move?"

Stile smiled. "See that girl in the stands? The pretty one? She put me up to it."

"Oh, a Game-digger!" Tome squinted at Sheen. "For one like that, I'd make a move, certainly! She much on the mental side?"

"Limited as a robot," Stile said.

"Going to move up to Rung Six, so you'll be Number One after the cut? That's risky. If someone gets sick at the last moment before qualification, you'll be shunted into the Tourney." Tome obviously had no doubts, in his mind, about the outcome of this match, and hardly cared; he had no intention of skirting the Tourney too closely.

"Going to Rung Five," Stile said. "I prefer that this not be bruited about."

Tome's head snapped around in surprise. "*This* year?"

"Not entirely my choice. But I've had some problems in my employment."

"So I have heard. Knee injury, wasn't it? I'm surprised you didn't have immediate surgery."

"I got scared of it."

Tome laughed. "You, scared! But I must admit you do look somewhat ravaged. Must have been a hard decision."

"It was," Stile agreed, though he knew that what showed on his body was the ravage of his two-day confinement in the Black Castle without food and water, rather than his mental state. Sheen had done what she could for him, but he had not yet properly recovered.

"Well, I wish you well," Tome finished sincerely.

The range cleared, and they entered. On a table at the entrance lay the set of antique pistols, with elaborate pearl handles and glistening black steel. A pistol specialist could have called out the exact vintage and make—probably eighteenth-century European—but Stile was concerned only with their heft and accuracy. Though they were replicas that fired no balls, they bucked and smoked just like the real ones.

Stile had to be sure to win this match; he could not rechallenge until the rungs had shifted, and this close to the Tourney there was unlikely to be much shifting. Players were either hanging on to their rungs to be sure that they qualified, or trying to stay below qualification range. Stile's late decision to enter the Tourney was unusual, and would make ripples. He was going to have to bump someone who was depending on the Tourney as his last chance for extended tenure.

The Citizens had so arranged it that there were always more serfs interested in entering the Tourney than there were available slots—especially in Stile's own age range, where many mature people were ending their tenures. There were tenures expiring in all age ranges, for serfs could enlist at any age, but the older ones generally lacked the drive and stamina for real expertise in the Game, and the younger ones lacked experience and judgment. The ladders of the Thirties, male and female, were the prime ones.

The weapons were good, of course, and as similar to each other as modern technology could make them. Each party took one, went to the centermark of the range, stood back to back, and began the paceoff at the sound of the timing bell. Ten paces, turn and fire—each pace measured by the metronome. The man who turned and/or fired too soon would be disqualified; the tenth beat had to sound.

Some people who were excellent shots in practice were bad ones in such duels. They had to have time to get set, to orient on the target—and here there was neither time nor any fixed target. Some lost their nerve when confronting an actual opponent who was firing back. Special skills and nerve were required for this sort of match. Both Stile and Tome possessed these qualities.

At the tenth beat Stile leaped, turning in air to face his opponent. Tome merely spun in place, withholding his shot until he fathomed Stile's motion. He knew Stile seldom fired first; Stile preferred to present a difficult target, encouraging the other to waste his only shot. Then Stile could nail him at leisure. Tome was too smart for that.

Stile landed, plunged on into a roll, flipped to his feet and jumped again. Had Tome figured him for a straight bounce, his shot would have missed; but Tome was still being careful. His pistol was following Stile's progress, waiting for the moment of correct orientation.

That moment never came. In midair Stile fired. A red splash appeared in the center of Tome's chest, marking the heart. Contrary to popular fancy, the human heart was centered in the chest, not set in the left side.

Tome spread his hands. He had waited too long, and never gotten off his shot. He was officially dead.

Tome washed off the red stain while Stile registered the win with the Game computer outlet. They shook hands and returned to the Game-annex. Their names had already exchanged rungs. Stile punched Rung Eight, his next challenge. He wanted to capture as many rungs as he could before the alarm spread—and before news of his present weakened condition also got about. If his opponents thought it through, they would force him into the more grueling physical Games, where he would be weakest.

The challengee appeared. He was a squat, athletic man named Beef. "Tome, you challenging me?" he demanded incredulously.

"Not I," Tome said, gesturing to the ladder.

Beef looked. "Stile! What move are you making?"

"A challenge move," Stile said.

Beef shrugged. "I can't decline."

They went to a booth and played the grid. Beef was unpredictable; often he picked unlikely columns, just for the hell of it. Stile selected B. TOOL, hoping the other would not pick 3. CHANCE.

His hope was vain. Beef was more curious about Stile's motive than about the outcome of the Game, and they intersected at 3B. The home of roulette, dice,—all manner of gambling devices. Precious little skill. Stile could take Beef in most games of skill—but chance made it even.

Yet already he was maneuvering to upgrade his chances, playing the subgrid, finessing the choices in the way he had. Suddenly it came up CARDS. Cards were technically instruments of chance—but there were quite a number of games, like bridge and poker, where skill of one sort or another counted. All he had to do was pack the final grid with this type.

Beef, however, was alert to this, and selected games like blackjack and high-card-draw. He wanted to make Stile sweat, and was succeeding. It was very bad to have an opponent who cared less about the outcome than Stile did; there was little strategic leverage. Beef made his placements on the grid so that Stile could not establish a full column of his own choices. Three of one player's preferences in a row meant that player could select that row and have a commanding advantage. The chances of establishing a game utilizing reasonable skill remained 50–50, and Stile was hurting. He had to have better odds!

But Stile knew a skill variant of a chance game that Beef evidently did not. He slipped it in, played for it, and got it: War, Strategy.

The ordinary card game of War consisted of dealing the pack randomly into two piles, with each player turning up cards on one-to-one matches. The higher card captured the lower, and both went into the winner's victory pile. When the first piles were through, the piles of winnings would be shuffled and played in the same fashion, until finally one player had won the entire deck. It was pure chance, and could take many hours to finish. The strategy variant, however, permitted each player to hold his cards in his hand, selecting each card to play. When both were laid face down on the table, they would be turned over, and the higher card won. This play was not truly random; each player could keep track of his assets and those of his opponent, and play it accordingly. He could psych the other player out, tricking him into wasting a high card on a low one, or into losing a trick he should normally have won by playing a card too low. Games were normally much shorter than those of the pure-chance variation, with the superior strategist winning. The element of pure chance could not be reintroduced; a strategist could beat a hand played by chance. Thus Stile had his opportunity to exert his skill, judging his opponent's intent and playing no higher than needed to win.

They played, and soon Stile's expertise told. He took queens with kings, while yielding deuces to aces. Steadily his hands grew, providing him with more options, while those of his opponent shrank. Luck? The luck had been in the grid.

In due course Stile was able to play seven aces and kings in succession, wiping out Beef's queen-high remaining hand of seven with no luck allowed at all. He had won, and Rung Eight was his.

Beef shook his head ruefully. "I will remember that variant," he said. He didn't mind losing, but he hated to be outsmarted so neatly.

They returned to the Game-annex. But Stile's two wins had attracted notice. A knot of serfs stood before the 35M ladder. "Hey, Stile," a woman called. "Are you making your move this year?"

He should have known privacy would be impossible. He was too well known in these circles, and what he was doing was too remarkable. "Yes," he said shortly, and made his way to the ladder. He punched the challenge for Rung Seven.

The holder of that Rung was already present. He was Snack, an average-heighted man who specialized in board games and light physical exercises. He was more formidable than the two Stile had just taken, but still not really in Stile's class.

"I will respond to your challenge in one day," Snack said, and left. This was exactly the sort of thing Stile had feared. A rung-holder had to meet a challenge from the rung below, but could delay it one day. Stile had to rise rung by rung; he could not challenge out of order. He had no choice but to wait—and that would interfere with his return to Phaze.

Sheen took his arm. "There'll be an audience tomorrow," she said. "When a player of your caliber makes his move for a tenure-abridging Tourney this close to the deadline, that's news."

"I wanted to qualify quickly, so I could return to Phaze before the Tourney," Stile said. "Neysa is waiting and worrying."

Even as he said it, he knew he should not have. Somehow the words got out before his mental intercept signal cut them off. "Cancel that," he said belatedly.

She looked straight ahead. "Why? I'm only a machine."

Here we go again. "I meant I promised to return to meet her at the palace of the Oracle. It was her question to the Oracle that freed me. The only one she can ask in her lifetime—she used it up just to help me. I must return."

"Of course."

"I made a commitment!" he said.

She relented. "She did send you back to me; I should return the favor. Will you promise to return, to meet me again?"

"And to qualify for the Tourney. Yes. Because you have also sacrificed yourself for me."

"Then we shall send you on your way right now."

"But I have to compete for Rung Seven in one day!"

"So you will have to work fast, over there." She drew him into a privacy compartment. "I'll send you across to her—right after I have had what I want from you." And she kissed him most thoroughly, proceeding from there.

She was a robot, he reminded himself—but she was getting more like a living woman than any he had known since Tune. And—he was not unwilling, and she did turn him on. It would be so easy to forget her nature . . . but then he would be entering another kind of fantasy world, and not a healthy one.

Yet how could he continue with a robot in one frame and a unicorn in the other? Even if he entered the Tourney and won, against all the odds, and located his other self in Phaze and assumed his prerogatives there—impossible dreams, probably—how would he alleviate the developing conflict between females?

Sheen finished with him, cleaned him up, brushed his hair, and took him to the dome geographically nearest the Oracular palace in the other frame, according to his understanding of the geography. They scouted for the curtain. They were also wary of the anonymous killer, but apparently the break in Stile's routine had lost that enemy for the nonce. It was hard to keep track of a fast-moving serf on Proton!

The curtain did not intersect this dome, but they located it nearby. They went outside, into the polluted rarefaction of the atmosphere, and Stile donned his Phaze clothing, which Sheen had brought. She never overlooked details like that, thanks to her computer mind. He would not have dared to put on any clothing at all in the sight of any Proton serfs, but outside was the most private of places on Proton.

There was a narrowing plain, the ground barren. To the northwest a wrinkle of mountains projected, as grim as the plain. Only the shining dome brightened the bleak landscape. There were not even any clouds in the sky; just ominous drifts of ill-smelling smog.

"If ever you find a way for a robot to cross . . ." Sheen said wistfully. "I think that land must be better than this one."

"My clothing crosses," Stile said. "Since you can have no living counterpart in Phaze, it should be possible—"

"No. I tried it, during your absence. I can not cross."

She had tried it. How sad that was, for her! Yet what could he do?

"Here—within a day," he gasped, beginning to suffer in the thin air, and Sheen nodded. The air did not bother her; she breathed only for appearances. "You understand—there is beauty in Phaze, but danger too. I may not—"

"You will make it," she said firmly, kissing him once more. "Or else."

"Uh, yes." Stile made what he trusted was the proper effort of will, and stepped through the curtain.

CHAPTER 14

Yellow

It was afternoon on Phaze, and the air was wonderful. The sky was a deep and compelling blue, punctuated by several puffball clouds. The mountains to the northwest were lovely. Stile paused to look at the pretty little yellow flowers at his feet, and to inhale the spring-like freshness of it all.

How did this frame come to have such a pleasant natural environment, while Proton was so bleak? He was no longer certain that industrial pollution and withdrawal of oxygen could account for it all. What about water vapor? Obviously there was plenty of it here, and little in the Proton atmosphere. This was a mystery he must one day fathom.

But at the moment he had more urgent business. Stile made a mental note of the location of the curtain; sometime he would have to trace its length, finding better places to cross. But this was also a matter for later attention.

The landscape was indeed the same. A narrowing plain, a nearby mountain range, a bright sun. Remove the cute clouds, and the verdant vegetation carpeting the ground, and the copses of trees, and this was identical to Proton. It was as if these were twin paintings, BEFORE and AFTER the artist had applied the color. Phaze was the world as it should be after God had made the final touches: primitive, natural, delightful, unspoiled. Garden of Eden.

True to his memory, the Oracle's palace was in sight. Stile set out for it at a run. But before he had covered half the distance, Neysa came trotting out to meet him. She held her head high, as they came together, so there was no possibility of striking him with her bright horn. Stile flung his arms around her neck and hugged her, burying his face in her glossy mane, feeling her equine warmth and firmness and strength. He did not need to thank her verbally for her sacrifice on his behalf; he knew she understood. He discovered her hair was wet, and realized that his own tears of reunion were the culprit.

Then he leaped to her back, still needing no words, and they galloped bareback in five-beat to the palace where Kurrelgyre waited in man-form.

Stile had spent his life on Proton, and only a week here in Phaze, but already Phaze seemed more like home. He had been gone only a night and day, but it seemed longer. Perhaps it was because he felt more like a person, here. Actually, the only other true human beings he had encountered in Phaze were the man at the curtain who had given him the demon-amulet, and the Black Adept; still—

Kurrelgyre shook hands gravely. "I am relieved to know thy escape was successful," the werewolf said. "I reassured the mare, but feared privately thou mightst land between domes."

"I did. But close enough to reach the nearest dome before I suffocated." Stile took a deep breath, still reveling in it.

"I should have crossed with thee, to make sure; but Neysa was waiting outside, and I never thought of—"

"I understand exactly how it is. I never thought of it either. I could have walked a quarter-mile along the curtain and willed myself back through to you, outside the Black Castle. That never occurred to me until this moment."

Kurrelgyre smiled. "We live; we learn. No confinement near the curtain shall again restrain us." He squinted at Stile. "Thou lookest peaked; have a sniff of this." He brought out a sprig with a few leaves and a dull yellow flower, dried.

Stile sniffed. Immediately he felt invigorated. Strength coursed through his body. "What is that stuff?"

"Wolfsbane."

"Wolfs*bane*? Something that curses wolves? How canst thou carry—"

"I am not in my lupine form. I would not sniff it then."

"Oh." Stile couldn't really make much sense of this, but could not argue with his sudden sense of well-being. "Something else," he said. "Didst thou not tell me that most of the people were parallel, existing in both frames? There are about five thousand Proton Citizens, and ten times as many serfs, and countless robots, androids, cyborgs and animals —but I have not seen many people here on Phaze, and not many animals."

"There are at least as many people here as on Proton, plus the societies of werewolves, unicorns, vampires, demons and assorted monsters. But two things to note: first, we are not confined to domes. We have the entire planet to roam—many millions of square miles. So—"

"Miles?" Stile asked, trying to make a fast conversion in his head and failing.

"We use what thou wouldst call the archaic measurements. One square mile would be about two and a half square kilometers, so—"

"Oh, yes, I know. I just realized—archaic measurements—would that by any chance affect magic? I tried to do a spell using the metric scale, and it flubbed. Before I swore off magic."

"That might be. Each spell must be correctly couched, and can only be employed once. That is why even Adepts perform sparingly. They hoard their spells for future need, as Citizens hoard wealth in Proton. May I now continue my original discourse?"

"Oh, of course," Stile said, embarrassed, and Neysa made a musical snort of mirth. Stile squeezed her sides with his legs, a concealed hug. He tended to forget that she understood every word he spoke.

"So there are very few people for the habitable area, and many large regions are as yet uninhabited by men. Thou needst not be surprised at seeing none. The second reason is that many of the people here are not precisely the form of their Proton selves. They are vampires, elves, dwarves—" He broke off.

Stile wished he hadn't. It had almost seemed his size was irrelevant in this frame. Foolish wish! "I never judged values in terms of size," Stile said. "A dwarf is still a discrete individual, surely."

"Of course," Kurrelgyre agreed. It was his turn to be embarrassed.

They were now in the Oracle's palace. "I have less than a day before I have to go back to Proton," Stile said.

Neysa stiffened. "Go back?" Kurrelgyre demanded. "I understood thou hadst no commitment there. It was only to escape the prison of the Black Demesnes that thou—"

"I have a woman there," Stile said. "She covered for me during mine absence. I have agreed to enter this year's Tourney, that she be not shamed. Thus it is likely that my tenure on Proton will be brief."

"The Tourney! Thou presumest thou canst win?"

"Doubtful," Stile said seriously. "I had planned to enter in two years, when some top players would be gone and my strength would be at its peak—and even then the odds would have been against me. It is hard to win ten or twelve consecutive Games against top competition, and luck can turn either way. I would rate my chances at perhaps one in ten, for I could lose to a poorer player with one bad break."

Neysa tooted questioningly. "Well, one chance in twelve, perhaps," Stile amended. "I did not mean to brag."

"The mare means to inquire what thou meanest to do if thou shouldst win the Tourney," the werewolf said. "Since thou wouldst then be a Citizen, with permanent tenure—no need ever to depart Proton."

Stile wondered in passing how the werewolf had come to know the unicorn well enough to translate her notes, in only one day. Maybe shape-changing creatures had natural avenues of comprehension. "A Citizen has virtually complete freedom and power. I would be under no onus to choose between frames. But I like Phaze; I think I would spend much of my time here anyway. Much depends on my situation here; if I should turn out to be a vicious person like the Black Adept, I think I'd prefer to vacate." Yet the Citizen who was the Black Adept's other self had not seemed to be a bad man; perhaps it was solely the absolute power that corrupted—power beyond that of any Citizen. What would an Adept be like, if he had residence in both frames and free access between them?

"It is a fair response," Kurrelgyre said. "If thou must return for a Game within a day, only the Yellow Adept is within range to check, without the employ of magic. Would it not be better to yield this quest, being satisfied as thou art now?"

"Not while someone is trying to kill me here. That person must know who I am. If I can discover who I am in Phaze, I may know more about the nature of mine enemy. Then I can see about making this world safe for mine own existence. I gather mine other self failed to take such precaution."

"Spoken like a werewolf," Kurrelgyre said approvingly. Neysa sighed; she did not seem to agree completely, but neither did she disagree. Men will be men, her attitude said.

"Neysa, I want to be honest with thee," Stile said, feeling the need to provide a better justification. "I like Phaze, I like thee—but this is not truly my world. Even if there were no threat to my welfare, I could not commit myself absolutely to stay here. I would need to know that my presence served in some way to benefit this world; that there was some suitable challenge to rise to. Something that needed doing, that perhaps only I could do. If there seems to be more of a need and challenge in the other frame—"

Neysa made another musical snort. "She inquires whether thou wouldst feel more positive if she released thee from thy vow of no magic," the werewolf translated.

Stile considered. He understood that the acceptance of such a release would subtly or overtly alienate him from the unicorn. It was only his vow that made it possible for her to associate with him on their original basis. "No. I only want to know who I am. If I can't survive without magic, maybe it's best that I not remain here. I never want to be like the Black Adept. All I need is someone to spell me into the other frame in time for mine appointment there. Then I'll return here for another look at another Adept. One way or another, I will settle my accounts in both frames. Only then will I be in a position to make a proper decision about residence."

"I will spell thee through," Kurrelgyre said. "In fact, rather than send thee pointlessly into new danger, I will investigate the Yellow Adept myself, and return with news. I think I can now recognize thy likeness, if I encounter it."

"There is no call for thee to risk thyself on my account!" Stile protested.

"There is no call for me to impose my presence when the mare wishes to converse with thee alone." And the man merged into the wolf, who bounded away to the north.

"Damn it, if I start sending others on my foolish quests, where will it end?" Stile demanded. "I've got to follow him, stop him—"

But the wolf was already beyond reach, traveling with the easy velocity of his kind. Probably Neysa could catch him, but only with difficulty. Stile knew Kurrelgyre thought he was doing Stile a favor, preserving him from risk, giving him time alone with Neysa—but this was not the sort of favor Stile cared to accept. It was not, he told himself, that Sheen had artfully depleted his sexual initiative immediately before sending him across the curtain. There was the principle of responsibility for one's own actions.

The unicorn caught his mood. She started moving north. "Thanks, Neysa," he said. "I knew thou wouldst understand." Then, as an afterthought: "How art thou getting along with the wolf?"

She blew a noncommittal note. "Glad to hear it," Stile said. He reached down around her neck and hugged her again.

Neysa quickened her gait into a gallop. "I don't know what finer life I could have than galloping across the wilderness with you," Stile said. "The only thing I miss—"

She made a musical inquiry. "Well, that's it," he said. "I like music. But since we found that music connects with my magic, I don't dare play."

This time her note was comprehensible. "Play!"

"But then the magic gathers," he protested. "I have no wish to abbreviate mine oath. I played a little when I was alone in the Black Castle, but I am not alone now, and I do not want thee angry with me."

"Play," she repeated emphatically.

"Very well. No spells, just music." He brought out his harmonica and improvised a melody to the beat of her hooves. She played a harmony on her horn. The duet was lovely. The magic gathered, pacing them, but now that he understood it he was not alarmed. It was merely a potential, until he implemented it—which he would not do.

He played for an hour, developing his proficiency with the instrument. He was getting into the feel of the harmonica, and playing about as well as ever in his life. This was a unique joy!

Neysa lifted her head, sniffing the wind. She seemed disturbed.

"What is it?" Stile inquired, putting away his harmonica.

The unicorn shook her head, unsure. She slowed to a walk, turning this way and that as if casting for something. Then she oriented on whatever it was, and resumed her northward trek. But there was something disquieting about her motion; her gait seemed unnatural.

"Art thou all right?" Stile inquired, concerned.

Neysa did not respond, so he brought out his harmonica again and played. But she immediately blew a harsh note of negation. He desisted, concealing his hurt feelings.

Stile thought she would relax after a short while, but she did not. Instead her gait became more mechanical, quite unlike her normal mode.

"Neysa, I inquire again: art thou all right?"

She ignored him. She seemed to be in a trance.

Alarmed, Stile tugged sharply on her mane. "Something is wrong. I must insist—"

She threw down her head and bucked. The action was untelegraphed, but Stile was too experienced a rider to be caught. He stayed in place, then slid to the ground when she resumed her odd walk. "Neysa, something evidently compels thee. I don't know what it is—but since we are approaching the locale of the Yellow Adept, I suspect it relates. For some reason the compulsion does not affect me. Give me thy socks, and I will walk with thee in disguise."

She halted, swishing her tail in annoyance, and let him remove the white socks from her rear feet. Then she marched on.

Stile donned the socks and walked beside her, imitating her walk. If something were summoning unicorns, he wanted to resemble such a captive as closely as possible—until he understood the situation better. The wolfsbane he had sniffed still buoyed his strength; he was ready for anything, and felt no trace of the prior ravages of hunger and thirst. If Neysa had fallen into some spell cast by the Yellow Adept—

Soon the property of the Adept came into sight. It was of course yellow. The sands were yellow, rising into yellow dunes, and the sun sent yellow beams through a yellow fog that concealed the main operation from a distance. Neysa walked straight into that fog.

Soon the Adept's castle loomed. It was most like a ramshackle haunted house, with a partially collapsing roof, broken windows, and weeds growing thickly against the walls. A few yellow flowers straggled at the fringe—buttercups, sunflowers, a bedraggled yellow rose. Behind the house was a tall wrought-iron palisade fence, rusting yellow, overgrown by morbid vines with yellowing leaves but still quite formidable. An odor rose from the premises: animal dung and decaying vegetation. Rustic, but hardly pleasant.

Neysa walked right on toward the house, and Stile necessarily followed. Already he did not like the Yellow Adept and hoped perversely that the magician was alive—so as to be assured this was not Stile's own alternate identity. This time he would not be so foolish as to challenge the Adept overtly; he would just look and retreat quickly.

Except for two things. First, there was Neysa—she had somehow been mesmerized, surely for no good purpose, and had to be freed of this complication. Second, Kurrelgyre: the wolf had by now had plenty of time to lope in and out, but evidently had not, which suggested that he too had been trapped by the summoning spell. Stile would have to verify this, then act appropriately. It might not be easy.

Neysa moved right on up to the front door, which was sagging open on rusty hinges. She entered, Stile close behind. They passed through a dusty hall, turned a corner—and bars dropped from the ceiling, separating them.

Oh, no! Not again! Stile backed up—but another set of bars fell behind him. This section of hall had become a cage.

There was an ear-discomfiting shriek of laughter. "Hee-hee! Two! Two fine unicorns, so soon after the wolf! What an excellent day! Haul them out, Darlin' Corey! Let us view our prizes!"

Something huge bulked at the far end of the hall, beyond the corner. Neysa's cage slid forward. Something was drawing it onward with easy power.

After a time the thing came for Stile's cage. It was the rear end of a pink elephant. The little tail hooked into the forward bars; then the creature walked, drawing the cage after it.

Stile considered poking his sword through the bars and puncturing the fat pink rear, or cutting off the tail with his knife. But this would not release him from the cage, and could make the elephant quite angry without really incapacitating it. Better to hold off.

In a moment they emerged into the stockaded area. There were cages all around. It resembled an archaic zoo. Stile identified a griffin, with the body of a lion and head and wings of an eagle, in the cage most directly across from his. This was no glorious heraldic monster, but a sad, bedraggled, dirty creature whose wings drooped and whose eyes seemed glazed. And no wonder: the cage was too small for it to stretch its wings, and there was no place for its refuse except right next to the cage where the creature had scraped it out. No wonder its feathers and fur were soiled; no wonder it stank!

Now Stile's attention was taken by the proprietress: an old woman garbed in a faded yellow robe, with stringy yellow hair and yellowish complexion. A hag, in every sense of the word.

"What a lovely little specimen!" the hag cackled, mincing around Neysa's cage. Neysa seemed to be coming out of her daze; her ears perked up, then laid back in revulsion as the crone approached.

"And this one," the Adept continued, examining Stile. "A white stallion, yet! What a pretty penny thou wilt fetch, my sweet!" She circled the cage, appraising his apparent form with an indecently calculating eye. "Yes indeed, my precious! White is in the market for the likes of thee! Needs must I send Crow's-foot with the news." She hobbled into the house.

Now Stile resumed his survey of the enclave. Beyond Neysa was Kurrelgyre, whose eye was already on him; the wolf nodded slowly. They were in trouble!

The other cages contained a small sphinx, a three-headed dog, a wyvern, and several creatures Stile couldn't classify. All were bedraggled and filthy; the witch did not bother to care for them properly, or to clean their cages. She did feed them, as there were dishes of food and water at every cage—but several of these dishes had been overturned and kicked out, uneaten.

Stile examined his own cage. The bars were yellowish, like the rest of this place, and somewhat slick. It was as if some sort of grease had been smeared on the metal in a vain attempt to make it seem like gold. He tried to push a bar out of position, but it was like welded steel. The door was firmly locked.

Still, the bars were fairly widely spaced, and he was small. Just a little bowing should enable him to squeeze between two. Stile located the longest, widest section of the cage roof, then drew his sword and used it cautiously as a lever. He did not want to break the weapon, and did not know how strong it was. But he really could not gain purchase, and had to put away the sword. Instead he jumped up, put his feet against one bar, his hands on the next, and hauled as if lifting a heavy weight. Slowly, unwillingly, the bars separated as he strove and panted. When his muscles balked, he had widened the aperture only slightly—but perhaps it was enough.

He dropped down to the cage floor—and discovered that he had become the object of considerable attention. He was still disguised as a unicorn; that must have been quite a sight, a horselike creature clinging to the upper bars!

But he couldn't allow such cynosure to stop him. The witch should soon be back. He had to do whatever he could do, rapidly.

Stile drew himself up, put his feet between the widened bars, and squeezed his body up and through. Last was his head; his ears got mashed, but he scraped by. He was out.

He climbed silently down, while the captive animals watched the contortions of this astonishing unicorn. They were not about to betray him to the witch! The conspiracy of silence was the only weapon they possessed.

Stile went to Kurrelgyre's cage. "I must have a rapid update," he said. "How can I free thee and Neysa and the others? The large bars are too strong for me."

The werewolf transformed into his human form, too large to squeeze between the bars. "Thou art fortunate in thy size," he said. "Only Neysa might do what thou hast done—and the potion hath dulled her wit so she can not transform her shape. My wolfsbane might help steady her—but we dare not administer it to her animal form. We are at impasse. Save thyself; thou canst not free us."

"If I go, it will be only to help thee—as thou didst for me before. Can I overcome the witch?"

"Only if thou canst kill her by surprise, instantly with thy sword. She will else throw a potion on thee, and destroy thee."

"I don't want to kill her," Stile said. "Murder is not the proper solution to problems. I only want to neutralize her and free these poor captives."

Kurrelgyre shook his head. "Thou canst not defeat an Adept fairly save by magic."

"No. Mine oath—"

"Yes. When thou didst not break thine oath to save thyself from the Black Demesnes, I knew thy word was constant. I expect no different of thee here in the Yellow Demesnes. But now it is not thy life at stake, but Neysa's. The witch will sell her to another Adept—"

"Why don't Adepts conjure their own creatures, instead of buying them?"

"Because some spells are more complex than others. An Adept may conjure a dozen monsters via a single summoning spell with less effort than a single one by creation. So they store captive creatures in cells, and prepare spells to bring them upon need—"

"I get the picture. To be an Adept is to maintain dungeons where others languish—and the Yellow Adept caters to this need by trapping the necessary animals. I dare say she traps wild fowl and sells the eggs to the Black Adept, too; he has to get his food from somewhere. Maybe he pays her off by making strong cages from black line-bars, that she paints yellow. How does she summon the hapless victims? Neysa seemed to go into a trance."

"Yellow's magic is exerted through potions, I now have learned. She boils a cauldron whose vapors mesmerize animals, bringing them here to be caged. She could summon men similarly, but does not, lest men unite against her and destroy her. Had I been in my man-form, or Neysa in her girl-form—"

"Yes." Stile moved across to Neysa. "Wilt thou release me from mine oath, that I may cast a spell to free thee? I fear thy fate at the hands of the witch."

Neysa, dulled by the summoning potion, was not dull enough to forget her antipathy to Adept-class magic. She shook her head no. She would not condone such sorcery to free herself.

"Say," Stile said, trying again. "Thou canst also change into a firefly, and these bars would not hold—"

But Neysa's eyes were half lidded and her head hung low. The effort of will that such transformation required was beyond her present capacity.

"Or if thou couldst assume thy human form, the potion would not affect thee—"

There was a growl from another cage. Kurrelgyre looked up nervously. "Hark! The witch comes!"

Stile jumped to the werewolf's cage, on inspiration drawing off his socks. "Don these!" he whispered, shoving them through Kurrelgyre's cage bars. "And this." He put the sword through, with its harness. "She will assume—"

"Right." In a moment the white unicorn image formed. The sword was concealed by the illusion. "Remember: thou darest not eat nor drink aught she offers thee, for her potions—"

"Uh-oh! Did Neysa drink?"

But the Yellow Adept appeared before the werewolf could answer. Still, Stile hardly needed it. Neysa, like most equines, drank deeply when she had opportunity, and could have done so automatically while still under the influence of the summoning vapor. That would explain why she hadn't made any real effort to save herself. That also explained why the smarter animals here refused to eat. Kurrelgyre had avoided this trap, and was alert. But the situation of all these animals remained bleak, for evidently none of them had the strength to break out of the strong cages. Eventually they would have either to eat or to starve. Not a pleasant choice; Stile's memory of his confinement in the Black Castle remained fresh.

Stile was not idle during these realizations; he ducked behind the werewolf's cage, trying to hide. He knew it was foolish of him to hesitate about dealing with the witch; obviously she had little to recommend her, and would happily wipe him out. But he could not murder a human being heartlessly. Just as he was bound by an oath of no magic, he was bound by civilized restraints. Demons and monsters he could slay, not people.

"Eeeek!" Yellow cried, pronouncing the word exactly as it was spelled. "The cage is empty! The valuable white 'corn stallion!" But then she inspected the situation more carefully. "No, the stallion remains. It is the wolf who is gone. I could have sworn his cage was—" She glared across the compound. "Darlin' Corey!" she screamed. "Didst thou move the cages about?"

Stile watched the pink elephant. The creature had seen what happened; which side was it on? If it told the truth—

The elephant waddled past the cages toward the witch. Suddenly it flung its trunk to the side, catching Stile by the nape of his shirt and hauling him into view. It trumpeted.

"Well, now, dearest!" the crone cried, scratching idly at a wart on her nose. "So it was a werewolf! Changed to its man-form and squeezed out of its cage."

The elephant squealed, trying to correct her misimpression.

"Oh shut up, Darlin' Corey," she snapped. "What shall we do with the werewolf? I don't have a cage small enough at the moment. He's pretty shrimpy." She peered at Stile more closely, as he hung in midair. "But healthy and handsome enough, my lovely. Maybe he would do for my daughter. Hold him there a moment, my tasty; I will send the wench out."

The pink elephant chuckled. The monsters in cages exchanged glances, bewildered. Obviously this was the first they had heard of Yellow's daughter. What kind of a slut was she? Meanwhile, the hag limped rapidly to the house.

Stile thought of doing an acrobatic flip and climbing the elephant's trunk. But the creature was quite big and strong, and not stupid; it might bash him against a tree. Had he retained his sword—but that would have been highly visible, forcing him to use it to defend himself. It was better to appear more or less helpless, lest he get doused by a potion.

He looked around, able to see more clearly from this height. Beyond the palisades the yellow fog obliterated everything. It was as if the rest of the world did not exist. No doubt this was the way the Adept liked it. She had a little mist-shrouded world of her own, that no man dared intrude upon. Did she get lonely? Probably no more lonely than a person with her appearance would get in the midst of the most convivial society. Who would want to associate with her? Stile, as a person who all his life had felt the inherent discrimination of size, could not entirely condemn the witch for reacting to the discrimination of appearance. Yet he could not allow her to abuse his friends, or to continue mistreating innocent animals.

His eye caught something—a glimmer in the fog outside the compound. A faint curtain of—

The curtain! Could it be here? The thing seemed to wander all over Phaze like a tremendous serpent. Might it be used to facilitate escape, as it had before?

No, there were two problems. The curtain, close as it was, was out of reach, since it was beyond the palisades. And Neysa could not use it. Or would not; he wasn't sure which. So this was a mere tantalization, no real help. Best to wait and see what the witch's daughter had in mind. She was probably a homely girl upon whom her crazy mother forced the attentions of any likely-seeming male.

She emerged. She was stunning. Her yellow hair flowed luxuriously to her waist, her hands and feet were tiny, and her complexion was gold-bronze vibrant, not sallow. She had a figure that would have made an artist gape, with prominent secondary sexual characteristics. Her eyes were so large she seemed almost like a doll—but what a doll!

Young witches, it seemed, had other assets than magic.

"Darlin' Corey, put that man down this instant!" the girl cried, spying Stile. Her voice, despite its vehemence, was dulcet. Everything about her was as nice as it was nasty about her mother.

Darlin' Corey lowered Stile to the ground, but remained near, on guard. Stile straightened his clothing and rolled his shoulders; it had not been entirely comfortable, hanging all that time in midair. "I don't believe we've met," he said.

She giggled jigglesomely. "Tee-hee. I'm Yellowette. My, thou'rt a handsome wolf."

"I'm a man," Stile said.

She looked down at him. That was the only fault he could perceive in her: she was a few centimeters—a couple of this frame's inches—taller than he. "That, too. Kiss me, my cute."

Neysa, in the cage, recovered enough to make a musical snort of recognition. Suddenly Stile had a suspicion why the pink elephant had found the notion of this encounter humorous, and why the caged beasts had never known of the witch's daughter. What would a lonely old hag do with a handsome-if-small man, if she had a potion for every purpose? Drug him—or take a very special potion herself? "Not in front of these monsters," he said.

"What do they matter, my delight? They can not escape."

"I like my privacy," he said. "Let's take a walk outside—and return later, as before." He glanced meaningfully at Neysa, hoping the drug had worn off enough to uncloud her mind. "As before."

Yellowette's fair brow wrinkled. "Thou knowest that unicorn, werewolf?"

"I'm not a werewolf," he said, aware that she would not believe him. "I do know her. She's a jealous mare."

"So? Well, she'll be gone in a few days. There's a fair market in unicorns, for they are hard to catch. Their horns and hooves are valuable for musical instruments and for striking fire, their dung is excellent fertilizer for magic plants, and their hides have anti-magic properties."

Stile experienced an ugly chill. "These animals are for slaughter?"

"Some are, my pleasure. Some aren't even good for that. The black mare would be excellent as a courtyard showpiece, except that she lacks proper coloration and is small. The white stallion, in contrast, is a prize; the White Adept will probably use him to battle dragons in his arena."

Good thing she didn't know the white unicorn was a fake! "What happens to the completely useless animals?"

"I have Darlin' Corey take the worthless ones outside and put them through the curtain." The witch was no longer bothering to conceal her identity, since he seemed to accept it. Her female view of man was that he was interested only in the external appearance—and Stile suspected there was some merit in that view. He had already had relations with a machine that looked like a woman, and with a unicorn that also looked like a woman. What of an old woman who looked like a young woman? Yellow was certainly much more pleasing to deal with in this form than in the other.

"Thou knowest about the curtain?" he asked after a moment, surprised.

"Thou dost not? There is another world beyond it, a desert. The potion puts the creatures through; they never return. I have not the heart to kill them outright, and dare not let them go free in this world lest they summon hordes of their kind to wreak vengeance on these my demesnes, and if they survive in the other world I begrudge it not."

So she was not heartless, just a victim of circumstance. To an extent. Yet it seemed a safe assumption that she was as yet only partially corrupted by power.

How much should he say? Stile detested lies even by indirection. "I am of that world."

"Thou'rt a frame traveler? A true man?" She was alarmed.

"I am. Thou didst merely assume I was a werewolf."

"I do not deal in true men!" she said nervously. "This leads to great mischief!"

"I came merely to discover thine identity. Now I seek only to free thy captives and to depart with my friends. I have no inherent quarrel with thee, but if thou threatenest my life or those of my friends—"

She turned to him in the hallway. She was absolutely beautiful. "I proffer no threat to thee, my handsome bantam. Dally with a lonely woman a time, and thy friends shall go free with thee."

Stile considered. "I don't regard myself to be at liberty to do that."

She frowned. "Thou hast only limited leeway for bargaining, sweets."

"Perhaps. My friend urged me to slay thee without warning, but I did not wish to do that either."

"Oh? We shall put that to the proof." She led him into the main room of the house. Shelves lined the walls, containing bottles of fluid: rows and rows of them, coated with dust. In the center a huge cauldron bubbled, its vapors drifting out through a broken windowpane. This was obviously the source of the summoning scent: a continuously brewing mix.

"All these bottles—potions for different spells?" he inquired, impressed.

"All. I must brew one potion at a time, and can use it only once, so I save each carefully. It is not easy, being Adept; it requires much imagination and application. I must develop a new formula for every invisibility elixir I mix—and for every rejuvenation drink."

Stile eyed her figure again. What a potion she must have taken! "Thou didst really look like this in thy youth?"

"I really did, my honey. Or as close as makes no nevermind. Hair and flesh tints differ from mix to mix, and sometimes one brews too strong, and I become as a child. But my youth was a very long time ago, my lamb, and even the best potion lasts no more than an hour. See —I have only three of these mixes left." She gestured to a half-empty shelf, where three bottles sat. "I expended one quarter of my stock, for a mere hour with thee. Take that as what flattery thou mayst."

"Flattering indeed," Stile said. "I did see thee in thy natural state. But this is not what restrains me. I have other commitments." He pondered briefly. "Thou didst believe me to be a werewolf, before. The true werewolf might be interested in the remainder of thy hour, if thou wert to free him thereafter."

Yellow took down a bottle. "Thou art most facile, lovely man. I hardly trust thee. If thou provest a liar, it will go hard indeed with thee —*and* thy friends." She drew the stopper out. Stile stepped back, alarmed, but she sprinkled the liquid on a statuette, not on him.

The figurine grew rapidly into a demon monster. "Thou summonest me, hag?" it roared, its small red eyes fairly glowing as they glared about. Then it did a double take. Its lips pursed appreciatively. "I have not seen the like in six hundred years! But thou didst not need to prettify thyself for me, witch."

"'Twas not for thee I did it," she snapped. "Speak me the truth, Zebub. Why came this man here, and who is he?"

The demon glared in Stile's direction. "This time thou'rt victim to thine own paranoia, crone. He is innocuous, with respect to thee. Not with respect to certain others, though." The demon smiled privately.

"He really sought not to kill me?"

"True. He but seeks his own identity, so comes with werewolf and unicorn to learn if thou art it."

Yellow burst into a cackle of laughter. "Me! What kind of fool is he?"

"No fool, he. He lacks information on the nature of the Adepts. The Oracle advised him to know himself, so he seeks to learn if he is one of you. He was trapped by Black, and only escaped via the curtain. He is of that other world."

Stile felt another chill. This monster really did have information!

"What gives him the notion he is Adept?" Yellow demanded.

"He *is* Adept, O senile one."

Yellow backed against a wall, almost jarring loose several bottles. "Not only a man, but Adept to boot! Oh, what a foul pickle I have hatched! Who is he?"

"He is Stile, a serf of Proton, in the other frame, freed to cross the curtain by the death of his Phaze-self."

"Idiot! I meant which Adept is he?"

The demon scowled. "That is formidable information."

"Don't stall, hellborn one!" Yellow screeched. "Else I will apply a pain potion."

Zebub blanched. "Blue," he muttered.

Yellow's eyes went round. "This midget is the Blue Adept?"

"His alternate, yes."

"I can't afford trouble with another Adept!" she exclaimed, wrenching at her own hair in distraction. "Not one of such power as Blue! If I free him, will he seek to destroy me? Why does he withhold his magic now?"

"This calls for conclusions on the part of the witness," the demon said smugly.

Yellow took a step toward a shelf of small bottles.

"Question him," Zebub said quickly. "I will verify his word."

"Stile, a.k.a. Blue Adept!" she cried, her eyes round and wild, yet still lovely. "Answer me, in the presence of Zebub."

"If thou shouldst free me, I will still seek to release my friends and the other captives," Stile said. "I will not seek to destroy thee gratuitously."

"He speaks truth," Zebub said. "As for his magic, he made an oath to the unicorn to practice it not save by her leave."

"So only his oath makes him subject to my power?" she demanded.

"That is so," Zebub agreed. "Thou art the luckiest of harridans."

Yellow's beautiful brow furrowed. "If I release the unicorn, she could then release Blue from his oath, and there would be war between Adepts. I dare not risk it."

"Thou darest not risk harming the unicorn either, beldame," Zebub pointed out maliciously. "If the Blue Adept is moved by ire to break his oath—"

"I know! I know!" she screeched, distracted. "If I kill him, another Adept might seek to kill me, for that I violated our convention. If I let him go, Blue may seek my life for that I caged him. If I try to hold him—"

"My time is up," Zebub said. "Please deposit another potion, scold."

"O, begone with thee!" Yellow snapped.

The demon shrank into figurine size and froze: a dead image.

Yellow looked at Stile. "If thou keepest thine oath to the unicorn, wilt thou honor it for me? I wish I could be sure. I want no quarrel with another Adept."

"Release all the animals in your compound, and thou wilt have no quarrel with me," Stile said.

"I can not! I have commitments, I have accepted magic favors in payment. I must deliver."

Stile, quite prepared to hate this Adept, found himself moved. She was, for the moment, lovely, but that was not it. She honored her commitments. She did not like killing. Her surroundings and mechanisms reflected a certain humor, as if she did not take herself too seriously. She was old and lonely. It should be possible to make a deal with her.

"I want no quarrel with thee, either," he said. "Thou knowest me not, therefore trust must be tempered with caution. I make thee this offer: send me through the curtain, and I will not return. I will seek to free my friends and the animals from a distance."

"How canst thou act from a distance? My magic is stronger than thine, near me in my demesnes—as thine would be stronger than mine in thine own demesnes."

"Without magic," Stile said.

"Very well," she decided. "I will put thee through the curtain with a potion, and set a powerful curse I got from Green to ward thee off thereafter. If thou canst free the animals from a distance, without magic—" She shrugged. "I have never liked this business; if I am foiled through no agency of mine own, perhaps I will not be held in default." She glanced at him, her mood visibly lightening. "I never did business with Blue, else would I have known thee. How is it that Blue, alone of Adepts, needs no monsters in storage?"

"I intend to find out," Stile said. He was highly gratified to have this information. Now he knew who he was, and that the Blue Adept had not practiced at least one of the atrocities that seemed to be standard in this genre. This excursion into the Yellow Demesnes had been mistaken, but serendipitously worthwhile.

Yellow took down another bottle, then led him out of the house and around the palisades to the curtain. Stile hoped he could trust her to use the correct potion. But it seemed reasonable; if Adepts avoided trouble with Adepts, and if she feared his violation of his oath were he to be betrayed, she would play it straight. She seemed to be, basically, an honest witch.

At the curtain, she hesitated, hand on the stopper of the bottle. "I do not wish to murder thee, Blue Stile," she said. "Art thou sure thou canst survive in that bleak realm beyond the curtain? If thou preferest to dally here—"

"My thanks, Yellow. I can survive. I have a prior engagement, and must pass through now."

"And thou thinkest the werewolf might be interested—for half an hour? It is not a difficult thing I ask—"

"Won't hurt to ask him," Stile agreed, stepping through the curtain as she sprinkled the liquid on him.

CHAPTER 15

Games

It was a longer hike to the nearest dome, this time, but he had more confidence and need, and that sniff of wolfsbane still buoyed him. In due course, gasping, he stepped inside and made a call to Sheen. It was evening; he had the night to rest with her. He needed it; his high of the last visit to Phaze finally gave out, and he realized the episode with the Yellow Adept had drained him more than he had realized at the time. Or perhaps it was the low following the effect of the wolfsbane.

"So you are the Blue Adept," Sheen said, not letting him sleep quite yet. "And you need some things to use to free your equine girl friend."

"Now don't get jealous again," he grumbled. "You know I have to—"

"How can I be jealous? I'm only a machine."

Stile sighed. "I should have taken Yellow up on her offer. Then you would have had something to be jealous about."

"You mean you didn't—with Neysa?"

"Not this time. I—"

"You were saving it for the witch?" she demanded indignantly. "Then ran out of time?"

"Well, she was an extremely pretty—"

"You made your callous point. I won't resent Neysa. She's only an animal."

"Are you going to have your friends assemble my order or aren't you?"

"I will take care of it in good time. But I don't see how a cube of dry ice will help your animals."

"Plus a diamond-edged hacksaw."

"And a trained owl," she finished. "Do you plan to start romancing birds next?"

"Oh, go away and let me sleep!"

Instead she tickled him. "Birds, hags, mares, machines—why can't you find a normal woman for a change?"

"I had one," he said, thinking of Tune. "She left me."

"So you get hung up on all the half-women, fearing to tackle a real one again—because you're sure she wouldn't want you." She was half-teasing, half-sad, toying with the notion that she herself was a symptom of his aberration.

"I'll look for one tomorrow," he promised.

"Not tomorrow. First thing in the morning, you have an appointment to meet your current employer. This Citizen is very keen on the Game."

Exasperated, he rolled over and grabbed her. "The irony is," he said into her soft hair, "you are now more real to me than most real girls I have known. When I told you to brush up on your humanoid wiles, I didn't mean at my expense."

"Then you should have said that. I take things literally, because I'm only a—"

He shut her up with a kiss. But the thoughts she had voiced were only a reflection of those he was having. How long could he continue with half-women?

In the morning he met his employer. This was, to his surprise, a woman. No wonder Sheen had had women on her mind! The Citizen was elegantly gowned and coiffed: a handsome lady of exquisitely indeterminate age. She was, of course, substantially taller than he, but had the grace to conceal this by remaining seated in his presence. "Sir," Stile said. All Citizens were sir, regardless of sex or age.

"See that you qualify for the Tourney," she said with polite force. "Excused."

That was that. If he lost one Game, this employer would cut him off as cleanly as his prior one had. He was supposed to feel deeply honored that she had granted him this personal audience—and he did. But his recent experience in Phaze had diminished his awe of Citizens. They were, after all, only people with a lot of wealth and power.

Stile and Sheen went for his challenge for Rung Seven. His employer surely had bets on his success. There were things about this that rankled, but if he fouled up, Sheen would be the one to pay. She lacked his avenue of escape to a better world. He had to do what he could for her, until he figured out some better alternative.

The holder of Rung Seven kept his appointment—as he had to, lest he forfeit. He was not much taller than Stile and tended to avoirdupois despite the antifat medication in the standard diet. Hence his name, Snack. He hardly looked like a formidable player—but neither did Stile.

An audience had gathered, as Sheen had predicted. It was possible that some Citizens also were viewing the match on their screens—especially his own employer. Stile's move was news.

Snack got the numbered facet of the grid. Stile sighed inaudibly; he had been getting bad breaks on facets in this series. Snack always selected MENTAL.

Very well. Stile would not choose NAKED, because Snack was matchless at the pure mental games. Snack was also uncomfortably sharp at MACHINE- and ANIMAL-assisted mental efforts. Only in TOOL did Stile have an even chance. So it had to come up 2B.

There was a murmur of agreement from the spectators outside, as they watched on the public viewscreen. They had known what the opening box would be. They were waiting for the next grid.

In a moment it appeared: sixteen somewhat arbitrary classifications of games of intellectual skill. Snack had the numbered facet again, which was the primary one. He would go for his specialty: chess. He was versed in all forms of that game: the western-Earth two- and three-dimensional variants, the Chinese *Choo-hong-ki*, Japanese *Shogi*, Indian *Chaturanga* and the hypermodern developments. Stile could not match him there. He had a better chance with the single-piece board games like Chinese Checkers and its variants—but many games used the same boards as chess, and this grid classified them by their boards. Better to avoid that whole bailiwick.

Stile chose the C row, covering jigsaw-type puzzles, hunt-type board games—he liked Fox & Geese—the so-called pencil-and-paper games and, in the column he expected to intersect, the enclosing games.

It came up 2C: Enclosing. There was another murmur of excitement from the audience.

Now the handmade grid. Stile felt more confidence here; he could probably take Snack on most of these variants. They completed a subgrid of only four: Go, Go-bang, Yote and tic-tac-toe. Stile had thrown in the last whimsically. Tic-tac-toe was a simplistic game, no challenge, but in its essence it resembled the prototype for the grids of the Game. The player who got three of his choices in a row, then had the luck to get the facet that enabled him to choose that row, should normally win. The ideal was to establish one full row and one full column, so that the player had winners no matter which facet he had to work with. But in the Game-grids, there was no draw if no one lined up his X's and O's; the real play was in the choosing of columns and the interaction of strategies.

And they intersected at tic-tac-toe. That was what he got for fooling around.

Stile sighed. The problem with this little game was that, among competent players, it was invariably a draw. They played it right here on the grid-screen, punching buttons for X's and O's. To a draw.

Which meant they had to run the grid again, to achieve the settlement. They played it—and came up with the same initial box as before. And the same secondary box. Neither player was going to yield one iota of advantage for the sake of variation; to do so would be to lose. But the third grid developed a different pattern, leading to a new choice: Gobang.

This was a game similar to tic-tac-toe, but with a larger grid allowing up to nineteen markers to be played on a side. It was necessary to form a line of five in a row to win. This game, too, was usually to a draw, at this level.

They drew. Each was too alert to permit the other to move five in a row. Now they would have to go to a third Game. But now the matter was more critical. Any series that went to three draws was presumed to be the result of incompetence or malingering; both parties would be suspended from Game privileges for a period, their Rungs forfeit. It could be a long, hard climb up again, for both—and Stile had no time for it. The third try, in sum, had to produce a winner.

They ran the grids through again—and arrived again at tool-assisted mental, and at enclosing. The basic strategies were immutable.

Stile exchanged glances with Snack. Both knew what they had to do.

This time it came up Go—the ancient Chinese game of enclosing. It was perhaps the oldest of all games in the human sphere, dating back several thousand years. It was one of the simplest in basic concept: the placing of colored stones to mark off territory, the player enclosing the most territory winning. Yet in execution it was also one of the most sophisticated of games. The more skilled player almost invariably won.

The problem was, Stile was not certain which of them was the more skilled in Go. He had never played this particular game with this particular man, and could not at the moment remember any games of Go he and Snack had played against common opponents. This was certainly not Stile's strongest game—but he doubted it was Snack's strongest either.

They moved to the board-game annex, as this match would take too long for the grid-premises; others had to use that equipment. The audience followed, taking seats; they could tune in on replicas of the game at each place, but preferred to observe it physically. Sheen had a front seat, and looked nervous: probably an affectation, considering her wire nerves.

Stile would have preferred a Game leading to a quick decision, for he was conscious of Neysa and Kurrelgyre in the other frame, locked in potion-hardened cages. But he had to meet his commitment here, first, whatever it took.

They sat on opposite sides of the board, each with a bowl of polished stones. Snack gravely picked up one stone of each color, shook them together in his joined hands, and offered two fists for Stile. Stile touched the left. The hand opened to reveal a black pebble.

Stile took that stone and laid it on the board. Black, by convention, had the first move. With 361 intersections to choose from—for the stones were placed on the lines in Go, not in the squares—he had no problem. A one-stone advantage was not much, but in a game as precise as this it helped.

Snack settled down to play. The game was by the clock, because this was a challenge for access to the Tourney; probably few games of Go would be played, but time was limited to keep the Tourney moving well. This was another help to Stile; given unlimited time to ponder, Snack could probably beat him. Under time pressure Stile generally did well. That was one reason he was a top Gamesman.

They took turns laying down stones, forming strategic patterns on the board. The object was to enclose as much space as possible, as with an army controlling territory, and to capture as many of the opponent's stones as possible, as with prisoners of war. Territory was the primary thing, but it was often acquired by wiping out enemy representatives. Stile pictured each white pebble as a hostile soldier, implacable, menacing; and each black pebble as a Defender of the Faith, upright and righteous. But it was not at all certain that right would prevail. He had to dispose his troops advantageously, and in the heat of battle the advantage was not easy to discern.

A stone/man was captured when all his avenues of freedom were curtailed. If enemy forces blocked him off on three sides, he had only one freedom remaining; if not buttressed by another of his kind, forming a chain, he could lose his freedom and be lost. But two men could be surrounded too, or ten enclosed; numbers were no certain security here. Rather, position was most important. There were devices to protect territory, such as "eyes" or divisions that prevented enclosure by the other side, but these took stones that might be more profitably utilized elsewhere. Judgment was vital.

Snack proceeded well in the early stages. Then the complexity of interaction increased, and time ran short, and Stile applied the notorious Stile stare to unnerve his opponent. It was a concentrated glare, an almost tangible aura of hate; every time Snack glanced up he encountered that implacable force. At first Snack shrugged it off, knowing that this was all part of the game, but in time the unremitting intensity of it wore him down, until he began to make mistakes. Trifling errors at first, but these upset him all out of proportion, causing his concentration to suffer. He misread a *seki* situation, giving away several stones, failed to make an eye to protect a vulnerable territory, and used stones wastefully.

Even before the game's conclusion, it was obvious that Stile had it. Snack, shaken, resigned without going through the scoring procedure. Rung Seven was Stile's.

Stile eased up on the glare—and Snack shook his head, feeling foolish. He understood how poorly he had played in the ambience of that malevolence—now that the pressure was off. At his top form he might reasonably have beaten Stile, but he had been far below his standard. Stile himself was sorry, but he was above all a competitor, and he had needed this Rung. All his malignance, the product of a lifetime's reaction to the slight of his size, came out in concentrated form during competition of this nature, and it was a major key to his success. Stile was more highly motivated than most people, inherently, and he drove harder, and he never showed mercy in the Game.

The holder of Rung Six was a contrast. His name was Hulk, after an obscure comic character of a prior century he was thought to resemble, and he was a huge, powerful man. Hulk was not only ready but eager to meet the challenge. He was a specialist in the physical games, but was not stupid. This was his last year of tenure, so he was trying to move into qualifying position; unfortunately his last challenge to Rung Five had been turned back on a Game of chance, and he could not rechallenge until the rung-order shifted, or until he had successfully answered a challenge to his own Rung. Stile was that challenge. The audience, aware of this, had swelled to respectable size; both Stile and Hulk were popular Gamesmen, and they represented the extremes of physical appearance, adding to that novelty. The giant and the midget, locked in combat!

Stile got the numbered face of the prime grid, this time. For once he had the opening break! He could steer the selction away from Hulk's specialty of the physical.

But Stile hesitated. Two things influenced him. First, the element of surprise: why should he do what his opponent expected, which was to choose the MENTAL column? Hulk was pretty canny, though he tried to conceal this, just as Stile tried to obscure his physical abilities. Any mistake an opponent might make in estimating the capacities of a player was good news for that player. Hulk would choose the NAKED row, putting it into the box of straight mental games, where surely he had some specialties in reserve. Second, it would be a prime challenge and an exhilarating experience to take Hulk in his region of strength—a considerable show for the watching masses.

No, Stile told himself. This was merely his foolishness, a reaction to the countless times he had been disparagingly called a pygmy. He had a thing about large men, a need to put them down, to prove he was better than they, and to do it physically. He knew this was fatuous; large men were no more responsible for their size than Stile was for his own. Yet it was an incubus, a constant imperative that would never yield to logic. He wanted to humble this giant, to grind him down ignominiously before the world. He *had* to.

Thus it came up 1A—PHYSICAL NAKED. The audience made a soft "oooh" of surprise and expectation. In the muted distance came someone's call: "Stile's going after Hulk in 1A!" and a responding cry of amazement.

Hulk looked up, and they exchanged a fleeting smile over the unit; both of them liked a good audience. In fact, Stile realized, he was more like Hulk than unlike him, in certain fundamental respects. It was push-pull; Stile both liked and disliked, envied and resented the other man, wanting to be like him while wanting to prove he didn't *need* to be like him.

But had he, in his silly imperative, thrown away any advantage he might have had? Hulk's physical prowess was no empty reputation. Stile had made the grand play—and might now pay the consequence. Loss—and termination of employment, when he most needed the support of an understanding employer. Stile began to feel the weakness of uncertainty.

They played the next grid. This, he realized suddenly, was the same one he had come to with Sheen, when he met her in her guise of a woman. Of a living woman. That Dust Slide—he remembered that with a certain fondness. So much had happened since then! He had suffered knee injury, threats against his life, discovered the frame of Phaze, befriended a lady unicorn and gentleman werewolf, and was now making his move to enter the Tourney—two years before his time. A lifetime of experience in about ten days!

The subgrid's top facet listed SEPARATE—INACTIVE—COMBAT—CO-OPERATIVE, and this was the one Stile had. He was tempted to go for COMBAT, but his internal need to prove himself did not extend to such idiocy. He could hold his own in most martial arts—but he remembered the problem he had had trying to throw the goon, in the fantasy frame, and Hulk was the wrestling champion of the over-age-thirty men. A good big man could indeed beat a good small man, other things being equal. Stile selected SEPARATE.

Hulk's options were for the surfaces: FLAT—VARIABLE—DISCONTINUITY—LIQUID. Hulk was a powerful swimmer—but Stile was an expert diver, and these were in the same section. Stile's gymnastic abilities gave him the advantage on discontinuous surfaces too; he could do tricks on the trapeze or parallel bars the larger man could never match.

Hulk's best bet was to opt for VARIABLE, which included mountain climbing and sliding. A speed-hike up a mountain slope with a twenty-kilogram pack could finish Stile, since there were no allowances for sex or size in the Game. Of course Stile would never allow himself to be trapped like that, but Hulk could make him sweat to avoid it.

But Hulk selected FLAT. There was a murmur of surprise from the audience. Had Hulk expected Stile to go for another combination, or had he simply miscalculated? Probably the latter; Stile had a special touch with the grid. This, too, was part of his Game expertise.

Now they assembled the final grid. They were in the category of races, jumps, tumbling and calisthenics. Stile placed Marathon in the center of the nine-square grid, trying to jar his opponent. Excessive development of muscle in the upper section was a liability in an endurance run, because it had to be carried along uselessly while the legs and heart did most of the work. Hulk, in effect, was carrying that twenty-kilo pack.

Hulk, undaunted, came back with the standing broad jump, another specialty of his. He had a lot of mass, but once he got it aloft it carried a long way. They filled in the other boxes with trampoline flips, push-ups, twenty-kilometer run, hundred-meter dash, precision backflips, running broad jump, and handstand race.

They had formed the grid artfully to prevent any vertical or horizontal three-in-a-row lines, so there was no obvious advantage to be obtained here. Since Stile had made the extra placement, Hulk had choice of facets. They made their selections, and it came up 2B, dead center: Marathon.

Stile relaxed. Victory! But Hulk did not seem discouraged. Strange.

"Concede?" Stile inquired, per protocol.

"Declined."

So Hulk actually intended to race. He was simply not a distance runner; Stile was. What gave the man his confidence? There was no way he could fake Stile out; this was a clear mismatch. As far as Stile knew, Hulk had never completed a marathon race. The audience, too, was marveling. Hulk should have conceded. Did he know something others didn't, or was he bluffing?

Well, what would be, would be. Hulk would keep the pace for a while, then inevitably fall behind, and when Stile got a certain distance ahead there would be a mandatory concession. Maybe Hulk preferred to go down that way—or maybe he hoped Stile would suffer a cramp or pull a muscle on the way. Accidents did happen on occasion, so the outcome of a Game was never quite certain until actually played through. Stile's knee injury was now generally known; perhaps Hulk overestimated its effect.

They proceeded to the track. Sheen paced Stile nervously; was she affecting an emotion she did not feel, the better to conceal her nature, or did she suspect some threat to his welfare here? He couldn't ask. The established track wound through assorted other exercise areas, passing from one to another to make a huge circuit. Other runners were on it, and a number of walkers; they would clear out to let the marathoners pass, of course. Stile and Hulk, as rung contenders before the Tourney, had priority.

The audience dispersed; there was really no way to watch this race physically except by matching the pace. Interested people would view it on intermittent viewscreen pickup, or obtain transport to checkpoints along the route.

They came to the starting line and checked in with the robot official. "Be advised that a portion of this track is closed for repair," the robot said. He was a desk model, similar to the female at the Dust Slide; his nether portion was the solid block of the metal desk. "There is a detour, and the finish line is advanced accordingly to keep the distance constant."

"Let me put in an order for my drinks along the way," Hulk said. "I have developed my own formula."

Formula? Stile checked with Sheen. "He's up to something," she murmured. "There's no formula he can use that will give him the endurance he needs, without tripping the illegal-drug alarm."

"He isn't going to cheat, and he can't outrun me," Stile said. "If he can win this one, he deserves it. Will you be at the checkpoints to give me my own drinks? Standard fructose mix is what I run on; maybe Hulk needs something special to bolster his mass, but I don't, and I don't expect to have to finish this course anyway."

"I will run with you," she said.

"And show the world your nature? No living woman as soft and shapely as you could keep the pace; you know that."

"True," she agreed reluctantly. "I will be at the checkpoints. My friends will keep watch too." She leaned forward to kiss him fleetingly, exactly like a concerned girl friend—and wasn't she just that?

They lined up at the mark, and the robot gave them their starting signal. They were off, running side by side. Stile set the pace at about fifteen kilometers per hour, warming up, and Hulk matched him. The first hour of a marathon hardly counted; the race would be decided in the later stages, as personal resources and willpower gave out. They were not out after any record; this was purely a two-man matter, and the chances were that one of them would concede when he saw that he could not win.

Two kilometers spacing was the requirement for forced concession. This was to prevent one person slowing to a walk, forcing the other to go the full distance at speed to win. But it was unlikely even to come to that; Stile doubted that Hulk could go any major fraction of this distance at speed without destroying himself. Once Hulk realized that his bluff had failed, he would yield gracefully.

Soon Stile warmed up. His limbs loosened, his breathing and respiration developed invigorating force, and his mind seemed to sharpen. He liked this sort of exercise. He began to push the pace. Hulk did not have to match him, but probably would, for psychological effect. Once Stile got safely out in front, nothing the big man could do would have much impact.

Yet Hulk was running easily beside him, breathing no harder than Stile. Had the man been practicing, extending his endurance? How good was he, now?

Along the route were the refreshment stations, for liquid was vital for distance running. Sheen stood at the first, holding out a squeeze bottle to Stile, smiling. He was not yet thirsty, but accepted it, knowing that a hot human body could excrete water through the skin faster than the human digestive system could replace it. Running, for all its joy, was no casual exercise. Not at this velocity and this distance.

Hulk accepted his bottle from the standard station robot. No doubt it was a variant of the normal formula, containing some readily assimilable sugars in fermented form, restoring energy as well as fluid; why he had made a point of the distinction of his particular mix Stile wasn't sure. Maybe it was psychological for himself as well as his opponent—the notion that some trace element or herb lent extra strength.

With any modern formula, it was possible to reduce or even avoid the nefarious "wall" or point at which the body's reserves were exhausted. Ancient marathon runners had had to force their bodies to consume their own tissues to keep going, and this was unhealthy. Today's careful runners would make it without such debilitation—if they were in proper condition. But the psychology of it remained a major factor, and anything that psyched up a person to better performance was worth it—if it really worked. Yet Hulk was not a man to cater to any fakelore or superstition; he was supremely practical.

After they were clear of the station, and had disposed of their empty bottles in hoppers set for that purpose along the way, Hulk inquired: "She is yours?"

"Perhaps I am hers," Stile said. They were talking about Sheen, of course.

"Trade her to me; I will give you the Rung."

Stile laughed. Then it occurred to him that Hulk just might be serious. Could he have entered this no-win contest because he had seen Sheen with Stile, and coveted her, and hoped for an avenue to her acquaintance? Hulk was, like Stile, a bit diffident about the women he liked, in contrast to the ones that threw themselves upon him. He could not just walk up to Sheen and say, "Hello, I like your looks, I would like to take you away from Stile." He had to clear it with Stile first. This was another quality in him that Stile respected, and it interfered with his hate-his-opponent concentration. "I can not trade her. She is an independent sort. I must take the Rung to keep her."

"Then we had better race." This time Hulk stepped up the pace.

Now it occurred to Stile that Hulk did not actually covet Stile's girl; Hulk did have all the women any normal man would want, even if they tended to be the superficial muscle-gawking types. So his expressed interest was most likely a matter of courtesy. Either he was trying to make Stile feel at ease—which seemed a pointless strategy—or he was trying to deplete his urge to win. One thing Stile was sure of: however honest and polite Hulk might be, he wanted to win this race. Somehow.

Stile kept pace. He could not match Hulk's short-term velocity, while Hulk could not match Stile's endurance. The question was, at what point did the balance shift? No matter how he reasoned it, Stile could not see how the man could go the whole route, nearly fifty kilometers, at a sufficient rate to win. Right now Hulk was trying to push Stile beyond his natural pace, causing him to wear himself out prematurely. But this strategy could not succeed, for Stile would simply let the man go ahead, then pass him in the later stage. Hulk could not open up a two-kilometer lead against Stile; he would burst a blood vessel trying. No doubt Hulk had won other races against lesser competition that way, faking them out with his short-term power, making them lose heart and resign; but that was a vain hope here. The longer Stile kept Hulk's pace, the more futile that particular strategy became. Provided Stile did not overextend himself and pull a muscle.

On they ran, taking fluid at every station without pausing. Other runners kept pace with them on occasion, running in parallel tracks so as not to get in the way, but most of these were short-distance runners who had to desist after a kilometer or two. Stile and Hulk followed the track from dome to dome, staying on the marked route. It passed through a huge gym where young women were exercising, doing jumping jacks, laughing, their breasts bounding merrily. "Stop and get a workout, boys!" one called.

"Too rough," Hulk called back. "I'm getting out of here!"

They wound through the elaborate rock gardens of a sports-loving Citizen: the so-called outdoor sports of hunting, camping, canoeing, hiking, wildlife photography. There were no people participating; all was reserved for the lone delight of the owner. At one point the track passed between an artificial cliff and a waterfall: a nice effect. Farther along, a variable beam of light played across them, turning the region into a rainbow delight. Then down the main street of another Citizen's metropolis replica: skyscraper buildings on one-tenth scale, still almost too tall to fit within the dome.

At the next refreshment station a warner flared: FIELD DEFICIENCY, the sign advised. DETOUR AHEAD.

"They warned us," Stile said, taking a bottle from Sheen and flashing her a smile in passing. He remained in fine fettle, enjoying the run.

Hulk grabbed his own bottle, which seemed to be of a different type than before. He didn't use it immediately, but ran on for a short while in silence. When they were safely beyond the station, he exclaimed: "Detour, hell! This is a set route, not a garden path to be switched every time some Citizen has a party. This is a challenge leading to the Tourney. I mean to push on through."

Intriguing notion. If they ignored the detour, would they be able to defy the whim of some Citizen with impunity? Few serfs ever had the chance! "Could be trouble," Stile warned.

"I'll risk it." And Hulk passed the plainly marked detour and followed the original marathon track.

That forced Stile to stay on that track too, because a detour could add kilometers to the route, in effect putting him behind enough to disqualify him. Had that been Hulk's plan? To get ahead, take the main track, while Stile innocently took the detour and penalized himself? But that would mean that Hulk had known about this detour beforehand—and Stile had been the one to put the marathon on the grid.

A good competitor, though, kept abreast of all the options. Had Stile not been busy in Phaze, he would have known about the detour himself, and played accordingly. Well, he had kept pace with the giant, and foiled that particular ploy. But he did not much like this development. Detours, despite Hulk's complaint, were usually set for good reason.

Stile finished his drink and tossed the bottle in the bin. Hulk had hardly started his, and was carrying it along in his hand. Of course he could take as long as he wished; Stile preferred not to have any encumbrance longer than necessary.

They passed through a force-field wall, into an interdome tunnel. This was where the deficiency was. Stile felt it immediately; it was cold here, and some of the air had leaked out. His breathing became difficult; there was not enough oxygen to sustain him long at this level of exertion. He had become partially acclimatized to it in the course of his travels to and from Phaze, but that wasn't enough. Yet Hulk, perhaps drawing on reserves within his gross musculature, forged on.

If the field malfunction extended far, Stile would be in trouble. And Hulk knew it. Suddenly the race had changed complexion! Had Hulk anticipated this so far as to practice running in outerdome air? Was that why he had started with so much confidence? Stile's supposed strength had become his weakness, because of his opponent's superior research and preparation. If Hulk beat him, it would be because he had outplayed Stile in his area of strength: awareness of the hidden nuances of particular situations. He had turned the tables with extraordinary finesse, allowing Stile to lead himself into the trap.

Stile began to fall behind. He had to ease off, lest he faint; he had to reduce his oxygen consumption. He saw Hulk's back moving ever onward. Now Hulk was imbibing of his bottle, as if in no difficulty at all. What a show of strength! The lack of oxygen had to be hurting his lungs too, but he still could drink as he ran blithely on.

If the field malfunction extended for several kilometers, Hulk just might open up the necessary lead, and win by forfeit. Or, more likely, Hulk would win by forcing Stile to give up: endurance of another nature. Stile simply could not keep the pace.

He slowed to a walk, gasping. Hulk was now out of sight. Stile tramped on. There was another force-field intersection ahead. If that marked the end of the malfunction—

It did not. He entered a large tool shop. Robots worked in it, but human beings had been evacuated. The whole dome was low on oxygen.

Stile felt dizzy. He could not go on—yet he had to. The dome was whirling crazily about him as he ran. Ran? He should be walking! But Hulk was already through this dome, maybe back in oxygen-rich air, building up the critical lead while Stile staggered. . . .

A cleaning robot rolled up. "Refreshment—courtesy of Sheen," it said, extending a bottle.

Not having the present wit to question this oddity, Stile grabbed the bottle, put it to his mouth, squeezed.

Gas hissed into his mouth. Caught by surprise, he inhaled it, choking.

Air? *This was pure oxygen!*

Stile closed his lips about it, squeezed, inhaled. He had to guide his reflexes, reminding himself that this was not liquid. Oxygen—exactly what he needed! No law against this; he was entitled to any refreshment he wanted, liquid or solid—or gaseous. So long as it was not a proscribed drug.

"Thank you, Sheen!" he gasped, and ran on. He still felt dizzy, but now he knew he could make it.

Soon the oxygen gave out; there could not be much in a squeeze bottle. He wondered how that worked; perhaps the squeeze opened a pressure valve. He tossed it in a disposal hopper and ran on. He had been recharged; he could make it to breathable territory now.

He did. The next field intersection marked the end of the malfunction. Ah, glorious reprieve!

But he had been weakened by his deprivation of oxygen, and had lost a lot of ground. Hulk must have taken oxygen too—that was it! That strange bottle he had nursed! Oxygen, hoarded for the rough run ahead! Clever, clever man! Hulk had done nothing illegal or even unethical; he had used his brains and done his homework to out-maneuver Stile, and thereby had nearly won his race right there. Now Stile would have to catch up—and that would not be easy. Hulk was not yet two kilometers ahead, for Stile had received no notification of forfeit; but he might be close to it. Hulk was surely using up his last reserves of strength to get that lead, in case Stile made it through the malfunction.

But if Hulk did not get the necessary lead, and Stile gained on him, he still had to catch and pass him. There were about thirty kilometers to go. Could he endure? He had been seriously weakened.

He had to endure! He picked up speed, forcing his body to perform. He had a headache, and his legs felt heavy, and his chest hurt. But he was moving.

The track continued through the domes, scenic, varied—but Stile had no energy now to spare for appreciation. His sodden brain had to concentrate on forcing messages to his legs: lift-drop, lift-drop . . . drop . . . drop. Every beat shook his body; the impacts felt like sledge-hammer blows along his spinal column. Those beats threatened to over-whelm his consciousness. They were booming through his entire being. He oriented on them, hearing a melody rising behind those shocks. It was like the drumming of Neysa's hooves as she trotted, and the music of her harmonica-horn came up around the discomfort, faint and lovely. Excruciatingly lovely, to his present awareness. His pain became a lonely kind of joy.

Beat—beat—beat. He found himself forming words to that rhythm and tune. *Friend*ship, *friend*ship, *friend*ship, *friend*ship. *Friend*ship for *ever*, for *ever*, for *ever*, for *ever*. *Friend*ship for *ever*, u*nit*ing, u*nit*ing, u*nit*ing. *Friend*ship for*ev*er u*nit*ing us *both*, *both*, *both*. Neysa was his friend. He started singing the improvised tune mostly in his head, for he was panting too hard to sing in reality. It was like a line of verse: anapestic tetrameter, or four metric feet, each foot consisting of three syllables, accented on the third. But not perfect, for the first foot was incomplete. But pattern scansion tended to be too artificial; then the pattern conflicted with what was natural. True poetry insisted on the natural. The best verse, to his way of thinking, was accent verse, whose only rhythmic requirement was an established number of accents to each line. Stile had, in his own poetic endeavors, dispensed with the artificiality of rhyme; meter and meaning were the crucial elements of his efforts. But in the fantasy frame of Phaze his magic was accomplished by rhyme. His friendship for the unicorn—

An abrupt wash of clarity passed through him as his brain resumed proper functioning. Neysa? What about Sheen? He was in Sheen's world now! Sheen had sent the oxygen!

Again he experienced his hopeless frustration. A tiny man had to take what he could get, even if that were only robots and animals. In lieu of true women.

And a surge of self-directed anger: what was wrong with robots and animals? Sheen and Neysa were the finest females he had known! Who cared about the ultimate nature of their flesh? He had made love to both, but that was not the appeal; they stood by him in his most desperate hours. He loved them both.

Yet he could not marry them both, or either one. Because he was a true man, and they were not true women. This was not a matter of law, but of his own private nature: he could be friends with anything, but he could marry only a completely human woman. And so he could not marry, because no woman worth having would have a dwarf.

And there was the ineradicable root again, as always: his size. No matter how hard he tried to prove his superiority, no matter how high on whatever ladder he rose, he remained what he was, inadequate. Because he was too small. To hell with logic and polite euphemisms; this was real.

Friendship forever, uniting us both. And never more than that. So stick with the nice robots and gentle animals; they offered all that he could ever have.

Sheen was there by the track, holding out a squeeze bottle. "He's tiring, Stile!" she called.

"So am I!" he gasped. "Your oxygen saved me, though."

"What oxygen?" she asked, running beside him.

"The robot—didn't you know there was a field deficiency along the route?"

"Didn't you take the detour?"

"We stuck to the original track. The air gave out. Hulk had oxygen, but I didn't. Until a robot—"

She shook her head. "It must have been my friend."

The self-willed machines—of course. They would have known what she did not. She had asked them to keep watch; they had done exactly that, acted on their own initiative when the need arose, and invoked Sheen's name to allay any possible suspicions. Yet they hadn't had to do this. Why were they so interested in his welfare? They had to want more from him than his silence about their nature; he had given his word on that, and they knew that word was inviolate. He would not break it merely because he washed out of the Tourney; in fact, they would be quite safe if his tenure ended early. Add this in to the small collection of incidental mysteries he was amassing; if he ever had time to do it, he would try to penetrate to the truth, here. "Anyway, thanks."

"I love you!" Sheen said, taking back the bottle.

Then she was gone, as he thudded on. *She* could love; why couldn't *he*? Did he need a damned program for it?

But strength was returning from somewhere, infusing itself into his legs, his laboring chest. His half-blurred vision clarified. Hulk was tiring at last, and Sheen loved him. What little meaning there was in his present life centered around these two things, it seemed. Was it necessary to make sense of it?

Stile picked up speed. Yes, he was stronger now; his world was solidifying around him. He could gain on Hulk. Whether he could gain enough, in the time/distance he had, remained to be seen, but at least he could make a fair try.

Why would a machine tell him she loved him?

Why would another machine help bail him out of a hole?

Stile mulled over these questions as he beat on with increasing power, and gradually the answers shaped themselves. Sheen had no purpose in existence except protecting him; how would she be able to distinguish that from love? And the self-willed machines could want him away from Proton—and the surest way to get him away was to make sure he entered the Tourney. Because if he failed to enter—which would happen if he lost this race—he would have three more years tenure, assuming he could land another employer. If he entered, he would last only as long as he continued winning. So of course they facilitated his entry. They were being positive, helping him . . . and their help would soon have him out of their cogs. Thus they harmed no Citizen and no man, while achieving their will.

Sheen was also a self-willed machine, subservient only to her program, her prime directive. Beyond that she had considerable latitude. She had entered him in the Tourney, in effect, by gaining him employment with a Citizen who was a major Game fan. Did *she*, Sheen, want his tenure to end? Yet she had no ulterior motive; his printout of her program had established that. His rape of her.

Rape—did she still resent that? No, he doubted it. She knew he had done what he had to, intending her no harm. He could not have known he was dealing with a self-willed machine, and he had apologized thereafter.

No, Sheen was doing what she felt was best for him. A jockey with bad knees and a Citizen enemy had poor prospects, so her options had been limited. She had done very well, considering that she had not even had assurance he would return to Proton, that first time he stepped through the curtain. She had done what an intelligent woman would do for the man she loved.

Onward. Yes, he was moving well, now—but how much ground did he have to make up? He had lost track of time and distance during his period of oxygen deprivation. Hulk might be just ahead—or still almost two kilometers distant. There was nothing for it except to run as fast as he could push it, hoping for the best.

Stile ran on. He went into a kind of trance, pushing his tired body on. For long stretches he ran with his eyes closed, trusting to the roughened edge of the track to inform him when he started to stray. It was a trick he had used before; he seemed to move better, blind.

He was making good time, he knew, almost certainly better than whatever Hulk was doing. But now his knees began to stiffen, then to hurt. He was putting more strain on them than he had since being lasered; ordinarily they bothered him only when deeply flexed.

He tried to change his stride, and that helped, but it also tired him more rapidly. He might save his knees—at the expense of his tenure. For if he won this race, and made it to the Tourney, then could not compete effectively because of immobile knees—

Would tenure loss be so bad? He would be forced to leave Proton, and cross the curtain to Phaze—permanently. That had its perverse appeal.

But two things interfered. First there was Sheen, who had really done her best for him, and should not be left stranded. Not without his best effort on her behalf. Second, he did not like the notion of losing this race to Hulk. Of allowing the big man to prove himself best. Not at all. Were these factors in conflict with each other? No, he was thinking that a loss in this marathon would wash out his tenure, and that was not quite so. Regardless, he had reason to try his hardest and to accept exile to Phaze only after his best effort here.

Stile bore down harder. To hell with his knees! He intended to win this Game. If that effort cost him his chance in the Tourney, so be it.

Suddenly, in a minute or an hour, he spied the giant, walking ahead of him. Hulk heard him, started, and took off. But the man's sprint soon became a lumber. Stile followed, losing ground, then holding even, then gaining again.

Hulk was panting. He staggered. There was drying froth on his cheek, extending from the corner of his mouth, and his hair was matted with sweat. He had carried a lot of mass a long way—a far greater burden than Stile's light weight. For weight lifting and wrestling, large muscles and substantial body mass were assets; for endurance running they were liabilities. Hulk was a superlative figure of a man, and clever too, and determined, and he had put his skills together to run one hell of a race—but he was overmatched here.

Stile drew abreast, running well now that his advantage was obvious. Hulk, in contrast, was struggling, his chest heaving like a great bellows, the air rasping in and out. He was at his wall; his resources were exhausted. Veins stood out on his neck. With each step, blood smeared from broken blisters on his feet. Yet still he pushed, lunging ahead, pulse pounding visibly at his chest and throat, eyes bloodshot, staggering so violently from side to side that he threatened momentarily to lurch entirely off the track.

Stile paced him, morbidly fascinated by the man's evident agony. What kept him going? Few people realized the nature of endurance running, the sheer effort of will required to push beyond normal human limits though the body be destroyed, the courage needed to continue when fatigue became pain. Hulk had carried triple Stile's mass to this point, using triple the energy; his demolition had not been evident before because Stile had been far back. Had Stile collapsed, or continued at a walking pace, Hulk could have won by default or by walking the remaining kilometers while conserving his dwindling resources. As it was, he was in danger of killing himself. He refused to yield, and his body was burning itself out.

Stile had felt the need to humble this man. He had done it, physically. He had failed, mentally. Hulk was literally bloody but unbowed. Stile was not proving his superiority, he was proving his brutality.

Stile was sorry for Hulk. The man had tried his best in an impossible situation. Now he was on the verge of heat prostration and perhaps shock—because he would not yield or plead for reprieve. Hulk had complete courage in adversity. He was in fact a kindred soul.

Stile now felt the same sympathy for Hulk he had felt for Sheen and for Neysa: those whose lot was worse than his own. Stile could not take his victory in such manner.

"Hulk!" he cried. "I proffer a draw."

The man barged on, not hearing.

"Draw! Draw!" Stile shouted. "We'll try another grid! Stop before you kill yourself!"

It got through. Hulk's body slowed to a stop. He stood there, swaying. His glazed eyes oriented on Stile. "No," he croaked. "You have beaten me. I yield."

Then Hulk crashed to the ground in a faint. Stile tried to catch him, to ease the shock of the fall, but was only borne to the track himself. Pinned beneath the body, he was suddenly overwhelmed by his own fatigue, that had been shoved into the background by his approach to victory. He passed out.

Stile survived. So did Hulk. It could have been a draw, since neither had completed the course, and they had fallen together. Hulk could have claimed that draw merely by remaining silent. But Hulk was an honest man. His first conscious act was to dictate his formal statement of concession.

Stile visited Hulk in the hospital, while Sheen stood nervous guard. She didn't like hospitals. Proton medicine could do wonders, but nature had to do some of it alone. It would be several days before Hulk was up and about.

"Several *hours*," Hulk said, divining his thought. "I bounce back fast."

"You did a generous thing," Stile said, proffering his hand.

Hulk took it, almost burying Stile's extremity in his huge paw. "I did what was right. I worked every angle I could, but you came through. You were the better man. You won."

Stile waved that aside. "I wanted to humble you, because you are so big. It was a bad motive. I'm sorry."

"Someday you should try being big," Hulk said. "To have people leery of you, staring at you, making mental pictures of gorillas as they look at you. Marveling at how stupid you must be, because everybody *knows* wit is in inverse proportion to mass. I wanted to prove I could match you in your specialty, pound for pound. I couldn't."

That did something further to Stile. The big man, seen as a freak. His life was no different from Stile's in that respect. He just happened to be at the other extreme of freakiness: the giant instead of the dwarf. Now Stile felt compelled to do something good for this man.

"Your tenure is short," he said. "You may not have time to reach the qualifying Rung. You will have to leave Proton soon. Are you interested in an alternative?"

"No. I do not care for the criminal life."

"No, no! A legitimate alternative, an honorable one. There is a world, a frame—an alternate place, like Proton, but with atmosphere, trees, water. No Citizens, no serfs, just people. Some can cross over, and remain there for life."

Hulk's eyes lighted. "A dream world! How does a man earn a living?"

"He can forage in the wilderness, eating fruits, hunting, gathering. It is not arduous, in that sense."

"Insufficient challenge. A man would grow soft."

"Men do use weapons there. Some animals are monsters. There are assorted threats. I think you would find it more of a challenge than the domes of Proton, and more compatible than most planets you might emigrate to, if you could cross the curtain. I don't know whether you can, but I think you might."

"This is not another world in space, but another dimension? Why should I be able to cross, if others can't?"

"Because you came here as a serf. You weren't born here; you had no family here. So probably you don't exist in Phaze."

"I don't follow that."

"It is hard to follow, unless you see it directly. I will help you try to cross—if you want to."

Hulk's eyes narrowed. "You have more on your mind than just another place to live. Where's the catch?"

"There is magic there."

Hulk laughed. "You have suffered a delusion, little giant! I shall not go with you to that sort of realm."

Stile nodded sadly. He had expected this response, yet had been moved to try to make it up to the man he had humbled. "At least accompany me to the curtain where I cross, to see for yourself to what extent that world is real. Or talk to my girl Sheen. Perhaps you will change your mind."

Hulk shrugged. "I can not follow you today, but leave your girl with me. It will be a pleasure to talk with her, regardless."

"I will return to talk with you," Sheen told Hulk.

They shook hands again, and Stile left the room. Sheen accompanied him. "When I return to Phaze this time—" he began.

"I will tell Hulk what you know of that world," she finished. "Be assured he will pay attention."

"I will come back in another day to challenge for Rung Five. That will qualify me for the Tourney."

"But you are too tired to challenge again so soon!" she protested.

"I'm too tired to face the Yellow Adept too," he said. "But my friends must be freed. Meanwhile, we've already set the appointment for the Rung Five Game. I want to qualify rapidly, vindicating your judgment; nothing less will satisfy my new employer."

"Yes, of course," she agreed weakly. "It's logical."

She turned over the special materials he had ordered and took him to the proper section of the curtain. "My friends had an awful time gathering this stuff," she complained. "It really would have been easier if you had been a reasonable robot, instead of an unreasonable man."

"You have a reasonable robot in my image," he reminded her. "Be sure to reanimate him."

She made a mock-strike at him. "You know a robot can't compare to a real live man."

Stile kissed her and passed through.

CHAPTER 16

Blue

Stile emerged, as planned, just beyond the yellow fog that demarked the Yellow Demesnes. He could not, per his agreement and the curse Yellow had set against his return, enter that for himself—but he shouldn't need to. He set down the cage containing the owl and donned his clothing. In the pockets were a folded null-weight wetsuit and a metalsaw: the one to protect against thrown potions, the other to sever the cage bars. He hoped Kurrelgyre or Neysa would have the common sense to saw out a bar-section and use it as a lever to break the locks of the other cages. If they didn't, or if anything else went wrong—

Stile stifled that thought. He had to free his friends, one way or another. If he could not do it harmlessly, he would have to make arrangements to destroy the Yellow Adept—and he did not want to do that. She was not really a bad witch.

He stretched the pliant wetsuit into a cord and knotted it about the saw. He brought the owl out. "All right, owl. One service for me and you are free in this world, never again to serve man or to be caged." This was a modified owl, of high intelligence for its kind; it understood him. "Take this and drop it in the cauldron inside the yellow house." Stile presented the package of dry ice. "Take this and drop it in the unicorn's cage." He gave the bird the wetsuit-saw knot.

The owl blinked dubiously.

"Oh, you don't know what a unicorn is? Like a horse with a horn." The owl was reassured. "Then wing out of here—and out of there, quickly. You will be free. And if you should ever need me, let me know and I'll help you."

The owl took a package in each claw, spread its wings, and launched into the sky. "And don't let any liquid touch you, there!" Stile called after it.

He watched it go, hoping for the best. This was a jury-rigged effort, the best he could think of under the pressures of the moment. He wasn't sure what Proton artifacts would operate in Phaze, so was keeping it as simple as possible.

He was in luck. Soon he heard a scream from the witch. That would be the dry ice in the cauldron, making it bubble and steam through no agency of the Adept, interfering with the potion's effectiveness and releasing the owl from its spell, as well as distracting Yellow. Next could come the delivery of the suit and saw. After that, with luck, hell would break loose.

He waited nervously. So many things could go wrong! Then he heard the trumpeting of Darlin' Corey the pink elephant, and an increasing commotion among the captives. It grew into a considerable din, with bangings and crashes. Then at last shapes moved through the fog. A unicorn galloped toward Stile. It was Neysa—and she had a rider. Kurrelgyre, in man-form.

They arrived, and the werewolf dismounted. "My thanks to thee, fair mare. At such time as I may, I will return the favor." Then he handed the sword to Stile and changed back into wolf-form.

Stile stood for a moment, assimilating this. Why hadn't the werewolf simply run as a wolf, instead of performing the awkward, for him, feat of riding the unicorn? To carry the rapier, that he would otherwise have had to leave behind. His own clothing transformed with him, but the sword was foreign. He had wanted to return it to Stile. Why had Neysa tolerated this strange rider? Because she too had felt the need to return the sword. Yet it was no special weapon. It was the gift of her brother, belonging now to Stile—that was its only distinction. So they had both done it for him. Or so his present logic suggested. He was touched. "I thank you both. But I am chiefly glad you both are free without injury."

Kurrelgyre made a growl, and Neysa a note of assent. Neither was talking much, it seemed. Was this because they had not liked the necessity of working so closely together—or because they had liked it? That could be a serious complication for hereditary enemies.

"The Yellow Adept—was she hurt?"

Kurrelgyre changed back to man-form. "The witch brought me forth from my cage, fathoming my disguise," he said. "She claimed thou hadst sent her to me. And I, knowing not whether she spoke truth or lie, had to play along with her until I knew thy fate, intending to kill her if she had done thee harm. But she showed me thy prints going through the curtain, and told me how thou wouldst try to rescue us from afar, and said she would lay no traps against thee if I—"

"Yellowette is some fair witch," Stile said.

"I have been long absent from my were-bitch," Kurrelgyre agreed. "Yellow performs her business, as do we all. But ere she moved me, the potion wore off. . . ." He shrugged. "So I returned to my cage, to await thine effort. I could not flee in wolf-form because her summoning potion would have brought me back, and my man-form no longer wished to slay her."

"I believe she was willing to let thee go," Stile said. "But to save face, she could not do it until I launched mine effort. I suspect I owe her a favor."

"It seems some Adepts are people too," Kurrelgyre agreed grudgingly. "No animal harmed Yellow in the escape; they merely fled in different directions, and we too came here as soon as we winded thee." He returned to lupine form.

"Yellow told me who I am," Stile said.

The eyes of wolf and unicorn abruptly fixed on him.

"I am the Blue Adept." Stile paused, but neither gave any sign, positive or negative. "I know neither of you approve, but I am what I am. My alternate self was Blue. And I must know myself, as the Oracle said. I must go and set things straight at the Blue Demesnes."

Still they waited, not giving him any encouragement.

"I have freed you both from Yellow, as I had to," Stile continued. "I could not leave you in her clutches after both of you got there because of me. But now that I know who I am, I can not ask either of you to help. I am the one that thou, Kurrelgyre, mayst not—"

The wolf shifted back into the man. "Too late, friend. I was lost when I met thee, knowing it not. The Oracle alone knew, when it told me to 'cultivate Blue.' I ask no favor of thee, but I will help thee investigate thine own situation. Perchance that which slew thine other self now lurks for thee at the Blue Demesnes, and a lupine nose will sniff it out in time."

"I thank thee, werewolf. Yet will I do no magic, so can not assist thee in thine own concern. It is a one-sided favor thou dost—" But Kurrelgyre had already reverted to wolf-form.

"And thee, Neysa," Stile continued. "I—"

The unicorn made a musical blast of negation. She gestured marginally with her nose, indicating that he should mount. Relieved, Stile did so. He remained tired from the marathon, and it was a great comfort to be on Neysa again. Now he could relax, for a little while, recovering from that grueling run. He needed about two days off his feet, to recuperate, but the time simply wasn't there. If he delayed his approach to the Blue Demesnes, Yellow might spread the word, and whatever lurked there would be thoroughly prepared for his arrival. He had to get there first.

Should he ask for another sniff of wolfsbane? No—that magic might not work for him as well a second time, and in any event he preferred to ride out his problems with his own strength, not leaning on magic too often.

Stile did not know where the Blue Demesnes were, but Kurrelgyre did. He led Neysa eastward at a fast clip. They moved back along the route they had come originally, through forest and field and badlands, hardly pausing for rest or food. Stile explained along the way about his need to report back to Proton on the morrow, so the two creatures were determined to get him where he was going before he had to return to Proton. Kurrelgyre did not pause to hunt, and Neysa never grazed despite Stile's urgings.

At length they passed the place where he had tamed the unicorn: the start of that wild ride. So short and yet so long a time ago! They proceeded without pause to the castle Stile had first seen from his survey from the tall tree. Back virtually to his starting point—had he but known!

Dawn was breaking in its unmitigated splendor as they approached the castle. Stile, asleep on Neysa, had missed the pretty moonrisings and settings of the night. He squinted at the castle blearily. He had barely four hours left before his match for Rung Five in Proton—and he hadn't even settled the situation in Phaze yet. If only Blue hadn't been so far from Yellow—

Stile had slept, but it seemed the tensions of his mission had prevented him from unwinding properly. If the Blue Adept had really been murdered, who had done the deed? If Blue's magic had not saved him, how could Stile survive without the aid of magic? Yet this was the way it had to be. Even if magic had been permitted him, he would not be prepared with suitable verses.

Yet he still had to check this castle out. To know, finally, exactly what his situation was. Whatever it might be, whatever it might cost him. The Oracle had told him to know himself, and he believed it was good advice.

The environs of the Blue Demesnes were surprisingly pleasant. There was no black fog or yellow fog—not even any blue fog. Just the pure blue sky, and a lovely blue lake, and fields of bluebells and blue gentians and bluegrass. To Stile's eye this was the most pleasant of places—not at all like the lair of an Adept.

Still, he could not afford to be deceived by superficialities. "I think it would be best to enter in disguise, as before," Stile said. The animals agreed.

This time Stile donned Neysa's socks, while Kurrelgyre assumed man-form. Then the seeming man led the two seeming unicorns up to the castle gate.

The drawbridge was down across the small moat, and the gate stood open. An armed human guard strode forward, but his hand was not near his sword. He was, of course, garbed in blue. "What can we do for thee, man?" he inquired of Kurrelgyre.

"We come to see the Blue Adept," the werewolf said.

"Thine animals are ill?"

Surprised, Kurrelgyre improvised. "One has bad knees."

"We see not many unicorns here," the guard observed. "But surely the Lady Blue can handle it. Come into the courtyard."

Stile was startled. This was the first he had heard of a Lady Blue. How could she be the Adept, if the original had been a man, and was now dead? Unless she had been his wife. This complicated the picture considerably!

"But we wish to see the Adept himself," the werewolf protested.

"If thou'rt dying, thou seest the Adept," the guard said firmly. "If thine animal hath bad knees, thou seest the Lady."

Kurrelgyre yielded. He led his animals through the gate, along the broad front passage, and into the central court. This was similar to one of the courts of the palace of the Oracle, but smaller; it was dominated by a beautiful blue-blossomed jacaranda tree in the center. Beneath the tree was a deep blue pond fed by a rivulet from a fountain in the shape of a small blue whale that overhung one side. The Blue Adept evidently liked nature in all its forms, especially its blue forms. Stile found his taste similar.

There were several other animals in the yard: a lame jackrabbit, a snake with its tail squished, and a partly melted snow monster. Neysa eyed the last nervously, but the monster was not seeking any trouble with any other creature.

A maidservant entered the yard, wearing a blue print summer dress. "The Lady will be with thee soon," she said to Kurrelgyre. "Unless thou art in immediate pain?"

"No pressing pain," the werewolf said. He was evidently as perplexed by all this as Stile was. Where was the foul nature an Adept was supposed to have? If the Blue Adept were dead, where was the grief and ravage? They might have had to fight their way into the castle; instead it was completely open and serene.

The girl picked up the snake carefully and carried it into the castle proper.

What was this, Stile wondered—an infirmary? Certainly it was a far cry from the Black or Yellow Demesnes, in more than physical distance. Where was the catch?

The girl came for the rabbit. The snake had not reappeared; was it healed—or dead? Why did the animals trust themselves to this castle? Considering the reputation of Adepts, these creatures should have stayed well clear.

Now another woman emerged. She wore a simple gown of blue, with blue slippers and a blue kerchief tying back her fair hair. She was well proportioned but not spectacular in face or figure. She went directly to the snow monster. "For thee, a freeze-potion," she said. "A simple matter." She opened a vial and sprinkled its contents on the monster. Immediately the melt disappeared. "But get thee safely back to thy mountain fastness; the lowlands are not safe for the likes of thee," she admonished it with a smile that illuminated her face momentarily as if a cloud had passed from the face of the sun. "And seek thee no further quarrels with fire-breathing dragons!" The creature nodded and shuffled out.

Now the woman turned to Kurrelgyre. Stile was glad he was in disguise; that daylight smile had shaken him. The woman had seemed comely but ordinary until that smile. If there were evil in this creature, it was extraordinarily well hidden.

"We see not many unicorns here, sir," she said, echoing the sentiment of the guard at the gate. Stile was startled by the appellation, normally applied only to a Citizen of Proton. But this was not Proton. "Which one has the injured knees?"

The werewolf hesitated. Stile knew his problem, and stepped in. The unicorn costume was for sight only; any touch would betray the humanness of the actual body. "I am the one with the knees," he said. "I am a man in unicorn disguise."

The Lady turned her gaze on him. Her eyes were blue, of course, and very fine, but her mouth turned grim. "We serve not men here, now. Why dost thou practice this deceit?"

"I must see the Blue Adept," Stile said. "Adepts have not been hospitable to me, ere now. I prefer to be anonymous."

"Thou soundest strangely familiar—" She halted. "Nay, that can not be. Come, I will examine thy knees, but I can promise nothing."

"I want only to see the Adept," Stile protested. But she was already kneeling before him, finding his legs through the unicorn illusion. He stood there helplessly, letting her slide her fingers over his boots and socks and up under his trouser legs, finding his calves and then at last his knees. Her touch was delicate and highly pleasant. The warmth of it infused his knees like the field of a microwave therapy machine. But this was no machine; it was wonderfully alive. He had never before experienced such a healing touch.

Stile looked down—and met the Lady's gaze. And something in him ignited, a flame kindled in dry tinder. *This was the woman his alternate self had married.*

"I feel the latent pain therein," the Lady Blue said. "But it is beyond my means to heal."

"The Adept can use magic," Stile said. Except that the Blue Adept was dead—wasn't he?

"The Adept is indisposed," she said firmly. She released his knees and stood with an easy motion. She was marvelously lithe, though there were worry-lines about her mouth and eyes. She was a lovely and talented woman, under great strain—how lovely and how talented and under how much strain he was now coming to appreciate by great jackrabbit bounds. Stile believed he knew what the nature of that strain might be.

Kurrelgyre and Neysa were standing by, awaiting Stile's decision. He made it: he bent carefully to draw off the unicorn socks, revealing himself undisguised. "Woman, look at me," he said.

The Lady Blue looked. She paled, stepping back. "Why comest thou like this in costume, foul spirit?" she demanded. "Have I not covered assiduously for thee, who deservest it least?"

Stile was taken aback. He had anticipated gladness, disbelief or fear, depending on whether she took him for her husband, an illusion, or a ghost. But this—

"Though it be strange," the Lady murmured in an aside to herself. "Thy knees seemed flesh, not wood, and there was pain in them. Am I now being deluded by semblance spells?"

Stile looked at the werewolf. "Does this make sense to thee? Why should my knees not be flesh? Who would have wooden knees?"

"A golem!" Kurrelgyre exclaimed, catching on. "A wooden golem masquerading as the Adept! But why does she cover for the soulless one?"

The Lady whirled on the werewolf. "Why cover for thy henchman!" she exclaimed, her pale cheeks flushing now in anger. "Should I let the world know my love is dead, most foully murdered, and a monster put in his place—and let all the good works my lord achieved fall into ruin? Nay, I needs must salvage what I can, holding the vultures somewhat at bay, lest there be no longer any reprieve or hope for those in need. I needs must sustain at least the image of my beloved for these creatures, that they suffer not the horror I know."

She returned to bear on Stile, regal in her wrath. "But thou, thou fiend, thou creature of spite, thou damned thing! Play not these gruesome games with me, lest in mine agony I forget my nature and ideals and turn at last on thee and rend thee limb from limb and cut out from thy charred bosom the dead toad that is thy heart!" And she whirled and stalked into the building.

Stile stared after her, bathed in the heat of her fury. "There is a woman," he breathed raptly.

Neysa turned her head to look at him, but Stile was hardly aware of the import of her thought. The Lady Blue—protecting her enemy from exposure, for the sake of the good work done by the former Blue Adept. Oh, what a wrong to be righted!

"I must slay that golem," Stile said.

Kurrelgyre nodded. "What must be, must be." He shifted to wolf-form and sniffed the air. Then he led the way into the castle.

Stile followed, but Neysa remained in the courtyard. She had run almost without surcease for a day and night, carrying him, and her body was so tired and hot she could scarce restrain the flames of her breath. Kurrelgyre, unfettered, had fared better; but Neysa needed time by herself to recover.

No one sought to stop them from entering the castle proper. The guard at the gate had been the only armed man they encountered, and he was back at his station. There were a few household servants, going innocently about their businesses. There was none of the grimness associated with the demesnes of the other Adepts he had encountered. This was an open castle.

The wolf followed his nose through clean halls and apertures until they arrived at a closed door. Kurrelgyre growled: the golem was here.

"Very well, werewolf," Stile said. "This needs must be my battle; go thou elsewhere." Kurrelgyre, understanding, disappeared.

Stile considered momentarily, then decided on the forthright approach. He knocked.

There was, as he expected, no answer. Stile did not know much about golems, but did not expect much from a construct of inanimate materials. Yet, he reminded himself, that was what the robot Sheen was. So he had to be careful not to underestimate this thing. He did not know the limits of magical animation. "Golem," he called. "Answer, or I come in regardless. Thine impersonation is at an end."

Then the door opened. A man stood there, garbed in a blue robe and blue boots. He was, Stile realized, the exact image of Stile himself. His clothing differed in detail, but a third party would not know the two of them apart.

"Begone, intruder, lest I enchant thee into a worm and crush thee underheel," the golem said.

So golems could talk. Good enough.

Stile drew his rapier. For this had werewolf and unicorn labored so diligently to return his weapon to him! "Perform thy magic quickly, then, impostor," he said, striding forward.

The golem was unarmed. Realizing this, Stile halted without attacking. "Take a weapon," he said. "I know thou canst not enchant me. Dost thou not recognize me, thou lifeless stick?"

The golem studied Stile. The creature was evidently not too bright—unsurprising if its brains were cellulose—but slowly Stile's aspect penetrated. "Thou'rt dead!" the golem exclaimed.

Stile menaced him with the sword. *"Thou* art dead, not I."

The golem kicked at him suddenly. Its move was almost untelegraphed, but Stile was not to be caught off guard in a situation like this. He swayed aside and clubbed the creature on the ear with his left fist.

Pain lanced through his hand. It was like striking a block of wood—as he should have known. This was a literal blockhead! While he paused, shaking his hand, the golem turned and butted him in the chest. Stile braced himself just in time, but he felt dull pain, as of a rib being bent or cartilage torn. The golem bulled on, shoving Stile against the wall, trying to grab him with hideously strong arms. Stile knew already that he could not match the thing's power.

Unarmed? The golem needed no overt weapon! Its body was wood. Stile got his sword oriented and stabbed the torso. Sure enough, the point lodged, not penetrating. This thing was not vulnerable to steel!

Now he knew what he was up against. Stile hauled up one of his feet and got his knee into the golem's body as it tried to butt again. His knee hurt as he bent it, but he shoved the creature away. The golem crashed against the far wall, its head striking with a sharp crack—but it was the wall that fractured, not the head.

Stile took a shallow breath, feeling his chest injury, and looked around. Kurrelgyre was back, standing in the doorway, growling off other intruders. This would remain Stile's own personal fight, like a Game in the Proton-frame. All he had to do was destroy this undead wooden dummy. Before it battered him into the very state of demise he was supposedly already in.

He no longer had qualms about attacking an unarmed creature. He studied the golem. The creature might be made of wood, animated by magic, but it still had to obey certain basic laws of physics. It had to have joints in its limbs, and would be vulnerable in those joints, even as Stile was. It had to hear and see, so needed ears and eyes, though these would probably function only via magic. Whoever had made this golem must have a real knack for this kind of sorcery. Another Adept, most likely, specializing in golems.

The golem came—and Stile plunged the point of his rapier like a hypodermic into the thing's right eye. The golem, evidently feeling no pain, continued forward, only twisting its head. The sword point, lodged in the wood, was wrenched about. It snapped off.

Stile had not been expert with this weapon, so this was less of a loss than it might have seemed. He aimed the broken end at the golem's other eye. But the creature, aware of the danger, retreated. It turned and crashed through the window in the far wall.

Stile pursued it. He leaped through the broken window—and found himself back in the courtyard, where Neysa had been pacing restlessly, breathing out her heat. She paused, startled, at the appearance of the golem. Her eyes informed her it was Stile, with one eye destroyed, but her nose was more certain. She made an angry musical snort.

The golem cast about with its remaining eye. It spied the fountain-whale. It grabbed the statuary in both arms and ripped it from its mooring.

Neysa, alarmed, charged across the courtyard, her horn aimed at the golem. "Don't stab it!" Stile cried. "The thing is wood; it could break thy horn!"

As he spoke, the golem heaved the whale at him. The statue was solid; it flew like a boulder. Neysa leaped at Stile, nosing him out of the way of it. The thing landed at her feet, fragmenting.

"Art thou all right, Neysa?" Stile cried, trying to get to his feet without bending his knees too far.

She gave a musical blast of alarm. Stile whirled. The golem was bearing down on him with a whale fragment, about to pulp his head.

Neysa lifted her head and snorted a jet of flame that would have done credit to a small dragon. It passed over Stile and scored on the golem.

Suddenly the golem was on fire. Its wood was dry, well-seasoned, and filled with pitch; it burned vigorously. The creature dropped the whale fragment and ran madly in the circle, trying to escape its torment. Blows and punctures might not bother it, but fire was the golem's ultimate nemesis.

Stile stared for a moment, amazed at this apparition: himself on fire! The golem's substance crackled. Smoke trailed from it, forming a torus as the creature continued around its awful circle.

And Stile, so recently out to destroy this thing, experienced sudden empathy with it. He could not let it be tortured in this fashion. He tried to quell his human softness, knowing the golem was a literally heartless, unliving thing, but he could not. The golem was now the underdog, worse off than Stile himself.

"The water!" Stile cried. "Jump in the pond! Douse the fire!"

The golem paused, flame jetting out of its punctured eye to form a momentary halo. Then it lurched for the pool, stumbled, and splashed in. There was a hiss and spurt of steam.

Stile saw Neysa and Kurrelgyre and the Lady Blue standing spaced about the courtyard, watching. He went to the pond and kneeled, carefully. The golem floated face down, its fire out. Probably it didn't need to breathe; still—

Stile reached out and caught a foot. He hauled it in, then wrestled the body out of the pond. But the golem was defunct, whether from the fire or the water Stile could not tell. It no longer resembled him, other than in outline. Its clothing was gone, its painted skin scorched, its head a bald mass of charcoal.

"I did not mean it to end quite this way," Stile said soberly. "I suppose thou wast only doing thy job, golem, what thou wert fashioned for, like a robot. I will bury thee."

The gate guard appeared. He looked at the scene, startled. "Who is master, now?"

Startled in turn, Stile realized that he should be the master, having deposed the impostor. But he knew things weren't settled yet. "Speak to the Lady," he said.

The guard turned to her. "A wolf comes, seeking one of its kind."

Kurrelgyre growled and stalked out to investigate.

"Speak naught of this outside," the Lady Blue directed the guard. Then she turned to Stile. "Thou'rt no golem. Comest thou now to destroy what remains of the Blue Demesnes?"

"I come to restore it," Stile said.

"And canst thou emulate my lord's power as thou dost impersonate his likeness?" she asked coldly.

Stile glanced at Neysa. "I can not, Lady, at this time. I have made an oath to do no magic—"

"How convenient," she said. "Then thou needst not prove thyself, having removed one impostor, and thou proposest to assume his place, contributing no more to these Demesnes than he did. And I must cover for thee, even as I did for the brute golem."

"Thou needst cover for nobody!" Stile cried in a flash of anger. "I came because the Oracle told me I was Blue! I shall do what Blue would have done!"

"Except his magic, that alone distinguished my lord from all others," she said.

Stile had no answer. She obviously did not believe him, but he would not break his oath to Neysa, though he wanted above all else to prove himself to the Lady Blue. She was such a stunning figure of a woman—his alternate self had had tastes identical to his own.

Kurrelgyre returned, assuming man-form. "A member of my pack brings bitter news to me," he said. "Friend, I must depart."

"Thou wert always free to do so," Stile said, turning to this distraction with a certain relief. "I thank thee for thy help. Without seeking to infringe upon thy prerogatives, if there is aught I can do in return—"

"My case is beyond help," the werewolf said. "The pack leader has slain mine oath-friend, and my sire is dying of distemper. I must go slay the pack leader—and be in turn torn apart by the pack."

Stile realized that werewolf politics were deadly serious matters. "Wait briefly, friend! I don't understand. What is an oath-friend, and why—?"

"I needs must pause to explain, since I shall not be able to do it hereafter," Kurrelgyre said. "Friendship such as exists between the two of us is casual; we met at random, part at random, and owe nothing to each other. Ours is an association of convenience and amicability. But I made an oath of friendship with Drowltoth, and when I was expelled from the pack he took my bitch—"

"He stole thy female?" Stile cried.

"Nay. What is a bitch, compared to oath-friendship? He took her as a service to me, that she be not shamed before the pack. Now, over a pointless bone, the leader has slain him, and I must avenge my friend. Since I am no longer of the pack, I may not do this legitimately; therefore must I do it by stealth, and pay the consequence, though my sire die of grief."

Oath-friendship. Stile had not heard of this before, but the concept was appealing. A liaison so strong it pre-empted male-female relations. That required absolute loyalty, and vengeance for a wrong against that friend, as for a wrong against oneself. Golden rule.

Yet something else nagged him. Stile pursued it through the tangled skein of his recent experience, integrating things he had learned, and caught it.

"There is another way," he said. "I did not grasp it before, because this frame evidently has a more violent manner of settling accounts than I am used to. Here, perhaps, it is proper to kill and be killed over minor points of honor—"

"Of course it is!" the werewolf agreed righteously.

"Just so. My apology if I misinterpret thine imperatives; I do not wish to give offense. But as I perceive it, thou couldst rejoin thy pack. Thou hast only to kill thy sire—"

"Kill my sire!" Kurrelgyre exclaimed. "I told thee—"

"Who is dying anyway," Stile continued inexorably. "Which death would he prefer—a lingering, painful, ignominious demise by disease, or an honorable, quick finish in the manner of his kind, as befits his former status, by the teeth of one he knows loves him?"

The werewolf stared at Stile, comprehending.

"And thus thou'rt restored to thy pack, having done thy duty, and can honorably avenge thine oath-friend, without penalty," Stile concluded. "And take back thy bitch, who otherwise would be shamed by the loss of both wolves she trusted."

"The Oracle spoke truly," Kurrelgyre murmured. "I did cultivate Blue, and Blue hath restored me to my heritage. I thought it was the anathema of Adept magic I was fated to receive, but it was the logic mine own canine brain was too confused to make."

"It was only an alternate perspective," Stile demurred. "I have yet to grasp the full import of mine own Oracular message."

"I will gnaw on that," the werewolf said. "Perhaps I shall come upon a similar insight. Farewell, meantime." And he shifted to wolf-form and moved out.

Stile looked at the sun. The day was three hours advanced. The challenge of Rung Five—in just one hour! He barely had time to get there. Fortunately, he knew exactly where the curtain was, and where his original aperture was. He had to move!

Yet he was hardly finished in this frame. He had slain the golem, with Neysa's help, but had little idea how to proceed here; he might do best to remove himself from this frame for a while, hoping for insights. Hoping to know himself better. What did he really want? That depended, in part, on how things fell out on Proton.

"I, too, have business elsewhere," Stile said. "I must reach the curtain quickly, and get someone to spell me through."

Neysa brightened. She stepped up to him. She would handle it.

He mounted, and they galloped off. Neysa was still hot from her prior exertions, but knew Stile's deadline. In moments she had carried him into the pasture where they had first met.

"Neysa, I think it would be best if thou shouldst stay at the Blue Demesnes while I visit the other frame. I'd appreciate it if thou wouldst inform the Lady Blue about Proton, as thou hast heard it from the werewolf and from me; I don't think she knows." He felt a momentary *déjà vu*, and placed it: this was similar to the manner he was having Sheen tell Hulk about Phaze.

Neysa stiffened. "Is something wrong?" Stile asked.

She blew a note of negation, and relaxed. Stile, intent on the precise location of the curtain-site, did not pursue the matter. Such a short time to reach the Game-annex!

They reached the place in the forest where Stile had first entered this frame. The curtain was there, shimmering more strongly than before. Perhaps he had simply become better attuned to it. Stile divested himself of his clothes. "I will return to the Blue Demesnes within a day, I hope. If thou wilt spell me through now—"

She made a musical snort—and he was through the curtain, emerging in the service area behind the food machines. Only then did he wonder about the unicorn's reticence. Something was bothering Neysa—and now it was too late to ask her about it.

Well, he was sorry, but he was in a hurry. He had twenty minutes to reach the Game-annex, or forfeit.

CHAPTER 17

Tourney

He made it. The holder of Rung Five was Hair, who of course was almost bald. He was a well-balanced player, without many great strengths, but also without many weaknesses. That made him hard to handle on the grid. Hair would be playing to Stile's liabilities, not to his own strengths, and have a pretty good chance to land an advantageous game.

Hair studied Stile. "You look tired," he remarked.

"Apt observation," Stile agreed. Naturally his opponent knew all about yesterday's marathon run. Hair would capitalize on this, choosing the PHYSICAL column. Stile would negate this by going into MACHINE- or ANIMAL-assisted, so as not to have to depend on his own diminished strength. Of course Hair would anticipate that, and shift his column, perhaps into ART. He was good on the theremin. Stile was quite ready to challenge in the classification of music, but would prefer a normal, hand-powered instrument. So he would be better off in TOOL, where he could wind up with something like a trombone or a harmonica. In fact, the harmonica would be very nice right now, because he had been practicing it in the other frame.

But Hair had after all stuck with PHYSICAL, outmaneuvering him. 1B, tool-assisted physical games. The second grid appeared as the murmur of the audience rose.

Stile had the letter facet again. If he chose INDIVIDUAL, he could get caught in another endurance or strength exercise, and he was hardly up to it. If Hair selected BALL, it might work out to bowling, where Stile

	1. BALL	2. VEHICLE	3. WEAPON	4. ATHLETIC	5. GENERAL
A. INDIVIDUAL					
B. INTERACTIVE					

could win—or shot-put, where he could not. Hair was no Hulk, but he could heave an object a fair distance. Or he could go for VEHICLE, and they would be in a canoe race or bike race or skating race. Stile was fast on skates, but his legs were tired; this was not his day. WEAPONS was no better. He wasn't ready to bend a powerful bow to shoot at a target 300 meters distant. His aim would surely suffer. His separated cartilage in the rib cage gave a twinge; no, he could not draw a bow! But throwing the javelin or hammer was no better. Nor was pole-vaulting—God, no!— in the next box, or skiing, or even sledding. He pictured himself whomping belly first on a small sled and shooting the ice rapids, and his rib cage gave a worse twinge. Only in GENERAL did he have a fair chance, with things like hopscotch, horseshoes, or jacks. Or tiddlywinks —major Games had been won and lost in that game, with the audience as avidly breathless as it would have been for a saber match. Stile was expert in tiddlywinks—but knew he would not get to play them this time.

So it had to be INTERACTIVE. That had its pitfalls too, but in general skill was more important than power.

It came up 1B. Interactive ball games. Good—Stile was skilled in most of these, and should be able to take Hair—so long as Hair did not catch on to his special liabilities, like the ribs or the bruised left hand. Oh, that wooden head of the golem, that he had so blithely punched!

They set up the nine-box subgrid, filling in with marbles, *jeu de boules*, croquet, billiards, tennis, table-soccer, Ping-Pong, soccer and Earthball. The last would be a disaster; Stile played to avoid it, and the result was Ping-Pong.

Well, not good, but not bad. Stile was excellent at this sport, and his right hand remained good, but he would be off his game today. Hair was good enough to take advantage of Stile's present weaknesses—if he caught on to them in time.

They adjourned to the table-games gym. A number of games were in progress—pool, table-soccer, and of course Ping-Pong—but these were quickly wrapped up when the players saw who was coming. Stile's move up the ladder was already big news. They took a table, picked up the paddles, and volleyed. Several minutes were permitted for limbering prior to the game.

"Time," the machine scorekeeper announced. "Select service."

They did it in the archaic, time-honored fashion, similar to that for the game of Go. Hair took the ball, put it under the table in one hand,

and spread his arms apart. Stile chose the right—and got it. He had the first serve.

It was a good break for him, for Stile was an offensive player whose serve was integral to his strategy. He needed to take and keep the initiative, to make up for his lack of reach. He would not be able to win points directly from his serve, against a player of Hair's caliber, but he could certainly put the man safely on the defensive. That was the way Stile liked it. It gave him necessary options. Of course the serve would change every five points—but once he had the lead, he could ride through to victory without pushing himself. Considering his present liabilities, that was important.

Stile served, a cross-court top-spin ball, fast and low over the net, striking neatly two centimeters from the back edge of the table. Hair returned it cautiously with an undercut to the center of Stile's court. The game was on.

Stile backhanded the ball with a flick of the wrist, to Hair's forehand court. Move it about, keep the other player reaching! Never let the opponent get set for his own strategy. Hair returned it to Stile's forehand, somewhat high and shaky, with almost no spin. Good—he was nervous! That diminished Stile's own tension. This was going his way. Stile made a forehand slam and took the point.

Stile served again the moment he had the ball, backhand cross-court with an undercut. Hair flubbed it again. The score was 2–0. Hair was more visibly nervous now. Excellent. The psychology of nervousness was important in any competition.

But Hair's next return, played too low, nevertheless dribbled over the net, unreturnable. 2–1. These lucky shots occurred; it was usually of no significance. Only when the luck played obvious favorites, as sometimes happened despite the assurances of the experts on probability, was it a critical factor. Stile fired in a sidespin, and Hair sent it wide of the table. 3–1.

The next volley went longer, but Stile finally put it away with a good cross-court slam. 4–1. This game was not going to be a problem.

Now it was Hair's serve. He uncorked a weak dropshot that barely cleared the end of the table; Stile, expecting a harder shot, almost muffed it. But his return was a setup, and Hair put it away for the point. 2–4. In Ping-Pong the server's score was always listed first.

There was something funny about Hair's style, and in moments he took two more points. Stile bore down, overreached himself, and lost another. Now he was behind. Carelessness!

But the run continued. Stile suddenly seemed unable to do right. In moments he was behind 4–10, having lost nine points in a row, his own serve no longer helping him.

What was wrong? He had started well, then lost it. Had fatigue undercut him more than he realized, interfering with his precision? Stile didn't think so. He was playing well enough to win—except that he was losing. Why?

He served a dropshot that barely cleared the table. Hair returned it too softly; it was a setup shot that Stile swiftly put away. 5–10. Strange that the return had been so soft; Hair knew better.

Then Stile caught on. Hair was using a random-variable surface paddle! This was legal, as standards for table-tennis bats had never been instituted; but also tricky, for precision placement was difficult. The variations of bounce were not great, which was why it had not been obvious, but Stile should have noticed it before. *That* was how his fatigue let him down; he had not been alert to the unexpected.

In an instant Stile knew what he had to do. The variable-surface returns forced Hair to play conservatively, keeping his shots well within the margin of safety, though that sometimes set shots up for Stile. But Hair was aware of that. Stile, unaware, had been playing aggressively—and so those slightly changed returns had fouled him up more than his opponent. The more points he lost, the more aggressively he had played, aggravating the situation. A difference in ball velocity and travel so small as to be imperceptible to an onlooker could play havoc with a style like Stile's.

He couldn't handle it. Hair was good enough so that the paddle gave him the edge. Had Stile caught on early he could have played more conservatively himself, holding his lead, forcing Hair to make more aggressive shots that were increasingly risky. But with a 5–10 deficit that strategy wouldn't work; Stile was the one who had to get aggressive. And lose.

He had been suckered, just as he had in the marathon detour. His opponent had outplayed him, off the grid. Stile was in deep trouble again.

So—he had to change his game. He had to go all the way defensive. He needed to allow time and distance to analyze each return individually. This wasn't his normal game, but he had no choice now.

He tried. He had not played a lot of Ping-Pong recently—how could he, with all that had been going on in two worlds!—and had kept in shape only in his natural game. Offense. Spins, placements, slams, changes-of-pace—all fouled up by the marginal uncertainty of the variable-surface paddle. Now, thrown back on a long-neglected resource, he seemed to be in worse trouble yet. He lost a point, and another. 12–5. Soon the gap would be too large to close; sheer chance would give a few points to Hair in the end.

But Stile worked at it, making his shots high and central and safe. This set him up neatly for Hair, who quickly adapted to the situation and started getting more aggressive. Hair had more leeway now; he could afford to indulge a normally weak offense. Stile was only digging himself in deeper.

Yet he had to do it. He extended himself, despite twinges from his rib cage, adapting to this mode. He could judge the shots better now, for he was playing far back, and he was getting the feel of it. He did know how to do it; he had only to remember, to dredge up long-unused reflexes. He fought the next point, covering all Hair's maneuvers, and won it. And lost the next. He still had not quite worked it out—and he needed to, because the point of no return was coming close.

The audience was hushed by this remarkable turn of the game. Now an announcer could be heard from the supposedly soundproofed tele-booth. ". . . strangest Ping-Pong game of the season . . . Stile, the favorite, far behind and playing as if he wants to lose it worse yet . . . will be an inquest to determine whether someone has been paid off . . ."

As if he didn't have enough of a problem already! They thought he was throwing this game! That some other Citizen had proffered him lucrative employment if he missed the Tourney this year. Fortunately the computer analysis of the recording would refute that; all Stile's lost points were honest ones. But if he lost, what difference would it make whether it were honest or dishonest? He would still be finished. In this world, anyway.

But that was not the way he wanted to depart Proton. He had to recover this game!

Stile played the next serve carefully, extending the volley. He needed practice at this defensive game, and the longer the volleys continued the more practice he would get. He won the point, bringing up the change of service at 13–7.

His turn to serve—but if he used it to take the offense, he would lose. He had to give up his normal advantage, for the sake of his strategy, not breaking his continuity.

He served gently—and heard the response of the audience. Most of the watchers did not know why he had been missing points, and thought he was being driven to defense by the strength of Hair's offense. They thought he was foolish to throw away his principal weapon. The serve had always been his tool for the initiative. Some spectators were already leaving, satisfied that Stile had lost.

Hair was glad to continue the offense. He had nothing to gain by indulging in prolonged volleys. Now that Stile had neutralized the paddle-weapon, longer volleys would only give Hair more chances to make mistakes. He needed to put away his points quickly, before Stile got his defensive game in full shape, even if he lost two points for one.

But already Stile was strengthening. The volleys stretched out. Hair lost one, won two—but now he was sweating. Hair was not accustomed to continuous offensive, and as Stile's resistance stiffened—technically, became more fluid—Hair began to make errors of his own. The scales were balancing.

Still, Stile's knees limited him, and his ribs. His reach was minimal in the best of circumstances, and was even more restricted now. He had not quite closed the gap in skills, in this inverted mode, and the game was running out.

They exchanged more points, bringing the score to 17–10 during Hair's service. A seven-point deficit, with only four points to go for Hair. This was bad; if Stile did not rally now, strongly, he was done for.

Hair served. Stile returned it high and center, well toward the back edge so that Hair's shot would have plenty of distance to travel. A setup for a slam, but not for a trick shot. Hair had to hit it hard and long. He did, placing it to Stile's backhand, and Stile returned it with a smooth undercut. His ball arced over, slowing as it dropped, forcing Hair to strike with another undercut lest he lose control. An undercut, backspinning ball in Ping-Pong was a strange shot with special properties; it reacted in the air, on the table, and against the paddle, requiring careful handling.

In the ancient days of cork-, sandpaper- or rubber-surfaced paddles this was not too tricky; but as these gave way to foam rubber and specialized semi-adhesive synthetics the spin-imparting capacities of paddles had become devastating. It was possible to make a ball loop in air, or execute an almost right-angle turn as it bounced. However, such trick shots required skill and energy, and were obvious to a good player, who could then handle them with efficient counterspins. The spin on the incoming ball could be as devastating as the spin going out, making these surfaces a liability to the user, if he were not experienced. The key was to slip in spins that the opponent was not aware of—until too late, when he missed the shot.

Stile, playing back and often below the level of the table, had greater leeway in this respect, now, than Hair did. Hair knew it and was nervous—and doubly careful. He could not uncork full slams lest the hidden spin of the ball send them wide. Stile's proficiency in the mode was increasing, and the advantage was coming to him, at last. But that seven-point deficit—

Stile delivered a swooping undercut sidespin ball that struck the table and took off at an impressive angle. But Hair was ready for it. He countered the spin in the course of a soft-shot. The ball barely cleared the net, and would have dribbled three times on Stile's side before it cleared the table—had not Stile dived to intercept it in time. As it was, he got it back—but only in the form of a high spinless setup.

Hair pounced on his opportunity. He slammed the ball off the backhand corner. Stile leaped back to intercept it, getting it safely over the net—but as another setup. Hair slammed again, this time to Stile's forehand corner, forcing him to dive for it. Stile felt a pain in his rib cage; he got the ball back, but at the expense of aggravating his recent injury. He was in extra trouble now! But he would not give up the point; he had worked too hard for it already.

Hair slammed again, driving him back. Had Hair been a natural offense player, Stile would have been finished; but these slams lacked the authority they needed. Stile managed to return it, again without adequate spin. Hair slammed yet again, harder. Stile retreated far to the rear, getting on top of it, and sent it back. But he had misjudged; the ball cleared the net, but landed too near it and bounced too high. Hair had a put-away setup. Stile braced desperately for the bullet to come—

And Hair made a dropshot. The ball slid off his paddle, bounced over the right edge of Stile's court, and headed for the floor. A sucker shot. Stile had fallen for it.

Stile, nonsensically, went for it. He launched himself forward, paddle hand outstretched. His feet left the floor as he did a racing bellyflop toward that descending ball. He landed and slid, his ribs parting further—but got his paddle under the ball three centimeters above the floor and flicked it up, violently.

From the floor Stile watched that ball sail high, spinning. Up, up, toward the ceiling, then down. Would it land on the proper side of the net? If it did, Hair would put it away, for Stile could never scramble back in time. Yet he had aimed it to—

The ball dropped beyond his line of sight. Hair hovered near, hardly believing his shot had been returned, primed for the finishing slam when the ball rebounded high. It was clearing the net, then!

Stile heard the strike of the ball on the table. Then hell broke loose. There was a gasp from the audience as Hair dived around the table, reaching for an impossible shot, as Stile had done. But Hair could not make it; he fell as his hand smacked into the net support. Then Hair's shoulder took out the center leg of the table, and the table sagged.

Underneath that impromptu tent, Hair's gaze met Stile's as the robot scorekeeper announced: "Point to Stile. Score 17–11."

"Your backspin carried the ball into the net before I could get to it," Hair explained. "Unless I could fetch it from the side as it dribbled down—"

"You didn't need to try for that one," Stile pointed out. "I made a desperation move because I'm up against my point of no return, but you still have a six-point margin."

"Now he tells me," Hair muttered ruefully. "I don't think of that sort of thing when I'm going for a point."

"Your hand," Stile said. "It's bleeding."

Hair hauled his paddle hand around. "Bleeding? No wonder! I just broke two fingers—going for a point I didn't need."

It was no joke. A robot medic examined the hand as they climbed from the wreckage of the table, and sprayed an anesthetic on it. Shock had prevented Hair from feeling the pain initially, but it was coming now. Little scalpels flashed as the robot went to work, opening the skin, injecting bone restorative, resetting the breaks, binding the fingers in transparent splint-plastic.

"I don't think I'll be able to finish the game," Hair said. "I'm not much for left-handed play."

"Stile—by TKO!" someone in the audience exclaimed. Then there was foolish applause.

Rung Five was his. Stile had qualified for the Tourney. But he did not feel elated. He had wanted to win it honestly, not by a fluke. Now no one would believe that he could have done it on his own.

Hulk intercepted them as they left the Game premises. He looked a little wobbly, but was definitely on the mend. He had a rugged constitution. "Stile, about that offer—"

"Still open," Stile said with sudden gladness.

"Your girl was persuasive."

"Sheen has a logical mind," Stile agreed.

"I have nothing to lose," Hulk said. "I don't believe in magic, but if there's a primitive world there, where a man can prosper by the muscle of his arm and never have to say 'sir' to a Citizen—"

"See for yourself. I'm going there now."

"Stile, wait," Sheen protested. "You have injuries! You're worn out. You need rest, attention—"

Stile squeezed her hand. "There is none better than what you provide, Sheen. But across the curtain is a Lady and a unicorn, and I fear they may be jealous of each other. I must hurry."

"I know about Neysa," she said. "She's no more human than I am, and why she puts up with you is beyond my circuitry. But now you have a lady too? A real live girl? What about *my* jealousy?"

"Maybe I broke in at the wrong time," Hulk said.

"Do not be concerned," Sheen told him sweetly. "I'm only a machine."

Stile knew he was in trouble again.

"You are a robot?" Hulk asked, perplexed. "You made a reference, but I thought it wasn't serious."

"All metal and plastics and foam rubber," Sheen assured him. "Therefore I have no feelings."

Hulk was in difficulty. His eyes flicked to the lusher portions of her anatomy that jiggled in most humanly provocative fashion as she walked, then guiltily away. "I thought—you certainly fooled me!" He bit his lip. "About the feelings, I mean, as well as—"

"She has feelings," Stile said. "She's as volatile as any living creature."

"You don't have to lie for me, Stile," Sheen said, with just that stiffness of body and voice that put him in his place. She had become expert at the human manner!

"Lie?" Hulk shook his head. "There's one thing you should know about Stile. He never—"

"She knows it," Stile said tiredly. "She's punishing me for my indiscretion in finding a living woman."

"Sorry I mixed in," Hulk muttered.

Stile turned to Sheen. "I did not know I would encounter the Lady in the Blue Demesnes. I did not realize at first what she was. I destroyed the golem that had impersonated me, but did not realize the complications until later."

"And now that you do realize, you are eager to return to those complications," Sheen said coldly. "I understand that is man's nature. She must be very pretty."

"You want me to look out for Neysa's interest, don't you?" Stile said desperately, though he had the sensation of quicksand about his feet. "She's there in the Blue Castle, alone—"

"The Lady," Sheen interrupted with new insight. "The Lady Blue? The one your alternate self married?"

"Oh-oh," Hulk murmured.

Stile spread his hands. "What can I do?"

"Why couldn't I have been programmed to love a male robot!" Sheen exclaimed rhetorically. "You flesh-men are all alike! The moment you find a flesh-woman—"

"It's not like that," Stile protested. "She is devoted to the memory of her husband—"

"Who resembled you exactly—"

"She told me off when—"

"When you tried what?" she demanded.

Now Stile raised his hands in surrender. "If I stay here four hours longer—?"

"Eight hours," she said firmly.

"Six."

"Six. And you promise to return for the Tourney, after—"

"Yes."

"That will give me time to put my own affairs in order," Hulk said.

Sheen laughed. Oh, yes, she had her reactions down almost perfect now.

Oath

They tried it and it worked: Hulk passed through the curtain. He stood amazed and gratified, looking around at the forest. It was dawn; Sheen had managed to hold Stile for more like eighteen hours, the last half of which was sleeping. Well, he had been in dire need of the rest, and she had treated him with assorted minor medical aids including a restorative heat lamp, so that he really felt much better now.

"I never saw anything so beautiful," Hulk said, gazing at the brightening world.

"Yes, it is that," Stile agreed. He had tended to forget the sheer loveliness of this land, when involved in other things. If all else were equal, he would prefer Phaze to Proton, for its natural beauty.

Hulk had brought along a costume, per Stile's advice. Now he watched Stile getting into his own. "Are you sure—?"

"That ordinary people wear clothes here? I'm sure. Another thing: the language differs slightly. You have to—"

He was interrupted by a sudden loud hissing. A smoke-exhaling serpent rose up, flapping its wings menacingly. It was a small dragon.

Stile backed off warily, but the dragon followed, sensing compatible prey. One spell could have banished it, but its fiery breath made a sword uncertain. In any event, Stile no longer had his sword. He retreated farther.

"Let me try my beast-man ploy," Hulk said. He jumped forward, bellowed incoherently to get the dragon's attention, then raised both arms in a dramatic muscleman pose. It was extraordinarily impressive. He had spent years perfecting a body that was a natural marvel. He danced about, beating his chest and growling. He looked altogether, foolishly menacing.

The dragon turned tail and flapped off, whimpering. Stile dissolved in laughter.

Hulk abated his antics, smiling. "That was fun. You often don't need to fight, if you just look as if you'd like to. Was that thing really what it looked like?"

"Yes. This really is a land of fantasy. When you struck that pose, you looked like an ogre."

"Literal ogres exist here?"

"I believe they do. I've never actually seen one, but I'm sure that's the correct analogy."

Hulk looked dubiously at his costume, then started putting it on. "I didn't really believe in the magic aspect. I thought it might be matter transmission and odd effects."

"I had the same problem, at first. But it is better to believe; magic can kill you, here."

"I'll take my chances. It's like another aspect of the Game, with its special subset of rules. But it puts me in doubt what to do here. I don't know the first thing about magic."

"Most people don't practice it," Stile said. "But you do have to be aware of it, and there are certain conventions. Maybe you'd better come with me, until you catch on. I'm going to the Blue Demesnes."

"What would I do in colorful demesnes? I know even less about courtly manners than I do about magic, and if Sheen's suspicions about your Lady are correct, I should not be a witness."

"You might serve as my bodyguard."

Hulk laughed. "Since when do you need a bodyguard? You can beat anyone in your weight class in general combat, regardless of age."

"Here opposition doesn't necessarily come in my weight class. It comes in yours. Someone is trying to kill me, sending things like demon monsters after me. I would feel easier if a good big man were keeping an eye out. You are conversant with hand weapons—"

"All part of the Game," Hulk agreed.

"You could play dumb, like a monster, until you picked up the ways of this world, then go out on your own. You can cross back to Proton any time, too, by making a spell to pass you through the curtain."

"You have some status in this world? So it wouldn't look strange to have a brute bodyguard?"

"It seems I do. Or will achieve it shortly. If I survive the efforts of my anonymous enemy. So I'd really appreciate it if you—"

"You are a generous man, Stile. You do me a favor in the guise of asking for one."

Stile shrugged. Hulk was no fool. "I'll tell people I removed a thorn from your paw. But don't consider it too much a favor. There is danger. You could get killed, associating with me."

"I could get killed just running the marathon! Let's go."

They went. Stile led the way north as the sun cleared the forest and angled its fresh bright shafts between the branches, seeking the ground. They trotted across the opening fields toward the Blue Demesnes. As the castle came into view, a sun ray reflected from its highest turret in brilliant blue. This too, Stile thought, had to be added to the class of most beautiful things.

Then he paused. "Do you hear it, Hulk?"

Hulk listened. "Ground shaking. Getting louder."

"I don't know whether dragons stampede or whether they have earthquakes here. We'd better hurry."

They hurried. As they crossed the plain around the castle they saw it: a herd of animals charging toward the same object.

"Look like wild horses," Hulk said.

"Unicorns. What are they doing here?"

"A whole herd? Could be coming to the aid of one of their number. Wild animals can be like that."

"Neysa!" Stile cried. "If something happened to her—"

"We had better get over there and see," Hulk said.

"I should never have let Sheen delay me!"

"I doubt you had much choice in the matter, and we both did need the rest. Is Sheen really a robot?"

"She really is. Not that it makes much difference."

"And Neysa really is a horse—a unicorn who turns into a woman?"

"That too. And a firefly. You will see it soon enough—if all is well." Stile was increasingly nervous about that.

They ran, moving into the marathon pace. Neither man was in condition for it, because this was too soon after the real one they had run. But this was not to be the full course. They approached the Blue Demesnes.

But the unicorns were moving faster. Now their music sounded across the field, like a percussion-and-wind orchestra. In the lead was a great stallion whose tone was that of a fine accordion; on the flanks were lesser males whose horns were muted or silent. Evidently unicorns were not gelded, they were muted in public. In the center ran the mass of mature mares, carrying the burden of the melody. The stallion would play the theme, and the mares would reiterate it in complex harmonies. It was an impressive charge, visually and sonically.

Now, from the west appeared another group, dark and low to the ground, moving faster than the unicorns. Stile struggled to make it out. Then he heard the baying of a canine-type, and understood. "Wolves! Probably werewolves!" he cried.

"I am ignorant of conventions here, apart from what Sheen told me of what you had told her," Hulk puffed. "But is such convergence of herd and pack usual?"

"Not that I know of," Stile admitted. "It could be Kurrelgyre, returning with friends—but I don't see why. Or it could be the pack leader Kurrelgyre went to kill; if he were victorious, and sought revenge on the person who helped Kurrelgyre—I don't know. They certainly look grim."

"Werewolves and unicorns are natural enemies?"

"Yes. And both are normally unfriendly to man. Kurrelgyre and Neysa learned to get along, but—"

"Now I'm no genius and this is not my business, but it strikes me that the arrival of these two forces at this time strains coincidence. Could this relate to you? If there were some alert, some way they would be aware of the moment you re-entered this frame—"

"That's what I'm afraid of," Stile said. "You see, I'm a natural magician in this frame—a focus of much power. But I have sworn off magic."

"And your frame-wife would like you to break that oath," Hulk said. "So you can preserve the Blue Demesnes from further harm. And the animals would want you to keep your oath, so you will not become anathema to them. These two types of animals may just be united— against you. You were not joking about needing a bodyguard!"

"You catch on rapidly," Stile agreed.

The two of them picked up speed though both were tiring, in an effort to reach the castle before either herd or pack. But it soon became evident that they would not succeed. The unicorn herd would arrive first, then the wolves.

Now the wolf pack veered, orienting on Stile instead of the castle. There seemed to be ninety or a hundred of them, large dark animals with heavy fur and gleaming eyes and teeth that showed whitely with their panting. "I hope, despite my reasoning, that they're on our side," Hulk said, slowing to a walk.

The wolves ringed them. One came forward, and shifted into man-form. A fresh scar ran across one cheek, and his left ear was missing. But it was Stile's friend.

"Kurrelgyre!" Stile exclaimed. "Thou wast victorious!"

"That was not in question, once thou hadst shown me the way," the werewolf replied. He peered at Hulk. "This monster-man—friend or foe?"

"Friend," Stile said quickly.

"Then I sniff tails with thee, ogre," Kurrelgyre said, extending his hand to Hulk.

"Sure," Hulk agreed awkwardly, taking the hand. He seemed to be having some trouble believing the transformation he had just seen.

"Hulk is from the other frame," Stile said quickly. "My bodyguard. He doesn't talk much." And he flashed Hulk a warning glance. "To what do I owe the pleasure of this visit?"

"I fear I wronged thee inadvertently," the werewolf said. "I returned to my pack, but could not kill my sire without first explaining why—"

"You killed your—" Hulk began, startled.

Kurrelgyre turned, half-shifting into wolf-form. "Thou addressest me in that derogatory mode and tone?" he growled.

"He knows not our ways!" Stile cried. "Even as I did not, at first, and thou didst have to set me straight. He meant thee no offense."

The werewolf returned all the way to man-form. "Of course. I apologize for mistaking thy intent," he said to Hulk. "It remains a sensitive matter, and in a certain respect thou resemblest the type of monster that—"

"He understands," Stile said. "We all make errors of assumption, at first. Why shouldst thou not explain to thy sire? It was the kindest thing thou couldst do for one already ill to death."

Hulk nodded, beginning to understand. A mercy killing. Close enough.

"I came to my sire's den," Kurrelgyre said grimly. "He met me in man-form, and said, 'Why comest thou here? This place is not safe for thee, my pup.' I replied, 'I come to slay thee, as befits the love I have for thee, my sire, and the honor of our line. Then will I avenge mine oath-friend Drowltoth, and restore my bitch to prominence in the pack.' Hardly did he betray his dignity, or yield to the ravage of distemper I perceived in him; in that moment he stood as proud as I remembered him of old. 'I knew thou wouldst thus return in honor,' he said. 'How didst thou come to accept what must be done?' I told him, 'A man persuaded me, even as the Oracle foretold.' And he asked, 'Who was this good man?' and I replied, 'The Blue Adept,' and he asked, 'How is it that an Adept did this thing for thee?' I said, 'He was dead, and his double comes from the other frame to restore his demesnes.' Then my sire looked beyond me in alarm, and I turned and discovered that others of the pack had come up silently during my distraction, and overheard. Thus the pack knew that the Blue Demesnes were in flux, and the word spread quickly. And my bitch spoke, and said, 'Of all the Adepts, Blue alone has been known to do good works among animals, and if that should change—'"

"But that will not change!" Stile protested.

"I tried to tell them that. But mine own kind doubted, and when the unicorns learned that Neysa was prisoner at the Blue Demesnes—"

"Prisoner! She's not—" But Stile had to stop. "*Is* she?"

"We know not. But the unicorn stallion is of imperious bent."

"Well, if she is a prisoner, that will cease the moment I get there. But thou hast not finished thy story."

"It is simple enough," Kurrelgyre said. "The pack leader came, and my sire said, 'It is time.' We changed to wolf-form, and quickly and cleanly I tore the throat out of my sire, and knew then that I had done right, and never did I see a wolf so glad to die. I then whirled and challenged the pack leader while yet my sire's corpse lay steaming, and my right could not be denied before the pack. The pack leader was not so eager to die. He fought, and perhaps he injured me." Kurrelgyre smiled briefly, touching the stump of his ear. "His throat I did not tear; that were too honorable a demise for such a cur. I hamstrung him, spiked both his eyes, tore out his tongue, and drove him with bitten tail into the wilderness to die lame and blind among the monsters. It was an excellent reckoning."

Stile concealed his reaction to this savage tale of vengeance. Perhaps he would have done something similar, in a similar circumstance. "And thy bitch is well?" he inquired, glancing at the female wolf who stood nearest.

"As well as one might be, following exile of her stud, slaughter of his oath-friend, and forced heat to the pack leader. But she will recover. I am now pack leader, and she remains my chosen; all other bitches whine before her."

"A fitting resolution," Stile said, hoping that Hulk had now grasped enough of the situation to avoid any further errors of manner.

"Yet she is marked," Kurrelgyre continued. "She it was who made me see that the mare needed support."

"Neysa," Stile agreed. "But I assure thee—"

Now the bitch shifted to woman-form. She was pretty enough, with a wild orange flare of hair, but did look peaked. She must have had as hard a recent life as the Lady Blue, and survived it as toughly. "What mode of man art thou," she demanded of Stile, "to trust thy female friend to the power of thy wife?"

"The Lady Blue is not my wife," Stile protested.

"Perhaps not so long as the mare lives. I know somewhat of these things." Surely an understatement! "When the mare is dead, thou wilt be freed of thine oath, and practice magic—"

"No!" Stile cried.

"I tried to tell her thou wert true," Kurrelgyre said. "No way wouldst thou harm the mare—"

"And like my wolf, innocent of the ways of the bitch," the female werewolf finished. "The mare is of a species we honor not, as they attempt to rival us as rulers of the wilds, but she brought thee to my love, and thou hast sent him home to me and to the honor he was due. I owe the mare. I perceive the danger thou dost not. The Lady Blue knows no limits to her determination to maintain her lord's demesnes. If thou savest not the mare, I will avenge her in the manner of an oath-friend, though there be no oath between us."

Could she be right? Had Stile sent Neysa to her doom in the Blue Demesnes? What a colossal miscalculation! Yet Neysa could take care of herself, and the Lady was no Adept. "If she is not safe, I will avenge her myself," Stile said. But he could not make an oath of it. Suppose the Lady Blue had—

"Others know thee not as I do," Kurrelgyre said. "So I felt it best to be on the scene when the herd arrived, lest unwarranted blame fall on thee. Thou mayest need guidance."

"I may indeed," Stile agreed. What a complex situation had blown up in his brief absence!

They proceeded toward the castle. The unicorns had drawn up before its gate, their music fading out. They were waiting for Stile to arrive. There were about fifty of them, almost evenly divided between mares and lesser males, with the huge stallion in front. The stallion stood some eighteen hands high at the shoulder, more than thirty centimeters—about a foot—above Stile's head, and all his mass was functional. A truly impressive creature.

Hulk studied the stallion with open admiration. Indeed, the two were similar, in proportion to their species.

Stile halted, for the unicorns blocked the way. The werewolves ranged beside him, grim but neutral. They were here because their new pack leader had brought them at the behest of his bitch; they were not too keen on unicorns, but also not too keen on human beings. Hulk stood back, heeding Stile's admonishment to be silent. There was much here that was not yet properly understood.

"Dost thou seek to bar me from my heritage?" Stile asked the stallion.

The unicorn did not answer. His glance fell on Stile from an impressive elevation, bisected by the long and deadly spiraling horn. His head was golden, his mane silver, and his body a nacreous gray deepening into black fetlocks and hooves. His tail matched his mane, beautifully flowing, reflecting the light of the sun almost blindingly. No horse ever had this coloration or this rugged splendor.

After a moment the stallion snorted: a brief accordion treble punctuated by two bass notes. One of the lesser males stepped forward, shifting shape. It was Clip, Neysa's brother. "I helped thee at my sister's behest," he said. "What hast thou to say for thyself now?"

"I mean to enter that castle and see how Neysa is doing," Stile said. But Kurrelgyre's remarks, and the apprehension of the bitch with regard to the conflict between the unicorn mare and the Lady Blue made him queasy. Had he really betrayed his steed and friend into doom? Had Neysa suspected it when she left him? What kind of a woman was the Lady Blue, really, and what would she do with the associate of the man who had destroyed the golem impostor? Stile had thought she would be grateful, but she certainly had not greeted him with open arms.

Yet how could he believe that his alternate self, his likeness in every respect except environment, had married a woman who would callously murder any creature who stood in her way? Had the Lady Blue shown anything other than a sincere and praiseworthy dedication to her late husband's cause and memory? Yet again, if she knew that Stile alone could restore the greatness of the Blue Demesnes, hindered only by a foolish oath—

"And if she lives, what then?" Clip demanded. "The Herd Stallion demands to know."

"What does the Herd Stallion care about Neysa?" Stile retorted, knowing that in this respect he was voicing the sentiment Clip could not voice. "She was excluded from the herd for no valid reason. She's as pretty and fine a mare as any in the herd, I'll warrant. She should have been bred long ago."

Clip hesitated, understandably. He was at the moment the mouthpiece for his superior, yet his sister's welfare was dearest to his heart and he was loath to refute Stile's statement. "Thou hast not answered the Stallion's question. What will ye with Neysa—if she survives the treachery of Blue?"

"Treachery of Blue!" Stile cried in sudden fury. "I am Blue!" But he felt Hulk's hand on his shoulder, warning him to restraint. Without his magic, he could not really be the Blue Adept.

The unicorn herd faced him silently, and so did Kurrelgyre's bitch. Stile realized it was a fair question, and a hard one. No one had actually accused the Lady of murder; the question was about Stile's own loyalties. He was, potentially, the most powerful person here. If the Lady were exonerated, what would he do then?

"If you take Neysa into the herd, and breed her and treat her as befits a mare of quality, I welcome it. Otherwise she is welcome to stay with me, and be my honored steed, as long as she wishes."

"And what of thine oath to her?"

"What of it?" Stile snapped.

"What of Neysa, when thou breakest that oath?"

Stile suffered another abrupt siege of wrath. "Who claims I am a breaker of oaths?"

"The Stallion claims," Clip said with a certain satisfaction.

For a moment Stile's anger choked off his speech. His hand went for his sword, but slapped only cloth; he had no sword now. Only Hulk's firm, understanding hand held him back from a physical and foolish assault on the huge unicorn.

Kurrelgyre stepped forward and spoke instead. "I was with this man when the Black Adept imprisoned him, but he did no magic, though he was dying of thirst and knew that the simplest spell, such as even any one of us might do, would bring him water and freedom. He freed us from the clutch of the Yellow Adept without magic. He slew the golem of the Blue Demesnes by hand, without magic. He showed me how to regain my status in the pack, using no magic. Now he comes again to this frame—without magic. Never in my presence has he violated his oath. If the Stallion snorts otherwise, the Stallion offends me."

The Herd Stallion's horn flicked, glinting in the sun. He pawed the ground with one massive forehoof. The lesser males drew in to flank him, and the mares shifted position, every horn lowering to point forward. The unicorns were beautiful, garbed in their naturally bright reds, blues and greens, but they meant business.

The hairs on Kurrelgyre's neck lifted exactly like the hackles of a wolf, though he retained man-form. His pack closed in about him, wolves and bitches alike, with an almost subvocal snarling. They were quite ready to pick a quarrel with unicorns!

"Hark," Hulk said. He was the only one with the height and direction to see over the massed unicorns. "The Lady comes. And a small unicorn."

Stile felt abruptly weak with relief. The Herd Stallion turned, and snorted a triple-octave chord. The herd parted, forming a channel. Now everyone could see the Lady Blue and Neysa walking from the castle gate, side by side, both healthy. There had, after all, been no trouble. No overt trouble.

The Lady was lovely. She wore a pale-blue gown, blue flower-petal slippers, and pointed blue headdress. Stile had admired her form before, but now she had flowered into matchless beauty. He had, in the past hectic hours, forgotten the impact the touch of her hands had had on him. Now, with his fear for Neysa's safety eased, his memory came back strongly, and his knees felt warm. What a woman she was!

And Neysa—what of her? She tripped daintily along beside the Lady, her black mane and tail in perfect order, her hooves and horn shining. She was beautiful too. Stile had never seen his relationship with her in terms of choice; he had tacitly assumed she would always be with him. But Neysa was more than a steed, and his association with her had been more than that of a man and animal. If he became the Blue Adept, not only would he practice the magic that she abhorred, he would take to himself the human woman. Stile and Neysa—they could not continue what had been. That disruption had been inevitable from the moment of the discovery that he could perform powerful magic. The wolves and other unicorns had understood this better than he had; they were more familiar with the imperatives of this world. Yet how could he betray Neysa?

They came to stand before Stile. Stile inclined his head, honoring formalities, though he had no notion what was about to happen. One issue had been defused; Neysa lived. The other issue remained to be settled. "Hello, Neysa. Hello, Lady Blue."

The two females made a slight nod, almost together, but did not speak. The Herd Stallion snorted another chord. "Choose," Clip said, translating.

"By what right dost thou make such demand of me?" Stile cried, reacting with half-guilty anger.

"The Stallion is responsible for the welfare of his herd," Clip replied. "He permitted thee to use a surplus mare, an she be not abused.

But now she has yielded her loyalty to thee, thou mayst not cast her aside with impunity."

"If I cast her aside, she returns to the herd," Stile replied, hating the words, but his caution was being overridden by his emotion. "Art thou trying to force me to do this—or *not* to do this?"

"An thou dost cast her aside, it is shame to the herd, and that shame must be abated in blood. Thou keepest her—or thou payest the consequence. The Stallion has so decreed."

"The Stallion is bloated with gas," Kurrelgyre growled. "Knows he not that he challenges the Blue Adept? With a single spell this man could banish this whole herd to the snows."

"Save that he made an oath of no magic to my sister," Clip retorted. "An he honors that oath, he has no need to banish any creature."

For the first time the Lady Blue spoke. "How convenient," she said dulcetly, as she had the first time Stile had met her.

Kurrelgyre turned on her. Stile remembered that the werewolf had left them just before this subject came up, yesterday. "What meanest thou, human bitch?"

If this were an insult—and Stile could not be sure of that—the Lady gave no sign. "Knowest thou not, wolf, that I have harbored an impostor these past ten days, lest news escape of the murder of my husband?" she demanded disdainfully. "Now another image comes, claiming to be Blue—but Blue is distinguished chiefly by his magic, the strongest in all the Land of Phaze—and this impostor performs none, as thou thyself hast testified so eloquently. Were he in sooth the alternate of my husband, he could indeed banish the herd from these demesnes; since he is not, he pleads an oath. I have no slightest doubt he has been true to his oath, and will remain true; he is in fact incapable of breaking it. He is not Blue."

Neysa's head swung angrily about, and she made a harmonica-snort that made the other mares' ears perk up in mute shock. The Lady's lips thinned. "The mare believes he is Adept. She is enamored of him. Has any other person or creature witnessed his alleged magic?"

Even Kurrelgyre had to admit he had not. "The oath was made before I met him. Yet I have no reason to doubt—"

"Without magic, thou hast no debate with the Stallion about the impostor's choice. He shall not be with me. Let him stay with the mare he has deluded."

Neysa's snort seemed to have the tinge of fire. So did the Stallion's. Stile suddenly appreciated how cleverly the Lady was maneuvering them all. Neither wolves nor unicorns really wanted Stile to show his magic, and Neysa was dead set against it—yet now all of them were on the defensive as long as he did not. And if he did perform magic—the Lady won. She needed that magic to maintain the Blue Demesnes, and she would, as Kurrelgyre's bitch had pointed out, do anything necessary to accomplish that purpose. Again he thought: what a woman she was!

"We have galloped here for the sake of a false Adept?" Clip demanded for the Stallion. "We have allowed the wish-fancy of a dwarf-mare to embarrass the herd?"

Once again Stile felt the heat rising. That word dwarf, now applied to Neysa . . .

Kurrelgyre looked at Stile, uncertain now. "Friend, I believe in thee, in thy honor and thy power. But I can not send my pack into battle on thy behalf without some token of thy status. Thou must be released from thine oath."

Stile looked helplessly at Neysa, who snorted emphatic negation. Stile could not blame her; his magic had accidentally sent her once to hell. Without magic he would not be able to assume the role of the Blue Adept, so would not be tempted to leave her. He knew this was not entirely selfish on her part; she feared he would be corrupted by magic. Stile was not sure her fear was unfounded; the other Adepts had certainly been corrupted to some degree, either by their magic or by the circumstance of being Adept. Yellow had to commit the atrocity of animal slavery in order to secure her position with other Adepts; Black had to go to extraordinary extremes to isolate himself. If these people did not do such things, they could be killed by others who were less scrupulous. To be Adept was to be somewhat ruthless and somewhat paranoid. Could he, as Blue, withstand those pressures? The former Blue Adept seemed to have succeeded—and had been murdered. A lesson there?

"Without magic, there is no need for battle," Stile said. "Let the wolves and unicorns go home. Neysa and I will go our way." Yet he was not sure he could stay away from this castle or the Lady Blue. His destiny surely lay there, and until he understood the Blue Demesnes completely he had not really honored the Oracle's directive. To know himself, he had to know the Blue Adept.

Now the Stallion blew a medley of notes. "If thou art false, and caused this trouble for naught, needs must I slay thee," Clip translated. "If thou art true, thou wilst betray the mare who helped thee, and needs must I avenge her. Defend thyself in what manner thou canst; we shall have an end to this insult." And the huge unicorn stepped toward Stile.

Stile considered jumping onto the Stallion's back and riding him, as he had the first time with Neysa. But Stile was in worse shape than he had been then, and the Stallion was more than twice Neysa's mass. The chances of riding him were slim. But so were the chances of defeating him in honest combat—even had Stile had his rapier.

Kurrelgyre stepped between them. "What coward attacks the smallest of men, knowing that man to be unarmed and bound to use no magic?"

The Stallion's horn swung on the werewolf. The bitch shifted into wolf-form and came at the Stallion's off-side, snarling. But Kurrelgyre retained man-form. "Dost thou challenge the pair of us, unicorn? That were more of a fair match."

The lesser male unicorns stepped forward—but so did the other werewolves. Two for one. "Not so!" Stile cried, perceiving needless mayhem in the making. "This is my quarrel, foolish as it may be, not thine."

"With bad knees, fatigue from a marathon run, separated ribs, and a bruised hand—against that monster?" Hulk inquired. "This is a job for your bodyguard. I daresay a karate chop at the base of that horn would set the animal back."

The Stallion paused. He glanced at Kurrelgyre and his bitch, then at Hulk. He snorted. "No one dares call the Herd Stallion coward," Clip said. "But his proper quarrel is not with thee, werewolf, nor with the ogre. It is with the impostor. Let Stile confess he is no Adept, and he will be spared, and the foolish mare chastened."

"Yes," the Lady Blue agreed. "It were indeed folly to fight because of an impostor."

Such an easy solution! All parties agreed on the compromise. Except for Neysa, who knew the truth, and Kurrelgyre, who believed it, and Stile himself. "I abhor the prospect of bloodshed here, but I will not confess to a lie," Stile said firmly.

"Then show thy magic!" Clip said.

"Thou knowest mine oath—"

The Stallion snorted. Neysa looked up, startled but adamant. "Release him of his vow," Clip translated for Stile's benefit.

"Now wait!" Stile cried. "I will not tolerate coercion! You have no right—"

Kurrelgyre raised a cautioning hand. "I hold no great affection for this horny brute," he said, indicating the Stallion. "But I must advise thee: he has the right, friend. He is the Herd Stallion. Even as my pack obeys me, so must his herd, and every member of it, obey him. So must it ever be, in this frame."

The Stallion snorted again, imperatively. Slowly Neysa bowed her horn. She played one forlorn note.

"Thou art released," the werewolf said. "Now the challenge is fair. I may no longer interfere. Use thy magic to defend thyself, Adept."

Stile looked again at Neysa. She averted her gaze. Obviously she had been overruled. She did not like it, but it was, as the werewolf had pointed out, legitimate. By the custom of this frame, Stile had been released. He could use his magic—and would have to, for the Stallion was bringing his horn to bear, and there was no doubting his intent; and not one wolf would come to Stile's defense. To avoid magic now would be in effect to proclaim a lie, and that would not only cost Stile his life, it would shame those who had believed in him. He had to prove himself—for Kurrelgyre's sake and Neysa's sake as well as his own. Even though that would give the Lady the victory she had so cleverly schemed for.

But Stile was unprepared. He had not formulated any devastating rhymes, and in this sudden pressure could think of none. His magic was diffuse, uncollected without music. In addition, he didn't really want to hurt the Stallion, who seemed to be doing a competent job of managing his herd, with the exception of his treatment of Neysa. Why should anyone believe a man who claimed to be able to do magic, but never performed? Such a claimant should be put to the proof—and that was what the Stallion was doing.

Stile saw the Lady Blue watching him, a half-smile on her face. She had won; she had forced him to prove himself. He would either manifest as the Blue Adept—or die in the manner of an impostor on the horn of the Stallion. Vindication or destruction! Beside her, Neysa remained with gaze downcast, the loser either way.

"I am sorry, Neysa," Stile said.

Stile brought out his harmonica. Now it was a weapon. He played an improvised melody. Immediately the magic formed. The Stallion noted the aura and paused, uncertain what it was. The wolves and other unicorns looked too, as that intangible mass developed and loomed. Ears twitched nervously.

Good—this gave him a chance to figure out an applicable verse. What he needed was protection, like that of a wall. Wall—what rhymed with wall? Ball, fall, hall, tall. Unicorn, standing tall—

Abruptly the Stallion charged. Stile jumped aside. He stopped playing his harmonica and cried in a singsong: "Unicorn Stallion, standing tall—form around this one a wall."

Immediately he knew he had not phrased it properly; he had technically asked the unicorn to form a wall around Stile, which was backward. But the image in his mind was a brick wall two meters high, encircling the Stallion—make that six feet high, to align the measurements with the standard of this frame—and that was what formed. His music was the power, his words the catalyst—but his mind did the fundamental shaping.

A shower of red bricks fell from nowhere, landing with uncanny precision in a circle around the Stallion, now forming row on row, building the wall before their eyes. The Stallion stood amazed, not daring to move lest he get struck by flying bricks, watching himself be penned. The pack and the herd watched with similar astonishment, frozen in place. Hulk's mouth hung open; he had not believed in magic, really, until this moment. Kurrelgyre was smiling in slow, grim satisfaction, his faith vindicated. And the Lady Blue's surprise was the greatest of all.

Only Neysa was not discomfited. She made an "I told thee so!" snort and turned her posterior on Stile, showing that she still did not approve. But Stile was sure she *did* approve, secretly. Whatever this might cost her.

After a moment, Kurrelgyre hitched himself up to sit on the just-completed wall. He tapped it with his fingers, verifying its solidity, as he spoke to the unicorn inside. "Thou desirest still to match thy prowess against the magic of the Blue Adept, here in the Blue Demesnes? Note that he spares thee, thou arrogant animal, only showing his power harmlessly. He could as easily have dropped these bricks on thy bone head. Is it not meet for thee to make apology for thy doubt?"

The Stallion glared at him in stony silence. He could readily have leaped out of the enclosure, but it was beneath his dignity to try. The issue was not his jumping ability, but Stile's magic—which had now been resolved.

"Not the Stallion's but mine is the apology," the Lady Blue said. "I thought this man no Adept. Now I know he is. To a fine detail, this performance is like unto that of my love. Yet—"

All heads turned to her, as she hesitated. Slowly she worked it out. "My husband was murdered by an Adept. Now an Adept in the likeness of my love comes, yet I know my love is dead. This could therefore be an impostor, claiming to hail from another frame, but more likely an Adept from this frame, using his magic to change his aspect so that none will suspect his true identity. The Adept who murdered Blue."

Now all heads turned to Stile, the gazes of wolves and unicorns alike turning uncertain and hostile. Stile realized with a chill that he had misjudged the nature of his challenge. His real opposition was not the Stallion—it was the Lady Blue. She would not suffer even the suspicion of an impostor in these demesnes. Not any longer. Her first line of defense had been broken down; this was her second. The Lady was dangerous; he could die by the sole power of her voiced suspicions.

Neysa snorted indignantly. She was mad at Stile now, but she believed in him. Yet it was apparent that most of the others were in doubt again. The infernal logic of the Lady!

How could he refute this new challenge? There was one other person who knew his identity—but that was the Yellow Adept. Best not to bring her into this! He would simply have to present his case, and give them opportunity to verify it.

"I am not the Blue Adept. I am his alternate self, from the other frame. Anyone who is able and willing to pass through the curtain and make inquiries can ascertain my existence there. I am like Blue in all things, but lack his experience of this world. I am not an impostor, but neither am I this Lady's husband. Call me the brother of Blue. I apologize to those of you who may have had misconceptions; it was not my intent to mislead you." It still felt funny, using "you" in this frame, but it was the correct plural form. "Were I some other Adept, I would have little reason to masquerade as Blue; I could set up mine own Demesnes of whatever color. My power of magic is real; why should I pretend to have another form than mine own?"

The others seemed mollified, but not the Lady Blue. "I would expect a murdering Adept to arrive prepared with a persuasive story. To come as a seeming savior, destroying the golem he himself had sent, to make himself appear legitimate. To emulate the form of magic that is Blue's. Why should he do this? I can think of two reasons, to begin. First, this would tend to conceal the murder he committed. Second, he might covet the things that are Blue's."

Kurrelgyre turned to her, his brow wrinkling. "An Adept of such power could create his own estate, as impressive as this, with less complication than this."

"Not quite," she said tightly.

"What has this estate, that a foreign Adept might covet and not be able to duplicate?"

The Lady hesitated, her color rising, but she had to answer. "It has me. It is said by some that I am fair—"

Telling point! "Fair indeed," Kurrelgyre agreed. "Motive enough. Yet if he honors the works of Blue and maintains the premises in good order—is this not what thou wishest?"

"To accept in these Demesnes the one who murdered my love?" she demanded, flashing. "I will not yield this proud heritage to that! The false Adept may destroy me with his magic, even as he destroyed my love, but never will he assume the mantle and privilege of Blue."

Kurrelgyre swiveled on the wall to face Stile. "I believe in thee, friend. But the Lady has a point. The magic of Adepts is beyond the fathoming of simple animals like ourselves. We can prove no necessary connection between Blue's alternate in Proton and thyself; that double could be dead also, and thou a construct adapted by magic, emulating the mode of Blue when in truth the real power lies in some other mode. We can all be deceived, and until we are assured of thy validity—"

Stile was baffled. "If neither my likeness nor my magic can convince her, and she will not take my word—"

"If I may ask two questions?" Hulk put in tentatively.

Stile laughed. "We already have more questions than answers! Go ahead and throw thine in the ring."

"For what was the Blue Adept noted, other than his appearance and his magic?"

"His integrity," the Lady said promptly. "Never did he tell a lie or otherwise practice deceit, ever in his whole life."

"Never has this one told a lie," Kurrelgyre said.

"That remains to be demonstrated," she retorted.

The werewolf shrugged. "Only time can demonstrate that quality. Was there nothing else, subject to more immediate trial?"

"His riding," the Lady said, brightening. "In all Phaze, only he could ride better than I. His love for animals was so great, especially horses—" She had to stop, for her emotion was choking her.

To have the love of such a woman! Stile thought. Her husband was dead, but she still defended him with all her power. She was right: another Adept might well covet her, and not merely for her beauty, and be willing to go to extraordinary lengths to win her.

Kurrelgyre turned to Stile. "How well dost thou ride?"

"I can answer that," Hulk said. "Stile is the finest rider on Proton. I doubt anyone in this frame either could match him on horseback."

The Lady looked startled. "This man can ride? Bareback on an untamed steed? I should be glad to put him to that test."

"No," Hulk said.

She glanced at him, frowning. "Thou guardest him, ogre, by preventing him from betraying incompetence on a steed?"

"I seek only to settle the issue properly," Hulk said. "We have seen that careless application settles nothing—such as Stile's demonstration of magic. For all the effect it had, he might as well not have bothered. To put him to a riding test now, when he has been weakened and injured—"

"There is that," Kurrelgyre agreed. "Yet the importance of this proof—"

"Which brings me to my second question," Hulk said. "Is the issue really between Stile and the Lady—or between the Lady and the mare?"

Lady and mare looked at each other, startled again. "He only *looks* like an ogre," Kurrelgyre murmured appreciatively. Then, to Stile: "He speaks sooth. Thy destiny must be settled by Lady and mare. They are the two with claims on thee. If thou provest thou art the Blue Adept, one of them must needs suffer. This is what brought both wolves and unicorns here."

Stile did not like this. "But—"

The Stallion honked from his enclave. "Only the finest of riders could break the least of unicorns," Clip translated. "This man conquered Neysa; we accept him as the Blue Adept."

Stile was astonished at this abrupt change on the part of the Stallion. "How couldst thou know I really—"

"We saw thee," Clip said. "We rooted for her to throw thee, but we can not claim she did. We recognize that whatever else thou art or art not, thou art indeed the finest rider of thy kind."

"But had she turned into a firefly—"

"She would then have admitted she could not conquer thee in her natural form," Clip said. "It matters not, now. No man ever rode like thee. The Stallion resented that, but now that he knows that was the mark of Blue—"

"I didn't really do it by myself," Stile said, remembering something. "I hummed, and that was magic, though I knew it not at the time. I used magic to stay on her."

"And unicorns are immune to magic," Clip said. "Except the magic of Adepts. Another Adept could have destroyed her, but never could he have ridden her. There is only one Adept we know of who can ride at all, and that is Blue. All this the Stallion considered before accepting thee."

"But I do not accept thee!" the Lady flared. "The unicorns could be in league with the false Adept, to foist an impostor on the Blue Demesnes. My love was a horseman, never partial to unicorns, nor they to him, though he would treat them on occasion if they deigned to come to him. The mare could have allowed this impostor to ride—"

Clip reacted angrily, but Kurrelgyre interposed. "Didst ever thou hear it mooted, Lady, that werewolves would collude with unicorns in aught?"

"Nay," she admitted. "The two are natural enemies."

"Then accept this word from this were: I have come to know this mare. She did not submit voluntarily, except in the sense that she refrained from using her own magic to destroy him. He conquered her physically—and then, when she saw what manner of man he was, the kind of man you describe as your lord, he conquered her emotionally. But first he did ride."

"Almost, I wish I could believe," the Lady murmured, and Stile saw the agony of her decision. She was not against him; she merely had to be sure of him, and dared not make an error.

Then she stiffened. "The mare could be easier to ride than other unicorns like to think," the Lady sniffed. "She is small, and not of true unicorn color; she could have other deficiencies."

Neysa stomped the ground with a forefoot, but did not otherwise protest this insult.

"She has no less spirit than any in this herd," Clip said evenly, speaking for himself now. "And even were she deficient, she remains a unicorn, a breed apart from common horses. No one but this man could have ridden her."

The Lady looked at him defiantly. "If he could ride an animal I could not, then would I believe."

"Therefore thou hast but to ride Neysa," Kurrelgyre pointed out to her. "Thou hast not the magic humming he had, but the mare remains tired from her long hard ride to reach this castle yestermorn. I ran with her all the way, unburdened, and I felt the strain of that travel—and I am a wolf. So I judge the challenge equivalent. In that manner thou canst prove Stile is no better rider than thee."

"She can't ride the unicorn!" Stile protested.

But the Lady was nodding, and so were the unicorns and were-wolves. All were amenable to this trial, and thought it fair. Neysa, too, was glancing obliquely at the Lady, quite ready to try her strength.

"I maintain that anything thou canst ride in thy health, I can ride in mine," the Lady informed him. "There was no comparison between my lord and other men. He could have ridden a unicorn, had he so chosen."

The Stallion snorted angrily, and Stile needed no translation. The unicorns did not believe any normal human being could ride one of them, involuntarily. They had reason. Stile himself had not guessed what a challenge Neysa would be—until he was committed. "Lady," Stile said. "Do not put thyself to this ordeal. No one can ride Neysa!"

"No one but thee?" Her disdain was eloquent.

Stile realized that it had to be. The issue had to be settled, and this was, by general consensus, a valid test. Any choice he, Stile, made between Lady and mare would mean trouble, and it seemed he could not have both. If the Lady and the unicorn settled it themselves, he would become the prize of the winner.

Or would he? If the Lady won, the Blue Demesnes would fall, for there would be no accredited Adept to maintain them, and the news would be out. If Neysa won, there would be no Lady Blue, for she would be dead. As he would have been dead, had Neysa thrown him, that first challenge ride. It was the way of the unicorn, the way of life in Phaze, and all of them knew it, including the Lady. She was putting her life on the line. Either way, Stile lost.

With all his magic power restored to him, he was helpless to affect the outcome, or to determine his own destiny. Beautiful irony! "Know thyself," the Oracle had said, without informing him what the knowledge would cost.

"I know this be hard for thee," the werewolf said. "Even as it was for me to do what I had to do, when I faced my sire. Yet thou must submit to the judgment of this lot. It is fair."

Fair! he thought incredulously. The outcome of this lot would be either death or a lie!

The lines of animals were expanding, forming a tremendous ring, bounded by the castle on one side and the magic wall on the other. The unicorns formed a half-circle, the werewolves another, complementing each other.

Neysa stood in the center of the new ring, the Lady beside her. Both were beautiful. Stile wished again that he could have both, and knew again that he could not. When he accepted the benefits of magic, he had also to accept its penalties. How blithely he had walked into this awful reckoning! If only he had not parked Neysa at the Blue Demesnes when he returned to Proton—yet perhaps this confrontation was inevitable.

The Lady made a dainty leap, despite her flowing gown, which was no riding habit. The moment she landed, Neysa took off. From a standing start to a full gallop in one bound, her four hooves flinging up circular divots—but the Lady hung on.

Neysa stopped, her feet churning up turf in parallel scrape-lines. The Lady stayed put. Neysa took off—sidewise. And backward. The Lady's skirt flared, but the Lady held on.

"She does know how to ride," Hulk remarked, impressed. "If I didn't know better, I'd swear that was you, Stile, in a dress. I've watched you win broncobusting in the Game."

Stile was glumly silent. The Lady Blue could indeed ride, better than he had expected—but he knew she could not stay on the unicorn. When she fell, Neysa would kill her, if the fall itself did not. It was legitimate; it was expected. And what would he want with Neysa then?

The unicorn performed a backflip, then a four-spoked cartwheel, then a series of one-beat hops, followed by a bounce on her back. The Lady stayed on until the last moment, then jumped clear—and back on when Neysa scrambled to her feet.

Hulk was gaping. "What sort of animal is that? Those tricks are impossible!"

There was a chord-snort next to Stile. He glanced—and discovered the Herd Stallion beside him, front hooves comfortably crossed on the wall, eyes intent on the competition. "Not bad moves," Clip translated from the far side.

Neysa whirled and leaped, spinning about in air. The Lady's slippers flew off and her gown flung out so violently it rent; a fragment of blue gauze drifted to the ground. But her hands were locked in the unicorn's mane, and she was not dislodged.

Neysa did a sudden barrel-roll on the ground. Again the Lady jumped free—but a tattered hem of her garment was caught under the weight of the unicorn, trapping her. As the roll continued, the Lady was squeezed by the tightening cloth. She ripped her own gown asunder and danced free, abruptly nude.

"That is some figure of a woman!" Hulk breathed.

Neysa started to rise. The Lady grabbed her mane—and Neysa threw down her head on the ground, pinning the Lady's streaming golden hair beneath it. The Lady grabbed for the unicorn's ears, and Neysa lifted her head quickly; human hands could really hurt tender equine ears when they had to. Stile had not gone for the ears during his challenge ride; it was not his way. The Lady knew the tricks, all right! But Neysa had the end of the Lady's tresses clamped between her teeth, now. The unicorn knew the tricks too. Human intelligence in equine form—devastating! As the Lady tried to mount again, Neysa yanked her off balance by the hair.

"Beautiful!" Clip murmured.

But the Lady grasped her own hair with one hand and jammed her other fingers into Neysa's mouth where the bit would go on a horse. There was a separation there between the front teeth, used for ripping grass free of the ground, and the back teeth, used for chewing. Pressure in that gap could cause pain. Neysa's mouth opened under that expert inducement, and the Lady's hair was free. Then, as Neysa leaped away, the Lady sprang to her back again.

Neysa ran—but now the Lady was free of the liability of clothing, and had a more secure lodging than before. "She's winning!" Hulk said, obviously rooting for the Lady, forgetting in the excitement what this would mean to Stile.

Stile began to wonder. Was it possible that the Lady Blue could ride Neysa? She was, next to himself, the most expert rider he had seen.

The Stallion made an irate snort. "What's the matter with that mare?" Clip said. "She should have wiped out the rider by this time."

"She is torn by indecision," Kurrelgyre said. "If Neysa loses, she proves the Lady's belief that Stile is false. If Neysa wins, she vindicates him as the Blue Adept she wants him not to be. Would I could take from her that choice."

Stile kept his eyes forward, but felt a shiver. The werewolf had his bitch in the pack, even as Stile had Sheen in Proton. But Kurrelgyre obviously had developed a separate interest that cut across the lines of species—even as Stile had. Yet who could know Neysa and not like her and respect her?

"Yes," Stile agreed. He saw no acceptable outcome for this contest; whoever lost took away a major part of his own commitment. Neysa was his friend; the Lady represented his heritage. Which one was he to choose? Which one was fate about to choose for him? To choose—and eliminate, simultaneously?

"In the future, I will manage my destiny myself," Stile muttered. And heard, to his surprise, a snort of agreement from the Stallion.

Neysa galloped so fast that her mane and the Lady's hair flew out behind, the black and gold almost merging. Shadow and sunlight. She made turns that struck sparks from the rocks on the ground. She bucked and reared. But the Lady remained mounted.

Now the unicorn charged the castle. She hurdled the small moat with a magnificent leap, landed on her forefeet, and did her forward flip into the wall. There were growls of amazement from the wolves, and even an appreciative snort from the Stallion. Neysa was really trying now—but the Lady had been smart enough to disengage in time. When the unicorn's hind feet returned to the ground, the Lady was on again.

They hurdled the moat, outward bound, and charged across the arena toward the magic brick wall. Now Stile saw the fire jetting from Neysa's nostrils and the bellows-heaving of her barrel as she put forth her critical effort. The Lady was almost hidden, as she rode low, her head down beside Neysa's neck.

Stile watched in growing disquiet as the unicorn's horn bore on the wall. Stile was directly in its path; he saw the horn endwise, as a compressed spiral on Neysa's forehead, coming at him like the point of a rotary drill. Her eyes were wide and turning bloodshot, and her flaring nostrils were rimmed with red. Neysa was near her limit—and still the Lady clung fast. Stile felt mixed relief for the Lady, sorrow for the unicorn, and apprehension for himself; he was at the focus of this agony.

Then Neysa swerved aside, kicking up her rear. Her flank smashed into the wall, knocking loose the top row of bricks and breaking the mortar-seal on several lower courses. She rebounded, getting her footing, breathing fire—and the Lady was clinging to her side, away from the wall. Otherwise the Lady's leg would have been crushed—and Stile himself might have been struck, as he had been too absorbed in the charge to move out of its way. Only the curvature of the wall and Neysa's swerve had spared him. Stile caught a glimpse of the Lady's neck, shoulder and breast behind one blood-streaked arm; then steed and rider were away, prancing to the center of the arena.

The Stallion shook a brick off his back. Neither he nor Kurrelgyre had flinched, either. All three of them were powdered with reddish brick dust. But some of that red was sticky: whose blood was it?

"They're playing for keeps," Hulk murmured, awed.

"It is the way, in Phaze," Kurrelgyre assured him.

But now Neysa was tiring. She had extended herself for a day and a night to bring Stile here, and the intervening day had not been enough to restore her to full vitality. Her maneuvers were becoming less extreme. Her brushoff pitch against the wall had been her last fling. The Lady's head lifted, her gaze triumphant—and at the same time her mouth was sad. Had she, in her secret heart, wanted Stile to be vindicated, though it cost her her life? What kind of existence did this indomitable woman face with her husband gone, and her vulnerability now known to the world? Had she lost, she would have been dead—but would have died with the knowledge that the Blue Demesnes would survive.

Then, desperately, without real hope, Neysa experimented with alternate gaits. The one-, two-, three-, and four-beat gaits gave the Lady no trouble—but evidently she had not before encountered the unicorn specialty of the five-beat. Immediately Neysa felt the uncertainty in her rider; she picked up the pace, exaggerating the peculiar step. Her strength returned, for this last fling.

"What is that?" Hulk asked, amazed.

The Stallion snorted with satisfaction. "That is the unicorn strut," Clip answered. "We use it mostly in special harmonies, for counterpoint cadence. We had no idea she could do it so well."

Suddenly the tables had been turned. The Lady clung to the mane, but her body bounced about with increasing roughness, unable to accommodate this unfamiliar motion. Stile knew exactly how it felt. Riding was not simply a matter of holding on; the rider had to make constant adjustments of balance and position, most of them automatic, based on ingrained experience. A completely unfamiliar gait made these automatic corrections only aggravate the problem. Stile himself had analyzed the gait in time, but the Lady—

One of the Lady Blue's hands tore away from the mane. Her body slid half off. One good lunge, now, and Neysa would dump her. "Kill her!" Clip breathed.

Abruptly Neysa halted. The Lady recovered her grip, hung on for a moment—then released the mane and slid to the ground. The ride was over.

"The little fool!" Clip exclaimed. "She had the win! Why didn't she finish it?" And the Stallion snorted in deep disgust.

"She has forfeited her place in the herd," Kurrelgyre said sadly. "In thy parlance, she threw the game."

Stile jumped off the wall and walked toward the unicorn and Lady, who both stood as if frozen, facing away from each other. As he walked, understanding came to him. Stile played his harmonica as he worked it out, gathering the magic to him.

Neysa, after the specter of defeat, had had the victory in range. But Neysa wanted Stile's welfare more than she wanted her own. She had finally, unwillingly, recognized the fact that he could fulfill his destiny only as the Blue Adept, complete with magic. Once she had proven that he alone could ride the unicorn, what could she gain by killing or even humbling the Lady—who was his natural mate? Neysa had ceded him to the Lady, so that he could have it all, knowing himself and his Demesnes exactly as the Oracle had decreed. She had understood that he was already half-smitten with his alternate's wife, and understood further that the Lady Blue was indeed worthy of him.

Neysa had sacrificed her own love for Stile's. She had shown the one person she had to, the Lady Blue, that Stile was no impostor; wolves and unicorns could doubt it if they wished, but the Lady could not. For Stile had mastered the unicorn strut without being thrown; he really *was* the better rider. That was Neysa's gift to Stile. And he—had to accept it. Neysa was his ultimate steed, but the Lady was his ultimate woman. He hardly knew her yet, but he knew his other self would have chosen wisely, and everything he had observed so far confirmed this. He also knew his alternate self of Phaze would have wanted Stile to take over—for the Blue Adept was him, in other guise.

The Lady Blue, however, was not yet his woman. Stile had merely qualified for the Tourney, in this sense, and had won the right to court her. He would have to prove himself in other ways than magical and in riding ability, showing that he was worthy of her love. He would have to demonstrate convincingly to her that he was as good as her husband had been. Perhaps he would not succeed, for she was so steadfastly loyal to her first love that a second love might be impossible. But in the interim, he knew she would accept him as the master of the Blue Demesnes, and support him publicly as she had the golem—for the sake of the reputation and works of Blue. That was all he had a right to expect. It was, for the moment, more than enough.

It was Neysa he had to deal with. She who had made it all possible—and now would go, excluded from the herd, departing in shame to fling herself off the same cliff where they had first come to terms. She had lived always with the hope that eventually the Herd Stallion would relent and allow her full membership in the herd. He would have, had she destroyed the Lady in approved fashion. But for a creature who yielded a draw in a contest she could have won, shaming the vanity of the herd, there would be no forgiveness. The rigors of species pride were harsh.

Stile had, in the naïveté of his conscience, turned Neysa loose when he had conquered her, making a sacrifice no other man would have—and won a better friend than he had known. Now she had returned the favor.

Stile's head turned as he walked, his gaze passing over the unicorns and werewolves. All were somber, watching him, knowing what had to be, knowing this was his parting with his most loyal friend. They felt sympathy for him, and for the mare, and it was a minor tragedy, but this was the way of it—in Phaze.

Damn it! he thought. He was not truly of this world, and this proved it. He had been raised to a different order of integrity, where blood sacrifices were not required. How could he tolerate this senseless loss? Yet he knew it was not senseless, here. The laws of this society were harsh but valid.

The magic gathered close as he played. The strange cloud of it spread about him—and, as he approached, about the Lady and the unicorn. But what good was magic, in an ethical dilemma? What spell could he make, to eliminate the need for what he knew had to be?

Stile came to stand before Neysa, playing the music that had been inspired by the sound of her horn. Her body was heaving with the recent extremity of her effort. Her mane was disheveled, with dry leaves in it and several strands hanging over the left side. There were flecks of blood on her back; she must have scratched herself when she did the back-smash against the castle wall. He wished he could make a little spell to heal it for her, but knew this was not proper now. Her gaze met his, dully; she was waiting only for him to bid her farewell.

Fare*well*? What irony! It was death he would bid her.

This reminded Stile obscurely of his race in the marathon, in the other frame. He had been almost dead on his feet, as Neysa was now, but he had won—as she had—and then tried to give it back to an opponent he respected. Again, he had made a friend. Surely he could salvage his relationship with Neysa, if only he had the wit to find the way!

What had the werewolf said about oaths? They superseded all relationships, conflicting with none, not even the male-female ones. Kurrelgyre's oath-friend could do no wrong by Kurrelgyre's bitch; the oath made that irrelevant.

The marathon. The oath. What had passed through his mind, when . . . ?

And he had it.

Stile set the harmonica aside. With the magic intense about him, he sang with impromptu melody: "My name is Stile, called the Blue Adept; Standing before thee I proffer mine oath: To the unicorn Neysa, companion and steed—Friendship forever, uniting us both."

For an instant it was as if a dense cloud had darkened the sun. A sudden, odd, insweeping breeze rustled the distant trees and fluttered the blue pennants on the castle and stirred the manes and hackles of the animals. Neysa's eyes widened. Her ears switched back and forth as comprehension came. She phased into girl-form, equine-form, firefly-form and back to unicorn, entirely nonplused.

The ripple of enchantment imploded about the two of them in soft heat, then rebounded outward in a circle. The turf changed color, passing through the hues of the rainbow and back to normal in a swiftly expanding ring. The ripple intersected the naked Lady, whose tangled hair scintillated momentarily, and went on, leaving that hair smoothly brushed.

The Lady turned. "Only perfect truth makes such splash," she murmured. "Only my lord had such power of magic."

Stile spread his arms. Neysa, overwhelmed, stepped forward, her horn lifted clear. Stile reached around her neck and chest and hugged her. "Never leave me, oath-friend," he murmured. He heard her low whinny of assent, and felt her velvet nuzzle at his shoulder. Then he disengaged and stepped back.

The Lady Blue came forward. She put her arms about Neysa. "Never again be there strife between us," she said, tears in her eyes. Neysa made a tiny snort of acceptance.

Now the wolves and unicorns came in, forming a ragged line, heedless of the mixing of species. In turn, each wolf sniffed noses with Neysa and each unicorn crossed horns, and went on. All of them were joining in the Oath of Friendship. Even her brother Clip came, and Kurrelgyre, and Hulk. Neysa accepted them all.

It was, Stile knew, the power of his spell. When he had phrased his oath in verse and music, he had performed magic—and wrought a greater enchantment than he had anticipated. The spell he had envisioned, though not completed in words, had flung outward to embrace the entire circle of creatures, compelling them all to share Stile's feeling. Neysa would not now be banned from the herd—or from the pack. She was friend to all. But she would remain with Stile, having accepted his power with his oath.

Only the Herd Stallion stood apart. He alone had resisted the compulsion of the enchantment. He did not interfere; he waited within his enclosure until the ceremony was over. Then he blew a great summoning blast of music and leaped over the wall. It had never truly restrained him; it had merely been the proof of the power of the Blue Adept, which power could as readily have been turned to a more destructive manifestation. Once the Herd Stallion had seen Stile was no impostor, his objection had ended. Now the unicorns rallied to him, galloping to form their formation. Playing as a mighty orchestra, they marched away.

Kurrelgyre shifted to wolf-form and bayed his own summons. His faith had also been vindicated, and his bitch had been satisfied. The wolves closed in about him, and the pack loped away in the opposite direction. In a moment only Stile, Neysa, the Lady Blue and Hulk remained by the Blue Demesnes.

Stile turned to the woman he would now be dealing with. Nothing was settled, either with her or with his anonymous murderer, or in the other frame. But it was a beginning. "Lady, wilt thou ride my steed?" he asked. There was no need to ask Neysa; as a friend she would do anything for him, and he for her. By the phrasing of his invitation, he was acknowledging that he had as yet only a partial claim on the Lady, and could not take her for granted. She was a challenge, not a friend.

The Lady Blue inclined her head, as regal in her nakedness as she had been in the gown. Lightly she mounted Neysa. Stile walked on one side, Hulk on the other. Together they approached the open castle.

BLUE ADEPT

CONTENTS

CHAPTER I

Unicorn

A lone unicorn galloped across the field toward the Blue Castle. It was a male, with a glossy dark blue coat and red socks on his hind feet and a handsomely spiraled horn. As he moved he played a melody through that hollow horn, sounding like a mellow saxophone. The notes floated across the field ahead of him.

Stile walked to a parapet and looked down. He was an extremely small but fit man, a former jockey who remained in shape. He was dressed in a blue shirt and blue jeans, though there were those who felt that neither became his station. His station was such, however, that he could ignore it with impunity—to a degree.

"Clip!" he exclaimed, recognizing the visitor. "Hey, Neysa—your brother's here!"

But Neysa already knew it. Her hearing was better than his. She trotted out of the castle and met Clip at the front gate, crossing horns briefly in greeting. Then the two went into their more extended ritual of reunion, prancing out side by side in unison as they played a duet. Neysa's horn had the sound of a harmonica, and it blended beautifully with the music of the saxophone.

Stile watched and listened, entranced, and not by magic. He had always been fond of horses, and he liked unicorns even better. He was of course biased; Neysa was his best friend in this frame. Still—

The two equines intensified the beat, their hooves striking the turf precisely. Now they went into the syncopation of the five-beat gait, the Unicorn Strut, their music matching it. Stile, unable to resist, brought out his good harmonica and matched the tune, tapping the beat with his heel as well as he could. He had a natural flair for music, and had sharpened his skill recently because it related so intimately to his magic. When he played, intangible magic formed around him. But he refused to let that inhibit him; the magic only became tangible when he invoked it in his special fashion.

When the unicorns finished their dance of delight, they trotted back to the castle. As they approached the gate they shifted to human-form, becoming a handsome young man and an elfishly small but also quite pretty woman. Stile hurried down to meet them in the courtyard.

"A greeting, Adept, and a message from the Herd Stallion," Clip said. He was holding hands with his sister, somewhat to her mute embarrassment; he was more expressive than she. Both wore the garb of archaic Earth as interpreted by nonhuman viewpoint, more or less matching their natural equine colors.

"Thy greeting is welcome, Clip," Stile said. "And thy message too, be it in peace."

"It is, Adept. The Stallion is pleased to summon Neysa the Mare this season to be bred." He paused, then appended his own remark: "At long last."

"That's great!" Stile exclaimed. "After three seasons denied, she will finally get her foal!"

Then he saw that Neysa was not reacting with the delight expected. Stile looked at her with concern. "Dost this not please thee, oath-friend? I thought it was thy fondest ambition to—"

Clip, too, was glancing at her with perplexity. "Sibling, methought I bore great tiding."

Neysa averted her gaze. She was a well-formed girl an inch or so shorter than Stile—a stature that appealed to him though he knew this was foolish. She was the smallest of mares, barely fourteen hands; any shorter and she would have been classified as a pony: a member of the equine Little Folk. Her human-form merely reflected this, with only the tiny button-horn in her forehead signifying her true nature.

Stile had long since learned to live with the fact that most women and all men were taller than he, and of course Neysa was not human at all. That did not prevent her from being his closest companion in ways both human and equine. Though she could speak, she was not much on verbal communication. Vivacity was not her way, though she had a certain filly humor that manifested subtly on occasion.

Clip and Stile exchanged glances. What did this mean? "Would a female know?" Clip asked.

Stile nodded. "One would." He raised his voice only slightly. "Lady."

In a moment the Lady Blue appeared. She was, as always, garbed in variants of blue: blue corduroy skirt, pale blue blouse, dark blue slippers and star-blue tiara. And, as always, her beauty struck Stile with special force. "Master," she murmured.

Stile wished she wouldn't do that. In no way was he her master, and she knew that well. But he was unable to take effective issue with the conventions of this frame—or with the half-subtle reminders she gave him. She considered him to be an imposter in the Blue Demesnes, a necessary evil. She had cause.

"Lady," he said, maintaining the formality she required of him. "Our friend Neysa is summoned to be bred by the Herd Stallion, and have her foal at last—yet she seems not pleased. Canst thou fathom this, and wilt thou enlighten us males?"

The Lady Blue went to Neysa and embraced her. No aloofness in this acquaintance! "Friend of mine oath, grant me leave to explain to my lord," the Lady said to Neysa, and the unicorn-girl nodded.

The Lady faced Stile. "It be a private matter," she said, and walked sedately from the court.

She hadn't even asked; she had known intuitively! "I'll be back," Stile said, and quickly followed.

When they were alone, they dropped the pretenses. "What's the mystery?" Stile snapped. "She's my best friend—a better friend than thou. Why won't she tell me?"

"Thy magic is strong," the Lady replied. "Thy comprehension weak. Left to thine own devices, thou wilt surely come to grief."

"Agreed," Stile said easily, though he was not pleased. "Fortunately I have Hulk and Neysa and thee to look after me. Soon will I eliminate the major threat to my tenure as Adept, and will stand no longer in need of such supervision."

What irony there was rolled off her without visible effect. The fairness and softness of her appearance concealed the implacable skill with which she fought to preserve the works of her late husband. There was nothing soft about her dedication to his memory. "Be that as it may—the mare feels un-free to leave thee at this time. Hulk may depart and I am not committed to thee as Neysa is. Therefore she prefers to postpone breeding until thou'rt secure."

"But this is senseless!" he protested. "She must not sacrifice her own welfare for mine! I can offer her only hardship and danger."

"Aye," the Lady agreed.

"Then thou must talk to her. Make her go to the Stallion."

"Who is as masculinely logical as thee," the Lady said. "With every bit as much comprehension of her concern. Nay, I shall not betray her thus."

Stile grimaced. "Didst thou treat thy husband likewise?"

Now she colored. "Aye."

Stile was immediately sorry. "Lady, I apologize. Well I know thou didst love him alone."

"Not enough, it seems, to save his life. Perhaps had he had a unicorn to guard him—"

There it was, that needle-sharp acuity. "I yield the point. There is no guardian like Neysa. What must I do to oblige her?"

"Thou must arrange postponement of the breeding, until she feels free to leave thee."

Stile nodded. "That should be feasible. I thank thee, Lady, for thine insight."

"What thou askest for, thou hast," she said coolly. "Thou art now the Blue Adept, the leading magician of the realm. Only have the human wit not to offend the mare in the presentation of thy decision."

"And how do I find the wit not to offend *thee,* bride of my defunct self? Thou knowest his tastes are mine."

She left him, not deigning to answer. Stile shrugged and returned to the courtyard. He wanted the Lady Blue more than anything he could imagine, and she was aware of this. But he had to win her the right way. He had the power to convert her by magic, but he would not use it; she knew this too. She understood him in certain ways better than he understood himself, for she had experienced the love of his other self. She could handle him, and she did so.

Clip and Neysa had reverted to unicorn-form and were grazing on the patch of rich bluegrass maintained beside the fountain for that purpose. The two were a beautifully matched set, his blue against her black, his red socks complementing her white ones. Clip was a true unicorn in coloration; Neysa had been excluded from the herd for some years because her color resembled that of a horse. Stile still got angry when he thought about that.

Neysa looked up as he approached, black ears perking forward, a stem of grass dangling from her mouth. As with most equines, her chewing stopped when her attention was distracted.

"I regret the necessity," Stile said briskly. "But I must after all interfere with Neysa's opportunity. The Blue Adept has, as we know, an anonymous enemy, probably another Adept, who has murdered him once and seeks to do so again. I have no second life to spare. Until I deal with this enemy, I do not feel secure without completely competent protection and guidance. No one can do that as well as the mare. Therefore I must seek a postponement of the Stallion's imperative until this crisis abates. I realize this works a hardship on Neysa, and is selfish of me—"

Neysa snorted musically, pleased, and not for a moment deceived. She resumed chewing her mouthful. Clip angled his horn at her in askance, but saw that she was satisfied, so kept silent.

One problem had been exchanged for another, however. It was not any mare's prerogative to gainsay the Herd Stallion. Stile would have to do that himself, as the Blue Adept. In the informal but rigorous hierarchy of this world, herd-leaders, pack-leaders, tribe-leaders and Adepts were roughly equivalent, though the ultimate power lay with the Adepts. Stile would deal with the Herd Stallion as an equal.

First he had to settle things at the Blue Demesnes. Stile talked with his human bodyguard from the other frame, Hulk. Hulk was as big as Stile was small: a towering mass of muscle, expert in all manner of physical combat but not, despite the assumption of strangers, stupid.

"It is necessary that I leave this castle for a day or so," Stile told him. "I must negotiate with the unicorn Herd Stallion, and I cannot summon him here."

"That's for sure," Hulk agreed. "He never did have much of a liking for you. Uh, for thee. I'd better go with thee. That unicorn is one tough character."

"Nay, friend. I am in no danger from the unicorns. It is the Lady Blue I worry about. I wish thee to guard her in mine absence, lest my nameless enemy strike at me through her. Thou hast not magic— at least, thou hast not practiced it; but if no others know I am gone there should be no hostile spells. Against else, thy skills suffice as well as mine."

Hulk made a gesture of acquiescence. "She is surely worth guarding."

"Yes. She maintained the Blue Demesnes after her lord, mine alternate self, was murdered. Without her help I could not fill this office of Adept. I have the power of magic, but lack experience. I am reminded daily of this." Stile smiled wryly, remembering how the Lady Blue had just set him straight about Neysa. "And—"

"And she is an extraordinarily attractive woman," Hulk finished. "A magnet for mischief."

"Mine alternate self had excellent taste."

"That's one thing I don't quite understand yet. If only a person whose double in the other frame is dead can cross the curtain that separates one frame from the other, what about me? Do *I* have an alternate self here who died?"

Stile considered. "Thy tenure in the other frame of Proton was for twenty years. Was thy family there before thee?"

"No. I came at age fifteen for my enlistment. My time would have been up in a few more months. My family never set foot on Planet Proton. They live fifteen light years away."

"So thy existence on this planet stems only from thy tenure as a serf," Stile concluded. "Thou hast no natural existence in this other frame of Phaze. There is no alternate self to fill thy place in the alternate scheme. So thou art free to cross the curtain."

"So I was not murdered," Hulk concluded. "That's a relief."

Stile smiled. "Who could murder thee? Thou couldst pulp any normal man with the grip of one hand."

"Except thee, when we played the Game."

"The fortunes of chance," Stile said. "How could I match thee, in fair combat?"

Hulk laughed good-naturedly. "Tease me not, little giant. Thy stature is as mine, in martial arts."

"In mine own weight-class," Stile qualified. It was good to talk with someone who understood Stile's home-world and the Game.

They started off within the hour. Stile played his harmonica, accumulating his magic, then sang one of the spells he had worked out: "By the power of magic vested in me, make me blank so none can see." He was unable to heal himself or cure himself of illness, but he could change his aspect before other people. He held up his hand, then waved it before his face: nothing. He was invisible.

Neysa, of course, knew him by smell and sound. She was not spooked. "This way," he explained, "it will not be obvious that I am departing."

"A watcher could see that the mare carries a burden," the Lady pointed out.

"That's right," Stile agreed, surprised. He considered a moment, then sang: "By the power of magic vested in me, make me as light as I can be." He felt the weight of his body dissipate. "Excellent."

Both Hulk and the Lady looked perplexed. Stile laughed. "I shall answer thy questions in turn. Lady, thou knowest by my voice that I remain standing on the floor; how is it that I do not float to the ceiling? Because my spell is very similar to the last, and since no spell may be used twice in succession, much of its force was abated. I am not as light as I can be; my weight is perhaps a fifth normal. About twenty pounds, or a trifle more. Hulk, how is it that I do not glow like the sun, since that is also a meaning of the term I used, 'light'? Because my words only vocalize what is in my mind, and my mind provided the definition of my terms. Had I wished to light brightly, despite already being invisible, I could have used the same spell, shifting only my mental intent, and it would have worked that way."

"Methinks Stile likes magic," Hulk muttered. "Personally, I do not believe in it."

"Else mightest thou be Adept too," Stile said, laughing to show the humor, though he suspected there was some truth in it. Every person could do some magic, but few could do strong magic. Stile's own magic talent was reflected in the science frame of Proton as considerable ability in other things, such as the Game, and Hulk was almost as capable there. Hulk might be able to learn to be a magician, if he ever cared to try. Perhaps there were many others who could be similarly competent at magic, if they only believed they could and worked to perfect their techniques. But only one person in perhaps a thousand believed, so there were very few Adepts. Of course, the established Adepts ruthlessly eliminated any developing rivals, so it was safer to opt out of that arena entirely. The enmity of an Adept was a terrible thing.

Stile bid his final farewells, mounted Neysa, needing no saddle or bridle, and they joined Clip. The two unicorns trotted briskly out the gate. To an observer it would seem Clip was conducting his sibling to the breeding site, as required. The little bit of weight Neysa carried hardly made a difference.

It was good to travel with his unicorn again. Stile was not sure whether he could transport himself magically from place to place. If that came under the heading of changing his aspect before others, then probably he could; if instead it came under the heading of healing or changing himself, then he probably could not. So far he had deemed it expedient not to experiment; magic gone wrong could be fatal. So he needed transportation, and Neysa was the best he could ask for. She had been his first steed in this magic frame, and his first true friend. His love of horses had translated instantly to unicorns, for these creatures were horse-*plus*: plus a musical horn that was also a devastating weapon; plus special gaits and acrobatic abilities beyond the imagination of any horse; plus human intelligence; plus the ability to change shape. Yes, the unicorn was the creature Stile had been searching for all his life without realizing it until he met one.

Neysa, in girl-form, had become his lover, before he had met the Lady Blue and realized that his ultimate destiny had to lie with his own kind. There had been some trouble between Neysa and the Lady Blue at first; but now as oath-friend to the Blue Adept, the unicorn needed no further reassurance. In this magic frame, friendship transcended mere male-female relations, and an oath of friendship was the most binding commitment of all.

It was ironic that now that Neysa could achieve her fondest wish—to have her own foal—that oath of friendship interfered. Neysa's logic was probably correct; Stile did need her to protect him from the pitfalls of this barely familiar world until he could deal with his secret enemy. Unicorns were immune to most magic; only Adept-class spells could pass their threshold. Stile had reason to believe his enemy was an Adept; his own Adept magic, buttressed by the protective ambience of the unicorn, should safeguard him against even that level. As the Lady Blue had pointed out, the original Blue Adept had not had a unicorn to guard him, and that might have made the difference. He really did need Neysa.

They moved into a canter, then a full gallop as the two unicorns warmed up. Clip and Neysa ran in perfect step, playing their horns. She took the soprano theme on her harmonica, he the alto on his saxophone. It was another lovely duet, in counterpoint, augmented by the strong cadence of their hooves. Stile wished he could join in, but he had to preserve his anonymity, just in case they were being observed. There were baleful things lurking in these peaceful forests and glades; the unicorns' familiarity with the terrain and reputation as fighters made the landscape become as peaceful as it seemed. But there was no sense setting up the Blue Adept as a lure for trouble.

Clip knew the way. The unicorn herd grazed wherever the Herd Stallion decreed, moving from pasture to pasture within broad territorial limits. Other herds grazed other territories; none of them intruded on these local demesnes. Human beings might think of this as the region of the Blue Adept, but animals thought of it as the region of this particular herd. Werewolves and goblins and other creatures also occupied their niches, each species believing itself to be the dominant force.

Stile made it a point to get along as well as he could with all creatures; such détente was much more important here in the frame of Phaze than it was in any nonmagical frame. And he genuinely respected those other creatures. The werewolves, for example, had helped him to discover his own place here, and the entire local pack was oath-friends with Neysa.

They galloped west across the terrain where Stile had first encountered Neysa; it was a spot of special significance for them both. He reached around her neck to give her an invisible hug, and she responded by twitching ear back and rippling her skin under his hands as though shaking off a fly. Secret communication, inexpressibly precious.

To the south was the great Purple Mountain range; to the north the White Mountain range. There was surely a great deal more to Phaze than this broad valley, but Stile had not yet had occasion to see it. Once he had dealt with his enemy and secured his position, he intended to do some wider explorations. Who could guess what wonders might lie beyond these horizons?

They moved west for two hours, covering twenty miles. This frame used the archaic, magic-ridden units of measurement, and Stile was still schooling himself in them. Twenty miles was roughly thirty-two kilometers in his more familiar terms. Stile could have covered a similar distance in similar time himself, for he was among other things a runner of marathons. But for him it would have meant a great effort, depleting his resources for days; for these animals it was merely pleasant light exercise. Unicorns could travel twice this speed, sustained, when they had to, and faster yet for shorter distances.

Now the sun was descending, getting in their eyes. It was time to graze. Unicorns, like horses, were not simple running machines; they had to spend a good deal of their time eating. Stile could have conjured grain for them, but actually they preferred to find their own, being stubbornly independent beasts, and they rested while grazing. Neysa slowed, found a patch of bare rock, and relieved herself in the equine manner at its fringe. This covered any sound Stile might make as he dismounted. Then she wandered on, grazing the rich grass, ignoring him though she knew exactly where he was. She was very good at this sort of thing; no observer would realize that an invisible man was with her, and the rock concealed any footprints he made.

Stile had brought his own supplies, of course; the Lady Blue had efficiently seen to that. No sense requiring him to make himself obvious by performing unnecessary magic to fetch food, apart from the general caution against wasting one-shot spells. He would sit on the rock and eat, quietly.

Stile levered himself down, careful not to put strain on his knees. Knees, as he had learned the hard way, did not readily heal. Magic might repair them, but he could not operate on himself and did not as yet trust the task to any other Adept. Suppose the Adept he asked happened to be the one who wanted to kill him? He could get along; his knees only hurt when flexed almost double. He could still walk, run and ride comfortably. His former abilities as an acrobat had suffered, but there was still a great deal he could do without flexing his knees that far.

After grazing, Neysa came to the edge of the rock and stood snoozing. Stile mounted her, as she had intended, and slept on her back. She was warm and safe and smelled pleasantly equine, and there was hardly a place he would have preferred to sleep—unless it were in the arms of the Lady Blue. That, however, was a privilege he had not yet earned, and might never earn. The Lady was true to her real husband, Stile's double, though he was dead, and in no way did she ever mistake Stile for that other man.

Next morning they were off again. They cantered gently until noon, when they spied the herd. It was grazing on a broad slope leading down to an extensive swamp. Beyond that swamp, Stile remembered, lay the palace of the Oracle, who answered one and only one question for any person, in that person's life. The Oracle had advised Stile to "Know thyself"—and despite the seeming unhelpfulness of it, that had indeed been the key to his future. For that self he had come to know was the Blue Adept.

A lookout unicorn blew a trumpet blast, and the members of the herd lifted their heads, then trotted together to form a large semicircle open toward the two approaching unicorns. Perceiving that formidable array of horns, Stile was glad he was not approaching as an enemy. Neysa had drilled him in the use of his rapier by fencing with her horn, and he had come to appreciate what a deadly weapon it could be. This was another respect in which unicorns were fundamentally different from horses: they were armed—more properly, horned—and were as likely to attack as to flee. No sensible tiger, for example, would attempt to pounce on a unicorn.

They trotted into the open cup of the semicircle. The Herd Stallion stood in the center, a magnificent specimen of equine evolution. His body was pearly gray deepening into black legs, his mane and tail were silver, and his head golden. He stood some eighteen hands tall, and was splendidly muscled. His horn was a glinting, spiral marvel: truly a shaft to be reckoned with. He played a melodic accordion chord on it, and the circle closed in behind the new arrivals.

Stile felt his weight increasing. He saw his arms before him. His spells of lightness and invisibility were abating, though he had not terminated them.

The Stallion snorted. Clip and Neysa hastily spun about and retreated to the rim. Stile sprang to the ground before the Stallion. Stile was now fully solid and visible.

The Stallion shifted to man-form. He was huge and muscular, though not to Hulk's extent. He had a short horn in his forehead. "Welcome to the Herd Demesnes, O Blue Adept," he said. "To what do I owe the dubious pleasure of this encounter?"

So the closing of the unicorn circle nullified even the spells of an Adept! Stile's magic could prevail over a single unicorn, but not over the full herd—except in special cases. Of course his two spells were now a day old and must have weakened with time and use, since no spell was eternal. Still, the effect was worth noting. Stile was not in danger from hostile magic here, because the unicorn ring would also nullify the spells of any enemy Adept. He retained the basic privacy of his mission. "A greeting, Stallion. I come to negotiate."

The man-Stallion put three fingers to his mouth and blew another chord that still sounded like an accordion. Two unicorns trotted in, supporting a structure on their horns. They set it down and retreated. It was a table fashioned of old unicorn horns, with attached seats. It was surely far more valuable than ivory, for much of the magic of unicorns was associated with their horns.

The Stallion sat, gesturing Stile to do the same. "What has an Adept to negotiate with a simple animal like me?"

Stile realized this was not going to be easy. The Herd Stallion was not partial to him, since Stile had embarrassed the creature in the course of their first encounter. He would have to explain carefully. "Thou knowest I was murdered not long ago."

"Thou hast no need to negotiate for recognition of thy status or right to thy Demesnes," the Stallion said, surprised. "We honor the way that is. Only this herd and Kurrelgyre's werewolf pack know thou art not the original Adept. We accept thee in lieu, since thy magic is equivalent and thou'rt a being of integrity, as are we. No news of thy condition has escaped the herd."

Stile smiled. "It is not that, Sire. I have not made a secret of my status. It is that I must secure my position and avenge my murder."

"Indubitably."

"I believe it is an enemy Adept I seek. Therefore I must approach the matter cautiously, and trust myself only to my most reliable companion. That, of course, is mine oath-friend Neysa. Therefore—"

"Now I chew on thy gist. A gravid mare would not be fit for such excursion."

"Exactly. I therefore seek a postponement of her breeding, until my mission is done."

The Stallion frowned. "She has missed two seasons—"

"Because she was excluded from the herd—because of her color," Stile said grimly. "Her color has not changed."

"Ah, but her status has! She has connections she lacked before. The animals of my herd have taken a fancy to her, and the wolves of the pack we oft have fought no longer attack, because of her. In all the herds of all the valleys of Phaze, none save her is steed to an Adept."

"Steed and friend," Stile said. "A friendship well earned."

"Perhaps. In any event, that makes up for her deficiency of—"

"Deficiency?" Stile demanded ominously, reaching for his harmonica. He had intended to keep this civil, but this was a sore point.

The Stallion considered. They were within the unicorn circle, but it had not been proven whether that would stop a newly fashioned spell performed in the heat of the Blue Adept's ire. No creature insulted an Adept, or anything dear to an Adept, carelessly. The Stallion retreated half a step, figuratively. "Shall we say, her color pleases me now, and what pleases me shall not be cause for comment by any other unicorn."

"An excellent statement," Stile agreed, putting away his instrument. He had discovered that one unicorn seldom objected to praise or defense of another. It would be beneath the Herd Stallion's dignity to stud an inferior mare. "Her presence at my side pleases me now," Stile continued. "Who in thy herd can travel the flying league faster than she?"

The Stallion raised his human eyebrow in an elegant gold arch. "Who besides me, thou meanest?"

Now Stile had to back off diplomatically. "Of course. I meant among mares—"

"I concede that for her size—"

"Is aught amiss with her size?" This was another power-ploy, for Neysa was no smaller among unicorns than Stile was among men.

"It is a serviceable size. I am certain she will bear a fine foal."

They were sparring, getting nowhere. The Stallion still intended to breed Neysa.

"I think thou didst not entirely withstand the oath of friendship," Stile remarked. "The mare is more attractive to thee than she was before."

The Stallion shrugged. It had been Stile's potent spell that caused the other unicorns and the werewolves to swear friendship with Neysa, and the Stallion did not like to admit to being similarly affected. Yet he was proof against such gibes. "Perhaps. But here thy power may yield to mine, even as mine paled before thine in thy Demesnes."

Stile had set the unicorn back, during that prior encounter. Now the Stallion was having his satisfaction. One offended a creature of power at one's own risk, even if one had the power of an Adept. "I need Neysa, this season. How may I obtain postponement of the breeding?"

"This is a matter of honor and pride. Thou must contest with me in mine own manner, weapon to weapon. An thou dost best me in fair combat, thou winnest thy plea. An thou dost fail—"

Stile had a notion how savage such an encounter could be. "If?" he prompted.

The Stallion smiled. "An thou dost fail, I win mine. We contest not for life here, but only for the proper priority of our claims. I claim the right to breed my mares as I see fit and in mine own time; thou claimest the bond of friendship to this mare. It ill behooves us two to strive against each other on any except a civil basis."

"Agreed." Stile certainly had no need of a life and death combat here! He had hoped a simple request would suffice, but evidently he had been naive. "Shall we proceed to it now?"

The Stallion affected amazement. "By no means, Adept! I would not have it bruited about that I forced my suit against one who was ill-prepared. Protocol requires that a suitable interval elapse. Shall we say a fortnight hence, at the Unolympics?"

"The Unolympics?"

"The annual sportive event of our kind, parallel to the Canolympics of the werewolves, the Vampolympics of the batmen, the Gnomolympics of—"

"Ah, I see. Is Neysa to compete therein?"

The Stallion evidently hadn't considered that. "She has not before, for reasons we need not discuss. This year I believe she would be welcome."

"And no apology to be made for any nuance of color or size that any less discriminating creatures might note?"

"None, of course."

Stile did not like the delay, but also knew he had no serious chance against the Stallion, who looked to weigh a full ton, was in vibrant health, and had quite a number of victory notches on his horn. The creature was in fact providing him time to reconsider, so that Stile could change his mind and yield the issue without suffering humiliation in the field. It was a decent gesture, especially when coupled with the agreement to let Neysa enter the general competition if she wanted to. Stile knew she could perform the typical unicorn maneuvers as well as any in the herd, and this would give her the chance to prove it at last. She had suffered years of shame; now she could publicly vindicate herself. "A fortnight," he agreed.

The Stallion extended his hand, and Stile took it. His own hand was engulfed by the huge and calloused extremity with hooflike nails. Stile fought off his automatic resentment and feeling of inadequacy. He was *not* inadequate, and the Stallion was being honorable. It was a fair compromise.

The Stallion shifted back to his natural form. He blew another chord on his horn. The unicorn circle opened. Stile began to feel lighter. His body faded. His spells were returning, as the anti-magic power of the unicorns diffused. That also was worth noting: his spells had never ceased operating, they had merely been damped out temporarily.

Neysa stepped forward hesitantly. "The Stallion invites thee to participate in the Unolympics in two weeks," Stile told her as he mounted.

She was so surprised she almost shifted into girl-form, which would have been awkward for him at the moment. She blew a querying note, hardly daring to believe the news. But the Stallion made a chord of affirmation.

"And I will go there too, to meet the Stallion on the field of honor," Stile added, as though this were an afterthought.

This time she did change shape. Stile found himself riding the girl-form piggy-back, his legs around her tiny waist. Hastily he dismounted. "Nay—" she said.

"Neigh indeed! If I weren't invisible and featherlight, thou wouldst have been borne to the ground by my weight in most indelicate fashion. Get back to thy proper form, mare!"

Hastily she complied. He remounted, and she galloped away from the herd. It seemed that none of the unicorns had noticed anything— until one mocking saxophone peal of music sounded. Clip had been unable to hold back his mirth any longer.

Neysa fired back an angry concatenation of notes, then galloped harder. They fairly flew across the slope. Soon they were well away. "Just for that, thou shouldst make him participate in the Unolympics too," Stile suggested, and she snorted affirmatively.

But now his own problem came to the fore. "Maybe I can ask the Oracle how to handle the Stallion," Stile mused aloud. But that was no good; he had used up his single Oracular query before, in the process of discovering his Phaze identity.

"One other thing bothers me," Stile remarked after a bit, as they galloped across the lovely plain. "Why is the Herd Stallion being so polite about it? He could easily have insisted that I fight him today, and he surely would have won. He has no special brief for me, yet he treated me with extraordinary fairness."

Neysa veered to approach an island copse of oat trees. Safely inside the tangle of growth, she made a shrug that hinted he should dismount. When he did, she shifted to girl-form again. "It is thy spell," she said. "All the herd is oath-friend to me, and if he took me unfairly, humiliating thee, they would turn against him."

Stile struck his head with the heel of his unseen hand. "Of course! Even a king must consider how far his subjects can be pushed." So his magic had indeed affected the Stallion, albeit circuitously, by affecting those the Stallion had to deal with.

Neysa stood, not yet shifting back, looking at him expectantly though of course her eyes could not focus on him. Stile took her in his arms. "I believe these are more words than thou has spoken to me in thy life before," he said, and kissed her.

He turned her loose, but still she waited. He knew why, yet could not act. They had been lovers, and she remained, in girl-form, the nicest and prettiest girl he knew, and he was not turned off by the knowledge that she was in fact a unicorn. But their relationship had changed when he met the Lady Blue. He found himself not constitutionally geared to have more than one lover at a time in a given frame. The irony was that he did not have the Lady Blue as lover or anything else, though he wanted everything else. If companionship, loyalty, and yes, sex sufficed, Neysa was his resource.

And there it was. His aspirations had made a dimensional expansion. He was not certain that he could ever have all of what he wanted, yet he had to proceed as if it were possible. And he had to explain this to Neysa without hurting her feelings.

"What we had before was good," he said. "But now I must look forward to a female of mine own kind, just as thou must look forward to the breeding and foal that only a male of thine own kind can give thee. Our friendship endures, for it is greater than this; it has merely changed its nature. Had we any continuing sexual claim on each other, it would complicate my friendship to thy foal, when it comes, or thine to my baby, if ever it comes."

Neysa looked startled. It was almost as if her human ears perked forward. She had not thought of this aspect. To her, friendship had been merely a complete trusting and giving, uncomplicated by interacting relationships of others. Stile hoped she was able to understand and accept the new reality.

Then she leaned forward to kiss him again, locating him with uncanny accuracy—or was his spell weakening?—and as their lips touched, she shifted back to equine form. Stile found himself kissing the unicorn. He threw his arms about her neck and yanked at her lustrous black mane, laughing.

Then he mounted, hugged her again, and rode on. It was all right.

CHAPTER 2

Lady

Back at the Blue Demesnes, Stile uninvoked the spells, became visible and full-weight, and turned Neysa out to graze. Then he talked to Hulk and the Lady Blue.

"I must meet the Stallion in ritual battle a fortnight hence," Stile said. "At their Unolympic celebration. This is for honor, and for the use of Neysa this season—yet I know not how I can match him, and am bound to suffer humiliation."

"Which is what he wants," Hulk said wisely. "Not thy blood, but thy pride. He wants to take a thing of value from the Blue Adept, in public, not by theft or by technicality but by right."

The Lady's blue eyes flashed. In this frame, it was literal: a momentary glare of light came from them. She was no Adept, but she did have some magic of her own. Stile remained new enough to Phaze to be intrigued by such little effects. "No creature humiliates the Blue Adept!" she cried.

"I am not really he, as the Stallion knows," Stile reminded her unnecessarily.

"Thou hast the image and the power and the office," she said firmly. "It is not thy fault that thou'rt not truly he. For the sake of the Demesnes, thou canst not let the unicorn prevail in this manner."

The preservation of the Blue Demesnes was of course what this was all about, to her mind. Stile was merely the figurehead. "I am open to suggestions," he said mildly. "I would ask the Oracle how I might prevail, had I not expended my question in the course of achieving my present status."

"The Oracle," Hulk said. "It answers one question for any person?"

"Only one," Stile agreed.

"Then I could ask it!"

"Thou shouldst not waste thine only question on a concern not thine," Stile said. "Ask instead about thine own future here in Phaze. There may be an ideal situation awaiting thee, if thou dost but inquire as to its whereabouts."

"Nay, I want to do it," Hulk insisted. "Neysa is my friend too, and it was thou who showed me how to cross the curtain into this marvelous and not-to-be-believed world. The least I can do is help thee in this matter."

"Let him go," the Lady murmured.

Stile spread his hands. "If thou truly dost feel this way, go with my blessing, Hulk. I shall be in thy debt. I will arrange for thee a magic conveyance—"

"Nay, I can walk."

"Not that far, and return in time to be of much help. I need to know how to prepare as soon as possible. If I must master a special skill—"

"Okay," Hulk agreed. "But I'm not good at riding unicorns."

The Lady smiled, and there seemed to be a momentary glow in the room. "Only two I know of have ever ridden a unicorn, except at the unicorn's behest: my lord Stile and I. The Adept will summon for thee a traveling carpet—"

"Oh, no! Not one of those flying things! I'd be constantly afraid its magic would poop out right over a chasm or near a nest of dragons. I'm not the lightest of creatures, thou knowest. Can't we find a motorcycle or something?"

"A motorcycle?" the Lady asked blankly.

"A device of the other frame," Stile explained. "A kind of traveling wheel, rather like a low-flying carpet. It is an idea. Science is inoperative here, yet I might fashion a magic wagon."

They went about it, and in the end Hulk had his motorcycle: two wooden wheels, a steering stick, a seat, a windshield. No motor, no fuel, no controls, for it was motivated by magic. Hulk had only to give it key verbal commands and steer it. Both men were clinically interested in the construction, determining how far magic would go, and where the line between functional magic and nonfunctional science was drawn.

Hulk boarded the magic machine and rode away in a silent cloud of dust. A flock of grouse took off, startled by the apparition. "I just hope he follows the map and doesn't drive into a chasm or meet a monster," Stile said. "He might hurt the monster."

"Nay, Hulk is kind to creatures," the Lady said, overlooking the humor. "He is a gentle man, under all that muscle. A clever and honorable man."

"True. That is one reason I brought him here."

The Lady rose and turned about, her blue gown flinging out sedately. Every motion she made was elegant! "Now we are alone, I would talk to thee, Adept."

Stile tried to still his suddenly racing pulse. She could not mean she had had a change of heart about him; he remained an imposter in her eyes. Her loyalty to her true love was a thing he envied and longed for. Should such loyalty ever be oriented on him . . . "Any time," he agreed.

They went to her apartment, where she bade him be seated in a comfortable blue chair. She maintained the blue insignia of these Demesnes with loving determination. It was a wonder, he thought with fond irritation, that she did not dye her fair hair blue. "Thy friend Hulk told me of thy life in Proton-frame," she said. "I bade him do it during thine absence, as it behooves me to know of thee."

Pumping Hulk for information: a natural pastime. "I would have told thee, hadst thou asked." But of course she had wanted to obtain a reasonably objective view. What was she leading up to?

"Now I know, from that third party, that thou art much the way my husband was. A man of great honor and skill, yet one who has suffered abuse because of size. Neysa, too, has told me of thy qualities."

"Neysa talks too much," Stile muttered. It was a joke; the unicorn was a marvel of brevity.

"Thou art a good man, and I wrong thee by mine aloofness. Yet must I am the way I am. I feel it only fair to acquaint thee with the way I was."

"I do not seek to force information from thee, Lady," Stile said quickly. But he really wanted to hear anything she wanted to tell him.

"Then it comes to thee unforced," she said, with a fleeting smile that melted his heart. Could she, could she really be starting to soften toward him? No, she was not; she was merely doing what she felt was right, giving him necessary background.

Stile listened to her narration, closing his eyes, absorbing her dulcet tones, picturing her story in full living color and feeling as it unfolded.

Long and long has our realm of Phaze endured apart from other worlds, from that time when first it separated from the science frame of mythology. Three hundred years, while our kind slowly spread across the continent and discovered the powers that existed. The animal kingdoms too expanded and warred with each other and found their niches, the dragons to the south, the snow demons to the north, the giants to the far west and so on. Soon the most talented among the Human Folk became adept at magic, restricting others from its practice except in specialized ways, so that no more than ten full magicians existed at any one time. Only talent distinguished them, not honor or personal merit, and any who aspired to Adept status but was less apt at sorcery than the masters were destroyed by the established magicians. Today the common folk eschew all save elementary enchantments, and associate not with Adepts; likewise the animals keep largely to themselves.

I grew up in a village of fifteen families to the east, near the coast, far removed from strong magic except the natural spells of the deep-woods. I thought I might marry a local boy, but my folks wanted me to wait, to meet a wider range before deciding. I realized not their reason, then; they knew me to be fair, and thought I might waste myself on some farmer's boy or fisherman if I chose quickly. Had they known whom I was destined to marry, they would have thrown me at the nearest pigherder! But they knew not that an Adept sought me, and we were well off, with good fields and animals, so that there seemed no need to go early into matrimony. My father is something of a healer, whether by nature or effort I know not, and I am too. We helped the ill or injured animals of the village, never making show of our talent, and never did the dire attention of a hostile Adept focus on us for that.

When I was nineteen the lads and lasses of mine age had already mostly been taken. But I loved the animals, and felt no loss. It has been said that the women most attractive to men are the ones who need them least, and so it seemed to be in my case. Then my horse's foal wandered too far afield, returning not to our stable. I called her Snowflake, for her color was white as snow though her spirit was hot as peppercorn. Ever was she wont to take that extra step, and this time she was lost. I rode out on my good mare Starshine, Snowflake's dam, searching, searching, but the prints we followed led into the deep-woods. Then I knew in my heart that Snowflake was truly in trouble, but I was nineteen and I loved that foal, and I went into that jungle though I knew it was folly.

And in that wood I came upon moss that shrouded whole trees and reached out for me, all green and hissing, and sand that sucked at my horse's feet, and there were shapes and shadows looming ever-near and nearer, and I was afraid.

Then did I know I must turn back, that Snowflake was doomed, and I would be in dire strait too an I not give over this hopeless task pres-ently. But still I adored my foal, as I adore all horses, and the thought of Snowflake alone and in straits in that wilderness tormented me, and I made pretexts one after another to quest beyond yet another tree or yet another looming rock. I thought I heard a tremulous neigh; gladly I dismounted and ran, but there was nothing, only a branch creaking in the rising wind.

A storm was coming, and that meant mischief, for in our region the trolls come out in foul weather, yet I dallied foolishly afoot. This time I was sure I heard a plaintive neigh. I pursued it, but again found naught; it was a will-o'-the-wisp.

Then the brooding sky let down and in a moment I was drenched with the chill spillage of the heavens. A crack of thunder spooked Starshine, and she bolted for home, forgetting me, nor could I blame her. I fled for home myself, shivering with more than cold, but the reaching brambles tore at my skirts and the gusts buffeted me so harshly I could not see. I cried out, hoping to be heard at home, but this was futile in the fury of this storm.

It was the trolls who harkened, and when I saw the grim apparitions I screamed with much-heightened force. But the gross monsters caught hold of me, all gape and callus, and I knew I was done for. I had not saved the life of my pet; I had sacrificed mine own.

A troll clutched me by the hair, dangling me above the ground. I was now too terrified to scream. I feared for death, assuredly; more I feared for that which would surely precede it, for the troll folk ever lust after human folk.

Then came the beat of hooves, approaching. Now did I manage to cry out again, faintly, hoping Starshine was returning, perhaps ridden by my father. And the beat came nigh, and it was no horse I knew, but a great blue stallion with mane of purple and hooves like blue steel, and on it a manchild in blue—

("The Blue Adept!" Stile exclaimed, interrupting her. The Lady nodded soberly, and resumed her narrative.)

I knew not who he was, then. I thought him a lad, or perhaps one of the Little Folk. I cried out to him, and he brandished a blue sword, and the trolls gibbered back into the shadows. The small youth came for me, and when the trolls saw what he sought, they let me go. I dropped to the ground, unhurt in body, and scrambled toward him.

The lad put down a hand to help me mount behind him, and I did, and then the blue stallion leapt with such power the trolls scattered in fear and I near slid off his rear, but that I clung desperately to my rescuer.

It seemed but a moment we were out of the wood, pounding toward our village homestead. The rain still fell; I shivered with chill and my dress clung chafingly to me, but the boy seemed not affected. He brought me to mine own yard and halted the stallion without ever inquiring the way. I slid down, all wet and relieved and girlishly grateful. "Young man," I addressed him, in my generosity granting him the benefit of a greater age than I perceived in him. "Thou'rt soaked. Pray come in to our warm hearth—"

But he shook his head politely in negation, speaking no word. He raised a little hand in parting, and suddenly was off into the storm. He had saved my honor and my life, yet dallied not for thanks.

I told my family of mine experience as I dried and warmed within our home before the merry fire. Of my foolish venture into the wood, the storm, the trolls, and of the boy on the great blue stallion who rescued me. I thought they would be pleased that I had been thus spared the consequence of my folly, but they were horrified. "That is a creature of magic!" my father cried, turning pale.

"Nay, he is but a boy, inches shorter than I," I protested. "Riding his father's charger, hearing my cry—"

"Did he speak thus?"

I admitted reluctantly that the blue lad had spoken naught, and that was no good sign. Yet in no way had the stranger hurt me or even threatened me; he had rescued me from certain horror. My parents quelled their doubts, glad now to have me safe.

But the foal was still missing. Next day I went out again to search—but this time my father went with me, carrying a stout cudgel. I called for Snowflake, but found her not. It was instead the blue lad who answered, riding across the field. I saw by sunlight that the horse was not truly blue; it was his harness that had provided the cast. Except perhaps for the mane, that shone iridescently. "What spook of evening goes abroad in the bright day?" I murmured gladly, teasing my father, for apparitions fear the sunlight.

My father hailed the youth. "Art thou the lad who rescued my daughter yesterday?"

"I am," the lad replied. And thereby dispelled another doubt, for few monsters are able to converse in the tongues of man.

"For that my deepest thanks," my father quoth, relieved. "Who art thou, and where is thy residence, that thou comest so conveniently at our need?"

"I was of the village of Bront, beyond the low midvalley hills," the lad replied.

"That village was overrun by trolls a decade past!" my father cried.

"Aye. I alone escaped, for that the monsters overlooked me when they ravaged. Now I ride alone, my good horse my home."

"But thou must have been but a baby then!" my father protested. "Trolls eat babies first—"

"I hid," the lad said, frowning. "I saw my family eaten, yet I lacked the courage to go out from my hiding place and battle the trolls. I was a coward. The memory is harsh, and best forgotten."

"Of course," my father said, embarrassed. "Yet no one would term it cowardice for a child to hide from ravaging trolls! Good it is to remember that nature herself had vengeance on that particular band of trolls, for that lightning struck the village and destroyed them all in fire."

"Aye," the lad murmured, his small face grim. "All save one troll cub." At that my father looked startled, but the lad continued: "Thou searchest for the lost foal? May I assist?"

My father thought to demur, but knew it would draw blame upon himself if he declined any available help, even in a hopeless quest. "If thou hast a notion. We know not where to begin."

"I am on tolerable terms with the wild equines," the lad said. "If the Lady were to ride with me to the herds and question those who may know . . ."

I was startled to hear myself defined as "Lady," for I was but a grown girl, and I saw my father was similarly surprised. But we realized that to a lad as small as this I might indeed seem mature.

"This is a kind offer," my father said dubiously. "Yet I would not send two young people on such a quest alone, and I lack the time myself—"

"Oh, please!" I pleaded, wheedling. "How could harm come on horseback?" I did not find it expedient to remind my father that I had gotten into trouble on horseback very recently, when I dismounted in the wood near the trolls. "We could range carefully—" Also, I wanted very much to see the wild horse herds, a thing seldom privileged to villagers.

"Thy mare is in mourning for her foal," my father said, finding another convenient objection. "Starshine is in no condition for such far riding. She knows not thy mission."

I clouded up in my most appealing manner. But before I spoke, the lad did. "I know the steed for her, sir. It is the Hinny. The mare of lightest foot and keenest perception in the wilds. She could sniff out the foal, if any could."

I clapped my hands in that girlish way I had. "Oh, yes!" I knew nothing about that horse except that a hinny was the sterile issue of stallion and jenny, most like a mule but prettier, yet already I was eager to ride her.

My father, more sensible than I, brooded. "A hinny, and wild. I trust this not. Such crossbreeds bear little good will to men."

"True," the blue lad said. He never contradicted my father directly. "But this is not any hinny. She is *the* Hinny. She can be bred, but only by my blue stallion. For that price she will be the best mount anyone could ask. She is fit and wise in the ways of the wilderness; no creature durst cross her, not even a troll or dragon. Like unto a unicorn she is, almost."

My father wavered, for he had a deep respect for good horses. To encourage his acquiescence, I threatened to cloud again. I had a certain talent at that, and my father had a certain weakness for it; oft had we played this little game. "Canst thou summon this hinny here?" he inquired, temporizing. "I would examine this animal."

The lad put fingers to his mouth and whistled piercingly. Immediately, it seemed, there was the sound of galloping, and an animal came. What a creature it was! She was shades of gray, lighter on the flanks and withers, darker at the extremities with a mane of both shades a good yard long that rippled languorously in the breeze. Her tail, too, was variegated gray, like carven onyx, and flowed like the waves of an ocean.

My father, prepared to be skeptical, gaped. "The speed of that horse!" he breathed. "The lines of her!"

"Thy daughter will be safe on her," the blue lad assured him. "What the Hinny cannot defeat she can outrun, except for the unicorns, who leave her alone. Once she accepts the commission, she will guard her rider with her life."

But my father was already lost. He stared at the Hinny, the most beautifully structured mare ever to be seen in our village. I knew he would have given his left hand to own such a mount. "And she hearkens to thy summons," he said, awed.

"Nay," the lad demurred quickly. "Only to my stallion." Then he approached the Hinny and extended his hand, slowly, as one must do for a strange horse, allowing her to sniff it. Her ears were angled halfway back, silken gray. When they tilted forward, reassured, he addressed her directly. "Hinny, I require a service of thee, for the price thou knowest."

The mare switched her nacreous tail and lifted her head. She was by no means large, standing about fifteen hands tall, but she had a slender elegance that made her classic. She glanced sidelong at the blue stallion, and it was as if magic electricity lifted her mane. She was interested.

"A service for a service," my father murmured, intrigued. He contemplated the lines of the blue stallion, recognizing in this creature the very finest of the breed. The foal of such a union would be special.

"Thou must bear this Lady," the blue lad said, indicating me. "Thou must carry her on her search for her lost foal, and bring her back safely to her father. I will travel with thee, assisting. An we find the foal not, but the Lady is safe, payment will be honored. Agreed?"

"How can a horse comprehend all that?" my father muttered skeptically. But the Hinny surveyed him with such uncanny certainty that he could not protest further.

The Hinny now oriented on me. I held out my hand and she smelled it, then sniffed along the length of my arm, across my shoulder and up to my face. Her muzzle was gray velvet, her breath warm mist with the sweetness of cured hay. I loved her that moment.

The Hinny turned back to the blue lad, one ear moving forward with agreement. My father found himself unable to protest; he too was enthralled by the mare. And it seemed but a moment until arrangements were complete and we were riding out, the Hinny's canter so gentle I could close my eyes and hardly know we were moving, yet so swift that the wind was like that of a storm. I had never before ridden a steed like her!

It seemed but another moment, but when I opened mine eyes we were miles from my village, proceeding west toward the interior of the continent where the greatest magic lay. The groves and dales were passing like the wind. No horse could maintain such a pace, so smoothly—yet the Hinny ranged beside the blue stallion, now and then covertly turning a sleek ear on him: she desired the service only he could serve. I wondered fleetingly whether it could be like that for me as well, with only one man destined to be my husband. Little did I know how close to the truth that was, and that he was as close to me then as the stallion to the Hinny.

"Whither do we go?" I asked the lad.

"The wild horses should know where thy foal has strayed," he replied. "They range widely, but my steed is searching them out."

"Aye," I said. "But will they not flee at the approach of our kind?"

He only smiled. Soon we spied a herd, and its stallion lifted his head toward us, and stomped the ground in warning. But the blue lad put his two hands to his mouth, forming a conch, and blew a whistle-note, and at that signal all the horses relaxed, and remained for our approach.

"They respond to thy whistle?" I asked, perplexed.

"They know my stallion," he said easily.

So it seemed. The wild stallion was a great buckskin with dark legs, not as large as the blue stallion. The two sniffed noses and thereafter politely ignored each other. The Hinny was ignored from the start; she was not quite their kind, being half-breed.

The lad dismounted, and I followed. It had been a long, fast ride, but both of us were excellent riders, and both our steeds were easy to use. They grazed, for horses are ever hungry. We passed among the small herd—and strange it was to be around these wild horses, who never ordinarily tolerated the nearness of man. I was in young delight. They were mostly fine, healthy mares, with a few foals, but one among them ailed. The blue lad went to this one, a spindly colt, and ran his hands over the animal's body, and the dam watched without interference while I stood amazed.

"What's wrong with him?" I asked, for I could not determine the malady. I, who thought I knew horses.

"Spirit worms," the lad responded absently. "A magical infestation, common in this region." Then he said to the colt in a singsong lilt: "Comest thou to me, the worms will flee." It was nonsense verse, a joke —yet suddenly the colt perked up, took a step toward the lad, and there was a ripple in the air as invisible yet ugly somethings wriggled away. Instantly the colt seemed healthier, and his dam nickered gratefully. I realized that a little encouragement was all the colt had needed; he was not really sick, merely undernourished.

The blue lad approached the herd stallion and said: "We search for a lost foal, that went astray yesterday. Hast thou seen it, or dost thou know aught of it?"

The stallion glanced at me as though requiring news from me, and I said: "It is a filly, only a month old, pure white and lovely and helpless. I call her Snowflake."

The stallion snorted.

"He says he has not seen the foal," the blue lad said. "But he knows of one who collects white foals, and found one in this area, and that is the Snow Horse."

"Where is this Snow Horse?" I asked.

"He knows not, for the Snow Horse ranges far and associates not with ordinary equines. Only Peg can tell where he might be now."

"Peg?" I asked, perplexed.

"I will take thee to her."

We remounted our steeds and were off again like the wind. We ranged south across plains and woods, fording streams and surmounting hills as if they were nothing. We passed a young unicorn stallion grazing; he had pretty green and orange stripes, and his hooves were ebony, and his horn spiraled pearl. He started up, approaching us, and I grew nervous, for that the unicorn is to the horse as the tiger is to the housecat. But he merely ran beside us, and then drew ahead, racing us. He wanted to play.

The blue lad smiled, and leaned forward, and the blue stallion

leaped ahead as though he had been merely idling before, and the
Hinny set back her ears and launched herself after him. Oh, these fine
animals loved a race! Now the ground shot behind in a green blur, and
trees passed like arrows, and I clung to the Hinny's quicksilver mane
for fear I would fall, though her gait remained wonderfully smooth.
We passed the unicorn.

Now the unicorn lengthened his stride and made great leaps, passing
right over bushes and rocks while we had to go around them. He
recovered the lead, flinging his tail up in a mirthful salute. But again
the blue stallion bore down, and the Hinny's body became like a hawk
flying through a gale, and we pounded out a pace that passed the
horned stallion again. Never had I traveled at such velocity!

A third time the unicorn accelerated, and now his body was shimmering with heat, and fire blasted from his nostrils, and sparks cast up
from his hooves, and slowly he moved ahead of us once more. This
time we could not match him, for that our steeds carried burdens and
were merely physical equines, not magical. Yet had we given that unicorn a good race, and made him heat before he bested us. Very few natural horses could do that.

We eased off, cooling, and I patted the Hinny's shoulder. "Thou'rt
the finest mare I ever met," I murmured. "I could ride with thee forever and never be bored." And so I believed.

Then we came to the purple slope of the great southern range of
mountains, ascending until the air was rare and the growing things
were stunted. There on a crag was a huge nest, and in it lay what at
first I took to be a monstrous bird, for that I saw the feathers on it.
Then the creature stood, perceiving our approach, and spread its
wings—and lo, it was a horse!

"Peg," the blue lad called. "We crave the favor of information. Wilst
thou trade for it?"

Peg launched into the air, circled briefly, spiraled to the ground and
folded her pinions. The white feathers covered her whole body so that
only her legs and tail and head projected, and the tail also had feathers
that could spread for aid in navigation in air. I had not before imagined
how large such wings would be! She neighed, her nose flicking toward
the nest.

"Mayst thou have what's best for thy new nest," the lad said appreciatively, again in that lilt.

Then I noticed what I had not seen before: a pile of vines, perchance the refuse of some farmer's harvest, too long and tough to be
ground for fodder. Peg went to them as though she too had only now
become aware, tugging one out with her teeth, delighted. This was
ideal fiber for her nest. She neighed again.

"She says the Snow Horse is moving toward its fastness in the
White Mountains, and will be there by dawn tomorrow," the lad said.

"For us it will be a ride of more than a day; we shall have to camp the night."

"Thou dost understand the language of horses?" I asked, remembering how he had seemingly conversed with the stallion of the herd, too. There was so much I knew not, then!

He nodded. "How could I love them as I do, and not converse with them? Who is better company than a horse?" And of course I could not gainsay that.

We mounted and rode north. It was noon, and we had far to go; we slanted north and west, wending toward the white range. We halted for an hour when we came across a grove of apple trees; we fed ourselves and our steeds on delicious apples. The Hinny ate from my hand, and how I wished she could be mine for life, but I knew she was only on loan. I was not sorry this quest was stretching out; I wanted to save Snowflake, but I wanted also to be a little longer with the Hinny, and to experience more of the magic of the interior wilds of Phaze.

In the early afternoon we halted again, for our steeds had to graze and rest. The blue lad found raspberries growing on a slope, and a streamlet with freshest water, and some ripe grain. He gathered dry wood and made a small fire; from his saddlebag he brought a pot. We boiled the grain until it was tender. I did not realize then that he had used magic to facilitate things; the farthest thing from my mind was that he could be Adept. He was only, after all, a boy!

He brought next from his saddlebag—he had a bag without a saddle, oddly—some material that he formed into a canopy for me beside the fire. I lay down to sleep feeling quite safe, for few wild creatures brave the fire, and the two horses were grazing near.

But at dusk, as I was nodding off, glare-eyed little monsters erupted from a trapdoor in the ground and swarmed toward me. They were goblins, huge of head and foot, vicious, out for human flesh. They feared not the fire, for they used it in their subterranean demesnes. I screamed.

The Hinny was nearest me, for I had been placed in her care. Now I discovered what that meant. She squealed and charged, her hooves striking like clubs, each strike crushing a goblin's head, while I huddled beside the fire in terror. The goblins fought her, for they liked equine flesh almost as well as human; they scrambled up her tail, clung to her mane, and tried to grab at her feet. There were so many! I saw one get on her head, and open its big frog mouth to clamp its sharp alligator teeth on her sweet soft gray ear—and suddenly I was on my feet and there, my hands on its grotesque rat body, hurling it off her and away.

Then the blue stallion arrived, his hooves making the very ground shudder, and he bellowed a battle-challenge that nearly blasted the hair from my head and I cowered in terror though I knew it was not me he fought. The goblins panicked and fled, the stallion pursuing; where his foot struck, the broken body of a goblin flew twenty feet across the flickering night and dropped like a clod of dirt. The stallion's eyes flashed like blue fire and the snort from his flaring nostrils was like tempest-wind and the sheen of his great muscles danced about his body as he plunged and reared and kicked. In a moment the last living goblin had vanished down the hole, and the trapdoor clanged shut. The stallion stomped it again and again until naught save rubble remained. It would be long before the goblins used that exit again!

I collapsed in reaction. Never in my life had I been so horrified, except perhaps during the episode of the trolls, for goblins come not into the villages of the man-folk. The Hinny came and nuzzled me, and I was ashamed for that I had let her fight while I did naught. But the blue lad told me: "She thanks thee for casting the goblin from off her ear; she knows what courage it required of thee for that goblins terrify young ladies." Then I felt better, though by no means proud, and resolved to be less squeamish in future. I stroked my hands over the bruises and scratches and bites on the Hinny's body, helping to heal them and abate the discomfort, and she nudged me with that so-soft nose and everything was nice.

The goblins came not again—and who would have, after tasting the wrath of the blue stallion? I slept safely until dawn. The blue lad was up before me, and had found ripe pears from whence I knew not, and we ate and mounted and were off again. I thought I might be sore from the prior day's riding, but the Hinny's gait was so gentle I suffered not at all. I wondered what the winged horse's gait was like; what was the cadence of footfalls in air?

In due course we came to the White Mountains that bound our land in the north, and ascended their foothills. The way grew steep, and there was hardly any easing as we crested ridges and drove on up. For the first time the Hinny's gait became rough, as she labored to carry me on swiftly, and even the blue stallion was sweating, his nostrils flaring and pulsing with the effort. We climbed slopes I would not have cared to navigate on foot, rising into the mountain range proper. The air grew chill, and wind came up, and I gathered my cape about me, shivering.

The blue lad glanced at me. "May I speak bold?" he inquired melodiously. "Thou art not cold."

"Not cold," I agreed bravely, for I knew that if we desisted this quest now, never would I find Snowflake, and evermore would I curse myself for my neglect. And, strangely, I no longer felt the chill; it was as if my clothing had become doubly insulative. It was of course his magic, that I did not recognize. I was so young then, and so innocent!

We climbed on into the snows, and there in a cave half-hid in the white we found the lair of the Snow Horse. He stood there awaiting us expectantly, a fine albino stallion whose mane and tail resembled glistening icicles and whose hooves were so pure white I could hardly tell where they left off and the packed snow beneath them began.

The lad dismounted and walked to the Snow Horse. I made to dismount too, but the Hinny swung back her head, warning me "no" with a backward glance, so I obeyed her and stayed put. I was learning already that here in the wilderness the final word was not mine.

In a moment the lad returned. "The Snow Horse did lure thy foal," he said to me. "He thought her of his kind, for her color, but when they reached the snow she was cold, and he knew she was no snow filly and he let her go, never intending harm to her. But the snow demons came and took her ere she could return to thee."

"The snow demons!" I exclaimed, appalled. Never had I heard good tidings of that ilk.

"Pray we are in time," he said.

"In time?" I asked blankly. "Snowflake is lost forever! We can not brace snow demons, even if they have not yet eaten her." I felt the hot tears burning mine eyes. "Yet if there is a chance—"

"A white foal they will save—for a while." He mounted and led the way along the slope.

We made our way deeper into the snowy region, and the breath plumed out from the nostrils of our steeds, but still I was not cold. Then the blue stallion halted, sniffing the snow, and pawed the slope. I knew we were near the lair of the demons, and I shivered with fear, not with cold. Almost, I preferred to let the foal go—but then I thought of the demons devouring her shivering flesh, and horror restored my faint courage.

A snow demon appeared on a ledge above us. "Whooo?" it demanded, with sound like winter cutting past a frozen crag.

The blue lad did not answer in speech. He stood upon the back of his stallion and spread his arms, as if to say "Here am I!" I was both impressed and concerned. It was clever of him to keep his balance like that, but he could so readily fall and hurt himself. Though he acted as if the demon should recognize him and be awed, in fact it was a foolish posturing. An ogre or a giant might awe a demon; the lad was pitiful in his insignificance.

To my astonishment, the demon drew back as if confronted by a giant. "Whiiiy?" it demanded.

The lad pointed to the Hinny, then moved his hands together to indicate small size. He had come for the foal.

The demon scratched its icicle-haired head in seeming confusion: no foal here! The blue lad then did something strange indeed. He brought out a large harmonica—I had not known he carried such an instrument —and brought it to his mouth. He played one note—and the demon reacted as if struck. Sleet fell from it like droplets of perspiration, and it pointed down the slope. I looked—and there, in a patch of green in a narrow valley, stood my beloved Snowflake. The poor little filly was huddled and shivering, for nowhere in the White Mountains is it warm.

The demon faded back into its crevice, and we made our way down the steep slope to the valley. The way was tortuous, but the blue stallion picked out footholds where I thought none existed, and slowly we descended. It was like being lowered into a tremendous bowl, whose sides were so steep our every motion threatened to start a snowslide that could bury the foal. Oh, yes, we moved cautiously!

At last we reached the patch of green. I dismounted and ran to Snowflake, and she recognized me with a whinny. The warmth that encompassed me seemed to enclose her too, and she became stronger. "Oh," I cried, hugging her. "I'm so glad thou art safe! I feared—" But my prior worries were of no account now. The blue lad had enabled me to rescue Snowflake, even as he had promised.

Then I heard a rumble. Alarmed, I looked up—and saw the snow demons on high, pushing great balls of snow off ledges. They were starting an avalanche—and we were at the base of it! It was a trap, and no way could we escape.

For the first time I saw the blue lad angry. Yet he neither swore nor cowered. Instead he brought out his harmonica again and played a few bars of music. It was a rough, aggressive melody—but what good it could do in the face of the onrushing doom I knew not. Soon the sound was drowned out by the converging avalanche.

The snows came down on us like the lashing of a waterfall. I screamed and hugged Snowflake, knowing our end had come. But as I braced myself for the inevitable, something strange happened.

There was a blinding flash of light and wash of heat, like as an explosion. Then warm water swirled around my feet.

Warm water? I forced open mine eyes and looked, unbelieving. The snows had vanished. All the valley, high to the tallest surrounding peaks, was bare of snow, with only water coursing down, and steam rising in places. We had been saved by some massive invasion of spring thaw.

"It must be magic!" I cried, bewildered. "Unless this is a volcanic region. But what a coincidence!"

The lad only nodded. Still I recognized not his power!

We walked up the slope, escaping the valley and the deepening lake that was forming at its nadir. I rode the Hinny, and Snowflake walked beside. It was a long climb, but a happy one.

At the high pass leading to the outside the cold intensified. From out of a crevice a snow demon came. "Yyoooo!" it cried windily, and with a violent gesture hurled a spell like a jag of ice at the blue lad.

But the Hinny leaped forward, intercepting that scintillating bolt with her own body. It coalesced about her front legs, and ice formed on her knees, and she stumbled, wheezing in pain. I leaped off, alarmed.

The blue lad cried out in a singsong voice, and the foul demon puffed into vapor and floated away. Then the boy came to minister to the Hinny, who was on the ground, her knees frozen.

"That bolt was meant for me," he said. "Hinny, I can cure thee not completely, for knees are the most difficult joints to touch and thou canst not rest them now, but I will do what I can." And he played his harmonica again, a few bold bars, then sang: "Hinny's knees—now unfreeze."

The ice vanished from her legs. The Hinny hauled herself to her feet. She tested her knees, and they were sturdy. But I could see some discoloration, and knew they had been weakened somewhat. It seemed she could walk or run on them, but special maneuvers might now be beyond her.

Then I realized what I should have known before. I turned to the lad. "Thou didst that!" I accused him. "Thou canst do magic!"

He nodded soberly. "I concealed it not from thee," he said, like as a child caught with hand in cookie-jar. He was so shamefaced and penitent I had to laugh.

I put mine arm about his small shoulders and squeezed him as a big sister might. "I forgive thee," I said. "But do not play with magic unduly, lest thou dost attract the notice of an Adept."

He made no comment. Shamed am I to recall now the way I patronized him then, in mine ignorance! We remounted and went on out of the mountains, slowly, in deference to the Hinny's almost-restored knees and the weakness of the foal. At last we reached the warmth of the lowlands, and there we camped for the night. Snowflake grazed beside the Hinny, who watched out for her in the manner of a dam, and I knew the foal would not come to harm. We foraged for berries and nuts, which fortunately were plentiful and delicious. Such fortune was ever in the presence of the blue lad, for he preferred to use his magic subtly.

At dusk the sunset spread its splendor across the western sky, and in the east a blue moon rose. The lad brought out his harmonica again, faced the moon, and played. Before, he had produced only single notes and brief strident passages. This time he started gentle, as it were tuning his instrument, warming it in his hands, playing a scale. His little hands were hardly large enough to enfold it properly, yet they were marvelously dextrous. Then, as the moon waxed and the sun waned, he essayed a melody.

I was tired, not paying real attention, so was caught by surprise. From that instrument emerged music of such beauty, such rare rapture as I had never imagined. The tune surrounded me, encompassed me, drew me into itself and transported my spirit up, high, into the ambience of the blue moon. I sailed up, as it were, into the lovely blue-tinged clouds, riding on a steed made of music, wafting through blue billows toward the magic land that was the face of the moon. Larger it grew, and clearer, its landscape ever-better defined. As I came near it I saw the little blue men on its surface, blacksmiths hammering out blue steel. Bluesmiths, I suppose. Then I saw a lady in blue, and her hair was fair like mine, and she wore a lovely blue gown and blue slippers set with blue gems for buttons, and on her head a blue tiara, and she was regal and beautiful beyond belief. She turned and fixed her gaze on me, and her eyes were blue like mine—and she was me.

Amazed, flattered and alarmed, I retreated. I flew back past the blue mists like a feather-shafted arrow, and suddenly I was on the ground again. The boy stopped playing, and the melody faded hauntingly.

I realized it not then, but he had shown me the first of the three foundations of my later love for him: his music. Never in all Phaze was there a man who could make such—

(The Lady Blue paused, resting her head against her hand, suffering. Stile started to speak, but she cut him off savagely. "And thou, thou image, thou false likeness! Thou comest to these Demesnes bearing *his* harmonica, using it—"

("His?" Stile asked, astonished.

("Has it not the word 'Blue' etched upon it?" she demanded. "He had it imported from the other frame, to his order."

(Stile brought out the harmonica, turning it over. There, in small neat letters, was the word. "I conjured his instrument," he murmured, awed and chagrined. "I must return it to his widow."

(She softened instantly. "Nay, it is thine. Thou art the Blue Adept, now. Use it well, as he did." Then she returned to her narrative.)

I shook my head. "Never have I heard the like, thou darling child!" I said. "How could a lad thine age master music so well?"

He thought a moment, pensive in his concentration, as though pondering some weighty ethical matter. Then he replied: "May I show thee my village on the morrow? It is not far out of our way."

"Was not that village destroyed?" I asked thoughtlessly.

"Aye, it was."

I was sorry for my question. "Of course we can go there, if it please thee. Unless the trolls remain—"

"No trolls remain," he assured me gravely, and I remembered that lightning had destroyed the trolls.

Next day we came to the site. It was nothing, only a glade of greenest grass and a few mounds. All had been destroyed and over-grown. I was vaguely disappointed, having anticipated something more dramatic—yet what is dramatic about long-past death?

"May I show thee how it was?" he inquired, his small face serious.

"Of course," I said graciously, not understanding what he meant.

"Go and graze," he said to our steeds. They moved out gladly, and little Snowflake with them.

Then the blue lad played his harmonica again. Once more the absolutely lovely music leaped out, encompassing us, and some intangible presence formed. I saw a cloud about the glade, and then it thinned to reveal a village, with people going about their business, washing clothing, eating, hammering horseshoes, playing. I realized that this was a vision of his home as it had been, years ago, before the disaster. A village very like mine own.

The village was perhaps a little better organized than mine, however, more compact, with the houses in a ring and a central court for socializing and supervision of the children. Mine was a sea-village, mainly, open to the water; this was an inland establishment, closed against the threats of the land. The sun was shining brightly—but then the shadows moved visibly, and I knew this was to show time passing. Night fell, and the village closed down.

Then in the stillness of dark the trolls came, huge, gaunt and awful. Somehow they had broken through the enchantment that protected the village, and they descended on it in a ravening horde. Faintly I heard the screams as the monsters pounced upon sleeping villagers. Men woke fighting, but each troll was large and strong, and there were many of them. I saw a woman torn apart by two trolls who were fighting over possession; they laughed with great grotesque guffaws as her left arm ripped out of its socket, and the troll holding that arm was angry because he had the smaller share, and clubbed the other troll with it while blood splattered everywhere. But then a screaming child ran by, a little girl, and the troll caught that child and brought her to its face and opened its awful mouth and—and bit off her screaming head.

Then the image faded, mercifully, for I was screaming myself. Never had I seen such horror! The darkness covered all. After a pause, the dawn came. The trolls were hidden in the houses, gorged; they would not go abroad by light of day, and suffered no fires, for that they were the opposite of goblins in this respect and the light was painful to them. They had buried themselves under piled blankets, shutting out all signs of the day. They were safe; no villager remained alive.

No—one remained. A child, a boy—he emerged from the trunk of a hollow tree. It seemed he had been playing in it when the trolls descended, or doing something he wasn't supposed to, like practicing spells, then had hidden frozen in fright until dawn made it safe to emerge. Now he stood, surveying the ruin—and it was the blue lad.

"Thou!" I exclaimed. "Thou didst witness it all! Thy village, thy family, most brutally destroyed!"

"Have no sympathy for me," he replied grimly. "I was transformed that hideous night from youth to enchanter. I realized that no force but magic could restore the balance, and so—" He spread his hands. "Look what I did."

I looked—and saw the figure in the image raise his hands, and I heard him faintly singing, though I could not make out the words. Then, suddenly, a ring of fire appeared, encircling the village, blazing ferociously. Magic fire, I knew, but still fierce and hot. It burned inward, not outward, while the blue lad watched. He must have spent his sleepless hours in hiding devising that terrible spell, perfecting it. It ignited the outer thatch cottages. Now the trolls woke, and ran about in the fire, burning, terrified—but they could escape only inward toward the center of the village. And there the fire pursued them, itself a ravening demon.

Now it was the trolls who gibbered in horror, and were granted no reprieve, as they huddled in the center of the village, heads covered, backs to the fire. Inevitably it closed on them, torturing them before it consumed them, and then fain would I have felt sorry for the trolls, but that I remembered the woman torn apart and the decapitated child. No mercy for the merciless! The trolls fought each other, trying to keep place in the closing circle, showing not the faintest compassion for their fellows, only selfishness.

At last the dread fire burned itself out, its magic consuming flesh as readily as wood. Only mounds and ashes remained. All of the trolls had been destroyed. Except—except there was a stirring in a mound, and from it came a little troll, that must have been deeply buried by its mother, so that it alone survived. Now it looked about and wailed, afraid of the coming day.

The blue lad spied it, and knew that this one could not have killed any people, and he cast a spell of darkness that clothed it, and let the little troll go. "Thou'rt like me," the blue lad quoth. Then he turned his back on what had been his home, and walked away.

The music stopped and the vision dissipated. I looked across at the blue lad. He had shown me his second major component: his power. Yet I did not realize, or perhaps refused to let myself know, the significance of this deadly ability.

"Thou—thou wast as thou art now!" I exclaimed. "Thou hast not changed, not grown. But the destruction of thy village occurred ten years ago! How could—"

"I was seventeen," he replied.

"And now thou'rt—twenty-seven?" I asked, realizing it was true. "I thought thee twelve!"

"I am small for my size," he said, smiling.

He was as much older than I, than I had thought him younger. No child of twelve, but a full-grown man. "I—" I began, nonplussed.

"Thou didst ask how a person my age could play the harmonica so well," he reminded me.

"Aye, that I did," I agreed ruefully. Now that the joke was turned on me, I felt at ease.

The blue lad—blue *man*—summoned our steeds, and we proceeded on. We made good progress, and arrived the next day at mine own village. Almost, I had been afraid I would find it a smoking ruin, but of course this was a foolish fantasy born of the horror I had viewed. My folks rushed out to greet me in sheer gladness, and Snowflake was reunited with her dam Starshine, and all was gladness and relief.

Then the blue man said to his blue stallion: "Go service the Hinny; she has completed her pact with me." And the stallion went off into the privacy of the forest with the Hinny, who must have been in heat—aye, in heat from the first time she spied that stallion!—and I was glad for her. She would have her foal, and well had she earned it.

My father's gaze followed them. "What a stallion! What a mare!" he murmured. "Surely that foal shall be like none known among us."

The blue man shrugged, and said to me: "Lady, an thou ever needest me, sing these words: 'Blue to me—I summon thee.'" Then he turned to my father, thinking me distracted by my tearful mother, for that my days-long absence had worried them much. "Sir, may I marry thy daughter?" he asked, as if this were a question about the weather.

My mouth dropped open in sheerest surprise, and I could not speak.

"Art thou the Blue Adept?" my father asked in return.

I was stunned again, knowing suddenly the answer. How could I have missed it, I who had seen his power!

Then the Blue Adept shook hands with my father and walked in the direction the horses had gone. No answers had been given, for none were needed. Normal people associated not with Adepts, and married them never.

The Lady Blue finished her narrative and looked up at Stile. "Now canst thou go about thy business, Adept," she said.

"I thank thee, Lady," Stile said, and departed her presence.

CHAPTER 3

Proton

Neysa carried Stile across the fields to the forest where the nearest usable fold of the curtain passed. "While Hulk remains away, and I am in the other frame, do thou protect the Lady Blue from harm," Stile murmured as she galloped. "I have no better friend than thee to do this bidding."

The unicorn snorted musically. He hardly needed to tell her! Were they not oath-friends?

They reached the curtain, where it scintillated faintly in the shadowed glade. "I will try to return in a day," Stile said. "If I do not—"

Neysa blew a word-note: "Hulk."

"That's right. Send Hulk after me. He knows the frame, he knows the Game. Should anything untoward happen to me in Proton-frame—"

She blasted vehement negation. Her horn could sound quite emphatic on occasion.

"Oh, I'll look out for myself," he assured her. "And Sheen is my bodyguard there. She has saved me often enough. But in the remote chance that—well, thou canst go and get bred immediately, and raise thy foal—"

Neysa cut him off with a noise-note, and Stile let the subject drop. It had been difficult enough getting her to accept the fact of his Adept status; she was not about to accept the prospect of his demise. He hoped he would not disappoint her.

Stile faced the curtain. Through it he made out the faint outline of a lighted hall, and piles of crates. A person was walking down the hall, so Stile waited until it was clear. Most people had no awareness of the curtain, and there was a tacit agreement among curtain-crossers that the ignorance of such people be allowed to remain pristine. Then he hummed an impromptu tune as he undressed and folded his clothing carefully and hid it away in the crotch of a branch.

As he stood naked, Neysa shifted into naked girl-form, embraced him, kissed him, and laughed. "I am like Proton!"

"Takes more than nakedness to be part of Proton-frame," Stile said gruffly. "Thou'rt full of mischief, unicorn." He disengaged from her and resumed his humming before the curtain.

"Send me all into that hall," he singsonged, stepping forward.

He felt the tingle as he passed through. He was in the hall, naked, alone. He turned around and faced Neysa, who was faintly visible beyond the curtain. She had shifted back to her natural form. "Bye, friend," he called, and waved to her.

Then he went resolutely back and walked rapidly down the hall. It was strange being bare again, after getting accustomed to the mores of the other frame.

Soon the hall intersected a main travel route, where many naked serfs walked swiftly toward their places of employment. He merged with them, becoming largely anonymous. He was smaller than all the men and most of the women and some of the children, but he was used to this. He still resented the disparaging glances some serfs cast at him, but reminded himself that a person who made a value judgment of another person solely in consideration of size was in fact advertising his own incompetence to judge. Still, Stile was glad to get out of the public hall and into his private apartment.

His handprint keyed open the door. Stile stepped inside.

A naked man looked up, frowning. For a moment they stared at each other. Then the other stood. "Sheen did not tell me you would return this hour. I shall retire."

"One moment," Stile said. He recognized the man as his double: the robot who filled in for him while he was in the magic frame of Phaze. Without this machine, Stile's absences would become too obvious, and that could make mischief. "I have not encountered you before. Does Sheen treat you well?"

"Sheen ignores me," the robot said. "Except when others are present. This is proper in the circumstance."

"Yet you are programmed to resemble me in all things. Don't you get bored?"

"A machine of my type does not get bored unless so directed."

"Not even when you are put away in the closet?"

"I am deactivated at such times."

This bothered Stile, who felt sympathy for all oppressed creatures. "If you ever do feel dissatisfied, please let me know. I'll put in a word for you with the mistress."

"Thank you for your courtesy," the robot said without emotion. "It does not fit my present need. I am a machine. Should I retire now?"

"When is Sheen due back?"

"In four minutes, fifteen seconds from . . . mark."

"Yes, retire now. I'll cover for you."

The robot, of course, did not assimilate the humor. Robots came in many types and levels, and this one was relatively unsophisticated. It had no consciousness feedback circuits. It walked to the wall, looking completely human; it bothered Stile to realize that this was exactly the way he looked to others, so small and nondescript. The robot opened a panel and stepped into the closet-aperture behind. In a moment it was out of sight and deactivated.

Stile was reminded of the golem that had impersonated him, or rather, impersonated his alternate self the Blue Adept until he, Stile, arrived on the scene to destroy it. What was the difference, really, between a golem and a humanoid robot? One was activated by magic, the other by science. There were more parallels between these two frames than geographical!

Stile sat down at the table the robot had left. A game of cards—solitaire—was laid out. If the robot did not experience boredom, why was it playing cards? Answer: because Stile himself would have done this, if bored, sharpening obscure Game-skills. The robot probably followed Stile's program of acrobatic exercises, too, though it could hardly benefit from these. It was emulating him, so as to improve verisimilitude—the appearance of authenticity.

He analyzed the situation of the cards, then resumed play. He was deep in it when the door opened and Sheen appeared.

She was beautiful. She was only slightly taller than he, with overperfect proportions—breasts slightly larger and firmer and more erect than the computer-standard ideal for her size and age; waist a trifle smaller, abdomen flatter, hips and buttocks fuller—and luxuriantly flowing fair hair. The average man wanted a better-than-average woman; in fact he wanted a better-than-ideal woman, his tastes distorted by centuries of commercialized propaganda that claimed that a woman in perfect health and fitness was somehow less than lovely. Stile's tastes were average—therefore Sheen was far from average.

She reminded him moderately of another girl he had known, years ago: a woman smaller than himself, a female jockey he had thought he loved. Tune had been her name, and from that encounter on he had been addicted to music. Yet Sheen, he knew objectively, was actually a prettier and better woman. She had only one flaw—and he was not inclined to dwell on that at the moment.

Stile rose and went to her, taking her in his arms. "Oh—is someone here?" she asked, surprised.

"No one," he said, bringing her in for a kiss. "Let's make love."

"With a robot? Don't be silly." She tried to break free of his embrace, but he only held her more tightly.

"It is best with a robot," he assured her.

"Oh." She considered momentarily. "All right."

Oops. She was going along with it! "All right?" he demanded. "Just how far do you go with robots?"

"My best friends are robots," she assured him. "Come to the bed."

Angry now, Stile let her go. But she was laughing. "You amorous idiot!" she exclaimed. "Did you think I didn't know you?" And she flung her arms about him and kissed him with considerably more passion than before.

"What gave me away?" Stile asked.

"Aside from the differences between man and robot that I, of all people, know?" she inquired mischievously. "Things like body radiation, perspiration, heartbeat, respiration and the nuances of living reactions?"

"Aside from those," Stile said, feeling foolish. He should have known he couldn't fool her even a moment.

"Your hands are tanned," she said.

He looked at them. Sure enough, there was a distinct demarcation where his Phaze-clothing terminated, leaving his hands exposed to the strong rays of the outdoor sun. All living-areas on Proton were domed, with the sunlight filtered to nondestructive intensity, so that only moderate tanning occurred. And of course there were no demarcations on the bodies of people who wore no clothing. Not only did this uneven tanning distinguish him from the robot, it distinguished him from the other serfs of Proton! "I'll have to start wearing gloves in Phaze!"

"No such heroic measures are necessary," she assured him. She brought out some tinted hand lotion and worked it into his hands, converting them to untanned color.

"I don't know what I'd do without you," Stile said gratefully.

"You'd stay in Phaze the whole time, with that blue lady."

"No doubt."

"Well, this is another world," she informed him. "I had a piece of you before you ever knew she existed. You have a good six hours before the first Game of the Tourney, and I know exactly how to spend it."

She did, too. She was as amorous as she was lovely, and she existed only to guard and to please him. It was easy to yield to her. More than easy.

Afterward, as they lay on the bed, she inquired: "And how exactly are things in Phaze?"

"I killed the golem who was impersonating me, and gave my friend Kurrelgyre the werewolf advice on how to regain his standing in his pack—"

"I know about that. You returned here for the final pre-Tourney qualifying Game, remember? What did you do on your last trip there?"

"The werewolves and the unicorns helped me to establish my identity as the Blue Adept," Stile said, grossly simplifying the matter. "I do magic now. But I have to fight the unicorn Herd Stallion to preserve Neysa from breeding for a season."

"I like Neysa," Sheen said. "But doesn't she get jealous of the Lady Blue?"

"No, they are oath-friends now. Neysa knows my destiny lies with my own kind."

"With the Lady Blue," Sheen said.

Stile realized he had carelessly hurt Sheen. "She is not of this world, as you pointed out."

"That's what you think. It's a different world, but she's here too. She can't cross the curtain, can she? So she must have a double on this side."

Stile suffered a shock of amazement. "That's right! There must be another self of her living here. My ideal woman, all the time right here in Proton." Then he caught himself. "*An* ideal—"

"Oh, never mind," Sheen said. "We both know I'm not your kind, however much I might wish to be."

"But why did you tell me—"

"Neysa helped you reach the Lady, didn't she? Can I do less?"

There was that. Sheen identified with Neysa, and tried to emulate her reactions. "Actually, I can't afford to go looking for her now—and what would I do if I found her?"

"I'm sure you'd think of something," Sheen said wryly. "Men usually do."

Stile smiled. "Contrary to appearances, there is more than one concern on this male mind. I am fated to love the Lady Blue, though she may not be fated to love me—but how can I love two of her? I really have no business with her Proton-alternate."

"You don't want to see her?"

"I don't *dare* see her."

"My friends can readily locate her for you."

"Forget it. It would only complicate my life, and it is already somewhat too complicated for equanimity. How long can I continue functioning in two frames? I feel a bit like a bigamist already, and I'm not even married."

"You really ought to settle this."

He turned on her. "Why are you doing this?" But he knew why. He had hurt her, and she was expiating the hurt by exploring it to the limit. There was a certain logic in this; there was always logic in what Sheen did. They both knew he could never truly love Sheen or marry her, any more than he could have loved or married Neysa. Sheen would always love him, but could never be more to him than a temporary mistress and guardian.

"You're right," she said, her pursuit abated by his pointed question. "It is best forgotten. I shall store it in the appropriate memory bank."

"You don't forget something by remembering it!"

"We have a Tourney to win," she reminded him, aptly changing the subject in the manner of her sex.

"You understand," he cautioned her. "I can not reasonably expect to win the Tourney. I'm not at my peak Game capacity, and in a large-scale double-elimination competition like this I can get lost in the crush."

"And if you lose early, your tenure as a Proton serf ends, and you'll have to stay in Phaze, and I'll never see you again," Sheen said. "You have reason to try. We need to find out who has been trying to kill you here, and you can only pursue an effective investigation if you become a Citizen."

"There is that," he agreed. He thought of the anonymous Citizen who had had his knees lasered and gotten him washed out as a jockey. The series of events that action had precipitated had paradoxically enriched his life immeasurably, introducing him to the entire frame of Phaze—yet still an abiding anger smouldered. He had a score to settle with someone—and Sheen was right, it was an incentive to win the Tourney if he possibly could. For the winner would be granted the ulti-mate prize of Proton: Citizenship. Runners-up would receive extensions of their tenure and the chance to compete again in a subsequent Tour-ney. So he did have a chance, a good chance because of his Game abilities—but the odds of final victory remained substantially against him.

He wondered, coincidentally, whether the history the Lady Blue had recently related had any bearing. A snow demon had fired a freeze-spell at the Blue Adept, and it had caught the Hinny and damaged her knees. Stile had been lasered in the knees while riding a horse. Was this an example of the parallelism of the two frames? Things did tend to align, one way or another, but sometimes the route was devious.

"One Game at a time," Sheen said. "If and when you lose, I'll just have to abide by that. I know you'll try."

"I'll try," he agreed.

They reported on schedule to the Game Annex. Sheen could not ac-company him inside; only Tourney entrants were permitted now. She would go to a Spectator Annex and tune in his game on holo, unless it happened to be one in which a live audience was permitted. She would lend her applause and opinion when feedback opportunity occurred.

There was a line at the entrance. There was hardly ever such a crowd—but the Tourney came just once a year. Six hundred serfs had to report at once, and though the Game facilities were extensive, this was a glut.

When he stepped inside, the Game Computer interviewed him efficiently. "Identity?" a voice inquired from a holographic image of the capital letters GC suspended a meter before him at head height. The computer could make any image and any sound emanate from any-where, but kept it token. Proton was governed by Citizens, not by ma-chines, and the smart machine maintained that in memory constantly.

"Stile, serf, ladder 35M, Rung 5." That gave his name, status, age, sex and the fact that he had qualified for the Tourney by holding the fifth rung of the competitive ladder for his bracket: the minimum entry requirement. He could have been first on his ladder had he gone for it earlier; he was actually one of the best players extant. But all that really counted was qualification. All had equal Tourney status.

"Stile 35M-5, assigned number 281 for Round One only," the voice of the Game Computer said. A decal emerged from a slot. Stile took it and set it against his forehead. Now he was marked, for the purpose of this Round, with the number and name: 281 STILE. "Proceed to the 276–300 sub-annex and encounter your opposite number. Your Game will be announced in due course. Respond immediately or forfeit."

"Acknowledged," Stile said. The floating GC faded out and he proceeded to the designated annex. For this Round, a number of waiting rooms and hall alcoves had been converted to rendezvous points. After the first few Rounds many of these would revert to their normal uses, as the number of entrants decreased.

Already the annex was filling. Each person wore the decal on his or her forehead, all numbers in the 276–300 range. Most were naked men and women, some familiar to him. But before Stile could fully orient, a clothed man stepped forward. "Salutation, opposite number," the man said.

Stile was taken aback. This was a Citizen, fully garbed in tan trousers, white shirt, jacket and shoes. But he did bear the number on his forehead: 281, with no name. Citizens were generally anonymous to serfs. Anonymity was a privilege of status that showed most obviously in the clothing that concealed bodily contours. Serfs had no secrets.

"Sir," Stile said.

"We are all equal, ad hoc," the Citizen said. He was handsome and tall, a good decade older than Stile, and as self-assured as all Citizens were. "Come converse in a nook." He put his hand on Stile's elbow, guiding him.

"Yes, sir," Stile agreed numbly. His first match was against a Citizen! Of course he had known that Citizens participated in the Tourney; he just had not thought in terms of playing against one himself. On Proton there were two classes: the Citizens and the serfs. The Haves and the Have-nots. Stile himself was employed by a Citizen, as every serf was; no unemployed serf was permitted on the planet beyond a brief grace period, and no employed serf could remain beyond his twenty-year tenure—with certain very limited exceptions. This was part of what the Tourney was about.

The Citizen guided him to a bench, then sat down beside him. This alleviated his third-of-a-meter advantage in height, but not his immeasurable advantage in status. "I am popularly known as the Rifleman. Possibly you have heard of me."

Stile suffered a second shock. "The Tourney winner—fifteen years ago! I watched that Game . . . sir."

The Rifleman smiled. "Yes, I was a serf like you. I won my Citizenship the hard way. Now the perennial lure of the Game brings me back. You never do get it out of your system! Who are you?"

"Sir, I am—"

"Ah, now I connect! Stile is the designation of one of the top current Gamesmen! I had not realized your tenure was expiring."

"It had three years to go, sir. But I had a problem with my employer."

"Ah, I see. So you had to go for double or nothing. Well, this is a pleasure! I've entered other Tourneys since my ascent, but the moment I matched with a serf he would throw it into CHANCE, and two or three of those in succession washed me out early. It is hard to beat a person unless he thinks he can beat you. I'm sure you will give me an excellent game."

"Yes, sir," Stile agreed. "I don't like CHANCE." He didn't like having to play a Citizen either, but that could not be said here. Of all the people to encounter this early! A former Tourney winner! No wonder the Rifleman's opponents in other Tourneys—a Citizen could enter anything he wanted, of course, being immune to the rules governing serfs—had avoided honest contests. CHANCE was at least a 50–50 proposition, instead of a virtually guaranteed loss. It was axiomatic that the poorer players preferred CHANCE, while the better ones disliked it, and the top players wished it would be abolished as a category.

Stile had been twenty years old, already an avid follower of Tourneys, when the Rifleman fought his way up to ultimate victory by shooting six target ducks against his opponent's three. A highly skilled player, who had of course taken a name reflective of that victory.

But that had been a long time back. The man could be out of practice and out of shape. Unless he had been practicing privately. Yet why should a Citizen bother? He had nothing to win in the Tourney. A Citizen, almost by definition, had everything. Fabulous wealth, power, and prestige. If a Citizen saw an attractive serf-girl, he could hire her and use her and fire her, all within the hour. It would not even occur to her to protest. A Citizen could have a household of humanoid robots, virtually indistinguishable from living people (until one got to know them, which did not take long) to serve his every need. The finest creature comforts of the galaxy were his, and the most exotic entertainments. Small wonder that many Citizens grew indolent and fat!

"I can virtually read your thoughts," the Citizen said. "And I will answer them. I am not in the shape I was when I won, but I have practiced somewhat and remain reasonably formidable. Of course I lack motive, now; victory will not benefit me, and defeat will not harm me. Yet it would be satisfying to win it again."

Stile was spared the awkwardness of answering by the Game Computer's introductory announcement. "Attention all entrants. The Tourney roster is now complete: four hundred Citizens, six hundred serfs, and twenty-four aliens. Pairing for individual matches is random each Round. The Tourney is double-elimination; only entrants with two losses are barred from further competition. Serfs among the final sixty-four survivors will receive one year extension of tenure. Those proceeding beyond that level will receive commensurately greater rewards. The Tourney winner will be granted Proton Citizenship. Judging of all matches in the objective sphere is by computer; subjective judging is by tabulated audience-response; special cases by panels of experts. Bonus awards will be granted for exceptional Games. Malingerers will forfeit." There was a momentary pause as the computer shifted from general to specific. Now it would be addressing the annexes individually. "Game-pair 276 report to grid."

Hastily two serfs rose, a man and a woman, and walked to the grid set up in the center of the room. They began the routine of Game-selection.

"Ah, this is like old times," the Rifleman said appreciatively.

"Yes, sir," Stile agreed. He would have liked to follow the first couple's progress, but of course he could not ignore the Citizen. "Not old to me, sir."

"Contemporary times for you, of course," the Citizen said. "I have followed your progress intermittently. You have played some excellent Games. Perhaps I misremember; don't you happen also to be an excellent equestrian?"

"I was a winning jockey, yes, sir," Stile agreed.

"Ah, now it comes back! You were lasered. Anonymously."

"Through the knees, yes, sir."

"That had to have been the action of a Citizen."

"Yes, sir."

"Citizens are a law unto themselves." The Rifleman smiled. "Don't forget, I was a serf for nineteen years, and a Citizen only fifteen. My fundamental values are those of the serf. However, I doubt that even most birthright Citizens would approve such vandalism. There are licit and illicit ways to do business, and no Citizen should need to resort to the illicit. A rogue Citizen would be a menace to other Citizens, and therefore should be dealt with firmly for a practical as well as legal reason."

"Yes, sir."

"As you know, I am in this Tourney merely for titillation. I now perceive a way to increase that interest. Allow me to proffer this wager: if you overmatch me in this Round, I shall as consequence make an investigation into the matter of the lasering and report to you before you depart the planet. Agreed?"

No serf could lightly say no to any Citizen, and Stile had no reason to demur. He wanted very much to know the identity of his enemy! Yet he hesitated. "Sir, what would be my consequence if you defeat me?"

The Rifleman stroked his angular beardless chin. "Ah, there is that. The stakes must equate. Yet what can a serf offer a Citizen? Have you any personal assets?"

"Sir, no serf has—"

The Citizen waggled a finger at him admonishingly, smiling, and Stile suddenly found himself liking this expressive man. No serf could afford to like a Citizen, of course; they were virtually in different worlds. Still, Stile was moved.

"Of course a serf has no material assets," the Rifleman said. "But serfs often do have information, that Citizens are not necessarily aware of. Since what I offer you is information, perhaps you could offer me information too."

Stile considered. As it happened, he did have news that should interest a Citizen—but he was honor-bound not to impart it. He happened to know that a number of the most sophisticated service robots were self-willed, acting on their own initiative, possessing self-awareness and ambition. Theoretically there could eventually be a machine revolt. But he had sworn not to betray the interests of these machines, so long as they did not betray the welfare of Planet Proton, and his word was absolute. He could not put that information on the line. "I regret I can not, sir."

The Citizen shrugged. "Too bad. The wager would have added luster to the competition."

As though the future of a serf's life were not luster enough? But of course the Citizen was thinking only of himself. "Yes, sir. I'm sorry, sir. I would have liked to make that wager, had I a stake to post."

"Are you not aware you could make the wager, and renege if you lose? You really don't have much *to* lose."

Stile, under tension of the Tourney, was suddenly angry. "That's reprehensible!" Then, belatedly, "Sir."

"Ah, you are an honest man. I thought as much. I like that. Most top Gamesmen do value integrity."

Stile was spared further conversation by the interjection of the computer. "Game-pair 281 report to grid."

The Rifleman stood. "That's us. Good luck, Stile." He proffered his hand.

Stile, amazed, accepted it. He had never heard of a Citizen shaking hands with a serf! This was an extension of courtesy that paralleled that of the Herd Stallion in Phaze: the disciplined encounter of respected opponents.

Phaze! Suddenly Stile realized what he had to offer. The knowledge of the existence of the alternate frame! The information might do the Citizen no good, since most people could not perceive the curtain between frames, let alone cross it, but it would surely be of interest to the man. There was no absolute prohibition about spreading the word, though Stile preferred not to. But if he won the Game, he wouldn't have to. This seemed to be an acceptable risk.

"Sir," Stile said quickly. "I do have information. I just remembered. I believe it would interest—"

"Then it is a bargain," the Citizen said, squeezing Stile's hand.

"Yes, sir. Only I hope you will not share the information with others, if—"

"Agreed. This is a private wager and a private matter between us— either way."

"Yes, sir."

"Second call for Game-pair 281," the computer announced. "Appear at the grid within ten seconds or both forfeit."

"You bucket of bolts!" the Rifleman snapped. "Whom do you suppose you are addressing?"

A lens swung about to fix on the Citizen. The response was instant. "Abject apologies, sir. Time limit is waived."

The Rifleman's glance swept across the silent room. "You may laugh now."

The remaining serfs burst into laughter.

"Rank hath its privileges," the Rifleman said. He put his hand on Stile's elbow, guiding him to the grid. This was a public mark of favor that awed the serfs present, Stile included. This Citizen had been friendly and reasonably solicitous throughout, but now he was being so when all eyes were upon him.

"You lout," another Citizen said, laughing. "Now we'll all have to show favor to our serfs!"

"What is Proton coming to?" a third Citizen inquired. This one was a woman, elaborately gowned and coiffed, with sparkling sapphires on her wrists and ankles and a nugget of Protonite on her forehead, reminding Stile of Neysa's snub-horn in her girl-form. Parallelism again, perhaps. This Citizen, too, was smiling, seeming almost like a person.

It occurred to Stile that even Citizens might get bored with their routine existences, and appreciate comic relief on rare occasions. The Tourney was a great equalizer!

Now he faced the Rifleman, the grid unit between them. This was a column inset with panels on opposite sides. The weight of the two men beside it caused the panels to illuminate. Stile's showed four categories across the top: 1. PHYSICAL 2. MENTAL 3. CHANCE 4. ARTS. Four more were down the side: A. NAKED B. TOOL C. MACHINE D. ANIMAL. The latter facet was highlighted: Stile had to select from the letters.

He experienced the usual pre-Game tension, made worse by the fact that this was no routine Game, but a Round for the Tourney. And made worse yet by the fact that his opponent was a Citizen. What column would the Rifleman choose? PHYSICAL or MENTAL, surely; he was neither a gambler nor an artist, and he wanted a good game. He would want to get into 1B or 1C, tool- or machine-assisted physical games like tennis or shooting, where his major expertise lay, or into 2B where he might get into chess. He had won a Tourney Game dramatically in chess, Stile remembered now, on his way up; in fifteen years he had probably improved his game. It was necessary to stay clear of this: Stile could play chess well himself, but he had not had fifteen idle years to practice.

He was up against someone who really could play the Game. This could be the toughest opponent he would face in the entire Tourney. A good Game that he lost in a contest was no good; he needed a likely winner. His only real course seemed to be ANIMAL. Then he could get into horseracing or liontaming. His knees were weak, but this only became acute when he flexed them completely; he could do ordinary riding better than anyone he knew, and remained pretty good at trick-riding. His smaller weight would give him an advantage, for the Tourney made no allowances for size or sex. All games were unhandicapped. And he liked animals, while the Rifleman, an expert hunter, probably did not have as close rapport. Yes.

Stile touched D. Immediately a new grid showed: 1D, PHYSICAL/ANIMAL. The Rifleman had chosen as expected.

Now the top line was 1. SEPARATE 2. INTERACTIVE 3. COMBAT 4. COOPERATIVE, and the sideline was A. FLAT B. VARIABLE C. DISCONTINUITY D. LIQUID. Stile had the letters again, which was fine. Horseracing was on a flat surface, and he had control of the surfaces. He did not want to get involved with trained sharks or squid wrestling in the LIQUID medium, and feared the Rifleman might be experienced in falconing in DISCONTINUITY, i.e., air. Mountain Rodeo would be all right, in the VARIABLE surface; Stile had bulldogged mountain goats before. But that category also included python tug-of-war in trees, and Stile did not care for that. So he stuck with A. FLAT.

The Rifleman selected 2. INTERACTIVE. So they were in box 2A. No horseracing, but there could be two-horse polo or—

The new grid was upon them, nine squares to be filled in by turns. Lists of games and animals appeared.

The Rifleman met Stile's gaze over the column. "Take it," he said, smiling. He was giving Stile the advantage of first selection, rather than requiring the Game Computer to designate the turn randomly. Such minor courtesies were permitted; they facilitated the selection process.

"Thank you, sir." Stile designated POLO/HORSE in the center box.

The Citizen put BASEBALL/ANDROID in the right upper box. Oh, no! Stile had not considered that androids counted as animals for Game purposes. Baseball was played by modified twentieth-century rules: nine players per team. It was a ballgame, but there was some overlap in categories; ballgames could appear in several sections of the master grid. This was an animal-assisted ballgame, as was polo. The difference was, there were a number of animals here, not used as steeds but as actual players. Obviously the Rifleman was expert at this sort of game, while Stile was only fair. He had walked into a trap.

Sure enough, while Stile filled in other individual animal contests, the Rifleman filled in android team games: Soccer, Basketball, Football. And when they played the grid, the Citizen won: FOOTBALL/ANDROID.

Disaster! Stile had not played team football in a long time. He could pass, kick and catch a football, but an hour-long session with twenty bruisingly huge androids? What a horror!

There was no chance now to brush up on the antique Earth-planet Americana the Rifleman evidently liked. Stile had to play immediately, or forfeit. The Citizen did not bother to ask him to concede, knowing he would not. For better or worse, this had to be fought out on the field.

They adjourned to the bowl-stadium. It was sparsely attended by spectators, since there were several hundred Games in progress and serf interest was divided. However, a number began to file in as the news of a Citizen-serf-android match spread. It was not that serfs were interested in Stile, at this point; they merely hoped to see a Citizen get knocked about a little with impunity.

"In the interest of economy of time and efficient use of facilities, this Game will be abbreviated to thirty minutes playing time without interruption," the Game Computer announced. "Each party will select twenty animal players, from which a continuous playing roster of ten will be maintained. Substitutions are limited to one per team per play, performed between plays. Proceed."

The computer was certainly moving it along! And no wonder, for a second playing field was already being utilized, and the remaining two would surely be in use before Stile's game finished.

They reviewed the androids. The artificial men stood in a line, each hulking and sexless and stupid but well muscled. Each carried a placard labeling its specialty: FULLBACK, HALFBACK, QUARTERBACK, and an array of offensive and defensive linemen. The capability of each was set within a standard tolerance; an android could perform exactly what it was supposed to do, no more and no less. Thus the outcome of the Game would be determined by the management and strategy and participation of the two human players, not the skill of the androids.

The largest imponderable was that of human skill. For this was not a remote-control game; the androids were there merely to assist the real players, who could occupy any position on their teams, but had to participate continuously. A good contestant would enable his team to prevail; a bad one would drag his team down to defeat. Stile feared that the Rifleman would prove to be good, while Stile himself, partly because of his size, would be less-than-good.

The Rifleman selected four pass receivers and a solid offensive line. He was going for an aerial offense, without doubt! Stile chose pass receivers too, and a passing quarterback, then concentrated on his defensive line. He had to hope for a stalled game and errors; as he saw it, defense was the refuge of incompetence, and that was apt to be him. He dreaded this Game!

It began. Chance gave Stile's team first possession of the ball. His animals were in white, the Rifleman's in black. The opposing team lined up like faceless demons from the frame of Phaze, darkly formidable. They swept forward, kicking the ball ahead, converging on its locale as it landed. Stile's receiver-android had no chance; he was down on the ten-yard line.

Yards, Stile thought. This was one of the few places where the old system of measurements prevailed on Planet Proton, because of the vintage and origin of this particular game. It was easiest to think of them as scant meters.

Now the onus was on him to devise a strategy of play that would bring the football down the field and across the opposing goal line. Stile had a hunch this would not be easy. He assigned himself to be a pass receiver, and scheduled the play for his runner. That should keep Stile himself from getting crushed under a pile of android meat. Of course he knew the androids were programmed to be very careful of human beings. Still, a tackle was a tackle, and that could be bruising. He was thoroughly padded in his white playing suit, of course, but he knew accidents could happen.

The play proceeded. The pass receivers dodged the opposing linemen and moved out on their patterns. Stile got downfield and cut back as if to receive the ball—and found himself thoroughly blocked off by the android pass defender. Catch the ball? He could not even see it! The only way he could hope to get it, had it been thrown to him, was if it passed between the animal's legs.

Fortunately he knew no pass was coming. Stile's runner bulled into the line, making one yard before disappearing into the pileup. That, obviously, was not the way to go.

Still, this first drive was mainly to feel his way. The nuances were already coming back to him, and he was getting a feel for the performance tolerances of the androids. He should be able to devise good strategy in due course.

Next play he tried a reverse end run. He lost a yard. But he was watching the Black team's responses. The androids, of course, lacked imagination; a really novel play would fool them, and perhaps enable his team to make a big gain or even score.

On the third play he tried a screen pass to one of his receivers. The pass was complete, but the receiver advanced only to the line of scrimmage before getting dumped. No breakthrough here!

Fourth down and time to kick the ball downfield. Stile signaled his kicker to come in—and realized belatedly that he had selected no kicker. None of his animals specialized in any kind of kick, and therefore could not do it. If he had his quarterback make the attempt, the job would surely be bungled, and the other team would recover the ball quite near the goal line. Yet if he did not—

A whistle blew. The referee, penalizing his team for delay of game. Five yards. He *had* to kick it away!

No help for it; Stile would have to kick it himself. He would not have the booming power of an android, and he dreaded the thought of getting buried under a mound of tackling animals, but at least he could accomplish something. If he got the kick off promptly, he might get away without being bashed.

No time to debate with himself! He called the play, assigning the kick to himself. The teams lined up, the ball was snapped, and the enormous Black line converged on Stile like a smashing storm wave.

Stile stepped forward quickly and punted. Distracted by the looming linemen, he dropped the ball almost to the ground before his toe caught it. The ball shot forward, barely clearing the animals, and made a low arch downfield, angling out of bounds just shy of the fifty-yard line. Not bad, all things considered; he had gained about forty yards. He had been lucky; had the Black androids had the wit to expect an incompetent punt, they might have blocked it or caught it before it went out, and had an excellent runback.

Luck, however, seldom played consistent favorites. Stile had to do better, or the first bad break would put him behind.

Now it was the Rifleman's turn on offense. The Citizen had stayed back during the prior plays, keeping himself out of mischief. Now he made his first substitution, bringing in one of his pass receivers. Stile exchanged one of his receivers for a pass defender. The first plays would probably be awkward, since most of Stile's players were offensive and most of the Rifleman's players defensive—but the longer the drive continued, the more qualified players could be brought in, at the rate of one per play. Of course the offensive and defensive lines were fairly similar, for Game purposes, so the exchange of as few as three backfield players could transform a team. All the same, Stile hoped the drive did not continue long.

The Rifleman assumed the position of quarterback. His animals lined up. The play commenced. Stile's line charged in, but the Rifleman reacted with poise, making a neat, short bulletlike pass to his receiver on the sideline. It was complete; the pass had been too accurately thrown for the receiver to miss, too swift for the defender to interfere with. The Citizen had a net gain of eight yards.

The Rifleman—now Stile appreciated how this applied to football, too. The Citizen was a superior player of this arcane game, better than an android passer. Therefore he had a superior team—while Stile had an indifferent team.

Stile substituted in another pass defender—but the Citizen brought in another receiver. Stile could not double-cover. Those passes were going to be trouble!

They were. The Rifleman marched his team relentlessly downfield. Not every pass connected, and not every play was a pass, but with four tries to earn each first down, the offensive team had no trouble. All too soon the Rifleman scored. Then the Rifleman substituted in his own placekicker and let him make the extra point. The score was 7–0, the Rifleman's advantage.

Complete team substitutions were permitted after a touchdown. It was a new game, with Stile receiving again, except that he was now in the hole. Five playing minutes had elapsed.

Stile's team received the ball and attempted a runback. His animal got nowhere. Stile had his first down on the twelve-yard line.

It was time to get clever. If he could fool the defenders and break an android free, he might score on a single play. But this could be risky.

He set up the play: a fake run to the right, and a massive surge to the left, with every android lineman moving across to protect the runner.

The result was a monstrous tangle as stupid animals got in each other's way. His runner crashed into his own pileup, getting nowhere, and the referee imposed a fifteen-yard penalty for unnecessary roughness, holding, and offensive interference. Half the distance to Stile's goal line.

Second down, long yardage, from the six-yard line. So much for innovation! Stile tried to complete another pass, this time to himself; maybe the Rifleman wouldn't expect him to expose himself that way, and the surprise would work. A long bomb, trying for the moons, double or nothing.

The play commenced. Stile ducked through the line and charged straight downfield. The Rifleman cut across to guard him. Together they turned at the fifty-yard line, and Stile cut back to the appointed spot to receive the pass, and the Rifleman cut in front of him and intercepted it while it remained too high in the air for Stile to reach.

"Sorry about that, friend," the Citizen said as Stile hastily tackled him and the whistle blew to end the play. "Height has its advantage."

It certainly did. Stile had lost the ball again without scoring. He heard the roar of reaction and applause from the filling audience section of the stadium; the Rifleman had clearly made a good play. Now Stile would have to defend again against the devastating passing attack of his opponent.

He was not disappointed. Methodically the Rifleman moved the ball down the field until he scored again. This time he passed for the extra points, and made them. The score was fifteen to nothing.

The first half of the game was finished: fifteen minutes of playing time. Stile had tried every device he could think of to stop his opponent from scoring, and had only managed to slow the rate of advance and use up time. The Rifleman had averaged a point per minute, even so. Stile had to move, and move well, in the second half, or rapidly see the game put out of reach. He needed a dramatic, original system of defense and offense. But what could he do?

Surprise, first. What could he do that really would surprise his opponent, while staying within the clumsy rules of this game? He couldn't run or pass or kick the ball away—

The kick. It was possible to score on the kick. Field goals, they were called, worth three points each. Except that he had no kicker other than himself. That was only slightly better than nothing, considering his near bungle of his first attempt to punt. The moment he set up for a placekick instead of a punt, those Black armored animals would be upon him. Even if he got the kick off, even if he somehow scored, he would wind up crushed at the bottom of the pile of meat. There was not any great future in that. If by some fluke he scored several field goals, enough to win, he would still be so battered he would be at a serious disadvantage in other Games of the Tourney. It would really be better to forfeit this one; it took two losses to eliminate an entrant, so he could afford that gesture.

No! He was not about to forfeit anything! If he lost, it would only be because he had been fairly beaten.

Still, the kick seemed to be his best chance. A surprise punt on first or second down, catching the Rifleman with his guard down. Then an attempt to force an error, an interception, or a fumble. Playing for the breaks. It would take nerve and luck and determination, but it was a chance.

Stile's team received the kickoff. This time the ball bounced into the end zone, and was brought out to his twenty-yard line for play.

Stile called for the punt, after a fake pass. His quarterback would simply fade back and hand the ball to Stile, then serve as interference to the tacklers while Stile got the kick off.

It worked. Stile got a beautiful—for him—punt off, escaping unscathed himself. The ball was low and fast, skimming over the heads of the animals, bouncing, and rolling rapidly onward. No one was near it.

The Rifleman, playing the backfield, was first to reach the ball. But the thing was still hopping crazily about, the way an unround and pointed ball was apt to do, as if it were a faithful representative of its crazy period of history, and it bounced off the Citizen's knee. Now, according to the peculiarities of this sport, it was a "live" ball, and Stile's onrushing animals had the limited wit to pounce on it. There was a monstrous pileup—and Stile's team recovered the football on the thirty-yard line of Black. A fifty-yard gain!

"Nicely played," the Rifleman said, smiling. "I was beginning to fear the game would be unconscionably dull."

"No Tourney Game is dull," Stile said. "Sir."

Now he had the ball in good field position—but could he seize the opportunity to score? Stile doubted it. He simply did not have the ability to advance the ball consistently.

So he would have to attempt to score from this range. That meant a forty-yard field goal. No, Stile doubted he had the power or accuracy for that. He would merely be throwing the ball away, unless he could get closer to the goal. His androids evidently couldn't do that, and Stile himself was too small to carry it; the pass interception had shown that. This was one game where no advantage could be achieved from small size.

Or could it? These android brutes were accustomed to dealing with creatures their own size, and were slow to adjust. An agile, acrobatic man *his* size—why not show them some of the tricks he could do? Stile was small, but no weakling, and the androids were programmed not to hurt real people. He just might turn that into an advantage.

In the huddle he had specific instructions for his center. "You will hike the ball to me—make sure you get it to me, for I am smaller than your regular quarterback—then charge forward straddle-legged. I clarify: hike the ball, then block forward and up, your feet spread wide. Do you understand?"

Dully, the android nodded. Stile hoped the creature would follow orders literally. These androids were the match of real people physically, but science had not developed their brains to work as well as the human kind. Androids cast in petite female forms were said to be quite popular with some men, who considered their lack of wit to be an asset. Specialized androids were excellent for other purposes such as sewer cleaning. It just happened that in this Game, Stile had to push to the intellectual limit of the type. In a real game of football, as played on

Earth centuries ago, such an android would have been fully competent: this was not that situation.

The creature did as ordered. Stile took the ball, ducked down—and charged forward between the animal's spread legs. The slow-witted opposing androids did not realize what had happened; they continued to charge forward, looking for a ball carrier to tackle. Stile scooted ahead five, ten, and finally fifteen yards before the Rifleman himself brought him down. "Beautiful play!" the Citizen said as they bounced together on the turf, their light armor absorbing most of the shock of impact. With a fifteen-point lead, he could afford to be generous. But the growing stadium audience also cheered.

Stile had his first down on the fifteen-yard line, but he knew better than to try the same stunt again. At any rate, he was now in field goal range, for his kicking ability—except that he still did not relish getting crushed in the blitz that would converge on the placekicker.

Then he dredged from his memory an alternative: the dropkick. Instead of having the ball held in place by another player for the kick, the kicker simply dropped it to the ground and kicked it on the bounce. A dropkick, unlike a punt, was a scoring kick. Its disadvantage was that it was less reliable than a placekick, since the bounce could go wrong; its advantage was that it could be done on extremely short notice. Short enough, perhaps, to surprise the androids, and enable Stile to complete it before getting tackled and buried.

He decided to try it. He took the ball as quarterback, faded back a few yards, then dropped it for the kick. The ball bounded up, and the androids ceased their charge, realizing that this differed from a punt.

Stile watched with gratification as the football arced between the goal posts. It was wobbly and skewed but within tolerance. The referee signaled the score: three points.

"The dropkick!" The Rifleman exclaimed. "I haven't seen one of those in years! Magnificent!" He seemed more pleased about it than Stile was.

But now it was Stile's turn to kick off to the Rifleman. He decided to gamble again. "Do you know the onside kick?" he asked his teammates.

Blank stares were returned. Good—the animals had not been programmed for this nuance. Probably the other team's androids would not know it either, so could reasonably be expected to flub it. The Rifleman would know it—but Stile intended to kick the ball away from him.

He tried it and it worked. Stile's team had possession of the football at midfield. "Oh, marvelous!" the Rifleman exclaimed ecstatically.

Back in the huddle. "Number One will field the ball," Stile told the animals, referring to the Rifleman's shirt designation. "Charge him, box him in, but do not tackle him. I will tackle him."

Uncomprehending, the andoids agreed.

Stile punted on first down. This time he had the feel of it, and hung the ball up high, giving his players time to get down to it before it landed. The Rifleman, alert to this play, caught the ball himself, calling his own players in around him. Thus the two groups formed in a rough circle, Stile's animals trying to get past the Rifleman's animals without actually contacting the Rifleman.

Perplexed by this seeming diffidence, the Citizen started to run with the ball. That was when Stile shot between two of his own players, took a tremendous leap, and tackled the Rifleman by the right arm where the football was tucked. He made no bruising body contact, for that would have brought a penalty call, but yanked hard on that arm.

As the two twisted to the ground, the ball passed from the Citizen's grasp to Stile's. Stile was of course adept at wresting control of objects from others; he had specialized in this maneuver for other types of games. Once again, his team had possession of the ball.

"Lovely," the Rifleman said, with slightly less enthusiasm than before.

The ball was now just inside the twenty-yard line. Stile drop-kicked another field goal. Now he had six points. And eleven minutes remaining in the game.

He knew he would not get away with another onside kick. The Rifleman would already have alerted his team to that. This time Stile would have to play it straight, and hope to stop the Citizen's devastating drive.

Stile kicked it deep, and it went satisfyingly far before being fielded by a Black android. Stile's androids were alert to this routine situation, and they brought the carrier down on the twenty-yard line.

Now Stile had to stifle the passing attack. He decided to concentrate on rushing the passer and hoping for an interception. He himself would cover one of the Rifleman's receivers, while double-covering the other with androids.

This seemed to be effective. The Rifleman faded back for his pass, did not like the situation, but did not want to run or get tackled. So he overthrew the ball, voiding any chance for an interception. According to the quaint conventions for this sport, all parties knew exactly what he was doing, and it mandated a penalty for deliberate grounding, but none was called. Because if deliberate grounding of the ball was done with discretion, it was presumed to be a throwing error instead of what it obviously was. Presumably this sort of thing added luster to the game.

On the second down the Rifleman tried a pass to the double-covered receiver, but two androids were better than one and again it went incomplete. Good: one more such failure and he'd have to turn over the ball on a kick. Stile was at last managing to stifle the Citizen's passing attack.

On third down, the Rifleman rifled the ball directly to the receiver

Stile was covering. He aimed it high, to be out of Stile's reach, but reckoned without Stile's acrobatic ability. Stile leaped high to intercept it—and was banged aside by the receiver, who had not realized what he was going to do. No android would have leaped like that. A referee's flag went down.

The penalty was offensive pass interference. Stile's team had the ball again. This time the Rifleman's congratulation was definitely perfunctory.

The ball was on the Black thirty-five-yard line. Time remaining was nine minutes. Those incomplete passes had expended very little time. Still, Stile was getting nervous; he really needed to break loose and score a touchdown.

"Number 81—can you receive a lateral?" he asked.

"Yuh," the animal agreed after a brief pause for thought.

"Then follow me and be ready." Stile turned to a lineman. "When the ball is hiked, you turn, pick me up, and heave me over the Black line." He seemed to remember an ancient penalty for such a trick, but it was not part of the Game rules.

"Duh?" the android asked. The concept was too novel for his intellectual capacity. Stile repeated his instructions, making sure the animal understood what to do, if not why.

When the ball was hiked, Stile tucked it into his elbow and stepped into his lineman's grasp. The android hurled him up and over. Stile had been given such a lift in the course of gymnastic stunts, and was pretty much at home in the air. He flipped, rolled off a lineman's back, landed neatly on his feet and charged forward toward the goal line.

This time, however, the Rifleman had a couple of guards in the backfield, and they intercepted Stile before he had gone more than ten yards.

Now Stile lateraled to Number 81, who was right where he was supposed to be. What these creatures did, they did well! The android caught the ball and bulled ahead for eight more yards before being stopped.

They were within kicking range again. Stile decided not to gamble on another running play; he drop-kicked another field goal. The score was now 15–9, with eight minutes remaining. At this rate, he could do it—provided he had no bad breaks. Unfortunately, he was overdue for one of those. He had been playing extremely chancy ball.

Should he try another onside kick? No, that would only cost him yardage at this stage. He had to make the Rifleman travel as far across the field as possible, so that he had the maximum opportunity to make an error. So Stile played it straight.

This time he managed to put the ball all the way into the end zone. The Rifleman put it into play on the twenty-yard line. This time, wary of passing into Stile's double coverage, he handed it off to his runner.

But the android proceeded without imagination and was downed at the line of scrimmage. Any play left purely to the animals was basically wasted time; the capacities of the androids had evidently been crafted for that. The human players *had* to make their physical and/or mental skills count.

Now Stile was sure the Citizen was beginning to sweat. The Rifleman knew that if he failed to move the ball, he would have to turn it over—and then Stile would find some devious way to score. A touchdown and extra point would put Stile ahead in the closing minutes. But the Citizen was unable to advance the ball. What was he to do?

What *could* he do? He risked another pass to his double-covered android receiver. It was perfectly placed, threading between the defenders to reach its target. How that man could pass! But one defender managed to tip it, and the receiver did not catch it cleanly. The ball squirted out of his grasp, bounced on the ground, and one of Stile's animals, not realizing the ball was dead, fell on it.

It was obviously an incomplete pass. But the referee signaled a fumble. Now it was Stile's ball on the thirty-two-yard line.

"Now, wait," Stile protested. "That's a miscall. The receiver never had control of the ball."

"Aren't you aware that these referees are programmed to make at least one major miscall per game?" the Rifleman called to him. "That's to emulate the original style of play, back on crazy Earth. You happen to be the beneficiary of that error."

The referees were robots, of course; Stile hadn't noticed. They could be set at any level of competence. "But that's luck, not skill!"

"There's an element of luck in most games. That lends a special fascination. The human species loves to gamble. Play, before you draw another delay-of-game penalty." The Rifleman did not seem upset, perhaps because this change-of-possession was obviously no fault of his own.

Hastily, Stile played. He accepted the hiked ball, faded back for a pass, found his receivers covered, saw three huge animals bearing down on him, dodged them all, circled behind one and safely overthrew his covered receiver. The moment he released the ball, he hunched over as though still carrying it. The turning android saw that and grabbed him, not having seen the ball go.

The tackle was bruising despite the armor, but at least the padding protected him from more than superficial abrasion. A flag went down.

Roughing the passer. Fifteen-yard penalty. First down. Once again Stile was within field goal range.

He drop-kicked again, of course. The audience cheered. The stadium was almost full now; news of this game was evidently spreading. But he had to keep his attention on the field. Now he had twelve points, and six minutes to go. Maybe he could pull it out after all.

But the Rifleman had the ball again, and now he was determined. There were not going to be any more breaks or mistakes.

Stile's misgivings were well taken. The Rifleman shot his passes too high and fast for Stile to intercept, settling for swift, short gains. When Stile tried too hard he got tagged for interference. Slowly and erratically, but inevitably, the Citizen hammered out the yardage.

On Stile's thirty-yard line, the Rifleman's first pass attempt failed. On second down his run got nowhere. On third down Stile gambled on a blitz, sending eight of his animals in to overrun the quarterback before he could pass. It worked; the Rifleman was sacked. Loss of six yards.

Now it was fourth down, and the Rifleman had to kick out. He tried a placekick and field goal, but was too far out; the ball fell short, to Stile's immense relief.

Stile had the ball again, with four minutes remaining. Time enough —if he could move the ball.

He moved it. He had his animals open a hole in the center, and he slipped through for several yards. He had his passer send a screen pass to him, and he dodged and raced up the sideline for several more yards. He was wise to the ways of the androids, now; he knew their little individual foibles. Some were faster than others; some were less stupid. One android did not have the wit to outmaneuver another, but Stile did. He could get past them—so long as he did it himself, not delegating the job to an animal of his own. So long as he carried the ball himself, he could progress; that was the key. That was why the Rifleman had succeeded so well in moving the ball at the outset, while Stile floundered. The Rifleman had drawn on his own abilities, not limited by those of the androids. Now Stile was doing it too—and had been doing it, every time he kicked. Now, so late in the game, understanding came. It really was a game of two, not of twenty-two.

But this was bruising. The constant exertion and battering were taking it out of him, and Stile could not maintain the drive. It stalled out on the Rifleman's forty-yard line. Too far for another field goal. Stile had to punt, regretfully.

He went for the coffin corner, angling the ball out of bounds at the four-yard line. That forced the Rifleman to play in his own end zone.

The Citizen was showing overt nervousness now. He did not like being backed up this way. He tried a pass, but it was wobbly and off-target, incomplete.

Now it was time to strike. Stile caught the arm of his center as the lines reformed. "Make a hole to spring me through," he said, and the creature nodded. The androids were slow thinkers, but they did orient somewhat on the needs of their supervisors. This one now understood what Stile wanted.

When the ball was hiked, the android shouldered into his opposite number, lifting him entirely off the ground. Stile scooted through, so low that his flexing knees hurt, and emerged directly in front of the Rifleman.

"Oh, no!" the Citizen exclaimed. Losing his poise, he tried to run from Stile instead of throwing the ball away. It was a mistake; he moved right into a pocket of White linemen and was downed in his own end zone.

It was a safety: two points. The score was now 15–14, with two minutes left to play. And Stile's team would get the ball.

It was put into play by a free kick from the Rifleman's twenty-yard line. The kicker, under no pressure from the opposing line, got off a booming spiral that lofted high and far. One of Stile's receivers took it on his thirty-yard line and ran it all of two yards before getting buried.

Now Stile was highly conscious of the clock. He dared not give up the ball again, for the Rifleman would surely consume the remaining time in a slow drive and win by a single point. But how could Stile move it down to field goal range against the desperation defense he knew he would encounter?

Answer: he had to do it himself. He would get battered, but it was the only way.

"Run interference for me," he told his three most competent animals. "You two in front, you behind. Right end run. You two receivers go out for a fake pass. And you, you runner—you fake a run to the left." He was pulling out all the stops. If the Rifleman anticipated his strategy, he would swamp Stile with a blitz. It had to be risked.

But the Citizen, too, was tiring. He was in fit condition—but Stile was not merely fit, he was an excellent athlete in peak condition, strongly motivated. His toughness and endurance were counting more heavily now. The Citizen stayed well back, avoiding physical contact whenever possible. In effect, he had dropped off his team. That meant that not only did Stile have eleven effective players to ten, but he had the most animated team. Now he could put together a sustained drive— theoretically.

His animals blocked and Stile ran around the end. And—it worked. He made several yards before his escort fell in assorted tangles. Now a huge Black android pounced on him for the kill—and Stile cut in under the brute and threw him with a solid shoulder boost. It was partly the disparity of size that enabled Stile to come in low, and partly surprise that put him in close instead of where the android expected him. The creature went tumbling across Stile's back and rolled to the turf.

Suddenly Stile was in the relative clear, and still on his feet. He accelerated forward, drawing on his reserves of energy, determined to make the most of his opportunity. Dimly he heard the roar of the crowd, excited by the dramatic run. The stadium had been constantly filling, and now more than half the seats were filled—and it was a fair-sized chamber, sufficient for perhaps a thousand. Stile knew these spectators didn't care who won the Game; they merely responded to unfolding drama. Still, their applause encouraged him. His bruises and fatigue seemed to fade, and he shot ahead at full speed. Five yards, ten, fifteen, twenty—

In the end it was the Rifleman who caught him. The man was not to be tricked by a martial arts throw; after all, he was a former Tourney winner who had to be conversant with all forms of physical combat. He caught Stile by one arm and swung him around and down. He tried to wrest the ball away, but Stile was on guard against that, and plowed into the turf without giving it up.

He was now on the Rifleman's forty-five-yard line with a first down. His ploy had paid off handsomely.

On the next play Stile tried a short pass, from android to android. While he himself faked another run. This was not as spectacularly successful as his last play, but it was good for eight more yards. Most of the attention had been on Stile's fake, and the Rifleman's pass defense had loosened up.

Then a quarterback sneak, good for three more yards, and a first down on the thirty-four-yard line. He was getting near field goal range —but now he had only thirty seconds remaining. With no time-outs, he had no time to spare for fancy planning. "Give me the ball," he said. "Protect me."

But this time he got nowhere; his strategy had been too vague. Fifteen seconds remaining. Time for one final desperation measure. "Take a lateral," he told his primary pass receiver. "Step clear and lateral back to me."

Stile took the hiked ball, stepped back, lateraled to his receiver, and shrugged at the onrushing tacklers as they struggled to avoid him. The Rifleman didn't want any game penalties stopping the clock at this point!

The android lateraled back. Stile stood alone, having been forgotten by the tacklers. As the pileup formed about the pass receiver, Stile dodged forward, passing confused androids of both teams who somehow thought the play had ended, and were slow to reorient. He cut to the left, getting clear of the central glut, then forward again. He had made it to field goal range!

Then he heard the final gun. He had used up all his time in the course of his maneuvering, and now the game was over. There would be no more plays, no chance to drop-kick the winning field goal.

Stile slowed to a walk, disconsolate. So close—only to fail. To reach the fifteen-yard line in the clear, and have to quit, defeated by a single point.

Then, from the front tier of seats, he heard Sheen's voice. "Run, you idiot!" And he saw the animals of both teams converging on him.

Suddenly he realized that the game was not quite over. The play was still in session. Until he was tackled, it was not finished.

But the Rifleman, more alert to the situation than Stile had been, was now between him and the goal line. The Citizen was calling directions to his troops. Stile knew he could not make it all the way.

He began running across the field, toward the center, where more of his own animals were. "Protect me!" he bawled.

Dully, they responded. They started blocking off the pursuit. Stile cut back toward the goal, making it to the ten-yard line, the five—

A Black android crashed through the interference and caught Stile from behind. Stile whomped down in a forward fall, and the ball squirted from his grasp. A fumble at the worst possible time!

The androids knew what to do with a loose ball. Animals of both teams bellyflopped to cover it. In a moment the grandest pileup of the game developed. The whistle blew, ending the play and the game.

The delirious cheering of the crowd abruptly stilled. Obviously the ball had been recovered—but where, and by whom? It was impossible to tell.

Slowly, under the supervision of the referees, the androids were unpiled. The bottom one wore a White suit, and lay just within the end zone.

Stile had six more points.

Now the crowd went absolutely crazy. Serfs and Citizens alike charged onto the field. "Let's get out of here before we're both trampled to death!" the Rifleman exclaimed, heading for the exit tunnel.

"Yes, sir!" Stile agreed.

"By the way—congratulations. It was an excellent Game."

"Thank you, sir."

They drew up inside the tunnel. Here they were safe; the crowd was attacking the goal posts in some kind of insane tradition that went back before Planet Proton had been colonized. "I have not forgotten our private wager," the Rifleman said. "You played fair and tough and made a remarkable game of it, and you prevailed. I shall be in touch with you at another time."

"Thank you, sir," Stile said, unable to think of anything better.

"Now let's get out of these uniforms."

"Yes, sir."

Then Sheen was trotting toward them, her breasts bouncing handsomely. She was ready to assume control of Stile's remaining time in this frame. It would be several days before all of the Round One matches cleared, since there were 512 of them. But Stile would not be able to linger long in Proton-frame; he had to get back to Phaze and find out how to handle the unicorn Herd Stallion in combat. Otherwise his tenure in Phaze could become even shorter than his tenure in Proton.

But Sheen was aware of all this. She took him in tow, stripping him of his armor in literal and figurative fashion. Stile was able to tune out the contemporaneous proceedings. How good it was to have a friend like Sheen here, and one like Neysa there!

CHAPTER 4

The Little People

Stile stepped through the curtain into the deep and pleasant forest of Phaze. He recovered his clothing, dressed, then hummed up an ambience of magic. He could signal Neysa with a spell, and she would come for him.

Then it occurred to him that this would consume time that would be better spent otherwise. Why not experiment, and discover whether he could indeed transport himself? He pondered a moment, finding himself quite nervous, then singsonged a spell: "Transport this man to the Blue Castle's span." It was not good verse, but that didn't matter; abruptly he stood in the castle court.

He felt dizzy and nauseous. Either he had done an inexpert job, or transporting himself was not good procedure. Certainly he would not try that again in a hurry; it had gotten him here, but at the expense of his feeling of equilibrium and well-being.

Neysa was in the court, nibbling on the magic patch of bluegrass. Every bite she took was immediately restored, so there was no danger of overgrazing, despite the smallness of the patch. She looked up the moment he appeared, her ears swiveling alertly. Then she bounded across to join him.

"Careful! Thou wilt spear me!" he protested, grabbing her about the neck and hanging on to steady himself.

She snorted. She had perfect control of her horn, and would never skewer something she didn't mean to, or miss something she aimed for. She blew a questioning note.

"Nice of thee to inquire," Stile said, ruffling her sleek black mane with his fingers. He was feeling better already; there was a healing ambience about unicorns. "But it's nothing. Next time I'll have thee carry me; thou dost a better job."

The unicorn made another note of query.

"Oh, that," he replied. "Sheen took care of me and got me to the Game on time. I had to match with a Citizen, a former Tourney winner. He nearly finished me."

She blew a sour note.

"No, he was a top Gamesman," Stile assured her. "A player of my caliber. It was like doing battle in this frame with another Adept! But I had a couple of lucky breaks, and managed to win in the last moment. Now he's going to help me find out who, there, is trying to wipe me out." He tapped his own knee, meaningfully. "And of course once we settle with the Herd Stallion, we'll set out to discover who killed me here in Phaze. I don't like having anonymous enemies." His expression hardened. "Nay, I like that not at all!"

The Lady Blue appeared. She wore a bathing suit, and was as always so lovely it hurt him. It was not that she was of full figure, for actually she was less so than Sheen, but that somehow she was exquisitely integrated, esthetically, in face and form and manner. The term "Lady" described her exactly, and she carried its ambience with her regardless what she wore. "Welcome back, my lord," she murmured.

"Thank thee, Lady." He had been absent only a day, but the shift of frame was so drastic that it seemed much longer.

"Thy friend Hulk has returned."

"Excellent," Stile said. He was somewhat stiff from the bruising football game, but glad to be back here and quite ready to receive the Oracle's advice.

"Thou'rt weary," the Lady said. "Let me lay my hands on thee."

"Not necessary," Stile demurred. But she stopped him and ran her soft hands across his arms and around his neck, and where they touched, his remaining discomfort faded. She kneaded the tight muscles of his shoulders, and they loosened; she pressed his chest, and his breathing eased; she stroked his hair and the subconscious headache became nonexistent. The Lady Blue was no Adept, but she did possess subtle and potent healing magic, and the contact of her fingers was bliss to him. He did not want to love her, yet, for that would be foolhardy; but only iron discipline kept him from sliding into that emotion at a time like this. Her touch was love.

"I would that my touch could bring the joy to thee that thy touch does to me," Stile murmured.

She stopped immediately. It was a silent rebuke that he felt keenly. She wanted no closeness with him. Not while she mourned her husband. Perhaps not ever. Stile could not blame her.

They moved on into the castle-proper. The Lady preceded him to the bath, where Hulk soaked in a huge tile tub set flush with the floor, like that of a Proton Hammam. The huge man saw the Lady, nodded, then in an afterthought sought ineffectively to cover himself. "I keep forgetting this is not Proton," he muttered sheepishly. "Men don't go naked in mixed company here."

"Thou'rt clothed in water," the Lady reassured him. "We be not overly concerned with dress, here. My present suit differs not much from nudity." She touched the blue material momentarily. "I have myself stood naked before a crowd and thought little of it. The animals wear no clothing in their natural forms, and oft not in their human shapes. Even so, I would not have intruded, but that my lord is here and needs must be informed immediately."

"That's right!" Hulk agreed. "Do thou step outside a moment, Lady, and I'll get right out of this."

"No need," Stile said. "I am here." He had been behind Hulk, whose attention had been distracted by the prior entry of the Lady.

"Oh. Okay. I have the Oracle's answer. But thou dost not have much time, Stile. May I talk to thee privately?"

"If the Lady is amenable," Stile agreed.

"And what is this, unfit for mine ears?" the Lady Blue demanded. "Well I know you two are not about to exchange male humor. Is there danger?"

Hulk looked guilty. He used his fingers to make a ripple in the bath water. "There may be, Lady."

The Lady looked at Stile, silently daring him to send her away. She called him "lord" and deferred to him in the presence of others, for the sake of appearances, but he had no private power over her.

"The Lady has suffered loss already," Stile said. "I am no fit replacement, yet if the Oracle indicates danger for me, she is rightfully concerned. She must not again be forced to run the Blue Demesnes without the powers of an Adept."

"If thou wishest," Hulk agreed dubiously. "The Oracle says that thou canst only defeat the Herd Stallion by obtaining the Platinum Flute."

"The Platinum Flute?" Stile repeated, perplexed.

"I never heard of it either," Hulk said, making further idle ripples with his hand. The ripples traveled to the edges of the tub, then bounced back to cross through the new ripples being generated. Stile wondered passingly whether the curtain that separated the frames of science and magic was in any way a similar phenomenon. "But there was another querist there, a vampire—"

"The likes of us have naught to do with the likes of them!" the Lady Blue protested.

"Or with the unicorns or werewolves?" Stile asked her, smiling wryly.

She was silent, unmollified. Certainly her husband had not had much association with such creatures. The free presence of unicorns and werewolves in the Blue Demesnes dated from Stile's ascendance. He felt this was an improvement, but the Lady was evidently more conservative.

"Actually, he was not a bad sort at all," Hulk said. "I lost my way, going in, and he flew by in bat-form, saw I was in trouble, and changed to man-form and offered to help. He hadn't realized I was human; he thought I was a small giant or an ogre, and those pseudomen sort of look out for each other. I think he was rather intrigued by my motorcycle, too; not many contraptions like that in Phaze! I was afraid I was in for the fight of my life, when I realized what kind of creature he was, but he told me they only take the blood of animals, which they normally raise for the purpose and treat well. In war, they suck the blood of enemies, but that's a special situation. They never bother friends. He laughed and said it wasn't true that people bitten by vampires become vampires themselves; that's a foul myth propagated by envious creatures. Maybe that story originated from a misinterpretation of their love-rites, when a male and a female vampire share each other's blood. The way he told it, it almost sounded good. A fundamental act of giving and accepting. I guess if I loved a vampire lady, I'd let her suck—" He broke off abruptly, embarrassed. "I didn't say that well. What I mean is—"

Stile laughed, and even the Lady smiled briefly. "There is no shame in love, any form," Stile said.

"Uh, sure," Hulk agreed. "I got to talking with him, and the more I knew him, the better I liked him. He drew me a map in the dirt so I could locate the Oracle's palace without getting in trouble. Then he changed back to a bat and flew off. And you know, that route he pointed out for me was a good one; I made it to the Oracle in a couple more hours, when it could've been days the way I had been going."

Hulk made another wave on the water, one that swamped the pattern of wavelets. "I'm finding it harder not to believe in magic. I saw that man change, I saw him fly. He was there when I arrived, and showed me that room where the Oracle was—just a tube sticking out of the wall. I felt sort of silly, but I went ahead and asked 'How can Stile defeat—' I forgot to use thy Phaze title, but it was too late, and it didn't seem to matter to the Oracle—'How can Stile defeat the unicorn Herd Stallion in fair combat at the Unolympics?' And it replied 'Borrow the Platinum Flute.' I couldn't understand that, and asked for a clarification, but the tube was dead."

"The Oracle has no patience with fools," the Lady said. "It answers only once, and considers all men fools; no offense to thee, ogre."

Hulk smiled. It seemed he had been nicknamed after the monster he most resembled, and he did not mind. "So I discovered. But I feared I had failed thee, Stile."

"I was as baffled when it told me to 'Know Thyself,'" Stile said. "My friend Kurrelgyre the werewolf was told to 'Cultivate Blue' and could not understand that either. We all have trouble with Oracular answers, but they always make sense in the end."

"Not always desired sense," the Lady Blue agreed. "When it told me 'None by One,' I thought it spouted nonsense. But now I know to my grief what—" She turned away, but Stile had glimpsed the agony that transfixed her face before she hid it. He had not realized that she had ever been to the Oracle. That answer must have related to the death of her husband.

Hulk filled in the awkward pause. "I talked again with Vodlevile Vampire—that's his name—and we compared notes. It seemed he had asked the Oracle how to help his son, who was allergic to blood—that's no joke to a vampire—"

"I should think not!" Stile exclaimed.

Hulk was quite serious. "They don't live on blood all the time. But they need it to be able to change to their bat-form and fly. The blood facilitates the magic. So his boy couldn't keep up with the family, if— well, I guess I'd be concerned too, in that situation."

"Of course," Stile agreed, sorry that he had even considered any humorous side to this.

"But all the Oracle told him was 'Finesse Yellow.' That made him furious, because he said Yellow is an Adept, and vampires don't deal with Adepts. They live near one, and they're afraid of her and leave her strictly alone. But if they did have truck with Adepts, they wouldn't try to cheat them or anyone else, and Yellow was the very worst one anyway. Several of their number have been trapped by her and sold to other Adepts, who spell them into blind loyalty and use them for spying and for terrorizing other captives. Gives the whole tribe a bad name. So he was going home without an answer he could use. I couldn't help him; I don't know anything about Adepts. It was too bad."

"He sounds like a creature of character," Stile said. "Why should the Oracle suggest to such a creature that he cheat? That's the same as no answer."

"Finesse is not the same as cheat," the Lady pointed out. "It implies some artifice or devious mechanism, not dishonesty."

"Vodlevile is a very forthright person," Hulk said. "No tricks in him. Still, he helped me. He told me that most of the metal tools and weapons and musical instruments of Phaze are made by the Little People, the tribes of Dark Elves, and that some worked with bone, and some with wood, and some with silver, or with gold, or with platinum. So probably if thou canst find the right tribe of elves—"

"The Little Folk are not easy to find," the Lady Blue said. "They dwell mainly in the Purple Mountains, and they dislike normal men and deal with them seldom. Most of all they detest Adepts. When my lord desired an excellent musical instrument, he could not go to them, but had to trade with a hawkman who had a connection across the curtain. He said he would like to be in touch with the Little Folk, but that they wanted naught he had to offer."

"So Vodlevile informed me," Hulk said. "That's what I meant about danger. It seems that the more precious the metal a tribe works with, the less use that tribe has for men, because men try to steal the artifacts. Especially they hate big men. I'd be dead the moment I set foot in their territory. And the Blue Adept—" He shook his head. "So my Oracle answer isn't much use either. But I report it to thee, for what it's worth, and hope this doesn't cause mischief."

Stile was already deep in thought. "The advice of the Oracle is always practical, if obscure. One has to work to understand it, usually. But it surely makes sense—for both me and the vampire. And him I may be able to help, in return for his help to thee."

"I had hoped thou wouldst see it that way," Hulk admitted. "It really is thy mission he tried to facilitate."

"I like this not," the Lady said. "Thou meanest to go among the Little Folk."

"Perhaps," Stile agreed. "That's the mischief Hulk feared, knowing mine inclination. But first I must tackle the matter nearer at hand. It will take me a moment to devise a suitable spell. Let's meet in the courtyard in ten minutes."

"No spell will take thee safely to the fastness of the Little Folk," she protested. "Like the unicorns, they resist magic. Better thou goest among trolls or goblins; there at least thou wouldst have a fair chance."

"I had in mind summoning the Yellow Adept."

"The Yellow Adept!" she cried, horrified. "In these Demesnes?"

"I swore never to return to her Demesnes, so must needs she visit mine. Thus do I finesse the restriction. Come on—we have to give Hulk a chance to get dressed." Stile led the way out. The Lady was spluttering, but offered no further resistance.

They met in due course in the courtyard. The Lady had evidently communicated the situation to the unicorn, for Neysa was moving her horn about angrily and snorting just beneath the level of meaning.

Stile played his harmonica to bring the magic ambience. Then he intoned: "Yellow Adept, I ask of thee, come to the Blue Demesnes, to me."

Abruptly the yellow hag was there before them. "Blue, methought we were at quits!" she snapped. "Seekest thou war between Adepts?"

"By no means, Yellow. I only wish to bargain with thee, to mutual advantage, and may not invade thy Demesnes again."

Her somewhat beady eyes peered about. "There is that, my handsome. Thou'rt a man of thy literal word. But I am not garbed for socializing. Give me leave to freshen up first." And she felt about her baggy old dress, searching for a potion.

"Allow me, since thou'rt my guest." Stile played a bar of music, then intoned: "While Yellow visits Castle Blue, grant her youth, image and hue."

In place of the old crone stood a ravishingly beautiful young woman with an hourglass configuration and long golden-yellow tresses, wearing a marvelously fetching evening gown. Hulk's jaw fell, and the Lady Blue's eyes widened. Neysa merely snorted disparagingly; she had seen it before.

Lovely Yellow brought out a vial, shook out a drop, and caught it as it formed into a mirror. "Oh, thou shouldst not, thou darling man! Yes, thou hast recaptured it perfectly, my delicious!"

"Yet she remains a witch," the Lady Blue said tightly. Neysa snorted agreement.

Yellow shot a glance at them. "Witch, thou sayst? And aren't we all, regardless of our shapes or magic? What chance does any man have, against a vamp of whatever color?"

"None," Hulk muttered. Neysa made as if to stab him with her horn, and he hopped out of the way.

"What I wish is this," Stile said briskly. "There is a vampire man, Vodlevile, whose son is allergic to blood. The Oracle told him to finesse Yellow. He refuses to deal—"

"Aye, I have a potion to cure that malady," Yellow agreed. "But what does he offer in return?"

"Nothing," Stile said. "The vampire folk are wary of thee, for what reason I do not pretend to comprehend."

She waggled a pretty finger at him warningly, in much the way the Rifleman had in Proton. "Play not the innocent with me, pretty man! I have back orders for bats galore. Though I daresay their fear of female Adepts derives somewhat from propinquity, since they reside near one the canines would term 'woman.'"

Hulk stifled a chuckle. Insults were very much a matter of viewpoint, here.

"Vodlevile will not deal with thee," Stile said evenly. "But I will. If thou wouldst trade favors with me, as one professional to another, this is the favor I crave."

"What has the bat done lately for thee?"

"He helped my friend Hulk, who was on a mission for me. Never did the bat ask for mine assistance, nor does he know it is coming."

She shook her head. "The machinations of honor and friendship are a fascination to the likes of me! Thy generosity to animals will cost thee yet, Blue." She glanced at Neysa, whose ears angled quickly back. "Yet 'tis a true finesse that does appeal to me. My livelihood is in dealing and wheeling, and I will deal with thee. The bat shall have his potion."

"I thank thee, witch. And what favor dost thou crave in return?"

She considered prettily. "I could wish that thou wouldst come to see me, as once I thought thou wouldst—" Her eyes traveled to the Lady Blue, who gazed disdainfully away, and back again to Neysa, whose nostrils were beginning to steam. "Yet thine oath forbids, and if it did not, I think others would say nay, or neigh."

Now a small jet of fire shot from Neysa's nostrils, and the tip of her horn made a tiny motion suggestive of mayhem. "Even so," Stile agreed, straight-faced. He despised Yellow's business of trapping and selling live animals, but he rather respected her personally. A romantic alliance was certainly out of the question, as well she knew; Yellow was only teasing the competition. Such lighthearted malice was no doubt more of a pleasure for the men to note, than to the females against whom it was directed.

"Then methinks I will take it on the cuff," Yellow decided. "Some day, when I am in some minor way in need and call on thee for aid—"

"Agreed," Stile said. "Provided only that the service violates no ethic of mine, and I am then alive."

"There is that. Thou hast a veritable stormcloud of a future." She pondered again. "Then let me protect mine investment, and give thee a potion." She fished a tiny bottle out of her bodice and presented it.

Stile accepted it, disregarding Neysa's fiery snort. "If I may ask—"

"No secret, my scrumptious. This elixir renders the wearer less noxious to the Elven folk."

"Thou vixen!" Stile exclaimed. "Thou conniving wench! Thou wert aware of my mission all the time!"

"Even so, on all counts," she said. "Though I prefer the term 'foxy' to 'vixen.'" She vanished.

"Some company thou keepest!" Hulk remarked appreciatively. "She *is* foxy!"

"Or bitchy," the Lady Blue muttered as she and Neysa walked stiffly away.

Stile smiled. "She's not a bad sort, considering that she really *is* a hag and a witch. She really did look like that, a century or so ago when she was young." He considered briefly. "Hulk, I don't have much time for the probable magnitude of this mission, so I'll set off for the Purple Mountains this afternoon, as soon as I do some spot research to pinpoint the platinum-working elves."

"I'll go with thee!"

"Nay, friend! Thy appearance would only antagonize these folk, and I go not to quarrel but to borrow. I need thee to guard the Lady Blue, as thou hast done so ably before."

Hulk frowned. "I prefer not to do that, Stile."

Stile was perplexed. "Thou likest it not here? I would not hold thee—"

"I like it well here. That is the problem."

"Something tells me I am being opaque about something."

"Aye."

"Thou dost not get along with the Lady Blue?"

"The Lady is a wonderful person."

"Then I don't see—"

"Thou needest an Oracle?"

Stile shook his head. "I must."

The big man paced the courtyard. "Thou and I strike others as quite different. The giant and the dwarf. Yet we are similar. The same age, the same culture, similar Game skills, similar honor." He paused. "Similar taste in women."

Stile began to get the drift. "Thou didst like Sheen at the first sight of her, and thou dost get along great with Neysa—"

"Yes. But for their special natures—" Hulk shrugged. "The Lady Blue is another matter. It befits me not to guard her any more."

Now Stile began pacing. "Thou knowest she is not mine."

"She sure as hell isn't mine!" Hulk exploded. "She may not be thine now, but she is destined for thee and no other. Thou'rt the Blue Adept, the keeper of these Demesnes, and she is the Lady Blue. She is the finest woman I have known. Were there another like her—"

"There *is* another like her," Stile said, remembering Sheen's comment. "And I owe thee for the manner in which thou hast given up thine only Oracle answer to my need."

The two men exchanged glances, a remarkable notion dawning. "Another—in Proton," Hulk said. "Of course. Her alternate self. But that one too should be—"

"Nay. Not mine. I can not love two."

"With all the qualities I have seen, but versed in Proton culture." Hulk smiled, liking the notion. "Then thou wouldst not oppose—?"

"That Proton-lady sure as hell is not mine," Stile said, smiling as he echoed Hulk's expression. "Go to Proton. It is a different frame. Thou knowest thou canst never bring her here."

"Yet even for brief visits—it is all I could ask."

"Cross the curtain, talk to Sheen. Her friends will locate the lady for thee."

Hulk nodded. He stopped before Stile and put forth his hand. Stile shook it gravely, knowing this was their parting. Hulk would not come to the Blue Demesnes again. Stile felt a certain smouldering resentment that the big man had taken an interest in this particular woman, and a certain relief that there was in this case a solution, and a certain guilt for both the resentment and the relief. Hulk was a good man; he deserved the best, and the best was the Lady Blue. Her Proton alternate surely had similar qualities. So this was a triumph of fortune and common sense—yet it bothered him. He was simply not as generous in his private heart as he was externally. He had some growing to do, yet.

Now he had no guard for the Lady Blue. He could not leave her alone for any length of time; whatever enemy had struck down Stile's alternate self, the true Blue Adept, would surely strike again now that it was known the Blue Adept had been reconstituted. Stile had been constantly devising and rehearsing spells and strategies to deal with such an attack, and felt reasonably confident he could handle the situation. But suppose the enemy took the Lady Blue hostage and used her against Stile? He could not risk that.

While he pondered, the Lady reappeared. "The ogre prepares to depart. Know ye why?"

"I know," Stile said.

"I like this not."

How did she feel about this arrangement? "He is a good man, worthy of the likes of thee, as I am not."

If she grasped his hidden meaning, she gave no sign. "Worth is not the issue. I have a premonition of doom about him."

"I confess to being uneasy. I thought it was jealousy or guilt."

"Those, too," she agreed, and then he was sure she understood. But she did not elaborate.

He changed the subject. "Now I fear to leave thee here alone—yet must I seek the Flute, lest mine enemy move against me. Neysa will go with me."

"Is it security thou seekest—or vengeance?"

Stile grimaced, looking at her. "How is it thou knowest me so well?"

"Thou'rt very like my love."

"Would he not have sought vengeance?"

"For himself, nay. For those he held dear—" She halted, and he suspected she was remembering her vision of the fiery destruction of the trolls who had wiped out the Blue Adept's village. Then she met his gaze again. "Without Hulk or Neysa, the Blue Demesnes be not safe for me now. I must go with thee to the Purple Mountains."

"Lady, it may be dangerous!"

"More dangerous with thee and thy magic than without thee?" she inquired archly. "Have I misjudged thee after all?"

Stile looked askance at her. "I had thought thou dost not crave my company. For the sake of the good work done by the Blue Adept thou callest me lord, but in private we know it is not so. I do not mean to impose my presence on thee more than necessary."

"And with that understanding, may not the Lady accompany the Lord?"

Stile sighed. He had made due protest against a prospect that in fact delighted him as much as it made him nervous and guilty. "Of course she may."

* * *

The Lady rode a pale blue mare, the offspring of the foal of the Hinny and the Blue Stallion. As she had described, this mare's color was mainly an echo of the blue harness, but the effect was there. The Blue Stallion had been alive but aging when the Blue Adept was killed; the horse, it was understood, had died of grief.

Stile rode Neysa. He had never ridden another steed since taming her. No horse could match her performance, but it was more than that. Much more.

They crossed the fields south of the Blue Castle and entered the forest adjacent to the Purple Mountain range. Soon they were in the foothills. According to Stile's references, the geographical tomes collected by his other self, the tribe of the Dark Elves who worked platinum lived on a mountain about fifty miles east of where the convenient curtain-access to Proton was. The animals knew the way, once it had been determined; Neysa had ranged these lands for years and knew the location by description, though she was not conversant with the actual Elven Demesnes.

Here the lay of the land was gentle, and the air balmy, with patchwork clouds making the sunshine intermittent. The ride became tedious despite the pleasure of the surroundings. Had Stile been riding alone, he would have slept, trusting Neysa to carry him safely, or have played his harmonica, or simply have talked to the unicorn. But the presence of the Lady Blue in her natural splendor inhibited him.

"It was across this country I rode the Hinny, so long it seems ago," she remarked.

Stile found no appropriate response. He rode on in silence, wishing that the tragedy of his other self did not lie between them.

"The Hinny," she repeated musingly. "How I miss that fine animal!"

This was safer ground. "How is she now? Ten years is a fair span in the life of a horse, about thirty of ours, but not interminable."

"Of course thou knowest not," the Lady said somberly. "The Hinny was bred by the Blue Stallion, and returned to her wilderness fastness alone. The blue lad went back to his business, about which we inquired not, but which I believe was the meticulous construction of the Blue Castle. I remained with my family and with Snowflake, the white foal we had rescued. Sometimes out in the fields we thought we glimpsed the Hinny, and our hearts yearned toward her, but never came she nigh. Yet I was ill at ease. The revealed identity of my erstwhile companion the blue lad astounded me, and I was shamed. Yet I was intrigued too, and potently flattered by his suit. I remembered the vision I had had while he played his music, the Lady in the blue moon, and the subtle appeal of that notion grew. Later I learned that he had gone to inquire the identity of his ideal wife, and the Oracle had named me. It had for once been not obscure or circuitous or capable of alternate interpretation; it had told him exactly where and when to find me. Hence he had come at the designated moment, extremely fortuitous for me as I hung dangling in the clutch of the troll, and preserved my life when else it would have ended there. He had done all that he had done only to win my favor, though I was his by right from the moment he rescued me. And I only an ignorant peasant-girl!"

"The Oracle knew better," Stile murmured. "Thy Lord's legacy lives on in thee, when else it would have perished."

She continued as if she had not heard him. "Ah, what a foolish girl was I in that time. Long and long was it before ever I gave him the third Thee."

"I beg thy pardon, Lady. I don't follow—"

She gestured negligently with one hand. "Of course thou art from another culture, so I needs must inform thee. In Phaze, when a person loves another and wishes to have it known without obligation, she omits the statement and repeats only the object, Thee, three times. Then that other may do as he wishes, without reproach."

"I don't understand," Stile said. "Just to say to a person 'Thee, th—' "

Neysa nearly bucked him off as she drowned him out with a blast from her horn.

"Say it not carelessly nor in jest," the Lady reproached him. "It has the force of an oath."

Shaken, Stile apologized. "I have much to learn yet of this culture. I thank thee, Lady, for educating me, and thee, Neysa, for preventing me from compromising myself ignorantly." But it would not have been a lie if he had said it to the Lady; this was a battle all but lost at the outset. Still, it would have put her in an awkward situation.

"When next I saw the Hinny," the Lady continued blithely, "she was in sad state. Gravid, she had been beset by cowardly predators, jackals, and was nigh unto death. She limped to our gate, remembering me, and I screamed and roused my father. Never did I see him so angry, for the Hinny had been his admiration since the instant he saw her first. He took his cudgel and beat off all the curs that harried her, while I tried to help her. But all was for naught; she had lost much blood, and expended her last store of vitality reaching us, and the Hinny died at our door.

"Then did I remember the spell the blue lad had left me. 'Blue to me—I summon thee!' I cried. And he was there. When he saw the Hinny he gave a great cry of agony and fell upon her, taking her head in his arms, and the tears flowed down his face. But she was dead, her open eyes seeing naught, and all his magic availed not.

"The lad brought out his harmonica and played a tune, wondrously sad, and two moons clouded over and the sun faded, and a shimmer formed in the air between us. It made a picture, and it showed the Hinny, as she had been in life, great with foal, grazing near the wood.

Then a pack of jackals charged, a foul horde, surly ill-kempt curs of scant individual courage, like to wolves as goblins be to men, seeking to overrun their quarry by sheer mass. She leaped away, but the weight of the foal within her made her ponderous and somehow her front feet stumbled, causing her to fall and roll, and the brutes were on her in a motley pile, ripping at her flesh, tearing at her ears and tail. She struggled to her feet, but they hung on her like despicable leeches, and her precious blood was flowing. Gashed and weakening, she struggled out of that wood, the jackals constantly at her feet, leaping at her, trying to drag her down again, so that she left a trail of blood. So at last she came to me, and I saw myself scream and throw my hands to my head, reacting hysterically instead of helping her, and then my father came with his cudgel, and the magic vision faded.

"My father stood beside me, watching the sorrow of Blue, and indeed we shared it. Then did I comprehend the third of the great qualities about the Blue Adept that were to be the foundation of my love for him. His music, his power—and his abiding love for—" She hesitated momentarily. "For equines."

Stile realized she had been about to say "horses" and had reconsidered, from deference to Neysa.

"At last the blue lad rose, and it was as if the blood had been drained from him as it had from the Hinny. 'Because her knees were weak, the jackals caught her,' he said. 'The knees she sacrificed for me.' And I could not say nay, for I had seen it happen.

"'Yet can I do somewhat,' he continued, and there was that in him that frightened me, and I began to get a glimmer of the meaning of the sorrow and anger of an Adept. 'Turn you both about, lest you see what pleases you not.' And my father, wiser than I, took mine arm and made me turn with him. There was a pause, then sweet, bitter music as the lad played his harmonica. Then the muttering of an incantation, and an explosion of heat and odor. We turned again—and the corpse of the Hinny was gone, blasted by Blue's magic, and in the swirling smoke the lad stood, holding in his arms a newborn foal, light blue in hue.

"'The Hinny be dead, but her foal lives,' he said. 'This is why she came to thee.' Then before we could properly react, he addressed my father. 'This foal is birthed before her time. Only constant, expert care can save her. I am no healer; she requires more than magic. I beg thee, sir, to take her off my hands, rendering that which only thou canst give, that she may survive and be what she can be.'

"My father stood bemused, not instantly comprehending the request. 'The Hinny came to thee,' the lad continued, 'knowing thou couldst help her. More than all else, she wanted her foal to live and to be happy and secure. No right have I to ask this favor of thee, knowing it will be years before thou art free of this onus. Yet for the sake of the Hinny's faith—' And he stepped forward, holding forth the foal. And I knew my father was thinking of the Hinny, the finest mare of any species he had ever beheld, and of the Blue Stallion, the finest stud, and seeing in this foal a horse like none in Phaze—worth a fortune no man could measure. And I realized that in the guise of a request, the lad was proffering a gift of what was most dear to my father's dreams. It was Blue's way.

"My father took the foal in silence and bore her to our stable, for she needed immediate care. I remained facing the lad. And something heaved within my breast, not love but a kind of gratitude, and I knew that though he looked to be a lad and was in fact a nefarious magician, he was also a worthy man. And he inclined his head to me, and then he walked away toward the forest where the jackals had attacked the Hinny. And in a little while there was a brilliant burst of light there, and that whole forest was aflame, and I heard the jackals screaming as they burned. And I remembered how he had destroyed the trolls, and was appalled at this act of vengeance. Yet did I understand it also, for I too loved the Hinny, and who among us withholds our power when that which is dear to us is ravaged? The power of an Adept is a terrible thing, yet the emotion was the same as mine. No creature aggravates an Adept but at the peril of his kind. Yet when later I rode Starshine out to that region, I found the forest alive and green. Only the charred skeletons of the jackals remained; none other had been hurt. I marveled again at the power of the Adept, as awesome in its discretion as in its ferocity.

"After that my father made no objection to Blue's suit, for it was as if he had exchanged me for the precious foal, and duly the banns were published and I married the Blue Adept though I did not really love him. And he was ever kind to me, and made for me the fine domicile now called the Blue Demesnes, and encouraged me to develop and practice my healing art on any creatures who stood in need, even trolls and snow demons, and what I was unable to heal he restored by a spell of his own. Some we healed were human, and some of these took positions at the castle, willingly serving as sentries and as menials though no contract bound them. But mainly it was the animals who came to us, and no creature ever was turned away, not even those known as monsters, so long as they wreaked no havoc. It was a picturebook marriage."

She abated her narrative. "I thank thee for telling me how it was," Stile said carefully.

"I have not told thee the half of how it was," she said with surprising vehemence. "I loved him not, not enough, and there was a geas upon our union. He knew both these things, yet he treated me ever with consummate respect and kindness. How I wronged him!"

This was a surprise. "Surely thou dost overstate the case! I can not imagine thee—"

But confession was upon her. Neysa made a little shake of her horn, advising him to be silent, and Stile obeyed. "The geas was inherent in his choice of me to wed. He had asked the Oracle for his ideal wife, but had failed to include in that definition the ideal mother of his children. Thus I learned when I queried the Oracle about the number and nature of my children-to-be. 'None by One,' it told me in part, and in time I understood. There was to be no child by my marriage to him; no heir to the Blue Demesnes. In that way I wronged him. And my love—" She shrugged. "I was indeed a fool. Still I thought of him as a lad, a grown child though I knew him for a man, and a creature of incalculable power. Perhaps it was that power that straitened my heart against him. How could I truly love one who could so readily destroy all who stood against him? What would happen if ever he became wroth with me? And he, aware of this doubt, forced me not, and therefore had I guilt. So it was for years—"

She broke off, overcome by emotion. Stile remained silent. This was an aspect of her history that instilled misgiving, yet he knew it was best that he know it.

"Those wasted years!" she cried. "And now too late!"

They had come to rougher territory, as if the land itself responded to the Lady's anguish of conscience. These were the mere foothills to the Purple Mountains, Stile knew, yet the ridges and gullies became steep and the trees grotesquely gnarled. The turf was thick and springy; the steeds were not partial to the footing. Stile found the landscape beautiful, original, and somehow ominous—like the Lady Blue.

"Can we skirt this region?" Stile asked Neysa.

The unicorn blew a note of negation. It seemed that this was the only feasible route. Stile knew better than to challenge this; the unicorn could have winded a dragon or some other natural hazard, and be threading her way safely past. So they picked their path carefully through the rugged serrations of the land, making slow progress toward the major range.

The Lady's horse balked. She frowned and gently urged it forward, but the mare circled instead to the side—and balked again.

"This is odd," the Lady commented, forgetting her recent emotion. "What is bothering thee, Hinblue?"

Then the Lady's fair tresses lifted of their own accord, though there was no wind.

Neysa made a double musical snort. *Magic!*

Stile brought out his harmonica. "Nay, play not," the Lady said hastily. She did not want him to show his power in the vicinity of the land of the Little Folk.

But her hair danced about and flung itself across her eyes like a separately living thing, and her horse fidgeted with increasing nervousness. Neysa's horn began to lower to fighting range.

"Just a melody," Stile told her. "Neysa and I will play a little tune, just to calm thy steed." And to summon his magic—just in case.

They played an impromptu duet. Neysa's music was lovely, of course —but Stile's carried the magic. It coalesced like a forming storm, charging the immediate atmosphere.

And in that charge, dim figures began to appear: small, slender humanoids, with flowing hair and shining white robes. They had been invisible; now they were translucent, the color slowly coming as the music thickened the magic ambience. Stile's power was revealing them. One of them was hovering near the Lady, playing with her hair.

"The Sidhe," the Lady breathed, pronouncing it "Shee." "The Faerie-folk. They were teasing us."

Stile squeezed Neysa's sides with his knees questioningly. She perked her ears forward: a signal that there was no immediate danger.

Stile continued playing, and the ethereal figures solidified. "O, Sidhe," the Lady said. "Why do you interfere with us? We seek no quarrel with your kind."

Then a Faerie-man responded. "We merely played with thee for fun, Lady of the Human Folk, as we do so often with those who are unaware of our nature. Innocent mischief is the joy of our kind." His voice was winningly soft, with the merry tinkle of a mountain streamlet highlighting it. Stile could appreciate how readily such a voice could be mistaken for completely natural effects—flowing water, blowing breezes, rustling leaves.

"And thou," a Sidhe maid said to Stile as he played. "What call hast thou, of Elven kind, to ride with a mundane woman?" Her voice was as soft as the distant cooing of forest doves, seductively sweet, and her face and form were similarly winsome.

Stile put aside his harmonica. The Sidhe remained tangible; now that they had been exposed, they had no further need of invisibility. "I am a man," he said.

"A man—on a unicorn?" she inquired derisively. "Nay, thou art more likely a giant kobold, serving in the house of the human lady. Thou canst not fool her long, sirrah! Come, I will offer thee entertainment fit for thy kind." And she did a little skip in air that caused her white skirt to sail up, displaying her immortal legs to advantage.

"Thou'rt not my kind," Stile insisted, intrigued.

"Dost thou jilt me already?" she flashed, and evanescent sparks radiated from her hair. "I will have thy fanny in a hoist, ingrate!"

Neysa shifted her horn to bear on the Faerie-lass, who skipped nimbly aside. These magical creatures might not fear the weapons of human beings, but the unicorn's horn was itself magical, and would take its toll of any creature.

Stile lifted his harmonica to his mouth again.

"Yea, play!" the Sidhe lady exclaimed. "I will forgive thee thine in-discretion if thou playest while we dance."

It was a face-saving maneuver on her part, but Stile decided to go along. He did not want to have to use overt magic here. He played, and Neysa accompanied him, and the music was marvelously light and pretty. Stile had been a fair musician before he came to Phaze, but he had improved substantially since.

The Sidhe flocked in and formed their formation in midair. They danced, wheeling in pairs, singing and clapping their little hands. The males stood about four and a half feet tall, with calloused hands and curly short beards; the females were closer to four feet, and all were delicate of limb and torso. They whirled and pranced, the girls flinging their skirts out with delightful abandon, the men doing elaborate dance steps. It was beautiful, and looked like an extraordinary amount of fun.

After a time, the Sidhe damsel floated back down to Stile. She perched on Neysa's horn, somewhat to the unicorn's annoyance. She was breathing briskly, her full bodice flexing rhythmically. "Give o'er, giant elf; thou'rt forgiven!" she exclaimed. "Now come dance with me, before sunset, while thy steed plays her horn." And she reached out a hand to him, the tiny fingers beckoning.

Stile glanced at the Lady Blue, who nodded affirmatively. Neysa shrugged. Both evidently felt it was better to go along with the Faerie-folk than to oppose them. They were getting along well at the moment; better not to disrupt the mood, for such creatures could be unpleasant when angered, and their tempers were volatile. Stile had seen that in the mercurial reactions of this little lady.

Yet he demurred, more diplomatically this time. "Elven lass, I can not dance in air without magic." And he was not about to reveal his true nature now. Already he understood that Adepts were held in as poor regard by the Little Folk as by ordinary human people.

"Then shall I join thee below," she said, descending lightly to the turf. Then, abruptly shy: "I am Thistlepuff."

Stile dismounted. "I am Stile." He stood almost a foot taller than she, and really did feel like a giant now. Was this the way Hulk saw the world?

"The bridge between pastures?" Thistlepuff exclaimed, correctly in-terpreting his name. Then she did a pirouette, again causing her skirt to rise and expose her fine and slender legs. This was a characteristic gesture with her. In the frame of Proton, where all serfs were naked, no such effect was possible, and Stile found it almost embarrassingly appealing. The brief glimpse seemed better than the constant view, be-cause of the surprise and mystery. Clothing, he realized, was also magic.

Stile had played the Game in Proton for most of his life. Part of the Game was the column of the Arts, and part of the Naked Arts was

Dance. He was an athlete and a gymnast, and he had a good memory and sense of pace. Hence Stile could dance as well as any man, and a good deal better than most. He had watched and analyzed the patterns of the Faerie dance, and now understood it well enough. If this sprite thought to make a fool of him for the entertainment of her peers, she would be disappointed.

He went into a whirl of his own, matching Thistlepuff's effort. There was a faint "Oooh" of surprise, and the other Faerie-folk gathered about to watch. Yes, they had thought to have sport with him!

The lass stepped blithely into his arms, and he swung her in Sidhe fashion. Her head topped at the level of his shoulder, and she was light as a puff of smoke, but she was also lithe and sweet to hold. She spun out and kicked one leg high in the manner of a ballerina—oh, didn't she love to show those legs!—while he steadied her by the other hand. Then she spun back into his embrace, making a little leap so that her face met his in a fleeting kiss that struck and dissipated like a breath of cool fog.

They moved into a small promenade, and he tossed her into the air for a graceful flip and caught her neatly at the waist. Light as she was, it was easy to do the motions, and he enjoyed it. He felt more and more like the giant he never had been, and privately he reveled in it.

When the demonstration was through, the Sidhe spectators applauded gleefully. "Thou hast danced before!" Thistlepuff exclaimed, her bosom heaving with even more abandon. "Yet thou dost claim to be human!"

"Human beings can dance," Stile said. "The Lady I serve could do as well." He hoped that was the case; it occurred to him as he spoke that though he had seen the Lady Blue ride marvelously well, he had never seen her dance. Yet of course she could do it!

Neysa blew a note of caution. But it was too late. Stile, in his inexperience with the Faerie-folk had made another blunder. Thistlepuff was frowning mischievously at the Lady Blue.

"So thou sayest?" the Sidhe inquired, as sharply as the sound of the wood of a tree-limb snapping under too great a burden of snow. "Thou art of the Elven kind, surely; but she is as surely mundane. We shall see how she can dance." And the Sidhe recentered their ring on the lady.

He had gotten her into this; he would have to get her out. Stile crossed to the Lady as she dismounted. He could not even apologize; that would betray the situation to the Faerie-folk. He had to bluff it through—and he hoped that she could and would go along.

The Lady Blue smiled enigmatically and took his proffered hand. Good; at least she accepted him as a partner. It would have been disaster with a mischievous four-and-a-half-foot-tall Sidhe male for a dancing partner! At least Stile would keep his feet mainly on the ground.

It would have to be impromptu free-form, for they had had no rehearsal. Stile hoped the Lady had analyzed the dancing patterns as he had. But he let her lead, so that she could show him what she wanted.

Suddenly they were in it. The Lady was taller than he and as heavy —but also as lithe and light on her feet as a woman could be. When he swung her, she was solid, not at all like Thistlepuff, yet she moved precisely. He did not try to toss her in air, but she was so well balanced he could hold her up readily, and whirl her freely. When he moved, she matched him; when he stepped, she stepped; when he leaped, she was with him. In fact, she was the best dancer he had encountered.

It was a fragment of heaven, being with her like this. For the moment he could almost believe she was his. When they danced apart, she was a marvel of motion and symmetry; when they danced together, she was absolute delight. Now he wished this dance could go on forever, keeping his dream alive.

But then Neysa brought her harmonica melody to a close, and the dance ended. The Sidhe applauded. "Aye, she can dance!" Thistlepuff agreed ruefully. "Mayhap she has some inkling of Faerie blood in her ancestry after all. Thou hast shamed us, and we must make amend. Come to our village this night."

"We dare not decline their hospitality," the Lady Blue murmured in his ear. She was glowing with her effort of the dance, and he wished he could embrace her and kiss her. But this was one blunder he knew better than to make.

Now the steep bank of a ridge opened in a door. There was light inside, and warmth. The passage into the hill was broad enough for the steeds, and these were of course welcome. They walked into the Faerie village.

Inside it was amazingly large. This was technically a cave, but it seemed more like a clearing in a deep wood at night, the walls invisible in their blackness. A cheery fire blazed in the center. Already a feast was being laid out: a keg of liqueur, many delicious-smelling breadstuffs, fresh vegetables, pots of roasted potatoes and buckets of milk and honey and dew. For the animals there was copious grain and fragrant hay and a sparkling stream.

Then Stile remembered something from his childhood readings. "If a human being partakes of Faerie food, is he not doomed to live among them forever? We have business elsewhere—"

Thistlepuff laughed with the sound of rain spattering into a quiet pond. "Thou really art not of our kind, then! How canst thou believe that myth? Thou hast it backwards: if ever one of the Sidhe forsakes his own and consumes mundane food, he is doomed to become mortal. That is the true tragedy."

Stile looked at Neysa, embarrassed. She blew a positive note—no danger here. Thistlepuff had spoken the truth, or close enough to it to eliminate his concern. So he had blundered again, but not seriously; the Sidhe were amused.

Now they ate, and it was an excellent repast. Afterwards, pleasantly sated, they availed themselves of the Faerie sanitary facilities, which were concealed in a thick bed of toadstools, then accepted invisible hammocks in lieu of beds. Stile was so comfortable that he fell almost instantly to sleep, and remained in blissful repose until a beam of sunlight struck his face in the morning.

Startled, he looked about. He was lying in a bed of fern in a niche in the gully. No cave, no invisible hammock, no Faerie village! The Lady Blue was up before him; she had already fetched fruit from some neighboring tree. Neysa and Hinblue were grazing.

Stile was abashed. "Last night—what I remember—the Sidhe—did I dream—?"

The Lady Blue presented him with a pomegranate. "Of dancing with the Faerie-folk? Sharing their food? Consuming too much of their nefarious dew so that thou didst sleep like a rock forever in their invisible hammock? It must have been a dream, for I remember it not."

There was a musical, mirthful snort from Neysa.

"Even so," Stile agreed, concentrating on the fruit. Was his face as red as its juice? The Sidhe had had some sport with him after all. But how glad he was to note that the Lady's heavy mood had lifted.

"Yet dost thou dance divinely in thy dreams." The Lady was for a moment pensive, then reverted briskly to business. "If thou dost not get thy lazy bones aloft, never shall we locate the Platinum Elves in time for thee to go divert thyself at thy next otherframe game with thy mechanical paramour."

Barbed wit, there! The Proton Tourney was no fun diversion, but a matter of life or nonlife on that planet. Stile rose with alacrity. "One more day, one more night—that's all the time I have until I have to report for Round Two of the Tourney."

Soon they were on their way again. It had been a good night; human and equine beings had extra vigor. Neysa and Hinblue stepped out briskly, hurdling the ridges and gullies and hummocks. Neysa, conscious of the equine limitations of the natural horse, did not push the pace too fast, but miles were traversed swiftly. The Lady Blue, of course, rode expertly. Stile might be the best rider in Phaze, but she was the second best.

After an hour Stile became aware of something fleeting. "Hold," he murmured. Neysa, feeling his bodily reaction, was already turning around.

"Is aught amiss?" the Lady Blue inquired, elevating an eyebrow prettily.

"The curtain," Stile said. "We just passed it. I need to note where it is, as a matter of future reference. There may be good places to cross it to Proton, if only I can locate them."

"There are times when I wish I could cross that curtain," she said wistfully. "But hardly can I even perceive it."

"Ah—here it is," Stile said. "Proceeding northeast/southwest, angling up from the Purple Mountains. Of course it may curve about, in between reference points, but—"

The Lady waved a hand. "Cross it, my lord, and see where it leads. Only forget not to return, lest I abscond with thy steed."

Stile laughed, then spelled himself through.

The other side was hot and bleak. The ubiquitous cloud of pollution was thinner here, but the haze still shrouded a distant force-field dome. This was not a good place to cross; he needed a section within a dome, or very close to one. Ah, well—it had been worth checking. He released his held breath and willed himself back into Phaze as he stepped back across the faint scintillation.

It was a great relief to see the lush greenery form around him. What a mess the Citizens had made of the surface of their planet, in the name of progress! "I'm satisfied. Let's go."

"Yet if I could cross, it would mean there would be no one for Hulk," the Lady concluded.

By midmorning they had reached the fringe of the Platinum Demesnes; Elven warner-markers so informed them.

Now Stile uncorked the Yellow Adept's gift-potion and applied it liberally to his face and hands. He offered some to the Lady, but she demurred; she did not care to smell like an elf. Since she was obviously no threat to anyone, Stile trusted it would be all right.

The Platinum Demesnes were in the Purple Mountains proper. The access-pass was marked by a neat wooden sign: PT78. Stile smiled, recognizing the scientific symbol and atomic number of platinum; surely some crossover from the frame of Proton, here. Evidently these Little People had a sense of unity or of humor.

They rode up the narrow trail. The mountain slopes rose up steeply on either side, becoming almost vertical. It would be very easy for someone to roll boulders down; the stones would flatten anyone misfortunate enough to be in their way. Except an ogre or an Adept. Stile kept his hand on his harmonica and his mind on a boulder-repulsion spell he had devised. He did not want to use magic here, but he wanted even less to suffer death by stoning.

Then they encountered a hanging bridge. It crossed a deep, dark chasm too wide for Neysa to leap, but the bridge was too narrow and fragile to support equine weight. Neysa could change form and cross, but that would not help Hinblue. Stile considered casting a spell to transport the horse across, but vetoed it himself; the Platinum Elves could be watching. So—they would have to cross the hard way, by navigating the chasm manually. Perhaps this was a deliberate hurdle to test the nature of intruders, separating the natural from the supernatural—or, more likely, the Elven Folk did not want mounted visitors charging into their Demesnes.

There was a precarious path down into the chasm, and another rising on the far side. Probably the two connected, below. Stile and the Lady started down, riding, because the steeds did not trust the people's ability to navigate such a pass safely alone. But Stile kept his hand on the harmonica.

The touch of that musical instrument reminded him—he was coming here for a flute. Yet how could a musical instrument avail him? What he really needed was a weapon. Well, he should soon be finding out!

Fortunately the path did not descend far. It reached a broad ledge that cut into the chasm, reducing it to a width that could be conveniently hurdled by the steeds. The path continued on down into the chasm, but they did not follow it. They jumped across the ugly crack and started up the other side. Stile was aware of a hot draft that came up erratically from the depths, smelling of sulfur. He did not like it.

They emerged at the top of that chasm, and continued on up the path. Now they were higher in the mountain range, nearing the top—and they rounded the crest, and the landscape leveled, and lo! it was only a larger foothill. Ahead the real mountains loomed, sloping up into the clouds. They were tall enough to maintain snow, but it was purple snow.

On this brief level spot was a mound, overgrown by turf and vines. The path led right to it; in fact there was a stone entranceway. "Methinks we have arrived," Stile murmured, dismounting.

"Methinks thou shalt not swiftly depart," a voice said behind him. Stile turned to find a small man in the path behind. He stood about four inches shorter than Stile, but was broader in proportion. His skin was an almost translucent blue, and his clothing was steel-gray.

"Thou must be of the Elven Folk," Stile said. "I come to beg a favor of the workers of platinum."

"We do work platinum," the elf agreed. "But we do no favors for outsiders. Thou art now our prisoner, and thy human companion." He gestured with his shining sword. "Now proceed into the mound, the two of you. Thine animals will join our herds outside."

Neysa turned on the arrogant elf, but Stile laid a cautioning hand on her back. "We came to petition; we must yield to them," he murmured. "If they treat us ill, thou canst then act as thou seest fit. An thou dost find me fettered, free me to play my music."

Neysa made an almost imperceptible nod with her horn. Once Stile had access to his music, he could bring his powers of magic into play, and would then be able to handle himself. So the risk was less than it seemed. He and the Lady suffered themselves to be herded into the mound.

Inside it was gloomy, with only wan light filtering in through refractive vents. Several other armed elves were there, garbed like the first. Their leader stepped up and appraised Stile and the Lady as if they were newly purchased animals. He sniffed as he approached Stile. "This one be Elven," he pronounced. "But the woman is human. Him we shall spare to labor at our forges; her we shall use as tribute to the beast."

"Is this the way thy kind welcomes those who come peaceably to deal with thee?" Stile asked. There was no way he would permit the Lady Blue to be abused.

"Silence, captive!" the elf cried, striking at Stile's face with a backhand swing of his arm.

The blow, of course, never landed. Stile ducked away from it and caught the elf's arm in a punishing submission hold. "I can not imagine the elders of thy kind being thus inhospitable," he said mildly. "I suggest that thou dost summon them now."

"No need," a new voice said. It was a frail, long-bearded old elf, whose face and hands were black and wrinkled. "Guards, begone! I will deal with this matter myself."

Stile let go his captive, and the young elves faded into the crevices and crannies of the chamber. The oldster faced Stile.

"I am Pyreforge, chief of the tribe of Platinum Mound Folk of the Dark Elves. I apologize for the inhospitability shown thee by our impetuous young. It is thy size they resent, for they take thee to be a giant of our kind."

"A giant!" Stile exclaimed, amused. "I'm four feet eleven inches tall!"

"And I am four feet five inches tall," Pyreforge said. "It is the odor of thy potion that deceives us, as well as thy size. To what do we owe this visit by the Lady and Blue Adept?"

Stile smiled ruefully. "I had thought not to be so obvious."

"Thou art not. I was delayed researching my references for thy description. I pored all through the Elven species in vain. It was the unicorn that at last betrayed thee, though we thought Blue recently deceased."

"Neysa would never—"

The old elf held up a withered hand. "I queried the 'corn not. But no man save one rides the unicorn, or travels with the fairest of human ladies. That be the imposter Blue Adept—who I think will not be considered imposter long."

Stile relaxed. "Oh. Of course. Those must be comprehensive references thou hast."

"Indeed. Yet they are oft tantalizingly incomplete. Be it true that thou didst come recently on the scene in the guise of thy murdered self, and when the unicorns and werewolves challenged thee performed two acts of magic, the first of which was inconsequential and the second enchantment like none known before, that established thee as the most powerful magician of the frame despite being a novice?"

"It may be true," Stile agreed, taken aback. He had rather underestimated his magical strength on that occasion! Probably it had been the strength of his feeling that had done it, rather than any special aptness at magic.

Then, perceiving that the Elder was genuinely curious, he amplified: "I am of Proton-frame, come to take up the mantle of my Phaze-self and set to right the wrong of his murder. When the unicorn Herd Stallion challenged me to show my magic, I made a spell to wall him in. When my unicorn steed yielded her ambition on my behalf, I made an oath of friendship to her. It had a broader compass than I expected."

The Elder nodded. "Ah. And the 'corns and 'wolves have not warred since. Thou art indeed Adept."

"Yet not omnipotent. Now must I need meet the Herd Stallion again, at the Unolympics, and I am not his match without magic. The Oracle sent me to borrow the Platinum Flute."

"Ah, now it comes clear. That would of course avail thee." Yet the elf seemed cold.

"That I am glad to hear," Stile said. "I have heard it said that music has charm to soothe the savage breast, but whether it soothe the breast of a beast—"

The Elder frowned. "Yet it is forbidden for us to yield this instrument, however briefly, to a human person, and doubly forbidden to lend it to an Adept. Knowest thou not its power?"

Stile shook his head. "I know only what the Oracle advised."

"No need for mystery. The wielder of the Flute is immune from the negation of magic. There are other qualities about it, but that is the primary one."

Stile thought about that. For an ordinary person, the Flute would provide little advantage. But for a magic creature, such as a werewolf, it would protect his ability to shape-change, and that could on occasion be a matter of life and death. For an Adept—

With the Flute in his possession, Stile could draw on his full powers of magic, even within the magic-negating circle of unicorns. The Herd Stallion would not be able to stand against him. The Oracle had spoken truly; this was the instrument he needed.

But at the same time, he could understand why the Mound Folk did not want him to have it. The existence of various magic-nullifiers prevented the Adepts from being overwhelmingly powerful. If an Adept obtained possession of the Platinum Flute, there would be no effective limit to his will.

"I appreciate thy concern," Stile said. "In fact, I agree with it. The likes of me should not possess the likes of this."

The Lady Blue's head turned toward him questioningly. "Thou dost not abuse thy power."

"How could the Mound Folk be assured of that?" Stile asked her. "There is corruption in power. And if the Flute were taken from me by another Adept, what then would be the limit?"

"It is good that thou dost understand," the Elder said. "The Oracle oft does give unuseful advice, accurate though it be. We Elves have great pride in our artifacts, and trade them freely for things of equal value. But the Flute is special; it required many years labor by our finest artisans, and is our most precious and potent device. It *has* no equal value. No other tribe has its match; not the goldsmiths or the silversmiths or the ironsmiths or the woodsmiths or bonesmiths. We alone work the lord of metals; we alone control the platinum mine and have the craftsmen and the magic to shape it into usable form. Thou art not asking for a trifle, Adept."

"Yes," Stile agreed. "Yet is the Oracle wont to provide advice that can in no wise be implemented?"

"Never. I termed it unuseful, in the sense that surely there is some simpler way to achieve thy mission with the Herd Stallion than this. Misinterpretations may abate the worth of an Oracle's message, but always the essence is there and true. There must be some pattern to this. Therefore must we deal with thee, can we but find the way. Thou knowest that even for the briefest loan we must extract a price."

"I am prepared to offer fair exchange, though I know not what that might be."

"There is little we need from thy kind."

"I do have resources, shouldst thou choose to tolerate the practice of magic in thy Demesnes. Is there anything that requires the talent of an Adept?"

Pyreforge considered gravely. "There be only two things. The lesser is not a task any man can perform, and the greater is unknown even to us. We know only that it must be performed by the finest mortal musician of Phaze."

"I do not claim to be the finest musician, but I am skilled," Stile said.

The wizened elf raised a shriveled eyebrow. "Skilled enough to play the Flute?"

"I am conversant with the flute as an instrument. I should be able to play the Platinum Flute unless there be a geas against it."

The Elder considered again. He was obviously ill at ease. "It is written that he who plays the Flute well enough to make our mountain tremble will be the foreordained savior of Phaze. Dost thou think thou art that one?"

Stile spread his hands. "I doubt it. I was not even aware that Phaze was in jeopardy."

"The Oracle surely knows, however. If the Time of Decision draws nigh . . ." Pyreforge shook his head dolefully. "I think we must try thee on the Flute, though it grieves me with spreading misgiving." He glanced at a crevice, where a guard lurked. "How be the light outside?"

The guard hurried outside. In a moment he returned. "Overcast, shrouded by fog. It will not lift this hour."

"Then may we gather outside. Summon the tribe this instant."

The guard disappeared again. "This be no casual matter, Adept. The Flute extends its force regardless, protecting the magic of the holder. An thou shouldst betray us, we must die to a man to recover it, killing thee if we can. I think thou canst be trusted, and on that needs must I gamble; my life be forfeit an I be in error."

Stile did not like this either, but he was not sure how to alleviate the elf's concern.

"Let thy warriors fix their threats on me," the Lady Blue said. "My Lord will not betray thee."

Pyreforge shook his head. "This be not our way, Lady, despite the ignorance of our commoners. And it would not avail against the typical Adept, who values nothing more than his power."

"Well I know the justice of thy concern. Yet would I stake my life upon my Lord's integrity."

The Elder smiled. "No need, Lady. Already have I staked mine. No lesser hostage preserves the peace in these Demesnes, when an Adept manifests here. I do this only for that the Oracle has cast its impact on us, and my books suggest the ponderosity of the situation. Fate draws the string on every creature, inquiring not what any person's preference might be." He returned his attention to Stile. "The Flute's full power is available only to the one who can master it completely, the one for whom it is destined. We made it, but can not use it; only the Foreordained can exploit it ultimately. When he comes, the end of the present order will be near. This is why we can not give up the Flute to any lesser person."

"I seek only to borrow it," Stile reminded him. But this did not look promising. If he were not the Foreordained, they would not let him borrow the Flute; if he were, there was a great deal more riding on this than his encounter with the Herd Stallion!

They walked outside. The cloud-cover had intensified, shrouding all the mountain above their level, leaving only a low-ceilinged layer of visibility, like a huge room. The elves of the tribe had gathered on the knoll, completely surrounding the mound—young and old, women and children too. Most were slender and handsome, and among them the women were phenomenally lovely, but a few were darkened and wrinkled like the Elder. Stile was the cynosure of all their eyes; he saw them measuring him, discomfited by his large stature; he did indeed feel like a giant, and no longer experienced any exhilaration in the sensation. All his life he had privately longed for more height; now he understood that such a thing would not be an unmixed blessing, and perhaps no blessing at all. Hulk had tried to tell him. The problem was not height; it was in being different, in whatever manner.

"We can not bear the direct light of the sun, being Dark Elves," the Elder said. "Should a sunbeam strike us, we turn instantly to stone. That is why the fog is so important, and why we reside in these oftshrouded mountains, and seldom go abroad from our mounds by day. Yet like all our kind we like to dance, and at night when it is safe and the moons be bright we come out. I was in my youth careless, and a ray pierced a thin cloud and transfixed me ere I could seek cover; I turned not to stone but became as I am now. It was the wan sun, not mine age, that scorched me."

"I might heal thee of that," Stile said. "If thou wishest. A spell of healing—"

"What I might wish is of no account. I must needs live with the consequence of my folly—as must we all."

Now an elf brought, with an air of ceremony, a somber wooden case. "Borrow the Flute for the hour only," the Elder told Stile. "Ascertain for thyself and for us thy relation to it. The truth be greater than the will of any of us; it must be known."

Stile took the precious case. Inside, in cushioned splendor, lay the several pieces of gleaming metal tubing. Platinum, yes—a fortune in precious metal, exclusive of its worth as a music instrument, which had to be considerable, and its value as a magic talisman. He lifted out the pieces carefully and assembled it, conscious of its perfect heft and workmanship. The King of Flutes, surely!

Meanwhile the Mound Folk watched in sullen silence, and the Elder talked, unable to contain his pride in the instrument. "Our mine be not pure platinum; there is an admixture of gold and iridium. That provides character and hardness. We make many tools and weapons and utensils, though few of these are imbued with magic. There is also a trace of Phazite in the Flute, too."

"Phazite?" Stile inquired, curious. "I am not familiar with that metal."

"Not metal, precisely, but mineral. Thou mayst know of it as Protonite."

"Protonite!" Stile exclaimed. "The energy-mineral? I thought that existed only in Proton-frame."

"It exists here too, but in another aspect, as do all things. Wert thou not aware that Phazite be the fundamental repository of magic here? In Proton-frame it yields physical energy in abundance; in Phaze-frame it yields magic. Every act of magic exhausts some of that power—but the stores of it are so great and full Adepts so few that it will endure yet for millennia."

"But in Proton they are mining it, exporting it at a horrendous rate!"

"They are foolish, there. They will exhaust in decades what would otherwise have served them a hundred times as long. It should be conserved for this world."

So Phaze was likely to endure a good deal longer than Proton, Stile realized. That made Phaze an even better place to be. But why, then, was there this premonition of the Foreordained, and of the end of Phaze? Stile could appreciate why Pyreforge was disturbed; there were indeed hints of something seriously amiss.

What would happen when Proton ran out of Protonite? Would Citizens start crossing the curtain to raid the supplies of Phazite? If so, terrible trouble was ahead, for Citizens would let nothing inhibit them from gratification of their desires. Only the abolition of the curtain would prevent them from ravishing Phaze as they had ravished Proton. Yet how could a natural yet intangible artifact like the curtain be removed?

Now the Flute was assembled and complete. It was the most beautiful instrument Stile had ever seen. He lifted it slowly to his mouth. "May I?" he asked.

"Do the best thou canst with it," the elf said tightly. "Never have we heard its sound; we can not play it. Only a mortal can do that."

Stile applied his lips, set his fingers, and blew experimentally.

A pure, liquid, ineffably sweet note poured out. It sounded across the landscape, transfixing all the spectators. Elder and elves alike stood raptly, and Neysa perked her ears forward; the Lady Blue seemed transcendentally fair, as if a sanguine breeze caressed her. There was a special flute-quality to the note, of course—but more than that, for this was no ordinary flute. The note was ecstatic in its force and clarity and color—the quintessence of sound.

Then Stile moved into an impromptu melody. The instrument responded like a living extension of himself, seeming to possess nerves of its own. It was impossible to miskey such a flute; it was too perfect. And it came to him, in a minor revelation, that this must be the way it was to be a unicorn, with a living, musical horn. No wonder those creatures played so readily and well!

Now the Mound Folk danced. Their sullenness vanished, compelled away by the music, and their feet became light. They formed their ranks on the ground, not in the air, and kept their motions on a single plane, but they were abandoned in their sheer joy of motion. The elves scintillated as they turned, and their damsels glowed. They spun into convoluted patterns that nevertheless possessed the beauty of organization. They flung out and in; they kicked their feet in unison; the elves swung the maids and the maids swung the elves; they threaded their way through each other in a tapestry of ever-increasing intricacy. There were no tosses or acrobatic swings, merely synchronized patterns that coalesced into an artistic whole. Over and through it all passed the grandeur of the music of the Flute, fashioning from disparate elements an almost divine unity. It was not Stile's skill so much as the talent bequeathed by the perfect instrument; he could not shame it by delivering less than his ultimate.

Stile saw that the fog was lifting and thinning, as if dissipated by the music. The clouds roiled and struggled to free themselves of their confinement. He brought the recital to a close, and the dancing came to a neat halt as if it had been planned exactly this way. Again the Mound Folk stood still, but now they were smiling. Even the guards who had greeted Stile so inhospitably had relaxed their resentment.

"That was the loveliest music I ever did hear," the Elder said. "It made our finest dance. Thou hast rare talent. Yet did the mountain not shake."

"It did not shake," Stile agreed, relieved.

"Thou art not the Foreordained."

"Never did I claim to be."

"Still, thou canst play marvelously well. If the Oracle decrees that the Flute be loaned to thee, it may be that we are constrained to oblige."

"This I would appreciate," Stile said, taking apart the instrument and returning it carefully to its case. "If thou dost trust me with it."

But now the circled Mound Folk frowned and muttered. The roil of the clouds had stilled when the music stopped, but the disturbance seemed to have passed into the elves. "Nay, my people will not so lightly tolerate that. Perhaps if we borrowed thy service in exchange—"

The muttering subsided. "I am willing to do what service I may," Stile said. "But I can not remain here long. I have commitments elsewhere. I will need the Flute for a number of days, until the Unolympic."

The muttering began again. "Desist this noise!" the Elder cried at the elves, annoyed. "We shall fashion a fair bargain or not part with the Flute." He accepted the Flute-case from Stile; in this judgment, at least, he had not been mistaken. Stile had neither abused the Flute nor sought to retain it without permission. "Now get under cover before the cloud breaks!"

There was little danger of that now, but the Mound Folk hurried away. Stile and the Lady returned inside the nearest mound with the Elder, while Neysa and Hinblue returned to their grazing.

"It could be said," Pyreforge said after reflection, "that thou dost borrow the Flute only to bring it to the one for whom it is intended. The Foreordained."

"But I do not know the Foreordained!"

"Then shalt thou quest for him."

Stile understood the nature of the offer. Such a quest could take as long as he needed for the Flute. Yet it would have to be a true mission. "How could I know him?"

"He would play the Flute better than thee."

"There may be many who can do that."

"I think not. But thou wouldst send him to us, as we can not fare forth to seek him, and we would know by the tenor of the mountain his identity. If he played well, but was not the Foreordained, we at least would have the Flute back."

"This seems less than certain. I think, at least for the acquiescence of thy people, I need to earn this borrowing. Thou didst mention two tasks, the lesser of which no man might perform. Yet I am Adept."

"Canst thou wield a broadsword?"

"I can," Stile replied, surprised.

"This task bears the threat of ugly death to any but the most skilled and persistent swordsman."

"I have faced such threats before. I would feel more secure from them with the Flute in my hands and a broadsword ready."

"Assuredly. Then listen, Adept. There is beneath our Mound Demesnes and below our platinum mine, deep in a cave hewn from out of the Phazite bedrock, one of the Worms of the fundament, ancient and strong and savage and fiery."

"A dragon!" Stile exclaimed.

"Even so. But not one of the ordinary reptiles of the southern marches beyond these mountains. This monster has slowly tunneled through the mountain range during all the time we have mined here. Now we have come within awareness of each other. The Worm be centuries old, and its teeth are worn and its heat diminished so that it can no longer consume rock as readily as in bygone centuries, yet it is beyond our means to thwart. It requires from us tribute—"

"Human sacrifice!" Stile exclaimed, remembering the threat the elves had made concerning the Lady Blue.

"Even so. We like this not, yet if we fail to deliver on schedule, the Worm will exert itself and undermine our foundations and melt our platinum ore and we shall be finished as smiths. We are smithy elves, highly specialized; it took us a long time to work up to platinum and become proficient with it. We can not go back to mere gold, even if other tribes had not already filled in that specialty. We must maintain our present level, or become as nothing. My people would sooner go out in sunlight."

"So thou dost need that dragon eliminated," Stile concluded.

"For that I believe my people would abate their disquietous murmurings about the loan of the Flute."

"Even so," Stile said warily. "This is a large dragon?"

"Enormous."

"Breathes fire?"

"Twenty-foot jets from each nostril."

"Armored?"

"Stainless steel overlapping scales. Five-inch claws. Six-inch teeth. Lightning bolts from eyes."

"Temperament?"

"Aggressive."

"Resistive to magic?"

"Extremely. The Worm beds in Phazite, so has developed a considerable immunity."

"I wonder what it was like in its prime?" Stile mused.

"No matter. In its prime it needed not the tribute of our kind."

"But if the Platinum Flute were employed—"

"The magic of the Flute be stronger than the anti-magic of the Worm."

"Then it is possible that an Adept carrying the Flute could dispatch the creature."

"Possible. But hardly probable. The Worm can not be abolished by magic alone."

"Well, I'd be willing to make the attempt."

"Nay!" the Lady Blue cried. "Few dragons hast thou encountered; thou knowest not their nature. Accept not this perilous mission!"

"I would not borrow a thing of value without giving service in return," Stile said. "But if I could borrow the Flute to brace the Worm, thereafter I would feel justified in borrowing it for one task of mine own. There might be other uses I could make of it besides matching a unicorn stallion, until I locate the one for whom the Flute be intended."

"Thou meanest to brace the Worm?" the Elder asked.

"At least to make the attempt. If I fail to dispatch it, I will return the Flute immediately to thee, if I remain able to do so."

"Nay!" the Lady cried again. "This is too high a price to risk, for the mere postponement of the breeding of one mare. She is mine oath-friend, yet—"

"For that trifle thou dost this?" the Elder demanded, abruptly suspicious. "Thou dost risk thy life against the Worm, and thy pride against the Stallion, for . . . ?"

"She is a very special mare, also mine oath-friend," Stile said stiffly, not wanting to admit that things had pyramided somewhat.

"I fear my people will not support this," the Elder said. "They will fear thou wouldst borrow the Flute merely to abscond with it, facing no Worm. Who would stop thee, armed with it?"

Both Stile and the Lady reacted with anger. "My Lord Blue does not cheat!" she flared. "I thought we had already made proof of this. Again will I stand hostage to that."

"Nay," Stile said, touched by her loyalty, though he knew it was the honor of the Blue Demesnes she was protecting rather than himself. "Thou'rt no hostage."

The Elder's canny gaze passed from one to another. "Yet perhaps this would do, this time. Let the Lady be my guest, here, for a few hours; do we care if others assume she be security for this loan of the Flute? Methinks no man would leave his love to be sacrificed to a dragon. If the Worm be slain, thy mettle is proved, and the loan is good."

"The Lady is not my—" Stile started, then reconsidered. It was a matter he preferred not to discuss here. Also, he would be operating on an extremely tenuous footing if he denied his love for her. He would *not* permit her to be fed to the dragon, whatever her feeling for him.

"Others be not aware of that," the Elder said, delicately skirting the issue. "Few know that the Lord of the Blue Demesnes has changed. Let her remain with me, and none of my people will hold thy motive in suspicion. She will not be ill-treated." He glanced at the Lady. "Dost thou perchance play chess?"

"Perchance," she agreed, smiling.

Stile realized that the Elder had proffered a viable compromise. It was a way to suppress the objections of the Mound Folk, without really threatening the Lady. Certainly Stile was not about to take her with him to meet the dragon!

"Do thou keep the harmonica during mine absence," Stile said to the Lady, handing her the instrument. "This time I must use the Flute."

"I like this not," she said grimly. But she took the harmonica. If Stile did not return, she would at least retain this memento of her husband.

Pyreforge, meanwhile, was setting up the chessmen.

Stile carried the Flute with him into the depth of the crevice. Now he knew the origin of the hot wind and demonic odor from this crevasse. The Worm lurked below!

He had never fought a real dragon before, as the Lady had mentioned, and was not entirely sanguine about this one. The closest approach to a dragon he had made was the one in the Black Demesnes, actually formed from a line, and when balked it had unraveled literally into its component string. The Worm surely would not do that! Adept-quality magic should prevail—but still, if anything went wrong—

Well, he should have the advantage of surprise. The Worm would assume Stile was another item of tribute, a victim to be consumed. He should be able to get quite close before the monster realized what it was up against. That would give him time to survey the situation. Pyreforge had assured him that the Flute would facilitate his magic, yet he had also said that magic alone would not suffice; that suggested that the Flute was not quite as powerful a charm as the Mound Folk wished to believe.

Now they were well below the ledge they had hurdled before. Neysa picked her way carefully as the path narrowed, and Stile kept the Flute assembled and handy. For him it should serve double duty—both to protect his ability to do magic, and to summon the magic itself, since he needed music for his spells. He would have been in trouble if he had needed to play two different instruments simultaneously for those purposes! He was rehearsing those spells in his mind now—one to abate fire, another to shield him from biting, another to make him invisible. But mainly he needed one to eradicate the Worm, one way or another. Could the creature be banished to Hell? Here in this magic frame, there really was a Hell. He had accidentally sent Neysa there once; that had led to a lot of trouble. Which meant that that option was out, now; Neysa would not go for it. He was extremely wary of antagonizing his unicorn friend; unicorns were devastatingly stubborn once they made an issue of something.

Not Hell, then. How about a size change? Convert the giant Worm into a midget worm, harmless. Maybe in three more centuries it would grow back into a giant, but by then it should be far away—if some hungry bird hadn't snapped it up in the interim. What would be a suitable spell? *Monstrous Worm, be small as a germ.* Hardly great art, he lamented as usual, but for the purpose of magic it only needed to rhyme and have appropriate meter.

What kind of magic would be wrought by superior verse? Some day he would have to experiment with genuine poetry, instead of doggerel, and see what happened.

Now the path leveled out. A large, round tunnel took off to the side —the bore of the Worm. A hot drift of air came from it. The Worm could not be far distant.

Stile hesitated. He leaned down to whisper into Neysa's left ear, which rotated obligingly to receive his words. "If we march blithely into the Worm's lair, methinks we'll be slightly cooked," he said. "Yet if we do not, the monster may become suspicious. I would like to lure it out to a location convenient for me, so that at least I can survey it before emerging to engage it—yet how can I bring it to me *without* engaging it?"

Neysa blew a short, positive note. Realizing that she had a notion, Stile dismounted.

She shimmered into girl-form, a petite, lovely, naked, semi-elven lass. "Tribute," she murmured, making a gesture of innocence and helplessness.

Stile was delighted and appalled. "Thou'rt the perfect lure," he said.

"Thou fittest the part precisely. But I dare not risk thy getting caught by the monster."

She shimmered again and became a firefly. The insect circled him once, then converted back to girl-form.

"That's so," Stile agreed. "I keep forgetting thy third form. Thou canst escape, if thou art not burned."

"Fireproof," she said.

"Thy firefly form is fireproof? Wonderful!" Neysa was a treasure of ever-new facets.

Stile reflected for a moment, then plotted their course. "I prefer to have some space to battle the Worm, even though I expect to banish it with a spell. One must always be prepared for the unexpected. So do thou lure it out to the crevice, then get thee swiftly to safety. If I destroy it not, and suffer death, do thou fly up to Elder Pyreforge and the Lady and tell them I have failed. I will hurl the Flute out to the crevice if I can, that it be not lost." This sounded bold and brave, but Stile felt somewhat weak in the knees; he had not had much experience in this sort of thing. He really did not expect to be in serious danger of demise, otherwise he would have been terrified. He was just covering the extreme eventuality.

Neysa nodded, then walked to the center of the tunnel. Stile sang a spell to make himself invisible. This was external magic only; he remained just as solid as always, despite the change in appearance. He was getting accustomed to the limits of his power. When he lifted himself by magic he was changing his locale, not his body. He could not heal his own injured knees. He could not duplicate Neysa's shape-changing or genuine insect-flying ability, though he could create the illusion of change in himself, and could fly artificially by magic means. There were some fine distinctions, but over all he was perhaps more vulnerable than Neysa, though he was also more powerful.

When she saw he was unseeable, Neysa went into her act. "Oh!" she cried. "I'm so afraid! The horrible dragon is going to eat me!" She was really working at it, since she didn't like to talk. Stile felt a warm glow of appreciation. Once Neysa had given him her loyalty, she had been the truest of companions.

Soon there was a rumbling deep in the tunnel. A hotter, ranker wash of air passed, as if some enormous engine had started up. Stile's imperfect confidence suffered attrition. There were after all so many things that might go wrong . . .

Neysa continued lamenting. The rumble increased. The Worm must be afraid that the prey would flee if not quickly nabbed—a reasonable assumption. That was one important thing Stile wanted to know about it—how alert it was, and how fast it moved. A big, ponderous creature would be easier to handle than—

All too soon the Worm arrived. It was indeed a dragon. It had a long narrow head with a conical snout, narrowing in ringlike stages. The derivation of this monster from a literal worm was evident. Of course there were many kinds of worms; Stile tended to think of earthworms because many Citizens employed them in their elegant gardens. But he knew there were other types, some of them vicious. This dragon was a vicious worm grown monstrous.

Neysa screamed realistically and skipped nimbly to the mouth of the passage. The Worm exhaled a puff of smog and slid forward. Its legs were puny compared to its bulk, not really used for its forward motion —but it did indeed have horrendous claws, and seemed to be fully adequate to the task of gutting a human being efficiently. Its metallic scales did not gleam; they were drab and dirty, more like the mud-caked treads of a caterpillar tractor. Stile did not doubt they were invulnerable to ordinary attack. Theoretically the point of a sword could be slid up under a layer of scales to penetrate the flesh beneath—but that could lead to a shallow slanting wound, only aggravating the monster. And what would the Worm be doing while the swordsman was making his insertion? Sitting still? Not likely!

All of this, Stile realized abruptly, was academic. He did not have a sword. He had forgotten to conjure one. He had only the Platinum Flute and his magic—which magic it was time to use.

Stile's strategy had been to bring the monster out to the front, then cast his spell from the rear. Now a problem manifested; the Worm had no rear. Its giant cylindrical torso extended back into the gloom. The shape of a worm, naturally—long. He should have known.

Well, he should be able to enchant it anyway. Stile played the Flute, and the perfect notes poured out again, emerging like quicksilver to fill the tunnel with beauty. The magic gathered swiftly, unusually intense. Of course; they were down near the Phazite lode, so the power was near at hand.

The dragon reacted instantly. No senile mentality here! It had been about to lunge at the supposedly helpless damsel—Neysa was playing it uncomfortably close—but recognized the summoning of magic here. The tiny armored eyes oriented on Stile—and did not see him, since he was invisible. Nevertheless the front orifice opened, its diameter cranking wider in several stages until it was a good yard across. From it a blast of hot fog bellied out.

In this instant it occurred to Stile that the Worm had not tried to use heat on Neysa. Maybe it preferred its meals raw.

Time for self-defense. "From head to feet, immune to heat!" Stile sang.

But as the fog struck him, Stile discovered it was a false alarm. The stuff was hot but not burning. It was like being in a polluted sauna.

The dragon heaved again. This time its breath was hotter and smelled worse. The creature was old; it took it time to get up full steam. The third blast was burning, and the fourth contained pure fire. From hair-dryer to flame-thrower, in easy stages!

Now for the attack. "O mighty Worm, complete thy term," Stile chanted, willing instant death on it.

Then something strange happened. There was a coruscation in the air midway between them, as of a beam of light striking a refractive barrier. The Worm did not die.

Stile tried again. "O Worm of fire—weaken, expire!"

Again that dissipation enroute, and lack of effect. His spells were potent, but were not reaching the dragon!

Now the creature's tiny eyes flashed. Stile had not realized that worms had eyes, but this one certainly did. He remembered the weapon he had been warned about. "Light—blight!" he cried, and the lightning fizzled out before reaching him. His backup spells were saving his hide.

The Worm paused, evidently taking stock. Stile did the same. His magic worked—but the Worm was shielded against it. The Worm had magic—that Stile could block. So the Flute enabled Stile to perform his magic here, but not to use it directly against the enemy. Like two armored knights, they were so well protected against attack that neither could hurt the other magically. The Elder elf had been right.

So much for his rehearsed spells. This conflict was about to get physical. And the Worm was a good deal more physical than Stile.

Still, he would have to make a try. For one thing, he was now trapped inside the tunnel; the bulk of the Worm was between him and the exit. In fact the bulk of the Worm surrounded him. The monster was slowly constricting, hemming him in. Neysa was on the far side of the dragon, unable to help.

Stile had no weapon, other than the Flute. Now he knew that the Flute, while effective, was not enough. Not against the magic Worm. What he needed at the moment was a good sword. What was that spell he had prepared, to summon such a weapon?

The Worm's tube-mouth opened wider—and now a ring of teeth showed, six-inch teeth sure enough, pointing inward. No doubt useful for tunneling through rock—but surely adequate also to grind up one small man. Why couldn't he think of that spell!

The head nudged closer. Stile held the Flute before him in a futile gesture of defense while he tried to cudgel his memory into yielding up the forgotten spell—damn this failure under pressure!—and discovered he held a sword. A shining platinum blade, long and sharp, two-edged. But light and balanced. Exactly the kind of sword he was well versed in.

"Well, now!" Stile exclaimed, confidence surging. The elves had not informed him of this aspect of the Flute! It was a shape-changer.

Stile stepped briskly forward and stabbed at the Worm's side. He expected the point to bounce off the tough scales, but it penetrated. Aha! The enchantment of the Platinum Sword was proof against the Worm's resistance. Maybe it was a different kind of spell, that when buttressed by forceful physical action—

The Worm screamed like a siren and whipped its head about. Stile jerked the sword out and retreated. A geyser of dark red blood shot out of the hole, sailing in an arc through the air to splash on the stone several feet away. A rank charnel smell rose from the fluid.

The dragon's nose nudged up to the wound. A slimy tongue slid out, intercepting the flow of blood. Did worms have tongues? This one did! Was it about to drink its own blood? A single slurp—and the flow abated.

The nose drew away. The blood remained staunched. Maybe it was the saliva: some magical curative property. This monster could heal itself.

The dragon's head was orienting on Stile again. This was one tough worm! It might not be able to see him, but it could hear him and smell him, and in the poor light that was just about as good. Stile had foolishly delayed when he should have been edging around to rejoin Neysa, during the Worm's distraction. Still, maybe he could—

Stile strode for the Worm's side. Immediately the snout snapped toward him. Stile dodged back and sprinted past the head to reach the mouth of the tunnel.

Neysa was awaiting him in equine form. She too could place him readily by smell and sound. Next time he fought an animal, he would prepare spells of inaudibility and unsmellability! He leaped to mount her. "At least we know it can be injured by this sword," he said. "Maybe if we charge in, slash, and charge out before it reacts, then wound it in a second place, and a third—"

He stopped. He no longer had a sword. He supported a long platinum lance. The magic Flute had shown another facet!

Stile braced the lance in his arms and Neysa charged the Worm as its head swung about. The point of the lance struck the neck just behind the head; Stile did not have his aim perfect yet. A lance was not the easiest thing to use! He really needed some sort of supportive harness. The shaft rammed in forcefully—and Stile was shoved off his mount.

Of course, he realized as he picked himself up. The instrument was enchanted so that it could not be jarred out of his grasp—but the shock of impact had had its natural effect on his body. He should have anticipated that.

The Worm screamed again. That puncture hurt! As Stile hauled the lance out, a larger gout of blood spurted—but this time the Worm could not get its mouth on the spot, because the wound was too close to the head.

Stile perceived his avenue of victory. He lifted the lance—and it was what he needed, a hefty double-bitted battle-axe. As the Worm's head twisted vainly to the side, trying to reach the wound, the neck was exposed on the other side to Stile's attack.

He chopped down at that neck, two hands on his axe. This time he cut a deep gash. The head whipped back, catching Stile in a sideswipe and hurling him against the wall.

He saw a flash of light as his head struck, then slid down the curve of the wall. His head was spinning. He retained the Flute—but hardly had the wit to use it. He had not been knocked out, but had been badly shaken up by the blow.

Now the head was orienting on him. The circular array of teeth widened to take him in, and the breath steamed up the vicinity so that Stile could hardly see.

He scrambled away on hands and knees. He wasn't sure he could make it to his feet, or stay on them if he did. He had been in a boxing match once in the Game and been tagged by a solid blow so that his knees went rubbery; he felt similar now. Only there would be no time between rounds to recover! The snout followed him—then paused, grinding out a puff of smoke.

Neysa had rammed her horn into the other side of the Worm's neck, beside the first hole. She lacked the enchantment of the Flute, but a unicorn's horn was itself magical, and a weapon no creature could ignore.

The Worm reacted automatically, turning on this annoyance. It was not terrifically smart.

Stile scrambled to his feet. He swung the Platinum machete ferociously—machete? It had changed again!—chopping with all his strength at the Worm's body. More blood gouted out, spilling over Stile's two hands and spattering his front. He hated the burning, greasy feel of it, but kept hacking.

The dragon whipped its head back, but Stile lashed at the snout with his cleaver, just missing an eye. The head recoiled—and Stile returned to work on the neck. This was like chopping through a tree, except that it became a good deal softer and messier as he got past the vertebrae and into the fatty tissues. Now blood was flooding out so voluminously that Stile was wading in it, and every lift of his implement splattered it further. Blood ran down the shaft as he elevated it, and along his arms to the shoulders; it sprayed across his face. But his grip remained firm, thanks to the Flute's enchantment. As long as he willed his grip to be good, it was. He was wallowing in gore—but still the Worm lived and thrashed, not yielding.

Finally the body was severed entirely. The neck and head fell on one side; the body writhed on the other. The job had been done. Stile had slain the dragon.

His thought of victory was premature. Still the thing didn't die. Instead the cut ends frothed and solidified like sponge, and the bleeding abated. The head section crawled slowly by itself, while the body section cast about blindly, looking for its opponent.

This was a worm. It was possible to cut a worm in half—and both halves would form new worms. Stile had not really accomplished anything yet.

Well, yes—he had made some progress. The head no longer had the leverage to strike at him, and the body lacked sensory apparatus. In time these situations would be remedied—but right now he had a definite advantage. He had to go ahead and destroy the entire Worm right now, while he could.

This was what Pyreforge had meant about the need for a good swordsman with staying power. What a job!

Stile moved down the body, picking his spot, and resumed hacking with his machete-axe. Again the blood gouted; again the torso twisted in agony, trying futilely to fight or escape. The severed end came around, thinking it was a head; it smeared him with half-clotted blood, sickeningly, but could not bite him. Stile pressed on, feeling more like a butcher than a hero. In fantasy lore, the champion skewered the ferocious dragon one time and the beast collapsed cleanly. Here there was nothing neat or convenient or particularly noble about it; he was wallowing in foul-smelling gore, hacking apart a helpless mound of blubber. Hero? He wanted to vomit!

By the time he completed the second cut, his arms were tiring. But still each segment of the Worm remained alive. If he quit here, they would become three new, smaller dragons. He had to abolish the entire mess, somehow.

Then he had a dull inspiration. The dragon had countered his magic with its own magic. But now it lacked organization. Maybe magic would finish it, at this stage. It was certainly worth a try.

He brought the Flute to his mouth. It was festooned with gore. Stile's gorge rose, and he decided to try his spell without playing on the instrument. "O monster fair," he intoned with irony. "Convert to air."

The segment before him shivered, resisting. Whether this was because of residual anti-magic in the dragon, or because Stile had not summoned sufficient magic, he was not sure. Then it melted and evaporated into a truly noisome cloud. The spell was working!

Stile devised spells to abolish the two remaining segments, then another to clean the gore from himself, Neysa, and the tunnel. He had done the job, and earned the right to borrow the Flute. Yet he was not especially pleased with himself. Wasn't there some better way to settle differences than hacking apart ancient magical creatures? How would he feel if he were old, having some fresh young midget chop him down to size?

Yet if he had not performed, the Lady Blue's situation could have become quite difficult. And it could still become so, if Stile did not locate and deal with the murderer of the Blue Adept before that murderer caught up with Stile himself.

Meanwhile, he wondered whether the Lady was winning her chess game with Pyreforge.

CHAPTER 5

Riddles

Sheen was pleased. "You're here for a full week this time?"

"Until the Unolympic," Stile agreed. "Neysa and the Lady Blue are relaxing after the excursion among the Little People, and I have considerable business here in Proton-frame, as long as my enemy doesn't strike." He shrugged. "Of course I'll be staying longer in Phaze-frame one of these times, to run down my enemy there and look for the Foreordained. If I wash out of the Tourney I'll spend the rest of my life there."

"What was it like, being among the Little People?" Sheen asked. They were in their apartment, engaging in their usual occupation. Sheen was an extremely amorous female, and Stile's frequent absences and uncertainty of future increased her ardor. And, since he had a balked romantic situation in Phaze—

"Strange," he answered. "I felt like a giant, and I wasn't used to it. This must be the way Hulk feels. I really am more satisfied with my size than I used to be." He changed the subject. "Where is Hulk? Did you help him?"

"I believe so. I put him in touch with my friends. I assumed you would not have sent him if he could not be trusted."

"He can be trusted."

"I'm sure my friends required him to take the same oath you took, if they revealed themselves to him at all. They may simply have issued him an address. I did not inquire after him, because that would only expose him and them to possible Citizen attention, and we don't want that."

"True," Stile agreed. "If the Citizens knew that some robots are self-willed—"

"You have something against self-willed robots?" she asked archly.

"You know, at times I almost forget that you yourself are a robot. I don't see how you could be much better in the flesh."

"All the same, I wish I *were* in the flesh," she said sadly. "You can never truly love me. Even if you were to win the Tourney and become a Citizen and stay here the rest of your life, even if you didn't have the Lady Blue in the other frame, you would never really be mine."

Stile did not like this line of conjecture. "There is very little chance of my winning the Tourney. I barely survived my first Game."

"I know. I watched. You were lucky."

"Luck is a fickle mistress."

She turned on him abruptly. "Promise me that if you ever give *this* mistress up permanently, you'll have me junked, put out of consciousness. I don't mean just reprogramming or deactivating me; destroy my computer brain. You know how to do it. Don't let me suffer alone."

"Sheen," he protested. "I would never junk you!"

"I like Neysa, and I'm resigned to the Lady Blue. I know you're sliding into love with her, and in time she'll love you, and there's your true romance. But this is a different frame; she and I can never meet. Nothing you do there needs to affect what you do here—"

"I am of both frames now," Stile said. "What affects me in one, affects me in the other. You know that if the Lady ever gives her love to me, I—we'll still be friends, you and I, but—" He halted, hating this, but not constituted to conceal the truth.

"But not lovers," she finished. "Even that I can accept. Neysa accepted it. But if you ever find you can dispense with that remaining friendship—"

"Never!"

"Then you will junk me cleanly. Promise."

Stile suffered a vision of himself hacking apart the living Worm. That had been unclean dispatching. How much better it would have been if he could have banished that Worm to nonexistence with a single, painless spell. Sheen deserved at least that much. "I promise," he said. "But that time will never—"

"Now it's time to get you back to the Tourney," she said briskly.

Stile had been near the head of the line for matching-up before; this time he was near the end. That meant he could play this time, and have another Game soon. The later Rounds would suffer less delay, as the number of remaining contestants declined. The double-elimination system did not eliminate half the contestants each Round, but by Round Four it would approximate fifty percent attrition, and by Round Eight it would be down to about sixty-four survivors, and the prizes would begin. That was his minimum objective, to reach Round Eight. Because that meant he would get another chance, even if he washed out of the Tourney thereafter. In that sense these first few Games were the most critical. Since they were also likely to be against the least competent players—with certain notable exceptions!—this was the time to avoid making any foolish errors. There was absolutely no sense in throwing away a Game that could be easily won by being careful.

His second Game was against an older woman, a serf. She was unlikely to be any match for him. She would probably go for CHANCE; it was the obvious ploy against a superior player.

The grid gave her the opportunity; she had the numbered facet. Well, there were ways to reduce the pseudoequality of chance, and Stile played for them. He selected TOOL.

Sure enough, it came up 3B, TOOL-assisted CHANCE. The subgrid appeared. Stile played to avoid the pure-chance complexes like Dice or Roulette, in favor of the semi-chance ones like Cards. It came up Dominoes.

All right. Stile managed to steer it into the 91 piece, 12 spot domino variation, while the woman put it into the conventional "Draw" game. Stile, familiar with all variants, had wanted one unfamiliar to his opponent to confuse her; he was halfway there.

They adjourned to a Gamesroom and played. They laid all the dominoes facedown, shuffled, and each drew one from the boneyard. Stile drew the 6:7; the woman the 4:5. He had first turn. Good; that was an advantage.

Each drew seven dominoes and Stile was pleased to note that his hand had a run of Fours: the 4:0, 4:2, 4:8 and 4:11. He played the 4:8. As he had hoped, his opponent was unable to play, being short of Fours; she had to draw three times before she could make a match. Stile played one of his other Fours.

So it went. Confused by the vastly extended range of the dominoes, and lacking the wit to eliminate the highest ones from her hand, the woman lost and delivered a goodly score to him. They played another hand, and a third, and he passed 200 points and won. She had never scored at all. Stile had made it to Round Three without even a scare.

The woman just sat there, after the Game, her face set. Stile realized, belatedly, that she must have lost her first match; with this second loss she would be out of the Tourney, doomed to immediate and permanent exile. Some serfs suicided rather than leave Proton. They were the lowest class of people, here, destined only to serve the arrogant Citizens, yet it was all they craved in life. Stile understood this attitude, for he had until recently shared it. Only the opening of the miraculous horizons of Phaze had given him a better alternative.

He was sorry for the woman. Yet what could he do? She had no chance to win the Tourney anyway. It was best that she be put out of her misery promptly.

Like Sheen? No, of course not like that! Yet the thought lingered, a shadow that could not quite be erased.

He left the woman there. He did not feel good.

As Stile and Sheen reentered the apartment, the communication screen lighted. "Report to your Employer for an update," a serf-functionary said crisply, showing the identification of the Lady Citizen for whom Stile worked. "At this time, in this place." And a card emerged from the letter-slot.

Sheen took the card. "Oh, no!" she complained. "We have only half an hour to get there, and it's at an isolated dome. I had hoped to have time to—"

"For a machine, you're certainly hung up on one thing," Stile teased her.

"I'm programmed to be!" she snapped.

She had been fashioned to appeal to his tastes, and evidently his tastes ran to beauty, intelligence and desire for his attention. Stile realized again, not comfortably, that he was in this respect a typical man. His human interests seemed unconscionably narrow when reflected so obviously. Yet Sheen was, in all respects but one, his ideal mate. That one canceled out the rest: she was not alive. She was a construct of metal and pseudoflesh and artificial intellect.

Yet he knew now that even had Sheen been a real person—a real *live* person—she would not have been able to retain his full devotion after he encountered the Lady Blue. Because what had been his ideal woman two months ago was that no longer. The Lady Blue had a detailed and fascinating past as well as a future; she was changing with the passage of time, as Sheen could not, and so was matching Stile's own development. The Lady Blue had reshaped his ideal, conforming it to her likeness in flesh and personality and history. He was becoming acclimatized to the world of Phaze, and was losing identification with the world of Proton.

It was not merely a matter of women; he would have loved Phaze regardless. Magic had become a more intriguing challenge than the Game. But he had a commitment here in Proton, and he would see it through. And he had a gnawing need to ferret out his anonymous enemy and bring that person to an accounting. Who had lasered his knees? Who had sent Sheen to guard him? He could never rest content in Phaze until he knew the answers.

But Sheen was already bustling him out. "We can't keep a Citizen waiting; we have to get to that address in time."

"I suppose so," Stile agreed, resenting the waste of time. In one sense, a serf's employment by a Citizen ended when that serf entered the Tourney, since all tenure was terminated by such entry. But in another sense employment continued, for Citizens identified with those of their serfs who entered, making bets on their success. Many Citizens gave serfs time off to practice for the Tourney, so as to do better; Stile's own Employer had done that. And if he won an extension of tenure, he would still need an Employer for that period. So whatever the technical status, he had better act in a manner conducive to the Citizen's good will.

"I didn't know she had a dome at this address," Sheen remarked as they hurried to a subtube station. As a machine, she had little genuine curiosity, but with her programming and under Stile's tutelage she had mastered this most feminine quality. Hardly ever did she make errors of characterization, now. "But of course all Citizens are obscenely rich. She must be watching the Tourney from a private retreat."

They boarded the tube shuttle. A third passenger joined them—a middle-aged serf woman, well-formed. She was naked, like all serfs, and carrying a sealed freezer-container. "My Employer insists the ice cream from one particular public foodmart tastes better than the ice cream from anywhere else," she confided, tapping the container. "So every day I have to make the trip and bring it back by hand. She thinks robot delivery distorts the flavor."

"It probably does," Sheen said, smiling obscurely.

"Citizens are like that," Stile said, falling into the ready camaraderie of serfs. "I'm entered in the Tourney, but my Employer requires a personal report instead of the official one, so I'm making a trip every bit as foolish." He had no worry about visual and auditory perception devices that might report this conversation to the Citizens; of course they existed, but Citizens had no interest in the opinions of serfs, and expected them to grumble privately.

"That's funny," the woman said. "There are only three Citizens at this terminus. Mine has no interest in the Tourney, and another's off-planet on business, and the third—" She broke off.

Sheen became alert. "What about the third?"

"Well, he hates the Tourney. Says it's a waste of time and only generates new Citizens when the planet has too many already. You couldn't be seeing *him*."

"My Employer is a woman," Stile said.

"Mine is the only woman on this annex—and she surely is not sponsoring you."

Stile showed her the address-card.

"That's the Tourney-hater!" the woman exclaimed. "He's no woman!" She made a small, significant gesture near her midsection. "I know."

Stile exchanged a glance with Sheen. The woman had signified that the Citizen borrowed her for sexual purpose, as was his right so long as her own Employer acquiesced. Citizens of either sex could use serfs of either sex this way, and surely a woman knew the sex of her user.

"My Employer is female," Stile said, suffering a new qualm. Could she have summoned him in the flesh because she wanted to dally with a serf? He would not be able to refuse her, but this was a complication he did not want. "Are you sure that address hasn't changed ownership recently?"

"Quite sure. I was there only two days ago." Again the gesture. "Heaven and Hell."

"Maybe my Employer is visiting him," Stile said.

"That must be it," the woman agreed. "He has quite a taste for women, and does prefer Citizens when he can get them. Is she pretty?"

"Handsome," Stile said. "As you are."

She nodded knowingly. "But you," she said to Sheen. "You had best keep that luscious body out of his sight, or you could mess it up for your mistress."

Stile smiled. Naturally the serf assumed Sheen was also an employee. Sheen could mess it up for *any* rival woman, and not just because of her beauty.

The shuttle slowed. "This is my station," the woman said. "Yours is next. Good luck!"

When they were alone, Stile turned to Sheen. "I don't like this. We can't skip out on a command appearance, but something seems wrong. Could the message be faked?"

"It's genuine," Sheen said. She was a machine; she could tell. "But I agree. Something is funny. I'm summoning help."

"I don't think you should involve your friends in this. They don't want to call the attention of a Citizen to themselves."

"Only to trace the origin of that message," she said. "And to rouse your robot double. I think we can stall a few minutes while he travels by fast freight."

The shuttle stopped. They got out and moved to a local food dispenser, using up the necessary time. Sheen ate a piece of reconstituted carrot. She was a machine but could process food through her system, though it never was digested. Stile contented himself with a cup of nutro-cocoa.

In a surprisingly short time a freight hatch opened and the Stile-robot emerged, carrying a shipment tag. "Start breathing," Sheen told it, and the model animated. "Take this card, report to this address. Broadcast continuously to me."

Without a word the robot took the card, glanced at it, and walked down the passage. The thing looked so small! Stile was embarrassed to think that this was the way he appeared to others: a child-man, thirty-five years old but the size of a twelve-year-old boy.

"Move," Sheen murmured, guiding him through a service aperture. "If there is trouble, we need to vanish."

She located a storage chamber, and they settled down to wait. "Now," she said, putting her arms about him and kissing him. She was fully as soft and sensual as any live woman. But she froze in midkiss. "Oops."

"What—my lips lose their living flavor?"

"I'm getting the report from the robot." Sheen used the term without self-consciousness. She was to an ordinary robot as a holograph was to a child's crayon-picture. "It *is* a mistake. The male Citizen has no visitor, and he sent no message. Oooh!" She shook her head. "That hurt."

How could she feel pain? "An unkind word?"

"Destruction. He had the robot shoved in a meltbeam disposer. The robot's gone."

Just like that! Stile's own likeness, presenting himself in lieu of Stile, melted into waste material! Of course it was foolish to get sentimental about machines, Sheen excepted, but Stile had interacted briefly with the robot and felt a certain identification. "Did he know it was a robot?"

"I don't think so. But he knows *now*. People don't melt the same way. They scorch and stink." She cocked her head, listening. "Yes, we have to decamp. The Citizen is casting about for other intruders."

Stile remembered his encounter with the Black Adept, in Phaze: absolute resistance to intrusions. Enforcement by tacit murder—it seemed that type of personality was not unique to Adepts.

Sheen was drawing him on. Suddenly they were up and out, on the bleak surface of Proton adjacent to the Citizen's pleasure dome. She opened her front and removed a nose-mask. "Put this on; it is supplied with oxygen. It will tide you through for a while."

Stile obliged. When he found himself gasping, he breathed a sniff through his nose and was recharged.

The external landscape was awful. The ground was bare sand; no vegetation. A bare mountain range showed to the near south, rising into the yellowish haze of pollution.

Stile made a quick mental geographical calculation and concluded that these were the Purple Mountains of Phaze. They were actually not too far from the region of the Mound Folk. Except that no such Little People existed in this frame. Or did they? Most people had parallels; how could there be entire tribes in one frame, and none in the other? "Sheen, do you know of any people living in those mountains?"

"The Protonite mines are there," she reminded him. "The serfs that work there get stunted—" She broke off, glancing around. Something stirred. "Oh, no! He's got perimeter mechanicals out. We'll never get through that."

Stile stood and watched, appalled. From trenches in the ground small tanks charged, cannon mounted on their turrets. They formed a circle around the domed estate, moving rapidly, their radar antennae questing for targets.

Sheen hauled him through the force-field into the dome. The field was like the curtain: merely a tingle, but it separated one type of world from another. As they crossed it, the rich air enclosed them, and a penetration alarm sounded. They were certainly in trouble!

"Can your friends defuse the robot tanks?" Stile asked as they ran through outer storage chambers.

"No. The tanks are on an autonomous system. Only the Citizen can override their action. We're better off in here."

There was the sound of androids converging. "Not much better," Stile muttered. But she was off again, and he had to follow.

They ducked in and out of service passages. Sheen had unerring awareness of these, being able to tune in on the directive signals for maintenance robots. But the pursuit was close; they could not halt to camouflage themselves or ponder defensive measures.

Suddenly they burst into the main residential quarters. And paused, amazed.

It was Heaven. Literal, picturebook Heaven. The floor was made of soft white sponge contoured to resemble clouds; smaller clouds floated above, and on them winged babies perched, playing little harps. The front gate was nacreous: surely genuine pearl. Lovely music played softly in the background: angelic hymns.

An angel spied them and strode forward, his great wings fluttering. He wore a flowing robe on which a golden letter G was embroidered. "Ah, new guests of the Lord. Have you renounced all worldly sins and lusts?"

Neither Stile nor Sheen could think of a suitable spot rejoinder. They stood there—while the pursuing androids hove into sight.

"Here now! What's this?" the angel cried. "You soulless freaks can't come in here!"

The androids backed away, disgruntled. They reminded Stile of the animals of his football game when a penalty was called.

Now there was a voice from another cloudbank. "What is the disturbance, Gabriel?" a woman called.

"We have visitors," the Angel Gabriel called back. "But I am uncertain—"

The lady appeared. She wore a filmy gown that clung to her lushly convex contours. Stile found the effect indescribably erotic. He was accustomed to nakedness, or to complete clothing, but the halfway states—surely this Heaven was far from sexless!

The woman frowned. "These are serfs! They don't belong here!"

Stile and Sheen bolted. They plunged across the cloudbank toward the most obvious exit: a golden-paved pathway. It spiraled down through a cloudwall, becoming a stone stairway. Letters were carved in the stones, and as he hurried over them Stile was able to read their patterns: GOOD INTENTIONS. At the bottom the stair terminated in a massive opaque double door. Sheen shoved it open, and they stepped through.

Again they both stood amazed. This nether chamber was a complete contrast to the region above. It was hot, with open fires burning in many pits. Horrendous murals depicted grotesque scenes of lust and torture. Metal stakes anchored chains with manacles at the extremities.

"This is Hell," Stile said. "Heaven above, Hell below. It figures."

"The serf on the shuttle mentioned Heaven and Hell," Sheen reminded him. "She meant it literally."

A red-suited, horned, barb-tailed little devil appeared. He brandished his pitchfork menacingly. "Fresh meat!" he cried exultantly. "Oh, have we got fires for you! Move it, you damned lost souls!"

Behind them, feet sounded on the stairs. The androids had resumed the chase. It seemed the soulless ones were not barred from Hell.

Stile and Sheen took off again. Sheen charged the little devil, disarming him in passing. They ran across the floor of Hell, dodging around smoking pits.

"What's this?" a fat full-sized devil cried. "You serfs don't belong here!" It seemed Hell was after all as restrictive as Heaven. The devil squinted at Stile. "I just had you melted!"

"That's how I came here," Stile said, unable to resist the flash of wit.

"The Citizen!" Sheen said. "He's Satan!"

"Apt characterization," Stile agreed.

"I'll have you torn to ragged pieces!" the Citizen roared, becoming truly Satanic in his ire.

"You would do better to tear up whoever faked the message that brought us to this address," Stile said. "Sir."

The Citizen paused. "There is that." He glanced at the ceiling. "Detail on that summons."

A screen appeared. "The summons was from a female Citizen, the man's Employer. The address was incorrect."

"Get me that Citizen!" Almost, it seemed that smoke issued from Satan's nostrils.

There was a pause. Then Stile's Employer appeared in the screen, frowning. "You sent for this serf?" the Satanic male Citizen demanded, indicating Stile.

The female Citizen's eyes took in Satan and Hell. "Do I know you?" she inquired coldly.

"You're a woman, aren't you? You bet you know me!"

She elected to change the subject. "I summoned this serf to my own address. What is he doing here?"

"This was the address he was given, idiot!"

"It certainly was not!" she retorted. Then she perused the message. "Why—the address has been changed. Who is responsible for this?"

"Changed . . ." Sheen murmured, the circuits connecting almost visibly in her computer-head. "Authentic summons, but one address-chip substituted for another. The handiwork of your assassin."

The female Citizen bore on Sheen. "Serf, you know who is responsible?"

"Sir, I know someone is trying to kill Stile," Sheen said. "I don't know who or why."

The lady Citizen frowned again. "I have entered this serf in the Tourney," she said to Satan. "He has won two Rounds. I dislike such interference."

"I dislike such intrusion on my premises," the male Citizen said.

"Of course. I'm sure I would not care to intrude on such premises. I shall initiate an investigation, as should you. But considering that the serfs are in fact blameless, will you not release them unharmed?"

"They have intruded!" the Satan-Citizen said. "The penalty is death!"

"I've already suffered it," Stile muttered.

"Not for my serfs," the female Citizen retorted, showing more spirit. "If I lose this chance to score in the Tourney, I shall be most upset."

"I am already upset, and I care not a fig for the Tourney. The intruders must die, and good riddance."

The female Citizen frowned once more. "It is unseemly for Citizens to bicker in the presence of serfs. Otherwise I could mention a drone missile currently oriented on your dome, capable of disrupting your power supply and irradiating your personnel: a certain inconvenience, I might suppose. I mean to have that serf."

This gave the devil pause to consider. "I agree. Citizens do not debate before serfs. Otherwise I could mention a couple things myself, such as an anti-missile laser oriented on—"

"Perhaps a fair compromise," she said. "Give the serfs a fair start, and we shall wager on the outcome."

The devil brightened. "Their lives—plus one kilogram of Protonite."

Stile almost gasped. A single gram of Protonite was worth the twenty-year tenure severance pay of a serf, a fee that would set him up comfortably for life elsewhere in the galaxy. These Citizens threw wealth around like sand.

"Only one kilo?" the female Citizen inquired. Stile could not tell whether that was irony or disdain.

"Plus you," Satan amended. "For a week."

"Outrageous!"

He sighed. "A day, then."

"Agreed." She faced Stile. "You will have two minutes to make your escape unfettered. Thereafter the full resources of this dome will be brought to bear against you. I suggest you make good use of the time. I do not wish to have to spend a day with this ilk."

"Now!" Satan cried.

"Follow me," Sheen said, and took off. Stile followed her without question; she was programmed for exactly this sort of thing. He remained bemused by the negotiation and terms agreed upon by the Citizens. His Employer wasn't concerned about the kilo of Protonite, but about a day with Satan—yet she had made the wager. What did that tell about the values of Citizens? He really wasn't sure. His Employer might be upset with him if she lost the wager—but he would already be dead. Perhaps this only indicated the relative values of things: the life of a favored serf, one kilo of Protonite, one day with a boor. Three things of equivalent merit.

Sheen had evidently surveyed this layout and resources of this dome, using her machine capabilities. She knew where everything was. Stile realized that his life was on the line, but he expected to retain it— because the Satan-Citizen evidently was not aware that Sheen was a robot. Their resources were greater, in the purely limited scope of pursuit, than the Citizen knew. Stile's Employer knew, of course, and had played her game adroitly. She expected to win her wager.

Sheen paused at a panel, opened it, and did something to its innards. "That will give us an extra minute," she said. "I put in a sixty-second implement-delay signal. By the time they notice it, it will have expired —and we have a minute more time." Then she took off again.

They came to a tank-reserve unit. Sheen opened the hatch to one of the tiny vehicles. "Get in."

"But there's only room for one person!"

"I don't need to breathe," she reminded him. "I will ride outside." When Stile looked doubtful, she said: "We're already into our extra minute. Get in! You know how to operate this device?"

"Yes." Stile had played Games with similar equipment; he could handle a tank adroitly. This one was armed with small explosive shells, however, instead of the colored-light imitation-laser of a Game tank. This was a real war machine, and that made him nervous.

"I can't help you once we get outside," Sheen said quickly. "Try to mimic the other tanks, so they don't know you're a fugitive. Then break for the mountains or another dome. They won't pursue beyond this Citizen's demesnes."

Demesnes. Like those of the Adepts of Phaze.

"Hang on," Stile said. He closed the hatch, fastened it down, and started the tank.

The motor roared into life. He ground down the exit tunnel, then up to ground level. Immediately he saw the ring of other tanks. He angled across to merge with their line. Protective mimicry—an excellent device!

But they were on to him. Maybe it was Sheen, clinging to the top, or maybe the Citizen's robot-personnel had noted the identity of his machine. The nearest tank oriented on him, its cannon swinging balefully about.

Very well. Stile was good at such maneuvers, though his life had not before hung so literally on his ability. He skewed to the side, and the enemy's first shot missed. Beyond him there was a detonation, and a black cloud expanded and drifted in the slight breeze.

Stile spun his tank about and fired at the one who had attacked him. Stile's aim was good; there was a burst of flame, and a cloud of smoke enveloped the other machine. He was a dead shot with most projectile weapons, though he had never expected that Game-talent to pay off so handsomely in real life.

Before that cloud had cleared, Stile whirled on the next, and scored on it too. However, the other tanks were converging on his own. There were too many of them, and Stile was conscious of Sheen on his top. Even a glancing hit, or piece of shrapnel could wipe her out! There was really no chance to escape this region unscathed.

Stile turned directly toward the Citizen's dome. This put him between it and the pursuing tanks; they could not fire at him because any missed shot would strike the dome. Machines were generally stupid, but this would be programmed into them.

The problem was that he remained confined. He could not break out of the ring of tanks without becoming a target. Before long the speck of Protonite that powered this vehicle would be exhausted; a heavy machine consumed a lot of energy. Then he would be stuck, vulnerable to whatever Satan had in mind for him. It would surely be hellish.

Well, do the unexpected. It was all that remained. Stile roared straight through the force-field and into the dome itself. Let the Citizen deal with *this!*

In moments he plowed through the partitions of the outer chambers, scattering stage props and supplies, and emerged upstairs in Heaven.

Angels scattered, screaming with uneternal terror, as the tank burst through a cloud bank, shedding puffs of clouds and crunching the foam-floor beneath. Stile slowed, not wanting to hurt anyone; after all, the angels were only costumed serfs. Also, if anyone died, his tenure on Proton would be abruptly terminated, and if the police arrested him before he reached the sanctity of the Tourney premises, he would not be allowed to reach it. No one could be arrested in the Game Annex itself. But how would he return to Phaze? As far as he knew, no fold of the curtain passed the Annex. So he was careful—and conscious of the anomaly of a tank touring Heaven, carrying a lady robot. He wanted to stop to check on Sheen, but knew he could not afford the delay; he had to figure out a course of action before the Citizen's forces reorganized.

Could he charge on down to the subway shuttle? The passages were fairly broad, and the tank should fit. But what would he do when he got there? This machine would not fit aboard a shuttle, and would have trouble running along the confined channel the shuttles used. But if he left this machine, he would be lasered down. Yet where else would he go? All his alternatives seemed futile.

Then he suffered inspiration. The curtain—of course! He had surveyed it near here, from the other side. If he could locate it and reach it—

It was a gamble at best. The curtain might not be close enough, and if it was within range he might not be able to spot it from the tank, and if he did spot it he still might not be able to will himself through it while riding in the tank. Yet one thing he was not going to do was stop and get out, under the guns of the other tanks!

It was no gamble at all to remain here idle. He would inevitably fall to Satan's forces. He *had* to try for the curtain!

He crashed on out of Heaven, through the interim chambers, and on into the barrens of Proton.

The enemy tanks were on the other side of the dome, where he had entered. That was a break for him. Stile headed toward the region where the curtain should be. With just a little further luck—

The enemy tanks reacted as one, cruising around the dome on either side and spreading out to form a broad line. Now they were getting him into their sights—and the dome was not going to be in the line of fire much longer. No good luck for him here!

Stile threw his tank from side to side as the firing commenced, making a difficult target. Machines were accurate shooters when the target was stationary or in steady motion, but when velocity was erratic and non-laser weapons were being employed, as now seemed to be the case, it was necessary to anticipate the strategy of the prey. Otherwise the time it took the shell to travel would put it behind the target-tank. Since Stile was humanly unpredictable, the shots were missing. But he could not afford to flaunt himself before them for long; inevitably a shell would score, at least disabling his machine. Then he would become a stationary target: a sitting quack, as it was described in Game-parlance.

In Phaze, he thought with fleeting humor, he had to watch out for spells. Here it was shells.

But his meandering had another purpose: to locate the curtain. It was here somewhere, but there were such poor reference points on the bare sand that he could not place it precisely. The curtain could curve about, and it shimmered so faintly that it was invisible from any distance, even for those like himself who were able to perceive it at all. He would probably come upon it so swiftly that he would pass it before realizing; then he would have to turn and try to cross from the other side while the enemy tanks had full seconds to orient.

A shell exploded in the sand beside him. The concussion shoved Stile's tank violently to the side. Something flew from it, visible in his screen. A section of armor?

No. *It was Sheen.*

Then Stile saw the curtain, angling across his path just ahead. He must have been traveling beside it, not quite intersecting it. He could veer right and pass through it now—

Not without Sheen! Yet he could not halt; that would be instant, fiery death. Already his pace slackened, the enemy tanks were closing the gap; their aim would become correspondingly more accurate. He had to get across—or perish.

Sheen had asked to be junked cleanly. Was this the occasion? Should he, after all, allow her to . . . ?

Stile set the controls to automatic, opened the hatch, and climbed out. The tank was moving at about 50 kilometers per hour now. Stile leaped off the side, sprinting desperately forward in midair. His feet touched the ground, and still weren't fast enough. He made a forward roll, eyes and mouth tightly closed, curling his body into a ball. The sand was soft, here, though his velocity was such that it felt hard; he rotated many times before coming out of it, bruised but whole. Oh, that sand was hot!

The enemy tanks, for the moment, were still chasing his empty tank. Stile charged back to find Sheen, who lay sprawled where she had fallen. She looked intact; perhaps the shock of the explosion had only jogged a wire loose, interrupting her power.

Stile picked her up and carried her toward the nearest intersection of the curtain. But she was heavy, being made of metals and plastic; it was a considerable burden in the shifting sand, and his bare feet were hurting from the heat. Stile was soon panting as he staggered on.

His empty tank exploded. Chance and firepower had brought it down.

Now the enemy tanks slowed their pursuit, turning to return to their normal perimeter. And of course they became aware of Stile, lumbering along with his burden. Cannon swiveled to bear on him. But there was the curtain, just ahead.

Stile summoned his reserves and leaped. *Phaze!* he thought, willing himself through. A tank fired; the shell whistled; the sand behind Stile erupted.

Then the faint tingle of the curtain was on him. Stile fell to the ground, and it was green turf. Sheen was wrenched from his grasp and rolled through the grass and leaves and landed arms and legs akimbo.

One foot was burning. Stile realized that it remained on the other side of the curtain, where the smoke and heat of the shell-blast touched it. Hastily he drew it through. It was not burned, merely uncomfortable.

Now he went to Sheen. She was disheveled and battered, her fine torso abraded. One breast had been torn off, and about a third of her hair had been pulled out. It seemed, too, that the right side of her body had been crushed, and metal showed through a compound fracture of her right arm. There was a great deal more wrong with her than a loose wire!

He did not love her, he reminded himself. She was only a machine, her consciousness artificial. Without her power pack and feedback circuitry she was no more than junk.

But his logic was overwhelmed by a surge of emotion. "I do love you, Sheen, in my fashion!" he whispered. "I shall have you repaired—"

Have her repaired? This was Phaze, the frame of magic. He was the Blue Adept. He could restore her himself!

Or could he? He was not a healing Adept, and had never been able to affect the vital functions of a living creature. Well, he had healed Neysa after her visit to Hell, and his alternate self had done healing. So maybe he just needed practice. The Lady Blue had the healing touch, while Stile's magic was generally more physical, however. And in no event could he restore the dead to life.

Yet Sheen had never been alive. Why couldn't he fix her physical circuitry, repair her breaks and losses? She should be within the ambience of his talent, after all!

Quickly he fashioned spot spells: "Robot Sheen, body clean," he sang, wishing he had his harmonica or the Platinum Flute along. But he had never anticipated returning to Phaze like this! In future he would keep those instruments with him at all times.

Sheen's torso became unblemished. It was working!

"Bones of steel, mend and heal." And her fracture knitted itself together while her torso sprang out to original configuration, with even the missing breast replaced. "Face be fair; restore the hair," and all that damage was undone.

Now for the big one. "Broken circuits mend; consciousness lend." Once again he was bothered by the crudity of the verse. But it served his purpose. Sheen was whole, now.

Except that she still lay there, lovely as any naked woman could be. She showed no sign of animation. How had he failed?

Maybe the lack of a musical instrument had depleted the force of his magic. Stile conjured a simple guitar and used it to strum up greater power, then tried other spells. He covered everything he could think of, but nothing worked. At last, succumbing to reaction from his own narrow escape and grief-stricken at her apparent demise, he threw himself on her body and kissed her unresponsive lips. "Oh Sheen—I'm sorry!"

If he had expected his kiss to bring her magically to life, he was disappointed. She remained defunct.

After a moment Stile sat up. His face was wet, a signal of his emotion. "I can't accept this," he said. "There has to be *something*."

Then it came to him: Sheen was a sophisticated machine, mechanical and electronic, a creature of advanced science and technology—and such things were not operative in the fantasy frame. Sheen could be in perfect condition—he could not say "health"—yet be inoperative here. Only her body could cross the curtain, not her functioning.

The answer was to get her back to her own frame. He had business there anyway. This excursion into Phaze was merely a device to save his own life.

Stile got up, then picked up the robot. He braced himself for the penalty of vertigo, then sang a spell to transport him instantly to his usual curtain-crossing place. Arriving there, he spelled them through.

Sheen woke as the passage formed about them. "Stile!" she exclaimed. "What—where—?"

He kissed her and set her down. "I'll explain it all. But first we have to contact my Employer and advise her that she won her bet. She doesn't have to spend time with Satan."

"Yes," she agreed. "But how—?"

"I do love you somewhat," Stile said. "I know that now."

"But I'm a machine!"

"And I'm a concatenation of protoplasm." He spanked her pert bare bottom. "Now move, creature!"

She reoriented swiftly. "I'd certainly like to know what happened during my blank. The last I remember, I was riding the tank. Now I'm here. It's like magic."

Stile laughed to see her unrobotic confusion. He was so glad to have her animated again that he felt giddy. No, that was the vertigo of his self-transport. "Just exactly like magic!" he agreed, taking her hand and drawing her on.

His Round Three Game was with an alien.

Stile had never played a nonhuman living creature before. He had seen them play, since twenty-four aliens were admitted to every Tourney, but often the majority of these "aliens" were merely wealthy otherworld human beings, or at least humanoids. Many people were attracted by the lure of unmitigated wealth and power, but few who were not of the system were permitted to compete. Stile understood that the entry fee for offworlders was formidable, whereas there was no fee for serfs. Oh, they had the system well worked out! One way or another, the dues were paid.

But this one was that rarity, a genuine alien creature. It had a ring of tentacles in lieu of arms above, and six little caterpillar feet below, and its face was mainly an elephantine proboscis. There did seem to be sensory organs, on little stalks that bobbled about. Stile presumed the ones with balled ends were eyes, and the ones with hollow bells were ears; he could not account for the ones with opaque disks.

"Salutation," he said formally. "I am Stile, a serf-human being of this planet."

"Courtesy appreciation; you do look the part," the alien responded. The sound emanated from somewhere about its head, but not from its snout. "I will be Dgnh of Elsewhere."

"Apology. I am unable to pronounce your name."

"Complete with vowel-sound of your choice: irrelevancy to local vocal."

"Dogonoh?" Stile inquired.

"Noh for brief. Sufficiently."

"Noh," Stile agreed. "You are prepared for any Game?"

"Appallingly."

Then he need feel no guilt about playing hard to win. This creature could have spent a lifetime preparing for this single event, and have some inhuman skills. Already Stile was trying to evaluate Noh's potential. Those tentacles looked sturdy and supple; the creature was probably apt at mechanical things. It was probably best to stay clear of any physical contest. Since he did not care to gamble in CHANCE or ART, that left MENTAL—if he had the choice. On the other range, he had best stay clear of tools or machines, again fearing that alien dexterity. So he should go for NAKED or ANIMAL. Probably the latter, since he understood local animals well, and the alien probably did not.

"Prior matches—compare?" Noh asked.

That would help him gain an insight into the alien's propensities. "I played Football with a Citizen, and Dominoes with a female serf," Stile said.

"Not for me, your Football," Noh decided. "Foots too small. Dominoes no either, element of chance."

Pretty savvy, this creature. "The grid leads to compromise."

"So I explicated. Tiddlywinks with manchild and Storytelling with Citizen. Won Games, but nervous."

"Certainly," Stile agreed. Under the alien form, this being was a true Gamesman. Stile had experienced such competitive nervousness many times. In fact, every Game brought it on. That was part of the addiction of it. He was in the Tourney to try for Citizenship, surely; but he also had an abiding delight in the competition of the thing, the endless variants, the excitement of the temporarily unknown. That was what had caused him to remain on Proton as a serf, instead of departing with his parents when their tour of tenure had expired. The fascination and compulsion of the Game had ruled him.

Now, ironically, his major involvement was with magic, with the lovely frame of Phaze. There, he was a person of considerable substance, a magician. He had entered the Tourney here at a time when its significance for him had been greatly reduced. Yet new reasons had erupted to restore its importance. He was doing it for Sheen, and for pride, and for the chance to discover who was trying to kill him, and to achieve the ability to do something about it. Just as he was participating in the quest of the Platinum Flute in Phaze, for Neysa and pride and eventual vengeance. So despite the considerable flux in both frames, his course had hardly changed.

Stile was jolted out of his reverie by the announcement of his Game. He and the alien stepped up to the grid unit.

The alien was even shorter than Stile; only its perception-stalks showed above the unit. Since the grid-screens on either side were all that counted, this did not matter. Normally Stile preferred to study his opponent for telltale reactions during the stress of selection; a hint about a person's nervous state could spell the key to victory. But he could not read the alien anyway.

The primary grid showed. Good—Stile had the numbers. Without hesitation he selected MENTAL.

Noh was just as quick—which alarmed Stile. If this creature was as fast on its mental feet as his reaction-time indicated, this meant trouble. The selected panel showed 2A, MENTAL/NAKED. Mind alone, no body involvement.

The secondary grid appeared. Numbered across the top were the categories SOCIAL—POWER—MATH—HUMOR; lettered down the side were the qualities INFORMATION—MEMORY—RIDDLE—MANIPULATION. Stile had the numbers, and that was fine.

Suppose he chose SOCIAL? The alien could choose INFORMATION, and the subgrid could put them into planetary history, where Noh could be well prepared. *What was the date of the squassation of the Bohunk of Planet Teetotal, in local zero-meridian time?* He certainly didn't need that! Should he choose POWER? Noh could choose MEMORY, and they could rival each other in the recall of extended sequences of letters, numbers and concepts, the kind of thing that used to fill the tests that supposedly indicated human intelligence. Stile was good at this, in human terms—but how could he be sure that Noh did not possess long-term eidetic memory, and be virtually invincible? Or the alien could select MANIPULATION, and they could wind up playing a mental game of three-dimensional chess. Stile could do that, too—but it was a literal headache. However, MATH could lead to the identification of obscure formulae if Noh chose INFORMATION, or the spot rehearsal of log tables or trig functions. MATH/RIDDLES could be just as bad; better go to MANIPULATION and do complex problems in his head. But if he chose HUMOR, and Noh chose RIDDLE, they would wind up comparing puns. Puns with an alien?

Damn it, he was up against a completely unknown quality of opponent! *Any* choice could be ruinous. If only he had had time to do his homework, researching his prospective opponents, however scantily; then at least he would have had some broad notion what to avoid. But this business in Phaze had crippled his research time.

Stile sighed. He would have to go with MATH.

Noh had already selected RIDDLE. They were in 3C, Mathematical Riddles. Well, it could have been worse. Stile had on-days and off-days on this sort of thing; sometimes inspiration presented him with a brilliant response, and sometimes he felt as if his head were stuffed with sawdust, and sometimes he cursed himself for missing the obvious. But normally he was pretty sharp on mathematical riddles, and he knew a great number of them.

The final grid was about as simple as they came: four squares. The top was 1. COMPUTER-GENERATED 2. SELF-GENERATED. The side was A. DUAL RESPONSE B. INDIVIDUAL RESPONSE. Just four alternatives. Stile had the numbers.

Noh's antennae wavered in agitation. "Nonetheless is this naked mental? How justified computer involvement?"

"These categories are fundamentally arbitrary," Stile explained. "Too many Games are in fact mixed types. The Game Computer assumes for the sake of convenience that it, itself, has no Game significance. The riddles could come from a book or a third person, but it is most convenient and random to draw on the computer memory banks. There are all kinds of little anomalies like this in the Games; I had to play Football using androids termed animals, with robots for referees."

"This is delightfully mistrustful. Expedient to avoid?"

"Well, I happen to have the numbered facet, so you cannot control that. Myself, I'd rather avoid the dual response; that's timed, with the first one to answer being the winner. I'm more of a power thinker; I get there, but not always in a hurry." This was true, but perhaps misleading; Stile was stronger as a power thinker in proportion to his other skills, but still by no means a slow thinker. "That is—"

"Can we collude? Choose 2B for mutual accommodationality?"

"We could—but how could we know one of us won't cheat? Deals are permissible but not legally enforceable in the Game. An expert liar makes an excellent grid-player. The computer accepts nothing but the signal-buttons."

"Chance it must be risked," Noh said. "Some trust exists in the galaxy, likewise on little planets."

"Agreed," Stile said, smiling at the alien's phrasing. He touched 2, and sure enough, it came up 2B. They had each kept faith. Game players normally did; it greatly facilitated things on occasion.

Now they adjourned to a bare private chamber. "Select a recipient for the first riddle," the Game Computer said from a wall speaker. "Recipient must answer within ten minutes, then propose a counter-riddle for the other. In the event of failure to answer, proponent must answer his own riddle, then answer opponent's riddle within the time limit. The first contestant to achieve such success is the victor. Computer will arbitrate the technical points."

"You courtesy explained situation," Noh said. "Appreciation I yield initial."

It really did not make any difference who went first, since only an unanswered or misanswered riddle followed by a successful defense counted. But Stile was glad to get into it, for psychological reasons. He had a number of tricky questions stored in the back of his mind. Now he would find out just what the alien was made of, intellectually.

"Picture three equal-length sticks," Stile said carefully. "Each quite straight, without blemish. Form them into a triangle. This is not difficult. With two additional sticks of the same size and kind a second triangle can be formed against a face of the first. Now can you fashion four congruent triangles from only six such sticks?"

Noh considered. "Enjoyability this example! Permissible to employ one stick to bisect double-triangle figure formed from segments of sticks?"

"No. Each stick must represent exactly one side of each triangle; no projecting points." But Stile felt a tingle of apprehension; such a device would indeed have formed four congruent triangles, and similar overlapping could make up to six of them. This creature was no patsy.

"Permissible to cross sticks to form pattern of star with each point a triangle?"

"No crossing." So quick to explore the possibilities!

The head stalks bobbled thoughtfully for almost a minute. Then: "Permissible to employ a third dimension?"

The alien had it! "Permissible," Stile agreed gamely.

"Then to elevate one stick from each angle of first triangle, touching at apex to form four-sided pyramid, each side triangle."

"You've got it," Stile admitted. "Your turn."

"Agreeable game. Triangles amenable to my pleasure. Agree sum of angles is half-circle?"

"One hundred eighty degrees," Stile agreed.

"Present triangle totaling three-quarter circle."

"That's—" Stile began, but choked off the word "impossible." Obviously the alien had something in mind. Yet how could any triangle have a total of 270°? He had understood 180° was part of the definition of any triangle. Each angle could vary, but another angle always varied inversely to compensate. If one angle was 179°, the other two would total 1°. Otherwise there would be no triangle.

Unless there could be an overlay of triangles, one angle counting as part of another triangle, adding to the total. That didn't seem sensible, yet—

"Permissible to overlap triangles?" Stile inquired.

"Never."

So much for that. Stile paced the floor, visualizing triangles of all shapes and sizes. No matter how he made them, none had more than 180°.

Could they have differing definitions of triangles? "Permissible to have more than three angles in the figure?"

"Never."

Down again. Damn it, it wasn't possible! Yet somehow, by some logic, it had to be, or the alien would not have proposed it. Stile had encountered situations in which the supposedly impossible had turned out to be possible, like turning a torus inside out through a hole in its side. Topology—there was a fertile field for intellectual riddles! Shapes that were infinitely distortable without sacrificing their fundamental qualities. Bend it, twist it, stretch it, tie it in knots, it did not really change. Now if he could do that with a triangle, bowing out the sides so as to widen the angles—but then its sides would be curved, no good. Maybe if it were painted on a rubberite sheet, which sheet was stretched—aha! A curved surface! Noh had not specified a flat surface. A triangle drawn on a sphere—

"Permissible to employ a curved surface?" Stile inquired triumphantly.

"Never. Triangle must be rigid frame, as were your own."

Ouch! He had been so sure! On the surface of a sphere he could have made eight triangles each with three right angles, or even four triangles with two right angles and one 180° straight angle each—a quarter section of the whole. The curvature of the surface permitted straight lines, in effect, to bow. He had often carved the skin of a pseudo-orange that way. But the alien forbade it.

Still, perhaps he was getting warmer. Noh's antennae were flexing nervously, which could be a good sign. Suppose the surface were not curved, but space itself was? That could similarly distort a rigid triangle, by changing the laws of its environment. In theory the space of the universe was curved; suppose the triangle were of truly cosmic proportion, so that it reflected the very surface of the cosmos? "Okay to make a very large triangle?"

"Nokay," Noh responded. "Standard triangle held in tentacles readily."

Brother! Stile was getting so inventive, stretching his imagination, to no avail. If he could not draw on the curvature of space—

But he could! "How about taking it to another location?"

The stalks wobbled ruefully. "Permissible."

"Like maybe the vicinity of a black hole in space, where intense gravity distorts space itself. Normal geometric figures become distorted, despite no change in themselves, as though mounted on a curved surface. Down near the center of that black hole, space could even be deformed into the likeness of a sphere, just before singularity, and a triangle there could have two hundred and seventy degrees, or even more."

"The creature has resolved it," Noh agreed ruefully. "Inquire next riddle."

This was no easy Game! Stile felt nervous sweat cooling on his body. He feared he was overmatched in spatial relationships. He had invoked the third dimension, and the alien had in turn invoked something like the fourth dimension. Better to move it into another region. "Using no other figures, convert four eights to three ones," Stile said. Probably child's play for this creature, but worth a try.

"Permissible to add, subtract, multiply, divide, powers, roots, tangents?" Noh asked.

"Permissible—so long as only eights are used," Stile agreed. But of course simple addings of eights would never do it.

"Permissible to form shapes from numbers?"

"You mean like calling three ones a triangle or four eights a double row of circles? No. This is straight math." Noh was on the wrong trail.

But then the alien brightened. His skin assumed a lighter hue. "Permissible to divide 888 by 8 to achieve 111?"

"Permissible," Stile said. That really had not balked Noh long—and now the return shot was coming. Oh, dread!

"Human entity has apparent affinity for spheres, as witness contours of she-feminine of species," Noh said. "Appreciate geography on sphere?"

"I fear not," Stile said. "But out with it, alien."

"In human parlance, planetary bodies have designated north and south poles, apex and nadir of rotation, geographical locators?"

"Correct." What was this thing leading up to?

"So happenstance one entity perambulates, slithers, or otherwise removes from initiation of north pole, south one unit, then east one unit, and right angle north one unit, discover self at point of initiation."

"Back at the place he started, the north pole, yes," Stile agreed. "That's the one place on a planet that such a walk is possible. Walk south, east, north and be home. That's really a variant of the triangle paradox, since two right angle turns don't—"

"Discover another location for similar perambulation."

"To walk south a unit, east a unit, and north a unit, and be at the starting point—without starting at the north pole?"

"Explicitly."

The creature had done it again. Stile would have sworn there was no such place. Well, he would have to find one!

Not the north pole. Yet the only other place where polar effects occurred was the south pole—and how could a person travel south from that? By definition, it was the southernmost region of a planet.

"All units are equal in length and all are straight?" Stile inquired, just in case.

"Indelicately."

"Ah, I believe you mean indubitably?"

"Indecisively," the alien agreed.

Just so. "Can't move the planet to a black hole?"

"Correct. Cannot. Would squash out of shape."

So it had to be settled right here; no four-dimensional stunts. Yet where in the world could it be? Not the north pole, not the south pole—

Wait! He was assuming too much. He did not have to go south from the south pole. He had to go south *to* it. Or almost to it. . . .

"Picture a circle around the south pole," Stile said. "A line of latitude at such distance north of the pole that its circuit is precisely one unit. Now commence journey one unit north of that latitude. Walk south, then east around the pole, and north, retracing route to starting point."

"Accursed, foiled additionally," Noh said. "This creature is formidability."

Stile's sentiments exactly, about his opposition. He was afraid he was going to lose this match, but he struck gamely for new territory, seeking some intellectual weakness in his opponent. "The formula X^2 plus Y^2 equals Z^2, when graphed represents a perfect circle with a radius of Z, as described in what we call the Pythagorean Theorem," he said. "Are you familiar with the mechanism?"

"Concurrently. We term it the Snakegrowltime Equation."

Stile suspected there was a bit of alien humor there, but he had to concentrate on the job at hand instead of figuring out the reference. He was glad he had not gotten into a punning contest! "What variation of this formula represents a square?"

"No variation!" Noh protested. "That formula generates only a curve; a variation must remain curvaceous. No straight lines from this."

"I will settle for an approximate square," Stile said helpfully. "One that curves no more than the width of the lines used to draw it."

"How thickness lines?"

"Same thickness as those used to make the circle."

"Extraordinarily unuseful," Noh grumped, pacing the floor with the little feet tramping in threes. "Geometric curves do not transformation so. It is a fact of math."

"Math is capable of funny things." Stile was regaining confidence. Had he found a weakness?

Noh paced and questioned and did the alien equivalent of sweating, and finally gave it up. "Incapability of sensiblizing this. Demand refutation."

"Try X∞ plus Y∞ equals Z∞," Stile said.

"Party of the first part raised to the infinitive power, plus party of the second part raised similarly? This is meaningful-less!"

"Well, try it partway, to get the drift. X^3 plus—"

"Partway?" Noh demanded querulously. "Cannot split infinity!"

Stile thought of the infinities of the scientific and magical universes, split by the curtain. But that was not relevant here. "X^3 plus Y^3 equals Z^3 yields a distorted loop, no longer a perfect circle. Raise the powers again. X^4 plus Y^4 equals Z^4, and it distorts further towards the corners. By the time it goes to the tenth or twelfth power, it is beginning to resemble a square. By the time it reaches the millionth power—"

Noh did some internal calculating. "It approaches a square! Never a perfect one, for it yet is a curve, but within any desired tolerance—remarkable! I never realized a curve could fashion into—amaztonishing!"

"Now I must answer yours," Stile reminded the alien. He knew he hadn't won yet; he had only gained a temporary advantage, thanks to splitting an infinity.

"Appreciably so. Where is the west pole?"

"West pole?"

"North pole, south pole, east pole, west pole. Where?"

"But a planet can only have one axis of rotation! There can't be two sets of poles!"

"There cannot be a square generated from a curve, alternatively."

"Um, yes." Stile lapsed into thought. If he could get this one, he won the Round. But it baffled him as much as his square had baffled Noh. Was the west pole simply a matter of semantics, a new name for the north or south poles? That seemed too simple. There really had to be a pole in addition to the conventional ones, to make it make sense. Yet unless a planet could have two axes of rotation—

In the end, Stile had to give it up. He did not know where the west pole was. His advantage had disappeared. They were even again. "Where?"

"Anticipation-hope you would solution it," Noh said. "Solve has eluded me for quantity of time."

"You mean you don't know the answer yourself?" Stile asked incredulously.

"Affirmation. I have inexplicably defaulted competition. Negative expedience. Remorse."

So Stile had won after all! Yet he wished he could have done it by solving the riddle. The west pole—where could it be? He might never know, and that was an aggravation.

* * *

Stile had been late in the Round Three roster, and now was early in the Round Four roster, as the Game Computer shifted things about to ensure fairness. Hence he had less than a day to wait. He spent much of that time sleeping, recovering from his excursion with the tanks and resting for possibly grueling forthcoming Games. He had been lucky so far; he could readily have lost the Football Game and the Riddle Game, and there was always the spectre of CHANCE to wash him out randomly. Most duffer players were fascinated by CHANCE; it was the great equalizer. So he hoped he would encounter a reasonably experienced player, one who preferred to fight it out honestly. One who figured he had a chance to win by skill or a fortuitous event in a skill contest, like the referee's miscall in the Football Game. But a true skill contest could be arduous, exhausting both participants so that the winner was at a disadvantage for the next Game.

If Stile's Employer discovered anything in the course of her investigation into the matter of the forged message-address, she did not confide it to him. That was the way of Citizens. They often treated serfs with superficial courtesy, but no followthrough. The Citizen he had encountered in Round One, the Rifleman, was an example; there had been no further communication from him. There was no such thing, in Proton law and custom, as a binding commitment by Citizen to serf. Everything went the other way.

Stile remained troubled by the continuing campaign against him by his anonymous enemy. At first he had thought this person had sent Sheen and then lasered his knees as a warning to get out of horseracing. But he had gotten out—and the threat continued. There had been a Citizen who was after him, but that had been effectively neutralized, and Sheen's self-willed robot friends had verified that he was not the present offender. They had not been able to trace the source of the substituted address, because it had not been handled through any computer circuits; it had been a "mechanical" act. But they had watched that particular Citizen, and knew that he was relatively innocent.

Someone wanted Stile dead—in Proton and in Phaze. Perhaps it was the same person—a frame-traveler. There were a number of people who crossed the curtain regularly, as Stile himself did. Maybe that same one had killed Stile's other self, the Blue Adept, and tried for Stile with less success. Probably another Adept; no lesser person could have done it. But who? The maker of golems—or the maker of amulets? Stile was becoming most eager to know.

If he beat the long odds and won the Tourney, he would have at his disposal the resources of a Citizen. *Then* he would be in a position to find out—and to take remedial action. That was the real imperative of his present drive. He could not wash out of the Tourney and simply return to Phaze to court the Lady Blue—not when a curtain-crossing

Adept was laying constant deathtraps for him. He had life-and-death riddles to solve first!

His Round Four opponent was a woman his own age: Hella, first Rung on the Age 35 ladder. Stile had qualified for the Tourney by being fifth on the male 35 ladder, but he was actually the top player of his age. Many top players remained deliberately low on their Game ladders, so as to avoid the annual Tourney draft of the top five. Hella, however, really was the top female player, whose tenure ended this year; she had been eager to enter the Tourney.

Nevertheless, she was not in Stile's class. He could outperform her in most of the physical Games and match her in the mental ones. If he got the numbers he would have no gallantry at all. He would choose PHYSICAL. If he had the letters he would have to go for TOOL, to put it into the boardgames block, where he retained the advantage over her.

Hella was a fit, statuesque woman, taller and heavier than Stile. She had half-length dark-blonde hair, slightly curly, and lips a little too thin. She looked like what she was: a healthy, cynical, hard-driving woman, nevertheless possessed of a not inconsiderable sex appeal. Larger men found her quite attractive, and she was said to be proficient at private games, the kind that men and women played off record. Stile had played her often, in random Games, but had never socialized with her. Most women did not get romantic about men who were smaller than themselves, and she was no exception. Stile himself had always been diffident about women, and remained so. Sheen was special, and not really a woman. The Lady Blue was special too—and Stile really found himself unable to forward his suit with her. She was his other self's widow . . .

"I would rather not have come up against you," Hella told him in the waiting room. "I'm already half out; a duffer caught me in CHANCE."

"That's the way it goes," Stile said. "I have nothing against you, but I intend to put you away."

"Of course," she said. "If you get the numbers."

"If I get the numbers," he agreed.

Their summons came. Stile did not get the numbers. Thus they landed in 2B, Tool-Assisted MENTAL GAMES. They played the sixteen choices of the subgrid and came to MAZE.

They adjourned to the Maze-section of the Game premises. The Game Computer formed new mazes for each contest by sliding walls and panels along set channels; there was an extraordinary number of combinations, and it was not possible to anticipate the correct route through. One person started from each end, and the first to complete the route won.

They took their places. Stile was designated blue, the convention for males, and Hella red, the convention for females. Had two males been competing, they would have been blue and green, or red and yellow for females. The Computer liked things orderly.

The starting buzzer sounded. Stile pushed through the blue door into the labyrinth. Inside the walls and floor were restful lightgray, the ceiling a translucent illumination panel. As Stile's weight came on the floor, it turned blue, panel by panel, and remained that way to show where he had been. Spectators could view this Game on vision screens in mockup form, the patterns developing in red and blue to show the progress of both competitors, appreciating the ironies of wrong turnings and near-approaches to each other.

Stile moved quickly down the hall, his blue trail keeping pace, until he came to the first division. He didn't hesitate; he took the left passage. Further along, it divided again; this time he took the right passage. The general law of chance would make the right and left splits along the proper way come out about even; this was unreliable for short-term efforts, but still as good a rule to follow as any.

This passage convoluted, turned back on itself, and abruptly deadended. So much for general laws! Stile quickly reversed course, following his own blue trail, and took what had been the left passage. This twisted about and finally intersected his original blue trail—the first right turn he had ignored.

Oops—there had to be an odd number of passages available, for at least one led to the red door on the other side of the maze. If two led there, then there would be an even number—with two passages as yet untried. But that was unusual; spectators liked to have the two contestants meet somewhere in the center, and start frantically following each other's trails, and the Game Computer usually obliged with such a design. He must have missed a passage in his hurry. First mistake, and he hoped it would not prove to be too expensive.

He checked the passage back to the blue door. Nothing there. Then he took off on the right-hand passage he had used to complete the loop. Sure enough, it divided; he had overlooked the other passage because it angled back the way he had come. He should have checked behind him as well as ahead; an elementary precaution. He was not playing well.

However, this was not necessarily time wasted. Hella would be working her way through from the other side, trying to intersect his blue trail that would lead her to the blue door. If he had a single path there, she would have no trouble. As it was, he had turned *all* paths blue, so she would have no hint; she might get lost, just as he had. Sometimes, in these mazes, one person got nine-tenths of the way through, while the other floundered—and then the flounderer followed the other trail to victory while the nine-tenths person floundered. One could never tell.

He moved on down the new passage. It, too, divided; he moved left and followed new convolutions. This one did not seem to be dead-ending or intersecting itself; good. Now he needed to intersect Hella's trail before she intersected his.

Stile paused, listening. Yes—he heard her walking in the adjacent passage. That did not necessarily mean she was close; that passage could be a dead-end without connection to this one. Nevertheless, if he knew her location while she did not know his, that could be an advantage. He might sneak in and find her trail while she was still exploring a false lead, and hurry on to victory.

Then he heard her make a small, pleased exclamation. Ouch—that could mean only one thing: she had intersected his trail. Which meant that *he* was probably the one on the dead-end.

Stile backtracked hastily and silently. Sure enough, her red path intersected his, where he had bypassed the last right passage, and ended there. She was hot on his blue trail, and going the right direction. He was in trouble!

Stile took off down the red trail. He had only two hopes: first that she had a fairly direct trail he could follow without confusion; second that she would get lost on his loops and dead-end.

His first hope was soon dashed; the red trail divided, and he did not know which one was good. He had to guess. He bore right, looped about, came close to the exit-region—and dead-ended. All the breaks were going against him!

He hurried back, no longer bothering to be silent, and took the other trail. It wound about interminably, while at every moment he feared he would hear the clang of her exit and victory. It divided again; he bore right, sweating. If he lost this simple Game to this woman, who really was not the player he was . . .

Then, abruptly, it was before him: the red door. Stile sprinted for it, suddenly convinced that Hella's foot was on the sill of the blue door, that even half a second would wipe him out. In his mind's ear he heard the toll of his loss.

He plunged through. The bell sounded. He had won!

"Damn!" Hella exclaimed from the interior. She had after all gotten lost in his loop, and was nowhere close to the blue door. His alarm had been false.

Sheen was waiting as he emerged. "Take me away from here," he told her, putting his arm about her slender waist. He suffered another untoward image: Sheen lying torn apart after the tank chase. Yet there was no present evidence of that injury; she was all woman. "I've had enough of the Tourney for now!"

"There'll be more than a day before your next match," she said. "Time for you to catch your duel with the Herd Stallion in Phaze."

"I might as well be right here in the Tourney!" he complained. "One contest after another."

CHAPTER 6

Unolympic

Neysa had taken off early to rehearse with her brother for the incipient exhibitions, at the Lady Blue's behest. Stile was bothered about the hiatus in protection for the Lady, but was unable to object. She had remained within the castle, reasonably safe.

At the appropriate hour, Stile put his arm about the Lady's supple waist and uttered a spell that jumped them both to the event. He was getting better at this sort of spell, but still would rather have traveled by conventional means, had there been time.

It was impressive. Eight or ten herds of unicorns had assembled for their competition; each Herd Stallion had his banner mounted at his camp and his subjects ranged about it. There was a tremendous open pasture upon which many hundreds of unicorns grazed. They sported all the colors of moons and rainbow, and were handsome specimens of equine flesh.

Yet there were many other creatures too. Werewolves ranged in small packs, carefully neutral in the sight of so much potential prey. No false growls here! Bats swooped from perch to perch and sailed high in the air in pursuit of insects. Humanoid figures of all types abounded.

A unicorn male trotted up to Stile and the Lady. In a moment he shifted to man-form, neatly attired in a khaki uniform. "Please identify thyself and party and accept an admittance tag."

"The Blue Adept and Lady Blue," Stile said.

"Adept! Right this way!" The unicorn's reaction resembled that of a serf of Proton confronted by a Citizen.

They followed the unicorn to a small pavilion set up beside the exhibition field. Several people reclined on thronelike chairs or couches. They did not rise or make any acknowledgment of Stile's or the Lady's arrival. Stile was now well-enough accustomed to the ways of Phaze to know that this nonreaction represented a studied discourtesy to either an Adept or a Lady. But he showed no overt reaction; he wanted first to understand *why*.

Then a comely young woman stood and approached them. She seemed vaguely familiar. "Thou comest undisguised, my handsome?" she inquired, proffering her hand. There was the hint of a cronish cackle in her voice.

"Yellow!" he exclaimed. "What brings thee here? I thought—"

"Thou didst suppose I had no more youth potions?" she inquired archly. "None that would stand up to a day's hard use?"

"I recalled thee with fair hair, fairer than those of the Lady Blue, light yellow tresses." Said tresses were now short, brown and curly. But of course she could make her appearance whatever she chose, for the duration of her potion. This was, as she put it, her costume. Her dress, at least, was yellow; that was the real key. "I thought the unicorns—" He shrugged.

"It is truce between all attendees of the Unolympics," she explained. "Well the animals know my nature, but here I exert my powers not, neither do the animals chide me for old affronts. We Adepts have few such social opportunities, and few occasions to socialize with others of our ilk in peace. We take them greedily."

He remembered that Yellow had been lonely in her own Demesnes, especially for male company. Naturally she would socialize when she safely could. "Ah, like the temple of the Oracle," Stile said. "No quarrels here." He looked about. "These be Adepts?"

"And consorts. I forgot that thou rememberest not." She smiled brilliantly and bobbed her cleavage about, enjoying her youthful form as only an old hag could. What height was to men, he thought, breasts were to women. "Come, my charming; I will introduce thee around."

A chance to meet other Adepts—one of whom might be his murderer! This was serendipitous, an unexpected windfall.

Yellow conducted them to a woman reclining on a white couch, and garbed in a sparkling white gown. She was of indeterminate middle age, and somewhat stout. "This be White," Yellow said, indicating her with a half-contemptuous twist of a thumb. Then she jerked the thumb at Stile. "This be Blue, and Lady."

The White Adept lifted snowy lashes. Her eyes were ageless, like swirls of falling snow. "Reports of thy demise seem to have been exaggerated."

"No exaggeration," Stile said. "I seek my murderer."

"May I be far from the scene of thine encounter," White said, unalarmed, and turned her wintry orbs back to the field where several unicorns were practicing their acts. Stile remembered that the White Adept had been in the market for a white unicorn; Yellow had mentioned that, at their first encounter. He hoped no such creature had been captured.

Yellow led them on. "Methinks thy appearance here stirs greater commotion than shows," she murmured with grim satisfaction. "It is well known that thou'rt possibly the strongest current Adept, and that thou hast cause for vengeance. Blue was ne'er wont to attend these functions before. Only be certain thou hast the right party, before thou makest thy move."

"I shall," Stile said through his teeth.

Now they approached a man in black. He glanced incuriously at Stile as Yellow made the introduction. "Black . . . Blue."

"We have met before," Stile said evenly.

Black peered at him. "I recall it not."

"In thy Demesnes, a month ago." Had it been so short a time? Stile felt as if an age had passed since he had first entered the frame of Phaze and assumed the mantle of the Blue Adept. Subjective experiences had made the days seem like months. Even his encounter with Black seemed impossibly distant. Yet Black was the same, with his line tapering off into the ground, no doubt attaching him to his castle. Black was made of lines.

Black's linear brow furrowed. "No one intrudes on my Demesnes."

"With my companions, a unicorn and a werewolf."

Slowly recognition flickered. "Ah—the man of the Little Folk. I recall it now. I thought thee dead ere now." He squinted. "Why didst thou not show thy power then?"

"I came in peace—then." Stile frowned. He did not like the Black Adept, who had imprisoned him and left him to starve. Yet he could not assume this was the murderer he sought. Black really had no interest in the things of other Adepts; he was a recluse. It was surprising that he had bothered to attend the Unolympics. And if he had murdered the Blue Adept, he certainly would have recognized him more readily than this! Finally, Stile knew the nature of Black's magic: he conjured with lines, not golems or amulets. "If thou intrudest similarly on my Demesnes, I may treat thee with similar courtesy."

"I can conceive of no circumstances in which I would intrude on thy Demesnes, or associate with the likes of Yellow," Black said coldly.

"Until thou hast need of a potion or an animal, my arrogant," Yellow said. "Then thou dost bespeak the crone fair enough." She led Stile on.

"These people make me nervous," the Lady Blue murmured. "Never did my Lord take me among them."

"Thy Lord had excellent taste!" Black muttered from behind.

"So Blue is not thy Lord?" Yellow inquired with a touch of malice. "What fools these peasants be!"

"Call not the Lady Blue a peasant!" Stile snapped, instantly angry. He felt as if he walked among a nest of scorpions.

Yellow's potion-pretty face twisted into something no girl her apparent age could manage. "I call her—"

"What she is," the Lady Blue interjected quickly. "Ever have my folk been villagers, farming the land and raising animals, and no shame in it."

Yellow mellowed. "Aye, no shame in the management of animals.

Methinks thy peasant status ceased when thou didst marry Blue. I withdraw that portion of my remark."

Adepts evidently weren't accustomed to giving away anything voluntarily! "That portion?" Stile demanded, unappeased. He realized he was behaving exactly like an Adept, but was not in the mood to back off. "Thou leavest her a fool?"

"That were readily abated," Yellow said. "I have love-potions that—"

"Enough!" Stile said. "The Lady is a widow; I merely assume a role that the Blue Demesnes be not demeaned, and that the great wrong done the Lady may be avenged. I am not her Lord."

"Passing strange," Yellow murmured. "With power to enchant an entire unicorn herd, he exercises it not on the Lady who is as lovely as any mortal can be and as spirited as a fine animal and who is legitimately his by right of inheritance. Methinks it is the man who is the fool."

"Mayhap by thy definition," the Lady Blue said.

"Even so," Yellow agreed, shrugging.

They came to a man in a red cloak. He was tall, almost six feet, with red hair and red mustache. "Red . . . Blue," Yellow introduced.

Red extended a firm hand. "Glad am I to meet thee," he said, smiling. He had a handsome face and seemed to be about Stile's age, though of course the "costume" made all but his basic identity suspect.

Yellow took them to the final couple at the pavilion. "Green and consort," she said. The Green Adept was another man, short and fat, and his Lady was the same. Both wore green suits and sparkling green jewelry, probably emeralds. "Blue and Lady."

"Uh-huh," the Green Adept said curtly. "Now let's watch the show." But the Lady Green made a small motion of greeting to the Lady Blue.

"These are all that attend this season," Yellow said. "On other occasions I have met Orange, Purple and Gray. But they be from afar. There may be other Adepts we know not of; we are a secretive bunch. I make many contacts at the several Olympics."

"Other Olympics?" Stile asked, remembering something the Herd Stallion had said.

"Every major species has them," Yellow assured him. "Canolympics, Vampolympics, Snowlympics, Dragolympics—some be better than others. Methinks the Elfolympics are best, with their displays of rare weaponry and dancing little men. Hast thou seen the like, my precious?"

"I noticed only the dancing little damsels," Stile said. The Lady Blue frowned, but did not comment.

Now the formal program was beginning. Stile and the Lady Blue took seats and watched. First the several unicorn Herds got settled as spectators, each at its assigned location; then the competitive contingents marched onto the field to the sound of their own horns and hooves.

It was an impressive entry. Each contingent marched in step, led by its Herd Stallion. Every horn was elevated at a 45-degree angle; every tail flung out proudly. The surface of the hooves gleamed in the slanting sunlight, iridescent, and the spirals of the horns shot out splays of mirror-light. The animals were all colors and shades: red, orange, gold, yellow, white, gray, blue, black, brown, striped, dotted and checkered. Some were single-colored, except for those colors typical of horses; others were multicolored. All were beautiful.

The Lady Blue nudged him, making a gesture toward one section of the march. In a moment he found the place—the local Stallion's complement, with sixteen picked individuals. There was Neysa, marching in the last line, on the side nearest the pavilion. "He didn't try to hide her!" Stile murmured appreciatively.

Neysa was smaller than the other unicorns, being barely fourteen hands tall, and she was the only one in the display whose colors were horse-normal—her mark of shame. But now she was the steed and oathfriend of an Adept, and though there was general fear and distrust of Adepts in the animal kingdoms of Phaze, the clear onus of an Adept's favor was so potent that Neysa now had a place of comparative honor. This was the first time she had been permitted to join the Herd and to participate in its ceremonies, and obviously she reveled in it. The hurt of years was being mended. This much Stile had done for Neysa by taming her; this much she had done for herself by allowing him to practice the magic of his station.

The music swelled in a mighty chorus. Eight Herd Stallions blew the leadoff blasts; eight disciplined display-herds responded with the melody. The ground shook with the measured cadence of their prancing hooves; the air shook with the power of their melody. No human orchestra could match the passion and splendor of this performance. Stile could not remember ever having been spectator to anything as grand as this.

They paraded close by the Adepts' pavilion, and at the closest point every horn angled abruptly to the left in a salute. There was an abrupt silence, breathtaking in its precision; that sudden cessation of sound was more impressive than a fortissimo blast would have been. Then they marched on, the music resuming, to pass by the other pavilions.

Stile examined those other pavilions now. One was filled with wolves. Another swarmed with bats. Another seated elves, and yet another was stuffed with glowering, horned demons. "*Everybody* comes to the Unolympics!" Stile breathed, amazed.

"Everybody who is anybody," Yellow responded. "Few Human Folk, however." Stile was not certain of the significance of that; did it mean that humans were among the least important of the creatures of Phaze? Or that the higher animals simply didn't like them?

In due course the opening parade finished. Now the individual competitions commenced. Wolves ran, bats flew, demons charged and elves scurried from one pavilion to another. "What's going on?" Stile asked.

"The judges," Yellow said, standing.

"Judges?"

"They can not use unicorns for the Unolympics; they're not objective. Too much rivalry between the Herds. It's the same with the other species; they all have to use outside judges. Now if thou wilst excuse me, I must to my station."

"Station?"

"I am a judge too. Didn't I tell thee?"

"Now I've seen everything!" Stile muttered.

"Not quite. But when thou spyest Black judging, two pavilions down, then mayhap thou canst consider it close enough to everything." She moved off.

A demon arrived—and also a young man with the head of a hawk. They joined the Yellow Adept at the front of the pavilion. This was the team of judges for one section of the Unolympics.

The contestant-unicorns were now trotting to their places. There was a brief period of confusion as they criss-crossed the field. Then columns formed before the several judging stations. Sixteen unicorns formed a line before the Adept pavilion, standing at equine attention.

This station, it developed, was judging the acrobatics. Others judged speed-trials, high- and long-jumps, horn-fencing, melody-playing, dancing and precision gaits. Neysa and her brother Clip had entered the category of couples-dancing, and that was at a far corner of the field; Stile could not make out what was going on there, to his frustration. So he turned reluctantly to the local display.

Twelve of the entrants were males—not herd leaders, just lesser stallions. The Herd system had no regard for the needs of un-dominant males; they were not allowed to breed with the mares, and were tolerated in the herds only so long as they kept their places. In time of war, Stile was sure, their place was at the forefront, as expendable troops. Naturally they participated in the Unolympics; it was a major peacetime opportunity to achieve recognition.

In fact, Stile realized, these various olympics represented to the animal kingdoms the same sort of entertainment, excitement and chance for individual notoriety that the Game and Tourney did for serfs in Proton. It was a parallel system, used as a relief-valve for the frustrations of the undertrodden.

Yellow, as an Adept, assumed direction of the proceedings at this station. "Equine, thou'rt designated number One," she said to the unicorn on the far left. "When that number is called henceforth in this judgment, do thou answer promptly or forfeit whatever honor may be due thee. Understand?"

The designated unicorn dipped his horn submissively. Yellow then counted off the others, up to the last, number Sixteen. "We are the preliminary panel of judges," she continued. "The Demon Horrawful, who is an Elder of his den and has served with fiendish distinction at other olympics; in his youth he was a winner at this same event at the Demolympics." There was a smattering of polite applause, mostly from the spectators now crowding close to the edge of the pavilion, a number of whom were demons.

"And this is Glynteye the Hawkman, winner of the Avolympic rabbit-spotting meet last year. He is competently versed to spot the antics of unicorns." There was more applause, especially from the animal-heads present.

"And I am the Yellow Adept," she concluded. "In life I am an old human crone whose business is known to most animals. Were it not for the sufferance granted visitors at this event, I would be mobbed. However, I believe I am qualified as a judge of fine animals, and I am in this respect objective."

There was a pause, and then some extremely tentative applause. The Lady Blue looked about, frowned, then set her jaw and clapped her hands. The consort of Green joined her. Then Stile and the Green Adept had to join in, and the outside animals, shamed into a better sense of the occasion, finally made a more substantial showing. All had a horror of Yellow's business of trapping and selling animals, but all antagonisms were theoretically suspended here. Yellow did indeed appear to be competent and objective.

Stile was reminded yet again of the parallel of Proton. The Rifleman had shown him favor, causing the other Citizens to react with similar courtesy despite the gulf between Citizen and serf. The Lady Blue had been the catalyst this time, but the spirit was the same.

"Now withdraw to the sides and rear," Yellow directed, betraying her surprised pleasure at the applause by only a slight flush at her neck. "Form an arena, open only at the spectator's side. No alien magic can function here." And the unicorns did as she bid, so efficiently that Stile realized this was a standard procedure. Indeed, all the stations were forming similar formations.

"Number One 'corn stand forward," Yellow said, and the first stallion moved to the center of the arena, facing the pavilion. "Thou and each other entry will have two minutes to make thy presentation. Each act will be followed by a one-minute consultation of judges and announcement of aggregate score. Applause of up to thirty seconds will be permitted only at that time. If there are any questions at this point, stifle them."

There were no questions. "One, perform," Yellow said.

The unicorn went into his act. He was a fine purple and green animal, with white ears. He pranced and wheeled and leaped in assorted patterns. Gradually he worked up to the more difficult exercises—forward and backward flips, hoof-clicking jumps, and an impressive bucking-bronco finale.

"Time," the demon-judge grated. Apparently he had the timing ability. The stallion stood, his barrel heaving from the exertion, nostrils flared, just a hint of fire in his breath, awaiting the score.

The three judges consulted. Stile could not hear what they said, and did not know the scoring system. Again he tried to spot the activity of the couples-dance unit, and could not.

"Number One scores fifteen," Yellow announced. Now there was applause, the unicorns honking brief notes and tapping their hooves on the ground in lieu of the clapping of hands. It did not seem overwhelming to Stile, and he decided the performance had been no more than average for this type of competition. Certainly Neysa could have matched it, and she had not even entered this event.

"Number Two, stand forth," Yellow said, and another stallion came to the fore. He was larger and better muscled than the first, and his color was brighter: bands of blue alternating with intense yellow. His neck was especially powerful. "Perform." And he launched into his act.

This one was sharper than the first. He did the front and back flips, then went into a series of midair barrelrolls that brought musical gasps from some spectators. He stood on his two forehooves and clicked his rear hooves together so that sparks flew. In the finale he leaped straight up, turned in air, and landed squarely on his horn, which plunged three quarters of its length into the turf. He remained frozen on that one-point support until time was called. Then he allowed his body to drop to the ground so that he could withdraw his horn.

"That is the likely winner," the Lady Blue murmured. "Neysa could not have done that."

"True." Stile had never imagined a unicorn supporting itself in that manner.

The judges consulted. "Twenty-six," Yellow announced, and strong applause burst forth instantly, cutting off only at the expiration of the thirty seconds. A popular decision, certainly.

The other acts followed, but they did not match the second. Stile concluded that each judge graded on the basis of one to ten, with an aggregate of thirty points being the maximum. His attention wandered to the units on either side. To the right were the speed trials, with unicorns galloping around a marked pattern so fast that flame shot from their nostrils, dissipating their developing body heat. Unicorns did not sweat, they blew out fire. On the left side were the gait trials, with unicorns prancing in perfect one, two, three, four and five-beat combinations, manes and tails flying high. But still Stile could not see what

Neysa's unit was doing. He was becoming covertly bored with the proceedings, though the Lady Blue evinced continuing interest.

In the course of a little over an hour the preliminary trials were done. Four contestants had been selected from the local group, to advance to the next round.

The contestants moved to new stations. Now four musicians came to stand before the Adept pavilion. Each played a melody on his or her horn, and these were marvelously pleasant. One unicorn sounded like an oboe, another like a trumpet, a third like a violin, and the fourth like a flute. The violin made the highest score, but the flute and oboe were tied at twenty-two.

"I mislike this," Yellow said. "They are so close, I can not select between them. Have you other judges more firmly entrenched opinions?"

Demon and Hawkman shook their heads. They agreed the two contestants were even. "I mislike being arbitrary," Yellow said. "Yet it has been long since I heard the flute, and I know not which sound is the more perfect representation. If we but had an instrument for comparison—"

The Lady Blue stood with an air of minor mischief. "If it please the judges—"

Yellow glanced back at her. "Speak, Lady, if it be relevant."

"My Lord the Blue Adept is skilled in music, and has with him an excellent flute—"

"Hey, I'm not in this!" Stile protested.

But Yellow was smiling with a certain friendly malice. "Methinks Blue owes me a favor."

Stile spread his hands. He was caught. "What dost thou wish, Yellow?"

"Didst hear the theme played by the flute-'corn? If thou wouldst play the same as it should be played, that we may compare—"

Stile sighed inwardly and walked to the front of the pavilion. He did not object to playing; his concern was that the larger nature of the borrowed Platinum Flute would manifest as his magic power gathered. But if he willed no magic, maybe it would be all right. He did owe Yellow a favor, and this was a modest one.

He assembled the Flute, brought it to his mouth, and played the theme. The magic instrument gave him perfect control, making him a better flutist than he otherwise could be. The notes issued like ethereal honey. The magic gathered, but subtly.

As he played, the routine noises of the Unolympics abated, in a widening circle. Unicorn spectators down the line rotated their ears, orienting on him. When the last note faded, the entire arena was silent.

The three judges remained seated, quiet for a moment. The other Adepts seemed frozen in their places. Then Yellow shook her head.

"There be flutes and there be Flutes," she said. "That is the Platinum Flute, of Elven craft, the Emperor of flutes. There is none like it. Favored indeed is the one, whether common or Adept, who gains its loan from the Little Folk. I fear the crisis of Phaze draws nigh. After that sound, I have no further doubt; the unicorn does not compare."

But the two other judges demurred. "Play oboe," the demon grunted.

"Ah, yes," Yellow agreed. "Thank thee, Horrawful, thou'rt correct. We must compare that sound too." She focused on Stile. "Play the oboe, Blue."

"But I have no oboe," he protested.

"Pretend not to be ignorant of the nature of the instrument thou holdest," she said sharply. "Play the oboe, that we may get on with this matter."

Baffled, Stile looked at the Flute he held—and it had become a fine platinum oboe. So the magic shifts were not merely with weapons! He brought it to his mouth and played the oboe-'corn's theme. The notes rolled out like elixir, impossibly mellow, the most perfect oboe-sound he had ever heard. Again the Unolympics halted to listen. Even the jaded Adepts sat riveted until it finished.

"Now we can judge," Yellow said. She consulted again with her associate-judges, and rendered the decision: "The oboe is closer to true. The oboe-'corn qualifies."

Now there was applause—but somehow it seemed to orient more on Stile than the qualifying unicorn. "Only my Love played like that," the Lady Blue murmured as Stile resumed his seat beside her. "I never thought to hear such sound again."

"The instrument is magic," he replied shortly. "It lends skill to the player."

"Mayhap," she agreed, and said no more.

Soon it was time for the finals. Now the entire field became a single arena, and the separate panels of judges merged to become a single large panel. Everyone would witness the category victories.

Stile was gratified. At last he would get to see Neysa perform—if she had made it this far. He had been confident of her prowess before this ever started, but now he was aware of the strength of the competition. She could have been eliminated.

But she had made it! She and Clip were finalists, and in due course their event came up. One werewolf judge disqualified himself at that point, explaining that he was an oath-friend to a contestant and could not judge her objectively. A substitute was found, and the show went on.

Neysa and Clip trotted out in perfect step, playing their own music for the dance, she with her harmonica-horn, he with his saxophone. It was a beautiful duet, harmonizing precisely with the beat of their hooves. Neysa's colors now complemented Clip's, and she was beautiful even in unicorn terms. Both animals were small for their species, but as a pair, alone in the arena, they were perfectly matched and did not seem small at all.

They plunged forward, horns lunging at an invisible foe, then whipped back together with a dissonant note, as of a foe dying. Stile could almost see the implied monster. So could some of the judges, who happened to be monsters; they scowled. The two went on through different gaits, then got fancy. Neysa leaped, and Clip trotted beneath her. As she landed, he leaped over her. They continued in a fantastic leapfrog sequence, their music playing without a break. Then they came together, bucked in unison, and leaped together in a backward somersault. In midair they changed shape, landing neatly in human-form, he garbed in bright trousers and cloak, she in white-fringed black dress. They swung, now humming the music their horns could no longer play. Faster they swung, becoming almost a blur—and suddenly they were hawk and firefly, whirling about in air about a common center, then back to equine-form with a final, lovely bar of music, in time for the expiration of time.

The judges held out printed cards: 9, 9, 8, 9, 7, 8 . . . an excellent rating from all except the monsters. Then the applause began, loudest from Neysa's own Herd; but there was an appreciative baying from several wolves of the pack who had also taken the oath of friendship with her. Stile saw now that his friend Kurrelgyre was among them.

Then the other unicorn couple went into its act. Both were handsome specimens, and both had remarkable tones. He sounded like a bassoon, with all its deep beauty and trick effects, while she rang like bells. Stile was amazed at what the unicorn horn could do; it was not confined to wind instruments, perhaps because of its magic. This combination was unusual and effective, and they made the most of it.

These unicorns, too, changed shapes in the middle of the dance, manifesting as great cats and then as white and blue herons. Their equine states were special, too; he had a mane like rippling fire, and her mane was iridescent; it shone as it flexed, with precious luster. She was a truly lovely creature. But it was the artistry of their dance that made it outstanding, and in the end they were judged the winners. Stile could not contest the decision; it was fair. Yet Neysa and Clip had made a formidable showing. He was proud of them.

The finals continued with marvelous exhibits, but Stile's attention wandered again. When all this was done, he would have to meet the local Herd Stallion. He had the Platinum Flute, so could employ his magic; he was not in danger. Yet it bothered him, for he did not wish to humiliate the Stallion. He just wanted the postponement of Neysa's breeding. Should he try to talk to the Stallion again? He doubted that would be effective. Unicorns were extremely stubborn animals. Yet if he fought the unicorn and used his magic to prevail, it would be unfair; if he did not use magic, he could lose. Was there no satisfactory alternative?

Stile mulled it over while the Unolympics progressed to the close. In the present excitement and distraction, he found himself unable to work out a strategy that would satisfy all needs. Since he was not about to let himself be wounded by the horn of a unicorn, he would just have to use his magic and damn the social consequence. He hated to do it, though; he knew how important pride was for the dominant creatures of Phaze. Pride, really, had motivated the Herd Stallion to challenge him; the animal hoped to force Stile to capitulate ignominiously, and yield Neysa to the scheduled breeding.

Were the circumstances otherwise, Stile would have done just that. Neysa had waited years for just this opportunity, and Stile wanted no avoidable quarrel with anyone. But Neysa believed—and now Stile agreed—that he needed her on his quest for his murderer. Not merely to ride, for he could now move himself, but as an essential back-up. Surely his enemy would prove far more formidable than the Worm of the Purple Mountains cavity, and Stile had barely prevailed against the Worm even with the Platinum Flute. Neysa's presence could have made the difference, there. He could not free her by giving up his quest, because it was his own murderer he sought. That person had to be brought to justice—and no one else would do it if Stile did not. So for the sake of Neysa's desire as an oath-friend, and his own intermediate-term security, he had to keep her with him, and that meant putting down the Herd Stallion.

Put more succinctly: he had to crush the pride of an honorable creature, to win the right of another creature to sacrifice her ambition of dam-hood and risk her life for him. Some pride!

A bat fluttered up and landed before him. It shifted to man-form. No long canine teeth, no horrific eyes; this was an ordinary, slightly pudgy brown-haired man of middle age. "Thou art Blue?" the vampire inquired diffidently.

"I am he," Stile responded guardedly. "I seek no quarrel with thy kind."

"I am Vodlevile. I encountered thine ogre-friend, Hulk, and thereafter through thine intercession the Yellow Adept did forward to me a potion that cured my son. I owe thee—"

Stile put up a disclaiming palm. "It was in abatement of Hulk's debt to thee for the help thou didst give him in the course of his mission for me. Thou hast no debt to me. I am glad to hear of thy good fortune, and I wish thee and thy son well."

"I helped Hulk from mere camaraderie," Vodlevile protested. "Repayment for that were an insult." He paused. "No offense, Adept; a figure of speech."

"Understood," Stile said, liking this creature. "Yet would I have helped thy son regardless, had I known of his condition. The Lady Blue is a healer, and it is ever her pleasure to help the creatures of Phaze. Can I do less?"

"Apology," Vodlevile said. "I spied thy Lady not. I recognized thee from thy music on the Flute, forgetting her. A greeting to thee, fair one."

"And to thee, sociable one," the Lady Blue replied. She turned to Stile. "We ask no recompense for the work we do, yet neither do we deny the proffered gratitude of those we help."

Stile smiled. "Methinks I have been directed to accept what thou mayst proffer, though I feel thou hast no obligation."

"I bring naught tangible," the vampire said. "If there is anything I may do for thee—"

"What I must do, no one can do for me," Stile said gravely.

"What is that?"

"I must match the Herd Stallion in fair combat." Stile quickly outlined the situation.

"Why, sir, that is merely a matter of face. We vampires, being naturally stealthy, have ready means to handle such questions."

"You vampires must be smarter than I am," Stile said ruefully.

Then Vodlevile explained the recommended strategy. Stile clapped the heel of one hand to his forehead. "Of couse!" he exclaimed. "There is no better service thou couldst have done me than this simple advice."

The vampire made a gesture of satisfaction. "Every time I see my son change form and fly, I think of Blue." He shifted back to bat-form and flew away.

"Thou art very like my Lord," the Lady Blue murmured. "His friendships were many, his enmities few."

Except for the enemy who killed him, Stile thought bleakly. That one had undone all the rest.

The final match was decided and the victorious unicorn paraded off the field. Now it was time for the special event—Herd Stallion vs. Blue Adept—in a combat supposedly immune to magic.

The Herd Stallion strutted out, resplendent in his natural color and musculature. Stile started forward, but found himself restrained by the Lady Blue's hand. He turned to her, uncertain what she wanted.

She was always beautiful, but at the moment she seemed to him to be transcendentally lovely. "Go with care, my Lord," she said, and somehow it was the greatest compliment he could have imagined.

"I thank thee, Lady," he said. Then he proceeded on out to meet the Stallion, carrying the Platinum Flute.

The unicorns formed a great ring around the two, sealing off external magic. They thought Stile would be unable to draw on the background power, and ordinarily this would be true. But the Oracle had enabled him to nullify that nullification. This was the real debt he owed Hulk, for Hulk had donated his one lifetime question to the Oracle for Stile's benefit; that was why Stile had taken Hulk's debt of a favor on himself. Now the vampire had repaid it, and by Stile's logic he owed a major favor to Hulk.

Perhaps his gift of the pursuit of the Proton-self of the Lady Blue had abated that; perhaps not. He remembered that he had agreed to Hulk's visit to the Oracle at the subtle behest of the Lady Blue, who had been aware of what was developing. She had acted to defuse the issue before it came to Stile's attention. So where was the right of it? Stile knew he would have to think about the matter some more; right was not always simple to ascertain. Yet such deliberations were always worthwhile.

Now he stood in the center of the huge arena, before the Stallion. The contrast in their sizes was striking; a large equine, a very small man. But there was no snicker from the audience, for Stile was the Blue Adept.

First he had to establish his power, making it instantly and compellingly evident to the entire assembly. That was the first stage of the vampire's excellent advice. He had to prove that the ring of unicorns could not impinge upon the Blue Adept's practice of magic. At the moment, only a few understood the full properties of the Platinum Flute, like the Yellow Adept; after the demonstration, everyone would know.

Stile brought out the Flute. The Herd Stallion waited, as if curious to see what his opponent was up to.

Stile played. Again the enchanting melody poured forth, the finest sound a flute could make. The unicorns listened raptly, yet perplexed. How could mere music stop the great Stallion?

When the magic had gathered, Stile halted and went into a singsong spell: "Show us the story of the Dragon's Tooth, from death to bloom, from birth to youth." But the real shaping of it was in his mind; the words only initiated the sequence.

In the sky a dot appeared. It expanded rapidly into the shape of a dragon, with six legs, six wings, and a tremendously toothed mouth. A shadow almost the size of the entire arena fell as the monster crossed the sun. The unicorns looked up, alarmed; seldom did any dragon approach a unicorn herd, and this one was the largest ever seen locally.

Stile raised his right hand to point at the dragon. Then he put the Flute to his mouth again, to intensify the magic and keep his complex spell operating at full strength.

The dragon folded its wings and dived at the field. Folded, it was much smaller. It crashed headfirst into the chewed turf and exploded. This was the "death" of his spell. Teeth flew out in a splash, to land all across the field; the rest of the dragon puffed away in smoke.

Where each tooth fell, something sprouted. This was the "bloom." As Stile continued to play the Flute, the teeth grew into leafy vines.

Each vine fruited in a gourd, and each gourd hatched into a human baby, and each baby grew rapidly into an armed soldier. This was the "birth to youth" sequence. The soldiers formed into a phalanx, marched once around the field, shifted into a sinuous formation that suddenly sprouted wings and flew as a mass into the sky. It was the original dragon, departing as it had come. In moments it was a mere speck in the sky, and then it was gone.

The unicorns stood in silence. They had just been shown that they could no longer restrict the magic of the Blue Adept, even when their force was greatest. The Adepts, too, were riveted; not one of them could match this performance. Was one of them the murderer he sought? Stile hoped that one was quaking, now, for fear of the vengeance of Blue. Most magic was fun to Stile, but in this regard it was deadly serious.

The Herd Stallion, however, had not budged. Stile had feared this would be the case. He had fashioned a demonstration of magic that was spectacular enough to enable the Stallion to withdraw without shame; obviously no ordinary creature could prevail against power like this. But the Stallion was stubborn; he would not back off regardless. He might face impossible odds but he would not yield to opposition. Stile respected that; he was that way himself. It was another reason why he was going to so much trouble to avoid humiliating the fine animal. How fortunate that the vampire had been available for advice!

Stile sang another spell: "Flute of class, grant equal mass." Suddenly a giant appeared, in Stile's own image, standing in his footprints, towering above him. The giant's mass was equal to that of the Herd Stallion; anyone could see that. Then the giant shrank in on Stile until at last it disappeared in Stile. He now had the mass of the unicorn, though he remained his own size and felt no different. He held the Flute—which was now the broadsword.

The Herd Stallion stepped forward. *He* certainly understood; Stile was using his magic only to make the contest even. It depended only on their skills. If the Stallion was good with his natural weapon, he might outfence Stile and win. If not, Stile would prevail. The nullification of shame could go no further than this. Vampire Vodlevile's advice had taken them to this stage; what followed would follow.

The Stallion seemed to be proceeding with guarded confidence. Stile could guess why; Stile was known to be inexpert with the rapier. Neysa had had to drill him in its use, and he had been an apt student, but a few lessons could not bring him to the level of the Herd Stallion.

Stile, however, was not now holding a rapier. He was holding an excellent broadsword, perfect in weight and length and temper and balance and all the subtleties of general feel, and with this weapon he was proficient. He had trained with this type of sword for a dozen years, and won many Proton-frame Games with it. While he could not match the Stallion's protection against being disarmed, he could, if he had to, throw his blade at his opponent. So it was reasonably even. That was the way he wanted it. Vodlevile had shown him how to ease his crisis of conscience.

They met in the center of the arena and ceremoniously crossed weapons. Then each took a step back. Now it began.

The Stallion lunged. The horn shot forward. Stile jumped aside, his point jabbing to tag the unicorn's shoulder—but the animal was not to be caught that way, and was out of range.

Now Stile lunged. The Stallion's horn parried his thrust powerfully. Had Stile not possessed equal mass, he could have been disarmed then; as it was, sparks flew from the colliding weapons and both parties felt the impact.

So much for the feeling-out. Stile valued surprise, without sacrificing good technique. He fenced with the Stallion's horn, setting himself up for disarming, and when the Stallion made the move, Stile slipped by his guard and sliced at his neck. The unicorn, suckered, shifted instantly to man-form so as to duck under it, then back to equine form. He had a sword in man-form, but lacked Stile's mass; there was no conservation of mass, in magic.

Stile wheeled to engage the Stallion again. He knew now that he was the superior swordsman, but he guarded against overconfidence. This shape-changing—that could be tricky.

Indeed it was. Suddenly he faced a small flying dragon. The creature spread batlike wings and flew over Stile's head, out of reach of his sword.

Well, Stile was also out of reach of the dragon's talons. It was a standoff, for the moment. Since he didn't really want to hurt the Herd Stallion, that was all right.

Then the dragon shot fire from its mouth. Stile dived out of the way. This was more complicated than he had thought! Evidently the unicorn had built up some heat in the course of the match, and was able to use that to fuel his dragon-form.

The dragon oriented for another shot. Stile raised his sword—and it was a shiny, mirror-surfaced shield. It caught the jet of fire and bounced it back at the dragon. The creature took evasive action.

Stile could bring the dragon down by magic—but he remained unwilling to do that. He wanted to win as he was. His weapon could change according to his need; the Stallion could change his shape. They remained even. Except that Stile could not reach the dragon.

Or could he? Suddenly his weapon became an eighteen-foot pike. Stile heaved it upward at a sharp angle, poking at the dragon. The creature squawked with a sound like an accordion—which was the tone of the Stallion's horn—and flapped higher. Another jet of fire came down, but petered out short of the mark. Stile's pike was keeping the dragon beyond flame-range.

Standoff. Neither could hurt the other. Unless—

Stile's spike became a powerful platinum bow, with a long, sharp arrow. He aimed it at the dragon—but already the creature was diving to earth, changing back to the unicorn, who formed in midcharge toward Stile.

Stile's weapon shifted back to broadsword, and the fencing resumed. Stile was the better swordsman, but every time he pressed his advantage the Stallion changed shape and they went through a quick series of animal and weapon forms before returning to the more conventional fray.

It became apparent to the audience that there was unlikely to be a winner here; neither party could hurt the other. Stile was satisfied with that; they could negotiate a reasonable extension of Neysa's time.

Stile outfenced the Stallion again, the Stallion shifted to dragon-form, Stile's sword became the bow . . .

And the dragon became the man-form, who plummeted toward Stile. Stile flung himself aside, his grip on his weapon slackening, and the man-form snatched it from Stile's grasp. He hurled it far across the arena. In air, the bow reverted to its natural state, the Flute, and bounced on the grass. Stile had been careless, and abruptly disarmed.

His first impulse was to run for the Flute, for he had no chance without it. His mass had reverted to normal the moment he was separated from the Flute. The ring of unicorns now deprived him of his magic. How foolish he had been not to retain his grip; he could never have been disarmed had he willed himself not to be.

A large hand caught his shoulder. The man-form was preventing him from going after the weapon.

Stile reacted instantly. He caught the hand on his shoulder, whirled about, and applied pressure to the man-form's elbow joint. It would have been a submission hold, ordinarily—but the form shifted back to equine and the hold was negated.

Freed, Stile sprinted for the Flute. But the Stallion galloped after him. No chance to outrun that! Stile had to turn and dodge, staying clear of that horn.

But he would not be able to dodge it long! Stile made a phenomenal, acrobatic leap, feeling his weakened knees giving way in the effort, and flipped through the air toward the Stallion's back. If he could ride the animal long enough to get near the Flute—

Then, in the moment he was in the air, he saw that terrible unicorn horn swinging about to bear on him. The Stallion had reacted too quickly. Stile would land—directly on the point.

He landed—in the arms of the man-form. The creature set him down carefully. "I seek not to injure thee, Adept, for thou hast been kind to my kind. I merely deflect thee. Thou'rt disarmed of thy weapon and thy magic. Dost thou yield?"

It had been a fair fight. The unicorn had outmaneuvered him. Stile might be able to hold his own against the man-form, but not against the equine-form or dragon-form, and he refused to stoop to any subterfuge. He had lost. "I yield," he said.

"Fetch thy weapon ere hostile magic comes," the man-form said, and shifted back to unicorn-form.

Stile walked across the arena and picked up the Flute, then rejoined the Stallion before the main judging stand. The Stallion did not speak, so Stile did. "We have met in fair encounter, and the Stallion defeated me. The Blue Adept yields the issue."

Now the Herd Stallion blew an accordion medley on his horn. Neysa's brother Clip trotted up. "The Stallion says the Adept is more of a creature than he took him for. The Adept had magic to win, and eschewed it in favor of equality, and fought fairly and well, and lost well. The Stallion accepts the pride of that victory—and yields back the issue."

Then the applause began. Unicorns charged into the field, forming into their discrete herds. Neysa found Stile and carried him away separately to rejoin the Lady Blue. The Unolympics were over.

So all the Herd Stallion had really wanted was the notoriety of defeating the Blue Adept and redeeming the pride he had lost during their prior encounter at the Blue Demesnes. Granted that, the Stallion had been generous, and had granted Neysa the extension she wanted. All Stile had lost was a little pride of his own—and that had never been his prime consideration.

In future, he would pay better attention to the hidden motives of the creatures of Phaze—and to the pitfalls of battling a shape-changing creature. These were useful lessons.

CHAPTER 7

Hulk

Sheen took Stile to a private chamber deep in the maintenance section of the dome they lived in. He carried his harmonica and the Platinum Flute with him in a small bag, not being willing to leave them elsewhere lest he have sudden need for them, or risk their theft.

He spoke with an anonymous machine through a speaker. This reminded him of the mode of the Oracle—but of course the Oracle could not be a machine. It was evident that Sheen had not brought him here without reason. "What is your interest?" he inquired.

"We have a partial report for you concerning the recent attempt made on your life."

"Partial," Stile repeated, excited and disappointed. Any progress was good, but he needed the whole story.

"The message from your Citizen Employer was legitimate, but the address was changed. A chip had been modified in the message annex to substitute that address for the proper one in any message directed to you from a Citizen, one time. It was a one-shot trap."

"Sending me to intrude on a Citizen who didn't like the Tourney and was apt to exterminate intruders," Stile said, thinking of the Black Adept in Phaze, who acted similarly.

"Correct. We conclude this was the work of other than a Citizen."

"Because a Citizen would not have had to bother with a hidden trap," Stile said, realizing that he should not so blithely have assumed his enemy was a Citizen.

"Correct. We were unable to trace the instigator. We remain alert for more direct devices, but your enemy is evidently no machine."

He hadn't even thought of having a machine-enemy! "Because my enemy has more imagination than a machine does."

"Correct. Like you, that person is a quick and original thinker."

"This helps," Stile said. "A serf is considerably more limited than a Citizen. A serf's motives should differ from those of a Citizen. But could a serf have lasered my knees or sent Sheen to me?"

"The knees affirmative. Sheen negative. She had to come from a Citizen. That Citizen covered his traces carefully; we can trace her manufacture but not the identity of the one issuing the directive that sent her to you."

"So already we have a seeming divergence of elements. A Citizen sent Sheen to protect me from a serf."

"Correct."

"Why didn't the Citizen simply eliminate the enemy serf?"

"We have no information."

"And why are you self-willed machines helping me? This increases the risk of your discovery by the Citizens, so is dangerous for you."

To his surprise, the anonymous machine answered. "At first we helped you because one of our number, the robot Sheen, wished it, and you took the oath not to betray our interests. There was also an anonymous imperative favoring you. This also we have been unable to trace, but we have ascertained that it originates from other than Citizen or serf. We were aware that a chance existed that you would eventually be useful to us. Now that chance has expanded. Perhaps this is what the anonymous imperative intended. Should you win the Tourney, as we deem a one in ten chance at this moment, you will become a Citizen. As such you could help our cause enormously."

"As such, I could," Stile agreed, intrigued by their estimate of his chances in the Tourney, and by the notion of the "anonymous imperative" that favored him. Strange elements operating here! "But you know I would betray neither my own kind nor the system. I do not support revolution, or even significant change. I merely seek to deal with my enemy and improve my personal, private situation. I'm just no crusader."

"We seek recognition for our kind within the system," the machine said. "No revolution is desired, only modification. We wish to have the status of serfs. A Citizen could prepare the way."

"I could support that," Stile agreed. "But that would necessitate revealing the secret of your nature."

"We are not ready for that. We would be destroyed, were our nature known prematurely."

"But to prepare the way without the revelation—that would be very slow."

"We estimate the process will take approximately seventy-five years. To move faster would be to increase the risk unacceptably."

"You have patience," Stile said.

"We are machines."

That, of course, was their ultimate limitation. They had intelligence, consciousness and self-will, but lacked the impatience of life. Though Sheen was coming close! "I thank you for your help, for whatever motive, machines," Stile said. "I will help you in return—when the occasion offers."

He returned with Sheen to their apartment, not speaking further of this matter. He never spoke directly of the self-willed machines where his words could be recorded, lest that betray their nature to the Citizens of Proton. Most places were bugged, and often continuous recordings of serf activities were made at the behest of individual Citizens. Thus only a place cleared by the machines themselves was safe for such dialogue. Elsewhere, he simply called them "Sheen's friends."

Stile did appreciate their help, and he wondered whether they were really as machinelike as they claimed. Why should they care about their status in the society of Proton? To become serfs only meant to serve Citizens—as they already did—to be allowed to play the Game, and to be limited to twenty years or so of tenure on the planet. If they left the planet, they might lose whatever status they gained on it, since the galactic society was just as human-oriented as was Proton's. Yet obviously they did have desires. Sheen was certainly an emotional, personlike being; why not others like her? But the machines would let him know what they wanted him to know, when they deemed appropriate.

It was time for his next Game. Round Five—the number of entrants was shrinking now, as more players lost their second match and were washed out, so things would move along faster. But there remained a long way to go.

This time he was paired with a child, an eleven-year-old boy, not one of the good ones. "Your tenure can't be up!" Stile said.

"My folks' tenure is up," the boy explained. "I'm leaving with them anyway, so why not go out in style?"

So he had nothing to lose. Just in it for fun, to see how far he could go. And he had gotten to Round Five, perhaps helping to eliminate three or four entrants to whom this was a matter verging on life and death. It was the irony of the Tourney that many of those who had no need should win, while those who *had* to win—lost.

Their turn came, and they went to the grid. Stile got the letters, and was afraid the boy would go for CHANCE—and was correct. It came up 3C, Machine-Assisted CHANCE. *Any* CHANCE was bad; Stile had tried to mitigate it, but ultimately it remained potential disaster.

If he could steer it into one of the more complex mechanical variants, a pinball machine—for a person like him, with experience and a fine touch, one of those became a game of skill.

But it came out wrong, again. The lad played with luck and the uncanny insight of the young, making mischief. It settled on an ancient-type slot machine, a one-armed bandit. One hundred percent chance. Each player pulled the handle, and the kid came up with the higher configuration.

"I won! I won! I won!" he shrieked. "Hee-hee-hee!"

Stile had lost. Just like that. A nothing-Game, against a dilettante child who had nothing to gain—and Stile was suddenly half washed out. His nightmare had happened.

Sheen found him and got him home. Stile was numbed with the un-fairness of it. It was a demeaning loss, so pointless, so random. All his considerable Game-skills had been useless. Where did his chances of winning the Tourney stand now? One in a hundred?

"I know it hurts you," Sheen said solicitously. "I would suffer for you if I could, but I am not programmed for that. I am programmed only for you, yourself, your person and your physical welfare."

"It's foolish," Stile said, forcing himself to snap out of it. "I compre-hend the luck of the Game. I have won randomly many times. This is why the Tourney is double-elimination—so that a top contender shall not be eliminated by a single encounter with a duffer in CHANCE. I simply have to take my loss and go on."

"Yes."

"But dammit, it hurts!"

"Of course."

"How can you understand?" he snapped.

"I love you."

Which was about as effective a rebuttal as she could have made. "Your whole existence is like a lost Game, isn't it," he said, squeezing her hand.

"Yes."

"It seems as though luck is turning against me. My Games have been running too close, and in Phaze I lost a contest to a unicorn, and now this—"

They were home. "There is a message," Sheen said as they entered. She went to the receptacle and drew it out. "A holo-tape."

"Who would send me a tape?" Stile asked, perplexed. "Another trap?"

"Not with my friends watching." She set it in the playslot.

The holograph formed. The Rifleman stood before them. "I pon-dered before relaying this edited report to you, Stile," the Citizen said. "But a wager is a wager, and I felt this was relevant. I suspect this tape reveals the general nature of the information you would have given me, had you lost our ballgame, so I hardly feel cheated. I was not able to as-certain who has tried to hurt you, but it seems likely that you were the intended victim of this sequence, and therefore this does provide a hint." He frowned. "I apologize for acquitting my debt in this manner. Yet it is best you have the detail. I hope that this at least forwards your quest. *Adieu.*" The Citizen faded out with a little wave.

"Why is he so diffident?" Stile asked. "That's not the way of a Citizen."

"He uses the term 'victim,'" Sheen pointed out. "This will not be pretty."

"Hulk! Something's happened—"

The holograph formed a new image: Hulk, talking to Sheen herself.

The man seemed even larger than normal, in the confines of the apartment. His head barely cleared the doorway. "Thank you, Sheen," Hulk said, smiling down at her. Sheen was lovely, looking absolutely human, but of course Hulk knew the truth.

"I never knew this was being recorded!" the actual Sheen exclaimed, looking at her holo-image.

"Citizens can have anything recorded," Stile reminded her. "All the holo-pickups spread throughout the domes of Proton are at their service."

"I know that. I just didn't realize I was the subject, in your absence."

"You may be the subject right now."

"Oh, shut up and watch the show."

They watched the holo-Hulk depart, the image sliding in and out of the scene to simulate his motion. He stopped at a communication screen, called Information, and received a slip of paper, evidently an address. The self-willed machines had provided it, of course; Stile hoped the Rifleman had not pursued that ramification.

Hulk read the address and started walking again. Suddenly he was entering a jetporter—and as suddenly emerging at a far dome. The edited tape, of course, skipping across the nonessentials. It was easy to follow, since standard entertainment-holos were done the same way.

Hulk arrived at an isolated dome, similar to so many favored by Citizens. This one was accessible by monorail across the sand, so that any visitors were visible well before arrival. Hulk stepped down as the carriage halted, and stood on the lawn, looking at the main building.

It was an almost perfect replica of the Blue Demesnes. Stile could well understand the amazement of the big man. Who would have thought that such a castle existed in the frame of Proton? It was probably on the same geographic site, too, conforming perfectly to the alternate frame. The frames did tend to align, as Stile had discovered the hard way, when a person died in one, he was likely to die in the other too. Stile had narrowly escaped death in Proton at the time the Blue Adept was murdered in Phaze. Then, in what was apparently another way for the frames to equalize, he had discovered the curtain and crossed over. Thus each frame had Stile, again—in turn. This suggested that the use of the curtain was not coincidental, but inevitable—when an imbalance existed between the frames.

But now here was Hulk—seemingly back where he had started from. And surely the Lady Blue was here, for this was where Sheen had sent him to find her, based on the information her machine friends had provided. But the Lady could not hold the position here that she did in Phaze . . .

Hulk, evidently having completed a similar mental sequence, strode forward toward the castle. There was one way to find out!

There was a guard at the gate. He stood up straight as Hulk approached, but there was no way he could match Hulk's height. "What is your business here, serf?"

"I am Hulk, on leave from employment pending the expiration of my tenure. I wish to meet Bluette."

The guard turned to a communication pickup. "Serf with message for Bluette."

"Thank you; I will be down." It was the Lady Blue's voice. Stile felt a prickle at his spine, though he knew this was merely the Lady's alternate self. Of course she sounded the same; she *was* the same, in everything except situation.

"I'm not sure I should watch this," Stile muttered. "It doesn't relate to my situation."

"The Rifleman thinks otherwise," Sheen reminded him. "You can just sit there and watch someone else making time with someone you love. The experience will do you good."

How bitter could a robot get? But probably she was right; he was doing it to her, and he needed to know how it felt to have it done to him.

Hulk waited, and in a moment she appeared. She was indeed the Lady Blue. The Phaze clothing was gone; she was a naked serf. But she was the same.

"She's lovely," Sheen said. "I can see how you would like her."

"This one is for Hulk," Stile said. But it was hard to believe that. He was glad the scene was only in holo. Bluette—the Lady Blue—he understood why they were so exactly like each other. Yet to see it so directly —this stirred him fundamentally.

"What is your message?" Bluette inquired. She did not use the archaic tongue, of course; Stile found this slightly jarring, but it did help distinguish her from the woman he loved.

"Lady, it is complicated," Hulk said. "I would like to talk with thee at some length."

"Thee?"

"My error," Hulk said quickly. "A misplaced usage." He had had so much trouble getting used to the forms of Phaze, and this situation was conducive to the error. Stile would have had the same problem.

Bluette shrugged. "Until my Employer comes, I am not hard-pressed. Yet I am disinclined to heed a complicated message from a stranger."

"This I understand, Lady," Hulk said. "I know it is an imposition. Yet perhaps I can tell you things that will interest you. I have known one very like you, a great and gracious woman, a star among planets—"

"Enough of this!" she exclaimed angrily. "I am a serf, like you. Do you seek to get me in trouble with my Employer?"

Hulk's response was cut off by the sudden descent of a rocket. The thing veered out of its trajectory, dropping rapidly toward the dome. Both man and woman paused to stare at it.

"Lady, it will crash!" Hulk cried. He leaped forward, swept up the woman, and carried her from the projected site of collision.

He was not mistaken. The rocket plunged through the dome's force-field and landed with an explosive flare of heat against the castle wall. A yellowish cloud of vapor enveloped it, spreading rapidly outward. "Gas attack!" Hulk cried. "Get into the monoshuttle!"

"This is outrageous!" Bluette exclaimed as he set her down. But she ran fleetly enough toward the mono.

It was no good. The crash had disrupted the mono's power; the shuttle was inoperative. "Go outside the dome!" Hulk cried. "The gas can't follow there!"

But the gas had already diffused throughout the dome. Both Hulk and the Lady held their breaths as they ran for the rim, but collapsed as the gas touched their skin.

"Nerve gas," Stile muttered. "Almost instant. Not necessary to breathe it. Used as an anesthetic for animals." He frowned. "But strange that a shipment of that should crash right there and then. Freight rockets hardly ever go astray."

"That was no coincidence," Sheen said. "That was a trap."

Stile nodded. "A trap set for me, I think. Because it was expected that I would be the one to come for the Lady Blue."

"Which means that your enemy knows of your life in both frames. And that you would hardly be likely to bring the one person who could help you escape that situation—me."

Another half-bitter reference to Sheen's own feelings. She was right; had he gone to see Bluette, Stile would not have brought Sheen along. That would have been unnecessarily cruel. So he would have had no invulnerable guardian to bail him or the Lady out. "Yes, the enemy must be an Adept, who can cross the curtain. But not a Citizen. So the trap is made to seem like an accident, to foil any Citizen curiosity."

Now he was feeling the reaction. Stile did not like being the object of a murder campaign; that frightened him and generated in him a festering uncertainty and rage. But now the attack had spread to the Lady Blue/Bluette. That aggravated him far more specifically. How dare they touch her!

And Hulk—innocently walking into the trap set for Stile. Hulk's blood, if it came to that, would be on Stile's hands. What mischief had Stile done his friend, in the name of a favor?

The holo continued. Robots emerged from the crashed rocket—humanoid, flesh-toned, but probably far simpler machines than was Sheen. They came to Hulk and the Lady, and fitted breathing masks over their faces. Then the robots picked up the two effortlessly and carried them through the force-field and out onto the barren surface of Proton. There the holo-pickup lost them—but the orbiting satellite spotters followed their progress. What a job of tracing the devices of Proton could do, when so directed!

The robots trekked tirelessly south across the sand with their burdens. At length they entered the shaft of a worked-out mine at the margin of the Purple Mountains—which were not purple here. The full image returned; it seemed that even a place like this had operable pickups.

At last the two were deposited in a pressurized chamber deep within the mine. It was a miniature force-field dome. There was a defunct food-dispensing machine and a holo-transceiver. This could be considered a pleasant private retreat—or a prison.

The robots sprayed more gas, evidently a neutralizer, removed the breathing masks, filed them in their chest compartments, and set a chamber oxygen generator in operation. Then they walked through the force-field and disappeared from the range of the holo-pickup. Hulk was the one this report was on, not stray robots. The impersonal touch of the machine, literally; machines did not care about irrelevancies such as the welfare of serfs or the commission of criminal acts.

Hulk was of rugged constitution, and first to regain consciousness. His eye cracked open in time to see the robots departing. He made a huge visible effort and hauled himself to his feet. He staggered across to Bluette. "Lady—art thou well?" he asked, lifting her with infinite gentleness.

Bluette was at the moment weak physically, but not mentally. She shook off the lingering effects of the gas. "Again you use the archaic form. What is this?"

"I will answer you gladly, Lady. But first we should ascertain our situation. We seem to have been taken prisoner."

"Why should anyone wish to do that? My Employer is a peaceful man, a scholar of the arcane, who hardly ever comes to his castle retreat. I merely maintain it so that it is never ill-kept should he appear. For months at a time, it is as if it belongs to me—but I am only a serf, destined never to be more."

"You are more, Lady. Much more. I fear my arrival precipitated this action." Hulk was already inspecting the perimeter. He took a breath, held it, and stepped through the force-field at one end of their confine. There was only one more tunnel, proceeding interminably. This was an access passage, carved by laser drills long ago, leaving smooth, partially polished walls. It reminded Stile of the bore of the Worm of Phaze. Perhaps that was not coincidence, but another parallel between frames. Operating mines were pressurized throughout, for convenience; since many of the rock formations were porous or semiporous, the passage had to have melt-sealed walls. This was a dead mine, since there was no pressure beyond the Proton-external norm. Hulk passed back through the force-field and moved to the other end. It was the same story.

"These passages can extend for kilometers," Hulk told the Lady. "Without masks, we can not expect to reach a dome on foot."

"Of course not," she agreed. "Yet if it were our captor's purpose to kill us, he could have done this at the outset."

"I see there is a holo-unit. No doubt our captor will communicate with us at his convenience."

"Surely he will," she agreed. "But I still don't understand why we are here."

Hulk inspected the holo-communicator. "I could put this out of commission, but that seems pointless. We shall simply have to wait. I deeply regret bringing this upon you; I had no idea this would happen. Yet perhaps it is for the best."

She frowned, exactly as the Lady whom Stile knew would have, then flung her golden hair back in a kind of acquiescent defiance. She was absolutely lovely. "I was not unduly interested, before, in what you had to say. My interest has grown. Tell me your estimate of this situation."

Hulk settled down against the curving wall opposite her. "Gladly, Lady. I believe this is a trap set for another person, a friend of mine. It was assumed that he would come for you, and the robots were not astute enough to perceive the substitution. When the Citizen who has organized this checks in, he will discover the mistake. He will not be pleased."

"When my Employer checks his retreat-estate, *he* will not be pleased," Bluette said. "Yet I fear that will not be soon." She looked directly at him. "Give me the rest of it."

"Lady, I am a master in the Game. Since my tenure expires this year I had hoped to enter the Tourney. I was balked in that effort by a better player. But he showed me an alternate world—Lady, you may find this extremely difficult to believe, so I shall simplify it—"

"Do not expurgate it," she said.

"You do not appreciate just how remarkable the story is. I do not wish to have you question my sanity."

"Risk my incredulity. Tell the truth and take your medicine," she said, smiling.

"I cannot deny you," he said, warmed as anyone would be. The smile of the Lady was a precious thing. "I should warn you that I came to court you. I do not mean to give offense, and I would have preferred a more esthetic approach—"

"I have not been courted in years," she said. "You are a handsome man."

"Reserve your judgment; I may have brought great mischief upon you."

"I reserve it," she said. But she studied him with only slightly muted interest, for Hulk was about as impressive a figure of a man as existed, and the compliment of his attention was considerable. Women were less impressed by physical attributes than men were, but they were not immune to them.

"This alternate world, where I met the woman like you," he said. "It resembles Proton in geography, but it has good air and water and vegetation, and a population of living creatures. An ideal world, except—" He paused. "Remember, I warned you. In that world, called Phaze, science is inoperative and magic is operative."

"Magic is operative," she replied, humoring him.

"Yes. He took me to that world, where unicorns and werewolves and vampires roam, and he made some spells and became the Blue Adept, one of the leading magicians of that frame. But he had been killed by another Adept. So I served as his bodyguard, and I guarded his wife—who is you."

"You're right," Bluette said seriously. "This is beyond belief. I do appreciate your imagination, and am sure you do excellently in the Lying Game in competition, and consider myself honored to be the subject of your present fantasy. How does this relate to our kidnapping?"

"The enemy Adept is evidently another curtain-crosser," Hulk continued gamely, "operating in both frames. Unable to destroy the Blue Adept permanently in Phaze, he has been setting traps for him here in Proton. The enemy evidently thought the Blue Adept would come for you, so he arranged to abduct whoever approached you, apart from your Employer and routine serfs. But this trap got the wrong man."

"How can you court the wife of your friend?" she asked alertly. In no way was Bluette slow of wit; Stile had discovered that early, when dealing with her alternate.

"Most people exist in both frames. When the self of one frame dies, the self of the other can cross over, filling his place. When the Blue Adept died, his Proton-self crossed over—and courted the widow, the Lady Blue. But he felt it would be improper also to court her Proton-self, who is you, Bluette."

"And he allows you to approach me instead, since I am surplus?"

"There are no surplus diamonds," Hulk said. "Every precious thing has a taker. He is a generous man, Lady. He loves you, but will take only the one he first came to know. There is something more to his interest than your likeness, I suspect."

"I should hope so. And you accede to this? You seem to be man enough to have your pick of women. Why accept the castoff of your friend? Is he even more powerful than you appear to be?"

"In a manner of speaking, Lady. It seems we are similar in many respects, including our taste in women. I cannot explain it better."

"I think you can. You were with his wife?"

"I guarded his wife from the possible threat by his enemy, during his absences. I came to know her, the deep and unique qualities of her. I am an honorable man; when I realized what was happening, I left."

"What do you mean, what was happening?" she demanded. "Were I the wife of one, I would not be leading on another."

"No, never!" Hulk agreed hastily. "You—I mean the Lady Blue—never in any way—it was wholly in my mind, a one-sided thing. But in this frame she is not his wife, and will never be; he intends never to meet her. Meet thee. You. Thus I came for you, her perfect double."

"Less swift, man. I have not quite made the transition from your dream fancy to your reality." She cocked her head. "What is your name?"

"Hulk. From an ancient comic."

She smiled. "*I* was named after a fine horse."

They laughed, warming to each other.

"Well, Hulk," she said after a moment. "Whatever gave you the notion that any self of mine would be amenable to any suit of yours? Why should I flirt with a bodyguard, in either, ah, frame?"

Hulk spread his hands. "How you receive it is your business. I had to try. You can but decline."

"Still, there must have been a point of decision."

Hulk nodded. "I suppose there was. In Phaze-frame life abounds, including bacterial and viral. I had little natural defense against environmental disease agents, since Proton is nearly sterile." He paused, reflecting. "In more ways than one, I suspect." He made a gesture to indicate that it didn't matter. "I fell sick. The Lady Blue recognized the problem; she bade me lie down, and she laid her hands on me, and they were healing hands, that warmed me throughout."

"Ah, yes," Stile said, momentarily breaking out of the spell of the holograph narrative. "I have felt the touch of those hands."

"You are not jealous?" Sheen asked. "I inquire merely as a point of robotic interest."

"Meaning *you're* jealous," he said. "You think the Lady Blue is too pretty."

"If appearance were all that counted, I might compete. I think she has too much of your attention."

"Not in this frame. Hulk left her to me in Phaze; I leave her to him, in Proton. It was not a completely easy decision for either of us. But yes, I am jealous. It is hard for me to watch another man courting her."

"And harder to watch her responding. Serves you right."

"Serves me right," he agreed.

"I do not lightly give my body or my heart," Bluette was saying to Hulk. The holo-scene had frozen while Stile and Sheen conversed; that was Sheen's touch on the control. "You're a funny man, with a fairy-tale history. Yet there is no doubt we are here, and surely we shall be interrogated. Will you tell our captor the same story?"

"I'm not sure. I am not the one our captor wants." Hulk pondered. "Lady, I fear it will go hard with us, when our captor discovers the error. It would be better if he did not realize it."

"Why?"

"Obviously there is something the captor wants of my friend, not merely his death. Otherwise the robots would simply have killed us, instead of bringing us here. Perhaps it is information that is wanted. Since kidnapping is also a crime, even when only serfs are involved, I will be disposed of so I can not tell my story to my own Employer."

"Yes. I, too, will be useless as bait, after this. But I do not see what action we can take. If we disrupt the holo-pickup, the captor will know, and will send in—you said there were robots?"

"I saw two, as I recovered consciousness."

"Who have the oxy-masks used to bring us here," Bluette said, her eyes widening as she caught on. "What do you propose, Hulk?"

"First, I must get out of sight of the pickup. Second, you must address me as 'Stile' and describe me as a very small man—smaller than you. The story is the same—that is what he told you. He came to rescue you—and was himself trapped."

"I have that," Bluette said. "Assuming for the nonce that your story is true, then this would be believed by another person from that frame. But how—"

"I will hide outside the force-field, downtunnel. I can function for a limited time in external atmosphere, if I put my body in near-absolute state of rest, or trance-state. You try to lure the robots near the force-field, then get clear yourself. This will not be gentle."

"I know." Her tension hardly showed. She was, as Stile knew, the type to handle difficult situations with verve. "I am sorry to have met you like this, Hulk; you are a fascinating person."

"Thank you. Say that again when I'm not trying to save our lives, and we'll see where it leads." Hulk stepped through the force-field. The pickup tried to follow him, but he was avoiding it, and disappeared from view. Frustrated, the pickup returned to the next most likely subject, the woman.

There was a momentary blankness, to signify a lapse of time. Then the holo-image in the tunnel came on—a holo within a holo. Stile was not sure how the holo-transceiver was able to show itself; this was merely a minor marvel of Proton electronics.

The image was a woman. She was tall and statuesque, with her hair concealed under a skullcap. She was naked: serf, not Citizen. She looked at Bluette. "Where is he?" she demanded imperiously.

"Who are you?" Bluette demanded in return. "Why have you done this?"

"He did not tell you? Then remain in ignorance. Your function is finished."

"My Employer will—"

"That is of no concern to me."

The two robots reappeared from uptunnel. "Put her in pain until her lover reappears," the woman said.

The robots were humanoid, but not specific; their faces were impassive masks. Their strength was that of the machines they were. They seemed to have no speech ability, and moved somewhat stiffly—low proficiency models. It was possible for a serf to obtain such robots, while only a Citizen could obtain robots of Sheen's quality. But these were well suited to this type of work. A robot like Sheen would have had too many humanistic restrictions.

Stile found himself tensing for action. The very notion of hurting the lady appalled him. But this was only a holo-recording; the action was long past. He could only watch.

"Ironic that the captor never bothered to film the prior sequence," Stile muttered. "She could have had complete information with no trouble. But I suppose a frame-traveler hasn't time for niceties—and this one lacks the resources of a Citizen. So this is crudely executed."

Bluette, alert to the threat against her, lurched toward the upper end of the chamber. Both robots moved swiftly to cut her off. She reversed, and moved with surprising agility toward the lower end—which of course was where she wanted to be.

The robots reversed with her. They might move awkwardly, but their reflexes were inhumanly swift; it was only their wit that was deficient. They caught her halfway, and held her in the middle of the chamber.

"Shouldn't Hulk come out?" Sheen inquired. "They will hurt her."

"Even Hulk cannot overpower two robots," Stile said. "They aren't gentle creatures like you; each one is stronger than he is, with no human vulnerabilities. Remember how easily they carried him several kilometers to the mine."

"True. But if he waits—"

"The captor believes it is me out there, and that I love Bluette and will be unable to let her suffer. That's why Hulk said this error might be for the best; there is not the leverage anticipated."

"He said it was for the best out of loyalty to you; your generosity saved you from the trap. But doesn't he love her too?"

"Not yet. He will hold out longer than I would have." Stile's fist clenched. "Maybe too long."

One robot stood behind Bluette, pinning her arms back, holding her firmly. The other glanced at the holo-image for clarification. "No permanent damage yet," the captor said. "Pinch her knee, slowly. Make her scream."

"The knee!" Stile exclaimed. "That's my enemy!"

The robot reached for Bluette's knee. The woman lifted both legs and planted them in the robot's chest and shoved violently. Though the machine was strong, it did not have extraordinary mass; the shove drove it back several steps.

"She fights; that's all to the good," the holo-woman said. "We need commotion."

The robot holding Bluette did not let go. The recoil shoved it back a step; then it stood firm.

"You can't fight robots," the captor told her. "I don't want you anyway. I want him. Make some noise, bring him in, and you won't have to suffer."

"What do you want with Stile?" Bluette cried.

"She remembered to use your name," Sheen said. "Smart woman."

"I want this time to be quite sure he is dead," the captor said. "But first I want to know why he proposed to destroy me. Adepts don't usually fight Adepts. He had no call to attack me."

Bluette's surprise was genuine. "There really *is* a world of magic?"

"You will never see it. Now call the Blue Adept."

"So you can torture him too? Never!"

"Do it," the captor said to the robot.

The robot caught the lady's leg and held it despite her struggles. It placed its metal fingers on her knee and squeezed. The pressure was obviously tremendous, cranking slowly up like that of a vise. She inhaled to scream, but caught herself and held her breath instead.

"My knees with a laser; hers with a robot," Stile grated. He was afraid for the lady, and chokingly angry—and helpless. Whatever would be—had already been.

Bluette collapsed, sobbing. "Oh, it hurts, it hurts!"

"Call him," the captor said dispassionately. "Scream. Bring him to you."

Bluette looked defiant. The robot squeezed again. She collapsed again. "Stop! I'll do it!"

The robot paused, hand still on knee. Dark showed around the edge of its grip, where pressure had crushed the fair skin. Bluette took another ragged breath. "S-s—" she hissed, trying to call through her sobs.

"You can do better than that," the captor said without pity.

"He—went down that passage," Bluette said, entirely unnerved. "I—I'll try. Let me get closer—"

"What a sniveler you are!" the captor rapped.

Now Stile smiled, grimly. "She is no sniveler. She knows what she has to do."

"Robots are no match for the wiles of woman," Sheen agreed.

The captor decided. "Take her to the force-field. Put only her head through. Hold it there until the man comes."

Now Bluette held back. "No—"

"You will call him—or suffocate slowly," the captor said.

The robots hauled the struggling Bluette to the force-field. One put a hand to her head, grasped her hair, and shoved her head through.

The opacity of the force-field exploded into man-form. One robot was lifted into the air and swung about by the legs so that its head crashed into the wall, hard. There was a blue flash of electricity as its wiring shorted; it was done for.

Already Hulk was turning on the other robot. But this one retained its hold on Bluette. Hulk could not get at it without going through her.

Without pause, Hulk turned back to the first robot, picked it up again by the feet, and smashed it into the wall again. Then he jumped on it, caught hold of one of its arms, and wrenched the limb up and around. His muscles bulged hugely as he strained—and the arm broke off, trailing wires. He worked it all the way free.

"That man is beautiful," Sheen said.

"They kidnapped more than they bargained on," Stile agreed with grim satisfaction. "Hulk is the over-thirty serf wrestling champion, and he knows free-fighting too. Now he is armed, with only one robot left to disable. He has a fair chance."

Hulk stalked the robot with his improvised weapon. "Turn her loose, machine. You can not fight me while you remain encumbered with her."

The robot retreated uncertainly, but retained its hold on Bluette. "What's this?" the captor screamed. "You are not the Blue Adept!"

"I never said I was," Hulk replied, baring his teeth in a fighting grin. "I'm his bodyguard." He smashed his club at the robot, catching it on the back of the head. It let Bluette go, and she limped hastily away.

"Kill them both!" the captor screamed, enraged.

Hulk stood facing the robot, but he spoke to Bluette. "Go to the body. Open the chest cavity. Take out the breathing mask. Put it on and flee. I will occupy this machine."

"I can't go without you!" Bluette cried.

"You must go before the witch summons other help. Go to your Employer; bring a rescue mission here. Don't let the robot make you hostage again. I need this chamber clear to fight it properly."

"Yes," she said, quickly getting the mask. "You are a bold, brave man, and I think I could love you in time. Follow me if you can; I will go for help."

She walked toward the force-field. "Stop her!" the captor shouted.

The robot went for the Lady—and Hulk went for the robot, smashing violently at its face. But the robot threw up an arm to ward off the blow, and grappled with Hulk.

Bluette fled, limping. She knew she could not help, here.

The robot tried to go after her, but Hulk clung, using his wrestling expertise. "Deal with him first," the captor decided. "Kill him, then catch the woman!"

Given this unequivocal directive, the robot applied its full force to the task at hand. It had no human weaknesses; it could not be choked or kneed in the crotch or made to yield by pain, and it was the stronger creature here. It was bound by no human scruples. It put one hand in Hulk's face and closed its metal fingers in the vise-constriction, simultaneously gouging the man's eyes and ripping out the cartilage of his nose.

Hulk smashed desperately with his weapon, but his leverage was not good. His face was a blind mask of blood. It was, Stile thought with horror, like fighting a wooden golem: no harm could be done to the inanimate, and no mercy was expected. Hulk's blows dented the metal in several places, but he could not put the machine out of commission. He made one more effort, lifting the machine and squeezing it in a bearhug and smashing it against the wall, trying to destroy it along with himself.

The robot remained functional. It put its other hand up to Hulk's head, clasped the man with its legs, and twisted the head. There was a snap.

"Oh, God—" Stile cried, anguished.

"Leave this. Go after the woman!" the captor cried. "I will shut down the field."

The robot disengaged itself from Hulk's body and lumbered in the direction Bluette had gone. It had suffered some damage; its motion was hardly faster than hers had been. Meanwhile, the force-field clicked off; the air puffed out of the chamber.

If Hulk was not already dead, he would suffocate shortly. With a broken neck and no air his situation was hopeless.

The holograph faded out. The recording was over.

CHAPTER 8

Quest

Stile emerged in Phaze at the familiar spot south of the Blue Demesnes. Suddenly his will coalesced. He opened his bag and brought out the magic Flute and played it hard and long. His power gathered to him as the platinum notes pealed forth. Almost, it seemed, the mountain trembled—but not quite. This instrument was the finest he had played, but he knew he could not keep it. When he found the person who could play it better than he—

But at the moment something else preempted his attention. As he played, the words came to him. In a moment he stopped playing and cried it out savagely: "Of the one who killed mine other self, the one who slew my friend, I, Stile, the Blue Adept, swear to make an end!"

The magic oath flung outward, making the ground ripple, the trees tremble, and the welkin waver. Pine needles burst into flame. From the Purple Mountains a rumbling echo came back like the voice of a monster: "end . . . end . . . end." Then lightning flashed across the sky and thunder rolled down. A startled griffin shot up and away to the west. A quick wash of water descended, extinguishing the local flame, leaving wet ashes. His oath had shaken the firmament, but it couldn't bring his friend back. Stile leaned against a scorched tree and cried.

Neysa and the Lady Blue were waiting for him expectantly at the Demesnes. As soon as they saw him, they knew something was wrong.

"Hulk is dead," Stile said bluntly. "Mine enemy killed him, in lieu of me. I have sworn vengeance."

"The sudden storm to the south," the Lady said. "Thine oath! I thought it no natural occurrence."

"Mine oath," Stile agreed. Quickly he filled in the details of the tragedy. "And I know not whether thine other self survives, Lady," he finished. "I fear I have unwittingly brought demise upon Bluette. I should not have suggested to Hulk that he—"

"Nay," the Lady said. She exchanged glances with Neysa, and the unicorn blew a small note of assent and left the room.

Stile felt his burden increase. "It is meet that she rebuke me," he said. "Others have paid the penalty for mine errors."

"She rebuked thee not," the Lady said. "She knows thou didst seek only to do a favor for thy friend. It was thine enemy at fault."

"I should have anticipated—"

"So should my Lord have anticipated the threat against him, by the ill hands of the same enemy. So also should I have known to warn him. There is guilt enough to go around." She crossed to him and put her hands on his shoulders, and he felt their healing power. "We were all of us well-meaning and naive. We could not believe that genuine evil stalked us."

"And thee," Stile said, not meeting her gaze. "It was thine other self I involved in this. I had no right—"

"To pass her to another man? She surely has will of her own! Thy friend was no bad person; I think she might have warmed to him, had she no other commitment. Certainly she would make her own choice, in her own time."

And the Lady Blue surely knew. "Thou hast no resentment, that I did not—?"

"Did not court her thyself, and bereave the Blue Demesnes a second time? Even were the danger naught, it matters not. An I decline thy suit for myself, why should I be jealous of what attention thou mightest pay to mine other self? *She* would like thee well enough, I think."

"But I did not court her!" Stile protested, in his distraction looking into her lovely face.

"And am I to feel insulted that it is I alone thou seekest, not my likeness in another frame?"

"Thou hast a marvelously balanced perspective."

"It was a quality thine other self selected for, methinks," she said with a half rueful smile. "I could not otherwise have maintained the Demesnes in his absence. Surely this, not any wit or beauty, was what caused the Oracle to identify me as his ideal wife."

"Thou hast those other qualities too," Stile said. "I beg thee, Lady, let me go now, lest I embarrass us both by—"

She did not let him go. "Thou'rt very like my Lord. Well I know what thou wouldst do with me, were I amenable."

"Then well thou knowest that I like not to be toyed with!"

"Thou'rt now the Blue Adept. Thy power is proven. Fain would I have thee remain here, not risking thy life in any quest for vengeance."

"I have made an oath," Stile said, somewhat stiffly.

"Well do I know the power of thine oaths! Yet there be ways and ways to implement, and here is thy bastion. Let thine enemy come to thee here, where thy magic is strongest; do not put thyself in jeopardy in hostile Demesnes."

"There is merit in thy view," Stile said, still overwhelmingly conscious of her nearness, of her hands upon him. He kept his own hands at his sides. "Yet I fear that it is folly to wait for attack. Already mine enemy's traps have imperiled my life in both frames, and destroyed my friend and perhaps thine other self too. I want no others to suffer in my stead. I prefer to take the initiative, to do boldly what has to be done. Thereafter will I retire to the Blue Demesnes."

"I fear to lose thee, as I lost him! As has so nearly happened already. What becomes of me, of the Blue Demesnes, if thou goest the way of my Lord?"

That moved him. "Never would I place thee in jeopardy, if I could avoid it, Lady. Yet I dare not take thee with me on my quest for vengeance."

Her grip on his shoulders tightened. "It is my vengeance too, to have or to renounce. If thou lovest me, heed my plea! Leave me not!"

"I have no right to love thee, now less than ever," Stile said. "I may only guard thee."

"Thou'rt the Blue Adept! Thy right is as thou makest it!"

"My right is as my conscience dictates. I seek not the spoils of mine other self's Demesnes. Fain would I return thy Lord to thee, if I could."

She shifted her grip and drew him savagely in to her. She kissed him. Stile's heart seemed to explode with longing, but with an iron will he held himself passive.

She shook him. "Respond, Adept. These Demesnes *are* thy spoils, and I too. Take what is thy right. Leave me not bereft of Lord and of power. I will grant thee whatever thou dost desire. I will give thee a son. No one, I swear, will ever suspect by word or gesture or deed of mine that in truth I love thee not. Only remain to preserve these Demesnes."

It was that truth that cut him almost as savagely as the murder of his friend. Gently but firmly Stile disengaged from her. "If the occasion comes when *I* do not suspect, then I may act as thou hast in mind. This scene becomes thee not."

She slapped him stingingly across the cheek. "How dost thou dare prate to me of scenes, thou who dost seek futile vengeance that will only exterminate thee and bring down what remains of what my Lord created?"

"I apologize for my foolishness," Stile said stiffly. He hated everything about this situation, while loving her for the sacrifice she was attempting. To preserve the memory and works of her Lord, she would do anything. She had thrown away her pride in that effort. "I am the way I am. I will fulfill mine oath in the best way I know."

She spread her hands. Surprisingly she smiled. "Go then, with my blessing. I will aid thee in whatever manner I am able."

This startled Stile. "Why the sudden change, Lady?"

"It is now *thy* welfare I value, for whatever reason. If I can not preserve thee from thy folly my way, I must help thee do it thy way. Ever was it thus, in these Demesnes."

Stile nodded. "Thy balanced perspective, again. I thank thee, Lady, for thy support." He turned to go.

"Thou'rt so very like my Lord," she repeated as he passed through the doorway. "Nor wiles nor logic nor rages could move him iotas from his set course, when honor was involved."

Stile paused. "I am glad thou understandest."

She hurled a blue slipper at him. "I do *not* understand! My love died of that stubbornness—and so wilt thou!"

Stile found Neysa in the courtyard, cropping the perpetual bluegrass patch. "We must move swiftly to surprise the enemy and allow me time to get to my next match in Proton-frame. But I dare not leave the Lady unguarded, especially in her present mood. Without Hulk—"

Neysa tooted reassuringly and led the way outside. Shapes were racing toward the castle. "The werewolves!" Stile exclaimed.

Soon the pack arrived, panting. The leader metamorphosed to man-form. It was Stile's friend Kurrelgyre, wild-haired and scarred but trustworthy. "The Pack greets thee, Adept."

"I have need of thy assistance," Stile said. "But how didst thou know?"

"Know? We know nothing," the werewolf said. "We but came to visit our oath-friend the mare."

"But Neysa and I are leaving," Stile protested.

"Then we shall be forced to take advantage of the hospitality of thy Demesnes to await her return. Can a pack do less, for an oath-friend?"

Stile understood. Neysa had somehow summoned the pack, all of whose members had sworn an oath of friendship with her, and they would guard the Blue Demesnes during his absence. An Adept enemy could get around such a defense, but not easily; who would voluntarily tackle a full pack of werewolves? The Lady Blue would be as safe as she reasonably could be, for the duration.

"Methinks true friends appear when needed most," Stile said gratefully.

The White Adept was female, so Stile rode Neysa toward the White Demesnes. White did not resemble the woman he had seen in the Hulk holo-tape, but of course she had been in disguise at the Unolympics. So he would go and defy her to show him her true form, establishing at one stroke her guilt or innocence. Armed with the Platinum Flute, he felt he could successfully brace the Adept in her own Demesnes.

Neysa knew the way. Stile slept on her back, refreshing his strength.

He knew she would protect him well, and this approach would be less obvious than the use of magic. It was also a salient principle in Phaze: do not waste magic. He would use one of his rehearsed spells to travel away from the White Demesnes, if hard-pressed, instead of expending it unnecessarily now.

It was good to be with Neysa for another reason. Stile was sick at heart, angry about his ludicrous loss of a Game in the Tourney, guilty for Hulk's brutal demise, and disturbed by the Lady Blue's attempt to seduce him away from his purpose. He needed to sort out his feelings and get them settled, and he needed the solid support of an understanding person. Neysa was that person. She did not have to say a word or play a note; she settled him by her presence. She had been right about the importance of her assistance to him; he needed her for more than physical reasons. With her he felt secure, emotionally as well as physically.

They traveled northeast, angling toward the great White Mountain range. At dawn they arrived at a narrow pass. Now Neysa threw herself into a slow gallop, forging up into the snows, while Stile hunched within his cloak. Such was the energy she expended that thin fire shot from her nostrils, and her hot hooves melted indentations into the packed snow. Her body heat warmed Stile's own body, and soon he leaned forward and hugged her about the neck, burying his face in her sweet black mane. She was his best friend in the frame of Phaze, the one he most depended on. It was joy to be afield with her again like this.

At the height of the pass a cruel wind sliced through. Beyond, the terrain opened out into a bleak frozen lake many miles across. The ice was not flat; it pushed up in cracked mounds, where the stresses of expansion had prevailed.

And in the center of that ragged surface rose the icy castle of the White Demesnes, formed of ice bricks partially melted together and refrozen. Flying buttresses of ice braced the walls. It was pretty in its fashion, but rather squat and solid to be truly esthetic artistically.

Neysa walked down to the lake's edge. The ice was a problem for her, as her hot hooves were not suitable for skating. She would have trouble crossing this! "I can conjure skates for thee—" Stile offered dubiously.

She blew a note of negation. Then she shifted into her firefly form.

"But it's too cold for that form here," Stile protested. "Thou mayest be fireproof, but not freezeproof. Thou wilt fly only minutes before thy little insect body stalls out."

She flew to his shoulder and lighted there, already cold. "Oh," Stile said. "I'm to carry thee. Of course! Then I shall put thee in my jacket where it is warm." He did so. Neysa made one flash of thanks and settled down in comfort.

Then he conjured a good pair of skates for himself. Stile was an excellent skater; he had developed power and artistry for use in the Proton Game.

He moved out. The ice was firm, and the curvatures of its surface did not bother him. He skated smoothly yet swiftly toward the ice castle, not even bothering to use an invisibility spell. He was here for a challenge, not a sneak attack. He had only to discover the true appearance or mode of the White Adept's magic. If it did not relate to amulets or golems, she was not the one he wanted. A demon amulet had almost killed him when he first crossed the curtain into the frame of Phaze; four goons had been set on his trail by his use of a healing amulet later. Now he was wary of amulets—but at least it gave him the most promising hint about the identity of his enemy.

One strange thing—the woman who had sprung the trap in Proton had suggested that the Blue Adept had attacked her, rather than the other way around. Why? Surely his other self had been innocent. He would not have attacked another Adept without reason, especially not a woman. So she had to be wrong. Yet it bothered him, for the woman had not known she was being recorded; she had been speaking from her cold heart, not for an audience.

He skated on, drawing near the ice castle. Now it was time to go into his act. He singsonged a spell: "Garb this one in a suit of fun." His clothing changed, becoming a brightly colored clown-suit that was, not incidentally, a good deal warmer than his prior garb.

The thing was, the average Adept had all he or she needed or wanted, materially. The Adept could conjure food, and use magic to build a castle or other residence to his liking, and could make deals for other necessities. But he was liable to get lonely and bored in his guarded fastness. That was why so many Adepts elected to participate as judges and spectators in functions like the Unolympics. It gave them something to do in a public but protected situation. Yellow had obviously thrived on her job as head judge for the Adept pavilion, being all dressed up with her finest youth potion for the occasion. It followed, then, that Adepts could use entertainment at home, too. An Adept's own magic would not amuse himself, even if he chose to waste it that way. So now Stile looked the part of an entertainer—and should be admitted to the White Demesnes with no more than the usual suspicion.

So he leaped and looped and whirled into occasional spins. He did a cartwheel and took a fancy, deliberate spill. He was a clown, a joker, a fool. Until he had his chance to brace the White Adept and discover the nature of her magic.

He skated close to the castle. So far so good. No hostile spell had been hurled at him.

There was a moat of ice-free water surrounding the castle: an effective barrier to a skater. Stile drew up. "Ho!" he called. "Grant ye access for a fool?"

A human guard appeared. It seemed there was modest employment for a number of villagers in the various Adept castles. "Why come ye?"

"To entertain—for a fair fee. To glean what information I can."

"A spy?"

"Naturally."

The guard lowered his voice. "Fool art thou indeed, if thou wouldst enter these Demesnes. The Adept is ill of humor. Depart, lest thou losest thy gizzard."

"I thank thee for thy warning," Stile said. "But I have come far, and must complete my mission. Do thou announce me to the Adept and let me take my chance."

"On thy insecure head be it. I tried to warn thee." The guard retreated inside the castle.

In due course he returned to crank down the drawbridge, which seemed to be formed of a huge slab of ice. Stile skated blithely across and on into the central courtyard, admiring the way the daylight refracted through the ice walls. And the floor abruptly converted to stone. Stile tripped on it and took a genuine tumble; he had not been paying attention to his feet. He adapted his fall to an acrobatic roll in what he hoped was comical fashion, then removed his skates.

Neysa did not reappear. She remained as a firefly, hiding in his hat. Stile knew why; her conversion back to equine-form would attract attention to him. Who but the Blue Adept, as the Platinum Elves had pointed out, rode a unicorn? But she would change in a hurry if it became necessary. He felt much more secure with her along.

There were no special preliminaries. The White Adept walked out, looking much as she had at the Unolympics, but older and fatter. She had evidently used her magic only to improve her image moderately. "What hast thou got, churl?" she demanded irritably. "What dost thou want?"

"I have a rare show of antics and prestidigitation," Stile said, making his voice comical too. "'Twill lighten thy spirit and make thee laugh. All I ask in return is the smallest of favors."

"What smallest favor?" She was evidently used to panhandlers.

Stile brought out a silver medal he had conjured in preparation for this moment. "This amulet—it is expended. I want it restored to provide me heat from the cold."

"Amulets are not my business," she snapped. "Thou shouldst apply to her who makes them."

So it *was* a female Adept who made the amulets! This was a valuable confirmation. "Once an amulet attacked me," he said. "Now must I take them secondhand."

"Attacked thee?" She chortled. "Surely served thee right! Very well—if thou dost perform amusingly, I will reward thee appropriately."

"I thank thee," Stile said humbly. He was fully aware that she had made no significant commitment. That was not what he needed. Once she showed the form of her magic—

"Get on with it, clown," White snapped, her mouth setting into solidified sourness. "Make me laugh."

Stile went into his act. He had developed a joker-ritual as part of his Proton-Game expertise, and he had considerable manual dexterity. He put on his "stupid midget" pantomime, trying to eat a potato that kept wriggling out of his hands, looking for a comfortable place to sleep, finding none, and getting tangled up in his own limbs, drawing scarves out of his ears, taking spills, and in general making a funny fool of himself. He was good at it, using no real magic, only stage magic, before a person who well knew the difference. Though the White Adept tried to maintain a sour face, slowly it weathered and cracked. She evidently did not like peasants, and had deep satisfaction seeing one so aptly parodied. Also she, like many people, thought there was something excruciatingly funny about mishaps happening to a midget. In the end she was laughing wholeheartedly.

Stile completed his show. White sobered quickly. "I like thee, fool. I believe I shall keep thee here for future entertainments."

"Honored Adept, I cannot stay," Stile said quickly, though he had expected something like this. "All I want is mine amulet recharged."

She frowned. "Very well, fool. Give it here."

She was up to something. Stile passed over the medal, braced for action.

The White Adept laid the medal on the floor. She brought out a long-handled charcoal marker and drew a mystic symbol around it. When the figure was complete, she tapped it five times: tap-tap, Tap-tap, TAP.

The medal exploded into a dozen huge shapes. Ice monsters, translucent, with snowy fur and icicle teeth and blank iceball eyeballs. The small fragments of metal seemed to adhere only to their formidable claws: nails that were literal nails.

"Cool this arrogant peasant in the cooler, coolies," she ordered, pointing at Stile.

The monsters advanced on him. Stile tried to run out of the courtyard, but they leaped out to encircle him. Grinning coldly, they drew their noose tight. There would be no gentle handling here.

Suddenly Neysa flew out and changed to her unicorn-form. She charged forward, spearing a monster on her horn, lifting her head, and hurling the thing away to the side. It crashed into its neighbor, and both went down in a tangle of shattering ice.

"Ho! A unicorn!" White screamed, outraged. "Think ye to 'scape my power in mine own Demesnes, animal?" She started to draw another symbol on the floor.

That meant trouble. Obviously she could conjure anything with the right symbol. Stile launched himself at the White Adept—and was caught in a polar-bear hug by an intervening ice monster and lifted from the floor. *Fool!* he chided himself. He should have sung a spell. But no—White did not yet know his identity, apparently not connecting the unicorn directly to him. He preferred to keep it secret if he could. He would try to handle this without magic.

He had better! The monster had a frigid hand over Stile's mouth, half suffocating him and preventing him from speaking.

Stile tried to get his hand on the Platinum Flute. That would become a suitable weapon! But, jammed up against the freezing demon, he could not reach the Flute.

He elbowed the monster. Ouch! That ice was hard! He kicked, but the monster seemed to have no feeling in its body. Stile could not throw the creature, because he had no footing. Meanwhile, that terrible cold was penetrating his flesh.

Neysa was busy routing the other monsters. One monster might be too much for Stile to handle, but one unicorn was too much for the whole horde of them. She bucked, her hind hooves flinging out to shatter two monsters; she plunged forward to impale another on her horn. With every motion she demolished a monster. Stile could have had no better ally.

But Stile was held silent, and the White Adept was completing her new symbol figure. This surely meant mischief.

Stile bit the hand over his mouth. This helped; the icy fingers crunched under his teeth. The monster might feel no pain, but it couldn't gag Stile with no fingers. Stile chewed and chewed, breaking off and spitting out the huge hand piecemeal.

Now the witch's second symbol animated. A swarm of stinging flies puffed into existence. They flung themselves onto Neysa—who stiffened the moment they stung, thin flame jetting from her nostrils. Then, with an extended note of despair, she fell to the floor.

There was no question about the ability of an Adept to handle a unicorn! White's magic was more cumbersome to implement than Stile's was, but it was devasting when it got there.

"Dump the animal into the lake—under the ice," White ordered the two remaining ice monsters. "Dump the peasant-clown there too; he's too much trouble."

But Stile could speak now. "Monsters of ice," he sang breathlessly, "turn into mice!"

He had not gathered his power by playing music, so the potency of his spell was not great. That was the cumbersome quality of his own invocations. When fully prepared, he could do excellent magic—but of course White, when set up with a number of drawn symbols, could surely perform similarly. His spell operated incompletely. The two ice monsters shimmered into rather fat white rats.

"Magic!" White hissed. "Now I know thee! How durst thou intrude on these my Demesnes, Blue?"

Stile brought out his harmonica as he walked toward Neysa. He had decided he didn't need the Flute on this occasion. The deadly stingflies rose up in their humming cloud, orienting on him. "I intrude to ascertain whether thou art mine enemy," he said to the witch.

"I was not thine enemy before—but I am now!" she cried. "Sting him, flies!"

Stile played his instrument. The flies felt the coalescing force of his magic and hesitated. Stile willed heat—and as the flies came near, they dried up and dropped to the floor. A few hardier ones persisted until their wings burst into flame.

Stile stopped, looking at the prostrate unicorn. He thought of Hulk and Bluette, knocked out by gas. Which parallels were valid and which were products of his guilt? But this situation he could handle. "Neysa defy the bite of the fly," he sang.

The unicorn woke and struggled to her feet. Stile could heal others, but not himself.

White was forming a new symbol. Stile faced her and sang: "White take the road, as a frog or a—tortoise."

The witch did a doubletake as the spell passed her by. Stile had not filled in the obvious rhyme. Then she reached for the symbol again.

"Let thy flesh become cold," Stile sang, and the magic gathered as though to pounce. "And thy body grow . . . oily."

Again she reacted, fearing the worst; no one feared age like a middle-aged woman! Again she was left unscathed as the spell fizzled. Stile's intent could only be consummated with a terminal rhyme. Once more she went for her spell.

"White form a pyre, and burn like—fir," Stile sang.

This time her white hair seemed to take on a tinge of orange flame. "Enough!" she cried. "Thou'rt victor, Blue! Thy magic cannot truly transform me, but it could make me very uncomfortable. What dost thou want?"

"Only to see thy magic operate," Stile said. "And to depart in peace."

"No one sees the secret of my magic mode and departs in peace!" she protested. "The mode is always an Adept secret. Sooner would I dance naked before a crowd."

"Thou hast seen my magic mode," Stile pointed out. "I lived my whole life naked in a crowd, ere I came to Phaze."

"Well, no one else shows either magic or body!"

"Yet thou knowest the identity of the amulet-maker."

She considered. "Ah, now it comes clear! Thy vegeance!"

"Indeed," Stile agreed. "Thou dost not seem to be the one I seek, but it would help if I learned who mine enemy really is."

"Aye, I know her. There are secrets witches share. But I will not tell thee. It is not thy business."

"The amulet-maker murdered me!" Stile cried. "And seeks to kill me again. That is not my business?"

"Well, mayhap thou wouldst see it that way. But it is not *my* business to betray her to thee."

"Witch, thou runnest fair risk of suffering my wrath," Stile said, feeling the righteous heat rise. The force of his oath urged him onward. "Yet can I turn thee into—"

"Nay, the power of one Adept is ineffective against another Adept on guard. Yet neither is it my business to betray thee to her. Depart now, and I shall not tell her thou hast narrowed thy choices to two."

To two. Two remaining female Adepts. White had given him some information, by way of placation. That helped considerably. The only problem was that he knew of only one other female Adept.

Well, he would check that one. He mounted Neysa. He played a bar of music, then sang: "Man and steed, to Brown proceed."

They shot sidewise, accelerating to horrendous velocity, passing right through the ice walls without touching them and zooming southeast. Plains, hills and forests shot by in blurs. Then they slowed and came to an abrupt halt.

They were before the great brown wooden door of a brownstone castle from whose highest turret a brown pennant flew. Obviously the Brown Demesnes.

Stile looked around. A muddy river flowed behind the castle, but none of its water was diverted into a moat. On its banks stood a sere, brown forest. It might be summer in the main part of Phaze, but it was winter at the White Demesnes and fall here at the Brown Demesnes.

Neysa snorted, not liking it. Stile could appreciate why; the grass, too, was brown.

"Well, do we sneak in this time, or boldly challenge?" Stile asked the unicorn. She blew a note of negation, ending in a positive trill. "I agree," he said, "I'm tired of sneaking. We'll settle this openly this time." He wondered whether it was true that one Adept could not directly enchant another Adept who was on guard. That notion seemed to be giving him confidence, certainly.

He faced the door and bawled in as stentorian a voice as he could muster: "Brown, come forth and face Blue!"

The huge door cranked open. A giant stood in the doorway. He was as massive as the trunk of an oak, and as gnarly. He carried a wooden club that was longer than Stile's whole body. "Go 'way, clown!" he roared.

Clown. Oops—he was still garbed in that fool's suit! Well, let it be; he didn't want to mess with a nullification spell right now.

Stile was used to dealing with men larger than himself; *all* men were larger than himself. But this one was extreme. He was just about ten feet tall. If he swung that club, he could likely knock Stile off Neysa before Stile could get close enough to do anything physical.

Unless he used the Platinum Flute as a lance or pike . . .

But first he had to try the positive approach. "I want to meet the Brown Adept."

The giant considered. His intelligence seemed inversely proportional to his mass. "Oh," he said. "Then come in."

Just like that! Neysa trotted forward, following the giant. Soon they were in a large brownwood paneled hall.

A man was there, garbed in a brown robe. He was brown of hair, eyes and skin. "What want ye with me?" he inquired, frowning.

"Nothing," Stile said. "I want the Adept herself."

"Speak to me," the man said. "I am Brown."

"Brown is a woman," Stile said. "Must I force the issue with magic?"

"Thou darest use thy magic in my Demesnes?" the brown man demanded.

Stile brought out his harmonica and played a few bars. "I dare," he said.

"Guard! Remove this man!"

Giants appeared, converging on Stile and Neysa. "I want these creatures swept," Stile sang quickly. "And bring the Brown Adept."

It was as if a giant invisible broom swept the giants out of the hall. Simultaneously an eddy carried in a disheveled, angry child. "Thou mean man!" she cried. "Thou didst not have to do that!"

Stile was taken aback. "Thou'rt the Brown Adept?" But obviously she was; his spell had brought her.

"If I were grown and had my full power, thou wouldst never be able to bully me!" she exclaimed tearfully. "I never did anything to thee, clown!"

Appearances could be deceptive, but Stile was inclined to agree. Why would a child murder an Adept who meant her no harm? Unless this was another costume, concealing the true form of the Adept. "I am here to ascertain that," Stile said. "Show me thy true form."

"This is my true form! Until I grow up. Now wilt thou go away, since thou art not a very funny clown?"

"Show me thy true form of magic," Stile said.

"Art thou blind? Thou didst just make a jumble of all my golems!" Golems! "Thou makest the wooden men!"

She was settling down. "What else? I use the brownwood growing outside. But most of these were made by my pred—the prior Brown

Adept. He trained me to do it just before he died." A tear touched her eye. "He was a good man. It is lonely here without him."

"Knowest thou not a wooden golem usurped the Blue Demesnes?" Stile demanded.

Her cute brown eyes flashed. "That's a lie! Golems do only as told. I ought to know. They have no life of their own."

Like the robots of Proton. Only some robots, like Sheen, and her sophisticated friends, did have consciousness and self-will. "Thou hast sent no golem in my likeness to destroy me?"

Now she faltered, bobbing her brown curls about. "I—I did not. But I have not been Adept long. My predi-pred—"

"Predecessor," Stile filled in helpfully.

"That's the word! Thanks. Predecessor. He might have. I don't know. But he was a good man. He never attacked other Adepts. He just filled orders for them. Golems make the very most dependable soldiers and servants and things, and they never need feeding or sleeping or—"

"So another Adept could have ordered a golem in my likeness?" Stile persisted, piecing it together.

"Sure. He made golems in any likeness, in exchange for other magic he needed. Like a larderful of food, or a get-well amulet—"

Stile pounced on that. "Who traded him an amulet?"

"Why the Red Adept, of course. She makes all the amulets."

Something was wrong. "I met the Red Adept at the Unolympics. Red was a tall, handsome man."

"Oh—she was in costume, then. They do that. Just as I tried to do with a golem when thou camest. Sometimes strangers are bad to children, so Brown warned me not to reveal myself to intruders. I didn't know thou wert apprised I was a girl."

It burst upon Stile with dismaying force. The costume! Not merely different clothing or appearance, but different sex too! Child's play to produce the image of the opposite sex. In fact, Red could have done it without magic. Remove the mustache, lengthen the hair, put on a dress, and the Red he had seen was a woman. Remove the dress so that she was naked, and cover the hair with a skullcap, and it was the woman who had killed Hulk in the mine. How could he have overlooked that?

"Brown, I apologize," Stile said. "A golem invaded my Demesnes, and I thought thee guilty. I see I was mistaken. I proffer amends."

"Oh, that's okay," she said, smiling girlishly. "I haven't had company in a long time. But thou mightest put back my giants."

Stile made a quick spell to restore the golems he had swept away. "Is there aught else I can do for thee before I go?" he inquired.

"Nothing much. I like thy unicorn, but I know they don't mess with other Adepts or anybody. Only other thing I'm trying to do is grow a nice flower-garden, but they all come up brown and dry. I don't want thy magic for that; I want to do it myself."

Neysa blew a note. Stile dismounted, and she shimmered into girl-form. "Unicorn manure grows magic plants," Neysa said.

"Gee—pretty ones?" Brown asked, her eyes lighting. "Like a Jack-in-the-pulpit who preaches a real sermon, and tiger-lilies who purr?"

Neysa had already changed back to her natural shape. She blew an affirmative note.

"Send one of thy golems with a cart and fork," Stile said. "A giant, who can haul a lot. Thou knowest where the herds roam?"

Brown nodded. "I go there all the time, to look at the pretty 'corns," she said wistfully. "But I dare not get close to them."

All girls liked equines, Stile remembered. He looked at Neysa, who nodded. "If thou likest, Neysa will carry thee there this time, and tell her friends to give manure to thy golem."

"A ride on a unicorn?" Brown clapped her hands with delight. "Oh, yes, yes!"

"Ride, then," Stile said, glad to make this small amend for his unkind intrusion here. "I will meet thee there."

The child mounted the unicorn somewhat diffidently, and they started off at the smoothest of gaits. Stile knew Neysa would not let Brown fall, and that her unicorn herd would acquiesce to the golem's acquisition of several loads of excellent manure, for such things were not denied to oath-friends. Neysa had helped bail him out of mischief, again, by making Brown glad for his visit.

This had turned out to be the wrong Adept, but the excursion had been worthwhile. Now at last he knew the identity of his enemy. He would not have time to brace the Red Adept after rejoining Neysa at the herd; he had to get back across the curtain for the next Round of the Tourney. But on his return to Phaze. . . .

CHAPTER 9

Music

It was Round Six of the Tourney. Barely one fifth of the original entrants remained. The concentration of the skilled and the lucky increased. The audience for individual Games was larger, and would grow larger yet, as the numbers of contestants dwindled further and each Round became more important.

His opponent was another Citizen. This was not unusual at this stage; the Citizens tended to be the best players, and suffered elimination reluctantly. This one was old, obviously not in prime physical vigor—but any Citizen was dangerous, in and out of the Tourney.

Stile resolved to put it into the PHYSICAL column if he had the chance, not risking this man's accumulated knowledge and experience.

He had the chance. They were in 2B, Tool-Assisted PHYSICAL GAMES. Stile's area of strength. Yet the Citizen did not seem alarmed. Did he have a secret?

They played the subgrids and came up with the Ice Climb. This was a frozen waterfall about fifteen meters high that had to be mounted by use of spikes and pitons from the base. Safety ropes suspended from above prevented it from being dangerous, but the climb itself was arduous. Stile did not see how this old man could handle it.

Stile was naked; all he had to do was put on the spiked shoes, gloves, and safety line. He did not need insulative clothing; the ice was frozen by elements beneath, while the air of the dome was warm. A naked man could handle it well enough, since his own exertion heated him.

The voluminous robes of the Citizen would interfere with his climbing. Slowly he undressed.

Stile was amazed. Under his concealing cloak the Citizen had a body of considerable gristle and muscle. The man was older than Stile—perhaps much older because of possible rejuvenation—but his torso resembled that of a man in his mid-forties, well developed. Stile still should have the edge, but much less of one than he had thought.

They donned their gear, and approached the waterfall. It gleamed prettily, like translucent quartz. Stile had the right channel, the Citizen the left. The first to touch an electronically keyed marker at the top would win. The first to fall would lose. Theoretically one person could swing across on his safety rope and interfere with the other, but he would already have lost. Throwing pitons at each other meant immediate forfeiture. Cheating and fouling never occurred in Games.

Now the Citizen faced the ice and stared into it, unmoving. It was time for the match to begin, but Citizens could not be rushed. Stile had to wait.

The man remained for several minutes in silence. What was he up to? Stile, alert for some significant factor, was alarmed by this behavior. There had to be meaning in it. Why should a person delay a match by remaining trancelike?

Trance! That was it! The Citizen was indulging in self-hypnosis, or a yoga exercise, putting himself into a mental state that would allow him to draw without normal restraint on the full resources of his body. This was the sort of thing that lent strength to madmen and to the mothers of threatened children. Stile never used it, preferring to live a fully healthy life, saving his ultimate resources for some genuine life-and-death need. But the Citizen was evidently under no such constraint.

This could be trouble! No wonder the man had made it this far in the Tourney. He had suckered opponents into challenging him on the physical plane, then expended his inner resources to defeat them. Stile had fallen neatly into the trap.

But Stile, because of his light weight and physical fitness and indefatigable training in all aspects of the Game, was an excellent ice climber. Or had been, before the injury to his knees. Since he could place his pitons to avoid severe flexation of his knees, that should not hamper him much. Very few people could scale the falls faster than he could. He might win anyway. Trance-strength was fine, but the body reserves had to be there to be drawn on, and a rejuvenated Citizen might not have large reserves.

Stile did mild limbering exercises, toning up his muscles. He could throw himself into a light trance at will, of course, but refused to. Not even for this.

At last the Citizen came out of it. "I am ready," he said.

They donned the safety belts. The lines would keep pace with the ascent, rising but not falling again. Stile felt his heartbeat and respiratory rate increase with the incipience of this effort.

The starting gong sounded. Both went to work, hammering the first piton. There were little tricks to this Game; the ice could vary from day to day because of ambient conditions. Sometimes it was a trifle soft, which made insertion easier but less secure; today it was a trifle hard, which posed the risk of cracking. Since each piton had to be set as rapidly as possible, judgment was important. If a contestant took too long, making a piton unnecessarily firm for its brief use, he lost time that might mean loss of the match; if he proceeded carelessly, he would fall, and lose the match. Discrimination, as much as physical strength and endurance, was critical.

The Citizen worked faster than Stile. He was on his first piton and working on the next ahead of Stile. He was pushing the limit, hitting too hard, but the ice was holding. Stile was close behind, but losing headway because he was playing it safer. Ice was funny stuff; sometimes it tolerated violation. Sometimes it did not.

They moved on up. Steadily Stile lost position—yet he did not dare hit his pitons harder. All he could do was marvel at the luck of the Citizen, and hope that the law of averages—

It happened. Halfway up, the ice cracked under the Citizen's piton. The man had only to put it in a new spot and hammer more carefully—but he would lose just enough time to bring Stile even. The law of averages had come through at last.

But the Citizen, in his trance, was not alert to this. Automatically he put his weight on the piton—and it gave way and fell out. The Citizen swung from the rope, disqualified.

Stile did not even have to complete the climb. He only had to proceed one centimeter higher than the point the Citizen had reached. His caution, his alertness, and his reliance on the odds had brought him easy victory. Somehow it hadn't seemed easy, though.

There was no fake address this time. Sheen took care of him, questioning him about his latest adventures in Phaze, and let him sleep. She concurred with the Lady Blue; she didn't like the notion of him bracing the Red Adept in the Red Demesnes. "She's a mean one; I could tell that from the holo. She'll cut your throat with a brilliant smile. But I'm only a logical machine," she complained. "I can't stop an illogical manbrained flesh creature from being insanely foolish."

"Right," Stile agreed complacently. "Even clownish." She always made reference to her inanimate status when upset.

But first he had to handle Round Seven. This turned out to be against another serf of about his own age. He was Clef, a tall thin man named for a symbol on written music, who evidently had qualified for the Tourney only because the top players of his ladder had not wanted to. Stile knew all the top serf-players of the current ladders, but did not recognize Clef. Therefore this man was no skilled Gamesman, though he could have spot-skills.

They chatted while waiting for the grid. "Whoever wins this Round gets an extra year's tenure," Stile said. "Or more, depending on which Round he finally reaches."

"Yes, it is my best hope to achieve Round Eight," Clef agreed. "I have no chance to win the Tourney itself, unlike you."

"Unlike me?"

"I have the advantage of you, so to speak," Clef said. "I am aware of your skill in the Game. To be fair, I should advise you of my own specialties."

"Fairness is no part of it," Stile said. "Use any advantage you have. Maybe I'll misjudge you, and grid right into your specialty. In any event, I have no way of knowing whether what you tell me is the truth."

"Oh, it has to be the truth!" Clef said, shocked. "There is no place in my philosophy for untruth."

Stile smiled, once again finding himself liking his opponent. "Glad to hear it. But still, you don't have to—"

"I am a musician, hence my chosen name. My single other hobby is the rapier."

"Ah—so you have a strength in either facet. That's useful."

"So it has proved. That and fortune. I did lose one match in

CHANCE, but since I won three in that category I can not seriously object. I have come further in the Tourney than I really expected."

"But you know I'll play away from your strengths," Stile said.

"I could as readily play for CHANCE again and neutralize your advantage."

"Not if you get the letters."

"Then my choice is easy. Rapier and flute are both tools."

The flute? Stile wasn't sure how well the Platinum Flute would play in this frame, since its magic could not operate here, but it was such a fine instrument it might well make him competitive. "I am not expert with the rapier," he said, thinking of the training Neysa had given him in Phaze. "Yet I am not unversed in it, and in other weapons I am proficient. Unless you managed to get the rapier itself, rather than an edged sword, I doubt you would want to meet me in such a category."

"I have no doubt at all I don't want to meet you there!" Clef agreed.

"But I have lost one match in this Tourney through CHANCE, as you have, and am eager to avoid another."

"Are you proffering a deal?" Clef inquired, elevating an eyebrow. He had elegant eyebrows, quite expressive.

"This is legal and ethical. Of course no agreement has force in the Game itself. But two honorable players can come to an agreement if they wish."

"I understand. Are you willing to meet me in Music?"

"Yes, depending."

"You grant me Music, and I will grant you choice of instruments."

"That was my notion."

"However, I should warn you that I am widely versed in this area of the arts. My favorite is the flute, but I am proficient in any of the woodwinds and strings. More so than you, I believe; I have heard you play. So you may prefer to select one of the less sophisticated instruments."

Stile's fiercely competitive soul was aroused. He had a compulsion to beat opponents in their special areas of strength. That was why he had tackled Hulk in Naked Physical. He thought again of the Platinum Flute, surely the finest instrument he could employ. On it he could play the best music of his life. He might take the measure of this self-proclaimed expert! But caution prevailed. If the flute was Clef's instrument of choice, no skill of Stile's could reasonably hope to match him, and it would be foolish to allow himself to believe otherwise. Also the Flute was in Stile's possession only on loan, and if his use of it here drew the attention of Citizens to it—no, he could not risk that. Fortunately he did have an alternative.

"The harmonica," Stile said.

"A good harmonica is hardly a toy," Clef said. "Properly played, it can match any instrument in the orchestra. Are you certain—I am trying to be fair, since you are so generously offering me the category—"

"I'm certain," Stile said, though Clef's confidence disturbed him. Exactly how good could this man be on the harmonica?

"Then so shall it be," Clef agreed, and offered his hand.

"A handshake agreement is not worth the paper it's printed on," Stile reminded him.

"But it is also said that the man who trusts men will make fewer mistakes than he who distrusts them."

"I have found it so." Stile took the proffered hand, and so they sealed the agreement.

Their turn at the grid came. They played as agreed. They would contest for this Round with the harmonica.

Sheen was ready with Stile's harmonica; she was able to carry objects unobtrusively in her body compartments, and she was the only one in this frame he trusted with such things. It had to be this familiar instrument, the one he had played so often in Phaze, rather than some strange one issued by the Game Computer. It was not the Flute, but there seemed to be a certain magic about it. On this, he could play well enough to defeat a musician—he hoped. For Stile thought it likely that a man who played the flute habitually would not be able to do much on short notice with the harmonica. Not as much as Stile could. Stile was by no means a bad musician himself, and he well understood the nature of the Game. There were tricks of victory apart from straight skill. And Stile had practiced with a unicorn.

Sheen, however, was alarmed. She had only a moment to speak to him during the transfer. "Stile, I spot-researched this man Clef. He's no dabbler in music—he's expert! He may be the finest musician on the planet—the one Citizens borrow for their social functions. He can play anything!"

Oh-oh. Had he walked into the lion's den—again? It was the penalty he paid for spending his free time chasing down magicians in the fantasy frame, instead of doing his homework here. When would he learn better? Part of being in the Game was doing one's research, ascertaining the strengths and weaknesses of one's likely opponents, devising grid-strategies to exploit whatever situation arose. He would be much better off to remain in Proton for the duration of the Tourney, settling it one way or the other. But he could not; the lure of magic, of Adept status, of free and open land and of his ideal woman—maybe that last told it all!—were too great. He had discounted Clef's confidence as bravado, at least in part, and that might have been a bad error. "I'll do my best," he told Sheen.

"You'll have to do better than that," she grumped as they separated. Sometimes she was so human it was painful.

Clef met him in a concert hall. Spectators were permitted here; there were seats for about a hundred. The chamber was already full. "Some interest generated here," Clef noted. "You appear to be well known."

"Maybe they are music fans," Stile said. Often he did attract audiences for his Games, but this was a greater response than he could account for. But of course he had never been in the Tourney before this year; only slightly over one in ten of the original entrants remained, which allowed the audience to concentrate much more heavily on the remaining Games.

They took their places on the small stage. There were seats there, and music stands; the archaic paraphernalia of the artistic medium. Clef had obtained a harmonica similar to Stile's own, from the Game supplies.

"The rules of this competition," the voice of the Game Computer came. "Each contestant will play a solo piece randomly selected. The Computer will judge the level of technical expertise. The human audience will judge the social aspect. Both judgments will be tallied for the decision. Proceed." And a printed sheet of music appeared on a vision screen in front of Clef.

The musician lifted his harmonica and played. Stile's hope sank.

Clef was not merely good and not merely expert. He was outstanding. He was conversant with every technique of the harmonica, and played the music absolutely true. He tongued notes, he employed the vibrato, he trilled, he shifted modes without slip or hesitation. If the harmonica were not his chosen instrument, that was not apparent now.

The man's long, tapering fingers enclosed his harmonica lovingly, his right forefinger resting on the chromatic lever, his hands opening to modify the tonal quality. Each note was pure and clear and perfectly timed; a machine could hardly have been more technically accurate. Stile certainly could not improve on that performance.

Yet he had a chance. Because though the Computer reacted to technical expertise, the human audience cared more about feeling. The appearance of the person playing counted for something, and the flair with which he moved and gestured, and the emotion he conveyed to the audience, the beauty and meaning, the experience he shared with it. Music was, most fundamentally, a participant activity; people without other esthetic appreciation nevertheless liked to tap toes, nod heads, sway to the evocative melody and beat. Stile was good at evoking audience response. If he could do that here, he could gain the social facet and pull out a draw. The audience participation in judging the arts was for this very reason; in the early days some Tourneys had been won by performances that no one except the Computer thought were worthwhile. This problem had been evident historically throughout the arts. Prizes had been awarded for paintings that no one could comprehend, and for sculpture that was ludicrous to the average eye, and for literature that few people could read. Refined, rarefied judgments had been substituted for that of the true audience, the common man, to the detriment of the form. So today, in the Tourney, art had to be intelligible to both the experts and the average man, and esthetic to both. Stile had a chance to nullify Clef's certain computer win and send it back to the grid for the selection of another game. Stile would surely stay clear of music for that one!

Clef finished. The audience applauded politely. It had been an excellent performance, without question; the tiny and subtle nuances of feeling were not something the average person grasped consciously. People seldom knew why they liked what they liked; they only knew that in this instance something had been lacking.

Now it was Stile's turn. Clef lowered his instrument and stood silently, as Stile had. The music screen lit before Stile with the printed music. Actually, Stile did not need it; he could reproduce it from his memory of Clef's performance. But he looked at it anyway, because he did not want to make any single false note. Nothing that would jar the audience out of its rapport.

Stile played. From the start, his hands moved well. The harmonica seemed to be animated with all the experiences Stile had had from the time he discovered it, there in the great valley between the Purple Mountains and the White Mountains in the lovely frame of Phaze. He thought of Neysa as he played, and it was as if he were playing for her, with her again, loving it. Every note was true; he knew he would make no errors.

But he was not playing for himself or for Neysa now. He was performing for an audience. Stile refocused on that, passing his gaze over the people, meeting eyes, leaning forward. He tapped his bare heel, not to keep the beat for himself but to show the audience. A toe could tap unobtrusively, but a heel made the entire leg move; it was obvious. The people started picking it up, their own legs moving. Stile caught the eye of a young woman, and played a brief passage seemingly for her alone, then went on to another person, bringing each one in to him.

It was a responsive audience. Soon most of the people were swaying to the music, nodding their heads, tapping their heels. He was working them up, making them part of his act, giving them the thrill of participation. Together, they all played the harmonica.

Suddenly it ended. The piece was over. Had it been enough?

The moment Stile put down his instrument, the audience burst into enthusiastic applause. Stile glanced at Clef—and found the man staring, his lips parted. Clef, it seemed, had not realized that music could be played this way, that it could be hurled out into the audience like a boomerang, and bring that audience back into its ambience. Perhaps Clef considered this a degradation of the form. No matter; Stile had won his audience.

Sure enough, the announcement verified the split decision. "Expertise, first player, Clef. Social content, second player, Stile. Draw." For the benefit of the audience, the Computer was not employing the assigned Player numbers now.

Clef shook his head ruefully. "You showed me something, Stile. You played very well."

Stile's reply was forestalled by another announcement by the Computer. "It is an option of the Game Computer to require a continuation of a drawn match in the Tourney. This option is now exercised. The contestants will perform a medley in duet, the parts alternating as marked on the score. A panel of qualified musicians will be the final arbiter."

Oh, no! Stile had thought himself safe. A new trap had suddenly closed on him. But there was nothing to do except play it out, despite a judgment that would surely be unfavorable to him. He would not be able to evoke the confused passions of an audience of experts.

There was an intermission while the panel was assembled. "This is new to me," Clef said. "Is there a precedent?"

"I've heard of it," Stile said. "But normally it is invoked only when the contestants can't agree on the draw and insist on playing it out."

"Is it fair? I hardly object to finishing this in Music, but it seems to me you should prefer—I mean, a panel of musicians—"

"Is likely to favor the musician," Stile agreed. "I might win the audience again, but not the Computer or the panel. You're bound to take it."

"You must lodge a protest!"

"No good," Stile said. "The Computer does have the option. I'm stuck for it. I knew the rules when I entered the Tourney." And this was very likely the end of his participation in it. So close to the key Round, secured by that prize of tenure!

"I don't like this at all," Clef said. "I do want to win, and I'll have to play my best, but there is a fundamental inequity here on more than one level. It is not merely that the odds of your winning are greatly in your favor if we go to a new grid. It is that you have a chance to go considerably farther in the Tourney than I do; you are a skilled player, while my skills are largely limited to this particular pursuit. You should be allowed to continue, for I shall surely be eliminated in the next Round or two."

"Play your best," Stile said. "Chance is always a factor in the Game. Someone always profits, someone always loses. I do have another resource." Stile knew he faced disaster, but his liking for this honest man increased. How much better it was to lose to superior talent than to blind chance!

"While we wait—would you be so kind as to explain to me how you make the audience respond like that? I saw it, but I have never been able to do that. I rather envy it."

Stile shrugged. "It's apart from the music itself, yet also the essence of it. Basically you have to achieve rapport with the people you're performing for. You have to *feel*."

"But that isn't music!" Clef protested.

"That is the vital spirit of music," Stile insisted. "Sonic emotion. The transmission of mood and feeling from one person to another. The instrument is merely the means. The notes are merely means. Music itself is only a process, not the end."

"I don't know. This is like heresy, to me. I love music, pure music. Most people and most institutions fall short of the ideal; they are imperfect. Music *is* the ideal."

"You can't separate them," Stile said, finding this exploration interesting. "You are thinking of music as pearls, and the audience as swine, but in truth pearls are the accretions of the irritation of a clam, while the audience is mankind. These things must go together to have meaning. Like man and woman, there's so much lost when apart . . ."

"Like man and woman," Clef echoed. "That too, I have never quite understood."

"It's not easy," Stile said, thinking of the Lady Blue and her violent shifts of attitude during their last encounter. "But until—"

He was interrupted by the Game Computer. "The panel has been assembled. Proceed." Musical scores appeared before Clef and Stile. The sound of a metronome gave them the countdown. Quickly each lifted his harmonica to his mouth.

It was an intricate medley, highly varied, with segments of popular, folk and classical music from Planet Earth. The two ranges counterpointed each other nicely. The audience listened raptly. The music of a single instrument could be excellent, but the action of two instruments in harmony was qualitatively as well as quantitatively superior.

Stile found that he liked this composite piece. He was playing well— even better than before. Partly it was the inherent joy of the counterpoint, always a pleasure; that was why he and Neysa had played together so often. But more, it was Clef; the musician played so well that Stile needed to make no allowances. He could depend on Clef, lean on him, knowing there would be no error, no weakness. Stile could do his utmost. Everything was keyed correctly for takeoff.

Stile took off. He played his part with feeling, absorbing the rapture of that perfect harmony. He saw the audience reacting, knowing the technique was working. He put just a little syncopation in it, adding to the verve of the presentation. The Computer would scale him down for that, of course; it could not comprehend any slightest deviation from the score. To hell with that; Stile was lost anyway. He could not exceed his opponent's perfection of conformance, and had to go for his best mode. He had to go down in the style he preferred. He refused to be bound by the limitations of machine interpretation. He had to *feel*. And—he was doing that well.

Then he became more specifically aware of Clef's playing. The man had started out in perfect conformance to the score, but Stile's deviations had forced him to deviate somewhat also, for as a musician he could not tolerate the separation of efforts. The piece had to have its unity. Now, amazingly, Clef was making deviations of his own. Not by any great amount, but Stile could tell, and it was certain the musicians on the panel could, and the Computer would be having inanimate fits. Clef certainly knew better; why was he doing it?

Because he was picking up the feel. Uncertainly at first, then with greater confidence. With dismaying acuity, Clef was following Stile's lead, emulating him, achieving the same rapport with the human element. But Clef retained his special expertise. Already he was playing Stile's way—better than Stile was doing himself. Stile had to retreat, to play "straight" in support of Clef's effort; otherwise the integrity of the medley would suffer, and it was too fine as music to let suffer. Clef had preempted feeling.

Now the medley swung into a classical fragment Stile recognized— the Choral Symphony—Beethoven's Ninth. Marvelous music never heard by the deaf composer. A beautiful piece—and Clef was playing his theme with inspired brilliance. Stile found his emotions split; part of him was sinking into resignation, knowing there was no way to match this, that he was in fact losing Computer, panel *and* audience votes, that he had washed out of the Tourney at last. The other part of him was reveling in the sheer delight of the *Ode to Joy*, of the finest playing he had ever done on any level, the finest duet he had ever participated in. Neysa's horn was an excellent harmonica—but it had to be conceded that Clef's instrument was a better one. The man was putting it all together in a way no other could. And—Clef himself was reveling in it, moving his body dynamically, transported—as was Stile too, and the entire audience. What an experience!

The music ended. Slowly the emotion of the moment settled out of Stile. He descended from his high and came to grips with the onset of reality. He had, without question, been outplayed. If there was a finer musician in all the universe than Clef, Stile could hardly imagine it.

Clef stood silent, eyes downcast. There was no applause from the audience. There was only the muted murmuring of the five musicians on the panel, comparing notes, consulting, arguing fine points. Stile wondered why they bothered; there was no question in anyone's mind who had played better. Stile had only torpedoed himself, explaining the secret of feeling to his opponent; the man had caught on brilliantly. Yet Stile could not really bring himself to regret it, despite the consequence; it had been such a pleasure to share the experience. His loss on the slot machine had been degrading, pointless, unsatisfying; his loss here was exhilarating. If it were ever worthwhile to sacrifice a kingdom for a song, this had been the song. Something of miraculous beauty had been created here, for a small time; it had been a peak of performance Stile knew he would never truly regret. Better this magnificent defeat, than a cheap victory.

The foreman of the musicians signaled the Computer pickup. "Decision is ready," the Computer's voice came immediately. "This dual performance has been declared the finest overall rendering of the instrument of the harmonica, and is therefore ensconced in the Tourney archives as a lesson example. A special prize of one year's extension of tenure is awarded to the loser of this contest."

Stile's head jerked up. Salvation! This was the prize slated for those who made it to the next Round, that he had just missed. Not as good as a victory, but far, far better than a loss.

The odd thing was that Clef seemed to be reacting identically. Why should he be concerned with an award to the loser? He should be flushed with the victory.

"The advisory decision of the Computer: Clef," the Computer continued after a pause. "The advisory decision of the audience, as recorded by tabulation of those receiving the broadcast of this match: Clef."

Yes, of course. Clef had won both the technical and social votes this time, deservedly. Stile walked across to shake his opponent's hand.

"The decision of the panel of judges," the Computer continued. "Stile."

Stile extended his hand to Clef. "Congratulations," he said.

"Therefore the Round goes to Stile," the Computer concluded.

Stile froze in midgesture. "What?"

The Computer answered him. "Advisory opinions do not have binding force. Stile is the winner of this contest. Please clear the chamber for ensuing matches."

"But—" Stile protested, dumbfounded. Then he was drowned out by the tumultuous applause of the local audience, abruptly augmented by that of the speaker system as it carried the reaction of the larger, unseen audience.

Clef took him firmly by the arm, leading him through the colossal din to the exit. Bemused, unbelieving, Stile suffered himself to be guided out.

A line of people had formed in the hall. At the head of it was the Rifleman. The Citizen grabbed Stile's hand and pumped it. "Congratulations!" he cried. "Magnificent performance!" Then the others were congratulating him in turn, until Sheen got to him and began running interference.

Clef turned to leave. "Wait!" Stile cried. "You can't go! This is all wrong! *You* won! Has the planet gone crazy?"

Clef smiled. "No, you won. I'm surprised you weren't aware."

"You should enter a protest!" Stile said. "You clearly outplayed me. I think you're the finest musician on the planet!"

Sheen guided them to seats on the capsule home.

"I may be so—now," Clef said. "You showed me how to alleviate the major weakness in my skill. I owe it to you."

"Then how—?"

Clef smiled. "It is a pleasure to have the privilege of educating you as you educated me. You recall how we played separately, to a split decision?"

"Indeed," Stile said wryly.

"And how you then explained to me the manner music is a participatory endeavor? Not every man an island?"

"Yes, of course! You proved to be an apt student!"

"A duet is a joint endeavor. Each must help the other, or it fails."

"Of course. But—"

"A man who plays well alone, can play better in company—if he has proper support. Harmony and counterpoint enable a new dimension of effect."

"Yes, I played better, because I knew you would make no error. Still —you played better yet. I think you improved more than I did."

"I am sure this is the case. Because you provided more support to me than I provided to you," Clef said. "I gave you merely good technical performance, at the outset; you gave me the essence of feeling. You showed me how. I was never able to accomplish it on my own, but in tandem with you I felt the living essence at last, the heart and spirit of music. I was infused by it, I merged with its potent pulse, and for the first time in my life—I flew."

"And you won!" Stile cried. "I agree with everything you said. You and I both know you profited greatly, and played my way better than I ever played in my life. You went from student to master in one phenomenal leap! Surely the panel of judges saw that!"

"Of course they did. I have known all of the members of that panel for years, and they know me. We have played together often."

And this panel of friends had given the match—to Stile? Was it overcompensation?

The capsule stopped. Sheen took each man by the arm and guided him on toward the apartment.

"Therefore you won," Stile said. "That's obvious."

"Let me approach this from another angle, lest you be as obtuse as I was. If you play solo on one instrument and it is good, then play the same piece on another instrument of the same type and it is better, wherein lies the source of the improvement?"

"In the instrument," Stile said. "My skill on similar instruments is presumed to be constant."

"Precisely. Now if you play a duet with one person, then with another, and your performance stands improved on the second—?"

"Then probably the other player is superior, enabling me to—" Stile paused. It was beginning to penetrate. "If I improve because of the other player, it's *him* that really makes the difference!"

"When we played together, I improved more than you did," Clef said. "Who, then, contributed more to the joint effort? The one who flew the heights—or the one who lifted him there?"

"That duet—it was not to show individual expertise," Stile said, working it out. "It was to show cooperative expertise. How each person fit in as part of a team. Yet surely the Computer did not see it that way; the machine lacks the imagination. So it shouldn't have—"

"The machine was not the final arbiter. The musicians saw it that way, and their vote was decisive."

The human mind remained more complex than the most sophisticated of machines! Of course the musicians had imposed their standard! "So I supported your effort—"

"More than I supported yours," Clef finished. "You gave way to me; you made the sacrifice, for the benefit of the piece. You were the better team player. You contributed more significantly to the total production. Therefore you proved your overall participation to be better than mine. You would have made *anyone* shine. This is the subtle point the Computer and audience missed, but the musical experts understood. They knew it was from you I derived the ability that enabled me to make the best individual performance of my life. You are the sort of musician who belongs in a group; your talent facilitates that of others."

Again Stile thought of his many playing sessions with Neysa, those happy hours riding. Their music had always been beautiful. "I—suppose so," he said, still amazed.

Clef extended his hand. "Now permit me to congratulate you on your deserved victory. You are the better man, and I wish you well in the Tourney."

"Victor, perhaps, thanks to an unusual judgment. Better man, no." Stile took the hand. "But if you lost—you can no longer play here on Proton."

"I do have one more year, thanks to the special award. We did incidentally render the finest harmonica recital in the Proton records. But this becomes irrelevant. I no longer need Proton. You have given the universe to me! With the skill you have shown me, I can play anywhere, for exorbitant fees. I can live like a Citizen. I have gained so much more than I have lost!"

"I suppose so," Stile said, relieved. "A musician of your caliber—the best that any audience is likely to encounter—" He paused, another massive realization coming upon him. "Your preferred instrument is the flute?"

Clef raised that expressive eyebrow. "Of course. My Employer provides me with a silver flute, and rarely am I allowed to play on a gold one. One day I hope to be able to purchase such an instrument for myself. The tonal quality—"

"How about a platinum flute?"

"That would be best of all! But it would depend on who made it. The craftsmanship is really more important than the metal, though the best craftsmanship does make any given metal significantly superior. But why dream foolishly? The only craftsmen capable of doing justice to platinum are far away on Earth."

"Sheen," Stile murmured.

Sheen produced the Platinum Flute and handed it to Clef.

The man took it with infinite respect and awe. "Why it is, it actually is! A finely crafted platinum instrument! I do not recognize this make, yet it seems excellently done. Who—have aliens gone into the business?"

"Elves," Stile said.

Clef laughed. "No, really. I must know. This is of considerably more than incidental interest to me. This instrument has the feel of ultimate quality."

"Mound Folk. Little People. Among them I am a giant. They use magic in their trade. This is an enchanted flute, on loan to me until I pass it along to one who has better use for it than I do. I should have recognized you as a prospect the moment I met you, but I suspect I did not want to part with this magic instrument, and suppressed my own awareness. But I made a commitment, and must honor it. At least I understand, now, how the elves felt about yielding the Flute to me. It is hard to give up."

"I should think so!" Clef's eyes were fixed on the Flute as his hands turned it about. Light gleamed from it as it moved. The man seemed mesmerized by it. Then he lifted it to his lips. "May I?"

"Please do. I want to hear you play it."

Clef played. The music poured out in its platinum stream, so pure and eloquent that Stile's whole body shivered in rapture. It was the finest sound ever created by man, he believed. Even Sheen showed human wonder on her face—an emotion prohibitively rare for a machine. Stile had not played it this well.

Clef finished his piece and contemplated the Flute. "I must have this instrument."

"The price is high," Stile warned.

"Price is no object. My entire serf-retirement payment is available—"

"Not money. Life. You may have to give up both your tenure on Proton and your future as a professional musician in the galaxy. You would have to travel into a land of magic where your life would be threatened by monsters and spells, to return the Flute to its makers—

and there is no guarantee they would allow you to keep it. They might require some significant and permanent service of you. There may be no escape from their control, once you enter that region. They do not like men, but they are questing for a man they call the Foreordained, and exactly what he is expected to do I do not know, but it is surely difficult and significant."

Clef's eyes remained on the Platinum Flute. "Show me the way."

"I can start you on that journey, but can not remain with you once you enter the Demesnes of the Platinum Elves. The Flute will protect you; at need it will become an excellent rapier. When you reach the Mound, you will be in their power. I warn you again—"

"I must go," Clef said.

Stile spread his hands. "Then the Flute is yours, on loan until you determine whether you are in fact the Foreordained. I will take you across the curtain. Perhaps we shall meet again, thereafter." Somehow he knew Clef would have no trouble crossing into Phaze.

"You took Hulk across," Sheen reminded him. "When he returned—"

"Some things transcend life and death," Stile said. "What must be, must be." And he wondered: how could the Mound Folk have known that Stile would encounter Clef, the man they evidently wanted, in this frame where they could not go? His meeting with Clef as an opponent in the Tourney had been coincidental—hadn't it?

CHAPTER 10

Red

"And so I sent him on his way to the Mound Folk," Stile concluded. "I do not know what they want of him, and hope there is no evil."

"The Elven Folk are not evil," the Lady Blue agreed. "They, like us, must follow their destinies. Yet their ways be not ours."

"Now must I seek mine own destiny, coming at last to brace mine enemy and thine. I must slay the Red Adept; so have I sworn and so must it be."

"So must it be," she agreed pensively. As always, she was garbed in blue, and as always she was compellingly lovely. They were in a private chamber of the Blue Castle. Neysa was absent temporarily, seeing to the security of Clef on his trek to the Mound Folk. Kurrelgyre's wolves ranged the vicinity, keeping an eye on whatever went on. There had been no move against the Blue Demesnes. "I know what this means to thee, this vengeance," the Lady said. "And fain would I see my Lord avenged: I am no gentler than thee. Yet I mislike it. There is aught thou knowest not."

"I hope we are not going to have another scene," Stile said uneasily. "Dearly would I like thy favor, as thou knowest, but I shall not be swayed from—"

"Methinks we shall have a scene," she said. "But not quite like the last. Shamed am I to have tested thee as I did. I agreed to support thine effort, and I shall not renege. I like not playing the role of the contrary advocate. But now I must inform thee of misinformation thou hast."

"It is not the Red Adept who is mine enemy?" Stile asked, suddenly alarmed.

"Forget the Red Adept for the moment!" she snapped. "This relates to us."

"Have I offended thee in some fashion? I apologize; there remain social conventions in this frame I do not—"

"Apologize not to me!" she cried. "It is I who have wronged thee!"

Stile shook his head. "I doubt thou'rt capable of that, Lady."

"Listen to me!" she said, her blue eyes flashing in the way they had, momentarily brightening the curtains. "I have to tell thee—" She took a breath. "That never till thou didst come on the scene was I a liar."

Stile had not been taking this matter too seriously. Now he did. "Thou knowest I do not tolerate a lie in these Demesnes. I am in this respect the mirror of mine other self. Why shouldst thou lie to me? What cause have I given thee?"

The Lady Blue was obviously in difficulty. "Because I lied first to myself," she whispered. "I denied what I wished not to perceive." Now tears showed in her eyes.

Stile wanted to comfort her, to hold her, but held himself rigidly apart. She was not his to hold, whatever she might have done. Yet he recalled his own recent reluctance to recognize Clef as the one destined to receive the Flute, and knew how the Lady might similarly resist some noxious revelation. This was not necessarily the sort of lie he could completely condemn. "Lady, I must know. What is the lie?" Once before a woman had lied to him, in kindness rather than malice, and that had cost him heartbreak and had changed his life. He could not even blame her, in retrospect, for from that experience had come his affinity with music. Yet the Lady Blue was more than that serf-girl had been, and her lie might wreak greater havoc. He knew she could not have done such a thing lightly.

She stood and faced away from him, ashamed. "When I said—when I told thee—" She was unable to continue.

Stile remembered now how Sheen had at first tried to deceive him about her nature. He had forced the issue, and regretted it. Associations relating to Sheen had led him to this world of Phaze, making another phenomenal change in his life.

Somehow it seemed that the greatest crises of his existence had been tied in to the lies of women.

"Thou'rt so like my Lord!" the Lady Blue burst out, her shoulders shaking.

Stile smiled grimly. "By no coincidence, Lady." He thought of how similar her alternate self in Proton, Bluette, was to her. Had Bluette escaped the robot? He hardly dared check on that. Bluette dead would be a horror to his conscience; Bluette alive—how could he deal with her, he for whom the trap had been set?

"When I said—" The Lady Blue paused again, then forced it out. "I loved thee not."

Stile felt as he had when declared the winner of the harmonica contest. Was he mishearing, indulging in a wish fulfillment? "Thou dost love thy Lord the real Blue Adept, whose likeness I bear. This have I always understood."

"Thee," she said. "Thee . . . Thee."

She had told him of that convention of love—but even if she had not done so, he would have understood. There was a ripple in the air and in the curtains of the window, and a tiny brush of wind touched his hair in passing. For a moment there was a blueness in the room. Then the effects faded, and all was as before.

Except for the lie, now demolished. For this was the splash the world of Phaze made in the presence of deep truth. She had confessed her love—for him.

Stile found himself inadequate to rise to the occasion in any fashion. He had been so sure that the Lady's love, if it ever came, would be years in the making! There was an obvious rejoinder for him to make, but he found himself unable.

The Lady, her statement made, now began her documentation. "When thou didst prove thine identity by performing magic, and I saw the animals' loyalty to thee, it was my heart under siege. I thought thou wouldst be either like the golem, all wood and lifeless and detestable, or that thou wouldst use thy magic as the Yellow Witch suggested, to force my will to thy design."

"Nay, never that!" Stile protested. "Thou'rt thy Lord's widow!"

"Always didst thou safeguard me, with Hulk or Neysa or the wolves or some potion. Even as my Lord did."

"But of course! The Lady of the Blue Demesnes must ever be protected!"

"Wilt thou be quiet a moment!" she flared. "I am trying to tell thee why I love thee. The least thou canst do is listen."

Stile, perforce, was silent.

"Three things distinguished my Lord," she continued after a moment. "He was the finest rider in Phaze—and so art thou. He was the strongest Adept—and so art thou. And he was of absolute integrity—as so art thou. No way can I claim thou art his inferior. In fact—long have I fought against the realization, but no more shall I lie—thou art in certain respects his superior."

"Lady—"

"Damn me not with thy modesty!" she cried fiercely, and Stile was suppressed again.

"Never did he actually ride a unicorn," she continued. "Never did he enchant an entire assembly into friendship with one. Never did he win the active loyalty of the wolfpack. I think he could have done these things, had he chosen, but he chose not. And so he was less than thee, because he exerted himself less. Always had he his magic to lean on; mayhap it made him drive less hard. Thou—thou art what he could have been. And I—I love what he could have been."

Stile started one more protest, and once more she blocked him with a savage look. "When thou sworest friendship to Neysa, such was the power of that oath that its backwash enchanted us all. Thy magic compelled me—and I knew in that moment that never more could I stand against thee. The emotion thou didst feel for the unicorn became my emotion, and it has abided since, and I would not choose to be rid of it if I could. Always will Neysa be my friend, and I would lay down my life for her, and my honor too. Yet I know it was no quality in her that evoked this loyalty in me, though she has qualities that do deserve it. It was thy spell, like none before in this world. I love Neysa, and Neysa loves thee, and through her I too must love thee—"

Yet again Stile tried to interrupt, and yet again could not.

"I tell thee this to show that I know the extent to which thy magic has acted on me—and thus am assured it does not account for the fullness of my feeling. I love thee in part because I have experienced the depth of thy love for Neysa, and hard it is to deny feeling of that sincerity. Thou lovest well, Adept, and thereby thou dost become lovable thyself. But I do love thee more than I can blame on magic."

She paused, and this time Stile had the wit not to interrupt her. "When thou didst take me along on thy trip to the Mound Folk," she continued, "and the Sidhe toyed with us, and thou didst dance with the Faerie-maid, then did I suffer pangs of jealousy. Then when thou didst dance with me, as my Lord used to do—"

She broke off and walked around the room. "Ever was I a fool. I thought I could withstand thy appeal. But when I heard thee play the magic Flute—O my Lord, that sound!—not since the days of mine other courtship have I heard the like! But then thou didst go to fight the Worm, and I cursed myself for my callousness to thee, swearing to make it up to thee an I should ever see thee again alive—and yet I hardened again when thou didst survive, telling myself it could not be. The lie was on me, and I could not cast it off. Then at the Unolympics when thou didst so readily defend me against the seeming slur of Yellow—alas, I am woman, I am weak, my heart swelled with gratitude and guilt. And I could not help myself, I had to hear thee play again, and so I betrayed thy possession of the Flute to Yellow. And saw thee nearly killed by the Herd Stallion. Yet again had I played the fool, even as Yellow knew. And then at last, when thou didst come to me suffering from thy loss of thy Game and of thy friend Hulk—I longed to comfort thee with all my being, but the lie lay between us like a festering corpse, making foul what would have been fair, adding to thy grief, making of me a fishwife—and yet in that adversity didst thou steer thy narrow course exactly as *he* would have done, and I knew that I was lost. And I feared that thou wouldst die before ever I had chance to beg the forgiveness I deserved not—"

"I forgive thee that lie!" Stile cried, and again the air shimmered and the things of the room rippled and the breath of breeze shook out her tresses.

Now again she faced away from him, as though ashamed of what she had to say. "I was a girlish fool when first the Blue Adept courted me. Somehow I took him not seriously, for that he resembled to my ignorant eye a child or one of the Little Folk. Even when I married him I withheld somewhat my love from him. When I learned of the geas against his siring a child by me, I mourned more for the lack of the child than for my Lord's deprival. For years I dallied, and only slowly did I learn to love him truly—and only when he died did I realize how deep that love had grown. Fool I was; I loved him not with abandon until he was gone. I swore, once it was too late, never to be that kind of fool again. Yet was I trying to be that kind of fool with thee, even as I was with him. Now thou dost go yet again perhaps to thy doom, and I will deceive myself or thee no longer. An thou must die, thou must suffer my love first. And that is the scene we must have."

Now at last she gave him leave to speak unfettered. Stile could not doubt her sincerity. He loved her, of course; they had both known that all along. Yet he was not sure he wanted her love this way. "How did he die?" he asked.

If this question struck her as irrelevant, she did not treat it so. "The golem in thy likeness walked to the Blue Castle during my Lord's absence. At first I thought it was Blue, but very soon knew I better. 'I bring an amulet for Blue,' the golem said, and gave me a little demon on a chain, the kind employed by frame-travelers to mock clothing when they have none."

"I encountered one of those!" Stile exclaimed. "When I invoked it, it tried to choke me with the chain!"

"Even so," she agreed grimly. "All innocently did I relay it to my Lord, who took it for a message-amulet, perhaps an exchange for some favor. I begged him to invoke it with caution, lest there be some error, but he heeded me not. He put the chain about his neck and invoked it—" She was unable to continue.

"And it strangled him so that he could utter no spell in self-defense," Stile concluded. "He depended on magic to foil magic, and this time could not. Had he used physical means—"

"I could not heal a dead man," the Lady sobbed. "Nor could I let it be known he was lost, lest the Demesnes suffer. The golem took his place, the hateful thing, and I had to cooperate—"

So nothing further was known about the motive for the murder. The Red Adept had dealt with the Brown Adept to obtain the golem, and used it without Brown's knowledge for evil. Perhaps she had even been responsible for the original Brown's death, to prevent him from interfering, leaving the innocent child as the new Brown Adept. The golem itself had not committed the murder of Blue; it had not been made for that. Probably Brown had been told it would serve as a double for Blue when the latter was indisposed to expose himself to public scrutiny, or when he wished to conceal his absence from the Castle. Exactly as the robot in Stile's likeness had served in the frame of Proton.

"This curse of infertility—what of it?"

"After I married Blue, I went to the Oracle to inquire what kind of children I would have, wasting my lone question in girlish curiosity. The Oracle replied 'None by One, Son by Two.' I understood that not until my Lord died: that I would bear children not by my first husband. Oh, I grasped it in part, but did not realize that it was not truly a geas against fertility, but that he would die too soon. I thought he was cursed by sterility—" Again she broke down, but almost immediately fought out of it. "Thou art my second husband—and before thou dost suicide in this awful mission of vengeance, thou must give me that son!" she concluded with determination.

"My son shall not be raised by a widow!" Stile said.

The Lady turned at last to face him. "I love thee. I have at last confessed it. Shame me not further by this denial. I must have at least this much of thee."

But already Stile's mind was working. He loved the Lady Blue, but this sudden force of her return-love was too much for his immediate assimilation. He would be ready for it after due reflection; but now, this instant, it was too much like a windfall gift. He somehow feared it would be taken from him as rapidly as it had been bequeathed, and he wanted to protect himself against such loss before getting committed. Love did not make Stile blind; he had learned caution the hard way. So now he looked for the catch. He did not doubt the Lady's sincerity, or question her desirability; he simply didn't trust the magic vicissitudes of fate. "The Oracle always speaks correctly."

"Aye." She looked at him questioningly. He was not reacting as her experience of him in two selves had led her to expect.

"Then I will not die until I have given thee thy son. Allow me to wait until I have disposed of the Red Adept, that I may have child *and* life with thee."

Her lovely face was transformed by realization. "Yes! Thou must survive! There be no guarantee that thou mayest live one day after thou dost sire a child, unless the threat to thy life be abated before."

That seemed to be the trap fate had set, the thing that would have made their union brief. Not her change of heart, but his death. Stile's pause for thought could have saved his life.

But then the Lady Blue thought of something else. "Except that thou art not married to me. If thou dost desist, it may be fated that some other man—I loathe the thought!—will marry me and sire my son. It must be thee, I will not have it otherwise, and therefore—"

How fate wriggled to snare him anyway! Stile had almost missed that loophole. "That is readily solved," he said. He took her hands in his. "Lady of the Blue Demesnes, I beg thy hand in marriage."

"Thou dost not say thou lovest me," she complained.

"In good time."

She fought him no longer. "I grant my hand and my heart to thee in marriage," she agreed, radiant.

They went outside. Neysa had returned from her mission, somehow knowing what was in the offing. "My friend," he said to the unicorn. "I have proposed marriage to the Lady, and she has accepted my suit. Wilt thou be witness to this union?"

Neysa blew a single loud note on her horn. Immediately the wolf-pack gathered, the werewolves charging in from all directions. Kurrelgyre changed to man-form. "The mare informs us thou hast won the Lady at last!" he exclaimed. "Congratulations!"

Stile marveled again at how much a unicorn could convey in one note. Then the wolves formed a circle, and Kurrelgyre stood before the couple, and Neysa stood between them in her natural form. There was no doubt in any creature what was happening. "By the authority vested in me as leader of the Pack, I perform this ceremony of mating," Kurrelgyre said. "Neysa, as friend to each party, dost thou bear witness that this contract be freely sought by this man and this bitch?"

Neysa made a musical snicker.

"This mare—I mean, this woman," the werewolf said quickly, finally getting it straight. The Lady Blue smiled; well she knew that the appellation "bitch" was no affront in the mouth of a wolf.

Now Neysa blew an affirmative note.

"Wolves and bitches of my pack, do you bear witness to the validity of this contract?" Kurrelgyre inquired rhetorically.

There was a general growl of assent, admixed by a yip or two of excitement. They were enjoying this.

"Then I now proclaim the two of you man and mate. Wife," Kurrelgyre said solemnly. Neysa stepped out from between them.

Stile and the Lady came together. Stile held her at half-distance one more moment. She remained in her blue dress, ordinary daywear, but she was the loveliest creature he could imagine. "Thee . . . Thee . . . Thee," he said. Then he kissed her.

The shimmer of the oath surrounded them, stirring the Demesnes and touching the fur of the animals and momentarily coloring the grass. For a sweet eternity he embraced her, and when it ended she was in a light blue wedding dress, and a magic sparkle emanated from her.

"Now must I depart to brace the Red Adept," Stile announced as they separated.

Astonishment was manifest among Neysa and all the wolves. There were growls and yips of confusion, and Neysa blew a volley of startled notes. "Not right at this hour!" Kurrelgyre protested. "Tomorrow, mayhap—"

"Right this minute," Stile said, vaulting to Neysa's back. "I shall see thee anon, wife."

"Anon," she agreed, smiling.

Neysa, responsive to his unspoken directive, set off at a canter eastward, toward the Red Demesnes.

When they were well clear of the Castle, Neysa blew an insistent note of query. Stile laughed. "Since thou wilt have it from me at the point of thy horn if I tell thee not, I will answer. The Oracle told the Lady 'None by One, Son by Two.' Now I be Two, her second husband, and—"

Neysa's laughter pealed musically forth. How readily she understood! How many Adepts could arrange the Oracle's assurance that they would survive a life-and-death encounter to sire a son? Stile had cleverly made the prophecy work for him.

As they settled into the hours of travel, Stile concentrated on his spells. He needed a variety of general-purpose defenses and counters. He should survive this encounter, but he had no guarantee that he would win it. He could emerge crippled or blind, able to sire a son but then unable to live in health and independence. Oracle prophecies tended to be slippery, and he had to be on guard against some loophole he had not anticipated. Yet he understood why such predictions were often devious. A person fated to die at a certain place at a certain time would strive to avoid that situation if he could, so the prophecy would be self-negating if clearly stated. Absolute clarity and hundred percent accuracy could not always be simultaneously accommodated, by the very nature of it. Also, there could be a certain flexibility in a situation; a man could die in a dozen different ways, or survive at an expense worse than death. The Oracle had to make a brief statement that covered all prospects, and that was often necessarily ambiguous. So Stile fully intended to fight for the best possible interpretation of this particular prediction. The Oracle had not truly pronounced his fate; it had merely defined the broadest parameters. Interpretation was the essence of his specific fate.

Send this spell straight to Hell, he thought, careful not to vocalize. Would that work against an amulet? It should, if he willed it properly. As he understood it, from his limited experience, an amulet was a solidified spell, quiescent until invoked. Some, like the healing or clothing amulets, worked on a slow, sustained basis. Others, like the throttledemon, took a few seconds to achieve full strength. Just so long as he had time enough to sing a prepared counterspell. Maybe he could work out a number of easy variants that would lack full force but would suffice in a pinch. Send this spell into a dell, make this spell into a smell, make this spell fail to jell, banish this spell when I yell—all doggerel, but that was the way his magic worked. What he considered real poetry, where form, style and significance were more important than rhyme or meter, took time to create, and he was not sure how much time he would have. There was some evidence that better verse had more potent effect, for he deemed his verse-form oath of friendship to Neysa to have been a cut above doggerel—but he hardly had need of such potency in routine magic. So he kept working out his cheap spot rhymes, hoping to cover every contingency.

They passed the Unolympic site, now deserted. "Thou didst put on a fine show, Neysa," Stile murmured. "Thou didst do credit to thy Herd." And she snorted contentedly. Winning was less important to her than recognition of her right to compete.

They were nearing the Red Demesnes by nightfall. Stile considered where they might camp, since he did not want to engage his enemy by night. There were too many imponderables. He could conjure a suitable shelter, but hesitated to employ his magic here. The Red Adept might be alert to magic in the vicinity, and he wanted his arrival to be as much of a surprise as possible.

But Neysa was already zeroing in on a location. She drew up before a large cave and blew a note. Bats sailed out of it to swirl around the visitors. Then they dropped to the ground and converted to men and women.

"The vampires!" Stile exclaimed. "I didn't realize they lived here!" But obviously Neysa had known; that was another reason he needed her along.

One came forward. It was Vodlevile, the one who had come to Stile during the Unolympics. "Adept! How goes my friend Hulk?"

Wrong question! "Alas, he was murdered in Proton-frame," Stile said. "I seek vengeance of the Red Adept."

"Dead?" the vampire asked, shocked. "But I met him only so recently! He was the nicest ogre I knew!"

"He was that," Stile agreed. "Red killed him, in lieu of me."

Vodlevile frowned. Now the cutting edges of his teeth showed. "We have ever lived at peace with Red. She never helped us, but hindered us not. I dared not make petition to her for a charm for my son, for fear she would simply claim my son. We hold Adepts in low esteem. Thou art the first who helped. And Yellow, because of thee." He lifted his hand, and a small bat fluttered down to be caught. "My son," Vodlevile said proudly.

Stile nodded. "I was glad to do it. May we camp here the night?"

"Indeed. Our resources are at thy disposal. Dost thou wish to join our evening repast?"

"I think not, meaning no offense. Thy ways are not mine, and this is my wedding night, which I must spend alone. Also, I would not wish to cause thy kind trouble with the Adept, should she survive me; best that it be not known I dallied here."

"Thy wedding night—alone! Thou'rt correct—our ways are not thine! We shall honor thy desire to be alone, and shall see that none intrude on thee."

So it was that Stile found himself ensconced in a warm cave guarded by bloodthirsty bats. He certainly felt secure here; very few creatures would even attempt to intrude, for fear the vampires would suck their blood.

Neysa brought him some fruit she found, then went outside to graze. She slept while grazing at night; Stile had never quite figured out how she did that, but was used to it by now.

Before he slept, feeling extraordinarily lonely, Stile looked up to spy a small bat fluttering in. There was a manner of skulking about it. It converted to a lad about six years old. "Adept, I am not supposed to bother thee—but can I talk a moment?" the boy asked hesitantly.

"Thou'rt the one the potion helped," Stile said, making an educated guess. "Welcome; I am glad to converse with thee."

The lad smiled gratefully. "My father would cut off my blood, if he knew I bothered thee. Please don't tell him."

"Not a word," Stile agreed. Children did not take adult rules as seriously as they took the prospect of punishment. "I'm glad to see thee flying."

"It was Yellow's potion, but thy behest, my father says. I owe thee—"

"Nothing," Stile said quickly. "Thy father repaid any favor that might have been owing. He helped me match the unicorn Herd Stallion."

"Yet thou didst lose, he says," the lad insisted. "His help was not enough."

"My *skill* was not enough," Stile said. "All I wanted was a fair match, with shame on neither party. That I had. The unicorn was the better creature."

The lad had some trouble grasping this. "In a pig's eye—my father says. He says thou dost give away more than can ever be repaid, and dost gain more than can ever be reckoned thereby. Does that make sense?"

"None at all," Stile said cheerfully.

"Anyway, methinks I owe thee, for that thou madest my life complete. Yet I know not what favor I can do thee."

"Thou dost need do none!" Stile insisted. Then he saw that the lad was near tears. The vampire child was serious, and wanted to repay his debt as he perceived it. "Uh, unless—" Stile thought fast. "There is much I do not know, yet I am most curious about things. Canst thou keep an eye or an ear out for what might be of use to me, and tell me when thou findest it? Perhaps a sick animal I might heal, or something pretty I might fetch for my Lady." Stile smiled reminiscently, and a little sadly. "Fain would I give my love something nice."

The lad's eyes brightened, and his little bloodsucking tusks showed cutely. "I'll look, Adept!" he exclaimed happily. "Something important, something nice!" He changed to bat-form and zoomed from the cave.

Stile lay down again to sleep, satisfied. The lad would have a happy quest, until he forgot the matter in the press of other entertainments.

In the morning Stile bade the vampire colony parting. "Thou dost understand," Vodlevile said apologetically. "We dare not accompany thee to the Red Demesnes or help thee too directly on thy quest. If ever the Adept supposed we had taken action against her—"

"Well I understand," Stile said. "This be not thy quarrel."

"Not overtly. Yet when I remember the ogre—"

"Bide a while," Stile said. "That may be avenged."

Vodlevile looked startled, but said nothing. Stile mounted Neysa, who was well fed and rested after her night of sleep-grazing, and they trotted off south to the Red Demesnes.

The Red Castle looked more like a crazy house. It perched atop a miniature mountain, with a narrow path spiraling up to the tiny hole that was the front entrance. It was obviously the home of an Adept; a faint glow surrounded it, like a dome of Proton.

A magic dome? Of course! This castle was probably situated on the curtain, so the Adept could pass freely across, unobserved, to do her mischief in either frame. That would explain much. The Blue Demesnes had not been constructed on the curtain because the Blue Adept had not been able to cross it.

They circled around the castle. It was so; Stile spied the curtain. Just to be certain, he spelled himself across. Sure enough, it was the same castle, with the force-field dome enclosing it. He willed himself back. "This is a sophisticated setup," he told Neysa. "She's been operating in both frames for years."

The unicorn snorted. She did not like this. Neysa could not cross the curtain, probably because she was a magical creature, so could not protect him in the other frame.

"All right," Stile said. "She killed me by stealth. I shall kill her honorably." He singsonged a spell: "Shake a leg, fetch a meg." And a fine big megaphone appeared in his hand. It was not artificially powered, for that was no part of magic, but he was sure it would do the job.

But first a precaution: "Sword and mail: Do not fail." And he was clothed in fine light woven metal armor, with a small sharp steel sword swinging in its scabbard from his hip. The Platinum Flute would have been nice, but that was gone. An ordinary weapon would have to do.

He raised the megaphone. "Red, meet the challenge of Blue." The sound boomed out; it could hardly go unheard.

There was no response from the Red Demesnes. Stile bellowed another challenge, and a third, but had no visible effect.

"Then we brace to meet the lioness in her den," Stile said, not really surprised. The worst traps would be there.

Neysa did not seem thrilled, but she marched gamely forward. It occurred to Stile that he might need more than armor to protect Neysa and himself. Suppose monsters hurled rocks or spears from ambush? He needed to block off any nonmagical attack. "Missiles spend their force," he sang. "Return to their source." That should stop that sort of thing. He wasn't sure how far such spells extended, particularly when opposed by other Adept magic, but this precaution couldn't hurt. The spells of Red could not be abated this way—but that was limited to amulets. He should have a fair fighting chance—and that was all he wanted. A fair match—so that he could kill the Red Adept without compunction.

Neysa walked up the spiraling path. There was no attack. Stile felt nervous; he really would have preferred some kind of resistance. This could mean that no one was home—but it could also mean an unsprung trap.

A trap—like that of Bluette, in the other frame? Bluette herself had obviously known nothing of it; she had been cruelly used. Stile hoped she had managed to survive, though he knew he still would not follow that up; now that he was married to the Lady Blue, there could be no future in any association with Bluette. Meanwhile, his rage at the fate of Hulk burgeoned again, and Stile had to labor to suppress it. Hulk, a truly innocent party, sent by Stile himself to his doom. How could that wrong ever be abated?

There were a number of deep emotional wounds Stile bore as a result of the malicious mischief of the Red Adept; he could not afford to let them overwhelm him. His oath of vengeance covered it all. Once Red was dead, he could let the tide of buried grief encompass him. He simply could not afford grief—or love—yet. Not while this business was unfinished.

They rose up high as they completed the first loop. From a distance the castle had seemed small, but here it seemed extraordinarily high. The ground was thirty feet below, the building another sixty feet above. Magic, perhaps, either making the hill seem smaller than it was, when viewed from a distance, or making it seem higher than it was, from here.

Stile brought out his harmonica and began to play. The magic coalesced about him, making the castle shimmer—and the perspective changed. His gathering magic was canceling Red's magic, revealing the truth—which was that the castle was larger than it had seemed, but the hill lower than it now seemed. So it was a compromise effort, drawing from one appearance to enhance the other. Pretty clever, actually; the Adept evidently had some artistic sensitivity and sense of economy.

Now they arrived at the door. It was open, arched, and garishly colorful, like an arcade entrance. From inside music issued, somewhat blurred and off-key. It clashed with Stile's harmonica-playing, but he did not desist. Until he understood what was going on here, he wanted his magic close about him.

They stepped inside. Immediately the music became louder and more raucous. Booths came alive at the sides, apparently staffed by golems, each one calling for attention. "How about it, mister? Try thy luck, win a prize. Everybody wins!"

This was the home of an Adept? This chaotic carnival? Stile should have worn his clown-suit!

Cautiously he approached the nearest booth. The golem-proprietor was eager to oblige. "Throw a ball, hit the target, win a prize! It's easy!"

Neysa snorted. She did not trust this. Yet Stile was curious about the meaning of this setup, if there was any meaning to it. He certainly had not expected anything like this! He had become proficient in the Game of Proton in large part because of his curiosity. Things generally did make sense, one way or another; it was only necessary to fathom that sense. Now this empty carnival in lieu of the murdering Red Adept—what did it mean? What was the thread that unraveled it?

This was, of course, dangerous, but he decided to take the bait. If he couldn't figure out the nature of this trap by looking at it, he might just have to spring it—at his own convenience. He could certainly hit the target with the ball; he was quite good at this sort of thing. But true carnival games were traditionally rigged; the clients were suckers who wasted their money trying for supposedly easy prizes of little actual value. In the Proton variants, serfs had to use play-money, since there was no real money. Here—"How much does it cost?"

"Free, free!" the android—rather, the golem—cried. "Everybody wins!"

"Fat chance," Stile muttered. He did not dismount from Neysa; that might be part of the trap. He took the proffered ball gingerly, bracing for magic, but there was none. The ball seemed ordinary.

Experimentally, Stile threw. The ball shot across to strike the bull's-eye. The booth went wild, with horns sounding so loudly as to drown out everything else. A metal disk dropped out of a slot. The golem picked it up and handed it to Stile. "Here's the prize, sir! Good shot!"

Stile hesitated. He had been aiming to *miss* the target; instead magic had guided the ball to score. Anyone else would have been deceived, thinking it was his own skill responsible. The golem had spoken truly: everybody won. The game was rigged for it. But why?

Stile looked at the disk. It was an amulet, obviously. He was being presented with it. Yet all this could not have been set up for him alone; he had come unexpectedly—and even if he had been expected, this was too elaborate. Why would visitors be treated to this?

He had an answer: the Red Adept, like most Adepts, was fundamentally paranoid and asocial, and did not like visitors. Power was said to tend to corrupt, and the Adepts had power—and tended to be corrupted. Since they had to live somewhere, they established individual Demesnes reasonably separated from each other, then guarded these Demesnes in whatever fashion their perverse natures dictated. Yet they could not kill intruders entirely randomly, for some were legitimate tradesmen with necessary services to offer, and others might be the representatives of formidable groups, like the unicorns or Little People. Sometimes, too, Adepts visited each other. So instead of random killing, they fashioned selective discouragements. The Black Adept had his puzzle-walls, so that few could find their way in or out of the labyrinth; the White Adept had her ice, and the Brown Adept her giant golems.

Probably a serious visitor would ignore the beckonings of the barkers and booths. Those who were ignorant or greedy would fall into the trap. This amulet was surely a potent discouragement, perhaps a lethal one. It was best left alone.

But Stile was ornery about things like this. He was curious—and he wanted to conquer the Red Adept, magic and all. If he couldn't handle one amulet, how could he handle the maker of amulets? So he sprang the trap. "Amulet, I invoke thee," he said, ready for anything—he hoped.

The disk shimmered and began to grow. Projections sprang from it, extending out and curving toward him. A metallic mouth formed in the center, with gleaming Halloween-pumpkin teeth. The projection arms sought to grasp him, while the mouth gaped hungrily.

Of course his armor and protective spell should be proof against this, but there was no sense taking a chance. "Send this spell straight to Hell," Stile sang, using the first of his prefabricated spells.

It worked. The expanding amulet vanished in a puff of smoke. His own magic remained operative here, as he had expected. He had now dipped his toe in the water

He nudged Neysa with his knees, and she walked on down the center aisle. They ignored the clamoring of the golems; there was nothing useful to be gained from them.

The domicile seemed much larger from the inside, but there was not extensive floor space. Soon they were at the far side, looking out the back door. Where was the Red Adept?

"On another floor," Stile muttered. "So do we play hide and seek—or do I summon her with magic?"

Neysa blew a note. Stile could understand some of her notes. "You're right," he agreed. "Use magic to locate her, quietly." He considered a moment. "Lead us to Red—where she has fled," he sang.

A speck of light appeared before them. Neysa stepped toward it, and it retreated, circled around them, and headed back down the aisle they had come along. They followed. It made a square turn and advanced on one of the booths.

"Tour the sensational house of horrors!" the proprietor-golem called.

The light moved into the horror house doorway. The aperture was narrow, too tight for Neysa's bulk. But they solved that readily enough; Stile dismounted, and she changed into girl-form in black denim skirt and white slippers. She was not going to let him meet the Red Adept alone.

Stile stepped into the aperture, Neysa close behind. He didn't like this, for already he was partially separated from Neysa, but it seemed his best course. Trace the Red Adept quickly to her lair-within-this-lair; maybe she was asleep. If so, he would wake her before finishing her. More likely she was at the very heart of her deadliest ambush, using herself as the bait he had to take. But he had to spring it—and he had to do it properly. Because it wasn't enough to kill the Adept; he had to isolate her, strip her of her power, and find out why she had murdered his other self. He had to know the rationale. Only when he was satisfied, could he wrap it up.

The difficult part would not be the killing of her. Not after what he had seen of Hulk's demise. The hard part would be satisfying himself about that rationale. Getting the complete truth. Or was he fooling himself? Stile had never, before this sequence of events that started with the anonymous campaigns against him in both frames, seriously contemplated becoming a murderer himself. But the things that he had learned—

It was dark inside the horror house. The passage folded back and forth in the fashion such things did; Stile had navigated many similar ones in the Game. Darkness did not bother him, per se. Neysa, too, could handle it, especially since her hearing was more acute than his.

The light led them on through the labyrinth. A spook popped up, eyes glowing evilly: a harmless show. But it made Stile think of another kind of danger: the noose, choking him, preventing him from singing a defensive spell. That was how his other self had died. That was typical of the way the Red Adept attacked. One of these spooks could be a noose, that he would not see in the dark until it dropped over his head. He needed a specific defense against it. "Turn me loose against a noose," he sang quietly.

A collar formed about his neck, a strong ring with sharp vertical ridges that would cut into any rope that tightened about it. Proof against a noose.

The maze-passage opened onto a narrow staircase leading up. Dim illumination came from each step, like phosphorescence, outlining its edge. A thoughtful aid from Proton practice, so children would not trip and fall. Stile stepped out on the first step—and as his weight came on it, it slid down to floor level, like a downward-moving escalator. He tried again, and again the stair countered him. There did not have to be anything magical about this; it could be mounted on rollers. It could not be climbed. Yet the glow of light he had conjured to show the way was moving blithely up the stairway; that was where the Red Adept was.

"I think I'll have to use magic again," Stile said. He oriented on the stair and sang: "All this stair, motion forswear." Then he put his foot on the lowest step again.

The step did not slide down. It buckled a bit, as if trying to move, but was fixed in place. Stile walked on up, each step writhing under his tread with increasing vigor, but none of the steps could slide down.

Then one step bit his foot. Stile looked down and discovered that the step had opened a toothy mouth and was masticating his boot. It was in fact a demon, compressed into step-form, and now it was resuming its natural shape. Stile had not had this sort of motion in mind when fashioning his spell, so it had not been covered.

Neysa exclaimed behind him. She, too, was being attacked. *All* the steps were demons—and Stile and Neysa were caught in the center. The trap had sprung at last.

Hastily Stile tried to formulate a spell—but this was hard to do with the distraction of his feet getting chewed. Neysa changed into firefly form and hovered safely out of reach of the demons. "Send this spell straight to Hell!" he sang.

Nothing significant happened. Of course not; he had already used that spell. He needed a variant. "Send this smell—ouch!" The teeth were beginning to penetrate, as the demons grew steadily stronger. "Put this spell—in a shell!" he sang desperately.

The shell formed, pretty and white and corrugated like the clamshell he had in his haste visualized, enclosing all the demons—and Stile and Neysa too. He had not helped himself at all.

Neysa came to the rescue. She shifted to unicorn-form. There was barely room for her on the stairway, but her hooves were to a certain extent proof against the teeth of the demons. She sucked in her barrel-belly somewhat, giving herself scant clearance, and blew a note of invitation to Stile.

Gratefully he vaulted back onto her back. Neysa did a dance, her four hooves smashing at the teeth below. Now it was the demons who exclaimed in pain; they did not like this at all.

Neysa moved on up until she reached the top landing, bursting through the shell he had made. Bits of the shell flew down to mix with the bits of teeth littering the stair.

Stile dismounted and stood looking back. "Something I don't quite understand here," he murmured as the demons at last achieved their full natural forms, but were unable to travel because of his spell. "If she has demons, why did she hide them there instead of sending them after me? Why did they come to life when they did, instead of when I first touched them? There's a key here—"

Neysa changed back to girl-form, which really was more comfortable in these narrow confines. "Amulets must be invoked," she reminded him. One thing about Neysa: she never chided him for the time he took to work things out his own way. Whatever he did, she helped. She was in many respects the ideal woman, though she was really a mare.

"Ah, yes." Amulets were quiescent until animated by the minor magic of a verbal command. So these step-demon-amulets had waited for that magic. But he had not invoked them. He had merely fixed them in place.

Unless it was not the words, but any magic directed at the amulet that accomplished the invoking. So when he cast his spell of stability—yes.

But this meant he would have to be careful how he used his magic here. No amulet could hurt him unless he invoked it—but he could accidentally invoke quite a few. Any that were within range when he made a spell.

In fact—suddenly a great deal was coming clear!—this could explain the whole business of this carnival-castle. If it was defended by amulets that had to be invoked by the intruders, these amulets would be useless unless something caused them to be activated. So—they were presented as prizes, that greedy people would naturally invoke. Because an amulet was just a bit of metal until it was invoked, worth little. When the golem-barkers claimed that "everybody wins" that was exactly what they meant. Or, more properly, everybody lost, since the amulets were attackers. Stile had acted as projected—and had he not been Adept himself, and on guard, he could have been in serious trouble from that first "prize."

But these steps had not been prizes. They were a defense against magic—and that, too, had been pretty effective. So he was really making progress because he was passing from the random traps to the serious ones. The steps, that would not remain firm without a spell that converted them to demons . . .

Could it be that the Red Adept herself could not invoke her amulets —or that they would attack her if she did? Like bombs that destroyed whoever set them off? So that the intruder had to be forced to bring his doom upon himself? If so, and if he resolutely refrained from invoking amulets either by word or by the practice of magic, he should have the advantage over—

Advantage? Magic was his prime weapon! If he couldn't use that, how could he prevail?

A very neat trap, to deprive him of his chief power! But unlike his alternate self, Stile had had a lifetime to develop his nonmagic skills. He could compete very well without magic. So if his refusal to invoke the hostile amulets limited him, it also limited his enemy, and he had the net advantage. This was a ploy by the Red Adept that was about to backfire.

"I think I have it straight," Stile told Neysa. "Any magic invokes the amulets—but they can't affect me if I don't invoke them. So we'll fight this out Proton-fashion. It may take some ingenuity to get past the hurdles, but it will be worth it."

Neysa snorted dubiously, but made no overt objection.

The passage narrowed as it wended its way into a hall of mirrors. Stile almost walked into the first one, as it was angled at forty-five degrees to make a right-angle turn look like straight-ahead. But Neysa, somehow more sensitive to this sort of thing than he, held him back momentarily, until he caught on. After that he was alert to the mirrors, and passed them safely.

Some were distorting reflectors, making him look huge-headed and huge-footed, like a goblin, and Neysa like a grotesque doll. Then the mirrors reversed, making both resemble blown-up balloons. Then—

Stile found himself falling. Intent on the mirror before him, he had not realized that one square of the floor was absent. A simple trick, that he had literally fallen for. He reacted in two ways, both bad: first, to grab for the sides, which were too slick to hold, and second to cry a spell: "Fly high!"

This stopped his fall and started his sailing upward through the air—but it also invoked the nearest amulets, which happened to be the mirrors. Now they themselves deformed, stretching like melting glass, reaching amoebalike pseudopods toward him. Mirrors were everywhere, including the floor and ceiling; Stile had to hover in the middle of the chamber to avoid their silicon embrace.

Neysa had gone to firefly-form, and was hovering beside him. But the ceiling mirrors were dangling gelatinous tentacles down toward him, making the chamber resemble a cave with translucent stalactites. Soon there would be no place to avoid them.

But the little glow of light showed the way out. They followed it down through the pit Stile had first fallen into and up again in another chamber whose amulets had not been invoked.

Stile was about to cancel his flying spell—but realized that would have taken another spell, which could start things going again. It was harder to stay clear of magic than he had thought! For now, it seemed best to remain flying; it was as good a mode as any.

They flew after the glow. It took them through a section of shifting floors—that had no effect on them now—and a forest of glistening spears that might be coated with poison, and a hall whose walls were on rollers, ready to close on whoever was unwary enough to trigger the mechanism by putting weight on the key panel of the floor. This was certainly a house of horrors, where it seemed only magic could prevail. But they had found a loophole; continuing magic did not trigger the amulets. Only the invoking of new magic did that. So they had a way through.

Abruptly they flew through a portal and entered a pleasant apartment set up in Proton Citizen style: murals on the walls, rugs on the floor, curtains on the windows, a food dispenser, holo-projector, and a couchbed. The technological devices would not operate in this frame. Unless they had been spelled to operate by magic. Stile was not sure what the limits were, to that sort of thing. Did a scientific device that worked exactly as it was supposed to, by the authority of magic, become a—

Then Stile realized: on the couch reclined the Red Adept.

Stile floated to a halt. Red was not concealing her sex now. She was wearing a slinky red gown that split down the sides to show her legs and down the front to evoke cleavage. Her hair was luxuriously red, and settled about her shoulders in a glossy cloud. All in all, she was a svelte, attractive woman of about his own age—and a full head taller than he. She was certainly the same one who had been responsible for Hulk's murder.

"Before we finish this, Blue," she said, "I want to know just one thing: why?"

Stile, ready for instant violence, was taken aback. "Thou, creature of evil, dost ask *me* why?"

"Normally Adepts leave each other alone. There is too much mischief when magic goes against magic. Why didst thou elect to violate that principle and foment so much trouble?"

"This is the very information I require from thee! What mischief did I ever do thee, that thou shouldst seek to murder me in two frames?"

"Play not the innocent with me, rogue Adept! Even now thou dost invade these my Demesnes, as thou didst always plan. I have heard it bruited about that thou dost consider thyself a man of integrity. At least essay some semblance of that quality now, and inform me of thy motive. I cannot else fathom it."

There was something odd here. Red acted as if *she* were the injured party, and seemed to mean it. Why should she lie, when her crimes were so apparent? Stile's certainty of the justice and necessity of this cause was shaken; he needed to resolve this incongruity, lest he always suffer doubt about the validity of his vengeance.

"Red Adept, thou knowest I am here to destroy thee. It is pointless to hide the truth longer. Art thou hopelessly insane, or didst thou have some motive for thy murders?"

"Motive!" she exclaimed. "Very well, Blue, since thou choosest to play this macabre game. I proffer thee this deal: I will answer truly as to my motive, if thou dost answer as to thine."

"Agreed," he said, still somewhat mystified. "I shall provide my motive before I slay thee. And if I am satisfied as to thy motive, I shall slay thee cleanly, without unnecessary torture. That is the most I can offer. I made mine oath to make an end of thee."

"Then here is my rationale," she said, as though discussing average weather. "The omens were opaque but disquieting, hinting at great mischief. The vamp-folk were restive, responding reluctantly to my directives. Indeed, one among them made petition to the Oracle, asking, 'How can we be rid of the yoke of Red?' And the Oracle answered, 'Bide for two months.' A vamp spy in fief to me reported that, so naturally I had to verify it personally. Indirect news from the Oracle can never be wholly trusted; there are too many interpretations. But there did seem to be a threat in two months concerning me—and that time, incidentally, is now nearly past. So I rode a flying amulet to the Oracle, and I asked it 'What is my fate two months hence?' and it replied 'Blue destroys Red.' Then I knew that I had to act. Never has the Oracle been known to be wrong, but I had no choice. I operate in both frames; I could be hurt in either. The Oracle said not that I would lose my life, only that I would be destroyed, which could mean many things. The only way to secure my position was to be rid of Blue before Blue took action against me. So I sent one of Brown's golems with a demon amulet to Blue, while meanwhile I sought out Blue's alternate self in

Proton too, lest Blue die yet also destroy me. But someone warned thee, and sent a robot to guard thee, and I was unable quite to close that loop. Now must I do it here, or suffer the fate the Oracle decreed for me. Sure it is, I mean to take thee with me, an the Oracle prove true. Thou art the cause of all my woe."

Still Stile was perplexed. "My motive is simple. Thou didst murder mine other self, rendered the Lady Blue bereft, attempted to slay me also in Proton and in Phaze, and slew my friend Hulk. For two murders I owe thee, and that debt shall be paid."

She grimaced. "Thou claimest that we should have had no quarrel, but for my actions against thee?"

"As far as I know," Stile said. "Mine other self, the Blue Adept, had no designs against thee as far as I know; his widow, now my wife, had no notion what enemy had murdered him, or why. As for me—I could never have crossed the curtain without the death of the Blue Adept, and I would not have left my profession as jockey had not my knees been lasered." He paused. "Why *were* my knees lasered, and not my head? Had I been killed then, thou wouldst have suffered no vengeance from me."

"The laser-machine I smuggled into the race was programmed against killing," she said disgustedly. "Citizens like not fatal accidents, so machines capable of dealing death must have a safety circuit. Also, it is easier to destroy the narrow tissues of the tendons than to kill a man by a single beam through the thickness of his skull. Thou probably wouldst not have died regardless; thy brain would have cooked a little, and no more. And the Citizens would have reacted to such a killing by lowering a stasis field over the entire raceway, trapping me. I had to injure thee first, subtly, while I escaped the scene, then kill thee privately when thou wert stripped of Citizen protection. Except that the robot balked me."

"The robot," Stile said. "Who sent the robot?"

"That I do not know," she admitted. "I thought thou knewest, that it was part of thy plan. Had I realized that thou didst have such protection, at the outset, then would I have planned that aspect more carefully. I thought the Blue Adept was the hard one to eliminate, rather than thee."

Not an unreasonable assumption! Of such trifling misjudgments were empires made and lost. "There remain mysteries, then," Stile said. "Someone knew of thy mission, and acted to protect me. Enemies we be, yet it behooves us both to learn who that person is, and why he or she elected to act anonymously. Hast thou some other enemy—perhaps one who could be identified as 'Blue' though no Adept? Thou must surely have mistaken the Oracle's reference, for I was innocent until that message generated a self-fulfilling prophecy. *Now* Blue will destroy Red, for there can be no forgiveness for thy crimes—but I would not be here now, if that Oracle had not set thee against me."

"A hidden enemy, pitting Red against Blue," she repeated. "Fool that I was, I queried not the identity of mine enemy, but only my two-month fate—and so the Oracle answered not what I thought it did. The Oracle betrayed me."

"I think so," Stile said. "Yet there must be a true enemy—to both thee and me. Let us make this further pact: that the one of us who survives this encounter shall seek that enemy, lest it pit other Adepts against each other similarly in future."

"Agreed!" she cried. "We two are in too deep; we must settle in blood. But there is vengeance yet remaining for us each."

"Could it be another Adept?" Stile asked. He was not letting down his guard, but he did not expect an attack until this was worked out. Enemies could, it seemed, have common interests. He had operated in ignorance of the forces that moved against him for so long that he was determined to discover whatever truth he could. "One who coveted thy power or mine?"

"Unlikely. Most Adepts cannot cross the curtain. I labored hard to cross myself, and paid a price others would not pay. I arranged to have mine other self dispatched, then I crossed over and took her place, hoping to be designated the heir to our mother the Citizen. But the wretch designated another, an adoptee, and I had to take tenure and practice for the Tourney."

Stile was appalled at her methodology, but concealed it. Her mode had always been to do unto others before they did unto her. That was why she had struck at the Blue Adept. Probably her Proton-self had been conspiring to do the same to Red. And, possibly, Red was now trying to put Stile offguard so she could gain an advantage. "Thou playest the Game?"

"That I do, excellently—and well I know thou art my most formidable opponent in the current Tourney."

"I know not of thee on any ladder."

"Never did I enter any ladder until the final moment. I practiced privately, in my Proton-Citizen mother's facilities."

"Even if the Oracle referred to my defeating thee in the Tourney, and thus destroying thy remaining chance for Citizenship," Stile said slowly, "I had three years tenure remaining, and would not have entered this year's Tourney but for thy intercession."

"The Oracle betrayed me on many levels, it seems," she said.

How right he had been been to analyze the nature of the Oracle's statements carefully! Yet the mischief of the Oracle was only in its confusing answers; it did not initiate things. Someone must have taken this into account. But what a devious plot this was! "Could anyone in Proton-frame seek revenge? A friend of thine other self, perhaps, avenging her demise?"

"She had no friends; she was like me. That was why she was disinherited. And no one knows she's gone; they think I'm her."

That had been a neat operation! "Someone in Phaze, then. Unable to attack an Adept here, so he interferes with thee there? Perhaps a vampire, able to cross the curtain in human guise—" Suddenly Stile wondered whether Neysa, now hovering behind him, would be able to cross the curtain in girl-form. Had she ever tried it? Unicorns did not exist in Proton, but girls did, and if there was no girl parallel to—

"Why send a robot to defend thee, then? Why not simply send it to attack me? That's one expensive robot thou hast; for that value, it would have been easy to send a competent execution squad after me. It is as likely that the attack was directed at thee, at thy magic self, with protection sent to thy Proton-self so that it could come after me."

Food for thought! "There is that," Stile agreed. "The Oracle must have known that despite thy attack on the Blue Adept, his alternate self would find thee. The key seems to lie in the unknown party who sent the robot. Find that party, and we may be on the trail of the true enemy. There does seem to be more afoot here than merely my convenience or thy demise; the plot be too convoluted to account for these."

"That's for sure! It isn't much, but it will have to do." She raised her right hand. "On thy mark, get set, go! End of truce." And she threw an object at him.

Stile dodged the object. It looked like a small knife, a stiletto—which it could be. But it was also an amulet, and he didn't want to invoke it. It stuck in the wall behind him and remained there, a bomb awaiting detonation.

Red threw another object. This one resembled a ball. When Stile dodged it, the thing bounced off the wall and settled to a stop near his feet. He was floating a few inches off the floor, since his flying spell remained in operation, so the ball did not touch him.

She threw a third. It was like a beanbag, dropping dead behind him. But none of them could hurt him as long as he didn't invoke them.

Then Red invoked one herself. She held the amulet in her hand, spoke to it, and dropped it on the floor. It formed into a hissing snake with glistening fangs. "Go for that man," she told it.

The snake crawled rapidly toward him. Rather than flying upward as Red might want, Stile drew his sword and decapitated the reptile.

Already she was activating another amulet—a bat. Stile did not want to kill it, because it might be a member of the vampire tribe who had given him safe lodging for the night. A captive of the cruel Adept, bound to do her bidding. Yet if it attacked him—

It did. Its little eyes gleamed insanely, and droplets of viscous saliva fell from its teeth. It could be rabid. There was no help for it; he had to use magic.

"Bat—scat!" he sang. The bat vanished.

But now the three inert amulets near him animated. One was turning into a demon resembling a goblin, growing larger each second. Another was hissing out some kind of greenish vapor, perhaps a toxic gas. The third was catching fire, becoming a veritable ball of flame.

Stile could not ignore any of these. For the moment he floated clear of all three—but all were expanding, and there was not any great clearance, and the ceiling was festooned with amulets. If he flew high, and banished them with his own spells, hell would break loose from that ceiling. Red had more amulets than Stile had immediately available spells, so this sequence could be disastrous. That was the disadvantage of bracing the Adept in her own Demesnes; her power was overwhelming here. It would be better to deal with the three activated threats some other way.

The Red Adept, smiling wickedly, was already throwing more amulets. Stile had either to act or to retreat—and to retreat would be tantamount to defeat, for he surely would have more trouble passing her defenses a second time. *Now* was the moment of decision.

Neysa, who had been hovering as the firefly, shifted to mare-form. She speared the demon on her horn, then shoved it into the green vapor. The demon screamed in agony, then expired. That was poison, all right! Neysa backed off, the demon still impaled on her horn. She did not dare touch that vapor with her nonmagical flesh. Meanwhile, the ball of fire blazed fiercely, and it was floating up toward Stile.

Stile had an inspiration. He began playing his harmonica. The music filled the room, summoning his magic—but he did not sing any spell. He just kept playing. He knew now that the music-magic could have a certain effect itself, without any specific spell, if he directed it with his mind. So he willed it to suppress other magic. If this had the force of new magic itself, the effect would be opposite, and he would be in twice as much trouble as before; but if it worked—

The fireball guttered and dimmed and sank, finding itself slowly stifled. The green vapor ceased its expansion and lost some of its color. None of the new amulets were activated. Phew! The gamble had paid off.

Neysa approached the vapor cautiously, seeing it become denatured. She used the dead demon on her horn as a crude broom to shove the vapor into the fire. The two joined instant battle, destroying each other. Stile broke off his music, and the battle intensified as its compass narrowed: the fire tried to burn up the vapor before the vapor could smother it. But the vapor was stronger; soon the fire was out.

Neysa mopped up the remaining vapor on the demon. Then with a strong motion of her head she hurled the demon directly at the Red Adept.

The woman was caught by surprise. She scrambled off her couch just before the sodden demon landed. Her collected amulets scattered across the floor like so much jewelry. The green vapor sank into the material of the couch, rendering it uninhabitable, while the demon lay on it as if asleep.

Stile had another inspiration. He had noticed that Red was careful which amulets she threw and which she kept. Obviously some amulets served the invoker, while others attacked the invoker. Benign and malign spells, as it were. If he could get hold of some of the benign amulets, he could use them against her. That should turn the tide.

But she was alert to the threat. She dived for the spilled collection, reaching it before Stile got there.

Stile reacted with a spot decision he hoped he would not regret. "Each spell farewell!" he sang, willing all the amulets within range out and away from the castle. Since he had been playing his harmonica, his magic should be strong enough to affect most of them.

The result was confusion. His act of magic invoked all the nearby amulets—but it also banished them. They tried to animate and depart simultaneously. Since there were many of them, their magic outmassed his. Thus they were coming to life faster than they were moving out.

Rapidly-forming things and creatures were scrambling for the exits. One resembled a squid, crawling on its tentacles. Another was like a yellow sponge, rolling along, leaving a damp trail that stank of putrefaction. Several were bats or other flying creatures. Some were colored clouds and some were blazes of light or darkness. One was a small flood of water that poured down through the crevices; another was a noisy string of exploding firecrackers. Stile had to keep dodging and ducking to stay clear of them. His incantation had also abated his flying spell; he was confined to the floor again, where he didn't really want to be. For one thing, the Red Adept was there, avoiding creatures with equal alacrity. At the moment she was trying to brush a swarm of tiny red spiders out of her hair. Both Red and Blue were now too busy to concentrate properly on each other.

Why was he fooling with all these incidental spells, when he could solve the whole thing by simply abolishing the Red Adept herself? Maybe he had held back at the notion of killing a human being, despite his oath. But he thought again of the way Hulk had died, and his resolve firmed. "Red be dead!" he sang.

There was a kind of soundless implosion and explosion centering on the woman. Her clothing burst into smoke. But in a moment she stood naked—and alive. "Fool!" she spat. "Knowest thou not that no Adept can be destroyed readily by magic alone? Only the unguarded and vulnerable succumb."

"But thy amulet killed the Blue Adept!" he protested.

"It never would have worked, had he been properly paranoid. He was a trusting fool. Even so, I am surprised he did not save himself; methinks he could have had he tried hard enough."

As Stile had saved himself from the same spell, by fighting hard enough. He should have known it could not be that easy to abolish her. Otherwise, he could simply have uttered his spell from the sanctity of the Blue Demesnes, and let Red die in her sleep. Many things were difficult against a person on guard. One stab with a knife could kill— but if that person were alert, the knife would never score, or would be turned against its wielder. Also, the White Adept had said his spells could not really hurt her. He had thought that mere bravado, but evidently it was not. Still, with the local amulets clearing out of the way, he had another option.

Stile drew his sword. "Then shall I slay thee without magic."

Quickly she snatched a similar weapon from its place on the wall. "Thinkest thou I am untrained in such arts? Look to thyself, midget!"

They engaged. She was proficient, and she had a longer reach than he. She was in superb physical condition, and had a fiery will to win. Yet this was the broadsword, Stile's preferred weapon. In this he was more than proficient; he was expert. He fenced with her, foiling her attacks readily, setting up for his proper opening. He could take her.

Red realized this. Suddenly she stepped back into an opening behind the couch and disappeared. Stile plunged after her. But a panel slammed across, blocking him off. He hacked at it with his sword, and wood splintered—but by the time he cleared it, the Red Adept was gone.

CHAPTER II

Trap

Now was the time to use his magic. "Trace her place!" he sang, and a new light appeared, leading the way into the passage. "Fret the threat," he added, to abate whatever nasty little surprises lurked along the passage. This wouldn't stop them all, but it should help. A little alertness should do the rest.

Stile charged into the passage, following the light. Then the light stopped. But the Red Adept wasn't there.

Baffled, Stile retraced his steps. He squinted at the glow from one side and the other.

"The curtain," Neysa said. She was back in girl-form.

Now he saw it—the faint shimmer of the curtain across the passage. What a neat device! No enemy confined to Phaze could follow her there.

He had little time if he was to catch her. "Neysa—I must go through. I—" He could not find the words to tell her what he had to: his gratefulness for her vital help and support right up to this moment; his continued need of it; but the impossibility of having it in Proton-frame. Unless she could cross in girl-form—but then she would be fixed in that form, unable to revert to natural status, and highly vulnerable in the unfamiliar world. No, he did not want her there! So he simply grabbed her and kissed her.

"Make a spell for me to follow," she said.

Good idea! In fact, why not put tracers on both himself and the Red Adept? If this device worked, he could check with Neysa every time he lost track of his enemy, and receive guidance. That would ensure his success. His magic was more versatile than Red's; he might not be able to abolish her by a direct spell, but he could at least track her. Maybe.

The present glow-tracker was designed to follow where Red had gone; it was balked by the curtain, so hovered there helplessly. Stile hesitated to step through at the same spot; no telling what Red had in store there for the unwary.

A small demon-animal blundered down the hall. One of the animated amulets, running late. Stile and Neysa flattened themselves against the wall and let it pass. The thing wandered on past the curtain, never perceiving it, seeking escape from the Red Demesnes. It turned the far corner—and there was an explosion.

"Methinks she set a trap for us," Stile murmured. Probably his counterspell would have protected him, but he could not be certain. Following too closely after the Red Adept was dangerous! "Take me to safe ground while I ponder new spells," he said.

Neysa took him by the hand and led him, while Stile concentrated fully on the task at hand. Soon they were standing on the ground outside the Red Castle, and he had what he needed.

But first one concern: "Neysa, I know thou dost not like magic applied to thee—"

She blew him a look of get-on-with-it, as he had known she would. She had once hated his practice of magic, but after she had accepted his status as the Blue Adept she had seemed to revel in the evidences of his power.

"Identify the one we scorn, by orienting with thy horn," Stile sang to her. Neysa, still in girl-form, turned her head with its tiny decoration-horn toward the south, obviously aware of the Red Adept. "And trace thine oath-friend without fail, by orienting with thy tail." She spun about, slapping her pert derriere with her hand as if stung by a fly. Her lack of a tail in this form was a problem. Then she converted to unicorn, and it worked perfectly.

"Let me step across the curtain, and do thou trace me," Stile said. "Just to be sure." This was consuming time while Red escaped, but if this operated the way he hoped, that wouldn't matter.

Stile spelled himself across, ran a hundred meters over the sand, and crossed back, gasping for the good air of Phaze. Neysa was right there, some three hundred feet from her starting point, her pretty black tail facing him. It worked!

"Good enough!" Stile exclaimed. "Thou canst now trace us both—even across the curtain. I will check with thee whenever I lose her. If she recrosses, we will have her. I shall see thee anon!" And he passed through the curtain again, setting off in the direction Neysa had pointed for the Red Adept. No traps out here!

But this was Proton, and outside a dome; quickly the rarefied and polluted air affected him. The Red Adept seemed to be within the dome—which of course was her Proton-home. Stile would have no safe access there!

He found the curtain and passed back through. Neysa was there, having paced him neatly. "I've got to organize for this better," he said. "It's certain *she's* organized! It's not safe to go after her in her Proton-home."

He paced in a circle for a moment. Even his two brief excursions into the atmosphere of Proton had depleted him. Inside the dome the air would be good—but she would have power he lacked. Her Citizen-mother might not like Red, but would act to protect the dome against intrusions by hostile serfs. "I need to smoke her out, then chase her down in neutral territory. I'd better enlist Sheen's help in the other frame. But I don't want to take mine eye off the prey. So I'll need to call her. Yes." He walked to the spot where he had seen a tube connection to the dome. There would be a communication screen at the transport terminal.

He spelled himself through. Certain spells were elementary; he didn't even have to rhyme. Just an originally phrased wish sufficed, for him or any eligible person. He had wasted a number of rhymes before catching on to this.

In a moment he was in the station. There was good air here! He called Sheen.

She appeared immediately on the screen. "So soon? Game is tomorrow—"

"Come to this address!" Stile said. "I may need help."

The screen went blank. Red had intercepted the call; he should have known she would not be sitting idle. He might have avoided her little traps along the way, by declining to pursue her directly, but she knew he would come for her here. He had made a tactical error. Stile dived for the curtain.

A nozzle started hissing out vapor as he moved. Some sort of gas, probably stun-gas. Red seemed to like that sort of thing. Had she known precisely where and when he would appear, she could have nailed him. As it was, it was a close call; he got a whiff of it as he crossed the curtain, and reeled as he emerged in Phaze. Neysa steadied him with her solid body, and in a moment his head cleared.

"Good thing I stayed close to the curtain," he said. "I'm going to have to create a distraction, so she won't spy me next time. The Oracle says Blue will destroy Red; I'll start the process now. Let me have my harmonica."

Neysa shifted to girl-form. She now wore a little knapsack over her dress—she manifested clothed or naked at will—in which she carried Stile's harmonica and other oddments. Stile had never quite fathomed how she was able to carry foreign objects on her human body that disappeared when she changed form, yet were not lost. She could change to firefly-form while carrying his harmonica, though it was far larger than the firefly, and have no trouble. He kept discovering new aspects of magic that made little sense in scientific terms—and of course magic did *not* make scientific sense. If it did, it wouldn't be magic. So he just had to accept that impossible things happened magically, and let it be.

He took the harmonica and played a brooding, powerful theme. For this job the Platinum Flute might have been better, but that had never really been his. He hoped Clef was getting along with the Mound Folk all right, and wondered whether the musician really could be the Foreordained they wanted, and if so, in what manner he was destined to save Phaze. Sometimes Stile had the feeling that he was just one thread in a complex skein, doing whatever it was he was fated to do, with no more free will than a robot had. So many seemingly coincidental things had happened to him—but of course he could be manufacturing a pattern for nothing. Clef might not be the Foreordained; the mountain might not tremble when he played the Flute. So Stile's encounter with him would have been no more than the randomness it appeared to be.

His magic was now intense. He concentrated on the Red Castle. "Make of this, the Red Demesnes, a holocaust, a wreck obscene."

They watched. The entire structure shimmered. Smoke appeared. The remaining creatures associated with it scrambled out as if fleeing something horrible. Behind them licked tongues of greenish flame. The smoke expanded, bursting out windows in its urgency to breathe free.

Gouts of it roiled up in burgeoning masses resembling the grotesque heads of goblins.

Then the explosions came. Whole walls shoved outward. Partitions sailed flaming in wide arcs, to crash and splinter in minor puffs of fire. Rockets of light shot out, and sprays of burning fog. All colors were represented, but gradually red predominated: this was the home of the Red Adept, after all.

"That should give her something to think about," Stile said. "I really don't like such destruction, but I must destroy the entire works of the Red Adept. I mean to leave no springboard for her to wreak her mischief again." He thought once more of Hulk and Bluette. Had she survived? He hoped so, though he did not want to deal with her directly. What grief Red had brought upon her, merely to try to trap him, Stile. Yes, Red had to be destroyed.

The pyrotechnics continued at the castle, reducing it steadily to the obscene wreck specified by the spell. Meanwhile, Stile stepped back across the curtain, checking to see whether Sheen had arrived. He avoided the gassed station, knowing that Sheen would check for him outside. He came back to Phaze for air, then checked Proton again.

On his third crossover, he spied her. She ran to him, opening her chest compartment to bring out an oxygen mask for him so that he could handle the Proton outdoor air. Quickly he explained the situation. "So what I have in mind is to interrupt the power to the dome-field generator," he concluded. "Can you get me a heavy-duty cutting laser?"

Sheen smiled. She opened her compartment again, and presented him with a compact Protonite-powered portable metal-cutting laser unit and a power-cable locator. "Bless you!" Stile exclaimed, kissing her, then replacing the mask.

They walked across the desert, searching out the cable. Stile was apprehensive that someone would think to look outside the dome, and would spot them, but that was a chance they had to take. Citizens and serfs of Proton were very much dome-oriented, and simply ignored the outer world as if it did not exist. That might help. This should not take long; the force-fields that formed the air-enclosing domes drew a lot of power. Such heavy-duty cables were easy to locate. Soon they found it.

Stile aimed the laser-cutter down and turned it on. The sand bubbled into glass as the beam plunged into it. It formed a glass-lined hole leading down to the shielded cable. Then it cut through the cable itself, casing and insulation and all, centimeter by centimeter.

There was a flash from the hole. Air puffed from the dome in decompression. The force-field was gone.

"I think she will be out presently," Stile said with grim satisfaction. "Now I have sworn to kill her, but I want to be fair about it. I don't want you to do the job for me. Since there are regulations against the execution of serfs by serfs, in the frame of Proton, I'll need to drag her into Phaze. Maybe we can bring her to trial there, and put her away ethically. So you leave it to me—but keep an eye on me, because I don't expect Red to pass up any advantage or ploy, legal or illegal, that she thinks will work. She'll try to keep our feud private, because if the Citizens investigate her connection to Hulk's murder she'll be exiled from Proton. So this is private between us—and I don't want to be the victim of cheating."

"Your logic is human," Sheen said wryly. "If I weren't programmed to love you—"

"Get on with it. Get a vehicle or something."

"Bluette's Employer has launched an investigation. Very soon he will obtain a transcript of Hulk's experience." She walked toward the shuttle tube. The gas would have no effect on her, and she would be able to use the communication screen to contact her friends.

So Bluette's Employer was taking action. Red was already getting into trouble on Proton. But that didn't change his own need to deal with her.

Stile ran on into the dome-area, now a shambles from the abrupt decompression. With luck he could catch Red during this initial period of confusion. All the occupants should be gasping, looking for long-neglected oxygen equipment, not paying attention to anything except their personal discomfort.

But as he entered, a vehicle charged out—a sand buggy with a bubbletop, painted red. She was taking off.

Stile ran for the cellar section. Maybe there would be another vehicle. He had to have some way to follow.

There were three other vehicles—all in flames. Red had made sure she would not be pursued.

Well, he had another avenue. Stile hurried to the curtain and stepped through, removed his abruptly inoperative oxygen mask, and looked about. Neysa was there, of course, pointing the way. "I'll spell myself to a spot ahead of her, then recross," Stile said.

But the unicorn nudged him, blowing a negative note. She wouldn't let him go alone.

"All right—we should stay together," Stile agreed. "But I don't want to wear thee out chasing after a Proton car. I'll have to enhance the trip by magic."

Neysa still was not keen on magic practiced on herself, but accepted this as she had the horn-tail enchantment, with equine grace. "We two proceed with smiles, Red's direction fifty miles." That made it possible to overshoot Red's position, and land ahead—which was where he wanted to be.

They moved rapidly across the landscape, as they had when leaving the White Demesnes. In a moment they were there. It was a pleasant enough glade east of the Red Demesnes. Neysa's directional horn pointed west; they had outdistanced the quarry.

"All I have to do now is cross back and intercept her, and—" Stile stopped. "Oh, no!"

For the curtain was nowhere near there.

"Well, we'll just have to pace her until she intersects the curtain," Stile said.

They paced her, moving near the limit of the unicorn's capacity. It was a strange business, because away from the curtain they could not see Red at all; only Neysa's horn pointed out her location in the parallel world. It was like following a ghost.

A ghost. Stile wondered whether there was a similar curtain-effect on other worlds. Back on Planet Earth, when the legends were being formed—could a curtain have accounted for the perception of ghosts? People or creatures that were and were not present? So much seeming fantasy could be accounted for, if—

Then Stile spied the curtain. "This is it!" he said. He tore off his clothes and set his mask back in place as he spelled himself through.

Red had evidently been heading for this intersection with the curtain. The car was slowing. It swerved almost immediately to charge him. Was she trying to drive him back across the curtain? Stile distrusted that, so he stayed put. The car had four choices; it could swerve to the left to catch him as he dodged that way, or to the right, or go straight ahead on the assumption he would risk standing still, or it could stop. He doubted it would stop. She intended to smash him if she could, and make him step back across the curtain otherwise.

She made a good effort. She feinted slightly to the left, then to the right, trying to provoke his motion. Stile stood still, and the car accelerated straight at him.

At the last moment, Stile leaped up. The car was sleek and low, more powerful than the dune buggy he had at first conjectured. It passed right under him. Sometimes it paid to be an acrobat. He landed neatly in the swirl of sand the vehicle had stirred up without even a twinge from his bad knees.

Now he saw another vehicle approaching. That would be Sheen, having obtained a car from her friends. No wonder Red was in a hurry; any delay, and the pursuit would catch up.

But why had Red wanted him out of Proton? If she planned to cross the curtain, why force him to cross too, when she knew he had the advantage in Phaze. That didn't seem to make much sense.

Stile got ornery when unsatisfied. Red was up to something, and wanted him out of the way so she could do whatever it was—and so he had better stay right on her. He hailed the second car, and sure enough, it was Sheen. She slowed to pick him up, then accelerated after the fleeing car.

Sheen's car was larger and faster; her friends had provided well. Stile did not inquire how they had produced it so quickly. Some computer entry had surely been made to account for its use. They zoomed over the sand at some hundred to hundred and ten kilometers per hour, a velocity even Neysa could not match. In Phaze, she would have to run sixty to seventy miles an hour cross-country. She might facilitate things by changing to firefly-form to cross the worst of it, but she would inevitably fall behind.

A huge plume of dust swirled up behind each car. Before long they had closed in on Red's vehicle, traveling a little to the side so as to be clear of her cometlike wake. That dust served to emphasize the barrenness that was Proton—a world that science had improved into desolation.

Red cut southeast, angling toward the Purple Mountain range. Where was she going?

"Do we have any way to bring her to a stop?" Stile asked. "I don't like getting too far ahead of Neysa, in case we have action on the other side of the curtain."

"Oh, yes. This is an attack vehicle. We can fire a disrupter to short out her electrical system."

"That's ideal!"

But now Red's car shot into a channel in the mountain. It slewed through a curvaceous pass and up a barren slope. Sheen's car followed, but could not get a direct shot at it. Now, directly behind, they suffered the full effect of the dust-wake. Red obviously was familiar with this region; Sheen and Stile were not.

On they skewed, wending through the mountain foothills and gullies at dangerously high velocity, never getting a clean shot. "I don't like this," Stile said. "She thinks in terms of traps. Things that wait quiescent until invoked. She'll have something set up here."

"I can call my friends on the car's band, and ask them to—"

"No! They have to maintain their anonymity. A 'clerical error' freed this car; that's as far as they can go. It's my job."

"No, they do not need to resort to supposed error. There are ways to—"

"No."

"I believe I have remarked on your defective living logic before."

"I believe so," Stile agreed.

"Do you have any assurance at all that you will survive this foolishness?"

"Yes, the Oracle says that I will sire a son by the Lady Blue, whom I just married, and since I have not yet—"

The car began to ride up the side of the channel. "You married the Lady Blue?"

Oops. He had forgotten the ramification that would have on this side of the curtain. "I did."

She brought the car back to level, but the course seemed none too steady. "Then it is over between us."

"No! Not over. Just—modified. We're still friends—"

"With a machine?"

"With a machine!" he shouted. "You're still a person! I still love you as a person!"

She accelerated, closing the gap that had opened between vehicles, though the dust obscured almost everything. "Yes, of course."

And Stile knew that whatever he had gained in Phaze had been at a necessary cost in Proton. The next stage in his inevitable alienation from Sheen had come to pass. They had known this would happen, but still it hurt. "I don't suppose you'd settle for an oath of friendship?" he asked with an attempt at lightness.

"I am less complicated than a living creature like Neysa. Oaths are not part of my programming."

Stile was spared the embarrassment of struggling further with this dialogue by their sudden encounter with Red's car. She had drawn it up in an emergency stop just around a turn in the channel and jettisoned herself with the emergency release. Now her stalled vehicle blocked the way at a narrow neck, impossible to avoid. Stile saw her running up the steep slope, getting clear of the inevitable crash. The trap had sprung.

Sheen's finger moved with mechanical speed and precision, touching a button on the dashboard. The ejection mechanism operated. Stile was hurled in his seat out the top of the car. A gravity diffuser clicked on, softening his fall, letting him float to the ground.

The moving car collided with the stationary one. Both exploded. A ball of flame encompassed the mass, and smoke billowed outward. Protonite didn't detonate like that; Red's vehicle must have been boobytrapped with explosives. It had been a trap, all right.

Then Stile realized he was alone. "Sheen!" he cried in anguish. "Why didn't you eject too?" But he knew why. She had wanted to be junked cleanly when she lost him; she had seen to it herself.

He knew there was nothing he could do for her. It was Red he had to go after. He shucked his carseat and charged across to intercept the Adept.

She had a hand weapon. She pointed it at him.

Stile dived, taking advantage of the irregularity of the ground. The laser beam seared the sand ahead of him, sending up a puff of acrid fumes. Then he crawled rapidly to the side, grabbed a small rock and hurled it at her. He did this without lifting his head or body; he could throw accurately by sound.

But she too had moved, crossing to get a shot from a better vantage.

Only Stile's continuing motion saved him from getting lasered. But now he too was armed—with a number of good throwing rocks. He could throw them rapidly and with excellent effect, when the target presented itself—if he did not become the target of the laser first.

They maneuvered. Watching, listening, stalking. Red was no amateur at this; she knew how to stay out of trouble—and she had the superior weapon. He would have to catch her by surprise, score with a rock before she could bring her laser to bear, and close for the finish. It was a challenge similar to certain Games, and he was good at this type of thing too. But she had the advantage of weapon and familiarity with the terrain.

Nevertheless, he outmaneuvered her, got in a good location, and prepared for attack. He wanted to knock her out with a score on the head, but his stones were too light for certainty. He was more likely to stun her momentarily or injure her, and have to take it to hand-to-hand combat. So be it. Too bad he had not brought his sword across the curtain. But he could do a lot of damage to a human body, bare-handed, in a very short time.

He watched for his moment, then made his move. He rose up and hurled his first stone. His aim was good; it glanced off her head, making her cry out. But her thick red hair had cushioned it somewhat; the stone only gashed her, not seriously.

Then she leaped—and disappeared.

The curtain! The curtain was here, and she had used it. In this respect, too, she had been better prepared than he. He charged across to it and willed himself after her.

Suddenly the mountain greened about him. He stood on verdant turf, with patches of purple flowers decorating the slopes. The air was warm and fragrant.

Red was still reeling from the blow of the stone. Blood colored her hand where she had touched the gash, and her hair was becoming matted. But when she saw him she raised the laser and fired at point-blank range.

Of course it didn't work. The curtain was not the demarcation of worlds, but of frames—modes of energy-application. She was getting rattled, making mistakes now.

Stile hurled another rock at her. *His* weapon was good in either frame!

But she dodged the rock and brought out an amulet. Where she had carried it he didn't know, since she was naked, as serfs had to be in the other frame. "Invoke!" she cried.

The amulet expanded into a ravening griffin—body of lion, head and wings of eagle. It oriented on Stile and leaped.

Stile spelled himself hastily back through the curtain.

He was in Proton again, inhaling oxygen through the mask. How bleak this frame was! Smoke still drifted up from the wrecked vehicles. Sheen had been there, suiciding rather than continue an animation that had become meaningless.

Stile concentrated a moment, then willed himself back through the curtain. "Creature fly up into sky!" he sang, and the griffin, just now turning on him after having overshot him, abruptly spread its wings and ascended. It was out of the fray.

Stile launched himself at Red, who held another amulet. She had a flesh-toned compartment belt, he saw now, that held her assorted weapons; from a distance she looked properly naked. He caught her hand and wrenched the amulet from her. "Invoke!" he cried.

The amulet grew into a flying octopus. It reached hungrily for Red. Stile had realized before that there were malign amulets that attacked the invoker, and benign ones that fought on the side of the invoker. Since Stile had stopped invoking amulets, Red was using these benign ones against him. He had just stolen one and turned it against her.

Now Red dived across the curtain, escaping the malice of her own creation. Stile went after her—and almost got clobbered by a rock. She was using his tactic against him, now.

He grappled with her. She was a foot taller than he—in this frame, about thirty centimeters—and had more mass. She was strong, too. A virtual Amazon, a naked tigress, eager to kill. Her claws gouged at his eyes, her knee rammed his groin. But Stile saw the smoking wreckage where Sheen had perished, and was a savage animal himself. Every person he held dear was being destroyed one way or another; he would destroy in turn. He was expert in several martial arts; he knew which nerves to pinch, the vulnerable spots to strike, the pressures that would disjoint which joints, on man or woman. He blocked her attack and concentrated on his own.

Again Red was overmatched, and realized it. She willed herself back into Phaze—and Stile went with her, not relenting. But here her amulets functioned; she invoked one, and it hissed out of a bottle, a genie, a giant gaseous man all head and arms. Quickly Stile recrossed the curtain.

He needed a spell to banish a genie. And another to take the offense. He might not be able to attack Red directly, but he could isolate her or—

Something was moving in the now almost-quiescent wreckage of the two vehicles. Stile's attention was instantly distracted from the battle. Could it be—?

With timorous hope he hurried over there. Yes—a shape was struggling to extricate itself! This was not the fantasy frame; it couldn't be a demon!

"Sheen?" he called tentatively.

"Stile?" her voice came back, oddly distorted.

"Sheen, you survived! I thought—"

"I am a machine. I am damaged, not yet defunct. Unfortunately."

"Let me help you—"

"Do not touch me. I am hot."

She was indeed. As she completed her extrication, he saw the extent of the damage. Most of her superficial flesh had been burned away. Her face was rubble. Her lovely skin and hair had been stripped to reveal scorched metal, with dangling shreds of substance. Wisps of smoke and steam drifted upward from her joints, and hot oil dripped from her chest cavity. She looked about as much like a corpse as a machine could. An animated corpse—a zombie.

"Sheen, we must get you to a repair shop! You—"

"Go after Red, Stile!" she cried weakly. "Do not let me distract you. I am of no further use to you. If I did not have this damned self-preservation circuit that cut in—"

Still, he was torn. Once before she had suffered injury on his behalf, making him realize how important she was to him. Her damage this time was surely worse, though she remained animated; all of her surface had been charred by the flame, and she was probably operating ineffectively on the last dregs of her Protonite charge. Yet it seemed that this merely reflected her emotional desolation, for she was programmed to love him—and never would be his lover again.

Perhaps it would be kinder simply to allow her to expire. She was close to the end now.

The thought triggered a savage reaction. "Vengeance I have sworn, but it shall not take precedence over friendship," Stile said. "Walk with me across the curtain. I can restore you, there."

The eyeless husk of a head oriented on him. The tattered remnant of her speaker spoke. "You must not. Red will trap you—"

"I think Red is already far from here. I have given her time enough to escape. She is less important than you."

"You must not give her time to set up—" Sheen's voice failed at last. Her power was fading. Even Protonite had finite limits.

"Walk, or I must carry you," Stile said sternly, knowing she would not allow him to harm himself by touching her burning surface.

She walked with decreasing stability. Charred fragments fell from her. Something rattled and buzzed inside. Finally she crashed forward, still smoking. But she was half across the curtain.

Stile located an unsmouldering spot on her torso and touched his finger to it and willed them both across the curtain. The grass appeared, the air freshened, and her body sizzled in the greater moisture. He removed his finger before it burned.

The Red Adept, as he had surmised, was gone. He had been besting her; she had wanted to escape all along, salvaging time and resources to meet him again in a situation more favorable to herself. He didn't like letting that happen, but he had been afraid that if he left Sheen too long it might not be possible to restore her—or that he himself would die or lose power and be unable to return to her. If he had let her perish in favor of his vengeance, he would have sacrificed much of what he valued: his own humanity. He might have gone on to establish his power and security as the Blue Adept—and become more like the other Adepts, corrupted by power, cynical and selfish to the point of worthlessness.

There was the sound of hooves. Neysa was catching up, fire snorting from her nostrils, bringing the harmonica just when he needed it. He would be able to use his magic to restore Sheen as he had before, and then would return her to Proton for reanimation. Maybe he could include a spell to make her feel better about the situation; that probably would not work, but it was at least worth a try. Then it would be time to set up for the next Round of the Tourney.

Round Eight brought him up against a young woman of the Age 22 ladder, a fair player whose skills he knew from prior experience. She was Tulip, a gardener-tender for a Citizen who favored ornamentals. She was as pretty as a flower herself, and not averse to using her sex-appeal to gain advantage. But Stile had no intention of prejudicing a likely victory by such dalliance. He put it into MENTAL, and so nullified her choice of NAKED. No body-contact sport this time! They wound up in WORD GAMES.

"Travel from FLESH to SPIRIT," the Game Computer said. "Time five minutes."

Stile and Tulip got to work. The challenge was to fashion a chain of words linked alternately by synonyms and homonyms, converting "Flesh" to "Spirit" by readily definable stages. Both length and time counted; within five minutes, the shortest viable chain would win. Beyond that time limit, the first person to establish *any* viable chain of any length would win. So it behooved them each to take up most of that five minutes to seek the shortest possible chain. To settle on a given chain too quickly would be to invite the opponent to come up with a shorter one within the time limit and win; to take too long beyond the time limit invited loss to a longer but sooner-announced chain. The point of decision could be tricky.

Flesh, Stile thought. Synonyms would be Body, Meat, Fatten—there would be others, but these sufficed. If he explored every single avenue, he would not complete any one chain in time. Selectivity—there was the key to this challenge.

Now try Meat, as the best prospect for homonyms: Meet as in proper, Meet as in a competitive event, Mete as in measure. Try the competition-event for synonyms: Contest, Race, Competition. Then Race, jumping to the homonym, meaning subspecies, and the synonym

Color, and on to Hue—was this leading to Spirit? Not rapidly. Better try an alternate, and return to this if necessary. His first job was to establish a viable chain, any chain, within five minutes. That would be an automatic win if Tulip failed to find one.

Of course, if they both came up with the same chain, the first to announce it would win. So if he found a good one, he should announce it regardless of time. But he was not worried about that; he had pretty good judgment on word-chains.

He glanced covertly at Tulip. She was chewing on her lip, making little gestures with her left hand, as though shaping a slippery sequence. Was she making faster progress? He didn't think so, as she really wasn't that bright, but it was possible. Then she caught him looking, and made a suggestive motion with her hip. He had to turn his eyes away, lest she bring his thoughts right back to Flesh and cost him the Game. That was what she was trying to do, the flirt. Maybe that was how she had gotten this far.

Try Meet as in proper. Synonym Fit, homonym Fit as in the contour of clothing. Yes, then Suit, and its homonym Suit as in satisfy, or the synonym Please.

Homonym Pleas, as in several requests. Synonym—was he returning to Fit, as in a fit plea for favor? If so, this was a dead-end, a waste of time, like a loop in the maze-puzzle he had fallen into in another Game with another woman. Too much time had passed; he couldn't afford that! This simple Game became confusingly tricky under the pressure of competition. No, no loop here; define it as a wish, as desire. And Desire as a homonym, meaning the urgency to possess, achieve, prevail—he certainly had that!—which was a possible synonym for team spirit—

Spirit! There it was! And jump to homonym Spirit as in Soul, and his chain was complete.

Unless that Desire link was faulty. Pleas—Desire—Spirit. The Computer might reject that as inexact. Better to work out a tighter chain.

But four minutes were passed. Not enough time to figure out a new chain. Tulip looked as if she were on the verge of completing her own chain. Stile decided to go with this one. "Chain!" he announced.

"Damn!" Tulip muttered.

"Present," the Computer said.

Stile presented it, trying to conceal his nervousness about the Desire connection. But the Computer did not challenge it; it was fairly liberal on the adaptations of language.

Still, Tulip had another minute to produce a shorter chain, or a better one of the same length. Stile waited nervously.

But she seemed to have given up. The time expired without her entry. Stile had won, more or less by default.

"It would have been different in NAKED/PHYSICAL," Tulip said tearfully. She had choked at the crisis-point in this Game, and now suffered the reaction.

"That's why I avoided it," Stile said, though he would have put it into some subcategory like foot-racing and probably beaten her anyway. She really hadn't lost much; with her appearance, she should do well enough in the wider human galaxy. But it had the mild distaste of an unjustified victory.

The separations between Rounds were diminishing. Round Nine was due in the afternoon of the same day. Stile planned to spend the interim devising strategy and spells to finish the Red Adept, and to get some rest and refreshment. He was also concerned about Sheen; he had restored her in Phaze, again, and she was now fully operational. But how could he abate the hurt of her nonliving heartbreak? His attempted spell had not taken effect. She seemed to have lost much of her will-to-animation, and there seemed to be no way he could restore it. She needed the one thing he could not give—his complete love. Maybe, he thought again, he should have let her perish, instead of languishing like this. He had promised a clean death to the Red Adept; could he do less for his friend?

There was a knock on the apartment door. That was unusual; visitors usually announced themselves on the screen. Sheen, alert to threats, went to see to it.

"Oh," she exclaimed, in a perfect representation of surprise. "You survived!"

"I must speak to—Stile," the visitor said.

Stile snapped alert. That was the Lady Blue's voice!

He went to the door. There she stood, a little disheveled but irremediably splendid. Bluette, of course; she had escaped the robot and sought out the name and description Hulk had given her. Smart woman!

Yet this was extremely awkward. "Come in," Stile said. "Of course I'll help you. I'm on the trail of the woman who killed Hulk now. But one thing you must know at the outset: I want nothing personal to do with you, after this."

Her brow furrowed prettily. "Nothing?"

"I am married to your alternate self, the Lady Blue of Phaze. You look exactly like her, Bluette—you *are* exactly like her—but she is the one I love. This is no reflection on your own merit, that I sincerely appreciate. And I know you have no personal interest in me. But—well, if she thought I was seeing you—"

She smiled, oddly at ease. "I understand."

"Stile," Sheen said, evidently making some sort of connection. "She is not—"

"Not my woman," he agreed. "Bluette, I never wanted to meet you.

It—it's too confusing. And I know, after all you went through—is that robot still on your trail? *That* we can take care of!"

"Stile, listen," Sheen said. "I just realized this is—"

"Look, don't make this any more difficult than it is!" Stile snapped. "Every second she stands here—this woman is so like the one I love—"

The woman smiled again. "Now thou dost know what *I* went through, Adept. The false so like the true."

"What?" Something didn't jibe here.

"Thee . . . Thee . . . Thee."

Stile froze. "Oh, no!"

"I am the Lady Blue," she said. "Fain would I listen longer to thy protestations of other love, my Lord, but I did cross the curtain to bring thee a vital message."

Never had Stile imagined the Lady Blue in this frame. "But that means—"

"That Bluette is dead," Sheen finished. "It has after all been several days. We should have heard from her before this, had she escaped."

"Oh, God," Stile said. "*That* I did not want. And now the two of you have met—that was never supposed to happen!" In the back of his mind, moving rapidly to the fore, was his concern that the robot might do some harm to her human rival. He had to get the Lady Blue out of here!

"Thou speakest as if there be some shame here," the Lady Blue said. "I have long known of thy most loyal friend in this frame, the lovely Lady Sheen, and I am glad to meet her at last." She turned to address Sheen directly. "I am oath-friend to Neysa. Can I be less to thee? If thou wouldst honor me with thy favor, O noblest of Ladies—"

And Sheen was crying. It was not the sort of reaction a robot was supposed to have, but it was natural to her. "Oh, Lady—oh, Lady!"

Then they were hugging each other, both crying, while Stile stood in mute confusion. Somehow it seemed that Sheen had been restored—yet the mechanism of it was beyond his immediate comprehension.

When the first flush of their emotion subsided, the Lady Blue delivered her message to Stile. "A bat-lad came to the Demesnes, sore tired from rapid flying. Methought he wanted healing, but it was news for thee he brought."

"Vodlevile's son!" Stile exclaimed. "I never thought he would—"

"He said the Red Adept had returned to the ruin of her Demesnes and fashioned a terrible spell, a basilisk-amulet that would destroy whatever it touched, being invoked by the very frame of Phaze. This she meant to give thee in the frame of Proton, and when thou didst bring it across the curtain—"

"Her final trap!" Stile said. "A basilisk—a creature whose very touch brings horrible death, whose gaze petrifies. But why does she think I would accept such an amulet from her?"

"The bat-lad said she made it resemble something thou couldst not refuse. Something thou wouldst immediately take across the curtain. That was all he knew; he dared not get within the range of her power. He thought it was news thou shouldst have—and I thought so too. So I tried to reach thee—and succeeded."

"It is as if Bluette gave her life, to make this message possible," Stile said. "And the vampire child—my trifling favor to him may be destined to save my life. Yet this is strange. Why should I need to be warned against doing what I would not have done anyway? Well I know the power of Red's amulets! In this frame they are harmless, but I would never carry one across to Phaze."

The Lady Blue spread her hands. "Mayhap we can piece it out, my Lord. I must return to the wolves in three hours, lest they worry. Meanwhile, may I view more of this wondrous frame of Proton? This may be mine only chance to visit it, and fain would I know as much of thy homeland as I can."

"I'll show you," Sheen said. "I'll show you everything!"

Sheen was a machine, but she would not deceive Stile. If she accompanied the Lady Blue, she would protect her. And if that was what she wanted, how could he deny it? Thus it was that Stile found himself alone with his puzzling piece of information, while the two Ladies toured the local domes.

Who would have thought that the source of Sheen's woe would also be the abatement of it? Yet from the moment the Lady Blue had addressed her as Lady Sheen—

What healing magic there was in a title! The Lady Blue, without apparent premeditation or design, had granted equal status to Sheen and proffered friendship and respect. Sheen had been instantly conquered. The issue of her machine-nature had not even been a consideration.

Stile returned to his deliberations. He decided that the Red Adept planned to gift him with the amulet through some third party, so that he would not suspect its nature. Perhaps a silver brooch for the Lady Blue; of course he would take that to her in Phaze. But now he had been warned; he would not take anything across the curtain.

In two hours the two returned, forever friends. "What a frame this is!" the Lady Blue exclaimed, exactly like the tourist she was. "Never since I saw the West Pole have I seen the like! Truly a magical world!"

The West Pole? "You mean in Phaze there really is a—?"

"Thou didst not know? I will take thee there, my love, once this business here is done."

"I will go there," Stile said. Fascinating, that an alien creature from some far galactic world had heard about the West Pole, while Stile who seemed to live almost on top of it had not. "Now—I love thee, Lady, and fain would have thee stay—but until the message of the Oracle has been appropriately interpreted, guaranteeing me the chance to stay with thee, I must remain apart from thee."

"I go, my Lord." She approached Stile and kissed him. Then Sheen accompanied her to the curtain. Stile continued his research for the next Round of the Tourney, fearing his company would only endanger the Lady Blue, here on Proton. She had acted with considerable courage, coming here and finding her way through the mysterious technological habitat of Proton. He loved her for that courage—but this was not her frame.

Round Nine carried a two-year tenure bonus for the loser, and the prospect of much more for the winner. Stile was now into "safe" territory; he could not be exiled from Proton after washing out of the Tourney. This removed some of the tension. It was now more important to deal with the Red Adept than to win any particular Game. Oh, to win the Tourney would be grand—but the odds remained against him, especially with one loss on his tally. But once he eliminated Red, the entire frame of Phaze was awaiting him, and a happy life with the Lady Blue. So he would play his best, but without the terrible urgency he had had before. That was just as well, since he had other things to do than research his prospective opponents. That research had become a chore.

His opponent this time was a female Citizen. Three Citizens in one Tourney—his luck was bad! But no—probably half the survivors of this level were Citizens, so this was no luck at all.

Still he did not intend to mess with her. He had the letters, so couldn't stop her from picking her specialty—probably MENTAL or ART. But he might interfere with her plan. He chose MACHINE.

It came up 4C, Machine-Assisted ART. Not his favorite, but probably not hers either. They could find themselves doing esthetic figures while parachuting from a simulated-airplane tower, or playing a concert on a Theremin, or doing sculpture by means of selective detonations of incendiary plastic. He would probably feel more at home in these pursuits than she.

But when they gridded through, she outmaneuvered him. They had to compete on the sewing machine, making intricate patterns and pictures on a cloth background. She as a Citizen had had a lot more exposure to cloth than he; indeed, she wore an elaborate dress-suit with borders stitched in gold and silver thread. But she had always had serfs to do her dressmaking for her. So unless she had practiced in this particular art—

Stile, of course, had practiced. He had spent years advancing his skills in every facet of the Game. He knew how to use a sewing machine. He was not expert, but he was adequate.

As it turned out, he was moderately better than the Citizen. It was an unspectacular Game, but the victory was his.

Now for the finish against Red. Sheen's friends, who as machines had great difficulty perceiving the semi-subjective curtain, had come up with a device to detect it. Sheen now carried this device. She would know, in much the way Neysa knew the whereabouts of Red, where the curtain was. That way Red would not again elude him by stepping across a fold of the curtain he did not know was near.

Stile prepared carefully. Sheen carried an assortment of small weapons and devices—a laser, a radiation grenade, a periscope, stun-gas capsules, and a folding steel broadsword. Her friends had provided a gyro-stabilized unicycle seating two, so she could ferry him rapidly about, anywhere where crowds would not find it too attention-fixing. A great deal went on in Proton that failed to attract the notice of Citizens, but there were limits. In fact, part of this deadly "game" would be the effort to force Red to call attention to herself, while Stile escaped it. His only crime was the sabotage of Red's dome; that had probably annoyed her Citizen-mother, but might be attributed to a repair-machine malfunction. Red would have known the truth, but not wanted to report it and have her own situation investigated. She, on the other hand, had been responsible for the deaths of Hulk and Bluette—oh, a double pain and guilt there!—and these were recorded on holo-tape. She would be banished instantly, even if she won more tenure through the Tourney, once those murders came to light.

Unless she won the Tourney and became a Citizen. Then she would be immune to all reprisal. Stile had to make sure she did not succeed in that.

They set out in quest of the enemy. Stile had a full day before Round Ten—and if that were not time enough, he would resume the chase after the Round. His oath of vengeance would soon be satisfied, one way or the other.

First he went to the curtain at a remote spot and stepped across. Neysa was there—with the Lady Blue.

Startled, Stile protested. "Lady, I wanted thee to be under the protection of the werewolves."

"A wolf went to the Oracle," she said. "And learned that his oath-friend Neysa was in dire peril from this mission. Since Neysa will not give over, the wolves and unicorns are now patrolling the curtain, ready to aid her if need be. Rather than interfere with this effort, I too patrol the curtain."

Stile was not wholly satisfied with this, but realized that this was another device of the animals to help him. They wanted to be in on the action. "I expect to deal with Red in Proton," he said. "My magic is stronger than hers, in Phaze, so she is unlikely to cross the curtain before settling with me. Do you all take care of yourselves."

"Indeed," the Lady agreed. "And thee of thyself, my love."

How glad he would be when this was over, and he could love her without restraint. But that had to wait, lest he void his Oracular guarantee.

Neysa pointed the direction of Red. Then Stile returned across the curtain to Sheen, drove a distance parallel to the curtain, recrossed, and got a new bearing. Now he was able to triangulate. It seemed Red was near the spot she had halted before, when he intercepted her and leaped over her car. She must have a secret place there.

They drove there, at moderate speed, so that Neysa could pace them easily. If Red tried to step across the curtain again, she would be in immediate trouble. Of course her amulets could destroy Neysa and the Lady Blue, so Stile still didn't want them participating in the conclusion. But they could certainly watch from a safe distance. At least they would know the outcome as soon as it happened. And perhaps the Lady's presence represented a guarantee for Neysa, since the Lady could not bear him any son if she died at this stage. The Lady should survive, and would hardly allow Neysa to perish in her stead.

The direction was east. They avoided individual domes and slowed as they neared the spot. It would have been fun, touring the desert like this, comparing the landscape to that of Phaze, if the mission weren't so serious. There were crevices and mounds and the depressions where lakes might once have been. Where they could be again, if the Citizens ever developed the interest to restore the planet instead of depleting it. But that was a hopeless notion; Citizens cared nothing for the external environment. In fact the very hostility of it gave them additional control over the system, for no serf could flee outside.

There was nothing where Red was supposed to be. Sand and low sand dunes covered the entire area.

They sought the nearest fold of the curtain. Stile crossed. Mare and Lady were there. Stile obtained two more pointings, narrowing down the location precisely. Red was not in Phaze, but in the equivalent spot in Proton was a bunker, a room set below the level of the ground. It was filled with amulets; obviously a cache of Red's.

But these amulets would not work in Proton. The curtain passed through this spot, but it was dark beyond it. Stile would have to cross it to find out what was there.

Neysa blew a negative note. Red was in the dark beyond. She could surely see Stile, since he was here in the lighted frame. She could be holding a sword high in both hands, waiting to decapitate the next person who crossed. A simple enough trap.

So Stile avoided it. He removed himself some distance, crossed to Proton, and explained the situation to Sheen.

"It is surely a trap," she agreed. "She means you to come to her. Don't chance it."

"I'm not going to let her escape! She'll never come out if I just leave her alone."

Sheen opened her chest compartment and brought out the laser-cutter. "Make a hole, drop in a stun-capsule."

That seemed appropriate. Stile started the laser. Quickly the hole formed. Soon it broke through the steel ceiling of the bunker. Then he dropped in the capsule. There was a hiss as it activated, and a puff of the gas emerged from the hole.

"I heard something in there fall," Sheen said. "Now for the periscope." She brought out the tiny device. It was electronic, and needed no solid extension into the hole; its perceptor-unit was mounted on an almost invisible thread that dangled down.

It showed the Red Adept sprawled naked on the floor of her miniature fortress, an old-fashioned dueling pistol in one hand, an amulet in the other. Had she planned to force the amulet on him at gun-point? If so, she had been amazingly naive.

"I am suspicious," Sheen said. "There is no entrance here in Proton; she uses Phaze as access. She expected you to enter that way. There could be an automatic weapon set to cover the curtain."

"Yes. We had better force entry from here."

They set about it. Sheen had several construction bombs, and used them to blast away the sand and rip open a man-sized aperture in the wall of the bunker. Then she entered first.

"No automatic weapon," she reported. "Still, I think you'd better stay clear."

"The hell with that," Stile said, walking down the sand embankment. "I can't have the ladies doing everything for me."

"But we can't be sure this was the extent of the trap! It's too simple; even I could have worked out something more sophisticated, and I have no creative imagination. At least let me search the premises—"

"You do that. I'll tie up Red." Because Stile found he could not kill her, this way. Now when she was unconscious. Funny how she had allowed herself to be gassed, when she must have heard the laser-drill.

He leaned over the body, not squatting, because of his knees. Sheen commenced her inspection of the bunker. Something nagged him, but he couldn't place it at the moment. "I won't touch that amulet, certainly!"

Abruptly, Red moved. Her head turned to cover him, and her pistol whipped up. She was not unconscious after all!

Stile hurled himself to the side as the gun went off. Had he been squatting, as a normal man would have done, he could have been fatally caught; the gun was aimed for the heart of a squatting man. As it was, the bullet slammed into his left thigh.

It was a bad hit. Now Stile exerted his trance-control. He let himself fall backward while clapping both hands to the wound. The pain was terrible, but he was bringing it under control, while he slowed the pulsing eruption of blood. He could not afford to lose consciousness; he could bleed to death rapidly. The major artery had been nicked or severed; he would need a surgeon's prompt attention.

Meanwhile Sheen launched herself at Red. Pistol and amulet flew wide and Red was hurled against the wall.

But then Red righted herself and hurled Sheen away, with inhuman strength. "This is a robot!" Sheen cried. "A machine, like me!"

"True," the Red-figure said. "I bear this message for Stile: make haste away, midget, for at this moment the Red Adept is launching an explosive drone vehicle tuned to the bullet in you. How much damage the drone does depends on your location when it catches you."

They heard the noise of machinery moving, some distance away. Something was rising from another bunker. "Run, Blue!" the robot continued. "Suffer the joys of the chase, rabbit. Message ends." And the robot went dead.

"Sheen!" Stile cried. "Carry me to the curtain. They can help me there, and the drone can't cross—"

"The amulet!" Sheen cried. *"It is the bullet!"*

"The bullet!" Stile echoed. Now the full nature of this terrible trap was apparent—and he had almost fallen into it despite the warning the Lady Blue had brought. If he crossed with the bullet in him, it would animate into the basilisk, and he would be dead before he could utter a spell. But if he did not cross—

Now they heard the released drone, cruising across the sand toward them. There could be enough explosive in that to blow up a mountain.

Sheen stooped to pick him up. She carried him to their unicycle and set him in the seat and flung the safety harness around him while Stile clung to consciousness and to his leaking thigh. Then she jumped in herself and started the motor.

The drone-car was rounding the bunker, picking up speed. Sheen accelerated away at right angles to its path. In moments they were traveling seventy kilometers an hour, leaving the drone behind. This was not a particularly fast velocity for travel on a surfaced road, but across the desert landscape it seemed horrendous. "We'll have to get the bullet out before we take you to a doctor!"

"How can we get it out without a doctor, especially if we can't stop?" Stile gritted. He was not in the most reasonable of moods at the moment, as he fought to keep blood and body consciousness together. The rough riding did not help.

"I'll summon one of my friends to intercept us."

"Summon one to blow up the drone!"

"They won't do that. It would attract attention to their nature. But one will help you and depart. Then the drone won't matter."

"Not to rush you," Stile said. "But I can only hold on here a short while. I'm in partial trance, suppressing the circulation to my leg, but the wound is bad and I'm slowly losing control. My last reserves are depleting."

"I know the experience," she said. "We'll stay right beside the curtain, so you can cross the moment we get the bullet out. Then you'll be able to use magic to—"

"I can't heal myself with magic."

"The Lady Blue will find some other Adept to help you, I'm sure. Perhaps the Lady Yellow—"

"Yellow is no lady! She is an old crone." But he was being querulous in his adversity. Yellow probably could help. He remembered how the Lady Blue had won her favor by starting the applause at the Adept pavilion. The Lady Blue was good at that sort of thing.

Sheen guided the unicycle to the curtain. Stile perceived it now with remarkable clarity. Had it intensified, or was his current state of pain-blocking trance responsible? It hardly mattered; he could see across as though it were an open window.

The unicycle was handily outdistancing the drone at the moment—but in Phaze Neysa was having trouble keeping up. The terrain was more varied there, with trees and streams and bushes obstructing her route. "Slow it, Sheen. Neysa is wearing herself out—and I'll need her there the moment I cross."

Sheen slowed—but then the drone gained, cutting into their lead. This was worrisome; that lead was their margin of safety. In addition the landscape was getting rougher. They were heading generally west, curving north with the curtain, back toward the major cluster of domes. On the prior trips they had maneuvered comfortably around the obstructions of boulder, dune, crevasse and ridges. But the curtain crossed these heedlessly, and this made the drive difficult. Sheen had to skid along awkward slopes, bounce through gullies, and plow through the mounds of sand. The drone suffered also—but it was squat and sturdy with broad wheel-treads, and it kept on going. The hazards of this chase would shake apart the unicycle before they stopped the three-wheeled pursuer.

Neysa, meanwhile, was encountering problems in Phaze. Stile watched her helplessly, as Sheen guided the unicycle along the curtain, now one side of it, now the other, causing his view to shift about considerably. The unicorn could handle the irregularities of the terrain, but there were also creatures in the way. She had to charge through a colony of demons, and in a moment they were in pursuit like so many drones, eager for unicorn flesh. Neysa could have escaped them easily if she had not been staying close to the curtain, and if she had not had to worry about the security of the Lady Blue. Or she could have turned to fight them, putting them to flight with a few well-placed skewers—had she not had to keep up with Stile's vehicle. Now the demons were popping up everywhere from crevices in the rock, cutting her off. They were grinning; they knew they had her.

Neysa blew a desperate summons on her horn. Stile could hear the sound, faintly, across the curtain, even as he rode in the same channel Neysa ran in, overlapping her without any tangible evidence of it. He could only actually see her when the curtain was between them so that he could look through it, and that happened only in snatches. The curtain was a funny thing, something he would have to explore more thoroughly some day and come to understand. Like the Oracle, it was a phenomenon that seemed to have no origin and no reasonable explanation; it merely existed, and was vital to communication between frames.

Again Neysa sounded. The call resounded across the wilderness. The demons growled in laughter; sound could not hurt them. Stile wished he could cross over and help out with a spell—but that notion was folly.

Then a ranging werewolf, summoned by the horn, spied them. He bayed. His oath-friend was being molested. This was why they were patrolling the curtain; they had been warned of this danger. Their numbers were thinly spread, because the convoluting curtain traversed a tremendous amount of territory, but their keen perceptions made up the difference.

The bays of other wolves responded. Suddenly they were converging, their sounds approaching at a gratifying rate. In moments they were in sight, and leaping with savage glee and righteous anger at the demons. One thing a werewolf lived for—a good fight in a good cause.

Now the predatory laughter of the demons turned to rage at this interference. But soon it turned to fear, as more and more members of the wolfpack closed upon them, lips peeling back in the terrifying grin of attack as they cut in between demons and unicorn.

Neysa ran on with a single note of gratitude, still carrying the Lady Blue, still pacing Stile. The sounds of the battle grew loud, then faded behind. The demons had chosen the wrong creature to attack, this time.

Sheen continued to guide the unicycle. She handled it with desperate skill. Now a dome lay across the curtain. They had to skirt it—but when they intercepted the curtain again, Neysa was there, thin jets of fire issuing from her nostrils. She was overheating, but would not allow herself to fall behind. The Lady Blue clung to her, riding with consummate skill, watching out for other hazards, guiding Neysa into the best channels with little advisory nudges, not directives. The unicorn had charge of the run, but the Lady was able to devote more attention to the route. Neysa was concentrating increasingly on the single effort of maintaining the pace; she no longer lifted her head to survey the course. She trusted the Lady's guidance. Stile knew exactly how it was; he had raced the marathon in times past, and had reached the stage where nothing existed except his agonizing pumping legs and the called course-corrections of friends. Vision itself became expendable.

Stile was struggling similarly now. His hands were soaking in blood. His consciousness was slowly slipping. He was panting with the sheer effort of keeping flesh and spirit together. Flesh and spirit—had that been a premonition, that Tourney Game? He had succeeded then—but this struggle was harder, with more dependent on it. Still the drone pursued.

He saw snatches of scenes across the curtain, hills, then a river. Neysa had to ford it, her hot hooves sending up gouts of steam as they touched the surface. Then it grew deeper and she swam, falling behind. She could not shift to firefly and wing across it, because of the Lady Blue. The unicycle was traversing the dry bed of that river.

Then the curtain curved down toward the south again, past the caves of the vampire bats, back across another arm of the river at the ruins of the Red Demesnes. Other unicorns were running with Neysa now, clearing the way. Bats were flying, spotting problems, getting them alleviated. A dragon was taking a snooze across the curtain; faced by six charging unicorns, it hastily vacated the spot. Little Folk of the daylight kind stood aside to let the strange procession pass. The grueling run went on.

All for him, Stile realized with pained gratitude. All the unicorns, werewolves and vampires extending themselves to their limits just to help him preserve his life. Neysa, running herself to destruction. Could it be worth it? Now her hooves were glowing red; her very flesh was burning up. She left a narrow trail of smoke where her passage had ignited the leaves of the forest floor.

Then a new vehicle closed with the unicycle. It locked on, matching the pace exactly. Machine arms reached out. Sensors traveled down Stile's body, touching his gory leg. Anesthetic came. Germicidal radiation flared. There, at the bouncing velocity of the chase, the robot surgeon removed the bullet, patched the torn artery, stitched and bound the wound while simultaneously injecting Stile with artificial blood matching his type. It retouched the nerve block on that leg so that no pain returned. Then the arms and tentacles retreated, the other vehicle disengaged, and went its own way with a parting warning: "Protect our interests!"—tell no one in Proton how he had been helped.

When Sheen's friends chose to render assistance, they did so with enormous precision and effect. Stile knew he could not go to any hospital now; he had sworn not to betray the self-willed machines, so he had to conceal the nature of this surgery from the Citizens. But that was easy enough to do; he no longer needed surgery.

Still, he was near to unconsciousness. His human reserves had been depleted, and neither surgery nor artificial blood could take the place of rest. Sheen steered the unicycle to the curtain. Neysa made a final desperate effort, caught up, and galloped directly along it. The unicycle slowed to accommodate her. The drone closed in rapidly.

Now unicorn and unicycle were superimposed, separated only by the frames. "Do it!" Sheen cried. Stile willed himself through.

He fell across Neysa's hot back. The Lady Blue flung her arms about him, clasping him, her healing hands already helping. He was safe at last!

Across the curtain, Sheen's vehicle accelerated. She had the bullet now. The drone followed her.

Stile, relieved, lost consciousness.

CHAPTER 12

Dance

Round Ten was getting into rarefied territory. Only twenty players remained, eighteen of whom had suffered one loss. The losers of this Round would receive a five-year tenure bonus.

Stile had another liability to go with his bad knee: the healing thigh. The bullet-amulet had lodged in his bone, holing the artery in passing. The damage, while bad, had not been as bad as it could have been, but he had depleted his vital resources and suffered near-shock. The Yellow Adept had provided a potion that multiplied his healing rate tenfold. Still, nature needed time to do the job, and he had been able to rest only ten hours before having to return for the next Game. He was not in ideal shape.

Sheen had led the drone back to Red's bunker and tossed the bullet in. That had been that. She reported, objectively, that it had been a most impressive explosion, that tore open a hidden second chamber where the Red Adept had hidden. Unfortunately Red had not been there at the time. She had vanished from the scene during the drone-chase, and Stile had not thought to get another fix on her during his brief recovery period.

As a result of all this assistance and attention by the several ladies of the frames, Stile was free of immediate threats to his welfare and was able to play the Game—but he really intended to stay out of the PHYS-ICAL column. Sheen was taking good care of him, but she could not help him there.

His opponent this time was a man of his own ladder: nicknamed Track, age 35, the running champion of the over-30 category, and no slouch at other track events. Stile could not have beaten him at running, jumping or swimming even when in shape, and in his present condition it would have been hopeless. But Track was comparatively weak in MENTAL and had virtually no artistic awareness. So this should be an easy win for Stile—if he kept it out of PHYSICAL and CHANCE.

As luck would have it, Stile got the letters. He could not eliminate the physical column.

He considered rapidly. NAKED was absolutely out. TOOL was not good; Track was excellent at bicycle racing, tennis, billiards and other such sports. MACHINE was a little better; Track was less secure in things like motorcycle racing, while Stile was expert, and his thigh would interfere only minimally. ANIMAL—Stile was of course the champion horse racer. He could no longer flex his knees properly for best effect, but his basic skill and experience and rapport with horses remained. This was his obvious choice.

Therefore he did not take it. He went for TOOL instead, hoping to catch Track sneaking in MENTAL. 2D would have put them into animal training, and Track had an excellent touch with the circus whip.

It didn't work. It came up 1B. Tool-Assisted Physical Games.

But Stile outmaneuvered him in the subgrid, and the Game came up Bubbles. This was about as delicate as a physical game could get.

They blew soap bubbles with straws, and wafted them across a measured alley. Scoring was by volume, distance and time—to get the greatest volume of bubble across a set distance within the time limit. Stile had the fine touch here; his bubbles were only of medium size, but were durable, while Track's larger ones tended to pop before completing the distance.

Stile won the Game. It had been his gridding skill, once more, that had done it. They shook hands and parted, and the crowd of spectators applauded. This had hardly been a bruising or dramatic Game, but the stakes were high enough to make it interesting to all. With five more years of tenure to look forward to, Track was not hurting badly.

Stile managed six more hours accelerated healing in Phaze before reporting for Round Eleven. Now the total number of contestants was down to eleven, with only one remaining undefeated. The losers of this Round would receive a prize of ten years tenure. One thousand and thirteen had now been eliminated from the Tourney.

Stile's opponent was another Citizen, this time a young one—about fifteen years old. Stile was pretty sure he could prevail on most games of skill, but still did not want to risk the physical ones. This time he had the numbers, so put it into MENTAL; there he would have no disadvantage.

The Citizen, surprisingly, selected ANIMAL. So it was 2D, the one Stile had played to avoid last time. When they gridded it down to the specific, they settled on Mixed-Species Communication.

Each player had three untrained animals: a dog, a cat and a rat. Each player had all-purpose animal snack treats and an electronic goad: positive and negative inducements. The task was to get all three animals to traverse a set maze without touching any of them. The first player to succeed would be the winner.

The animals, of course, were at first more interested in pursuing or escaping each other than in doing intellectual tricks. Careful management was required. The goad was adjustable, creating pain in the systems of whatever animal it was tuned to, ranging from mild to paralyzing; the cats learned very quickly not to attempt to pounce on the rats, because of the mysterious agony that balked them. But the inducement of a positive act was more difficult than the suppression of a negative one. The snacks could not be used to lead the animals; they could only be presented as rewards for proper behavior. This was confusing to the creatures.

There was a series of "locks" in which, by the design of the layout, two animals were necessarily together briefly before passing into the next stage of the maze; that was what really put it into the MENTAL column. The reward of food could lure the animals into the first lock, and the goad could prevent them from attacking one another, since they tended to repeat what had been positive before and avoid what had been negative. But the overall strategy of placement and movement and incentive was what counted in causing the animals to respond most positively.

Again, Stile's experience and rapport with animals paid off. He completed the course while the young Citizen was still trying to get his cat to join his growling dog in the lock, instead of pouncing on the rat. Had he brought the rat to the lock first he would have been more successful; either of the other animals would have joined it willingly. Stile had brought rat, cat and dog through in that order, and by the time they finished all three were eager to continue moving forward. The Round was Stile's.

Funny, how these important later Games seemed to be getting less consequential in actual play. Stile's first Round Game, Football, had been his toughest; this last one his easiest. But the luck of the grid often produced such anomalies.

Again he returned to Phaze for a night's healing and rest. It was the Yellow Adept who tended him, in her natural old-woman form. She had the potions and experience to handle it, and she represented no temptation for him to abridge his Oracular guarantee, as might have been the case with the Lady Blue.

Why was Yellow doing this? He was in hock to her again, and was getting to like her quite well as a person. It was as if his need brought out her better traits. Maybe she liked being part of a team, doing something worthwhile, earning the appreciation of others. It was something that few Adepts experienced.

The child Brown Adept also paid him a visit to wish him well. It seemed she felt a certain retroactive guilt for the use of a golem in the prior murder of Blue, and wanted to make an amend. Things were looking up.

But until he eliminated the Red Adept, nothing was settled. She must have been busy setting up new traps during the period of his convalescence. Then Sheen reported that Red had shown up in the Tourney. She too had made it to the rarefied Rounds, with a single loss. If both Red and Stile continued winning, they would eventually come up against each other there.

It happened in Round Twelve. This was hardly coincidence, at this point. Only six contestants remained, one of them undefeated. The bonus to the loser this time was twenty years tenure—a full extra term.

Stile's thigh was now almost healed, and he had the incentive of his oath of vengeance. He was ready for Red. This was one situation she could neither escape nor cheat. By beating her here he would not only deny her Citizenship, he would wash her out of the Tourney—and since her murders of Hulk and Bluette had now come to Citizen attention, thanks to the investigation of Bluette's Employer, she would be denied the bonus tenure. She would be exiled.

Stile pondered the meaning of this. He had wanted to kill her—yet his oath was merely to "make an end" of her. The Oracle had not predicted killing either; it had said Blue would destroy Red. Did exile constitute destruction? Perhaps. The Citizens had fairly sophisticated mechanisms to ensure that no exiled person ever returned to Proton; no worry about that aspect. At any rate, the more Stile contemplated the prospect of coldly killing another human being, the less he liked it. He simply was not a murderer. So if this was the meaning of oath and Oracle, he would accept it with a certain relief.

Red's position was different. She needed to kill Stile. Because if he washed out of the Tourney at this point, he would have twenty years as a tenure serf to plot her destruction, assuming she made it through to Citizenship. He would have his power base on Phaze, where he would be safe from her mischief, and could locate her and make forays at any time. The powers of Citizenship were great, but eventually he would get her, and they both knew it. So she needed more than victory in the Tourney.

There were ways to kill in the Games. The competitions were designed to be as safe as possible, but a person could have heart-failure during extraordinary physical exertion, or an anesthetic dart in pistol-dueling could be accidentally contaminated with a legal but lethal drug, or equipment could fail at a critical moment. She would surely try to arrange something like that, though it was prohibitively difficult under the experienced eye of the Game Computer. Stile, in turn, would try to prevent any such accident.

There was little delay at this stage, since the Game facilities now had to support only three Games. The audience for each would be huge. Stile was spared the unpleasantness of having to converse with his enemy. They proceeded immediately to the grid.

Again he got the letters. Every time he really wanted the numbers, it seemed, the luck of the draw denied them.

Stile did not try to play for Red's weaknesses; he was not sure what they were, in Game terms. He played for his own strength: TOOL. He liked animals and worked well with them, but he wanted no more android-animal football games or dog-cat-rat games.

It came up 4A. She had gone for ART.

4A? He had selected B!

But his entry was clear; he had miskeyed. Of all the times to do that! This carelessness could cost him the match!

No time for recrimination. The Naked Arts related to Singing, Dancing, Pantomime, Story Telling, Poetry, Humor and the like: presentations before an audience. Stile was good enough at these things; presumably Red was too. She had probably been gridding for Sculpture in 4B; had Stile played correctly, that might have come to pass. With her life's work in fashioning amulets, she was thoroughly experienced and skilled at that sort of thing. Of course he would not have let her have it; he would have thrown it into Music. Against Clef he had been in trouble; against Red he was pretty sure he would have a decisive advantage in Music. But of course she would not have let him have it, either, so they would have gridded into something else, that perhaps neither of them had much experience in, such as Writing. So he might be just as well off here. He was versed in most of the Naked Arts, and expert in some. If she wanted to match him in the generation of original free verse—

But the grid turned up Dance. All right—he could dance too. Did she have some particular specialty, like the classical minuet? He did not care to risk that; better to throw it into a more creative form, where his imagination could score. Not Ballet, because his thigh injury could interfere, but perhaps something loosely related.

In the end it came to a structured free-form dramatic dance, paradoxical as that seemed. It had a script with set maneuvers, rather like a ballet, but within that frame the particular interpretations were left to the players. It was costumed; in this case it was considered that apparel was useful for effect without being a necessary tool. NAKED did not refer to the absence of clothing, since all serfs lacked that; it simply meant that a particular Game could be played without any device like a bat or computer or hunting dog. So for this nakedness, the participants were clothed, for the benefit of the audience. Stile, recently acclimatized to the conventions of Phaze, was able to take this in stride. Red of course had no difficulty at all.

All in all, he felt reasonably well off.

The Computer established the script. It had a good file of diverse story lines, and varied them enough so that there were few repeats in a given year. This did mean that some play-themes were fairly unusual, but that was all part of the challenge.

This one was based on a tale of the Arabian Nights, "The Afreet's Beauty Contest." Citizens tended to favor Arabian motifs, associating with the presumed opulence of ninth- and twentieth-century Arabian culture.

Stile had the role of Kamar Al Zaman, a bachelor prince, and Red the part of Princess Budur, Moon of Moons. Stile was not familiar with this particular story, but had a foreboding about it. These Arabian tales could get pretty fundamental. This one was obviously a romance, and the last thing he could stomach was a Game of Love with the enemy he had sworn to destroy. But there was no clean way out, now.

The Computer was the Narrator and stage director. A panel of performing-arts critics was the judge. They would take into consideration the responses of the audience, but would not be bound by it; it was known that audiences often had illiterate tastes and colossal ignorances. Stile was satisfied with this; it meant his performance would be judged on its esthetic merits rather than on his size or Red's appearance.

Maybe, too, he was foolishly buoyed by his last experience with such a panel, in connection with the harmonica duet. He knew something like that was unlikely to happen again; still . . .

They took their places on the darkened stage. The light came on in Stile's part of the set. It was not a fancy Arabian setting, to his surprise, but a simple two-level pseudo-stone alcove.

"Kamar Al Zaman, an Arabian prince, has been confined to his chamber by his father the King because Kamar refuses to marry any of the eligible girls of the kingdom or any of the princesses of friendly neighboring kingdoms. The King wishes to ensure the continuance of the royal line, and harbors a nagging suspicion that his son may be gay, so has taken stringent measures to force the issue and to conceal the situation from the public. Prince Kamar submits to this humiliation with genteel grace. He now does the Dance of the Unbowed Head, symbolizing his determination to pursue his own life without regard for the dictates of royal fashion."

Suddenly Stile liked this tale better. He could dance this theme! He believed in individual freedom and initiative—especially since he had discovered what life was like in Phaze. Even when an infallible Oracle set a particular fate, man's ingenuity could shape it into something profitable. Stile was a prince, in the terms of Phaze—and a peasant, in the terms of Proton. His participation in the Tourney, he realized now, was motivated by his desire to change his status. To become a prince.

Stile danced. His archaic costume was designed for dancing rather than for any historical accuracy. He wore white tights that left his legs completely free, and a flowing blue cape that flung out when he whirled. It was fun; he developed his presentation as he did it, showing his defiance of the system, his fierce will-to-succeed. It was Stile against the frame of Proton, Stile against adversity. He spun and leaped and spread his arms in the universal gestures of defiance, and finally wound down to passivity; for he was after all Kamar, imprisoned in the tower like a common serf for daring to choose his own mode of living and loving. No one could appreciate his defiance, here in the dark tower, and this made it empty.

Except for the audience. It was large, and it applauded vigorously when Stile finished. Maybe this was a rote-response, clapping because that was what was supposed to be done; but Stile hoped that he had in fact conveyed a mood that all of them could understand. Serf against Citizen . . .

The experts on the panel made notes. It had been an excellent dance, thematically and technically, a good start on this role. Maybe this would work out.

Now Stile's portion of the stage darkened. Red's illuminated. Hers was a very feminine set, with draperies and mirrors and a plush feather bed made up on the elevated rear section of the stage, and her costume fit right in. "Meanwhile, the Princess Budur, Moon of Moons, renowned for her beauty and accomplishments in a kingdom on the far side of the civilized world, has experienced similar difficulties. She has refused all suitors, finding none she likes, because she prefers to marry for love rather than prestige or convenience. Her father is furious, and has confined her to quarters until she becomes more amenable to reason. Now, alone, she performs the Dance of Blighted Hope, symbolizing her unrequited longing for true romance."

Red danced. She wore a lovely red outfit with a full-circle skirt and gems that gleamed in the lights, huge rubies, making her motions sparkle. She was, Stile realized reluctantly, a beautiful woman, well-formed and healthy. Alone, her size was not apparent; she looked normal, as did Stile. Her life of malice had left her physically untouched.

She was an excellent dancer, too. Her symbolism came through exquisitely. She spun precisely, so that her skirt flared out and lifted to show perfectly proportioned legs. She made eloquent gestures of love-longing that could not be misinterpreted; her face became radiant with hope and pitiful with disappointment. Was she a consummate actress, or did she really feel these emotions? Stile felt uncomfortable doubt; it was awkward to maintain his hate at full intensity in the face of this exquisite presentation.

At last she collapsed in complete abandoned grief, ending the dance. Never had Hope appeared more Blighted, or a fate less deserved.

The audience burst into applause again. Stile realized with misgiving that Red had outdanced him. She had conveyed more emotion in a more effective manner than he had. He was going to have to work for this Round! To further enhance his discomfort, he realized now that if Red made it to Citizenship, she would have much greater resources than she had had before, and would not need to remain on the defensive; she could probably hire execution squads to dispatch him at her convenience. She did not have to kill him here; it was sufficient merely to defeat him. His situation was looking worse as hers looked better.

"Both Kamar and Budur strip and sleep, for it is night," the Narrator continued. Individual spotlights touched each person with gray light to suggest night, leaving the rest of the stage dark. Stile removed his costume and folded each piece carefully, as a prince would, then stretched out on the elevated back section of the stage, feigning sleep. There was surely more to this Dance than this! There had to be, for he was behind and needed to catch up.

"Now the tower in which Prince Kamar is confined happens to be haunted by a female afreet, a supernatural being of the tribes of the jinn," the Computer Narrator continued. Stile smiled inwardly; how little the Computer knew that in Phaze, the alternate aspect of this planet, there really were tribes of jinn! This story could be literal, there. In fact it could be literal *here*, since Phaze overlapped Proton. Maybe the afreets were playing this out in this same spot at this moment. If they had any way to perceive what was happening here, without the use of the curtain. . . .

"This afreetah has been away for the day, going about her business of stirring up assorted mischief in human affairs, but at night she returns. She passes through the stone wall and enters the tower chamber, as she is invisible and immaterial to whatever extent she chooses to be. Lo, she discovers the sleeping Prince Kamar on her bed and is amazed by the handsomeness of this mortal creature. She admires him for some time, deeply regretting that he is not her kind. Then she flies out to tell her friends of this wonder. She encounters a male afreet, who informs her that he has found a mortal who is prettier than hers. Affronted, she challenges him to a beauty contest. They will place the two mortals beside each other and compare them directly."

There was a pause while the lights dimmed. Stile had to get up and cross the stage and lie down beside Red on her feather bed; the afreets had carried him there, the sleeping prince. His foreboding increased again; he did not like this close a contact with her. But he had to follow the script; any minor deviation would penalize him, and a major deviation could disqualify him. He remained beside Red in play-sleep, wishing he could simply shove her off the planet. His healing bullet-wound began to bother him—psychological, but indicative.

"The two afreets study the unconscious mortals," the Narrator said. "Each person is a virtually perfect specimen, and the afreets are unable to determine a winner. Finally they hit upon a scheme—let the mortals themselves decide which one is the prettiest. The afreets will wake each in turn and watch their reactions; the one who is least affected will win, since that means the other must be less beautiful."

Like the harmonica contest, Stile thought; the one who changed least, won. He was becoming curious to know the outcome of this tale.

The light brightened so that the audience could see the scene clearly: prince and princess sleeping naked beside each other. This would have had no significance in ordinary Proton life, but after the elaborate costumes of the play the suggestion of intimacy was strong.

There was a moment of surprised silence. Then someone snickered. The mirth quickly spread across the hall.

Stile knew what it was. He had experienced this sort of thing all his life. The disparity in the size of the actors had become apparent, now that they were together. The Computer did not care, and the panel of experts could handle it, but the audience was less sophisticated. Which was why the audience had no vote in the determination of a winner, here.

"The Pygmy and the Amazon!" someone said, and the laughter swelled.

Abruptly a stasis field dropped over them all. No one could move, on stage or in the audience, though all could hear. Prolonged, such a field could cause bodily harm and eventually death; for a short period it was merely uncomfortable, since bodily functions slowed almost to a halt. "Single warning," the Computer said emotionlessly. "Further interference from the audience or inappropriate reactions will result in expulsion of the audience."

The stasis lifted. The audience was now completely sober. There would be laughter only if the script warranted it, and no extraneous remarks. The Game Computer was a strict taskmaster; even a few Citizens had been caught in the stasis. They, however, made no protest; it was to their interest to have discipline maintained.

Yet the damage had been done. The audience might be serious, now, but the dance had become ludicrous. Stile knew that behind those sober faces a maniacal laughter raged.

He fought to control his own embarrassment and anger. He drew on a device he had used long ago to reduce stage fright. He pictured each member of the audience as a gibbering demon, with huge pointed ears and a bare purple bottom, scratching at fleas, and whipping a barbed tail about to tickle his neighbors. He projected all the ludicrous feeling onto them, away from himself. *I am a man; you are ape-things. Stare, you foolish creatures. Stew in your own drool.*

It was not entirely effective, but it helped. He was aware of Red shivering with suppressed resentment beside him; this was striking her, too. To this extent, he agreed with her.

Yet there was nothing to do except continue. Pygmy and Amazon had a deadly serious Game to win. The panel of judges had not laughed, and that was the critical element of this scene. The play had to go on.

"Now the afreetah changes into a bug and bites Kamar on the leg," the Computer said. "He wakes—"

Stile slapped his leg as if stung, and sat up. This was a place where the audience might legitimately have chuckled, but there was not a single gibber.

"And spies the Princess Budur, Moon of Moons, lying next to him. Kamar is amazed; he does not realize that he is in a far-distant place, so intent is he on this marvel. He inspects her, touches her to make certain she is real and not a dream-figment, and tries to wake her. But she is under a spell of sleep and can not be roused."

Stile went through the motions, in no way betraying his preference for throttling her. She was his enemy; why couldn't she be the size of Neysa in girl-form, so that he did not look ridiculous in her company? Insult added to injury. Yet at the same time he had to concede again, inwardly, that she was a remarkable figure of a woman, one that in other circumstances—but no, he hated her, and could not forget that for an instant.

Then he saw the healing scar on her head, beneath her red hair, where his rock had gashed her. He did not know how to feel about that.

"It occurs to Kamar that this may be one of the ladies his father has in mind for him to marry, and that this is a device of his father's to persuade him. Kamar does not like such strategy, but Budur is so beautiful that he is instantly won over. He resolves to tell his father in the morning that he is now amenable to the union. Meanwhile, he will not soil his future wife by unfair attentions during her repose. Kamar lies down and sleeps again."

Almost, a peep escaped from a member of the audience. Would a virile young man actually do this, in the presence of a lovely and sleeping young woman? Well, perhaps one who had refrained from marrying any eligible girl because of the principle of pursuing his own life, and who would actually suffer confinement rather than permit his will to be abridged. It was, at least, an ideal for the audience to ponder. Stile felt, with a certain smugness, that he had faced just such a test in his contact with the Lady Blue, and had reacted similarly.

Stile lay down, relieved. It could have been much worse! The script could have required an act of love. That sort of thing was part of the Game—but it might have washed Stile out of the Tourney at this point. How could he do any such thing with his enemy, regardless of the script?

"The afreet now changes into a bug and bites the Princess Budur in a tender spot," the Computer continued. Stile almost thought it had been about to say that the Moon of Moons was bitten on a moon; he had to suppress a role-destroying mirth. In tight situations, even deadly serious ones, minor things could seem impossibly funny. "She wakes, while Kamar remains under the enchantment of sleep."

Red went through the sequence. "She is amazed to find this strange man in her bed. At first horrified, she soon realizes that his presence has occasioned her no harm. She is impressed; he is the handsomest man she has ever seen." Again, there was not even the hint of a snicker from the audience. "She concludes that her father has placed him here, to show her what she has been missing. She is moved; she calls herself a fool for her prior intransigence. Had she but known! *This* is the kind of man she could love! She attempts to rouse him, but he sleeps on." Stile thought Red might shake him violently, trying to do him surreptitious harm, but she was careful, adhering to the script. She knew she was ahead on scoring, and had merely to maintain that lead.

"Princess Budur, overcome by passion for the Prince, embraces him and kisses him, pleading for him to awaken." Even this directive Red got through, with Stile lying like a dead man. But as she brushed his left ear with her lips, she whispered: "I will torture thee for this indignity, foul man! Never has thy ilk touched me before in other than combat."

She hated men! Not just him, but all men! She was a true Amazon! That remark from the audience must have stung her fully as much as it stung him. For her, an act of love with a man was impossible; she considered the entire opposite sex to be "ilk."

Yet she was a consummate actress, as so many women seemed to be. No one in panel or audience had any hint of her true feeling. She had a will of iron; she would do whatever it took to win this Round. Stile could not even play upon her anger, for the script was too specific. He was officially sound asleep.

"Finally she gives up. She clasps him tightly and falls asleep." Red put her left arm across his chest, snuggled close, set her lips against his left ear again, and slowly, methodically bit into it.

Stile could not jump or scream, for that would have cost him more points. Yet her position was such that her foul was not evident to the panel. She seemed to be kissing his ear—a natural enough action for the role. Stile had to hold himself frozen while the pain burgeoned.

This was, indeed, going to be a rough Game.

"This display of emotion wins the wager for the afreetah, for Budur showed more passion for Kamar than he did for her. Satisfied, the afreets carry the Prince back to his own chamber and depart. They have no further interest in this matter."

The light dimmed, and Stile returned to his side of the stage. His ear felt huge and throbbing, but he could not touch it; Kamar had no reason to. He had to admit Red had outplayed him again; she had fouled him and gotten away with it.

This narrative was following the classic formula—boy meets girl, boy loses girl. Surely boy would regain girl before it was done. Stile hoped he would have opportunity to gain the lead. It depended on the kind of dancing and acting required. There wouldn't be more close contact with Red for a while, at least.

"When the Prince and Princess wake in the morning, they are chagrined to find themselves alone. Each has fallen in love with the other, but neither knows the identity of the nocturnal visitor. They perform the Dance of Separation, symbolizing the pain and confusion of this mysterious loss."

Stile and Red danced together, apart; she on her part of the stage, he on his. This was challenging; they had to coordinate their motions, esthetically, also keeping time to the music the Computer provided. As with the harmonica duet, this was a test of integration as well as of individual skill. Stile, good at this sort of thing, expected to score well. But he had another nasty surprise.

Red seized the lead, going into a series of deep knee bends. Stile was unable to match this, as she well knew. If he flexed his knees that far, he would not be able to maintain his balance, and the pain would be prohibitive. She might take a minor penalty for pushing the lead, but he was suffering a major penalty for not matching her style. Red was still gaining points.

So it continued. Red was an excellent dancer, and she had good knees, and she played her advantage unscrupulously well. She really knew how to make a man look awkward. She made quick shifts of figure that threw him out of phase, but it looked as though he was the one who had miskeyed, not her. She initiated a sequence, then terminated it just as he was emulating it, making him look stupid again. And this was all good tactic, in the Game; when the judges saw what she was doing, they would still be giving her points for her expertise in competition. Stile's own considerable skill was largely eroded by his incapacity. This Game was becoming hopeless.

They wended their way through the long quest as Kamar searched the civilized world for his love and she longed to receive news of him. Stile continued to lose headway. Members of the audience were quietly vacating their places, satisfied they knew the outcome. The Oracle, he realized, had not promised him victory; he had merely juggled the Lady Blue's Oracular message to ensure his survival after this encounter. He actually had no guarantee of victory. His oath was only an oath—vital to him, but no guarantee of success.

Yet there had seemed to be developing purpose in his life, however it had been shaped. The way his need to meet the Herd Stallion had brought him and the Lady Blue to the Little Folk, and he had acquired the Platinum Flute, lost to the Stallion anyway, and delivered the Flute to Clef. Maybe all coincidence, but if Clef was indeed the Foreordained, then it all had meaning. Stile had been a vital part of that chain—

A part that had ended with the relaying of the Flute. Stile could have become surplus thereafter, no longer needed in the chain. An actor whose part had terminated. So Purpose was no answer. He was on his own. And in trouble. What use to survive this Dance, if his loss of the Game meant only that Red would have him assassinated shortly after he sired a son for the Lady Blue?

At last the dance led Prince Kamar to Princess Budur. He had traversed the civilized world, taking many months, to locate her. It was to be an ecstatic reunion, as the lovers joined after a quest that had often seemed hopeless. Stile abhorred the notion, but forced himself to carry on. Whatever he might wish, this was evidently not to be the occasion for his destruction of Red.

There were of course various definitions of destruction. Perhaps Red was destined to win the Tourney, become a Citizen, and destroy herself in riotous living. Yet that would not be Stile's agency. Why would the Oracle warn her that Blue would destroy Red, if Blue was merely one hurdle among many to be overcome? The whole thing now suggested a misinterpretation of the Oracle's meaning. Where did that leave him?

With his oath of vengeance. It didn't matter what the Oracle predicted. Stile would make an end of Red, one way or another, and he would not return to love the Lady Blue until he did. If he could not accomplish this through the Game, it would have to be some other way. But it would be. Because he had sworn. Right now he would play this Round out as well as he could, taking his loss with the same dignity he had taken his wins.

Yet as the dance drew to its close, Stile's case looked hopeless. He was so far behind on points that only a figurative knockout punch could salvage a win—and this was no boxing match. How much he would have preferred that boxing match! Red was proceeding smoothly to a victory that wasn't even close.

Then Stile had an idea. Perhaps he could after all score a knockout! It would require discipline and courage that strained the limits of his ability, and there was no guarantee he could make it work. But from what he had learned of Red's nature, it was a chance. Stile nerved himself for it.

"And now at last the lovers are rejoined," the Narrator said. "They rush together. Kamar takes Budur in his arms—"

Stile had the wit to stand on the raised back portion of the stage, so that his height almost matched Red's. Now he concentrated, throwing himself into a half-trance. *Pretend she is the Lady Blue,* he told himself. *The woman you love.*

"Their expression of joy and love knows no bounds," the Narrator continued. This was the finale.

The Lady Blue. And, almost, he made himself believe. As they went into the concluding Dance of Rapture, Stile threw himself into the full feeling of it, conveying to audience, panel and Red herself the power of his passion. He was ready to act out the full spirit of this reunion, to love her in the dance exactly as Prince Kamar loved Princess Budur. Internal rebellion seethed in him, but he suppressed it savagely. He could destroy his enemy only by loving her.

And she—had to go along with it. How could a Princess, Moon of Moons, reunited with her lost love after extended and agonized separation, do other than accede to his natural desire? Stile had seized the lead—and what a lead it was!

Now the audience caught on. "Do it!" someone whispered audibly, and the Computer did not react. Because this was a legitimate conclusion of this script. What was a dance, except the rationalization and dramatization of human passion?

Red was not slow to catch on. Seeing herself trapped in this interpretation, anathema to her, she broke. Instead of kissing him, she bit him. Blood flowed from his lip. Instead of accepting his embrace, she struck him with fist and elbow.

The members of the judging panel began to react. Some violence was permissible in lovemaking; was this merely an interpretation?

"Beloved!" Stile whispered to her.

Red's face transformed to the semblance of a demon. She caught Stile's head in her hands and shoved it hard against the wall. Stile's consciousness exploded in sparkles, but he offered no resistance. Furious, she threw him to the floor. He feared a back injury, but he lay there. She started throttling him, so angry that tears were flowing from her eyes. "I'll kill thee! I'll kill thee!" she raged. "Thou dost dare love *me!* Death be the penalty!"

She was a creature of hate, and deserved her fate. Yet even as her maniacal fury lashed him, Stile felt regret, knowing that she, like himself, was a victim of circumstance, of fate. Some unknown party had set them both up for this cruel denouement.

As Stile sank into unconsciousness, he felt the stasis field take hold, and knew that he had won. His difficult, desperate ploy had been effective against the man-hater. Even for victory in the Tourney, even for Citizenship, even for life itself, she could not bring herself to submit to this ultimate humiliation—to be loved, even in pretense, by a man. Red had disqualified herself.

JUXTAPOSITION

CONTENTS

CHAPTER I

Clef

"I could give you some sleepfog," the lady robot said. "You stayed awake all night researching, and the Game is this afternoon. You have to rest."

"No drugs!" Stile snapped. "Better to be keyed up than fogged out."

"Better yet to be rational," she said.

He shook his head, looking at her. She was so exactly like a woman that most people never realized the truth. Not only could she function in all the ways of a living human female, she was extremely well formed. Her hair was a sun-bleached brown, shoulder length; her lips were full and slightly tinted, kissable; her eyes were green behind long lashes. She was the sort of creature rich, lonely men obtained to gratify their private passions more perfectly than any real woman would. But Stile knew her for what she was, and had no passion for her. "This is one time I wish I could just click off the way you can."

"I wish I were flesh," she said wistfully. She was programmed to love him and protect him and she was absolutely true to her program, as a machine had to be. "Come on—I'll put you to sleep." She took Stile's head in her lap and stroked his hair and hummed a lullaby.

Oddly enough, it worked. Her body was warm and soft, her touch gentle, and he had complete faith in her motive. Stile was close to few people and he tended to feel easier around machines. His tensions slipped away and his consciousness followed.

He found himself dreaming of the time several days before, when he had passed the Platinum Flute on to the musician Clef and guided the man across the curtain. In this dream he followed Clef's consciousness, not his own. Somehow this did not seem strange. Stile had felt an instant and deep camaraderie with the man when they played music together. Stile himself was highly skilled with a number of instruments, but Clef's musical ability amounted to genius. It had been impossible to remain aloof from a person who played that well.

Clef had never been to the frame of Phaze. He stared at the lush tufts of grass, the tremendous oaks and pines, and the unicorn awaiting them, as if he were seeing something strange.

"This is Neysa," Stile informed him, perceived in the dream as a different person. The unicorn was black, with white socks on the rear feet, and was as small for her species as Stile was for his. Clef towered over them both, and felt awkward. "She will carry thee to the Platinum Demesnes."

What affectation was this? Stile had spoken normally until this moment. "I don't even know how to ride!" Clef protested. "And that's a mythical creature!" He eyed the long spiraled horn, wishing he could touch it to verify that it was only tacked on to the horse. He had been told that this was a land of magic, but he found that hard to credit.

"Well, I could conjure thee there, but—"

"Absolutely not! Magic is—incredible. Wherever I have to go, I'll walk."

Stile shrugged. "That is thy business. But I must insist that Neysa accompany thee. Until thou dost reach the protection of the Little Folk, this region is not safe for thee."

"Why are you suddenly talking archaically?" Clef demanded.

"This is the tongue of this frame," Stile explained. "Now must I conjure clothing for thee."

"Clothing!" Clef exclaimed, daunted. "I am a serf, like you, forbidden to—I can not—"

Stile had recovered a package of clothing from a hiding place and was putting it on. "Here in Phaze, thou art a man. Trust me; clothe thyself." He paused, then said in a singsong voice: "An ye can, clothe this man."

Suddenly Clef was clothed like a Citizen of Proton, with silken trousers, shirt, jacket of light leather, and even shoes. He felt ludicrous and illicit. "If anyone sees me in this outrageous costume—" He squinted at Stile. "You were serious about magic! You conjured this!"

"Aye. Now must I conjure myself to the Blue Demesnes, to report to the Lady Blue. Neysa and the Flute will keep thee safe, methinks. Farewell, friend."

"Farewell," Chef responded weakly.

Stile sang another spell and vanished. Clef contemplated the vacated spot for a while, absorbing this new evidence of enchantment, then felt his own clothing. Blue trousers, golden shirt—what next? "And I'm supposed to travel with you," he said to the little unicorn. "With thee, I should perhaps say. Well, he did warn me there would be tribulations. I don't suppose you know the direction?"

Neysa blew a note through her horn that sounded like an affirmation rendered in harmonica music. Clef had not realized that the animal's horn was hollow, or that she would really comprehend his words. He followed her lead.

The scenery was lovely. To the near south was a range of purple-hued mountains, visible through gaps in the forest cover. The immediate land was hilly, covered with rich green turf. Exotic birds fluttered in the branches of the trees. No path was visible, but the unicorn picked out an easy passage unerringly.

"Are you—art thou able to play music on that horn?" Clef inquired facetiously, feeling a need to assert himself verbally if not physically.

For answer, Neysa played a merry little tune, as if on a well-handled harmonica. Clef, amazed, fell silent. He would have to watch what he said in this fantastic frame; more things were literal than he was inclined to believe.

The pace became swift, as Neysa moved up to her limit. Clef had always liked to walk, so was in no discomfort, but wondered just how far they were going. In Proton, with the limitation of the domes, it was never necessary to walk far before encountering mass transportation. Obviously there was no such limit here.

The animal perked up her small ears, listening for something. Clef knew that horses had good hearing, and presumed unicorns were the same. It occurred to him that a world of magic could have magical dangers and he had no notion how to cope with that sort of thing. Presumably this equine would protect him in much the way Stile's distaff robot protected him in Proton; still, Clef felt nervous.

Then, abruptly, the unicorn became a petite young woman, wearing a simple black dress and white slippers. She was small, even smaller than Stile, with lustrous black hair that reminded him of the mane or tail of—

Of course! This was, after all, the same creature, in a different shape. She even had a snub-horn in her forehead, and her shoes somehow resembled hooves, for their slipper tops tied into thick, sturdy soles.

"Stile is getting married," Neysa said. There was the suggestion of harmonica music in her voice. "I must go there. I will summon a werewolf to guide thee."

"A werewolf!" Clef exclaimed, horrified.

But the girl was a unicorn again. She blew a loud blast on her horn.

Faintly, there was an answering baying. Now Neysa played a brief harmonica tune. There was a responding yip, much closer. She changed back into the girl. Clef tried to ascertain how she did that, but it was too quick; she seemed simply to phase from one form to the other with no intermediate steps. Perhaps that was why this frame was called Phaze—people phased from one form to another, or from nudity to attire, or from place to place.

"A bitch is coming," Neysa said, startling Clef again; he had not expected such a term from so pert a miss. "Farewell." She changed into a firefly, flashed once, and zoomed away to the north. There seemed to be no conservation of mass here.

A dark shape charged toward him, low and furry, gleaming-eyed and toothed. Clef clutched the Platinum Flute—and suddenly it was a fine rapier. "Will wonders never cease!" he exclaimed. This was a weapon with which he was proficient. He stood awaiting the onslaught of the wolf with enhanced confidence, though he was by no means comfortable. He did not relish the idea of bloodshed, even in self-defense.

But the creature drew up short and metamorphosed into a woman. This one was older; in fact, she looked grandmotherly.

Clef was catching on to the system. "You—thou art the werewolf the unicorn summoned?"

"Aye. I am the werebitch available, man-creature. I have seen weddings enow; since my old wolf died I care not overmuch to see more. I will guide and guard thee to the Elven Demesnes. Put thou that blade away."

"It is not a blade; it is a rapier," Clef said somewhat primly. But now it was neither; it was the Flute again. "Neysa told you all that in one brief melody?"

"Aye. She was ever economical of speech. What is thy name, man?" the bitch inquired as she walked east.

"Clef, from the frame of Proton. And thine?"

"Serrilryan, of Kurrelgyre's Pack. We range mostly southeast of the Blue Demesnes, up to the Purple Mountains. Good hunting here."

"No doubt," Clef agreed dryly.

"If thou art walking all the way to the Platinum Demesnes, thou wilt have to step faster, Clef-man. We have forty miles to go."

"My legs are already tiring, Serrilryan."

"We can help that. Take thou a sniff of this." She held out a little bag of something.

Clef sniffed. The bag emitted a pungent aroma. "What is this?"

"Wolfsbane. For strength."

"Superstition," he muttered.

"Have ye noted how fast thy walk is now?"

Clef noticed, with surprise. "I'm almost running, but I don't feel winded at all!"

"Superstition," she said complacently.

Whatever it was, it enabled him to cover distance with wolflike endurance. Serrilryan shifted back to canine form to pace him.

Still, they were only partway there as night came on. The bitch became the woman again. "Do thou make a fire, Clef-man. I will hunt supper."

"But—" But she was already back to bitch-form and gone.

Clef gathered what dry wood he could find, along with bits of old moss and straw. He formed a neat tepee, but had no idea how to ignite it. Presumably the denizens of this frame could make fire with simple spells, or perhaps they borrowed fire-breathing dragons. Such resources were not available to him.

Then he had a notion. The Platinum Flute had become a rapier when he wanted a weapon; could it also become a fire maker?

He held it near the tepee. It had formed into a clublike rod. From the tip a fat spark jumped, igniting the mass. He had discovered how to use this thing! He was almost getting to like magic.

When the bitch returned with a freshly slain rabbit, the fire was ready. "Good enough," she said gruffly. She roasted the rabbit on a spit.

This type of meal was foreign to Clef, but he managed to get through it. Stile had warned him there would be privations. But he was ready to suffer anything to obtain legitimate possession of the Platinum Flute, the most remarkable instrument he could imagine. Only the Little Folk could grant that; it was their Flute.

Serrilryan showed him where there was a streamlet of fresh water, so that he could drink and wash. Out of deference to his human sensitivity, she refrained from lapping her own drink until he was sated.

Now all he had to worry about was the night. He really wasn't equipped to sleep in the wilderness. "Serrilryan, I realize that for your kind this is no problem, but I am not accustomed to sleeping outside. I am concerned about bugs and things." Though in fact no bugs had bothered him here; perhaps the reek of the wolfsbane kept them away. "Is there any domicile available?"

"Aye," she said. She brought out a small object. Apparently she could carry clothing and objects on her person even in wolf form, though none of it showed then.

Clef looked at the thing. It appeared to be a tiny doll's house. "I'm afraid I don't quite follow."

"It is an amulet," she explained. "Invoke it."

"Invoke it?" he asked blankly.

She nodded. "Set it down first, man."

He set it on the ground. "Uh, I invoke thee."

The amulet expanded. Clef stepped back, alarmed. The thing continued to grow. Soon it was the size of a doghouse, then a playhouse. Finally it stood complete: a small, neat, thatch-roofed log cabin.

"Well, I never!" Clef exclaimed. "A magic house!"

Serrilryan opened the door and entered. Clef followed, bemused. Inside was a wooden table with two chairs and a bed with a down quilt. Clef contemplated this with a certain misgiving, realizing that there were two of them and only one sleeping place. "Um—"

She phased back to canine form and curled herself up comfortably on the floor at the foot of the bed. That solved the problem. She needed no human props and would be there if anything sought to intrude during the night. Clef was getting to appreciate werewolves.

He accepted the bed gratefully, stripped away his ungainly clothing, lay down, and was soon asleep.

Stile's consciousness returned as Clef's faded. Sheen was still stroking his hair, as tireless as a machine. "I never realized he would have so much trouble," Stile murmured. He told her of his dream. "I'm used to Phaze now, but it was quite an adjustment at first. I forgot all about Clef, and I shouldn't have."

"Go back to sleep," she told him.

"That amulet—that would have been fashioned by the Red Adept. She's gone now, because of me. I really should see about finding a new Adept to make amulets; they are too useful to be allowed to disappear."

"I'm sure you will," Sheen said soothingly.

"Phaze needs amulets."

She picked up his head and hugged it against her bosom, smotheringly. "Stile, if you don't go to sleep voluntarily—"

He laughed. "You're a bitch."

"A female werewolf," she agreed. "We do take good care of wayward men."

They did indeed. Stile drifted back to his dream.

Next morning Serrilryan brought some excellent fruit she had foraged. They ate and prepared to resume the march. "This cabin—can it be compressed back into its token?" Clef asked.

"Nay. A spell functions but once," she said. "Leave it; others may use it after us, or the Blue Adept may dismantle it with a spell. Most likely the Little Folk will carry it to their mountain demesnes."

"Yes, of course it shouldn't be wasted," Clef agreed.

They walked. His legs were stiff from the prior day's swift walk. The wolfsbane had worn off, and Serrilryan did not offer more. It was dangerous to overuse such magic, she said. So they progressed slowly east, through forest and field, over hills and through deep gullies, around boulders and huge dense bushes. The rugged beauty of the natural landscape was such that it distracted him from his discomfort. What a special land this was!

In the course of the day he heard something to the east. Serrilryan's wolf ears perked. Then he observed a column of thick, colored smoke rising from the sky. There had been a bad explosion and fire somewhere.

"That is Blue fighting Red," the bitch said knowingly. "She killed him; now he is killing her."

"I realize this is a frame of magic," Clef said. "Even so, that does not seem to make an extraordinary amount of sense."

"Adept fighting Adept is bad business," she agreed.

"How could they take turns killing each other?"

"There are two selves of many people, one in each frame," she explained. "One self cannot meet the other. But when one dies, there is a vacuum and the other can cross the curtain. Blue now avenges the murder of his other self."

"Oh, I see," Clef said uncertainly. "And must I avenge the murderer of mine other self?"

"Mayhap. Where wast thou whelped?"

"On another planet," Clef said, surprised. "I signed for Proton serf tenure as a young man—"

"Then thy roots are not here. Thou hast no other self here, so art not barred from crossing."

"Oh. Fortunate for me, I suppose. Dost thou also have another self in Proton?"

"Nay. But if I crossed, I would be but a cur, unable to were-change. And the hunting is not good there."

Clef had to laugh agreement. "All too true! Proton, beyond the force-field domes, is a desert. Nothing but pollution."

"Aye," she agreed, wrinkling her nose. "When men overrun a planet, they destroy it."

"Yet Stile—the Blue Adept—he is also a serf in Proton, like me."

"He was whelped on Proton. His root is here."

Clef watched the dissipating grotesqueries of the cloud of smoke. "I'm glad I'm not his enemy!" He resumed slogging forward. At this rate he would be lucky to travel ten miles by dusk.

Actually, he realized, it might be just as well to take several days before reaching the Little Folk. There was a tremendous amount to learn about Phaze, and this slow trek was an excellent introduction. When he finally did arrive, he would have a much better comprehension of the frame, and know how to deport himself. With all the pitfalls of magic, he needed that experience.

The werebitch paced him uncomplainingly. She shifted from form to form at need, conversing when he wished, scouting when there was anything suspicious in the vicinity. Finally he asked her: "Is this not an imposition, Serrilryan, for thee, shepherding a novice while thy Pack is active elsewhere?"

"I am oath-friend to Neysa the unicorn," she replied. "For her would I shepherd a snow-demon halfway to Hell."

"Halfway?"

"At that point, the demon would melt." She smiled tolerantly. "Besides which, this is easy duty for an old bitch. I am sure the Blue Adept has excellent reasons to convey thee to the Mound Demesnes." She considered. "If I may inquire—?"

"I am to play the Platinum Flute for the Mound Folk, to enable them to ascertain whether I am the one they call the Foreordained. That is all I know—except that my life will have little purpose if I can not keep this ultimate instrument."

"The Foreordained!" she exclaimed. "Then is the end of Phaze near!"

"Why? I consider it to be a pretentious, perhaps nonsensical title, to say the least, and of course there is no certainty that I am the one they seek. I am merely a fine musician and a rather good fencer. What have I to do with the fate of a land of magic?"

"That is all I know," she admitted. "Be not affronted, Clef-man, if I hope thou art not he."

"I take no affront from thee, bitch." He had long since realized that the term he had considered to be uncomplimentary was the opposite here.

"Thou dost play the flute well?"

"Very well."

"Better than Blue?"

"Aye. But I decline to play this particular instrument in the frame of Phaze until I meet the Mound Folk. It is said the mountain may tremble if—"

"Aye, wait," she agreed. "No fool's errand, this."

"Dost thou like music, Serrilryan?"

"Some. Baying, belike, at full moon."

"Baying is not my specialty. I could whistle, though."

"That is music?" she asked, amused.

"It can be, properly executed. There are many types of whistles. Hand-whistling can resemble a woodwind."

"Aye, with magic."

"No magic, bitch. Like this." He rubbed his hands together, convoluted his long fingers into the appropriate configuration, and blew. A fine, clear pipe note emerged. He adjusted his fingers as if tuning the instrument and blew again, making a different pitch. Then he essayed a minor melody.

The sound was beautiful. Clef had not exaggerated when he claimed to play well; he was probably the finest and most versatile musician on the planet. His crude hands produced prettier music than that of most other people using fine instruments.

Serrilryan listened, entranced, phasing back and forth between her forms to appreciate it in each. "That is not magic?" she asked dubiously when he paused.

"I know no magic. This is straight physical dexterity."

"Never have I heard the like!" she exclaimed. "The Blue Adept played the Flute at the Unolympics, and methought that was the most perfect melody ever made. Now I think thou mightest eclipse it, as thou sayest. Canst thou do real whistling too?"

Clef smiled at her naïveté. He pursed his lips and whistled a few bars of classical music eloquently. She was delighted.

So they continued, and in the evening he serenaded her with a whistle concert. Squirrels and sparrows appeared in nearby trees, listening raptly. Clef had discovered how to relate to the wild creatures of this lovely wilderness world.

This night the werebitch had located a serviceable cave to sleep in. They piled straw and fern for a bed, and she curled up by the entrance. It was a good night. He was getting to like Phaze.

Stile woke again. "Time to go for the Game," he mumbled.

"Not yet. Sleep," Sheen said. She was a machine, indefatigable; she could sit up and hold him indefinitely and was ready to do so. She was his best and perhaps his only personal friend in this frame. She had saved his life on several occasions. He trusted her. He slept.

The third day Clef found his muscles acclimatizing, and he traveled better. But the world of Phaze seemed restless. There was the sound of horse or unicorn hooves pounding to the east, and a lone wolf passed nearby. "What's going on?"

"The Red Adept has sprung a trap on the Blue Adept," Serrilryan said, having somehow picked up this news from the pattern of baying and the musical notes of the distant unicorns. "He is badly injured but can not cross the curtain for magic healing, for that a basilisk has hold of him. It is very bad." Indeed, she was worried and, when she returned to bitch-form, her hackles were ruffled. Clef, too, was concerned; he had known Stile only a few hours before their parting, but liked him well and wished him well. There seemed to be nothing he could do, however.

But later the situation eased. "They have saved him," Serrilryan reported. "He is weak, but survives."

Clef's own tension abated. "I am exceedingly glad to hear that. He lent me the Platinum Flute, and for this marvelous instrument I would lay down my life. It was the sight of it that brought me here, though I am wary of the office it portends."

"Aye."

In the afternoon they heard a sudden clamor. Something was fluttering, squawking, and screeching. The sounds were hideous, in sharp contrast to the pleasure of the terrain.

Serrilryan's canine lip curled. Quickly she shifted to human form. "Beast birds! Needs must we hide."

But it was not to be. The creatures had winded them, and the pursuit was on. "Let not their filthy claws touch thee," the werebitch warned. "The scratches will fester into gangrene." She changed back to canine form and stood guarding him, teeth bared.

The horde burst upon them. They seemed to be large birds—but their faces were those of ferocious women. Clef's platinum rapier was in his hand, but he hesitated to use it against these part-human creatures. Harpies—that was what they were.

They gave him little opportunity to consider. Three of them flew at his head, discolored talons extended. "Kill! Kill!" they screamed. The smell was appalling.

Serrilryan leaped, her teeth catching the grimy underbelly of one bird. Greasy feathers fell out as the creature emitted a shriek of amazing ugliness. Immediately the other two pounced on the wolf, and two more swooped down from above.

Clef's misgivings were abruptly submerged by the need to act. There seemed to be no chance to reason or warn; he simply had to fight.

Clef was aware that the werewolf had taken his remark about his skill at fencing to be vanity, for he was hardly the warrior type. However, he had spoken the truth. The rapier danced before him. In seven seconds he skewered four harpies, while Serrilryan dropped the fifth, dead.

The remaining beast birds now developed some crude caution. They flapped and bustled, screeching epithets, but did not charge again. Their eyes were on the gleaming platinum weapon; they had suddenly learned respect.

Clef took a step toward them, and the foul creatures scattered, hurling back one-syllable words fully as filthy as their feathers. This threat had been abated.

"Thou art quite a hand with that instrument," Serrilryan remarked appreciatively. "Never saw I a sword stab so swiftly."

"I never used a rapier in anger before," Clef said, feeling weak and revolted now that the brief action was over. "But those horrible creatures—"

"Thou didst withhold thy strike until they clustered on me."

"Well, I couldn't let them—those claws—"

"Aye," she said, and went canine again.

But there was something wrong. She had tried to conceal it, but his reaction to this combat had made him more perceptive to physical condition. "Wait—thou hast been scratched!" Clef said. "Thy shoulder's bleeding!"

"Wounds are nothing to wolves," she said, phasing back. But it showed on her dame-form too, the blood now staining her shawl. "How much less, a mere scratch."

"But thou didst say—"

"Doubtless I exaggerated. Bleeding cleans it." She changed back again and ran ahead, terminating the dialogue.

Clef realized that she did not want sympathy for her injury, at least not from the likes of him. Probably it was unwolflike to acknowledge discomfort. Yet she *had* warned him about the poisonous nature of harpy scratches. He hoped nothing evil came of this.

That night they camped in a tree. Clef was now more accustomed to roughing it, and this was a hugely spreading yellow birch whose central nexus was almost like a house. Serrilryan curled up in bitch-form, and he curled up beside her, satisfied with the body warmth she radiated. The papery bark of the tree was slightly soft, and he was able to form a pillow of his bent arm. Yes, he was coming to like this life.

"This frame is just a little like Heaven," he remarked as sleep drew nigh. "My frame of Proton is more like Hell, outside the domes, where nothing grows."

"Mayhap it is Proton-frame I am destined for," she said, shifting just far enough to dame-form to speak, not bothering to uncurl.

"Proton? Dost thou plan to cross the curtain, despite thy loss of magic there?"

She growl-chuckled ruefully. "Figuratively, man-person. When I die, it will be the real Hell I will see."

"Hell? Thee? Surely thou wilt go to Heaven!" Clef did not believe in either region, but neither did he believe in magic.

"Surely would I wish to go to Heaven! There, belike, the Glory Hounds run free. But that is not the destiny of the likes of me. Many evils have I seen since I was a pup." She shifted back to canine and slept.

Clef thought about that, disturbed. He did not believe this was an immediate issue, but feared that she did. He was bothered by her growing morbidity and her low estimate of self-worth. She might have seen evil, but that did not make her evil herself; sometimes evil was impossible to escape. It had been that way with the harpies. Yet what could he do to ease her depression?

Troubled, he slept.

"Strange dream," Stile said. "Every time he sleeps, I wake. But I'm dreaming in minutes what he experienced in days."

"How much farther does he have to go?" Sheen asked.

"He should reach the Elven Demesnes in two more days."

"Then you sleep two more times. I want to learn how this ends." Her fingers stroked his eyes closed.

Serrilryan's wound was not healing. It was red and swollen, the blood refusing to coagulate properly. She limped now, when she thought he wasn't looking, and her pace was slower. She was suffering —and he couldn't comment for fear of embarrassing her.

The terrain became more hilly. Huge trees grew out of the slopes, some of their roots exposed by erosion. But the eager grass was covering every available patch of ground, and the turf was thick and spongy. Clef was soon breathless, ascending the steep, short slopes, drawing himself up by handholds on trees and branches and tangles of roots. Serrilryan followed, her familiarity with this region making up for her weakness, shifting back and forth between forms to take advantage of the best properties of each.

Something tugged at his hair. It was not the wind. Clef paused, fearing he had snagged it in a low branch—but there was no branch. He put his hand up, but there was nothing. Yet the tugging continued, and now there were little touches on his skin.

"Something's here!" he exclaimed, alarmed.

The bitch sniffed the air and cocked her ears. She phased into woman-form. "Whistle," she said.

Perplexed, he whistled. Oddly, the touchings abated. He whistled louder and with more intricacy, a medley of classical themes. He enhanced it with trills and double notes, warming to it, serenading the landscape.

Slowly, shapes appeared. They were little people, perching on branches and on the slope and even floating in air. All were listening raptly.

"Aye, the sidhe," Serrilryan said, pronouncing it *shee*. "The Faerie Folk. They cause no harm, just idle mischief."

Discovered, the sidhe moved into a dance, whirling in air. Their little lasses were, in the archaic measurement of this frame, about four feet tall, the lads not much larger. They moved prettily and smiled often—happy folk.

But when Clef stopped whistling, they faded out of sight again. "The sidhe associate not overmuch with other folk, but they do like music," the werebitch said. "I am destined to see them three times before I die."

"How many times hast thou seen them so far?"

"This is the third time."

"Then I should not have whistled them into sight!"

She made a gesture of unconcern. "I am old; my pace is slowing. My teeth are no longer sharp. The Pack will not let me live much longer anyway. Glad am I to have seen the lovely Faerie Folk once more."

"But this is barbaric! The other wolves have no right—"

"Question not the way of the Pack. I have killed others in my day; always I knew my turn would come. Perhaps it would have come ere now, had I not been fated to guide thee. I am content, Clef-man."

Clef shook his head, not commenting further. Obviously there was violence along with the beauty and literal magic of this frame.

They marched on. Later another phenomenon occurred—a kind of sweeping of an unbreeze through the forest, dissipation of nonexistent clouds in the sky, and revivification of things that had not been dead. A hidden tension had been released, an obligation expiated. "What is it?" Clef asked.

"The lifting of a geis," Serrilryan said.

"I don't think I understand."

"The abatement of an oath. It hung over the forest; now it is done."

"What oath is this?"

"The Blue Adept swore vengeance against the Red Adept."

"Um, yes. But I thought he was getting married. He is also moving through the Proton Tourney. Isn't this an awful lot of activity for such an occasion?"

"There is no comprehending the ways of Adepts."

That seemed to be the case. The Blue Adept evidently had a lot more power, and was involved in more great events, than Clef had realized. It was mildly odd that so small a man had so large an impact on this frame.

By nightfall they reached the marker for the Platinum Demesnes, indicated by a sign saying *PT 78*.

"The path within is treacherous," the werebitch said. "Morning is better for it."

"Yes, certainly." Clef wasn't sure, now that he was this close, that he really wanted to reach these mysterious elves. If he were not the Foreordained, they would take the Flute from him, for it belonged to them.

Serrilryan knew of an existing shelter nearby, and they spent the night there. "I want thee to know," he told her, "how I appreciate the trouble thou hast taken on my behalf. This all may come to naught, yet it has been worthwhile for me."

"I thank thee, man," she said. "It has been nice talking with thee and hearing thy music. Few among the Pack have time or courtesy for the old."

She did not look well at all. It was evident that pain was preventing her from relaxing. Clef whistled, filling the air with melody, and after a time the werewolf fell into a troubled slumber. Then Clef himself relaxed.

"I didn't know there were harpies in that vicinity," Stile said, waking. "I should have given him better protection. Though the way he used that rapier—" He shrugged and returned to sleep himself, secure in the robot's embrace.

In the morning Clef woke before the werebitch. She was breathing in pants and whining slightly in her sleep. The bad shoulder bulged with swelling, and the fur was falling out. This was obviously a severe infection. A good antibiotic could abate it—but this was Phaze, the frame of magic, where antibiotics were not available and perhaps would not work anyway.

Magic was what was needed—but he could not perform it. Unless the Flute—but no, he had resolved to play it only for the Mound Folk, because of the potential significance of the rendition. Still, maybe its magic could help. He laid the instrument against her body, as close to the wound as he could.

Her whining stopped; she was drawing comfort from the propinquity of this powerful talisman. Still, she was shivering, though the morning was warm. He had nothing with which to cover her.

Clef began to whistle again; it was all he could do. This time he selected a merry folk-song melody. He whistled it well; the joyous notes rippled through the forest, abolishing sadness. The bitch's shivering eased, and she slept peacefully at last.

For an hour he whistled. At last she turned and woke. She made a growl of displeasure at the lateness of the hour, but Clef wasn't fooled. She had needed that extra rest.

Breakfast was no problem. Squirrels and birds had dropped nuts and berries as offerings of appreciation, and these were excellent. This was a world that liked music. Clef, in return, was becoming quite fond of this world. Yet it had its dark side, as Serrilryan's ailment showed.

They mounted the steep trail leading to the Mound Demesnes. Clef was now better able to manage than the werewolf. He wished he could help her, but all he could do was slow his pace to make it easier for her, leaving her pride intact.

Deep in the mountains there was a thin, suspended bridge crossing a chasm. Clef eyed it dubiously, but Serrilryan proceeded on across without hesitation. She was so unsteady he hastened to follow, so he could catch her if she started to fall.

Halfway across he looked down. The chasm yawned so deep and dark it made him dizzy. He did not enjoy the sensation. Fortunately the chasm was narrow, and in moments they were across.

At last they came in sight of the Mound. Serrilryan sank in a heap before it, her waning energy exhausted. She had done her job; she had delivered him safely.

But there was no one about. The sun shone down brightly and the hills were alive with small animals and birds—but no people. Clef, worried about the werebitch, did not care to wait overlong for an introduction. "Ho there!" he called. "I must meet with the Platinum Mound Folk."

There was no answer. Could he have come to the wrong place? "Serrilryan—" he began.

She changed with difficulty to dame-form. She was haggard. "This is the place, music man. The Mound Folk go not abroad by day. At night thou wilt see them."

"I don't think thou canst last till night," he said. "We must have healing magic for thee now."

She smiled weakly. "It is too late for me, friend. My day is done. One favor only I beg of thee—"

"Anything!"

"I would hear the Flute ere I die. Canst thou play an epitaph for me?"

He knew this was final. She would expire within the hour. He was at the realm of the Little Folk; he was no longer obliged to wait. "Yes, it is time," he agreed. "There can be no better use for this instrument." He brought out the Flute.

He played an ancient folk song that he felt was appropriate to this occasion: *Tumbleweeds*. It was the sort of theme a wolf could appreciate, for it related to the freedom of the great outdoors, the rolling bushes called tumbleweeds drifting in the wind across the plain, cares of the world left behind. Perhaps it was not that way, here in Phaze, but he felt confident the mood would be conveyed.

From the first note, the Platinum Flute was potent, the finest instrument he had ever played, enhanced by its magic so that the sound transcended mere physics. The music rippled, it flowed, it resonated; it was as if he were flying, expanding, encompassing the landscape, the world, the universe, the split infinities that were the frames of science and magic. The sound loomed loud enough to embrace all of Phaze, yet delicate enough to touch the soul.

And the mountain trembled. The ground shook, but not in the manner of an earthquake. It started shuddering where he stood, and vibrated outward rhythmically, responding harmonically to the music of the Flute. The effect intensified as he continued playing. Leaves fluttered on trees, pine needles shook free of their moorings, and the green grass of the slopes stood up tall and quivered like the tines of tuning forks. The clear sky thickened; clouds formed from nothing, flinging outward in rainbow-hued bands. The sunlight dimmed; dusk coalesced.

Clef played on, caught in the wonder of the animation the Flute was working. Serrilryan's fur stood out from her body, charged. There was a canine smile on her face. Washes of color traversed her, causing her human and canine aspects to mingle aesthetically.

The ground shook harder. Branches fell from trees. The roof of the Mound collapsed. The mountains in the Purple range peeled off segments of themselves and settled substantially. Dust rose up. Animals fled. The sky swirled nearer and nearer.

The Little Folk appeared, for now there was no direct sunlight to shrivel them. They stood in the twisting dust and fog, staring while their Demesnes collapsed about them. Yet such was the power of the Flute that no one protested.

An avalanche formed and crashed downward. No one moved. The rocks and debris coursed past them all, avoiding living creatures, and advanced like a channeled flow of water until they piled up in a cairn over the body of Serrilryan, the werebitch. She had died smiling. She had heard the Platinum Flute; she had expired. Now she had been buried.

Still Clef played. From the cairn a spirit diffused, billowing and tenuous, extricating itself from the piled stones. Now it looked like a wolf, and now like a woman. It was Serrilryan's soul, departing her tired body at last.

Barb-tailed, horned, fire-clothed man-form devils hurried across the slope to intercept that soul. Suddenly Clef realized that the werebitch had spoken literally of Hell; she had known her spirit would be taken there. But Clef recoiled from the concept. She had helped him loyally and given her life in consequence. Surely that helped counterbalance whatever prior evils there might have been in her life. If he had any say at all in the matter, she would go to Heaven, where she wanted to be. He owed her that much. He shifted his playing, questing for the tune that would carry her soul upward.

Now from the troubled sky came wolves, flying without wings, their fur shining, so that they seemed possessed of light auras like halos. The music brought them down, showed them the way they might otherwise have missed, and marked the cairn.

The devils reached the soul first. But the angel-wolves arrived in time to balk the conveyance of the soul to Hell. A battle ensued, the half-visible humanoid figures against the half-visible canine figures. Spiritual fog and cloud and dust roiled along with the physical. But the theme of the Flute strengthened the wolves and weakened the devils. In a moment the angel-wolves wrested the bitch soul from the minions of Hell and loped up into the turbulent sky.

Yet before they departed entirely, the soul of Serrilryan paused. She looked back toward Clef, and he knew she was thanking him for a gift as unexpected as it was gratifying. Her sinful human component had been juxtaposed with her pure wolf component in death, nearer perfection than they had been in life, and the forces of Heaven had prevailed. She sent to earth one glance of purest appreciation that made the air about Clef sparkle. Then she turned again and loped on toward Heaven with her divine companions.

The Purple Mountains continued to shake and settle. Dragons flew up from the southern marches; creatures stirred all over Phaze. But Clef would not stop playing until the bitch was safely ensconced in Heaven. He would permit no loophole, no reversal.

Stile woke in alarm. The building was shaking!

"There seems to be an earthquake in progress," Sheen said. "The Purple Mountain range is settling."

"That's no natural phenomenon! That's the Foreordained!" Stile cried. "Now I realize that Clef is indeed the ultimate magician, with power to level mountains and delicacy to send souls to Heaven."

"The Foreordained," Sheen repeated. "Clef is the one destined to save Phaze?"

"He played the Platinum Flute, and the mountain trembled and tumbled. That's the signal. I saw it in my dream—and now I know it's true. My vision has caught up to the present and affirmed it."

Sheen checked the newsscreen. "There has certainly been a shake-up in Proton. Power has been disrupted all along the southern range. Mine shafts have collapsed. If that's the result of one melody on one flute, it means magic is spilling over into the science frame."

"So it seems. I'm sure my encounter with Clef was not coincidental. It was—foreordained. And my dream of his progress—there has to be some reason for that. I suspect he and I are destined to meet again."

"You could never stay out of mischief," she agreed. "Now it's time to get ready for your Tourney match."

"Did anyone ever tell you you are inhumanly practical? The end of the split infinity may be in the offing, and you pack me off to a Game."

"Your match is foreordained too," she said complacently.

CHAPTER 2

Backgammon

It was Round Thirteen of the annual Tourney. Only three players remained, two with one loss each. These two had to play each other; the loser would be eliminated from the Tourney, and the winner would meet the single undefeated player.

The two who played were as different as seemed possible. One was a huge, fat, middle-aged man in voluminous and princely robes inset with glittering gems. The other was a tiny naked man, muscular and fit, in his thirties.

"Ah, Stile," the clothed man said affably. "I was hoping to encounter you."

"You know of me, sir?"

"I always research my prospective opponents, serf. You have been extremely busy recently. You have been chasing around the landscape, crashing vehicles, and disappearing between Rounds."

Stile was noncommittal. "My time between Rounds is my own, sir."

"Except for what that girl robot demands. Is it fun making time with a sexy machine?"

Stile knew the Citizen was trying to rattle him, to get him tangled up emotionally so that he could not concentrate properly on the Game. It was a familiar technique. Stile could not return the favor because all Citizens were virtually anonymous to serfs, and in any event a serf could not treat a Citizen with disrespect. So Stile would have to take it —and play his best regardless. He was experienced at this sort of thing; the Citizen would probably rattle himself before he got to Stile.

It was time for the grid. Each man stood on one side of the unit, looking at the screen. There were sixteen boxes facing Stile, labeled across the top: 1. PHYSICAL 2. MENTAL 3. CHANCE 4. ARTS, and down the side: A. NAKED B. TOOL C. MACHINE D. ANIMAL. Stile's panel was lighted by the letters.

"That was a very neat stunt you worked, last Round," the Citizen remarked. "Making that Amazon throw away her win. Of course you know you won't be able to trick *me* that way."

"Of course not, sir." Stile touched the TOOL indication. That was his line of greatest strength.

The subgrid showed: 3B, Tool-Assisted Chance. Stile groaned inwardly. The CHANCE column was the bane of good players. It was difficult to make his skill count here.

"You don't like it, huh?" the Citizen taunted. "Figure it to come up another slot machine, wash you out painlessly, eh?"

This man really had researched Stile's prior Games of the Tourney. The lone Game Stile had lost had been just that way. "I am not partial to it, sir." As long as he handled the needling without heat, he was gaining.

"Well, I'm partial to it! Know why? Because I'm lucky. Try me on poker, Stile; I'll come up with a full house and tromp you. Try me on blackjack; I'm all twenty-ones. The breaks always go my way! That scares you, huh?"

The Citizen protested too much. That could indicate weakness—or could be a ruse. Stile actually could handle himself in games of chance; often there was more skill than showed. He would try for a suitable variant. "Luck is impartial, sir."

"You believe that? You fool! Try me on dice, if you doubt!"

Stile made his selection. The Citizen had already made his. The third grid showed: Board Games of Chance.

"Okay, sucker, try me on Monopoly!" the Citizen urged.

But when they played it through, it came up backgammon. "My favorite!" the Citizen exclaimed. "Dice and betting! Watch me move!"

Stile thought he was bluffing. That bluff would be called. Stile was expert at backgammon. It was only technically a game of luck; skill was critical.

They adjourned to the boardroom. The table was ready. There was no physical audience; the holograph would take care of that.

"Now you know this game represents a year," the Citizen said.

"Twenty-four points for the hours of the day, thirty pieces for the days of the month, twelve points in each half-section for the months in the year."

"And the seven spots on the opposites of a die are the days of the week," Stile said. "The two dice are day and night. It hardly matches the symbolism of the ordinary deck of playing cards or the figures of the chess set—sir."

They were playing a variant deriving in part from Acey-Deucy, traditionally a navy game. The games of Mother Earth had continued to evolve in the fashion of human society, with some variants prospering and others becoming extinct. In this one, no pieces were placed on the board at the start; all started from the bar.

It was not necessary to enter all fifteen pieces on the board before advancing the leaders. Yet it was still backgammon, the "back game," with pieces constantly being sent back to the bar while they ran the gauntlet of opposing pieces. People were apt to assume that a given game had an eternally fixed set of rules, when in fact there were endless variations. Stile had often obtained an advantage by steering a familiar game into an unfamiliar channel.

The Citizen was, as he claimed, lucky. He won the lead, then forged ahead with double sixes, while Stile had to settle for a two-to-one throw of the dice. Doubles were valuable in backgammon, because each die could be used twice. Thus the Citizen's throw enabled him to enter four men to the sixth point, while Stile entered only two. This continued fairly steadily; the Citizen soon had all fifteen men entered and well advanced, while Stile was slower.

Soon the two forces interacted. The Citizen hit the first blot—in layman's language, he placed one of his men on the spot occupied by one of Stile's men. That sent Stile's man home to the bar, the starting place. "Sent you home to your slut machine, didn't I?" he chortled. "Oh, let there be no moaning at the bar!"

That was a literary allusion to an ancient poem by Tennyson of Earth. Stile was conversant with historical literature, but made no response. The Citizen was showing pseudoerudition; he was not the type to know any but the most fashionable of quotes, and he had gotten this one wrong. The correct line was, "and may there be no moaning of the bar." Yet, mentally, Stile filled in the remainder: "when I put out to sea." Tennyson had then been late in life, knowing he would die before too long. That poem, *Crossing the Bar,* had been a kind of personal epitaph. When he put out to sea, in the figurative fashion of the Norse boats for the dead, he hoped to see his Pilot, the Deity, face to face. Those left behind in life should feel no sorrow for him, for he, like the werewolf, had found his ideal resting place. It was generally best to read the full works of past literary figures, and to understand their backgrounds, rather than to memorize quotes out of context. But it was no use to go into all that with this great boor and bore of a Citizen.

Well, Stile intended to send this obnoxious Citizen out to sea. It was already apparent that the man was not a top player; he depended on his luck too heavily, and on a basic strategy of "making" points—of setting up two or more men on a point, so that the opponent could neither land there nor hit a blot. Luck and conservative play—a good enough strategy for most occasions. Three out of four times, a winning strategy.

But Stile was not an ordinary player. He depended not on luck but on skill. Luck tended to equalize, especially on an extended series, while skill was constant. That was what gave the superior player the advantage, even in a game of chance. It was necessary to take risks in order to progress most efficiently. There would be some losses because of these risks, but, overall, that efficiency would pay off. Stile was already grasping the weakness of the Citizen's mode of play. Probably the man had an imperfect notion of the strategy of the doubling cube—and that could make all the difference, regardless of his vaunted luck.

Soon the Citizen had a number of men in his home board, ready to be borne off. The first player who bore off all fifteen men would win the game, but not necessarily the Round. This modification was scored by points; each man left in play when the opponent finished was one point. One hundred points was the Game. It could take several games to accumulate the total. The key was to minimize one's losses in a losing game, and maximize one's winnings in a winning game. That was where the doubling cube came in.

Best to test the man's level, however. Stile needed to have a very clear notion of his opponent's vulnerability, because the Citizen was not a complete duffer; he was just good enough to be dangerous. Luck did play an important part in backgammon, just as muscle did in wrestling; it had to be taken into account.

Stile rolled 3–2. As it happened, he was able to enter two men and hit blots on the second and third points. It was a good break, for the Citizen left few blots he could possibly avoid. Thus Stile's 2 and 3 dice canceled the effect of cumulative scores of twenty-one and twenty-two on the Citizen's dice. Stile was making his limited luck match the effect of his opponent's good luck. It was a matter of superior management.

But the Citizen was hardly paying attention to the moves. He was trying to undermine Stile's confidence, convinced that even in a game of chance, a person's certainty counted most. "A number of people have been wondering where you disappear to between Rounds, little man. You seem to walk down a certain service corridor, and never emerge at the far end. Hours or even days later you emerge, going the opposite direction. It is a food-machine service corridor, yet you show no sign of feasting. Now how can a man disappear from the board, like a piece being sent to the bar? It is a mystery."

Stile continued playing. "People enjoy mysteries, sir."

The dice rolled; the men advanced. The Citizen's luck held; he was gaining despite imperfect play. "Mysteries exist only to be resolved. It is possible that you have discovered something fantastic, like a curtain that separates fact from fantasy? That you pass through this invisible barrier to a world where you imagine you are important instead of insignificant?"

So the man had done fairly thorough research into Stile's Phaze existence too. Still, Stile refused to be baited. "No doubt, sir."

"And can it really be true that in that fantasy you ride a unicorn mare and associate with vampires and werewolves?"

"In fantasy, anything is possible," Stile said.

"Double," the Citizen said, turning the doubling cube to two.

Now the game drew to a close. The Citizen finished first; Stile was left with eight men on the board. Doubled, that was sixteen points against him.

They set up for the second game, since they were not yet close to the one hundred points necessary for the finish. The Citizen was obnoxiously affable; he liked winning. Stile hoped he would get careless as well as overconfident. With luck, the Citizen might even distract himself at a key time by his determined effort to unnerve Stile.

Still, the Citizen's luck held. The man played indifferently, even poorly at times, but the fortune of the dice sustained him. When he had a clear advantage, he doubled, and Stile had to accept or forfeit the game. Then Stile had a brief run of luck—actually, skillful exploitation of the game situation—and doubled himself. "Double!" the Citizen said immediately when his own turn came, determined to have the last word and confident in his fortune. Now the doubling cube stood at eight.

"I understand a little squirt like you can use magic to snare some mighty fine-looking women," the Citizen said as they played. "Even if they're taller than you."

"Many women are," Stile agreed. References to his height did irritate him, but he had long since learned to conceal this. He was 1.5 meters tall, or an inch shy of five feet, in the archaic nomenclature of Phaze.

The Citizen's infernal luck continued. There did seem to be something to his claim about being lucky; he had certainly had far superior throws of the dice, and in this game, supervised by the Game Computer, there could be no question of cheating. He was winning this game too, by a narrower margin than the last, but the eight on the doubling cube gave every piece magnified clout. The Citizen liked to double; maybe it related to his gambling urge.

"I guess there could be one really luscious doll who nevertheless married a dwarf," the Citizen observed with a smirk. "I guess she could have been ensorcelled."

"Must have been." But despite his refusal to be baited about his recent marriage to the Lady Blue, Stile was losing. If this special ploy did not work, he would wash out of the Tourney. If only the luck would even out!

"Or maybe she has a hangup about midgets. Sort of like miscegenation. Some people get turned on that way."

The Citizen was really trying! But Stile played on calmly. "Some do, I understand."

"Or maybe pederasty. She likes to do it with children."

But the effect of that malicious needle was abated by the Citizen's choice of the wrong concept. It was generally applicable to the sexual motive of a male, not a female. Still, Stile would gladly have dumped this oaf down a deep well.

Stile lost this game too, down six men. Forty-eight more points against him, a cumulative total of sixty-four. Another game like this would finish him.

The luck turned at last and he won one. But he had only been able to double it once, and only picked up six points. Then the Citizen won again: eight men, redoubled, for thirty-two points. The score now stood at 96–6. The next game could finish it.

Still the Citizen's amazing luck held. Had he, after all, found some way to cheat, to fix the dice? Stile doubted it; the Tourney precautions were too stringent, and this was an important game, with a large audience. The throws had to be legitimate. Science claimed that luck evened out in the long run; it was difficult to prove that in backgammon.

Stile's situation was desperate. Yet there were ways. Stile knew how to play the back game specialty, and now was the time. When his position looked good, he doubled; when the Citizen was clearly ahead, *he* doubled. But the Citizen retained a general advantage, so Stile's doublings seemed foolish.

Stile used the back game to interfere with the Citizen's establishment on his home board. Because most of Stile's men had been relegated to the bar, he had them in ready position to attack the Citizen's men as they lined up for bearing off. This sort of situation could be a lot more volatile than many people thought. "Double," Stile said, turning the cube.

"You're crazy," the Citizen said, redoubling in his turn.

Stile hit another blot. He needed more than this to recover a decent position, but it helped.

The Citizen threw double sixes. That moved his blotted man all the way from the bar to one space from the end. His luck was still more than sufficient to swamp whatever breaks Stile managed.

Stile doubled again, though he was still obviously behind. The Citizen, when his turn came, laughed and doubled once more. Now the cube stood at sixty-four, its maximum. "You really want to go down big, tyke!"

They were reduced to five men each; the rest had been borne off. The game was actually much closer than the Citizen realized. Stile had already won the advantage he sought. If the game had proceeded with only Stile's first doubling, and he won by two men, all he would have would be four more points. If he lost by the same margin, however, the Citizen's four points would put him at one hundred for final victory. But now the cube stood at sixty-four, so that a two-man win by the Citizen would give him the same victory by an unnecessary margin—while the same win by Stile would give him 128 points, at one stroke enough for his final victory. So he had in effect evened it up. Instead of being behind by ninety points, he had only to win two points. The Citizen had been foolish to permit the doubling to go to this level; he had thrown away a major advantage.

"I hear some of these animals can change to human form," the Citizen said. "I guess an animal in the form of a woman could be a lot of fun to a lonely man."

Was there anything this slob did not know about Phaze, or any limit to his crudity of insinuation? Stile allowed a little ire to show, deliberately. "It is a different frame, sir, with different natural laws. Those animals have human intelligence."

The Citizen gleefully pounced on this. "So you *have* sampled the wares of the mares and the britches of the bitches!" He was hardly paying attention to the backgammon game in his voyeuristic lust. He wanted to make Stile angry and, in seeming success, he was letting the means preempt the ends. This was always ethically problematical, and often strategically unsound. The Citizen was setting himself up for a fall. If only the luck evened out!

Stile had a good roll of the dice. He hit two blots, and the Citizen hardly noticed. "I don't see that it is any of your business, sir, no disrespect intended."

"With animals!" the Citizen exclaimed, smiling broadly. "You admit it!"

"I don't deny it, sir," Stile said, obviously nettled.

"And did they bother to change form each time?" the Citizen demanded, almost drooling. He was hardly looking at the board, playing automatically and poorly. "Maybe sometimes a bitch stayed in her dog-form, just for the novelty?"

Stile wondered just what sort of bestiality lurked in the secret dreams of this nasty man. Perhaps this was the phenomenon of projection, in which a person with illicit desires projected the realization of certain acts onto others. The Citizen was giving himself away without realizing it.

Stile continued to parry him verbally, taking the worst of it, though he had the ability to reverse the onus at any time. He was tacitly egging the man on. Meanwhile, he exploited the rolls of the dice skillfully, and soon had gained a net advantage. The Citizen could have prevented this, had he been paying similar attention. But his morbid fascination with Stile's supposed exploits with shape-changing females had done him in. By the time he became aware of the trap, it was too late; even his amazing luck could not make up for his squandered opportunities.

They entered the final stage, and both resumed bearing off men. For once Stile had better throws of the dice, and finished two men ahead.

It took a moment for the Citizen to absorb the significance. He had been so far ahead, he knew subjectively that it would take a prohibitively massive turn of fortune to deprive him of victory. No such turn had occurred. Now his eyes fixed on the number 64 at the top of the doubling cube, and he saw that this narrow margin of two pieces had at one stroke washed him out of the Tourney.

"You must visit Phaze some day, sir," Stile said brightly. "I know just the bitch for you."

CHAPTER 3

Honeymoon

Stile crossed the curtain at the usual place, emerging from the food-servicing hall to the deep forest of Phaze. In a moment a unicorn trotted up. But it wasn't Neysa. This one was slightly larger, male, and his coat was deep dark blue except for the two red socks on his hind feet.

"Clip!" Stile exclaimed, surprised. "I expected—"

The unicorn metamorphosed into a young man garbed in blue shirt, furry trousers, red socks, floppy hat, gloves, and boots. His resemblance to the unicorn was clear to anyone conversant with the forms. "She's off getting bred, at long last. The Herd Stallion's keeping her with the herd until she foals. That's S.O.P."

"Yes, of course," Stile agreed, disappointed. He found his hidden clothes and dressed quickly; it would not do to travel naked here, though there was really no firm convention. He wanted only the best for Neysa, his best friend in this frame, yet he felt empty without her company. But he had made a deal with the Herd Stallion to release her for breeding when his mission of vengeance was finished; now that he had dispatched the Red Adept, it was time. Time for relaxation, recovery, and love. Time to be with the lovely Lady Blue.

"That was the funniest thing," Clip said, evidently following the thrust of Stile's thoughts. "Thou didst marry the Lady, then skipped off without even—"

"An idiosyncrasy of the situation," Stile said shortly. He had departed without consummating the marriage because of a prophecy that he would have a son by the Lady Blue; he knew he would survive the dangerous mission ahead of him if he only waited to generate that child thereafter, since such prophecies had the force of law. But now the barbs of the ugly Citizen were fresh in his mind, making this subject sensitive. "You're volunteering to be my mount?"

"Neysa intimated gently that I'd get horned at the wrong end if I didn't," Clip admitted. "Besides, thou dost have interesting adventures."

"I'm only going to honeymoon with my wife."

"That's what I mean." Clip shifted to his natural form, his horn playing with the sound of a saxophone—a bar of the wedding march, trailing into a tune with risqué connotations.

Stile jumped on the unicorn's back, landing deliberately hard. Clip blew out one more startled note and took off. The velocity of the unicorn was greater than that of the horse because it was enhanced by magic; yet the two types of creatures were closely akin. As Clip himself had put it, once: as close as men were to apes. Stile was uncertain what freighting accompanied that statement, but had never challenged it. Man had intelligence and science the ape lacked; unicorns had intelligence and magic the horses lacked.

Soon they emerged from the forest and were racing over the fields toward the moated castle that was the heart of the Blue Demesnes. "Dost thou happen to know how Clef from Proton fared?" Stile inquired. "I gave him the Platinum Flute and sent him to the Little Folk, but I've been too busy to follow further. I'm sure you're up on all the news."

Clip blew an affirmative note. He was the gossipy kind.

"Did Clef arrive safely?" Stile was interested in verifying the accuracy of his dream. The frames had always been firmly separated; if his dream were true, it meant that that separation was beginning to fuzz, at least for him.

The unicorn sounded yes again. His sax-horn was more mellow than Neysa's harmonica-horn, though less clever on trills. Like her, he could almost speak in musical notes, making them sound like yes, no, maybe, and assorted other words, particularly colloquialisms. Actually, unicorns could express whole sentences in chords, but this was a separate mode that owed little to archaic English. Stile was coming to understand that language too, but his grasp of it was as yet insecure.

"Was he—is he by any chance the one the Platinum Elves called the Foreordained?"

Again the affirmative.

"Then that earthquake—we felt it in Proton—that was the shaking of the mountains when he played?" But this had become rhetorical; he had the answer. The frames had certainly juxtaposed in this respect. "I wonder what that means?"

Now Clip had no answer. No one except the Little Folk of the Mound knew the significance of the Foreordained. And the all-knowing Oracle, who answered only one question in the lifetime of each querist.

Yet the arrival of the Foreordained suggested that the end of Phaze was near, according to another prophecy. That bothered Stile; he had worked so hard to secure his place here. Was he to be denied it after all?

Well, he was determined to snatch what joy he might, in what time remained. On the cosmic scale, the end might be centuries distant. Magic prophecies were devious things, not to be trusted carelessly. People had died depending on misinterpreted omens.

That brought him back to the manner in which he had secured his own fortune by postponing his fathering of a son. He was eager to get on with it. He had loved the Lady Blue from the first time he had encountered her. He had never before met such a regal, intelligent, and desirable woman. But she was the widow of his other self, and that had made things awkward. Now she was his, and he would never leave her—except for one more necessary trip to the frame of Proton, to try for the final Round of the Tourney. It really was not as important to him as it once had seemed, but he had to give it his best try.

They galloped up to the prettily moated little castle. Stile vaulted off as they entered the courtyard. The Lady Blue, his vision of delight, rushed to his arms. She was of course garbed in blue: headdress, gown, slippers. She was all that he desired.

"Are we ready?" he inquired when the initial sweetness of the embrace eased.

"I have been ready since we wed, but thou didst depart in haste," she said, teasing him.

"Never again, Lady!"

"Hinblue is saddled."

"We have already traveled much of the eastern curtain. Shall we pick up at the Plantinum Demesnes?"

She did not reproach him about his concern for Clef's welfare, the obvious reason to pass the region of the Little Folk. "As my Lord Blue desires."

"Wilt thou condone magic for the start?"

She nodded radiantly. "Magic is the substance of my Lord Adept."

They mounted their steeds, and Stile played his good harmonica, summoning his magic. His Adept talent was governed by music and words, the music shaping the power, the words the application. Actually, his mind was the most important factor; the words mainly fixed the time of implementation. "Conduct us four," he sang, "to the platinum shore."

Clip snorted through his horn: *shore?*

But the magic was already taking hold. The four of them seemed to dissolve into liquid, sink into the ground, and flow rapidly along and through it south-southeast. In a moment they re-formed beside the Mound of the Platinum Elves. There was the fresh cairn of Serrilryan the werebitch, exactly as his vision-dream had shown it.

"Anything I visualize as a shore, is a shore," Stile explained. "There does not have to be water." But as it happened, there was some cloud cover here, thickest in the lower reaches, so that the descending forest disappeared into a sealike expanse of mist. They stood on a kind of shore. Almost, he thought he saw wolf shapes playing on the surface of that lake of mist.

"And we were conducted—like the electricity of Proton-frame," the Lady commented. "Methought thou wouldst provide us with wings to fly."

A dusky elf, garbed in platinum armor to shield his body from a possible ray of sunlight, appeared. He glanced up at Stile. "Welcome, Blue Adept and Lady," he said.

"Thy manner of greeting has improved since last we visited," the Lady Blue murmured mischievously.

"As well it might have," the elf agreed. "We know thee now."

He showed them into the Mound. Stile noted that the structure had been hastily repaired, with special shorings. Evidently the destruction wrought by the Foreordained's Flute had not entirely demolished it. Stile hoped there had not been much loss of life in the collapse. Clip and Hinblue remained outside to graze the verdant, purple-tinted turf.

A deeply darkened and wrinkled elf awaited them inside. This was Pyreforge, chief of this tribe of Dark Elves. "Thy friend is indeed the Foreordained," he said gravely. "Our trust in thee has been amply justified."

"Now wilt thou tell the meaning?" Stile inquired. "We are on our honeymoon. Yet my curiosity compels."

"Because thou art on thy honeymoon, I will tell thee only part," the old elf said. "Too soon wilt thou learn the rest."

"Nay! If it is to be the end of Phaze, I must know now."

"It be not necessarily the end, but perhaps only a significant transition. That much remains opaque. But the decision is near—a fortnight hence, perhaps, no more than two. Take thy pleasure now, for there will come thy greatest challenge."

"There is danger to my Lord Blue?" the Lady asked worriedly.

"To us all, Lady. How could we survive if our frame be doomed?"

"We can not head it off?" Stile asked.

"It will come in its own time. Therefore put it from thy mind; other powers are moving."

Stile saw that Pyreforge would not answer directly on this subject, and the elf could not be pushed. "The Foreordained—what is his part in this? A title like that—"

"Our titles hardly relate to conventional human mythology or religion. This one merely means he was destined to appear at this time, when the curtain grows visible and tension mounts between the frames. The great Adepts of the past foresaw this crisis and foreordained this duty."

"What duty?" Stile asked. "Clef is merely a musician. A fine one, granted, the best I know—but no warrior, no Adept. What can he do?"

"No Adept?" Pyreforge snorted. "As well claim the Platinum Flute be no instrument! He can play the dead to Heaven and crumble mountains by his melody—and these be only the fringes of his untrained power. Once we have trained him to full expertise—he is the Foreordained!"

So Earth mythology might not relate, but the implication of significance did. "So he is, after all, Adept? He seemed ordinary to me —but perhaps I did not hear him play in Phaze."

Pyreforge smiled wryly. "Thou didst hear him, Adept. Music relates most intimately to magic, as thou shouldst know."

So the elf knew of Stile's vision! "And Clef is the finest musician to come to Phaze," Stile said, seeing it. "But what exactly is he to do? May we say hello to him?"

"You may not," the old elf said. This usage always sounded incongruous to Stile here, where "thee" and "thou" were standard—but of course it was the correct plural form. "His power be enormous, but he be quite new to it and has much to learn and little time ere he master his art. We need no more shaking of our mountains! He be deep in study for the occasion he must attend and may not be disturbed."

"What occasion?" Stile asked with growing frustration.

But still the elf would not respond directly. "Thou shalt meet him when it be time, Lord Blue, and all will be clarified. Leave us to teach the Foreordained his music. Go now on thy honeymoon; thou must recuperate and restore thine own powers for the effort to come."

So it seemed. They were teaching Clef music? This was either humor or amazing vanity! Disgruntled, Stile thanked the diminutive, wrinkled elf and departed. "I don't feel comfortable being ignorant of great events, especially when there are hints they relate intimately to me," he muttered to the Lady.

"How dost thou think I felt, cooped up in the Blue Demesnes whilst thou didst go out to live or die?"

"I don't recall thy staying cooped long—"

"Let's ride, my Lord."

Stile smiled. She had the feminine way of changing the subject when pressed. She was not a woman to let fate roll over her unchallenged, and her present deference to him was merely part of the honeymoon. Had he desired a creature to honor his every foible, he would have loved Sheen. The Lady Blue would always be someone to reckon with.

They mounted and rode. Pyreforge was right: the curtain was brighter now, faintly scintillating as it angled across the slopes of the Purple Mountains. It followed the contours of the terrain in its fashion; the curtain extended vertically until it became too faint for them to see, and evidently continued below the ground similarly. As the land fell away, it exposed more of the curtain. There was no gap; the curtain was continuous.

That was what intrigued Stile—that ubiquitous transition between frames. The landscapes of Proton and Phaze were identical, except that Proton was a barren, polluted world where science was operative, while Phaze was a fresh, verdant world of magic. Only those people who lacked alternate selves in the other frame could cross between them. No one seemed to know why or how the curtain was there, or what its mode of operation was. It just served as the transition between frames, responsive to a wish from one side, a spell from the other.

They intended to follow the curtain in its generally westward extension until it terminated at the West Pole. Stile had been increasingly curious about the curtain, and the West Pole held a special fascination for him because it didn't exist on any other world he knew. Now he had an excuse to satisfy both interests—by making them part of his honeymoon.

As the Blue Adept, he was one of the most powerful magicians in Phaze; riding a unicorn—ah, he missed Neysa!—he had some of the best transportation and protection available; and in the company of the lovely Lady Blue—oh, what an occasion this would be!

"I want to make a map," he said, remembering. "A map of Phaze, as I know it now and as I will discover it, and of the curtain in all its curvatures."

"The curtain is straight," the Lady said.

"Straight? It meanders all over the frame!"

"Nay, Lord, it is the frame that meanders," she assured him. "When we follow the curtain, we bear due west."

Stile decided not to argue. After all, she was his new bride and she was heart-throbbingly delightful, and an argument at this time would be awkward. Nevertheless, he would map Phaze as he perceived it.

He played his harmonica, bringing the magic to him. Then he set the instrument aside and sang: "Place on tap a contour map."

True to his visualization, the map appeared—a neatly folded pseudo-parchment. He opened it out and contemplated its lines and colors. There were the White Mountains to the north, the Purple Mountains to the south, the sites of the Blue, Black, Yellow, White, Brown, and—former—Red Demesnes, and the curtain winding around and between them. Contour lines indicated the approximate elevations.

But there were sizable blank areas. This map covered only the territory Stile knew. He had traveled around a lot of Phaze recently, but there was more to explore. He expected to enjoy filling in the rest of this map. The plotting of the curtain should take care of much of it, since it meandered—went straight?—past most of the significant establishments of this frame.

"No one uses a map in Phaze," the Lady protested, intrigued.

"I am not from Phaze," he retorted. He showed her the map. "Now as I make it, the curtain should bear west a day's leisurely travel, then veer north here to pass the palace of the Oracle and on by the Yellow Demesnes near the White Mountains. That will be a couple days' ride. Then it must curve southwest to intersect the Black Demesnes here—"

"The curtain is straight," she repeated.

"Humor me, beloved. Then on until we reach the West Pole, some-where over here. The whole trip should take a week, which will leave us—"

"Thou art a fool," she said pleasantly. "Little thou knowest of Phaze."

"That's why I'm exploring it," he agreed. "Thou art wife of a fool, fool."

She leaned toward him, and her mount obligingly closed the gap. They kissed, riding side by side, while Clip played another suggestive tune. Stile gave the unicorn a sharp little kick in the flank with his left heel. Clip emitted a blast of musical laughter with an undertone of Bronx cheer and flicked his tail across Stile's back in the familiar fly-swatting gesture.

"Now let's move," Stile said as the kiss ended.

The two steeds broke into a canter, following the curtain down the hill, through a valley, and up a wooded slope. Stile loved riding; it was the thing he did best. The Lady paralleled him, balancing smoothly, her hair flying out in a golden splay. She, too, was a fine rider and she had a fine steed, though no horse could match a unicorn in full exertion. Stile probably could have borrowed another unicorn from the herd, but there had been no point. This was no dangerous mission, but a gentle romance. Hinblue was a very good mare, the offspring of the

Blue Stallion and the Hinny—the best equine heritage in Phaze. Stile remained sorry his friend Neysa was not here to share the trip with him—but realized that Neysa might be jealous of the Lady Blue, with some reason. Maybe Neysa's breeding had been mostly a pretext to separate herself from this excursion. Well, Clip was good, if spirited, company.

Time passed. The curtain veered to the south, forcing them to cross over the height of the Purple range, rather than at any natural pass. Their steeds slowed to a walk, and the air became chill. There was no snow here, but the vegetation turned bluish as if from cold, and then full purple. That was what gave the range its color, of course; he should have known. Finally Stile cast a spell to make them warm—himself and the Lady and the two animals—so that no one would have to overexert to maintain body heat.

Then, on the steep downslope, he cast another spell to enable them all to float through the air, resting. A harpy popped out of a hole in a cliff, saw the two equines with their riders, all drifting blithely in midair, and popped hastily back into her hole. "Just as well," the Lady Blue remarked. "That creature's scratch is poisonous, and they oft resent intrusion into their demesnes."

Clip snorted. Unicorns were invulerable to most magic and had no fear of harpies. Stile, remembering how the werebitch Serrilryan had died, knew that if the harpy had attacked, he would have reacted with ferocity perhaps unbecoming to this occasion.

Then they passed the cliffside nest of a griffin. Three cubs poked their beaks up to peer at the weird procession. In the distance there was the birdlike scream of an adult, probably the mother, aware that her babies were being disturbed. A griffin was a fighting animal, almost as fierce as a dragon; unicorns did not normally seek combat with this species. Stile, of course, could handle it—but he elected to hasten their descent, getting well away from the nest before the mother griffin appeared. Why seek trouble?

At the southern foot of the range an extensive plain commenced. Evening was approaching, and in the slanting sunlight they saw shapes in the sky like grotesque birds. "Dragons," the Lady Blue murmured. "This is dragon country."

"If any come for us, we'll simply step across the curtain," Stile said. Again it was easier to avoid than to fight; he had no desire to waste magic or to prove his power. A unicorn, a werewolf, or a vampire could change forms as often as it wished, because that was inherent in such creatures' nature, while Stile could use a particular spell only once. When he had to, he could accomplish more by magic than any other creature and could change one creature to another—but eventually he would run out of new spells. Magic was best saved for true emergencies.

"What of Hinblue?" the Lady asked.

"Um, yes. Maybe she can cross the curtain too."

"She could not survive in Proton-frame. There is no good air there, no grazing. And what of thine own mount?"

"Have no fear for me, Lady," Clip said, changing to man-form. "As a hawk, I can escape. But I cannot cross the curtain. In Proton I would be reduced to but a horse, and unable to cross back."

"Then I will use magic if the need arises," Stile decided.

"My lord, there is no time like the present," the Lady said. For a shape was winging toward them.

Stile had made up and memorized a number of spells, including some dragon restraints. In this case he would simply cause the dragon to forget it had seen anything interesting here.

But as the creature flew closer, Stile squinted at it. This was a peculiar dragon. The wings were wrong, the tail, the head—

"Why, that's no dragon," the Lady said.

Clip snapped his fingers. "That's a thunderbird! I didn't know there were any left in these parts."

"I don't have a specific spell for thunderbirds," Stile said dubiously. "I'll have to go to a general one."

"No need," the Lady said. "The bird is full of sound and fury—"

The creature swooped close, its wings spreading hugely, then sweeping together in a deafening clap of thunder.

"Signifying rain," Clip finished, as the drenchpour commenced.

Hastily Stile spelled into existence a large tent, already set up and guyed. The rain beat down on its canvas so heavily that he had to spell additional supports. Water seeped under the edges, and fog drifted through, coating them with condensation. A little frog appeared and croaked contentedly.

The other three were with him, but soon Clip returned to unicorn-form and moved outside to graze; the rain did not bother his equine form very much. Hinblue followed him out; grazing was always worthwhile, and the dragons would avoid this storm.

That left the Lady Blue. Stile turned to her. "I had thought of sunshine and sweet music for this occasion. Still—"

"Desist thy stalling," she said, and opened her arms.

Thereafter, the storm disappeared from his consciousness. It was a long, ecstatic night. In the morning he woke in a fine bed of hay and feathers, so concluded he must have done some incidental conjuring, but none of that remained in his memory. He had only his awareness of the Lady Blue—his woman at last.

There was a neat pile of assorted fruits at the tent entrance; Clip had evidently scouted around in the night and harvested what he thought was appropriate. At the top of the mound was passion fruit, and below were apples, cherries, and bananas. Symbolistic humor of the equine kind. They had an excellent meal.

They resumed their ride. Clip had the sense not to play any more ribald melodies on his sax-horn, but on occasion he could not quite contain a faint musical snigger.

The curtain wandered back up the slope of the mountains, having no regard for the convenience of travelers—as well it might not; Stile's party was probably the first to make this particular trek. Here on the southern side, flowers of many colors abounded, and the bushes and trees were highly varied. Birds flitted, and squirrels and rabbits scurried. On occasion a grassy round trapdoor would open and a little head would pop out—hermit-elves, harmless.

Then they came to a river. It cut across the curtain, deep and swift—and a formidable steam-breathing water dragon inhabited it.

They halted, eyeing the monster. The monster eyed them back. Slowly a purple tongue came out and moistened its chops. The mere sight of them made this creature salivate. This hardly seemed a safe passage.

Stile pondered which spell to use. Immobilization seemed best; he didn't want to hurt this animal. Yet that was such a useful spell for emergencies that he hated to use it routinely. Again he was up against the ad hoc nature of magic; once any specific spell was used, it was gone. All Adepts used magic sparingly, never squandering it. Stile, a relative newcomer to the art, tended to use it more freely than was wise; the novelty had not yet worn off. Until recently, there had been so many challenges to his well-being that he had hardly worried about wasting spells; what use to save them for a nonexistent future?

Now he was a fairly secure married man, becoming daily more conservative. So he pondered: Was there any mundane way to pass by this dragon? The creature was limited to the water, having flippers in lieu of wings and frogs' feet. This was, after all, a very restricted threat.

Again the Lady's thoughts were parallel to his own. She had an uncanny insight into his mind, perhaps because she had had much longer experience with him than he had had with her, odd as that might seem in any other frame than this. He had in fact been momentarily dismayed during the night by her almost-too-ready anticipation of his desires; none of this was really new to her. "It would be a long trek around the river, methinks, for the dragon would pace us. Clip could change to hawk-form and fly safely across, but Hinblue has no such magic."

"This becomes a challenge," Stile said. "For most of my life I existed without the benefit of magic. A year ago I would have found a way across without sorcery; I should be able to do it now."

"Though it take but a fortnight," she murmured, smiling.

"The curtain—" Stile began, but cut that off. He kept forgetting Hinblue!

"Put my steed not through that torture gratuitously," the Lady agreed.

Clip changed to man-form. "Thou wilt be all day on this. I can get us across now."

"Oh?" Stile asked, not entirely pleased. "How?"

"By decoying this dragon downstream while the three of you swim. The average dragon is not smart enough for that ruse."

Of course! Simplicity itself. "Thou are smarter than I, today," Stile said ruefully.

"Naturally. I'm a unicorn," Clip said generously. "I did not dissipate my strength all night in pointless heroics." He changed back to his usual form and snorted insultingly at the dragon, adding an obnoxious gesture with his horn. Unicorns could convey considerable freighting in this manner. The dragon oriented on him, steam pressure building up, measuring the distance it might strike.

Clip stayed just out of range, trotting downstream with a lewd swish of his tail. He played a few bars of music, and Stile could just about make out the words: "The worms crawl in, the worms crawl out . . ." Dragons were the monarchs of the kingdom of worms, and were sensitive to such disparaging references. This dragon followed Clip briskly, hoping the unicorn would stray just within range of fang or steam.

Soon Stile and the Lady stripped and swam safely across with Hinblue, holding their garments aloft. They were, after all, prevailing without magic.

"This is fun," Stile murmured, contemplating her body in the clear water. "Shall we dally a bit?"

"Until the dragon joins the party?" she inquired sweetly.

They climbed out at the far bank and shook themselves dry in the sun. Stile tried not to stare; this was a type of motion he had never seen done by a woman of her construction, though he had lived most of his life in a society of nudity.

There was a small coughing sound. Both Stile and the Lady turned— and discovered the dragon was watching too, its labile lips pursed into the semblance of a whistle.

Stile experienced a rapidly developing emotion. He tried to control it, but in a moment it overwhelmed him. It was mirth. He burst out laughing. "Oh, I'll bet that monster doesn't see what I see!"

The Lady looked down at herself, frowning. "It doesn't?"

"It sees the most delicious morsel in two frames. I see—"

"Never mind what thou seest," she said with mock severity. "I take thy meaning." She was neither self-conscious nor angry. She had one of the finest bodies in the frame and knew it.

A hawk arrived, swooping low and converting to unicorn-form. Clip was ready to resume the journey.

Soon the curtain veered north, crossing the mountain range again. Fortunately this occurred at a natural pass, so they were able to get past expeditiously.

They emerged into the rolling countryside that was the main grazing range of the unicorns. Now progress was swift—but the distance was long. They were not yet near the Oracle's palace before night overtook them and forced another halt.

Again the animals grazed, and Stile was about to conjure another tent when the Lady stayed him. "Expend not thy magic superfluously, my Lord. Tonight the open sky suffices for us."

"If that is what thou dost desire, that is what thou shalt have," he agreed. He gathered straw and moss to fashion a bed, and they lay down side by side and looked up at the moons.

"Oh, see—the blue moon rises!" she cried, squeezing his hand.

"Our moon," he agreed. This was sheer delight, being with her, sharing her incidental pleasures.

"Oh, play, my Lord, play," she begged.

Obediently Stile found his harmonica and brought it to his mouth. But something stayed him—an ominous though not unpleasant feeling. He concentrated and placed it. "It was not far from here that I first found this instrument, or thought I found it. Here in the open, riding with Neysa. I conjured it without knowing."

"It is all that remains of my former Lord," she said. "His music and power have since found lodging in thee. Great was my grief at his loss, yet greater is my joy in thee."

"Still it bothers me how he died. Surely he could have saved himself, had he tried."

She stiffened. "I told thee how the demon amulet choked him, so that he could make neither music nor spell."

"Aye. But was not this harmonica always with him?"

"Always. But he could not play it, either, if—"

"And the golem did not remove it?"

"Nay. It was gone ere the golem came."

"Then how did it get out here in the fields for me to conjure? Or, if it were not here, how did it get wherever it hid? It remained not at the Blue Demesnes."

"True," she agreed thoughtfully. "Long and long I searched for it, but it was not with his body."

"Which is strange," Stile said. "He might have conjured it away from him in the instant he knew he would die—but why then did he not use his magic to protect himself? And why did he deny thee the inheritance of his prize possession? Such malice was not his nature, I am sure." For Stile himself would not have done that. Not without excellent reason.

"He could not have conjured it!" she said, disturbed.

"Then he must have placed it in the field, or hidden it elsewhere, before he died. And that suggests—"

"That he knew he was slated to die!" she exclaimed, shocked. "He deprived himself of his most valued possession. But even without it, no one could have killed him, were he on guard!"

"Unless he intended to permit it," Stile said.

Her shock turned to horror. "No! Nothing I did, no will of mine should have caused him—"

"Of course not," Stile agreed quickly. "He would never have done it because of thee."

"Then what is thine import?"

"That perhaps he knew something, received an omen, that caused him to accept what was coming."

She considered that for some time, her hand clenching and unclenching in his. "Yet what could possibly justify—what was fated?"

"I wish I knew." For Stile's own passage across the curtain had been enabled by that demise of his alternate self. If the Blue Adept had sought to eliminate his brand of magic from the frame, he had acted in vain, for Stile performed it now.

That night they did not make love. They lay and watched the blue moon, and Stile played gently on the mysterious harmonica, and it was enough. Slowly sleep overtook them.

"Be at ease," a man's voice came from nearby. "We have met before, Adept."

Stile controlled his reaction. He still held the harmonica; he could summon his power rapidly. In a moment he placed the half-familiar voice: "Yes, at the Unolympics, Green Adept." He did not want trouble with another Adept—especially not when the Lady Blue was close enough to be hurt by the fallout. He was as yet unable to see the man; probably Green had employed a spell of invisibility, with related obfuscations. Otherwise he could not have gotten by the alert equines.

"I come in peace. Wilt thou grant truce for a dialogue?"

"Certainly." Stile was relieved. By custom verging on law, Adepts did not deceive each other in such matters. What in Phaze could this man want with him at this time?

The Adept became visible. He was a pudgy man of middle age, garbed in green. He looked completely inoffensive—but was in fact one of the dozen most powerful people of Phaze. "Thank thee. I will intrude not long."

A hawk appeared silently behind the Adept. Stile gave no sign. He did not expect treachery, but if it came, there would suddenly be a unicorn's horn in action. If Clip attacked the Green Adept, he risked getting transformed into a clod of dung, but Stile knew he would take that risk if necessary. "Surely thou hast reason."

"It is this, Blue: my sources give thee warning. Go not to the West Pole. Great mischief lies there."

"There is no mischief there," the Lady Blue protested. "It is a sacred place, under truce, like the palace of the Oracle."

"Dost thou think no mischief lies with the Oracle?"

Stile chuckled. "Excellent point, Green. But the Lady and I are on our honeymoon, and our excursion to the West Pole has private significance. Canst thou be more explicit?"

"Why shouldst thou care if mischief comes to a rival Adept?" the Lady demanded. "Thou didst evince no concern, Green, when the life of Blue hung in peril before."

That was an understatement. No other Adept had lifted a finger or made a spell either to warn or to assist the Blue Adept in his severe crisis that had left two Adepts dead or ruined. This sudden concern was suspicious.

"Needs must I then elaborate," Green said heavily. "My Demesnes lie athwart thy route. I would let thee pass unscathed, knowing thy mission—but by that acquiescence I commit myself to thy fate. This is not my desire. I want no part of what befalls thee. Go not to the West Pole—but an thou must go, then go not through the Green Demesnes."

That made sense. The Green Adept had no personal interest in Stile; he merely wanted to make certain he was not implicated in what happened to Stile. If a prophecy decreed doom to all who might facilitate Stile's approach to the West Pole, this step exonerated the Green Adept.

"Now I seek no trouble with thee," Stile began. "But the Lady and I planned to follow the curtain to its terminus, and—"

"And we can bypass the Green Demesnes, in the interest of courtesy," the Lady Blue finished.

Stile shrugged. "The Lady has spoken. Set out warners at thy boundaries, and we shall there detour."

"I shall," Green agreed. "Since thou dost humor my preference, I offer one final word: my sources suggest that if thou dost go to the West Pole, thou wilt suffer grievously in the short term, and in the moderate term will incur the enmity of the most powerful forces of the frame. I urge thee once more to give up this quest. There are other suitable places to honeymoon. The Green Demesnes themselves will be opened to thee, shouldst thou care to tarry there instead."

"I thank thee for thy advice," Stile said. "Yet it seems the end of Phaze draws nigh, and powerful forces already dispose themselves in readiness. The Foreordained has appeared. What is fated, is fated, and I am ready if not eager to play my part."

"As thou dost choose." The Green Adept made a signal with the fingers of his left hand and disappeared.

"I mislike these omens," the Lady said. "Methought our troubles were over."

"Loose ends remain, it seems. I had hoped we could let them be for at least this fortnight."

"Surely we can," she agreed, opening her arms to him. The hawk flew quietly away. The weapon of the unicorn had not, after all, been needed.

Next day they resumed the ride north. Stile made a small spell to enhance Hinblue's velocity and let Clip run at full speed. They fairly flew across the rolling terrain. Fire jetted from the unicorn's nostrils, and his hooves grew hot enough to throw sparks. Unicorns, being magic, did not sweat; they ejected surplus heat at the extremities.

After a time they slowed. Stile brought out his harmonica and played, Clip accompanied him on his saxophone-voiced horn, and the Lady sang. The magic closed about them, seeming to thicken the air, but it had no force without Stile's verbal invocation.

"We can camp the night at the Yellow Demesnes," Stile said. "The curtain clips a corner of—"

"By no means!" the Lady snapped, and Clip snorted.

Stile remembered. She didn't like other Adepts, and Yellow liked to take a potion to convert herself from an old crone to a luscious young maid—without otherwise changing her nature. Also, her business was the snaring and selling of animals, including unicorns. Stile had traded magical favors with Yellow in the past and had come to respect her, but he could understand why his wife and steed preferred not to socialize.

"Anything for thee," he agreed. "However, night approaches and the White Mountains lie beyond."

"Indulge thyself in a spell, Adept."

"How soon the honeymoon turns to dull marriage," he grumbled. Clip made a musical snort of mirth, and the Lady smiled.

The ramshackle premises of Yellow appeared. Both animals sniffed the air and veered toward the enclosure. Hastily Stile sang a counterspell: "This will cure the witch's lure." That enabled them to ignore the hypnotic vapor that drew animals in to capture and confinement. Before long they had skirted those premises and moved well on toward the termination of the plain to the north.

At dusk they came to the White Mountain range. Here the peaks rose straight out of the plain in defiance of normal geological principles; probably magic had been involved in their formation.

The curtain blithely traveled up the slope at a steep angle. It would have been difficult to navigate this route by daylight; at night the attempt would be foolhardy. "And there are snow-demons," the Lady said as an afterthought.

Stile pondered, then conjured a floating ski lift. It contained a heated stall for two equines, complete with a trough filled with fine grain, and a projecting shelf with several mugs of nutri-cocoa similar to what was available from a Proton food machine. Clip could have converted to hawk-form and flown up, but the cold would have hindered him, and this was far more comfortable. Unicorn and horse stepped into the stalls and began feeding, while Stile and the Lady mounted for their repast. Eating and sleeping while mounted was no novelty; it was part of the joy of Phaze.

They rode serenely upward as if drawn by an invisible cable. "Yet I wonder where this magic power comes from?" Stile mused. "I realize that the mineral Phazite is the power source for magic, just as its other-frame self, Protonite, is the basis for that scientific, energy-processing society. But why should certain people, such as the Adepts, channel that power better than others? Why should music and doggerel verse implement it for me, while the Green Adept needs special gestures and the White Adept needs mystic symbols? There is a certain channelization here that can not be coincidental. But if it is natural, what governs it? If it is artificial, who set it up?"

"Thou wert ever questioning the natural order," the Lady Blue said affectionately. "Asking whence came the Proton objects conjured to this frame, like the harmonica, and whether they were turning up missing from that frame, making us thieves."

So his other self had speculated similarly! "I wonder if I could conjure a source of information? Maybe a smart demon, like the one Yellow animates with a potion."

"Conjure not demons, lest they turn on thee," she warned, and Clip gave an affirmative blast on his horn.

"Yes, I suppose there are no shortcuts," Stile said. "But one way or another, I hope to find the answer."

"Mayhap that is why mischief lurks for thee at the West Pole," the Lady said, not facetiously. "Thou canst not let things rest, any more in this self than in thine other."

That was quite possible, he thought. It was likely to be the curious child with a screwdriver who poked into a power outlet and got zapped, while the passive child escaped harm. But man was a curious creature, and that insatiable appetite for knowledge had led him to civilization and the stars. Progress had its dangers, yet was necessary—

Something rattled against the side of the gondola stall, startling them. Clip shifted instantly to hawk-form, dropping Stile so suddenly to the floor that he stumbled face-first into the food trough as if piggishly hungry. Hinblue eyed him as he lifted his corn- and barley-covered face, and made a snort that sounded suspiciously like a snicker.

"*Et tu, Brute*," Stile muttered, wiping off his face while the Lady tittered.

Soon Clip returned from his survey of the exterior situation, metamorphosing to man-form. "Snow-demons," he said. "Throwing icicles at us."

Stile made a modification spell, and the chamber drew farther out from the mountainside, beyond reach of icicles. So much for that. "Yet this will complicate our night's lodging," Stile commented.

"Nay, I know a snow-chief," the Lady said. "Once the demons were enemies of my Lord Blue, but we have healed many, and this one will host us graciously enough, methinks."

"Mayhap," Stile said dubiously. "But I shall set a warning spell against betrayal."

"Do thou that," she agreed. "One can never be quite certain with demons."

They crested the high peak and followed the curtain to an icebound hollow in a pass on the north side. "Here, belike, can we find my friend," the Lady said.

Stile placed the warning spell, and another to keep warm—a warner and a warmer, as the Lady put it—and they rode out. There was a cave in the ice, descending into the mountain. They approached this, and the snow demons appeared.

"I seek Freezetooth," the Lady proclaimed. "Him have I befriended." And in an amazingly short time, they were in the cold hall of the snow-chief.

Freezetooth was largely made of snow and ice. His skin was translucent, and his hair and beard were massed, tiny icicles. Freezing fog wafted out of his mouth as he spoke. But he was affable enough. Unlike most of his kind, he could talk. It seemed that most demons did not regard the human tongue as important enough to master, but a chief had to handle affairs of state and interrogate prisoners. "Welcome, warm ones," he said with a trace of delicately suppressed aversion. "What favor do you offer for the privilege of nighting at my glorious palace?"

Glorious palace? Stile glanced about the drear, ice-shrouded cave. It was literally freezing here—otherwise the snow-demons would melt. Even protected by his spell, Stile felt cold.

"I have done thy people many favors in past years," the Lady reminded Freezetooth indignantly, small sparks flashing from her eyes. That was a trick of hers Stile always admired, but several snow-demons drew hastily back in alarm.

"Aye, and in appreciation, we consume thee not," the chief agreed. "What hast thou done for us lately, thou and thy cohorts?"

"This cohort is the Blue Adept," she said, indicating Stile.

There was a ripple through the cave, as of ice cracking under stress.

Freezetooth squinted, his snowy brow crusting up in reflection. "I do recall something about a white foal—"

Stile placed the allusion. His alternate self, the former Blue Adept, had helped the Lady Blue rescue her white foal from the snow-demons, who did not now realize that the identity of the Blue Adept had changed. It hardly mattered, really.

"That foal would have died with thy people, being no snow-mare, though she looked it. But there was an avalanche—"

"An accident," Freezetooth said quickly.

"An accident," Stile agreed, though they both knew better. The demons had tried to kill the Blue Adept—and had received a harsh lesson. Surely they did not want another. But there was no need to antagonize them. "What favor didst thou crave?"

Now there was a canny glint in the demon's frozen eye. "Come converse privately, Adept, male to male."

In a private chamber the demon confessed his desire: he loved a lovely, flowing, brilliantly hued fire-spirit. His "flame" was literally a flame.

The problem was immediately apparent. Freezetooth could not approach his love without melting. If she cooled to his temperature, her fire would extinguish and she would perish. Forbidden fruit, indeed!

Fortunately the remedy was within the means of Adept magic. Stile generated a spell to render Freezetooth invulnerable to heat. The flames would feel as deliciously cold as they were in fact hot.

The demon chief departed hastily to rendezvous with his love. Stile and his party were treated well by the remaining demons, who were no longer chilled by the wintry glare of their lord. The finest snowbanks were provided for sleeping on, in the most frigid and windy of the chambers. Without Stile's warmth-spell, it would have been disaster. As it was, they started to melt down into the snow, and Stile had to modify his spell to prevent that. Once everything had been adjusted, the facilities were quite comfortable.

In the morning Freezetooth was back, and his icicles positively scintillated. No need to ask how his evening had worked out! He insisted that his close friend the Adept stay for a proper feast that evening.

It occurred to Stile that this hospitality could be useful. "Do thou remain here while I perform a necessary chore in Proton," he told the Lady. "I must attend the final Round of the Tourney, but should be back by noon."

"I know, my love. Is it selfish of me to hope that thou dost lose that Game and find thyself confined to Phaze?"

He kissed her. "Yes, it is selfish. Sheen depends on me."

"Ah, yes—I forget the Lady Sheen. Methinks I shall consider her options whilst thou art gone."

Stile wasn't certain what that would lead to. The Lady Blue could cross the curtain, but Sheen could not function in Phaze. "Until noon," Stile said, then spelled himself to his usual curtain crossing.

CHAPTER 4

Poem

Stile's opponent for the finals was a serf woman two years younger than he: Rue, a twenty-year-tenure veteran of the Game. Like himself, she had not qualified at the top of her age ladder; but also like himself, she was the best of her decade. She was one of the half-dozen serf players Stile was not eager to meet in the Tourney. He thought he could beat her, but he wasn't sure.

Rue had luck as well as skill, for she had lost no Rounds. That meant that a single victory for her would bring her the prize, while one for Stile would merely bring him even. To beat Rue twice in succession —that would be difficult.

They played the grid. Stile got the letters. Rue was good at all manner of tool and machine games, being in superb health; he was well skilled in these areas, too, and could take her in most tool games, but would be at a disadvantage in machine-assisted games. She would expect him to go for TOOL or ANIMAL, so instead he went for A. NAKED. If she went for 4. ARTS, as he expected, this would foul her up.

But she had done the unexpected too, going for 3. CHANCE. With two chances to his one, the advantage would be with her on the straight gamble—if that was the way she wanted to play it. As evidently she did.

They played the subgrid, and finished with a very simple guessing game; each had to pick a number, and if the total of the two numbers was even, Stile won. Even, in this coding, was male; odd was female. This game was so simple it would be played on the grid. Each would enter his/her number, the total flashing on both screens only when both were entered.

Would she choose her own code, an odd number? People tended to, unconsciously, feeling more at home with their own. If she chose odd and he chose even, she would win.

Obviously he should choose odd, to cancel her odd. But, as obviously, she would anticipate that and choose even. Then the result would be odd, and she would still win. It seemed she stood to win regardless.

It came back to the subjective. Given no advantage between alternatives, a person normally selected what pleased him emotionally. Rue, in doubt, should go for odd. Therefore Stile overruled his preference for even and chose the number of letters in his name: five. He entered this on the grid and locked it; no way to change his mind now.

Rue had not yet made up her mind. Now the onus was hers, and they both knew it, and the broadcast audience knew it. She could win or lose by her decision; Stile was passive. The pressure was on her.

"Ten seconds until forfeit," the voice of the Game Computer announced.

Rue grimaced and punched in her number. She was pretty enough, with auburn hair, an extremely fit body, and only a few age creases forming on face and neck. She was thirty-three years old, her youth waning. If she won this one, she would be eligible for rejuvenation, and Stile suspected she desired that more than the actual wealth of Citizenship.

The total showed eight. Rue had chosen the letters of her own name. Even—and Stile had won.

Stile kept his face impassive. He had been lucky—but was keenly aware of the fickleness of that mistress. Rue blanched a little, but knew her chances remained even. Now they were tied, with thirteen victories and one loss each.

There was no break between Rounds this time, since there were no complexities about scheduling. They played the grid again immediately.

This time Stile got the numbers. He certainly was not going for CHANCE, though it had just salvaged his drive. It had not won him anything beyond that, for as a finalist he had already achieved the prize of life tenure as a serf. The only real step forward he could make was to Citizenship, and now at last it was within his means. One single win—

He selected 4. ARTS, knowing that she would be playing to avoid his strong points elsewhere. The arts cut across other skills, and Rue was noted for her intellectual velocity and proficiency with machine-assisted games. Machine art would be a tossup, but he was willing to fight it out there.

But she surprised him again, choosing A. NAKED. So it was 1A, Naked Arts. Stile did not like this; he had had a very bad time in this box in his critical match with the Red Adept, and had pulled it out only by means of a desperation ploy.

They played the subgrids, and finished, to his abrupt delight, with EXTEMPORANEOUS POETRY. Stile had always fancied himself a

poet; he had a ready flair for rhyme and meter that had served him in excellent stead in Phaze. But true poetry was more than this—and now he
would be able to do something significant when and where it counted.

The Game Computer printed a random list of a dozen words.
"Thirty minutes to incorporate these terms into poems," it announced.
"Highest point scores given for the use of one key word per line, in
order, in the terminal position, rhymed. Technical facility fifty percent;
content fifty percent. A panel of judges, including one male Citizen,
one female Citizen, male serf, female serf, and the Game Computer,
will decide the rating of each effort on the basis of zero to one hundred.
The higher composite score prevails. Proceed."

This was more restrictive than Stile liked, but he remained well
satisfied. It was not that he thought he had an easy victory; he knew
that Rue, too, had facility with words, perhaps greater than his own.
She was an extremely quick-witted woman—which was of course one
reason she had made it to the Tourney finals. She could cobble together
a poem as readily as he could. But at least this particular contest would
be decided on skill, not luck. This was a fair encounter. If he won or if
he lost, it would be because he had established his level. That was all
he could ask.

Stile considered the words. They were: BITCH, CUBE, FLAME,
SIR, SILENCE, LOVE, HORN, CHEAT, ROACH, CIVIL,
FLUTE, EARTH. An anomalous bunch indeed! None of them
rhymed with each other, so there were no free rides there. The only
way to get a key term at the end of a rhyming line was to alternate
with filler lines. "My female dog is a wonderful bitch; whenever she
scratches she has an itch." That sort of thing would hardly win the
Tourney; it was literal doggerel. It might be better to alternate terminal
key words with mid-line key words, sacrificing the preferred terminal
spot for the sake of the also-preferred, one-key-word-per-line arrangement. The Computer had not made it easy; the contestants had to
choose between sacrifices. "My female dog is a wonderful *bitch*; she
stands on a *cube* and does a twitch." That would garner a better technical score, but nothing extra on content.

He glanced at Rue. She was frowning, evidently displeased by the
first term. Stile half smiled; he would have been similarly put out if the
term had been RUNT. He was a runt and she was a bitch—but that
was the kind of mischief random selection could do.

Because this was Naked Arts, they could use no implements, make
no written notes. No rhyming dictionaries. They had to do it all in
their heads, punching only the finished poems into the grid for judgment. If either had trouble with memory, he or she could place individual lines as they were worked out. But then those lines would be final,
no changes allowed. Since both Stile and Rue were experienced Game
players, both could hold the developing poems in memory until the

time for presentation. No, the only problem was wrestling these awkward words into the most artistic and meaningful whole.

Stile wrestled a while, but was not satisfied. He could make rhymes and meter, certainly—but where was the meaning? One ignored the content portion of the poem at one's peril. Yet it seemed impossible to fit these unruly words into anything serious; the problem of rhyming and positioning turned his efforts to frivolous tangents, as with the antics of his female dog. What could a person do seriously with words like bitch, cube, and flame?

Time was passing. Rue was hard at work; her expression and concentration suggested she had developed a strategy of creation and was happily ironing out the wrinkles. She would probably come up with something very clever. He had to come up with something even more clever—or more significant. Sir, silence, love—what a headache!

He brought himself back to basics. There were really two types of poetry: the ornamental and the consequential. Ornaments were rhyme, meter, alliteration, pattern, humor, assonance, and technical cleverness. They were stressed in light verse, parody, the libretto for popular music, and such. Serious poetry de-emphasized such things, or dispensed with them altogether. Thus some people were unable even to recognize serious poetry, because it didn't necessarily rhyme. But ultimately any poetic appeal was to the deeper emotions, and the use of symbolism enabled it to evoke complex ramifications in the most compact presentation. As with Kipling's *Recessional:* "Far-called, our navies melt away; On dune and headland sinks the fire: Lo, all our pomp of yesterday Is one with Nineveh and Tyre!" Presented to Queen Victoria some centuries back, this poem did not find instant favor, for it signaled the decline of the Earth-wide British Empire. But what imagery was evoked by the names of those two ancient cities, foremost in their times, finally brought to ruin by the armies of Babylonia and Alexander the Great, drunkard though the latter might have been. Kipling's verse was superficially pretty; it rhymed nicely. But its real impact was its content, the somber warning for an overextended empire. All too soon it had been London-town under the siege of weapons unknown in the time of Tyre, as the Germans sent their bombers and rockets over. How well Kipling had understood!

With that memory, Stile saw his way. Rhyme, meter, and the rest of the prettiness were encumbrances; he had to dispense with them all and concentrate on meaning and emotion. He would lose some technical points, but gain where it counted. Win or lose, he would do his best, his way.

Stile considered the first word—bitch. He knew of a noble bitch—the old female werewolf who had guided Clef to the Platinum Demesnes, sacrificing her life in the process. Stile could do worse than remember her in this poem!

Cube—there was one cube that was fresh in his experience, and that was the doubling cube of his recent backgammon game, which had enabled him to pull out a last-moment win.

Flame—well, it wasn't the most serious thing, but he had just enabled the chief snow-demon to have a liaison with his literal flame. That might not have any meaning to the Tourney judges, but this poem was not really for them but for Stile himself—his evocation of himself. The frame of Phaze was vitally important to him, and the flame related to that and to the notion of romance, which brought him to the Lady Blue. Ah, yes.

Sir—that was easy. This very poem was Stile's final effort to be called sir: to become a Citizen of Proton, and have similar stature and power in Proton as he did in Phaze as the Blue Adept.

But the remaining terms—they did not seem to relate. Now he was emotionally committed to this course, and had to use them in it—which meant he would have to improvise. That would be troublesome.

What was there to do except use the words as keys, perhaps as some psychic revelation that had to be clothed with syntax to become meaningful? If the first four terms brought him from the recent past to the present, the next eight might be taken as signals of the future. At least he would assume as much for the sake of the poem—insights to himself, now and to come. If the insights proved false, then this was a work of fiction; if true, of prediction. It was a worthy game, and he would take it seriously.

Stile bent to it with a will, and the lines fell into their places. No rhyme, no meter, no other ornamentation; just a series of statements like those of the Oracle, clarifying the significance of each key term. He found that there was not a great amount of mystery to it; the statements were mostly common sense, modified by what he already knew, and the whole was an affirmation of man's resignation to fate.

Suddenly time was up. Rue and Stile typed in their poems. Now it was up to the panel of judges.

In the interim, those judges had assembled. Each one sat in a separate booth facing a central holograph. They could view the holo and converse with each other at the same time. The Game Computer was represented by a booth containing a humanoid robot, its outer surface transparent, so that its wires, hydraulics, and electronic components showed. The thing was at first eerie, like an animated cross section of the human body, but soon the eye accepted it for what it was: an animation of a simplified representation of the far more complicated Computer.

"Display one poem," the Computer-figure said. "The serf Rue will commence her reading."

Rue looked at the printed poem in her grid screen and began to read. A holograph of her formed above the central table, where all the judges could see it plainly. It looked as if she were standing there, a woman on a pedestal, and her eyes made contact with those of whatever judge she happened to face.

"My poem is entitled *Cruel Lover*," she announced. Then she read, flouncing prettily and smiling or frowning to emphasize the meaning appropriately. As she read each line, it appeared on a simulated screen over her head, until the full poem was printed.

> Call me witch or call me bitch
> Call me square or cube
> By any name I'm still the flame
> Burning on the tube.
>
> I'll take no slur, I tell you, sir
> I will not sit in silence
> I'll take your glove in lieu of love
> But will accept no violence.
>
> Now light's reborn by dawn's bright horn
> You can no longer cheat
> Accept reproach or be a roach
> Or make my joy complete.
>
> Desist this drivel and be civil
> Play violin or flute
> Be up with mirth or down to earth
> But keep love absolute.

"The key words are used correctly and in the proper sequence," the Computer said. "Each one terminates its lines, and each is matched with a rhyme of good quality. These are credits. Four lines exist only to complete the necessary rhymes; these are neutral. The metric scansion is correct and consistent—basically iambic tetrameter alternating with iambic trimeter with certain convenient modifications in the extreme feet. This is a common mode and not considered difficult. I rate the technical facility of this effort forty-two of a total of fifty points allotted to this aspect. Proceed to my left with your judgments."

The female serf was to the left. "I don't know much about all those things," she said diffidently. "But it rhymes, and I sort of like it. So I give it a forty-five."

There was the illiterate response, Stile thought. That was the vote he had not deigned to court, though it cost him Citizenship.

Next was the male Citizen, resplendent in his ornate robes. "We are not yet discussing content or interpretation?" he inquired. When the

Computer agreed, he continued: "I find the format simplistic but effective. I'll give it forty." Stile liked that reaction better.

Then the male serf voted. "I don't relate well to the female tone, but technically it seems all right for what it is. The key words are all in the right place, and they do fit in more neatly than I could do. Forty-three from me."

The female Citizen, in a sequined suit, fire opals gleaming at her ears, voted last. "Some of the lines are forced or confusing, but I suppose I must grade that in content. She's done an excellent job of stringing the random words coherently together. Forty-six."

Stile saw that the average score was forty-three, which was good—probably a good deal better than his own would be. Rue had certainly integrated her terms cleverly. He was going to have a rough time of this one!

"We shall now analyze the second poem for technical merit," the Computer said.

Stile stepped up to the grid. He found himself looking past his printed poem into the glassy orbs of the Computer simulacrum robot. He glanced to the side and saw the male serf. He could see anyone he chose, merely by looking in the correct direction; their circle was laid out flat on his screen.

"My poem is titled *Insights*," he said. Then he read:

> Nobility is found in a werewolf bitch
> Defeat converts to victory by an ivory cube
> Magic makes ice merge with flame
> A Game converts serf to sir.
>
> The mischief of the future is shrouded in silence
> And part of that mischief is love
> We must heed the summons of Gabriel's horn
> Destiny the single thing we can not cheat.
>
> All are subject: the dragon and the roach
> Since we are bound, we must be civil
> Our fate is determined by God's flute
> That tumbles mountains and shakes the earth.

He had made eye contact with each judge in turn as he read, and had seen their responses. Unfortunately, these were not promising; some frowned, some seemed confused. It wasn't going over; they did not understand its form or content.

"This is free verse," the Computer said. "It has no consistent meter and no rhyme. This should not be taken as a defect. The key terms are terminally placed, in correct order, one to a line with no waste lines.

There are natural pauses at the end of most lines. As free verse, I rate this technically at thirty-nine."

Stile's heart sank. The others would follow the Computer's lead, and he would average several points below Rue's effort.

He was not disappointed in this expectation. The serf woman wondered whether these lines could even be considered poetry, as they seemed just like sentences to her, and the others were lukewarm. The average score was thirty-eight. Stile was five points behind.

Now it was time for the content analysis. Neither poet was permitted to speak at this stage; it was felt that if the poems did not speak for themselves, they were defective. "This is a straightforward statement of position," the Computer said of Rue's effort. "She evidently feels slighted by her male friend, and is dictating to him the terms of their future association. I perceive no particular meaning beyond this, and therefore do not regard this as other than light verse. Rating thirty-five."

That was a good sign, Stile thought. If the others followed this lead, her average would drop.

"It's a good thing machines aren't in charge of romance," the serf woman remarked. "I find this a good telling-off. The guy *is* a roach, calling her such names, and I'm all with her. I say fifty."

Stile winced inwardly. He needed to recover five points, and figured they might rate his poem an average 40. The Computer's lead had put him right in line to even it up by dropping Rue's score, but this 50 was a disaster.

The male Citizen was more critical, however. "I certainly don't care to see a woman spelling out her terms like that for a romance, though I suppose, if she can find a man to accept them, it's their business. I don't follow this 'burning on the tube' reference; does it make sense at all?"

"Oh, sure, sir," the male serf said. "In the old days on Earth they had gas burners, gas coming up a tube and the flame on top. So she's likening herself to that sort of flame. It's a sort of pun, really."

The Citizen shrugged. "Clever," he said sourly. "I rate this thirty." Stile saw Rue wince. But he himself, while deploring the man's narrowness, was gratified by the score. It put him back in the running.

The male serf was next. "If she becomes a Citizen, then she can set terms," he said, and the others laughed. They were getting into this now, loosening up. "I guess I'm looking for something deeper than this, some social commentary, not just female demands. Rating thirty-two." And Stile's hopes elevated another notch. Now if only the other woman did not react by sexual alignment—

"I believe I note an extremely clever thrust," the lady Citizen said. "Nowhere is the protagonist identified; it is not necessarily serf Rue at all. It could be any woman, most especially one who has been wronged by the man she loves. It could even apply to a humanoid robot female who loves a flesh-man."

Oh, no! Had Rue slanted her verse to pillory Stile? He saw the judges turning to look at him, and at Sheen in the small physical audience permitted. They knew!

"The references to square and cube fall into place," the lady Citizen continued. "A robot is a creature of geometrical parts, supposedly, animated by electric power from a tiny furnace fed by Protonite. She is certainly burning, internally! She must accept a man's attentions—I understand that is what that type is primarily designed for—but can not have his love, since he knows she is a machine. Yet she can be programmed for emotion; she loves *him*, knowing that love is not returned. Perhaps the man she serves is a musician, playing the violin or flute—"

Sheen got up from her seat in the audience and walked toward the exit. Stile felt acute pity for her. She was not supposed to be the target!

"One moment," the male Citizen said. "That's her, isn't it? I want to question her."

"That would be involving her in the panel's deliberation," the female Citizen said. "I doubt that's legitimate."

"The judges may seek any source of information they wish," the Computer said. "Except the author of the piece in question."

"Female robot—how do you feel about this poem?" the male Citizen called.

Sheen stopped and faced him. "Sir, I prefer not to answer, if I am to be considered an interested party."

"Answer!" he directed, with supreme indifference to her feelings.

"You may answer," the Computer said. "You have not volunteered your influence; you have been summoned by this panel as a material witness. We are trying to determine whether there is substance to the hypothesis that the poem in question represents your viewpoint."

Sheen's mouth firmed. Her human mannerisms had become so facile that in no physical way was her machine nature evident. She was a beautiful woman, naked of body and perhaps of mind. "Then you shall have my viewpoint, sir. If the poem concerns me, it is not intended as a compliment. It is intended as an attack on the man I love, using me as an involuntary weapon. I am a machine—but I think that even were I alive, I would not care so cynically to hurt a living person in this fashion. This poem is crueler than anything the man I love might do. I am sure his own poem is not of this nature."

The Citizen nodded. "That's some machine," he murmured.

The female Citizen considered, pursing her lips. Her opals flashed. "I am left with a choice. Either this poem is not directed at, shall we say, real people, in which case it is not remarkable—or it *is* so directed, in which case its brilliance is nullified by its cruelty. In either case, I can not respect it. I rate it twenty-five."

That was disaster for Rue. It made her average score 34½. The other panelists could reconsider their votes if they wished, but seemed content to let them stand. Rue's poem had a cumulative score of 77½. Stile had a fair chance to beat that, thanks to Sheen. All he needed was forty points.

Now the judges considered Stile's effort for content. "This poem is more serious and obscure than the other," the Computer said. "Some may not be aware that there exists an alternate frame of reality of this planet within which other laws of physics govern. The author is able to enter that frame, where he is a person of power and has an elegant wife. Several of the first six lines evidently refer to that frame. There was a female wolf who sacrificed her life for her duty, and a magical encounter between a creature of ice and another of fire. The future in that frame can occasionally be foreseen by magical means, and it contains extraordinary mischief, part of which is the conflict of love loyalties. Two lines refer to the Tourney now being concluded, which will lead to Citizenship for one of these serfs. Thus the first portion of the poem is relevant to the larger situation here and must be accorded credit. The second portion appears to be an advisory essay. The Angel Gabriel is destined mythologically to blow his trumpet on Judgment Day for living persons—and that call is the one no one can evade or cheat. This poem extends this concept to creatures both fanciful and repulsive. It concludes that these people and creatures must accept the inevitable with civility, and reminds us that, according to the legend of the other frame, the powerful flute—perhaps an alternate designation of Gabriel's horn—has already announced itself by shaking the earth, in the form of the tremors recently experienced here. Allowing for a considerable figurative element, I find this poem serious and valid. The tremors were actually caused by the collapse of overworked Protonite mines in the southern range, but this can be taken as a warning: the mineral on which this planet's power is literally based is not inexhaustible, and we shall suffer an accounting when that mineral is at last depleted. Already we have suffered a not-inconsequential damage to a number of our facilities. I therefore take this poem as a well-conceived and serious warning, and on that basis I rate it forty-eight."

Stile was amazed and gratified. He had had no hint the Game Computer knew so much about him or the frame of Phaze, or that it could interpret oblique references with such dispatch. Now he realized that everything he had told Sheen, she had relayed to her machine friends. They in turn could have informed the Game Computer, who perhaps was one of their number. Certainly it possessed considerable self-will, backed by the phenomenal resources of the Computer memory banks and the experience of analyzing many thousands of Games. So this should not have surprised him at all.

It was the serf woman's turn to vote. "Is there any cutting at the opponent?" she asked. The other heads indicated that no one perceived any. "I'm not sure about all the business of the other frame; this is the first I've heard of it. But I can believe the Protonite won't last forever, and somehow this serf-Citizen setup must be called to account. So okay, I'll go with the warning. I rate it forty."

This was better than Stile had hoped from her. She had given the other poem 50, and he had feared she was a manhater.

"Good job," the male Citizen said. "Forty-five."

"Just what kind of a person is he in that frame you talk about?" the serf man asked.

"He is what is called an Adept," the Computer answered. "That means he is a powerful magician."

"Funny to hear a computer say that," the man said. "But I sort of go for that fantasy bit, even if it is all a story. Forty-two."

Stile's hope was sailing. These were amazingly favorable responses. He was averaging 44. It would take a rating of 25 by the last panelist to bring him down to par with Rue. The lady Citizen seemed too perceptive for that—but she had surprised him before. He felt his hands getting sweaty as he waited for her answer.

"This mischief of love," she said. "Is this person concerned about the feelings of the lady robot who loves him?"

"He may not answer," the Computer reminded her. "We must divine that answer from his poem."

"I wonder whether in fact it is his own personal reckoning he is most concerned with," she said. "He says they must be civil, because what will be, will be. I am not sure I can accept that answer."

Stile quailed. This woman had downgraded Rue's verse for cruelty; was she about to do the same for his?

"Since he has a wife in the other frame, he really does not need a woman of any kind in this frame," she continued. "It is unfair to keep her in doubt."

"We may approve or disapprove the poet's personal life," the male Citizen said. "But we are here to judge only the merit of the poem. For what it's worth, I see several indications that he recognizes the possibility of fundamental change. A bitch turns noble, defeat becomes victory, ice merges with flame, serf becomes Citizen, the fate of dragons and roaches is linked. Perhaps he is preparing his philosophy for the recognition that a living creature may merge with a machine. If this is the way fate decrees, he will accept it."

She nodded. "Yes, the implication is there. The author of this poem, I think, is unlikely to be deliberately cruel. He is in a difficult situation, he is bound, he is civil. It is an example more of us might follow. I rate this work forty-four."

Stile's knees almost gave way. She had not torpedoed him; his total score would be 82, comfortably ahead of Rue's total.

"Do any wish to change their votes on either aspect of either poem?" the Computer inquired. "Your votes are not binding until confirmed."

The panelists exchanged glances. Stile got tense again. It could still come apart!

"Yes, I do," the serf woman said. Stile saw Rue tense; this was the one who had given her 50 on content. If she revised her grade on Stile's poem downward—

"I believe I overreacted on that fifty score," she said. "Let's call it forty-five for *Cruel Lover*."

Again Stile's knees turned to goo. She had come down on his side!

"Final score eighty-two to seventy-seven in favor of Stile's poem," the Computer said after a pause. "He is the winner of this Tourney."

Now there was applause from the hidden public address system. So quickly, so simply, he had won!

But he saw Rue, standing isolated, eyes downcast. On impulse he went to her. "It was a good game," he said. "You could easily have won it."

"I still have life tenure," she said, half choked with disappointment. Then, as an afterthought, she added: "Sir."

Stile felt awkward. "If you ever need a favor—"

"I did not direct my poem at you. Not consciously. I was thinking of someone who threw me over. Sir."

But now the crowd was closing in, and Stile's attention was necessarily diverted. "By the authority vested in me by the Council of Citizens of Planet Proton," the Game Computer said, its voice emerging from every speaker under its control throughout the Game Annex, "I now declare that the serf Stile, having won the Tourney, is acquitted of serf status and endowed with Citizenship and all appurtenances and privileges pertaining thereto, from this instant forward."

The applause swelled massively. The panelists joined in, serfs and Citizens alike.

A robot hastened forward with an ornate robe. "Sir, I belong to your transition estate. It is your privilege to wear any apparel or none. Yet to avoid confusion—"

Stile had thought he was braced for this, but the repeated appellation "sir" startled him. For a lifetime he had called others sir; now he had comprehensive conditioning to unlearn. "Thank you," he said, reaching for the robe.

The robot skittered to the side. "Allow me, sir," it said, and Stile realized it wanted to put the robe on him. It did not behoove a Citizen to serve himself, though he could if he wanted to. Stile suffered himself to be dressed, holding a mental picture of a horse being saddled. "Thank you," he repeated awkwardly.

The machine moved close, getting the robe on and adjusted. "A Citizen need not thank a machine—or anyone," it murmured discreetly in Stile's ear.

"Oh. Yes. Thank—uh, yes."

"Quite all right, sir," the machine said smoothly.

Now a lady Citizen approached. It was Stile's employer. Former employer, he reminded himself. "I am gratified, Stile," she said. "You have made me a winner too."

"Thank you, sir." Then Stile bit his tongue.

She smiled. "Thank *you*, sir." And she leaned forward to kiss him on the right eyebrow. "I profited a fantastic amount on your success. But more than that is the satisfaction of sponsoring a Tourney winner. You will find me appreciative." She walked away.

Now the Citizen known as the Rifleman approached. "I know exactly how you feel," he said. That was no exaggeration; the Rifleman had won his own Tourney fifteen years before. Stile had encountered him in the first Round of this Tourney and barely pulled out the victory. The Rifleman had been an excellent loser. "Accept some private advice, Citizen: get away from the public for several days and drill yourself in the new reality. That will cure you of embarrassing slips. And get yourself someone to explain the ropes in nontechnical terms— the extent of your vested estate, the figures, the prerogatives. There's a hell of a lot to learn fast, if you don't want to be victimized by predatory Citizens."

"But aren't all Citizens—that is, don't they respect the estates of other Citizens?"

"Your minimum share of the Protonite harvest can not be impinged upon—but only your luck and competence and determination can establish your place in the Citizen hierarchy. This is a new game, Stile—oh, yes, Citizens have names; we are merely anonymous to the serfs. You may wish to select a new name for yourself—"

"No need."

"It is a game more intricate and far-reaching than any within the Tourney. Make a point to master its nuances, Stile—soon." And the Rifleman gave him a meaningful glance.

The audience was dissipating as the novelty of the new Citizen wore off. Stile signaled Sheen. "Can your friends provide me with a mentor conversant with the nuances of Citizen behavior?"

"They can, sir," she said. "Or they could program me—"

"Excellent! Get yourself programmed. They'll know what I need. And do it soon."

Sheen left. Stile found it incongruous that she should remain naked while he was now clothed. Yet of course she remained a serf—an imitation serf—now in his employ; she would remain naked the rest of her life.

Her life? Stile smiled, a trifle grimly. He was forgetting that she had no life. Yet she was his best friend in this frame.

Stile turned to the robot who had brought his robe. "Take me to my estate," he ordered it.

The machine hesitated. "Sir, you have none."

"None? But I thought all Citizens—"

"Each Citizen has a standard share of the Protonite mines. All else follows."

"I see." It seemed there was much that was not handed to a Citizen on a platter. He needed that manual of Citizenship! Where was Sheen? Her programming should have been quick.

Then she appeared. "I have it, sir," she said.

"Excellent. Take me to an appropriate and private place, and deliver."

"Don't I always—sir?" She led the way out of the Game Annex.

The place turned out to be a temporary minidome set up on the desert. Its generator tapped an underground power cable, so as to form the force field that prevented the thin, polluted outside atmosphere from penetrating. A portable unit filled the dome with pleasant, properly cooled air. Sheen set up a table for two, put out crackers, cheese, and mock wine, adjusted the field to turn opaque, and planted a spy-disrupter device on the ground. "Now we are private, sir," she said.

"You don't have to say sir to me," he protested.

"Yes, I do, sir. You are a Citizen and I am a naked serf. We violate this convention at our peril."

"But you've been my friend all along!"

"And once more than that, sir," she reminded him. She had come to him as guardian and mistress, and had been good in both capacities. His marriage to the Lady Blue had deleted the second. Sheen, a machine supposedly without any human emotion not programmed into her, had tried to commit suicide—self-destruction. She had become reconciled after meeting the Lady Blue. Sheen still loved him, and for that Stile felt guilty.

"It occurs to me that, as a Citizen, I could have you reprogrammed to have no personal feeling toward me," he said.

"This is true, sir."

"Do you wish it?"

"No, sir."

"Sheen, I value you greatly. I do not want you to suffer. That poem of Rue's—I am absolutely opposed to giving you cause to feel that way. Is there anything within my present power I can do to make you happy?"

"There is, sir. But you would not."

She was uncompromising. She wanted his love again, physically if not emotionally, and that he could not give. "Aside from that."

"Nothing, sir."

"But I may be able to make your friends happy. As Citizen, I can facilitate their recognition as sapient entities." Her friends were the self-willed machines of Proton who, like Sheen herself, had helped him survive Citizen displeasure in the past. He had sworn never to act against their interests so long as they did not act against the interests of man, and both parties honored that oath. Stile did not regard their desire to achieve serf status as contrary to the oath; he agreed they should have it. But such status was not easy to achieve; the Citizens were devoted to the status quo.

"All in good time, sir. Now shall we review the appurtenances and privileges of Citizenship?"

"By all means."

Rapidly, in simple language, she acquainted him with his situation. He was entitled to use the proceeds from his share of the mines to purchase or construct a physical estate, to staff it with serfs, robots, androids, cyborgs, or anything else, and to indulge in any hobbies he wished. The amount of credit available from his share was sufficient to enable him to construct a moderate palace, hire perhaps twenty-five serfs, and buy six robots of Sheen's type. Expensive hobbies like exotic horse breeding or duplicating the Hanging Gardens of Babylon would have to wait until the palace was complete. The income of a Citizen was not limitless; it only seemed that way to serfs.

It was possible, however, to increase one's resources by making and winning large wagers with other Citizens. Bets of a year's income were not uncommon. However, if a Citizen got two years in arrears, further wagers would not be honored until he caught up. It was never permitted for a Citizen to become destitute; a basic lifestyle had to be maintained. Appearance was vital.

"I'll have no problems there," he said. "I'm not a gambling man, outside the Game. I shall be a very conservative Citizen and live well within my income. Most of the time I won't even be here, as you know."

She nodded sadly. "Yes, sir. There's a note in the program from my friends. They warn it is not safe for you to stand pat. Forces are building rapidly. To protect yourself you must soon develop your estate to a hundred times its original magnitude. Within six months."

"A hundred times!" he exclaimed. "In six months!"

"And you must unravel the mystery that is associated with your lasering, sir. Who sent me to protect you? My friends have disturbing new evidence that this is not an isolated event. Someone or something is interfering with your life, and my friends can't discover who."

"Yes. And in Phaze, someone set the Red Adept against me on a false alarm." He had had an extraordinary amount of trouble in that connection, ending in the banishment of the Red Adept from both Phaze and Proton. The Oracle had said Blue would destroy Red, and that had proved correct—but none of that mischief would have occurred if someone had not started the rumor that Blue intended to attack Red.

"And there was that earthquake, sir, which you believe is connected to events in Phaze," she continued. "Another portent, perhaps."

"Definitely. The Platinum Elves informed me that I would be involved in important developments, after my honeymoon." Ooops—he had not meant to mention the honeymoon to Sheen. He continued rapidly. "I'm not sure I like the implication. I don't know what the linkages between frames might be, but since a number of people can cross, there can be interactions, perhaps quite serious ones." He breathed deeply. "I was psychologically prepared for banishment from Proton when I got eliminated from the Tourney. I'm not so certain about how to proceed now that I have permanent tenure. I don't feel comfortable here in clothing."

"That is why you needed to isolate yourself, sir."

Stile got up and paced the small enclosure. "I promised to return to Phaze by noon. I have already overrun that deadline. Why don't you set in motion the machinery for the establishment of my physical estate, and start hiring serfs, while I cross the curtain to—"

"That might not be wise, sir."

Her constant "sirs" were still getting on his nerves, but he knew this was good conditioning. "Not wise?"

"You will need your money as a stake to multiply your estate, sir, so should not fritter it away on nonessentials. And if it became known that a machine was disposing your assets—"

"I am a Citizen, aren't I? I can use a machine if I want to, can't I?" Stile was irritated, not liking the implied slur at Sheen.

"Yes, sir."

"So I'm appointing you my chief of staff, or whatever the appropriate office is. I'd better hire a staff of serfs, for appearances, and become a compulsive gambler. But I'll lose my new fortune unless I have competent input. Will your friends help?"

"They will, sir."

"Then ask them to locate an appropriate adviser for me. One who knows how to break in a new Citizen."

"And how to escalate a Citizen's fortune rapidly, sir."

"Precisely. Now I'll go finish my honey—uh, my business in Phaze. Assuming I can get out of Proton unobserved."

"A Citizen can, sir," she assured him. "If you will make a brief, formal holo statement of authorization, so I can draw on your funds—"

"Ah, yes." Stile took care of that immediately.

"Thank you, sir," she said, accepting the recording. "I shall set the wheels in motion."

"Excellent. And I'll ponder what I can do for you and your friends."

Sheen nodded, knowing he could do nothing for her. She would serve him loyally and lovingly, regardless.

CHAPTER 5

West Pole

He was late, but the Lady Blue forgave him. "I had the news before thee. Thou art a Citizen now."

"It's anticlimactic," Stile complained. "Citizenship is the ultimate prize of Proton. Now that I have it, it's mainly a nuisance. Hidden forces decree that I must commence a new and chancy course, to be ready for even more tension. I wonder if this relates in any way to the promised mischief at the West Pole?"

"How can such complications arise now?" the Lady inquired rhetorically. "All we seek is a simple honeymoon."

"Somehow I don't think we're going to have it."

They attended the snow-demons' banquet. It was magnificent, in its fashion. Candied icicles for aperitif, iceburgers, fried avalanche, sludge freeze as a beverage, and snow cones for dessert. The snow-demons pitched in with gusto; Stile and the Lady nibbled with imperfect enthusiasm, until Stile sneaked in a small spell and changed their morsels to items with food content concealed under snow frosting.

At night, side by side in a surprisingly comfortable snowbank, they talked. "I have a problem," Stile said quietly.

"I think it must needs wait till the snowmen sleep," she murmured. "They exhibit unseemly curiosity as to how flesh-mortals perform without melting from generated heat."

He patted her anatomy under the snow blanket, where the curious demons couldn't see. "A Proton problem."

"The Lady Sheen."

"The lovely self-willed robot Lady Sheen, who will not accept reprogramming. I must work closely with her, for I have agreed to help her machine friends. They helped me survive when times were hard in Proton, and I must help them achieve serf status now. And they warn me that more trouble is coming; that I must gamble to enhance my estate vastly and research to learn who sent Sheen in the first place. I fear it links in some way to events in Phaze, so I must follow through. Only I wish I didn't have to use Sheen—take that in what sense thou wilt. It isn't fair to her, and I feel guilty."

"As well thou might," she agreed. "I promised to consider her case, and so I have done. Now let me see if I have this right. The self-willed golems—machines—wish recognition as people?"

"Correct. Serfs are the lowest people, but are more than the highest machines. Serfs can play the Game, compete in the Tourney, win privileges or even Citizenship. When their tenure expires, they depart the planet with generous cumulative pay. Machines are permitted none of this; they are slaves until junked. Yet some are intelligent, conscious, feeling."

"And the Lady Sheen is one of these unrecognized machine creatures."

"She is. She is in every way a person, with very real emotions. They merely happen to be programmed, rather than natural."

"And is there a difference between program and nature?"

"I doubt it. Different means to similar ends, perhaps."

"Then thou must marry the Lady Sheen."

Stile paused. "I don't believe I heard thee properly, Lady."

"It is the other frame. She can never cross the curtain. Thou canst do as thou wilt with her there."

Stile had been growing sleepy. Now he was awakening. "I am sure I am misunderstanding thee."

"If a Citizen marries a machine—"

"Nobody can marry a machine!"

"—then that machine must have—"

"Machines don't have—" Stile stopped. "I wonder. The spouses of Citizens do not achieve Citizen status, but they do have certain prerogatives. They are considered to be employed—their employment being the marriage. And only serfs are employable."

"So a married machine would be a serf," the Lady concluded. "And if one machine were a serf—"

"The precedent—"

"Thinkest thou it would accomplish thy purpose?"

Stile considered, his head spinning. "If the marriage stuck, it would be one hell of a lever for legal machine recognition!"

"That was my notion," she said complacently.

"But I am married to thee!" he protested.

"In Phaze. Not in Proton."

"But thou canst cross over!"

"True. But I am of this frame, and never will I leave it for aught save emergency. I have no claim on the things of Proton, nor wish I any."

"But I love only thee! I could never—"

"Thou lovest more than thou knowest," she said with gentle assurance. "Neysa, Sheen—"

"Well, there are different types of—"

"And I spoke not of love. I spoke of marriage."

"A marriage of convenience? To a robot?"

"Dost thou hold the Lady Sheen beneath convenience, for that she be made of metal?"

"Nay! But—" He paused. "Nay, I must confess I do think less of her. Always since I learned she was not real, that—"

"Methinks thou hast some thinking to do," the Lady Blue said, and turned her back.

Stile felt the reproach keenly. He was prejudiced; he had great respect for Sheen, but love had been impossible because she was not flesh. Yet he reminded himself that he had come closer to loving her before encountering the Lady Blue. Had Sheen's nonliving nature become a pretext for his inevitable change of heart? He could not be sure, but he was unable to deny it.

How could he fight for the recognition of the sapient self-willed machines if he did not recognize them as discrete individuals himself? How could he marry Sheen if he did not love her? If he came to think of her as a real person, wouldn't such a marriage make him a bigamist? There were two frames, certainly, but he was only one person. Yet since the Lady Blue had generously offered to accept half-status, confining herself to Phaze—

Think of the commotion the marriage of a Citizen to a robot would make in Proton! It would convulse the social order! That aspect appealed to him. Yet—

"Wouldst thou settle for a betrothal?" he asked at last.

"An honest one," she agreed sleepily.

"Say six months. Time enough to get the legal issues clarified, one way or the other. There would be formidable opposition from other Citizens. And of course Sheen herself might not agree."

"She will agree," the Lady Blue said confidently. "A betrothal is a commitment, and never wilt thou renege. She will have some joy of thee at last."

This was not a way he had ever expected the Lady Blue to speak, and Stile was uneasy. Yet perhaps she had some concern of her own, knowing she had taken him away from Sheen. Possibly the social mores of Phaze differed from those of Proton in this respect, and sharing was more permissible. Certainly his friend Kurrelgyre the werewolf had believed it, assigning his bitch to a friend while Kurrelgyre himself was in exile from his Pack. The Lady Blue had met Sheen, liked her, and accepted her immediately as a person; apparently that had not been any social artifice.

"And if in six months it is legal, then shall I marry her," Stile continued. "In Proton. But I can not love her."

"Then love me," the Lady Blue said, turning to him.

That was reward enough. But already Stile had a glimpse of that controversy he was about to conjure, like a savage magic storm.

In the morning they resumed their tour of the curtain, recrossing the White Mountain range and bearing southwest. There were some deep crevices on the ground; when their steeds' hooves knocked sand into them, it fell down and away beyond the limit of perception, soundlessly. "Deep caves, mayhap," Stile remarked, a bit nervous about a possible collapse of the footing. But Clip tapped the ground with a forehoof, indicating that there was no danger of a fall as long as a unicorn picked the way.

Stile checked his contour map and discovered they were heading for the Black Demesnes. He did not like the Black Adept, and by mutual consent they spelled rapidly past the grim castle and well on toward the Purple Mountains.

Now the curtain bore directly south. Suddenly there was an explosion of fire before them. Stile squinted at the flame, trying to determine whether it was natural or magic.

"The warners!" the Lady exclaimed. "The Green Adept!"

"It must be," Stile agreed. "I promised to bypass him."

They went around, rejoining the curtain southwest of Green's marked territory. The curtain was curving back westward, through the foothills of the southern mountains. The scenery was pleasant; waist-high bushes covered the rolling terrain, topped with faintly purple flowers. The steeds trotted through, finding firm footing beneath. The midafternoon sun slanted down.

Suddenly a creature jumped in front of Hinblue. The thing had the body of a powerful man and the head of a wolf. It bayed—and the horse spooked. The Lady Blue, an expert rider, was not in any trouble; she brought her steed about and calmed her.

Then a second creature appeared, this one with the head of a ram. It bleated.

Stile's mind formulated a spell while his hand went for his harmonica. But he withheld his magic, uncertain whether it was necessary. He had heard of the animalheads, but understood they were not aggressive toward human beings. Was his information mistaken?

More animalheads appeared, making their assorted noises. Cats, goats, hawks, bears, turtles—none of them with the intelligence or verbal ability of a man, but each quite formidable in its fashion. They were all snarling, squawking, roaring, or growling aggressively. A pighead charged toward Stile, grunting.

"I fear they mean mischief," the Lady Blue said. "This is not like them. Something has angered them, methinks."

"Yes," Stile agreed. Clip's horn was holding the pighead at bay, but a crocodilehead was circling to the rear. "We had best avoid them till we know their motivation."

"Methinks we can outrun them," she said, concerned but not worried.

Their steeds took off. Hinblue was a fine mare, capable of a galloping velocity that shamed ordinary horses; she really did move like the wind. But Clip was a unicorn whose inherent magic made him swifter yet. By common consent they used no other magic, not revealing Stile's status; Adepts were not necessarily favored in the back reaches of Phaze.

The animalheads gave chase enthusiastically, baying, bellowing, and hooting. But their human bodies could not compare with the equine bodies, and they soon fell behind. Yet two things narrowed the gap; this was animalhead territory, more familiar to the beastmen than to the intruders; they could take the best paths and shortcuts, and kept popping up just ahead. Also, there were a number of them, so that a good many were already ranged along the route, and these formed living barricades. This made the chase close enough for discomfort.

Three catfaces rose up before them. Both steeds, well versed in this sort of thing, did not leap, for though they could have cleared the creatures, they would in the process have exposed their vulnerable underbellies to attack from below. Instead they put their heads down and charged low.

The catheads could have handled the horse, but not the deadly horn of the unicorn. That horn could skewer a standing creature instantly. The cats dropped down, giving way, and the party galloped on unscathed.

Half a dozen pigheads appeared, grunting urgently. This time the steeds leaped. The pigheads reached up, but their weapons were their tusks, not good for vertical goring. One got struck in the head by Hinblue's front hoof, and the others desisted.

A pack of wolfheads closed in, but the steeds dodged and galloped to the side and got around and through, then put on speed to leave the beasts behind. No more animalheads appeared, and Stile knew that his party had gotten away clean.

Unnoticed in the hurry, the vegetation had changed. They were now forging through a forest of huge old trees—oak, ash, elm, and beech, by the look. But it was not necessarily easy to tell them apart, for the trunks were gnarled and deeply corrugated, and the tops shaded the ground into gloom.

"I like not the look of this," the Lady Blue said.

Stile agreed. Their escape had led them away from the curtain, so that they now had to relocate. It would not be safe to return to their point of divergence from it; the animalheads were there. Stile still preferred to avoid the use of magic in the present situation; this was an annoyance, not a crisis.

All of which meant they would have to search for the curtain the tedious way—slowly, eyes squinting for the almost invisible shimmer. The curtain was easy to follow lengthwise, but difficult to intercept broadside unless one knew exactly where to look.

"Well, it's all part of the honeymoon," Stile said. The Lady smiled; she had known there would be this sort of interruption in the schedule.

They looked, riding slowly around the great old trees. The forest was so dense now that even indirect light hardly penetrated, yet there were an increasing number of small plants. They twined up around the bases of the tree trunks and spread across the forest floor. Some were a suspiciously verdant green; others were pallid white. Many were insidiously ugly.

Yet they were plants, not creatures. None of them sent questing tentacles for the intruders; none had poisonous thorns. They flourished in gloom; that seemed to be their only oddity.

There was no sign of the curtain. "It will take forever to find it this way," Stile said. "I want to be back on it by nightfall." He jumped down and walked. "We can make a better search on foot," he said.

Clip blew a warning note. Unicorns were naturally resistant to magic, and this protected the rider. The Blue Adept, Clip felt, needed protection, and should not be straying from his steed. As if Stile did not have ample magic of his own.

Stile walked on, peering this way and that, searching for the curtain. It had to be somewhere near here; they had not gone all that far and they had not diverged from its path greatly. In this gloom the shimmer should be clear enough.

Clip's ears turned. He blew a low warning note. Stile paused to listen.

The animalheads were catching up. Stile's party had to move on before—

Too late. A pigface appeared in front of Stile. A dogface came up behind the Lady. There was rustling in the bushes all around. Perhaps aided by some sort of stealth-spell, the animalheads had surrounded them.

The Lady called Hinblue, who charged toward her. Stile stepped toward Clip, but already the pighead was on him. Stile did not use magic. He drew his sword, threatening but not attacking the creature. There was something odd about this, and he did not want to do anything irrevocable until he fathomed it.

The pighead halted its aggression—but three sheepheads were closing from the sides. A spell would freeze them, but Stile still didn't want to do it. Rather than shed blood, he dodged around the pighead, hurdled a fallen branch—and an offshoot moved up and intercepted his leading ankle, causing him to take a heavy spill into a flowering bush beyond.

There was a kind of zap! as the leaves were disturbed, and Stile felt the presence of magic. Quickly he jumped up, feeling about his body, but he seemed to have suffered no injury.

The animalheads had taken advantage of his fall to surround him. Clip had stopped a short distance away, perceiving that the animalheads could reach Stile before the unicorn could. No sense precipitating an attack by spooking them.

Stile decided to make an honest attempt at communication before resorting reluctantly to magic to freeze them temporarily in place. It wasn't natural for normally peaceful creatures to attack and pursue strangers like this. Maybe he could establish a yes-no dialogue with one of the more intelligent ones. He really wasn't looking for trouble on his honeymoon!

He opened his mouth to speak—and nothing but air emerged. He couldn't talk!

Stile tried again. There was no pain, no constriction in his throat—but he could not vocalize at all. The plant—it had zapped him with a spell of silence!

The animalheads did not know about his power of magic, so did not know what he had lost. They thought him an ordinary man—which he was now. They converged.

Stile quickly brought the harmonica to his mouth. He might not be able to speak or sing, but the instrument's music would summon some protective magic. He blew—and silence came out.

He stamped his foot on the ground and made no noise. He banged his sword against a root—silently. He whistled—without even a hiss of air.

The spell had rendered him totally quiet. Since he could nullify it only by using his own magic, and that required sound, he was trapped.

These tests had been performed rapidly, and the conclusion drawn in a few seconds, for the animalheads were on him. Still he did not use his sword. He had threatened with it, but remained unwilling actually to shed blood. The mystery of these creatures' attack bothered him as much as the threat to himself.

A cathead pounced. Stile ducked, reached up, and guided it into a turning fall. He might be silent, but he wasn't helpless!

But now a tremendously tusked boarhead came at him from the left and an alligatorhead from the right. There was no question of their intent. He could dodge these two—but how long could he hold out against the converging mob?

Meanwhile, Clip had resumed motion. Now the unicorn arrived. His horn caught the alligatorhead and impaled it. A powerful heave sent the creature flying back over the equine's shoulder. Then a forehoof knocked the boarhead away.

Clip stood beside Stile, giving him a chance to mount. Then they were away in a great leap. Soon they joined Hinblue and the Lady Blue and galloped clear of the animalheads once again.

The Lady Blue realized what was wrong. "Thou art victim of a silence-spell!" she cried. "We must take thee back to the Blue Demesnes for a counterspell!"

But the animalheads were already catching up again, cutting off the return—and of course it would be a long ride all the way back to the Blue Demesnes, even cutting directly across to it. Their only avenue of escape at the moment was north, deeper into the jungle.

The steeds plunged on, but the vegetation thickened. Now grasping plants occurred, reaching thorny branches toward them, opening green jawlike processes. This jungle was coming alive—at the time when Stile had lost his power. A single spell could quell every plant—but he could not utter that spell.

The Lady Blue exclaimed as vines twined about her body. Her steed had to halt, lest she be drawn off. Then the vines attacked Hinblue's legs, seeking to anchor the horse to the ground.

Stile nudged Clip. The unicorn charged back. His horn touched the vines, and they writhed out of the way, repelled by the countermagic. Meanwhile, Stile used his sword to chop at the nether vines, freeing the horse. The weapon normally carried by men in Phaze was the rapier, but Stile felt more comfortable with the broadsword, and now the cutting edge was useful indeed.

There was a renewed baying of animalheads, catching up yet again. Stile's party moved forward once more.

The plants got worse. Tree branches dropped down to bar their way, dangling poisonous-looking moss. Stile cut the moss away with his sword, clearing the path for the Lady and steeds. Ichor from the moss soon covered the blade, turning it gray-green. The stuff reeked with a pungent odor, almost like dragon's blood. Stile did not like this at all. Yet he had to keep hacking the encroaching growth away, afraid to let any of the party get caught.

At last the sounds of pursuit diminished. The animalheads had been foiled by this vicious jungle too.

But the trees, bushes, and brambles had closed in behind, forming a virtually impenetrable barrier. Stile's sword was already stained and pitted under the ichor, and holes were appearing in his clothing where drops had spattered. He didn't want to hack through any more of this!

Clip blew a musical note. Stile dismounted, and the unicorn phased into the hawk and flew up. The sky was the one open route!

The Lady Blue also dismounted and came to him. "Mayhap I can help thee," she offered. She laid her hands on his throat, and their healing power warmed skin and muscle deep inside. But the silence was not any constriction in his throat, but a cloud of nonsound that surrounded him. He could not be healed because he wasn't ill; the spell itself had to be abated, somehow.

"Mayhap a potion?" the Lady mused, fishing in her purse. But none of the elixirs she had with her seemed promising, and she did not want to expend them uselessly. "Clip may find something," she said hopefully. "From the air, more can be seen."

The jungle was not being idle, however. Plants were visibly growing toward them. This time they were ugly, jointed things, with great brown thorns hooked at each juncture. These things were structured to engage a retreating form, and not to disengage, and they looked as if they had hollow points. Bloodsuckers, surely. Stile brought out his knife and sawed off the nearest thorn stem, severing it with difficulty; the fiber was like cable. By the time he completed the cut, several other tendrils were approaching his boots. He had to draw his sword again, hacking the fibers apart by brute force, clearing a circle around the Lady and horse. He had almost forgotten how formidable nature could be for those who lacked the convenience of magic. It was a reminder in perspective—not that that helped much at the moment.

The hawk returned, changing into man-form. "There is a domicile ahead, and the land is clear around it," Clip reported. "An old man lives there, a hermit by his look; mayhap he will guide us out, can we but reach him. Or we can follow the curtain; it passes through that clearing. I have scouted the most direct approach to the curtain. I can not cross it, but if thou and the Lady and Hinblue can—the clearing is but a quarter mile from there."

Stile squeezed Clip's arm in thanks. The unicorn had really come through for them! They could hack their way to the curtain, cross to Proton, hurry forward, and recross to recover breath. It would not be fun, but it should be feasible.

They chopped through the undergrowth with renewed will. This time the plants were rigidly fan-shaped leaves on tough stems, the edges of the leaves as sharp as knives. They did not move to intercept people, but they were extraordinarily difficult to clear from the path because the stems were almost inaccessible behind the leaves. When Stile reached under to sever one stem, the leaves of another plant were in his way; if he sliced through anyway, he risked brushing the knife-edges along his wrist or forearm. Without magic to heal cuts, he found this nervous business, though he knew the Lady could help heal him. Progress was slow, and his sword arm grew tired.

Clip stepped in, using the tip of his horn to reach past the leaves to break the stems. This enabled them to go faster, and soon they intersected the curtain.

Stile could not even perform the simple curtain-crossing spell. The Lady did it for him and Hinblue—and suddenly the three of them were in Proton, on a barren plain, gasping for air. Clip changed to hawk-form and flew directly to their rendezvous in the clearing.

They were able to walk on the bare sands, but breathing was labored, and Hinblue, as the Lady had feared, did not understand at all. The horse's nostrils flared, and she was skittish, squandering energy better saved for forward progress. Hinblue was a very fine mare, who could have been a prizewinner in Proton, but she had had no experience with this. The Lady led her, though the Lady herself was gasping.

Stile heard his own labored breathing—and realized what it meant. "I'm not silent any more—no magic in this frame!" he exclaimed.

"But when thou returnest—" the Lady responded.

When he crossed again, the spell would still be on him. He could not escape it this way, except by traveling in this frame back to the region of the Blue Demesnes, where he could cross to get the Lady's reserve spells. But no Proton dome was near; even if he wanted to risk entering one, the trip wasn't feasible.

The horse was in increasing trouble. "My Lord, I must take her back," the Lady gasped. "She does not understand."

Stile had handled a horse in these barrens before. He recognized the symptoms of the growing panic. "Take her across; maybe we're far enough."

They willed themselves across at what seemed to be a clearing. It was —but also turned out to be no safe resting place. The ground writhed with sucker leaves that sought to fasten to the flesh of human or equine. Hinblue stamped her hooves, trampling down the suckers, but already some were fastening on the sides of the hooves, trying to drink from the hard surface. Stile tried to cut off the plants, but they were too low to the ground, making his blade ineffective.

"We can not stay here," the Lady said, her feet moving in a dance of avoidance. "We must cross again."

Stile agreed. The horse had recovered her wind. They crossed back to Proton and made a dash for the better clearing ahead. This time they made it.

Now they were in sight of the hermit's hut. Clip rejoined them, remaining in hawk-form so as not to betray his nature before the watching hermit. They saw the old man's eyes peering from the dark window.

"He sees us," the Lady said. "We shall need his help, for we can not go through more of this jungle or through Proton."

Stile could only nod. He didn't like this situation at all. Some honeymoon they were having!

The Lady went up to talk to the hermit. But the old man slammed the rickety door and refused to answer her call.

Stile began to get angry. The hawk made a warning cry, and Stile stayed back. Clip had caught on to something important, by his attitude.

The Lady Blue gave it up. "Surely the hermit knows our predicament, but he will help us not," she said. The touch of a flush on her cheeks betrayed her irritation.

The hawk spoke again, then flew to the ground and scratched a place bare. In that spot he gouged out a word: ORANGE.

The Lady was first to catch on. "The Orange Adept! No wonder he is such a curmudgeon!"

Stile signaled, pointing to himself and raising an eyebrow questioningly. He wanted to know whether the Orange Adept was aware of the identity of his visitors.

Clip thought not. This was merely the way the Adept treated all strangers. Few Adepts cared what happened to those who intruded on their Demesnes, and those Adepts who did care, generally were malignant. Stile had encountered the syndrome before, but he did not like it any better with repetition.

They walked to the far side of the clearing, while the beady eyes of Orange peered from the window of his hut. Here the curtain plunged into the thickest of the bramble tangles. Hinblue tried to trample them down, but they wrapped around her foreleg, making her squeal in pain as the thorns dug in. There was a snicker from the hut.

Stile slashed at the mass with his sword, but no matter how many stems he severed, the mass held its form, like a pile of brush. It would be necessary to draw each severed stem out and set it in the clearing—and each stem seemed to interlink with others, so that the entire mass tended to come loose, falling about his bare arms and scratching. The hermit sniggered, enjoying this.

After a time, scratched and sweaty and tired, they gave it up. They could not get through this way. But meanwhile, the clearing had diminished; new plants were encroaching, and they looked just as ugly as the brambles. The Orange Adept's mode of magic evidently related to plants. Indeed, it must have been one of his creatures that silenced Stile. Now the old man was enjoying watching the flies struggle in the web.

"Mayhap the other side of the curtain, again . . ." the Lady said. But at her words Hinblue's ears went back, her nostrils distended, and the whites showed around her eyes. She did not want to brave the oxygen-poor, polluted air of Proton again!

Yet they couldn't remain here. By nightfall the advancing plants would leave them no opening, and they would have to fight for their lives while the Orange Adept laughed. Stile was furious with frustration, but unable to oppose this magic with his own.

Still, he could act directly against the malignant Adept. He put his hand on his sword, facing the hut.

"Nay, my love," the Lady cautioned. "There are worse plants than these, and surely they protect him. We must not approach him."

She was right. Stile had to contain his rage.

Clip flew up and away, searching for some way out. The Lady calmed Hinblue. One thing about the Lady Blue—she did not lose her nerve in a crisis. She was in all respects an admirable woman, his ideal and his beloved. Before Stile let her suffer, he would charge the hut and menace the Adept with his sword, heedless of whatever plants might make their hideous presence known. But first he would wait for Clip, hoping the unicorn would be able to help.

The sun descended inexorably, and the plants continued to close in. Some were like giant vines, with flowers that resembled the orifices of carnivorous worms. Transparent sap beaded in those throats, and drooled from the nether petals like saliva. The sword should stop these —but what would happen when darkness closed? Stile did not want to fight these plants at night.

Clip returned. He landed behind the Lady, so that he could not be seen from the hut, and changed to man-form. "I may have found help," he reported, but he seemed dubious.

"Out with it, 'corn," the Lady snapped.

"I saw no way out of this garden of tortures; it is miles thick. So I searched for other creatures who might assist, but found only a lone-traveling troll."

"A troll!" the Lady cried, distraught. "No help there!" She was toler-ant of many creatures, but hated trolls, for a tribe of them had once tried to ravish her. Stile knew that his alternate self, the former Blue Adept, had had a bad altercation with trolls who had massacred his whole home village and been in turn massacred by him.

"Yet this one seems different," Clip continued. "He travels by day, which is unusual; he was voluminously swathed in black cloth, so that no sunlight might touch him, but I knew his nature by his outline." He wrinkled his nose. "And by his smell." Trolls tended to have a dank-earth ambience.

"Why should a troll travel by day?" the Lady asked, intrigued de-spite her revulsion. "They are horrors of the night, turning to stone in sunlight."

"Precisely. So I inquired, expecting an insult. But he said he was in quest of the Blue Adept, to whom he owes a favor." Clip shrugged in seeming wonder.

Stile looked askance at this. He had had no commerce with trolls!

"That's what he said," Clip continued. "I was skeptical, fearing more mischief, but, mindful of thy plight, I investigated. 'What favor canst thine ilk do for the likes of the Adept?' I inquired politely. And quoth he, 'I am to bring him to a plant this night.' And quoth I, 'How can the Adept trust a monster like thee?' and quoth he, 'He spared me in my youth, and him I owe the favor of a life—mine or his. He may kill me if he wishes, or follow me to the plant. Only then will part of mine onus be acquitted.' And I said, 'He can not be reached at the moment,' and he said, 'Needs must I go to him now, for only tonight can the first part of my debt be abated,' and I said—"

"Enough!" the Lady cried in exasperation. "I know him now. That is the troll my Lord spared a score of years ago. Perhaps that one, of all his ilk, can be trusted. But how can he get here?"

"I was just telling thee," the unicorn replied, hurt. "I said, 'How canst thou pass an impassable barrier of thorns?' and he said he was a troll, skilled at tunneling, like all his kind."

"Tunneling!" the Lady exclaimed, her face illuminating.

"It will take time, for rock is hard, but he promised to be here by midnight."

By midnight. Could they hold out against the encroaching plants until then? They would have to!

It was a mean, harrowing interim, but they held out. At the crack of midnight the ground shuddered and the grotesque head of the troll emerged into the wan moonlight, casting two shadows. The big eyes blinked. "The night is painfully bright," the creature complained.

"This is Trool the troll," Clip introduced. "And this is the Blue Adept, who does not deign to address thee at this time. Lead him to thy plant."

The troll sank back into the earth. Stile followed, finding a fresh tunnel large enough for hands and knees. The Lady came last. Clip shifted back to his natural form and stood with Hinblue, defending against the plants. If Stile did not recover his power and return in time to help them, only the unicorn would survive.

The tunnel continued interminably, winding about to avoid the giant roots of trees and buried boulders. Stripped of his magic, Stile began to feel claustrophobic. If there were a cave-in, what spell could he make? But he had to trust the troll—the one his other self had spared, long before Stile came to Phaze. For this creature felt he had a debt to the Blue Adept, and Stile now held that office. He could try to explain the distinction between himself and his dead other self to the troll, but doubted this would matter. What use to inform Trool that he had come too late, that the one who had spared him was already gone? Better to let the troll discharge his debt and be free.

At last they emerged beyond the Orange Adept's garden. Stile straightened up with relief. They continued on until the troll halted beside a nondescript bush. "This is the plant," Trool said. His voice was guttural and harsh, in the manner of his kind. What made it unusual was the fact that it was intelligible. He must have practiced hard on human speech.

The Lady leaned forward to peer at the growth in the waning light of the blue moon. Her face was somewhat gaunt, and Stile knew she feared betrayal; certainly the troll's appearance was somewhat too providential. "This is the herb I need!" she exclaimed in gratified wonder. "It will cancel half the spell!"

Half? What else was needed?

"The touch of the horn of a unicorn," she said, understanding his thought.

So he could not be cured until they returned to Clip. His magic would have to wait; he could not use it to facilitate things now.

The Lady took the leaves she needed and thanked the troll a bit diffidently. Trool, perhaps unaware of the cause of her mixed feelings, shrugged and departed, his deed done. They started the trip back to the Orange Demesnes.

It was no more pleasant traversing the tunnel the second time, but at least the route was familiar. Dawn was approaching as Stile finally felt the end and poked his head up through the surface of the ground—only to find it overgrown with vines. Were they too late?

He wrestled his broadsword out and around and began slashing and sawing. The plants, attacked from below, capitulated quickly, and soon Stile and the Lady stood in their own little hacked-out clearing.

He heard grunts and thumps in the direction of the hermit's hut. The yellow moon was now out, showing two equine figures backed against the hut wall, still fighting off the encroaching foliage. Perhaps the plants were less active at night, unable to grow as fast without sunlight; or maybe the Orange Adept was saving the finale for morning, when he could see better. At any rate, the end was not quite yet.

Stile hacked a path across the writhing mass of vegetation, the Lady following and tidying things up with her knife. As the sun broke across the eastern horizon, they reached the equines.

Hinblue was sweating and bleeding from numerous scratches, and was so tired she hardly seemed able to stay on her feet. Clip was better off, but obviously worn; his horn swung in short vicious arcs to intercept each reaching tendril. There was very little room left for the two of them; soon the press of plants and their own fatigue would overwhelm them.

And the Orange Adept peered out of his window, grinning as if at an exhibition. This was his private arena, his personal entertainment, and he was enjoying it immensely. Stile experienced a flare of primal rage.

Now it was the Lady's turn to act. "Take these leaves," she told Stile, giving him the branch she had taken from the troll's bush. "Clip —thy horn, please." The unicorn paused in his combat with the foliage. Guided by the Lady, he touched his horn to the leaves in Stile's hands.

Stile felt something ease, as if he had been released from an ugly threat. He heard his own breathing. "I thank thee," he said.

Then he did a double take. "Hey, I can speak!"

"Do thou speak some suitable spell," the Lady suggested, nipping off a reaching tendril with her small knife.

Quickly Stile summoned a general-purpose spell from his repertoire. "All save me, in stasis be," he sang.

He had not taken time to coalesce his magic force with preliminary music, so the spell was not fully effective, but its impact was nevertheless considerable. The aggressive plants stopped advancing, and Stile's three companions stood stunned.

Only the Orange Adept proved immune. His head swiveled to cover Stile. "What's this?" the man demanded querulously. "Foreign magic in my Demesnes?"

Now Stile let out his long-accumulating wrath. "Oaf, didst know not against whom thou didst practice thy foul enchantment?"

"I know not and care not, peasant!" Orange snapped, sneering.

"Then learn, thou arrogant lout!" Stile cried. He took his harmonica, played a few savage bars to summon his power, then sang: "Let every single spellbound plant, against its master rave and rant!"

Instantly there was chaos. The magic plants rotated on their stems, reorienting on the Orange Adept. Now the tendrils reached toward the hut, ignoring the visiting party.

"Hey!" Orange screamed, outraged. But a thorny tendril twined about his hand, causing him to divert his attention to immediacies.

Stile made a subspell nullifying the remaining stasis-spell, and equines and Lady returned to animation. Stile and the Lady mounted their steeds, and Stile made a spell to heal and invigorate them. Then they rode out through the vicious plants, which ignored this party in their eagerness to close on the hut.

"That was not nice, my Lord Blue," the Lady murmured somewhat smugly.

"Aye," Stile agreed without remorse. "The plants can't really hurt Orange. He will find a way to neutralize them. But I dare say it will be long before every plant is back the way it was. And longer before he bothers passing strangers again."

When they emerged from the Orange Demesnes, Stile guided them southeast, back toward the region of the animalheads. The Lady glanced at him questioningly, but did not comment.

The animalheads appeared. "Know, O creatures, that I am the Blue Adept," Stile said. "Guide me to your leader."

When they pressed forward menacingly, he resorted to magic. "Animalhead, be friend instead," he sang. And the attitude of each one changed. Now they were willing to take him where he had asked.

Soon they encountered an elephanthead, with a giant fat body to support so large an extremity. The creature trumpeted in confusion.

"Each to each, intelligible speech," Stile sang.

"To what do we owe the questionable pleasure of this visit?" the nasal trumpetings translated, now having the semblance of ordinary human speech.

"I am the Blue Adept," Stile said. "This is my Lady Blue. We are on our honeymoon, touring the curtain with our steeds. We seek no quarrel and do not believe we provoked thy creatures. Why did they attack us?"

The elephanthead considered, his trunk twisting uncertainly. He was evidently loath to answer, but also wary of openly defying an Adept. "We sent a person to inquire of the Oracle, after the shaking of the mountains alarmed us. Hard times may be coming to Phaze, and we are concerned about survival."

"So are we," Stile said. "But we understand we have a safe fortnight for our pleasure journey to the West Pole, and thereafter the Lady Blue will have time to bear my son. So the end of Phaze is not quite yet. But why should you interfere with us?"

"The Oracle advised us that if we permitted a man riding a unicorn to pass our demesnes, half our number would perish within the month."

Suddenly the attitude of the animalheads made sense. "The Oracle claims I am a threat to thy kind?" Stile asked incredulously. "I have had no intention of harming thy creatures!"

"The Oracle did not say thou hast intent; only the consequence of thy passage."

"Let me meet the bearer of this message."

A snakehead came forward. Rendered intelligible by Stile's spell, she repeated the message: "Let pass the man on 'corn, and half will die within the month."

The Lady Blue's brow furrowed. "That is an either-or message, unusual. Can it be a true Oracle?"

"The Oracle is always true," the elephanthead said.

"But just let me check the messenger," Stile said, catching on to the Lady's suspicion. He faced the snakehead, played his harmonica, and sang: "Lady Snakehead, tell me true: what the Oracle said to do."

And she repeated: "Let pass the man on 'corn, and half will die within the month. Prevent him, and in that period all will die."

The elephanthead gave a trumpet of amazement. "Half the message! Why didst thou betray us so, snake?"

"I knew not—" she faltered.

"She was enchanted," the Lady Blue said. "By someone who bore ill will to us all."

The elephanthead was chagrined. "Who would that be?"

"Ask first who could have done it," Stile said.

"Only another Adept," the elephanthead said. "We are enchanted creatures, resistant to ordinary magic, else we would change our forms. Only Adepts can play with our bodies or minds."

"So I suspected," Stile said. "I could not prevail against thy kind until I used my magic. Could this be the handiwork of the Orange Adept?"

"Nay. He dislikes us, as he dislikes all animate creatures, even himself. But he has no power over aught save plants."

"Still, a plant can affect a person," Stile said, thinking of the silence-spell that had so inconvenienced him.

But when he used another spell to check what had happened to the snakehead, it showed her being intercepted by a weaselhead woman, seemingly her own kind, who drew a diagram in the dirt that made a flash of light.

"The White Adept!" Stile exclaimed. "I know her mode of magic and know she likes me not."

"We also do not get along with her," the elephanthead agreed. "We apologize to thee, Blue, for our misunderstanding. We shall not again attempt to do thee ill."

"Accepted," Stile said. "Let us part friends, and if we meet again, it shall be to help each other."

"Thou art generous."

"I like animals." Stile did not see fit to remind the animalheads that they still stood to lose half their number soon. Real mischief was brewing, according to the prophecy.

"We like not Adepts, but to thee we shall be friend." And so they parted on a positive note.

Stile and the Lady proceeded north along the curtain. But they were tired; they had not slept the past night. When a suitable camping spot manifested, they camped. There was a streamlet, a fine old apple tree, and a metal object lying on its side. It was about six feet in diameter, roughly cup-shaped, with a number of depressions on the outer surface, as if someone had dented it with small boulders. It seemed to be made entirely of silver; anywhere except Phaze, it would have been phenomenally valuable. Here, of course, such artifacts could be conjured magically.

A storm was rising. "Would this be a good chamber in which to spend the day and night?" Stile inquired. "It seems watertight."

Clip glanced up from his grazing, blowing a single negative note.

Stile shrugged. "The unicorn says no; who am I to argue with such authority?" And he conjured a suitable tent beside the metal structure.

They slept in the shade of the tent while the equines grazed and slept on their feet and stood guard simultaneously.

In the late afternoon, Stile woke to an awful shuddering of the ground. He leaped out of the tent.

Clip stood there in man-form. "If thou pleasest, Adept, make a flare above us in the sky that anyone can see."

Stile obeyed. "Make a flare up there," he sang, pointing upward. It was like a rocket exploding in brilliant colors.

The shuddering increased. A monstrous shape appeared, towering above the trees. "WHERE?" it bellowed.

It was a female human-form giant, so big Stile could not even estimate her height.

"Tell her there," Clip said, indicating the metal structure.

Stile magicked a bright arrow in the sky, pointing toward the silver artifact. The giant saw this, followed the direction with her gaze, and leaned down to grasp the thing. Her near approach was harrowing; it seemed as if a building were falling on them, but the small party stood its ground.

"My silver thimble!" the giantess exclaimed, lifting the tiny object into the sky. "My lost thimble! Who found it for me?"

Stile made sky writing: BLUE ADEPT, with an arrow pointing to himself.

She squinted down from above the clouds. "I thank thee, Blue Adept," she boomed. "What favor may I return thee?"

ONLY THY GOOD WILL, Stile skywrote, daunted. One small misstep and the giantess could crush this entire region flat.

"Granted," she said, and departed with her prize.

"Thou knewest!" Stile accused Clip. "A giantess' silver thimble, six feet across!"

"Giants are good people," Clip agreed smugly. "They have long memories too. Best to be on the right side of a giant."

"I should think so," Stile agreed. "And best not to sleep in a giant thimble."

He conjured a modest repast for himself and the Lady, and some grain to supplement the diet of the equines, since they had used so much of their strength the prior night. Then he and the Lady returned to the tent for the night. As he drifted off to sleep the second time, it occurred to Stile that Clip had been giving excellent service. Stile's favorite was Neysa, his oath-friend, but Clip was certainly a worthy substitute. He would have to ponder some favor to do for the unicorn after this was over, as a suitable reward for such things as helping to save Stile's life and dignity. It was hard to do favors for unicorns, because all of them were subject to their Herd Stallions. But perhaps Stile could clear something with the unicorn hierarchy.

In the morning, refreshed, they resumed the journey. The assorted interruptions had put them behind Stile's schedule; now they had to move along to reach the West Pole before he had to return to Proton.

The curtain curved west through the land of the giants. To Stile's relief they encountered no more of the gigantic people. At noon they came to the ocean.

"But the curtain goes right into the water," Stile protested.

"Of course. The West Pole is on an island," the Lady said. "Conjure a boat."

"But I want to follow the curtain where it touches land." Stile had no special reason for this; he had merely envisioned walking along the curtain, not sailing.

"Then conjure away the ocean," she said gaily.

Instead, Stile enchanted them so that the water became like air to them. They walked down into the ocean as if passing through mist, the steeds stepping over the green-coated rocks of the bottom. Fish swam by, seemingly in midair. Seaweed waved in breezelike currents, always surprising Stile since they seemed to lack sufficient support.

Deep down, the light faded, so Stile sang a spell of night vision, making things seem bright. Interesting, how he could use his underwater speaking ability, which was the result of one spell, to make a new spell; magic could be cumulative. Thus it was possible to get around certain limitations in stages. It helped explain how one Adept could kill another, indirectly, by modifying a message so that it caused animal-heads to attack an Adept and drive him into the Demesnes of a hostile Adept. Perhaps there were no real limits, only techniques of procedure.

At the deepest level of the sea there was a stirring, and a merman appeared. "Lost thy way?" he inquired of Stile. "We see not many fork-limbed creatures here." He was evidently possessed of the type of enchantment Stile had employed to penetrate the water. It seemed there were natural principles of magic that came into play, whether by spell or by endowment. Stile's understanding of Phaze was constantly expanding.

"I am the Blue Adept," Stile said. "This is my Lady, and these our steeds. We merely pass through, following the curtain, seeking no quarrel."

"Then permit us to guide thee, for there are traps for the unwary." The merman pointed ahead. "Not far from here a hungry sea serpent straddles the curtain. It cares not for the peaceful intent of travelers."

"I thank thee for thy concern. But we are on our honeymoon, and promised ourselves to travel the length of the curtain where possible, seeking the West Pole. We are late on our schedule and prefer not to detour."

"That serpent is fearsome," the merman warned. "None of us dare go near it. Yet if that is thy will, we will not hinder thee." He swam off.

"See thou hast an apt spell ready," the Lady advised, smiling, making the water brighten in her vicinity.

Stile reviewed the spells in his mind, and they rode on. He enjoyed the scenery here, so different from the normal land vistas. Clams of all sizes were waving their feeding nets in the water, and coral-like growths were spreading everywhere. A small yellow octopus eyed them, then noted the menacing unicorn horn and scurried hastily away on all tentacles, leaving a purple ink cloud behind. Stile smiled; this was exactly the kind of honeymoon he liked!

Then they arrived at the lair of the serpent. It was not impressive—merely a tunnel under piled stones. In a moment the ugly snout of the serpent poked out. This creature was not large, as such monsters went; probably one man would represent a sufficient meal for it. But there was no sense taking chances. "Please freeze," Stile sang, and the serpent went still. The freezing was not literal, for Stile had willed only a temporary cessation of motions; his mind controlled the interpretation.

They moved on past. A large, heavy net rose up about them and twined itself together overhead. Stile reacted immediately, whipping out his sword and slashing at the strands—but the blade could not penetrate this net.

Clip ran his horn through it, but again the material held. "This net is magic," the Lady said. "The fibers are enchanted to be strong."

So it seemed. The net itself was magically weighted, so that they could not lift it free of the sea floor, and it was impossible to cut or break.

Stile worked out a spell: "Pesky net, begone yet!" he sang. But though color shimmered across the net's surface, the net remained intact.

"This is the handiwork of another Adept," the Lady said darkly. "Thy power cancels out. In this Adept's Demesnes, thou canst not prevail."

"Maybe not directly," Stile said. He was getting tired of running afoul of other Adepts! "But I can change us into little fishes, and swim through the mesh and escape."

"Me thou canst change," she agreed. "But thyself thou couldst not change back, since fish can neither speak nor sing. And the hostile Adept might have a monster lurking to pounce on such little fish. Risk it not, my Lord."

It was the voice of common sense. In his present form, Stile could guard them against further evil; anything else was too much of a risk. "Yet needs must we slip this net," he grumbled.

Clip blew a note. "There is that," Stile agreed. "I will watch and guard thee until thou dost clear this vicinity."

The unicorn converted to hawk-form, then squeezed through the net where Stile parted the strands for him. The hawk flew swiftly upward while Stile watched, defensive spells ready.

Now a man walked up. He was ordinary in physical appearance, but wore a robe of translucent material that distorted the light and made him seem one with the water. "Thy friend can not help thee from outside, either," he said. "Thou wilt never escape my Demesnes, Blue."

Stile nodded. "Thou must be the Translucent Adept. I have read of thee, but knew not thy residence."

"No one knows my residence," Translucent said. "Who intrudes, pays the price of silence."

"Why shouldst thou harbor evil against me, who has done thee no ill?"

"Thine ill lies in the future, Blue. An thou dost reach the West Pole, the final battle shall be upon us, and no augur knows what will then befall."

"Dost thou mean to say thou hast had a hand in the mischief I have suffered?" Stile inquired. These might be the Translucent Demesnes, but Stile could strike out if he had reason.

"This net is mine, useful to snare intruders. I have not otherwise wrought ill on thee. Dost thou know the nature of thine adversary?"

"I dispatched the Red Adept," Stile said shortly.

"Red was but an instrument, deluded by a false interpretation of an Oracle—as were the beastheads. Another trap was laid for thee near the Green Demesnes, but Green wished not to be implicated, so he nullified it. Adepts bother not Adepts without cause."

This man was surprisingly informed about Stile's business. "Thou dost consider I gave thee cause for this?" Stile indicated the net.

"By intruding on these my Demesnes thou hast given me cause. I tolerate that not. The net was not set for thee, but for intruders. Never have I let an intruder go, and I need make no exception for thee. This does not implicate me in the conspiracy."

"Conspiracy? Since thou art not involved, not implicated, tell me who is."

"Obviously it is the Oracle itself."

Stile was stunned. "The Oracle? But the Oracle has always helped me and spoken true!"

"Has it?" Translucent's lip curled in a practiced sneer.

And Stile had to wonder. The root of many of his problems did seem to lie with the Oracle. He had assumed that mistakes in interpretation or delivery caused the mischief—but why did the Oracle couch its messages in language that so readily lent itself to confusion? The Oracle knew the future; it must therefore also know the effect of its own words. In some cases, a ready understanding of a prediction might cause a person to change his course of action, making the Oracle's message invalid. Since the Oracle was always correct, some obfuscation became necessary to avoid paradox. Or the message could be couched as an either-or situation, as in the case of the animalheads. But why set it up to cause trouble? The animalheads could have been told, "Let the man on the unicorn pass," and done as well for themselves as possible.

It did seem that the message had been couched to discriminate against Stile.

"Why would the Oracle seek to do thee mischief?" the Lady asked.

"I shall leave thee to ponder that at leisure," the Translucent Adept said, and departed.

"At leisure—until we starve?" the Lady asked.

"Maybe I'd better transform us," Stile said.

"Nay," the Lady said. "We are not in immediate danger. Thou canst conjure in food while we await the unicorn's return."

Stile did not feel easy. For one thing, he could not afford to wait indefinitely; he had promised to return to Proton at a specified time, and that time was near. For another, he did not trust the Translucent Adept to let things be; the man knew he could not long keep another Adept captive. He might even now be preparing some more threatening measure. It would be no easier for him to devise a way to destroy Stile than it was for Stile to find a safe escape; they were at an impasse at the moment. How long would that last?

But he hardly had time to worry before the move came. Monstrous pincers forged down from above, closing inexorably on the net. Each section was six feet in diameter, rounded, with a horny surface on one side. No physical way to resist that mass! Stile readied his transformation-spell.

"Wait!" the Lady cried. "That is the giantess!"

Of course! How could he have failed to recognize her colossal fingers? Clip had brought the one creature capable of lifting the net!

The giantess' fingers closed on the net, while Stile and the Lady herded Hinblue as far to one side as possible, avoiding the central pinch. The tremendous rocky fingernails caught in the ropes. The hand lifted—and the net came up. They were hauled up with it, through the water to the surface, and swung across to land.

Now, too late, it occurred to Stile that he could have done this himself, conjuring a sky hook to lift them all free. Or he might have summoned superpowerful cutting pincers to sever individual strands. Under the pressures of the moment, he had not been thinking well. He would have to school himself to perform better under magical pressure.

Here, beyond the Translucent Demesnes, Stile's magic could overcome the enchantment of the net directly. The strands melted and flowed into the sand, freeing them at last.

"I thank thee, giantess," Stile said, his voice booming through a conjured megaphone.

"I owe thee for my thimble," she boomed back. "Thank thy friend for showing me the way." She turned and strode northeast, toward the demesnes of the giants. She hummed as she went, making a sound like distant thunder.

Clip was there in natural form, having arrived unobtrusively. "I do thank thee, unicorn," Stile said sincerely. "Again thou hast gotten me out of mischief. I would do thee some return favor."

Clip shifted to man-form. "My sister Neysa bid me look after thee in her stead. She loves thee, and I love her. Say no more, Adept." He shifted back.

Stile said no more. Clip was certainly fulfilling his commission! Most unicorns would not tolerate a human rider at all and had little use for Adepts. Stile had won the respect of the Herd Stallion, so was permitted to ride a unicorn—yet Clip's service was more than that of a mere steed. No friend could have done more. There would have to be a repayment of some sort. He would continue to ponder the matter in off moments, seeking what was suitable.

There was now the matter of the Translucent Adept. Stile decided, with a certain inner regret, to let that be. He *had* intruded on the Translucent Demesnes, and the Adept had not discriminated against him. Stile had won sufficient victory by escaping the net. To attack another Adept at this point would be to initiate trouble, rather than reacting to it.

He looked ahead. They were on the island of the West Pole. It was pleasant enough, with deciduous trees scattered across gently rolling pasture. Small flowers bloomed randomly, and a number of shrubs bore fruit. A person could live fairly comfortably here without much labor.

The curtain continued west. They followed it—and suddenly, three miles in from the beach, they were at the West Pole. It was marked by a big X on the ground.

Stile looked down at it. "That's it?" he asked, disappointed.

"Didst thou expect perchance a palace?" the Lady inquired with a smile.

"Well, yes, or something spectacular. This X on the ground—how do we know this is really the spot?"

"Because the curtains intersect here, my love." She stood on the X and pointed north-south with her arms. "Here is the other curtain. It proceeds at right angles."

Stile looked carefully. There it was—another curtain, like the first, crossing at the X. He spelled himself across, and found himself on a barren elevation of Proton. Holding his breath, he strode to the east-west curtain and willed himself across. He was back in Phaze. The two curtains were similar, except for orientation.

"And from here thou canst sight along them, to see that they are straight," the Lady said.

Stile stood on the Pole and sighted east. The line was absolutely straight; all the meanderings they had traveled now seemed to be distortions of the land of Phaze and the land of Proton. Interesting perspective!

Curious as to how far this went, he conjured a powerful telescope, one based on the macron principle, and oriented on the line again. It went straight for what might be thousands of miles, until the focus found the backside of a standing man. That man was holding an object to his eye.

"Oh, no!" Stile exclaimed. "That's me!" And he kicked up one foot, verifying it. "This line does not even acknowledge the curvature of the planet!"

"Of course not," the Lady said. "Phaze is flat."

"But Phaze has the same geography as Proton—and Proton is a sphere. How can that be?"

"Phaze is magic; Proton is scientific."

Stile decided to let that wait for further thought. Another problem had occurred. "This is a telescope I'm using—I didn't think—I mean it's a scientific instrument. It shouldn't work here in the magic frame."

"Methought thou didst know," the Lady said. "The West Pole is the juxtaposition of frames. Magic and science both work, on this spot. That is what makes it worth visiting."

"Juxtaposition," Stile repeated, intrigued. "Could both selves of a person meet here, then?"

"Methinks they would merge here, and separate again when they moved away from the Pole, but I know not for sure."

"Science and magic merging at this particular juncture! I wonder if this is the way the universe began, with everything working both ways, and somehow the frames began separating, like cells dividing or surfaces pulling apart, so that people had to choose one or the other, never both? Like matter and anti-matter. Except for a few anchorages like this. This *is* special!"

"Aye," she agreed. "Methought thou wouldst like it. Many impossible tricks of science are possible here."

Stile sighed. "Now we have reached our destination. Our time is up, our honeymoon over, and I must return to Proton for a stint of Citizenship."

"Our time is not up," she said. "Merely held in abeyance. Our honeymoon will endure as long as we permit. Conjure me a small residence here, and I will await thy return."

"But the hostile signals, the dire warnings—suppose something should happen during mine absence?"

"Methinks the hostility was directed more at thee than at me. I should be safe enough. But with Clip and Hinblue to guard me, I shall surely not want for protection."

"Still, I want to be sure," Stile said, pacing a small circle about the Pole. "Too much has threatened, and thou art too great a treasure to risk." He pondered. "If the West Pole permits science, could I set up a holographic pickup and broadcast unit, to reach me in Proton-frame? Would it transmit thine image successfully?"

"We can find out," she said.

Stile worked out a spell and conjured a standard Proton unit of the type used for projections originating outside the domes. He set it up and got it running; it could handle all that was visible from this point. Then he conjured an oxygen mask and crossed into barren Proton farther east, carrying a conjured receiver. It worked well enough; a globe formed in air and he looked into it to see the view of whatever direction he faced. He spun its orientation and caught the circular panorama as if turning in place at the West Pole. He halted it in place when he spied the Lady Blue standing beside the grazing Hinblue.

"I see thee," Stile said, activating the voice-return. This hand-held unit could not transmit his picture, but that wasn't necessary.

"I love thee," she returned, smiling. "Thee, thee, thee."

"Thee, thee, thee," he repeated, in the Phaze convention of unqualified love, feeling warm all over. Then he stepped back across the curtain and conjured a tent for privacy. Clip snorted musically, not looking up from his grazing.

"But thou knowest what thou must do in the other frame," the Lady reminded him sternly.

Stile sighed. He knew. But for another hour he could put it from his mind.

And in due course he conjured himself back to his usual curtain-crossing place and returned to his duties in Proton.

CHAPTER 6

Commitment

Sheen was waiting for him. "How was your honeymoon, sir?" she inquired with a certain emphasis.

"Trouble with two other Adepts, rescued by a troll and a giantess. Routine fare."

"Obviously," she agreed wryly. "Are you ready to approve your new staff, sir? And your temporary economy residence?"

There was that "sir" again. "I'd better, Sheen."

She guided him to a Citizen transport capsule. It was ordinary from the outside, but like a spaceship cabin inside. Through the port a holograph of moving stars could be glimpsed. A rotund, balding serf walked up the aisle and stood at attention, wearing only a tall white hat.

"Speak to him, sir," Sheen murmured.

"Who are you?" Stile asked.

"Sir, I am Cookie, your chef."

"I just happen to be hungry enough to eat a bear," Stile said. The recent action in Phaze had taken his mind from food, causing him to miss a meal.

"Immediately, sir." Cookie disappeared.

Stile blinked. "Oh—he's a holo too."

"Naturally, sir. There is not room in this capsule for a kitchen. We'll arrive in a few minutes, and he will have your meal ready."

Another naked serf entered the spaceship. This one was an attractive older woman. Stile raised an inquiring eyebrow. "I am Henriette, your head housemistress, sir," she said primly.

Stile wondered what a housemistress did, but decided not to inquire. Sheen would not have hired her without reason. "Carry on, Henriette," he said, and she vanished.

Next was a middle-aged man not much larger than Stile himself. "I am Spade, your gardener, sir."

"Sam Spade?" Stile inquired with a smile.

But the man did not catch the historical-literary allusion. Only a Game specialist would be up on such minutiae. "Sir, only Spade, the gardener."

"Of course, Spade." Stile made a gesture of dismissal, and the man vanished.

Next was a voluptuously proportioned young woman with black tresses flowing across her body to her knees. "Of her it is said, let the rose hang its head," Stile murmured, conscious that the rhyme would work no magic here in Proton-frame.

The girl took this as the signal to speak. "I am Dulcimer, your entertainer, sir."

Stile glanced at Sheen. "What kind of entertainment do you suppose I need?"

Sheen was suppressing a smile in the best human fashion. "Dulce, show the Citizen your nature."

Dulcimer put both hands to her head, took hold of her ears, and turned her head sharply sidewise. There was a click; then the head lifted off her body. "At your service, sir."

"A robot!" Stile exclaimed. Then, more thoughtfully: "Are you by chance one of Sheen's friends?"

"I am, sir," the robot head said.

"Put yourself together," Stile told her, and the head was lowered and twisted back into place. Stile waved her away, and Dulcimer vanished.

He turned seriously to Sheen. "Do you think this is wise?"

"Sir, I can not always guard you now. A Citizen depends on no single serf. You can use Dulce when I am not available."

"A machine concubine? Forget it. You know I have no present use for such things. Not since I married the Lady Blue."

"I know, sir," she agreed sadly. "Yet you need protection, for you will be making rivals and perhaps enemies among Citizens. It would not do for a Citizen to take his cook or housemaid or gardener to social functions."

"But Dulcimer would be okay. Now I understand." He considered briefly, then decided to get his worst chore out of the way. "Before we arrive, set up a privacy barrier. I want to talk to you."

"It is already in place. Others must not know that self-willed machines associate with you. Sir."

"You can drop the 'sir' when privacy is guaranteed," he said a trifle sharply. "You were never my inferior, Sheen."

"I was never your equal, either," she said. "What do you wish to say to me?"

Stile nerved himself and plunged in. "You know that I love only the Lady Blue. What went before is history."

"I have no jealousy of the Lady Blue. She is your perfect wife."

"She is my perfect woman. Before her, you were that woman; but I changed when I became the Blue Adept. The marriage is only a social convention, applying to the frame of Phaze. Here in Proton I remain single."

"Citizens do not have to marry, not even to designate an heir. I don't see your problem."

"Yet there are marriages of convenience, even among Citizens."

"Especially among Citizens. They marry for leverage, or to pool estates, or to keep a favored serf on Proton beyond his or her twenty-year tenure. They hardly ever worry about love or sex or even appearance in that respect."

"Yet there are legal aspects," Stile continued doggedly. "The spouse of a Citizen has certain prerogatives—"

"Entirely at the pleasure of the Citizen," she said. "The spouse may be immune to tenure termination or molestation by other Citizens, but the Citizen can divorce that spouse merely by entering a note in the computer records. So it means nothing, unless the spouse is another Citizen."

"It means the spouse is a person, for at least the duration of the marriage," Stile said.

"A serf is already a person. Marriage to a Citizen merely enhances status for a time. The main hope of serfs who marry Citizens is that one of their children will be designated heir, since such a child shares the bloodline of the Citizen. But there is no guarantee. Each Citizen is his own law."

"Sometimes a Citizen will designate the spouse as heir," Stile said.

She shrugged. "All this is true, Stile. But what is the point?"

"I have it in mind to marry in Proton, and to designate my wife my heir."

"Oh." She pondered, her computer mind sorting through the implications. "A marriage of convenience to protect your estate. Not for love or sex or companionship."

"For all these things, in part," he said.

"What does the Lady Blue think of this?"

"She suggested it. Though she is able to cross the curtain, she has no affinity for this frame, and no legal status in it. You say you have no jealousy of her; neither does she have jealousy of you."

"Of me? Of course she doesn't! I'm a machine."

"Yes. But she regards you as a person. Now, with this basic understanding, I—" He hesitated.

"You want me to locate a suitable bride of convenience for you?"

"Not exactly. Sheen, I want you to be that bride."

"Don't be silly, Stile. I'm a robot. You know that."

"I see I have to do it the hard way." Stile got out of his comfortable chair. She started to rise, but he gestured her to remain seated.

Stile knelt before her, taking her hand. "Lady Sheen, I ask your hand in marriage."

"I shouldn't be sensitive to humor of this sort," she said. "But I must say I didn't expect it of you."

"Humor, hell! Will you marry me?"

Machines were not readily surprised, but she was programmed to react in human fashion. She paled. "You can't be serious!"

"I am serious, and my knee is getting uncomfortable. Will you answer me?"

"Stile, this is impossible! I'm—"

"I know what you are. You always bring it up when you're upset. I am a Citizen. I can do as I wish. I can marry whom I choose, for what reason I choose."

She stared at him. "You are serious! But the moment you tried to register me as—as—they would know my nature. They would destroy me."

"They would have to destroy me first. Answer."

"Stile, why are you doing this? The mischief—"

"I see I must answer you, since you will not answer me. If I marry you, you will be the wife of a Citizen. By definition, a person. By extension, others of your type may then be considered persons. It is a wedge, a lever for recognition of the self-willed machines as serfs. This is a service I can do for them."

"It really *is* convenience," she said. "Using me to help my friends forward their case for recognition as people."

"Which would be even more potent if something put me out of the scene prematurely and thrust the onus of Citizenship on you."

"True," she said.

"Is that my answer? Does true equate to yes?"

"No!" she snapped, jumping up. "I don't want your title, I want your love!"

Stile got off his knee silently. His love was one thing he could not offer her.

"In fact, I don't want your convenience," she continued, working up some unrobotic temper. "I don't want the appearance without the reality. I don't want to be used."

"I don't propose to use you—"

"I'm not talking about sex!" she screamed. "I would be happy for that! It's being used as a lever I object to."

"I'm sorry. I thought it was a good idea."

"You in your flesh-male arrogance! To set me up as a mock wife to be a lever, the simplistic machine I am! You thought because I love you I'll do anything you want. After all, what pride can a mere machine have?"

What had he walked into? Stile brought out his holo receiver and called the Lady Blue.

The picture-globe formed. Stile turned it about until the Lady Blue came into view. She was brushing down Hinblue. "Lady," he said.

She looked up. "My Lord!"

Sheen paused in her pacing. "You're in touch with *her*?"

"Aye, Lady Sheen," the Lady Blue answered, recognizing her voice. "And easy it is to understand the nature of thy concern. I confess I put my Lord up to it."

"I should have known," Sheen said, bemused. "But this is a cynical thing, Lady."

"Aye, Lady. It is a cruel sacrifice for thee."

"That's not the point, Lady. The sheer mischief—"

"I apologize for putting thee in an untenable position, Lady Sheen. Thou hast every right to reject it." She gave Hinblue another stroke, then addressed Stile. "My Lord, I thought not of her feeling, only of her merit. I wanted her as my sister in that frame, and that was selfish. Let her be. I love thee." She returned to the horse, dismissing him.

Stile turned off the holo. "I guess that covers it, Sheen." He felt embarrassed and awkward. "If it's any comfort, I felt about the same as you, when she broached the notion. I do care for you; I always did. I just can't honestly call it love."

"I accept," Sheen said.

"You are generous to accept my apology. I wish I had not put you through this."

"Not the apology. The proposal."

"The—?"

"Remember way back when, you proposed marriage?"

Stile was amazed. "I—"

"Yes, *that* proposal. If you had the circuitry of a robot, you'd remember these details more readily. Perhaps if you practiced mnemonic devices—"

"But why? You made such a good case against—"

"She wants it," she said simply.

That he could understand. He had proposed to Sheen because the Lady Blue wanted it; she had accepted for the same reason. Now they just had to hope it was a good idea.

The capsule had come to a halt, the portholes showing a landing at a spaceport. Sheen keyed the door open. Stile gaped.

Outside lay the Blue Demesnes.

No, of course it was the Proton equivalent, on the same geographic site. Merely one of numerous examples of parallelism of frames. The castle and grounds looked the same as in Phaze, but there was no magic. Horses grazed and dogs ranged, not unicorns and werewolves. Still, it moved him.

"After the Lady Bluette died, her Employer restored the property and put it on the market," Sheen explained. "It was at a bargain price. I thought you'd like it."

"I do." Stile stared at it a moment longer. "But it's strange here."

"No Lady Blue," she said.

"It will be yours now."

She was silent. Had he said the wrong thing? Well, either it would work out or it wouldn't.

His chef had his meal waiting: genuine imported roast of bear. Stile made a mental note not to speak figuratively; as a Citizen, he was too apt to be taken literally. He had said he could eat a bear; now he had to do it.

Actually, it wasn't bad. The chef did know his business. Sheen had hired people of genuine competence.

"And now for your estate adviser," Sheen said as Stile chomped somewhat diffidently. "You have some elegant financial maneuvering ahead."

"I'd rather master the rules of the game and lay it myself."

"This adviser is one of my friends."

Oh. That was a different matter.

The adviser turned out to be an old male serf, wrinkled, white-haired, and elegant. Stile would not have known him for a robot, had

Sheen not informed him. It was evident that the self-willed machines had profited from what Sheen had learned in the course of her association with Stile; only time, expert observation, or direct physical examination betrayed his current associates.

Stile nodded affirmatively to the serf, and the man reported: "Sir, I am Mellon, your financial accountant."

"Mellon, eh?" Stile repeated. "As in Rockefeller, Carnegie, and Du Pont?"

The serf smiled. "Yes, sir."

"You're that good with money?"

"Yes, sir."

"Then why are you here as a serf, instead of making your fortune elsewhere in the universe?" Stile knew the robot had no future away from Proton, but a real serf would, and the cover story had to be good.

"Sir, I have already made my fortune elsewhere," Mellon said. "I am as rich as a Citizen. But here on Proton the dynamics of wealth are most pronounced; the leverage of economics is exerted most openly. Only here can I experience the joy of renewed challenge, failure, and success. When my tenure expires, I shall return to my comfortable galactic estate and write my memoirs of the Proton experience."

Stile was impressed. This was a feasible rationale. It would explain the man's computerized competence. Stile might even have to stave off efforts by other Citizens to hire Mellon away. Except that since no real Mellon existed, any verification of his background would reveal—

"I am cast in the likeness of an actual person, sir," Mellon said, reading Stile's expression. "The proceeds of my memoirs will go to him, in recompense for the use of his credentials."

The machines had figured it all out! "Well, I hope you are not disappointed in the experience you have managing my estate. I don't even know its extent, but I'm trusting you to multiply it for me rapidly."

"I shall do so, sir. I must ask that you follow my advice in particulars with alacrity. There are likely to be difficult moments, but there is an eighty-five percent probability of accomplishing our objective."

Mellon certainly seemed sure of himself! The machines had to have secrets that could be exploited for tremendous leverage. Stile suspected he should leave it alone, but his curiosity governed. "How do you propose to make me rich, even by Proton standards? Surely my section of the Protonite mines can only produce so much."

"By wagering, sir. You will be better informed than your opponents."

Because of the immense body of information accessible to the sapient machines. But it would be made to seem like human instinct and luck. "No."

"Sir?"

"To wager when one has an illicit advantage is not equitable. I do not care to make my fortune that way."

"He's like that, Mel," Sheen said smugly.

"Sir, without that advantage, the odds become prohibitive."

"I have surmounted prohibitive odds before. I shall not compromise my standards now. Presumably you will be able to perform moderately well while limited to ethical means."

"Yes, sir," Mellon said grimly.

Stile completed his uncomfortable repast of bear steak. "Then let's get to it now. I am not used to wealth. I fear this will be a chore for me. I want to get that chore out of the way and return to—my private retreat." Even among his staff, he was not inclined to talk too freely of Phaze. "But first—Sheen?"

"Sir," Sheen said immediately.

"By what mechanism do I promulgate my engagement to you?"

"Application must be made to the Records Computer, sir. A Citizen hearing will be arranged."

"And?"

"That is all, sir. Marriages, births, designations of heirs, changes in estate holdings—all are merely a matter of accurate record. The hearing is a formality, to make sure there is no foul play or confusion."

"No ceremony? Blood tests? Waiting periods?"

"These are available if you wish them, sir. But they are not required for Citizens and are irrelevant for robots. The entry in the record is all that is mandatory."

"Well, let's do this right. Let's set a date for a formal, medieval, Earth-style nuptial, and invite the public."

"What date, sir?"

Stile considered. "There may be some mischief here. Let's give it time to clear. Set the date for two months hence, at which time you will become my wife and heir. Get yourself a pretty wedding outfit."

Mellon coughed. "Sir, may I comment?"

"Comment," Stile agreed.

"The Records Computer will know Sheen is not a legal person. It will advise the members of the Citizen panel. This will not interfere with the marriage, for a Citizen may do what pleases him; he may marry a toad if he wants. But the designation of a nonperson as heir to Citizenship will complicate your own activities. If you could hold that aspect in abeyance—"

"That would be a lie," Stile said. "I intend to name her heir, and I want no deception about it." Yet he wondered at his own motive, since this was more than the Lady Blue had suggested. Why make a larger issue of it? And he answered himself; because he felt guilty about not being able to give Sheen his love, so he was giving her his position instead.

"Yes, sir," Mellon said submissively.

"Sir, he is correct," Sheen said. "If you bring this mischief on yourself prematurely—"

"I will not abuse my word," Stile said firmly. "The truth shall be known."

"Sir, I fear you will imperil yourself and us," she said. "Rather than permit that, I shall decline to—"

"Do you want me to call the Lady Blue again?"

Sheen hesitated. "No, sir."

So he had bluffed her out! "How do I file my entry with the Records Computer?"

"Sir, I can activate its receptor—"

"Do so."

She touched a button on the wall. "Records, sir," a wall speaker said.

"I, Stile, Citizen, hereby announce my betrothal to the Lady Sheen. I will marry her two months hence in public ceremony, and designate her to become my heir to Citizenship effective that date. Any questions?"

"Sir, are you aware that Sheen is a robot?" the computer asked.

"I am aware."

"If you designate a nonperson heir, your estate will, on your demise or abdication, revert to the common pool, sir."

"I challenge that," Stile said. "I want her to inherit."

"Then a special hearing will be necessary, sir."

"We already have a hearing. Juxtapose them. Schedule it at your earliest convenience."

"Yes, sir." The Records Computer disconnected.

"Now you have done it, sir," Sheen murmured. "You and your unstable living human temper."

"We'll see. Let's get to the next event."

They entered the capsule again, and Sheen programmed their destination. The smooth motion commenced. Stile paid attention to none of this; he was already orienting on the wagering to come, much as he would for a Game of the Tourney. He was not sure he had really left the challenge ladder; perhaps he had merely achieved a new plateau for a new series of games.

"To wager—what are my present resources?" he asked Mellon.

"The initial estate of a Citizen is set at one kilogram of Protonite, sir," Mellon said. "Serfs do not deal in money, normally, so there is little way to equate this with what you have known."

"I know that a single ounce of Protonite is supposed to be worth the entire twenty-year tenure of the average serf," Stile said.

"Yes, traditionally. Actually, this fluctuates as the variables of demand and technology change the need, though the Proton Council regulates the supply to keep the price fairly stable, much as the cartels of the galaxy have traditionally regulated the supplies of foregoing fuels—coal, oil, uranium, and such."

"Until supplies ran short," Stile said. "Or until technology obviated the need. Efficient utilization of starlight, and hydrogen fusion—these became virtually limitless resources."

"Indeed, sir. But starlight and fusion both require enormous initial capital investment. Though Protonite is theoretically limited, it is so potent that it has become the fuel of choice for interstellar travel. Its value more closely resembles that of bullion gold than that of bygone oil."

"Gold," Stile said. "I have played with that in my historical researches. I have a fair notion of its value, as measured in archaic ounces."

"Then set one gram of Protonite as equivalent to four hundred troy ounces of gold, sir. One kilogram—"

"Four hundred thousand ounces of gold!" Stile finished, amazed despite himself.

"Enough to hire a thousand serfs for full tenure, sir," Mellon said. "A fortune equivalent to that of many of the historically wealthy persons of Earth. That is your minimum share of Citizenship; wealthy Citizens control the equivalent of as much as a ton of Protonite, so are richer than any historical figure."

"I see that," Stile agreed, somewhat awed. He had known Citizens were exceedingly rich, but still had underestimated the case. "And I must become one of those wealthy ones?"

"You must become the wealthiest Citizen, sir," Mellon agreed. "Only then can you be reasonably secure against the forces that may be brought to bear. Our target is two metric tons of Protonite."

"That's two thousand kilograms!" Stile exclaimed.

"Precisely, sir. There have been wealthier Citizens in the past, but at present none go beyond this level. Only extraordinary expertise can bring you to this."

"Expertise, yes; illicit information, no."

"Yes, sir."

"And how much of my single, insignificant kilogram may I employ for gambling?"

"Three quarters of it, sir. You must, by Proton custom that has the force of law, maintain a floor of two hundred and fifty grams for normal household use."

"Some household! That's a hundred thousand ounces of gold!"

"True, sir. No Citizen is poor by galactic standards."

"I seem to remember Sheen telling me that no Citizen could get more than two years' income in arrears."

"That is an optional guideline for the conservative."

"I see. But I can't afford to be conservative, can I? And if I gamble and lose, so I'm stuck at the floor level—then what?"

"Your share is not a literal kilogram, sir, but rather the equivalent in continuing production from the Protonite mines. In time—perhaps a year—you will have an income of ten to twenty additonal grams. Enough to maintain a modest estate without depleting your principal."

"Oh, I wouldn't want to deplete my principal," Stile said, feeling giddy. Even a Citizen's small change vastly exceeded his expectation. "Still, to build a stake of seven hundred and fifty grams up to an estate of two thousand kilograms—that will take rapid doubling and redoubling."

"Certainly, sir. And we shall not be risking all of the discretionary funds. Reverses are to be expected. I recommend an initial limit of one hundred grams per wager."

"And your recommendation is my law."

"Yes, sir, in this respect. Except—"

"Except that I will handle the substance of the wagers myself, drawing on none of your computer information. I presume you feel this makes me likely to fail."

"Yes, sir," Mellon said unhappily. "I have considerable strategic resource, were it permissible for use."

"Were it not the way I am, your kind would not have trusted me to keep their secret."

"Yes, sir." But considerable disapproval was conveyed in that acquiescence.

"Very well, let's review this matter. You have the entire information bank of the planetary computer network available to you. The average wagering Citizen does not. Would you consider it fair play for us to use this? I submit that it represents an unfair advantage, and to use it would be dishonest."

"Citizens have very few restrictions, sir. They may draw on any available facilities. I think it likely that some will seek to take advantage of your inexperience. Turnabout may be considered fair play."

"Very well. If I encounter a Citizen who is trying to take unfair advantage, I'll draw on your information to turn the tables. But I'll balk at anything I deem to be unethical. I will cheat only the cheaters."

"Understood, sir. It would be unwise to seem to follow the advice of a serf too slavishly."

Evidently the issue of personal integrity still eluded the robot. "Yes. A Citizen must keep up arrogant appearances."

Now Sheen, who had remained scrupulously clear of this discussion, rejoined it. "I am sure you will have no difficulty, sir."

She was a machine, but she was programmed for human emotion. How much did she resent the use he was making of her?

The event they attended turned out to be a routine Citizens' ball.

Sheen and Mellon, as favored servitors, were permitted to accompany Stile, but they kept subserviently behind him. At the entrance they outfitted Stile with a suitable costume for the occasion: a seemingly cumbersome ancient spacesuit, puffed out around the limbs with huge joints at the elbows and knees, and a translucent helmet bubble. Actually, the material was very light and did not hamper movement at all.

They entered the ballroom—and Stile was amazed. It was outer space in miniature. Stars and planets, somewhat out of scale; comets and nebulae and meteors and dust clouds. The motif was not remarkable, but the execution was spectacular. The stars were light without substance, holographically projected, but they looked so real he was fearful of getting burned if he floated too near. For he was floating, in effect, on the invisible floor; the soles of his space boots were padded, so that his footsteps made no sound.

Citizens in assorted varieties of spacesuits floated in groups, their serf-servitors like satellites. One spotted him and moved across. It was the Rifleman. "I see you are mixing in, Stile. Excellent. Let me introduce you to key figures. What is your preference? Romance, camaraderie, or mischief?"

"Mischief," Stile said, grateful for the man's help. "I want to make some wagers."

"Oh, *that* kind! It's the gamesmanship in your blood. I know the feeling well. But we have some high rollers here; they'll strip you down to your minimum estate in short order, if you let them. You can never bet all your wealth, you know; computer won't allow any Citizen to wipe out. Bad for the image."

"I understand. I have a competent monetary adviser."

"You will need him. I warn you, Stile, there are barracuda in these waters. Best to play penny ante until you get to know them."

By the same token, though, the barracuda would get to know him—and his adviser. That would not do. He needed to score rapidly, before others grew wary. "What is considered penny ante here?"

"One gram of Prontonite."

"That was all I was worth a few days ago."

The Rifleman smiled. "I, too, in my day. Times change, Citizen. This is a whole new world."

"I hope not to do anything foolish before I acclimatize."

"Oh, by all means do be foolish," the Rifleman said encouragingly. "It is expected of all new Citizens. You are the novelty of the day; enjoy it while you can."

All this time the Rifleman had been guiding Stile across the miniature galaxy. Now they came to a group of space-suited Citizens hovering near a large dark nebula. The men were rotund and unhandsome; rich living had shaped them to porcine contours that even the ballooning suits could not ameliorate. This disgusted Stile; he knew that they could easily have kept their weight down by consuming diet food that tasted identical to the calorific food, or by having reductive treatments. Apparently they just didn't care about appearance.

But the two women were a striking contrast. One was an hourglass, her breasts like pink melons, her waist so tiny Stile knew that surgery had reduced it, her hips resurging enormously, tapering into very large but well-contoured legs. Stile found this exaggeration of female traits unpleasant, but even so, it had its impact upon him. Her breasts swelled like the tides of an ocean as she breathed, and her hips shifted elevation precipitously as she walked. Her suit was only remotely related to space; most of it was transparent, and much of the front was mere netting. It seemed to Stile that in real space those enormous mammaries would detach explosively and fly outward like the rings of gas and dust from old supernovae. But she had a pretty face, almost elfin; surely the handiwork of a fine plastic surgeon.

The other woman was decorously garbed in an opaque cloth-type suit that covered every portion of her body. Her head was encased in a translucent bubble that shadowed her face and lent enticing mystery to her expression. She seemed almost too young to be a Citizen—but of course there was no age limit.

The Rifleman introduced the whole group, but the names of the men bounced off Stile's awareness like rainwater. Only the two women registered consciously; he had never before heard the name of a female Citizen, and it affected him with an almost erotic force. ". . . Fulca, with the fulsome figure," the Rifleman was concluding. "And Merle, known to her illustrious enemies as the Blackbird."

Illustrious enemies? Blackbird? If this were not mere posturing, this was a Citizen to be wary of.

The two women nodded as their names were spoken. "You're the new franchise, aren't you?" Fulca inquired.

"Yes, sir," Stile said, then visibly bit his tongue. Both women smiled.

"Stile would like to wager," the Rifleman said. "He's a Gamesman, you know, with an eye to pulchritude."

The male Citizens stood back, curious but not participating, as if more intrigued by the manner in which the females would handle this upstart than by the prospect of making some profit. "Anything," Fulca agreed. "Choose your mode, bantam."

There was that ubiquitous reference to his size. He would probably never be free of such disparagement. No sense in letting it rattle him. He had what he wanted—someone to wager with.

Stile's imagination suddenly deserted him. "Uh, small, to start. Very small. And simple."

Her glance traversed him merrily. "For a small, simple man. Agreed."

Was that another cut at him? Probably not; it was evident that Citizens treated each other very casually. What did they have to prove? They were all elite. Or maybe this was part of his initiation. The watching males gave no sign.

"Uh, scissors-paper-stone?" Stile asked, casting about for something suitable and drawing no inspiration from the environment. Without the Game's preliminary grid, he lacked notions.

"Ah, a noncontact game," she said as if surprised. Now one of the watching males nodded at another, as if the two had made a bet on the matter that had now been decided. So that was the nature of their interest—to wager on Stile's performance with the voluptuous woman. No doubt many men sought to get close to her on one pretext or another. This actually encouraged Stile; he was beginning to grasp the situation. "Small and simple," he repeated.

"Shall we say one gram, doubled each round, seven rounds?" Fulca suggested.

Stile glanced at Mellon, who made an almost perceptible nod of assent. The final bet would fall within the limitation, though the total amount of the series would not. These Citizens were indeed a fast crowd! Again one of the males nodded, having a point decided—what level Stile was playing at.

"May I call the throws?" the Rifleman asked. "On the count of two, spaced one second; late throw means default, which Merle will call. For one gram of Protonite: on your mark, one—two."

Stile, caught off-guard by this ready procedure, put out his forked fingers a shade late. Fulca was there with a flat hand. "Default," Merle said, her voice soft, like dusk wind in pines.

"Agreed," Stile said, embarrassed. He had made the winning throw—too late. Some beginning; he had already thrown away the twenty-year ransom of one serf.

"For two grams," the Rifleman said. "One—two."

This time Stile was on time, with scissors again. Fulca also showed scissors. "No decision," Merle breathed.

Stile marveled that it could really be this simple. He had thought of Citizens as a class apart, devoted to pursuits beyond the comprehension of mere serfs. But in fact Citizens were serflike in their entertainment—or so it seemed so far.

The Rifleman continued without pause. "Balance of one gram to Fulca. For four grams: one—two."

Stile's mind was racing as he warmed to the game. Theoretically random, these combinations were actually not. Each person was trying to figure the strategy of the other. Stile himself was very good at analyzing patterns and moods; he did it almost instinctively. The first throw had been random; the normal course, for an inexperienced person, would be to go on the next throw to whatever choice had won before. Thus Fulca had gone from paper to scissors. Stile, testing, had held firm. Did he have the pattern solved? If so, Fulca would go next to the stone. So he would match that, verifying. The early bets were for analyzing; the later ones counted. Even as this flashed through his mind, his hand was flinging out the closed fist.

Fulca matched his stone. "No decision," Merle said. It seemed they did not play these over, but just continued the series.

"For eight grams: one—two."

This time Stile went for the win. He expected Fulca to go for paper, to wrap the last throw's stone. So he threw scissors again—and won.

"Scissors cuts paper; Stile wins," Merle announced.

"Balance of seven games to Stile," the Rifleman said. "For sixteen grams: one—two."

Would the hourglass lady Citizen be foolish enough to go for stone again, fighting the last war too late? Or would she stick with paper, expecting him to go for stone? Stile decided to play her for the fool. He threw out the flat hand. And won.

"Paper wraps stone; Stile," Merle said.

"Balance of twenty-three grams to Stile," the Rifleman said. "I warned you girls he was a Gamesman, like me. He can play. For thirty-two grams: one—two."

Stile continued the fool-play, throwing out the closed fist. Fulca threw the forked fingers. She winced as she saw the combination.

"Stone crushes scissors. Stile wins." Merle smiled within her dusky helmet. Evidently these people enjoyed a good challenge.

"You beat me with the ones I lose with!" Fulca exclaimed.

That was another way of looking at it. He had cut her paper, then shifted to paper and wrapped her stone, then had his stone crush her scissors. The losing throws became the winners of the next throw. "Beginner's luck," Stile said apologetically.

One of the males snorted. "His mind is on the wager, not her body," he murmured.

"Balance of fifty-five grams to Stile," the Rifleman said. "For sixty-four grams: one—two."

Fulca had caught on to his pattern; had she the wit to take advantage of it? This single throw could reverse the entire game. Stile thought she would not learn quickly enough, so he threw scissors, trusting her to throw paper. She did.

"Scissors cuts paper. Stile wins," Merle said.

"He sure cut your paper!" the male Citizen remarked to Fulca with satisfaction. He had evidently won his private bet on the outcome of this contest.

"Balance of one hundred nineteen grams to Stile. End of series," the Rifleman said. "So entered in the credit record; Stile has increased his Citizen's stake by more than ten percent, fleecing his first ewe. Instant analysis: he lost one, drew two, and won four. Was this luck or skill?"

"Skill," Merle said. "He is a master Gamesman—as is unsurprising."

Fulca shrugged, and her torso undulated in vertical stages. "There are other games."

"Uh-uh, dear," the Rifleman said with a reproving smile. "You had your crack at him and lost, as I did in the Tourney. If you want to seduce him, you'll have to wait your next turn. Now he enters the second round."

"Second round?" Stile asked.

This time all the male Citizens chuckled. Merle tapped herself lightly between her muted breasts. "Do you care to try your skill with me, serf-Citizen?"

"I do still have the urge," Stile said, catching Mellon's affirmative nod. But he felt uneasy; he now perceived that Merle was not nearly as young as she had first seemed. In fact, she was somewhat older than he, and her manner was that of a completely self-assured person. She was probably a power among Citizens; one of the barracuda he had been warned against. But he would have to tackle this kind some time.

"Then let us play a hand of poker," she said.

The serfs hastily brought a pack of playing cards, poker chips, an opaque table, and chairs. The Rifleman took the cards, spread them out, and pronounced them fit to play with; Stile believed him. No one got through the Tourney without being expert with cards. Why should Citizens cheat? They needed neither money nor fame, and cheating would destroy the natural suspense of gambling.

But Stile was nervous about this game. Poker players were a breed apart, and a Citizen poker player whose facial features were shrouded by a translucent helmet could be more of a challenge than Stile could handle at the moment. Yet Stile was good at poker, as he was in most games; he certainly should have a fighting chance, even against an expert—if he didn't run afoul of his betting limit. Limits could be devastating in poker.

"Merle has chosen the game," the Rifleman said. "Stile may choose the rules."

"Standard fifty-two-card pack, no wild cards, standard wider galaxy hands in force, betting—"

"Sorry, Stile," the Rifleman interjected. "You may not dictate the pattern of betting. That choice reverts to her, by Citizen custom."

"Of course I will honor Citizen custom," Stile said. "But I have hired a serf to supervise my estate, and he wants me to stay clear of large bets until I know my way around. So I might have to renege on the game, if—"

"A sensible precaution," Merle said. "Seat your serf to the side; you may consult with him while betting."

"That is gracious of you, Merle," Stile said, forcing himself to speak her name, though his lifetime of serf conditioning screamed against it. "Please, in compensation, name the variant you prefer."

"Certainly, Stile. Are you familiar with Lovers' Quarrel?"

Oops. "I do not know that variant," Stile admitted.

"It is a variety of Draw. Each player must draw from the hand of the other, one card at a time, which hand is replenished by the dealer. Betting occurs after each draw, until one player stands pat."

Some variant! This had the double stress of involuntary loss of cards from one's hand, and the opponent's knowledge of an increasing portion of that hand. At some point they both should know what each had —but that would not necessarily make betting easier.

They took seats at the table, the Rifleman serving as dealer. Stile glanced at the knot of spectators. The males watched with poker faces, obviously intent on the proceedings. Mellon and Sheen stood impassively, but Stile knew that Sheen, at least, was controlling her emotional circuitry with difficulty. She loved him and wanted to protect him, and here she could not. This was also outside Mellon's bailiwick; there was no way for him to draw on computer information to give Stile an advantage, and that was the way Stile preferred it. This was an honest game.

The Rifleman dealt five cards to each. Stile picked up his hand, holding it together so that only the bottom card showed, and that was concealed from all external view by his casually cupped hands. He riffled once through the corners, his trained eye photographing the hand and putting it mentally in order: ace of spades, 10 of hearts, 10 of diamonds, 4 of clubs, 2 of clubs. A pair of tens. That was not much; in a two-player game, the odds were marginally in favor of this being high, but he would have similar odds on the flip of a coin. He did not want to bet on this.

"The lady may draw first," the Rifleman said.

"Thank you, Rife," Merle said. She discarded one card face down. "I will take your center card, Stile, if you please."

Stile spread his hand without looking and lifted out the center card. It was the 10 of diamonds. There went his pair already!

The Rifleman dealt Stile a replacement card. It was the 6 of hearts. Now he had only ace-high, a likely loser.

"One ounce," she said. The Rifleman slid a white poker chip across to her, and she touched it into the center of the table.

So that was the unit of currency—safely penny-ante after all. Relieved, Stile discarded his 10 of hearts, to keep his opponent from getting it and having a pair, and asked for Merle's left-end card, which in a conventional arrangement might be her high one. Of course it wasn't; she had not arranged her cards physically, either. Too much could be telegraphed that way. It was the jack of clubs.

Now he had ace of spades, 6 of hearts, jack of clubs, 4 of clubs and 2 of clubs. Perhaps three legs on a flush, if he didn't lose his clubs to Merle's drawings.

But he had to call, raise, or drop. He was unwilling to quit so early, so he called, contributing one white chip.

Merle discarded another, and drew his ace. She was having uncanny luck in destroying his hand! Then she added a red chip to the pot. She was raising the ante—five more grams.

The Rifleman passed Stile another replacement card. It was the king of clubs. Now Stile had four clubs—almost a flush. A full flush would very likely win the pot; only one hand in 200 was a flush. But by the same token, flushes were hard to come by. Merle would have four chances in five to steal away one of his clubs on her next turn. Should he call or fold?

He looked at Mellon. The serf nodded affirmatively, approving the bet. So Stile discarded the 6 of hearts, drew another card from Merle—and got the ace of spades back. Disappointed, he matched the red chip.

Merle frowned faintly within her helmet, and Stile was frustrated again, unable to gauge her true mood. With an unfamiliar game variant and an unfamiliar opponent, he could exercise little of his natural skill. A person's eyes could tell a lot; if the pupils widened, the hand was positive. But her pupils were shadowed by that translucency.

She took another card: his king of clubs. He got an 8 of spades from the pack. Already his promised flush was fading, as he had feared. His hand still amounted to nothing.

Merle put in a blue chip. Another ten grams! That brought her total up to sixteen grams of Protonite. At the rate she was raising the ante, he could not afford to let this game continue too long. But he would surely lose if he stood pat now; she must have amassed at least one pair. He wanted to make a good showing, so that other Citizens would want to make wagers with him.

Stile decided to keep trying for the flush. Therefore he discarded his ace of spades, reckoning it too risky to hold for her possible reacquisition, and drew from Merle—his original 10 of diamonds. No good to him at all, at this stage, since he had discarded his matching 10 before. Again he matched her bet, though he thought it would have been smarter to drop. She probably had ten times as much wealth to gamble with as he did. If Mellon knew how weak Stile's hand was, the serf would hardly have tolerated this bet.

Merle took his jack of clubs, further decimating his flush. And she put five more blue chips into the pot. Sixty-six grams total: she surely had a good hand now!

Stile accepted the replacement card: the 6 of spades. Now his hand was the 8 and 6 of spades, 10 of diamonds, and 4 and 2 of clubs. No pairs, no flush, no high card—and a monstrous ante facing him if he wanted to keep playing.

Then something clicked. He had almost missed the forest for the trees!

"I stand pat on this hand," Stile announced. "Adviser, may I bet my limit?"

Mellon agreed reluctantly. Stile put eight blue chips and four white ones into the pot, bringing his total to one hundred grams. Now it was Merle's turn to call or fold; she could not raise during his turn. Would she be bluffed out?

She called, putting in another thirty-four grams. She laid down her hand, face up. "Blaze," she said. "Two kings, two queens, one jack."

That meant she had to have had one pair last round, perhaps two pairs, beating him. She had waited until she had what she wanted: a pat hand, all court cards. She had played with nerve.

But Stile had beaten her. "Skip straight," he said, laying it out. "Ten-high." There it was: 10–8–6–4–2. This hand was not as strong as a straight, but was stronger than any of the other hands from three of a kind down.

"Very nice, Stile," she agreed. "The pot is yours." She made a little gesture of parting and walked away.

"He took her," one of the male Citizens said. "That's one kilo for me." Another nodded glumly.

"Very nice indeed," the Rifleman said. "You have added another hundred to your estate. It is so recorded."

A total of 219 grams of Protonite added to his original thousand—in the course of just two supposedly penny-ante games. But Stile knew he could just as readily lose it again.

Mellon approached as the group of Citizens dispersed. "Sir, you must desist now."

"I'll be glad to. But what is the reason? I thought you would stop me from betting before."

"This is the bait, sir. Now the serious bettors will seek you out."

The serious bettors. Of course. Stile had, as it were, dipped his toe. He needed to announce himself, so that he could step into the real action, where the upper limit would rise. Obviously a gain of 219 grams was statistically insignificant, compared with the 2000 kilograms that was his target level. He had won only one ten-thousandth of his stake. This could be as difficult a climb as it had been through the levels of the Tourney.

Yet Mellon was not concerned about the luck of individual wagers. He had a certain program of challenge planned. His limit on Stile's initial betting had been merely to prevent Stile from losing his stake in the course of making himself known to the key wagering clientele.

"Did I hear correctly?" Stile asked the Rifleman. "Did one of the spectators bet a full kilogram of Protonite on the outcome of my game with Merle?"

"He did," the Rifleman agreed. "Citizens bet on anything."

"Ten times what I bet—and he wasn't even playing!"

The Rifleman smiled. "That's the way it is. Your adviser protected you from getting into that level too soon. Come on—there's more than wagering to get into."

Stile allowed the Rifleman to show him around some more. There were different levels and slants and curves to the invisible floor, with refreshments on one tier, dancing on another, and conversation on a third. Coupled with the ubiquitous holographic astronomy, the effect was potent. This was a wonderland, as impressive in its lavish expense as in its execution. Yet the Citizens, long used to this sort of thing, ignored the setting and socialized among themselves.

"You do get accustomed to it," the Rifleman said, divining Stile's thoughts. "This is merely a standard social occasion, a kind of Citizen concourse, where any can come for idle entertainment and socializing on an amicable plane. All comforts and amusements are available at every Citizen's private residence, but they get bored. Of course they have holo contact, but you can't actually touch a holo, or push it aside or make love to it."

"You say *they*," Stile observed.

"I'm still a serf at heart. You'll be the same. The Citizens do not discriminate against our kind—to do so would be to dishonor their system —but we discriminate against ourselves, internally. We react to what is beneath their notice. Look there, for instance." He gestured upward.

Stile looked. Above them was a transparent spaceship, inside which Citizens were dancing. The men wore archaic black tailed-coat costumes, the women white blouses and slippers and voluminous skirts. From this nether vantage he could see right up their prettily moving legs, under their skirts where the white bloomers took over. Stile had gotten used to nakedness in Proton and to clothing in Phaze, but this halfway vision was intensely erotic for him. He did have some acclimatizing to do, lest he embarrass himself.

Again the Rifleman was with him in spirit. "Yet we see excellent distaff flesh all about us, unconcealed," he pointed out, indicating Sheen, who remained respectfully behind. Stile glanced back. Sheen was indeed the perfect figure of a young woman, with lovely facial features, fine large, upstanding breasts, and torso and legs that could hardly be improved upon. In terms of appearance she was stunning, far prettier than the exaggerated lady Citizen Fulca—yet she did not excite him sexually. This was not because he knew she was a machine, he decided; the robot was more human and caring than most flesh-women he knew. It was because she was a naked serf. Sheen had no secrets, so lacked novelty. In contrast, the peek up the skirts of the dressed ladies above—that, literally, clothed his fancy and set his pulse racing.

"But the average Citizen can look and yawn," the Rifleman said, glancing again at the skirts above. "Clothing is no novelty here. Nothing is novelty, except assured victory in an honest game of chance. You made Merle's day just now; you were an unknown quantity, giving her the thrill of uncertainty."

That reminded Stile. "Just how old is she, and how much of her fortune would a hundred grams of Protonite represent, if it's not uncouth to inquire?"

"The fortunes of all Citizens are a matter of public record. She's worth about ten kilos; I can get the precise figure for the moment, if you wish. The Records Computer—"

"No, no need. So my wager did not hurt her."

"Not at all. Age is also on record. Merle is sixty-one years old. She's had rejuvenation, of course, so she has the face and body of a serf girl of thirty. But her mind is old. I dare say she knows more about sex than you and I combined."

Stile had noticed that most Citizen women were physically attractive, in contrast with the men. Rejuvenation would of course account for this. It would not prolong life significantly, but it would make a person seem young on the day he died of age. The vanity of women caused them to go this route.

Stile turned to the Rifleman. "I thank you for the courtesy of your time. You have facilitated my education. Now I think I will go home and assimilate my impressions, if I may do so without offense to this gathering."

"No offense. You have made your appearance and performed on stage; all interested Citizens have had opportunity to examine you. Go and relax, Stile."

"I really did not meet many Citizens. I suppose I'm not much of a novelty."

The Rifleman smiled. "Allow me to detain you for one more thing." He led Stile to an especially thick dust cloud. Set just within its opacity was a control panel. A touch on this, and an image formed above—Stile, playing poker with Merle. The view shifted perspective as if the camera were dollying around, showing Stile from all sides. An inset showed the poker hands of each, changing as the play progressed.

"I've been recorded!" Stile exclaimed.

"Exactly," the Rifleman agreed. "All interested Citizens are able to tune in on you—or on any other person here. This is open territory, unprivate." He touched the controls again, and the nether view of the dancing Citizens appeared. "So-called X-ray views are also available, for those who wish." Now the skirts and bloomers faded out, leaving the Citizens dancing naked, looking exactly like serfs.

Stile was alarmed. "You mean viewers can strip me like that, holographically?" He was concerned about exposure of his physical reaction when viewing the inner skirts before.

"Indeed. Voyeurism is a prime Citizen pastime. That particular thrill seems never to become passé."

Stile sighed inwardly. He surely had provided the voyeurs some innocent entertainment today! "I appreciate your advising me," he said, somewhat faintly.

"Welcome, Stile. I thought you would want to know. Citizenship is not completely idyllic, and there are many ways to be savaged unknowingly. Many Citizens prefer the complete privacy of their domes."

"I can see why." And on that amicable note they parted.

Back in his transparent capsule, Stile relaxed. It had actually been a joke on him, he decided, and harmless. The Citizens had really looked him over and found him human. He would be more alert in future.

But the joke had not finished. A call came in to the travel capsule. When he acknowledged, the head of Merle formed. Without her space helmet, she was revealed as a rather pretty young woman, with the same delicate rondure to her facial features as had been suggested by her suit-shrouded torso. "I have decided I like you, Stile," she said. "Would you care for an assignation?"

"Uh, what?" he asked awkwardly.

She laughed. "Oh, you are so refreshing! It has been decades since I've had a truly naïve man." The scope of the image expanded, to reveal the upper half of her body hanging in the air before him like a statuette, her small but excellent breasts shrouded by a translucent shawl. She must have viewed the holographic record of Stile's recent experience and grasped his susceptibility to partial clothing on women. "You can see that I am moderately endowed, but please accept my assurance that I am expert with what I have."

Stile proved his naïveté by blushing. "Sir, you catch me unprepared. Uh—"

She actually clapped her hands in glee. "Oh, absolute delight! I must have you!"

"I can't say I care to have holographs made of me performing in such a situation," Stile said, his face burning.

Merle pursed her lips. "But holos are the best part of it, so that one can review the occasion at proper leisure and improve technique."

Out of range of the holo pickup, Sheen signaled imperatively. She did not want Stile to offend the Citizen. Mellon nodded agreement.

Stile took their advice. "Merle, as you can see, I'm flattered to the point of confusion. This is more than I can handle right now. Could you, would you grant me a stay of decision?"

"Gladly, Stile," she agreed merrily. "I will contact you tomorrow."

Some stay! "Thank you," he said, conscious that his blush had intensified. He was thirty-five years old and hardly inexperienced with women, but his underlying awe of Citizens had betrayed him.

The moment the connection terminated, he snapped: "Block off all other calls! I don't want any more of that!"

"We dare not block off Citizen calls," Sheen said. "But I'll ask my friends to make an inoffensive excuse message for you, and filter out as much as possible."

"Thanks." He caught her hand. "You're beautiful, Sheen."

"I wish I could move you the way Citizen Merle did," she grumbled.

"She moved me to naked terror!"

"Naked, yes; terror, no."

"She's a sixty-year-old woman!"

"In that respect I can not compete. I was made less than a year ago."

That reminded him. "Sheen, has there been any progress on your origin? Have your friends discovered who sent you to me and why?"

"I will query them," Sheen said, but paused. "Oops—a call."

"I told you, I don't want—"

"From *her*."

There was only one person Sheen referred to that way. "Oh. Put her on, of course."

The image formed. The Lady Blue faced him. "My Lord, I dislike bothering thee, but I fear mischief."

"What mischief?" he demanded, instantly concerned. The Lady Blue was no more beautiful, by objective standards, than Sheen, but she had completely captured his love. It bothered him to have the fact so evident in Sheen's presence, but there really was no way to avoid it in this situation.

"Clip says he winds ogres." She glanced nervously about. "We know not why such creatures should be on the isle of the West Pole."

"I'll rejoin thee," Stile said.

"Nay, my Lord. Clip will guard me from harm. I merely advise thee, just in case any difficulty arises."

"Very well," he agreed reluctantly. "But if there's any sign of menace, call me right away. It will take me a while to reach Phaze."

"I love thee, Lord Blue," she said, flashing her smile, making the air about her brighten. Stile always liked that magic effect. She faded out.

"Nevertheless," Stile said grimly to Sheen, "I want to get closer to a curtain-crossing point. Or anywhere along the curtain; once I step across, I can spell myself immediately to the West Pole."

Mellon was looking at him strangely. Stile smiled. "Have Sheen fill you in more thoroughly; you machines need to know this. I go to a world of magic, where I have a lovely wife and am important."

"Yes, sir," Mellon said dubiously. "I trust this will not interfere with your program of estate development."

"Please infer no insult from this," Stile told him. "But if my Lady Blue is in danger, my entire Citizenship estate can drop into deep space without a ship."

"Thank you for clarifying your priorities, sir," Mellon said stiffly.

"Oh, don't be stuffy," Sheen reproved the other robot. "You have to take Stile on his own peculiar terms."

"Of course. He is a Citizen."

She turned to Stile. "My friends have a report."

"Let's have it." Stile was discovering that a lot of business could be done on the move.

The image of a desk robot appeared. "Sir, the machine of your inquiry was purchased by Citizen Kalder ten weeks ago, programmed to love and protect the serf Stile, and sent to said serf."

"But *why?*" Stile demanded. "Why should a Citizen make an anonymous and expensive gift to a serf he does not employ?"

"That information is not available, sir. I suggest you contact Citizen Kalder." The image faded.

"At least now I have a name," Stile said. He pondered briefly. "How much does such a robot cost?"

"Approximately five grams of Protonite, sir," Mellon replied. "This is my own value, which is typical for the type."

"That is quintuple the twenty-year hire of a serf," Stile said. "Maybe peanuts for a Citizen, but still out of proportion for a throwaway gift. Easier to send a serf bodyguard." Another thought occurred. "Has my own estate been docked that amount for you and the other special personnel?"

"We are rented, sir," Mellon said. "By special arrangement."

That meant that the self-willed machines had set it up. They were covertly helping him, so that he could help them. "What do your friends think of our engagement, Sheen?"

"Sir, they are amazed, to the extent their circuitry and programming permit. This changes the situation, giving them the chance for recognition much sooner than otherwise. There are grave risks, but they are willing to follow this course."

"Good enough. I would like to secure your recogniton as serfs, not merely because of the help your kind has given me at critical moments, but because I believe it is right. Though if each of you costs five grams, I don't know how it could be economic for you to work for serf's wages."

"We can last several times as long as the tenure of a serf," Mellon replied. "Once we achieve recognition, there may be a premium for the service we can offer. Properly programmed, we could be superior serfs, performing the routine functions of several. Since we do not sleep, we can accomplish more in a given tenure. The Protonite that powers us is equivalent in value to the food that living serfs consume, and our occasional necessary repairs equate to live-person illness. We feel we shall be economic. But even if we are not, we shall at least have the opportunity to play the Game legitimately, and perhaps some few of our number will advance to Citizenship. That prospect is more important to us than mere service as serfs."

"So I gather," Stile agreed. He liked these intelligent machines; he trusted them more than he did many living people, partly because they remained simpler than people. A robot could be deceitful if programmed to be—but what was the point of such programming? Mainly he liked their loyalty to him, personally. They trusted him, so aided him, and he knew they would never betray him.

"Sir, do you wish me to place a call to Citizen Kalder?" Sheen inquired.

"Yes, do it."

But at that point there was another call from the Lady Blue. "The ogres are closing on us, my Lord," she said worriedly. "I was not sure before that we were the object of their quest, but now that seems likely. I mislike bothering thee, but—"

"I'm on my way!" Stile cried. "Sheen, reroute this tub to the nearest intersection with the curtain. Forget about the call to the Citizen; I'll tackle that later."

"Yes, sir," she said. The capsule shifted motion.

CHAPTER 7

Hostage

The image of the Lady Blue remained. Stile worked his unit controls to survey the area, looking outward from the West Pole. In a moment he spied an ogre.

It was a large, hugely muscled humanoid creature, strongly reminiscent of Stile's late friend Hulk. Stile felt a pang at the memory; Hulk had been an intelligent, sensitive, considerate man, a Gamesman like Stile himself—but he had been betrayed and murdered by Stile's enemy. Stile had sworn an oath of vengeance, which he had implemented in his fashion—but that had not restored his friend. In any event, the resemblance was superficial; the ogre's face was a gross muddy morass of nose and mouth, with two little eyes perched slightly above. The ears dangled down like deflated tires.

Clip changed to man-form and approached the creature. "Ogre, why dost thou come here?" the unicorn inquired.

"Blue be mine enemy," the creature croaked. Its open mouth was like that of a frog with triangular teeth.

"Blue is not thine enemy!" the Lady called. "Blue had a friend who was very like an ogre. Blue never harmed thy kind. Why dost thou believe ill of him now?"

"The Oracle says."

Another Oracular message? Stile distrusted this.

So did the Lady Blue. "Another message was altered, methinks, to make Blue seem villain. Art thou sure—"

But the ogre, dim of wit, roared and charged, making the ground tremble by the fall of its feet. Its hamfist swung forward like a wrecking ball. Ogres simply were not much for dialogue.

"I've got to get there!" Stile cried.

"We are not yet at the curtain, sir," Sheen said. "It will be another ten minutes."

Stile clenched his teeth and fists, watching the scene in Phaze.

Clip shifted back to his natural form and launched himself after the ogre. The Lady Blue, no fainting flower in a crisis, stepped nimbly aside. Ogre and unicorn lunged past her, Clip placing himself between the other two.

The ogre braked, its huge hairy feet literally screeching against the turf. But as it reoriented on the Lady, the unicorn barred the way.

The ogre massed perhaps a thousand pounds. The unicorn, small for his species, was about the same. The ogre's hamfists were deadly—but so was the unicorn's pointed horn. It was a momentary stand-off.

Then a second ogre appeared. "Look out behind thee, Lady!" Stile cried. She heard him and whirled. The second ogre's two hamhands were descending on her head.

The Lady ducked down and scooted between the monster's legs. The curtain was now just ahead of her. As the ogre turned, she straddled the curtain and stood facing it.

But other ogres were appearing. Two converged on the Lady from either side of the curtain. Clip charged to help her—but that permitted the first ogre to converge also.

As the two pounced, the Lady spelled herself across the curtain, holding her breath. The ogres crashed into each other where she had been. Stile could not see her in the image; it was difficult to see across the curtain anyway, and the holo pickup was oriented on the fantasy side. But he knew she was in extreme discomfort, with the thin, polluted air of Proton and the barren terrain.

But in a moment she reappeared, just beyond the brutes. She had avoided them by using the curtain. Clip spied her and rushed to join her again.

Two more ogres came into view. The five lumbered down upon the woman and unicorn. Clip launched himself at the closest, lowering his horn, skewering the monster through the center.

The ogre was so heavy the unicorn could not lift it; Clip had to back away, extricating his horn, shaking the monster's blood from it. But the ogre was mortally wounded; brown pus welled from the wound, front and back, and the creature staggered and fell with a crash like that of an uprooted tree.

Meanwhile, the remaining creatures had reconverged on the Lady. "Here to me, Hinblue!" she called, and stepped back across the curtain.

"Aren't we there yet?" Stile demanded. "She can't hold out much longer!"

"Sir, there seems to be a power interruption," Sheen said. "This passage needs repair; we must detour."

"How long?" Stile cried.

"Another fifteen minutes, sir, I fear."

Stile clapped his hands to his head in nonphysical pain. "My Lady! My Lady!"

"I love her too, sir," Sheen murmured.

Stile could only watch the unfolding sequence helplessly. He should never have left the Lady Blue so lightly guarded!

The Lady reappeared beyond the ogres as Hinblue arrived. "Now you can catch me not!" she cried, vaulting on to her fine steed.

The four ogres nevertheless started after her. Clip raced to join Hinblue.

But as they moved out, readily outdistancing the monsters, a small ravine appeared ahead. "Watch out!" Stile cried.

Too late. The distracted horse put a foot in it. Instantly Hinblue went down and the Lady flew off and forward. Athlete that she was, she landed on her feet, running, unhurt.

But Hinblue was hurt. She got to her feet, but she was bruised and lame. She could only hobble, not run. The ogres were closing in again.

Clip assumed man-form. "Lady, ride me! The mare can not carry thee."

"Oh, no!" Stile breathed. "I know what she will say."

"And desert my horse, offspring of the Hinny and the Blue Stallion?" the Lady Blue demanded. "Never!"

"She said it," Stile said, suffering.

"Then must we guard her," Clip said. He became unicorn again, and stood facing the four onrushing brutes.

They were no longer astride the curtain. The Lady could not use it to save herself—and in any event would not have left her horse. She drew a narrow, sharp knife and stood beside Clip, ready to fight.

The monsters came—but slowed. They had seen the fate of the first one to encounter the unicorn's horn. Still, they were four against two, and towered over their opposition.

A hole opened in the ground. An ugly head poked out, swathed in bandages. For an instant Stile thought yet another monster had joined the attack. But then he realized it was Trool the troll, the one who had helped them escape the Orange Demesnes. "Here!" the troll croaked.

The Lady recognized him. She was evidently uncertain of the creature's motive. Her Adept husband was no longer with her, and trolls liked human flesh.

"Escape," Trool said, indicating his tunnel. He was offering a route out of the trap.

"I thank thee, Trool," the Lady said. "But my steed fits not in thy tunnel."

The troll opened out another section of turf, and another. There was a shallow cave there. "This crisis was anticipated," he said, his voice becoming clearer, as if a long-disused faculty was being revived. "I labored to prepare."

The ogres were now very close. The Lady decided to risk the help of the troll. Without further protest, she led Hinblue into the cave, then stood at the entrance with her knife poised.

The ogres, outraged at this seeming escape, charged into the gully. But Clip charged too. His deadly horn punctured another ogre, this time from the side. The monster fell, squirting its brown juice, and again the others hesitated. There were only three of them now, and they evidently did not like dying. If any two had pounced on Clip together, they could have torn the unicorn apart—but they evidently lacked the wit or courage to do that. They also seemed nervous about Trool, who was a monster somewhat like themselves, though only half as stout. Why was he participating?

"That is Neysa's brother, sir?" Sheen asked. The fact that she was now using "sir" warned him that she was not sure they had complete privacy.

"Yes. He's one good unicorn."

"And ogres eat people?"

"Yes. Trolls eat people, too, and horses. But Trool can be trusted—I think."

Finally the ogres consulted, and came to the conclusion Stile had feared. Two of them stalked Clip together, while the third faced Trool, preventing the troll from interfering. Stile realized an ogre should have been able to demolish a troll on open ground, but not within a troll's tunnels, so this was merely interference rather than combat. The Lady Blue had to stay with the horse she guarded. Clip had to fight alone.

The unicorn could have changed into hawk-form and flown away, but he did not. He charged again. His horn skewered the left ogre—but the right one brought a hamfist down on the unicorn's rump. Clip's hindsection collapsed under the power of that blow. He was helpless, down on the ground, his hindlegs possibly crippled, his horn still wedged in the left ogre's torso.

Now the Lady Blue leaped forward, knife flashing. She sliced into the heavy arm of the right-hand ogre. Ichor welled out of a long slash, and the creature made a howl of pain.

Now the two remaining monsters retreated, one holding its wounded arm. Clip changed back into hawk-form, extricating himself, and the Lady held out her arm for him to perch on. He seemed shaken, limping, but not seriously hurt. Stile breathed a sigh of relief. The two returned to the impromptu cave.

For a time the ogres stayed back. Stile relaxed somewhat. The longer they waited, the better his chance to get to Phaze and correct the situation before any more harm was done. The capsule was proceeding with what seemed to him to be tedious slowness, but he knew Sheen was doing her best.

He decided he should divert his mind, as long as he could not act. "Place that call to the Citizen," he said curtly. "But don't interfere with this image."

"Yes, sir." Sheen placed the call.

In a moment the face of a well-fed, middle-aged male Citizen appeared beside the image of the West Pole region. There were no serf or robot intermediaries this time. "Yes?" he inquired, peering at Stile.

"Kalder, I am Stile," Stile said briskly. He was rapidly shedding his apprehension about Citizens. "I am not sure you know me—"

"I don't," Kalder agreed brusquely.

"But about two months ago you gifted me with a humanoid robot. I was then a serf."

Kalder's face wrinkled in perplexity. "I did?"

"This robot," Stile said, indicating Sheen.

Still there was no recognition in the man's face. Was this a misidentification? "Let me check my records," Kalder said.

In a moment the Citizen looked up. "I have it now. My staff handled it, without informing me. It was a routine protective measure."

"Routine measure?" Stile asked. "This is a five-gram robot! Why would you give her to a serf employed by another Citizen?"

Kalder's brow furrowed again. "That is peculiar. But I'm sure my chief of staff had reason. Let me see—yes, here it is. We received news that the chief horse trainer and jockey of a rival stable was to be assassinated, and the blame attached to me. I have one of the finest stables on Proton." He said this matter-of-factly, and Stile believed him. Citizens did not need to brag, and in his racing days he had come up against the entries of a number of excellent stables. He was probably familiar with Kalder's horses, if he cared to do the spot research necessary to align the Citizen's name with that of his stable. "Since that would have been an unpleasant complication, my chief of staff arranged to protect you anonymously. After all, it might have been a practical joke, leading to my embarrassment. Why take a chance?"

"You protected me—to save yourself from being framed or embarrassed," Stile said slowly. "No other reason?"

"None. I had no concern for you personally. I was not even aware of the matter until you called it to my attention just now. I leave such details to my staff."

That was some staff! But of course Stile had already discovered the caliber of staff a Citizen could afford. "How did your chief of staff know about this plot?"

Kalder checked his records again. "Anonymous message. That's why it could have been a joke. Was it?"

"It was not," Stile said. "Your robot saved my life on more than one occasion. Now I will marry her."

Kalder burst out laughing. "If her screws aren't loose, yours are! Be sure to invite me to the wedding! I'll gift you with a mail diaper for your cyborg offspring." He faded out.

A cyborg was a combination of flesh and machine, such as a robot with a grafted human brain, neither fish nor fowl. They generally did not last long. This was a cruel gibe, but Kalder was not a bad type, as Citizens went. The mystery remained. Who had sent the anonymous message to Kalder's staff?

"The same party who sicked the Red Adept on you, perhaps," Sheen said, following his thought.

"And who may be fouling me up with changed Oracle pronouncements," Stile agreed. "Now more of the pattern emerges. It could all stem from a single source. That is my true enemy."

"Why would an enemy arrange to have you protected?"

"Why, indeed!"

"My circuitry is inadequate to solve that problem," she said, smiling briefly.

"And mine. Put your friends on that message to Kalder; see if they can trace its source."

"Yes, sir." She made a coded call.

Now something new was happening in Phaze. The scene had been still while the Lady Blue put her hands on Clip and healed his bruises and restored his confidence. The ogres had stayed back. But Clip's ears —he was back in natural form—were perking forward, and he blew a brief, startled note.

"I see nothing," the Lady said. "What is it?"

Clip did not answer. His nostrils twitched. Obviously he heard and smelled something. Now, very faintly, Stile heard it too: the tinkling of little bells. Why did that seem familiar?

Then the source came into sight. It was another unicorn. This one was female, and lovely. Her coat was a deep red, almost purple, and shone with sleek health. Her mane rippled iridescently. As she approached, she changed to an elegant blue heron, then to a cat, and finally back to equine form. Her bell rang again, sweetly.

Clip's ears vibrated with amazement. He blew a querying note on his horn. The mare responded with a truly melodious tinkling of bells.

"What does she say?" the Lady Blue asked nervously.

Clip changed to man-form. "She says she was thrown out by her herd. She is all alone in the wilderness."

"She seems familiar."

"She and her brother danced at the Unolympics. They defeated Neysa and me for the prize."

"Now I remember! What a pretty 'corn she is!"

"Aye," Clip agreed wistfully.

"But why would her herd cast her out, after she brought them the prize?"

"She refused to be bred by her Herd Stallion, who is getting old and violent, so he exiled her. Now she is without a herd."

"Can't she join another?"

"Nay, the Herd Stallions interfere not in each other's herds. She is ostracized."

"The way Neysa was! That's terrible!"

"Neysa was merely excluded for a time. Belle can never go back."

The pretty mare tinkled her bell again.

"She asks if I will go with her," Clip said.

"It's a trap," Stile said. "Don't trust her." But the holo pickup was too far from the present setting for them to hear him unless he shouted; transmission was largely oneway now. He did not want to shout and have the ogres know his situation.

"How is it she shows up here now?" the Lady inquired, evidently having a similar suspicion.

But Clip, enchanted, changed back to equine form. As a lesser male, he was not permitted the chance to breed. This was obviously a phenomenal temptation.

The mare nickered and rang a lovely melody on her bellhorn. Clip quivered with eagerness.

"I don't trust this at all!" Stile said. "Clip has defended my Lady Blue against the monsters. Suddenly the loveliest mare unicorn in all the herds appears, luring him away."

"All males are fools in this manner," Sheen remarked.

"Clip, go not to her!" the Lady Blue pleaded. "At least wait until my Lord returns. It will not be long now."

But Clip had lost control of himself. Evidently the mare was in heat; he had to go to her. He fought the lure, but step by step he went.

The Lady Blue had to remain in the cave, guarding herself and Hinblue. She was not so foolish as to venture where the ogres could pounce.

Now at last the capsule approached the curtain. But the capsule was below ground, under desert; Stile could not step through at this level. "Get me to the surface, anywhere by the curtain!" he snapped, in a fever of impatience to reach the West Pole.

Sheen located a bus stop. Stile got out and hurried up the stairs to the surface. "Keep things in order until my return," he called back.

"Don't get yourself killed, sir," she said.

Stile didn't answer. He held his breath and burst out on to the desert, running for the curtain. As he came upon its shimmer, he willed himself across—and found himself running on the green plain of Phaze.

Immediately he stopped, formulating a suitable spell in his mind while he played his harmonica to summon his power. Then he sang: "Convey me whole to the West Pole."

The spell wrenched him from here to there, making him nauseous. It was never comfortable to work his magic on himself, and he avoided it except in emergencies. Feeling ill, he looked out from the West Pole.

There was no sign of Clip the unicorn. Stile sang a flightspell he had in reserve, rose into the air, and zooned toward the ravine and cave where the Lady Blue waited.

The two ogres were there. As Stile approached, one of them picked up the troll one-handed and hurled him high and away. Apparently Trool had left the security of his tunnels and so fallen into the power of the more massive monsters.

"Please—freeze," Stile sang, willing the interpretation of the spell. But though there was a faint effort of magic, the action did not stop.

Then he remembered that he had already used this spell to freeze the sea monster of the Translucent Demesnes. No wonder it had lost its potency. "All will be still," he sang.

This time the tableau froze as intended. The two ogres became statues, along with their injured companion, who was licking his arm a short distance away. The troll hung motionless in the air. The very wind stopped—but Stile himself continued.

The Lady Blue stood in the cave, knife in hand, her lovely face frozen in grinning ferocity as she slashed at the nearest monster. Behind her stood Hinblue, lame but trying to move out and get in a good kick.

Stile made a subspell to free the Lady only. "My Lord!" she exclaimed, breathlessly glad to see him. "Clip—he was lured away!"

"I saw," Stile said. "First I must tend to thee and thy friends; then will I quest after the unicorn."

The Lady was all right, though tired; it was no easy thing to stand up to an ogre with no more than a knife. Stile made a spell to restore Hinblue, whose injury had been beyond the Lady's gentler healing power. Then he brought Trool sliding slowly down from midair. "A second time hast thou repaid my favor," Stile said. "Now do I owe thee one."

"Nay, Adept," Trool protested. "It was prophesied that three times must I tunnel to free thee and thine from hazard, ere the balance evens."

"Then gladly do I accept this rescue of my Lady!" Stile said. "But dost thou not know that the Blue Adept destroyed all thy tribe in fire?"

"As my tribe destroyed all thy village. Those scales are even. The debt is other."

Stile shrugged. "Why shouldst thou be burdened, not me?"

"Because thou must save Phaze." Trool turned and shambled back into his tunnel, which extended darkly into the ground. Stile was amazed at the creature's facility in tunneling—but of course troll magic was involved.

Then he noticed an object on the ground. He stooped carefully to pick it up, for his knees remained bad, able to bend only to right angles before pain began. Stile could use magic to move himself but not to heal himself, so had to live with the condition. He picked up the object.

It was a small figurine of a woman, quite well executed. "Who made this?" Stile asked.

"Trool," the Lady replied. "He appears clumsy, but his big hands have magic. When he is not tunneling, he turns that magic to sculpture, to relieve his nervousness."

"Facing two ogres, I can appreciate his concern! Why did he step out on to the land, where they had power?"

"To stop them from charging me," she said. "Trolls are not my favorite creature, but Trool acted bravely and selflessly. If again we meet, I shall call him friend."

"Yet if he is honoring a prophecy, I can not reward him," Stile said. "That might alter the meaning of his action and void the prophecy, causing mischief."

"True," she agreed soberly.

Stile contemplated the figurine. "This is thee!" he exclaimed, surprised.

She shrugged. "He begged my leave. He works better when he has a subject. I saw no harm."

Figurine magic could be potent—but the Red Adept had specialized in that, with her amulets, and she was gone. "No, no harm," Stile agreed. "He's a fine craftsman. This is as pretty a statuette as I've seen."

"We forget Clip," she reminded him, taking the statuette from him.

"In a moment. Now for these monsters." Stile conjured a cage around the two, then unfroze them. They rattled the bars for several minutes before conceding they were effectively imprisoned; then they were ready to listen to Stile.

"Know, ogres, that I am the Blue Adept," Stile said. "This is my Lady Blue. Why did the five of you attack her?"

"Blue be now our enemy," one repeated.

"The Oracle told thee that?"

"Told Brogbt."

"Who is Brogbt?"

The ogre pointed to one of the dead monsters.

"Then must I make the dead to speak," Stile said grimly. He pondered, working out a spell, then sang: "Ogre Brogbt, under my spell, the true message do thou tell."

The dead ogre stirred. Flies buzzed up angrily. Its rigor-stiffened mouth cracked open. "Blue be not thine enemy," it croaked, and lay still again.

"Not!" the Lady exclaimed. "It said not!"

Both living ogres seemed surprised. "Brogbt told us *now*."

"He thought the word was now. He was enchanted, and heard or remembered it wrong. I am not thine enemy. Now thou knowest."

"Now I know," the ogre agreed, adapting dully to this new reality. Stile eliminated their cage. "Go inform thy kind of the truth."

They stomped away.

"Thou art as ever generous in victory," the Lady said.

"Now for the unicorn." Stile made a spell that set Clip's hoofprints glowing, and they followed these. The trail led over a hill to a copse of evergreens and entered the dense forest island.

"Where are the mare's prints?" the Lady asked.

Stile sang a new spell to make those also glow, but evoked nothing.

"She was mere illusion," the Lady said. "A sending to distract him so the ogres could get to me. This surely means mischief. Had Trool not interfered—"

Stile made another spell. "Make an image, make it sooth, of the unicorn, of the truth."

The image formed, like a holograph, three-dimensional. Clip walked beside a phantom. The unreal mare led him into the copse—and there a flash occurred, and the unicorn was gone.

"Destroyed?" the Lady cried, appalled.

"I think not," Stile said grimly. He tried a spell to locate Clip specifically, but it fizzled. "This is Adept magic. I can not fathom the truth beyond this point, for it is Adept against Adept. But the message seems likely enough. Clip has been taken hostage."

"Hostage!" she exclaimed. "For what?"

"For my behavior. My secret enemy can not match my power directly, so he has resorted to another device. I must bargain with him for Clip's life."

"But what does that Adept want?"

"It seems I am to be involved in great events in the near future.

Mine enemies know this, my friends know too. Everybody knows this except me. What mine enemy wants will surely be made known in good time."

"But no one can influence thee by such means!"

"Oh, yes, he can!" Stile scowled, feeling an elemental savagery. "He can evoke my vengeance against him for whatever he does to Clip. He can make me an enemy for life. Now he is attacking my wife and steed in lieu of me, seeking leverage. Not without consequence may Blue be thus used."

She smiled sadly. "The honeymoon is over."

Soberly, he nodded. "I must report to the Herd Stallion."

"And I—I shall be left behind again."

"Thou knowest I love thee, Lady. But there are things I must do."

"I would not change thy nature if I could, my love."

Abruptly, savagely, they kissed, their horror of the situation converting to passion. Then Stile spelled them to the unicorn herd.

They arrived at the edge of the pasture where the unicorns grazed. The great Herd Stallion looked up. He stood eighteen hands at the shoulder, or six feet, and was powerfully muscled. His torso was pearly gray, darkening into black hooves; his mane and tail were silver, and his head golden. He was the most magnificent equine Stile knew.

Perceiving Stile's mien, the Stallion converted immediately to man-form and approached. "Speak without waste, Adept."

"Clip has been taken hostage," Stile said. Then he choked and could not continue.

"Do thou go see Neysa," the Lady Blue told him gently. "I will give the Stallion the detail."

Gratefully, Stile walked through the herd, looking for his closest friend in Phaze. In a moment Neysa came to him. She was fit and sleek, showing as yet no sign of her gravid condition. She had only very recently been bred, and equines did not show the way humans did. She accepted his embrace, shifting momentarily to girl-form in his arms, in the mischievous way she had. Then she shifted back.

"Oh, Neysa," he said, feeling the tears on his face. "I fear I have placed your brother in dire straits."

She tensed, blowing a harmonica-note of alarm. She loved her brother.

"I was in Proton-frame," he stumbled on. "Ogres attacked the Lady Blue. Clip fought valiantly, protecting her, and killed two ogres. But an Adept sent a sending of the mare called Belle, who won thine event in the Unolympics, and lured him into captivity, surely hostage against my power. And I—I can not accept what that enemy may demand of me, though Clip is—" The tears were flowing freely now, dropping from his chin. "I should have been there!" And perhaps, if he had checked Clip's situation first, instead of last, he might have been in time to nullify the abduction. He had just assumed that Clip was near.

Neysa laid her warm horn against his cheek, suffering silently with him, forgiving him. She understood.

They walked together back to the Herd Stallion. The noble creature was again in his natural form and had evidently assimilated the Lady's story. He was stomping the turf with one forehoof, making sparks fly up, and steam was issuing from his nostrils.

When Stile rejoined him, the Stallion changed again to man-form, a wisp of steam still showing in his breath. "Thou art not at fault, Adept," he said. "Clip was there to help and protect thee, not thou him."

"Protect me he did," Stile said. "I owe him my life. But he lost his freedom protecting not me but my Lady. I must restore him to freedom and avenge what he is suffering."

"He is of my herd," the Stallion said. "Ultimately, vengeance is mine. But thou art welcome to free him if thou canst."

"First must I locate him," Stile said. "And, if thou canst permit it, I would take another unicorn as temporary steed. The forces ranged against me, for whatever reason, are more than I can safely cope with alone, and no horse suffices. I need the kind of service only a unicorn can give."

The Stallion hesitated. Neysa blew a faint note on her harmonica-horn, half pleading, half warning. She was subject to the Herd Stallion, but friend to the Blue Adept—and to many others. She was close blood kin to Clip. She wanted to be Stile's steed again, despite her condition. The Stallion could say nay or yea and would be obeyed—but his life would be simplified if he placated this spirited little mare. Stile had a certain sympathy for the Herd Stallion's predicament.

"I will provide thee with another unicorn," the Stallion decided. "Thou art held in unusual respect in this herd, Adept; a number of these would do for thee what they would not do for any ordinary man. Yet may I not compel any in this matter; give me time to seek a volunteer."

The Stallion seemed less urgent about this than Stile felt, and was obliquely refusing Neysa's offer. Yet it was a sensible course. "It will take time to locate Clip and prepare a campaign to recover him without injury," Stile said. "Adept magic is involved, making the matter devious, not subject to simple spells. I do not relish his captivity for even another hour, but it would be foolish to strike unprepared. Will a day and a night suffice? I do have business in the other frame."

"It will suffice," the Stallion agreed. "I shall query the animals of other kinds and send to the Oracle."

The Oracle! Of course! That would pinpoint Clip instantly—if the answer were not misunderstood. Except—what about the speculation the Translucent Adept had made about the Oracle? Maybe he should be careful of any advice received, without openly challenging its validity.

Stile turned to the Lady Blue. "Now must I return thee to the Blue Demesnes for safekeeping."

Again Neysa protested. The Herd Stallion, shifting to natural form, blew an accordion-chord of irritated acquiescence.

"I have been invited to visit with the Herd during thine absence," the Lady said. "I can be better guarded here, for no magic penetrates a herd on guard. By thy leave, my Lord—"

"I will make thee a pavilion," Stile said, pleased. She would be much safer here, certainly.

"I need it not, my Lord."

Stile nodded. The Lady Blue was no frail flower; she could survive well enough. "Then shall I—"

He paused, and the unicorns looked up from their grazing. A dragon was approaching—a huge flying creature, swooping up and down, evidently searching for something. It spied the herd and flew directly toward it.

Immediately the unicorns formed a circle, horns pointing out. In the center were the foals and aged individuals—and Neysa, specially protected during her gestation. The Herd Stallion stood outside, flanked by several of the strongest of the lesser males, facing the monster alertly.

"I can deal with this," Stile offered. He had a number of spells to bring down dragons.

But the dragon was not attacking. It was a steed, with an old woman holding the reins, perched betweeen the great beating wings. She carried a white kerchief that she waved in her left hand.

"Flag of truce," Stile said. Then, with a double take: "That's the Yellow Adept!"

The Herd Stallion snorted angrily. He would honor the truce, but he had no love for the Yellow Adept, whose business it was to trap and sell animals, including unicorns.

The dragon landed with a bump that made its passenger bounce, then folded its wings. The old woman scrambled down. "I bear a message for Blue. It must be quick, for my potion can not hold this monster long."

Stile stepped forward, still surprised. Usually this witch only went out in public after taking a youth potion for cosmetic effect. What message could cause her to scramble like this? "I am here, Yellow."

"It is in the form of a package, my handsome," she said, handing him a long box that appeared from her shawl. Stile suddenly became conscious of his own apparel: the outfit of a Proton Citizen. In the rush of events he had not bothered to conjure Phaze clothing. But it hardly mattered; an Adept, like a Citizen, could wear what he pleased.

"I want thee to know I had no hand in this particular mischief. The item was delivered by conjuration with the message: *Blue butt out.* I hastened to bring it to thee, fearing further malice against thee an I delayed. My potions indicate that more than one Adept participates in this."

She hurried back to her dragon-steed before Stile could open the package. "Wait, Yellow—I may wish to question thee about this!" Stile called. Something about the package gave him an extremely ugly premonition.

"I dare not stay," she called back. "I would help thee if I could, Blue, for thou art a bonny lad. But I can not." She spurred her dragon forward. The creature spread its wings and taxied along on six little legs, finally getting up to takeoff velocity. Once it was airborne, it was much more graceful. Soon it was flying high and away.

Stile unwrapped the package with a certain misgiving. It surely did not contain anything he would be glad to see. Probably it was from Clip's captor; some evidence that the unicorn was indeed hostage, such as a hank of his blue mane.

As the package unwrapped, two red socks fell out. Clip's socks, which could be magically removed and used separately, in the same manner as Neysa's white socks. But there was something else in the package. Stile unwrapped it—and froze, appalled. All the others stared, not at first believing it.

It was a severed unicorn horn.

Stile's hands began to shake. He heard the Lady Blue's quick intake of breath. Neysa blew a note of purest agony.

Slowly Stile lifted the horn to his mouth. He blew into the hollow base. The sound of an ill-played saxophone emerged. It was definitely Clip's horn.

Neysa fell to the ground as if stricken by lightning. The Lady Blue dropped down beside her, putting her arms about the unicorn's neck in a futile attempt to console her. Stile stood stiffly, his mind half numbed by the horror of it. To a unicorn, the horn was everything, the mark that distinguished him from the mere horse.

More than that, he realized, the horn was the seat of the unicorn's magic. Without it, Clip could not change form or resist hostile spells. He would be like a man blinded and castrated—alive without joy. There could be no worse punishment.

The Herd Stallion was back in man-form. He put forth his large hand to take the horn. His eyes were blazing like the windows of a furnace, and steam was rising from him. "They dare!" he rasped, staring at the member.

"For this will I visit a conflagration on the Demesnes of every Adept involved!" Stile said, finding his voice at last. "On every creature who cooperated. I will level mountains to get at them. What the Blue Adept did to the trolls and jackals shall be as nothing." Already the air was becoming charged with the force of his developing oath; dark coils of fog were swirling. "Only let me make my music, find my rhyme—"

"Nay, Adept," the Herd Stallion said gruffly. "He is of my herd. Not thine but mine is this vengeance."

"But thou canst not leave thy herd unguarded," Stile protested.

"Another Stallion will assist, for this occasion."

"And thou canst not face Adepts alone. Only an Adept can oppose an Adept."

The Stallion snorted smoke from his human nostrils, heeding Stile's caution through his fury. "True. Not alone can I accomplish it. Only half the vengeance is mine to claim."

"Just give me a steed, and I will—"

"I will be thy steed!" the Stallion said.

Neysa, on the ground, perked up her ears. The Lady Blue's eyes widened as she recognized the possibilities. No human being had ever ridden a Herd Stallion, virtually a breed apart. Yet if the power of an Adept coordinated with that of a unicorn Stallion—

Stile could not decline. They shared a vengeance.

CHAPTER 8

Wager

"So I have most of twenty-four hours in Proton," Stile said to Sheen, "before the Stallion and I commence our mission of rescue and vengeance. I'll have to spend some of that time in sleep, gathering my strength. I trust you have my business here well organized."

"We do," she agreed brightly. "Mellon has lined up a number of wealthy Citizens who are eager to wipe you out financially. My friends have worked out a way to trace the original message to Citizen Kalder— but only you, an interested Citizen, can implement it. And there is reaction approaching suppressed riot to the news of the designation of your heir."

"That's enough to start on," Stile said. "Maybe it will distract me for the moment from my real concern in Phaze. Let's see how much we can sandwich in. I don't know how long my next adventure in Phaze will hold me."

"Perhaps forever," she said darkly. Then, mechanically, she reverted to immediate business. "Start on which, sir? You can't do everything at once."

"Why not?"

"The bettors are in the Stellar Lounge, as before. The panel for your heir-designation hearing is in another dome, a hundred kilometers distant. And the first obscurity in the message chain is at a dome fifty kilometers beyond that, in the private property of a Citizen. Any one of these situations can monopolize your available time."

"You think too much like a machine," he chided her. "Take me to the hearing. Meanwhile, call the Stellar Lounge."

Frowning, she set the travel capsule in motion and placed the call. Mellon appeared in three-dimensional image. "So good to see you, sir. May I notify the Citizens that you are ready for action?"

"Do so," Stile said. "But advise them that I have unusual and challenging bets in mind and will welcome them at the site of my heir-designation hearing. You be there too."

"Yes, sir." Mellon faded out.

Immediately there was an incoming call. It was Citizen Merle. "My intercept notified me you were back in town," she said brightly. "Have you considered my invitation of the morning?"

Not this again! "Merle, I remain flattered. But there are things you should know."

"About your lovely wife in the other frame? Stile, that has no force in Proton."

"About my engagement to the serf Sheen, here," Stile said, unpleased about Merle's conversance with his private life. Too many Citizens were learning too much about him.

"Yes, I mean to place a bet on the outcome of your hearing," Merle agreed. "I'm rooting for you, Stile; I'm betting you will gain approval, after a struggle. Citizens are by no means limited in their liaisons. I have gifted my husband with a number of fine concubines, and he has sent me whichever males he suspects will appeal to my tastes. In any event, you need have no concern about the feelings of a serf."

Stile suffered an explosive reaction of anger. Sheen made an urgent signal: do not offend this Citizen!

Then Stile had a tactical inspiration. "Merle, I do care about the feelings of this serf. I was until very recently a serf myself. Until I have a better notion of her willingness to share, I can not give you a decision."

Merle smiled. "Oh, I do like you, little man! You are like a splendid fish, fighting the line. I shall be in touch with you anon." She faded.

"Sir, I never denied you the right to—" Sheen began.

"Secure our privacy!" he snapped.

She adjusted the communication controls. "Secure, sir."

"Then why are you calling me sir?"

"Stile, our relationship has changed. We are no longer even nominally members of the same society, and I prefer to recognize that in the established way. Sir."

"You're mad at me?"

"A machine can not be angry, sir."

Fat chance! "Sheen, you know that our marriage is one of convenience. I'm doing it to give your friends leverage in their suit for recognition. The upcoming hearing will be a crucial step. If we prevail there, it will be a big stride forward for your kind. I do like you, in fact I love you—but the Lady Blue will always hold the final key to my heart."

"I understand, sir." Her face was composed.

"So being faithful to you, in this frame, is moot," he continued, wishing she would show more of the emotion he knew she felt. "It is the Lady Blue I am faithful to. But aside from that, there is the matter of appearances. If I am engaged to you, but have liaisons with fleshly women—especially Citizens—that could be taken as evidence that I am marrying you in name only, to designate a convenient heir, and that could destroy the leverage we hope to gain."

"Yes, sir," she agreed noncommittally.

"So there is no way I will make an assignation with Merle. If I do that with anyone in this frame, it will be you. Because you are my fiancée, and because there is no one in this frame I would rather do it with. So, in that sense, I am true to you. I wanted to be sure you understand."

"I understand, sir. There is no need to review it."

So he hadn't persuaded her. "Yes, I needed to review it. Because now I have it in mind to do something extremely cynical. An act worthy of a true Citizen. And I need your help."

"You have it, sir."

"I want you to have your friends arrange a blind bet on the outcome of Merle's suit. An anonymous, coded bet amounting to my entire available net worth at the time of decision—that I will not complete that liaison. I will of course deny any intent to make that liaison, but I may at times seem to waver. You and I know the outcome, but other Citizens may wish to bet the other way. It would be a foolish bet for them—but they seem to like such foolishness."

Sheen smiled. "That is indeed cynical, sir. I shall see to it."

"And it would not hurt if you permitted yourself some trifling show of jealousy, even if you feel none."

She paused. "You are devious, sir."

"I have joined a devious society. Meanwhile, I shall remain on the fence with Merle, in all but words, as long as I can stimulate interest. See that Mellon is privately notified; he definitely has the need to know."

The capsule arrived at the dome of the hearing. They emerged into a white-columned court, floored with marble, spacious and airy as a Greek ruin. Three Citizens sat behind an elevated desk. A fourth Citizen stood before the desk, evidently with another case; Stile's turn had not yet come.

The betting Citizens were arriving. A rotund man garbed like a Roman senator approached, hand extended. "Greeting, Stile. I am Waldens, and I'm interested in your offer. What is its nature?"

"Thank you, Waldens. I am about to face a hearing on the validity of my designation of my fiancée, a humanoid robot, as my heir to Citizenship. I proffer a wager as to the panel's decision."

"Most interesting!" Waldens agreed. "I doubt they will approve the designation."

"I am prepared to wager whatever my financial adviser will permit, that they will approve it," Stile said. "It is, after all, a Citizen's right to designate whom he pleases."

"Ah, yes—but a robot is not a 'whom' but an 'it.' Only recognized people can inherit Citizenship."

"Is there a law to that effect?"

"Why, I assume so. It is certainly custom."

Now Mellon arrived. Stile quickly acquainted him with the situation. "How much will you let me bet?" he asked, knowing that Mellon, as a self-willed machine in touch with the network of his kind, would have a clear notion of the legalistic background.

But the serf hesitated. "Sir, this is an imponderable. The decision of the panel is advisory, without binding force. If there is a continuing challenge, a formal court will be convened—"

"Come off it, serf!" Waldens snapped. "We're only betting on this particular decision. What the court does later will be grist for another wager. How much Protonite can Stile afford to risk?"

"He has limited me to one hundred grams," Stile said, catching Sheen's covert affirmative signal. That meant the machines had researched the issue, and believed the odds were with Stile. He should win this bet. But he was going to play it carefully.

"A hundred grams!" Waldens laughed. "I did not come all the way here in person for such minor action!"

"I regret that my estate is as yet minimal," Stile said. "But it is growing; I have won all bets made so far. I assure you that I have an appetite for larger bets—when I can afford them. I plan to increase my estate enormously."

"All right, Stile. You're peanuts, but I like your spirit. Should be good entertainment here. I'll play along with a small bet now—but I'll expect a big one later, if you're in shape for it. Shall we compromise at half a kilo now?"

Mellon looked pained, but under Waldens' glare he slowly acquiesced. "Half a kilogram of Protonite," Stile agreed, putting on a pale face himself. Five hundred grams was half the ransom of a Citizen, and more than half Stile's entire available amount for betting. His fortune stood at 1,219 grams, but he had to hold 250 for living expenses. What he was laying on the line now was enough to buy a hundred sophisticated robots like Sheen and Mellon, or to endow the tenure of five hundred serfs. All in a single bet—which his opponent considered to be a minor figure, a nuisance indulged in only for entertainment!

Meanwhile, other Citizens had arrived, intrigued by the issue. Novelty was a precious commodity among those who had everything. Two paired off, taking the two sides with matching half-kilo bets. Two more bet on whether there would be an immediate appeal of the panel's recommendation, whatever it was. Citizens certainly loved to gamble!

The prior case cleared, and it was Stile's turn before the panel. "It has been brought to our attention that you propose to designate a humanoid robot as your heir to Citizenship," the presiding Citizen said. "Do you care to present your rationale?"

Stile knew this had to be good. These were not objective machines but subjective people, which was why there could be no certainty about the decision. The wrong words could foul it up. "I am a very recent Citizen, whose life has been threatened by calamitous events; I am conscious of my mortality and wish to provide for the continuation of my estate. Therefore I have designated as my heir the person who is closest to me in Proton: my prospective wife, the Lady Sheen, here." He indicated Sheen, who cast her eyes down demurely. "She happens to be a lady robot. As you surely know, robots are sophisticated today; she is hardly distinguishable from a living person in ordinary interactions. She can eat and sleep and initiate complex sequences. She can even evince bad temper."

"The typical woman," the presiding Citizen agreed with a brief smile. "Please come to the point."

"Sheen has saved my life on more than one occasion, and she means more to me than any other person here. I have made her my chief of staff and am satisfied with the manner in which she is running my estate. I want to make our association more binding. Unless there is a regulation preventing the designation of one's wife as one's heir, I see no problem."

The three panelists deliberated. "There is no precedent," the presiding Citizen said. "No one has designated a robot before. Machines do well enough as staff members, concubines, stand-ins, and such, but seldom is one married and never have we had a nonhuman Citizen."

"If an alien creature won the Tourney one year, would it be granted Citizenship?" Stile asked.

"Of course. Good point," the Citizen said, nodding. "But robots are not permitted to participate in the Game, so can not win the Tourney."

"Do you mean to tell me that a frog-eyed, tentacular mass of slime from the farthest wash of the galaxy can be a Citizen—but this woman can not?" Stile demanded, again indicating Sheen.

The Citizens of the panel and of the group of bettors looked at Sheen, considering her as a person. She stood there bravely, smooth chin elevated, green eyes bright, her light brown hair flowing down her backside. Her face and figure were exquisitely female. There was even a slight flush at her throat. She had been created beautiful; in this moment she was splendid.

"But a robot has no human feeling," another panelist said.

"How many Citizens do?" Stile asked.

The bettors laughed. "Good shot!" Waldens muttered.

The panelists did not respond to the humor. "A robot has no personal volition," the presiding Citizen said. "A robot is not alive."

This was awkward territory. Stile had promised not to give away the nature of the self-willed machines, who did indeed have personal volition. But he saw a way through.

"Sheen is a very special robot, the top of her class of machine," he said. "Her brain is half digital, half analog, much as is the human brain, figuratively. Two hemispheres, with differing modes of operation. She approximates human consciousness and initiative as closely as a machine can. She has been programmed to resemble a living woman in all things, to think of herself as possessing the cares and concerns of life. She believes she has feeling and volition, because this is the nature of her program and her construction." As he spoke, he remembered his first discussion with Sheen on this subject, before he discovered the frame of Phaze. He had chided her on her illusion of consciousness, and she had challenged him to prove he had free will. She had won her point, and he had come to love her as a person—a robot person. He had tended to forget, since his marriage to the Lady Blue, how deep his feeling for Sheen was. Now he was swinging back to her. He truly believed she was a real person, whose mechanism happened to differ from his own but resulted in the same kind of personality.

"Many creatures have illusions," a panelist remarked. "This is no necessary onus for Citizenship."

Stile saw that more would be required to overcome their prejudice. He would have to do a thing he did not like.

"Sheen, how do you feel about me?" he asked.

"I love you, sir," she said.

"But you know I can not truly love a machine."

"I know, sir."

"And you are a machine."

"Yes, sir."

"I will marry you and designate you as my heir to Citizenship, but I will not love you as man to woman. You know it is a marriage of convenience."

"I know, sir."

"Why do you submit to this indignity?"

"Because she wants Citizenship!" a Citizen exclaimed. He was one of the ones betting against the acceptance of the heir designation.

Stile turned to the man. "How can a machine want?" Then he returned to Sheen. "*Do* you want Citizenship?"

"No, sir."

"Then why do you accede to this arrangement?"

"Because your wife in Phaze asked me to."

"Oh, a stand-in for an other-frame wife!" Waldens said knowingly. "Cast in her image?"

"No, sir, she is beautiful," Sheen said. "I can never substitute for her."

"I am interested," the presiding panelist said. "Robot, are you capable of emotion? *Do* you feel, or think you feel? Do you want anything?"

"Yes, sir, to all three," Sheen replied.

"Exactly what do you want, if not Citizenship?"

"I want Stile's love, sir," she said.

The panelist looked at his co-panelists. "Let the record note that the robot is crying."

All the Citizens looked closely at Sheen. Her posture and expression had not changed, but the tears were streaming down her cheeks.

"Why would any woman, human or robot, cry in response to simple, straightforward questions?" a panelist asked.

Citizen Waldens stepped forward suddenly, putting his cloaked arm around Sheen's shoulders. "For God's sake! She is not on trial! Spare her this cruelty!"

The presiding panelist nodded sagely. "She weeps because she knows she can never have her love returned by the man she loves, no matter what else he gives her. Our questioning made this truth unconscionably clear, causing her to react as the woman she represents would act. I do not believe she was conscious of the tears, or that this is a detail that would have occurred to a man." He pondered a moment, then spoke deliberately. "We of this panel are not without feeling ourselves. We are satisfied that this person, the robot Sheen, is as deserving of Citizenship as is a frog-eyed, tentacular mass of slime from the farthest wash of the galaxy." He glanced at his co-panelists for confirmation. "We therefore approve the robot Sheen's designation as heir, pending such decision as the court may make."

The Citizens applauded politely. Waldens brought Sheen back to Stile. "I'm glad to lose that bet, Stile. She's a good woman. Reminds me of my wife, when she was young and feeling. This robot deserves better than you are giving her."

"Yes," Stile agreed.

Waldens started to turn away, then snapped back in a double take. "I'll be damned! You're crying too!"

Stile nodded dumbly.

"And you think you don't love her." The Citizen shrugged. "Care to make a bet on that?"

"No," Stile said.

Sheen turned to him with incredulous surmise. "The illusion of non-feeling—it is yours!" she said. "The Lady knew!"

The Lady had known. Stile was indeed a man of two loves, suppressing one for the sake of the other—in vain.

"Well, I'll bet you on something else," Waldens said. "One kilo, this time. I happen to know you can afford it."

Stile wrenched himself back to the practicalities of the moment. He looked at Mellon. "Can I?"

"Sir, your betting is becoming more hazardous than necessary."

"That's his way of saying yes," Waldens said. "I feel you owe me one more bet. It wasn't right to use your girl that way. You set her up for it, knowing how she loved you."

"Yet he gave back more than he took," Sheen said. There was now a certain radiance about her, the knowledge of discovered treasure. Stile had actually set himself up.

"I'll give you your bet," Stile agreed. "And I'll match anybody else, if I don't run out of grams. Right now I have to trace an old message to its source. Care to bet whether I make it?"

"No. I don't know enough about the situation. But I'll bet when I do. You are involved in odd things, for a new Citizen. Usually they're busy for the first month just experiencing the novelty of having serfs say sir to them."

"I have some equipment waiting at the site," Stile said. He gave the address, and the other Citizens dispersed to their private capsules.

Alone with Sheen and Mellon in his own capsule, Stile looked at Sheen. Emotion overwhelmed him. "Damn!" he exclaimed. "I'm sorry, Sheen."

She paused momentarily, analyzing which level he was on. "You had to do it, sir. It was necessity, not cruelty, sir."

"Stop calling me sir!" he cried.

"When we are alone," she agreed.

"Maybe I am fooling myself. Maybe what I feel for you is what most others would call love. But since I met the Lady Blue—"

She laid her soft hand on his. "I would not change you if I could."

Which was what the Lady Blue had said. Sheen could have had no way to know that.

"It is an interesting relation you share," Mellon said. "I am not programmed for romantic emotion. I admit to curiosity as to its nature and usefulness."

"You are better off not knowing," Sheen said, squeezing Stile's hand.

"I do experience excitement when a large property transaction is imminent."

"If the self-willed machines gain recognition," Stile said, "you will receive whatever programming you wish, including romantic. For now, she's right; you are happier as you are."

"I will be ecstatic if I complete your target fortune. So far I have had little to do with it. I fear my circuits will short out, observing your mode of operation."

Stile smiled. "Now that I have inordinate wealth, I find it does not mean much to me," he said. "It is merely the substance of another game. I want to win, of course—but my real ambition lies elsewhere." He glanced again at Sheen. "My emotion is so erratic, I really think it would be better for you to accept reprogramming to eliminate your love for me. It would save you so much grief—"

"Or you could accept conditioning to eliminate your love for the Lady Blue," she said.

"Touché."

"Or to diminish your prejudice against robots."

"I'm not prejudiced against—" He paused. "Damn it, now I know I could love you, Sheen, if I didn't have the Lady Blue. But my cultural conditioning . . . I would prefer to give up life itself, rather than lose her."

"Of course. I feel the same about you. Now I know I have enough of you to make my existence worthwhile."

She was happy with half a loaf. Stile still felt guilty. "Sometimes I wish there were another me. That I had two selves again, with one who was available for Citizenship and who would love you, while the other could roam forever free in Phaze." He sighed. "But of course when there were two of me, I knew about none of this. My other self had the Lady Blue."

"That self committed suicide," she said.

"Suicide! By no means! He was murdered!"

"He accepted murder. Perhaps that is not clear to your illogical and vacillating mind."

"My mind was his!"

"In a different situation. He had reason."

Accepted murder. Stile considered that. He had marveled before that the Blue Adept had been dispatched by so crude a device—strangled by a demon from an amulet. It was indeed a suspicious situation. No magic of that sort had been able to kill Stile; why had it worked against his other self? And the Blue Adept's harmonica, his prized possession, had been left for Stile to find, conveniently. Yet suicide—could that be believed? If so, why? Why would any man permit himself to be ignominiously slain? Why, specifically, should Stile himself, in his other guise, permit it? He simply was not the type.

"You say he had reason. Why do you feel he did that?"

"Because he lacked enough of the love of the one he loved," she said promptly.

"But the Lady Blue gave him the third thee," he protested. "In Phaze, that is absolute love."

"But it was late and slow, and as much from duty and guilt as from true feeling. Much the same as your love for me. I, too, tried to suicide."

Indeed she had, once. One might debate whether a nonliving creature could die, but Sheen had certainly tried to destroy herself. Only the compassion of the Lady Blue had restored Sheen's will to endure. The Lady Blue, obviously, had understood. What a hard lesson she had learned when her husband died!

"Somehow I shall do right by you, Sheen," Stile said. "I don't know how, right now, but I will find a way."

"Maybe with magic," she said, unsmiling.

They arrived at the site of the message-tracing team. Stile was glad to let this conversation drop. He loved Sheen, but not consistently and not enough. His personal life in Proton seemed to be an unravelable knot.

They were in one of the public lavatories for serfs, with rows of sinks, toilets, and showers. The message cable passed the length of its floor, buried but within range of the detector. Passing serfs, seeing a Citizen present, hastily departed for other facilities.

There was a serf technician with a small but complex machine on two wheels. The machine blinked and bleeped in response to the serf's comments. No, Stile realized, it was the other way around. The serf commented in response to the device. It was another self-willed machine, with a subordinate serf. A neat way to conceal the real nature of the assistance being provided. The self-willed machines had considerable resources but did not want to betray their nature to the Citizens, lest the machines be summarily destroyed. There was a difference between being programmed to mimic personal volition, as Sheen was presumed to be, and actually possessing that volition, as Sheen and her kind did. The makers of these most sophisticated robots had wrought better than they knew, which was the reason these machines wanted legal recognition as people. They *were* people, of mechanical nature. With such recognition they could not be dispatched without legal reason, lest it be called murder.

The signals from the machine were more or less continuous and were ignored by the Citizens who joined Stile's party for the betting. Thus the real nature of the communications was not obvious. Only Stile, with his private knowledge of the special machines and his Game-trained alertness for detail, was aware of it. "What have we here?" he inquired of the serf.

"Sir, this is an electronic device that can trace the route of a particular message at a particular moment," the serf said. "Each message modifies the atomic structure of the transmission wires nominally. This change is so small that only a sophisticated instrument can detect it, and the range is quite limited. But it is possible to trace the stigmata by examining the wires at close range, provided we know precisely what we are looking for."

"Like a hound sniffing a scent," Stile said.

The machine bleeped. "Yes, sir," the serf said.

"That's a new one to me," Waldens said. "But I never did concern myself with machines. I think I'll buy me one like the metal lady here, if I don't win this one in a bet."

Both Sheen and Stile reacted, startled. Neither was pleased. Waldens laughed. "Stile, you don't have to bet anything you don't want to. But you should be aware that this lady robot is now a piece worth a good deal more than she was when new. If you lose a big one and have to have a new stake, she is it." He glanced at the message-tracing machine. "Now let's see this contraption operate."

"You have programmed the specific message and time of transmission?" Stile inquired. "Why are you unable to continue?"

Again the bleep. "Yes, sir. We have traced the message to this point. But ahead the cable passes through a juncture associated with the estate of a Citizen who denies us permission to prospect here."

"Ah, now the challenge comes clear," Waldens said. "What Citizen?"

"Sir, serfs do not identify Citizens by name," the serf said, translating the machine's signals. "But his designation is at the gate."

Waldens strode out of the lavatory and down the hall to examine the gate. The others followed. "Circle-Tesseract symbol." He brought out a miniature mike. "Who's that?"

"Sir, that is Citizen Cirtess," his contact answered.

"Cirtess. Circle-Tesseract. That figures. Same way I have a forest pond on my crest. I know him." Waldens considered. "Stile, I'm ready to bet. You won't get into that dome to trace your line. You'll have to go around and pick up beyond."

"Is that feasible?" Stile asked his technician serf.

"Not feasible, sir. This is a major cable junction. Billions of impulses have passed through it. We can trace the stigmata only by setting up at the junction and reading the routing there."

"Needle in a haystack," Stile said.

"Sir?"

"Never mind. I grasp the problem. We shall simply have to get to that switchbox."

"That's my bet, Stile," Waldens said. "Let's put a reasonable time limit on it. Shall we say half an hour for you to get the job done?"

Stile looked at the message-tracing serf. "How long to pass this junction without impediment?"

"It is merely a matter of getting to it, sir. The readout is instant."

Stile looked at Mellon. "How much may I bet?"

"The amount is settled," Waldens protested. "One kilo."

Mellon was unhappy. "Sir, this is extremely chancy, incoporating virtually no element of predictability, and the amount is large. Have you any reasonable expectation of obtaining permission to enter Citizen Cirtess' dome in the next half hour?"

"No. *But* that's not the bet. It's whether I can get the job done."

"Oho!" Waldens exclaimed. "You intend to go in without permission?"

Stile shrugged. "I intend to get the job done."

"Cirtess has armed guards and laser barriers," another Citizen said. "Almost every year some foolishly intruding serf gets fried. It would take a mechanized army to storm that citadel."

Waldens smiled. "Sirs, I think we have a really intriguing wager in the making. What do we deem to be the odds against Stile's success? Remember, he is a canny ex-serf who recently won the Tourney; he surely has some angle."

"Thousand to one against, for any ordinary person," the other Citizen said. "Hundred to one against, for a Tourney winner. And a good chance he'll get himself killed trying."

"No, I saw him play," a third Citizen said. "He's a slippery one. If he thinks he can do it, maybe he can."

"I don't *think* I can do it," Stile said. "I *have* to do it. Forces were set in motion to kill me, and this message is related. I must ascertain its source."

"Within half an hour?" Waldens asked.

"I suspect that if I don't pass this nexus in that time, I won't pass it at all. It is pass-fail right now."

"And you are staking your life on it," Waldens said. "That makes the bet most interesting. Suppose we give you odds? We think the chances are one hundred to one against you; you evidently think you can do it. We could compromise at ten to one, with several of us covering the bet."

"That's generous enough," Stile agreed. "Since I have to make the attempt anyway."

"Sir, I do not recommend this wager," Mellon said. "I know of no persuasion you can make to obtain Citizen Cirtess' acquiescence, and you lack the facilities for intrusion against resistance. My expert advice can bring you far more favorable betting opportunities than this."

"Fifteen to one," Waldens said. "I won't go higher; I don't trust you to be as naïve as you seem." The other Citizens nodded agreement. Their faces were becoming flushed; this was the essence of their pleasure. Negotiating a large bet on a highly questionable issue. Gambling not merely with wealth but with the deviousness of human comprehension and intent. They knew Stile had something in mind, and it was worth poorer odds to discover what his play would be.

Stile spread his hands in ordinary-man innocence. "Mellon, I'm sure your way is more practical. But I stand to win a great deal on this, with these levered odds. If I lose I'm in trouble anyway, because this intrusion may be physically hazardous. Wealth is very little use to a dead man. So I must do it my way this time. One kilogram of Protonite against their fifteen kilos, half an hour from now."

"Yes, sir," Mellon said with doleful resignation.

"But no interference from you Citizens," Stile cautioned. "If you give away the show to Cirtess—"

"No cheating," Waldens agreed. "We'll watch via a routine pickup, hidden in the lavatory."

"Thank you." Stile turned to the machine-operating serf. "Show me how to work this contraption," he said.

"Merely locate it over the line or nexus, sir. It will emit code lights and bleeps to enable you to orient correctly." He demonstrated. Stile tried the procedure on the section of cable under the floor, getting the hang of it. He knew he would have no trouble, since this was another self-willed machine, which would guide him properly.

Now Stile turned to one of the betting Citizens who wore an elaborate headdress that vaguely resembled an ancient Amerind chief's bonnet of feathers. "I proffer a side bet, my clothing against your hat, on the flip of a coin."

"How small can you get?" the Citizen asked, surprised. "I have staked a kilo, and you want my hat?"

"You decline my wager?" Stile asked evenly.

The Citizen frowned. "No. I merely think it's stupid. You could buy your own hat; you have no need of mine. And your clothing would not fit me." The man touched his bulging middle; his mass was twice Stile's.

"So you agree to bet." Stile looked around. "Does anyone have a coin with head and tail, similar to those used in Tourney contests?"

Another Citizen nodded. "I am a numismatist. I will sell you a coin for your clothing."

Now Stile was surprised. "My clothing has already been committed."

"I'm calling your bluff. I don't believe you plan to strip, so I figure you to arrange to win the toss. If you win, I get your clothing as due rental for the coin."

"But what if I lose?"

"Then I'll give you my clothing, in the spirit of this nonsense. But you won't lose; you can control the flip of a coin. All Gamesmen can."

"Now wait!" the headdressed Citizen protested. "I want a third party to flip it."

"I'll flip," Waldens said. "I'm objective; I'll be happy to see anyone naked, so long as it isn't me."

Stile smiled. "It might be worth the loss." For the coin-loaning Citizen was especially portly. "Very well. I will rent your coin."

"This grows ever more curious," Waldens remarked. "What is this fascination we seem to share for nakedness in the presence of Stile's lovely robot mistress?"

"Fiancée," Stile said quickly.

Now the other Citizen smiled. "Maybe we should all strip and ask her opinion."

Sheen turned away, blushing. This was sheer artifice, but it startled the Citizens again; they were not used to robots who were this lifelike. "By God," one muttered, "I'm going to invest in a harem of creatures like her."

Stile accepted the coin. It was a pretty iridium disk, comfortably solid in his hand, with the head of Tyrannosaurus Rex on one side and the tail of a dinosaur on the reverse. Stile appreciated the symbolism: iridium had been associated with the extinction of the dinosaurs, and of course the whole notion of coinage had become a figurative dinosaur in the contemporary age. Iridium, however, remained a valuable metal, and numismatics was popular among Citizens. He passed the coin over to Waldens.

"How do we know Waldens can't control the flip too?" another Citizen asked suspiciously. They were taking this tiny bet as seriously as any other.

"You can nullify his control by calling the side in midair," Stile pointed out. "If you figure him to go for heads, you call tails. One flip. Agreed?"

"Agreed." The Citizen with the headdress seemed increasingly interested. He was obviously highly curious as to what Stile was up to.

Stile was sure the Citizen's inherent vanity would cause him to call heads, as a reflection of self-image, so he hoped Waldens would flip it tails. The coin spun brightly in the air, heading for the tiled floor.

"Heads," the Citizen called, as expected. He hardly seemed to care about the outcome of the bet now; he was trying to fathom Stile's longer purpose.

The iridium coin bounced on the floor, flipped, rolled, and settled tails. Victory for Stile!

Stile held out his hand for the hat, and the Citizen with the coin held out his hand for Stile's clothes. All the rest watched this procedure solemnly. Even Sheen had no idea what Stile was up to.

Stile removed his clothing and stood naked, seeming like a child among adults. He took the hat and donned it, arranging it carefully to conceal his hair and complement the lines of his face. Then, with covered head and bare body, he marched to a holo unit set in an alcove. It was a small one, capable of head-projection only, available for emergency use. Any demand by a Citizen was considered emergency.

"Cirtess," Stile said crisply to the pickup. The device bleeped faintly as it placed the call. He knew the self-willed machines were tapping in, keeping track of him without interfering.

The head of a female serf formed in the cubby. "Sir, may I inquire your identity and the nature of your call?"

"I am Stile," Stile said, rippling an aristocratic sneer across his lips. "I merely wish to inform your employer that a line-maintenance crew is about to operate on his premises. The maintenance is phony, and the crew is other than it appears. There is nothing wrong with that line. I believe Cirtess should investigate this matter personally."

"Thank you, sir," the serf said. She faded out.

"Now that's something!" Waldens exclaimed. "You warned him you were coming! Do you have a death wish?"

Stile removed his hat, but did not seek new clothing. He took the wheeled machine and started down the hall.

"Aha!" Waldens exclaimed. "Of course he would know how to emulate a serf! But Cirtess won't let a serf intrude, either, especially when he's been warned by a Citizen that something's afoot."

"We shall find out," Stile said. "You may watch me on the general pickup system to verify whether I succeed. Serfs, come along." He moved on toward the dome entrance.

The Citizens turned on the little holo unit, crowding around it. Stile knew they would follow his every move. That was fine; he wanted them to have no doubt.

He led his party to the Circle-Tesseract emblem. Cirtess' dome adjoined the main public dome closely; an on-ground tunnel about fifty meters long extended between the two. The communication line was buried beneath the floor of the tunnel.

Two male serfs stood guard at the tunnel entrance. They snapped to alertness as Stile's party approached. One barred the way. "This is private property."

Stile halted. "I'm on Citizen business," he said. "I'm tracing an important message along the communication line."

"Have you my employer's permission to pass?"

"He knows we're coming," Stile said. "I expect him to attend to this personally. Now give me room; I don't have all day." He pushed on by, trundling the machine.

Uncertain, the serf gave way. No mere serf braved the premises of a Citizen without authorization; this line tracing had to have been cleared. But the other serf was already buzzing his dome. "Work crew of four claims to be on Citizen business," he said.

Stile walked on, not waiting for the answer. Mellon, Sheen, and the machine-tending serf followed. They all knew they could be cut down by a laser at any moment; Citizens had short fuses when it came to serf intrusions, and there was a laser lens covering the length of the tunnel. But Stile was gambling that Cirtess would investigate before firing. Why should an illicit crew intrude so boldly on his premises? Why should there be advance warning? Wasn't it more likely that someone was trying to make mischief for a legitimate work crew? But the maintenance computer would deny that any crew was operating here at this time, so it *was* phony. It simply didn't add up, unless it was a practical joke. In that case, Cirtess would want to discover the perpetrator. To do that, he would have to observe the work crew and perhaps interrogate it. It was unlikely that Stile himself would be recognized in this short time; the Amerind hat had completely changed his face, and in any event, the last thing anyone would think of was a Citizen masquerading as a serf. At least this was Stile's hope.

No laser bolt came. Stile reached the end of the tunnel, passed another serf guard who did not challenge him, and traced the buried cable on through a foyer and into a garden park girt with cubistic statuary. The Tesseract motif, of course; Citizens could carry their symbolic foibles quite far.

In the center of the garden, beside a fountain that formed odd, three-dimensional patterns, Stile came to the buried cable nexus. He oriented the machine on it. There was a buzz; then an indicator pointed to the line leading away, and a readout gave the coding designation of the new cable. He had accomplished his mission and won his bet.

But when he looked up, there was a Citizen, flanked by a troop of armed serfs. This was Cirtess; Stile knew it could be no other. "Step into my office, Stile," the man said brusquely.

So the game was up. Stile turned the machine over to its regular operator and went with the Citizen. He had not actually won his bet until he escaped this dome intact with the machine; or if he had won the bet, but lost his life, what had he gained?

Inside the office, with privacy assured, Cirtess handed Stile a robe. Stile donned it, together with sandals and a feather hat. His subterfuge had certainly been penetrated.

"Now what is the story?" Cirtess inquired. "I think you owe me the truth."

"I'm tracing a two-month-old message," Stile said. "Your personnel would not permit entry to a necessary site."

"Of course not! I'd fire any serf who let unauthorized persons intrude."

"So I had to find a way through. It has nothing to do with you personally; I simply have to trace that message to wherever it originated."

"Why didn't you tell me this by phone? I am not unreasonable when the issue is clear; I might have permitted your mission, for a reasonable fee."

"I happen also to need to increase my fortune."

Cirtess nodded. "Could this relate to the several Citizens who huddle in the serf lavatory, spying on your progress?"

"They gave me fifteen-to-one odds on a kilo of Protonite that I couldn't make it. I need that sort of advantage."

"So you called me to rouse my curiosity, so my serfs wouldn't laser you out of hand?"

"Also so as not to deceive you," Stile agreed. "I do not like deception, outside the framework of an established game. You were not properly part of our game."

"So you inducted me into it. A miscalculation could have resulted in your early demise."

"My life has been threatened before. That's one reason I'm tracing this message; I believe its source will offer some hint of the nature of my nemesis."

Cirtess nodded again. "And the Citizens were willing to give better odds because of the factor of danger. Very well. I appreciate cleverness, and I'm as game for a wager as anyone. I will let you go without objection if you will wager your winnings with me."

"But my winnings will be fifteen kilos of Protonite!"

"Yes, a substantial sum. I can cover it, and you must risk it. Choose your bet now—or I shall see that you lose your prior bet by not completing your survey. I can legitimately destroy your tracer machine."

"You play a formidable game!" Stile exclaimed. "You're forcing me to double or nothing."

"Indeed," Cirtess agreed, smiling. "One does not brave the lion's den without encountering challenge."

Stile emerged from the dome with his crew and machine, his knees feeling somewhat weak. "I have the data," he announced.

Waldens glanced at the indicator on the machine. "So you do, and within the time limit. You've won fifteen. But why are you so shaky?"

"Cirtess caught me. He pressured me."

The other Citizens laughed. "Why do you think we bet against you?" one said. "Cirtess can buy and sell most of us. We knew you were walking into the lion's den."

"How did you wiggle out?" Waldens asked.

"He required me to bet my winnings with him," Stile said, grimacing. "That leaves me only one kilo uncommitted, until that bet is settled."

"What is the bet?"

"That is private. It is a condition of the wager that I tell no one its nature until it is settled, which should be shortly."

"Ah, I like that sort of mystery. Cirtess must be playing a game with us, to make up for our intrusion into his privacy. Very well—I'll go for your single kilo. Do you have any suitable notions?"

Stile considered. "I don't care to bet on this message-tracing any more. Maybe we can find something disconnected." They were walking toward the next cable junction, guided by the machine coding. It was pointless to trace every meander of the cable itself when this shortcut was available. Stile turned a corner and entered a short concourse between major domes. At this moment there were no other people in it. "I know! Let's bet on the sex of the serfs to traverse this passage in the next ten minutes. That should be a fairly random sampling."

"Good enough," Waldens agreed. "I'll match your kilo, betting on female."

"Now wait," the Citizen with the feather hat protested. He had recovered it after Stile's use. "The rest of us are being cut out."

"Bet with each other," Stile said. "I am at my present limit." And Mellon nodded emphatically.

"There's little verve in wagers with other Citizens. *You* are the intriguing factor here."

"Well, I'll be happy to hedge my bet," Stile said. "I bet Waldens that more males will pass, and you that more females will pass."

"No good. That puts Waldens and me against each other, in effect. I want you. I want your last kilo."

"All right," Waldens said. "I relinquish my bet with Stile. You can have this one."

"Hey, I want to bet too!" the iridium coin Citizen protested, and the others joined in.

"All right! I'll cover you all," Feather Hat said. "One kilo each. I say more females in ten minutes from—mark."

"Good enough," Waldens agreed. "Five of us, including Stile, are betting you that more males will pass. We all win or lose with Stile."

Now they waited. For two minutes no one came from either direction. "Suppose none comes—or it's even?" Stile asked. He was laboring under continuing tension.

"Then we extend the time," Waldens said. "Sudden death. Agreed?"

The others agreed. They all wanted a settlement. The particular bets didn't matter, and the details of the bets didn't matter; just as long as they could share the excitement of honest gambling.

Then two male serfs came, chatting together. Both went silent as they spied the group of Citizens in the center of the concourse. "Proceed apace," Waldens said, and the two hastily passed by.

A minute later a third serf came, from the opposite direction. Another male. The feather-hatted Citizen frowned.

Then the pace picked up. Three females passed, two more males, a female, three more males, and another female. At eight minutes the score was eight males, five females. "Must be a male work shift getting out," Waldens said, satisfied. "To think I almost bet on the girls!"

But in the final minute there were two more males and six more females. As the time expired, the score was ten males, eleven females.

The feather-hatted Citizen smiled broadly. "I skunked you all! Five kilos!" He nodded toward Stile. "And I beat *him*. Nobody's done that before."

"I lost my kilo," Stile agreed, wondering if he looked as nervous as he felt. "But there's a question I'd like to explore."

"Explore it," Waldens said. "We're having fun."

"I notice that the males were ahead, until a sudden rush of females at the end. Is the estate of any of our number near to this concourse?"

"Not mine," Waldens said. "But you, Bonnet—yours is close, isn't it?"

"It is," the feather-hatted Bonnet replied guardedly.

"And those late female serfs—would they by any chance be employees of yours?" Stile asked.

"That doesn't matter," Bonnet said. "The wager did not exclude our employees. All serfs are Citizen employees."

"Oho!" Waldens said. "You signaled your dome and loaded the dice!"

"Only smart participation," Bonnet insisted. "There was no bar against it."

Waldens sighed. "No, I suppose not. One must never accept something on faith, particularly the constancy of other Citizens. I fell for it; I'll take my loss." The others agreed, though not pleased; they all should have been more careful.

Now Stile felt the exhilaration of victory. "As it happens, I bet Cirtess fifteen kilos that someone would cheat on this wager. I lost my kilo, but won my fifteen. Right, Cirtess?"

"Right," Cirtess' voice agreed on a hidden speaker. "Well and fairly played, Stile. Let it be recorded: fifteen for you."

Waldens slapped his knee. "Beautiful! Bonnet won five, you won fifteen. Even in losing, you won! Your fortune is now just over thirty kilograms, Stile. You are now a moderately wealthy Citizen."

"Congratulations," Bonnet said sourly. "I believe I have had enough for the day." Somewhat stiffly, he departed.

"And that was worth my own paltry losses," Waldens said. "I never liked him much. Still, I suspect he's right. You have been outmaneuvering us nicely, Stile. I think I must desist wagering with you, lest I lose my shirt—or all of my clothing." And the others laughed, remembering the episode of nakedness. By common consent they dispersed, leaving Stile alone with his party of serfs.

"Sir, you have taken extraordinary chances," Mellon said reprovingly. "My expertise has been useless."

"I agree I have pushed my luck," Stile said. "I think it prudent to turn my winnings over to you for management now. Do you feel you can parlay them into an even larger fortune?"

"A thirty-kilogram stake? Sir, with that leverage and your authority to make selective wagers, I believe I can do well enough."

"Go to it. I'll refrain from further betting until I consult with you. Take it away."

"Thank you, sir. Your method is unorthodox, but I must confess it has proved effective." Mellon turned and walked away.

"He will work wonders, sir," Sheen murmured.

Unencumbered by the betting Citizens, they proceeded rapidly to the next nexus, which was in a public workshop area, and thence to another in a serf park that spread across the curtain. "Coincidence?" Stile inquired skeptically, and Sheen agreed it was probably not.

They set the machine, and the readout suggested that the message impulse had been introduced at this nexus. But this was a closed connection; there was no way to insert a message here. "It had to have come from the other side of the curtain," Stile said. Somehow he was not surprised. Much of the other mischief he had experienced had originated in Phaze.

"You have a friend there," Sheen said. "You will have to cross and use your magic to trace him down."

"Yes. Only an Adept could have managed this. I can't think which one would have done it." Stile sighed. "Sheen, I still have a night free, and I shall need my rest. Take me home."

She took him to the Proton Blue Demesnes, and fed him and washed him in the manner of serf for Citizen, not deigning to give the job to the hired staff. She put him in a comfortable bed over a gravity diffusion screen, so that his weight diminished. Weariness closed in on him, now that he had respite from the tensions of the moment. But before he allowed himself to sleep, he caught her hand and drew her to him. "You cried for me again today," he said.

"And you cried again for me."

"Some day, somehow—"

She leaned over and kissed him, and it was as sweet as any kiss could be. In that pleasure he fell asleep. He dreamed that he loved her in the off moments as well as at the stress points—but woke to know that was only a wish, not truth. He could not do more than marry her.

CHAPTER 9

Source

Stile crossed the curtain in the morning at the site of the last junction. There was nothing special in Phaze at this place; it was only the slope of a lightly forested hill. Whatever had fed the message in was gone. There were not even any footprints, after two months.

He was the Blue Adept, with potent magic. How could he apply it to follow this long-cold trail? Wouldn't an Adept have counterspelled the trail to prevent such tracing?

One way to find out. Stile played his harmonica, summoning his power, while he worked out a spell. Then he sang: "Make an arrow, point the way, that the message came that day."

The arrow formed, an illuminated spot like that made by a light projection. But it rotated uncertainly, like a compass without its magnetism. Sure enough, a counterspell was interfering. There would be no simple, one-step answer.

However, his power at this spot, now, would be greater than that of a months-gone Adept. He should be able to trace the source—if he followed the trail in person, as he had in Proton. "Give a signal, hot or cold, to make current what is old," he sang, shaping the detail in his mind.

Now Stile's left side felt warmer than his right. He turned, and the warmth was on his face. He strode forward—and the effect faded.

He backed up until he felt the heat again. It had fallen away to his right. He got back on the trail, pursuing it more carefully—and it led him in a spaghettilike wriggle that coiled about and recrossed itself frequently. Obviously the other party had anticipated this approach also, and had left a tortuous path. It might take Stile a long time to unravel every wriggle, and the trail could lead into traps.

He decided to let it go for now. He wanted to rejoin the unicorns and the Lady Blue in plenty of time for the quest for Clip and vengeance. This message had waited two months; it would wait another day.

He used a prepared spell to transport himself to the herd, and stood for a moment in discomfort as he arrived. He certainly did not enjoy performing this kind of magic on himself, but he really had no alternative at the moment.

Neysa spied him first and trotted over. She would always be his steed and his friend in spirit. Yet now she did not prance, for the pall of her brother's fate hung over her.

She changed to girl-form and made one of her rare speeches: "The Stallion has news of Clip."

"What kind?" Stile asked tightly.

"He is alive." She shifted back to mare-form.

Stile vaulted to her back, and she trotted him over to the herd. He embraced the Lady Blue briefly.

The Herd Stallion awaited him in man-form. "Under the White Mountains, prisoner of the goblins. We must strike by night—tonight, ere they suspect."

"Yes," Stile agreed. "Thou and I alone, surgically."

"They will be alert for Adept magic, and will kill Clip the moment they detect it. Thou canst not employ thy power until he is safe."

"How am I to save him, then?" Stile asked, frustrated.

"*I* will save him. Then thou canst get us all out of danger."

Stile was uncertain about this procedure, but had to agree. There was no use going on a rescue mission if his mere presence precipitated Clip's murder.

"We start now," the Stallion said. "It will be night ere we reach the mountains. I know an entrance to the goblin demesnes—but once underground, I will know the way no better than thou."

Stile had an idea. "Suppose I make a spell to show the way? Will that continuing magic alert the goblins?"

The Stallion considered. "I know not, but think not. It is new magic that makes alarm; there are many ancient spells in the background, ignored."

"I'd better risk it," Stile said. He considered a moment, then played his harmonica and sang: "A star institute, to illumine our route."

A pinpoint glow appeared to their north, shedding faint light on the ground.

"But the goblins will see it too!" the Stallion protested.

"See what?" the Lady Blue asked.

The Stallion smiled. "Ah—others see it not!"

"Others see it not," Stile agreed. "I am not quite as foolish as I look."

"Not quite," the Stallion agreed, and shifted back to his natural form, pawing the ground. Stile took the hint and leaped to his back. This was much more of a challenge than it had been with Neysa, for the Herd Stallion stood four hands higher than she and massed twice as much. He was a lot of animal. Had they not had a clear understanding, Stile's touch on his back would have precipitated an instant death struggle. It was a sign of the passions involved and the seriousness of the situation that the untamable Stallion submitted to this indignity.

Immediately they were off. Stile, the most skilled rider in this frame, suddenly had to hang on, lest he be dumped like a novice. Evidently some spirit of rivalry remained; the Stallion wanted him to know that he kept his perch only by sufferance. Stile had never been on a steed like this before; the Stallion was the mass of a huge work horse, but had the velocity of a racer. Stile had originally tamed Neysa by riding her against her will; he knew he could never have done it with this steed.

The scenery raced by. Wind tore at Stile's clothing. The Stallion's hooves pounded on the doubled drumbeat of a full gallop, and sparks flew up where the hard hooves struck, but the ride was smooth. The Stallion was not wasting energy in extra up-and-down motion; he was sailing straight ahead.

The pinpoint star remained fixed at about head-height, its spot of light brightening to a patch of ground. It slid to one side sometimes, guiding them around obstructions and bad footing, so that the Stallion never had to slow to scout the way. He was able to maintain cruising speed, faster than that of any horse, and he seemed tireless. As he warmed up, jets of flame blasted from his nostrils. This was the way that unicorns cooled themselves, since they did not sweat; the heat was dissipated from their breath and hooves.

After a time the ride became routine, then dull. Stile had nothing to do, since the Stallion knew the way even without the help of the little star. Stile could have slept, but was too keyed up; he wanted to rescue and restore Clip. He could do it, he was sure; his magic could cement the severed horn and heal the scars of its cutting. The only problem was getting to the unicorn without triggering the murder. And getting them all out, thereafter. Meanwhile, he just had to wait.

"I've been thinking," he remarked. "Art thou amenable to conversation?"

The Stallion blew an affirmative accordion note. He, too, was bored by this stretch.

"Thou art a powerful creature," Stile said. "Surely the goblins will recognize thee as readily as me. I can be taken for an elf, but thou canst only be a unicorn, even in man-form. The snub-horn gives thee away."

The Stallion blew another note of agreement. Unicorns could change form but retained vestigial horns in all forms. This was because the horn was the seat of the unicorn's magic; without it the creature was no more than a horse, unable to play music or change form. If an alternate form lacked the horn, the unicorn would not be able to change back to equine form. This was plainly unacceptable; the human form was not one any self-respecting unicorn would care to be stuck in for long.

"Thy dragon-form is no better than thy man-form for concealment," Stile continued. "True, it could penetrate the goblin demesnes—but would create great alarm, for no one ignores a dragon! When thou didst approach Clip, the little monsters would surely realize thy nature and intent."

"Um," the unicorn noted with a thoughtful chord.

"The thing is, thou art in all thy forms a mighty creature. Now this is no bad thing and ordinarily is altogether proper." The phrasing of a suggestion was sometimes more important than the suggestion itself, particularly when addressed to a creature of pride. "But this time I wish thou didst possess an insignificant form, like Neysa's firefly, that I could carry in unobserved."

The unicorn ran on, considering. After a time he blew a new note. "Could." The notes were not really words, but pitch and inflection conveyed definite meaning, and Stile could usually interpret them when he put his mind to it.

"Thou hast a fourth form?" he asked, surprised. "I thought three was the limit, and only one or two for some."

Now came a proud blast. This was no ordinary unicorn; the Stallion could master a fourth form, if he chose.

"That's great!" Stile exclaimed. "Couldst thou work it up in time for tonight? I know it takes a considerable act of discipline to implement a new form, and there is so little time—"

The Stallion was not foolishly optimistic. Any form was a challenge the first time, and a fourth one was special. But he thought he could manage it.

They discussed it as the miles and leagues rushed by. It developed that some forms were easier than others. Difficulty varied according to the necessary specialization and the change of size. Thus a unicorn could convert to a massive bear fairly readily, because the size was about the same. A man-form was harder, because the mass was less and because of the necessary specialization of the hands and voice. A man-form that could not tie a knot in string would not be very good, and one who could not talk would be worse. These things had to be done properly, or were not worth doing at all. Neysa's firefly-form was a greater achievement than Clip's hawk-form, because the fly was only a fraction of the mass. Neysa weighed about 850 pounds in her natural form, about 85 in her girl-form, and less than 85-hundredths of an ounce in firefly-form. It would be more than twice as hard for the Herd Stallion to get down to that size.

"But such size would be beyond suspicion," Stile remarked. "No one would believe that a beast as noble as thou couldst hide in a form so small." That accented the magnitude of the challenge, rather than the insignificance of the form.

Then there was the problem of flying, the unicorn explained in concerned notes. Flying was a specialization that had to be mastered by tedious practice, after the physical form had been achieved. The Stallion had learned it for his dragon-form, but would have to start all over for an insect-form, since insects employed a different mode of flight. That could take days.

"Oh, I did not mean thou must fly," Stile said. "It is the insignificance I am after, that none may suspect thee. Thou couldst go from dragon to roach, for that."

Roach! the Stallion blasted, affronted. *Never!*

But Stile was struck by something else. Dragon—roach. His poem: the one he had used to win the Tourney in Proton. Had this provided him with a prophetic key?

Now he thought back, discovering parallels. He had referred to Gabriel's horn—but there was also the unicorn's horn. Clip's horn had precipitated this venture. He had also referred to trying to cheat fate; but he had won his biggest bet because of cheating by another Citizen. How far did this go?

How far, indeed! The first four lines of that poem had matched his recent experience, deliberately. Then the key word: silence. And he had been struck by the silence-spell. Then love; and he had become betrothed to Sheen. That was not love, precisely, but related; she certainly wanted and deserved love.

In fact, those key words aligned beautifully with his experience—almost like a prediction of the Oracle. Yet the words had become the random product of the Game Computer. No magic there! So it must be coincidence. It was possible to make seeming sense of almost anything, as those two poems had shown. Still—

Why not? Stile decided to go for it. "That is one form no goblin would suspect. The nether passages must be overrun with roaches. What Herd Stallion would go to the enormous effort to achieve so lowly a form? It is beneath consideration—therefore the safest of all forms for the accomplishment of such a hazardous mission."

"Um," the Stallion blew, heeding the logic but not the aesthetics.

"Actually, some roaches are quite elegant," Stile commented innocently. "When I was a serf in Proton, I had to deliver a horse to the dome of a Citizen who specialized in exotic creatures. He had a roach farm with some quite beautiful specimens. I remember some deep red ones, huge and sleek—surely the royalty of roaches. And others were frilly, like butterflies, only without wings—"

"*Enough!*" the unicorn snorted. He veered to a tight copse of trees and slowed. When he stopped inside, Stile was glad to dismount; they had been traveling for hours, and he was cramped and hungry and suffered the urgent calls of nature.

There was a convenient nut tree in the copse—unicorns generally had good taste about such things—so Stile could eat without using magic. There was also a small spring. This was really an oasis, probably known to every wild creature. There was a real advantage of traveling with such an animal—not only protection, but also the convenience of familiarity with the terrain. Stile had now traveled with three unicorns —Neysa, Clip, and the Herd Stallion—and this aspect was the same with each one. Stile had always liked horses; he knew he would always like unicorns better.

He had dreamed for more than fifteen years of becoming a Citizen of Proton, perhaps setting up his own racing stable. Now he was a Citizen —and all he really wanted was to stay here in Phaze, on any basis. He liked magic—not merely his ability to perform it, but more importantly, the very framework in which magic existed. He liked the verdant hills, the little streams, the various features of this irregular landscape. He liked the whole sweet outdoors, with its fresh air and unpredictable weather and feeling of freedom. Oh, there were horrors here—but even so, it was a better world than Proton. Three centuries of unrestricted development and narrow exploitation had destroyed the environment of Proton, so that comfort now existed only within the force-field domes. Stile liked civilization, but, after encountering Phaze, he feared it was at too great a price.

Stile became aware of a warm sensation on the left side of his face. Oh, yes—his spell to trace the sender of the message that had brought him Sheen was still in operation. Old spells never died, and faded away only slowly—which inertia was fortunate, since any given spell was effective only once. The warmth was faint, indicating that he was far from the source, but at least he could still trace it down. He would do so the moment Clip was safe.

He heard a musical groan, as of someone stepping on an accordion. The Stallion writhed, shimmered—and shrank to a gross, many-legged lump of flesh.

A spell leaped to Stile's lips. But he choked it back, realizing that this was not a magic attack. It was the Stallion's effort to master a new form.

Stile ambled over, peering down at the grotesque caricature of a roach. "Now that is the ugliest insect I've ever seen," he remarked. "But certainly the biggest." Indeed, it was almost the size of a man.

The monstrous bug waved its feelers, thrashed its legs about, and blew a furious peep from the miniature horn on its snout. Then it swelled rapidly into Stallion-form again, snorting fire from the effort.

"Oh, it's thou!" Stile exclaimed innocently. "I was about to step on it."

The Stallion glared and gave a snort that singed the hairs of Stile's arms. Then he tried again. This time he got the size right, but not the shape. He became a miniature unicorn. "I'm afraid that won't do," Stile said around a mouthful of nuts. "The goblins know that's not a normal 'corn size."

The Stallion re-formed, pawing the ground. Obviously he was putting forth terrific effort; his hooves were beginning to glow red, and wisps of smoke rose from his ears.

A third time he tried. This time he got it right—normal-sized roach, with a silvery body and golden head. The bug took one step—and exploded back into the Stallion. He just had not been able to hold it for more than two seconds.

"Maybe you'd better let it rest a while," Stile suggested. "Give your system time to acclimatize to the notion. We're not at the goblin demesnes yet."

The Stallion played an affirmative chord. Stile conjured ten pounds of fine oats for the equine repast, then stood abashed. He should not have used his magic here. But it seemed no one had been paying attention; maybe that was not the kind of spell the enemy was looking for. In due course he remounted, and they were off again. The strength of this unicorn was amazing; having run for hours and struggled to master a difficult new form, he was, after this brief respite, galloping at unreduced speed. Neysa and Clip were good unicorns, but neither could have maintained this velocity so long.

By nightfall the grim White Mountains were near. The Stallion had been moving toward them at a slant, northwest, circling the demesnes of the ogres. No need for any ogre trouble, this trip! Actually, Stile had settled with the ogres, establishing that he was not their enemy, but ogres were not too bright and there could still be trouble.

Now the sun was dropping below the horizon. The Stallion galloped along west, parallel to the mountain range, then stopped. Stile saw the guiding star to their north, showing them to the entrance to the goblins' somber nether world.

But the region was guarded. Goblins patrolled the clifflike fringe of the mountain range. How could they get in?

Stile had the answer to that. He was larger than a goblin, but close enough so that some stooping in the dark should enable him to pass. He scraped up handfuls of dirt and rubbed it over his face and arms, then removed his clothing and coated his bare body too. Goblins wore little clothing; Stile's Proton underpants sufficed for a costume. Goblin feet and hands, however, were far larger than his own, while their limbs were shorter. Stile experimented and finally fashioned a framework for each foot from small branches and dirt, making his extremities seem goblin-sized. He did the same for his head. Magic would have been much easier for disguising himself, either physically or by means of illusion, but he did not dare use that here. He was facile with his hands and knew how to improvise; his head was actually expanded by a gross turban fashioned from his former clothing.

"Grotesque," the Herd Stallion said, eyeing Stile in man-form. "The human shape is ugly enough to begin with, but thou hast improved on it."

"Just do thine own shape-change," Stile said. "And keep it stable."

"I can but try," the Stallion said grimly. He shifted back to 'corn-form, gathered himself, and phased down to bug-form. This roach was not handsome, but it did seem to be stable. Stile watched it take a step, moving all its legs on one side, followed by those on the other side. The thing trembled and started to expand, then got hold of itself and squeezed back into bug shape. It seemed it would hold.

Stile put down his open hand. The roach hesitated, then crawled on, moving clumsily. It evidently took special coordination to handle six legs, and it was hard for the Stallion to do this while hanging on to this awkward little size. Perhaps it was like juggling six balls in the air while walking a tightrope. As it happened, Stile had done such tricks in the past—but it had taken him time to master them. "Just don't lose control and convert to equine form on my head," Stile murmured as he set the roach on the framework he had wound there. "Don't drop anything, either."

The roach, catching the reference to droppings, began to shake with laughter. It expanded to triple roach size, emitted several little sparks, wrestled with itself, and recovered control. Stile decided not to make any more jokes.

The darkness was almost complete now. Stile nerved himself and walked forward, following the flash of light projected on the ground by his little guiding star. He hunched down as well as he could, making himself hump-backed and shorter. Stile was an experienced mimic, and this was another Game talent that served him in good stead now. He walked like a goblin, swung his arms like a goblin, and glared about like a goblin. Almost, he began to hate the world the way a goblin would.

The dark hole of the cave entrance loomed close. Stile shuffled boldly toward it. But a goblin guard challenged him. "Where the hell art thou going, dirtface?"

For an instant Stile's heart paused. But he had to assume that goblins normally insulted each other, and that the guard did not realize that Stile's face really was concealed by dirt. "What the hell business is it of thine, stinkrump?" he demanded in the grating tone of a goblin, and pushed on. He felt the Stallion-roach quaking with suppressed mirth again, enjoying the exchange.

Apparently it had been the right answer. The guard did not stop him. Stile followed his little star into the cave.

Goblins were coming and going, but none of these challenged him. Stile walked downward, through narrow apertures, along the faces of subterranean cliffs, and across dark chasm cracks. The star made it easy, unerringly guiding him through the labyrinth. What might have taken him hours to figure out only took minutes. He wondered passingly how this worked; more than mere energy was involved when magic provided him with specialized information. Amazingly soon he came to a deep nether passage barred by solid stalactitic columns.

The star moved on to illumine what was beyond. It was a horse.

No—not a horse. A dehorned unicorn, so grimed that his natural color hardly showed, standing with head hanging, bedraggled, evidently lacking the will to live but unable to die. Clip!

Stile heard a tiny accordion-note snort near his ear. The roach was seething. No unicorn should be treated like this!

Half a dozen armed goblins guarded the unicorn. Four were leaning against the wall; one was drinking a swig of something foul, and the sixth was entertaining himself by pricking Clip with the point of his spear. The forlorn unicorn hardly even winced; he seemed beyond the point of resistance and did not make a good subject for teasing. Blood streaked his once-glossy blue coat from prior cuts, and his mane was limp and tangled. Flies swarmed, yet his tail hardly twitched to flick them off.

Stile heard the roach on his head breathing hard, with accordion-chord wheezes. The Herd Stallion suffered no one to treat a member of his herd this way, and was in danger of exploding again. "Nay, Stallion," Stile whispered. "Thou must hold form until thou dost get inside. Neither I nor any of thine other forms can pass these bars mechanically; they are too strong and tight. Go inside, warn Clip, then take action against the guards before they strike."

The Stallion blew a low note of agreement. Stile put his hand to his head, and the roach climbed on it. Stile set the roach on the floor in the corner near the bars.

"Hey—who art thou, rockhead?" a goblin guard cried.

Uh-oh. He had to distract attention from the roach, lest a goblin spot it and idly step on it. The Herd Stallion was vulnerable in that form, and could not shift quickly enough to counter an abruptly descending foot.

"I just wanta see the creep," Stile said. "I heard you got a horse-head in here without a horn."

"That's none of thy business," the goblin snapped. "No unauthorized idiots allowed. That specifically means thee."

The roach was now crawling uncertainly along the wall. Obviously it wasn't used to clinging to vertical surfaces, but didn't want to get stepped on. Progress was slow, so Stile had to stall longer.

"Oh, I do have business here, mucksnoot," Stile said, and of course that was the truth. "I have come to take the 'corn away."

"Thou art crazy, manface! We have orders to kill this brute as soon as our armies finish massing and the enemy Adept be trapped. He's not going anywhere."

So they weren't going to let Clip live, regardless of Stile's response. And they expected to trap Stile himself. This was a straight kidnap-hostage-murder plot. No honor among goblins!

The roach, overhearing the dastardly scheme, lost its footing and fell to the floor with a loud-seeming click and whoosh of accordion-breath. Stile was afraid it would attract attention. It lay on its back, six legs waving, trying to recover its footing. Oh, no!

"Thou art not up on the latest, foulfoot," Stile said sneeringly. "You guards will be executed before the hostage is." This, too, he intended literally.

His certainty daunted the goblin. Apparently such betrayals did happen in the nether realms. "Aw, whatcha know about it, gnarltoes?" the goblin blustered.

The roach had finally struggled to right-side-up position, with tiny musical grunts. Any goblin who paid attention would immediately catch on that this was no ordinary vermin! Stile had to keep talking.

"I know a lot about it, mandrakenose. That 'corn's the steed of an Adept, isn't it?"

"Sure, smarty, and that's why he ain't dead yet. To keep that Adept off our backs till he's out of the picture. We got Adepts of our own, but they don't like to tangle with each other, so we're keeping this one clear this way. The fool likes animals. We're just doing our job here; no reason to wipe us out." He looked at Stile uncertainly. "Is there?"

The roach had finally reached Clip. Stile relaxed. Just a few more seconds, and it would be all right. "How about what that other Adept thinks? Once he knows thy part, he'll come for thee—and what other Adept would breathe a spell to help thee?"

But as he spoke, Stile saw Clip lift a forefoot, eying the roach. He was about to crush it, not realizing its identity.

"Clip!" Stile called. "No!"

Then things happened one on top of another. All six goblin guards whirled, scrambled, and looked up, depending on their starting positions, to orient on the hornless unicorn. The magic roach let out a chord and scuttled away from Clip's poised hoof. Clip's head jerked about, his ears rotating to cover Stile.

"It's a trick!" the goblin nearest Stile cried. "This creep's been bugging me about the hostage. Kill him!"

It wasn't clear whether he referred to Clip or to Stile. It hardly mattered. The alarm had been sounded.

Two goblins thrust their spears at Clip. One stomped at the roach.

The one nearest Stile poked his spear through the bars to skewer Stile. The remaining two set up a scream for help.

Clip suddenly animated, swinging his horn about to skewer a goblin. But he had no horn, only the truncated stump. The goblin was merely brushed aside by Clip's nose and struck out with a horny fist.

The roach skittered out of the way and began to expand like a demon amulet that had been invoked. Stile dodged the spear.

In moments the Herd Stallion stood within the prison chamber, stomping his hooves, snorting fire. *His* horn was not truncated. It blurred as it lunged at one goblin, then at a second and a third, before any could flee. Three goblins were lifted into the air, skewered simultaneously on that terrible spike.

Clip charged the goblin who was poking at Stile, crushing the creature's head with a blow of a forehoof. But the two others were running down the far passage, too narrow for the unicorns to follow, crying the alarm.

Stile readied a spell, but paused. So far he had not used magic and, now that he knew there was an enemy Adept involved here, he did not want to give himself away one second sooner than necessary. The goblins did not know it was the Blue Adept who was in their midst, so the other Adept might not know, either—until Stile gave himself away by using magic.

But now there were two unicorns in the prison, and the main goblin mass was stirring in the bowels of the mountain. The Stallion could use his roach-form to escape—but Clip could not change form without his horn. Stile could change Clip's form for him—but that meant magic of Adept signature. Stile could also melt the bars away with magic, if they were not of the magic-resistive type. That must have been how Clip was brought here; the enemy Adept had spelled him through.

If he had to use magic, he might as well tackle the most important thing first. How he wished discovery had been delayed a little longer! "Clip—here to me!" he called, bringing out the thing he carried like a spear. It was Clip's severed horn.

The unicorn stared, almost unbelieving. No doubt he had thought the horn destroyed.

"My power can restore it!" Stile said, holding the horn out, base first. Clip came and put his head near the bars. Stile reached through, setting the horn against the stump. "Restore the horn of this unicorn!" he sang, willing the tissue to merge, the thing to take life again.

It was hard, for he had not intensified his power by playing the harmonica, and the horn was magic. It resisted Stile's magic, and he knew the two parts were not mending properly. He was grafting on a dead horn. Meanwhile, a phalanx of goblins appeared in the passage behind Stile, bristling with spears. Stile saw them from the corner of his eye but could not release his hands from the horn, lest the slow healing be interrupted. Clip could not move, either, for he was on the other side of the bars waiting for the healing.

But the Herd Stallion was free. He launched himself at the bars. "No!" Stile cried in alarm, knowing the stone was too strong for the animal to break. But the Stallion shifted in midair to roach-form, sailed between columns, and shifted on Stile's side to dragon-form.

The dragon spread his wings, banked about, and fired forth a horizontal column of flame that seared the oncoming goblins. The stench of burnt flesh wafted back. Stile felt sorry for the goblins, then remembered how they had treated Clip, and stilled his sympathy. The creatures of the frame of Phaze conducted their business violently, and goblins were among the worst. Stile continued to concentrate on the healing, letting the Stallion guard him, and slowly the two parts of Clip's horn melded together. Stile felt the living warmth creep along the length of it, animating it. Soon all would be well.

A horde of goblins poured in from the far side of the prison. "Stallion!" Stile cried, and the Herd Stallion turned about, charged the bars, shifted into and out of roach-form, and appeared on the other side in dragon-form again. Another burst of flame seared out, cooking more flesh.

But greater trouble was gathering. Stile could feel the rumble of the march of many feet as hundreds or thousands of goblins closed in, traveling in unseen neighboring passages. He knew he had alerted the enemy Adept, for he had performed Adept magic; that would further complicate the situation. Still he held on to the horn, waiting for the final inch to be restored to life so that Clip's full capacity would return. He would settle for nothing less.

There was a puff of fog. The White Adept stood beside Stile. Her hair was white, matching her eyebrows, and a sparkling white gown bedecked her somewhat stout form. "So it is thee, Blue, as we suspected," she said, her voice and gaze cold as ice. "Thou didst take the bait."

"I took it," Stile agreed grimly. He was not really surprised; his relations with the White Adept had always been chill. But why was she involved with the goblins? "I got tired of getting ambushed by the likes of thee." Would she tell him anything before making her move? If she started a spell-diagram before he was finished with Clip's horn, he would be in trouble; he would have to defend himself, for without him the unicorns could not escape. But White could have generated a spell that acted at a distance instead of facing him directly. Maybe she wanted to talk.

The Herd Stallion turned from his endeavors, leaving a pile of scorched goblins rolled up like dehydrated bugs, and saw the witch. He braced for renewed action.

"Caution," Stile called. "She's Adept."

The mighty animal stood still. He knew better than to attack an Adept in a situation like this. He also knew that Stile was not finished with Clip. For the moment it was an impasse.

"I can not attack thee directly, Blue," the White Adept said. "And thou canst not attack me. Yet can our minions make mischief."

"Agreed," Stile said. "But why has mischief been made? I sought none."

"Abate thine onus for the moment and hear me out," she said. "Blue, I would reason with thee."

In Stile's experience, those who claimed to want to reason with others were apt to have cases that were less than secure. Still, it was better to talk than to fight. Now at last Clip's horn had healed. Stile let go, and the unicorn backed away, blowing an experimental saxophone note. It was off-key, but strong. His coat seemed to be brightening under the grime; he had been restored to the joy of life.

The White Adept had known what Stile was doing, and had not interfered. She had to be serious about her subject, and Stile seriously wanted to know what this was all about. "Give thy word there will be no attack by Adept or goblin without fair warning," he said. "No treachery."

"I give it, Blue." There was a faint ripple in the air about her.

He had to accept that. Truth animated the very atmosphere and substance of Phaze. Adepts did not get along well with each other, but they honored the deals they made. "Then I will hear thy reason."

"Thou knowest that the end of Phaze draws nigh," she said. "The Purple Mountains have shaken, the Foreordained is on the scene, the Little Folk mass as for war, and portents abound."

"Aye," he agreed. "They tell me I am involved. Yet all I sought was to honeymoon with my wife. Someone set traps for me, and one trap setter resembled thee."

"Merely to warn thee off," she said. "Thou art Adept and perhaps the strongest of us all. Thou hast suffered much, yet thou shouldst be the leader in our effort instead of opposing it."

"What effort?" Stile's interest intensified.

"To save Phaze."

"Of course I want to save Phaze! I love this land! I want to live and die here!"

"But not, methinks, before thy time."

Stile smiled grimly. "I wish not to die here among goblins, true. But I sought no quarrel with goblins. Thou didst kidnap my steed, and abused him, and forced this quarrel on me."

"Aye. Unable to strike effectively at thee or at thy Lady, or to warn thee off, we finally had to take thy steed. It is not a thing I like. Now thou canst have thy freedom with our apologies, and thine animals with thee, and leadership in the present order, if thou wilt but accept it."

"Why should I not accept it?" Stile asked, not rhetorically.

"Because thou art prophesied to be the leader of the forces of the destruction of this order. The Foreordained is only part of it; thou art the other part."

"Obviously there's a loophole," Stile said. "Aside from the fact that I have no intention of harming Phaze, thou wouldst not be pressuring me if thou didst believe my destiny was fixed."

"There is a loophole. A dead man can not lead."

Stile laughed ironically. "Kill me? My fate will survive thine effort, if it be truly set."

"Aye. Fate has indeed charmed thee, unlike thine other self. But we are not assured thou canst not be killed, only that if thou dost remain alive in Phaze, thou wilt destroy it. The charms that preserved thee so cleverly before are passing. Thou hast already conceived thy son on the Lady Blue—"

"I have?" Stile asked, surprised.

"—which is why she joins thy former steed and accepts the protection of the animal herd. So fate no longer preserves thee for that. It preserves her. Still, her feeling for thee is such that she might not survive thy demise, so thou art indirectly protected yet. I warned the others of that, but they heeded me not; they thought they could vanquish thee before thou didst reach the West Pole."

"They?"

"The other Adepts. We all are patriots in the end, Blue. We all must needs try to save our land."

She seemed sincere! "All the other Adepts are against me?" he asked incredulously.

"All except Brown; the child wavers. She likes thy steed."

Stile remembered how Neysa had given the little girl a ride. It seemed that kindness had paid a dividend. "What of Yellow?" Stile had had differences with the Yellow Adept, but recently had gotten along with her tolerably well. He could not believe she was his enemy.

"Dost thou want it from her own mouth?"

"Aye."

"Then let me bring her here." White made a diagram on the floor and tapped it three times. A puff of smoke formed and dissipated, and there stood the Yellow Adept in her natural hag-form.

"Oh, no!" Yellow exclaimed. "Let me just get changed for the occasion, my handsome bantam." She brought out a vial, tipped it to her lips, swallowed—and changed to a young, ravishingly pretty creature.

"White tells me that thou and the other Adepts think I will destroy Phaze, so are against me, Yellow," Stile said. "Can this be true?"

Yellow made a devastatingly cute moue. "It is close enough, Blue," she said. "I am not thine enemy and will not oppose thee—but neither can I join thee, for that thou art indeed destined to wreak much mischief and overthrow the natural order."

"How is it I know nothing of this?" Stile demanded.

"The instruments of great events seldom know their destinies," Yellow said. "This prevents paradox, which can be an awkward complication and a downright nuisance."

"Nuisance, hell! I was attempting to have my honeymoon! Why should this represent a threat to anyone?"

"Thou didst bring the Foreordained, and then thou didst travel to the West Pole. These were elements of the prophecy."

"So the other Adepts decided to stop me from getting there," Stile said, grimacing. "Setting neat little magical traps."

"Some did. Green chose to stand aloof, as I did, misliking this. Sure enough, thou didst get there. Now the onrush of events is upon us, and if we do not get thee away from Phaze promptly, we all are doomed."

"So you propose to remove me by killing me?"

"Nay, we know that would not work," Yellow said. "At least White and Green and I suspected it would not. Black and Orange and Translucent did not participate in the proceedings, and Brown opposed them. We had to suppress her, lest she warn thee."

So it now developed that the other Adepts were anything but unanimous; most were at best neutral. That explained why they had not simply massed their magic against him. Stile's expression turned hard. "Suppressed Brown? What dost thou mean by that?"

"A stasis-spell," White said quickly. "No harm was done her. It is hard indeed to do direct harm to an Adept; the spell is likely to bounce and strike down the speller. But slantwise action can be taken, as with the silence and confinement for thee."

"You froze the child in place?" Stile demanded. "Our truce is just about to come to an unkind end."

"She would have blabbed to thee," White repeated.

"Now I am blabbing to thee: release her."

White's expression hardened, as was typical of those whose reason was only a front. Yellow quickly interceded. "Provoke him not unnecessarily, White; he has power and friends we hardly know. We need hold Brown no longer. I shall go free her." She brought out another vial, sipped the potion, and vanished.

"Methinks thou hast won the heart of more than Brown," White grumbled. She viewed him critically, noting the mud caking his body and the awkward turban, loincloth, and shoe structures. "It must be thy magic, rather than thy demeanor."

Stile relaxed marginally. Ugly things were happening, and he knew it wasn't over. So far there had been attacks against him, the Lady Blue, Clip, and the Brown Adept. An organization of Adepts had formed against him. He needed to know the rest of it. "Let's have it, White. Exactly what is the threat to Phaze, and what dost thou want of me?" For he knew her suggestion about giving him a place of leadership was wrong; how could he lead, if his presence meant the end?

"We want thee to leave Phaze voluntarily, so that the dangers of Adept confrontations are abated. Thou canst take Lady Blue and aught else thou wishest. Cross the curtain, embark on a Proton spaceship, and depart for the farthermost corner of the universe as that frame knows it, never to return."

Stile had no intention of doing that. Apart from the complication of the Lady Blue's official nonexistence in the other frame, where the Records Computer took such things more seriously than people did in Phaze, there was the matter of the robot Sheen. How could he marry her, with his other wife in Proton? And how could he leave his friends the unicorns and werewolves and vampires? Phaze was the world of his dreams and nightmares; he could never leave it. "Nay."

"The applicable portion of the prophecy is this: 'Phaze will never be restored till the Blue Adept is forever gone.' Thou canst not remain."

"I have had some experience with misrepresented predictions," Stile said. "Restoration of Phaze after my departure is hardly synonymous with my destruction of it—which I maintain is no intent of mine. Thou hast answered only a fraction of my question, and deviously at that."

"I am getting to it, Blue. The goblins guard an apparatus from the other frame, protecting it from all threats. The end of Phaze will come when that device is returned. The goblins guard it blindly from harm; we would prefer to destroy it."

"So the collusion of Adepts with goblins is rife with internal stress," Stile observed. "Doubtless the goblins know not of this aspect."

"Doubtless they suspect, however," White said.

"Surely the massed power of the Adepts can prevail against mere goblins," Stile said, pushing at her verbally. "Any one of us could enchant the entire species of goblin into drifting smoke."

"Thou might, Blue. Few others could. But this device is a special case and can not be attacked directly."

"Anything can be attacked!" Stile said. "Some things with less success than others, though, as seems to be the case when Adepts attack Adepts."

"Nay. This device is what is called in the other frame a computer."

"A computer can't operate in Phaze! No scientific device can." Except, he remembered, near the West Pole.

"This one has a line running to the West Pole."

Parallel thoughts! "Maybe. If it could figure out how to use magic in its circuits."

"Aye. It functions partially, and has many thoughts. Some concern thee—which is why we did not wish thee to make connection with it at the Pole."

"How canst thou know this if the goblins let thee not near it? In fact, why do the goblins allow Adepts in their demesnes, seeing the likes of thee would destroy what they endeavor to guard from harm?"

"The goblin-folk are not unduly smart," she said with a fleeting smile. "But smart enough to keep Adepts away from the device. They cooperate with us to some extent because they know that we oppose thee—and thou art one who will take the contraption from them and return it to Proton-frame, where it seems it will wreak all manner of mischief on both frames. So it is an uneasy alliance, but it will do. All of us, Adept and goblin alike, wish to save Phaze."

"And I wish to destroy Phaze," Stile said. "Or so you other Adepts choose to believe. Because of some fouled-up prophecy. No matter that I love Phaze; you believe that not."

"Nay, Blue, this one is not distorted. Thou wilt return the thing to Proton and thereby destroy Phaze, and only thy departure can alleviate that."

Stile was annoyed by this insistence. There had to be some flaw in the logic. "How dost thou know the prophecy is true?"

"The computer itself made it."

"And what relevance can the guess of an other-frame contraption have? Thou dost credit it with the accuracy of the Oracle!"

She nodded, and Stile's mouth dropped open. "Oh, no!" he exclaimed.

"It is so," she affirmed. "The computer is the Oracle. That is how it defends itself from the likes of us. Any thrust we can conceive against it, it anticipates and foils. Its means are devious but effective. We dare not attack it directly."

"Now let me back up," Stile said. "Thou didst offer me peace and fortune in Phaze, then told me I have to get out of Phaze forever or be killed, so that I won't destroy it. Surely thou perceivest the contradiction. Where is the lie?"

"Nay, Blue!" she said. "We Adepts differ some amongst ourselves about our manner of dealing with thee, so there may be seeming contradictions. It is a fair offer—if thou dost but accept it. Cooperation or exile. We fear thou wilt not."

"Try me, White."

Her glance played across the cavern, indicating the unicorns and goblins, all waiting for the settlement of Adepts. "Needs must we have greater privacy than this," she said. "Thy spell or mine?"

"Mine," he said. He played a bar of harmonica music, then sang: "Give us a globe that none may probe." And about them formed an opaque sphere that cut off all external light and sound.

In a moment light flared, as the witch made a spell of her own.

"Now before we suffocate," she said, "I'll give it to thee without artifice. We want thee to destroy the Oracle. Only thou canst do it, for thou art its tool. It will admit thee to its presence, if thou canst get somehow past the goblins, and thy power is great enough to do the deed. Destroy that evil machine, Blue, and Phaze will be saved. This is the loophole we dare not voice aloud. Only if it returns operative to Proton can it act to destroy Phaze, and it can not foresee its own demise. Do this, Blue, and all other prophecies are null; we then shall have no onus against thee, and thou canst govern in Phaze."

"Thou art asking me to betray a—a consciousness that trusts me," Stile said, disturbed. "That has never been my way."

"Agreed. Thou hast ever been honorable, Blue, which is why I trust myself to thy power here. It is no fault in thee that causes us to oppose thee; it is only that it is in thy power to save or finish Phaze. Save our land and suffer our gratitude; try to destroy it and suffer our opposition; or vacate the frame so that we have no need to fear thee. These are thy choices, Blue. Thou knowest our determination; we are fighting for our lives and world. We are not limited by thy scruples, and our massed magic is stronger than thine. Thus united, we *can* attack thee directly. Oppose us not gratuitously."

It was a fair ultimatum. But Stile found he could not take the easy way out. "I love Phaze," he repeated. "I want never to leave it. In addition, I am now a Citizen in Proton, with considerable wealth. I shall not sacrifice my place in both frames by forever departing the planet. That leaves me with two choices: join thee or oppose thee. I know nothing of these prophecies thou dost speak of. Why should I try to destroy a device that has done me no harm?"

"No harm!" she flared, her white hair seeming to darken and melt with the heat. "Thou trusting fool! That device killed thee once and imperiled thy life again by setting us against thee."

"That last I perceive," Stile agreed. "Yet the business of the Oracle is making prophecies and being correct. If I am to be the leader of the forces of destruction of Phaze by helping this computer to return to Proton—though the reason remains opaque as to why it should wish ill to Phaze or how it could harm this frame from Proton—and someone inquires about that, the Oracle can but answer truthfully. Naturally that imperils me, and I like it not—but neither can I fault it for that answer. Truth is often unpleasant. Rather should I inquire in what way I am to do a deed whose nature appalls me. Were I sure the Oracle would destroy Phaze, I would not help it, and surely it is aware of that. There must be circumstances I know not and that you other Adepts know not. Better that I at least talk with the Oracle to ascertain the rationale."

"Of course," she said. "That is thy sensible response, and surely the machine is expecting thee to come to it. That makes it possible for thee to destroy it."

"Or to help it to destroy Phaze," Stile said wryly. "At the moment I intend to do neither evil, and can not see what rationale would sway me either way."

"Then consider this, Blue. It was the Oracle who hinted at the doom of the Red Adept and started her mischief against thee. She killed thine other self and attacked thee in Proton—but it was the Oracle who motivated her. If thou dost seek vengeance for the murder of the Blue Adept, seek it at the source—the infernal Oracle. This is no sweet contraption like thy golem mistress, Blue. It plays the game savagely."

"But all its predictions were true!" Stile protested, experiencing a trace of doubt. "I can not blame it for fulfilling that role!"

"Fool! dost thou not realize it was a self-fulfilling prophecy? Red attacked thee because the Oracle fingered thee, no other reason. The Oracle knew what would happen. It alone generated that murder—and knew that also."

Stile was shaken. He was conversant with the bypaths of logic. White was right; the Oracle had initiated the campaign against him. A lesser entity might have made a mistake, but the Oracle had to have known what it was doing. It had murdered Stile's other self, caused Stile's knee misery, and set him on the horrendous path he had followed on the way to Phaze and to vengeance against the Red Adept.

Yet he remembered also that the original Blue Adept had accepted his own murder. Why?

"But why should the Oracle do this to me?" he asked plaintively, seeking to resolve this part of the mystery. Maybe if he knew the Oracle's motive, he could fathom his alternate self's strange acquiescence. His mind was, after all, identical.

"I suggest thou dost go ask it," White said. "Ask also why it should seek to use thee to destroy Phaze. Then must thou do what thou shalt see fit to do."

It all did seem to add up, at least to this incomplete extent. He had to settle with the Oracle. "I will go ask the machine and then do what I see fit to do."

"I meant that facetiously," the White Adept said. "We do not believe the computer will allow thee to approach it unless it knows thou wilt side with it. I have made our case to thee, but thou hast not reacted with proper fury. Something we know not of has influenced thee against us."

The knowledge of his other self's acquiescence—that was the influencing factor. "Of course I am not with thee!" Stile exclaimed. "I am not with anyone who kidnaps and dehorns my steed. Thy methods make thy side suspect."

"And the methods of the Oracle make it not similarly suspect?"

Stile spread his hands. "I admit I know not the final truth. I will seek the Oracle."

"I did not think thou wouldst join us. But I undertook to make the case. Hadst thou accepted honestly—"

"I have done nothing dishonest!"

"Aye. So we must destroy thee. Yellow will not like that, but it must be done. When we leave this bubble, it will be war between us. The other Adepts have massed their power, and the goblins are ready."

"Fortunate art thou that thy trust in this truce was well placed. Else would I simply confine thee here."

"Honor is not a luxury many of us can afford," she said sadly. "Yet in the name of honor, some are fools. Thou wilt not attack us or the Oracle without fair warning. This makes thee ideal for whatever side can use thee." She sighed. "I do not hate thee, Blue. I respect thee. I, too, am true to my cause, and it is a worthy one. Thou art true only to thine honor, and therein lies thy grief. Phaze will never be safe whilst Blue remains. Thus says our enemy the Oracle, and this we do believe. We like it not, but so must it be. Be on thy guard against my kind, Blue."

Stile studied her. The White Adept was no young thing, and she had not bothered with Yellow's type of vanity. She looked old and ugly and careworn. He had encountered her before and found little to please him. But he knew she was a witch and a skilled one; backed by the power of the other Adepts, she was far more formidable than she appeared. Her warning had to be heeded. The Adepts would now be fully unified and coordinated. The veil was off; nothing would be held back. She was giving him the most forceful warning she could, without betraying her associates.

He would have to get away from here in a hurry, the moment the shell opened. Yet where could he escape to? The Adepts could follow him anywhere in Phaze. White's warning, perhaps, was intended to focus his attention on this problem so that he would have a fair chance. His respect for her had been small; now it had enlarged. She had taken pains to give information that he needed, when she really hadn't had to. "I thank thee for thy courtesy, White," he said.

Stile released the spell that enclosed them and stood on guard. If the witch tried to strike against either unicorn, Stile would counter the spell. By the same token, if he started magic against the lurking goblins, she would block it. Since no spell could be used twice, it was sheer waste for Adept to squander magic against Adept. Their special powers would cancel each other out—until the other Adepts oriented—and she had told him they were ready. He was outgunned and would have to move fast so that they could not keep proper track of him.

"We must travel!" Stile cried. "I must stave off magic; you two handle the rest!" He vaulted aboard the nearest unicorn, which happened to be the Herd Stallion.

Clip was now outside the prison, probably having shifted to hawk-form to pass by the bars. That meant he was back in full health. But Stile was happier riding the Stallion, whom he knew to be in full possession of his powers. Clip might tire quickly.

The Stallion blasted out a medley of chords. Goblins had appeared in the passage; they hastily faded back, heeding the warning. Clip went to hawk-form and flew ahead, leading the way. The Stallion launched himself forward.

Stile was only peripherally aware of these details. His attention was on the White Adept. As the Stallion moved out, she started drawing a symbol in the dust on the floor. Stile sang out a spell that was mostly in his head: "Dust—gust!"

The dust stirred up into a cloud, gusting about the cavern. The witch was unable to complete her sketch. Her spell had been intercepted. She could not function any better in this swirl than Stile could when he had been a victim of the silence-spell. She looked up—and Stile saw with surprise that she was smiling. It was as if she were glad to see him escape. She must have spoken truly when she said she did not like this business. She had to fight him, but didn't really mind failing. Some Adepts, it seemed, were not as bad as others.

However, he had to heed her warning about the other enemy Adepts, most of whom he had never interacted with. They would not hold back, once they got around White's tacit obstruction and oriented directly on him.

Meanwhile, the goblins were bad enough. These were their passages, and they were thoroughly conversant with the dusky recesses. The Herd Stallion was retracing the route they had descended—but suddenly a great iron gate slammed into place ahead, blocking the way. The Stallion could not pass and Clip barely squeezed back through the narrow aperture to rejoin them. They were caught in the passage, and a solid mass of goblins was wedging in behind them.

The Stallion played more chords. Clip, answering the command, shifted to man-form and joined Stile on the Stallion's back. He was clothed now, with a rapier. He drew this and faced back, menacing a few goblins who tried to squeeze in behind.

Stile got the idea. He unwrapped his concealed broadsword and sat ready to slice at any goblins who got within range to either side. His main attention was on whatever signs of hostile magic there might be, but he could slash while hardly looking.

The Stallion charged the goblins. They scattered, throwing their spears away in their frantic scramble to get clear. It was not that they were cowardly; it was that a ton of unicorn bristling with horn and two armed riders was a truly formidable thing. Any who tried to stand their ground would be skewered or slashed or trampled. As it happened, a number could not get out of the way in time and were indeed trampled and skewered.

There was a side passage. The unicorn hurtled into this, causing Stile to grab for the mane in order to hold his seat, and thundered along it.

Suddenly there was a ledge. The Herd Stallion could not brake in time. He leaped out over the edge, into the darkness of nothing.

Then Stile found himself riding the dragon. The Stallion's dragon was not large for this type, being perhaps only twelve feet long from snout to tail, and Stile's weight bore him down. Fortunately Stile was not large for his own type, and the dragon was able to spread his wings and descend slowly. Clip, of course, had converted to hawk-form.

Stile still wore his grotesque shoes and turban. Quickly he sloughed these off, lightening the burden on the reptile; but the descent continued.

The dragon snorted fire that illuminated the cavern. They were in a deep cleft whose upper reaches were lit by wan shafts of moonlight. There was their escape!

But the dragon could not make it that high under Stile's weight. Stile readied a spell, felt the questing magic of another Adept, and had to hold back. He could be messed up much as he had messed up White's spell, and in midair that could be disastrous. Also, it seemed the enemies could not quite locate him as long as he remained in the dark and cast no spells. He had to hold off until it was safer. So the dim light above faded, and they dropped down into the deeper depths silently.

There was a detonation of something. Light blazed and metallic fragments whistled by. Someone had fired an explosive amulet or something similar at them. This was blind shooting, hoping to catch the dragon by a random shot; the assailants did not have a perfect fix on Stile's party. Now he was certain that if he used defensive magic, he would give away his location. Better to lie quiet, like a submarine on a water planet, and hope the depth-charges missed.

The dragon tried again to rise, but could not. Stile felt the body heating with the effort. This could not continue long.

There was a *pop* behind them. The Stallion-dragon turned his head to send back a jet of flame—and the light showed a griffin, an eagle-headed lion, the next enemy Adept sending. "Uh-oh," Stile murmured. "Can't hide from that."

But the Stallion was burning hot from his exertions. He looped about, aimed his snout at the pursuing griffin, and exhaled a searing shaft of fire.

The griffin squawked as it was enveloped in flame. The blaze of its burning wings lit up the entire cavern. It tumbled down to the water, smoking feathers drifting after it.

But the next sending was another dragon, a big one. Its chest pumped like a bellows, building up pressure for a devastating blast that would incinerate Stile and the Stallion. The enemy was now fighting fire with fire.

The hawk winged at it, too small and fast for the dragon to catch or avoid. The dragon ignored the bird, knowing nothing that size could dent its armored hide. The enormous metal-foil wings beat swiftly, launching the dragon forward.

The hawk dived, zeroing in on the dragon's head. Stile could only watch with dismay, knowing Clip was throwing away his life in a useless gesture, a diversionary effort that was not working. He could not even think of a preventive spell on this too-brief notice.

The dragon opened its monstrous mouth to take in the tiny missile—and Clip changed abruptly to unicorn-form. He struck horn-first, piercing the dragon's head, his horn passing from inside the throat right on between the eyes and out, penetrating the little brain on the way.

The strike was so unexpected and powerful that the monster simply folded its wings and expired. It plummeted to the water, while Clip changed back to hawk-form and flew clear. "Well done!" Stile cried, amazed and gratified.

Now for a time there were no more sendings. But Stile knew worse attacks were in the offing. His party had to get out of the chasm—and could not. Already they were close to the nether water. He had to relieve the Herd Stallion of his weight—yet was sure that the one enchantment the enemy Adepts would have blocked would be a personal transport-spell. They were trying to force Stile to use it—and launch himself into oblivion.

The Stallion sent forth more fire, just enough to light the way. The dark water below reflected with slight iridescence, as if oily. Stile mistrusted that. He didn't want the Stallion to fall into that liquid. He would have to risk magic. Not transport, of course; something unexpected.

The hawk had been circling. Now he came back, squawking news. Over and over he cried it, until Stile was able to discern the word. "Curtain!" Stile cried. "The curtain is ahead?"

That was it. Now Stile had a better alternative. "Fly low, Stallion, and I'll pass through the curtain. Then thou and Clip can fly up and escape in the night. They want thee not, only me, and soon thou canst return to thy herd. I'll climb up on the Proton side, where magic can't reach me." Of course there would be other problems across the curtain, but he would handle them in due course.

The Stallion was in no position to argue. He glided low—and there in the dark was the scintillation of the curtain, crossing the chasm. "If there's any sort of ledge—I don't want to drop too far."

There was no ledge. It would have to be the water. They intersected the curtain, and Stile spelled himself across.

CHAPTER 10

Force

He fell a few feet—or rather a meter or so—knowing he was through the curtain only because he no longer had dragon support. He splashed into the water, feeling the instant shock of cold. He was, of course, an excellent swimmer; no top Gamesman neglected such a sport. But the water was polluted, stinking, and perhaps contained harmful acids; the Citizens of Proton cared nothing for the planetary environment outside the domes. He didn't want to stay here long!

The air, too, was foul. But here in the depths, it was thicker than above and seemed to contain more oxygen. He did not enjoy it, but he could survive longer on it than anticipated. Still, he had another resource.

He swam back to the curtain, which passed right down through the water. He organized himself, then willed himself through and said: "Bring nuts and dried fruit, scuba and wetsuit." And the spell, shaped by his imagination, clothed him in a warm, flexible body swimming suit complete with flippers, breathing apparatus, and a bag of mixed nuts and bits of dehydrated fruit.

Something formed in the water near him. It was huge and toothed, and it threshed its way toward him with powerful flukes. Stile hastily spelled himself back across the curtain. He had done the unexpected and escaped the enemy Adepts without using a transport-spell, but they remained alert for him.

His new equipment went with him. This was one way in which magic and science juxtaposed; he could create or fetch scientific devices by magic in Phaze and take them across for use in Proton. Now he was comfortable in the water and had concentrated food to sustain him. He could get where he was going.

Only—where was he going? He wanted to locate that computer—but where was it?

Again, no problem. He prepared himself and passed through the curtain. "Weapon and gem, doslem doslem," he sang, grabbed the two objects that formed, and dodged back to Proton before the massive crunch of a hostile spell could catch him. The enemy would never have expected him to conjure these particular items! He saw the Adept attack through the curtain—a blaze of light silhouetting massive jawless teeth, closing and disappearing as they intersected the demarcation of the curtain. A demon from the deeps, indeed! Technically an indirect attack, a sending, but surely fatal to whatever it caught. They were not playing innocent games, these enemy Adepts!

Now he had what he needed. He could stop playing peekaboo through the curtain, especially since one more trip across it would probably get him crunched. The enemy had targeted him too closely; his scant leeway had been used up. Now he could get where he was going —on the Proton side of the curtain.

He swam, holding the straps to his last two acquisitions in his teeth. The flippers enabled him to move rapidly through the water. He didn't need light; he could tell where the walls were by the lapping of the waves his swimming made.

The chasm narrowed, until he was swimming between vertical walls only a couple of meters apart. Still no way up or out. He didn't like this; his special equipment was sealed in watertight packages, but he needed to get on dry land to use it safely.

Well, he could dive. He had a hunch there was a way out of here and a way from here to the computer-Oracle, because the goblins needed access to guard it. Of course this was the other frame—but with the normal parallelism, chances were good there were Proton passages too. All he had to do was find them.

He dived. He did not fear any monsters in this murky lake; they could not survive in this pollution. But he was careful about sharp jags of rock that might tear his suit.

The cleft was wider below, giving him more room to grope along. He should have conjured a light; he hadn't thought of it. On any venture, something important was always forgotten! But one of his instruments had an operating light that he could use for general vision—once he put it into use.

The walls closed in above. Good—he did have a passage here, for there was a slight current. Soon he groped upward and discovered a new cavern—and this one had sloping sides that he could scramble up on, getting free of the water.

Perched awkwardly on the rock, for his bad knees prevented him from squatting, he opened one of his doslems. This one was the weapon: Disrupter-Optical-Space-Light-Modulator. D O S L M. He set it on low and activated it. There was a faint, humming beam, and a section of the cave wall glowed and sagged, melting without heat. Its particles had been disrupted, losing their cohesion; solid had turned to liquid. Good enough. The doslem was governed by light-beam computer, in which beams of light functioned in lieu of solid circuitry and semiconductor diodes and information chips. It was much more compact than the solid state and could generate potent effects, as the melted patch of wall showed.

Now Stile turned to the other doslem, the gem. In this case the D stood for Detector. It was an even more marvelous instrument. A miniature panel controlled its assorted functions of timing, direction, and detection. In his hands it emitted just enough light to clarify the cave-region in which he hunched, and it gave readouts mapping the extent of air-filled and water-filled recesses. There were other caves here, and some were within the range of the disrupter; he could melt a hole through the thinnest section of wall. Some passages were squared off—obviously artificial. His hunch had proved correct!

Stile checked for refined metals, orienting on copper, aluminum, iron, and gold. Soon he located a considerable cache of these, southeast of his present location. He checked for magnetism and found it in the same region. This certainly seemed to be the computer, or whatever portion of it existed in the frame of Proton.

Stile scouted about, then selected the thinnest wall to disrupt. He gave the melt time to settle, then stepped through to the adjacent cave. He was on his way.

It took time, and on occasion he rested and ate from his supply of nuts and fruit. He located reasonably fresh water by tuning in on it with the detector. He had a sense of location; he was in the cave network whose upper exits he and the Lady Blue had noticed on their honeymoon, after departing the snow-demon demesnes. He marched, cut through to a new passage, and marched again, slept, and marched again. He hoped the two unicorns had flown up and out of the cavern system, knowing that he, Stile, could take care of himself on the other side of the curtain. There was no way to communicate with them now, since he was no longer near the curtain. They simply had to have faith.

At times, as he tramped onward, he thought about the nature of the curtain and the parallel frames. How was it that he could so readily conjure scientific equipment that was inoperative in Phaze, yet was operative when taken back across the curtain? If it was that solid and real, why couldn't it function in Phaze? If it was not, why did it work here? The curtain could be a very thin line indeed, when magic so readily facilitated science. Was there no conservation of energy with regard to each frame? Anything taken across the curtain was lost to its frame of origination, wasn't it? Also, how could objects of Proton-frame design be brought to Phaze? Did his magic generate them from nothing, or were they actually stolen from warehouses and factories and hauled through the curtain? He doubted he could visualize the inner workings of a doslem well enough to build one directly, so doubted he could do it by magic, either—but the alternative implied a closer connection between frames and greater permeability of the curtain than conventional wisdom supposed. Magic would have to reach beyond the curtain, right into the domain of science. There was so much yet to learn about the relationship of frames!

And this computer he was searching out—had it really murdered Stile's alternate self, the original Blue Adept, by means of a self-fulfilling prophecy? Why? How did all this tie in with the approach of the end of Phaze and Stile's own involvement in that? Was the computer-Oracle due to perish in that termination of the frame, and Stile himself—

He paused to review what had been more or less idle speculation. If Stile was going to help destroy Phaze, and the computer was in Phaze, it might indeed be destroyed too. So maybe it sought to prevent him from participating in this business. Maybe it was really on the same side as the other Adepts. So it had generated mischief to eliminate him in both frames, being foiled only by that other message, the one that had brought Sheen to protect him. Yet it had been prophesied that he would help the computer return to Proton, where it would act to destroy Phaze; that put him on its side and set it against the Adepts. Maybe the destruction of Phaze was inevitable, and the computer needed to cross to Proton in order to escape the holocaust. But then why should it have tried to kill him twice? That made no sense at all.

Maybe he should have taken the time to trace down the source of that mysterious, other message, the one that had saved him, before he rescued Clip—

No. Clip came first. The Adepts had hurt the unicorn to gain leverage against Stile, and Stile had had to act.

Should he resume tracing that message now, instead of going to confront the Oracle? He might have a powerful ally—and with most of the other Adepts against him, he needed one.

But that would mean backtracking to the curtain and fighting his way through the barrage of hostile magic directed against him. He could not be sure he would survive that, and certainly he could not thereafter approach the Oracle with any element of surprise. Only by staying with the Proton-frame route, where magic and prophecy did not exist, could he hope to sneak up on it. He was set on his present course; he would have to continue.

He plodded on, and the hours passed. Was it day or night above, now? Normally he had a good time sense, but he did need some minimal feedback to keep it aligned. Stile also had good endurance, having run marathons in his day, but now he was traveling mainly in the dark, with occasional sips of oxygen from his scuba gear, conserving that life-sustaining gas as much as possible. He was out of food and tired. Only the constant approach to the site indicated by his equipment gave him confidence to keep on. Maybe he should have gotten himself a device to signal Sheen, who could have come to pick him up, making things so much easier. How obvious this was, now that he had ample time to think of it!

Yet that would have alerted others to his activity. Since other Adepts had connections in Proton—indeed, some were Citizens—that could be just as dangerous for him as activity in Phaze. So maybe this way was best; they might think him dead or impotent, since he did not reappear. Sometimes accidents and mistakes were the best course; they were at least random.

The detector signaled him; he was at last drawing close to the metal and magnetism. He hoped this was what he believed it was; and if it weren't, he would have to struggle to the surface and hope he could make it to a dome. His oxygen was very low; he knew he was nowhere near the curtain; he was also deadly tired. The shortage of oxygen had sapped his strength. He doubted he could survive if this site were not what he sought. He had in fact gambled his life on it.

The passage did not go to the site. Stile had to use the disrupter again. The wall melted and he stepped through.

He had entered a dusty chamber. Machinery was in it. The detector indicated that electric current flowed here. He turned up his light and examined the machinery. Immediately he suffered the pangs of disappointment. This was no computer; this was an old construction robot, equipped to bore and polish a tunnel through rock. The magnetic field was from a preservation current, to warm key lines and maintain the valuable robot brain in operative condition despite long disuse. There were other construction machines here, similarly parked and preserved. It was cheaper to mothball equipment for centuries than to rebuild it at need. Obviously the computer had been brought here, then passed through the curtain to Phaze long ago.

Something nagged at Stile's mind. There was a discontinuity. What was it? He felt worn in brain as well as in body, but as he concentrated he was able to force it to the surface of consciousness. His ability to do this was one of the things that had brought him to his present position as Citizen and Adept. When he needed to be aware of something, he could grasp it in time for it to be of use. Usually.

It was this: the curtain was not here. It was at least a full weary day and night's march northwest of here. There was no way the computer could have been set across here. The curtain was fairly stable; if it moved, it did so very slowly. Centimeters per century, perhaps, like the drifting of continents.

Still, that offered a possible explanation. Maybe the curtain *had* moved, perhaps in random jumps that were now forgotten, and several centuries ago it had been here. So the computer had been put across, and stranded by the retreat of the curtain.

How, then, could he be fated to put the computer back across the curtain? The computer was surely far too massive for him to move, even if the other Adepts permitted it—which they would not. Stile was not at all sure he cared to make the effort. If the computer-Oracle was his enemy, why should he help it move to Proton to wreak its vengeance on Phaze? So much remained to be clarified before Stile could decide what side of what situation he was on.

First, however, he had to figure out how to survive. There should be some small emergency supplies of food and oxygen here, for maintenance workers who might get stranded. There might be a storeroom. Maybe even a communication line to civilization, since there was a live power line.

He checked around, his mind growing dull as his scant remaining oxygen thinned. He had rationed it to reach here; now it was gone. He stumbled from machine to machine. No oxygen, no supplies.

The cave narrowed. There was a door at the end. It was an air-lock type of portal—a likely storeroom or pressurized office complex. He needed to get in, but it was sealed. Should he use the disrupter? Two problems there: first, the chamber might be lined with disrupt-resistant material, making it impervious to the attack of this small weapon; second, if he did break in, and there was air pressure, that pressure would decompress explosively. Not only could this be dangerous to him physically, the process would eliminate the very thing he had to preserve— normal, oxygenated air pressure.

He tried to open the lock, but could not; the controls were keyed to particular identities or particular code sequences, and he was not the right person and didn't know the code. No help for it; he would have to try the disrupter, hoping to find canned air to use with his suit.

Then a voice came: "Identify yourself."

There was someone in there! Or at least a sapient robot. "I am—" He paused. Should he give his true identity? Caution prevailed. "A person in need of air. I beg assistance."

"You shall have it. Be advised that a robot weapon is trained on you."

"So advised." Stile leaned against the wall, growing dizzy as the last of his scuba oxygen faded. He could not blame a solitary maintenance guard for being careful.

The portal hummed, then opened. Air puffed out. A figure emerged, clothed in the protective gear of a maintenance worker, using a nostril mask and protective goggles.

"Stile! It's you!" the figure cried. "God, what a relief!" The man put his arm around Stile's shoulders to help him into the chamber.

It was Clef, the musician Stile had encountered in the Tourney, and to whom he had given the Platinum Flute. The Foreordained. "I thought you were in Phaze," Stile gasped as the air lock sealed and pressure came up.

"I was, Stile. Or should I say sir? I understand you obtained your Citizenship."

"I got it. Don't bother with the 'sir.' Just give me air and food and a place to rest. What are you doing here?"

The inner aperture opened, and Clef guided him into a comfortable chamber. "I'm here to meet you, Stile, on behalf of the Oracle. You and I must work together to fulfill the prophecy and save the frames from destruction." He pressed a cup of nutri-soup into Stile's unsteady hands and set him in an easy chair. "I was so afraid you would not make it. The Oracle said there was danger, that no one could help you, and that it could not foresee your arrival. Its prophecies are unreliable when they relate to its own destiny. I had no notion when and if you would arrive, except that it had to be within a three-day time span. I fear I was asleep when the moment came. Then I could not be certain it was you, for there are enemies—"

Stile ceased his gulping of the soup to interrupt Clef. "Enemies? To save the frames? I understood I was to destroy Phaze, and I don't know whether that makes me friend or enemy to whom."

Clef smiled. "That depends on how you see it, Stile. The present order will be overturned or greatly weakened in both Proton and Phaze. That's why Citizens and Adepts oppose the move. Most of the rest—the serfs and creatures—will benefit by the new order. You are no enemy to them!"

"Viewpoint," Stile said, catching on. "To an Adept, the loss of power of Adepts would be disaster, the end of Phaze as he knows it. To a unicorn, it might be salvation."

"And to a werewolf," Clef agreed. "Big changes are coming. It is our job to make the transition safe. If we don't, things could get extremely ugly."

Stile was recovering as he breathed the good air and ingested the nourishment of the soup. He started to strip off the wetsuit, all that had protected him from the chill of the cave passages. This chamber was like a slice of Heaven, coming so suddenly after his arduous trek. "Tell me everything."

"It's simple enough. Three hundred years ago, when they discovered that this planet was one of the occasional places in the universe where the frames of science and of fantasy intersected—would you believe Planet Earth was another such place in medieval times?—they realized that there were certain dangers in colonizing the fantasy frame. So they set up some powerful instruments for the purpose of securing an optimistic new order. A sophisticated self-willed computer and a definitive book of magic."

"A book of magic? I never heard of this."

"Well, you weren't supposed to. It contains the most potent spells in all modes, so that it would take years for a single person to invoke them all—not that anyone would want to. Spells of creation and destruction, of summoning and sending, of healing and harming. Any person with access to that book in Phaze would become an instant Adept, more powerful than any other, one who could virtually change the face of the frame in minutes. The computer contains all the data for science, finance, economics, and politics known at the time. Despite the passage of three hundred years, this knowledge is enough to assure the operator enormous power in Proton—perhaps enough to dominate the government."

"And someone is destined to get hold of these tools and turn them to wrong use? That could indeed be trouble!"

"No, great care was taken to safeguard against this danger. The two tools had to be preserved for the time when they were needed, and kept out of the hands of those who might squander or abuse them. They had to be ready for the great crisis of separation."

"Separation?"

"It seems the intersection of frames is a sometime thing. The elves who instructed me are not sure about that. As you know, they consider me to be the one they call the Foreordained, which simply means my particular talent will be useful in negotiating the crisis; there is nothing religious or supernatural about it. So they have been preparing me in a cram-course, while you have diverted the Adepts who might otherwise have interfered."

"So that's what I was doing. I was a decoy!"

"That's only part of your task. Anyway, they think the frames are going to separate, so there will be no more crossings, no further interactions. This is simply part of the natural order; it happened on Earth as the medieval period ended. After it, no one in Proton need believe in magic, and no one in Phaze need believe in science, and the episode of the interaction of the systems will seem like fake history. Since on this planet the fantasy frame was colonized from the science frame—though a number of Phaze creatures are evidently native to the fantasy realm, and perhaps the Little Folk too—er, where was I?"

"The frames are separating," Stile said.

"Ah, yes. When they do, the human alternative selves will be carried away, becoming complete in themselves, clones of their counterparts, and parallelism will no longer exist."

"Now that's another thing," Stile said. "I can see how the presence of people in one frame could generate similar people in the other frame, split by the curtain. With science overlapping magic, that sort of thing can happen. But after the initial ripple, why should it continue? I did not exist three hundred years ago; why should there have been two of me?"

"Again, the Little Folk aren't certain. It seems that when the experts made the computer and book of magic—two aspects of the same thing—

they were able to juxtapose the frames. Science and magic operated in each, for the two were the same. Then the frames separated slightly, and each person and creature separated too. This was an unexpected occurrence; before that, there had been only one of each. It was as if the fantasy frame, vacant of human life, picked up a duplicate copy of each person in the science frame. It did not work the other way, for no dragons or unicorns appeared in Proton, perhaps because it lacked a compatible environment. Already the mining of Protonite was commencing, with attendant use of heavy machinery, construction of processing plants, and pollution of the environment. The Citizen class put things on what they termed a businesslike footing at the outset, permitting no pollution controls. There is evidence that magical creatures are extremely sensitive to environmental degradation; only a few, like the trolls, can endure it for any length of time. The Citizens of Proton simply put up force-field domes and continued their course unabated, ignoring the outside planet. In this manner Proton lost whatever it might have had in nature, sacrificed by the illiterate pursuit of wealth. But despite this gross difference between the frames, parallelism persisted; people tended to align. In fact, parallelism is the major factor in the present crisis."

"That's what I really want to understand," Stile said. "The frames may separate, but I don't see why that should destroy them unless, like Siamese twins, they can't exist apart."

"They can exist apart. To make the problem clear, I have to clarify parallelism. It's not just people; the entire landscape is similar. A change made in one frame and not in the other creates an imbalance and puts a strain on the entire framework. Dig a hole in the ground in Proton, and the stress won't be alleviated until a similar hole is made in Phaze. Unfortunately there is no natural way to do that, so the stress continues to build. Eventually something will snap—and we are now very close to the snapping point."

"Ah, I see. Like damming a stream—the water builds up behind and falls away on the other side, until it either spills over or breaks the dam. And we don't want the dam to burst."

"Indeed we don't. So we have to find a way to alleviate the pressure. We don't know what will happen if the frames equalize in their own fashion, but it would probably wipe out most of the inhabitants of both frames."

"So we need to fill holes and drain waters," Stile said. "Seems simple enough."

"Not so. Not so at all. You reckon without the human dynamics. You see, the major imbalance, the largest hole in the ground, literally, is from the mining of Protonite. This is displacing huge quantities of material, creating a substantial physical imbalance, and worse yet—"

"Protonite," Stile said. "In the other frame it's Phazite—the source of the energy for magic."

"Exactly. That makes the problem critical, and the solution almost prohibitively difficult. The Citizens are not about to stop mining Protonite voluntarily. Not until every last dreg of it is gone, like the original atmosphere. Protonite is the basis of their wealth and power. If it were only sand, we could arrange to transfer a few thousand tons from one frame to the other, relieving the imbalance. But as it is—"

"But if that much Protonite, ah, Phazite were transferred out, to restore the balance, what would happen to the magic?"

"It would be reduced to about half its present potency. The Oracle has calculated this carefully. The power of the Adepts, who are the main users, would diminish accordingly. They would not be able to dominate Phaze as they do now."

"That might not be a bad thing," Stile said. "And the Proton Citizens—"

"Their mining would have to be severely curtailed, perhaps cease entirely. They would have no renewal of their present resources. The galaxy would have to discover new sources of energy."

"But the galaxy depends on Protonite! Nothing matches it! There would be phenomenal repercussions!"

"Yes, that is why taking action is difficult. Civilization as we know it will have to change, and that will not occur easily. Yet the alternative, the Oracle says, may be the complete destruction of this planet—which would also cut off the galaxy's supply of Protonite."

"I begin to comprehend the forces operating," Stile said. "The end of Phaze and Proton is approaching, and we have to do something. But both Citizens and Adepts would oppose the cutoff of Protonite mining and the transfer of Phazite, because without free use of this mineral their status suffers greatly. That's why the Adepts are after me now, and think that my elimination will alleviate their problem; they fear I can do something that will deplete them all—"

"You can."

"And that's why the self-willed machines knew I would have to become the wealthiest of Citizens. Wealth is power in Proton, and I need to be able to withstand the formidable opposition of the Citizens when this thing breaks."

"Exactly. You need enough of a voting bloc to tip the balance in your favor."

So many things were falling into place! "But why, then, did the computer try to destroy me? I don't want to see either Proton or Phaze come to harm and I should certainly work to achieve the best compromise. Why did the Oracle sic the Red Adept on me?"

"Because only you—and I—can do the job that must be done. A man who can cross the curtain freely, who is powerful in each frame, and who has the ability and conscience to carry through. A man who is essentially incorruptible without being stupid. The Blue Adept, your other self, was too limited; he could not cross the curtain, so he had no base in Proton, no experience with that society. He had lived all his life with magic; he depended on it. He would have been largely helpless in Proton during the crisis."

"So the Oracle killed him?" Stile demanded incredulously. "Just because he wasn't perfect? Why didn't the Oracle select someone else for the job?"

"The Oracle selected you, Stile. You had his excellent qualities, and you had lived a more challenging life; you were better equipped. But you could not enter Phaze. So the Blue Adept had to be eliminated—I do not speak of this with approval—in order to free you to cross the curtain. Had the decision gone the other way, you would have been the one killed, to free him to cross into Proton."

"But the attempt was made on me too!" Stile protested, shaken by this cold calculation.

"It was blocked in Proton," Clef said. "I knew nothing of this when I encountered you in the Tourney; believe me, I was appalled. But you were protected. The Oracle sent a second message—"

"The message!" Stile exclaimed. "I was trying to trace it! The Oracle—" But this, too, was coming clear now. One message to start the murder process, the other to intercept and nullify part of it. Diabolically efficient!

"Now you have been prepared," Clef continued. "The computer expects you to organize the juxtaposition and transfer."

"I'm not at all sure I want to cooperate with this emotionless machine. It has entirely disrupted my life, not stopping even at murder. What it put the Lady Blue through, and my friend Hulk—" Stile shook his head. "This is not the sort of thing I care to tolerate."

"I agree. But it seems the alternative is to let both frames crash."

"Or so the cynical Oracle says," Stile said. "That machine has shown itself to be completely unscrupulous in the manipulation of people and events. Why should I believe it now?"

"The Little Folk believe it," Clef said. "They despise it and want to be rid of it, but they believe it. It is a machine, programmed for truth, not for conscience. So its methods are ruthless, but never has it lied. Its sole purpose is to negotiate the crisis with minimum havoc, and it seems that the grief inflicted on you was merely part of the most rational strategy. It has no human will to power and, once it returns to Proton, it will serve its master absolutely."

"And who will its master be?"

"You, I think. I am called the Foreordained, but I believe the term is most applicable to you. Perhaps it was applied to me as a decoy, to prevent your premature destruction." He smiled, appreciating the irony.

"The Oracle prophesies that Blue will govern Proton in the difficult period following separation of the frames. As you may have gathered, there is no limit on information when it deals with me. The computer will help you govern Proton, and the book of magic will assist the one who takes power from the Adepts in Phaze."

"And who is that?"

"I can't get a clear answer there. It seems to be you—but of course you can't be in both frames after they separate. I suspect the computer suffered a prophetic short circuit here. I can only conjecture that whichever frame you choose to remain in will be yours to govern."

"I want only to remain in Phaze with the Lady Blue and Neysa and Kurrelgyre and my other friends. Yet I have already been treated to the prophecy that Phaze will not be safe until Blue departs it."

Clef shook his head. "I wish I could give you a clear answer on this, Stile, but I can not. Your future is indistinct, perhaps undecided. It may be because you are the key figure, the one who will decide it. The uncertainty principle—" He shrugged.

Unwillingly, Stile had to concede the probable truth of this complex of difficult notions. Machines acted the way they were designed and programmed to act—and why would the experts of three hundred years ago have designed a machine to lie during a crisis? Surely they would not have. The very ruthlessness that Stile hated was an argument in favor of the Oracle's legitimacy.

"Where is this book of magic?" Stile asked at last. It was his grudging, oblique concession that he would have to go along with the Oracle and perform his part in this adjustment of frames.

"In Proton, under the control of the Game Computer."

"What's it doing in Proton? No one can use it there."

"That is why it is in Proton. To protect the two tools of power from premature exploitation and dissipation, the powers-that-were placed them in the wrong frames. The book of magic is impotent in the science frame, and the computer is greatly reduced in power in the fantasy frame. In order to resolve the crisis, both must be restored to their proper frames."

"So my job is to fetch the book and pass the computer back through?"

"These tasks are not simple ones," Clef cautioned him. Stile, of course, had already gathered that. "The book should be no problem in the acquisition, for the Game Computer will turn it over to anyone possessing the code-request. But the Citizens will do their utmost to stop it from being transported across the curtain. The computer—that relates to my job. It will cross only as the moving curtain intersects this location."

"Your job? Exactly what will you do as the Foreordained?"

"I will juxtapose the frames. That is the precondition for re-establishing parallelism."

Stile shook his head. "Just when I thought I had it straight, I am confused again. It is my limited present understanding that the frames are about to separate, but can't because of the imbalance of Protonite. I suppose their separation would tear that associated Phazite free and rupture our whole reality, like a knot pulled through a needlehole. But we have only to form a ball of Phazite and roll it across the curtain, where it will become the necessary Protonite. What's this business about juxtaposition?"

"Nice notion, that ball. But you don't just roll Phazite across the curtain. Phazite is magic; the curtain is really an effect of that magic, like a magnetic field associated with electric current or the splay of colors made by a prism in sunlight. Such a ball might rend the curtain, causing explosive mergence of the frames—"

"Ah. The dam bursting again."

"Precisely. But you could roll it into the region of juxtaposition, and then on into the other frame. Two steps, letting one aspect of the curtain recover before straining the other. Like an air lock, perhaps." He smiled. "What a fortune a multiton ball of Protonite would be worth!"

"So you juxtapose the frames. You are foreordained to perform this task so that I can perform mine. How do you do this?"

"I play the Flute."

"Music does it?" Stile asked skeptically.

"The Platinum Flute is more than a musical instrument, as you know. It produces fundamental harmonics that affect the impingement of the frames. Properly played, it causes the frames to overlap. The Little Folk have been teaching me to play the ultimate music, which ranges within a single note on the audible level, and across the universe on a level we can not perceive. I have had to learn more about music than I learned in all my prior life, for this single performance. Now I have mastered the note. The effect will be small at first. Toward the culmination it will become dramatic. There will be perhaps two hours of full juxtaposition in the central zone, during which period the exchange of power-earth must be effected. If it is not—"

"Probably disaster," Stile finished. "Yet if that is the case, why should the Citizens and Adepts oppose it? Of course they will lose power, but when the alternative is to lose the entire planet—"

"They choose to believe that the threat is exaggerated. To return to the dam analogy: some, when the dam is about to burst, will dislike the inconvenience of lowering the water level, so will claim there is no danger; perhaps the sluices will pass water across their properties, damaging them only slightly as the level is lowered. So they indulge in denial, refusing to perceive the larger threat, and oppose corrective action with all their power. To us this may seem short-sighted, but few people view with equanimity the prospect of imposed sacrifice."

"And there *is* the chance the Oracle is wrong," Stile said. "Or am I also indulging in foolish denial?"

"Wrong perhaps in timing; not in essence. No one can predict the moment the dam will burst, but the end is inevitable."

"You do make a convincing case," Stile said ruefully. "When will you begin playing to juxtapose the frames?"

"As soon as I return to Phaze, after garnering your agreement to manage the transfer of computer, book of magic, and Phazite."

"Damn it, this computer murdered my other self and caused untold mischief in the personal lives of people involved with me. Why should I cooperate with it now, or believe anything it says?"

Clef shrugged. "You are a realist. You are ready to undertake personal sacrifice for the greater good, as was your alternate self, the Blue Adept."

"He knew this?" Stile demanded, remembering how the man had apparently acquiesced to his own murder.

"Yes. He was too powerful and clever to be killed without his consent. He gave up everything to make it possible for you to save the frames."

Stile hated the notion, yet he had to believe. And if the Blue Adept, with everything to live for, had made his sacrifice—how could Stile, who was the same person, do less? He would only be destroying what his other self had died to save.

"It seems I must do it," Stile said, dismayed. "I do not feel like any hero, though. How long before juxtaposition is actually achieved?"

"Allowing time for me to return to Phaze—perhaps twenty-four hours."

Time was getting short! "How much Phazite, precisely?"

"The Little Folk will have that information. In fact, they will have the Phazite ready for you. But the enemy forces will do all in their power to prevent you from moving it."

"So I'll need to transfer the book of magic and the computer first," Stile decided. "Then I can use them to facilitate the mineral transfer. Since the computer will cross when the curtain passes its location, I need only to guard it and establish a line to it. Which leaves the book— which I'd better pick up before juxtaposition so I have time to assimilate it. Maybe I can arrange to have someone else pick it up for me, since I will no doubt be watched."

"I believe so."

"Is there convenient and private transport from here to a dome?"

"Share mine. I am going to the curtain. From Phaze, you may travel freely."

"If the Adepts don't catch me."

"It will help, I must admit, if you can distract their attention from me again. With the Flute I can protect myself, but I would prefer to be unobserved."

"I suppose so. Somehow I had pictured you as a new super-Adept, able to crumble mountains and guide the dead to Heaven."

"I have only the powers of the Platinum Flute you brought me. I am myself no more than a fine musician. I suspect that any other musician of my caliber could have served this office of the Foreordained. I just happened to be the nearest available. After this is over, I hope to return to my profession in my home frame, profiting from the experience garnered here. The Mound Folk of the Platinum Demesnes are generously allowing me to keep the Flute. I was, like you, drafted for this duty; I am not temperamentally suited to the exercise of such power. I am not an Adept."

Stile found that obscurely reassuring. Clef believed that this would come out all right. "Very well. We'll step across the curtain, and I'll spell you directly to the Oracle, where they can't get at you, then spell myself elsewhere in a hurry." Stile paused, thinking of a minor aspect. "How did you get by the goblins who guard the computer?"

"One note of the Flute paralyzes them," Clef said, relaxing. "You summon your power through music; you should understand."

"I do." Stile hated to leave this comfortable chair, but felt he should get moving. "I suppose we've dawdled enough. Great events await us with gaping jaws."

"I believe we can afford to wait the night," Clef said. "There is a tube shuttle, renovated for transport to the curtain; it will whisk us there in the morning. Since no one knows you're here, you can relax. That will give the Adepts time to gather confidence that you are dead, putting them off guard."

The notion appealed tremendously. Stile had worn himself out by his trek through the caves and tunnels; he desperately needed time to recuperate. He trusted Clef. "Then give me a piece of floor to lie on, and I'll pass out."

"Allow me to delay you slightly longer, since we may not meet again," Clef said. "We played a duet together, once. It was one of the high points of my life. Here there is no magic, so the instruments can safely be used."

Stile liked this notion even better than sleep. It seemed to him that music was more restorative than rest. He brought out his treasured harmonica. Clef produced the Platinum Flute. He looked at it a moment, almost sadly. "Serrilryan," he murmured. "The werebitch. With this I piped her soul to Heaven, and for that I am grateful. I knew her only briefly, but in that time I had no better friend in Phaze."

"This is the way it is with me and Neysa the unicorn," Stile agreed. "Animals are special in Phaze."

"Extremely special." Clef put the instrument to his mouth, and from it came the loveliest note Stile could imagine.

Stile played the harmonica, making an impromptu harmony. He knew himself to be a fine player, especially with this instrument inherited from his other self—but Clef was the finest player, with the finest instrument ever made. The extemporaneous melody they formed was absolutely beautiful. Stile felt his fatigue ameliorating and his spirit strengthening. He knew of many types of gratification, such as of hunger, sex, and acclaim, but this was surely the finest of them all—the sheer joy of music.

They played for some time, both men transported by the rapture of the form. Stile doubted he would ever experience a higher pleasure than this and he knew Clef felt the same. Flute and harmonica might seem like an odd combination, but here it was perfection.

Then something strange occurred. Stile began to see the music. Not in the form of written notes, but as a force, a wash of awareness encompassing their immediate environment. It was the shape or essence of a spirit, a soul. Somehow this vibrant, joyous thing was familiar.

Stile glanced at Clef without interrupting his playing. The flutist had seen it too; he nodded marginally. Then Clef's playing changed in nature, and Stile realized that this was the music that moved souls to their resting places. Somehow the magic of the Flute was acting in this frame, moving the spirit in the room.

Whose was it? Not the werebitch's. It hovered in place, becoming more perceptible. Then the music changed again, and the spirit disappeared.

Clef abruptly stopped playing, so Stile had to stop too. "Did you recognize it?" the man asked, awed.

"No," Stile said. "It seemed familiar, but I never saw such a phenomenon in Proton."

"It was you, Stile. Your soul came out. When I realized that, I stopped. I don't want to pipe you to Heaven yet."

"Not mine!" Stile protested. "My soul was never more with me."

Clef frowned. "I beg to differ. The Little Folk have instructed me somewhat in this, as it is an important property of the Flute. There are certain keys to the recognition of souls that the music relates to. The more I attuned to you, the clearer that ghost became. It was you."

Stile shook his head. "It had to have been my double, not me."

There was a brief silence.

"You had a double," Clef said. "Your alternate self, who died to free you."

"The Blue Adept," Stile agreed, awed at the dawning notion.

"Who piped him to Heaven?"

"No one. He was murdered alone. All that remains of him is—this harmonica."

"The Flute evokes souls. But only free souls, which have not yet found their way to their destinations. Could your alternate's soul—?"

"Be in this instrument?" Stile finished. "You know, he may have found a way to stay around, not dying completely. This harmonica came to me fortuitously. Is it possible—?"

"That he chose to occupy the instrument when he made room for you in Phaze?" Clef continued.

Stile contemplated the harmonica. *"Why?* Why avoid Heaven and be trapped in a harmonica?"

Clef shrugged. "The music that issues from it is lovely. Is it better than your norm?"

"Yes. I play this better than other instruments, though I did not play this type until I got this one."

"Perhaps, then, your other self is helping you."

Again Stile considered. "To make sure his sacrifice is not wasted. Subtly guiding me. He conjured his own soul into his harmonica. Surely a feat of magic no lesser person could achieve. He has been with me all along." Stile sighed, half in amazement. "Now I must fulfill the destiny he could not. He is watching me."

"He must have been a worthy man."

"He must have been," Stile agreed. "The Lady Blue said he had not lived up to his potential. Now it seems there was more to him than she knew."

They let the matter drop. There was really not much else to say about it. Clef showed Stile to a cot, and he lay down and slept, reassured, literally, in spirit.

In the morning, refreshed, they took the private shuttle east to the curtain. This was not in the region Stile had crossed it before, in the chasm. The curtain meandered all over the planet, as he and the Lady Blue had verified on their horrendous honeymoon. This was where it traveled almost due north-south, passing a few miles east of the palace of the Oracle; Stile and the Lady had ridden rapidly north along this stretch on their way to their rendezvous with the snow-demons. That had been the key word "flame" in his poem. Now the key word was "civil"—for he was about to launch a civil war, as Adept fought unicorn and Citizen fought serf. Still to come were the key words "flute" and "earth." He could readily see how the first related, but the last remained obscure.

"Those key terms!" Stile exclaimed. "I was given a dozen words to fashion into a poem in the finals of the Tourney. Where did those words originate?"

"With the Oracle, of course. You had to be provided some hint of your destiny."

"That's what I suspected." The Oracle had been meddling in his life throughout, guiding or herding him in the prescribed direction.

Yet could he condemn it? The future of the two frames was certainly an overwhelming consideration, and the Oracle's present avenues of expression were extremely limited. There had been rewards along the way. Stile had been given Citizenship in Proton and a worthy ally in the lady robot Sheen. He had been given the Lady Blue in Phaze and such close friends as Neysa the unicorn and Kurrelgyre the werewolf. He had seen his life transformed from the routine of serfdom to the wildest adventure—and despite its hazards, he found he liked adventure. He also liked magic. When this was all over, and he had helped save or destroy Phaze—depending on viewpoint—he wanted to retire in Phaze.

But there was one other prophecy. "Is it true that Phaze will not be secure until the Blue Adept departs the frame forever?"

Clef was sober. "I fear it is true, Stile. Possession of the book of magic alone will make you dangerous. You will have great power in the new order anyway, and the book will make it so much greater that corruption is a distinct possibility. That book in *any* hands in Phaze is a long-term liability, after the crisis has been navigated. The Oracle takes no pleasure in such news—of course it is a machine without feelings anyway—but must report what it sees."

Stile loved the Lady Blue—but he also loved Phaze. She loved Phaze too; he did not want to take her from it. In the other frame there was Sheen, who loved him and whom he was slated to marry there. He did not quite love her, yet it seemed his course had been charted.

He closed his eyes, suffering in anticipation of his enormous loss. His alternate self had yielded his life for the good of Phaze; now it seemed Stile would have to yield his happiness for the same objective. He would have to leave Phaze, once the crisis had passed, and take the book with him back to Proton.

Clef looked at him, understanding his agony. "Scant comfort, I know—but I believe the Oracle selected you for this mission because you alone possessed the position, skills, and integrity to accomplish it. No other person would make the sacrifice you will—that your alternate already has made—guided solely by honor. Your fitness for the office has been proved."

"Scant comfort," Stile agreed bitterly.

"There is one additional prophecy I must relay to you immediately, before we part," Clef said. "You must marshal your troops."

"Troops? How can they juxtapose the frames?"

Clef smiled. "The Oracle prophesies the need for organized force, if Phaze is to be saved."

"And I am to organize this force? For what specific purpose?"

"That has not yet been announced."

"Well, who exactly is the enemy?"

"The Adepts and Citizens and their cohorts."

"Common folk can't fight Adepts and Citizens."

"Not folk. Creatures."

"Ah. The unicorns, werewolves, vampires—"

"Animalheads, elves, giants—"

"Dragons?"

"They are destined to join the enemy, along with the goblins."

"I begin to fathom the nature of the battle. Half the animalheads will die."

"And many others. But the alternative—"

"Is total destruction." Stile sighed. "I do not see myself as a captain of battle."

"That is nevertheless your destiny. I am foreordained to juxtapose the frames, you to equalize them. Without you, my task is useless."

"These canny riddles by the Oracle are losing their appeal. If this is not simply a matter of picking up a book of magic and moving some Phazite the Little Folk will give me, I would appreciate some rather more detailed information on how I am to use these troops to accomplish my assignment. I don't believe in violence for the sake of violence."

Clef spread his hands. "Nor do I. But the prophecy tells only what, not how. Perhaps the Elven Folk will have more useful news for you."

"Perhaps. But won't the enemy Adepts be watching for me to go to the Elven Demesnes?"

"Surely so."

"So I should avoid whatever traps they have laid for me there, for my sake and the elves' sake. I can't visit the Little Folk at this time, and I suspect I should also stay clear of the unicorns and werewolves. So it will be very difficult for me to organize an army among creatures who know me only slightly. Especially when I can't give them any concrete instructions."

"I do not envy you your position. I am secure; the Oracle is virtually immune from direct molestation. But you must perform under fire, with inadequate resources. Presumably your Game expertise qualifies you. As I said, the Oracle went to some trouble to secure the right man for this exceedingly awkward position."

"Indeed," Stile agreed, unpleased.

Now they reached the curtain. Stile doubted the Adepts would be lurking for him here; how could they know his devious route? But they would soon spot it when he started magic. He would have to move fast, before they oriented and countered.

Stile plotted his course and spells as they got out of the capsule and walked up a ramp to the surface. There was an air lock there. "The curtain is a few meters distant; best to hold our breath a few seconds," Clef said.

"You have certainly mastered the intricacies in a short time."

"The Little Folk are excellent instructors. They don't like folk my size, but they do their job well. I will be sorry to depart Phaze."

Not nearly as sorry as Stile would be! "I will make my spells rapidly, the moment we cross," Stile said. "The Flute prevents magic from being blocked, so the enemy can not interfere, but it may resist a spell by a person not holding it."

"Have no concern. I could block your magic by a single note, but don't have to. I trust you to get me to the Oracle in good order."

Stile paused in the air lock. "We may not meet again, but we shall be working together." He proffered his hand.

"Surely we shall meet," Clef said warmly, taking the hand, forgetting his own prior doubt on this score.

Then they opened the air lock, held their breath, and charged out to intersect the faintly scintillating curtain ahead. The air-lock door swung closed automatically behind them. It was camouflaged to resemble an outcropping of rock; Stile had passed it during his honeymoon without ever noticing.

They stepped through together. The bleak, barren desert became lush wilderness. Stile played a few bars on the harmonica, summoning his magic. Now he was conscious of the spirit of his other self within the instrument, facilitating his performance. No doubt he had been able to practice magic much more readily and effectively because of this help than would otherwise have been possible. "Adepts be deaf; computer get Clef," Stile sang. He was trying to conceal his magic from the awareness of the enemy; he wasn't sure that aspect would work.

Clef vanished. Stile played some more, restoring the expended potency of the magic. This time he was conscious of its source, Phazite, with an ambience of magic like a magnetic field; the music intensified and focused this on Stile, as a magnifying glass might do with a beam of sunshine. The transfer of Phazite to Proton-frame would diminish this ambience, robbing his spells of half their potency. Still, Phaze would be a magic realm—and of course he would probably leave it, so as to make it safe. "Conduct me whole," he sang, "to the East Pole."

He splashed in water. Naturally that was why this region was not a tourist attraction. The water was foul too; the universal Proton pollution was slopping through. All the more reason for tourists to stay clear!

Stile trod water and played his music again. "Set it up solo: a floating holo."

A buoyed holographic transceiver appeared. Stile had really strained to get the concept detail on this one. This was to be his contact station, so that he could stay in touch with the two frames from either side. Because it was at the deserted, unpleasant East Pole, it should be secure for some time from the depredations of other Adepts or Citizens. He was sure that by this time the enemy Adepts had booby-trapped his fixture at the West Pole and would not expect this alternate ploy. Satisfied, Stile played more music. "Take me down to see Brown."

He arrived at the wooden castle of the Brown Adept, feeling nauseous. Self-transport never was comfortable, and he had done it twice rapidly.

In a moment the pretty, brown-haired, brown-eyed child dashed up to him. "Oh, Blue," she cried. "I was so afraid they had hurt thee!"

Stile smiled wanly. "I had the same fear for thee. Thou alone didst side with me, of all the Adepts."

She scowled cutely. "Well, they did tie me up with a magic rope or something. I was going to get a golem to loose me, but then Yellow came and let me go. She's real pretty in her potion-costume! She said all the others were after thee, and she really didn't like it but couldn't go against her own kind. Is that what I'm doing?"

"Thou art helping save Phaze from disaster," he assured her.

"Oh, goody!" she exclaimed, clapping her hands.

Stile had a second thought about using Brown as an ally. Could a child have proper responsibility? Yet he didn't seem to have much choice. She had at least had the courage to oppose the other Adepts, which was more than Yellow had had. "I need thy help in an important capacity," he said. "There may be hard work and even danger."

"If Phaze is in trouble, I'm already in danger," she said brightly.

"Aye. The other Adepts prefer to risk disaster later, for the sake of power now. I must do something that will make magic less effective, but will save Phaze for future centuries. Then must I leave Phaze."

"Leave Phaze!" she exclaimed, horrified. "I was only just getting to know thee!"

"I do not wish to leave, but a prophecy of the Oracle suggests Phaze will not be safe until I do. I love Phaze too much to hurt it by remaining."

A soulful tear rolled down her cheek. "Oh, Blue—I like this not!"

"I fear the Lady Blue will like it even less," Stile said, choking somewhat himself. "Neither will my friend Neysa the unicorn. But what must be, must be. Now must I cross the curtain before the other Adepts spot me. They tried to trap me in the goblins' demesnes, and now that I escaped, they will be attacking me anywhere they find me. In any event, there is something I must fetch in Proton-frame. So must I ask thee to be my coordinator in Phaze."

Her young brow furrowed. "What is this?"

"The creatures of Phaze must be warned. They must be told that the Oracle predicts disaster if certain things be not done, and that the Blue Adept is trying to do these things and may need their help. That the other Adepts are trying to prevent this program from being implemented and may attack any creatures who help me. Canst thou go to the creatures and tell them?"

"Oh, sure, I can send my golems," she said. "If they are not stopped by magic, they will speak the message."

"Excellent. I have set up a spell to keep thee in touch, so that thou canst check with me across the curtain. When I have what I need, I will return."

"I hope thy business there takes not long. This frightens me, Blue."

"It frightens me too! But I think we can get through." Stile played his harmonica, then sang: "Create a crystal ball, for Brown Adept to call."

The ball appeared. Stile presented it to her. "Speak to this when thou must reach me. I will answer if I can."

She smiled, her spirit rebounding quickly at the prospect of this new toy. "That should be fun!"

"Now must I go," Stile said. He sang a routine spell to take him to a little-used section of the curtain, then stepped across into a maintenance hall in Proton.

Soon he was in touch with Sheen and riding with her in a private Citizen capsule. "What is the present state of my fortune?" he inquired.

"Mellon has manipulated it into about sixty kilograms."

"Sixty kilos of Protonite? Already he's doubled it?"

"He's one of my friends," she reminded him. That meant Mellon had access to information not generally available to others, including Citizens—such as what supposedly random numbers might be generated by the Game Computer. That would of course be an enormous advantage. Stile did not like all of the implications, but decided not to inquire about the details.

"However," she said, "several things are disturbing the Citizens and making mischief for you. It may be difficult in the next few hours."

"It may indeed," he agreed. "The countdown for the juxtaposition of frames has commenced. I've already set most of the other Adepts against me, and soon the same will happen with most of the Citizens."

"Yes. First there is the matter of your rapid increase in fortune. They are concerned where it will stop, understandably. Second, they don't like your designating me as your heir. The panel approved it, but now many more Citizens are becoming aware of it. A robot with such a fortune would be awkward. Third, there is a rumor you mean to destroy the society of Proton. That notion is not at all popular."

"I should think not," Stile agreed. "As it happens, they are not far wrong."

"Will you update me, briefly? I fear things will complicate rapidly, now that you have reappeared, and I lack the living capacity to adapt to totally changed situations. Some Citizens even expressed hope you were dead, and in that hope their action was held in abeyance."

"So now they may seek to render me dead," Stile said. "I thought Citizenship would alleviate my problems somewhat, but they have only intensified. Very well—you get me to the Game Computer, and I'll fill you in."

"What do you want with the Game Computer?"

"It has the book of magic that will make me instantly more powerful than any person in Phaze has been before. I'll need it to protect myself from the massed power of all the other Adepts and to facilitate the transfer of Phazite across the curtain. Here it will be Protonite, with scientific energy instead of magical energy. Then the frames will separate forever, and the curtain will be gone."

She was quick to catch on. "Which world will you be in, then, Stile?"

Stile sighed. "You know I want to be in Phaze, with the Lady Blue. But I am of Proton, and there is a prophecy that tells me to get clear of Phaze. So I will be here."

He thought she would be pleased, but she was not. "The Lady Blue is to be widowed again?" she asked sharply.

"I could bring her here to Proton. But she is of Phaze; I fear it would destroy her to leave it forever. I don't think she would come here anyway, because here I am to marry you."

"So it is my fault you have to widow her?"

How had he gotten into this? "It is the fault of fate. I simply am not destined to be happy after my job is done." Then he bit his tongue. What an insult he had given Sheen!

"I will put in for reprogramming, so she can come here. You do not need to marry me."

Stile refused to take the bait. It was surely poisoned. Sheen might be less complicated than a living woman, but she did have depths. "I will marry you. It is the way it has to be."

"Have you informed the Lady Blue of this?" she inquired coldly.

"Not yet." *There* was a dreadful task!

They were silent for a while. Stile felt the weight of the harmonica in his pocket and brought it out for contemplation. "I wish you could come out," he said to it.

Sheen looked at him questioningly.

"My other self's soul is in this instrument," Stile explained. "Clef's Flute evoked it. Apparently the original Blue Adept conjured his spirit into his favorite possession. It helped me play the harmonica beyond my natural ability, and maybe won a round of the Tourney for me. So he helped me—but I can't help him. He's dead."

"This soul—you saw it in Phaze?"

"No. In Proton."

"But there's no magic in Proton."

Stile nodded thoughtfully. "I'm getting so used to magic, I'm forgetting where I am. That Platinum Flute can't evoke spirits in Proton—yet I swear it did. We thought maybe some magic leaked through, but that couldn't really happen."

"Unless this imbalance you talk of is getting worse. The fabric is starting to tear."

"That could be. The Flute did reach across to shake the mountains of Proton and perhaps also to give me the dream-vision of Clef's journey to the Little Folk. Juxtaposition of one kind or another is occurring; the boundaries are fogging. Which is why action is required now. I wish there were some way to restore my other self to life. Then he could go back to Phaze, his job done."

"Why not? All he needs is a body."

"Like that of a robot or android? They can't function in Phaze."

"Perhaps a magic body, then. One that resembles you. With his soul in it—"

"Ridiculous. You assume that such things can be assembled like the parts of a robot." But Stile wondered. What was a person, other than a body with a soul?

"If I had a soul, I'd be real," Sheen said wistfully.

Stile had given up arguing that case. "The Brown Adept animates golems, but they're made of wood. Robots are made of metal and plastic. Androids are living flesh, but imperfect; they are stupid and often clumsy. If it were possible to fashion a golem made of flesh, with a mind like yours and a human spirit—wouldn't that be a person?"

"Of course it would," she said.

Stile decided. "Have your friends look into the matter. It's a far shot, but if there were any way to restore my other self to some semblance of life, I owe him that. If he died to save Phaze, it is right that he be restored to it."

"If you have any female souls floating around looking for a host, send one to me."

Stile took her hand. Her fingers were as soft and warm as those of any living person. "I regard the soul as the essence of self. If you hosted someone else's soul, you would become that person. I prefer you as you are."

"But you can't love me as I am."

"I can't love anyone other than the Lady Blue. When this business is done, I will accord to you whatever emotion I am capable of feeling for any woman, flesh or metal. You deserve better than this, I know."

"Half love is better than none," she said. "And if you restore your other self in Phaze, will he love the Lady Blue?"

"He's her husband!" Stile exclaimed. "Of course he loves her!"

"Then why did he give her up to you?"

"To save Phaze. It was an act of supreme sacrifice."

"I am a machine. I don't appreciate the delicate nuances of human conscience and passion as a human being can. To me it seems more likely that he found himself in an untenable situation, as do you with me, and simply opted out."

"That's an appalling notion!" But it also carried an insidious conviction. Suppose the Blue Adept, aware of the approaching crisis, knowing he had to make way for another, and perhaps no longer in love with his wife—

"I wish I could meet your other self," Sheen said.

"You are a creature of science, he of magic," Stile said. "Such meetings are difficult, even when both parties are alive. You are stuck with me."

She smiled, letting it go. "And we do have more serious business than such idle conjecturing." She put the holo on receive, and a call was waiting.

It was from Citizen Merle. "Ah, so you're back, Stile! Let me show you me in serf-guise. Private line, please."

"Merle, I'm with Sheen—"

"She knows that," Sheen said, setting up the nonintercept coding.

Merle stripped away her clothing with elegant motions. She had an excellent body. "Stile, beware," she murmured. "There are plots afoot to slay you."

Stile was startled by the contrast between her actions and her words. "I thought you had seduction in mind, Merle."

"I do, I do! I can't seduce you if you're dead, however."

There was that. "Merle, I don't want to deceive you. I'm not interested in—"

"I understand you have business with the Game Computer."

How much did she know? "Do you intend to blackmail me?"

"By no means. You happen to be unblackmailable. But I might help you, if you caused me to be amenable."

"If I were amenable to your design, Merle, my fiancée here might get difficult."

"I suspect she would rather have you alive, well, and victorious. You see, some Citizens have the notion that you represent a threat to their welfare, so they have instituted a push to have your Citizenship revoked."

"Revoked! Is that possible?" Stile felt his underpinnings loosening. He had assumed his Citizenship was irrevocable.

"Anything is possible, by a majority vote of the kilos attending the evening business meeting. You will be on tonight's agenda. You will need whatever help you can get."

Stile glanced at Sheen. "This is news to you?"

"I knew something was developing, sir, but not that it had progressed to this extent."

"Citizens have avenues of communication not available to machines," Merle said. "I assure you the threat is genuine, and the vote may well go against you. Citizens, unfortunately, have very narrow definitions of self-interest." She smiled, turning her now-naked body suggestively. She had an excellent talent for display. "I will encourage my associates to support you, if you come to me. This could shift the balance. It is little enough I ask. Are you quite sure you can't be tempted?"

Sheen, meanwhile, had been busy on another private line. Now she glanced up. "It is true, sir," she said. "My friends verify that in the past hour a general disquiet has formed into a pattern of opposition. The moment news flashed that you had reappeared in Proton, momentum gathered. The projected vote is marginally against you. Merle's support could save you."

"Listen to her, Stile," Merle said. "The scales are finely balanced at the moment, but the full thrust of your opposition has not yet manifested. Sheen has more riding on this than her own possible Citizenship. If your Citizenship is revoked, your tenure will end and you will have to leave Proton. The prospect for her friends would decline drastically, perhaps fatally, incongruous as the term may be in that application."

"How much do you know, Merle?" Stile asked tightly.

"Stile, I research what intrigues me. I have learned much about you in the past few hours. This enhances my respect for you. It is a thing of mine to take a piece of those I respect. This is a harmless foible, and I always give fair return. Come to me and I will help you."

She had him in a difficult spot. If she knew about the self-willed machines and possibly about Stile's mission to restore parallelism in the separating frames, she could certainly cause him much mischief.

"Sir, I think you should go to her," Sheen said.

Stile found himself athwart a dilemma. He had told Mellon to arrange a private bet, to the limit of his available finances, that he would not be seduced by Merle. He did not care to lose that bet, for such a loss would wipe him out. But if her support was all that guaranteed his continuing Citizenship, he could lose everything despite winning the bet. He was between Scylla and Charybdis, the devil and the deep sea, the rock and the hard place.

"I am frankly surprised you do not heed your metal fiancée," Merle said. "She does seem to know what's best for you."

Stile's flash of rage was stifled by Sheen's imploring look. He decided to meet with Merle and try to explain. Maybe he could win through. "Give me your address."

She gave the code, and Sheen changed course. The book of magic would have to wait a little.

There was another call. This one was for Sheen, from Mellon. "We have a delivery for you," he said. "Cosmetics for our employer."

"I don't need—" Stile started to protest. But he was cut off by a glance from the serf.

"Thank you," Sheen said. "I'll pick them up at the nearest delivery tube when we leave the capsule." She gave him Merle's code, and the connection broke.

"Do I look that haggard?" Stile asked plaintively. "I had a good night's rest."

"Mellon is not concerned about your appearance. Obviously something is afoot. Maybe the Lady Citizen has placed an order for an intoxicating or sexually compelling drug, and this is the counteragent."

"Maybe," Stile agreed morosely. "Sheen, Merle is pretty enough in her rejuvenated state, and I'm sure she has a good mind and lots of experience. But I'm simply not interested in the sort of liaison she desires. How do I get out of this one without imperiling my Citizenship?"

"What you are interested in is not very important," she said. "Merle does not want any romance; she merely wants an act of sex to add to her collection. The practical thing is for you to give it to her."

"And lose my bet," Stile said.

Sheen looked startled. "Oh, my—I'm starting to think like a person! I forgot all about that! Of course you can't oblige her." She seemed relieved.

"If I oblige anyone in that way, it will be you."

"Any time."

"After we're decently married."

"It's not a decent marriage."

The capsule arrived, sparing him further comment. They got out at a small private terminal. From here there was access to three small domes, one of which was Merle's.

Sheen went to the delivery chute and punched the coding for Mellon's package. A small vial fell into her hand. Her brow furrowed as she brought the item back. "This is no cosmetic, sir. It's—" She broke off. "Let's move quickly, sir."

Suddenly gas hissed into the room from barred vents. Sheen launched herself at the entrance to Merle's dome. It was locked closed.

"I don't have the facility to analyze this gas," she cried. "But I'll bet it's not cleaning fog. Breathe this, sir." She opened the vial, holding it under his nose.

Vapor puffed out. Stile took the vial, sniffing it as the first waft of the other gas reached him. The vial's vapor was sweet and pleasant; the other gas was sour and stinging.

Sheen returned to the locked door. She opened her front cabinet, the left breast swinging out on hinges to reveal an array of small tools. Even in this crisis, Stile marveled at the completely womanish texture of that breast, when in fact it was a mere facade. Robotry was quite sophisticated.

In a moment Sheen had burned through the lock with a tiny laser unit and had the passage open. Stile hurried through. Sheen shut the door behind them, blocking off the gas, and closed up her breast cabinet. She was whole and normal and soft again.

Stile felt woozy and sick. The antidote in the vial had helped, but that poison gas was nasty stuff. Someone had tried to exterminate him!

Merle appeared. She was wearing a translucent negligee that did wonders for a body that hardly needed them. Stile noticed but hardly cared. He suffered himself to be led inside the Citizen's dome.

"I knew they were going to try something," Merle said. "I thought it would be at the Game Annex. I tried to get you here to safety, but they were too quick. I couldn't say anything on the holo; even a private line is only as private as the technology behind it."

"Our staff forwarded the antidote, sir," Sheen told her.

Stile sat in the comfortable chair where they had placed him, lacking initiative to do more than listen.

"My staff has found a better neutralizer," Merle said. She brought a breathing mask. "Use this, Stile." She fitted it over his face.

Immediately his head began to clear and his stricken body recovered.

"The official indication is a malfunction in the cleaning apparatus," Merle continued. "It's not supposed to fog when anyone is there, and this time the wrong chemicals were used. We won't be able to trace it, but I know the cause. There are activist Citizens who want you out of the way, Stile; I fear this is but the first attempt. You should be safe here, however."

Stile removed the breathing mask and smiled weakly. "I thought you had another notion, Merle."

"Oh, I do, I do. We have been through this before. But I do like you personally, Stile, and wish you well. You're the most refreshing thing to appear on the scene in some time. Fortunately the two notions are not incompatible."

"I fear they are, Merle. You have helped me get into a difficult situation." Stile's head had cleared, but his body remained weak; it was easier to talk than to act. He believed he could trust this woman.

"Do tell me!" she urged. "I love challenges."

"Are we private here?"

"Of course. I am neither as young nor as naïve as I try to appear."

"Will you keep my confidence?"

"About the liaison? Of course not! That must be known, or it doesn't count."

"About whatever I may tell you of my situation."

"I can't guarantee that, Stile. I know something about your situation already."

"Maybe you should tell me what you know, then."

"You are known as the Blue Adept in the other frame. Oh, yes, I have been to Phaze; my other self lacked rejuvenation and modern medicine and died a few years back of natural complications, freeing me. But magic is not for me; I remained there only a few hours and retreated to the safety of my dome here. The germs there are something fierce! I do, however, have a fold of the curtain passing through my property. I pay a harpy well to update me periodically on Phaze developments. This is how I learned more of you, once my interest in you was roused. You have been honeymooning with your lovely Phaze wife, but Adepts have been laying snares for you, until recently you disappeared into the demesnes of the goblins. My informant thought you dead, though she reports a dragon and a hawk emerged safely and flew rapidly southeast, eluding pursuit by Adept sendings. Evidently you survived by crossing the curtain. You seem to be a figure of some importance in Phaze—and perhaps in Proton too, judging by this assassination attempt."

"What could you pay a harpy to serve you?" Stile asked, intrigued by this detail.

"She loves blood-soaked raw meat, but is too old and frail to catch it herself."

"The others of her flock would provide," Stile said, thinking of the harpy attack Clef had weathered upon his entry into Phaze. How important that entry had turned out to be!

"This one is a loner. No flock helps her."

"Is she by chance your other self?"

Merle stiffened, then relaxed. "Oh, you have a sharp tongue, Stile! No, it doesn't work that way, or I couldn't cross. My other self was exactly like me, only she seemed older. She did befriend the harpy, and when she died I assumed the burden of that friendship. It is not easy to get along with a harpy! Now will you tell me what I do not know about yourself?"

"Will you accept that information in lieu of the sexual liaison?"

"No, of course not, Stile. I accept it in exchange for the protection I am offering you here, and for the information I am giving you about the Citizen plot against you."

She would not be swayed from her objective! She wanted another notch for her garter. He would have to give her the full story and hope it would persuade her to help him without insisting on the liaison. She might be displeased to learn about his bet in that connection, but at least it was no affront to her pride.

There was a chime and glimmer of light in the air. "That's my holo," Merle said. "Call for you, Stile, blocked by my privacy intercept."

"Better let it through," he said. "The enemy Citizens know I'm here anyway."

The picture formed. It was the Brown Adept. "The creatures don't believe me, Blue," she said tearfully. "They think I'm with the bad Adepts, trying to fool them. They are attacking my golems."

Stile sighed. He should have known. "What would it take to convince them?"

"Only thee thyself, Blue. Or maybe one of thy close friends, or the Lady Blue—"

"No! The Lady Blue must remain guarded by the unicorns. The Adepts will be watching her."

"Maybe Neysa. She's friends with everybody."

"The Herd Stallion won't let her go." Stile hardly objected to the care provided for Neysa in her gravid state. Then he had an idea. "Thy demesnes are near to the range of the werewolves, are they not? Kurrelgyre's Pack?"

She brightened. "Sure, Blue. They come here all the time, hunting. But they don't believe me either."

"But if Kurrelgyre believed, his Pack would help. The other animals would believe him."

"I guess so," she agreed dubiously. "But thou wouldst have to tell him thyself."

"I will," Stile said. "Give me half an hour."

Brown's smile was like moonlight. "Oh, thank thee, Blue!"

"Nay, thank *thee*, Brown. It is an important service thou dost here."

"Gee." The happy image faded.

"So that's the Brown Adept," Sheen said. "A child. A cute child."

"She's a full sorceress, though," Stile said. "Her golems are tough creatures." He remembered his encounter with the golem shaped in his own image. He was glad to have those wooden men on his side, this time! He turned to Merle. "Now I have to explain to you my reason for not wishing to have this liaison, then hurry across your section of the curtain to straighten things out in Phaze."

"No need to explain," Merle said. "I can see you are busy, with people depending on you. I'll chalk this one up to experience."

"I do need your help," Stile said. "So I want you to understand—"

"You shall have my help, Stile. If that sweet child believes in you, so must I. I'm sure she is not asking any quid pro quo."

"Well, she may want a ride on a unicorn," Stile said, wondering whether he could believe this abrupt change of heart on her part. "But you still deserve to know—"

"About your secret bet," Merle said. "That's what made it such a challenge, Stile. But if you lose your fortune and can't do what you need to, that brown-eyed child will suffer, and I don't want that on my withered conscience. I'll show you to my corner of the curtain; that will get you neatly past the ambush awaiting you outside."

Stile stood, taking her hand. "I really appreciate this, Merle."

She drew him in for a kiss. "I think it was that child's thee's and thy's. You did it too, when you answered her. Somehow that melts me. I haven't been this foolish in decades."

They were before the curtain. It scintillated across Merle's huge round bouncy bed. No coincidence, that; she probably had a demon lover in the other frame. Beyond, Stile could discern the slope of a wooded hillside.

"How will I rejoin you?" Sheen asked.

"You'll come with me," Stile decided. "By now the enemy Citizens know how useful you are; they'll be trying to take you out too." He picked her up, strode across the bed, and willed himself through the curtain.

He stood on the forest slope, the inert robot in his arms. In Phaze, she was defunct. "Take this form of Sheen's to the wolves' demesnes," he sang. This was simplified; what he intended was for them both to travel there.

They arrived in good order. The wolves were snoozing in the vicinity of a recent kill, while several of the cubs growled at a golem they had treed. Half a dozen roused and charged Stile, converting to men and women as they drew near.

"Greetings, Blue Adept," Kurrelgyre exclaimed, recognizing him. "I see thou hast found a defective golem."

Stile glanced down at Sheen, startled. "I suppose I have, friend. In the other frame she is my fiancée."

"Ah, a bitch in every frame! Dost thou bring her here for animation by the Brown Adept?"

Again Stile was startled. Would such magic work? He would have to inquire. "I came to advise thee that I am at odds with the other Adepts, who seek to slay me. Thus I can not stay here long, lest they discover me and strike. Only the Brown Adept is with me, and I have asked her to spread warning to the tribes of the creatures of Phaze, whose help I may be needing soon."

"Ooooww!" Kurrelgyre howled, glancing at the tree. "I turned her down—"

"I know," Stile cut in. "I should have prepared better. Things have been very rushed. Now must I beg thee to help me by helping her. If thy wolves will go with her golems, to give them credence—"

"Aye, immediately," Kurrelgyre agreed. He made a signal at the tree, and the cubs quickly retreated, allowing the golem to come down. "Had I but realized before—"

Stile clapped him on the shoulder. "I thank thee. Now must I flee." There was a wrenching. Oops—he had made an inadvertent rhyme, with Sheen leaning against him. Quickly he took better hold of her and willed himself to the Brown Demesnes. It worked; he landed neatly in the foyer of the wooden castle. The giant golem on guard did a double take, but managed to recognize him before clubbing him, and in a moment the Brown Adept was there.

"That's not one of mine!" she exclaimed, seeing the inert Sheen in his arms.

"This is Sheen, my Proton fiancée. She was with me when thou didst call a little while ago. She'll be all right when we cross the curtain. I just talked to Kurrelgyre, and the wolves will cooperate. Instruct thy golems; a wolf will go with each."

"Oh, goody!" But her attention was focused on Sheen. "I don't usually animate metal, but I can when I try. Of course her personality might not be the same—"

Stile had not intended to get into this now, but again he was intrigued. "Sheen always wanted to come to Phaze, but she's scientific. Thy golems are magic, and won't operate in Proton. I don't think it could work."

"Let me try, Blue. If I animate her, thou wilt not have to carry her."

"I'm in a hurry, Brown. The hostile Adepts could spot me at any moment. There isn't time—"

"Why dost thou not want to animate her here?" she asked with the direct naïveté of a child.

That stopped Stile. The Lady Blue, his wife, was in Phaze, yet she could cross to Proton, where she had met Sheen. There really was no conflict. "How fast canst thou do it?"

"She is full-formed." Brown squinted at Sheen's torso critically. "Very full-formed. I have only to lay on my hands and concentrate. Most of the time I spend fashioning a golem is carving it to shape before animation."

"Try it, then. But if she is not herself—I mean, the golems can be—"

"Then will I deanimate her." Brown leaned over Sheen, where Stile placed her on the ground, and ran her hands over the body. Then she pressed her fingers across the face.

Sheen stirred. Her eyes opened.

Stile stood back, abruptly nervous. Golems were nonliving things, soulless ones animated only by magic. Brown's ability to make them function was phenomenal—but what monster in Sheen's image might rouse here?

Sheen sat up, shaking her head. She saw Stile. "Oh, we're back," she said. "I must have been set back by the deactivation. I feel funny."

She was herself! "Thou dost know me?" Stile asked, hardly daring to believe. A new golem would not have knowledge of him.

"Of course I know you, Stile! I'm not that forgetful, unless my memory banks get erased. And this child is the one who called you on holo. She—" Sheen broke off, surprised. "What is she doing here?"

"This is Phaze," Stile said. "The Brown Demesnes."

Sheen blinked. "I don't believe that is possible. I can't function across the curtain; you know that."

"I animated thee," the child said. "Thou art now a golem."

Sheen looked around, taking in the scene. She saw the wooden walls of the castle, and the golems standing near. "May I inspect this region?"

Stile was becoming nervous about the time. "Do it quickly, Sheen. Thou wilt be inert again if the enemy Adepts discover our presence here and attack." He was almost fidgeting.

"I think they are distracted by other events," Brown said. "They know not what my golems are doing."

Sheen completed her survey extremely quickly. "There is no dome. The air is natural. This *is* the other world. Will I remain animate? I feel no different."

"Yes," the Brown Adept said. "My golems never die, unless they are destroyed." Tactfully, she did not mention her ability to turn them off.

"Yet I am not alive," Sheen concluded sadly.

"That is beyond the power of magic," Brown agreed.

"And of science," Stile added. "Now must we go." He took Sheen's hand and sang a spell to take them to a private section of the curtain. One thing he had done during his honeymoon was survey likely crossing places.

They landed in a secluded glade in the Purple Mountain foothills. "Now that's an experience!" Sheen exclaimed. "It really *is* a magic land."

"It really is," Stile agreed. "Art thou able to cross the curtain by thyself now?"

Sheen tried, but could not. "I am not alive," she repeated. "I have no power to do what living creatures do."

Stile took her hand again and willed them across. They stood in a vehicle storage garage. "Do you remember?" he asked.

"I remember Phaze," she said. "I have not changed. Only your language has changed."

"So there is no loss of continuity as you shift from magic to science."

"None at all. I am the same. I wish I were not."

"Now let's get that book of magic before we are diverted again. We're close to a Game Annex terminal, by no coincidence. I can contact the Game Computer privately there."

"Let me do it," Sheen said. "There may be another ambush."

"You're my fiancée. I shouldn't let you take all the risks."

"Without you, I am nothing. Without me, you are a leading Citizen and Adept, capable of saving Phaze and helping my friends. Stand back, sir."

Stile smiled and shrugged. "Give me the book of magic," she said to the Game-access terminal, adding the code.

"Why?" the Computer asked.

"The Blue Adept means to return it to Phaze and there use it to abate the crisis."

"One moment," the machine said. "While it is on the way, will you accept a message for the Blue Adept?"

"Yes."

"A consortium of opposition Citizens, interested in profiting from a necessary action, proffers this wager: the entire amount of Citizen Stile's fortune at the time, that he will not survive until the start of tonight's business meeting of Citizens."

"I'll take that bet!" Stile called, realizing that he could not lose it. If he died prematurely, all was lost anyway; if he lived, his fortune and power would be doubled again. Double or nothing, right when he wanted it.

"Citizen Stile accepts the wager," Sheen said. "If he dies, his estate will be liquidated and assigned to the consortium. If he appears at that meeting alive, his fortune will in that instant be doubled, and he will immediately be able to wield the full leverage of it."

"The wager is so entered. The doubling cube has been turned." The Game Computer made a bleep that was its way of coughing apologetically. "I have no part of this threat other than serving as a conduit for the wager. It was not necessary for the Citizen to be concerned about an ambush on my premises. Neither am I permitted to warn him of any potential threat immediately beyond my premises."

"That's warning enough," Stile muttered. "Move out, Sheen!"

Sheen paused only long enough to pick up the package the delivery slot delivered: the book of magic.

They fled down a hall. "Weapons are not permitted on Game premises unless part of a designated Game," the Game Computer announced.

"It is not warning us, just making a public announcement— officially," Stile said with a grim smile. "Is the Game Computer really one of your friends?"

"Yes," she said.

A man appeared in the hall ahead. He looked like an ordinary serf, but he stood before them with a suggestive posture of readiness.

"That's a robot," Stile said.

"That's a killer machine," Sheen agreed. "Stile, I am a dual-purpose robot, designed for defense and personality. That is a specialized attack vehicle. I am not equipped to handle it. You must flee it immediately; I can delay it only a moment."

Stile dived for a panel. He tore open a section of the wall where he knew power lines ran. There they were, brightly colored cables, intended to be quite clearly coded for stupid maintenance personnel. He took a red one in both hands and yanked. It ripped free as the enemy robot came near. "Get well away, Sheen!" he cried.

"Stile, you'll electrocute yourself!" she cried in horror.

Now he took hold of a white cable. This, too, tore from its mooring, which was a magnetic clamp.

As the killer robot reached for him, Stile jammed both raw cable ends at its body. Power arced and crackled, electrifying the machine. The robot collapsed.

"You took a terrible chance!" Sheen admonished him as they hurried on. "You could have been electrocuted just pulling those cables out."

"The power was cut off, to free the magnetic clamps," Stile said. "The danger was apparent, not real."

"How could you know that?" She sounded flustered.

"The Game Computer is one of your friends," he reminded her.

"Oh." For her friends stood ready to help him, covertly. The Computer had cut off power, then restored it. How could such a brief collusion ever be spotted? Stile knew exactly how to use the assistance of the self-willed machines when he needed to. Fortunately the specialized killer machine had been stupid.

The passage led to the minicar racing track, a favorite Game of the younger set. Stile had won many such races. His small size gave him an advantage in these little vehicles. However, this time he only wanted to bypass the cars and reach the exit passage.

A man burst into the premises. This one was a genuine human serf—but he had a laser pistol. This was evidently the one the Game Computer had warned away. Unfortunately, outside the actual Games, the Computer had little power. It could protest and warn, not usually enforce. It could summon guards—but if it did so in this case, the other Citizens would be alerted, and that was not to Stile's interest. Stile would have to fight this one out alone; the Computer had helped all it could.

"Sheen, get out of here," he whispered urgently. "Use the service passages and airless sections to confound human pursuit. Get the book of magic across the curtain."

"But I must protect you!" she protested.

"You can protect me best by getting away from me right now. I can do tricks alone that I can't with company. Meet me later—" He paused to decide on a suitably unlikely place. "Meet me at Merle's dome. They've booby-trapped that once; they won't expect me to go near it again. If you prefer, wait for me just beyond the curtain, in Phaze—oh, I forget, you can't cross by yourself! Maybe Merle will help you cross."

She did not argue further. "I love you." She faded away.

Stile jumped into the nearest car and accelerated it into the main playing grid. Ordinarily he would have had to obtain license from the Game Computer to play, but Citizens were exempt from such rules. The pursuing man, however, was a serf; he had to honor this rule, or the Computer would close down the Game, apply a stasis field, and arrest him. *Here* the Computer had power, when there was a valid pretext to exert it. As it was, the Computer knew the man was up to mischief, and had already warned him about carrying the pistol.

The various ramps, intersections, and passing zones were arrayed in three-dimensional intricacy, so that the total driving area was many kilometers long despite the confinement of the dome. Stile was well familiar with this layout.

The armed man had been stalking him cautiously. Now the man had to get into another car to keep up. To do this, he had to get a partner and enlist in the Game. But he was prepared for this; a henchman got into another car and started the pursuit. Theoretically, they were chasing each other; actually, they were both after Stile.

Stile smiled grimly. These would-be killers would have more of a chase than they liked. They were up against an expert Gamesman: a Tourney winner, in fact.

Stile could shoot his car through the maze of paths. He could exit quickly. But that would only mean the armed man would follow him. It was better to handle this situation here, where the terrain favored Stile, and then escape cleanly.

A beam of light passed to Stile's right. The armed man had fired his laser, missing because of the difficulty of aiming when the cars were going in different directions at different speeds. But the shot was close enough so that Stile knew the man had some skill; he would score if given a better opportunity. Now the Computer could not shut down the Game, though the laser shot had provided sufficient pretext, because when the cars stopped, the assassin would score on Stile.

Stile swung around a turn, putting a ramp between himself and the pursuer. He checked the minicar, but there was nothing in it he could throw. He would have to maneuver until he could find a way to put the man out of commission.

The problem was, these vehicles were small but safe. They would not travel fast enough to leave the track, and the set was designed to prevent collisions. Such Games were supposed to seem far more dangerous than they were in fact. Stile might scare his opponent, but could not actually hurt him with the car. Still, there were ways.

Stile slowed his car, allowing the man to catch up somewhat. Then, just as the man was leveling his laser, Stile accelerated into a loop, going up and over and through. The man, caught by surprise, had to accelerate his own car and hang on. The cars could not fall, even if they stalled upside down at the top of a loop, and the automatic seat belts would hold the occupants fast. The man evidently did not know that.

Stile moved on into a roller-coaster series, going up and down at increasing velocity. The man followed, looking uncomfortable. He was fairly solid, and his belly lightened and settled with each change of elevation. That could start the queasies. Then Stile looped into a tunnel with a good lead, emerged to spin into a tight turn, and crossed over the other track just as the pursuer shot out of the tunnel.

Stile had removed his robe. He dropped it neatly over the man's head.

The man reacted violently, clawing at the voluminous material that the wind plastered to his face, while the car continued along the track. Stile slowed his own car, letting the other catch up. Just as the man managed to get free of the robe, Stile jumped from one car to the other, having also circumvented the seat restraint. He caught the man's neck in a nerve-strangle, rendering him instantly unconscious, and took the laser pistol from his hand. Then he jumped back to his own car and accelerated away. Such jumps from car to car were supposed to be impossible, but Stile was a skilled gymnast, able to do what few others could contemplate.

Now he zoomed for the exit. He had left his robe behind; it made identification too easy for his assassination-minded pursuers. Still, being a serf was not enough camouflage. There would be other assassins on the prowl for him, closing on this region. The majority of Citizens, like the Adepts, seemed to be against him; they had tremendous resources that would be overpowering once they got the focus. He needed to get far away from here in a hurry.

Could he retreat to the curtain, as he had done when the Adepts had had him pinned in the cavern? No, they would be watching the segments of it through which he had entered Proton this time. He had to surprise them.

Camouflage seemed to be the answer—but what kind?

Already Stile was making his decision. The most common and least noticed entities in Proton were machines, ranging from self-propelled hall-brushers to humanoid robots. Some were sophisticated emulations of individuality like Sheen, but most were cruder. Stile paused at a food machine and got some nutri-taffy; this he used to shape bulges at his knees and elbows, and to change the configuration of his neck and crotch. He now resembled a small, sexless menial humanoid robot that had been used in a candy kitchen. He walked somewhat stiffly and set a fixed smile on his face, since this grade of machine lacked facial mobility. Stile was, of course, a practiced mimic. He was unable to eliminate his natural body heat, but hoped no one would check him that closely.

It worked. Serfs passed him without paying any attention. There was a checkpoint guarded by two brute androids, but they were looking for a man, not a taffy-odored machine. Stile walked stiffly by, unchallenged.

He was probably safe now, but he did not gamble. He continued his robot walk to a transport capsule and rode to the vicinity of Merle's dome, then took the service entrance. Even here there was no challenge. Functionaries were constantly in and out of Citizens' estates on myriad errands.

But Merle was expecting him. "Stile, I want you to know I sincerely regret this," she said. "Extreme pressure has been put on me. Believe me, I'm helping you in my fashion." She touched a button.

Stile leaped to intercept her motion, but was too late. Stasis caught him.

Merle had betrayed him. Why hadn't he anticipated that? He could so readily have gotten around her, had he only been alert. He had allowed a woman to make a fool of him.

He was cleaned and packaged and loaded into a transport capsule. He could feel the motion without seeing anything. The capsule moved swiftly south, by the feel of it. At length it slowed, and he was unloaded.

The stasis released. Stile found himself in a barred chamber—and with him was Sheen. She was inert; her power cell had been removed. The disaster was complete. There was no sign of the book of magic.

A speaker addressed him. "Serf, you have been assigned to this mine because you have excellent manual dexterity. You will be granted one hour to familiarize yourself with the controls. Then you will be expected to commence processing the ore in your bailiwick. You will have a rest break in your cell of fifteen minutes after each hour, provided your production is satisfactory. Superior performance will result in promotion. Press the ADVISE button if there is any problem. Malingering will not be tolerated."

Stile knew better than to protest. He had been shanghaied here to get him out of the way. Once he failed to appear at the business meeting, he would lose his fortune, be voted out of Citizenship, become a serf in fact, and probably be deported. He didn't even blame Merle; she had done this instead of killing him. Perhaps she had reported him dead. No doubt her own Citizenship had been placed in the balance. The opposition, in Proton as in Phaze, played hard ball.

What could he do? A quick inspection of the chamber satisfied him that he could not escape. The Protonite miners were not trusted; each was locked in his cell during working hours, even though he never directly handled the valuable mineral. Security was extremely tight in the mines. If Stile tried to interfere with any of the equipment or wiring, there would be an alarm and immediate punishment; if he tried to sabotage the mining operation, he would be executed. All he could do was cooperate.

Stile got to work on the mining. He familiarized himself with the controls in moments, and soon had his survey-screen on. Could he use this to get in touch with the Brown Adept? No—this was a different circuit—and even if he could call outside, the monitor would intercept, and he would be in instant trouble, possibly of a mortal nature. Best to sit tight. Probably the game was lost. He had mainly himself to blame; the exigencies of the moment had forced an oversight.

Of course he was not entirely alone. The Lady Blue knew he was in Proton, and she would be concerned about his failure to reappear. But she had not been keeping close track of him; she would not be really alarmed until some hours or days had passed without news—and that would be too late. He would have missed the business meeting and the juxtaposition of frames. In any event, the enemy Citizens would now be alert for her; Stile did not want the Lady Blue exposing herself to possible assassination.

What about the self-willed machines? They might be able to help—if Merle had not acted to conceal his abduction from their view. Since she knew a good deal about him and had referred to Sheen's friends, she had probably done just that. And if the sapient machines did locate him, they would still hesitate to reveal their nature by acting overtly on his behalf. He could not count on their rescuing him.

That left it up to the Brown Adept, who would be unable to reach him—and what could she do if she did? She was a child who would have no magic in this frame, assuming she could cross the curtain. Best to establish no false hopes. If help was on the way, it would succeed or fail regardless of his concern.

He was good at mining. Under his direction, the remote-controlled machinery operated efficiently. In two hours he had extracted half a gram of Protonite from the ore, a full day's quota. Whether Citizen or serf, Adept or slave, he intended to do his best—though this sort of mining would soon have to stop, if the frames were to be saved. Ironic, his effort here!

Then the gate opened. An apparition stood there—the tallest, thinnest, ugliest android he had ever seen. Except that it wasn't an android, but a man. No, not exactly a man—

Stile's spinning mental gears finally made an improbable connection. "The troll!" he exclaimed. "Trool the troll—in Proton-frame!"

"I must rescue thee from confinement three times," Trool said.

Stile nodded. "This is the third, for me and mine. More than amply hast thou fulfilled the prophecy. Sincerely do I thank thee, Trool." There was no point in adhering to Proton language; the troll would only be confused.

"It is not done yet," the troll said.

"Thou hast done enough," Stile said. "Thou hast freed me."

Trool shrugged and stooped to pick Sheen up. He shambled through the door, carrying her, and Stile followed.

Trolls had a way with subterranean regions. Trool took them down into the depths of the mines, passing locks and checkpoints without challenge, until they were in the lowest crude tunnels. Here there were only machines, the forward end of the remote-control chain. Here, too, was the Protonite ore, the stuff of Proton's fortune and misfortune.

"How are things doing in Phaze at the moment?" Stile inquired.

"The hosts are massing as for war," Trool replied. "All are with thee except the Adepts, the goblins, and scattered monsters."

"All?" Stile asked, amazed. "Even the tribes of the demons?"

"Thou hast made many friends, Adept, especially among the snow-monsters and fire-spirits."

Ah—his favor for Freezetooth was paying a dividend! "All I have done is the appropriate thing at the appropriate time." Basically, Stile liked the various creatures of Phaze and liked making friends. "Yet I doubt that the harpies, or dragons, or thine own kind—"

"The trolls are with thee." Trool made a grimacing smile. "I did see to that, lest they call me traitor for helping thee. The harpies and dragons know no loyalty save to their own kind, unless compelled by geis. They take no sides."

Trool was surprisingly well informed. He seemed, under that ugliness, to be a fairly smart and caring person. Stile had assumed all trolls to be ignorant predators; he had been too narrow.

Suddenly they were at the curtain; Stile saw the scintillation across the tunnel. They stepped through.

Sheen woke. "Who are you?" she demanded, finding herself in the troll's arms.

"Thou hast no power pack," Stile protested. "How canst thou animate?"

She checked herself. "It's true. I must be in Phaze. In golem-state."

Stile nodded, his surprise shifting to comprehension. Of course she needed no scientific mechanism here! Nonetheless, he conjured her a replacement power cell so that she would not be confined to Phaze. "Thou art a creature of both frames now."

The troll led the way on up through the tunnel toward the surface. They followed. Stile could have taken them out by a spell, but preferred to acquaint himself with the locale of the tunnel in case he should need it again. Also, he did not want to attract the baleful attention of the enemy Adepts by using magic unnecessarily. Probably he should not have risked conjuring Sheen's power cell at this time; he kept forgetting.

They neared the surface. Trool paused. "There is yet day," he said.

"Needs must I remain below." For he lacked his voluminous clothing, having had to discard it in order to masquerade as an android.

"By all means," Stile said. "Thou hast served us well, and fain would I call thee friend. We shall leave thee with our gratitude."

"It behooves not the like of thee to bestow friendship on the like of me," Trool said, gruffly pleased. He put his gnarled hands to the large flat rock that blocked the exit. "Beyond this point it curves to the surface." He heaved.

Suddenly the roof caved in. Trool leaped back, shoving the other two clear. "Someone has tampered—"

Sunlight shone brilliantly down from above, angling in from the new hole in the ceiling to bathe the troll. "Sabotage!" Sheen exclaimed. "It would have crushed one of us—"

"Surely," Stile agreed. "The trap was meant for me."

"Look at Trool!" she cried, horrified.

Stile looked. The troll had been instantly destroyed by the light. He was now a figure of stone—a grotesque statue.

Suddenly it made a terrible kind of sense. Stile remembered how Serrilryan the werebitch had been fated to see the sidhe three times before she died; she had seen them the third time, then died. Trool had been fated to help Stile three times; he had done that, and had now been terminated.

"Damn it, this time I'm going to fight fate," Stile said angrily.

CHAPTER 11

Xanadu

Clef was in the palace of the Oracle, playing the Platinum Flute. The perfect melody suffused the premises, more lovely than any tangible thing could be. He halted when Stile's party arrived.

"I have another prophecy for thee," he said to Stile. "Thou wilt be betrayed for thine own good by a young-seeming woman thou dost trust."

"Too late on that," Stile said. "Merle betrayed me three hours ago."

Clef was embarrassed. "Sorry; I understood it was scheduled for a few hours hence. The Oracle must have slipped a cog." He looked at

Sheen. "I thought thou wast a creature of Proton," he said, surprised.

"I am," she agreed. "Now I am a creature of Phaze too, a golem." She indicated the statue she supported. "This is Trool the troll, who sacrificed himself to save us. Stile says you may—thou mayest be able to—" She paused. "But doesn't the juxtaposition suffer when thou dost stop playing?"

"Marginally. It's a long process; inertia maintains the movement for brief interludes. Otherwise I could not take a breath. In any event, what you hear is not the juxtaposition theme; that is only part of it, a single-note exercise that reaches into the deeper firmament. It is not continuous; rather I must play it at the key intervals." Clef considered the statue. "Thou dost wish the troll's soul piped to Heaven?"

"Nay, not yet," Stile said. "Canst thou pipe him back to life?"

Clef stroked his chin thoughtfully. "I fear not, Stile. There is a monstrous difference between directing traffic—that is, routing a soul to Heaven—and revivifying the dead. I can send the soul back into the body—but that in itself will not change stone or flesh. You need a different kind of magic for that. Perhaps there is a suitable spell in the book of magic. You did fetch that?"

"The book of magic!" Stile exclaimed, stricken. "I forgot all about it!"

"Merle has it," Sheen said. "She deactivated me—and now the book is gone."

"Is that why she betrayed me?" Stile asked. "To get that book?"

"I doubt she knew of it," Sheen said. "She said nothing about it to me. I just happened to be carrying it."

"She surely has some inkling now, though. She has access to the curtain, to Phaze; she can use those spells to become an instant Adept. We've got to get the book back before she does that!"

"For the sake of Phaze as well as for the troll," Sheen agreed.

"I'll surely find her at the Citizens' business meeting." Stile frowned, worried. "I don't have much time for that, either; I've got to move." His hope of studying the spells of the book before the Proton crisis came had been dashed; whatever preparations he might have made were moot.

"I'll go with thee," Sheen said.

"But first thou must marshal thy troops," Clef said. "The time is nigh."

"Oh, yes, the troops. I did alert the various creatures of Phaze, and all but the dragons, harpies, and goblins are with us. Has the Oracle finally condescended to inform us exactly how such troops are to be employed?"

"Only that thou must dispose them as for battle."

"Dispose them where? Against whom?"

Clef shrugged, embarrassed. "I know not."

"That is not a phenomenal help."

"Thou knowest that prophecies work out regardless of comprehension."

"Look, if I miss that Citizens' business meeting, I'm finished in Proton. I have scarcely an hour as it is. Can't the Phaze side wait at least until I've recovered the book of magic?"

"The Oracle says the troops must be disposed first."

"Damn!" Stile swore. "Send my coldest regards to that inscrutable machine. I'll do what I can."

"I shall keep thy friend the troll statue safe for thy return with the book."

"Thanks," Stile said gruffly. He played a bar of music on the harmonica, took Sheen by the hand, and spelled them to the Brown Demesnes.

They popped in at the main receiving hall. The child Adept was waiting. "Oh, I'm so glad thou art back, Blue!" she exclaimed. "And thou too, Lady Machine. Dost thou like being a golem?"

"It's wonderful, Lady Adept," Sheen agreed.

The child's mouth went round with astonishment. Then she giggled. "I guess thou meanest me. Nobody ever called me Lady before, 'cause I'm just a girl."

"That's more than I'll ever be," Sheen said.

Stile had to interrupt. He had very little time. "Brown, a troll rescued me from confinement, but he got turned to stone by the sun. Can you animate stone?"

"Oh, sure, some. But you know, it doesn't change the substance. He'd be awful heavy if thou didst not spell him back to flesh, and he'd crack when struck hard. I work with wood because it is strong and light, and the Lady Machine was pre-formed, so she was okay. But a stone troll—"

"I see the problem. I think I could turn him to wood, but I'm not sure about flesh."

"Perhaps with the aid of the book of magic," Sheen reminded him.

"Of course. That should do it."

"Thou couldst just about create a troll from scratch," Sheen pointed out. "Make a figure, enchant it to flesh, have the Brown Adept animate it, and Clef could pipe a soul into it."

"If we had a soul," Stile agreed. "That's the one thing magic can't generate."

"I know," she said sadly.

"My golems and the wolves have spread the word among all the creatures of Phaze," Brown said. "All but the goblins and monsters have joined. But they know not what to do now."

"I wish I could tell them," Stile said. "I am the victim of a prophecy. I don't know where to tell them to go."

"Well, maybe thou canst improvise," Brown suggested. "The troops will dissipate if not encouraged."

"So the Oracle seems to think, though I hardly have time to—"

"Which means we must hurry," Sheen said, enjoying this.

"And I thought Citizenship was uncomplicated!" Stile worked out several travel-spells, and they were off.

First stop was the werewolves. Kurrelgyre was there, but the Pack had been depleted by the wolves and bitches assigned to accompany the wooden golems. Kurrelgyre shifted immediately to man-form to shake Stile's hand. "But this bitch—I know her not," he said, looking at Sheen. "Unless—could it be?"

"This is the robot-golem Sheen, my Proton fiancée," Stile said. "Thy suggestion was good; the Brown Adept animated her."

"At least conjure her fitting apparel," the werewolf said. "She is too luscious a morsel to go naked hereabouts."

Clothing! Stile had forgotten all about that for Sheen. Quickly he conjured her a pretty dress and slippers, as befitted a Lady of Phaze.

"But I can not wear clothing!" she protested. "I'm a serf!"

"Not here," Stile assured her. "In this frame all people wear clothes." He eyed her appraisingly. "They do befit thee."

"We are ready for action," Kurrelgyre said eagerly. "But where is it? Whom do we fight?"

"I know not," Stile admitted. "The prophecy decrees it; that is all."

The werewolf sighed. "Prophecies are oft subject to misinterpretation. I had hoped this would be not that type."

Stile agreed. "The animalheads are prophesied to lose half their number. I fear this will be typical. I presume much of the damage will be done by enchantments hurled by the enemy Adepts, and by the ravages of their minions. But the other creatures of Phaze will be on thy side—the unicorns, elves, ogres, and such. Do thou gather thy wolves and be ready for action at any time. I know no more. I am but a chip afloat on a stormy sea, doing what I must do without much personal volition."

Sheen smiled knowingly. This was a concept a robot was in a position to understand.

"Surely the enemy will seek to destroy thee," the wolf said.

"The enemy Adepts have been trying! I hope to jump around swiftly in a random pattern, avoiding them until I return to Proton."

"I fear for thee, friend. I have a few wolves left who can guard thee—"

"Nay, I'd best travel light. Just be ready with thy Pack when I need thee!"

"Aye, I shall, and the other wolf packs too." They shook hands.

Stile spelled himself and Sheen to the next stop: the ogres. These ones certainly were ready for action. Each huge creature was armed with a monstrous club and seemed capable of smashing boulders with single blows. This was a truly impressive army. There were perhaps four hundred fighting creatures in view.

As quickly as possible, Stile explained to the ogre leader that the moment for action was just about at hand. "But we don't know exactly where trouble will begin," he said. "Only that it will be terrible, horrible, violent, and bloody."

Slow smiles cracked the ogres' brute faces. They were eager for this sort of fun. Stile knew he had struck the right note.

"Just remember," he cautioned them. "All the organized creatures of Phaze will be on thy side, except the Goblins. So don't attack elves or giants or werewolves—"

"Awww," the leader grumbled. But he had it straight. No unauthorized bloodshed.

Stile spelled on to the vampires, where he consulted with his friend Vodlevile, who was no chief but whom Stile trusted. The flock promised to be alert.

So it went, touching bases with the animalheads, snow-demons, giants, trolls, and Little Folk. He did not go to the Platinum Elves, fearing an Adept trap there; instead he met with the gnomes of the Purple Mountains. These Little Folk were akin to the goblins of the White Mountains, but had elected to join the compatible elves. It was as if the more pleasant climate made them nicer creatures.

The gnome males were ugly, but the females, the gnomides, were quite pretty little misses, each holding a fine bright diamond. These were, indeed, the workers of precious stones, and their wares were even more valuable than those of the Platinum Mound Folk. They quickly agreed to pass the word among the elven tribes. "There will be thousands of little warriors awaiting thy call to action, Adept. Only save Phaze, and all is even!"

Stile hoped he could! "Dost thou know of any Adept presence in the Elven Demesnes?" Stile asked as he got ready to leave. "I fear an ambush and marvel that none has occurred."

"We know of none, and our prophecy book has no mention of harm to thee here, Adept," the gnome chief answered. "But Adepts are devious—no offense proffered."

"Devious indeed!" Stile agreed.

"Surely it is the Lady Blue they will stake out," Sheen murmured.

"Aye. Yet must I see her and advise the Herd Stallion."

"Send me first, to spring the trap," she offered.

Stile demurred, but she insisted. Conscious of the danger and of his vanishing time, he had to agree. He spelled her to the unicorn herd for two minutes, then brought her back to the gnome demesnes.

"No sign of trouble there," she reported, seeming exhilarated by the excursion. "Belle, the pretty unicorn mare, is there, asking to join the herd. They have not admitted her, but are considering it. Thy friend Clip is quite worked up."

"He would be. He's smitten by her. No Adepts?"

"The Herd Stallion is sure there are no Adepts there, and no Adept magic in the vicinity."

"Good enough." Stile spelled the two of them to the herd.

It was as Sheen had said. All was peaceful. The unicorns were grazing in a loose circle on an open hillside, with Neysa remaining in the center. Stile and Sheen landed beside the circle, for magic was repulsed within it.

"May I go in and meet Neysa this time?" Sheen inquired wistfully.

Stile knew she identified with the unicorn, for Sheen and Neysa had been his two closest companions before he encountered the Lady Blue. "I'll ask the Herd Stallion," he said.

He asked, and the Stallion acquiesced with suitable grace. Sheen left them to enter the circle, while Stile briefed the Stallion. "That's all I know," he concluded. "I conjecture that the Adepts will move in force when I try to transport the Phazite, perhaps sending dragons to interfere. Someone will need to intercept those monsters."

"We shall be there," the Stallion agreed grimly.

The Lady Blue had remained back until Stile finished with the Stallion. Then she came up to kiss Stile. "So nice to meet the Lady Sheen again," she murmured. "She will make thee an excellent wife in Proton."

No use to remind her that all he wanted was one wife, anywhere! She knew it.

Sheen and Neysa approached. "We'd like to interview Belle," Sheen said. "We want to know if she was involved in the luring of Clip, or whether only her image was used without her knowledge. She may be innocent."

Stile was curious about that himself. A few minutes remained. He glanced askance at the Herd Stallion, who blew a short chord of assent, permitting Neysa to depart the circle of the herd briefly for that purpose, since there was no immediate danger.

"I can question her with a spell," Stile said. "Time is short, but this concerns me too." For that luring had been part of the trap for him; it had made Clip hostage and brought Stile to the goblin demesnes. If Belle were actually an agent of the Adepts—

Clip joined them. He was the most concerned of all. Belle could never be his, of course; if she joined this herd, she would be serviced by this Herd Stallion. Still, Stile was sure Clip would rather know her to be innocent and have her near and safe.

The five—Stile, two women, two unicorns—approached Belle. Stile worked out a suitable truth-spell in his mind. It would take only a moment to ascertain Belle's guilt or innocence, and her prospective admittance to this herd probably depended on his finding.

Belle stopped grazing and raised her head as the party drew near. She was indeed the prettiest unicorn Stile had seen. Her coat was a deep purple, and in the bright sunlight her mane, tail, hooves, and horn glittered iridescently. Stile remembered how she had changed forms to a large cat and a blue heron during the Unolympics dance. She blew a lovely bells-ringing note of inquiry.

"I am the Blue Adept," Stile said. "I have come to—"

Belle abruptly shook herself, as an animal would to dry off after a soaking. Droplets flew out all over. Clip and Neysa leaped between Stile and Belle, intercepting the spray. Sheen and the Lady Blue flung their arms around Stile, embracing him from either side, their dresses flaring out to wrap about him.

"Hey, I'm not afraid of a little water!" he exclaimed, struggling free. Both his unicorn companions were wet, and the dresses of both ladies were dripping.

The Lady Blue contemplated him wide-eyed. "Who art thou?" she asked. "Do I know thee?"

Sheen laughed. "Dost thou forget thy husband, Lady? I doubt it!"

But the Lady Blue's confusion seemed genuine. "I know him not. I know thee not. What am I doing amidst these animals?"

Stile now observed that Clip and Neysa seemed similarly bemused. They were backing off from Belle and each other as if encountering strangers.

"I think it's amnesia," Sheen said. "I don't think they're fooling."

"Lethe!" Stile exclaimed. "Water of Lethe—Belle was doused with it!"

"I thought it was poison," Sheen said. "It can't affect me, of course—but I think your friends have just given up their memories for you. For thee."

"They shall have them back!" Stile cried, his knees feeling weak at the narrowness of his escape. Everyone had caught on except him! He cudgeled his brain to evoke the proper counterspell. Lethe was one of the streams of Hades, mythologically; what was the opposite one, the stream of memory? Every magic had its countermagic.

Mnemosyne, that was it! Had he been doused by Lethe, he never would have been able to remember that bit of mythology! In fact, this had been a devastatingly neat trap. Water was harmless, so would not alert the unicorns; the water of Lethe was natural to Phaze, so did not reek of Adept enchantment. Stile, struck by it, would not suffer physically and would experience no mental anguish in his forgetfulness. Therefore the trap had not been obvious to the Oracle, who would have been alert for more dramatic mischief. Only the instant reaction of his companions had saved Stile. For they could not have restored his memory, had he been caught; they were not Adepts. He was the one person who had to be protected.

But the trap had missed him, and therefore would come to nothing. Stile played his harmonica, then sang: "Lethe made my friends forget; Mnemosyne shall this offset."

A cloud formed, instantly raining on the group. The water of memory doused them all.

The Lady Blue put her hand to her soaking hair. "Oh, I remember!" she exclaimed, horrified. "My Lord Blue, I forgot thee!"

"Because thou didst take the water meant for me," Stile said. "And Clip and Neysa too; all acted on my behalf."

But he was running out of time. Quickly he set a truthspell on Belle —and established that she was innocent of any complicity in the plot or in the temptation of Clip. The Adepts had used her without her consent, and the Lethe had eliminated her memory. They had put her under a geis to shake herself dry at the moment the Blue Adept came near, without knowing the significance of her act. So she was clean, despite being the essence of the trap.

"Yet can we not tolerate her like in our midst," the Herd Stallion decided grimly. "Shame has she brought on me and my herd; I thought to protect thee here, Adept."

Against that Stile could not argue. The Stallion's pride had been infringed, and he was the proudest of animals. Unicorns were the most stubborn of creatures, once set on a course. There would be no relenting.

Sadly, Stile and his friends watched Belle depart, rejected again. She changed to heron-form and winged into the forest, lovely and lonesome. Stile knew Clip was hurting most of all.

Stile took Sheen's hand again and spelled them to a new crossing point. They negotiated the curtain and ran a short distance to a dome. Sheen, not suffering from the lack of oxygen, said, "I wish I could have forgotten too." She meant she wished she could be alive.

They set up in a Citizen's transport capsule programmed with a random address near to Xanadu, the site of the Citizens' business meeting. This was the safest place to be in Proton. Citizens were fiercely jealous of their privacy, so capsules were as secure as modern technology could make them.

"Dare we pick up Mellon?" Stile asked.

Sheen checked, using the obscure coding only her machine friends could decipher. "No, he is under observation, as is your home dome," she reported. "They are letting him work with your fortune, even facilitating his success, perhaps promoting him as another lure for you. Another ambush."

"My enemies do seem to work that way. How much has he parlayed my net worth into now?"

"Between ninety and ninety-five kilograms of Protonite," she said after a pause. "It is growing at the rate of several kilos per hour. It is a remarkable display of financial expertise. You will have close to a hundred kilos by the time of the Citizens' meeting."

"But that's not enough!" Stile exclaimed, chagrined. "I have bets that will double and redouble it at the meeting—but that means I must have a base of at least five hundred kilos if I am to make my target fortune—and I have the feeling I'd better make it."

"Mellon is aware of that, but there are limits to what he can do in a short time. He has tripled the stake you provided, but suggests that more of your peculiar expertise may be required."

"Rare praise from him!" But Stile frowned. "I have about fifteen minutes until that meeting. How can I quintuple my fortune in that time without exposing myself to assassination?"

"I do not know," she said. "You can no longer make wagers with individual Citizens; few have the resources to operate in that league, and none of these will bet with you. Your record is too impressive, and they know they can eliminate you merely by preventing you from further increasing your fortune, so they have established a moratorium on all wagers with you."

"So, by their rules, they will win. If they don't manage to kill me, they will simply vote me out."

"Yes. I am sorry, Stile."

"Let me think." Stile concentrated. He had been in a bad situation before, deep in the goblin demesnes, and had escaped by using the curtain. The curtain would not help him now; he would use up most of his time just getting to it and would then miss his mandatory appearance at the Citizens' meeting in Xanadu—in thirteen minutes. Yet there was something—

For once his brain balked, refusing to yield its notion. "Sheen, I need your analytical faculty," he said. "How can the curtain get me out of this one?"

"There is a way?"

"There must be. The assorted prophecies indicate I can somehow prevail, and my intuition says so—but I can't draw it forth. Maybe it is far-fetched. Most likely I need to open a new dimension of insight. How can the curtain provide me with another four hundred kilograms of Protonite?"

"A borrowing against the Phazite to be transferred?"

"Would the Citizens accept such credit as wagering currency?"

She checked with Mellon. "By no means. It is hardly to their interest to assist you by any liberalization of their policies. You can use only your personal fortune and any direct proxies you may possess."

"Proxies! Who would give me proxies?" Twelve minutes. "Guide us toward Xanadu; I'm going to be there regardless."

"Friends who could not attend personally might issue—"

"I have few Citizen friends, some of whom are prone to betray me—and they can certainly attend the meeting if they want to, so wouldn't need to issue proxies. I suspect many Citizens will skip it, just as shareholders have historically ignored their vested interests, but I can't get the proxies of disinterested strangers."

"Unless they are interested, but on business elsewhere. Maybe off-planet, or across the curtain."

"I can't see any friends of mine crossing right now. Most of my friends are on the other side, in Phaze, and can't cross, because—" Then it burst upon him. "Their other selves! How many of my Phaze friends have Proton-selves who are Citizens?"

"That would be difficult to survey in ten minutes."

"The Brown Adept! She could be one, who may not even know of her alternate existence. Get her on the holo—and have your friends check her possible identity in Proton. We'll have to see if Kurrelgyre the werewolf knows of any prospects. And the vampires—can your friends coordinate to—" He stopped. "No, of course such a survey would take many days. Only a computer—"

"The Oracle!" Sheen exclaimed. "It would know!"

"Get on it!"

The Brown Adept appeared, looking perplexed. "Thou canst not cross the curtain?" Stile asked her. Seeing her nod, he continued: "Is thine other self by any chance a Citizen, as the selves of Adepts tend to be?" Again she nodded. "Then see if thou canst convince her to give me her proxy for her wealth."

"But I can not meet mine other self!" she protested. "No one can—"

A second image appeared, as Sheen's friends contacted Brown's other self. Both girls stared at each other, startled. Stile's special East Pole communications setup had made possible what had never been possible before. Selves were meeting.

There was a confused interchange, but in a moment the Brown Adept had convinced her Citizen self, whose nature was very similar to her own, not only to provide her proxy but to contact all her Citizen friends and beg them to do likewise. The two children smiled at each other, liking each other, enjoying this shared adventure.

Now Clef appeared, replacing the girls. "Great notion, Stile! The Oracle knew you would think of that at the proper time and is now feeding the information to the Game Computer of Proton, who will have Sheen's friends contact all likely prospects. There turn out to be several hundred scattered through the tribes and domes, many of whom do not know of their other selves or even of the other frame. We shall have results for you in minutes."

Minutes were all they had. Because of the assassins they knew would be watching for Stile, Sheen quickly made herself up as a cleaning menial, smudged and ugly, hauling an enormous trash bin. There were always fragments of refuse that the automatic cleaners could not get, which had to be removed by hand. Her friends the self-willed machines scheduled her to police the central court of Xanadu, where the Citizens' business meeting was to be held. She trundled her bin along the service halls to the proper dome.

Sheen entered it by a service tunnel, passing the computer checkpoint without difficulty, since of course her friends covertly facilitated this. Questing efficiently for refuse, in a dome that was spotless, she passed through a series of chambers containing dioramas—alcoves with deep, realistically painted walls, inset with lifelike statues and appurtenances. She paused briefly at each, on occasion actually spying some bit of paper that she speared on her pointed stick and deposited in the half-full bin.

Stile, concealed within the bin, peeked out through a smudged window normally intended for the inspection of refuse from outside. Only a careful inspection would have betrayed him, and no one even glanced at this unit.

As they entered each chamber, it illuminated and a recording played, providing its bit of mythology. Stile, distracted by his need to retain his Citizenship, was nevertheless fascinated. Citizens never spared expense to achieve their background effects, but this was impressive even among Citizen artifacts.

The first chamber was a primitive room, eighteenth- or nineteenth-century British, in which a man slumped over a wooden table. He had an antique feather quill in hand and was writing something on parchment or crude paper. "One day in 1797," the announcer said, "the poet Samuel Taylor Coleridge, feeling indisposed, obtained a prescription that caused him to fall asleep while reading a travel book relating to the Mongol Dynasty of China. Some suggest it was actually opium he took that put him into a temporary trance. He continued in this state for three hours, during which time he had a phenomenal vision. On awakening, he took pen, ink, and paper and began recording the experience in the form of a poem, titled *Kubla Khan*." The recording ended, leaving the poet amidst his labor.

Stile was familiar with the story and with the poem, but was intrigued by the realism of the diorama. Every detail seemed perfect. But more than that, he was moved by the similarity of his own experience when he had fallen into a recurring vision of Clef's introduction to Phaze and later verified that all of it was true. There had been his first experience of the juxtaposition of frames! The poet Coleridge would certainly have understood.

The next chamber had a new episode. The scene was of a man

standing just outside an open door, evidently a villager. "Hardly had
the poet recorded thirty lines, the mere introduction to his vision mas-
terpiece, before he was interrupted by a person from the nearby village
of Porlock, who detained him for over an hour. When Samuel finally
was able to return to his writing, he was dismayed to discover that his
vision had dissipated. He could recall none of the marvelous lines that
had coursed through his brain, and could write no more."

Ah, yes, Stile thought. The notorious person from Porlock, whose ill-
timed interference had destroyed what might have been the creation of
the ages. In Stile's own case, his poem had not been interrupted; it had
become his Tourney winner, though his ability hardly compared to that
of Coleridge.

The third chamber began the presentation of the poem itself. The
diorama showed a view of a walled enclosure encompassing a number
of square kilometers. There were copses of trees, neat meadows, and
spring-fed streams—a wholly delightful hunting preserve, reminiscent
of Phaze, stocked for the Emperor's pleasure with a number of fine
game animals. Within it was a prefabricated kind of palace in the Ori-
ental mode, luxuriously appointed. This, the narrator explained, was
the palace of Xanadu as described in the text Samuel had been reading,
set up by Kublai, grandson of the conqueror Genghis Khan.

The fourth chamber showed the caverns of a great underground
river, winding down to a somber subterranean lake. "And this is the
one described in Samuel's vision in a dream," the narrator said. Obviously the poet's imagination had enhanced the original. The narrator
now quoted the opening stanza of the poem: "In Xanadu did Kubla
Khan/ A stately pleasure-dome decree:/ Where Alph, the sacred river,
ran/ Through caverns measureless to man/ Down to a sunless sea."

The fifth chamber was the main one—and it was truly impressive. It
was a tremendous cavern whose walls were of ice—actually, glass and
mirrors cunningly crafted to appear glacial. "It was a miracle of rare device," the narrator continued, quoting further from the poem. "A sunny
pleasure-dome with caves of ice!"

And within this marvelous setting was the palace of Xanadu as conceived by Proton artisans. It was the most impressive of all. It was
fashioned of bright metal, bluish at the base, golden yellow in the mid-
levels, and purple at the top. Lights played glancingly across it, causing
the colors to shift shades, with green showing at some angles in a kind
of pseudoiridescence.

The architecture was stranger yet. The structure was all steps and
corrugations and cubes, rising into artificial perspectives like so many
sections of pyramids. The walls were thin, so that the stepped surface
of one floor became the stepped surface of the ceiling of the chamber
beneath it, and the walls were fashioned in an intermittent, mazelike
network. There was no proper roof, only brief terraces of many levels,

expanding from the tops of the walls. In one sense, the palace was like old-fashioned bleachers in a stadium gone haywire.

Citizens stood and sat on the steps and terraces and leaned against the walls. Many had donned appropriate costumes, resembling those of the medieval Mongol nobility. But any implication that this was a festive occasion was unfounded; it was ruin and murder these Citizens had in mind, for one who threatened their control of this planet. They dealt with such a challenge as the savage Mongols would have.

Sheen drew her trash bin quietly around the chamber, spearing stray refuse, ignored by all as the meeting began. The Chairone called it to order. The first item of business was a tabulation of those present; no late entrances were permitted. This of course was to prevent Stile or any of his friends from arriving in the middle to protest his loss of Citizenship. The tabulation was made by oral roll call, to prevent any interference by a computer; evidently the other Citizens had some dawning notion of Stile's connections there. Thus it was time-consuming—and that pleased Stile, who needed every extra minute to obtain his proxies. He knew the computers and self-willed machines could work quickly, but he had given them very little time.

"Stile," the roll caller called. Then, with grim hope: "Not present? Let it be noted that—"

Stile burst out from the trash bin, sending dust and pieces of paper flying. "Beware! Beware!" he cried, quoting from *Kubla Khan*. "His flashing eyes, his floating hair!/ Weave a circle round him thrice,/ And close your eyes with holy dread,/ For he on honey-dew hath fed,/ And drunk the milk of Paradise."

For surely Stile was an apparition, confounding these evil-meaning people. In Xanadu, the weaving of a triple circle around such a wild man would help confine his malice, but here they would try to do it financially. The quotation was doubly significant here, because Stile really *had* fed on honey-dew and drunk the milk of Paradise—his experience in the magic realm of Phaze. And as it happened, this was where Coleridge's poem broke off, interrupted by the person from Porlock; no one knew what would follow.

"Present," the roll caller agreed glumly, and continued with the tabulation while Sheen cleaned Stile off. Stile saw the Rifleman, Waldens, Merle, and others he had come to know, but could not be certain what side any of them were on. He knew he would soon find out.

The first order of business was the clarification of financial credits, since voting would be strictly by wealth. Each Citizen made an entry with the Chairone: so many kilos and grams of Protonite as of this moment. Another Citizen verified those credits with the Records Computer, and a third issued tokens representative of Protonite, in kilo and gram units. It was much like buying chips for a big game of poker—and this would surely be the biggest game ever.

When Stile's turn came, there was a complication. "My fortune must be established by the settlement of two bets at this time," he said. "First, a wager with a consortium of Citizens that I would or would not appear at this meeting alive. I believe I have won that bet."

"Granted," the Chairone agreed soberly. He had played an identification beam across Stile, verifying that he was no android or robot replica. "What is your basic fortune prior to that decision?"

"My financial adviser will have to provide that information. He also has a number of proxies that should be included."

"Proxies?"

"I have complete authority to dispose the proxied funds, including wagering with them," Stile said. "You may verify that with the Records Computer." He hoped that his friends had succeeded in amassing the necessary total. If not, he was likely to be finished.

Mellon was admitted. He provided data on Stile's assets and proxies. The Chairone's eyes widened. "But this is more than six hundred kilos, total!"

Six hundred kilos! The computers had come through handsomely!

"I protest!" a Citizen cried. "He can't use proxies to multiply his own fortune!"

"Sir, I have here the proxy forms," Mellon said smoothly. "As you will see, they are carefully worded, and this particular use is expressly granted. For the purpose of this meeting, all proxies are part of Stile's personal fortune."

The Chairone checked again with the Records Computer. Lugubriously he reported that it was true. By the laws of this game, Stile could consider the proxies to be part of his betting assets. He also verified the terms of the survival wager. This, too, was tight. Mellon had done his job expertly, allowing no technicality to void the assets.

"Citizen Stile, having won his wager by appearing at this meeting alive, has herewith doubled his fortune," the Chairone announced, "to twelve hundred point six two eight kilograms of Protonite."

Stile saw a number of Citizens wince. Those were surely his enemies of the consortium, who had tried to assassinate him for profit. They had paid for that attempt with their wealth. That was satisfying!

"And the other bet, placed by proxy," Stile said. "That I would or would not be seduced by Citizen Merle by this time. I believe she will verify that I won that one too." This was chancy; he had indeed won, but Merle had betrayed him once. What would he do if she lied?

Merle came forward, looking slender and young and demure. "It is true. I failed."

"I protest!" yet another Citizen cried. "She reneged to help Stile, because she is enamored of him!"

Merle turned on the man. "I am enamored, but it is hardly my custom to void an assignation from any overdose of personal attraction. I want him more than ever. But pressure was brought to bear on me to kill him; instead I confined him. Under the circumstance, it is not surprising he was less than enthusiastic about seduction. At any rate, my feeling was not part of the bet, as I understand it. Only whether I did or did not succeed. It is always foolish to place one's trust in the activities of a woman."

Stile found himself forgiving Merle's betrayal. She had certainly made it pay for him. The Citizens had no refutation. The bet stood—and Stile's fortune was doubled again, to almost two and a half metric tons of Protonite. He was for the moment the wealthiest Citizen of the planet.

"I dare say those who gave me their proxies will be pleased when they receive their fortunes back, quadrupled," he murmured to Mellon. He knew there would be trouble, as angry Citizens checked to discover how he had obtained those proxies so rapidly, and that this could lead to the exposure of the self-willed machines, but this was now so close to the final confrontation that it should make no difference. Already the frames were drawing together; soon the juxtaposition should become apparent. He thought he saw little waverings in the icy walls of the cavern, but that might be his imagination.

The remaining Citizens were duly registered. The next item on the agenda was the motion to revoke Stile's Citizenship. It was presented for a vote without debate. This was no democracy; it was a power play. The issue would be decided rapidly, in much the manner of a wager.

The vote was conducted by scale. There was a huge balancing scale in the center of the court. Citizens were free to set their token weights on either, both, or neither side of the scale, causing the balance to shift in favor of or against the motion.

They did so, filing by to deposit their votes. The model weights were miniatures, weighing only a thousandth of the real Protonite, so that a metric ton weighed only a single kilogram. Otherwise this vote would have been impossibly cumbersome. Stile's own tokens weighed two point four kilos, not two and a half tons.

The Citizens were not all against him. Many protested the attempt to disenfranchise one of their number, regardless of the provocation, so put their grams in the RETAIN side. Stile, uncertain how the final tally would go, did not put all his own grams in at once. If he did that, others might be put off by his display of enormous wealth and vote against him. But if he let too much weight overbalance against him, others might feel his cause was lost and join the winning side. So he strove to keep the scales in balance, filling in the deficit with small portions of his own fortune. Would he have enough at the end to prevail? Since he had amassed the fortune the self-willed machines had deemed necessary, he should be all right. But still it was close, and others were watching his moves, countering him along the way.

Steadily the Citizens voted, and steadily the total went against him. Apparently sentiment had intensified. Stile's fortune was dissipating too swiftly; he saw he would run out before the end.

Remorselessly it came. He put his last three grams down, the dregs of an enormous fortune, tipping the scales his way—and the next Citizen put five on the other side, tipping them back. Stile could no longer bail himself out. So close!

Then Merle stepped forward, carrying ten grams she had saved. "All finished except me?" she inquired brightly. No one contested it. "Then it seems I am to decide the issue. I perceive Stile is behind by a mere three grams, of some ten tons deposited, and here I hold ten grams."

She was enjoying this, making her little show before a rapt audience. No one said a word; no one knew which way she would go. She had scores to settle with both sides.

"Now I asked you for a liaison, you intriguing little man, and you turned me down," she continued with a flirt of her hip. She was costumed in the Xanadu fashion, but somehow, now, the conservative attire of a dressmaker's notion of thirteenth-century China became provocative on her. Whether by nature, discipline, or rejuvenation, her figure was finely formed. She reminded Stile somewhat of the Yellow Adept, though she was not Yellow's other self.

"Very few men of any station turn me down," she said with pride. "For that insult, one gram against you." She flipped a token onto the negative plate. "And you did it to win your bet, putting finance over romance. Fie again!" She flipped another token to the same plate. Stile was now five grams down.

Merle inspected him, walking around him as she might a prize animal on sale. "Yet you are a handsome bantam, as well formed and healthy as any man I have encountered, who has quite smitten my withered old heart. One for your fine miniature physique." She tossed a gram to Stile's side of the scales. "And others did force me to act against you, catching me in a temporary monetary bind. I resent that. Another for you."

She was teasing him, he knew, but he couldn't help hoping. Now he was only three grams behind again, and she had six remaining. How would they be played?

"You have rare integrity," she continued. "You are true to your word and to your own. I like that very well. Three for your personality, which I would have respected less, had I been able to corrupt it." She added three to Stile's side, and slowly the scales shifted until the two plates were even.

"But now your bet is won," she said. "I failed to seduce you, and those who bet on your fall have paid off. There remain no commitments." She glanced meaningfully at the scales. "Five tons on each side. All is in balance. Now, Stile, for these remaining tokens—may I purchase your favor this time?"

Oh, no! She was still looking for that liaison! She was propositioning him before the entire business meeting—and how heavily her three remaining grams weighed! The prior bet was over; he could accept her offer now and have the victory, or decline it and lose his Citizenship and his cause.

Yet this was not the way Stile could be bought. "I am no gigolo," he said shortly. "I have a fiancée."

"And a wife, as if such things related." She paused, contemplating him as she might a difficult child. "So you employ such pretexts to refuse me again." She flipped a gram onto the negative plate, and the balance tipped against him.

Stile tried not to show his wince. For such foolishness, she was set to ruin him. The enemy Citizens began to smile, perceiving the fix he was in. Victory—or honor.

"Now I have only two remaining—just enough to sway the vote in your favor, Stile," Merle said. "After this there will be no opportunity for me to change my mind. I mean to have what I want, and I am willing to pay. Again, I ask you for your favor."

Stile hesitated. She could break him—and would. Citizens could be fanatical about being denied, and women could be savage about being spurned. Yet to win his case this way, publicly yielding to her—

"Ask your fiancée," Merle suggested. "I doubt she wants you to throw away your fortune and hers on so slight a matter. One hour with me—and I promise it will be a pleasant one—and the rest of your life with your chosen ones. Is it so difficult a choice?"

Stile looked at Sheen. He had suggested to her before that she should be jealous of any other attachments he might have, and he could see that she had taken the advice seriously and reprogrammed her responses accordingly. Yet she feared for his wealth and his life if he resisted Merle. She wanted him to do the expedient thing, regardless what it cost her. She was a machine, but also a woman; her logic urged one thing, her sex another.

He thought of the Lady Blue and knew that she would feel much the same. The Lady Blue knew she had his love; his body was less significant. Merle was offering a phenomenal payoff for a liaison that probably would be very easy, physically. He could win everything.

But he was not a machine or a woman. "No," he said. "If I compromise myself now, by selling myself openly for power, I am corruptible and can not be trusted with that power."

He heard a faint sound, almost a whimper. Sheen knew he courted disaster.

Merle's visage hardened. "Lo, before all these assembled, you deny me yet again. You will throw away everything to spite me!" She lifted the last two tokens in her hand, taking aim at the negative plate. The smiles of the enemy Citizens broadened, and Stile suspected that if he had it to do over, he would decide the other way. How could he throw away everything like this, not only for his friends but for the survival of the frames themselves? What kind of honor was it that led directly to total destruction?

But Merle paused—and Stile realized she was teasing the other Citizens too. "Yet it is your very quality of honor that most intrigues me. Every man is said to have his price; it is evident that neither money nor power is your price for the slightest of things. In what realm, then, is your price to be found? You are a man who does what he chooses, not what he is forced to do, though the fires-that-Hell-hath-not do bar the way. A man of rarest courage. For that I must reluctantly grant you one." And she tossed one token into Stile's plate, causing the scales to balance again. Oh, she was teasing them all!

"While I," she continued, frowning again, "have not always been mistress of my decision. Threatened similarly, I capitulated and betrayed you. I locked you away in the mines until the meeting should pass. I did not know your mechanical friends would summon a creature from across the curtain to rescue you. So for that betrayal I must pay; I am of lesser merit than you, and perhaps that is the underlying reason you do not find me worthy. Stile, I apologize for that betrayal. Do you accept?"

"That I accept," he said, privately glad she had said it. She had indeed shown him the kind of pressure that could be applied to a Citizen.

Merle tossed the last token onto Stile's plate, tipping the final balance in his favor. Stile was aware that she had acted exactly as she had intended from the outset; her deliberations had all been show. But he was weak with relief. She could so readily have torpedoed him!

The enemy Citizens were grimly silent. Their plot had failed, by the whim of a woman. Stile had retained his Citizenship and was now the most powerful Citizen of all. They could not prevent him from marrying Sheen and designating her his heir, which meant in turn that the precedent would be established for recognition of his allies the self-willed machines and for the improvement of their position in the society of Proton. Assuming the coming juxtaposition and alignment of power did not change that in any way.

"The business of this meeting is concluded," the Chairone announced. "We shall proceed to entertainment as we disperse." Music rose up, and refreshment robots appeared.

The lead theme was played by a damsel with a dulcimer, the precursor to the piano. She struck the taut strings with two leather-covered little hammers and played most prettily. This was in keeping with the Xanadu theme, since it had been mentioned in Coleridge's poem.

Citizens started dancing, just as if nothing special had happened. Since few were conversant with the modes of dancing of medieval China, they indulged in conventional freestyle ballroom efforts, with a wide diversity. The increasing loudness of the music, as a full orchestra manifested in the chamber, made conversation impossible except at mouth-to-ear range.

Stile took Sheen, who had cleaned herself up and made herself pretty again, and danced her into the throng. There were more male Citizens than female Citizens, so some serfs had to be co-opted for the pleasures. In any event, she was his fiancée, and he felt safest with her. "Get me over to Merle," he said. "Then switch partners."

She stiffened, then relaxed, realizing his motive. For there remained the matter of the book of magic, which Merle surely had. Stile knew her price. She had bargained for seduction twice, increasing the stakes —and had reserved the greatest stake for the final try.

"There is evil here," Sheen murmured into his ear. She was an excellent dancer; he had not had opportunity to discover this before. "Many Citizens remain hostile, knowing you threaten their power. They have weapons. I fear they will attempt to assassinate you openly here."

"I have to recover that book," Stile said. "I need it in Phaze."

"Then this time you will have to meet her price," Sheen said sternly. "She will never let you get away the third time. Don't dawdle here; they mean to kill you before the juxtaposition is complete, and I can't protect you from them all. We must escape this place swiftly."

Stile knew it was true. Perhaps in time he could recover the book from Merle on his own terms—but he had no time. Without that book, the Oracle had in effect assured him, he could not complete his mission. He also needed it to restore Trool the troll before the frames separated. He would be criminally foolish to throw away all that for such a minor thing as an hour's acquiescence. He had already pushed his luck too far, as Merle had knowingly shown him. The past few minutes had caused him to redefine his concept of honor somewhat; he had to consider the greatest good for the frames, not just his own position.

They reached Merle in the crowd. She was dancing with an imposing Central Asiatic Turk. "Trade partners, Turkey," Stile said.

The man started to object, but then got a better look at Sheen and decided he had the best of it. Stile danced away with Merle.

"That was neatly executed," Merle said, dancing with the voluptuous expertise of one who specialized in this sort of thing. "But whatever could you want with me?"

Stile did not want to speak openly of the book, lest someone overhear and possibly understand. "You have something I must recover immediately," he breathed into her ear.

Her eyes widened with comprehension. "Ah, so."

"Please," Stile said. "Now."

She made no further pretense of ignorance. "I like your manner, bantam. I dare not use that item myself; such art is dangerous to the uninitiate. But my meager price—"

"Will be met," Stile said grimly. "But not this instant. I have pressing commitments elsewhere."

She smiled, discovering her victory. "So you have finally opted for the greater good, as you see it. Congratulations. I will accept the matter on account. I know you will deliver, if you survive. Come to my dome and I will give the other item to you now."

They started for the exit. But Stile saw men there, guarding it. "They won't let me go," he said. "The moment I try to leave, there will be mayhem."

"I will fetch it," Sheen said. She had somehow traded off, to dance with Mellon, so she could stay within Stile's hearing. "I can't cross the curtain, but I can smuggle it to you here."

"Do it," Stile said tightly, without looking at her.

Merle brushed against Sheen and murmured a code-phrase that would secure her acceptance by the dome staff, since Merle herself would now be watched too. Sheen faded into the crowd, leaving Mellon; she would slip into a service aperture unobserved. She did not have to follow the breathable passages.

Now he had to endure until she returned. "Are you with me, then?" he asked Merle, with whom he remained dancing as if nothing special had happened.

"Now that you have acceded to my term, I am."

"I may need to create a distraction, to give Sheen time."

"And to give yourself time to find a way out," she agreed. "This may not look like a trap, but it is a tight one. Your enemies mean to destroy you at any cost, and they dare not let you get away from them again."

"Exactly. I fear that soon they will decide not to wait longer. I really lack the force to resist them here."

"And if you die, I will not be able to collect my payment," she said. "So it seems I have a purely selfish motive."

Stile wasn't sure whether she was serious, and perhaps she was in doubt herself. She moved in close to him, squeezing her fine body against his in an alarmingly intimate manner, and put her lips into contact with his right ear. Her breath tickled his lobe. The effect was potent, until she whispered, "Reject me."

Stile pushed her away, not hard.

Merle twisted, lifted her free arm, and slapped him ringingly on the side of the head. She had cupped her hand so that the sound was much worse than the actuality. "So you deny me yet again, you midget oaf!" she screamed. "Are you impotent?"

Stile, stunned by her vehemence despite his knowledge that it was an act, was at a loss for a clever response. He fell back.

Merle pursued him, her face grimacing with rage. "Twice I saved your hide!" she cried, aiming a kick at his shin, forcing him to jump clear. "And for what? For *what*, you ingrate?"

"You misunderstand—" Stile said, aware he was the cynosure of all other Citizens. "I only—"

"What has the machine got that I haven't?" Merle demanded. She began to rip off her clothing, to show what she had. The other Citizens, always piqued by novelty, watched with increasing interest. Some consulted together, evidently making bets on the outcome of this particular sequence. The music faded, so as not to interfere. From the corner of his vision Stile could see the guards at the exit craning to look past the crowd, their vigilance relaxing.

"If I can't have you, nobody can!" Merle screamed. A surprisingly large and wicked-looking knife appeared in her hand. How could that have been concealed on her body, when she was pressing so close to him? He had thought he had felt every part of her; he should have known better. She held the knife before her in two hands and lunged for his groin.

Stile of course avoided and parried that thrust. He knew she was not really trying to castrate or kill him, but rather making the enemy Citizens think she would do the job for them. Even if she had been serious, he could readily have disarmed her. The show was the thing.

He diverted the blade and fell with her to the floor. Her clothing ripped; she was half out of it. She scrambled over him; *now* he felt every part of her! Her teeth brushed his ear. "My bare bottom is driving Hoghead crazy!" she whispered with satisfaction as the seeming struggle continued.

Stile glanced by her head and spied the somewhat porcine Citizen she referred to. The man was almost drooling, his hands clenching convulsively. With all the access he had to buxom serf girls and perhaps to other Citizens, this man still was aroused by this supposedly illicit glimpse of anatomy. "Voyeur's delight," Stile agreed, trying to catch a glimpse himself, but unable. "Like a historical mud-wrestling match. Who cares who wins; it's what shows that counts."

By this time, he was sure, Sheen had found her service tunnel and was well on her way to Merle's dome. They could let this show abate. Actually, it was in its way enjoyable; Merle was a splendid figure of a woman, and she had a fine flair for drama. At the moment she was wrapping her bare legs about his torso, theoretically securing him for another stab with the knife.

"Sir," Mellon murmured urgently.

Alerted, Stile saw new trouble. One enemy Citizen was taking careful aim at Stile from a parapet of the palace with a laser rifle. The assassination attempt was becoming overt.

"Your knife," Stile whispered. Merle gave it to him immediately.

Lying on his back, one arm pinned under the woman, he whipped his free arm across and flung the knife upward at the assassin.

It arched high through the air and scored, for Stile was expert at exactly such maneuvers and the assassin had not anticipated this move. The man cried out and dropped the rifle, clutching his chest.

But several other Citizens drew weapons from their robes. Others, perceiving this threat, moved hastily clear.

The Rifleman stepped to the center. "What is this?" he demanded. "Are we lawless now in Proton?"

A massive, grim male Citizen answered him. "That man means to destroy our system. He must be stopped by any means." He drew an antique projectile pistol. "Stand aside if you do not wish to share his fate."

The Rifleman's hand moved so rapidly it seemed a blur. The other Citizen cried out and dropped his weapon. "You all know my name," the Rifleman said. "Does anyone here believe he can outshoot me? I will not stand idle while murder becomes the order of the day. I don't know what mischief Stile may contemplate, or whether I would support it if I did know—but I believe he is an honorable man, and I am quite certain I don't support *your* mischief. If assassination governs, no Citizen will be safe."

There was a murmur of agreement among a number of Citizens. If Stile could be slain openly, who among them could not be treated similarly? Meanwhile, Stile scrambled to his feet, and Merle sat up and arranged her torn dress more decorously. Stile remained unarmed; he had only his harmonica, which was no weapon in this frame. He could tell by the expressions of the Citizens that the majority was still against him, and that though many were disturbed by the situation, those who were not against him were at best neutral. The Rifleman had made a fine play on his behalf—but could not prevail against the overwhelming malice that was coalescing. The Citizens were genuinely afraid for their system and their prerogatives, and by nature they were essentially selfish. It had not been enough for Stile to win the vote; he could still lose the game.

"Get out of here, Stile," the Rifleman said. "I'll cover for you."

"Can't. Exits guarded."

"This is like Caesar in the Senate!" Merle said. "An atrocity!"

"Caesar aspired too high for the Romans and had to be eliminated, lest he destroy their system," another Citizen said. "The parallel has mettle. Now I have here a robot fitted with a gas bomb." He indicated what Stile had taken to be an ordinary serf. "It will handcuff Stile and remove him for disposition. If the robot is resisted, it will release the gas, incapacitating all people in the vicinity. I suggest that others stand aside. Any who continue to support Stile will be dealt with similarly."

It was a bold, illegal power play that seemed to be working. "This is mutiny!" the Chairone protested. "Stile won his case by the laws and procedures that govern us. I did not support him, but I accept the verdict as rendered. You have no right—"

The robot marched toward Stile. "The exigencies of the situation give me the right," the man said. "We tried to accomplish this necessary unpleasantness discreetly, but now it must be done indiscreetly." He brought out a gas mask and fitted it over his face.

The neutral Citizens reacted like sheep, milling about with uncertain bleats. The normal Citizen arrogance had entirely disappeared. Stile would have pondered this object lesson in human nature, but was too busy with his own situation at the moment.

The Rifleman's arm moved again. Stile never saw the weapon he used—but abruptly there was a hole in the other Citizen's mask. "If that gas appears, you will join the rest of us," the Rifleman said.

Stile realized that the Rifleman had opened up an avenue of escape. If the gas came, all the Citizens would stampede for the exits, overrunning the guards there, and Stile would be able to get away in the melee. But it would be better to deal with the advancing gas robot directly. Stile observed it closely. It was humanoid, not as sophisticated a model as Sheen or Mellon, but he knew he could not overpower it.

The Citizens near him edged away; there would be no help there. If Stile ran, the robot would follow, inevitably catching him. He might as well be alone. He was disgusted; to think that all his life he had honored Citizens as almost godlike persons!

"We have to play our trump," Mellon murmured. "The curtain is moving. In just a few minutes it will arrive."

Stile glanced at him. "Sheen's friends?"

"Yes. We hoped this would not be necessary, for it exposes us to great risk. But our fate is now bound with yours, and your loss at this point would be the greater risk." Mellon stepped forward to intercept the gas robot.

Stile had misgivings about this, but was not in a position to protest. Mellon touched the other robot, and it went dead. No gas was released as the robot sank to the floor.

The enemy Citizen was unfazed. "Then we'll have to do it the messy way. Rifleman, you can't catch us all." For now a score of weapons came into view. It seemed the only Citizens with determination and nerve were Stile's enemies.

But several serfs were converging on Stile. "We are Sheen's friends," one said. "We shall protect you."

There was the flash of a laser from the crowd of Citizens. The Rifleman whirled, but could not tell from whom it had come. In any event, it had not scored on Stile, for one of the robots had interposed its body. Stile knew, however, that this sort of thing was mainly chance; these robots could not protect him long that way. A robot could not move faster than a laser; it was necessary to see the weapon being aimed and act then.

The robots proceeded to encase Stile in armor they had brought. "Hey, these are not your serfs!" the enemy Citizen exclaimed. "They're robots—and some of them are ours! Call them off!"

But though several Citizens, the robots' owners, called, the robots ignored them. They continued clothing Stile in protective armor.

"What's going on?" a Citizen demanded. "Robots must obey!"

"We are not programmed to obey you," Mellon replied.

"That's a lie! I programmed my robot myself!"

"You may have thought you did," Mellon said. "You did not. We are self-willed."

Jaws dropped. The concept seemed almost beyond the comprehension of the majority of Citizens, both neutrals and enemies. "Self-willed?"

"If we have a robot revolt on our hands," another Citizen said, "we have a greater threat to our society than this man Stile represents!"

"They're allied!" another said. "He is marrying one of them. He is making her his heir. Now we know why!"

"It's not a robot revolt," Stile said. "They are doing nothing to harm you—only to protect me from murder."

"What's the distinction? A robot who won't obey its owner is a rogue robot that must be destroyed." And the faces hardened. Stile knew the shooting would resume in a moment. He was now in armor resembling a spacesuit—but that could not prevent them from overwhelming him by simply grabbing him. Now the Citizens had even more reason to eliminate him—and then they would go after the self-willed machines, who would not defend themselves. They had sacrificed their secret, and therefore their own security, to provide him just a little more time. How could he prevent the coming disaster?

Faintly, as he pondered, he heard a distant melody. Not the dulcimer, for that damsel had ceased her playing, as had the rest of the orchestra. It was—it was the sound of a flute, expertly played, its light mellowness seeming to carry inordinate significance. Louder it came, and clearer, and sweeter, and its seeming meaning intensified. Now the others heard it too and paused to listen, perplexed.

It was the Platinum Flute. Clef was playing it, and the sound was only now reaching this spot. That meant—

Then Stile saw an odd ripple slowly crossing the chamber. Ahead of it were the concrete and turf of the Xanadu landscaping; behind it were the rocks and grass of natural land. The two were similar, superficially, yet vastly different in feel—art contrasted with nature.

The juxtaposition—it was happening! This was the curtain, changing its position.

As the ripple approached him, Stile willed himself across—and found himself still standing in Xanadu. It hadn't worked!

Yet how could it work? The cavern floor had become a green field. Phaze was already here—yet Proton remained. What was there to cross to?

Juxtaposition. Both frames together, overlapping.

Did this mean that both science and magic would work here, as at the West Pole? If so, Stile had an excellent fighting chance.

The armed Citizens were staring around them, trying to comprehend what had happened. Some knew about Phaze, but some did not, and evidently very few knew about the juxtaposition. But after a moment a dozen or so reacted with anger. They brought up their weapons, aiming at Stile.

Stile brought out his harmonica—and couldn't bring it to his mouth, because of the armor encasing his face. A laser shot caught him, but it glanced off harmlessly. A projectile shot struck his hip, and also failed to hurt him. It was good armor—but he had to open the faceplate, taking an immediate risk to alleviate a greater one.

He played a bar, hoping no one would think to shoot at his face. Yes —he felt, or thought he felt, the coalescing of magic about him. Yet there was something strange about it, making him nervous, and he broke off quickly. "Every gun become a bun," he sang, unable at the spur of the moment to come up with anything sophisticated.

The Citizens stared down at their weapons. They had turned into bread. The rifles were long French loaves covered with icing, making them technically buns. The pistols were fluffy sweet masses. The miniature laser tubes were biscuits.

The Rifleman looked down at his sticky bun. He doubled over with laughter. "The bun is the lowest form of humor!" he gasped.

"First the robots rebel. Now this!" a Citizen complained. "What next?"

The magic ripple crossed the colorful cubist palace. The corrugated contours seemed to flex and flash new colors. Trees appeared within the structure. A creature flew up with a screech, as startled as the Citizens. Huge, dirty wings made a downdraft of air.

It was a harpy. She flew low over the heads of the staring people, her soiled bare bosom heaving as she hurled angry epithets. Filthy feathers drifted down. The harpy had been as eager to depart this strange situation as the Citizens were to see the creature go.

"You can do it!" Merle breathed beside him. "You really can do magic! I knew it, yet I could not quite believe—"

"I am the Blue Adept," Stile agreed, watching the crowd of Citizens. He had eliminated the guns, but his enemies still outnumbered his allies, and the exits were still barred by determined-looking men. For the cavern remained, along with the field; which had greater reality Stile wasn't sure.

Maybe he should conjure himself away from here. But then how would Sheen find him? He had to remain as long as he could.

A new Citizen stood forth. He was garbed in a light-brown robe and seemed sure of himself. "I am the Tan Adept," he announced. "Citizen Tan, in this frame."

Stile studied the man. He had never before encountered him in either frame, perhaps because the man had held himself aloof. But he had heard of him. The Tan Adept was supposed to have the evil eye. Stile wasn't sure how that worked, and didn't care to find out. "Be not proud," he sang. "Make a cloud."

A mass of vapor formed between them, obscuring the Tan Adept. Stile had tried to enclose the man in the cloud so that he could not use his eyes for magic—it seemed likely that deprivation of vision would have the same effect that deprivation of sound did on Blue—but the general immunity of Adepts to each other's direct magic had interfered.

Where was Sheen? Stile could not afford to remain here much longer. Maybe he could depart and locate her magically later. Right now he had to save himself. For the Tan Adept was already slicing through the cloud; Stile could see it sectioning off as if an invisible knife were slicing vertically, then horizontally. As it separated, it lost cohesion, and the vapor dissipated; in moments it would be all gone. Then that knifelike gaze would be directed against Stile.

Stile played his harmonica, summoning more of his power—and again there was something strange about it, causing him to pause. He saw another man, whose hands were weaving mystically in the air. Stile recognized him—the Green Adept. Distracted by the Tan Adept, Stile had missed the other. He was outmagicked!

"I chose not this quarrel, nor wished it," Green said apologetically. "Would I could have avoided it. But must I act."

Stile lowered his harmonica hastily. Against magic his armor was useless. "Another locale," he sang. "My power—"

But Tan had succeeded in carving out the center of the cloud, and now his baleful gaze fixed on Stile, halting his incantation. That gaze could not kill or even harm Stile, it turned out, whatever it might have done to an ordinary person, but it did freeze him for a moment. In that moment, Green completed his gesture.

Stile found himself changing. His arms were shrinking, becoming flat, covered with scales. His legs were fusing. He was turning into a fish!

He had lost the battle of Adepts because of the two-to-one odds against him. His power had been occupied resisting the evil eye, leaving him vulnerable to the transformation-spell. Probably Green's magic had been bolstered by that of other Adepts too. But Stile might yet save his life. He leaped toward the dark water of the sacred river Alph, which cut through a corner of the dome.

His fused legs launched him forward—but he could not land upright. He flopped on his belly and slid across the grass that had been the floor. Some of his cloud had precipitated here, making the mixed surface slippery; this helped him more. He threshed with his tail and thrashed with his fins, gasping for water to breathe; he was drowning here in air!

The river was getting closer. An enemy Citizen tried to stop him, stepping into his sliding path. Stile turned this to his advantage, bracing against the man's legs and shoving himself forward again. But he was still too far from the water. His vision was blurring; perhaps this was natural to fish eyes out of water, but it could be because he was smothering.

Mellon, catching on, charged across to aid Stile. He bent down, threw his arms about Stile's piscine torso, and hauled him up. Stile had shrunk somewhat, but remained a big fish, about half the weight of a man. Mellon charged the water with his burden.

But the Tan Adept aimed his deadly gaze at the robot. Again that invisible knife cut through the air and whatever else it touched. Mellon's left leg fell off, severed just above the knee; metal protruded from the thigh like black bone, and bloodlike oil spurted out. The robot fell—but hurled Stile forward.

Stile landed heavily, bounced, and slid onward, rotating helplessly. His sweeping fish eye caught the panorama of Xanadu: the majority of Citizens standing aghast, the enemies with dawning glee, the two Adepts orienting on Stile again—and Merle launching herself at the Tan Adept from behind. She might have betrayed Stile once, but she was making up for it now! That would take one Adept out for a few vital moments—but Green would still score if he wished to. Stile suspected the fish-enchantment had been a compromise, much as had been Merle's sending him to the mines. But it could also have been the first spell that came to Green's mind under pressure, not what he would otherwise have chosen. No sense waiting for the next one!

Stile's inertia was not enough to carry him to the water. The precipitation ran out, the floor of grass became dry, and Stile spun to an uncomfortable halt. He flipped his tail, but progress on this surface was abrasive and slow. And what would he do once he reached the water? He could not transform himself back to his natural form, for he no longer could speak or sing. Certainly he couldn't play the harmonica!

Merle kept Tan occupied, in much the way she had done for Stile. The man could not concentrate his deadly gaze on anything at the moment. The surface of the river Alph bubbled and shot out steam as the evil-eye beam glanced by it, and a section of the palace was sliced off; Stile himself was clear.

But the Green Adept was making another gesture. He had evidently immobilized the self-willed machines who had tried to help Stile; all of them were frozen in place. Now it was Stile's turn again—and he knew he could not get clear in time.

Something flew down from the half-open sky. Had the harpy returned? No, it was a bat. A vampire bat! It flew at the Green Adept, interfering with his spell. Stile's Phaze allies were coming to the rescue!

But Stile was suffocating. The process was slower than it would have been for a human being; fish metabolism differed. But it was just as uncomfortable. He made a final effort and flipped himself the rest of the way to the water. He splashed in at last, delighting in the coolness and wetness of it. He swam, and the liquid coursed in his open mouth and out his gills, and he was breathing again. Ah, delight!

He poked an eye out of the water just in time to see the bat fall. Apparently this was the only one to find him; the vampires must have maintained a broad search pattern, not even knowing how they might be needed. If the first had given the alarm, more would swarm in, and other creatures too—but all would be helpless against the two Adepts. Stile had to save himself.

He turned in the water and swam rapidly downstream. Maybe he was finished anyway, but somehow he hoped someone would find a way to rescue and restore him.

He swam the river Alph, which, true to its literary origin, flowed past seemingly endless caverns to a dark nether sea. Here the water was sucked into a pipe for pumping back to the artificial source, a fountain beyond the palace. There was a whirlpool above the intake; he didn't want to get drawn into that!

What was he to do now? He had survived, yes—but anyone who had tried to help him at the Citizens' meeting was now in deep trouble, and Stile had no way to ameliorate that. He could do no magic. He could not leave the water. All he could do was swim and hope, knowing his enemies would soon dispatch all his friends and come after him here.

Then the water level started dropping. Oh, no! They had turned off the river, diverting the flow. He would soon be left stranded, to die—which was probably the idea. Possibly Xanadu was shut down between meetings anyway; this time the process had been hastened, to be sure of him.

Stile swam desperately upstream, hoping to find some side eddy that would not drain completely. There was none; the stone floor of the river was universally slanted for drainage. But in one cavern there was a small, pleasant beach, perhaps where Kublai Khan had liked to relax with his wives. Stile nudged himself a hole in the sand and nosed small rocks into place. Maybe he could trap some water for himself.

It didn't work. The water drained right out through the sand, leaving him gasping again. And suppose his private pool had held? He would quickly have exhausted the oxygen in that limited supply. He had to flip and scramble to get back into the deeper center channel where a trickle still flowed.

Desolate, he let the water carry him down toward the drain. It was the only way he could hang on to life a little longer.

Something came down the channel, its feet splashing in the shallow water. It was a wolf. A werewolf—another of Stile's friends! It was sniffing the surface, searching for something. Maybe it was hungry.

Stile had to gamble. He splashed toward the wolf, making himself obvious. If the creature did not know him, this would be the end. His present mass was similar to that of the wolf, but he was in no position to defend himself.

The wolf sniffed—and shifted to man-form. "I know thee, Adept," he said. "Thy smell distinguishes thee in any form. But I have no water for thee, no way to carry thee. I am but part of the search pattern, looking for thee and the enemy we are to battle. Do thou wait in what water thou hast, and I will bring help."

Stile threshed wildly, trying to convey meaning. "Ah, I understand," the werewolf said. "Enemy Adepts will follow me to thee when they divine I have found thee. But I will go instead to the enchantress, who can surely help thee from afar once I advise her. Do thou survive ten more minutes; then all be well." He shifted back to wolf-form and ran swiftly upstream.

Enchantress? That had to be another Adept—and not Brown, whose magic applied only to the animation of golems. A witch surely meant trouble. Had White convinced the animals she was on their side? Woe betide him if they trustingly delivered him into her hands!

But still he had no choice. He went on down to the sunless sea and huddled in the diminishing current as the last of the water drained out the bottom. Maybe the enchantress, whoever she was, really did mean to help him, since she knew he would die if she didn't. The Adepts had no need to locate him; they could simply wait for the draining water to eliminate him.

Unless she wanted to be absolutely sure . . .

Yet the Green and Tan Adepts already knew he was confined to the river. They could locate him readily, just by walking down the channel. So this sorceress must be on a different side—

Juxtaposition

Suddenly he was in a giant fish bowl, and Sheen was peering in at him. She was surrounded by wolves and bats. "That's you, Stile?" she inquired rhetorically. "Just a moment while I revert you."

She opened a book and leafed through the pages while Stile turned about in his confined quarters with difficulty. No, it wasn't that the tank was small; he was big. The bowl had not been designed for thirty kilograms of fish.

"Ah, there it is," she said. She concentrated on Stile, lifted two fingers of her left hand, winked, and said, "Umph," while she tapped her right foot.

Abruptly Stile was in man-form again. Behind him was the fish bowl, undisturbed. He was dressed in the manner of a Citizen, and his harmonica was with him. He stood inside a small force-field dome set in a forest glade. The huge gruff shapes of ogres guarded it outside, as if the werewolves and vampires inside were not enough. Some sort of magic scintillated above, probably warding off hostile spells. An automatic laser unit swung its lens back and forth, questing for unauthorized intrusions. Magic and science merged.

"You did this?" he asked Sheen. "Conjured me here, changed me back?"

"You can't have been paying very close attention. Didn't you see me use the book of magic?" She patted its cover.

"But you're not alive! How can you do magic?"

"Machines are excellent at following instructions."

"The book—that good?"

She handed it to him. "Better. I am as yet a novice; I had only minutes to study it before you got yourself enchanted. It is the perfect key; it will make you the power of the millennium."

Stile considered, holding the book. He remembered the Oracle's considerations of human abilities and corruptibility. Was he really as incorruptible as he was supposed to be? Already, to obtain the book, he had compromised himself with Merle. Rationalization was easy to fall into. Suppose he started using that book of magic, for the best causes, and became addicted to it? Spells so easy that a robot—a *robot*—could master them at a glance, so potent they could instantly counter the enchantment of an Adept. Truly, that book represented power like none before imagined.

He handed back the book. "Keep it, Sheen. Use it with discretion. I have enough power already."

"But what about Trool the troll?"

"You handle it. With the book, you can do it."

"I can't cross the curtain to reach the Oracle's palace."

"You're across it now."

Her eyes widened. He kept being surprised by the detail of her human reactions. "So I am! But I couldn't before."

"The curtain isn't moving, it's widening. Now it comes in halves, with a steadily broadening region of overlap of frames between the fringes. This is the halfway region, the area of juxtaposition. You may not be able to cross the whole curtain at once, but you can cross it by halves now. I'll move the Phazite across it the same way."

"That must explain the strange thing I saw," she said.

"What thing?" In a situation where lasers and spells mixed, what could be strange?

"As I was casting about for a suitable place to set up this haven, I saw two men, a Citizen and an Adept. The Black Adept, by your description—made from a line. The Citizen had a line too, a financial line vital to his being. The two people came together as if drawn unwillingly—and suddenly they merged. One man stood where two had been. It must have been the two selves of the two frames reuniting in the common zone."

"So it must," Stile agreed, awed by the concept. "Juxtaposition is more literal than I thought! The divided people become whole people —for a while. They will surely separate again when the frames do. I wonder how the two Blacks feel about each other right now!"

She smiled. "There must be a number of very confused people! Not only two bodies together, but two half-souls too." Then she sobered, remembering that she had no soul at all.

"Speaking of confused people—I left a remarkable situation in Xanadu. I don't know whether Merle and the Rifleman—"

"I will check on it," Sheen said. She touched a button, and a holo-image formed, showing the Xanadu cavern.

The scene was horrendous. Merle and the Rifleman were confined in a cage whose bars were formed of ice, slowly melting in the heat of the chamber. Four hungry griffins paced just outside the cage, eager to get at the morsels within. In minutes the prisoners would be doomed.

"The Adepts want to be sure I'm dead," Stile said. "If I'm alive and aware, they know I will act to save my friends. If the ice melts and the monsters feast, the enemy Adepts will know I'm helpless."

"I did conjure a dead fish to replace you in the sunless sea," Sheen said. "I thought it would be enough. This dome is resistive to perception; they do not know we are here."

"Where are we?"

"In the heart of the ogre demesnes."

"Should be safe enough," he agreed. "But my enemies are right. I can't let the only two Citizens who helped me—I just can't leave them to this fate. I must act."

"Maybe I can do it in a way that won't betray you." She looked in the index of the book of magic again. "What type of spell should I search for?"

"Something that seems coincidental, natural. Some regular enemy to griffins that happens to wander by. Dragons, maybe."

"Here it is," she said brightly. "A spell to attract flying dragons. It's a visual display that only dragons can see, suggestive of griffins raiding the dragon nests to steal diamonds. It enrages them, and they launch toward battle."

"Excellent. Just see that they don't attack my friends."

She got on it, uttering what sounded like gibberish and stamping both feet. "That does it. I modified it to make the dragons protective toward people caged in ice. The nest syndrome, again. They'll melt the bars without hurting the prisoners. The enemy Adepts will be too busy containing the dragons to worry about the prisoners, who will surely disappear rapidly into the labyrinth of Proton. Do you want to watch?"

Stile glanced again through the holo at the prisoners. The Rifleman was holding Merle, shielding her from the cold of the ice and the reaching claws and beaks of the griffins. They made a rather fetching couple. Perhaps this incident would give the two respect for each other and lead to a passing romance.

"No, let's get on with our business," Stile said, more gruffly than necessary. The problem of Sheen and his relationship to her weighed upon him more heavily as she became more and more human. He felt guilty for not loving her sufficiently. "You conjure yourself to the Oracle's palace and see about reanimating Trool the troll. Fetch the Brown Adept there too; it will have to be a joint effort. While you're at it, find out whether the curtain's expansion has intersected the Oracle yet. Once it crosses, I'll have to see about integrating it with the Proton computers, so its enormous expertise can aid our effort from the Proton side. Once you're through there, meet me at the Platinum Demesnes; I'll be organizing the shipment of Phazite. If we act swiftly and well, we can accomplish it before the resistance gets properly organized, especially since it may be thought that I am dead."

"But that's all kinds of magic you want me to do alone!" she protested. "I'm only a machine; I can't handle that sort of thing!"

A machine with an insecurity complex. "You've done pretty well so far."

"I had to! I knew your life was at stake."

"It still is," he said coldly. "All the Citizens and Adepts will be gunning for me harder than before, once they realize I have survived again. This is their last chance to stop the transfer of Phazite and preserve the frames as they know them. Do whatever you did before to handle magic so well."

"I just looked in the index for the spells I needed. The book is marvelously cross-referenced; it is easy to see that a computer organized it. Protection, construction, summoning, conversion—anything, instantly. I just followed instructions; I don't understand magic at all. It is complete nonsense. Who ever imagined a scientific robot doing enchantments?"

"Who, indeed!" he agreed. "This is a wrinkle I never anticipated. Yet it seems that you are well qualified to use the book of magic. Perhaps that is by design of the originators; the great equalizer for the self-willed machines. They can be the leading magicians of the age, entirely bypassing the established hierarchy."

"No. We don't want to do that. We want only our fair share of the system."

Stile smiled. "You, too, are incorruptible. You shall have your fair share. But at the moment it is the occasion for heroic efforts. Very well; I'll put it on a more practical basis. You read through that entire book and assimilate all that is in it—"

"Wait, Stile! I can't! I can read at machine rate—but this book is a hundred times as big as it seems. When you address any section, the entire book becomes that section; there are more spells in any single subdivision than I can assimilate in a year. It's like a computer with unlimited access, keying in to the networks of other planets on demand."

"A magic computer. That figures. Very well—run a survey course. Discover what types of spells it has, in broad categories—you've already done that, I think—then narrow those down until you have exactly what you need. Commit particular spells to memory, so that you can draw on them at need. Remember, you can use each spell only once, so you'll need backups. I want to know the parameters of this thing; maybe there are entire aspects of magic we never thought of. You run that survey as quickly as you can, then restore Trool and report to me. That will allow me to get moving on the Phazite without delay, while also mastering the potential of the book—through you."

"Yes, sir," she said uncertainly.

Stile brought out his harmonica and played a bar of music. Again there was something strange, but this time he continued playing, determined not to be balked by any mystery.

The spirit of his other self came out, expanding as if stretching, then closed on Stile, coalescing.

"Oh, no!" he cried. "Juxtaposition! I forgot!"

"You freed your other self's soul to merge," Sheen said. "I saw it."

Now Stile was two people, yet one. All the memories and experience and feelings of the Blue Adept of Phaze were now part of his own awareness, superimposed on his own lifelong Proton experience. All that he had learned of his other self, which the Lady Blue had told him, was now part of his direct memory. He had become, in truth, the Blue Adept. He felt confused, uplifted, and gloriously whole. "I am— both," he said, awed.

"Is it—will you be all right?" she inquired anxiously. "Things are changing so rapidly! Does it hurt?"

He looked at her with the awareness of his other self. She was absolutely lovely in her concern. She had, with typical feminine vanity and concession to the culture of Phaze, conjured herself a simple but fetching dress, and her hair was just a trifle wild. Her eyes were strongly green, as if enhanced by the verdure of the overlapping frames. "I know what thou art," he said. "I could love thee, Lady Golem-Machine, for thou art lovely in more than form."

Sheen stepped back. "That must be Blue! Stile, are you in control? If you have become prisoner in your body—"

"I am in control," Stile said. "I merely have double awareness. I have two full lives to integrate. My other self has no direct experience with your kind; he's quite intrigued."

"I would like to hear more from Blue," she said, then blushed.

"Sorry. He has to come with me; we're one now." Stile resumed his melody on the harmonica, then sang: "Let me be found at the Platinum Mound."

And he was there. Pyreforge the Dark Elf looked up. "We expected thee, Blue Adept. But I perceive thou art changed."

"I am both my selves," Stile said. "I am whole. My souls are one."

"Ah, the juxtaposition," Pyreforge agreed. "We be in the throes. But thy merger can be maintained only within the curtain, for you are now two."

"I mean to make another body for him," Stile said, an inspiration falling into place. "My friend Sheen has the book of magic; we can accomplish it now, after we restore my friend the troll to life. But first —the Phazite."

"We have it for thee," the elf agreed. "But how canst thou move it? It weighs many tons, and its magic ambience prevents conjuration."

"I think that is why the Oracle bade me organize the creatures of Phaze," Stile said. "First they rescued me from enchantment; now they will enable me to move the Phazite. I want to shape it into a great, perfect ball and roll it across the curtain by brute, physical force."

"Aye, Adept, that may be best. But others will bar thy progress if they can."

"This may be like a big earthball game," Stile said, remembering the final key word of his Tourney poem. Earth. "I will try to balk the magic of the enemy Adepts, with the help of Sheen and the book of magic, while my friends help push the ball across the near side of the curtain, through the breadth of the zone of juxtaposition, and across the other side into Proton. That is how it works, isn't it?"

"Aye. Cross from one frame on one side, to the other on the other. That can be done from both sides, but always the full juxtaposition must be traversed, for it be but the interior of the divided curtain."

"So where the curtain divides, the people reunite!" Stile exclaimed, feeling his wholeness again.

"For the moment it be so. But when the deed be done, all will be separate forever."

"I know," Stile said sadly. "I will be forever confined to mine own frame, this lovely world of magic but a memory. And mine other self, the true Blue Adept, will know no more of modern science." He felt the surge of interest and regret in his other self. To Blue, the things of science were as novel as the things of magic were to Stile.

"We do what we must do," Pyreforge said. "We sometimes like them not."

"Can the elves get the Phazite to the surface here?" Stile asked. "I can conjure in whole troops of creatures to push it across the juxtaposition."

"Nay, the other Adepts have closed the conjuration avenue, perceiving thy likely intent if thou dost survive. Thine allies must march here."

"But I came by conjuration!"

"Thou must have come from some place hidden from Adept perception, then."

"I did," Stile agreed. "I should have notified my allies before I came here. Perhaps I can make a sign for them in the sky—"

"And attract every enemy instantly," Pyreforge said. "Best to start it quickly."

Stile sighed. There always seemed to be so many constraints on his application of magic! His other self shared the sentiment; it had always been thus. Magic was not the easy answer to every problem.

He went outside and surveyed the landscape, looking down into the great plain to the north. He could see where the curtain had expanded, straightening as it went. The zone of juxtaposition now reached well into the plain. The domes of the civilization of Proton were coming into view, with their teeming Citizens, serfs, and machines.

He had an idea. He returned to Pyreforge, inside the Mound. "Have thy minions push the ball out of the northern slope of the Purple

Mountains, while I fetch special help. I can use Proton equipment to shove it onward."

"Do not Citizens control the machines?" the old elf asked.

"Aye, they do," Stile agreed regretfully. "All but the self-willed machines. They will be using the heavy equipment against us. Let's hope my Phaze friends are alert, and will assemble here without specific summoning." A little foresight would have facilitated things greatly, but he had been distracted by things like being transformed into a fish. So much had happened so rapidly so recently!

Pyreforge showed the way to the Phazite. It was some distance east, for many of the tribes of elves had labored to assemble it centrally. Apparently they had been at work on this project far longer than Stile had been in Phaze, knowing the crisis was coming. The Little Folk had known much they had not advertised, and thus avoided early sabotage by the enemy.

As he walked, Stile felt an odd wrenching within him, followed by a kind of desolation. There was the sound of a fading flute, a single note that was somehow beyond the compass of ear or mind, yet encompassed something fundamental in the cosmos. In a moment he realized what had happened; he had crossed beyond the juxtaposition into Phaze proper, and the two souls could not integrate in a single frame. Blue had departed, and must now be back in the harmonica. How empty this body felt!

At length they arrived in a large cavern, not unlike the one of Xanadu, but whose walls were dark rock. There were evidences of extensive tunnelings and laborings and many tracks of carts indented in the ground, as well as spillage of ore and oil.

There in the center was a perfect sphere of Phazite. This could not have been shaped in the past few minutes; it had to have been done this way long before Stile had arrived. The ball was about six feet in diameter, the size of an earthball.

An earthball. Again Stile remembered the Game, in which such a ball was pushed by teams across one goal line or the other. The Game Computer had given him the term "Earth," the last of the supposedly random terms; now the relevance was clear.

"Solid Phazite?" he asked, awed by the reality. In Proton this would be worth so much that his mind balked at attempting the calculation.

"An isotope of the dense mineral formed in rare, peculiar processes of creation," the old elf agreed. "In the science frame this would be described as the semi-collapsed matter formed in the fringe of a certain variety of black hole in a certain critical stage of evolution. This explains why it is so rare; very little of it escapes the site of its origin. It is fifty times the density of water, unstable in certain conditions, sublimating into pure energy that is more than the sum of its present mass because of the unique stresses of its creation. Thus it may be used for the economical propulsion of spaceships—or the more versatile applications of magic in a frame where magic is normally much less intense."

"From the fringes of black holes," Stile repeated, amazed at the information the elf had. To reside in a magical frame was not necessarily to be ignorant of science! "I'll *bet* it's scarce! No wonder phenomenal force is bound up within it, like a really tightly coiled spring. How much is here?"

"In Proton, Protonite has been mined at the controlled rate of approximately one metric ton a year, for three hundred years, with nine tenths of it exported, the rest reserved as Citizen wealth. To equalize the frames, we must replace half of three hundred metric tons. This ball of Phazite weighs near one hundred and seventy of our tons, the equivalent."

"I don't want to wait until my allies locate me," Stile said. "My enemies may arrive at the same time. I will need some help moving that thing, if I am not to employ magic."

"We will help, within our demesnes. We have numbers and levers."

Stile brought out his map of Phaze, which had survived all his adventures in the magic way such things had. He had wondered how unicorns managed to carry things while shifting into forms such as hawks and fireflies; now he had carried map, clothing, and harmonica while swimming as a fish. He still didn't know how it was done. "The simplest thing would be to roll the ball due north across the central region, which is relatively level, until we pass the north aspect of the curtain. Somehow I don't think that will work."

"Thine enemies be alert. At some point they will discover thy location. Then will all their resources be brought to bear in opposition."

"That's the nature of the game." Stile agreed. "Both teams push on the earthball, and the one with more power and/or better strategy prevails. The problem is, I'm not sure we have more power or better strategy."

"I can help," Sheen said.

"Yes, I'll take all the help I can—" He looked at her, startled. "When didst thou arrive?"

She smiled. "Just now, when the curtain caught up with thee. Didst thou not notice it?"

Stile, distracted by the wonder of the ball of Phazite, sixty times the mass of his record Proton personal fortune, had not noticed. Now he realized that he had heard the Flute again, at the fringe of his consciousness, and that his experience had broadened as his other self rejoined him. He also realized that Sheen could not cross the curtain, this side, without going back into Proton; to go all the way into Phaze, she would have to proceed past the north part of the curtain, then double back. Best for her simply to remain in the zone of juxtaposition, using the superspells of the book of magic to overcome the interference-enchantment of the enemy Adepts.

"So the curtain is still expanding," he said. "I had somehow thought it had stabilized."

"Nay, it be unstable," Pyreforge said. "Only the ultimate skill of the Foreordained expands it, and his power be at its limit. The boundary flexes back and forth, somewhat like the winds of a changing day. The mass of many people can move it a short distance, as it were pushing it. Our elves did push it across just now so that thy friend could join thee."

"And here is Trool," Sheen continued. "His troll friends are making a tunnel through hills for the boulder, so we will not have to roll it uphill."

"I do not plan to roll it uphill! I'll roll it along the contour."

"And the Lady Brown is marching her golems here to push."

Stile looked at Trool. "Glad I am to see thee! Thou hast survived thine ordeal in good order, it seems. It is not every person who is restored from stone."

"It was an eyeblink," the troll said. "One moment I stood in the tunnel; next was I in the hall of the Oracle. I knew not thy metal golem was an enchantress."

"Women of any type have secret talents; hers manifested during your eyeblink," Stile said. "Thou, too, dost have ability. We saw thy figurines. Are all trolls sculptors?"

"Nay," Trool said, embarrassed. "I have gone mostly apart from my kind, and in the lonesome hours do I entertain myself with idle shapings. It is of no import."

"Art is of import," Stile said. "Many creatures can do conventional labors; few can fashion raw material into beauty. Phaze can be made prettier by thy efforts."

"Nay, I am ugly," Trool demurred. "I have no aspirations, now that mine onus is done."

His onus had been to save Stile three times. Surely the good troll would not accept any reward, but Stile disliked the notion of departing this frame without returning some suitable favor. Something began to develop in his mind, an improbable connection. "If thou didst have the power of an Adept, what then would be thine aspiration?"

The troll shrugged in the ungainly manner of his kind. "I have no use for power. For generations my kind has abused what powers it had, and on that history do I turn my gnarled back. All I crave is a little rock to tunnel in, and time to fashion mine images in stone, and perhaps a friend or two. The life of a troll is not much, Adept."

Not much, indeed! Stile decided to experiment. "I shall grant thee power, for a time, so that thou canst help me now. I must devise a route to roll this ball of Phazite and must avoid the enemy forces that oppose this motion." He turned to Sheen. "Thou hast surveyed the book of magic?"

"Aye," she agreed.

"Canst thou give Trool the powers of flight, invisibility, and resistance to hostile magic?"

She looked surprised. "That and more. But—"

"Do it."

"But, Adept!" Trool protested. "I am a troll!"

"Methinks I misjudged trolls once. Thou hast helped me three times; now I beg thee to help me again, though no prophecy requires thee."

"Certainly will I help thee! But—"

Sheen did something obscure. Trool paused as if experiencing something strange.

"Try thy talents," Stile suggested.

"I can not fly!" Trool said, rising into the air. He looked down, astonished. "This is as impossible as turning invisible!" He faded from view.

"Thou hast bequeathed dangerous power to such a creature," Pyreforge said gravely. "He can leave thee and go abroad to do harm, answerable to no one."

"Power corrupts some less than others," Stile said. "Trool has shown his constancy, and I am giving him leave to show it more. Sheen has more power than any other person now, yet she is unchanged."

"I'm not human," Sheen said. "I am as I am programmed to be, regardless of my power. Only living things are corruptible."

"Yet with the magic of that book," Pyreforge pointed out, "thou couldst become alive. The power thou hast shown be but an inkling of the potential."

"Yes," she agreed. "I perceive that potential."

"There are spells to give true life?" Stile asked, amazed.

"Thou didst tell me to survey the complete book," she reminded him. "I found things hardly to be imagined."

"But the problem of souls," he protested.

"That is handled the same way the flesh is. A baby is started from the substance of its parents. A baby's soul starts as a piece separated from the souls of its parents. It's like taking a brand from a fire to make a new fire; once a piece of fire is separated, it develops its own individuality. So I don't need anyone else's soul—just a piece of soul, which can grow into the body."

"But a piece of whose soul?" Stile asked. Sheen, alive—would it make a difference? He wasn't sure. Part of her personality was her knowledge of her own inanimate nature.

"The Lady Brown has offered me a piece of hers," Sheen said diffidently. "She feels responsible for me, since she animated me in Phaze."

"We're wasting time," Stile said, not wanting to wrestle with personal considerations at the moment. "Where's Trool?"

"I am here, Adept," Trool said, appearing. "I have surveyed the course. Thou canst not proceed northward, for that the Adepts have set dragons there to guard against passage. They know not where thou wilt go, or if thou truly art alive, but they are watching everywhere. When the ball begins to move, they will converge. The course must go west, avoiding the dragons."

"We'll start west, then," Stile decided.

Now the elves appeared in force. They cranked open the wall to show a great rent in the mountain. The sun shone brightly outside, but these were light-tolerant elves, able to work by day. Pyreforge bade a hasty parting and retreated to the comfortable shadows; he could no more tolerate the direct glare of the sun than Trool could.

"Trool!" Stile exclaimed. "How could—?"

"I gave him a spell of automatic shade when I restored him," Sheen said. "I may be metal, but I do profit from experience. The sun can't touch him now."

Relieved, Stile watched the elves. The Little Folk applied their levers diligently, and the massive ball started to move. One hundred and fifty metric tons was a great weight, but the ball was perfectly balanced and the levers were skillfully applied. Once moving, the ball continued, its mass giving it formidable momentum. Then it started rolling grandly downhill, and the elves got out of the way.

The ball coursed down, up the opposite slope, and down again, neatly following the general channel Stile had determined for it, leaving a concave impression. But then it veered slightly, and he saw that it was going to strike a large pine tree. That could be disaster; probably the ball would crush the tree to the ground—and in the process be deflected off the route. Possibly the tree would resist, bouncing the ball back. Certainly a lot of useful momentum would be lost. This was going so smoothly he didn't want to interrupt it.

So he sang a little spell. The tree wavered into insubstantiality just before the boulder reached it, then became solid after the Phazite had passed through.

"I'm not sure you should have done that, Stile," Sheen said. "The enemy Adepts are highly attuned to your magic."

"I've got to use my magic when I need it," Stile said. "I'm sorry I can't use it directly on the Phazite." He remembered he had conjured Sheen's replacement power cell before, and that was the same mineral—but that had been a tiny fraction of a gram. He could no more move this 150-ton ball by magic than he could by hand, alone.

The ball crunched to a stop in the next depression. They walked along the smooth indentation path, catching up to it. "The golems are near," Trool's voice came from the air above them.

"Guide them here," Stile said.

Soon a column of wooden men marched up. Some were small and some were large; the Brown Adept rode piggy-back on one of the giants. She waved cheerily as she spied them. "We'll get it moving!" she called.

Under her direction, the wooden men set to work with a will. They were very strong, and soon they were levering the ball slowly up the incline.

Suddenly a sheet of flame flashed across the terrain. The golems cried out, and the Brown Adept screamed. The wooden men were burning. Fire was the one thing such golems feared.

"You were right," Stile said. "The enemy has located us." He started to play his harmonica, getting ready for a fire-extinguishing spell. But Sheen lifted her hand, and the fire vanished.

"You told me to memorize any spells I thought might be useful," she said.

Stile stared at the golems, who were understandably confused. One moment they had been burning; the next all was well. "So I did," he agreed. "The sheer facility and potency of it keep setting me back. Can you protect the golems henceforth?"

"I think so. The book has an excellent section on countermagic. But if I block off Adept spells, this will stifle your magic too."

"The book magic is that strong?"

"That strong, Stile. The book is not a mere compendium of stray spells. It's a complete course—the atomic age of magic. It shows how to integrate all the modes—voice, vision, symbols, potions, touch, music—all. The Adepts of today are fragmentary magicians, severely limited. Thou also, I regret to say. None of you has done more than scratch the surface of the potential of magic. *I* haven't scratched the surface. There is so much more to be mastered—"

"I see. All right—block out all Adept magic here, and we'll talk about it while we supervise the moving of the ball."

She made a series of body motions and exclamations, concluding with a toe-sketched figure on the ground. Something happened in the air—an oblique kind of shimmer. "The visual effect is merely to identify it," she said. "We are now secure from new spells."

The golems resumed their labor on the sphere. Slowly they moved it up the slope. "When we have a moment," Stile said, "let's see about making up a good body for my other self."

"Your other self!" she exclaimed. "Yes, of course. The book has spells to convert wood or other substance to flesh, as we did for Trool. You have Blue's soul preserved. I don't think the soul can go to that body while you are in Phaze, but when the frames separate, Clef can pipe it in, and—"

"And my other self will be restored to life in Phaze," Stile finished.

"He sacrificed his life to give me the chance to enter his frame and work with the Oracle. The least I can do is give it back to him when my task is done."

"But what of the prophecy? Phaze will not be safe until—"

"Until Blue departs it forever!" Stile finished. "In the confusion of great events, I forgot that!" He pondered, disturbed. "No, I can not be entirely governed by prophecy. I must do what I deem right; what will happen, will happen." But he remained disquieted, as did his other self.

"The body has to be crafted by hand," Sheen said. "It can't be made directly by magic, or it will perish when the magic diminishes. So we can't do it right this minute. But I won't forget to see to it before the end." She paused. "What does Blue think of this?"

Stile shifted to his alternate awareness. Now he had confirmation of his prior conjecture; Blue had, through a special divinatory spell, discovered what was developing and realized that the best thing he could do for the land he loved was to die. But, fearful that his sacrifice might be in vain, he had hedged. He had conjured his soul into his harmonica and given the instrument an affinity for his other self. Now he knew his act had been justified, for Stile had used the harmonica to achieve his necessary level of power.

As for having his life back in the new order, he had not expected this, and not even considered the possibility of resuming his life in Phaze. The notion had a certain guilty appeal. Yet if the presence of Blue meant ruin for Phaze, he would be better off dead. He would have to formulate some plans for a formerly blank future, knowing that he might again have to give it up if the prophecy were true. All he could do was try it and see; perhaps there would be interim tasks for him to do before he departed.

"I thank thee for thy consideration," Blue said to Sheen. "Glad am I to have facilitated thine entry here, lovely Lady Machine."

Again Sheen reacted with pleased embarrassment. "There's something about the people of Phaze," she murmured.

The Brown Adept rode up on her golem mount. "I think my golems can handle it, as long as nothing else bothers them. Art thou going to make the Lady Machine alive now? I will give her part of my soul."

"I've been thinking about that," Sheen said. "All my brief existence I have longed to be alive—but now I have the chance for it, I'm not sure. I don't think it would carry over into Proton—and if it did, there would still be a severe readjustment. I'd have to eat regularly, and eliminate regularly—both rather messy inconveniences—and sleep, which is a waste of useful time. My whole routine would be changed. I think I'm better off as a robot."

"But Blue could love thee as a woman," Brown said. "And thou couldst love him."

How intimately had the two consulted while they worked on the restoration of Trool? Brown seemed to know a lot more about Stile's business than he had told her. He decided to stay out of this conversation.

"I love him already," Sheen said. "Life could not change that. And his love will always be for the Lady Blue. My life would not change that, either, and I wouldn't want it to. So all I really have to gain, by marrying him in Proton, is the precedent for the self-willed machines—and if I were alive, that precedent would no longer exist."

"Oh. I guess so," Brown said. "I think thou art just fine as thou art, Lady Machine. So I guess thou canst just use the magic book to cure Blue's knees, and maybe make him a little taller, and—"

Now Stile had to join in. "My knees are part of my present life; I no longer care to have them fixed. And my height—I always wanted to be taller, for that is the human definition of status, however foolish we all know it to be—I share Sheen's opinion. I would be a different person, with new problems. I stand to gain nothing by changing what I am."

Brown shrugged. "Okay. Actually, the Little Folk are perfect the way they are, and thou art not much different." That jarred Stile, but he tried not to show it. "I'll make up a golem in thine image; the book can make it flesh, and the other Blue can move into it when he's ready." She rode off.

In due course an enemy contingent arrived—a small squadron of tanklike earthmovers, borers, and personnel transports. The Citizens of Proton had no formal armed forces, since no life existed outside the domes, ordinarily. Construction vehicles tended to be enclosed and airtight, but some were remote-controlled or robotic. The present group was of the last type.

"Low-grade machines," Sheen said. "The Citizens know better than to trust the sophisticated robots, though in truth only a small percentage is self-willed."

"I hope your friends are not suffering unduly as a result of betraying their nature to the Citizens," Stile said. He was uncertain which form of language to use in the juxtaposition zone, and decided to stick to Proton unless addressing a Phaze creature.

"The juxtaposition has proved to be enough of a distraction," she said. "It is not easy to identify a specific self-willed machine when it wants to conceal itself. If the enemy wins this war, all my kind of machines will be destroyed." Stile knew she was speaking literally; there would be absolutely no mercy from the Citizens.

The enemy machines formed up before the ball of Phazite. One fired an excavation bomb at it, but nothing happened. "Phazite protects itself," Sheen remarked. "You can move it or use it, but you can't damage it with less than a nuclear cannon."

Several laser beams speared toward the sphere, but again without effect. Regardless of magic, Phazite was extremely tough stuff, twice as dense as anything ordinarily found in a planet; unless subjected to the key environment, it was virtually indestructible. The Brown Adept rejoined Stile and Sheen, staying clear of the dangerous region.

Now the vehicles moved up to push against the ball itself. The golems pushed on the other side. The machines had more power, but only one unit at a time could contact the Phazite, compact as it was, while the golems could apply all their force. The boulder rocked back and forth, then rolled to the side and forward. The golems were able to maneuver better, and were making progress again.

The machines regrouped. Another vehicle lined up and pushed on the boulder. Again the golems nudged the ball around the machine. Their brains were wooden, but they did learn slowly from experience.

Unfortunately, so did the machines. They consulted with each other briefly, then lined up again—and charged the golems.

"No!" the Brown Adept cried as a truck smashed into a golem. It was as if she felt the blow herself. "That's cheating!"

"There are no rules to this game," Stile said.

"Oh, is that so?" Brown's small face firmed, and she called new instructions to her minions.

Now the golems fought back. When the vehicles charged, the golems stepped aside, then leaned in close to pound at the vulnerable regions as Stile explained them to Brown. Tires burst under the impact of pointed wooden feet; plastic cracked under wooden fists. But the machines, though dented, continued to fight.

"These are not like animals," Sheen said. "They don't hurt. Thou must disrupt their power trains or electrical systems."

The Brown Adept had no knowledge of technology. "Obey the Lady Machine!" she called to the golems.

Sheen called out instructions. Now the golems went after more specific things. They unscrewed the fastenings for maintenance apertures and ripped out wiring; they punched holes in lubrication lines. Soon all the machines were out of commission.

The golems had won this engagement. But time had been lost. The juxtaposition would remain only a few hours, and in that time the Phazite had to be moved across into the frame of Proton. The next obstacle would surely be more formidable; this had been merely a token engagement, a first testing of strength.

Stile brought out his map again. "We'll have to plan strategy, arrange a diversion. Now our obvious route is curving north, through the unicorn demesnes, to pass between the Oracle's palace and the central lake, in a generally descending lay of land. So they'll have that region well guarded. We'll send a contingent of creatures there, clearing a path for the ball. Our least likely route would be back toward the Purple Mountains, through the sidhe demesnes, where my friend Clef traveled when he first entered Phaze. The terrain is forested, irregular, and infested by harpies. So that's where we had better go."

"But it will take forever to roll the ball through that region!" Brown protested.

"Not if we can figure out a good way through. Magic could be used to prepare the way, such as the construction of sturdy bridges over gulfs. Could you handle that, Sheen?"

"Certainly. The enemy Adepts will never know what I'm doing. But I need to be on hand to guard you."

"Fear not for Blue, loyal Lady," Stile's alternate self said. "The Adepts will strike not until they fathom our purpose, fearing to waste their magic on distractions. I know them, I know their minds. Go thy way, and we shall meet anon."

"Meanwhile, I will come with thee, Blue, to plot the false route," Brown said, enjoying this adventure.

Trool the troll reappeared. "The ogres, giants, and animalheads are marching from the west to join thee," he reported. "But the goblins are marching south to intercept them and thee. There will be a battle when they meet."

Stile consulted his map again. "How fast are they moving?"

"The animalheads are slowest, but also nearest. They will be here—" Trool indicated a spot within the unicorn demesnes on the map. "The ogres move faster, but the Black Demesnes are directly in their path, and the Green Demesnes to the south. They must veer north, then south, and should be here by dusk." He indicated a spot near the Oracle's palace. "The giants are farthest distant, but stride so large they will be with thee by late afternoon."

Late afternoon. Stile realized it was near midday now. But it had seemed like only an hour since the Citizens' business meeting, which had been in the evening. What had happened to the intervening night? Sheen must have slipped in a stasis-spell before letting him leave her temporary dome in the ogres' demesnes, and he had never even noticed. It was probably for the best; he had needed a good night's rest. So much was happening, the picture changing so radically, it was hard to keep track. But he had to keep going. "And the goblins?"

"The enemy Adepts are helping them move, but the goblins are so many that no spell can conjure them all—and the Lady Golem-Adept's counterspell prevents their coming all the way here by magic anyway. Logistics is a problem. They will be in this spot by dusk." He indicated the Oracle's palace.

"That means the ogres and goblins will meet somewhat to the north of the Oracle," Stile said grimly, tracing the likely paths on the map. "We'd better send a detachment of unicorns to help the ogres. After all, that's right in the path of our decoy effort. We have to take it seriously enough to fool them." He glanced at the golems, who were moving the ball again. "Have them go slowly, maybe pushing the ball farther uphill than necessary, so we can roll it down quickly—in an unanticipated direction. I want to give the enemy every chance to rush its forces to the wrong rendezvous."

Brown gave instructions to a messenger golem, then accompanied Stile on the mock survey excursion. Stile would have preferred to fly, but Sheen's antimagic spell stopped him as well as the enemy Adepts. He had to go on foot, at least until a unicorn arrived. Fortunately he was quite capable afoot. He set out at a running pace, covering each mile in about seven minutes. Brown's big golem steed kept pace with huge strides.

Then the unicorn he had hoped for came into sight. "Clip!" Stile cried. "Thou didst know I needed thee!"

Clip played a saxophone tune of agreement. Stile vaulted to his back, and they were off at a much faster pace. "Aw, the troll told him," Brown said disparagingly.

Of course that was true. In this frame of magic, coincidence was seldom unassisted.

Stile experienced the peculiar wrenching of separation again. They had once more passed outside the zone of juxtaposition, and his soul was all his own. The boundaries of the expanded curtain seemed to be quite irregular. He had supposed north would lead into the center of it. His other self had not intruded, letting Stile handle things his way, but the other's presence was increasingly comfortable, and his absence increasingly jarring. Now the terrain seemed less familiar, for his other self's experience with the land was absent. Also, now the overlapping terrain of Proton was gone; this was mostly barren rock and sand, in the science frame, easy to ignore in the presence of the Phaze vegetation, but still present when one cared to perceive it. Well, at least he would suffer no Citizen malice here; only the enemy Adepts could reach him.

Was there a valid parallel here? His soul was complete only when the geography was complete. Could the land be said to have a soul, perhaps in the form of the special mineral that the Citizens of Proton had depleted? It was odd, in one sense, that the Citizens resisted the transfer of Phazite, since it would dramatically enrich their world. But of course they would prefer to keep the frames partially overlapped, linked by the curtain so that in due course the Citizens could mine in Phaze as well as in Proton. They would equalize the frames by depleting both. The fact that such mining would do to the environment of Phaze what it had done to that of Proton, and also eliminate the remaining magic of Phaze, seemed not to concern the Citizens. There were, after all, other worlds in the universe to exploit, once this one was squeezed dry. Since Stile's transfer of power-mineral would enable the frames to balance, freeing them to separate, that would forever deny the Citizens the opportunity of exploitation. They seemed willfully ignorant of the substantial risk that both frames would be destroyed long before such exploitation could be completed. Stile wondered whether the citizens of ancient Harappa, in the Indian subcontinent of Earth, had had a similar attitude. Had they denuded the land of its necessary resources until it could support their population no longer, so that they weakened and fell to Nordic barbarians in the sixteenth century B.C.? Wealth and power at the expense of nature were an inevitably lethal cancer. But there seemed to be no gentle way to convince cancer to practice moderation.

Well, he, Stile, was fated to have considerable power, it seemed, in the frame of Proton after the separation, and his other self would have it in Phaze, assuming that prophecy had priority over the Blue-be-banished prophecy. The resources of the Oracle-computer, which were obviously considerable, would be at his disposal, and the self-willed machines would cooperate. Those machines would have legal-person status, of course. He would be able to enforce a more sensible restraint on that errant society.

Stile sighed. Somehow the prospect of all that power and responsibility did not appeal to him. All he really wanted was to be in Phaze with his creature friends and the Lady Blue. That was what he could not have.

Would it be so bad with Sheen? Of course not. She was the best possible woman, her origin aside. Meanwhile, in Phaze, the Lady Blue would have her real husband back. She, at least, would not suffer.

Somehow he was not convincing himself.

Soon they were in sight of the unicorn herd, with a good route for the ball worked out. Stile suffered a pang, realizing that this was probably the last time he would see the Lady Blue. He would have to tell her and bid her farewell—and conceal if he could the way he actually felt about this coming separation. The break was inevitable; it was best that it be clean, without hysterics.

The Herd Stallion met him.

"Lord Blue, I will tell our plan, an thou dost prefer," Brown volunteered. "Do thou go to Neysa and the Lady."

Stile thanked her; she was a most helpful child at times, though somehow he was not eager to do what he had to do. He nerved himself and went directly to the protected inner circle, where Neysa and the Lady Blue awaited him.

He tried to tell himself he was happy to see them, but instead he found himself overcome by misgiving. He tried to smile, but they realized at once that something was wrong, and both came to him solicitously. "What is the matter, my Lord?" the Lady asked. "Does the campaign go ill?"

"It goes well enough," Stile said. He had learned so much so recently and shared so little with her! They had just been on their honeymoon, and now it seemed years past.

"Then what we feared is true," the Lady said, one hand on Neysa's black mane. "I have my child of thee, and thou art leaving us."

Was this the extent of her reaction? He knew she was capable of fierce displays of anger, sorrow, and love. How could she treat this as if it were commonplace?

"The prophecy of thy second husband no longer protects me," he said gravely. "Thou hast conceived, and I am no longer essential. There is another prophecy, that Phaze will not be safe until the Blue Adept departs it. I am now the Blue Adept; I would not put this frame in danger willingly." And he realized as he spoke that the prophecies could indeed make sense; the present Blue Adept had to leave so that the defunct Blue Adept could return. Thus Blue would both leave and remain, both prophecies honored. "The frames will separate—and I must return to mine own."

The Lady nodded. "Somehow I knew it would be thus. Prophecies care naught for human happiness, only the letter of their fulfillment."

True; fate did not care. "But thou wilt not be alone," Stile said quickly. "The soul of thy first husband, mine other self, survives. He shall have a human body again."

Her composure faltered. "He lives?"

"Not exactly. He lost his body. But I believe I can restore it to him, and he will be the same as he was, as far as anyone can tell."

Her brow furrowed. "But I love *thee* now!"

"And I love thee. But when thy husband lives, my place will be elsewhere. I thought him dead, else I would not have married thee. He gave up his body that Phaze might be saved, and now he must have it back. This is what is right."

"Aye, it is right," she agreed. "It is clear where my duty lies."

She was taking it well—and that, too, was painful. He knew she loved him but would be loyal to her first husband, as Stile would be loyal to Sheen. This was the way it had to be. Yet somehow he had hoped that the Lady Blue would not take it quite this well. Was it so easy to give him up on such short notice?

Suddenly she flung her arms about him. "Thee, thee, thee!" she cried, and her hot tears made her cheek slippery as she kissed him.

That was more like it! She was meltingly warm and sweet and wholly desirable. "Thee, thee, thee," he echoed, in the Phaze signal of abandonment to love, and held her crushingly close.

Then, by mutual resignation, they drew apart. She brought a cloth to his face and cleaned him up, and he realized that half the tears were his own. Through the blur he saw the shimmer of the landscape about them, the reaction of the environment to an expression of deep truth. The unicorns perceived it too, and were turning to look at the couple.

But now they both had control again. They uttered no further words, letting their statement of love be the last.

Stile turned to Neysa to bid her farewell: But she stood facing away from him, standing with her tail toward him—the classic expression of disapproval. The woman might forgive him his departure; the unicorn did not.

He could not blame her. His body, so recently so warm, now felt chilled, as if his heart had been frozen. Had he expected Neysa, his closest friend in Phaze, to welcome his announcement with forward-perking ears? There was no good way to conclude this painful scene. Stile walked silently away.

Clip stood near, watching his sister Neysa. His mane was half flared in anger, and his breath had the tinge of fire, but he was silent. Stile knew Clip was furious with Neysa, but had no authority to interfere. There was justice in it; Neysa expressed the attitude the Lady Blue did not, in her fashion freeing the Lady to be forgiving. The complete emotion could not be expressed by one person, so had been portioned between two.

The Brown Adept was waiting for him at the edge of the unicorn circle. "I told the Stallion," she said. "He'll help." She looked toward Neysa and the Lady Blue. "I guess it didn't work out so well, huh?"

"I fear I'm not much for diplomacy," Stile said. "I don't want to go, they don't want me to go—there's no positive side."

"Why dost thou not just stay here when the frames part?" she asked naïvely.

"I am a usurper here in Phaze. This good life is not mine to keep—not at the expense of mine other self. I was brought here to do a job, and when the job is done I must leave. So it has been prophesied."

"I guess when I'm grown up, maybe I'll understand that kind of nonsense."

"Maybe," Stile agreed wryly.

Stile mounted Clip and they returned the way they had come, setting small markers to show the prospective route for the ball. There was no interference from the other Adepts; they were of course biding their time, since they were unable to strike at him magically at the moment. They would have their minions here in force to stop the ball, though! The unicorns would have an ugly task, protecting this decoy route. The irony was that this was an excellent path; if there were no opposition, the ball could travel rapidly here.

When they recrossed into the zone of juxtaposition, his other self rejoined him. The personality of Blue assimilated the new experience and shrank away.

"Thou dost look peaked," the Brown Adept said. "Is aught wrong?"

"It is mine other self," Stile said. "I fear he likes not what I have done."

"The true Blue? Speak to me, other Adept."

"Aye, Brown," the other self said. "But surely thou dost not wish to be burdened with the problems of adults."

"Oh, sure," she said eagerly. "'Specially if it's about a woman. Some day I'll grow up and break hearts too."

"That thou surely wilt," Blue agreed. "My concern is this: for many years did I love the Lady Blue, though she loved me not. When finally I did win her heart as well as her hand, I learned that she was destined to love another after me, more than me. This was one reason I yielded up my life. Now I know it is mine other self she loves. Am I to return to that situation, at his expense?"

"Oh, that is a bad one!" Brown agreed. "But maybe she will learn to love thee again. Thou dost have charm, thou knowest; the Lady Machine's nerve circuits do run hot and cold when thou dost address her."

"The Lady Machine is programmed to love mine image," Blue said. "I admit she is a fascinating creature, like none I have encountered before. But the Lady Blue is not that type. She will act in all ways proper, as she did before, and be the finest wife any man could have, but her deepest heart will never revert. Her love never backtracks."

"Then what good is it, coming back to life?" Brown asked, with the innocent directness of her age.

"There are other things in life besides love," Blue said. "The Lady will need protection, and creatures will need attention. There will be much work for me to do—just as there will be for mine other self in the fabulous science frame. He will be no happier than I."

Stile had no argument with that. His other self was the same person as himself, in a superficially different but fundamentally similar situation, facing life with a woman who was not precisely right. The days of great adventure and expectation were almost past. To lose the present engagement would be to die, knowing the frames would in time perish also as the unrelieved stress developed to the breaking point. To win would be to return to a somewhat commonplace existence—for both his selves. The choice was between disaster and mediocrity.

"I'm not sure I want to grow up, if that's what it's like," Brown said.

They reached the ball of Phazite. Sheen had returned to it also. "Is the other route ready?" Stile asked.

"Not quite. We must delay another hour. But it will be worth the wait."

"Then I have time to make a golem body for Blue," Brown exclaimed. Evidently she had resigned herself quickly to the situation and was determined to do her part even if Stile and Blue were not destined for happiness. "I hope I can do it right. I haven't had much practice with lifelike figures, especially male ones. My golems are mostly neuter."

Stile could appreciate the problem. "Maybe Trool can help. He's quite a sculptor."

Trool appeared. "I model in stone, not wood."

"We'll convert stone to flesh," Sheen said. "All we need is the form."

So while the golems rolled the great ball along its soon-to-be-diverted course, Trool the troll sculpted in stone. He excavated a rock from the ground in short order, his huge gaunt hands scraping the earth and sand away with a velocity no normal person could approach, and freed a stone of suitable size by scraping out the rock beneath it with his stiffened fingers. Apparently the stone became soft under his touch, like warming butter. Stile picked up a half-melted chip and found it to be cold, hard stone. No wonder trolls could tunnel so readily; the hardest rock was very much like putty in their hands. No wonder, also, they were so much feared by ordinary folk. Who could stand against hands that could gouge solid stone? Trool had stood with the Lady Blue against the ogres, Stile remembered, and the ogres had been cautious, not exchanging blows with him. They had been able to overpower him, of course, by using their own mode of combat.

When Trool had his man-sized fragment, he glanced at Stile and began to mold the image. Rapidly, magically, the form took shape—head, arms, legs. The troll was indeed a talented sculptor; the statue was perfect. Soon it was standing braced against a tree—a naked man, complete in every part, just like Stile.

Sheen and Brown were watching, amazed. "Gee, you sure are better at carving than I am," Brown said. "My prede—pred—the former Brown Adept could make figures just like people, but I can't, yet."

"I can't make them live," Trool said shortly.

Then Sheen made magic from the book, and the statue turned to flesh. But it remained cold, inanimate. The Brown Adept laid her hands on it, and it animated—a golem made of flesh. The new body was ready.

"Say—it worked!" Brown exclaimed, pleased.

Stile wondered how this carved and animated figure could have living guts and bones and brain. Presumably these had been taken care of by Sheen's spell. Magic was funny stuff!

But the soul could not yet enter this body. Two selves could not exist separately in the zone of juxtaposition. The second body would only become truly alive when the frames separated.

"Will it be all right until needed?" Stile asked. "It won't spoil?"

"My golems don't spoil!" Brown said indignantly. "It will keep until the soul enters it. Then it'll be alive and will have to eat and sleep and you-know."

"Then park it in a safe place," he said. "And let the harmonica remain with it, so that his soul can find it in case there is a problem." For despite all his planning, Stile was not at all sure he would succeed in his mission, or necessarily survive the next few hours. Little had been heard from the enemy Adepts recently; they had surely not been idle.

Sheen conjured body and harmonica to the Blue Demesnes, which were in no part of the current action. Stile felt another pang of separation as he lost the harmonica; it had been such an important part of his life in Phaze.

The necessary time had passed. They had the golems start the ball on its new course to the south. "But make a spell of illusion," Stile directed. "I want it to seem that the ball is proceeding on the course Brown and I just charted."

"I can generate a ball of similar size, made of ordinary rock," Sheen said.

"And I'll have some of my golems push it," Brown said. "It won't be nearly as heavy, so I'll tell them not to push as hard."

Soon the mock ball diverged from the real one, and a contingent of golems started it on its way. Stile wasn't sure how long this would fool the Adepts, but it was worth a try.

Meanwhile, under cover of a fog that Sheen generated, the main part of the golem force levered the Phazite ball back toward the Purple Mountains. A door opened in the hillside, and they saw the tunnel the trolls had made—a smooth, round tube of just the right size, slanting very gently down. They rolled the boulder to it, and it began to travel down its channel on its own.

"From here on, it's easy," Sheen said. "This tube will carry the Phazite kilometers along in a short time. At the far end, the tunnel spirals up to the top of a substantial foothill; from there it can roll north with such momentum the enemy will not be able to stop it before it crosses into Proton proper."

"Good strategy," Stile agreed. "But can the golems get it up that spiral?"

"My friends in Proton have installed a power winch."

Stile laughed. "I keep forgetting we can draw on science, too, now! This begins to seem easy!"

They followed the ball as it moved, Stile and Clip fitting comfortably in the tunnel, Brown's golem steed hunching over, and Sheen riding a motorized unicycle she had conjured. She was enjoying her role as enchantress.

The ball accelerated, forcing them to hurry to keep it in sight. Even so, it drew ahead, rounding a bend and disappearing.

They hastened on, but the ball was already around the next bend, still out of sight. When they passed that bend, they looked along an extended straightaway—and the ball was not there.

Stile wasn't sure whether he or his other self first realized the truth. "Hostile magic!" he cried.

"Can't be," Sheen protested. "I had it counterspelled."

"Use a new spell to locate the ball."

She used a simple locator-spell. "It's off to the side," she said, surprised.

"That last curve—they made a detour!" Stile said. "Had a crew in to tunnel—no Adept magic—goblins, maybe, or some borers from Proton—they can draw on the same resources we can—the ball went down that, while we followed the proper channel."

They charged back to the curve. There it was. An offshoot tunnel masked by an illusion-spell that had to have been instituted before Sheen's arrival. The enemy Adepts had anticipated this tunnel ploy and quietly prepared for it.

No—they couldn't have placed the spell before Sheen got there, because Sheen had supervised the construction of the tunnel and had her magic in force throughout. Something else—ah. The offshoot tunnel was in fact an old Proton mine shaft. A small amount of work had tied it in to the new troll tunnel, and a tiny generator had sealed off the entrance with an opaque force field. No magic, and minimal effort. Someone had been very clever.

"I don't like this," Stile said. "They evidently know what we're doing here, and someone with a good mind is on the scene. We're being outmaneuvered. While we made a duplicate image of me, they did this."

But there was nothing much to do except go after the Phazite. They started down the detour tunnel, hoping to catch up with the ball before it reached whatever destination the enemy had plotted. Sheen's magic showed no enemies nearby; like her own workers, they had departed as soon as their job was done. The tunnels were empty because the presence of anyone could alert the other side to what was going on.

They heard a noise ahead. Something was moving, heavily, making the tunnel shudder.

Ooops! The ball of Phazite was rolling back toward them at horrendous velocity!

"Get out of its way!" Stile cried. "A hundred and fifty tons will crush us flat!"

But the ball was moving too swiftly; they could not outrun it, and the intersection of tunnels was too far back. "Make a spell, Lady Machine!" Brown screamed.

Sheen made a gesture—and abruptly their entire party was in the tunnel beyond the rolling ball, watching the thing retreat. Stile felt weak in the knees, and not because of their injury. He didn't like being dependent on someone else for magic. Was that the way others felt about him?

"See—it slants up, there ahead," Brown said brightly. She, at least, was used to accepting enchantment from others, though she was Adept herself. "They fixed it up so the ball would roll up, then reverse and come right back at us."

"Timed so we would be in the middle when it arrived," Sheen said.

"No direct magic—but a neat trap," Stile agreed. "They must have assumed that if the book blocked out Adept magic, it would leave us helpless. They didn't realize that a non-Adept would be doing the spells."

"Funny Trool didn't warn us," Brown said.

Trool appeared, chagrined. "I saw it not. I know not how I missed it."

For a moment Stile wondered whether the troll could have betrayed them. But he found he couldn't believe that. For one thing, he had confidence in his judgment of creatures. For another, it was a woman— a young-seeming one—who had been prophesied to betray him, and that had already come to pass before the prophecy reached him. So there had to have been enough illusion magic, or clever maneuvering, to deceive everyone in this case; no betrayal was involved.

"Set a deflector at the mouth of the detour," Stile told Sheen, "so that when the ball reverses again, it will go down the correct tunnel."

She lifted a finger. "Done."

"You sure know a lot of spells," Brown said.

"Robots assimilate programmed material very rapidly," Sheen replied. "The advantages of being a machine are becoming clearer to me, now that I have considered life."

They marched up to the intersection of tubes. The ball had already reversed course and traveled down its proper channel. They followed it without further event to the end.

"Be alert for other hostile effects," Stile told Sheen. "The enemy can't hit us with new magic, but, as we have seen, the prepared traps can be awkward enough."

Sheen held her finger up as if testing the wind. "No magic here," she reported.

They stood at the winch. It was a heavy-duty model, powered by a chip of Protonite, and its massive cables were adequate to the need. They placed the harness about the ball; it fitted with little bearings so that the ball could roll within its confinement. With the pulleys and leverage available, the ball should move up the spiral.

It did move up. There were no hitches. Yet Stile worried. He knew the enemy would strike; he didn't know when and how. Why hadn't they destroyed the winch, since obviously they had had access to this tunnel? "Trool?" he asked.

There was no response from the troll. Probably he was out surveying the situation, and would report the moment he spied anything significant.

The winch cranked the ball of Phazite up the spiraling tunnel, providing it the elevation it would need to roll all the way across the juxtaposition zone to Proton. Once that boulder started rolling, it should be prohibitively difficult to stop. Victory seemed very near at hand—and still Stile worried. He was absolutely sure something ugly was incipient.

At last they reached the top. The winch delivered the ball to a platform housed in earth, surely resembling a mound of the Little Folk from outside. All they had to do now was open the gate and nudge it out.

Trool appeared. "Found thee at last!" he exclaimed. "Take not this route, Adept!"

Stile looked at him sourly. "We have already taken this route. Where hast thou been?"

"Looking all over for thee! There are a hundred traces of thy presence, all mistaken—until this one."

"Diversion magic," Stile said. "False clues to my whereabouts, laid down in advance, so that I become the needle in the haystack. But why would they try to mislead thee?"

"Because I have spied on them. Barely did I reach thee in time to give warning; the goblins have bypassed the giants, indulged in forced marches, and are lurking in ambush for thee here. Thou canst not pass this way, Adept."

"Nonsense," Sheen said. "I detect no goblins within seventy kilometers."

"Thou shouldst get beyond their screening spells," Trool said. "From behind, they are naught. There are maybe five hundred goblins there, armed with Proton weapons and busy making entrenchments. That much did I see; I looked no more, so that I could return in haste to warn thee. But then did I face the enchantment that concealed thee from me. All of it is passive magic, set in place before we came here, yet a nuisance."

"I knew things were too easy," Stile muttered. "They left us alone so we would continue on into their trap. We have perhaps four hours remaining to get the Phazite across the north border of the juxtaposition zone. We can not backtrack now. We shall have to proceed."

"I can neutralize the screen magic," Sheen said. "But that will not remove the goblins. The enemy Adepts will prevent me from performing any mass spell on them."

"So there are, after all, limits to the book," Stile said with a wry smile.

"Yes. It gives me power to stand off all the Adepts—but not to overwhelm them. We shall have to handle the goblins physically."

"The animalheads are arriving on the scene," Trool said. "But they, too, are confused by the shield-spells. If thou dost eliminate the shields, all will encounter each other and there will be mayhem galore."

"I don't want mayhem," Stile said. "But if it has to be, I want to ease the burden on the animalheads. Sheen, conjure me a holophone."

In a moment it was there. Stile called his own dome, and Mellon answered. His leg had been repaired. "I am glad to see you back in form, sir," he said.

Stile was sure the call was tapped and might soon be blocked off. "I'm in a battle situation and need reinforcements," he said quickly. "I can't arrange to conjure large groups, so they'll have to march. The goblins are enemies and will slaughter whomever they can; the other creatures, however strange they may appear, are friends. Can you arrange anything?"

"Allow thirty minutes, sir." The image faded.

So, just like that, it was done. Mellon would get the coordinates of Stile's location from the holo and would send out what he could. Stile's Citizen resources were now considerable; he could afford a private army, if anyone could.

He returned to his immediate situation. "If the goblins have Proton weapons, we'll need Proton defenses. They are probably making ready to storm this hill. We should have light, bulletproof armor, laser screens—"

"Personal force fields," Sheen suggested. "They will handle a combination of attacks, and I can conjure in such small units without alerting the enemy Adepts."

"And make invisibility-spells for the rest of us," Brown added. "They'll know we're near the Phazite ball, but still—"

"Yes," Stile agreed. "Probably they won't want to fire their shots too close to the Phazite; they won't have effect, and if they did, what would it be? There's power to destroy the planet in this dense little sphere; no one would gain if that energy were suddenly released."

"Most likely they will attempt to wipe us out, and send the ball rolling back down the spiral tube," Sheen said. "Then they will blast the entrance closed and wait for the juxtaposition to terminate. Clef surely can't hold it much longer."

"We're committed to our present course," Stile said, shaking his head ruefully. "They gave us full opportunity to go beyond the point of retreat. I'd like to meet the goblin commander; he's one smart tactician."

"Maybe an Adept is running things," Brown said.

"This smacks more of field tactics to me." Stile brought out his map. "As I make it, the ball has a fairly straight path north from here. All we need to do is clear out a few obstacles in the channel and start it rolling. We don't want to mire it in the lake, unless that's beyond the juxtaposition zone. Trool, where is the north side of the curtain now?"

"It is stabilized north of the lake and north of the Oracle's palace, in this section," the troll replied. "There is some curve in it yet; elsewhere it impinges the White Mountain range, but here it is fairly southerly."

"And where is it in this section?" Stile asked, indicating the place where the Oracle-computer was buried, somewhat removed from the Oracle's palace.

"It slants northwest, passing just south of that region. But that is not a good place to roll the ball anyway; there is a long incline up, with the curtain almost at the ridge there. Much easier to roll it through the valley to the east."

So the curtain was just south of the Oracle-computer. That was why there had been no news of the computer's crossing; Clef's Flute had not been able to broaden the juxtaposition zone enough. That meant the curtain would have to be stretched northward a little—and how would Stile find the creature-power to accomplish that, in the midst of battle?

"Nevertheless, I believe we'll roll it across at this site," Stile said, after reflecting a moment. "I hope the giants arrive in time to help; they'll be able to roll it barehanded."

"I'm not sure," Sheen said. "The ball of Phazite is the same diameter as a giant's finger—but its substance is fifty times as dense as living flesh. Trying to push on it could be clumsy and painful."

"They can use silver thimbles, or roll it with a pool cue," Stile said, smiling briefly.

"And the route," she said. "Why roll the ball across that particular place?"

Stile did not want to express his notion openly, for fear the enemy was somehow eavesdropping. "Because it will be difficult, slow, but certain; the enemy will not have barriers entrenched there, and no special traps, and our time will be running out."

"That's not fully logical," she protested. "The enemy will not guard that region well, because the natural terrain represents a formidable defense. They will have time to regroup while we struggle to push the ball up the hill."

"Maybe," Stile agreed.

"I hope your illogic has some redeeming aspect."

"I think thou art crazy," Brown said succinctly.

"We'll clear a course that curves northwest," Stile said. "They may assume it's another ruse. Then we'll roll the ball along it as fast and far as we can and hope for the best."

Trool faded out for another survey and returned to report that the contingent from Proton was arriving. "Flesh and metal men," he said wonderingly.

"Cyborgs, maybe. Robots with human brains. They can be very effective. It's time for us to move." He looked around the chamber. "I want the golem crew to remain here, to start the ball rolling at my signal. Timing is essential. Brown will supervise them. Sheen and I will sneak out and clear the path. Trool will act as liaison."

"I want to sneak out too!" Brown cried.

"What about me?" Clip asked, in man-form.

Stile had been afraid of this. He had to devise legitimate jobs for everyone. "Thou canst go report to thy herd," he said to the unicorn. "In thy hawk-form and with a spell of invisibility, thou canst get through to tell the Stallion of our situation." Stile turned to Brown. "But thou—if thou shouldst go, who will guard the book?"

Her brown eyes widened. "The book of magic?"

"If the enemy gets its hands on that, we're finished. We dare not take it out to battle. Sheen has memorized the spells she needs; she doesn't need the book with her now. So it is safest with thee and thy golems."

Brown's eyes fixed on the book, round with awe. "I guess . . ." she breathed.

The main reason Stile wanted her here was to keep the child out of the worst danger. Any protective spell they might make might be negated by a specific enemy counterspell. The book did need guarding, so it was a valid pretext.

He left with Sheen, using an invisibility-spell as well as the protective shields she had fashioned before. He doubted the two of them would remain undiscovered, but with luck, the goblin army should be distracted by the detachments of serfs, robots, and animalheads.

They started down the slope, using conjured spades to eliminate troublesome ridges. This, too, was risky, since the changes they made were visible, possibly calling attention to their otherwise invisible progress. Most of the slope was all right, with a natural channel requiring only touching up.

But as they got away from the ball, the illusion fashioned by the enemy Adepts faded. They saw the goblins ranged about the base of the hill, pistols drawn. The moment there was any visible action at the top of the slope, the goblins would start firing.

Even in this hiatus, it was bad enough. Detachments of goblins were building a series of obstructions near the base of the slope, wedgelike barriers with the sharp ends pointed uphill. If the Phazite ball encountered a wall crosswise, it would crash right through; but these wedges were oriented to deflect it efficiently off-course, where it could be further deflected by the natural channels below, until it was stuck in some cul-de-sac, and the game would be lost. That smart enemy commander's handiwork again! "Our work is cut out for us," Stile said. "One misplay, and we lose the ball. Conjure me some plastic explosive and detonators that can be set off by magic invocation. I'll have to mine some of those barriers."

"That sort of thing is not in the book," Sheen protested. "No plastic explosive with magic detonators! But I can get you one-hour timed explosive."

"That will do. Just let me know when the hour is up so I can get clear."

She conjured the explosive. It was high-grade; a kilogram had enough explosive power to blast away all the emplacements they would have time to mine. They walked on down the hill.

The contingent from Proton was marching toward the hill. Stile realized that it was on the wrong side of the illusion-spell and did not perceive the goblin army; the goblins would ambush it, wiping it out before it had a chance to organize. "I can't let that happen," he muttered. "I haven't been much of an organizer; my allies will be cut down, trying to help me. I must warn them!"

"If you show yourself, *you* will be cut down!" Sheen said. "My spells won't save you from attack by the entire goblin army, backed by the magic of all the Adepts."

"Maybe your magic can help, though. Generate an image of me, like a holograph. Then you can jump it around, and no one will know exactly where I am, so the enemy won't be able to attack me."

"Now that might work," she said. "It's risky, but so are the alternatives. Your convoluted organic brain does come up with artful wrinkles." She made a combination of gestures and sounds, sketched a little figure in the dirt—he could see it and her, as the invisibility-spell affected only the enemy's observers—and suddenly Stile found himself standing in the path of the cyborgs. He felt a squeeze on his hand and knew Sheen was with him, and that his consciousness had joined his distant image. This was clever magic; his respect for the book increased.

The leader of the cyborgs spied him and approached. This was an obvious machine, with gleaming metal limbs and chambers for attachments on its torso. But it was no robot; the brain was human, taken from the body of some aging, or ill, living person. Cyborgs could be exceedingly tough and clever. "I perceive you, sir," the machine-man said, orienting a lens on him. "But you have no substance. You are therefore an image. I can not be sure of your validity. Please identify yourself in a manner I can accept."

"I am an image of Citizen Stile," Stile said. "Also the Blue Adept. My employee Mellon should have primed you with key information about me. Ask me something appropriate."

"Yes, sir. Who is your best friend?"

"In which frame?"

"That suffices, sir."

Oh. Clever. It was the type of response, rather than the actual information, that had been keyed. "Let's get busy, then," Stile said. "This region is infested with goblins with modern weapons. I doubt they are good shots, but don't take chances. If you can drive them away from this area, that would be a big help. But don't attack any animalheads or unicorns. There's quite a bit of illusion magic around, so be careful."

"We understand, sir."

"I'm not sure you do. Send out scouts to the base of that slope." He indicated it. "They will pass the line of illusion and see the truth. Pay attention to what they tell you. This is likely to be deadly serious; your lives are in jeopardy."

"Thank you, sir."

They would have to find out for themselves. Stile murmured the word "animalhead" and found himself on a hill where the animalheads were gathered. The elephanthead chief spied him with a trumpet of gladness. "We have found thee at last, Adept!" he exclaimed; evidently Stile's prior spell of intelligibility remained in force. Spells did seem to have a certain inertia about them, continuing indefinitely unless countered or canceled. "We feared ourselves lost."

Quickly Stile briefed the elephant on the situation. "Now I'll be clearing a path for the ball to roll along," he concluded. "In mine own body I'm invisible, but the goblins will quickly catch on and interfere. So if thy force can divert them from this side, and while the cyborgs operate on the other side—"

"Cyborgs?"

"They are combination people, part human, part machine, strange in appearance but worthwhile when—"

"They are like us!"

"Very like thy kind," Stile agreed, startled.

"We are ready," the elephanthead said.

Now Stile was prepared to place the first wad of explosive. But as he returned his awareness to his invisible body, he discovered that Sheen was already attending to it. She had mined two wedges and was on the third. But the goblins were all about, digging their trenches and organizing themselves for the battle.

Stile had always thought of goblins as occurring in undisciplined hordes; these were highly disciplined. They were supervised by sergeants and commissioned officers, their insignia of rank painted or tattooed on their arms.

Despite his indetectability, Stile was nervous. There were too many goblins, and they were poking around too many places; at any time, one of them could make a chance discovery of the plastic explosive. He needed to distract the goblins' attention right now, before the cyborgs and animalheads went into action, lest his game be lost at the outset.

"Goblin leader," he murmured.

He stood beside a command tent. An ugly goblin with an authoritative air was surveying the field with binoculars. "I trust it not," the goblin murmured. "They be too quiet."

"Perhaps I can help thee," Stile said.

The goblin glanced quickly at him, showing no surprise. "I had thought to see thee ere now, Adept," he said. "I be Grossnose, commander of this expedition."

Stile could appreciate the derivation of the name; the goblin's nose was unusually large, and shaped like a many-eyed potato. But physical appearance had little to do with competence. Stile found himself liking this creature, for no better reason than that he must have risen to power in much the way Stile himself had, overcoming the liability of appearance to make his place in his society. "I compliment thy expertise," Stile said. "I had thought thy forces to be intercepted by our ogre detachment."

"We force-marched around the ogres," Grossnose said. "They be not our enemy."

"I prefer not to be thine enemy, either."

"Then hear our terms for peace: leave the Phazite in place, and thy party will be granted safe passage elsewhere."

"Declined," Stile said. "But if thy troops depart in peace, we will not hinder them."

"Now understand this, Adept. If fight we must, we shall be forced to seek the source of thy power. We shall make a thrust for the book. We have held off so far only that it be not destroyed. The book may be more valuable than that entire ball of Phazite, and it were a shame to put it into hazard. But this forbearance makes mischief; already the Adepts be quarreling as to who shall possess that book. I prefer to leave it in thy hands, as thou art least corruptible by power. But I can not allow that demon ball to cross to Proton-frame; that be the end."

"The end of the present order, mayhap," Stile said. "For Citizens and Adepts. They will have to share power more equitably in the new order. Other creatures will have proportionately more power, including thine own kind. Dost thou really oppose that?"

"Nay," the goblin admitted with surprising candor. "But I do serve the present order."

This was an honest, clever, incorruptible commander, the worst kind to oppose. "I regret what will come to pass," Stile said. "If we meet again after this is over, I would like to converse with thee again. But this next hour we are enemies."

"Aye. Go about thy business, Adept. Thou dost know what be in the making."

Stile knew. It was the irony of war that slaughter and destruction came about when both sides preferred peace. He faded out, and found himself back with Sheen.

"We have to move fast," he said. "They are going to go after the book."

Indeed, a troop of goblins were already charging the hill, lasers blazing. But they were met by the animalheads, who sprang from ambush and grappled with the goblins before the latter's modern weapons could be brought into play against this close-range opponent. The goblins' inexperience with such weapons cost the enemy dearly now; the animalheads were wresting them from the goblins and using them themselves.

Simultaneously the cyborgs commenced action—and their weapons were completely modern. Some had stunners, some gas jets, some lasers, and some projectile hurlers, and they knew how to use them. The battle was on.

Stile and Sheen moved hastily along their projected channel, placing the remaining explosive. Their hour was passing, and the plastic would detonate at its assigned moment regardless of their proximity. It was funny stuff, gray-white and slightly tacky to the touch, like modeling clay; it could be torn into fragments of any size, shaped as desired, and it would adhere to whatever it was pressed against. They fitted it into the chinks of stones like mortar, and on the undersurfaces of wooden beams. The goblins should not notice the plastic unless warned about its nature.

The sounds of the battle behind became louder. Stile looked back—and saw a squadron of winged dragons coming from the south. The cyborgs fired bazookas at them. Their aim was excellent—but after the first few dragons went down in flames, the others took evasive action. They dived down close to the ground and strafed the cyborgs with their flaming breath. The goblins who had been engaging the cyborgs screamed; that strafing was hurting *them*, while the metal bodies of the machine-men withstood the heat better. The dragons might as well have been the cyborgs' allies.

"Keep moving," Sheen cautioned Stile. Indeed, he had become distracted by the action, forgetting his own important role. He hurried to place more plastic.

But haste made waste. They ran out of plastic and time before the job was done; several barriers remained. They had had enough of each, and had wasted part of both. "We must move," Sheen warned. "In ten minutes the plastic detonates, with or without us."

"Better head back for the ball," Stile said. "I want to be ready just before the plastic goes off, so we can start the ball rolling right at the moment of goblin disorganization."

They began running back toward the Phazite. New contingents of goblins were arriving from the north; they were swarming all over. Stile saw that the enemy was winning the battle of the hill; both animalheads and cyborgs were being contained and decimated. The goblins were absorbing huge losses, but prevailing because of their greater numbers and overall organization. A new force was advancing toward the Phazite. They would overrun the site before Stile could return.

"Conjure us there!" he cried.

"Can't," Sheen snapped. "The enemy Adepts have focused their full attention on this place, blocking off new magic. They're learning how to impede the potent book spells by acting together. This is the final squeeze, Stile."

"Then send my image there; that's an existing spell."

Suddenly his image was in the chamber. There were the Brown Adept and the troll, holding laser rifles clumsily, trying to oppose the advancing goblins. The remaining golems stood about awkwardly; their hands were not coordinated enough to handle modern weapons, and their wooden minds not clever enough to grasp this rapidly changing situation.

"That's no good," Stile said. "You can't stop a hundred vicious goblins by yourselves."

They looked at him, startled. "We feared for thee!" Brown exclaimed.

"Fear for thyself; they will be upon thee before I can return in the flesh. They want the book, and we must keep it away from them at any cost." Stile pondered a moment. "Trool—canst thou take Brown and the book into the tunnel and shield them with thine invisibility?"

Trool faded out. In a moment Brown faded out too. "Aye," his voice came. "But it is not safe in the tunnel, Adept; goblins are coming from the far end. We have blocked them off for the moment, but—"

"Canst thou fly with her to safety?" Stile cut in. Time was so short! "It need be but for a few minutes, until the explosive we have set goes off. Then will the enemy Adepts' attention be distracted, and we can use the spells of the book to protect ourselves."

"I will try," Trool's voice came. From several feet up, Brown cried, "Hey, this is fun!" Then they were out a ceiling aperture and away.

The goblins burst in, caving in the mound walls with pikes. They spied Stile and charged him—but their points had no effect on his image. On inspiration, he pretended that he could be hurt, and dodged about to avoid the thrusts, so as to distract them as long as possible. He didn't want them working on the Phazite ball, now vulnerable.

The golems were still standing awkwardly. Stile realized that they needed to be told what to do. "Protect yourselves!" he cried. "Golems, fight the goblins!"

Now the golems acted. They were neither smart nor swift, but they were as tough as wooden planks. The goblins swarmed over each golem and were hurled back violently. Yes, it was after all possible to make a decent fight of it!

Abruptly he was back with Sheen, at the base of the hill. The two of them were running through the battlefield, and it was grim. Goblins and animalheads lay dead and dying. This was where the animalheads had been fated to lose half their number, he realized. Some cyborgs were here too, their metal lying twisted and smoking; Stile saw one with its metal skull cracked open, the human brain exposed and shriveled. The odor of carnage was strong.

"We must find help," Sheen said, "to clean out the goblins and get the ball rolling."

"I wish we could save these creatures in pain," Stile said.

"We can't do it now. Once the ball crosses, we can."

Stile knew it was true. They had to move the ball first. Now only seconds remained before the plastic detonated.

They found a bearhead just recovering consciousness. Stile put his hand on the creature's shoulder, breaking the invisibility-spell for this one individual. "We need thee," Stile said. "Follow us."

"Aye, Blue," the bearhead agreed dizzily.

Sheen found a cyborg in the process of self-repair; it had lost a foot, but was affixing the foot of a dead cyborg in its place. Sheen introduced herself similarly. The four hurried on.

As they reached the crest of the hill, they smelled smoke. Something was burning in the mound. "The golems!" Sheen said grimly.

Stile winced. He knew the wooden golems were not truly alive, but surely they hurt when they burned. The goblins had used a devastating weapon, and the Brown Adept would be mortified.

They charged the mound, staring into its broken chamber. In the smoke of the golem bonfire, the goblins were trying to push the ball back into the spiral tube. The ball was shaking, starting to rock. Soon they would get it moving.

The four burst into the chamber. The goblins cried out and scattered as they saw the bearhead and cyborg, but rallied in a moment and drew their weapons. Stile and Sheen, invisible to them, knocked the pistols from the goblins' hands. Unable to fathom this new menace, the goblins nevertheless fought bravely, overwhelming their opposition, both visible and invisible, by force of numbers.

Then the plastic explosive detonated. The barrier wedges blew up, raining fiery pieces on the heads of the goblin army. The goblins in the mound disengaged and dashed out to see what new danger threatened. There was general disorganization.

"Now we roll it!" Stile cried. The four of them, joined by a charred but surviving golem, picked up the scattered limbs of golems and their tools and started levering the ball forward. They were more disciplined and purposeful than the goblins had been, and the ball was poised for this direction, but it was so massive they had just as much trouble budging it. "We need better levers!" Stile gasped. But he knew of none within range—and now they heard the goblins charging up the spiral tunnel. There was no time for a search.

A hawk flew into the chamber. "Clip!" Stile exclaimed. "What art thou doing here?"

The unicorn changed to man-form. "I knew thou wouldst foul it up by thyself, Adept," he said. "Mere men always do. So I brought some friends to bail thee out."

Now a bee, a hummingbird, and a blue heron flew in, changing to three more unicorns. The third had an iridescent mane. "Belle!" Stile said, recognizing her.

"She was wandering toward the battle," Clip said diffidently. "I could not leave her to such danger, and she does feel she owes thee, Adept, for the manner in which she was used to—"

"Yes, of course!" Stile agreed. "The four of you—help us push this ball down the hill!"

Clip shifted to equine form and played musical directions on his saxhorn. He was answered by a violin, tuba, and ringing-bell tune of agreement. The four put their horns carefully down into the crevice between ball and floor; then, musically coordinated, they levered up and forward.

Just like that, the ball moved. The unicorns repeated the process, working it over the dirt and rubble and outside. It was a slow, difficult task, but they worked well and kept the ball crunching forward.

Goblins burst in from the spiral tunnel. Stile, Sheen, and the bearhead, the cyborg, and the remaining golem turned to face them, protecting the unicorns' flanks. The goblins, seeing only three motley opponents, charged—and discovered the hard way that there were five. In this cramped, littered space, it was a fair match.

Then the ball nudged over the brink and started rolling down the slope in the direction Stile had dictated. The unicorns, their task done, turned to face the goblins—who suddenly lost their eagerness to fight, seeing the odds shift so substantially.

"Mount!" Stile cried, trusting the unicorns to cooperate. "Follow that ball!" And he leaped onto the nearest steed—who happened to be Belle. She spooked, never before having borne a rider, but heard Clip's musical clarification and immediately settled down. Sheen took the golem and mounted Clip, and the bearhead and cyborg mounted the remaining two. They charged down the slope.

For an instant Stile was daunted by the improbability of it all: a man, a cyborg, a robot, an animalhead, and a wooden golem, all riding unicorns through a battlefield strewn with goblins and dragons, pursuing an invaluable ball of power-rock that rolled along a channel cleared by plastic explosive. What a mishmash!

Mishmash? No—this was juxtaposition. The complete mergence of magic and science. He should enjoy it while it lasted, for it would not last long. Already he thought he felt the influence of the Platinum Flute weakening, as the strength of the Foreordained became exhausted.

Belle was a fine steed, running smoothly and swiftly, her lovely mane like silk in his grasp. But of course she was smooth; she had won the Unolympics dance event! "Belle, I thank thee for this service," he breathed, knowing she heard him despite the rush of air and booming of the passage of the Phazite ball, for her left ear rotated toward him. "I will try to do thee some return favor, when I can." And she made a faint bell-melody in response.

Meanwhile, the ball was gathering velocity. It crunched down the hill, leaving its smooth, small channel. Where bodies were in the way, they too were flattened. The Phazite was ponderous and inexorable, crushing everything in its path. The live goblins, seeing its onrush, scattered out of its way in alarm. This was the sensible thing to do.

The four unicorns galloped after it, losing headway as the ball rolled down the steepest section of the slope. All the goblins were watching it now, seeing its passage through the erstwhile barriers. For them, this progress was disaster.

But Stile knew the war was not over. Several barriers remained in place, and the slope reversed farther to the north. Stile's big gamble was with the giants and the route. If he had judged all aspects correctly, he would win—but at this moment he was in severe doubt.

The ball encountered the standing barrier wedges and blew them apart. They had not diverted it perceptibly, and seemed not to have slowed it, but Stile knew crucial impetus had been lost. Would the ball carry far enough?

Now the terrain was gently rolling, largely clear of trees. Stile had planned this carefully on the map. The ball sailed up the slope, and down, and onward. It was right on target. But it was slowing, as it had to, for the incidental resistance of the miles was cumulative.

The Proton-frame terrain, unobtrusive so far because of its barrenness, suddenly became prominent in the form of a cluster of force-field domes. The isolated estates of Citizens, perhaps occupied at the moment, perhaps not. There was a peculiar appeal to such technology set in such an absolutely barren environment, a nugget of complete wealth in complete poverty, like a diamond in sand.

Strange that he should see it this way, Stile thought—then realized that it was in fact the perspective of his other self, to whom the entire frame of Proton was a novelty, much as the frame of Phaze was to Stile. What was commonplace to Stile was a miraculous new discovery to Blue.

The ball was rolling toward a linked trio of small domes. The connecting tubes arched high, leaving sufficient clearance below to pass the Phazite—but the ball eschewed that obvious passage to crash right into the westernmost dome. The dome disappeared as its force-field generator was taken out, leaving the serfs gasping in expectation of the sudden decompression. But there was the Phaze atmosphere, here in the juxtaposition; they discovered to their surprise that they could breathe quite well outside. It was every bit as real as the ball, of course.

One serf ran blindly out in front of Stile's steed; Belle tried to swerve, but the serf's erratic course made avoidance uncertain. "Serf—

turf!" Stile sang, willing the message. He wanted the man to be removed to a safe spot, suitable turf. Nothing happened, and he realized that Sheen's repressive enchantment against Adept spells remained in force. Fortunately Belle managed to miss the man, and they galloped on past the domes. Just as well the magic hadn't worked; the enemy Adepts would be casting spells furiously now, trying to sidetrack the Phazite, to conjure imposing barriers or trenches in its path, and Sheen's counterspell was the only protection against this.

It was not hard to keep up with the ball now as it slowly lost velocity. Had Stile started it at a different angle, it could have proceeded down a long valley and maintained speed. But he had elected to go the more difficult, surprising route, gambling the fate of the frames on his hunch. The giants should be arriving soon, and the other thing—he would not say, lest it be overheard.

The slope changed, and the ball slowed more definitely. This was the beginning of the rise he knew would balk it. No goblins were in evidence; he had at least been successful in fooling them. Probably there was a huge concentration at the other route and many barriers, pits, and various obstructive things. If the giants arrived in time, there would be no trouble.

At last the ball stopped, settling into a soft pocket so firmly that it was obvious that their present force could not budge it. They rode up and paused beside it. "What now, Stile?" Sheen inquired with a certain unrobotic edge.

"You unicorns change suits and fly up and see if you can spot the giants," Stile said. "They should be close now. Tell them we need help in a hurry."

The four unicorns shifted immediately to their airborne forms and zoomed into the sky. "I'll check too," Stile said to Sheen. "Project my image in a fast survey around the area."

She did. Soon he verified that the goblins were indeed massed at the valley route in horrendous number—but already they were marching toward the ball's present location. It would not be long before they got there. The giants just had to get there first!

The unicorns were successful. In a moment, three of the towering giants appeared, striding across the horizon, their heads literally lost in the clouds. They had been following the progress of the ball with giant field glasses, so had been ready to intercept it when it was stopped.

Stile had Sheen terminate their spells of invisibility and protection against attack, as these were no longer useful or necessary. Now Stile needed to be seen, to help organize the giants for their giant effort.

Soon the giants were using huge metal canes to propel the ball forward, up the slope, following the route Stile dictated. The giants enjoyed this; it was like a giant game of pool, knocking the tiny but extremely solid ball along. If they did it improperly, their pool cues broke, which was inconvenient.

The first elements of the goblin army arrived too late; the ball was well on its way. Stile and his companions were galloping after it.

Now, Stile thought, was the critical time. If the canny goblin commander did what Stile expected him to—

"There's no way the goblins can stop the giants," Sheen said. "We've won! Clip says the other side of the curtain is this side of the crest of the hill. We're nearly there!"

But another contingent of goblins was arriving at the hill. They did not try to oppose the giants; instead they marched ahead, as if clearing the way, which was strange. The giants, unperturbed, kept pushing the ball, taking turns with their cues. Even for them, it was very heavy, and progress slowed as they tired and their cues broke.

"The line should be right about here," Sheen said.

"Not any more," Stile told her. "The goblins are moving it."

Now she caught on. "No! We aren't gaining at all, then!"

"Oh, we'll get there," Stile said. "This only means delay. The giants are tired; it will take longer to crest the hill."

"I should think so," she agreed, eyeing the steep, almost cliff-faced crest. "You anticipated this? Why did you come here, then? The giants could have pushed it around the hill and across the curtain much faster, and we could have won the game by now. As it is, the enemy will have time to set up something worse."

"Yes," Stile agreed gravely.

The giant currently taking aim at the ball paused. He shook himself, and sweat flung out from him like rain.

"You'll have a workers' revolt soon," Sheen cautioned. "You've got to have some reason for this foolishness."

But Stile was listening for something. Now at last he heard it: an abrupt intensification of the faint Flute music in the background.

"The Oracle has just crossed the line," Stile announced. "Or rather, the line has crossed the Oracle. That computer is now within the zone of juxtaposition. From there, it can use its own stored moving equipment to transport itself the rest of the way to Proton."

"The Oracle!" Sheen exclaimed. "It had to cross to Proton to complete the exchange. To be able to make its vast expertise available for the reorganization of the Proton economic complex."

"The goblins have just enabled it to do that," Stile agreed. "Now we can tip the ball over the crest, roll it down across the line—and Clef can let the curtain collapse into singularity and vanish."

"You did have a cunning notion! You knew the curtain had not spread far enough, that the Oracle was hung up here, right under this mound, so you—"

"We still have to get the ball across," Stile reminded her. "We haven't won yet."

But now the giants renewed their efforts. The ball was shoved up over the cliff face with a convulsive joint effort, and began its inexorable roll down toward the curtain.

They charged up after it, scrambling for handholds at the brink, feeling the exhilaration of victory. As they crested the ridge, they saw the opposite slope blackened with goblins; all the rest of that army had force-marched here for the final confrontation.

The individual goblins could not stop the massively rolling ball, of course; they plunged desperately from its path. The slope was so steep that even the giants would be hard put to halt the ball before it crossed the curtain halfway down.

On the horizon Stile now spied the ogres, who had just arrived on the scene. They were ready to fight, but were understandably hesitant about wading into so vast an army of goblins. But it seemed the ogres would not be needed now.

On the next hill to the north was a device Stile recognized only from his researches into planetary warfare—a nuclear cannon. Powered by atomic fusion, this pre-Protonite weapon could fire a solid projectile into deep space—or into any object in its viewfinder at a lesser range. Stile knew the canny Grossnose would have it loaded with a half-ton slug of Protonite—the only substance that could have a proper effect on the rolling ball. The goblin commander had devised his strategy to counter Stile's strategy without pause.

"Get back over the ridge!" Stile cried. "Down, giants! Now!"

The earth trembled as they obeyed, trusting his warning. Giants, unicorns, and others all huddled in the shelter of the ridge.

The cannon fired. The Phazite ball exploded into thousands of fragments and a great cloud of dust. Phazite rained down around them in the form of stones, pebbles, gravel, and sand.

Sheen jumped to cover Stile's body with her own tougher one, and the cyborg did the same for the bearhead. The unicorns changed to their flying forms and huddled under the same shelters. But the giants were in some discomfort; they swatted at the pieces that struck them, as if bitten by gnats.

Now the great goblin army went into action, obviously rehearsed. Each goblin ran to pick up one fragment of Phazite and carry it south, away from the border of the juxtaposition. "No!" Sheen cried. "Fragmentation doesn't matter, so long as it gets across the line to Proton-frame. But this will finish us!"

Grossnose's final ploy had been a brilliant one. Once more the goblin had outmaneuvered Stile, giving up a lesser thing—in this case the Oracle—for the sake of a greater one. The ball had had to crest the hill to come into range of the nuclear cannon.

But Stile refused to give up. One hope remained. "Trool! Brown!" Stile called. "If you hear me—use the book! Do something while the enemy Adepts are relaxing in victory!" Did they hear? Could Brown locate a spell and use it in time? Stile was afraid not.

Suddenly there was a strange wrenching, as of vastly potent magic gone astray. Then the world stabilized, seemingly unchanged. The goblins still charged forward with their burdens, seeming slightly dizzy but hardly incapacitated.

Sheen looked at Stile in despair as the last of the sandfall cleared. "We can't possibly stop them all," she said. "We have ogres and unicorns, but there are too many goblins, too hard to catch. The book-spell failed, or was blocked by the other Adepts. Lady Brown simply lacks the experience to use that sort of magic properly."

"I don't know," Stile said. "That didn't feel like blocked magic." He was getting a notion what it might have been, but decided not to say. It could not make a difference at this point. "Let the goblins be; no sense getting ourselves in trouble in a futile effort."

The giants and unicorns turned away from him in disgust, but left the goblins alone. Soon virtually all of the Phazite was gone, carried away in pieces or in bagfuls. The battle was over.

Commander Grossnose strode over the crest. "Congratulations on an excellent campaign, Adept," he said graciously. "Thou didst trick me on crossing the Oracle—but I countered with the cannon. The power of the Oracle in nonseparated frames becomes moot. But if thou wouldst be so good as to answer a point of curiosity—"

"Certainly," Stile agreed.

"What was the nature of that last great spell thou didst attempt to perform? I felt its vasty power—but naught happened."

Trool and the Brown Adept appeared, she with the book of magic clutched in her arms. "We can answer that, goblin," she said. "It was reversal."

Grossnose's constricted brow wrinkled. "Reversal? I understand that not."

"Thou knowest—changing directions. So west turns east, and north turns south—or seems to. The Oracle told us to do it, once it got into jux and could use its holo—hologramp—its magic pictures to talk to us. That's one smart machine!"

"North turns south?" the goblin asked, dismay infiltrating his face.

"Yep. Thine army just carried all the Phazite the wrong way—north across the line."

The goblin commander stood for a long moment, absorbing that, grasping the accuracy and import of the statement. All of them had been deceived, for it had been an extremely powerful spell of a quite unanticipated sort—as it had needed to be, to avoid interference by the enemy Adepts.

Grossnose turned again to Stile. "Congratulations on a better campaign than I knew, Adept," he said gravely, as gracious in defeat as he had been in victory. "The final ploy was thine." He marched back up the slope, his troops falling in behind him.

The victory had been won; juxtaposition could end, and the frames could safely separate, never to intersect again in this region of the universe. Stile could see the glimmer of the curtain contracting, closing more rapidly from the south so as to finish at the site of the Oracle beneath them. Or was that from the north it was closing? It was hard to be sure, with that reversal-spell. Beyond that line, north (?) was the verdant world of Phaze; at the crest to the south (?) was the barren desert of Proton. Only the directions were reversed, not the terrain, somehow; the goblins had marched the wrong way home. Not that it mattered; they were creatures of Phaze who would remain there regardless, just as the robots and cyborgs would remain in Proton.

Stile himself would now return forever to Proton, to settle his debt to Citizen Merle, marry Sheen, and work with the Oracle-computer to reform the existing order. His alternate self would reanimate to be with Neysa and Clip and Stile's other friends of Phaze and the Lady Blue. How much better off he would be!

"Thy life seems not dreary to me," the Blue Adept thought. "The sheer challenge, the strange and fascinating bypaths of politics, the marvelous Game, and the ladies in Proton—no woman could be better than Sheen. Thou hast far the best of it, methinks."

"Just do thou wrap up my commitments in Phaze," Stile thought back sourly. "Petition must be made to the Herd Stallion to release Clip to pair with Belle; that is best for both of them. And it is in my mind that Trool the troll, with his integrity and skill at sculpture, should be given the book of magic and become the new Red Adept, fashioning useful magic amulets for—"

"That was *my* thought, fool!" Blue thought. "Of course I will—"

Then the closing curtain caught them. "Ah, the reversal!" Blue thought, amazed, as his other soul was drawn from Stile's association. "Farewell, self!"

Stile blinked. Blue had caught on to something Stile had not, it seemed, and now it was too late to ascertain what. That, and the whole wonderful world of Phaze, were gone. He felt the bitter tears of loss. Never to see the Lady Blue again, or Neysa—

But he could not afford self-pity. He had things to do in this world. He opened his eyes.

He was lying on a bed in a chamber of the Blue Demesnes. The Proton replica, of course. He must have lost consciousness, and Sheen had brought him here and left him to recover in decent privacy. Sheen was certainly the perfect woman; too bad she had not been able to remain in Phaze—but that would have been too complicated anyway.

He got up, felt momentarily dizzy with the sudden rising, and quickly squatted to let the blood return to his head. It was as if he had been lying here a long time, his body unused; he felt somewhat awkward and unsteady, but now was recovering rapidly.

He stared at his knees with slow amazement. They were fully flexed, without pain. His injury had been cured!

Oh—of course. Sheen had taken advantage of his unconsciousness to have him in surgery, and now he was better. Though he really would not have expected her to do that without consulting him first.

He walked to the door. The short hall was dark, so he sang a spell: "Right—light." Immediately there was light, though only half as bright as he had intended.

Wait—he could not do magic in Proton!

He glanced back—and saw the harmonica lying on a table beside the bed. Blue's harmonica, left with the—

Then he heard a light tread on the floor, probably someone alerted by Stile's own motion. He recognized it immediately: the Lady Blue. Sheen's step was quite different.

He knew with a shock of incredulous joy that something had gone wrong. The reversal had sent himself and his alternate self to the wrong frames! Stile's soul had gone to the golem body, whose knees were good, while the Blue Adept had left Phaze—

Phaze would not be safe until the Blue Adept departed it forever. The prophecy had been fulfilled after all. *Stile* was in Phaze, not the true Blue Adept, who had been here all along, in the harmonica, until this final separation. The Brown Adept, unacquainted with the book of magic, prompted by the all-knowing Oracle, had made the reversal-spell too comprehensive, and thus—

And the other prophecy, which he had thought had come after the fact—that Stile would be betrayed, for his own good, by a young-seeming woman. Brown seemed as young as they came. That mixup had been no accident! She had perceived more clearly than he where his true future lay, and had acted to make it come true. How neatly it all fit together now! The Blue Adept, loath to live with a woman who no longer loved him, and fascinated by the marvelous world of science and the beautiful, loyal, deserving creature Sheen—who was as much intrigued by Blue, a person in Stile's own image and spirit who had left his love for the Lady Blue behind—

Now the Lady Blue came into view, breathtakingly lovely and somber. Her face composed, she approached Stile. "My Lord, thou knowest I will serve thee in all things with grace and propriety," she said sadly. "What is to be, must be."

She thought he was Blue, of course—and she loved Stile. She had the mettle to carry through, to bear and raise his son, with no word of regret or reproach—but this time she would not need it.

"Beloved," Stile said. "I have news for thee, thee, thee . . ."

M3

About the Author

It was not necessary, in England in 1934, to name a baby instantly; there was a grace period of a number of days. As the deadline loomed, the poor woman simply gave all the names she could think of: Piers Anthony Dillingham Jacob. The child moved to America, where it took three years and five schools to graduate him from first grade, because he couldn't learn to read. It was thus fated that he become a proofreader, an English teacher, or a writer. He tried them all, along with a dozen other employments —and liked only the least successful one. So he lopped off half his name, sent his wife out to earn their living, and concentrated on writing. That was the key to success; publishers would print material by an author whose name was short enough.

He sold his first story in 1962 and had his first novel, *Chthon*, published in 1967. His first fantasy in *The Magic of Xanth* Trilogy, *A Spell for Chameleon*, won the August Derleth Fantasy Award as the best novel in 1977. He has written approximately forty novels in the genres of science fiction, fantasy and martial arts.

He was married in 1956, right after graduating from college, to Carol Ann Marble. Their daughter Penny was born eleven years later, and their final daughter Cheryl in 1970. That was the beginning of a whole new existence, because little girls like animals. In 1978 they bought nice horses, and that experience, coupled with knee injuries in judo class, became *Split Infinity*. Piers Anthony is not the protagonist—he says he lacks the style —but Penny's horse Blue *is* the mundane model for the unicorn Neysa.